IN HER NAME:
THE LAST WAR

By
Michael R. Hicks

This is a work of fiction. All of the characters and events portrayed in this novel are products of the author's imagination or are used fictitiously.

WHAT READERS ARE SAYING

Drawn straight from some of the reader reviews of the collected works in *The Last War*:

On *The Last War* trilogy itself:

"Normally I'm not a big fan of a "prequel" type series but this one kicked some major butt."

"The three books that make up The Last War are a masterpiece of setting the tale of how an alien civilization seeks its' survival by waging war on one more group of space-going people - that happen to be humans! The author is one of a very few that can make this alien race's mission of seemingly killing every last human one of a tale of their races survival - and have you rooting for them! It's great!"

"This book is a great read. Will keep you going to the end. I would recommend reading this before reading the Empire trilogy, just for a time sense and mystery. The characters are well established and everything has enough believability and background info to keep the readers interested."

"I do not normally read sci-fi, especially military sci-fi but this was a fantastic read... The author has a way of making this series as much about the Kreelans and their survival as it is about the human race surviving. I even shed a tear or two when a favorite character, on either side of the conflict, died."

On *First Contact*:

"I have read a lot of science fiction books over the years but have gotten away from them because they did not seem as good anymore. This book brought me back to the fold, was a very good read. I am now re-reading it a second time because I wanted to find out what happen and quickly read to the end the first time around. Highly recommend this to any lover of science fiction."

"Michael Hicks is one of the bright stars in the new generation of Sci-Fi writers today. This is book four of the "In Her Name" series of novels and it is an exciting and well written story about the interstellar war that will occur with the Kreelans."

"This one's a page turner. Couldn't put it down. Read it all night without sleep. Really a great read."

"I highly recommend this whole series, truly a remarkable story. The alien culture is rich and nuanced, as are the characters. Warning, this will suck you in!"

"Probably the best series of science fiction I have read. I only regret there is no fourth volume."

"This is an excellent book, and I highly recommend it!! I found myself reading late into the night, past when I normally go to bed just to see what happened next."

On *Legend Of The Sword*:

"I've now read six of his books and I am about to start my seventh. I took my time reading this one because I think subconsciously I want to make sure there is another book ready for me to buy. Whether it's this series, or his "Season of the Harvest", which a sequel is on it's way (can't wait), his writings just pull you into the story like few authors can."

"This is an outstanding series out of the mind of Michael R. Hicks who is a new star in the Sci-Fi community. I have purchased and read all of his books and enjoyed every one. If you like Sci-Fi you will love this book!"

"I found this story to be engrossing and I couldn't put it down. I drove my wife to anger by reading it in bed late at night after she came home at midnight from work and wanted to sleep. I tend to talk to my books as I read a great story by saying things like, "Wow." I found this story to be one truly worthy of being placed on the best library shelves in all of America, and I mean America as in the Continent, not the USA!"

"Loved these books and the female warriors and the story of their interaction with humans. Hick's ability to present the soul and motivations of each race was fantastic, although I must admit siding with the aliens more often than not such was his skill in creating understanding of an alien mindset. Well, I for one can not wait for the next book in the series and hope that Hick's is thinking about the one to follow that!"

On *Dead Soul*:

"The In Her Name series stands at the top with some of the best SF I have ever read. All six books will draw you in and leave you wanting more."

"Loved this as much as the other books in the series. I love the characters, the tie in to the other books and the ability of the author to take us to an entirely new world!!"

"I have been reading SF ever since my Dad brought home E.R. Burroughs books when I was ten, I'm 60 now. I've read really good SF {and some not so good). This group of books by this new author has just become one of my favorites! These books will be bought bound and will be read and re-read for a long time to come!"

"I highly recommend this book to anyone interested in a Military/Science Fiction tale that is not only fast moving, but accurate in portrayal of the cast of characters. This book has been a complete joy to read and I look forward to more."

"I like this author's work so much that I have just brought his newest book to read, ~~Season~~ *Of The Harvest*. I hope it is just as good!"

DISCOVER OTHER BOOKS BY MICHAEL R. HICKS

The *In Her Name* Series
First Contact
Legend Of The Sword
Dead Soul
Empire
Confederation
Final Battle
From Chaos Born

"Boxed Set" Collections
In Her Name (Omnibus)
In Her Name: The Last War

Thrillers
Season Of The Harvest

Visit *AuthorMichaelHicks.com* for the latest updates!

FIRST CONTACT

ONE

Captain Owen McClaren was extremely tense, although a casual observer would never have thought so. Commanding the survey vessel *TNS Aurora*, he was one of the best officers in the fleet, and to his crew he had never appeared as anything but calm and in control. Even when one of the ship's newly refitted reactors had suffered a breach during their last run into dry dock, McClaren's deep voice had never wavered, his fatherly face had never betrayed a hint of fear or apprehension as he personally directed the engineering watch to contain the breach. A man of unusual physical and moral courage, he was the perfect captain for the exploratory missions the *Aurora* and her sister ships mounted into distant space, seeking new homes for humanity.

McClaren had made thousands of jumps in his twenty-year career, but every one was like the very first: an adrenaline joyride. As the transpace sequence wound down to zero, his heart would begin to pound and his muscles tensed like spring steel. It wasn't fear that made him react that way, although there were enough things that could go wrong with a jump to make fear a natural enough reaction.

No, what made the forty-three-year-old former middleweight boxing champion of the Terran Naval Academy hold the arms of his command chair in a white-knuckle grip wasn't fear. It was anticipation. To *Aurora's* captain, every jump, particularly out here in uncharted space, was a potential winning lottery ticket, the discovery of a lifetime. No matter where the *Aurora* wound up, as long as she arrived safely, there was bound to be a wealth of astrogational information to help human starships travel ever farther from Man's birthplace: Earth.

On rare occasions, precious habitable planets were to be found. Finding such systems was the primary goal of the survey ships. McClaren was currently the fleet's leading "ace," with twelve habitable planets to his credit in return for nearly fifteen years of ship-time, sailing through uncharted space.

"Stand by for transpace sequence," the pilot announced, her words echoing through every passageway and compartment in the *Aurora's* five hundred meter length.

McClaren tensed even more, his strong arm and back muscles flexing instinctively as if he were back in the ring, preparing to land a solid upper cut to the chin of an imaginary opponent. But his calm expression never wavered. "Very well," he answered, his dark brown eyes drinking in the growing torrent of information on the navigation display.

"Computer auto-lock engaged," interjected a faux female voice reassuringly. McClaren always had to suppress a grimace: the one thing he had never liked about *Aurora* was the computer's voice. It reminded him too much of his first wife.

For the next few seconds, the crew was little more than excess baggage as the ship's computer guided the transition from hyperspace back into the Einsteinian universe with a precision measured in quadrillionths of a second. While the bridge, which was buried deep in the *Aurora's* core habitation section, had no direct observation windows, the wraparound display depicted the eerie streams of light that swirled around the ship in complete detail. But what the human eye saw in the maelstrom of quantum physics beyond the ship's hyperdrive field was an illusion. It was real in one sense, but in another it wasn't. Space and time as humans commonly understood it did not exist in this realm. As the captain of a starship, McClaren had to understand both the theory and the practical application of hyperspace and the means to travel through it. But he was content in the knowledge that he never could have come up with the breakthroughs that allowed this miracle to happen: he stood on the shoulders of the scientific giants who had made the first test jump into hyperspace long before he was born.

While in hyperspace, the display would normally show the computer's assessment of the relative location of stars and other known celestial waypoints as the ship moved along its straight-line (relatively speaking) course. But McClaren always cleared the display to show what was really outside the ship just before they dropped back into normal space. It was a sight he never tired of.

"Ten seconds..." the computer's voice began counting down to the transition. "Five...four...three...two...one....sequence initiated. Hyperspace Engines disengaged."

The display suddenly shifted, the swirling light streams condensing into a bright yellow sun against a background of stars. McClaren knew that the system had several planets; gravitational perturbations observed from their last jump point had confirmed that much. The question was whether there were any orbiting at a distance from the star where water could exist as a liquid. For where there was liquid water, there was the possibility of carbon-based life. The trick now was to find them. Planets were huge close up, but in the vast expanse of a star system they seemed incredibly small.

"Engineering confirms hyperspace engines are secure, sir," the executive officer, Lieutenant Commander Rajesh Kumar, reported. "Engineering is ready to answer all bells, and the ship is secured for normal space."

Nodding his thanks to his exec, McClaren turned to the most important person currently on the bridge: the navigator. "Raisa, what's the word?"

The navigator looked like she would have given McClaren a run for his money in the boxing ring. Big-boned and heavily muscled, Lieutenant Raisa Marisova had in fact been a champion wrestler in her college years. But it was her genius at stellar astrogation that had won her a place on the *Aurora's* all-volunteer crew.

"Well..." she murmured as she rechecked her readings for what McClaren knew was probably the fifth time in the few moments the ship had dropped back into normal space. Raisa was always able to confirm the ship's emergence point so quickly because her calculations for pointing the various telescopes and other sensors at known stars to make a positional fix were always so precise. "It seems we are...right where we are supposed to be," she said as she turned and smiled at her captain, "give or take a few meters. We're above the ecliptic plane based on our pre-jump survey information. Now it's up to the survey team to find your next habitable planet, captain."

McClaren grinned, then opened a channel to the entire ship. "Well, crew, it looks like we've made another successful jump, and emerged right on target. The bad news is that we're even farther out in the Middle of Nowhere. But that's what they pay us for. Great job, everyone." The last few words were more than just a token verbal pat on the back: he truly meant it. Unlike most transits that took regular ships into hyperspace for a few days or even a week or two, the *Aurora* routinely made jumps that lasted for weeks or months. While McClaren's crew made it look easy, he knew quite well that an amazing amount of planning and preparation went into every jump, and his crew followed it up with painstaking diligence every moment they were in hyperspace. It wasn't just that they didn't want to wind up somewhere other than where they had planned, or because their captain expected perfection. It was because they had no intention of settling for second best. Period. "Everybody gets an extra round on me when we get back to the barn. Carry on."

The bridge crew grinned at one another: the captain ran up a huge bar tab on every mission, but he never failed to deliver when the ship made port.

They had no way of knowing that all but one of them would be dead in a few short hours.

* * *

The stranger's arrival was no surprise to the Imperial warships that orbited the Settlements on the third and fourth planets from the star. While even the greatly advanced technology of the Empire could not track ships while in hyperspace, they could easily detect the gravity spikes of vessels about to emerge in normal space. The stranger had been detected many hours before, as measured in the time of humans.

While this system was at the distant edge of the Empire, far from the Homeworld and the Empress, its defenses were not lacking: of the dozens of starships in orbit around the two settled worlds and the hundreds plying the asteroid belt, four were battlecruisers built within the last century. Humans might have considered them old, until they understood that the warriors of the Empire had sailed among the stars for over one hundred thousand of Earth's years. Even the most ancient of Her warships still plying the void between the stars was tens of thousands of years more advanced than the arriving stranger. Humans would barely have recognized them as starships.

But the warriors charged with protecting this far-flung system had no way of knowing the primitive nature of the incoming stranger. Nor would they have cared. The Empire had encountered other sentient races over the millennia, and the first contact protocol was no different now than it had been in ages past: the stranger would be greeted with overwhelming force.

In unison, the four enormous battlecruisers left orbit for the gravity anomaly at maximum velocity, safe behind shields that could protect them from titanic energy discharges and made them all but invisible to anything but direct visual observation.

Behind them, smaller warships and the planetary defense systems prepared to welcome the new arrival should it prove more than a match for the great warships sent to greet it.

* * *

"Bridge, this is Survey..."

Captain McClaren frowned despite himself. He knew that Lieutenant Amundsen's survey team worked fast, but they had been in-system less than fifteen minutes. It often took days for them to identify the orbits of any planets in the temperate zone unless they had extensive perturbation data on the star or stars in the system. And that they rarely had: humanity's rapid expansion to the stars didn't allow for years-long observations of any given star. His frown deepened as he took in the expression on Amundsen's face in the comms display. The normally very reserved man was uncharacteristically excited. And just as frightened. "What is it, Jens?"

"Sir..." Amundsen began, his pale blue eyes darting away momentarily to another display. "Captain...we've confirmed not just one, but *two* planets in the temperate zone..."

"Hot damn!" McClaren couldn't help himself. One planet that might have liquid water was miracle enough. Their pre-jump analysis had suggested there was one, but two had been too much to hope for. "That's fantastic!"

"Sir...they're both inhabited," Amundsen said in hoarse whisper. Normally a quiet man, often more at home with the stars and planets than his fellow human beings, the volume of his voice dropped with every word. "We didn't have to find their orbits. We found them from their neutrino and infrared readings." He paused. "I've...I've never seen anything like this. Even Sol system doesn't have this level of activity. The two planets in the temperate zone are highly industrialized. There are other points of activity throughout the asteroid belt, and on several moons orbiting a solitary gas giant. We have also observed ships through the primary telescope. Hundreds of them. They are...nothing like ours."

The captain sat back, stunned. *First contact*, he thought. Humans had explored thousands of star systems and endless volumes of space, but had never once encountered another sentient species. They had found life aplenty on the hundred-odd discovered worlds that would support human life or could be terraformed. From humble bacteria to massive predators that would have been at home with Earth's dinosaurs, life in the Universe was as expansive as it was diverse if you looked long and far enough. But no one had discovered a single sign of sentient life beyond the mark *homo sapiens* had left behind in his celestial travels.

Until now.

"Jesus," the captain breathed, conscious now of the entire bridge crew staring at him. They hadn't heard Amundsen's words, but they immediately picked up on the captain's reaction. "XO," he ordered, pulling his mind back to the here and now, "let's have the first contact protocols." He looked pointedly at Kumar. "I want to make damn sure these folks understand we're harmless."

"Aye, sir," Kumar replied crisply as his fingers flew over his terminal. "Coming up on display one." A segment of the bridge wraparound screen darkened as the standing orders for first contact appeared.

"Lieutenant Amundsen," McClaren ordered, "let's see some of these ships of yours on display two."

"Sir." Amundsen's face bobbed about slightly in the captain's comms terminal as he patched the telescope feed to another segment of the main bridge display.

"Lord of All," someone whispered. The *Aurora*'s primary telescope was nearly ten meters across, and dominated the phalanx of survey instruments mounted in the massive spherical section that made up the ship's bow. Normally used to search for and map stellar and planetary bodies, it could also be pressed into service to provide high magnification visuals of virtually anything, even moving objects that were relatively close, such as nearby (in terms of a stellar system) ships.

But what it showed now was as unlike the *Aurora* as she herself was unlike a wooden sailing ship. While the *Aurora* was largely a collection of cylindrical sections attached to a sturdy keel that ran from the engineering section at the stern to the instrumentation cluster at the bow, the alien ship displayed on the bridge display was insectile in appearance, her hull made up of sleek curves that gave McClaren the impression of a gigantic wasp.

"Why does the focus keep shifting?" Marisova asked into the sudden silence that had descended on the bridge. The alien vessel shimmered in the display as if a child were twisting an imaginary focus knob for the primary telescope back and forth, taking the image in and out of focus.

"That's what I was about to say," Amundsen answered, McClaren now having shifted the survey team leader's image onto yet a third segment of the bridge display. Before he had seemed both excited and frightened. Now it was clear that fear was crowding out his excitement. "That is one of at least four ships that is heading directly toward us from the outer habitable planet. The reason you are seeing the focusing anomaly is because the ships are moving at an incredible velocity, and the telescope cannot hold the image in alignment. Even what you see here has been enhanced with post-processing." He visibly gulped. "Captain, they knew we were coming, hours, possibly even a few days, before we arrived. They knew right where we were going to be, and they must have left orbit before we arrived. They *must* have. It's theoretically possible to predict a hyperspace emergence, but...we now know that it's not just a theory." He looked again at one of his off-screen displays, then back to the monitor. "I don't know exactly what their initial acceleration rate was, but they're now moving so fast that the light we're seeing reflected from their hulls is noticeably blue-shifted. I estimate their current velocity is roughly five percent of C."

Five percent of the speed of light, McClaren thought, incredulous. Nearly fifteen thousand kilometers per second. And they didn't take much time to reach it.

"I'm trying to estimate their acceleration rate, but it must be-"

"A lot higher than we could ever achieve," McClaren cut him off, looking closely at the wavering image of the alien vessel. "Any idea how big she is?"

"I have no data to estimate her length," Amundsen replied, "but I estimate the beam of this ship to be roughly five hundred meters. I can only assume that her length is considerably more, but we won't know until we get a more oblique view."

"That ship is five hundred meters *wide*?" Kumar asked, incredulous. *Aurora* herself was barely that long from stem to stern. While she was by no means the largest starship built by human hands, she was usually the largest vessel in whatever port she put into.

"Yes," Amundsen told him. "And the other three ships are roughly the same size."

"Christ," someone whispered.

"Raj," McClaren said, turning to his exec. "Thoughts?"

"Communications is running the initial first contact sequence now." He turned to face the captain. "Our signals will take roughly thirty minutes to reach the inner planets, but those ships..." He shook his head. "They're close enough now that they should have already received our transmissions. If they're listening." He looked distinctly uncomfortable. "If I were a betting man, I would say those were warships."

McClaren nodded grimly. "Comms," he looked over at Ensign John Waverly, "keep stepping through the first contact communications sequence. Just make sure that we're listening, too."

"I'm on it, sir," the young man replied. Waverly seemed incredibly young, but like the rest of *Aurora's* crew, he did his job exceptionally well. "I'm well versed in the FCP procedures, sir. So far, though, I haven't come across any emissions anywhere in the standard spectrum, other than what Lieutenant Amundsen's team have already reported. If they use anything anywhere in the radio frequency band, we're sure not seeing it. And I haven't identified any coherent light sources, either."

So, no radio and no communications lasers, McClaren thought uneasily. Even though the aliens knew that company was coming, they had remained silent. Or if they were talking, they were using some form of transmission that was beyond what *Aurora* was capable of seeing or hearing. Maybe the aliens were beyond such mundane things as radio- and light-based communications?

"How long until those ships get here?" McClaren asked Amundsen, whose worried face still stared out from the bridge display screen. *Aurora* herself was motionless relative to her emergence point: McClaren never moved in-system on a survey until they knew much more about their environment than they did now. And it made for a much more convenient reference point for a rapid jump-out.

"At their current velocity, they would overshoot us in just under three hours. But, of course, they will need to decelerate to meet us..."

"That depends on their intentions," Kumar interjected. "They could attack as they pass by..."

"Or they could simply stop," Marisova observed quietly. Everyone turned to gape at her. "We know nothing about their drive systems," she explained. "Nothing about those ships registers on our sensors other than direct visuals. What if they achieved their current velocity nearly instantaneously when they decided to head out to meet us?"

"Preposterous," Amundsen exclaimed. "That's simply not possible!"

"But-"

"Enough, people," McClaren said quietly. "Beyond the obviously impressive capabilities of the aliens, it all boils down to this: do we stay or do we go?" He looked around at his bridge crew, then opened a channel to the entire ship. "Crew, this is the captain. As I'm sure most of you are now aware, the system we've entered is inhabited. We're in a first contact situation. The *only* first contact situation anyone has ever faced. So what we do now is going to become part of The Book that will tell others either how to do it right, or how not to do it if we royally screw things up. I'll be completely honest with you: I'm not happy with the situation. We've got four big ships heading toward us in an awful hurry. They could be warships. I don't blame whoever these folks are for sending out an armed welcoming committee. If it were my home, I'd send some warships out to take a look, too.

"But I'd also make sure to send some diplomats along: people who want to talk with their new neighbors. What bothers me is that we haven't seen anything, from the ships or the two inhabited planets, that looks like any sort of communication. Maybe they're just using something we can't pick up. Maybe the ships coming our way are packed with scientists and ambassadors and they want to make it a big surprise. I just don't know.

"What I do know is that we've got about three hours to make a decision and take action. My inclination is to stay. Not to try and score the first handshake with an alien, but because...it's our first opportunity to say hello to another sentient race. We've been preparing for this moment since before the very first starship left Earth. It's a risk, but it's also the greatest opportunity humanity has ever had.

"So here's what we're going to do. We've got a little bit of time to discuss our options before our new friends reach us. Department heads, talk to your people. Get a feel for what they're thinking. Then all department heads and the senior chiefs are to meet in my ready room in exactly one hour. I'll make the final decision on whether we stay or go, but I want to hear what you all have to say. That is all." He punched the button on the touchpad, closing the circuit.

"In the meantime," he told Kumar and Marisova, "get an emergency jump sequence lined up. Pick a destination other than our inbound vector. If these ships come in with guns blazing, the last thing I want to do is point them back the way we came, toward home."

On the display screen, the alien ship and her sisters continued toward them.

* * *

The four battlecruisers sailed quickly to meet the alien vessel, but they hardly revealed their true capabilities. While it was now clear that the alien ship was extremely primitive, those who guarded the Empire took nothing for granted. They would reveal no more about themselves than absolutely necessary until they were sure the new arrival posed no threat. The Empire had not lasted through the ages by leaving anything to chance.

Aboard the lead ship, a group of warriors prepared for battle with the unknown, while healers and other castes made ready to learn all there was to know about the strangers.

They did not have much longer to wait.

* * *

There was standing room only in the captain's ready room an hour later. At the table sat the six department heads, responsible for the primary functional areas of the ship, the *Aurora's* senior chief, and the captain. Along the walls of the now-cramped compartment stood the senior enlisted member of each department and the ship's two midshipmen. The XO and the bridge crew remained at their stations, although they were tied in through a video feed on the bridge wraparound display.

The emotional tension ran high among the people in the room, McClaren could easily see. But from the body language and the expressions on their faces it wasn't from fear, but excited anticipation. It was an emotion he fully shared.

"I'm not going to waste any time on preliminaries," he began. "You all know what's going on and what's at stake. According to the Survey Department," he nodded at Amundsen, who was the only one around the table who looked distinctly unhappy, "the ships haven't changed course or velocity. So it looks like they're either going to blow by us, which I think would probably be bad news, or their technology is so radically advanced that they can stop on a proverbial dime."

At that, the survey leader's frown grew more pronounced, turning his normally pale face into a grimace.

"Amundsen?" McClaren asked. "You've got something to say. Spit it out."

"I think Lieutenant Marisova was right," he said grudgingly, nodding toward the video pickup that showed the meeting to the bridge crew. But McClaren knew that it wasn't because Marisova had said it. It was because he was afraid to believe that what she said could possibly be true, or even close to the truth. "I don't believe they could accelerate to their current velocity instantaneously, but even assuming several days' warning - even weeks! - the acceleration they must have achieved would have to have been...unbelievable." He shook his head. "No. I believe those ships will not simply pass by us. They will slow down and rendezvous with us sometime in the next two hours, decelerating at a minimum of two hundred gees. Probably much more."

A chill ran down McClaren's spine. *Aurora* had the most efficient reactionless drives in service by any of the many worlds colonized by Mankind, and was one of the few to be fitted with artificial gravity, a recent innovation, and acceleration dampers. She wasn't nearly as fast as a courier ship, certainly, but for a military survey vessel she was no slouch. But two hundred gees? Not even close.

"Robotic ships?" Aubrey Hannan, the chief of the Engineering Section suggested. "They could certainly handle that sort of acceleration."

"It doesn't matter," McClaren interjected, gently but firmly steering the conversation from interesting, but essentially useless, speculation back to the issue at hand. "From my perspective, it doesn't matter how fast the aliens can maneuver. We're not a warship, and I have no intention of masquerading as one. It's clear they have radically advanced technology. That's not necessarily a surprise; we could have just as easily stumbled upon a world in the pre-atomic era, and we would be the high-tech aliens. Our options remain the same: stay and say hello, or jump out with what I hope is a fat safety margin before they get here." He glanced around and his gaze landed on the junior midshipman. "Midshipman Sato, what's your call?"

Ichiro Sato, already standing ramrod straight against the bulkhead, stiffened even further. All of nineteen years old, he was the youngest member of the crew. Extremely courteous, conscientious, and intelligent, he was well respected by the other members of the crew, although his rigid outer shell was a magnet for good-natured ribbing. Exceptionally competent and a fast learner, he kept quietly to himself. He was one of a select few from the Terran Naval Academy who were chosen to spend one or more of their academy years aboard ship as advanced training as junior officers. It was a great opportunity, but came with a hefty commitment: deployed midshipmen had to continue their academy studies while also performing their duties aboard ship.

"Sir..." Sato momentarily gulped for air, McClaren's question having caught him completely off-guard.

The captain felt momentarily guilty for putting Sato on the spot first, but he had a reason. "Relax, Ichiro," McClaren told him. "I called this meeting for ideas. The senior officers, including myself, and the chiefs have years of preconceived notions drilled into our heads. We've got years of experience, yes, but this situation calls for a fresh perspective. If you were in my shoes, what would your decision be? There's no right or wrong answer to this one."

While Ichiro's features didn't betray it, the captain's last comment caused him even more consternation. He had been brought up in a traditional Japanese family on Nagano, where, according to his father, everything was either *right* or it was *wrong*; there was no in-between. And more often than not, anything Ichiro did was *wrong*. That was the main reason Ichiro had decided to apply for service in the Terran Navy when he was sixteen: to spite his father and escape the tyranny of his house, and to avoid the stifling life of a salaryman trapped in the web of a hegemonic corporate world. Earth's global military services accepted applicants from all but a few rogue worlds, and Ichiro's test scores and academic record had opened the door for him to enter the Terran Naval Academy. There, too, most everything was either right or wrong. The difference between the academy and his home was that in the academy, Ichiro was nearly always *right*. His unfailing determination to succeed had given him a sense of confidence he had never known before, putting him at the head of his class and earning him a position aboard the *Aurora*.

That realization, and his desperate desire not to lose face in front of the captain and ship's officers, gave him back his voice. "Sir. I believe we should stay and greet the ships."

McClaren nodded, wondering what had just been going on in the young man's mind. "Okay, you picked door number one. The question now is why?"

"Because, sir, that is why we are here, isn't it?" Loosening up slightly from his steel-rod pose, he turned to look at the other faces around the room, his voice suddenly filled with a passion that none of his fellow crew members would have ever thought possible. "While our primary mission is to find new habitable worlds, we really are explorers, discoverers, of whatever deep space may hold. With every jump we search for the unknown, things that no one else has ever seen. Maybe we will not find what we hope. Perhaps these aliens are friendly, perhaps not. There is great risk in everything we do. But, having found the first sentient race other than humankind, can we in good conscience simply leave without doing all we can to establish contact, even at the risk of our own destruction?"

The captain nodded, impressed more by the young man's unexpected burst of emotion than his words. But his words held their own merit: they precisely echoed McClaren's own feelings. That was exactly why he had spent so much of his career in survey.

"Well said, Ichiro," he told the young man. The two midshipmen on either side of Sato grinned and nudged him as if to say, *Good job.* Most of those seated at the table nodded or murmured their agreement. "So, there's an argument, and I believe a good one, for staying. Who's got one for bailing out right now?"

"I'll take that one, sir," Raj Kumar spoke up from the bridge, his image appearing on the primary screen in the ready room. "I myself agree with Midshipman Sato that we should stay. But one compelling argument for leaving now is to make sure that the news of this discovery gets back home. If the aliens should turn out to be hostile and this ship is taken, or even if we should suffer some unexpected mishap, Earth and the rest of human space may never know until they're attacked. And we have no way to let anyone know of our discovery without jumping back to the nearest communications relay."

That produced a lot of frowns on the faces around the table. Most of them had thought of this already, of course, but having it voiced directly gave it more substance.

Kumar went on, "That's also a specification in the first contact protocols, that one of the top priorities is to get word back home. But the bottom line is that any actions taken are at the captain's discretion based on the situation as he or she sees it."

"Right," McClaren told everyone. "Getting word back home is the only real reason I've been able to come up with myself for leaving now that isn't tied to fear of the unknown. And since all of us signed up to get paid to go find the unknown, as the good midshipman pointed out, those reasons don't count." He turned to the woman sitting to his left. "Chief, what's your take?"

Master Chief Brenda Harkness was the senior enlisted member of the crew, and her word carried a great deal of weight with McClaren. Completely at odds with the stereotype of someone of her rank, she was a tall, slim, and extremely attractive woman in her late thirties. But no one who had ever worked with her for more than five minutes ever took her for granted: she was a hard-core Navy lifer who never dished out bullshit and refused to tolerate it from anyone else. She would move mountains to help anyone who needed it, but her beautiful deep hazel eyes could just as easily burn holes in the skin of anyone foolish enough to cross her.

"I think we should stay, captain," she said, a light Texas drawl flavoring her smooth voice. "I completely agree with the XO's concerns about getting word of this back home, but with the alien ships so close now..." She shook her head. "I can't imagine that they'd be anything but insulted if we just up and disappeared on them."

"And the crew?" McClaren asked.

"Everyone I had a chance to talk to, and that was most of them, wanted to stay. A lot of them are uneasy about those ships, but as you said, we just happen to be the 'primitives' in this situation. We'd be stupid to not be afraid, sir. But I think we'd be even more stupid to just pack up and go home."

All of the other department heads nodded their agreement. Each had talked to their people, too, and almost without exception the crew had wanted to stay and meet with the aliens.

It was what McClaren expected. He would have been shocked had they come to any other conclusion. "Okay, that settles it. We stay." That brought a round of bright, excited smiles to everyone but Amundsen, whose face was locked in an unhappy grimace. "But here's the deal: the XO and navigator have worked out an emergency jump sequence, just in case. We'll spool up the jump engines to the pre-interlock stage and hold them there until we feel more confident of the aliens' intentions. We can keep the engines spooled like that for several hours without running any risks in engineering. If those ships are friendly, we get to play galactic tourist and buy them the first round at the bar.

"But if they're not," he looked pointedly at Amundsen, "we engage the jump interlock and the navigation computer will have us out of here in two minutes." That made the survey leader slightly less unhappy, but only slightly. "Okay, does anybody have anything else they want to add before we set up the reception line?"

"Sir..." Sato said formally, again at a position of attention.

"Go ahead, son."

"Captain, I know this may sound foolish," he glanced at Amundsen, who was at the table with his back to Sato, "but should we not also take steps to secure the navigation computer in case the ships prove hostile? If they took the ship, there is probably little they would learn of our technology that would be of value to them. But the navigation charts..."

"It's already taken care of, midshipman," Kumar reassured him from the bridge with an approving smile. Second year midshipmen like Sato weren't expected to know anything about the first contact protocols, but the boy was clearly thinking on his feet. Kumar's already high respect for him rose yet another notch. "That's on the very short list of 'non-discretionary' actions on first contact. We've already prepared a soft wipe of the data, and a team from engineering is setting charges around the primary core." He held up both hands, then simulated pushing buttons down with his thumbs. "If we get into trouble, *Aurora's* hull is all they'll walk away with."

And us, Amundsen thought worriedly.

* * *

The alien ship had activated its jump drive. While primitive, it was clearly based on the same principles used by Imperial starships. Such technology was an impressive accomplishment for any species, and gave the warriors hope that once again they had found worthy adversaries among the stars.

But the aliens would not - could not - be allowed to leave. Together, the battlecruisers moved in...

* * *

"Jump engines are spooled up, captain," Kumar reported from his console. The jump coordinates were locked in. All they had to do was engage the computer interlock and *Aurora* would disappear into hyperspace inside of two minutes.

"Very well, XO," McClaren replied, his eyes fixed intently on the four titanic ships, all of which were now shown clearly in the main bridge display.

Suddenly the ships leaped forward, closing the remaining ten million kilometers in an instant.

"What the devil..." McClaren exclaimed in surprise, watching as the alien vessels just as suddenly slowed down to take up positions around his ship.

"Sir," Kumar exclaimed, "they must've picked up the jump engines activating! I recommend we jump-"

"Execute!" McClaren barked, a cold sliver of ice sliding into his gut. Then he jabbed the button on his command console to open a channel to the crew. "General quarters! Man your battle stations and prepare for emergency jump!"

"Interlock engaged," came the unhurried and unconcerned voice of *Aurora's* navigation computer. "Transpace countdown commencing. Primary energy buffer building. Two minutes remaining."

McClaren looked at his command console, willing the countdown to run faster. But it was a hard-coded safety lock. There was no way to override it.

"Navigation lock confirmed-"

"*Captain!*" someone shouted.

McClaren looked up at the screen as a stream of interwoven lightning arced from the bow of the alien ship that had taken up position in front of them, hitting *Aurora's* spherical sensor section. Its effect was instantaneous.

"*Jesus!*" someone screamed as what looked like St. Elmo's fire suddenly exploded from every control console and electrical system on the ship. The dancing display of electric fury went on to cover everything, even the clothing of the crew. The entire ship was suddenly awash in electrical discharges.

But it clearly wasn't simple electricity. There was no smoke or heat from overloaded circuits, and no one was injured by whatever energy washed through the ship and their own bodies. Surprised and frightened, yes. But hurt, no.

Then every single electrical system on the ship died, plunging *Aurora's* crew into silent, terrifying darkness.

* * *

Having subdued the alien ship's simple electronic systems, the lead warship made ready the boarding party that had been awaiting this moment. While the great warship's crew now knew the layout of the alien ship and all it contained, including the aliens themselves, down to the last atom, the boarding party would be sent without this knowledge. They would give themselves no advantage over the aliens other than the surprise they had already achieved; even that, they would have given up if they could. They wished as even a field as possible, to prove their own mettle and to test that of the strangers. In this way, as through ages past, they sought to honor their Empress.

As one, the thirty warriors who had bested their peers in fierce ritual combat for the right to "greet" the strangers leaped into space toward the alien vessel. Thirty warriors pitted against seven times as many aliens. They hoped the odds would challenge their skills.

* * *

"*Calm down!*" Chief Harkness's voice cut through the sudden panic like a razor. At her assigned jump station in the survey module inside the spherical bow section, Harkness had immediately clamped down on her own fear in the aftermath of the terrifying electrical surge that apparently had killed her ship. She had people to take care of, and she was too much of a professional to panic. "Listen to me," she told the seven others in the cramped compartment. There were still a couple of them moaning in fear. "Listen, goddammit!" she snarled. That finally got their attention. Of all the things in the ship they might be afraid of, she would be the first and foremost if that helped them hold it together. "Get your heads screwed on straight. The ship's hull hasn't been ruptured. We've still got air. That's priority number one. All the electrical systems must've been knocked out, which is why the artificial gravity is gone, along with the lights." The darkness was disorienting enough, but being weightless on top of it was a cast iron bitch. She was actually more worried that the emergency lighting hadn't come on. Those weren't powered by the main electrical system, and their failure meant that something far worse had happened to her ship than a simple, if major, electrical blowout. "You've all experienced this before in training. So relax and start acting like the best sailors in the Navy. That's why you were picked to serve on this ship." She paused to listen, relieved to hear that the sniveling had stopped, and everyone's breathing had slowed down a bit.

"Now, feel around for the emergency lockers," she told them. "There should be three in here. Grab the flashlights and see if the damn things work." While they could survive for some time on the available oxygen, the total darkness was going to give way to fear again if they didn't get some light.

"Found one, chief," someone said off to her left. There was a moment of scrabbling around, the sound of a panel opening, then a bit of rummaging.

Click.

Nothing.

"Fuck," someone else whispered.

"Try another one," Harkness grated.

"Okay-"

Suddenly she could see something. But it wasn't the ship's lighting or one of the emergency flashlights. It was like the walls themselves had begun to glow, throwing a subdued dark blue radiance into the compartment.

"Chief, what is this stuff?" one of the ratings asked quietly, her eyes, visible now in the ghostly light, bulging wide as she looked at the glowing bulkheads around her.

"I don't know," Harkness admitted. "But whatever it is, we can see now." The compartment was now clearly, if softly lit. "So let's use it and find out what the hell's happened to the ship."

Then something else unexpected happened: the gravity returned. Instantly. All eight of them slammed down on the deck in a mass of flailing limbs and passionate curses. Fortunately, they all had been oriented more or less upright, and no one was hurt.

"Shit," Harkness gasped as she levered herself back onto her feet. "What the *hell* is going on..."

That's when she heard the screaming.

* * *

The warriors plunged toward the alien ship. They wore their ceremonial armor for this ritual battle, eschewing any more powerful protection. They soared across the distance between the ships with arms and legs outstretched, enjoying the sight of the universe afforded by the energy shields that invisibly surrounded them and protected them from hard vacuum. They needed no devices to assist in maneuvering toward their target: theirs was a race that had been plying the stars for ages, and their space-borne heritage led them to a fearless precision that humans could only dream of.

They were not concerned about any pathogenic organisms the aliens carried, as the healers who would be sent once the ship had been subdued would take care of such matters. The scan of the alien vessel had revealed an atmosphere that, while not optimal, was certainly breathable.

There was no warrior priestess in this system to bear the honor of leading them in this first encounter, but no matter. The senior warriors were well experienced and had the blessing of the Empress: they could sense Her will in their very blood, as She could sense what they felt. It was more a form of empathic bonding than telepathy, but its true essence was beyond intellectual understanding.

As they neared the ship, the warriors curled into a fetal position, preparing to make contact with the alien hull. The energy shields altered their configuration, warping into a spherical shape to both absorb the force of the impact and force an entry point through the simple metal rushing up to meet them.

The first warrior reached the hull, and the energy shield seared through the primitive alien metal, instantly opening a portal to the interior. The warrior smoothly rolled through to land on her feet inside, quickly readjusting to the gravity that the crew of the warship had restored for benefit of the aliens. The energy shield remained in place behind the warrior, sealing the hole it had created in the hull plating and containing the ship's atmosphere.

In only a few seconds more, all the other warriors had forced themselves aboard the hapless vessel.

* * *

The screaming Chief Harkness heard was from Ensign Mary Withgott. Her battle station was at a damage control point where the spherical bow section connected to the main keel and the passageway that led to the rest of the ship. The damage control point was on the sphere's side of a blast proof door that was now locked shut. She could open it manually, but wouldn't consider it unless she got direct orders from the captain.

"Ensign!" one of the two ratings with her shouted as a shower of burning sparks exploded from the bulkhead above them. The two crewmen stared, dumbstruck, as someone, some alien *thing*, somersaulted through a huge hole that had been burned through the hull and into the damage control compartment.

A blue-skinned nightmare clad in gleaming black armor, the alien smoothly pirouetted toward the two crewmen, exposing fangs between dark red lips. Its eyes were like those of a cat, flecked with silver, below a ridge of bone or horn. The creature's black hair was long and tightly braided, the coils wrapped around its upper shoulders. The armored breastplate had two smoothly contoured projections over what must be the alien equivalent of breasts. While Withgott had no idea what the alien's true gender (if any) might be, the creature's appearance was such that Withgott had the inescapable impression that it was female, a *she*.

The alien stood there for a moment, meeting Withgott's frightened gaze with her own inscrutable expression. Then the sword the alien held in her right hand hissed through the air, cleanly severing the head from the nearest crewman. His body spasmed as his head rolled from his neck, a gout of crimson spurting across the bulkhead behind him.

Withgott screamed, and kept on screaming as the alien turned to the second crewman with the ferocious grace of a hunting tigress and thrust the sword through the man's chest.

Then the fanged nightmare came for Withgott.

TWO

Amundsen knew that he would probably receive a court-martial for abandoning his post in the face of the enemy. But he had few doubts that any of the crew, particularly himself, would survive long enough to have to worry about such technicalities.

While he was the survey section leader, his assigned jump and battle station wasn't in the survey module itself, but in the main damage control point just forward of and two decks below the bridge. Amundsen was a "plank owner" of the *Aurora*, having been with the ship since she was launched, and in addition to being a first-rate astronomer, he was also an engineer who had intimate knowledge of the ship's systems. His job was to help the XO manage the ship's damage control parties during any sort of emergency, and to act as something of an insurance policy for the ship during its many hyperspace jumps.

The compartment they were in, which in everyday use served as the lower crew galley, had one peculiarity that was shared by only a few other compartments in the ship: it had a real viewport, a window to the universe outside the ship, and not just a video display.

After the inexplicable electrical hurricane had swept through the ship, killing all the electrical systems and leaving *Aurora's* crew in darkness without gravity, Amundsen had pushed himself over to the viewport to look outside. He could see the huge alien warship off of *Aurora's* bow. His eyes, which reflected more anger now than fear, took in the thing's smoothly curving flank, which was adorned with great runes that stretched from the pointed prow toward the slim-waisted stern. He guessed that the ship must be at least four, if not five, kilometers long. It would have been a beautiful marvel of engineering if its purpose had not been so openly malevolent.

That's when he saw them: roughly two dozen tiny forms that launched themselves from a bay that had opened like a biological sphincter. Sailing across the few hundred meters that now separated the two ships, he had no doubt as to their purpose.

"Commander Kumar!" he called out to the XO, who had been trying to locate an emergency locker in hopes of finding a light that worked. "Sir, you need to look at this!"

"What is it, Jens?" he replied quickly, making his way over to the viewport.

"Look..." Amundsen pointed at the figures who drew rapidly closer. Over a dozen were going to land on the main habitation section, with the others spreading out to cover the rest of the ship. "Boarders."

Kumar stared, openmouthed, at the approaching aliens. He didn't want to believe it, but there could be no other explanation after what had just happened to the ship. "Bloody hell," he whispered. He turned and leaped away across the compartment, back toward the still-dead damage control console, just as the walls, floor, and ceiling began to glow.

"What the devil?" Amundsen gasped as he pushed himself back from the bulkhead, wondering at this latest horrific display of alien technology. Outside the viewport, the boarding party rapidly approached.

Then the gravity came back on. Amundsen heard a loud thump and a brief cry of pain from Kumar as the man slammed down on the deck. Amundsen fell awkwardly, but managed to roll on his back to absorb most of the impact as he landed. He looked across the compartment and saw the XO sprawled next to one of the tables, his right leg twisted under him. A gleaming white sliver of bone protruded from his left calf muscle: a compound fracture.

He quickly made his way to Kumar's side.

"Commander..." It was then that he saw the pool of blood spreading from beneath Kumar's head. He felt for the man's pulse and was rewarded with a faint but steady beat: he was still alive, but clearly badly injured and in need of immediate medical attention.

Kumar's condition left Amundsen in a very difficult situation. In a battle, which this clearly had become, his duty was to stay at his post until or unless relieved: if engineering could get the electrical system back up, he needed to be here to help the damage control parties get to where they were most needed. Or do what he could to help repel boarders.

He was normally the only one posted here during a jump sequence, to act as a partial backup to the bridge and engineering in case something went wrong with a jump. Kumar had only been here because the captain had wanted a bit of extra human redundancy for this particular jump contingency. But none of the half dozen ratings who had their battle stations here had arrived after the captain had hurriedly sounded general quarters. Amundsen figured they had either become lost when the lights and gravity went off-line, had been trapped by the sealed compartment doors, or had been injured like Kumar.

For now, at least, Amundsen was on his own.

He knew that he should first try to get help for Kumar, but he also desperately wanted to get in contact with the captain. Despite the mysterious blue glow that provided enough light to see by, and the convenience the return of artificial gravity afforded, there was no doubt that these were engineered somehow by the aliens. There was absolutely no question that they were now *Aurora's* masters.

The thought suddenly made him uncharacteristically angry. No, more than that: he was enraged. Amundsen had never been an excitable man, nor had he ever been prone to anger, even in the most provocative situation. But these aliens had attacked *his* ship, the ship he had been with since her keel had been laid. The ship they were playing with like a toy and treating her crew, men and women who, while not really his friends, he had come to deeply respect, like rats. And now they had the balls to send over a boarding party...

Something in him suddenly melted and flowed away like white-hot steel. He hated to leave Kumar and knew that he was doing what The Book clearly said he shouldn't. He knew he could be shot if a court-martial found him guilty of abandoning his post in the face of the enemy.

But when he heard the shouts that suddenly rang out down the passageway that led to the rest of the ship, he knew that he had no more time to consider. The boarders had arrived.

Moving quickly, he left the galley compartment and headed down the passageway in the direction opposite from where he heard the shouting. He knew exactly where he needed to go.

The ship's armory.

* * *

"Damage report!" McClaren's voice cut through the sudden darkness and eerie sensation of weightlessness. He didn't shout, nor did his voice contain any trace of fear. He had always been a problem solver. This was a problem, albeit an incredible one, and he focused himself on finding a way to solve it.

"Everything's off-line, captain," Raisa Marisova reported quickly from somewhere in the absolute darkness. With Kumar down in damage control, she was the acting first officer on the bridge. Her voice expressed her nervousness, but she was on top of it. "All systems, including the battery-powered backups, are dead." She paused. "No communications, nothing. As far as I can guess, the hull hasn't been ruptured. I can't hear any air escaping."

Despite himself, McClaren smiled. *Here we are*, he thought, *in a ship that's a marvel of modern technology, and in the blink of an eye we've been reduced to relying on some of Mankind's oldest sensors.* He knew that engineering would be working on trying to get the ship's power back up, but he had to reestablish contact with the crew. And find out what the devil the aliens were up to.

"Captain!" the yeoman at the communications station yelped. Her console, followed by every surface of the bridge, began to radiate a deep blue glow.

It gave McClaren the creeps, but at least it peeled back the darkness as he floated next to his command chair. "Take it easy," he soothed. "Maybe the aliens are just giving us a hand-"

The return of gravity came as an unwelcome surprise. Some of the crew had been strapped into their positions, some hadn't. There were several meaty thumps as those like McClaren, who hadn't been strapped in, unceremoniously fell to the deck. Fortunately, no one had any injuries more serious than bruised dignity.

"Let's get the door open," he ordered gruffly as he stood up with as much grace as he could manage, "and find out what's going on in the rest of the ship."

Marisova led two of the other bridge crew to the door and directed them in removing the manual access panel on the wall near the floor. It was a cumbersome, if straightforward process of first unlocking the door (all the major compartments of the ship automatically sealed themselves when the hyperspace jump interlock had been engaged), and then turning a crank to open it.

The door was open almost enough to squeeze through when McClaren heard angry shouts and screams of fear coming from both directions down the passageway that led fore and aft. He shoved himself sideways into the still-widening gap in the doorway, determined to find out what was happening. Looking down the passageway toward the bow, he couldn't see anyone. They'd be in the compartments, not running around in the passageways, but that's where most of the screaming was coming from.

Suddenly he felt what could only be Marisova's powerful grip around his arm, yanking him bodily from the doorway, back into the bridge.

"What the devil-" was all he had time to say as the blade of a sword cleaved the air where he had just been.

"Close the door!" Marisova barked at the two stunned crewmen who were still cranking the door open. *"Shut it now!"* She had seen the alien rush up behind the captain as he struggled in the doorway, and hadn't paused to think. She had just reacted, grabbing her skipper and using her considerable strength to pull him back just as the creature attacked.

McClaren faced the thing that stood on the other side of the doorway, baring its fangs at him. It pointed its sword at his chest, and he noticed the black rapier claws on its hands flexing just as the door slid closed.

* * *

Ichiro Sato fought to control his fear. It was an oily, slippery sensation that coiled and uncoiled in his gut. It wasn't because of whatever had happened to the ship that had cast them into darkness and shut down the artificial gravity. It wasn't the fear that the aliens might be hostile.

It was the dark. It was always the dark. His roommates at the academy had always thought him strange for keeping a tiny flashlight by his bedside. He claimed that it was simply in case of emergency, a prudent preparation for the unknown. He rarely used it anymore, but even at the age of nineteen the fear would sometimes come back. He would wake up in a cold sweat, panic welling in his chest until his hand found the comforting shape of the light, itself no bigger than his thumb. Just touching it would usually reassure him enough that he could control his raging fear, but sometimes he had to turn it on. Just to peel away the darkness.

When he was a young boy and his father was particularly displeased with him, which was often, he would lock Ichiro in a tiny closet in their apartment. His father had gone to great trouble to ensure that there was enough air, but that absolutely no light penetrated his son's prison. And there Ichiro would have to sit, silently, until his father chose to release him. If the boy made so much as a whimper, his father would drag him out and beat him and then throw him in for even longer. Breaking the unwritten law of female submission that was typical for many families on Nagano, his mother had tried to stop her husband once. He had beaten her savagely, and she had been greatly shamed when she had to go out in public. Until the bruises healed. After that...

Ichiro shook himself. *The past is gone,* he told himself. *Focus on now.* Reaching into his tunic with a shaking hand, he removed the tiny flashlight he always kept with him. He squeezed it to turn it on, but nothing happened. Like everything else electrical in the ship, it was dead.

He felt a wave of panic rise like bile in his throat.

"Ichiro, are you okay?" a disembodied voice asked quietly from the darkness. He suddenly found a comforting hand on his arm. It was Anna Zalenski, the senior of the three midshipmen. Ichiro was a second year at the academy, she was a fourth year. He felt her hand move down to take his. Ashamed that he needed such comfort, he nonetheless returned the reassuring squeeze she gave him. He also silently thanked her for not bombarding him with any reassuring *it'll be all right* platitudes.

He got his breathing under control. He told himself firmly that it would indeed be all right. The captain would know what to do.

A burst of what was no doubt a very poetic curse in Chinese filled the compartment as Petty Officer Yao struggled in the dark to get the hatch from auxiliary engineering open. While China and Japan on Earth had never exactly gotten along famously, Ichiro had taken an immediate liking to Yao Ming. It was a feeling that was echoed by the older enlisted man toward the young midshipman, although Yao would never have publicly admitted it. A human encyclopedia of curses (in Mandarin, of course, with happily provided translations into standard English, which had come to be known simply as "Standard") who always wore a smile, Yao was also a genius with computers. He had been offered the chance to go to officer candidate school numerous times, but had politely declined. "If I did that," he had said in his very formal Standard grammar, "I can no longer do that at which I am best." The logic was irrefutable. He had no higher ambitions than to be just what he was.

Not surprisingly, his post was in the computer operations center, which itself was separate from the physical computer core, down toward the engineering section. And since Ichiro and Zalenski had demonstrated very high aptitudes for applied computing, it had only made sense for the captain to assign them to Yao as a mentor. "Just don't repeat anything he teaches you in Mandarin in a bar," the captain had warned them with a smile, "or you'll wind up with somebody swinging a chair at your head."

Yao had taken on the youngsters eagerly, teaching them all he could and enjoying their company immensely. Over the six months they had been together, the three had become close friends (although Ichiro still hid his feelings). The midshipmen reminded Yao of his own children, whom he missed terribly.

The compartment suddenly began to glow as if it were radioactive, and Yao uttered another passionate stream of expletives.

Ichiro could see him now, crouched down by the door. The access panel was open, and he carefully cranked the handle a few times, opening the door just a hair.

"I wished to verify that the passageway was still holding atmosphere," he told them, almost as an aside. "I had not heard any sounds of decompression, but one may never be too careful."

He began to vigorously crank the handle, and the hatch began to smoothly open.

Ichiro made to get out of his chair (Yao always insisted that both midshipmen strap in for every jump) when the older petty officer admonished him, "Remain in your seat, please, young sir." It was as if he had eyes in the back of his head.

"Right, Ming," Ichiro said sheepishly, calling Yao by his given name as he relaxed back into his combat chair. He noticed Anna smiling at him, and a hot flush of embarrassment crept up his neck as he realized they were still holding hands. With a shy smile, he squeezed her hand once more and then released it. He saw her smile back.

"Ah!" Yao exclaimed suddenly as the gravity returned. He was already in a semi-crouch next to the panel, holding himself in place with one hand braced against the access panel while he cranked the door open with the other. His feet flexed as they took up his weight, almost as if he had been somehow prepared for it.

Ichiro felt his weight return, of course, but because Yao had kept them strapped in, he hadn't been at any risk of injury. Yao looked after his midshipmen like a mother, and of all the duties the man had, it was the one he took most seriously.

"Perhaps our illustrious engineers have managed to partially repair the ship's systems," he said with a big grin as he stood up and turned toward them, the door now fully open. "Now let us seek out the rest of the crew-"

"*Yao!*" Anna screamed in warning, pointing past him into the passageway.

Ichiro, who had momentarily been preoccupied with unfastening his combat harness (even though Yao hadn't yet given his permission to do so), snapped his head up in time to see a humanoid apparition smoothly step into the compartment. It looked much like one of the pictures of Samurai warriors his grandfather had been fond of showing him. And this warrior, for she could be nothing else in any civilization, was as frightening to Ichiro as fully armored Samurai must have been to simple peasants in long-ago Japan. Clad in shimmering black armor with a sword clutched in her right hand, she fixed the two young midshipmen with the predatory gaze of a big cat.

Suddenly realizing that Yao was standing right beside her, she spun with unbelievable speed, bringing her sword up to slash at his neck.

Ichiro watched in awe as Yao, standing still with a serene expression on his face, suddenly *moved*. Stepping fluidly toward the alien like fast-flowing and deadly water, he blocked her sword arm with his own left arm, breaking her attack. At the same time, he pushed out with his right hand against her upper left arm and chest, momentarily pinning her arm, neutralizing it, before sweeping his hand up to hammer the elbow of her sword arm, causing her to lose her grip on the weapon. His left hand smashed into the side of her face in a brutal open-handed attack that stunned her, followed by an open-palm strike by his right hand straight into her face that snapped her head back. Then Yao grabbed her sword arm with both hands and yanked her down along his right side, exposing the base of her skull to a savage strike from his left forearm.

The alien crashed to the floor, unconscious or dead, her sword clattering to a stop at Yao's feet. The fight had lasted little more than a second.

Anna and Ichiro gaped at Yao, completely stunned. "Ming..." Ichiro managed, "...how?"

The little man, his face still bearing a serene expression, ignored him for a moment as he knelt down to pick up the alien's sword. Standing up, he assumed a fighting pose, then swung it through the air with professional interest. "Magnificent," he conceded quietly, impressed by the weapon's balance and, in truth, its beauty. The craftsmanship that went into making the weapon was astonishing.

"Ming?" Anna urged, now free of her combat harness. She and Ichiro moved next to the older man, who held the alien's sword carefully down by his side.

"It is what I have been teaching you, of course," he chided gently as he searched the alien for any other useable weapons. She had a long knife and what looked like some sort of *shuriken*, commonly known as throwing stars. But these alien weapons were different, something that clearly required considerable skill to use. Ignoring them, he took the knife. "Not all the forms of *t'ai chi ch'uan* are slow and gentle," he explained as he gracefully stood up. Yao had taken to instructing them in *t'ai chi* as a way to help them stay in good shape, and as something enjoyable to do together. But he had never let slip the fact that he was, and had been for quite some time, a *t'ai chi* master whose close-quarter combat skills were lethal.

Without hesitation, Yao handed the alien's knife to Zalenski. She was senior to Ichiro, and also had some limited close-combat training.

While he felt a momentary flush of shame, having grown up in a very male-dominated society, Ichiro knew that Yao had made the right choice. It was one of the many ironies of his own youth that he had grown up on a world where ancient martial arts were nearly worshipped. But his father had never bothered to teach his "worthless offspring" any of what he knew, and Ichiro purposefully showed no interest. While he would have treasured having such skills now, he doubted he would have survived his father's methods of instruction. His grandfather had tried to pass on what he could, but what Ichiro remembered from those days was little more than pleasant memories.

"Come," Yao said, leading them out into the main passageway that wound its way through the ship. He turned left, heading toward the bridge, then stopped.

Three alien warriors, swords drawn, blocked their path.

Yao, his face serious now, turned to the young midshipmen. "Run, children," he said quietly, before turning his attention back to the enemy.

* * *

The screaming suddenly stopped.

A few moments later, Harkness could see the alien moving toward them up the passageway from the damage control point, the strange blue glow that illuminated the ship's interior glinting from the thing's black armor. Harkness saw the sword and knew that the dark streaks running its length must have been from blood. Human blood.

Like most of the other members of the crew, Harkness had never had any formal close-combat training. The closest thing she'd ever had to that was brawling in seedy bars. When she was new to the Navy she had started her share of fights. As she'd risen in the enlisted ranks, she'd broken up her share. But her style of fighting was limited to in-your-face punches and smashing beer bottles over the head. And the last thing anyone had ever worried about in the list of potential situations *Aurora* might encounter was a hostile boarding. But here they were. Aliens. On her ship. Killing her crew.

"Fuckers," Harkness hissed, her fury boiling away any trace of fear she might have had.

"Chief," Seaman First Class Gene Kilmer asked, "what do we do?" A big man who'd done his share of brawling and more, Kilmer's ham-sized fists were clenched tight, his eyes fixed on the approaching apparition.

"We take back our fucking ship," she replied. Turning to the others, she said, "Grab anything you can use for a weapon. There's seven of us and one of them. Some of us are going to get tagged," she watched the alien raise its sword as it approached, "but we can take this one easy."

The rest murmured agreement and quickly scattered through the module, grabbing whatever they could to throw at or strike the alien.

Harkness had a sudden inspiration. She reached under one of the consoles and grabbed a miniature fire extinguisher. It was small, about the size of a beer bottle, and didn't have anything harmful in it. But it might give them just a second of surprise.

"Let it come in here," she told the others, spreading them around the module away from the doorway.

Without hesitation the alien stepped into the module, surveying her planned victims with what Harkness was sure could only be boredom.

Keep thinking that, you bitch, Harkness thought as she stepped toward the alien. Three meters. Two. The alien began to raise her sword. Then Harkness darted in just a bit closer and triggered the fire extinguisher in the creature's face.

The alien closed her eyes and whirled away, trying to avoid the white spray.

"Now!" Harkness yelled, and the six other crewmen, led by Kilmer, leaped at the alien, swinging or thrusting whatever they had chosen as a weapon.

The alien blindly lashed out and caught Seaman Second Class Troy Fontino across the ribs with her sword, slicing muscle and bone as if it were paper. He collapsed to the deck, howling in agony.

But that was the only chance the alien got. Kilmer slammed into her, knocking her to the deck, and the others dog-piled on top of them. Kilmer was holding a heavy lead-lined isotope container, and started slamming it into the alien's head, over and over, while the others kept the alien's arms and legs pinned. He kept hammering at her, reducing the left side of her face to pulp, until he heard Harkness call out to him.

"Kilmer," she said in an oddly subdued voice, "that's enough."

He smashed the container into his lifeless opponent one last time, then turned to look up at Harkness, his face spattered with alien blood.

Three more aliens had suddenly appeared, and one of them held a wicked looking knife at Harkness's throat.

* * *

At first the warriors found nothing but hapless creatures that were as meat animals before their swords and claws, crying piteously for what must be mercy. But it was a mercy they would not be shown. The warriors understood the concept, but no mercy would be shown to those who would not fight.

Moving through the alien ship, they sought not to simply slaughter these beasts that largely mimicked their own form, but to bring them to battle, to see if they were worthy of the honor of the arena. Other species in millennia past had proven worthy opponents for Her Children, and it would be a great blessing to find another.

Such encounters were momentous events in the history of the Empire, and the Empress had decided to send a warrior high priestess to act as Her eyes and ears, Her sword and shield. This priestess was the Empire's greatest warrior.

She had not come by ship, but had simply materialized on the command deck of the lead warship, transported from the far side of the Empire in what was purely an act of will by the Empress. Such were the least of Her powers.

Standing quietly aboard the great vessel, the warrior priestess cast her mind outward to the alien ship, noting with quiet satisfaction that the aliens were beginning to pose a challenge to the warriors. They were starting to fight back.

Perhaps they would be worthy opponents, after all.

* * *

McClaren still stood staring at the closed door, trying to believe what he had just seen. *Alien boarders with swords*, he thought. *What the devil?* "So much for first contact," he muttered hoarsely.

"Captain," Marisova said quietly, "what do we do?"

For the first time in his career, McClaren didn't have an answer to that. Marisova's question really got to the heart of what being a captain was all about: showing or telling people what needed to be done. Letting them use their brains to figure out things as much as possible, but when all hell broke loose, it all came down to that one question, and the captain was always expected to have an answer. He had to have the answer, because the captain was one step down from God.

For all that, McClaren was first and foremost an honest man. He was lousy at poker and couldn't tell even the smallest white lie without giving himself away. Besides, the people he worked for, his crew, deserved only his best.

"I don't know, Raisa," he told her, loud enough for the others on the bridge to hear. He swept his gaze over them in the strange blue light the aliens had somehow provided. "But here's what I *do* know," he told them firmly. "Yes, we're in a bloody pickle," that was as close as he ever got to cursing, "but we're not going to panic. We've lost control of the ship, and our first priority is to try and regain control, at least long enough to make sure the computer is destroyed and our navigation records are kept out of enemy hands." He didn't bother calling them *aliens* any longer. "To do that, we've got to somehow reestablish contact with the rest of the crew to make sure someone else does the job, or somehow get past those...things out there," he gestured toward the closed door, "so we can make sure it's done ourselves." He paused. "Without power, that's the only option I can think of, unless someone else has some bright ideas?"

The others were silent. The bridge only had one exit. As for weapons, unlike some of the other compartments that had some items handy that could be pressed into service as weapons, there was really nothing on the bridge they could use but their own bodies.

"Okay, then," he said quietly. "Let's get the door open. There won't be any finesse to what we do after that, because we don't have a lot of options. Just-"

He saw the pilot's eyes go wide, looking past him, and McClaren whirled around just as the door, hardened alloy that was ten centimeters thick, suddenly glowed white and then just disintegrated into a pile of coarse black powder on the deck.

Beyond stood the alien that had tried to attack him earlier, and one of its companions, wearing nearly identical armor. The first one darted forward, raising its sword to strike.

McClaren didn't even pause to think. He had grown up in a tough neighborhood in a gray-hearted city on the world of Bainbridge, and had managed to channel his violence into boxing. He probably could have made it as a professional on the Bainbridge circuit, but that wasn't where he wanted to take his life. He had always been captivated by the stars, by all the worlds that humanity had found and colonized, and by the new ones that appeared in the news reports. He wanted to be an explorer. As it turned out, he managed to get accepted to the Terran Naval Academy because of his "sports" abilities. He wasn't the most promising of the plebes that year, but he graduated second in his class four years later, with the additional title of world college middleweight champion. Not bad for a kid with skinned knuckles who'd grown up fighting his way out of the slums.

Those instincts and the many hours he had devoted since then to keeping in top shape served him well now. As the alien's sword reached the top of its deadly arc, he danced forward - *fast* - and faked a left hook that drew the alien's attention, just as he'd hoped. It dropped its sword arm, the right arm, to try and block his strike, and lashed out with the claws of its left hand just as McClaren twisted his body, throwing all his power into his trademark right cross. His fist slammed into the alien's jaw, rocking its head back. He could hear and feel the *crunch* as the creature's jawbone broke under his knuckles, but he didn't stop there. The alien's armor limited the options he had for punches, but when it lost its balance, reeling backward, its right arm, still clutching the sword, windmilled upward, exposing the armpit. McClaren had no idea if the alien's physiology was anything like a human's, but he wanted to take the sword out of the equation and it was a target of opportunity. His left arm swept up in a powerful jab that landed squarely under the alien's arm where there was no metal armor to protect the bundle of nerves that served the arm, only what looked like smooth leather.

With a grunt of agony, the alien dropped its sword and slammed against the bulkhead next to the door. McClaren was going to move in and finish it off, but suddenly Marisova was there. She grabbed the warrior's right arm, paralyzed from McClaren's left hook, and snatched it up in a fireman's carry. McClaren watched, wide-eyed, as his navigation officer tossed the alien over one shoulder, then smoothly dropped to a kneeling position on the same side. Marisova had one arm still wrapped around the alien's neck, guiding its spine down to the navigator's bent knee. McClaren clearly heard a wet *crack* as the alien slammed down, its head bent back at an extreme angle over Marisova's leg.

He was no surgeon, but to him that sounded like a broken neck. *Score one for the home team*, he thought grimly, turning to the other alien behind him.

The creature simply stood there, its outstretched sword keeping the other members of the bridge crew at bay for the few seconds he and Marisova had taken to finish off its partner. While he couldn't read the alien's body language or expressions, if he had to guess, he'd say it looked satisfied.

"Your turn," he growled as he moved toward it, fists raised in their ready position, with Marisova moving off to one side to flank the creature.

But he never got a chance for a second round. The alien casually brought its free hand to the collar around its neck, from which hung a dozen or so glittering pendants, and touched it in a peculiar fashion.

McClaren's vision exploded in a white flash before darkness took him.

* * *

Ichiro sprinted down the passageway, Anna right behind him. His gut boiled with fear and self-loathing, feeling like a coward for abandoning Yao Ming. But his friend's quiet order to run had left no room for doubt or argument.

And so the two of them ran. At first, Ichiro had no idea where they were going, except to get away from the three aliens who had confronted Yao Ming. The ring of sword against sword still echoed in his head, and tears threatened to burn his eyes at the thought of Ming being killed. But Ichiro's subconscious was guiding him with a purpose, even if it was one he didn't understand or recognize.

He and Anna, breathing hard with the exertion of running and fear of what must be somewhere behind them, suddenly found themselves standing in front of the doors to his quarters. These doors weren't designed to be airtight, nor were they normally locked. Taking the alien knife from Anna's hand, he shoved it into the center slot of the door and pried it open enough to get a grip with his fingers. Then he simply shoved it open enough for them to enter.

"In here," he breathed, grabbing her arm and leading her inside.

"We can't hide here, Ichiro," she gasped, trying to catch her breath as he handed the knife back to her. He could run like a greyhound, and she'd had trouble keeping up. "The door..."

"We didn't come here to hide," he told her as he quickly rummaged around in the closet at the end of his bed. *Aurora* was a naval vessel, but her accommodations were far more luxurious than any warship designed strictly for combat: even the midshipmen had their own tiny cabins, and plenty of storage space. It was a small tradeoff for deployments that could last a year or more.

"Ichiro..." Anna said worriedly, keeping her eyes on the door.

"Ah..." he said finally. She watched as he pulled something out of the closet that was over a meter in length, and that at first glance looked like a shiny black tube several centimeters across, slightly curved...

"Is that a *sword*?" she asked, incredulous. Personal weapons like that were not normally allowed aboard ship.

"Yes," he told her as he held the *katana* by its handle, then reverently drew the gleaming blade from the polished black scabbard. He had been tempted to show it to Yao Ming once, but had chastised himself for wanting to show off. He had no idea how impressed his friend would have been with the quality of the weapon. "It belonged to my grandfather." He glanced at her as if reading her mind. "The captain gave me a waiver for it. It is the only thing I have to remember my family by."

He had no time to tell her about the old man, and about how much he'd loved him. His grandfather had been the only thing to keep Ichiro's father in check, at least until he was paralyzed from the neck down in a freak transportation accident when Ichiro was only five years old. After that, bedridden in a closet-sized room at the back of his family's apartment, the father of Ichiro's mother endured his own special form of hell. But it was a hell he and Ichiro shared, and the old man was the boy's childhood hero. His grandfather had been a great swordsman, his mother had told him, and the old man had told his grandson what he could of his former life, and showed him pictures from books and the information network, when his father was not around, of what it meant to be a warrior. He couldn't train the boy in the way of the sword, but he could teach him what it meant to have a sense of honor.

"He never had a chance to teach me to use it," Ichiro explained softly. "But he always told me that it was the spirit of the warrior that mattered most." He looked at her, fierce determination lighting up his eyes even as tears streaked down his face. "I accept that I will die here. But I will *not* dishonor him. Nor will I dishonor my shipmates."

She leaned forward and gently kissed him on the lips. Anna had entertained fantasies about being more than friends with Ichiro, but she realized now they would never have the chance. "Let's go," she said quietly.

They left his quarters and moved quickly down the main passageway that would eventually lead them toward the bridge, Anna still clutching the alien knife, Ichiro holding his grandfather's *katana* at his side.

Turning a corner that would lead them to a set of stairs that would take them up to the level the bridge was on, they nearly collided with two aliens coming in the opposite direction.

Ichiro, simply reacting on instinct, brought his sword up over his head for an overhand slashing attack, while Anna backed away slightly: her knife had no business in this particular fight.

The alien easily parried his amateurish attack with her own sword, then casually moved in close to slam her opposite elbow into his jaw.

Dazed, Ichiro was sent flying to the deck. The only thing he was conscious of was that he had managed not to drop his grandfather's sword. Anna moved to a position between him and the two aliens, holding her knife in an underhand grip.

"Come on," she hissed at them. "*Come on!*"

As one of the aliens made to step forward, an ear-splitting roar filled the passageway, and her head disappeared in a spray of bone and gore.

Quick as a cat, the other alien went for something on her shoulder that looked like some sort of throwing weapon, with several wicked blades attached to a central hub, but she never reached it.

There was another roar, and the second alien pitched forward, a hole the size of a dinner plate in her chest.

Her ears ringing, Anna looked around to see what, *who*, had done this, when Lieutenant Amundsen stepped around the corner from the direction the aliens had come, smoke streaming from the muzzle of the M-22 Close-In Assault Rifle he was holding. Pausing just long enough to give each of the aliens a spiteful kick, Amundsen quickly made his way to Ichiro and helped him up.

"Lieutenant..." Anna said, so grateful to see him that she nearly burst into tears.

"Are we ever glad to see you!" Ichiro finished for her, his jaw aching fiercely.

"You're the only two I've found so far who are alive," he told them grimly. "The rest..." He shook his head slowly.

After leaving Kumar behind, an act that threatened to crush him with guilt, particularly once he saw what had happened to most of the rest of the crew, he had gone to the ship's small armory. Amundsen couldn't fight worth a damn with his hands, but he knew how to handle a rifle. He wasn't an Olympic marksman by any stretch, but at the ranges afforded by the ship's passageways and compartments, he didn't have to be.

The main problem had been getting into the armory, which was no more than a small locked closet inside one of the ship's storage holds that held a few "just in case" weapons and ammunition that the ship's designers had put in as an afterthought. But he didn't have to use his knowledge of astronomy, physics, or engineering to open the armory. Some problems yield themselves quite satisfactorily to the judicious application of a crowbar and hammer.

After that, moving through the ship had been a nightmare. He hadn't gone through all the compartments, of course, but from what he'd found so far, *Aurora* had become an abattoir. He had vomited after stumbling across the first butchered bodies, and periodically had been beset by dry heaves ever since. He had never seen a dead body before, let alone one of someone he'd known and worked with. Some bodies had been decapitated. The heads were strewn about the deck, expressions of terror forever fixed to their faces. Some bodies had arms or legs hacked off...

He shuddered, then went down to one knee as he felt his gorge rise again.

"Lieutenant?" Anna asked worriedly, putting a hand on Amundsen's shoulder.

"I'll be all right," he said hoarsely, trying to regain his composure. A genius in many ways and aware of the fact, he had never claimed to be a leader of men. But he realized that he had a responsibility now to these two younger almost-officers. While his rage at what the aliens had done was as fierce as ever, he wasn't on a quest for vengeance anymore. He had to try and look after these two. And find the captain. "It's just..." he shook his head and chuckled mirthlessly. "Never mind." He forced himself to stand up. "Come on, let's see if we can get to the bridge and find the captain."

They made their way back to the stairs leading up to the next level, only to find another pair of aliens standing halfway up the steps, as if they had been expecting the humans.

Amundsen reacted instantly, bringing the rifle to his shoulder and sighting down its length at one of the alien horrors, but he never had a chance to pull the trigger.

One of the aliens already had her hand on her collar, touching it *just so* as Amundsen raised his weapon to fire.

The last thing he saw was a blinding flash of white. He hit the floor, unconscious, the two midshipmen collapsing beside him.

THREE

"Sir? Captain, are you all right?"

McClaren heard the voice as if from far away, through a dull ringing in his ears. He tried to open his eyes, and was rewarded with a thousand hot needles lancing into his optic nerve. He hissed with the pain.

"It'll pass in a minute, captain," the voice said again, closer this time. Chief Harkness. "You must've gotten a big jolt," she went on quietly, her hand on his shoulder. Her touch felt very warm. "Fucking alien bitches," she suddenly spat.

He smiled grimly. Whatever had happened to the ship, he was glad Harkness had made it. This far, at least.

"How many," he asked her, squinting up into her worried face. "Do you know how many of the crew...are okay?"

For a moment she didn't answer, but looked up at someone else. His eyes followed her and found Amundsen, kneeling at his other side.

"Twenty-three survivors, sir," he said quietly. "Including yourself."

McClaren couldn't hide his shock. "*Twenty-three?* Out of a crew of two hundred eight?" They helped him sit up. The aliens had gathered the human survivors in *Aurora's* main galley.

Amundsen was only grateful that it hadn't been the lower galley where he had been forced to abandon Raj Kumar. The ship's XO was not among the survivors, and Amundsen had seen enough in the rest of the ship to know what must have happened to him. "Yes, sir," he said. "That's all. Everyone else is..." He shook his head slowly.

McClaren didn't have to hear the word to know that all the other men and women of his crew were gone. Dead. Amundsen's haunted eyes told him that they hadn't gone down easily. He remembered the swords that the aliens who attacked the bridge had been armed with, and imagined the havoc that such weapons could cause in the close quarters of a ship. *Fucking alien bitches*, Harkness had said. He couldn't have agreed more. "Get me up," he ordered. Harkness and Amundsen helped the captain to his feet, where he stood, swaying. His inner ears were playing tricks with his balance, and he smelled the sharp scent of ozone. But his vision was clearing, and he took a look around the galley.

The members of his crew, what was left of it, all stood to attention. Marisova and the rest of the bridge crew. Yao and two of the midshipmen. The half dozen sailors from the forward survey module. Another half dozen from the engineering section. Harkness. Amundsen. And himself.

Then he saw the blood. The left side of the galley was covered in it, with pools of it among the tables. He stared at the streaks and sprays of crimson that stained the dark gray deck tiles and the white walls. Even the ceiling. So much blood. He couldn't tear his eyes away.

"They allowed us to move the bodies, captain," Amundsen explained, nodding toward the four aliens who stood wary guard at the galley's entrance. "Six crewmen were cornered in here. We...moved the remains into the storage closet in the back and covered them."

McClaren turned back to Amundsen. That was when he noticed the blood on Amundsen's uniform. On his hands and arms. On his face. McClaren imagined, *knew*, that this is what the entire ship was like. It had become a slaughterhouse. His stomach suddenly dropped away into a bottomless abyss, and he felt his sanity starting to follow down after it. *No*, he told himself desperately, trying to reassert control of himself. *No! The crew needs you. You're not taking the easy way out. You can't.*

Forcing his eyes shut, he blocked out the horror for a moment. He took a deep breath to calm himself, but the smell of blood suddenly poured through the stench of ozone he had been smelling. The coppery scent threatened to overwhelm him, and he started to lean over, about to vomit.

He suddenly felt a steadying hand on his shoulder again, squeezing tightly. Chief Harkness. He covered her hand with his, squeezed it tight in return. He willed away the tears as anger began to replace despair.

At last regaining his composure, he let go of the chief's hand and turned back to his crew. *Back to business*, he told himself. "Does anyone know if the engineering crew was able to destroy the navigation computer core?"

"No soft wipe was performed, captain," Petty Officer Yao told him immediately, his eyes downcast. That would have been his responsibility had the order been given. He knew intellectually that there was no way he could have wiped the core after the aliens overwhelmed the electrical system, even had he been given orders to do so. The order had never come, but he felt a sense of shame nonetheless.

Beyond that, Yao was not even sure how he had survived to be here. After he had told the two midshipmen to run, he had turned back to fight the aliens confronting them. They surprised him by refusing to fight him as a group, only singly. But after he had managed to kill two in a set of fierce sword fights, the last one had somehow paralyzed him and rendered him unconscious. He remembered nothing else until waking up here, maybe fifteen minutes ago.

"There was nothing you could have done about that, Yao," McClaren reassured him. "If anyone is to blame, it's our blue-skinned hosts."

"Captain," Amundsen interjected, "I went through the computer core compartment before I met up with the midshipmen," he nodded to Anna and Ichiro, who stood next to Yao. "The engineers weren't able to set off any charges because of whatever the aliens did to our power systems. They opened the core manually and tried to destroy the primary crystals. Some of them were destroyed, but..."

"There would have been far too many to destroy in such a fashion in the moments they had before the enemy arrived," Yao finished for him. He had spent more time in and around the primary computer core than anyone else in the ship, and he knew better than most the futility of trying what the engineers had done. But he gave them great credit for making the attempt, and said a silent prayer for their spirits. He and Amundsen had talked briefly before the captain woke up from the stun he had received, and the computer core had been their first topic of conversation. The younger officer had described the carnage he had found in the compartment, where three young engineers armed only with basic tools had fought against some of the alien warriors. The engineers had died, but they had taken one of the aliens with them, a long screwdriver shoved through her neck. The alien's killer, a young woman Amundsen had barely recognized, lay dead beside her, the alien's knife still buried in her chest. "They will have destroyed some information," Yao went on, "but the chances are great that most of the navigation data remains intact. The system is holographic and redundant. Critical data is stored and phased across multiple crystals."

"People," McClaren told them through gritted teeth, "the aliens *must not* be allowed to retrieve our navigation data. We cannot allow these...*things* to discover where we came from." He swept his gaze over the blood stains left on the galley walls and floor. "We can't allow this to happen to our home planets-"

"Captain," Harkness interrupted softly, "look."

McClaren turned to see half a dozen warriors enter the galley, taking up positions next to the four already standing guard. They were accompanied by four more aliens who wore no armor, but simple white robes and collars around their necks. Aside from their mode of dress, they looked identical to the warriors. Looking more closely, he noticed that these aliens didn't seem to have claws on their hands. Then he took a close look at what each of them was holding.

"What the hell is *that*?" one of the crewmen behind him said, a thread of fear twisting through his voice as he saw the same thing that McClaren had noticed.

Each of the robed aliens held an amoebic mass of what could only be living tissue. Roughly the mass of a grapefruit, each of the gelatinous blobs was dark green and purple, slowly writhing in their bearer's hands.

McClaren felt an immediate visceral revulsion toward the things, and almost in unison the humans stepped back, away from their captors.

The warriors took that as a cue to move forward, spreading out with their swords held at the ready to deter their captives from doing anything rash. Two moved over to one of the young female ratings from engineering, roughly grabbing her arms and dragging her toward the waiting robed figures and their undulating pets. She screamed and struggled, kicking fiercely at the warriors' legs. One of them raised her sword hand to smash her in the face-

"Stop!" McClaren boomed. The aliens may not have understood the word, but they certainly seemed to understand a command voice when they heard it. The warrior about to strike the woman paused, turning to look at him, as did the others of her kind. McClaren calmly walked over to them. "Let her go," he said quietly, gesturing at the young woman the two warriors held. "Take me instead." He pointed at himself.

The warriors paused, still holding the woman, when one of the other warriors standing near the robed aliens spoke. "*Ka'ana te lath.*" The young woman was immediately released, and her captors looked expectantly at McClaren.

"Go on, Ramirez," he told the woman, "get back with the others."

"But captain..." she whispered hoarsely, her frightened eyes darting to the robed aliens and what they held waiting for him.

"It's okay," he reassured her with a confidence he didn't feel. He glanced at Amundsen, and the younger man nodded sadly. *You're in charge now, lieutenant,* he told himself. But he didn't trust his voice to speak the words aloud.

With that, he turned and walked toward the galley table the four robed aliens had gathered around. One of the warriors stopped him, then in a few swift motions with an incredibly sharp knife cut off his uniform, even his boots. The robed aliens gestured for him to lay on the table, and he did so, the cold metal burning against the skin of his naked body. Then the four robed aliens gathered around him and one of them began to knead the mass of pulsating tissue she held.

The crew watched in horrified fascination as the alien worked the strange tissue like it was pizza dough, expertly kneading, pressing, and twirling it until it was no thicker than a piece of paper, but large enough to cover McClaren's entire body. With one last twirl, she let go of the thing, and it settled through the air to land on him.

As the hideous shroud touched him, McClaren suppressed a scream. It wasn't because the thing was causing him pain, because it wasn't. But he felt such a primal *wrongness* as it touched his flesh. It was cool and slimy against his skin, covering him from head to toe, and he desperately held his breath, because the thought of that thing falling into his mouth was a nightmare come to life.

Then he felt it start to move. It began to wrap itself tighter about him. It wasn't constricting him, but seemed to be making a better fit for itself, like a self-shaping glove. He even felt it somehow working its way under him, insinuating itself between his body and the table. The sensation of being completely encased in oozing, living slime was hideously unpleasant even before it began to probe his nostrils and ears. Then it started on his eyes, forcing itself between his tightly shut eyelids. Nothing being sacred to this alien horror, it pressed against his anus, even the opening of his penis.

Between that and his burning lungs, McClaren had had enough. He tried to move his arms to clear the thing from his mouth and nose, but any movement he made was futile: this thing seemed slimy and malleable, but when he tried to move it hardened like concrete. He was totally immobilized.

He willed himself to hold his breath until he was unconscious, but his body betrayed him. With a soundless scream on his lips, he opened his mouth wide as his body forced him into a last-ditch attempt to gather in some air. As if it had been waiting for this, the thing rushed into his mouth, then down his throat as the tendrils invading his nostrils suddenly pulsed through his sinuses, then expanded down his trachea into his lungs.

On the verge now of blacking out, McClaren was sure he was going to die. Absolutely, positively sure.

But as the slime entered his lungs, the strangest thing happened: the urge to suck in huge breaths abated, and the stars that were forming in his vision as his brain ran out of oxygen disappeared. He wasn't breathing, but he was clearly getting oxygen now. The slime was somehow doing it.

Then he felt a sensation of pleasant warmth. It wasn't localized to one spot, but was throughout his body. He'd never felt anything like it before. It was as if someone had taken a magical heating pad that didn't just lay on a part of his body, but actually became a part of it, warming and massaging every cell. He was afraid to admit it, but aside from a brief flare of hot pain in his lower back, this part of this bizarre experience was actually pleasant.

Suddenly he became aware that he could move his arms again. Not only that, but his eyes seemed clear. He blinked them open to see the four robed aliens looking at him attentively. He held up one of his hands to look at it, and saw the last traces of slime as it sank into his flesh, as if it had melded with him on a cellular level. He ran his hands over his chest, his upper thighs: the slime had disappeared. *Right into his skin.*

He lay there for a few more moments before he felt a tremor in his chest. The terror suddenly returned, with visions of some nightmarish apparition bursting from his rib cage, but fortunately he was disappointed. Another moment of increasing discomfort passed, and then suddenly the entire mass of slime forced itself back out of his lungs, oozing out of his mouth.

"Agghhh!" he gagged as the thing's keeper retrieved it. He had no idea how the whole thing had managed to get into his lungs. It was as if it had somehow penetrated his body like some sort of biological scanning device, then gathered in his lungs for convenient extraction.

The robed alien, who seemed distinctly more pleasant than the warriors, gestured for him to get up. He made to return to the others, but she gently stopped him. Standing behind him, she ran her hands professionally (he had no other word for it) along his lower spine. Then she gripped one of his hips and put her opposite hand on a shoulder, gently pushing him forward, apparently trying to get him to bend forward at the waist. He did so, and after she ran her fingers over a few of his lumbar vertebrae, she gestured for him to straighten up, which he did. She exchanged a few quiet words with the warrior who had spoken earlier, and then gestured for him to return to the others.

As McClaren rejoined his elated crew, who pointedly ignored his nakedness, something struck him as odd: his lower back, where he had felt the surge of painful heat earlier, now felt fine. Better than fine. It felt perfect. And he knew that it shouldn't, because he had a very mild case of arthritis in his lumbar region that the ship's surgeon had warned him would ground him at the end of this deployment. It didn't interfere with his duties, and consistent exercise helped keep it at bay, but it was a constant source of mild discomfort. Now it was gone. And the robed alien had known it would be; that's why she examined that particular area. Somehow, that blob of slime had communicated to her whatever it had done, or seen, in his body.

The fucking alien bitches, as Harkness had called them earlier, had completely cured him.

* * *

The warriors looked on as the animal who was dominant convinced the others to come to the healers without further struggle. One by one, and then in groups of four, they came to be tended. The healing gel was the only instrument used by the healers other than some specialized potions; it was the only instrument needed. A product of forced evolution millennia long past, the gel was at once an organism unto itself, yet also a part of the healer to which it was bonded. It had no intelligence of its own, yet could perform the most complex tasks to heal or repair another organism, even a completely alien species.

Through this unique symbiont, the healers could "see" the bodies of the aliens down to the sub-cellular level. While the purpose of the healers here was primarily to learn all there was to know about the aliens' physiognomy, they also employed the gel to seek out any pathogenic organisms and compounds that could be harmful to Her Children. At the same time, the gel immunized the aliens against potentially harmful pathogens carried by the denizens of the Empire, and also did for them what it was normally meant to do: heal disease and repair injury.

Once the healers had finished their task with the living humans, they communed with another group that had studied the remains the warriors had left behind. Pooling the gel together, each symbiont exchanged its information with the others. The healers, their minds conditioned to assimilating such information, now understood the human body and its inner workings far better than all of humanity's physicians combined.

In the human sphere, such information would have to be communicated elsewhere by technology. But an outside observer would have seen no technology in evidence here: once the symbionts had digested the information about the aliens and been merged together, other symbionts throughout the Empire began to spontaneously mutate, reflecting this new knowledge.

The final task of the healers was to transfer the genetic knowledge from the symbionts to the members of their own race to immunize them. This was accomplished for the warriors and other castes simply by placing a small piece of the symbiont on any convenient patch of skin: it merged into the flesh of the patient and made any necessary alterations. The symbiont regenerated itself by merging with its parent healer, whose body provided the necessary nutrients for recovery. This immunization was accomplished quickly throughout the Empire, not just to those here in this system.

For while the final test of the aliens had yet to be performed, the Empress had sensed enough through the blood of Her Children here to know what lay ahead: war.

FOUR

"Lord of All," McClaren breathed as the alien gently shoved his naked body through the perfectly circular hole, about three meters across, that they'd cut in the side of his ship. He had thought at first that they were going to push him into hard vacuum through some sort of invisible barrier, for there was nothing visible between the *Aurora's* hull and that of the enemy vessel that now stood very close alongside. But he had seen that there were warriors at a few spots along the invisible gangway that somehow linked the ships, and that had held his fear in check. Barely.

But my God, the view, he thought as he crossed over the threshold from the metal deck into the void. Suddenly leaving the ship's artificial gravity behind, his stomach momentarily dropped away as he became weightless. He could see down the *Aurora's* flank, noting the holes where the enemy warriors had burned through the hull to board his ship.

Then there was the enemy ship - *huge!* - that didn't look a thing like any spacecraft ever made by humankind. The smooth metal (he assumed it was metal) of the hull gleamed a deep but brilliant green, with contoured dark gunmetal-colored ports and blisters where he assumed some sort of hatches or weapons were mounted. Unlike a human ship, which was a patchwork of plates, the surface of the alien ship's hull was as smooth as a still pond: he couldn't see any joints or welds, rivets, screws or other fastenings as he got closer. It was as if the hull was one gigantic sheet of...whatever it was made of. The craft was all graceful curves, as if it were designed to fly in an atmosphere, with none of the boxy fittings and other angular projections typical of human ships. Looking forward, he saw that giant runes were inscribed along its raked prow, perhaps proclaiming the ship's name, whatever it might be.

And all around him: the stars. As if his hand had a will of its own, he reached out to touch them. He knew they were billions of miles away, but they seemed so close. The alien sun burned brightly mere millions of miles away, and a point of light far brighter than the other stars proclaimed itself the planet from which the four warships had come. He had been on plenty of spacewalks, but this wasn't the same. Maybe it was the emotional exhaustion of the last few hours since the alien ships had been spotted. So little time on the scale of his life, but an eternity for those who had lived through it.

The stars. Part of him knew that this would be the last time he would ever see them. He looked outward, and the unfeeling Universe returned his gaze.

He felt one of the warriors take his arm, amazingly gently, he thought, to propel him onward to his destination. With one last heartbroken look at *Aurora*, he turned toward the open maw of the alien ship that awaited him.

Behind McClaren, the other survivors of the *Aurora* were ferried along, naked and still dazed from the emotional and physical trauma of the healing gel. Even though a number of them had performed spacewalks countless times, they gawked in awe at the great Void around them, and felt a deep tremor of fear at the huge alien warship that seemed in their eyes as big as a planet.

As McClaren approached the "hatch" of the alien ship, he looked closely at the smooth petals of the material (he was less and less convinced that anything on this ship was metal as he understood it) that had irised open. He had no doubt that when this aperture was closed, it would be totally invisible against the hull. Or maybe the aliens could open an aperture like this anywhere, if needed.

His professional curiosity warred with the fear of what would happen to humanity if these creatures were able to trace the path *Aurora* had taken here. His failure to ensure the navigation computer core had been destroyed ate at him like a bitter acid in his gut. And with his crew now removed from the ship, any opportunity - *Not that there really had been any,* he thought bitterly - to somehow break free of the warriors and destroy the core had been lost. His only hope now was that the *Aurora's* computer technology was sufficiently alien that they couldn't figure it out. But after seeing what the aliens with the goo did with his body, and the heart-stopping technology he saw in this ship, he knew that hope was truly a vain one. It was a disaster of literally stellar proportions, and he knew his name would go down in history as the man who had unwittingly opened the human sphere to invasion. The thought was a crushing blow to his soul.

He floated across the threshold into the alien ship, and a gentle artificial gravity gradient allowed him to land gracefully on his feet. There was a phalanx of warriors waiting for the humans to arrive, and a pair escorted McClaren down the connecting passageway that, like everything else on this ship, was huge: it could have easily accommodated a pair of elephants walking side-by-side, with room to spare.

As on the *Aurora* after the aliens had attacked, the walls themselves gave off a soft light. Unlike the dark blue glow on the *Aurora*, however, this was near the color humans viewed as normal sunlight, although tinged with magenta. It gave him the impression of an everlasting sunrise, a thought that struck him as supremely ironic given the very questionable nature of his fate.

The deck felt soft and warm to his bare feet, its dark gray surface pebbled to provide a superior grip. Like the rest of the hull, he had the impression that this wasn't any sort of metal, and he was struck by the thought that perhaps the ship was semi-organic. The thought of such radically advanced technology chilled McClaren to the bone.

By contrast, the walls and ceiling appeared to be nothing more sophisticated or high-tech than stone, perhaps a type of granite that was a very pale rose color. He thought for a moment of the ancient burial places like the Pyramids on Earth, where the walls and rooms of the dead were decorated with ancient writing. For that's exactly the way these walls appeared: there was writing everywhere in the form of alien runes, as if the walls and even the ceiling were part of a giant book that someone had written. Chancing that his guards wouldn't notice or perhaps care, he drifted to one side of the passageway and stretched out a hand to touch the wall's surface. While it could certainly be artificial, to his touch it felt like nothing more sophisticated than very finely polished granite. But how the aliens made it give off light to illuminate the passageway, and why they would have something like stone for the interior of a starship, he couldn't even guess.

Making sure he kept pace with the warriors, who seemed content not to harass him, he glanced back to check on the other members of his crew. Like him, each of them had a pair of warriors as escort, except for Yao Ming, who was surrounded by four warriors. McClaren's people were spaced out evenly behind him at five meter intervals. Those who saw him looking nodded back, fear written plainly on their faces. After the slaughter on the *Aurora*, there was no reason to think anything pleasant awaited them here.

* * *

Like the rest of the crew, Yao Ming had been appalled at the wanton murders of the rest of the crew. But unlike the other survivors, he had seen such horrors before. The colony world on Keran where he had been born and raised had been settled by an unlikely mix largely made up of ethnic Chinese and Arabs. The two communities, while maintaining distinct cultural identities, interacted peacefully and had rapidly expanded from the original towns they established on landing to intertwining cities and villages. While not a rich world compared to many, it was prosperous and generally peaceful.

But when Yao Ming was eleven years old, an ethnic Chinese gang that had been brutalizing the local Arabs and that local authorities in his town had been unable to control finally went too far: they kidnapped, gang-raped and murdered three young Arab girls. What turned out to be the final insult that made a violent confrontation inevitable was that they stuffed the girls' mouths with pork before they killed them.

Citizens of both communities were shocked and horrified. A local mullah wasn't satisfied with the claims by the police that the gang would be brought to justice, since they never had before. He led the grief-stricken worshippers in his mosque, nearly two thousand of them, including the parents of the murdered girls, on a rampage through the adjacent Chinese district.

While the violence was localized and didn't affect the overall population, Yao Ming's neighborhood became a killing ground as the frenzied mob surged through the narrow streets. Armed with everything from fists and knives to assault rifles (authorities later determined that more than a few of the perpetrators had gone to the mosque bearing concealed firearms), they grabbed, mutilated, and killed anyone in their path who couldn't run away fast enough. They surged into shops, homes, and apartments, leaving a trail of bloody carnage: nowhere was safe. Some of the Chinese tried to stand and fight, but they were simply overwhelmed by numbers.

Yao Ming's parents were among the victims, caught in the local marketplace as they did their daily shopping. Both of them were masters of *t'ai chi*, a skill they had been passing on to their only son, but even that couldn't save them from the mob. As Yao himself had told the midshipmen to run when he turned to face the aliens who had boarded *Aurora*, his parents had said the same to him that day before plunging into the seething mob, fists and feet flying. His escape had been a harrowing flight through blood-filled streets that still haunted his dreams. He never saw his parents again, for they were among the hundreds who died that day.

Now, walking through this alien ship, he had the honor of having not just two, but four warriors as escort. Unlike those escorting the others, these had their swords drawn and were exceptionally alert. Having killed three of them in close combat earlier, the first with his hands and the other two with the sword from the first one, Yao took some measure of grim satisfaction that they felt he was more of a threat than the others. But he had no illusions about what probably awaited them. Just like McClaren, he had taken a last longing look at *Aurora* before stepping aboard the alien warship, because he knew in his heart that he would never see her again.

After moving through what Yao estimated to be nearly half a kilometer of twisting and turning passageways, they came to a huge door. Like most of the other doors they had passed, this one was deep black in color, polished to a reflective shine, with runes similar to those carved in the stone-like material of the passageway walls. However, these runes were much larger, and inlaid with a material similar in appearance to lapis lazuli.

The door stood partway open, and Yao's guards ushered him in, following the remaining human survivors. Inside, there were more aliens of what he assumed was another caste. Like the ones who had applied the healing gel earlier, these wore robes, black, this time, and also lacked the lethal claws of the warriors.

This group, numbering perhaps fifty individuals, wasted no time carrying out their task. Two quickly approached each human and began to take measurements with what Yao realized was nothing more ominous than a tailor's cloth measuring tape. While these had no numbers or other markings that he could discern, the way the two aliens stretched it along various parts of his body left no doubt. After his parents had been killed, he had gone to live with his uncle, his father's only brother, who worked as a tailor and taught young Yao Ming his craft, along with continuing his education in *t'ai chi*.

"Mister Yao..." he heard young Sato call to him quietly from off to one side.

"*Kazh!*" one of the boy's escorting warriors hissed. The aliens hadn't harassed the humans coming here, but they had refused to allow them to speak to one another.

Yao met the young midshipman's gaze and nodded, adding a wry smile as a small gesture of reassurance. Whatever was to come, at least they would not have to die naked.

* * *

The armorers worked quickly, as was their custom. While their caste was known for its great skill in handling the living steel from which their weapons were forged, they also created the other clothing and accessories in which their race was attired. Ignoring the strange coloring and pungent scent of the strangers, but welcoming the fact that they were amazingly similar to Her Children in form, they measured their bodies in the time-honored fashion. Like their sisters throughout the Empire, in all the castes, perfection was the goal toward which they strived from birth until beyond death, and they allowed themselves no room for error. Measuring several times, they left the main hall for a series of anterooms where their materials waited. The strangers would not receive any armor, for the priestess had determined that they did not wear such things, and thus would not be accustomed to it.

Instead, the aliens were given only the undergarments worn by all the castes, be it beneath armor or robes. Like virtually all things made by the hands of their race, it was the essence of perfection and would last indefinitely if given a small amount of care. The armorers fashioned close-fitting long sleeve shirts and long pants of a black gauzy material that was perfectly smooth against the skin. It would keep the wearer cool in the heat, and warm when it was cold, and this batch of the material had been specially prepared to accommodate the strangers' unique thermal requirements. Each piece would fit the individual wearer perfectly, tailored only for them. It would stretch effortlessly, but would never bind or lose its shape. Since it had been created to be worn under armor, it never interfered with a warrior's movements when in combat.

Once the armorers finished covering the aliens' pale bodies, they shod their feet in traditional black sandals, open-toed with wraps that secured them above the wearer's ankles.

* * *

Amundsen wasn't sure what bothered him more, the overt advanced technology such as the ship, or the almost supernatural craftsmanship of everything the aliens made. The clothing in which he now found himself, as the humans were once again herded down the labyrinthine passageways, fit, literally, like a custom-made glove. He had owned tailored clothes, but they were nothing like this. The material itself would be worth a fortune for its clearly advanced properties, and the fit was astonishing. The footwear, in particular, felt like part of his body. This was no small achievement, for Amundsen had a slight deformity in his left foot that required custom-made shoes. But, like his tailored clothes, they were nothing compared to this.

The reason it bothered him was that these aliens seemed to do what they did, be it healing or making clothes, almost by instinct. They did it perfectly, every time, apparently without the assistance of anything he could recognize as technology as he understood it: there were no machines, no computers; only simple tools like the cloth measuring tape. From the looks he had exchanged with the other members of the crew, particularly the captain, it was clear that everyone else was equally awed by the clothes they now wore. Most of them even wore smiles at the incredibly pleasant feel of the garments, at least until they remembered how they had come to be here.

The warriors, certainly, had more advanced technology available to them, such as whatever device they used to stun a number of *Aurora's* crew. Yet their preferred weapons would have been at home on any battlefield on Earth before the widespread use of gunpowder weapons.

That and the lack of claws among the robed castes, which appeared to be natural, and not a surgical modification, as best he could tell, made him think that this species was likely far older than humanity. Yet how much older, and how much more advanced, he couldn't hazard a guess.

But the biggest puzzle was that they had seen no males. He didn't want to make any assumptions about why that might be. They knew almost nothing about this species, except for their predilection for violence, but he found it extremely curious. Since he and his shipmates hadn't exactly had a chance to do a full physiological examination of the aliens, perhaps they were hermaphrodites. But something in his gut told him otherwise: even though their paths of evolution had followed somewhat different courses, his own race and the aliens shared far more similarities than differences. He was convinced that all of the aliens they had seen so far were biologically female.

His internal analysis was interrupted when the humans were herded through yet another massive door, far larger than the others they had passed. Inside was a gigantic compartment hundreds of meters across that reminded him of an amphitheater, with concentric rows of steps for spectators to stand on so all could clearly see what transpired on the "stage" below.

The humans were positioned in the last row, behind two other rows of perhaps three dozen aliens. Spaced wide apart in a semicircle around the stage, these aliens also wore robes, but of a dark blue color. The aliens stood erect, staring at the stage, holding their hands out in front of them as if they were pushing something away. While he couldn't read their body language, it was clear that they were concentrating intently on the stage below.

As he looked down at the dark surface, he discovered that it was more akin to a huge liquid pool whose surface had been completely still when they first walked in, with whatever it contained merely mimicking a solid surface.

Suddenly the material in the pool below began to morph, and he watched with growing horror as it took shape.

* * *

"That's impossible," McClaren breathed as he watched the apparition begin to rise and take shape in the alien cauldron that lay below. He tore his gaze from the thing and looked first at Amundsen, then Yao. Both of them were staring back at him, eyes wide with shocked disbelief.

McClaren, in what was a major act of will, turned back to look at what was taking form, somehow being created, cloned, using the black material in the pool: the *Aurora's* central computer core. Next to it the navigation core began to take shape. Just like with the healing goo, the black material in the pool was being used as a matrix to create whatever the blue-robed controllers willed. The components were still taking shape, with the various assemblies supported by tendrils of the shimmering black material. McClaren had no idea how the aliens did it, but they must have made an incredibly detailed scan of his ship, probably as part of whatever happened to the electrical system. And now, as humans could model a three-dimensional object in a computer and have a machine produce an exact physical replica, the aliens were recreating the computer systems here. He realized with a sinking feeling that it wouldn't have mattered if they had blown the computer hardware to bits. The aliens already had what they needed. And he no longer entertained any hopes that they would have difficulty interpreting the computer data. They would get whatever they wanted, and there wasn't a bloody thing he could do to stop them.

Before his eyes, the computer systems continued to take shape. While he only saw the exterior of the components, he knew with cold certainty that the memory crystals, which were custom grown in a zero gee environment, were forming inside, and that the data held in their matrices would be completely intact. Threads of the black substance connected to the extruded human technology where optical links and power conduits entered the system, providing power and input/output streams that the human design could interact with.

He chanced another glance at Yao. The brilliant petty officer's face was ashen. Yao would know better than anyone, even Amundsen, the implications of what they were seeing. None of them were good.

In a few minutes, the entire array of hardware and necessary peripheral systems had been created. McClaren heard a series of soft clicks, and then the telltale lights on the core casings flashed on: the system was booting up.

* * *

The priestess watched silently from the shadows, invisible to the aliens, as the builders performed their work recreating the alien ship's control system. While primitive, she nonetheless granted them respect for the achievement of creating systems that took them to the stars, and courage for relying on such simple machinery to take them there.

The matrix in the formation pool below was an analog of the symbiont used by the healers. Advanced as it no doubt appeared to the aliens before her, it was a feat achieved in what were now very ancient times, and was one of the many examples where the lines between technology and biology had become blurred. The builders, those who created that which the Empress required, from tiny things invisible to the naked eye, to entire worlds, no longer used the interfaces that were once required to control the matrix material. Their evolution was shaped by the Empress over the ages, and the power to control the creation of inanimate objects was now an effort of will, guided by the mental vision of what was desired. Like the healers, the minds of the builders could grasp the totality of a thing, see its construction on a subatomic level. Her race did not use computational devices, computers, as the aliens might understand them, for her people had no need. The use of such things had long ago faded into the Books of Time.

But that did not prevent the builders from understanding and creating what was needed. The alien machines quickly took form, and the matrix was guided into providing the necessary electrical input and other connectivity. The major challenge the builders faced was to recreate it exactly as they had memorized it when the alien vessel had been scanned, and not to improve upon it. Otherwise they would have finished much more quickly.

The system activated, and they monitored its initiation sequence. In their perception, time was variable: they could slow down events relative to the actual timescale. In this way they analyzed each function undertaken by the machine. They did not learn the language the machine used, exactly, but they understood on a fundamental level how it worked, much as the healers understood the aliens' bodies after they had been treated with the healing gel. Following the machine's primitive processing routines was a laborious, excruciatingly painstaking experience, but the builders excelled at such things. And with the priestess looking on, her Bloodsong echoing strongly in their veins, the builders' usual obsession with perfection was taken ever higher.

At last they understood what they needed to know about the machine and the data it contained. Others would be required to interpret most of it, but one thing they could show the priestess now...

* * *

"Oh, *fuck.*"

McClaren heard the words, but didn't know or care who said them. He wasn't a man who used foul language, but in this case the words exactly fit his feelings.

Above the pool, where the clones of the ship's computer systems hummed with unnatural life, a stellar chart began to form. It was hologram, incredibly realistic, that spread across the entire breadth of the huge theater. It displayed the series of waypoints tracing *Aurora's* path to reach this system, and after a moment additional data began to appear for each waypoint. Much of it was visual, with realistic representations of the system stars and planets, but some of it was also being translated from Standard into the aliens' language, judging by the runes that began to appear next to a number of the systems and waypoints.

He thought his sense of horror couldn't get any worse until he saw the first colony world on the Rim, the last friendly port of call before *Aurora* had jumped into the unknown, appear in the rapidly expanding course the ship had taken. Much more data in the aliens' language suddenly appeared next to it, suspended in the darkness above the renegade computers. Then onward to the next, and the next.

Finally, there was Earth itself, the home port from where they'd sortied months ago. The home of Mankind.

And then came the final insult: the navigation trace shifted to show Earth at the center, and outward from there every single human colony and settlement was displayed. The aliens might not have everything sorted out yet, for a great deal of information was stored away in files that they would have to learn Standard to interpret, but McClaren had no doubt they would: among its other wonders, the computer contained a complete educational library. And then every single human being would be at the mercy of these monsters.

He turned again to look at Amundsen and Yao, but instead caught a fleeting glimpse of a towering figure detaching itself from the shadows along the wall at the rear of the theater. Clearly a warrior, and the largest he had seen by far, she silently disappeared into the passageway, her black cloak swirling behind her.

FIVE

Ichiro marched along between his two guards as the humans were once more paraded through the ship. He had been trying to keep careful track of the turns and distances, and he guessed that they must be somewhere close to the center of the great vessel. He had been shocked by what he'd seen in the theater they'd just come from, his fear hammered deep by the ashen looks on the faces of the officers and Yao Ming.

Beside him, one of his guards carried his grandfather's sword. It was clear that she was handling it very carefully, as if it were her own treasured heirloom. She wore a weapon that bore more than a passing resemblance to the *katana*: a gently curved blade, somewhat longer than his grandfather's weapon, that ended in an elaborate but functional guard plated in what appeared to be gold, and an equally elaborate grip. That, of course, wasn't the only weapon she carried: there were three of the throwing-style weapons clinging to her left shoulder, and a wicked-looking long knife with a crystal - *Diamond?* he wondered - handle strapped to her side. Most of the other warriors were similarly equipped, although every single weapon except for the throwing stars, for lack of a better term, appeared to be custom-made. While sometimes similar, no two were exactly alike.

His reverie ended quickly as they passed through a portal that was even larger than the one to the theater. As the humans were escorted in, a chill ran down Ichiro's spine. This, too, was a sort of theater, but not one he wanted to be in: it reminded him all too clearly of the Colosseum of ancient Rome that they had studied as part of their military history lessons. In fact, had Roman gladiators been snatched through time and dropped onto the sandy arena that must have been nearly a hundred meters in diameter, he had no doubt that they would have felt completely at home. It was built from tan-colored stone, the finely set blocks polished to a smooth finish. While it wasn't dilapidated like the Colosseum, Ichiro couldn't shake the uneasy feeling that this alien version was terribly old, perhaps older than Rome itself.

The seating was arranged in two dozen or more rising tiers, and Ichiro wondered at the size of the crew this vessel must carry: if this was designed purely for those aboard this ship, there must be thousands of aliens aboard, yet they had seen so few. There were arched portals arranged around the sand of the circular arena, and above...

He paused, another wave of awe momentarily suppressing his fear. Above him was a blue sky, slightly tinged with magenta, and a bright sun. It didn't just look like it was outdoors, as if it were a good projection or hologram, it felt like it, too: the radiant warmth on his face from an alien star, just the touch of a breeze, and faint odors from what must be some type of alien flora, and not the scents they had noticed thus far on the ship , which had mostly reminded him of cinnamon. There was a palpable sense of scale that he had only ever felt planetside, almost as if they'd been teleported off the ship and onto an alien world.

But when he turned around to look behind him, the passageway and the portal through which they'd entered were still there.

After a moment of allowing the humans to gawk freely, their guards again ushered them onward. Descending through a set of wide, curved steps, Ichiro followed the others into a large anteroom that let onto the sands of the arena through one of the portals that he'd seen earlier. He half expected there to be torches on the walls and gladiators preparing themselves for combat.

When black-robed aliens entered the room, he realized that while the light was coming from the walls and not ancient torches, there were indeed gladiators here: he and his shipmates.

The warriors took up positions along the walls as the robed ones brought in a veritable arsenal of weapons, from daggers and throwing knives to spears and pikes, and swords of a bewildering variety. They arrayed them carefully on several low benches clearly tailored for the purpose, then stood off to one side.

* * *

The ritual had its origins in time before legend, and the aliens were not expected to understand. As with many things in the lives of those who served Her, tradition and ritual reminded the living of the past, and were a mark of the personal discipline and obedience of Her Children.

These aliens, the survivors of the original crew, would fight for the honor of their race. They likely would not comprehend why they were about to die, and win or lose, it would not avert the fires of war that would soon descend on their worlds. It was for the sake of honor, and honor alone. The outcome was inevitable, for in this ritual there were no survivors, save one: the Messenger, who would be spared to tell the tale of what had happened here. And to tell of what was soon to come.

After the armorers had laid out a suitable assortment of weapons the aliens could arm themselves with, should they choose, the bearers of water brought food and drink. The builders had replicated samples of the food and liquids aboard the ship, based on what the healers had told them would be appropriate. Fearing a trick, no doubt, one thing they need not have feared from their hosts, some of the aliens refused the refreshments; others consumed what they would.

The priestess watched them with her second sight, content to let the aliens eat in peace. When they had finished, she nodded to her First, who commanded that the warriors and clawless ones enter the arena and take their seats, spectators to the ritual combat that was soon to begin.

As they quickly filed into the arena's stands, the priestess decided that it was time to greet the aliens herself, and guide them in what must be done.

* * *

McClaren had forced himself to eat and drink something, not so much because he was hungry or thirsty, but because he suspected he would need the energy soon. He was also trying to lead by example, as some of the crew feared that the food or drinks, which included water, coffee, and beer, of all things, might be poisoned. But McClaren figured that the aliens could kill them a million different ways, and poisoning didn't seem to be their style. Their preferred methods of mayhem and murder seemed a bit more direct.

The other officers had joined him in taking at least a token bite to eat of some of the fruit and other food the aliens had offered. At first he had thought the food must have been taken from the *Aurora's* galley, but on further inspection he decided that the aliens had probably replicated it, just as they had the ship's computer systems. As much as anything, he was curious about the taste, and wasn't disappointed when he sampled one of the apples. It was delicious, and he quickly ate it down to the core, then drank some water.

He noticed Yao moving slowly along the tables holding the weapons, looking at them carefully, and walked over to join him. He knew more about Yao's background than anyone, except possibly Harkness, and he wanted his insights. "What do you think, Yao?" he asked quietly. Since they had arrived in this room, the aliens had relaxed their ban on the humans speaking to one another. He was keeping his voice down because he didn't want the other members of the crew to hear.

Yao paused and looked up at him with troubled eyes. "You realize what is coming, do you not, captain?" He glanced at the others, most of whom stood huddled in a fearful group near the center of the room, watching the warriors along the walls. "The crew...there is no way to prepare them."

McClaren's mind had been grasping at possibilities, at outcomes that would at least give them a chance of survival. "I can't accept that they're just going to kill us," he grated, "not after all this. What would be the point?"

"The point may be irrelevant, captain," Yao replied. "I believe we are to face a test of character," Yao told him. "We will never know the reason behind it, for the aliens cannot communicate it to us, even if they wanted to, and we must accept that. But I do not believe that any of us are destined to leave this place alive." His gaze hardened, revealing the warrior who dwelled within. "The best we may do is to earn their respect."

"I agree," Amundsen said softly from behind them, having quietly moved over to join the discussion. Marisova, Harkness, and the two midshipmen stood with him. "I don't see a positive end-game in this, captain. I realize that I'm usually considered a pessimist, and often enough that's true. But this," he gestured around them, at the weapons, at the portal that led onto the sands of the arena, then shook his head. "I see nothing here that gives me any hope. We're sacrificial lambs."

"Kuildar mekh!" one of the warriors suddenly barked, startling the human survivors. As one, the other warriors lowered their heads and brought their left arms up to place an armored fist over their right breasts in some sort of salute. The clawless ones did the same.

McClaren looked up toward the warrior who had spoken, wondering what was going on, when behind her a huge warrior *walked right through the wall into the room*. Had he not seen it with his own eyes, he would never have believed it.

"Jesus fucking Christ!" someone cried, and the group of crew members clustered toward the center of the room darted away from the apparition like a school of terrified fish.

McClaren realized that it was the same warrior he had caught a glimpse of leaving the theater where they had reconstructed the ship's computers. She was something different from the others, over and above however she had managed to walk through a solid wall. She was easily the tallest being in the room, standing a full head taller than McClaren, with the most impressive physique he had ever seen on a female (if inhuman) form. While her armor was a gleaming black just like the others, hers had some sort of rune of blazing cyan in the center of her breastplate. Her collar was also different, holding some sort of ornamentation at her throat that bore the same marking as her breastplate, and a dozen or more rows of the strange jeweled pendants that the other aliens, including the robed ones, wore from their collars. Only this warrior had far more than any of the others. The claws that protruded from her armored gauntlets reminded him of the talons of an eagle, and were the longest he'd seen by far. Her hair was also much longer than that of the others, but like theirs was carefully braided, with the long coils looped around her upper arms. Her face struck him as regal, with deep blue skin that was as smooth as porcelain. Had her features been translated into the form of a human woman, she would have been a thing of beauty. But here, now...

Ignoring the other humans, she walked straight toward him, bearing a staff in one hand that he knew he would have had difficulty lifting off the ground with one arm.

Mustering his courage, he stepped forward to meet her, gesturing for Yao and the others to get behind him.

She stopped an arm's length away, appraising him with silver-flecked feline eyes that pierced his soul, and he felt as if he was staring into the eyes of a hungry tiger.

In a way, he was not far wrong, for she was the ultimate predator among a race of predators.

* * *

Tesh-Dar, high warrior priestess of the Desh-Ka order and blood sister of the Empress, looked upon the alien in silence. She was the Empire's greatest living warrior, a legend among her fellow warriors, her peers, and had been sent by the Empress to observe these beings. Aside from the Empress Herself, Tesh-Dar was also the most sensitive to the song of the spirit, the Bloodsong, that bound her people together, and to the Empress herself. She had studied the aliens closely in this short time, and while she could sense their minds and their churning emotions, she could hear nothing of the spiritual chorus that might reveal their souls to her questing senses. Without the Bloodsong, they were but animals in Her eyes, beyond Her grace and love. Yet they could still serve the needs of the Empire.

For the way of their race, the *Kreela*, was forged in the fires of battle, and Tesh-Dar knew that they had at last found another worthy foe among the stars. The last such enemy had been defeated and its flame extinguished from the galaxy many generations before she was born. It had been a worthy race that had fought well for hundreds of great cycles until, exhausted at last, their civilization had collapsed in defeat. Unwilling to fight on, no longer able to challenge Her Children in battle, the Empress had swept their race from the stars. All that remained to prove they had existed were the accounts of the war collected in the Books of Time, and samples of stone and flora taken from their worlds, which had long since been reduced to molten rock and ash.

The Bloodsong. It was an ethereal thing, unmeasurable by any instrument or technology, but was as real as the ten thousand suns of the Empire. If the aliens' blood could be made to sing, they would be spared, for they would be one with Her. But if not...

Tesh-Dar nodded to one of the warriors and held out her staff. The warrior took it reverently, and another warrior handed her a small urn whose mouth was large enough for an alien hand to reach inside. Turning to the dominant alien, she offered the urn to it. After a moment of deliberation, the creature took it, holding it in unsteady hands. It peered inside to find it empty.

One of the armorers, a clawless one robed in black as were all her sisters, stepped forward. She held a small disk in each hand: one was black, the other cyan. Tesh-Dar first took the black one in her ebony talons, holding it up to the alien. She gestured with her free hand at the disk, then at the alien, then the weapons, then the sands of the arena beyond. The creature's face began to turn pale, and she could sense its heart beating faster. It suppressed its fear from the others of its kind, but it could not do so against her heightened senses.

She dropped the black disk into the urn, and the armorer produced twenty-one more, dropping them in slowly so that the creature could count them.

Then she handed Tesh-Dar the cyan disk. Tesh-Dar again gestured at the disk, then at the alien, and then she projected an image of the alien ship in the air around them, and pointed to it; the image morphed to show the ship returning to its point of origin, which the priestess now knew was where this species had first been born. As tradition demanded, whichever alien chose the cyan disk would be the Messenger. She dropped the disk into the urn, held in the alien's unsteady hands.

Twenty-three disks.

Twenty-three aliens. Twenty-two would die, and one would live to bring the tidings of war to its people.

She did not have to know their language or read their thoughts to know that the dominant animal and its companions understood.

* * *

"It's a fucking lottery," someone choked in the shocked silence that followed the innocent sounding *clink* made by the last disk, the one McClaren thought of as *the ticket home*, as it fell into the urn he was holding.

"Throw the goddamn things back at them!" Gene Kilmer, the brawny rating who'd been with Harkness when the aliens attacked, shouted angrily.

"No," one of the enlisted men said quietly, his eyes wild. "I'm not going to die here. *I'm not going to die here, do you hear me!*" he shrieked, his eyes a mask of undiluted fear as he backed away from the tall alien woman who now speared him with a rapacious gaze. In a blind panic, he tried to bolt toward the entrance they'd come through earlier, oblivious to everyone and everything around him.

Before the warriors could react, Marisova darted sideways and deftly grabbed the younger man in a full nelson hold, her arms wrapped under his armpits and locked behind his neck, totally immobilizing him.

Harkness was there an instant later, her hands clamped to either side of his face, her nose a centimeter from his. "Listen to me, Lederman!" she shouted, but he continued to struggle, trying to kick her and drive Marisova off balance. Harkness let go of him with her right hand and slapped him hard enough to snap his head back before turning his dazed face toward hers again, her eyes boring into his. "Listen, damn you!" she hissed. "You are not going to panic, you bastard. You are *not!*" She shook him, her hands in his crew cut hair now, holding on so hard her knuckles were white. "Do you hear me? *Do you?*"

Lederman's eyes slowly focused on hers and his struggles eased, then stopped. He sagged in Marisova's grip, and she suddenly found herself not having to restrain him, but to keep him from collapsing to the deck. He suddenly burst into tears. "I don't want to die, chief," he said miserably. "Not like this." He shook his head. "Not like this..."

"We all die, Lederman," Harkness told him, her voice softening as she released her death grip on his hair, her hands moving now to his shoulders, giving a gentle squeeze of comfort. "And most times we don't get to pick how we go. But listen," she told him, leaning to touch her forehead against his, "if we have to die, I don't want to give these fuckers the satisfaction of seeing us afraid. They attacked our ship. They murdered our friends and shipmates in cold blood, Lederman. I don't know about you, but I want some goddamn payback. If they kill me, fine. But I plan on kicking some of their blue-skinned asses before I go down." She lifted his chin with one hand so their eyes met again. "What do you say?"

With an obvious effort, she could see that Lederman was getting it together. He was still terrified, but she could see the spark of anger she'd planted growing in his eyes. "You're right, chief," he rasped, nodding. "Shit, I'm sorry."

"Just use it, Lederman," she told him as she stepped away. "Get pissed at what these bitches did and use it."

He nodded, and Marisova released him. "I'm sorry, captain," he told McClaren. "I...lost it–"

"It's okay, son," McClaren said, nodding his thanks to Marisova and Harkness. "You just said and did what most of us would like to." He looked around at the others. "Petty Officer Yao told me a theory, that this is a test of character, and an opportunity to gain the respect of the aliens. Now that we know what's in store," he gestured to the urn, "I think he's right."

"Captain," one of the others asked, "what if we just refuse?"

Glancing at the tall warrior who stood watching them intently, he said, "We'd be slaughtered where we stand," he said bluntly, "just like the rest of the crew." He paused, thinking of what Harkness had said, and suddenly he felt the fear start to slip away from him. Part of the fear of death lay in uncertainty, the fear of when, or where, or how you would die. But that was gone now. He knew that he was going to die here, in a time probably measured in minutes from now, at the hands of one of these alien warriors. In that moment, he accepted death's inevitability as something more than an intellectual understanding. He looked over to see Yao looking at him, a knowing look on his face. "No," McClaren went on firmly. "We're going to stand and fight. Aside from Yao, most of us don't have extensive martial arts training, so we're at a big disadvantage. But our goal here isn't to win. Our goal is to do what we can to make them pay for what they've done." He could see that his resolution was beginning to take root in the others. Most of them were still clearly afraid, and he didn't blame them a bit. But they were good men and women. The best. And he could think of worse ways to die. "Are you with me?" he asked them quietly.

Each of them met his gaze as he looked around the room, nodding their agreement.

"Okay, then," he said with a grim smile. "So much for the tough breaks. Now for the lucky sod who gets to go home." He gave the urn a good shake, mixing the disks it contained. Then he went to the lowest ranking survivor of the crew, a young African woman who had been plucked right out of advanced training to serve on the *Aurora*. It was to be her first and only deployment. "Subira," he said softly, calling her by her first name, "you get first shot at the golden ticket."

Subira, whose skin was nearly as black as the armor the aliens wore, slowly shook her head. "I'm not leaving, captain," she told him firmly, her face proud and defiant, not toward him, but their hosts. "Let someone else pick first."

He nodded, not trusting his voice as tears began to form in his eyes. He was so proud of her. So proud of them all. One by one, they refused to reach into the urn.

Finally, Ichiro, the youngest among them, spoke. "Captain," he said formally, drawing himself to attention. "Sir, none of us are leaving. We are your crew, and we are staying together. Staying with you."

"Is that what you all say?" McClaren asked them softly. "As honored as I am to have you here, one of us has the chance to get home and tell them what happened here."

"If they want, I'm sure they have the means to send the ship back with the bodies of the crew," Amundsen said darkly. "That should tell the story close enough, sir."

The rest of them nodded agreement. They were staying. All of them.

McClaren turned back to the tall warrior and stepped up to her, his fear gone now. The die was cast. He pointed at himself, then the others, then at the weapons and the sands of the arena where he could see what must be thousands of aliens now.

He held out the urn to her, and she took it. Her expression was unreadable, but if he had to guess, he would have said she was pleasantly surprised.

* * *

As she took the urn back from the dominant alien, Tesh-Dar was indeed pleased. These creatures had demonstrated resilience and a will to survive that would challenge Her Children in the war-to-be, and she eagerly awaited the coming combat.

While the aliens had declined the lottery, a Messenger would still be chosen. A Messenger was always chosen, for that was the way of things since ages long past. She did not know yet which one to choose, but she was content in the certainty that she would when the moment came.

In the meantime, the aliens began to choose their weapons from among those the armorers had provided. And beyond the wide portal to the arena, the peers continued to gather.

SIX

Reduced from the captain of one of humanity's most advanced starships to a gladiator with only modest skills, Captain McClaren stood in the center of the line formed by *Aurora's* survivors in the sands of this strange arena. The stands were packed with alien spectators, thousands of them, who murmured amongst themselves in their own language. As he and a number of the others in the crew had noted earlier, every single one of them appeared to be female: armored warriors or those that wore robes of a bewildering variety of colors, there was not a single male among them that he could see. He realized this would no doubt be important to the xenobiologists back home, but it was purely academic to a man about to die.

Unlike most of the rest of his crew, he had chosen to forego any of the many weapons they had been offered. He was trained as a boxer and knew how to use his fists as weapons. He wasn't as young or as strong as he once was, but he felt better than he had in a long time. He couldn't say that his soul was at peace, exactly, but he was determined to send a clear message to the aliens that, despite their advanced technology and the massacre aboard the *Aurora*, humans weren't going to let them have a free ride. He only hoped that the aliens would meet him and the others on roughly equal terms, or the coming bloodbath would be an extremely brief affair.

He had already said his goodbyes to the others just before they'd been herded out here and formed into a line facing the far side of the arena. He had shaken everyone's hand and told them that it had been an honor to serve with them, and he meant it down to the bottom of his heart. It had taken all his willpower not to break down and cry, not in fear, but in pride at their courage and resolution. If the aliens wanted a showing of the best humanity had to offer, they would find it here among his crew, his comrades.

When the alien warriors gestured for them to move out to the arena, Harkness called the crew to attention, and the men and women of the *Aurora* fell into formation as if they were in a fleet inspection. After a glance at the warriors to make sure they didn't plan to interfere, she turned her attention back to the crew. She cast a critical eye over them to make sure their formation was nothing less than perfect. Then she did an about face, waiting for her captain to take charge.

As McClaren stepped to the head of the formation, he came to attention and she rendered a sharp salute. "Ship's company ready for..." she paused, her face hardening, "...ready for battle, sir."

McClaren returned her salute, snapping his arm up, fingers at his brow. "Post, chief," he ordered her quietly before snapping his arm down to his side.

Her eyes held his for a long moment before she replied, "Aye, aye, sir!" in her best deck formation voice, her words echoing off the stone walls. Then she pivoted on her heel and took up position at the rear of their little formation.

With one last look over the men and women of his command, McClaren marched them out in single file onto the waiting sands of the arena.

* * *

Ichiro stood to his captain's right, holding his grandfather's *katana*. After the captain had given in to the crew's desire to stay, everyone had begun choosing weapons. Ichiro had started toward one of the tables when the alien warrior who had taken his grandfather's sword stopped him. She held it up before him in both hands, arms outstretched, and bowed her head to him as he took it from her, grasping the black lacquered scabbard in shaking hands. She held his gaze, and for just a moment he thought he detected a trace of empathy in her inhuman eyes. She murmured something to him in her language, her long ivory canines flashing behind her dark ruby lips, and then she turned away to join her fellow warriors.

He had left the scabbard behind in the weapons room, for he knew he would never need it again. The weapon felt good in his hands, the carefully wound leather of the handle easy to grip, despite the sweat pouring from his palms. Because he had never had any training in swordsmanship, he knew that he would only last a matter of seconds against any of the alien warriors, who were clearly trained from childhood in combat. But the *katana* represented his heritage, and as his grandfather had often told him, the true nature of the warrior rested in his spirit, not in his knowledge of technique or the weapon he held. He would die, but he would die a man, and with honor.

He hadn't completely mastered his fear, but as the captain himself had discovered, removing the unknowns had allowed him to control it. He hoped it would be quick, but he also hoped that he would give a good accounting of himself before he died, that he would make his grandfather's spirit proud.

* * *

Standing at the far right of the human line, Amundsen had chosen an alien version of the quarterstaff. He had no experience with any of the other types of weapons, but as a child he and his brother had often engaged in sparring with poles not unlike this. He would have been much more comfortable with a rifle, but that wasn't one of the options they had been given, and he was completely useless at unarmed combat.

Like the captain, he had noticed the complete lack of males among the gathered spectators. It was indeed an academic question at this point, but those were the types of things he had spent his life exploring. If he lived only a few more minutes, then it was worth spending them analyzing the aliens. To satisfy his own curiosity, if nothing else. He just wished that he would have been able to pass on the information to someone who could have put it to use.

He guessed there were probably upward of twenty thousand of them packed into the arena to see the coming slaughter. The warriors, so far as he could see, appeared to be a completely homogenous group: all wore gleaming black armor, all wore a black collar around the neck with some number of the gleaming pendants (this adornment appeared to be common to all of the aliens), and all were armed to the teeth with completely customized weapons. The only exception had been the huge alien who had faced off with McClaren in the strange lottery business. She was clearly a warrior, but was not one of the rank and file: aside from her size, she wore that strange adornment on her throat that echoed the rune on her breastplate, carried that huge staff that looked like it probably weighed twenty kilos, and wore a black cloak. Unlike the other warriors, she only carried a single weapon, a short sword, although he suspected that she was more dangerous than a dozen of the others, particularly in light of that walking-through-walls stunt she had pulled earlier. The other crewmen were sure that it had been some sort of illusion using holographic projection. Amundsen hadn't argued, but he was completely convinced that what they had seen had been real: she had somehow walked right through a stone wall that was probably a full meter thick. How she had done it, he couldn't even guess. He didn't believe in magic, but the level of technology this civilization had achieved was so far beyond humanity's that it may as well have been a form of sorcery.

As for the other aliens, they had two common features that were distinct from the warriors: they wore robes and they didn't have any claws on their fingers. It was clear to him now, having seen several of them in action in the last couple of hours, that the color of the robe identified the functional caste (for lack of a better term) of the wearer. What he took to be physicians wore white; the ones who worked on weapons and personal garments and armor wore black; then there was the dark blue of the ones who recreated the *Aurora's* computer systems. All of them were highly specialized, and in some cases, particularly with the physicians and the ones who recreated the computer systems, they apparently were able to interface with other "systems" (if one could consider such things as the healing goo and the black matrix in the tank of the theater as systems) without any visible intervening technology.

Looking through the crowd, he identified at least two dozen different colors of robes being worn. On the surface that seemed like a lot of specialized castes, but on the scale of human technical specialization it was nothing: everything from fixing a toilet to designing a starship required some sort of specialized skills, and it often took years to learn them. Surely the aliens still had need of a a similar variety of skills, far more than the two dozen or so castes here represented. But perhaps their people didn't need nearly as long to learn such skills, or maybe each caste could do many things in a given area. The physicians, for example, replaced in a single caste hundreds of different types of specialists among their human counterparts. They also did a far better job, even having known nothing about their human guinea pigs prior to a few hours ago.

While the others were more concerned about the next few moments, Amundsen's reflections on the nature of the aliens chilled him in more abstract terms: if what he thought was even close to being correct, the aliens would have an incalculable advantage against humanity in a conflict. With warriors like these, backed up by legions of their robed sisters who could create or do virtually anything, they would be unstoppable.

Gripping the quarterstaff in his hands so tightly that his knuckles were bled white, Amundsen for the thousandth time cursed the fate that had brought them to this system.

* * *

Yao Ming stood to the right of young Sato, with Midshipman Zalenski on his own right. By tacit understanding with the captain that was made with no more than a quick look and a nod, he had positioned himself between the two young cadets, with Marisova on the other side of Zalenski, in what he knew was the vain hope of providing them some protection in the coming ordeal. No one doubted the outcome of this alien duel, but Yao was determined that the two youngsters would not be among the first to die.

While Yao had considered one of the finely crafted alien swords, like the captain and a few of the others he had decided that his most trusty weapons were those provided by his own body. He was an outstanding swordsman, but he was even better with his bare hands and feet. And those were the weapons he would use.

While the others stood upon the sands and tensely watched the alien crowd, wondering what would happen next, Yao was thinking of...nothing. Having assumed the standing meditation, or *Wu Ji*, posture, he stood with his feet shoulder width apart, toes pointed forward, and a slight bend in his knees. His hands dangled loosely at his sides, all the tension having been drained away from his shoulders and upper body. Head held suspended as if by a string, his eyes were closed, and he was perfectly relaxed. He focused on the union of his feet to the alien sand, imagining that it was the Earth, and drew power from it as he slowly inhaled its energy, then exhaled the tension from his body. He imagined the energy flowing upward from his feet, filling his entire body as he swept everything else away.

His companions, looking at him, might have thought he was in a trance. Nothing would have been further from the truth: he was totally alert. In fact, he was far more alert than the others, for he had eliminated all distractions, all fear, all doubt.

With a contented sigh, he continued his meditation, only opening his eyes when the alien challengers stepped into the arena.

* * *

Harkness gritted her teeth as a stream of warriors emerged from one of the portals on the opposite side of the arena. She counted them, noting with no surprise that there were twenty-three. One for one.

On her right stood the captain; on her left stood Kilmer. He had muscled over one of the other ratings who had taken the spot first, insisting he be next to her.

"Chief," he said awkwardly as the aliens formed up into a line and began to slowly advance toward them, "it's...it's been an honor."

Harkness turned to stare at him. He had always been a monumental pain in the ass and she'd always put up with him only because he was so damn good at his job. When it came right down to it, pain in the ass aside, he'd been a good sailor and a good shipmate. She smiled at him, brushing away a tear that threatened to race down her cheek. She never in a million years would have expected him to say something so sentimental. "Fuck you, you big ape," she said hoarsely.

He gave her a huge smile in return, and quipped, "You know chief, I'd love to take you up on that offer, but your timing really sucks."

She made a very unladylike snort as she suppressed a laugh. Then, seriously, she told him, "Good luck, sailor boy."

He nodded, his roughly chiseled face grinning eagerly as he casually slammed a fist into his open palm. "You, too, chief," he told her. "Let's kick some fucking alien ass."

As she turned her attention back to the approaching aliens, she saw that they had removed their armor and were now dressed identically to the humans, wearing only the black garment and sandals, plus their collars. *Evening the odds a bit for us*, she thought. They bore weapons similar to what each of *Aurora's* crew members had chosen, with each warrior squaring off opposite her human counterpart.

Harkness studied the woman, the enemy, who came to stand in front of her, looking at how she carried the weapons Harkness herself had chosen: two sticks made of something that was like wood (but probably wasn't, Harkness thought), each a bit less than a meter in length and maybe as big around as her thumb. A practitioner of *Eskrima*, a Filipino martial art, would have been quite comfortable using them, but Harkness had never heard of *Eskrima*. She knew nothing about martial arts except the hopped-up sequences she'd seen in the holo-vids, and figured she'd probably only last two seconds with a bladed weapon in her hands. But the two sticks were at least easy for her to hold and swing, and having one in each hand gave her a small illusion of being able to defend herself. She might even be able to give her opponent a whack or two.

She spared a glance at Kilmer's opposite number: a husky warrior who held no weapons. Kilmer had fondled just about every sword and other killing contraption they'd had to choose from, but in the end had decided, like the captain and Yao, that he was most comfortable fighting with his fists. He was a brawler, and a good one: Harkness could attest to that from the times she'd seen him wallop landlubbers in planetside bars, just before she'd had to drag him and any others out before the modern day shore police arrived.

She looked toward the captain, wondering what was supposed to happen next. He only shook his head and shrugged.

The tall warrior chose that moment to enter the arena, and the babble of the thousands of aliens gathered in the stands of the arena stilled.

* * *

Tesh-Dar strode through the portal the other warriors had used to enter the arena. Unlike them, her sandals made no imprint upon the sand as her long and powerful legs carried her to the stone dais set at one end of the arena. Last of the great warrior priestesses of the Desh-Ka, the oldest order that had ever served the Empress since a time before legend, Tesh-Dar was as much spirit as she was flesh. Her powers were beyond the understanding of most of her own race, let alone the wide-eyed strangers who now watched her with a mixture of awe and fear. She no longer wore her short sword, an ancient weapon many generations-old, or her cloak, but was armed for combat: she wore a wicked longsword in a scabbard sheathed at her back; another sword, not unlike the one brought by one of the young aliens, hung from her left waist; and her favorite weapon, the *grakh'ta*, a seven-stranded barbed whip, was coiled at her right waist. Three of the lethal throwing weapons, known as the *shrekka*, were clipped to the armor of her left shoulder in the traditional position.

As she entered, the gathered peers stood and saluted, left fists over their right breasts and heads bowed, the crash of the warriors' armored gauntlets against their breastplates echoing as though from a single giant hammer. This was the way of things throughout the Empire wherever Tesh-Dar went, for she had no living equals: she stood upon the first step below the Throne itself, upon the great pyramid of steps that defined the status of each and every one of Her Children. Even the few remaining great warrior priestesses of the other orders climbed no higher than the third step from the Empress. Only the Empress held a higher place in the hierarchy of their people. Had Tesh-Dar not been who and what she was, no doubt the Empress would have come Herself to oversee this Challenge, such was the importance of what was to take place here. But She was closely linked to Her blood sister, and instinctively trusted Tesh-Dar's judgement and feelings. For with Tesh-Dar here, the Empress could concentrate fully on the changes even now sweeping many parts of the Empire to prepare for war with the strangers. Such trust was a singular privilege and honor for the great priestess, but her towering status among the peers made for a lonely aerie, even for one whose soul was bound to countless billions of others.

Standing upon the dais, the stone of which had been quarried from the Homeworld thousands of human years before, she gestured to the gathered peers, the crews of the squadron of ships that still hung in space around the alien vessel, and they silently took their seats. She looked upon the two lines of warriors: one of her own kin, whose blood sang clearly with want of battle; and the strangers of pale flesh who were silent, soulless creatures to her spiritual ears. She knew that they would not understand any of what was to come, or why it was so important to Tesh-Dar's people. Few even among Her Children truly understood the importance of these rare encounters with other civilizations. For they did not realize that their own race had been slowly dying for over a hundred thousand years as marked in the time of the orbit of the aliens' homeworld around its parent star. With every encounter with another race that Tesh-Dar's people had experienced in past millennia, the Empress and those who knew the heart-wrenching truth behind some of their ancient legends built up their hopes that they would find among the strangers that which they had sought for tens of thousands of great cycles: one not of Her Own kind whose blood would sing, one who could save Tesh-Dar's people from eventual extinction.

But their hopes had thus far been in vain. The dozen spacefaring species encountered in past ages had been given every chance for the blood of even a single one among them to sing, but none had. Truly, they had served in glorifying the Empress through battle, but in the end the defeat of the strangers of old had left nothing but more pages in the Books of Time. And Tesh-Dar knew as well as the Empress that there were few enough pages left before Her Children would be no more. Centuries, perhaps, but no longer.

Such were Tesh-Dar's thoughts when she began to speak. "Long has it been, my sisters, since we have encountered strangers among the stars," she told the gathered thousands in the New Tongue, her powerful contralto voice echoing across the arena. While her words carried no farther than the stone walls around her, her Bloodsong cast her emotions and sensations in a wave that swept through the Empire. As she spoke, the toil and labor of the billions of Her Children across ten thousand star systems came to a halt as they rode the emotional tide experienced by Tesh-Dar and the peers gathered here as witness. "Coming to us of their own purpose, of their own accord, they do not know the Way of Her Children, for their blood does not sing. Soulless they may be, but as in ages past, in the time since the First Empress left us, they will be given the right of Challenge, to give them every chance for their blood to sing.

"For as the warriors of Her Blood well know, the Bloodsong echoes in our veins the strongest when in battle, just as it sings most clearly from the hearts of the clawless mistresses when achieving perfection in form. For this is our Way. So has it been-"

"-so shall it forever be," the crowd replied as one.

"The warriors chosen to fight this day I have carefully matched to the strangers," Tesh-Dar went on. "For while it is a battle to the death, we seek no advantage, for that brings Her no glory, no honor. For the Way of Her Children is not a path easily traveled, and honor is not given, but must be earned." She paused to look closely at the strangers who stared at her, uncomprehending. "None of the strangers may leave, save the Messenger, whom I shall choose." Looking at each of the warriors arrayed against the aliens, she added, "Should all of our sisters fall at the hands of the strangers, I shall complete what they began with my own hand." She raised her staff a hand's breadth and then hammered it down onto the dais, the sound reverberating like a gunshot. "In Her name," she called to the warriors standing ready in the arena, "let it begin."

SEVEN

Captain McClaren listened to the speech made by the commanding warrior, although of course he couldn't understand her. It infuriated him, because his crew had been murdered. The few of them here were walking dead now, he knew, and he couldn't even ask her why.

When she rapped her staff on the stone dais, he knew it must be time for the fun to begin. For with the last few words she spoke, the warriors facing his crew went from simply being wary and alert while they listened to their leader to being as tense as spring steel under a heavy load.

The warrior opposite him was just a bit shorter than he was and probably weighed less by a good ten or more kilos, but he had no intention of underestimating her. It was abundantly clear that her people trained their entire lives for whatever skill they would have as adults. That was okay by him, because many humans did, too.

He assumed the classic boxer's stance, hands raised up to guard his face with his arms protecting his upper body, with one leg forward, knees bent. He felt light on his feet as he began to move toward his opponent to test her skills and see what he was really up against. Adrenaline surged through his arteries, now that the fight was upon them. He almost hated to admit it to himself, but he felt oddly ready for this. He felt *good*.

As captain, he wanted to be the one to land the first blow (or take the first hit); this was part of the "first in, last out" philosophy that had been one of the guiding principles of his style of leadership. But he refused to let himself rush in like a fool: he was too experienced for that, and while he knew he would die on these sands, he wanted to take out at least one of the enemy, one of Harkness's "fucking alien bitches", with him.

But the first blow wasn't to be his: he suddenly saw Ichiro Sato rush toward his opponent, his bellow echoing across the arena as their swords crashed together.

* * *

Ichiro had stood silently, eyeing his opponent as the big warrior spoke. Unlike the other alien warriors, who were roughly similar in size (and presumably age, although that was impossible to tell) to their human counterparts, Ichiro's was clearly smaller than himself. If he had to guess, had she been a human girl she might have been twelve or thirteen, if that. She held a sword similar to his (it seemed that the *katana's* form was a universal constant in bladed weapons) and he had no doubt she knew how to use it far better than he did.

Nonetheless, it was a maddening insult. He had reconciled himself to dying, but had imagined he would be cut down by a warrior like the one who had handed back his grandfather's sword: he clearly would have been no match for someone like her, and he would have been content with that.

But this was simply too much. In the brief moment of uncertainty that took hold in the arena after the big warrior had spoken her final words, Ichiro's indignity overrode any pretense of logic or sense.

Whipping the gleaming *katana* above his head, holding it high with both hands, he charged his opponent, roaring his undiluted rage.

* * *

Tesh-Dar watched intently with both her physical and spiritual senses as the battle was joined. The rash young alien was the first to strike. Tesh-Dar noted with satisfaction that Li'an-Kumer, the young warrior chosen to face the human, did not kill him right away, as she easily could. Instead, she parried his spirited but foolish attack, then twirled in closer to deliver a cut that left only a minor flesh wound. The alien animal howled, more in indignation than in pain, Tesh-Dar thought, and slashed ineffectively at Li'an-Kumer with his sword.

Content that the young warrior had this creature well in hand, she swept her gaze over the other combats that were developing. Some of the combatants had not yet actually closed with their opponents in these first few seconds, but were still sizing up their opposition.

And then, as if a secret signal had been given, they all crashed together in a mass of snarling fury.

Tesh-Dar focused her attention on the one about whom she was most curious, one of the older animals whose inner strength radiated like a beacon...

* * *

For a fleeting instant as Sato charged forward, Yao Ming prepared to save the young man from his impetuosity. But there was something about the stance of the alien girl opposite him that told Yao that he need not intervene. Yet. As Yao stood, no longer in the *Wu Ji* posture, but simply standing calmly, he watched Sato's attack in slow motion, and was content with the young alien's reaction. She seemed happy to play with Sato for now, and that would allow Yao some time to deal with his own opponent.

The warrior facing him wore many more of the pendants around her collar than the other aliens, which Yao assumed meant she was far more accomplished. She also had silver claws, which perhaps a third of the others had, as well; the remainder had black claws. He had no idea if this was an adornment of some sort, or if it was physiological. He had also recognized her fluid grace in step and posture as she had strode forward into the arena. All of the warriors possessed a sort of feline grace, but this one was different, more like the great warrior who now stood watching the proceedings. For in her he had seen a grace and power, quite apart from her size, like he had never seen before.

His opponent calmly stared at him, her form a mirror image of his own, radiating confident strength. Yao had considered going on the attack, and would have if he had perceived an immediate major threat to either of the midshipmen. But Sato appeared to be all right for the moment, and on Yao's other side, Midshipman Zalenski was sparring confidently with her own opponent, armed with the alien equivalent of a saber. This gave Yao the choice of going on the offense or letting the alien do so. While *t'ai chi* could certainly be used in the attack, its roots were in defense, and he lost nothing by ceding the initiative to her. In fact, that gave him a certain advantage in his own fighting style, allowing him to use her own energy against her.

So he stood there, relaxed, staring into the alien's eyes as the battle was joined around him in a frenzied cacophony of curses and cries of pain, of metal striking metal, striking flesh. One second passed, then two.

And then she attacked.

* * *

Harkness reeled from the agonizing pain in her left thigh and right breast. The simple sticks were not as glamorous, or gory, perhaps, as a sword, and not as swiftly lethal, but she had never felt such agony as she was feeling now: it felt like her flesh had been seared by white-hot metal.

She had managed to stave off most of the blows the alien had rained down upon her since the match began, at least until the bitch had grown tired of playing around and decided to systematically attack Harkness's right hand, breaking three of her fingers in a savage strike. Then the alien smashed both of her sticks against Harkness's right breast, and whirled around to do the same to her left thigh as Harkness reflexively brought both hands up to try and protect her chest from another attack.

Her left leg collapsed under her, effectively paralyzed from the pain. As Harkness went down, the alien slammed her sticks down in a brutal one-two strike on the chief's exposed shoulders. Harkness screamed as she fell face-first into the sand, her body quaking from the pain. She tried to roll over and free her left hand, which still clung desperately to one of the sticks, to defend herself, but she couldn't. It felt as if the muscles in her shoulders had been severed with a knife, and she couldn't move her arms. The best she could manage was to turn her head enough to spit out the sand from her mouth.

She suddenly felt the alien slip a foot under her belly and lift, flipping her over onto her back like a turtle. The alien stared down at her impassively as she brought her weapons up to deliver the *coup de grâce.*

"Fuck you, you bitch," Harkness spat, staring the alien in the eye.

Suddenly a hulking figure swept across Harkness's vision, and with a surprised grunt the alien warrior was literally carried away. Harkness watched in wonder as Kilmer, his face already a tattered mess, slammed her tormentor into the sands of the arena and straddled her chest. Grabbing her by the neck with one hand, he began to rhythmically pound her in the face with his other bloodied fist. The warrior frantically beat at him with the sticks, hitting him in the head, in the side of the ribs, in the legs, but he seemed impervious to what Harkness knew must have been blinding pain.

Then the warrior abandoned the sticks and used the weapons she was naturally equipped with. Snarling in fury and pain, one of her fangs snapped off by one of Kilmer's hammer-blows, she stabbed him in the throat with the talons of her right hand, while using the left to claw at his face.

He contemptuously swatted away the hand she tried to claw him with and simply ignored the fact that he'd been stabbed. With blood streaming from his torn throat, the alien's hand still desperately slashing and tearing, his right fist became a jackhammer against the alien's face, battering her down to the bone.

After a few more seconds, her hand fell away from his throat, and she stopped struggling. Whether he had strangled her or had fractured her skull, or both, it was clear that she was done. Dead.

Kilmer turned to Harkness and gave her a smile through his bloody lips. Then he slowly sank down on top of the second warrior he'd killed.

Harkness managed to crawl over to him, her own injuries seeming like trifles in comparison. "Kilmer," she rasped, tears flowing freely down her cheeks, "you didn't have to do that, you damn fool."

"Couldn't stand...to see...my chief scream," he whispered, the sound more of a wet whistle as it passed through what was left of his throat, "except at me."

Harkness cradled his head gently against her chest. Turning to where Kilmer's original opponent lay still in the sand, Harkness saw that the warrior's jaw was misshapen, no doubt smashed to splinters by one of his fists, and her face was a patchwork of bloody flesh. He must have fought like a lion to defeat her so quickly so he could help defend Harkness.

She held him tenderly the few remaining moments until he died. Then, grasping one of the sticks with her good hand, she struggled to her feet. If she was going to die, she wasn't going to do it whimpering in the sand.

* * *

McClaren was holding his own, but that was about as much credit as he could give himself. The alien was simply a better fighter, although not by much. But in a battle to the death, it didn't necessarily take much. He had seen Kilmer and Harkness go down, but they weren't the first. About half a dozen others had died already, and the battle had become one of exhausted attrition.

Most people who had never engaged in a real fight didn't realize just how much physical stamina it required. While most of his crew, including himself, were in good shape, only a handful had the athletic conditioning for combat that the aliens clearly had. Even those who had close-combat training were simply being worn down.

McClaren dodged another open-handed strike from his opponent. Her fighting style would have been interesting if he wasn't in a fight for his life. It was similar to boxing, but instead of using clenched fists, she struck with her hands open, using the heels of her hands instead of her knuckles. It made sense, since it would be difficult for her to clench her hands like he did: her claws would cut right into her palms.

Regardless, her style was quite effective: the blows she'd landed felt like he'd been hit with a small sledge hammer. He had managed to give her some satisfaction in return, but she was faster than he was, and equally tough. He had snapped her head back a few times and gotten solid hits on her torso, but it felt like he was hitting a leather punching bag packed with sand and solid as a rock.

She dropped low and made a quick jab for his midsection, and he twisted his torso slightly to deflect part of the blow while lashing out with a right hook. Luck was with him this time, and he made a solid connection with her jaw. She spun away from him, blood spraying from her mouth, but it was only a momentary victory. Stepping back from him, not letting him pursue the advantage, she shook her head vigorously, regaining her bearings as she warded off his jabs.

Then, baring her fangs in anger, she bored into him with those feline eyes and moved back into the attack, driving him back with a blinding flurry of open-handed strikes.

* * *

While Yao was anything but a sociologist, he was able to tell a great deal about the aliens' culture from the way his opponent fought. As with many human martial arts that emphasized hand and foot strikes in the attack, the alien's style of fighting clearly was based on the offense, at expressing aggression. Considering the humans' experience with their hostesses thus far, that came as no surprise.

But she was clearly surprised, and growing increasingly frustrated, at Yao's employment of a variety of moves based on the fundamental *t'ai chi* principle known as *pushing hands*. Her arts had certainly endowed her with great skill in a variety of attack and defense techniques, but she simply could not get through Yao's fluid deflection and absorption of her attacks. In a civilization like that of the aliens where combat was the centerpiece of the society's existence and aggression was the rule, Yao suspected that it would be very unlikely for martial art forms like *t'ai chi* to evolve, for it was fundamentally based on the ideals of self-defense and compassion toward one's enemy. And thus his opponent had no effective counter but frustration. And frustration inevitably leads to mistakes.

She suddenly lashed out with a high roundhouse kick aimed at his head, and Yao decided he had learned enough. He sank back on his legs, easily avoiding the kick, and suddenly surged forward while her leg was still following through, leaving her lower body dangerously exposed and her balance fixed on only one leg. While *t'ai chi* had its foundations in quiet strength, certain offensive variations that Yao had been taught long ago were quite lethal: he landed a crippling strike with his right closed fist against her lower abdomen, then followed it up with a brutal attack with his right shoulder, concentrating all of his internal energy into a thrust against her lower ribs. He grimaced inwardly at the *crunch* several ribs made as they shattered, the splintered ends spearing several of her internal organs as his attack lifted her from the ground and sent her flying backward. Her part in this battle was finished.

Without further thought of his vanquished foe, Yao quickly moved to help the others.

* * *

Sato knew he should have been dead a dozen times over. The alien imp who faced him was toying with him, humiliating him. He hadn't managed to make a single blow against her: all he had for his efforts was a dozen flesh wounds and at least as many gouges along the razor sharp blade of his grandfather's *katana* where it had slammed ineffectively against the alien's sword. He was shaking with exhaustion and pain, gasping for breath, and wished that the young fiend would finish him off and be done with it.

He had tried to keep track of Yao Ming and Anna, but if he let his attention wander at all, he was brought back to reality by yet another bloodletting from his tormentor.

She darted forward again in what he knew must be a feint, but he didn't know enough to counter it effectively. She jabbed her sword at his left leg, goading him into defending it with his own sword, then she twirled and slashed at his shoulder.

Ichiro braced himself for the pain, but it never came. As on the *Aurora* when the aliens first boarded, Yao was suddenly *there*. In a brief flurry of powerful blows from his hands, the alien girl fell to the sand, unconscious or dead.

Collapsing to the ground himself, Ichiro gasped, "Thanks, Ming...I don't think I could've lasted-"

His words were cut off by a scream from only a few feet away. He looked up in horror to see Anna Zalenski clutching an expanding red spot on her stomach where her opponent had stabbed her. Her face growing pale as blood flooded out of the severed abdominal aorta, the major artery that carried blood to her lower body, she slowly sank to her knees.

Her opponent raised her sword to take off Anna's head, but never got the chance. Yao snatched up the weapon Ichiro's tormentor had been using and hurled it like a spear, the blade stabbing clean through the neck of Anna's killer.

"*Anna!*" Ichiro screamed as he ran to her side, catching her in his arms as she collapsed.

"Ichiro..." was all she said as she reached up to caress his face. He held it tightly, bringing it to his lips to kiss her fingers.

But she was already dead.

* * *

McClaren staggered backward, putting some distance between himself and his opponent. He had evened up the odds slightly with a few lucky blows to her head and what he hoped had been an extremely painful punch to the kidneys (assuming she had kidneys), but he was exhausted. He had gone a full twelve rounds a couple of times in unofficial fights, and knew just how grueling it could be. But that was when he had been a young man in prime shape. Even with whatever the alien healers had done to fix him up, he still wasn't young anymore. Even their miraculous powers couldn't turn back time.

Looking around through his one good eye - his right, since his left had swollen shut after the warrior had gotten through his defenses and clobbered him good - he saw that the battle was almost over. He had no idea how long they'd been fighting; it was probably only a matter of minutes, but it felt like hours. Everyone who had been off to his left, except Harkness, was down, and she was barely able to move, limping badly on her left leg as she slowly made her way toward him. On his right, Yao and Sato were still up and moving, and he noted with an amused grin from his bloodied lips that Amundsen was still alive, too. He wondered how the brilliant pessimist was dealing with that turn of events. But the others, including Midshipman Zalenski and Lieutenant Marisova, were gone.

They hadn't gone down without a fight, though. At least half of the aliens were either dead or crippled, and the only ones still actively fighting were his own sparring partner and the alien Amundsen was fending off. The other warriors, after finishing off their victims, had backed away from the action and taken up position in front of the dais where the huge warrior still stood watching. McClaren didn't think they were going to get out of this alive, but it was nice to see that they were at least playing fair. Sort of.

He glanced at Yao as he fended off another flurry of punches from his personal alien training assistant, and shook his head slightly. While he hadn't won every match he'd fought, he'd never been carried out of the ring, and he didn't intend to start now. He knew Yao could make short work of his opponent, but that wasn't how McClaren wanted it.

With one last surge of adrenaline, buoyed up by the fact the others were still alive, he moved in on his lighter opponent. He was done trading blows with her: they were going to finish it now, one way or another.

The warrior had come to the same conclusion. They crashed together, and McClaren used his weight advantage to push against her, keeping her slightly off balance as he sent a series of right uppercuts into her abdomen. She slammed the heels of her hands into the side of his head, sending him to the verge of unconsciousness before he put everything he had left into a punch to the side of her ribcage that actually lifted her from the sand. With a grunt of agony, the fight suddenly went out of her, and she collapsed to her knees, clutching her left side.

McClaren staggered for a moment, ready to collapse himself, but he wasn't going to let the job go undone. He took a shaky step toward her, grabbed her hair with his right hand, and smashed the bloody knuckles of his left fist into her temple as hard as he could. Once. Twice. Three times, until he could tell that he was just holding her up by the hair. He let go, and her body flopped limply to the ground.

He managed to turn toward where Amundsen was still fighting and took two wavering steps before falling unconscious into Yao's arms.

* * *

No one was more surprised than Amundsen that he was still alive. He could only assume that the aliens had made a mistake in choosing his challenger, because from what little he'd been able to see of the other fights around the arena, the others were fairly evenly matched. He had no other explanation for how he had lasted this long. He had even managed to deal some damage to his opponent, landing a completely accidental hit that broke some of her fingers early on, denying her the use of that hand. He hated to admit it to himself, but he was even holding out some hope that he might actually beat her.

The alien made another jab at him with her quarterstaff. Only able to use one hand now, her movements were very awkward, and Amundsen easily fended off her attack, sweeping her quarterstaff to the side. He hated to get fancy, but he decided to take a risk and spun around, dropping low as he swung the quarterstaff like a baseball bat, hoping to hit the warrior's legs.

To his amazement, he did. She wasn't able to get her weapon around in time to stop his attack, and his staff was too high to jump over and too low to drop under. Amundsen had put all the power he could into the blow, and it hit her right in mid-thigh, sending her tumbling into the sand with a yelp of pain.

He lunged after her, raining down a series of frenzied blows on her exposed back and head before she could get back up. He kept hitting her, over and over, his quarterstaff hammering her body.

Suddenly, Harkness was next to him, her hand on his shoulder. "Lieutenant," she said shakily, "you can stop now. You won."

Amundsen felt like he'd just snapped out of a trance. He blinked at her, then got a look at the quarterstaff he held. The end of it was covered in blood. He looked down at the warrior he'd been fighting. He must have hit her dozens of times. Her head looked like a smashed melon, and her torso was misshapen from the bones he'd broken.

"Lord of All," he whispered as he tossed the quarterstaff aside. Falling to his knees, he vomited into the sand.

Harkness knelt beside him, rubbing his back gently as she might to soothe a child. "It's okay," she murmured. "It's okay, lieutenant."

* * *

The culling is complete, Tesh-Dar thought as she surveyed the carnage of the arena. Of the twenty-three aliens who had begun, only five remained. Of the warriors who had fought them, eight had died, and another seven had been badly wounded. The aliens had displayed great spirit in their fighting, and she knew they would be worthy opponents in the coming war.

But the end of this first battle had come. Tesh-Dar left the dais and strode toward the remaining humans.

* * *

Yao watched as the huge warrior approached the battered human survivors. Amundsen, recovered now, and Sato stood on either side, with Harkness on the ground behind them, the captain's head propped up on her knees. He had not yet regained consciousness, and Yao feared he never would.

The alien stopped a few paces away and looked them over for a moment. Then she held out her left hand. In her palm lay the cyan disc. The ticket home.

"Take it."

Yao turned to see the captain staring at him with one eye that looked like a bloody cue ball from the burst capillaries.

"Take it, Yao," McClaren rasped. He had regained consciousness, but was clearly fighting to remain awake. "We've made our stand. One of us...one of us has to get back. To tell what happened here."

"I cannot take it, captain," Yao told him. "I-"

"Give it to Ichiro," Harkness suggested, and McClaren nodded weakly.

"Captain, no!" Ichiro begged him. "I'm not going to be the one to leave. I couldn't fight, I couldn't do anything to help anyone. Please don't send me home in shame-"

"It is not dishonorable or shameful to live, Ichiro," Yao told him softly.

McClaren nodded. "Listen, son," he said, struggling to get out the words, "you're young and deserve a chance to really live, if you can get out of here. You've also paid attention to everything you've seen: the people back home need to know what they're up against." He paused, drawing in a painful breath. "If they don't, all of this, the deaths of your shipmates, will have been for nothing. And our worlds will burn."

"Why not Lieutenant Amundsen?" Ichiro countered, turning to look hopefully at the lieutenant. Ichiro never would have thought that he would do everything he could to avoid having to go on living. "Why not send him?"

"Because those are the captain's orders, Midshipman Sato," Amundsen replied. Managing a tired grin that looked more like a grimace, he went on, "I wouldn't mind living another day. But I joined the service late, Ichiro; I'm nearly as old as Yao. And you're at least as observant as I am. I wish I had time to tell you my thoughts," he glanced at the warrior, sensing her patience was coming to an end, "but you'll come to your own conclusions."

"I'm not going," Ichiro said resolutely, standing up and coming to attention. "I refuse those orders, sir."

"Yao..."

Ichiro didn't even feel the blow that knocked him unconscious a moment after the captain had uttered the petty officer's name. Yao carefully laid his young friend down on the sand beside the captain.

"Now get the goddamn disc," McClaren ordered, "while we still have time."

Yao saluted, did a smart about-face, and stepped up to the huge alien, who still held the cyan disc in her outstretched palm. He took it, then knelt next to Ichiro. Holding it up for the warrior to see, he placed it inside the young man's alien-made shirt, carefully sealing it closed.

* * *

Tesh-Dar watched as one of the aliens slide the Sign of the Messenger inside the upper garment of the youngest among them. She did not understand their methods, but was in agreement with the one they had chosen. Had she been forced to choose among them, she would have made the same choice, although likely for different reasons. The young animal's spirit burned brightly in her mind's eye, his aura brighter than the others. He would do.

As for the others, it was time...

* * *

Ichiro's eyes fluttered open. Laying on his back, staring straight up into the sky, he didn't realize where he was until he noticed the color wasn't quite the right tint of blue, but was tinged with magenta.

With an electric surge, he suddenly remembered where he was. He rolled over onto one side, his neck pounding with pain - had Yao hit him? - only to see the captain staring at him with one bloodshot eye. He was dead. Harkness lay on top of him, having tried to protect him with her own body. Her back had been opened up like she'd been hit with a giant meat cleaver. Her beautiful face hung slack and pale in death.

Next to them lay Amundsen. He was on his back, as Ichiro had been, his face turned up to the alien sky above. One might have thought him sleeping, except for the pillar of gleaming alien metal sprouting from his chest: the great warrior's longsword.

"Ichiro..." a voice rasped from his other side.

He turned to find Yao, clutching the shimmering blade of the alien's other sword, the one that looked like a *katana*, that had speared through him, just below the heart.

"*Yao!*" Ichiro cried as he scrambled over to his friend and mentor. "No! No, you can't die...you can't-"

"Remember what I told you," Yao whispered, gripping Ichiro's hand tightly. "There is no dishonor...in living." With a final squeeze of his powerful but gentle hand, Yao Ming was gone.

The big warrior stood a pace or two away, her hands at her sides, intently watching Ichiro.

"Why?" he screamed at her. "*Why?* Goddamn you! *Goddamn you to hell!*" Without thinking, he reached back and picked up his *katana*, a weapon he'd never learned how to use, a weapon that had gone unblooded while his friends and shipmates had died around him. The blade of his grandfather's sword held before him, he charged the alien in his last great act of defiance.

* * *

Tesh-Dar did not have to understand his words, for she was beginning to sense the emotions of the aliens, and to understand them. Her comprehension was far from perfect, but what this young creature was feeling now, she understood all too well. This one gift she could give him.

As the alien charged, she made no move to step aside. Instead, as he came within range she reached out, faster than the eye could see, and guided the tip of the human's blade toward a weak spot in her armor, just under the breastplate and to one side. The sword pierced the underlying leatherite armor and stabbed through her abdomen. Carried by the young alien's momentum, the tip emerged out her back.

She hissed at the pain, but it was not a new sensation for her: she had endured far worse many times in her long life.

* * *

For a moment, Ichiro simply stood there, frozen in time as he held the handle of the *katana*. His eyes were wide in shock, fixed on where the blade had entered the alien warrior's body. His momentum had run the sword all the way through her, the warrior's blood running in a dark crimson stream from the wound. He looked up to meet her eyes, sure that she must be about to kill him. But she met his gaze with what he knew must be understanding, and perhaps even a trace of empathy. He wasn't sure how he knew that, for he couldn't read her facial expressions. But he knew that's what she felt. He had absolutely no doubt.

She brushed his hands away from the sword's handle, and then in a single smooth motion pulled it free of her body. It was slick with her blood, and he could see blood running down the armor on her legs from the wound. But if she felt any pain, she certainly wasn't showing it. With a practiced twist of her wrist, she flicked off most of the blood from the blade onto the sand. One of the other warriors stepped forward with the scabbard, and the big warrior slid the sword's blade home. Then she held it out to Ichiro.

He reached out and took it with shaking hands, still unable to believe that she was going to let him live. Blinking away the tears that came to his eyes, tears of shame that he had lived while the others had died, tears of joy that he might be able to go on living, he looked up at her once more.

But there was nothing for him to see but the contemplative faces of the thousands of aliens still crowding the arena. The huge warrior had simply vanished.

EIGHT

Kneeling in the sand, flanked by a pair of alien warriors, Ichiro watched silently as the funeral pyres consumed the remains of his friends and shipmates. After the huge warrior had mysteriously disappeared, a procession of warriors had poured through the portals into the arena bearing kindling wood. Where it had come from, Ichiro couldn't guess, even had he been of a mind to try. They built a pyre for each of the victims of the bloody fight, alien and human alike, using practiced ritual motions that made it appear as if he were watching a well-rehearsed play. Part of his dead heart warmed as he saw a group of healers enter, and carefully, reverently, even, prepare his dead shipmates for their final voyage. Wrapping each of them in a pure white shroud that didn't allow any of the blood to show through, they carried the bodies to their individual pyres and placed them carefully on top, all at once.

In what Ichiro thought was an odd thing for the aliens to do, they removed the dog tags from his dead shipmates. After washing the tags in a clay bowl, carefully cleaning off any blood and then drying them, one of the warriors stepped up to him and bowed, then handed the plastic tags to him. All twenty-two sets. He noticed absently that the same ritual was being performed using the collars from the dead warriors.

His gut churning in a mix of anger, shame, fear, and uncertainty, Ichiro forced himself to read every one of the tags, burning the names into his memory. The alien garment he wore had no pockets, so he simply slid them inside his shirt with the cyan disk, trusting that the elastic material would hold it all in place.

When all the bodies were prepared, one of the warriors barked an order, and the assembled thousands stood up as one. After a moment, Ichiro did, too: he came to attention and saluted. Flames suddenly sparked to life under all of the pyres, and the wood, if that's really what it was, began to burn bright and hot. Watching the smoke from the flames rise high into the sky above, it was hard for him to believe he was on a starship.

In only a few minutes of fierce burning, the fires generating so much heat that Ichiro felt like he was in an oven himself, the pyres collapsed into flickering coals. The bodies that had been upon them were nothing more than ash and smoke. Ichiro, his right arm trembling from holding it up the entire time, dropped his salute.

As the aliens in the seats began to file out, his two guards, one of whom was the same warrior who had handed him his sword before the fight, gestured for him to head toward the portal through which he'd entered a lifetime ago. It was time to leave.

With one last look at the charred remains of the *Aurora's* captain and crew, he turned and followed them out of the arena.

* * *

The two warriors led him down a different set of passageways than before, although they were as big. The main difference now was that they were filled with aliens bustling to and fro. Their reactions to seeing him were universal: a slight bow of the head, as if he were someone of at least modest importance.

Despite the leaden weight of the survivor's guilt that had settled onto his shoulders and the crushing physical and emotional exhaustion he felt, Ichiro automatically absorbed everything he saw, everything he smelled, everything he heard and could touch. He wanted to catalog every sensation so that he could recall it when he returned home, if that truly came to pass, and help humanity mount a defense against these monsters. Any and every detail might be vital.

But most importantly, focusing on what was around him took his mind away from his battered soul. He was only nineteen, but he had aged decades in the few hours since they'd first seen the enemy ships. Only a few hours. It had been an eternity.

His escorts made no detours this time, showed him no rooms pulsing with mysterious technology. They took him straight back to the semi-organic airlock through which he and the others had originally been brought into the ship.

The huge warrior was waiting for him. He glanced at her side, expecting to still see the wound made by his sword and traces of the blood she had lost, but there was nothing: the leather-like armor was like new, and so was the gleaming metal armor. It was as if his stabbing her had never happened.

Feeling no fear, for that had been burned out of him, he approached the towering warrior who stared at him with her silver-flecked eyes.

* * *

Tesh-Dar watched as the youngling was brought before her. He had proven to be a hardy creature, for which she was thankful: the task of the Messenger was a difficult one, and while she knew little yet of his species, she suspected his worst trials were yet to come.

In her right hand she held out a sphere that was roughly the same size as the young animal's head. It was the physical image of one of the worlds of his race, captured and held in an energy capsule. She held it forth for him to see, and it was evident he immediately understood what it represented. The image was of a planet that she had chosen for the first large-scale battle between their civilizations. After her warriors and the builders had studied the records of the primitive alien computing machines, they identified all the worlds the animals had colonized. After a great deal of consideration, they had presented Tesh-Dar with several choices, and she had picked this one. It was not so important that its loss would shatter their will, nor was it so small that it would pose no challenge. It was heavily industrialized, yet not located too near their primary core systems. It had a large population, but not so large that its loss would strike a crippling blow to their ability to repopulate.

"What do they call themselves in their own tongue?" Tesh-Dar had earlier asked those who now worked to understand the language of the aliens.

"They have many tongues, my priestess," one of the builders, a senior mistress, had replied, "although one is dominant. In that tongue, the animals refer to themselves as *human*."

"And this world," Tesh-Dar asked, staring at the image of the planet that she had chosen, "what is its name?"

"They call it *Keran*, priestess."

Now, standing before this young human, Tesh-Dar saw that he recognized the planet, for his lips made the sound of the word the builder had spoken to her.

* * *

"Keran?" Ichiro said out loud as he looked at the incredibly lifelike globe the warrior held in her huge hand. It was as if the planet had been shrunken down to the size of a bowling ball. He recognized it, because that was Yao's home planet, and the older man had spent many hours regaling Ichiro and Anna with exceedingly unlikely tales of his youth, usually to explain the origins of one of his poetic expletives. Ichiro felt his eyes burn again, but willed the tears away. "Is that where I'm to be sent?" He didn't expect the alien to understand him, but he had to ask the question.

She seemed to understand, or perhaps just guessed. She reached forward and put the palm of her free hand on his chest, right where the cyan disk was, then gestured out the circular hatch toward where the *Aurora* waited for him. Then an image of the Earth, as lifelike as the globe of Keran she held in one hand, appeared over one of her shoulders, and she pointed to that.

Then she held up the globe and drew her palm across the face of it, as if her hand was the curtain of a play, and he watched in horror as the bright blue and comforting browns of the seas and land were suddenly stricken with what could only be the smoke and ruin of burning cities, with ships overhead, blasting at the surface and at one another.

She was telling him what planet they were going to invade first. "No," he murmured, shaking his head. "No. You can't..."

Taking her hand away, the replica of Keran returned to the way it had been before, the land, seas, and sky at peace.

With trembling fingers, he reached out to put his hand on the sphere, but he couldn't feel anything. It wasn't solid; it was simply as if his hand was being repelled. He'd never felt anything like it. But the flames of war didn't ignite under his touch as it had hers.

"When?" he asked her. "How long do we have?"

She only looked at him, her eyes narrowed. After a moment of consideration, she moved her hand over the globe in a different fashion, her hand flat as if she were pressing down on something. Starting at the north pole of the globe, her hand held just beside it, she slowly moved her hand toward the equator, then the south pole. As her hand moved, the planet's image took on the ravages of war.

Suddenly, he understood. *The globe is a countdown timer.* The alien couldn't, or wouldn't, tell him how long they had in any measure of time he would understand. But he knew now that when the globe she held had fully transformed into a world at war, the aliens would come. The invasion would begin.

* * *

Tesh-Dar could tell from his emotional reaction that the alien, the *human*, understood the meaning of the sphere. Their people would be given some time to prepare, although if the legends of past encounters in the Books of Time were to be believed, they likely would not use it wisely. The Messenger was never believed at first. In the meantime, the preparations now beginning in the Empire for waging war against this new race would be at their peak. The human could not know it, but the sphere was attuned to the will of the Empress, and was not a mere mechanical timer in a sophisticated case.

She handed it to him, and he took it with obvious care, no doubt concerned that it might break. She smiled inwardly, knowing that little could disturb the device short of a release of energy on a scale that would sear half a planet.

For the last time, she looked in the young human's eyes. "Far must you travel, young one," she said to him, "and much have you to do. Go now..." she paused, nodding to him, "...in Her name."

* * *

Ichiro took the globe of Keran from the warrior's hand as if he were a timid god holding the planet itself. He looked at the globe, amazed at the clouds that slowly swirled across the surface, their shadows passing across the land and seas.

Looking up at her once more, she spoke to him in her language for a moment, then paused. Nodding to him, she then said "...*uhr Kreela'an.*"

He had no idea what any of it meant, but he knew he had heard that particular phrase several times before in the arena. Was it important? He had no way of knowing.

The two warriors who had come this far with him gently took his arms and launched themselves into the invisible energy bridge between the two ships. Looking at the *Aurora*, Ichiro saw with some amazement that the holes the enemy boarders had made were gone. The one in the side of the hull that was their destination was still there, but the rest of the ship somehow looked newer. He thought it was only an illusion, but then it struck him: just like some of his comrades whose physical ailments had been cured by the healing goo, the aliens had done something to the *Aurora*. The pitting left by small particle impacts that had dulled the gloss of her hull over time was gone. It was as if she had just been launched from the yards.

His two escorts expertly landed him in the hatchway burned into the ship's flank, but he hung back, unwilling to step farther into the ship. What lay before him was suddenly striking home: a months-long voyage alone in a death ship. He began to shiver, remembering the blood and gore strewn about the galley where they had been herded together after the boarding. And Lieutenant Amundsen's gruesome description of what had happened to the rest of the crew. He didn't want to be trapped in here with *Aurora's* rotting bodies, with her ghosts.

The aliens weren't concerned with his fears. Taking him gently, but firmly, by the arms, they led him down the passageways that led to the bridge.

Soon, he began to relax. The interior of the ship was just like the outside: pristine. The lights were on as they normally would be, and the strange blue glow of the walls after the aliens had killed the ship's power was gone. There was no sign of struggle, no traces left of the homicidal mayhem that had taken place only a few hours before. No smell of blood and death. Except for what he remembered, the ship was like new.

They led him to the bridge, where one of the aliens in the dark blue robes, one of the ones who had recreated the ship's computer systems, stood waiting. She gestured at him, and then the primary command console, then made pushing motions with her hands toward him, as if warding him off.

"Don't touch, I assume," he said aloud. The alien made no reply, but simply repeated her gestures. Then she bowed her head to him, and the warriors turned him about and led him off the bridge.

They walked him through the whole ship, although he wasn't really sure why. Possibly to see that they cleaned up all the mess. Not only was everything clean, but even a few minor imperfections, like some dents that had been made in one of the bulkheads from an accident two years before with some heavy repair equipment, were gone. He wondered how deep this "fixing" went, and if some of the ship's systems hadn't been improved.

Finally, the warriors led him back to the hole cut in the hull. The alien in blue robes hovered in open space outside the hull as if she were pinned in place. Turning to him, the two warriors bowed their heads, and then stepped outside the hull, taking up position next to the blue-robed woman. He wasn't sure how they managed that, because their momentum should have kept them moving once out of the hull's gravity distortion field. But apparently the basic laws of physics didn't apply to these people. Humanity's enemy.

The alien in the blue robes closed her eyes and raised her hands, palms out, toward the edges of the hole. Ichiro watched in wonder as what looked like dust motes from the hull of the alien vessel suddenly began to flake off and float toward the *Aurora*. Soon it was like a blizzard of tiny particles heading toward the robed alien, and they swirled around her before coming to rest on the edges of the hole.

He suddenly realized that he was seeing a form of the black matrix material they had used to recreate the ship's computers, and this woman was taking mass from the hull of the gigantic warship and converting it for use to patch this hole in the *Aurora*. But it wasn't just a patch: she was actually recreating the missing section of the hull, all the way through. The outer metal alloy, the insulation layers, the cabling and conduits: all of the bits and pieces of technology that was buried in this segment of *Aurora's* hide was being remade.

In only a few minutes it was done. He stood gaping at a solid bulkhead and the lettering on a small hatch that read, *Pressure Valve 87*. There was absolutely no trace of there ever having been a hull breach here. No seams. No marks. Nothing.

He was suddenly startled by a familiar voice.

"Interlock engaged," *Aurora's* navigation computer suddenly announced. "Transpace countdown commencing. Primary energy buffer building. Two minutes remaining."

Still clutching the tiny effigy of Keran, Ichiro ran for the bridge. He made it in plenty of time. "Bridge display, full," he ordered the computer. The wraparound display sprang to life, showing the alien ships now moving off to give the *Aurora* a wider berth.

"Primary energy buffer threshold achieved," the navigation computer told him. In a way it reminded him of Chief Harkness's voice, from the times when she had sat down with Anna and himself to teach them the finer points of being leaders. "Transpace sequence in ten...nine..."

He clutched the globe of Keran tighter as the sequence wound down.

"...three...two...one. Transpace sequence initiated." Pause. "Jump."

On the bridge display, the alien ships and the bright stars that were the planets that originally drew his captain here suddenly swirled into nonexistence as *Aurora* disappeared into hyperspace, headed for home.

NINE

Terran Navy Commander Pavel Leonidovich Sidorov had a splitting headache. The shift commander for coordinating customs inspections for starships inbound to Earth, he was responsible for orchestrating the actions of over three dozen cutters that shuttled dozens of inspection parties from one merchantman to another, looking for contraband. Even with that many inspection parties, it was a daunting task: Earth had more ships to handle than any two other planets, with hundreds of ships arriving and departing every day. Customs control had several gateways at different orbital nodes spread around the equator, but all the inspection operations were run from this one command center, located at the primary Earth-orbit transfer node located over Africa. Attached to the "bottom" of Africa Station's massive docking and embarkation facility, Sidorov and his crewmen were located in an expansive enclosure of clearsteel that gave them an unrestricted view of the space around them: Earth below, and dozens of starships spread out in orderly rows pointing toward the station.

While this type of duty was normally performed planetside by civilian customs officers or the wet-fleet Coast Guard, outside the atmosphere it was a Terran Navy show. Funded by the Terran Government, which was loosely based on the ancient United Nations but with funding and executive authorities that never would have been conceived for the UN, the Terran Navy had exclusive purview for security matters beyond the atmosphere. Ironically, that had come to include customs inspections after a few nasty incidents of incoming "merchantmen" turning out to be armed raiders. So rather than form a new bureaucracy, the Terran Government simply expanded on the existing one. As a general rule, it had turned out to be a good compromise: the customs inspections were run with Navy efficiency, and there was only one major tax burden to be maintained for exo-atmospheric defense.

But Sidorov wouldn't have minded shoving the job onto someone else on occasion, like right now. "Negative," he grated, his Russian accent barely creeping into his otherwise excellent Standard as he spoke into his microphone to the captain of the bulk cargo transport *Manzanar*, "you are not cleared to maneuver beyond customs until you have been cleared by one of the inspection teams. This has already been explained to you, captain." *About fifty times already*, Sidorov added to himself.

"This is outrageous!" the captain of the other vessel sputtered. "We have been waiting here for two days, and have precious cargo that must be delivered immediately! You have no idea what an inconvenience this is for us, commander."

Sidorov put his face in his hands and shook his head, eliciting grins from the other members of the inspection control crew and the civilian harbor masters who directed the ships in and out of Earth space. The *Manzanar's* captain had been ranting at customs control every two hours on the dot since the ship had arrived two days before, with the man cursing the Navy and customs through both shifts. *The man must never sleep*, Sidorov lamented. And according to the ship's manifest, the cargo that had to be delivered "immediately" was a load of old-growth lumber that had been harvested on Kelsey's World and had been in transit for a month. Chances are it could wait a few more hours. With a sigh, Sidorov said, "Captain, as you have been told repeatedly, you *will* stay in queue, you *will-*"

"*Holy shit!*" one of the senior harbor masters shouted as he and several others suddenly stumbled back away from the massive viewports around the cylindrical command hub.

Outside, not more than one hundred meters away from where Sidorov stood gaping in shock, a ship had emerged from hyperspace almost directly below Africa Station. Such a navigational feat was unheard of, and coming out of hyperspace this close to a planetary gravity well was not only suicidal, it should have been mathematically impossible.

After the slightest pause where everyone was in utter shock, total pandemonium broke out. The comm panels were suddenly flooded with frightened or angry calls from the ships in queue, a hundred, and quickly far more, calls from passengers in the station who'd seen the ship appear, and the station commander, who had a dedicated channel.

"*Chyort vozmi!*" Sidorov cursed in his native Russian. "Get cutters 12 and 17 over to that ship, and I want her captain on the comm *right now!*"

"Aye, sir!" one of the controllers replied, still in shock.

"Sidorov," the station commander, Captain Rhonda Burke, demanded from his primary video console, "what the hell is going on?"

"You know exactly as much as I do, captain," Sidorov told her. "I've got two cutters on the way and am trying to raise her captain. I'll let you know as soon as I have something."

"Understood. Out." With a brusque nod, Burke signed off so he could get to work.

"Harbor masters," he shouted above the din, "make sure those merchant ships understand that if they break out of line they'll be fined until doomsday and if we catch them I'll throw their captains into the brig!"

"Commander," another controller called, "her telemetry's active. It's the *Aurora*, sir."

Sidorov didn't need the telemetry to tell him what ship it was. He could see the house-sized letters of her name from where he stood: *TNS Aurora*. "That's Captain McClaren's ship, isn't it?" he asked. The controller who was monitoring the ship's signals nodded. "What the devil is she-"

A face suddenly appeared on the central video monitor. It belonged to a young man, but his eyes had the distant look Sidorov had once seen on the faces of the old veterans of the war twenty years before on the Russian colony of Saint Petersburg. Those eyes, set in a gaunt face that wore a haunted expression, gave him a bone-deep chill. His hair was far too long for a man serving in the Navy; while it was clean and brushed out, it looked like it had been growing wild for months.

"Africa Station," the young man said, "this is...I am Midshipman Ichiro Sato of the *TNS Aurora*...commanding. I..."

"What do you mean, 'commanding,' Midshipman Sato?" Sidorov demanded. "Where is Captain McClaren?"

"Captain McClaren is dead. As is the entire crew. All but me. Sir." He struggled a moment for control of his emotions.

"Midshipman, if this is some sort of joke, you'll wish you were never-"

"Sir," Sato interrupted, his voice choked with emotion, "I wish to report that *Aurora* made first contact with a sentient race..." He paused again, his face assuming a cold mask of hatred before continuing, "and that human space is about to be invaded."

There was total and utter silence on the control deck as everyone suddenly tuned in to what Sato was saying. Not just there in customs control, but throughout the station and among the waiting merchantmen, for Sato was communicating on an open channel.

For a second time in as many minutes, pandemonium erupted.

* * *

Stephanie Guillaume was standing in line with all the other human geese who were waiting for the next orbital transfer shuttle to take them down to the surface when the call came through on her vidphone.

"Stephanie!" her editor and boss at TransCom News, Simon Whyte, shouted at her from the tiny high definition screen. She always went by Steph. He never called her Stephanie unless she was about to get a bonus or a major ass-chewing. "Where are you?"

"What do you mean?" she asked sarcastically. "I'm still stuck on Africa Station because the Transit Authority boneheads can't make the shuttles run on time."

"Thank God," Simon breathed, practically in tears.

"Simon," she said, suddenly concerned, "what the hell's going on?" She had never particularly liked the man, but he'd given her a chance when she'd been stiffed by most of the other news organizations she'd tried for. An attractive, if not quite beautiful, brunette with inquisitive brown eyes and a personality to match, she knew she was good enough, both in terms of looks and brains, for a spot on one of the major news-zines. The only real challenge was getting the break she needed to get into the big leagues. Simon was a pushy jackass, but she knew she could do a lot worse. At least he had never tried to push her toward his bed or pulled any other crap on her. As jackasses went, he really wasn't so bad. *Maybe one of his fifty thousand relatives has died or something*, she thought, trying to come up with a reasonable facsimile of sympathy. It was hard.

"Listen," he went on in a rush, completely ignoring her, "something's happened. Something big. *Right there on the station.* We got a tip - shit, a pile of tips now - that a mystery ship suddenly appeared and there's talk of an alien invasion."

"*What?*" Steph exclaimed. "Oh, come on! How many times have we been sent on wild goose-"

"It's the *Aurora*," he said, cutting her off. "The research guys say it's one of the newest survey ships that went out almost a year ago. Go find her. Find out what happened."

Fuming, Steph grabbed her bags and stepped out of line, tossing them angrily against a nearby wall. That's when she noticed that a lot of people were on their vidphones. More people than usual. Listening closely, she made out phrases that sounded an awful lot like what Simon had told her: "ghost ship" and "alien attack" among them. She saw a growing number of perplexed, amused, and even frightened expressions.

"Listen, Simon-"

"Just do it, dammit! This could be the biggest story since Christ got nailed to the cross-"

Her vidphone suddenly went blank. Then her vid screen filled with an unfamiliar message: "Network connectivity lost."

Around her, everyone else who was using their phones must have experienced the same "connectivity problem," because she heard a lot of cursing and people just staring into their blank vidphones.

"Network problem, my ass," she muttered. Their connection had been cut off intentionally.

"Information," she demanded of the console embedded in the wall. It still was working. "What can you tell me about an inbound ship called *Aurora?*"

"I'm sorry," the disgustingly deferential female voice replied, "that information is restricted."

Steph felt her pulse quicken with excitement. *There might really be something to this!* "Okay, who do I need to talk to for information on inbound ships?"

That information apparently *wasn't* restricted. After she got what she needed, she bolted down the corridor toward the central elevators as fast as her high heels could carry her. She left her bags behind, completely forgotten.

* * *

"Cutters 12 and 17 are in position, sir," one of the harbor masters reported through the din of frantic pleas and threats being made by the other controllers to keep the merchantmen from scattering in the wake of *Aurora's* spectacular arrival and Sato's equally spectacular claims of invading aliens. The two small vessels, looking like remoras alongside the much larger survey ship, had approached the main port and starboard gangway airlocks.

"Commander..."

Sidorov shifted his attention from updating the station commander back to the face of the midshipman who appeared to be *Aurora's* only survivor.

"Sir," Sato told him, "I strongly recommend that you consider first contact safety protocols before boarding. I don't believe the aliens left any contamination. That wouldn't fit with what I saw of how they do things, but..."

"Don't worry, Sato," Sidorov told him, "the boarding parties will be wearing full vacuum gear." *And weapons*, he added silently. He didn't know whether to believe the young man or not. He had said little before Sidorov had gotten him switched over to a secure circuit, but first contact? Alien invasion? He sounded delusional, and Sidorov half expected the boarding parties to find some sort of massacre that would wind up being made into a holo vid show for lunatic teens.

On the other hand, Sidorov couldn't take any chances. If the midshipman's wild story did seem to check out, things were going to get dicey very quickly. The station commander had already put through a call to the customs fleet commander, who wanted verification before he woke up the Chief of Naval Staff half a world away. Everyone was thus far taking the story with a big grain of salt, but one thing was indisputable: *Aurora's* reappearance simply should not have happened the way it did, and they wanted an explanation. Fast. "I hate to say it, but you'll probably be in quarantine for a while if this story of yours checks out."

"Understood, sir," the young man replied. "Sir, I have opened the outer gangway hatches and the inner hatches are unlocked. The cutters may send in their boarding parties."

Sidorov noticed the change in Sato's speech as he said *boarding parties*, almost as if he were gritting his teeth.

"Thank you, midshipman," Sidorov told him. He glanced at the tactical controller who sat before a wide-screen console, who nodded in return: he had contact with the boarding parties, and both teams reported they were aboard and moving quickly to secure the bridge and engineering.

After a few minutes the team leader from Cutter 12 reported in. "Sir, so far as we've seen, there's nobody here. Not a soul. No sign of a struggle, no bodies, no nothing. Just a spanking new-looking ship." His video feed confirmed it. Empty passageways. Empty cabins. Empty work spaces. Nothing.

"Same here, commander," the leader of Cutter 17's team reported as he reached engineering. "There's nobody home but the kid on the bridge."

Sidorov could hear the stress in their voices. There were always people aboard a ship in orbit. The passageways might not be teeming with people, but a Navy ship returning from a long cruise would have half her crew at the airlocks, chomping at the bit to get off to shore leave. And there was *always* someone on the engineering watch, even if a ship was in space dock. Always. But this ship had just completed a hyperlight journey of who knew how long with no one but a midshipman aboard. It gave Sidorov the creeps.

"We're at the bridge, sir," the leader from Cutter 12 said quietly. There was Sato in the man's video display, standing rigidly at attention. Sato saluted the ensign who stood before him. "Midshipman," the ensign told him as he saluted, "you stand relieved."

"Aye, aye, sir," Sato replied hoarsely, tears suddenly welling from his eyes. "I stand relieved. The *Aurora* is yours."

With that, Sato collapsed to his knees and wept.

* * *

Steph stood at the back of the command deck near the access portal from the central elevator shafts, staring in disbelief at the drama playing out on the video monitors around her. Dressed in a tight red dress that didn't leave all that much to the imagination - she was damned if she'd look like a frump while traveling first class on the company's dime - she stood out like a collision beacon among the starched khaki uniforms of the Navy crewmen. But that dress and her press ID had gotten her past some tough gatekeepers before, and certainly hadn't failed her this time: the Navy security people she had to get past to get in here had both been men, and had been easily manipulated into believing that she'd been summoned there by the commanding officer, but she was to keep a low profile until he had a free moment to speak with her. She figured it wasn't *too* far from the truth. The dress and her curves distracted them, while the ID and a sharp tongue gave her credibility. She looked harmless enough, so they let her through.

She watched as the young man on the main screen, the sole survivor of the ship's crew, broke down in tears after the space-suited figure of a member of one of the boarding teams officially assumed control of *Aurora*. For a while she simply stood against the back wall of the command center, about a dozen paces behind where the person in charge, Commander Sidorov, one of the guards had said, stood watching the main monitor. She could see and hear everything, and so could the mini vid-cam array that was clipped to her ear, the video array and microphone on a wire-thin boom that extended forward next to her cheek. With the network shut down she couldn't get her data off the station, but an idea was churning in her brain to not only get around the little problem of censorship, but to make it work to her advantage. She added audio notes quietly, whispering so as not to draw attention to herself too soon.

* * *

A part of Sato was ashamed for breaking down and crying like a child in front of everyone who might be watching him, but the greater part of him pushed it away. It was an emotional release from the burden he had borne alone for the last few months. He hated to admit it to himself, but it was the first time since the slaughter of the ship's crew that he had felt a positive emotion of any kind. In this case, it was simply relief. Relief that he was back among his own kind. Relief that he was no longer alone on a ghost ship with the nightmares that plagued his sleep each and every time he laid down.

The voyage back had been entirely uneventful and mind-numbingly boring. As he had suspected, the aliens had made more than simply cosmetic changes to the ship: they had modified some of her systems to allow her to function entirely on her own. The things the crew normally had to do to keep her systems in good working order were no longer required, at least for the months it had taken to get back to Earth. *Aurora* had sailed for six months from her last port of call on the Rim to reach the alien system, but had taken about four months to return to Earth. It should have been impossible for the ship to go that far in only four months, even taking a direct transit. So the aliens must also have altered the ship's engines in some way, making her faster in hyperspace than should have been possible. He had tried to learn about the course settings and what the ship was doing, but while the blue-robed alien had warned him away from the command console, the warning appeared to have been unnecessary: he could get no navigation information from the ship's computer at all, no matter what he tried. He couldn't retrieve any information that could even corroborate his story of where the *Aurora* had been since she left the Rim: all evidence of the aliens had apparently been stripped from the ship's records. And the aliens had locked him out of everything that had to do with the ship's drives, navigation, sensors, everything. About the only thing he had free access to were the educational and entertainment sections.

And their sense of navigation...Sato had cried out in surprise when the ship had emerged from hyperspace, literally right next to Africa Station. It was impossible for at least half a dozen reasons. Not just the accuracy - how could they have known that *Aurora* wouldn't intersect another ship when she emerged? - but because of how close they were to the Earth's gravity well. The formulas were complex and handled directly by the navigation computer, and of course varied depending on the gravity index of a planetary or stellar body, but the nearest safe jump radius for Earth was well beyond the orbit of the moon. But the aliens had somehow brought the ship right *here*, matching the orbit with a moving object from an unimaginable distance. It wasn't just a coincidence. It wasn't luck. They had done it intentionally.

At the start of the lonely months aboard the ship, after he realized that he had been locked out of everything he wanted so desperately to know, he became listless, falling into a dark depression. Had there been liquor aboard, he had no doubt he would have spent most of the trip in a drunken stupor, even though he didn't normally drink alcohol.

What shocked him out of it was his obsession with watching the replica of Keran. Three months after leaving the alien system, he noticed that the northern pole had turned from its previous pristine white to a dirty gray as it had when the big warrior had shown him how the globe would change as the time for war drew closer. That's when it struck him that he had only four pieces of evidence to prove what had happened: the alien clothes he'd worn back aboard; the changes the aliens had made to the ship; the cyan-colored disk that had been his "ticket home"; and the replica of Keran. There appeared to be nothing in the ship's computer memory, and certainly no trace that aliens had been aboard the ship.

That meant that everything else, *everything*, was in his head. Everything to show how his shipmates had died. And that was when he finally got a grip on himself again and started acting like the young Navy officer he wanted to become. He started to log all his impressions, everything he could remember, down to the tiniest detail. Then he broke it down into sections, organizing the information into logical categories and cross-checking it for accuracy and consistency. He drew diagrams of what he could remember of the alien ships, outside and inside; of what the warriors and the robed aliens looked like, and how many different kinds of robed aliens there were. Sights, smells, sounds, the taste of the food they'd been given, the texture of things he had touched. Everything. In the end, it was not only a vital exercise in giving humanity some intelligence information on the foe they would soon face, but helped him deal with the crushing survivor's guilt he felt, and the penetrating sense of loneliness and isolation.

But that horrible voyage was finally over. His tears expended now, he stood up and faced the ensign who led the forward boarding party. "My apologies, sir," he said, gathering himself again to the position of attention. "It has been a...difficult trip home."

* * *

Steph watched as several Navy officers suddenly burst into the room, led by a stern-faced female officer who was all business. Steph frowned to herself, because women like this one were almost impossible to manipulate. She sometimes felt guilty about pulling strings on people, but it wasn't a question of morality, it was a question of getting the job done. It was a part of her job that she wished she didn't have to do, but that's not the way life was. Not hers, at least.

She directed the microphone pickup toward the woman and waited to see what would happen next.

* * *

"I'm not sure how to handle this, captain," Sidorov told Captain Rhonda Burke quietly as the boarding teams quickly finished scouting through the rest of the ship. He had muted the audio channel with *Aurora* so they could speak in relative privacy in the hubbub of the harbor masters working around them.

"I don't see the problem," Burke replied sharply. "You've implemented the first contact quarantine protocols, and fleet is up to speed on the situation for now."

Sidorov didn't take offense, because he knew that she wasn't impugning his judgement, just making a direct observation. She was direct about everything. But sometimes she didn't see problems that came at her from an oblique angle. "I'm not worried about that part, ma'am," he told her. "I'm worried about containment of any sensitive information. I don't want to speculate, but if news of some sort of 'alien invasion' gets out, there could be some ugly repercussions."

"I'm sure there's a perfectly logical explanation to what's happened that doesn't involve aliens," Burke said, shaking her head and rolling her eyes. "We've had stranger things than this happen over the years. There's not going to be any alien invasion. That's ridiculous."

"Excuse me, but how can you possibly assume that?"

Burke and Sidorov turned to see a civilian woman in an eye-popping red dress stalk forward as if she wore the stars of an admiral.

"And who the bloody hell are you?" Burke demanded hotly. "Security! Get this civilian out of here!"

"Captain," Steph said quickly, recognizing the woman's rank and knowing she only had seconds before she would be bodily thrown out of the command center, "I'm a journalist," she quickly flashed her press ID, "and I can tell you that the secret's already out of your hands. The best you can do is control it and spin it the way you want. And I can help you do that."

"Bullshit!" Burke spat, motioning to the same two guards who had let the mystery woman into the command center. The captain's expression left no doubt that they would get the ass-chewing of their lives later.

"I was up in one of the transit lounges when *Aurora* came in," Steph rushed her words out as the two men gently but firmly took her by the arms and started hauling her out, "and there were dozens of people on their vidphones a minute later talking about it, with their noses pressed up to the observation windows, *looking at the fucking ship and talking about an alien invasion!*"

Burke glanced at Sidorov and saw the indecision on his face. Again, if she was anything, she was direct. "Commander?"

"Ma'am, she may have a point," he said as the guards continued to haul the woman out. "If she's a legit journalist..."

"Hold it!" Burke suddenly ordered the guards. "Take her in there." Burke pointed toward a small briefing room at the rear of the command center. "We'll join you in a moment."

* * *

Steph's heart was hammering, not with fear but with excitement. She didn't have a "yes" from the captain, but she had at least put off being tossed out on her ass.

The guards led her into the conference room and left her there for a few minutes before the captain, Burke was her name, according to the name placard embedded in her khaki uniform, and Commander Sidorov came in. The guards closed the door and waited outside.

"You've got precisely one minute to convince me why I shouldn't put you under arrest," Burke ordered brusquely.

A minute, Steph thought. *Please*. "Captain, *Aurora's* arrival is news already. Look at any of the info channels and I'm sure you'll see it. And somebody heard something to make them worry about an alien invasion. I don't know where that angle came from, but that's why my bloody editor called me: because he'd gotten wind of it from someone else!" She leaned closer. "And even if the invasion bit isn't true, people are thinking and talking about it. The cat was already out of the bag before you took the station data networks down."

That elicited a stage-perfect "I-told-you-so" look from Sidorov to the captain.

Her frown deepened. "Thirty seconds."

Thirty seconds, my ass, Steph thought. *You know I'm right*. "Listen. I'm a legitimate journalist," she flashed her ID again, holding it right under the captain's nose, "not some idiotic independent blogger. I can help you spin this the way you want, tell the story the way you want it told. Otherwise," she nodded her head back toward the station core where thousands of people were still gawking at the *Aurora* and murmuring angrily about their lost network connectivity, "those idiots out there are going to fuck it up royally for you. I'll bet there are a hundred journalists and five thousand bloggers who just bought tickets to come up and visit Africa Station to see for themselves."

"Give me a break, lady," Burke growled, not impressed. "No news hound is going to give us a free ride. What's in it for you?"

"All I want," Steph said in a rare moment of total and absolute truth, "is exclusive access. I'll agree to any conditions you want, as long as they're legal, but I get access to the ship, your personnel, the survivor," her mind conjured up the image of the haunted-looking young man, wondering at the tale he had to tell, "and whatever else I may need to tell the story that wouldn't normally be classified. Your way. In exchange, you keep all the other newsies out."

"And why shouldn't we just hold the usual press conferences and not tell any of you anything?" Burke countered.

"Because you won't have control of shit," Steph replied bluntly. "People are going to talk, and you can either make it look like the Navy is being up front and honest, or we can play the usual stupid government cover-up game. And you know how those end up."

Burke looked at Sidorov, who only nodded. The captain suddenly leaned down and slapped the controls of a nearby comms terminal.

"Yes, ma'am?" a young navy rating answered.

"Get me Admiral Schiller," Burke told her, directing the call to the commanding officer for public relations at Terran Navy Headquarters. "He's expecting my call." She turned toward Steph, her lips twitching upward in what might loosely be called a smile.

Steph's eyes widened as she realized that Burke had played her. The bottom line hadn't changed: Steph would still get the exclusive access that she had wanted. But instead of negotiating from a position of strength and possibly getting out from under a pile of restrictions that Burke would probably slap on her story, she had practically begged for it. She felt a flush of anger and embarrassment at being manipulated so easily by the captain. It was a sensation she wasn't used to, and definitely didn't like.

"Schiller." A middle-aged man with an olive complexion and a hawk nose appeared on the screen. "Has she agreed?"

"Yes, sir." Burke glanced at Steph again. "We've got what we need."

"Then get moving, captain," Schiller ordered. "We've got to get on top of this situation before we have an interstellar panic." He leaned closer, his eyes narrowing. "We need to know exactly what happened out there. And fast."

TEN

Once over the initial shock, the Navy moved quickly. Burke decided to keep Sato on board *Aurora* for now, both to contain any further revelations and to quarantine him physically until they could make sure the ship hadn't brought back any pathogens or other alien oddities that could pose a direct threat. Two tugs arrived and quickly maneuvered the big ship to a berth in a space dock that had been hurriedly emptied. Several compartments in the dockway were quickly converted over to sterile rooms to accommodate a team of military medical and hazardous materials specialists. And a small team of psychiatrists and physicians had been assembled to debrief and examine Sato.

As all this was going on, Burke, Sidorov and Steph sat around the table in *Aurora's* main briefing room. It was uncomfortable wearing full vacuum gear, but until the biohazard team arrived with more appropriate suits, it would have to do. Admiral Patrick Tiernan, Chief of the Terran Navy Staff, had given Burke direct orders to start debriefing Sato immediately and determine if the whole thing was some sort of bizarre hoax, or if his claims of possible alien invaders were real. They didn't have time to waste.

No one else was present as Sato told his story for the first time. Burke and Sidorov knew that he'd be telling it a hundred more times to the debriefing team and others later on. But for now it was a closed first-time session.

Steph listened, enraptured as the young midshipman told his tale in a briefing that he'd carefully prepared during the long months he'd been alone on the ship. Burke had ordered that they all hold their questions until Sato had gone through his briefing the first time. As he spoke, Steph noticed that the expressions of both Navy officers grew more and more intense. Despite their initial incredulity, Sato's briefing was extremely convincing. Despite her own natural skepticism, Steph found she believed him, especially when he brought out the dog tags of the captain and crewmen who had died in the arena. She could see him fighting for emotional control as he detailed the ordeal that left him as the sole survivor.

And then he showed them the artifacts, which he'd intentionally saved for last.

"This is the disk," he told them, taking the shimmering cyan disk, his "ticket home," from a pocket in his uniform and passing it to Captain Burke. He had kept it with him the entire trip, and he only gave it to the captain with the greatest act of will.

Burke took it gingerly, finding it difficult to hold while wearing the bulky gloves. "Did you run any tests on it?" she asked him as she handed it to Sidorov.

"Yes, ma'am," Sato told her. He tapped a few buttons on the briefing console and a close-up of the disk appeared on the main screen. "I ran a full battery of basic tests, using everything I either knew how to do or could learn in the time I had, and came up with almost nothing." He nodded at Burke's frown. "I realize that such testing isn't my specialty, ma'am, but basic spectrographic analysis, which is one of the first tests I ran, with the equipment we have aboard is something I was taught early on by Lieutenant Amundsen. But look at the results."

A chart appeared on the display. Most materials were made up of a variety of basic elements, each of which would appear as a line of data showing each element and the amount of that element as a percentage of the whole. But in this case, there were only two lines. The first indicated *Fe*, or iron, with a composition of 0.05183%. The remainder of the material was lumped under the ominous heading of *Unknown*.

"That doesn't make sense," Burke told him as she passed the disk to Sidorov. After turning it over gingerly in his hands, he passed it to Steph, who stared at it, fascinated.

"I know, ma'am," he replied. "But I assure you, it's accurate. I ran it a dozen times, using different equipment, calibrating everything carefully. I also performed as many other tests as I could think of that were non-destructive, all with the same results." He shook his head. "I know someone here will conduct many more tests, but I will be surprised if the results differ. This," he retrieved the disk from Steph, who parted with it only reluctantly after becoming transfixed by the shimmering cyan surface, "is a completely new material to our science."

Steph noticed that he automatically put the disk back in the pocket of his uniform tunic. *He's going to have a tough time parting with that little souvenir*, she thought.

"But it's nothing compared to *this*." An insulated box that was big enough to hold a basketball had been on the table the entire time. He removed the lid, setting it aside on the table. Then he reached in with both hands and pulled out the globe of the planet Keran.

His audience gasped.

"This is what is most important now," he told them, holding it up so they could look at it closely. "I believe this represents the planet Keran, and is some sort of countdown timer to an invasion there." He handed it to Burke.

"Goddamn suits," she grumbled, having difficulty holding it. "I can't seem to get a grip on it."

"It's not the suit, captain," Sato told her. "It's what the globe is made of. Or, perhaps, what it is *not*."

"What do you mean?" Steph asked, fascinated by the incredibly sharp detail of everything shown on the globe, from the lights of the larger cities showing on the planet's dark side, to the deltas of the major rivers emptying into the seas.

"I don't believe that it is a physical object," he explained. "It is more like an...energy capsule of some sort. That is why it's so difficult to hold. It seems to have mass, but I haven't been able to measure it accurately. And you can't actually touch it:

it's almost like trying to handle some sort of self-contained repeller field." He shook his head. "I've tried everything from pressing against it with my hand to a low-intensity laser to try and get an accurate measurement of its size. But the results are all inconsistent. The harder you press against it, the harder it presses back. I don't have the necessary physics knowledge to explain, but I believe that what we're seeing here *is* Keran, perhaps reflected in some sort of space-time bubble, and we are seeing it in real-time."

"Impossible," Sidorov breathed, gingerly taking the object.

"What do you mean, 'we're seeing it in real-time'?" Steph asked.

"I believe that the cloud formations and other phenomena you see here on this object, at least the parts that aren't reflections of what the aliens want us to see of the invasion, are actually happening, now, on Keran," he replied, taking the globe back from her. He set it on a ring on the table that acted as a stand. "I have actually studied the cloud patterns, and in the months it has taken me to return home they haven't repeated. I don't think this is some sort of replica that the aliens produced from the ship's navigational records. It is real."

"How can you be sure?" Burke asked.

"It should be simple," Sato told her. "I have made three-dimensional recordings of the object, and the files have been dated. If we can get meteorological data from Keran for those times, comparing them should be a trivial matter." He tapped a few buttons on the console, bringing up the information on the files.

The thought sent a chill snaking down Burke's spine. "If what you're saying is true, the bastards must have a ship in the Keran system, spying on us and relaying this somehow."

Reluctantly, Sato shook his head. "That is a possibility, captain, but..."

"Spit it out, midshipman," she told him. "Now isn't the time to hold back any ideas."

"As I said, ma'am, I think this is more than some sort of transmitted image from a ship or sensor platform in the system. I think what we are seeing here really *is* Keran, as if it was contained in a separate bit of space-time."

"You're not making me feel any better, Ichiro," she said in a softer voice, the implications suddenly striking home. *If the aliens had technology that was that advanced*, she thought, *what chance would we have against them?*

"I want confirmation of this right now," Burke ordered Sidorov. "Get Sato's data to *Hecate* and have her jump for Keran immediately." Direct communications between the far-flung star systems occupied by humanity was, as yet, impossible. Instead, a fleet of courier ships spent their operational lives jumping between systems, gathering up data from special communications buoys that buffered outgoing information. In turn, the incoming couriers dumped their communications files into the buoys for distribution into the local system, or to be held for couriers heading to systems further on. It was a cumbersome and slow way to communicate, but until some of the highly experimental, and incredibly expensive, direct communications systems long in development had been perfected, it was all humanity had.

In the unusual case of *Aurora's* return, the Navy had anticipated the need for priority interstellar communications and had pulled several Navy courier ships off of their regular runs and put them at Burke's disposal. They were small and unarmed, but with their massive engines, they were the fastest ships in human space.

Sidorov spoke for a few moments on a private channel, his voice muted in his helmet. "Done," he told Burke. "We won't have anything back for nearly two weeks, though."

Burke shrugged, the gesture nearly lost in the bulk of the vacuum suit. "We're stuck with what we've got," she said stoically as she eyed the blue globe that sat on the table. "And this thing is going to start changing the closer we get to the time the aliens will arrive?"

Sato noted that Burke's original skepticism, which he had certainly expected, had fled. She believed him. In one way, it was a huge relief that at least someone believed his tale. But it also frightened him: it confirmed that this was a nightmare from which he would never awaken. "Yes, captain." He brought up a view of the globe that he had taken soon after *Aurora* had left alien space that showed it in pristine condition. "This is what it originally looked like. But if you look here," he pointed toward the northern pole, which was a sooty gray, "you can see that it has already changed significantly. It will continue to alter its appearance from the northern to the southern pole as time runs out, sort of like an hour glass. In the four months it took me to return here, this much has run out." He leveled his hand, much as the huge warrior had, at what was roughly fifty degrees northern latitude, which was the northern boundary of where the larger towns and cities began. While the more spectacular visions of war were not yet apparent, the clouds of smoke from burning cities were already swirling into the air of the northern pole. "Again, I have studied its progression, and it seems to be constant. If my projections are correct, we have roughly eighteen months to prepare."

Burke and Sidorov exchanged a look. *Eighteen months.*

"Shit," was all Burke could think of to say.

"But Ichiro," Steph asked, "what of the aliens themselves? We have these two bits of their technology," she nodded toward the globe and implied the disk in his pocket, as well, "but there's nothing about them. No physical evidence-"

"But there is," he said, bowing his head to her. He reached under the table and withdrew a long curved black tube that was carefully sealed in plastic.

"Jesus," Steph breathed. "That's your grandfather's sword, isn't it? The one you stabbed the alien with?"

"The same," he told her. "After I realized its value," he made an apologetic nod toward Captain Burke, "I hermetically sealed it in plastic. The aliens may have erased all traces of what happened from the ship's computers, but I assure you that there is physical evidence here." He slowly slipped the blade from the scabbard to reveal some dried blood along the blade's edge. "I ran some basic DNA testing on it as well as I was able with some of the bio-survey team equipment. Not surprisingly, it is not human." He carefully slid the blade back in the scabbard and set down the sword.

"Midshipman Sato," Burke began, then paused. "*Lieutenant* Sato, I can't express to you the value of what you've done, not just in surviving, but in having the presence of mind to do all the work you did on the trip back to give us a jump start on this thing. You're going to have a rough time for a while answering endless questions from the debriefing team, and you'll also have to sit for a formal inquiry. I apologize for that, but I'll be straight with you: a lot of people in high places aren't going to want to believe any of this, and the inquiry might help with that. It's going to be hell, but not nearly as bad as the hell you've already survived. And if there's anything I can do for you, anything, just ask, and I'll go straight to the bloody Chief of Naval Staff to get it if I have to."

"Thank you ma'am," Ichiro told her, bowing his head in respect. She had just spot promoted him up three grades. "I do have one request..."

"Name it," she told him.

"When the defense plan for Keran, whatever it might be, is put into operation, I want to be there," he told her, his eyes burning with a cold fury as he remembered Chief Harkness's words. "I want to welcome those fucking alien bitches to human space."

* * *

Steph was deep in thought as she watched Ichiro eat. Burke and Sidorov had left the ship. After going through the strict decontamination procedures in a temporary airlock set up outside the entrance to the space dock, they had been able to get out of their vacuum suits and get back to Africa Station. Burke had put Sidorov in overall command while she went planetside to confer with the brass. Steph already had most of her initial story put together, and had already run it by Sidorov. With a few minor changes, he had loved it.

But one thing was missing: their enemy didn't have a name. Ichiro had tried to make sketches of what the aliens looked like, and no doubt one of the members of the growing debriefing team who waited impatiently in the space dock compartments set aside for the purpose would be a profile artist to help refine Sato's rough vision. But no one had really come to grips with what to call them; they were simply "the aliens."

That just wouldn't do, and she wanted to be the one to set the standard, not some egghead on the debriefing team who'd come up with some idiotic appellation.

The problem was that she couldn't just make up something. Well, she could, she reflected, but the Navy probably wouldn't approve it if she didn't have some basis for it. And it had to have a decent ring to it. She knew that she just needed a bit more time, and had pleaded with Sidorov to give her a while alone with Sato. He had finally agreed, knowing that Burke already had the most critical information, and all the debriefing team was really going to do was polish and further substantiate what Sato had already told them. But they still needed to get a story out, and fast.

Something tickled her mind, some small bit of information, but she couldn't latch onto it. So she let her mind wander as she scrolled through the text and video files that Ichiro had put together.

The next file that came up was a video of Ichiro recounting those things he could recall from the aliens' speech, from what little they had spoken.

"...one of the things that was repeated during the ceremony in the arena, and that the lead warrior said to me before I was put back aboard *Aurora*, was what sounded like *uhr kreelan,*" his image said, trying to carefully pronounce it. "I believe there were a couple of other variations, but what sounded like *kreelan* was a common ending of some of what was clearly ceremonial speech. It sounded similar to what you might hear in some religious services, with the congregation answering the clergyman..."

Kreelans, she thought, mulling over the term in her head. Humans might never know what they were really called, but at least this was something that had a basis in fact, and was certainly better than what some of the idiots waiting their turn at Ichiro were going to come up with.

"Ichiro," she asked, leaning forward on her elbows in the increasingly uncomfortable vacuum suit, "we really need a name for these...creatures, other than the 'sword-wielding, blue-skinned bitches from hell.'"

He almost choked on his dinner as he burst out laughing, the first time since before first contact. He had rarely exposed that much emotion to others, but there was something about this woman that made him want to open up to her. He knew that it was probably just the fact that she was a very attractive woman and he was a young man who hadn't seen a human female for months. *Hormones*, he counseled himself. But it was more than that. From the moment he'd met her, he'd felt a strange kinship with her that he was at a loss to explain. "Well," he told her after he'd managed to bring his laughter under control, "that would certainly get some headlines, wouldn't it?"

She smiled at him, genuinely warmed by the fact that she'd been able to inject a little humor back into his life. Feelings like that didn't come often to her as part of her work: she was usually a cause of angst to others in the course of her job, and this was a nice change. It didn't hurt that he was attractive and extremely intelligent, if a little on the young side. She frowned inwardly. Definitely not her type, to judge by her previous history with boyfriends. But this wasn't a social call. She had a story to write, and she set that train of thought aside.

"Okay, so that might make the tabloids happy, but for something serious, how about we call the aliens 'Kreelans'? It's not quite as sexy, I know, but it's something the average Joe can pronounce and remember in between beers, and is something you remember them saying-"

"Yes," he said, interrupting her. The light of humor had left his face, and his eyes were dark pools of thought. "We have no idea what that term means, of course. But yes, I think that would fit the bill." He shrugged. "Not that I really have anything to say about it."

Steph shook her head. "Listen to me, Ichiro," she told him. "You've already made history, no matter how anybody looks at this whole thing, no matter what else happens. And you're going to make more before it's over. You're the only expert we really have, and that counts for a lot." She leaned back, making some more notes on her comp-pad. "Okay, so we'll go with that. For all I know, it might mean 'moron' in their language..."

That elicited another uncontrolled guffaw from Ichiro.

"...but it'll work. The next question, though, is what the hell are they? Their civilization, I mean."

"The first thing that I thought of when we walked into the arena," Ichiro said after a moment of thought, "was that it reminded me of Earth's Roman Empire. We studied that a bit at the academy. I know it doesn't necessarily fit, but that's how it felt to me, like we'd been transported back in time to an alien version of Rome." He shrugged. "We don't know anything about their government, of course, unless some of the wizards on the debriefing team can puzzle something out. So the analogy is probably completely wrong. But that's how I felt," he finished quietly, trying to turn away from the memories of the slaughter that arose unbidden in his mind.

Steph saw him involuntarily shiver, and reached a hand across the table to take hold of his. He tried bravely to smile. "Well, we're not really trying to get all the details straight at this point," she told him. "We're just trying to come up with something that we can use to help tell people the story."

The Kreelan Empire, she thought. Perfect.

* * *

Four hours after *Aurora* flashed into existence above Earth, the senior civilian and military members of the Terran Planetary Government were gathered in the main briefing room of the Presidential Complex in New York. They had just seen the first report that Stephanie Guillaume had prepared and that the Navy had approved. The woman had effectively summarized not only the facts, such as they were at this point, of *Aurora's* voyage, but had also turned it into an expertly crafted propaganda piece that gave "the enemy" a face and a name.

Admiral Tiernan, the Terran Navy Chief of Staff, nodded to an assistant to bring the lights back up. With fiery red hair long since faded to gray and piercing green eyes that missed nothing, Tiernan was a sailor's sailor who had started his career as an enlisted man and worked his way up to the highest uniformed position in the Terran Navy over the course of his forty year career. While he could play the political game as well as anyone, his heart and mind were always focused on the ships of his fleet, and the men and women who served on them. "That's what we plan to let TransCom News run through the newswire, Madam President." Tiernan had been briefed personally by Captain Burke, and despite his misgivings - who would want to believe such a story? - she had been extremely convincing. He also knew her reputation as a hard-nosed no-nonsense officer, and if the young man who was the sole survivor on *Aurora* had convinced her, Tiernan felt compelled to believe the story. But he knew he wouldn't be in the majority.

President Natalie McKenna was still staring at the now-blank screen. She was leaning forward in her chair, with her elbows on the table. Her hands covered the lower half of her face as if she were trying to hide her expression. Tiernan knew that wasn't the case; it was simply one of her habits when she was concentrating hard.

"Josh," Vladimir Penkovsky, the head of the Terran Intelligence Service asked Joshua Sabine, the civilian Defense Minister, "Do you really believe this?"

Sighing, Sabine nodded. He'd been present when Burke gave her briefing. He had asked some hard, hard questions, and she'd had straight answers for him. And none of them were encouraging. "Yes, Vladimir," he said, almost grudgingly. "I believe it." He raised a hand as Penkovsky opened his mouth to interrupt him. "I know that it's not ironclad until Sato is debriefed and the engineering team goes over the ship with a fine tooth comb. But I think we've got enough solid evidence to feel confident that *Aurora* did indeed have a first contact encounter, and that this so-called 'Kreelan Empire' poses a clear and present danger to the human sphere."

Several other members of the council began to talk at once.

"Enough," President McKenna said quietly, immediately stilling the babble. A tall black woman from what had once been the state of Mississippi in the United States, she never had to raise her voice. Born in poverty, orphaned at an early age, and raised in a series of foster homes, no one would have ever thought she would make it to the highest leadership position on the face of planet Earth. But her resolution was as solid as her intellect was keen, and she had overcome every obstacle that life had ever placed before her. This one, while potentially greater by unknown orders of magnitude, was no different in her mind. "Like most of the others in this room and elsewhere," she went on, "I don't want to believe this. But we've always known that there might come a day when we encountered another sentient race. Everyone has always hoped that such a civilization would be a peaceful one." She glanced at Tiernan. "But we also knew that it might not be. And we can't afford to ignore what Sato brought back. Not with only eighteen months to prepare for an invasion."

"Our options are limited, Madam President," the Secretary of State, Hamilton Barca, rumbled. Looking more like a professional football linebacker than a top graduate of New Harvard's law school, Barca's appearance often put his counterparts off-balance in negotiations, while his endless patience in diplomatic discussions could wear down even the most difficult negotiator. "Earth has a trade relationship with Keran, of course, and full diplomatic ties, but no military treaties," he explained. "Even if they believe this," he nodded at the screen where they had just seen the proposed press report, "we don't have any mutual support agreements with them, and they don't even have a real spacegoing navy. It's going to take a lot of time to-"

"Hamilton," McKenna interrupted, something she almost never did to anyone, "I'm aware of what you're going to be facing on the diplomatic front. But if we believe the information we have, and I do, based on what Admiral Tiernan has presented today, we simply don't have time for normal negotiations. And if we don't act, and act decisively, the invasion won't stop at Keran. They showed us with *Aurora* that they could as easily attack Earth."

"It's a deception," Penkovsky interjected. "What if they want us to do exactly that? They can lead us into pouring our resources into defending a second-string colony world, and then just appear here and gut one of the core worlds."

The room once again descended into a babble of arguing.

"We need to dust off the Human Sphere Defense Agreement," Barca's voice boomed out.

His remark not only silenced the argument, but elicited a series of groans from around the table. The Human Sphere Defense Agreement, or HSDA, had been proposed years before after a similar scare that had turned out to be a false alarm. While the details of the proposal were complex, it basically would put all the spacegoing navies of the human sphere under unified military control and create an independent force of marines. The main sticking point, of course, was who would then be in control of the new joint military structure. Just like the countries of Earth had been a few centuries before, not all human-settled worlds were democracies, and not all of the world-states got along well (even many of the democracies did not get along well). The HSDA would never come about unless a unified political structure to control it was formed. None of the world-states, including Earth, wanted to give up any of their sovereignty to an inter-system government, and many planets had weak or nonexistent planetary governments, as well. The only reason Earth's Terran Planetary Government functioned as well as it did was that the nation-states that had guided Earth's destiny for so many years were greatly weakened in the series of wars before the Diaspora, when much of Earth's population fled the turmoil to found new colonies. Earth's surviving governments realized that the only hope of long-term survival and renewed prosperity lay in forming a strong global government. It was not an easy or bloodless process, but eventually had put Earth diplomatically and economically far ahead of the colonies whose governments remained decentralized.

"I agree," President McKenna said, much to the chagrin of most of the members of the cabinet. "This is what the HSDA was meant for, but before there wasn't a real threat to make it stick. This time there is."

"If anyone else buys this story," Penkovsky said under his breath.

McKenna fixed him with a burning glare. "I don't care if anyone else believes it," she grated. "If half of what Admiral Tiernan said was true, if the aliens, these Kreelans, have technology that advanced, our entire species is at risk. We will spare no effort, *none*, to protect both ourselves and other human-settled worlds to the best of our ability."

"And that, Madam President," Defense Minister Sabine said, "is the next big question. We've only got about one hundred warships with jump capability, ranging from corvettes on up to light cruisers and a handful of troop transports. Most of them are engaged in anti-piracy patrols in systems that don't have their own navies, with three dozen or so in Earth space at any given time on home patrol or in refit."

Admiral Tiernan nodded in agreement. While the Terran Navy sported a big league title, it wasn't nearly as large as any of the old major wet-fleet navies had been. Earth had never really had to fight anyone since the Diaspora, and so had never allocated a huge budget for defense.

"We have quite a few ground troops," General Jaswant Singh, Chief of the Terran Army Staff said. "We could easily deploy several divisions without seriously affecting our own defenses."

"It's the same with us," General Sharine Metz, commander of the Terran Aerospace Defense Force, said. "We could deploy at least six squadrons of interceptors for near-space defense, and cover the gap in Earth's defenses by activating some reserve units to fill in."

Tiernan frowned. "The main obstacle is going to be lining up enough transport capacity to get our forces there and then keep them supplied," he said. "We've only got a few assault carriers, enough to hold two full heavy divisions. The interceptors," he glanced at Metz, "we'd have to take in on civilian freighters, so we'd have to get prior approval from Keran to get the squadrons on the ground and prepare them for combat."

McKenna nodded. None of this was a surprise to her. Everyone was still just trying to get used to the idea that there was another intelligent species out there that had decided to wage war on humanity for no apparent reason, and all they had right now were problems without solutions. She could listen to those who wanted to wait for more information, to see if this would just go away, but she wasn't about to waste any time. Thinking about the strange "hourglass" of the planet Keran and the millions of people there, she knew they had precious little as it was. "Here are my orders," she said formally, "and they are not subject to debate." Everyone nodded. They'd heard that tone of voice before during the major economic crisis that McKenna's first administration had faced, when the global economy was in deep peril and she had redefined the meaning of personal leadership. "First," she said, turning to Tiernan, "I want you to run the story your pet journalist has put together. We'll have a certain amount of apprehension among the populace, but I want to let our people know what we're up against. I'll hold a press conference immediately after the first story runs, and I want periodic updates as we learn more.

"Second, we will make all of our findings from the survivor's debriefing public once the next of kin of the *Aurora's* crew have been notified, and we will honor any reasonable requests by other governments to send observers for independent study of whatever the ship brought back." That raised a few eyebrows, but no one said anything.

"Third, we will offer any and all assistance that we can to Keran. And even if they won't accept direct military assistance, I want an expeditionary force prepared for a rapid insertion into the system if things go south and they need help. If we can help stop the Kreelans there, so much the better.

"Fourth, we will call a special session of the Interstellar Forum and refloat the HSDA. I don't expect it's going to be adopted, but I want it out there again, fresh in everyone's mind. Because if Keran falls, everyone's going to be worried about who will be next and how they can defend themselves, and HSDA will at least give us something to start with.

"Fifth, I want a plan to get our economy on a wartime footing. The red tape and all the rest of the *bullshit* goes out the door." Several members of the cabinet flinched at the expletive. McKenna rarely cursed. "We need ships, weapons, and manpower, and we need them fast. We also need public support for this, both financially and politically." She paused, her face turning grim. "And when we have the plan together, I'm going to go before the Terran Congress and petition for a draft."

Defense Minister Sabine whistled through his teeth. "That's going to be an awfully tough sell, Madam President," he said quietly. The president had complete authority to do everything she'd said except for instituting a draft for obligatory military service. For that, congressional approval was required in the form of a two-thirds majority vote. *And that was tough to get on the* easy *legislation*, Sabine thought sourly. "And if we get into a massive arms buildup, a lot of our neighbors are going to wonder if we're not thinking of doing a little empire-building ourselves."

"Good," McKenna said. "If we can leverage their fear of us, then so be it. But I want us to be transparent about what we're doing. I want other governments to know why we're doing it, and we'll offer to help them do the same. But I don't care if they build ships and weapons for the wrong reason; it will still help our collective defense when the enemy comes. As for Congress, that's up to me." She looked around the room. "Let me be perfectly clear, my friends," she told them in a voice laced with steel. "This is not a time for half-measures. I'll accept the resignation now from anyone who feels they can't get behind this one hundred percent from the start. Because as of today, after learning of the unprovoked attack on *Aurora*, the systematic murder of her crew, and the direct threat made to a human world, even if not our own, I plan to ask the Terran Congress for an official declaration of war against the Kreelan Empire."

ELEVEN

Among the countless planets that orbited the ten thousand suns of the Empire, many were such as this: great barren rocks that were host to gigantic seas of the matrix material controlled by the builders. From this they created the smallest to the greatest of the Empire's physical constructs, even entire worlds. For if the Empress willed it, it would be done.

A great task had She given the builders here and on other worlds, even as the strangers, the *humans*, were fighting and dying before Tesh-Dar's eyes. A new fleet would be created for Her warriors, to carry them forth into battle with their new enemy among the stars.

But this fleet was not meant to seek out and expunge the human animals from the Universe, for even a small task force of Her modern warships could accomplish that menial task. Instead, the builders had to reach back into the Books of Time, far back, to recall the designs created by their ancestors over one hundred thousand human years before. They sought designs that predated even the founding of the First Empire, for that was the level of technology that they sought to match. The bulk of the Imperial Fleet would remain as it was, the physical sword and shield of the Empire, but the new fleet would be roughly equal to the human ships they expected to face. And if the humans brought more advanced technology to bear in the coming encounter, so much the better for the added challenge Her Children would face.

Standing on the crest of a low mountain that held a great underground city, Tesh-Dar looked out across a giant lake of the black matrix. Above her the sky was bright with the artificial sun created aeons ago to light and warm this barren planet. It was a sterile wasteland of a world, useless for colonization, but ideal for the purposes to which it had been put. Much of its surface mass had been converted to the black matrix millennia before, and had been used as She required. A jarring landscape of violently upthrust rocks and ancient impact craters, the builders and the others of Her Children who labored here found solace and beauty in the monumental city beneath Tesh-Dar's feet, where the graceful domes and spires of buildings and dwellings lay under open skies and were surrounded by forests as if they were still on the Homeworld.

While Tesh-Dar's own powers were beyond the comprehension of any builder ever born, their powers left her with a keen sense of respect and awe. She watched as thousands of them stood in a rough oval nearly a human kilometer in length and half as wide, their arms out with palms turned inward to the center of the oval. She could sense the buildup of energy as the builder mistresses, those oldest and most powerful among the builders here, harnessed and guided the power of the acolytes. Other such groups of builders stood in similar ovals farther out; some groups were larger and some smaller, depending on the type of ship they had been called upon to build, with all of them near the shore of the matrix lake.

Tesh-Dar gasped as the power of the nearest group surged, and the surface of the nearby matrix lake began to stir. Its black, featureless surface suddenly began to ripple, and then the first particles began to separate from the depths of infinite black and float into the air. Moving faster and faster, the particles flew toward the center of the oval, the stream of airborne matrix becoming thicker until it blocked her view of the other groups of builders who worked beyond.

After momentarily hanging in the air in a nebulous cloud, the particles began to coalesce, and Tesh-Dar saw the first translucent shapes appear in mid-air where the ship's internal systems would be. At first only as thick as a single matrix particle, the primitive internal components of the ship gradually took form, even as more particles began to form some of the outer hull segments.

The great priestess marveled at the sleekness of the emerging design. Even with primitive spacecraft as ancient as this Her Children had fused the beauty of form with function, so unlike the designs of human ships she had seen from the extracted logs of the human craft. Unlike the boxy and cylindrical utilitarian shapes of the human vessels, this craft was formed with elegant curves and shapely proportions pleasing to the eye, as well as deadly to its foes. Kreelan engineering was as much art as it was science in all that they did, and warships were no exception.

"In Her name," breathed Tesh-Dar's First, a fiery young warrior named Kamal-Utai. This was her first visit to such a place, and Tesh-Dar smiled inwardly at the fascination felt by her apprentice, for she found it no less enthralling after seeing similar scenes countless times before. "Even before the days of the First Empress were we masters of the stars."

Tesh-Dar knew that it would take the builders weeks of painstaking labor to finish the ship that was now taking form, and even more time to complete the others being built for the new fleet, but she was satisfied with their interpretation of the Empress's will. It would take yet more preparation to train the warriors who would crew the ships, for they would have to learn everything anew. She did not envy the task of the ship mistresses who now studied the Books of Time translating from the Old Tongue the information on how to operate these primitive vessels. But she herself would be among the many to receive their tutelage, for Tesh-Dar was to lead this first campaign. Piloting the ships, operating the weapons, learning appropriate battle tactics: there was so very much to learn, and she looked forward to every moment of it.

In the coming war with the human horde, Her warriors would be evenly matched against the enemy. It would be a glorious opportunity to bring honor to the Empress for the warriors chosen to fight. Even now, countless arenas around the Empire were filled with cries of fury and the clash of steel as warriors fought in ritual combat for the right to slay, or be slain by, the human animals. Such combats would continue for many weeks, for many tens of thousands of warriors would be involved in the invasion of the human world, *Keran*, and many more would fight in the cycles to come. The attack on this first world had no particular strategic value, but was merely to provoke the humans into a fierce response. For this was not a battle or a war to be won or lost: it was simply to be fought for the honor and glory it brought to Her, to the Empress. And Her warriors would keep on fighting through the remaining centuries left to their dying race, should that be the will of the Empress.

With the Bloodsong burning in her veins and her body tingling with the energy unleashed by the builders, Tesh-Dar watched in silent wonder the birth of the fleet that would soon be hers to command.

* * *

Seated behind a lavish teak desk in his main office at the Keran Embassy, Ambassador Faisul bin Sultan, Keran's diplomatic representative to Earth, listened quietly as Secretary of State Hamilton Barca explained the situation as it was viewed by the Terran Government. Less than twenty-four hours had elapsed since *Aurora* flashed into existence next to Africa Station, and the shock waves of Stephanie Guillaume's news report and the president's press conference were spreading through human space with every successive jump of the communications couriers that carried the broadcasts. Ambassador bin Sultan had, of course, seen both the news release and the president's press statements: Barca had called him beforehand to make sure the news did not catch him by surprise, and to schedule a meeting as quickly as possible at the Keran Embassy.

"...and so, Mr. Ambassador," Barca concluded, "we would like to offer our unconditional support in the defense of your world, including direct military assistance should you so desire. The president made it very clear to me that there were absolutely no strings attached, no *quid pro quo*."

Bin Sultan's eyebrows shot up in surprise. There were always strings, always conditions, he thought, even though they were often invisible.

"When the enemy invades," Barca told him, "we want to try to stop them cold."

Leaning back in his chair, bin Sultan regarded Barca for a moment before he spoke. "Mr. Secretary," he said finally, his mellifluous voice carrying only the hint of an accent of his native Arabic through his Standard English, "I do not wish to appear ungrateful, because the offer made by your president is truly generous. I also wish to express condolences, on behalf of my government and myself, for the loss of your ship's company, among which was a citizen of our world, as I am sure you know. As with ships that sail upon the seas, the loss of a crew or a vessel on such a long and perilous journey is always a terrible tragedy. All that aside, Mr. Secretary, I will of course convey your government's kind offer immediately to my government." He paused for a moment, clearly grappling with what he was to say next. "But I also cannot help but feel that President McKenna may be reacting with, if you will forgive me, some small haste in the matter. It has barely been a full day, and complete analysis of the information has barely begun. I feel very strongly for the young man who returned alone from this ill-fated expedition, but asking us to go to a war footing based solely upon his account and some interesting artifacts is...precipitous, let us say."

Barca grimaced inwardly at the diplomat's choice of words. In diplo-speak, it was the rough equivalent of bin Sultan shouting that he thought the president was fucking crazy. But Barca couldn't help but agree to some extent with what bin Sultan was saying: the president had been incredibly quick off the mark on this one, and two cabinet members had already resigned after her little in-house pep talk. But to Barca, she was still The Boss, and if she wanted to go balls to the wall to prepare for an alien invasion, he would do everything in his power to help her. Because, God forbid, she just might be right.

"I completely understand, Mr. Ambassador, believe me," Barca said. "We fully realize how much of a shock this must be, and how...well, how incredible it all seems. But the president is fully convinced by the available evidence and is committed to having Earth do whatever we can, as quickly as we can, to prepare for whatever may come. Eighteen months leaves us very little time."

"Thank you, Mr. Secretary. And please rest assured that I will contact you personally the moment I have a response from my government." The ambassador smiled and stood up smoothly, signaling an end to the meeting, and Barca did the same. Shaking the bigger man's hand, bin Sultan told him, "I appreciate your coming here, Mr. Secretary. Please keep us apprised of your findings, and I will contact you soon."

"Always a pleasure, Mr. Ambassador," Barca replied formally.

A few minutes later, Barca settled into the limousine that would take him on to the next of half a dozen visits to other embassies to try and drum up support for the war effort against an enemy that only one man had encountered and survived. Sighing, he put a call through to the president to give her an update. He expected one of her executive assistants, but his call was answered immediately. It was the president herself.

"How did it go, Ham?" she asked him expectantly.

"He said, in a most dignified manner, of course, that he thinks you're a loon and that we're making a mountain out of a molehill," he told her bluntly. "He's going to pass the offer along to his government, of course, but..." He sighed and shook his head.

She puffed out her cheeks and rubbed her temples. "I know," she said, trying to rein in her frustration, "and I don't blame him. And the others will be the same, I'm sure, at least right now. There are huge questions that we can't answer, and precious little evidence-"

Barca snorted. "Ma'am, a five hundred meter ship with a missing crew is plenty of evidence of *something*. It's just that people don't want to believe Sato's story about the aliens. Not so much that there *are* aliens, although there are a lot of folks who won't believe that, either, but that they don't even know us and yet they're coming to look for a fight. If the ship's records had been intact and had shown some reflection of the attack, anything to support Sato's story other than the physical artifacts, it might be different. *Might* be. But even at that," he shrugged, "people have an incredibly powerful sense of denial."

"I know," she said, a trace of strain in her voice, "I know. But I feel this in my gut, Ham. We can't afford to be wrong. We've somehow got to make them see that there's a threat. And get them to do something about it."

He paused before he answered. He had known Natalie McKenna for over twenty years, and had found her to be one of the most noble, intelligent, sensible, and downright tough human beings he had ever encountered. He also remembered that she'd had quite a few "gut feelings" in the time he'd known her, and she had never once been wrong. Not one single time. Call it intuition, call it blind luck, call it whatever you want. It all boiled down to the same thing. If something inside her was telling her that this was the real deal, something beyond the incontrovertible evidence embodied in what the *Aurora* had brought back, then he believed it. And it was starting to scare him to death.

"I'll do my very best, Madam President," he told her solemnly as he flexed his massive arms, stressing the seams of his suit. "Even if I have to pound it into their thick heads."

That won him a tentative smile from his commander-in-chief. "I know you will, Ham," she replied. "And thanks…"

* * *

Three weeks later, Ichiro Sato was finally released from medical quarantine aboard the *Aurora*. He had stoically endured the endless poking and prodding for blood samples and biopsies, provided urine and stool samples every few hours, had a variety of two- and three-dimensional scans done every week, and suffered even more intrusive and humiliating tests to satisfy the army of doctors and nurses in biological warfare suits. He knew it was in a good cause, both for himself and for his fellow humans, but being released from quarantine was almost as emotional an experience as had been his return to Africa Station.

With the scientists and engineers finally losing interest in him or, in the case of the doctors, having no excuses to continue holding him, Sato had finally been freed from quarantine aboard the ship. But as soon as he stepped out the airlock, he first had to sit through some very tough questioning from the board of inquiry about what had happened to the ship and her missing crew. After surviving that, he was plunged into an endless series of meetings planetside with senior officers and civilians who demanded his story in person. As he was shuttled from venue to venue, he discovered that his image was plastered everywhere. He was an overnight celebrity across the planet, and that was spreading rapidly to the other planets of the human sphere. Some pundits considered him a heroic survivor, but some weren't so kind. A few even went so far as to accuse him of somehow engineering the deaths of the crew so he could return home, overlooking the fact that Earth wasn't his home, and the navigational feat of *Aurora* appearing right next to Africa Station was simply impossible with available human technology. Others were convinced that his body secretly harbored some sort of alien parasite that would suddenly burst forth and begin the process of eliminating his fellow humans.

The only saving grace in his time planetside was Steph. She and her network, which had shot to the top of the ratings charts, had an exclusive, and no other reporters were allowed access to Ichiro unless her network agreed to it. They had made some exceptions, but for the most part Steph had kept them out of his now properly cut hair. She went with him to all of the sessions with the senior brass, and made it all look good in the public eye. While she was doing it for obvious professional reasons and Sato essentially had no choice, they found each other to be pleasant company and had become good friends. In a way, Sato wished it might become something more, but he found that there was a deep emotional emptiness inside him that concealed a sense of guilt that the psychologists and psychiatrists had been unable to expunge. On balance, he was happy enough just having a friend who seemed to understand him.

Today, though, was something special: the courier had finally returned from Keran with the meteorological data he had requested to compare with the images he had taken of the cloud formations circling the alien replica of the planet. That information was what the powers that be had been waiting for before holding the final review of what had come to be called the "*Aurora* Incident."

Sitting at the front of the main briefing complex at Terran Naval Headquarters with the other presenters, Sato listened as Admiral Tiernan, Chief of the Terran Naval Staff, delivered short opening remarks before a battery of experts, including Sato, was called upon to deliver their findings to a joint council that included everybody who was anybody in the Terran military. The meeting was chaired by Tiernan, but representatives from every service were present, as were Defense Minister Joshua Sabine and several other key cabinet members. The president had decided to wait for the executive summary version from her cabinet representatives: in the meantime, she had more battles to fight with congress.

"Because we have a lot of ground to cover," Tiernan told the attendees, "I'd like to ask that you hold your questions until the breakout sessions after the main presentation. And with that, I'll turn it over to Dr. Novikov to begin."

Dr. Anton Novikov was the director of the medical staff that had examined Sato. "After the most exhaustive test battery we've ever run," Novikov explained, "our findings on examining Lieutenant Sato were completely negative in terms of any identifiable pathogens." On the main screen in the expansive conference room, a bewildering list of tests, dates, results, and other information scrolled from bottom to top. But no one paid it any attention: everyone's eyes were riveted on Sato.

"However," Novikov went on, "we did find clear evidence of physiological manipulation." On the screen, the blinding list of tests disappeared, replaced by side-by-side bioscans of Sato's jaw line. "In this case," Novikov went on, "the cracks that Lieutenant Sato had in two of his lower teeth, sustained during his first year at the academy-" the hairline fractures were highlighted in the bioscan on the left, "-have disappeared, as you can see in the bioscan on the right." The audience murmured as they examined the two images. While the cracks were subtle in the "before" image, they were nonetheless clear. And they were plainly gone in the "after" image. "We examined them extremely closely, and they are definitely the original teeth, not replacements. But there are no indications of any type of repair: no fusing or any other technique. It's as though they were never damaged in the first place."

A new set of bioscans flashed onto the screen, this time of Sato's left ankle. "Lieutenant Sato had mild scarring of his left achilles tendon from a childhood accident," the doctor continued. An easily visible mass of tissue at the base of his achilles tendon was highlighted in red. "Again, the evidence of this injury is completely gone in the bioscans we made after his return." The image on the right showed Sato's achilles tendon again, but this time in pristine condition. "Ladies and gentlemen, there is no medical application or science we have available to us today that would repair these injuries and leave absolutely no trace behind. There are also other, more subtle, differences that we detected in Lieutenant Sato's physiology that indicate some sort of medical intervention." He paused, looking across the audience. "Without a sample, we obviously cannot corroborate Lieutenant Sato's report of an alien 'healing gel.' However, based on our findings, we can certainly say that *something* happened to him that is beyond our ability to satisfactorily explain. And that, ladies and gentlemen, concludes the medical portion of this briefing."

"Thank you, Dr. Novikov," Admiral Tiernan told him. "And now I'd like to move on to-"

"What about psychological aberrations?" someone interrupted.

Tiernan frowned. Someone always didn't get the message about what "hold your questions" meant, but he let the question stand. Novikov hadn't touched on the psychological aspects, and Tiernan himself was curious.

Novikov shook his head. "We ran an extremely intensive series of psychological tests," he said. "The reason I did not include the results here is that, aside from some understandable emotional trauma, we could detect no unexpected or unreasonable variations from normal."

There were some sidelong glances around the room, Sato noticed. More than a few people were concerned that he might have been psychologically influenced or brainwashed by the aliens and made into a spy or assassin. He didn't really blame them: it was a lot easier to believe that than face the truth.

"Any other questions?" Tiernan asked, the tone of his voice making it clear that there had better not be. Heads shook around the room. "Very well. Captain Bennett, if you please."

The woman sitting next to Sato rose and took up a position behind the podium. Captain Leona Bennett was the chief engineer that had led the team that had taken *Aurora* apart from stem to stern. When she looked at the audience, she didn't smile. She had not liked what her team had found.

"As Dr. Novikov's team did with Lieutenant Sato himself," she nodded at him from the podium, "we conducted extended forensics tests of the *Aurora*, including her hull, interior, and all ship's systems.

"We found that *Aurora* herself was completely free of any suspicious microorganisms, particles, or devices. However," she went on, "as Dr. Novikov found with his patient, there were a number of oddities about the ship that we are at a complete loss to explain.

"The first," she said as a projection of the ship appeared on the screen, the camera panning from the bow toward the stern, "is that there was no evidence at all of any holes having been cut anywhere in the hull. Even microscopic examination of several specific areas that Lieutenant Sato pointed out to us revealed nothing.

"However," she went on, "the microscopic scans revealed something completely unexpected, and led to a detailed metallurgical sampling of the hull and interior components." She flashed a chart up on the display screen. "These are spectrographs of samples of the ship's outer hull plating during her last refit. As you can see, there are tiny variations in the composition of the alloy. This is normal from slight imperfections in the production processes. *This*, however," she said as she changed the display to a new chart, "is not." Where the previous chart showed slight differences among the samples, the samples in the new chart were eerily identical. "These samples were taken from the same plates in the hull as those in the chart you just saw. Not only are they all identical, but they're all slightly different than the samples taken during *Aurora's* last refit." She paused, her face taking on a grim expression. "Ladies and gentlemen, this is flat-out impossible unless someone completely remade, on a molecular level and with a precision that we cannot match - the entire ship."

That sparked an uproar until Tiernan ordered everyone to silence so Captain Bennett could continue.

"That's not all," she told them. "More perplexing to us were the findings from the analysis of the ship's engines. As most of you know, certain components have a limited operational life because of heat, friction, or a variety of other factors and must be periodically replaced.

"But everything in *Aurora's* sublight and hyperdrive systems looked brand new," she explained. "And I have to emphasize that some of the components are normally extremely difficult to get to, and require very special tools. It took my engineers a full week working around the clock to pull the hyperdrive core. And it was clear from the part identification markings and three-dimensional scans that they weren't replacements: *they were the very same parts as installed on the ship's last refit*. But somehow made new."

Looking directly at Admiral Tiernan, she summed up her findings and her fears. "Sir, I can't confirm Lieutenant Sato's story from what we found on the ship. But I can definitely confirm that something incredibly strange happened to that ship, something that's centuries beyond our current engineering capability."

Those around the room fell silent. Bennett had a reputation for being an engineering genius, and many had long thought her talents wasted in the Navy. Her last words sent a haunting chill through the senior military officers and civilian officials who sat around the table at the center of the room.

"Thank you, captain," Tiernan said into the resounding silence. He had already read the summary and most of the details of Bennett's findings, but was nonetheless disturbed. While she made it clear that there was no indication that the ship itself posed any danger, whoever had manipulated the vessel was clearly in a league of their own in terms of technology.

"Dr. Larsen will now present the results of the study of the substance, believed to be blood, found on Lieutenant Sato's sword," Tiernan said, nodding toward a tall, thin man with thinning blonde hair who sat on the other side of Sato. "Doctor, if you would, please."

Larsen was nervous as he took the stage. Unlike many academics who had a lot of experience in front of people, even if just students in a classroom, Larsen had very little: his life was spent in the laboratory. He was widely published, but had generally avoided giving public talks himself. Instead, he almost always trusted it to one of his understudies.

Sato grimaced inwardly, expecting a droning catalog of esoteric genetic technobabble, but he, along with most of the rest of the audience, was surprised as Larsen's stage fright was overcome by enthusiasm for his topic.

"You have already seen many incredible things in the various reports from the analyses of *Aurora* and young Lieutenant Sato," Larsen began, reading from his notes after clearing his throat several times. "But I believe that those revelations pale in significance to the findings I bring before you now." He groped around on the podium for a moment, finally finding the control to bring up his first display.

"Here you see the double-helix that we are all familiar with," he explained as a strand of DNA slowly turned on the screen behind him. "While it varies depending on the species used for comparison, human DNA - a reconstruction of which you see on the screen behind me - is much more similar to other Earth-descended life forms than it is different. For example, we share roughly ninety-five percent commonality in our DNA with chimpanzees." A second strand of DNA appeared on the screen next to the first, with a watermark of a chimp behind it. To the untrained eye, the two strands were identical.

"Now, ladies and gentlemen," Larsen said, for the first time glancing up from his prepared notes, clearly excited, "I know that you expected me to ramble on about gene sequences and such. But there is no need once you've seen *this*."

The chimp DNA disappeared, and was replaced by the image of a new double helix. It was nearly twice as long as the human DNA strand, and had strange protrusions from the helix at regular intervals along its length. The audience made a collective gasp: Larsen's team had only just finished their analysis, and no one, not even Tiernan, had yet seen the results until now.

"Yes, ladies and gentlemen," Larsen told them, turning to look admiringly at the image. "This is something entirely new to our science! Nowhere in all the worlds we have surveyed have we seen anything like it. Some parts of it, we understand; others, such as these strange extensions-" he pointed to one of the protrusions, "-continue to baffle us. There is much controversy among those of us looking at the samples brought back by Lieutenant Sato. But there are two incontrovertible facts. First, that this gene sequence can encode vastly more information than our own DNA; and second, that it is not from any known species of life that humanity has ever encountered and sampled.

"While this is all still very preliminary," he went on, turning back to his stunned audience, "I feel compelled to point out that a majority of my colleagues are convinced that the species or sub-species that this sample came from was genetically engineered, that there is far too much data in the structure to have been encoded naturally, even over an extended period of evolution. Others believe differently. I myself am not yet decided on the matter. But we are all in agreement that it is of completely unknown origin."

"I don't bloody believe it," someone murmured.

I wish I could say that, Tiernan thought. Whether Sato had really found blue-skinned alien women from hell out in deep space or not, *something* was out there. "Thank you, Dr. Larsen," he told him, relieved that the haunting image of that alien DNA had been taken off the screen.

As Larsen shuffled off the stage, Tiernan turned to look directly at Sato. "Okay, son, it's your show."

Sato took his place at the podium, facing his audience. In his earlier life, he would have been terrified of briefing such an assembly of senior officers and civilians. But he had already come to know many of them fairly well over the last few weeks through an endless series of vidcom calls, and what he had experienced on the *Aurora* had forever changed his threshold of fear. His eye caught Steph sitting in the back row, again wearing her "killer red dress," as she liked to call it. He didn't acknowledge the wink she gave him, but her confidence warmed him nonetheless.

"Thank you, sir," Sato said, his strong voice carrying well without the need for artificial amplification. "Since most of you already know the background on what you're going to see, a comparison of the cloud formations on the alien artifact representing Keran with time-matched meteorological records sent back from the Keran government, I'll skip over the preliminaries and get to the bottom line." He pressed a button on the tiny remote he held, and the massive screen at the head of the room suddenly showed an image of a planet that looked much like Earth, with a set of time and date information at the bottom. "This is satellite data that was delivered to us this morning by courier from Keran," Sato explained. "Please note the date and time information, which is shown in Universal Standard to correspond with the times of the images I took while returning on *Aurora*." The view of the planet suddenly changed from that of a typical sphere, expanding to show a two-dimensional display of the entire planet, as if it had been converted to a wall map. Three red circles flashed on, illuminating some large cloud masses. "These three major storms are good points of reference for what we're about to see in this first sample."

He clicked the remote again, and that image shrank to half the screen, while another image of what looked like the same planet appeared, except that it was suspended on a metal ring in an image capture stand. Identical time and date information to what was on the first image appeared at the bottom. "This is the alien artifact that appears to represent Keran, taken at the same relative time." Another click, and the sphere was reformed to show a rectangular display of the entire planet's surface as Sato had done a moment before with the satellite imagery, with three red circles around major storm systems.

"These cloud formations look similar, but the question is, are they the same? I had the computer highlight any differences between them in bright red." Sato clicked the remote again. The two images came together and were merged. "As you can see, they appear to be the same. Closer analysis revealed, however, that the two images are not just similar, but are *identical*." He paused. "This means that the alien artifact is showing not just some random representation of Keran, but is actually echoing an image of the planet in real-time, even from hundreds of light years away."

"That's impossible," someone blurted.

"To us, perhaps," Sato said. "But this isn't a fluke. I made a dozen different recordings over the four months of the journey back to Earth. Every single one of those recordings was a perfect match with the imagery from Keran."

"So what does this mean?" the Minister of Defense, Joshua Sabine, asked pointedly. "I've heard the arguments both ways about there being a Kreelan ship in Keran space somehow broadcasting to this...artifact. But how does it influence our strategy?"

"It means, Mr. Secretary," Tiernan pointed out, "that, aside from the implications such advanced technology has in general, the enemy has unparalleled reconnaissance and communications capabilities compared to our own forces. They'll know about anything that goes on in Keran space instantly, while we have to rely on couriers for inter-system communications. And, of course, if the Keran government doesn't allow us to preposition any forces in the system when the clock is about to run out, we'll have nothing in the way of reconnaissance to help us if the president orders us in." He tossed the pen he'd been idly twirling in his fingers onto the table. "We'll be going in completely blind."

"It's actually worse, admiral," Sato told him quietly, although his voice still carried easily through the hush that had settled on the room.

"How can it be worse?" Sabine growled.

"Sir," Sato went on, "it's something that we discovered this morning. I never thought to check for this myself, but Miss Guillaume," he nodded toward the back of the room toward Steph, "happened to be doing some video recording of the artifact, and had the idea of taking some very close-up macro shots. What she found prompted us to turn a high resolution microscope onto the artifact. Here are the results of some of the images we took."

With another click of the remote, a seaside city suddenly sprang into view. But it wasn't a typical landscape scene as taken from someone on the ground; it was as if it had been taken from the air. Oceangoing ships, vehicular traffic, even large groups of people could clearly be discerned in the video image. The scene shifted to what was clearly a military facility, with armored vehicles aligned next to vehicle sheds and rows of barracks nearby. It shifted again to show a major airport, with aerospace vehicles taking off and landing, shuttling people and cargo to low orbit.

"Dear mother of God," Sabine whispered. "Are you telling me that what we're seeing here is - was - really happening at the time these images were taken of the artifact?"

Sato nodded grimly. "Yes, sir. We haven't confirmed it directly, of course, because that would require another courier run to Keran for additional data. But based on our analysis this morning of both the meteorological and ocean wave data that we were able to compare with the artifact, we believe that what you are seeing here actually took place, and is not a random simulation of the activity on the planet." He paused. "And these images are really limited by the equipment we had available at the time. I believe that it would be theoretically possible to go to street level and see the individual people there as clearly as we see each other around the table here."

"Anything else to cheer us up with, Sato?" Tiernan sighed. He knew it wasn't the boy's fault, but this was all news that he definitely did not want to hear.

"Actually, yes, sir, there is some good news." He clicked the remote again, clearing the troubling close-ups of Keran from the screen. "As you know, I believe the artifact is a countdown timer for the invasion." Several heads around the table nodded. Very few had been inclined to believe his claim before, but he saw that much of the doubt about his story had faded quickly in the last half hour. "It is gradually changing what it shows over time, I believe morphing from a real-time image to some sort of artificial projection of what may happen." A recent view of the artifact showed the smoke from the northern continent swirling into the polar region, and a variety of ships orbiting, apparently in combat. "So, using what Miss Guillaume discovered this morning, we turned our attention to the ships we periodically see passing across the northern pole of the artifact, as well as to some of the surface areas that appear to have been attacked. It was very difficult in the short time we had to do the analysis this morning, so these results must be considered preliminary, but..."

He clicked again, and suddenly a rakish vessel, what could only have been a warship, swam into jittery focus. To those in the room who had knowledge of such things, it clearly was not of any human design. Where human warships, regardless of the builder, tended to be very utilitarian in nature, made up largely of basic shapes and sharp angles with a variety of antennas and weapons arrays poking out into space, this one looked almost like a super-sized aerospace fighter aircraft. It fired what looked like a brace of missiles and followed up with a salvo of what appeared to be lasers at a target that was outside the field of view. "While we'll need more exact measurements," Sato said as his audience sat, transfixed by the scene, "we believe this particular ship to be roughly on a par in size with our heavy cruisers. It is nothing close to the size of the ships that attacked *Aurora*. And from what little we were able to tell this morning, reflected in what you see here, the weapons this ship is using appear to be roughly similar to those in general use by human warships."

"Has this information been turned over to my analysts for further study?" Vladimir Penkovsky, head of Terran Intelligence, asked pointedly.

Sato opened his mouth to respond, but was cut off by Vice Admiral Mary "Bunny" Richards, the Commander-in-Chief, Orbital Systems Command. Her command was responsible for all the orbital platforms like Africa Station, and she was at the top of Sato's current command chain. Sato had always wondered if anybody really ever called her Bunny. He knew that he certainly never would.

Eying Penkovsky with evident distaste, Admiral Richards told him in her heavily accented native British, "Lieutenant Sato and his team sent a report out this morning at oh-eight-forty, along with a request for support from TIA." TIA was Penkovsky's Terran Intelligence Agency.

"Listen, Joshua," Penkovsky told the Defense Minister, "we need better integration on the intelligence side of this. We've been kept at arm's length-"

"With all due respect, sir," Richards interjected. "TIA was invited from the very beginning to participate in the debriefing and on the analyses of *Aurora*, but you declined."

"Enough," the Defense Minister held up his hands. "Vlad, we'll take this up later off-line. On the one hand you're right: we do need better integration between operations and intelligence, particularly in light of these recent revelations." He nodded toward the screen, which now showed blurry images of what appeared to be some sort of assault boats disgorging from a larger vessel, probably an alien troop carrier, before they plunged toward the surface. "But let's count our blessings, people, what few of them we've got. I don't know if we can accept what we see here as valid - maybe the enemy is trying to deceive us - but at least we've got *something* to work with, and that's where we need to start." He looked at Sato. "Lieutenant, this is damn good work." Turning toward the back of the room, he nodded at Steph. "You, too, Miss Guillaume."

Steph smiled her thanks, grateful for the notice.

Sitting back in his chair, Sabine said, "Ladies and gentlemen, I'm going to be candid here: does anyone *not* believe that we have a real reason to be worried? Does anyone still think this is some sort of hoax, and if so, do you have any plausible story to back it up? I'm not looking for people to hit in the head, I just want to make sure we're not overlooking some other plausible explanation."

The faces around the table, along with the back-benchers, were uniformly grim. Those who had come into the presentation scoffing at the whole affair were now believers. They didn't even have to believe all of Sato's story: the evidence presented today was terrifying enough.

Sabine turned back to Sato. "How much time does Keran have left?"

Sato answered without hesitation. They had confirmed that the progression of the depiction of war southward across the artifact's surface was at a constant rate, and had refined his own original estimates. Unfortunately, the confirmed rate left them with less time than Sato had originally predicted. "Four hundred and eighty-three days from today, sir," he told him. "A little over sixteen months."

A lot of heads shook at that number, and Sato heard several groans and curses. No one in this room had really, truly believed it until then. But seeing an image of what was clearly an alien ship made it a lot more real than the word of an emotionally devastated midshipman-turned-lieutenant.

"All right," Sabine went on, "that's what we have to work with. Ladies and gentlemen, I can't emphasize enough how important it's going to be to pull what we can together as fast as possible. This is the president's number one priority. We're probably going to go through some rough changes in how we do things, so be flexible and remember what's at stake. Because if they can hit Keran, they can hit Earth. They proved that with how they sent *Aurora* back to us."

"Which brings up the question of why they even bothered to send you back," Penkovsky said, looking at Sato. "Why not just attack out of the blue and wipe us off the map? Why go to all this trouble of warning us?"

Sabine turned to look at Sato, too, as if the young lieutenant had all the answers.

"I believe," he said slowly, "that it is their sense of honor."

"Explain," Admiral Tiernan told him.

"I am only speculating, sir. But consider: only the members of the crew who fought back, or were in a group that collectively fought back, survived the original boarding attack. I believe the only exception was the engineers tasked with destroying the computer core, who apparently died fighting. From what Lieutenant Amundsen said, it sounded as if they forced the Kreelans to kill them before they could be stunned. But that is only a guess." He glanced at Steph, and saw her nod. It didn't matter how many times he'd thought or spoken of what happened in the arena, it was still impossible to talk about it without having to seize firm control of his emotions. "Then those of us who were herded into the arena faced off against warriors who were clearly chosen to be roughly equal to ourselves. We were given a choice of weapons, and they fought without the armor that they normally wore. Petty Officer Yao believed that it was a test of our character, and everything the aliens did seemed to be aimed at making the contest as equal as possible." He nodded toward the images on the screen, now showing the alien warship again. "The lottery was also clearly intended to choose one of us to send back, to bear witness to what happened. I believe that sending the *Aurora* back tells us that they are intentionally giving us a chance to prepare. I believe that they *want* us to put up a good fight." He shrugged. "It would have made my job much easier for them to have left the ship's sensor and navigational records intact, but perhaps that was all part of the test of our character, as well."

"What if we refuse to give them a fight?" Penkovsky mused. "What if they jump into Keran and are welcomed with open arms?"

"The people on the planet will be slaughtered," Sato said bluntly, "to the last man, woman, and child. Just like the Kreelans cut down everyone on *Aurora* who didn't fight back."

"You have no doubt of that?" Admiral Tiernan asked softly.

"None, sir," Sato told him, fists clenched at his sides. "I saw enough to convince me."

Tiernan nodded sadly. He had known Owen McClaren well, and his death and that of his crew hit him personally.

"All right, then, people," Sabine told them. "If the president can get us the money and the people, we've got a fleet to build and a war to prepare for. And we don't have much time..."

TWELVE

"So that's the best we can do?" President McKenna said quietly as she stood at the windows of her private office in the Presidential Complex, staring out over the water toward where the Statue of Liberty still stood. While the United States technically no longer existed, its constitutional values had evolved into the foundation for the Terran Government, and Lady Liberty was as much an icon of the planetary government as she had once been of the nation for which it had originally been created. But statues would not help defend Keran or the rest of the human sphere from the Kreelan Empire. "Forty-seven ships and two heavy ground divisions?"

"Yes, ma'am," Joshua Sabine told her, feeling ashamed that he had not been able to do better. But in the time they had been given, and with the incredibly stiff resistance the president had faced from Congress, he was amazed they had been able to accomplish that much. "That's what we'll be able to deploy in the expeditionary force, while maintaining roughly two-thirds of the fleet here. We've altered the refit cycle to have nearly one hundred percent readiness for a three-week window, long enough to find out what happens at Keran. We could provide a lot more ground troops if the Keran government would allow us to send them ahead of time, but two divisions is all we can embark at one time on the carriers without using civilian liners. And if we have to do that, there's no way we can deploy those troops in a combat environment. It's the same with the aerospace squadrons we'd wanted to send: there's simply no way to bring them in under combat conditions. So we settled for two interceptor squadrons carried on one of the fleet's support ships, along with enough logistics support for a month." He sighed in frustration. "But they won't be able to get into the fight unless we can get them down to the planet. And we can't do *that* unless we have permission from the government or, if the Kreelans do show up, control of the system so we can protect the support ships as they bring in the interceptors."

She turned to face him, and once again Sabine was stunned at how much of a toll the last year had taken on her. Her close-cropped black hair was now streaked with gray, and her forehead was creased with wrinkles from the enormous burden she had taken upon her shoulders: literally, the fate of humanity. A fate that so few still believed involved alien invaders from across the galaxy, even after the evidence the government had presented from the *Aurora* investigation.

But the president did believe it, and she had suffered for her perceived heresy at the hands of the press and from the Terran Congress. After the initial sensation of *Aurora's* return started to wear off, the public and the congressmen suddenly paid closer attention to exactly what the president was asking for, and it didn't take them long to start screaming bloody murder. President McKenna had enjoyed an extremely good working relationship with Congress, but the massive appropriations bill her staff had hammered together in an amazingly short time was met with shocked disbelief. The sale of war bonds, tax increases, possible federalization of key industries, and other measures brought a howl of indignation from the public and their elected representatives. The president had invited further attacks with an appeal for a vote to institute a draft that she sent to both houses. The resulting public uproar plunged her popularity into a tailspin. More than one critic had commented that had the Terran democratic institutions been based on a parliamentary system, McKenna would have been kicked out of office in a very one-sided vote of confidence.

On the diplomatic front, the story was equally bleak. The local diplomats were completely unsupportive, and the official government positions, delayed by weeks due to the communications time lag, were the same.

But there was a ray of hope. The one diplomat who took Hamilton Barca's entreaties seriously was Ambassador Laurent Navarre from the planet Avignon. Unlike most of the other ambassadors, Navarre was a former naval officer who had seen extensive combat during the St. Petersburg intervention, and he had taken a very keen interest in what had happened with the *Aurora*. After his initial meeting with Barca, he had taken the bold step of asking to speak directly with Sato. At Barca's request, the Navy had quickly provided a secure vidcom terminal, and Barca sat in Navarre's office while the French diplomat bombarded Sato, who at the time was still quarantined on *Aurora*, with very pointed questions. Impressed with the young man's responses, Navarre told Barca that not only would he recommend that his government support Earth's position, but that he would also recommend that Avignon and the other members of the Francophone Alliance offer to send military assistance to Keran. It was a huge diplomatic victory, particularly since the Francophone Alliance represented a major bloc of the human sphere. But it was the only such victory they had enjoyed.

Now, only six weeks were left before the invasion was to occur. A lot of people were becoming curious again as the day approached, drawing the populace away from the general apathy that had replaced the initial surge of reaction to *Aurora's* return. "Are they going to be ready in time?"

Sabine shrugged. "They'll be as ready as we can make them, Madam President," he told her. "Admiral Tiernan has been running them through a tough training cycle, trying to get the new ships and crews in shape. He's got a lot of challenges trying to pull everything together, but everyone's pushing as hard as they can. I think the ground forces are fine, as General Singh decided - wisely, I believe - to take two of our best divisions and tailor them for the deployment. So if we can get them on the ground, they'll be ready to go." He sighed. "Part of it is that we just don't know what we're going to be facing. For all we know, the Empire could throw a thousand ships at us in the first wave. Aside from the things we see from the crystal ball..."

That's what everyone had taken to calling the alien artifact showing Keran, which had almost completely transformed into a raging world at war.

"...we have absolutely no intelligence information to go on."

"And the Keran government still hasn't budged?" McKenna asked.

"No, Madam President," Hamilton Barca sighed. "I've done everything I can think of, short of wringing bin Sultan's princely neck to get them to accept our help, even humanitarian assistance. They simply refuse to allow a Terran military presence in the system, even a single military vessel." It wasn't a surprise, of course: part of the reason for Keran's odd mix of Chinese and Arabic cultures was due to the last round of wars that were fought on Earth before the Diaspora. The old United States, together with India and Russia, had been heavily involved on the "opposite side." The inhabitants of Keran viewed the Terran Planetary Government, which was largely dominated by constituencies from the old United States, Russia, and India, with a great deal of circumspection, if not outright distrust.

"Then how the devil are we supposed to know if the invasion takes place?"

"That, at least, we have covered," Barca told her, nodding toward Vladimir Penkovsky.

"We've arranged the diplomatic courier shuttle schedule so that there are at least two courier ships in-system at any given time," Penkovsky explained, "with one in orbit and the other transiting in- or out-system. We've equipped all the courier ships with enhanced sensor packages that will augment their normal navigation and collision-avoidance systems to provide us with data on what is happening in local space and on the planet itself." He held up a hand to forestall the question he saw the president about to ask. "No, Madam President, none of the equipment is classified or in any way compromises the diplomatic integrity of the couriers in the unlikely event one of them should be examined. Everything is off-the-shelf and commercially available. The upgraded systems will not provide information as detailed as we could get from our military systems, but it will be close."

McKenna nodded, satisfied. The last thing she needed now was a major diplomatic incident with the Keran government. "What about the French?" she asked.

Barca smiled. When she said *French*, she meant the Francophone Alliance. Like virtually all the major nation-states since the formation of the Terran Planetary Government, the country once known as France still existed as an administrative entity. But in Terran Government circles, "France" referred to the group of worlds settled by refugees from France, Belgium, their former African colonies, and even some of the *Quebecois* from Canada, during the Diaspora. Unlike some of the other worlds that were settled during that period, they had benefitted from amazing luck in colonizing Avignon, La Seyne, and several other planets that were very compatible with humans and were rich in natural resources. Collectively they had become one of the major economic and military forces in the human sphere, and generally shared common interests with Earth. Fortunately, the Francophone Alliance also enjoyed very good relations with Keran that weren't tainted by unpleasantness from the past.

"That's still our best news," Barca told her, "although it has its warts, too. The Alliance is preparing to deploy roughly one hundred warships to Keran, along with ten ground divisions. Ambassador Navarre indicated that the only real sticking point was the ground forces: the Keran Government is only going to allow them to deploy a single division planetside until or unless the enemy fleet actually materializes. The Kerans still don't think there's anything to worry about, and while they don't mind having a bunch of French warships in orbit, they don't want three full heavy corps of troops running amok on the streets."

"But the French don't have enough carriers to get their divisions deployed quickly from orbit," Sabine pointed out, incredulous. "Are they just going to hold the troops on starliners until the attack comes and then shuttle them down?" Barca nodded, shrugging. "Good, God," Sabine said, rolling his eyes, "they're going to be sitting ducks!"

"They don't have any choice," Barca pointed out. "Believe me, Navarre wasn't happy with the plan when he heard about it, either. But the Alliance approved it, so that's what they're going with."

"So which division are they allowing the French to land ahead of time?" the president asked.

"They're deploying the entire combat contingent of the Foreign Legion," Barca told her, "which is technically a division-plus. They're sending all twenty field infantry regiments, plus the Legion's independent armored brigade. Navarre said the decision is already raising hell with peacekeeping operations where they had to pull out some of the regiments, but they did it anyway."

Sabine grunted. "The Keran government would have been better off letting them deploy the other nine divisions and keep the legionnaires in orbit if they were worried about troops getting wild on the ground," he said. "On the other hand, they're a bunch of tough bastards. Good call. But they won't have any heavy artillery support outside of the armored brigade."

"So," the president asked, "what major problems do we have left, aside from the obvious ones."

"Command and control," Sabine said immediately. "We've been talking to the French about inter-operability, but we've gotten an ice-cold shoulder." The president gave him *the look*, the one where she seemed to promise that she'd rip the heart out of someone's chest if he or she hadn't been giving something their all. "Ma'am," Sabine said, leaning forward to emphasize his point, "we even offered to give them a set of our systems to look over and modify - no questions asked! - to be compatible with theirs so our ships and ground troops can communicate effectively. But they're so paranoid about their system security that they simply won't do it. They refused to even take the equipment and software that we offered them, even to just look at it."

"So when the attack comes and our ships jump in to assist," she asked him, a look of pained incredulity on her face, "they won't be able to communicate with the French fleet?"

"No, Madam President," Sabine told her grimly. "Aside from the normal basic communications that all ships have, we'll have no way of integrating our battle management capabilities. The ships will be able to talk to each other with normal voice and video, but other than that both fleets will be fighting completely on their own..."

* * *

Aboard the recently commissioned destroyer *TNS Owen D. McClaren*, Lieutenant Ichiro Sato found himself far more worried about the survival of his own ship in the current fleet exercise than the strategic concerns guiding the president's cabinet discussion. What troubled him wasn't the complex targeting and maneuvering problems the exercise controllers were throwing at the ships. It was the ship's captain.

"*Goddammit, Sato!*" Commander Scott Morrison, the ship's captain, cursed, making half the bridge crew cringe. Glaring at his young tactical officer, he practically sneered, "I ordered you to fire on target Delta with the pulse cannon. Are you deaf or just incompetent?"

"Sir," Sato said, trying not to grit his teeth, "as I explained to you earlier, the pulse cannon has a thirty second recycle rate under optimal conditions." The pulse cannon was a highly modified laser that was mounted in the ship's keel. It could deliver a massive punch, but the entire ship had to be aligned on the target, and it took virtually all of the ship's energy reserves to fire. It was a powerful weapon, but had some serious tactical drawbacks. The *McClaren* was one of only two of the expeditionary force's ships that had been built with one. "You had already ordered a laser salvo against targets Alpha and Bravo, which depleted the energy buffers. Every time that happens, the recycle sequence for the pulse cannon resets-"

"Enough," Morrison snapped, waving his hand dismissively as he turned back to the primary bridge display. "The bottom line is you fucked up."

"Sir, I-"

"I said that's enough," the captain hissed. Getting out of his combat chair, which was strictly prohibited during exercises except for safety reasons, he stalked over to Sato's position. Pointing a finger in Sato's face, he went on, "The reason - the *only* reason - you are on this ship, mister, is because you managed to stuff your head up Admiral Tiernan's ass so far that you could look out his ears. All I ask from you, if it's not too much, is that you just sit there, keep your bloody mouth shut, and *do your fucking job!*" He paused, staring at Sato and clearly expecting the younger man to cave in. Tall but still gangly even in early middle age, Morrison normally towered over Sato. But now the captain's face, which could only be described as grossly ordinary, was a mere hand's breadth from Sato's nose. "Do I make myself clear?"

"Perfectly, captain," Sato replied stonily, his gaze unwavering, although his hands were digging into his armrests. He wasn't intimidated; he was disgusted and heartsick that such an awful man had been given command of one of the few ships humanity had to send against what Sato knew must be heading toward Keran even now. And it was an insult that someone like Morrison had been given command of the ship that bore Captain McClaren's name.

Sato had only come aboard two weeks earlier as the ship was finishing up her initial space trials, and had been immediately appalled by the state of the crew: sullen and quiet, the various departments of the ship in fierce competition to avoid the captain's ire. Morrison had effectively cowed all of the officers, including the exec, except for the chief engineer, Lieutenant Commander Vedette Pergolesi. But while Pergolesi stood as a human heat shield between the captain and the crewmen of the engineering department, the rest of the crew had to fend for themselves. After having their hides flayed a few times after he'd come aboard, even the senior chiefs stayed out of the path of the captain's vitriol. Most of them had seen his type before and kept their distance as much as possible. And that, as much as anything else, was devastating for the crew.

"We've just been hit by a brace of kinetics," the XO said in a matter-of-fact voice. While Morrison had been berating Sato, an enemy ship had fired the equivalent of giant shotgun shells at them. Since no one else on the bridge was about to interrupt his tirade to ask for maneuvering orders, or take the initiative to change the ship's course and avoid the incoming projectiles, the exercise computer declared five hits along the length of the hull.

"*Goddammit!*" Morrison cried disgustedly, stomping back to his command chair.

"And the captain has been declared a casualty because he wasn't in his combat chair," the XO added meekly, waiting for the spontaneous human combustion that he knew would result.

Morrison didn't disappoint him.

"Incoming from Commodore Santiago, sir," the communications rating announced in the middle of the captain's impressive stream of invective. Her voice was perfectly neutral, but Sato had no trouble identifying the underlying tone of vicious glee.

Morrison threw himself into his chair and snapped, "On my console." Sato knew that normally the captain took any calls from senior officers in private in his ready room adjacent to the bridge, but he couldn't get away with that in an exercise, especially since he'd just become a casualty for being out of his command chair. Even on the small console screen that was embedded in the chair, the entire bridge crew would be able to hear the admiral, even if they couldn't see his expression. All exercise communications were recorded for later analysis during the debriefing and lessons-learned discussions, and no one had any doubt that the recording of this particular discussion would make its way to the entire crew.

"Scott," Commodore Rafael Santiago, who commanded the flotilla to which *McClaren* was assigned, appeared on the vidcom and demanded, "what the devil is going on over there?"

"My apologies, sir," Morrison answered evenly. "We're having some difficulties adapting the pulse cannon to our tactics. It's playing hell with our energy buffer allocation, and our tactical officer lost the shot on target Charlie. I was trying to get that sorted out when the kinetic attack came in, but the XO failed to maneuver clear." He put a sympathetic but determined look on his face. "We've only had a couple weeks to hammer this crew together, commodore. We're not as tightly integrated yet as the other ships." *McClaren* was the only newly-launched ship in Santiago's flotilla; the other five ships had captains and crews that had served together for more than a year.

Santiago frowned. "I realize that, Scott," he sighed. "And training is where we're supposed to make our mistakes. Let's just make sure we all learn from them, because we won't get a second chance at this."

"Aye, aye, sir," Morrison replied, resolution evident in his voice. "We won't let you down."

"Good enough," Santiago said. "Carry on." The screen went blank.

* * *

Sato and some of the other junior officers from *McClaren* sat around the table at the back of Nightingale's, one of Africa Station's less reputable bars, enjoying their last bit of off-ship time before the expeditionary force prepared to deploy. While open twenty-four hours a day, the bar's schedule was really slaved to Universal Standard Time, which was now sixteen-hundred. Before the dinner hour the bar was fairly quiet and not too crowded, but business would pick up soon, with raucous music blaring over the bodies packed onto the dance floor and seated at the surrounding tables.

"We're fucked," Ensign Kayla Watanabe sighed. She was the ship's junior navigation officer, and had more than once been on the receiving end of a rebuke from her captain for things that weren't her fault. That didn't bother her so much; she could take the tongue lashings. What she couldn't take was the certain knowledge that their ship couldn't fight worth a damn.

Heads around the table nodded glumly. They had managed to do better during the rest of the exercise, but Sato attributed that to luck as much as anything else. Commodore Santiago had positioned *McClaren* in a support role during the following engagements, giving the other ships the lead in the flotilla's attacks while *McClaren* cleaned up the scraps. The ship had managed to survive, but the entire crew felt humiliated.

"What do you think, Sato?" Watanabe asked. "Are we going to get our asses reamed by the Kreelans?" In unison, the others turned to him, dejected, but eager to hear what he had to say.

It was odd, Sato thought, that here he was, again the youngest and least experienced officer on the ship, much as he had been on the *Aurora* as a midshipman. Yet, they were looking to him for an answer, for leadership. It was true that he outranked most of those around the table, but there was more to it than that. He was the only one aside from Pergolesi, the chief of engineering, who continued to stand up to the captain. Even during the shit-storm of their after-action review, when the captain had found fault with virtually every one of his officers, Sato had stood firm and said what needed to be said about his perceptions of the crew's performance - both the things they had done well, and those they hadn't - respectfully but firmly. *For the record, if nothing else*, he'd thought at the time. He had absorbed a lot of abuse from the captain after making contradictory observations on the actions of some of the other members of the bridge crew. It had been incredibly difficult to not spell out all the captain's mistakes, but he knew that wouldn't help. There was no way the commodore would replace Morrison at this late date unless he made some sort of flagrant violation, and the captain was too savvy for that. As with his conversation with the commodore during the exercise, he was an expert at taking just enough blame to make himself look responsible, while shoving the bulk of it off on the alleged inadequacies of his junior officers.

Sighing, Sato looked around the table at their expectant faces, the faces of people he'd only known for a couple weeks, but on whom his life would depend in the coming battle. He wished he had some good news for them, some way to give them some confidence. "Look," he told them, "I'll be honest and say that I don't think the expeditionary force is going to be nearly enough to stop them when they come, even if we had the best captain in the fleet. I don't think the Kreelans will be using ships like the ones that attacked *Aurora*, but they don't have to. Somehow they're going to level the playing field with us, but..." He shook his head. "I think Keran is going to be a much bigger version of the arena that my old crew fought and died in. I don't think they're going to let us win this battle."

"So all this is for nothing?" one of the others asked, disgusted. "We just go out there and get our asses kicked by an enemy we can't touch?"

"No," Sato replied forcefully. "That's not what I meant. I don't think we'll be able to save Keran from whatever the aliens plan to do. But I do think that they're going to give us a chance to show them what we're made of. I think if we fight hard and well, we'll buy humanity extra time to build its defenses. If we don't..." He shook his head. "If we don't meet their expectations, I believe they could wipe us from the universe without even trying."

"But what the hell do we do about Captain-fucking-Queeg?" someone asked.

"Nothing," Sato sighed in resignation. "The only thing we can do is our very best as individuals, and to try and work hard as a team. The captain's used to playing the department heads against each other, instead of having them work together." It was common knowledge that very few officers aboard a ship would ever qualify for command in what was a relatively small fleet. So the competition for top ratings on their first ship tour was critical: only the officers in the top one or two slots stood a chance at ever earning command wings. And the way most captains accomplished this winnowing of their junior officers was to pit them against each other, promoting those who wound up with the fewest marks against them. It was generally a divisive and corrosive way to run a ship, but only a few captains, such as Ichiro's old skipper, Owen McClaren, saw beyond it to cultivate a close sense of teamwork, basing officer evaluations primarily on how well they worked with one another. Almost all of McClaren's former junior officers qualified for command later in their careers, and

Ichiro knew that the Navy was very shortly going to wish it had a great many more command qualified officers. "So," Ichiro went on, "we've *got* to do our best to work together. Forget all the career advancement garbage. That's not going to mean a thing if we get vaporized a few weeks from now."

Everyone agreed with that: what was the point of coming out in the top one or two position on your ratings when you were dead?

Sato picked up his glass and drained it, savoring the cold tea. Unlike the others, he didn't drink alcohol. "Okay, I've got to go." Standing up, he said, "I'll see you all back aboard tomorrow morning."

Watching Sato leave, Watanabe remarked, "Well, maybe when we go into combat the first time, the captain will forget to stay in his chair..."

* * *

Ichiro was covered in a fine sheen of sweat as he went through the various *katas* he had been taught, the movements to attack and defend with the *katana*. It had become an obsession, and the closest thing he had now to religion.

One of the first things he had done to fill up what little free time he had after being released from quarantine aboard the *Aurora* was to seek out a *sensei* to teach him how to use his grandfather's weapon. It was a difficult task for two reasons: he had no idea even where to look for someone with the right skills, and among those he found very few were really willing to offer what he truly wanted: a crash-course in how to kill with a sword. He wasn't interested in the finer points of swordsmanship, because he knew that he would never make a great, or probably even good, swordsman: that process took many years, and he only had a little over one year to learn what he could. The teachers he spoke to didn't understand that he didn't want to learn for sport or for some higher personal purpose. He wanted to learn how to kill.

Then one day a man appeared at the door of his cabin on Africa Station. When Sato opened the door, the man, who was of Japanese descent, bowed and then gestured for Sato to go with him. The man refused to say a word. Frustrated by the man's bizarre behavior, Sato was nonetheless curious and decided to follow him. The man took him to the station's sports complex, where they entered one of the many exercise rooms. It was empty except for two items: a pair of wooden swords, *bokken*, that lay in the center of the floor.

The man, who Sato judged to be in his late fifties, knelt gracefully on one side of the two *bokken*. Sato, shrugging, knelt opposite him. Giving in to ingrained habit from his childhood, he lowered himself to the floor in a deep bow, and the older man did the same. Then he handed Sato one of the *bokken*, and wordlessly began to teach him how to use it.

The scene repeated itself every day that Sato was on the station. Regardless of whether he was there early or late in the day, the old man magically appeared on his doorstep. Sato had tried everything he could think of to get some sort of information from him about who he was and what he was doing there, beyond the obvious of teaching Sato swordsmanship, but the old man calmly ignored him and simply got down to business as soon as they arrived at their designated workout room. Sato tried to find out who scheduled the room, but in every single case, it was listed as open. He tried finding out who the man was from the shuttle transit services, but they couldn't release passenger information, and even Steph couldn't dig her way to the bottom of it. It was maddening.

But aside from the strange circumstances, Sato could clearly see that the man, his silent *sensei*, knew what he was doing. The many hours they spent together were hard and challenging, and more than once Sato went back to his quarters sporting a number of welts where the *sensei* had underscored some of Sato's shortcomings. But that only made Sato want to train harder, because he knew that if his teacher had been a Kreelan wielding a real sword, Sato wouldn't just be bruised, he'd be dead.

After about eight months, they began to train with real *katanas*, but with their edges blunted. Sato knew that he didn't have the refinement or overall abilities of someone who had trained for years, but he now had confidence that he could fight. He knew that he would lose against a Kreelan warrior who had probably been trained since birth for combat, but he would never again be completely helpless as he had been in the arena aboard the Kreelan warship, seemingly so long ago.

Then, two weeks ago, his *sensei* suddenly stopped coming. Sato was worried that something had happened to the man - he still didn't even know his name - until a package arrived. It was a tube about fifty centimeters long and maybe fifteen in diameter. Carefully opening it, he was stunned at the contents: a *wakizashi*, the shorter companion sword that samurai warriors traditionally carried with the longer *katana*. But this wasn't just any *wakizashi*. It was the companion to his grandfather's sword.

Wrapped inside the tube was a brief handwritten note in flowing Japanese characters:

I regret the odd circumstances of our relationship, young Ichiro. But after your journalist friend sent word to Nagano of your adventures and mentioned your wish to learn the ways of the sword, your mother sent me. She swore me to silence, for she did not wish your father to find out for fear he might somehow learn what your mother had done. He is a most unworthy man, unlike his son.

She knew me through your grandfather, you see, who was an honored friend, and my sensei long ago. She wanted you to have this, your grandfather's wakizashi, when you completed the training I could give you. Your father had spitefully hidden it before you left home, but your mother found it again soon after, and kept it safe since then.

You are a fine young man, Ichiro. Your mother is so very proud of you, as would be your honored grandfather.

- Rai Tomonaga

It was a revelation for which Ichiro was totally unprepared. He simply sat in his quarters for most of that evening, staring at the note and the short sword that had come with it. Finally, he spent the next few hours, well into the night, composing a note to his mother, the first he had sent since he had left home.

Now, on his last free evening station-side, he had spent a full two hours practicing the moves Tomonaga had taught him when the door chime rang. Then he heard the door open. Only one person had his access code. Steph.

"Hey, kid," she called to him as she came in, the door automatically swishing closed behind her. She always called him that when they were alone, although she was only ten years older.

Steph leaned against the wall near the door, watching as Ichiro went through the remainder of a ballet of lethal moves with his grandfather's sword. Bare above the waist, the muscles of his upper body rippled as he slashed and thrust with the glittering weapon, and she marveled at how hard and chiseled his body had become. He hadn't exactly been in bad shape physically when she'd first met him on the *Aurora*, but he had totally transformed himself in the last year with the help of the mysterious Tomonaga-san. *Admit it, woman*, she chided herself, trying to look away but failing, *he's goddamn beautiful.*

After a few more moves, Ichiro sheathed the sword, making even that move graceful and deadly-looking. Holding the *katana* in both hands, he bowed his head to it, then carefully placed it on a small wooden stand that held the matched pair of swords.

"It's too bad the Navy didn't take you up on your suggestion to make close combat training and swordsmanship mandatory," she sighed. "Then they'd all be hunks like you."

Ichiro grinned at her as he toweled off the sweat. "Don't you wish," he quipped. "So, what's going on?"

She folded her arms at him and gave him a look that he knew from experience meant that he'd just said something incredibly stupid. "Gee, I don't know," she told him, stepping up to take the towel to rub down his back. "Maybe this'll be the last time I see you before you deploy, you moron." She paused, then added, "Although maybe I'll get to see you while you're on station at the rendezvous point."

Ichiro whipped around and took her wrists, not altogether gently. "What?" he exclaimed. "I thought you were staying back here to cover the president."

Steph's career had taken off into the stratosphere after her coverage of the *Aurora*, and she had been able to pick any assignment she'd wanted. She'd chosen a lead position on the press team that covered the president, and hadn't been disappointed by the massive battle that had been waged in the following months between the executive and legislative branches. While the fighting had only been waged in words and manipulation of governmental processes, it had been as fierce in its own way as men and women grappling on a battlefield.

"I know, Ichiro," she told him, reaching her hands up to touch his face, his own hands still wrapped around her wrists. "But I asked for an embed position in the expeditionary force. That's where the action's going to be, and I want to be in the middle of it."

"Stephanie," he nearly choked, looking as if he'd been sucker-punched, "you mustn't go. Please." He had never called her by her full name since she had told him she went by Steph.

She smiled up at him. "Trying to be Mister Chivalrous, are you?" she told him gently. "Listen, I know how to take care of myself." She moved closer, her nose almost touching his. "You don't have to worry about me."

"Most of us won't be coming back, Steph," he whispered, his dark almond eyes glittering. "Maybe none of us. I don't want...I don't want anything to happen to you."

"Nothing will," she whispered before bringing her lips to his. For just a moment, he didn't react. They had always been "just friends," never thinking that their relationship would ever be anything more. Then he returned her kiss, tentatively at first, and then with growing passion. When Steph felt his powerful arms wrap around her, drawing her body tight against his, a wave of heat rushed through her core. Suddenly, she wished that they'd done this a long time ago.

Without another word, Ichiro effortlessly picked her up and carried her to the bedroom.

THIRTEEN

Communications between ships, like everything else that was taken for granted in the normal universe, was impossible in hyperspace. But Tesh-Dar needed no machines to communicate with the warriors and shipmistresses of the fleet that now approached the end of the voyage to the human world of Keran. Distance and space were immaterial to the Bloodsong that linked her with the billions of her sisters and to the Empress. It was not the same as the spoken word, but Her will was clear. War was upon them.

Tesh-Dar thought back to the time before her fleet was launched, to the gathering of the warrior priestesses and mistresses of the guilds and castes on the Empress Moon. Orbiting above the Homeworld, the Empress Moon was the home of the Imperial City and dwelling place of the Empress, a physical monument to Her power. In the heart of the city lay the Great Tower, atop which was the throne room. Kilometers high in terms of human measure, the Great Tower was thousands of years beyond anything humans could build, yet it had been created by Kreelan hands untold centuries before. The throne room itself surpassed any human's imagination of magnificence: larger than all the palaces ever built by humankind and enclosed in a pyramidal ceiling of diamond-hard crystal, the room itself was a breathless work of art with giant frescoes and tapestries telling the great tale of the First Empress and the Unification.

This gathering was the first of its kind in many great cycles of the Empress Moon about the Homeworld, for this was one of the rare events that affected the entire race of *Kreela*. Upon the hundreds of steps to the great throne stood representatives of all the castes of Her Children, from the lowliest bearers of water to Tesh-Dar herself, greatest of the Empire's warriors. It was a trek the Empress made, from step to step, taking into account the needs of each and every caste, of all of Her Children from the lowliest to the mighty.

On this special day, She sat upon the throne as Her Children knelt before Her, Tesh-Dar foremost among them, kneeling upon the first step from the throne.

"My Children," the Empress began, Her voice carrying clearly across the great expanse of the throne room to the multitudes who knelt below, the crews and warriors of the ships that were about to go into battle against the humans, "today is a day that long shall be remembered in the Books of Time. For once again we have found a race worthy of our mettle, an alien species that in flesh is like us in many ways, but is yet soulless. Make their blood burn, My Children, in the fires of war. For if their blood sings to us, they may be saved. If it does not, then let them perish as animals without knowing the light or the love that awaits us among the Ancient Ones.

"You are led this day," the Empress went on, "by Tesh-Dar, high priestess of the Desh-Ka and a living legend of the sword. Thrill to the song of her blood in battle, My Children, and great honor shall be yours." She paused, and Tesh-Dar could feel a warm wind stir in her soul as the Empress said, "So has it been, so shall it forever be. Let the Challenge begin."

"In Thy name, let it be so," Tesh-Dar echoed along with the thousands below her.

Returning her thoughts to the present, Tesh-Dar watched the globe of the human world they sought in a twin of the energy capsule they had sent back with the Messenger. On and above the surface of the planet, fierce battles raged, a simulacrum of what was to begin only moments from now. The great priestess sat in her command chair, her talons scoring the metal of one of the armrests as she absently drummed her fingers on it. She had no idea what awaited them in the system, and her body tingled with eager anticipation at what they might find. Had her instincts been right, and the Messenger well-chosen? Did a war fleet await them, or would these *humans* succumb to utter obliteration because they refused to rise to battle?

She was not concerned about dying or even her entire fleet being destroyed, as long as it was lost in battle against a worthy adversary. For that would accomplish what she and her sisters lived and died for: to honor their Empress in battle. In the millennia-long interludes when they had no external enemies to fight, Her Children sought honor through combat in the multitude of arenas throughout the Empire, in ritual battles that were rarely fought to the death.

That was why this contest brought such a sense of excitement to Tesh-Dar and the warriors she led: this was not simply a ritual contest, but truly *war*. She could imagine no more terrible, no more glorious pursuit, and her blood raged with expectant fire.

Holding her breath in anticipation, she watched as the globe of the human world quickly began to darken...

* * *

What to do with the artifact had sparked a long and fierce debate throughout the Terran defense community, all the way up to the president. Some had wanted to keep it in Earth space, both to study and to use as an indicator of the progress of the battle in hopes that what would be reflected on the globe after the attack began would show what was really happening, and thus provide real-time intelligence. Others argued that it would make more sense for the expeditionary force to have the artifact for the very same reasons.

The decision had eventually wound up on the president's desk. She took less than thirty seconds to decide. "Send it with the fleet," she ordered as commander-in-chief. "If it provides any sort of warning, they'll need it a lot more than we will. It won't do us any good when it would take us a week and a half to get ships there. Assuming we had any more to send."

Once that had been determined, others raised concerns about whether it was a bomb. But after a great deal of discussion that essentially went nowhere, Admiral Tiernan decided that if it had been some sort of weapon, the Kreelans could have used it to good effect long before. He ordered that a special instrumentation enclosure be built aboard the flagship to record any emissions or changes in the artifact, and a close watch had been kept every moment since the fleet had jumped from Earth space.

The fleet had gathered at a point that was a two-hour hyperspace jump from Keran. That was as close as they felt they could come without alerting the colony or the French fleet in-system and creating a diplomatic mess. The Keran and French governments knew, of course, that the Terran expeditionary force had left Earth space, but as long as it stayed clear of the Keran system, no one was likely to complain too loudly.

Admiral Tiernan was now on the flag bridge of the heavy cruiser *Ticonderoga*. The flag bridge was a special compartment, separate from the ship's bridge, that had all the systems his staff needed to help him control the fleet's operations.

"What the hell?" someone yelped "Something's happening!"

Tiernan snapped his head up to look at the three-dimensional image of the alien orb that was being projected on one of the flag bridge view screens. The globe was quickly darkening, the scene of a world at war being swallowed by infinite black. Then it started to shrink. But it didn't appear to be just getting smaller. It looked more like it was moving away from them. Tiernan thought it was a trick of the view screen display, but wasn't sure.

"What's happening to it?" He asked one of the battery of scientists who had been monitoring the artifact.

"Admiral..." the lead scientist replied, then paused as he conferred with the others. "Sir, this is impossible..."

"Dammit, man, what's happening?"

"It's moving away from us, sir," the man said, shaking his head. In the view screen, the globe was now the relative size of a marble, and growing smaller by the second. "It can't be doing what the instruments are saying," he said, looking up at Tiernan with a helpless expression, "but it is. And it's accelerating-"

"Damn!" someone in the background shouted as a thunderous boom echoed from the instrumentation chamber.

"What was that?" *Ticonderoga's* captain interjected worriedly. "Did that thing explode?" The ship's executive officer was already moving a damage control party in. They weren't taking any chances on something that, even after all this time, was still a complete unknown.

"No..." the scientist said, shaken. "That was a sonic boom from within the chamber from displaced air. The globe just...vanished."

* * *

Admiral Jean-Claude Lefevre stood in a moment of tense quiet on the flag bridge of the heavy cruiser *Victorieuse,* the flagship of the *Alliance Française* fleet that had been deployed to Keran. Because of the prevailing political conditions, the deployment had been conducted under the guise of joint exercises with the Keran Navy, although everyone knew the cover explanation was a farce. Lefevre twisted his mouth into an ironic grin: any one of his five squadrons, with a total of one hundred and fifty-three naval vessels, was larger than the entire Keran fleet in terms of tonnage. And when one considered that most of the Keran ships were small corvettes with little real combat capability, the "joint" label became rather ludicrous. Nonetheless, the Alliance had taken the Terran information of an alien threat seriously, and Lefevre was trying to do the same.

Unfortunately, he was terribly frustrated by the total lack of intelligence information. His government believed the possibility of an alien attack was credible, as difficult as he himself found it to believe. But he had no idea of what size force he might be facing, where they might appear in the system, or even what their objective might be, other than the occupation of Keran. And if any of the information he had received about the enemy's technical capabilities were true, his ships would be so grossly outclassed that the presence of his fleet, the largest assembled since the St. Petersburg war, would be little more than a token gesture of defiance.

The only concrete information he had was when the attack was to take place. The Terrans had some sort of device that they believed was a countdown timer, an artifact from these so-called "Kreelans." Terran military authorities provided Avignon's military attaché on Earth with a digital countdown timer that would approximate the time left, calibrated to the changes shown by the alien device. The time remaining on that digital timer was displayed on every bridge in the Alliance fleet, and he now watched it closely as it wound down to zero.

"Thirty seconds," his flag captain said quietly into the mounting tension on the flag bridge. All the ships of the fleet had been at general quarters for the last two hours, as no one was sure how accurate the timer might be. Lefevre's mouth compressed into a thin line as he stared at the flag bridge tactical display that showed the disposition of his ships. Without having any idea of what the enemy planned or was capable of, his tactical options were very limited. He didn't want to put his ships in low orbit, deep inside Keran's gravity well, because even with reactionless drives gravity was a source of drag on a ship's acceleration potential: ships farther away from the planet were subject to far less gravity influence and had a tactical advantage when maneuvering. But he also couldn't put his ships too far out from the planet, or they might not be able to respond rapidly in case the enemy was planning on an orbital bombardment rather than an assault on the surface with ground forces. Having no information about their intentions and capabilities was maddening.

So he had been forced to compromise. He had divided his fleet into five task forces and placed them around the planet in high orbit to cover the most important population centers on the surface. In low orbit were twenty-four civilian starliners, each carrying a heavy combat brigade and tended by dozens of shuttles that would get the troops down to the surface as quickly as possible if he received permission to deploy them. A flotilla of six destroyers was tasked with protecting the starliners, forming a protective globe around the formation of huge civilian vessels.

"Fifteen seconds," the flag captain breathed. Lefevre shot the man a look, more bemused than annoyed, and his flag captain rewarded him with a sheepish grin. None of them wanted to believe anything was going to happen, but the Alliance was deeply worried, or they would not have been willing to absorb the enormous cost of deploying this many ships here. Lefevre watched as the timer counted down: *three...two...one...*

"Zero," he said to himself. "*Capitaine* Monet," he said into a comms screen to the ship's captain who stood tensely on the ship's bridge, "there are no changes in sensor readings, I assume?"

"*Non, mon amiral,*" he replied. "Nothing but merchant traffic coming into the normal inbound jump zones. Three ships in the last two hours."

Lefevre sighed. *All a wild goose chase*, he thought. *But it's just as well.* "Very well," he said. "We will remain at general quarters for another two hours, then resume our planned training-"

"*Amiral!*" the flag captain shouted, pointing at the flag bridge tactical display. The ships of the fleet were tied together in a data net, with the sensor readings and targeting data from each ship automatically distributed to the others to maximize situational awareness and coordinate their attacks. One of the task forces on the far side of the planet had picked up a set of bogies - unidentified contacts, presumed hostile - jumping in.

Lefevre looked up at the display and paled at what he saw. "*Oh, mon Dieu...*"

* * *

Aboard the two-person Terran *Hermes* class diplomatic courier ship *Alita*, pilot Amelia Cartwright was just settling down to a delicious dinner of reprocessed steak and potatoes from a foil packet when her copilot, Sid Dougherty, suddenly stiffened like he'd been hit with about ten thousand volts. They were on the modified courier run that had been established a number of weeks before, where at least one courier ship was in orbit and one was in transit at all times. *Alita* had just arrived the previous day, where she was supposed to remain for a week until their relief arrived.

"Sid?" she asked, then turned to see what he was staring at. On the monitor that had been installed a few weeks before as part of the ship's instrumentation upgrade, a wave of red icons had suddenly materialized roughly half a million kilometers from Keran. Inbound enemy ships.

"Shit!" she exclaimed, tossing her food onto the deck and strapping herself in. "Come on, Sid! Get on the departure checklist and let's get the hell out of here." They should be able to get underway in only a couple of minutes. She only hoped they had that long.

"Got it," Sid replied, tearing his eyes away from the screen. A tall, lanky Texan who always insisted on wearing a ridiculous-looking cowboy hat, she had never seen him rattled before. "Damn," he drawled as he quickly punched up the remaining preflight checks, "I just never believed this would happen. Look at all those bastards! There must be two hundred ships!"

"Keran control," Cartwright called over the planetary navigation network, "this is Terran diplomatic courier ship *Alita*, requesting emergency departure clearance, outbound vector radial three-five-one mark zero." The ship's computer was also sending the information in a more detailed format to its counterpart at Keran control, but it was longstanding tradition to establish positive human-to-human contact, as well.

"*Alita*, this is Keran control," a heavily accented but very pleasant voice replied immediately. "Please hold current position. Alliance fleet elements are on exercise in your sector, and have requested all vessels to remain clear. We will notify you immediately when we can grant departure clearance."

Sid glanced at her and shook his head. *No goddamn way*, he mouthed silently.

Cartwright paused for just a moment. In the fifteen years that she had been in the diplomatic courier service, she had never once disobeyed a controller. But this time she had no choice: her orders were very explicit, and they were signed by the Secretary of State himself. "Negative, Keran control," she said as Sid completed the last of the checklist items and gave her the thumbs-up that the ship was ready. She took the controls and poured power to the massive engines, breaking out of her assigned orbital position for open space. "My sincere apologies, but we have to depart immediately. Please inform the Alliance fleet that we're an outbound friendly. They have enough targets to worry about without wasting munitions on us."

She broke off the connection before the controller could reply. "Get me the ambassador," she told Sid.

"Already done," he told her, nodding to a secondary view screen on the console, where the face of a regal-looking older woman calmly looked out at them.

"Madam Ambassador," Cartwright said formally, "this is *Alita*. Be advised that a Kreelan fleet has - repeat, *has* - arrived in-system, and Alliance fleet units are maneuvering to engage. As you know, we have orders to jump out immediately. You should be receiving a download of all the data that we get until we jump, and if you have any last-minute information you want to send out with us, I request you transmit it immediately."

"Thank you, *Alita*," Ambassador Irina Pugachova replied. "Our final communiques are being uploaded as we speak, and I thank you for the sensor data. I have instructed our military attaché to provide it directly to the Keran military liaison. What is your assessment of the situation as it stands now?"

Cartwright tried not to cringe. "Ma'am...there are roughly two hundred enemy ships now in the system. I don't know how they stack up against what the Alliance has in terms of tonnage and weapons, but the Frenchies are going to have their hands full."

Ambassador Pugachova nodded gravely. She looked to the side briefly as someone spoke to her, then turned her attention back to Cartwright. "The invasion alert is being broadcast on the media. At least that did not take too long." She looked back at Cartwright. "Get to the fleet rendezvous as quickly as you can. Good luck and godspeed, pilot."

"Same to you, ma'am," Cartwright said. The ambassador's face disappeared as the screen went blank. The connection was closed.

"Five minutes to jump," Sid informed her as *Alita* fled toward open space. Fortunately, the vector Cartwright had chosen was largely free of Alliance ships, and the Kreelans were on the far side of the planet. She watched the sensor display as two of the Alliance task forces that were closest to the mass of Kreelan ships maneuvered, trying to optimize the geometry for deploying their weapons. Two of the other task forces were quickly accelerating around the planet to join the fray, while the last task force remained on station opposite the battle, probably in case the Kreelans tried to flank them with another inbound force.

In low orbit, the cloud of shuttles hovering around the starliners began to plunge toward the surface, desperately trying to ferry nine heavy divisions to the ground as quickly as possible.

"One minute," Sid said quietly, and Cartwright could hear the low thrum of the hyperdrive capacitors spooling up.

On the sensor screen, the nearest of the Alliance task forces had closed to within weapons range, and ships began to die. The sensor suite was not powerful enough to tell them anything about the weapons being employed, but icons representing both Alliance and Kreelan ships began to flare on the screen, then disappear.

Just before her ship jumped, Cartwright saw another cloud of red icons appear right on top of the lone Alliance task force guarding the far side of the planet.

* * *

Tesh-Dar's blood burned like fire as she felt the emotional surge from her sisters throughout the fleet as they began to engage the humans. Having no information on how many forces the humans may have gathered or how they might be deployed, she had settled on a simple strategy that was most likely to ensure rapid contact with at least some of the human ships, assuming there were any. While they knew a great deal about the humans after fully absorbing the information contained in the data of the primitive vessel on which the Messenger had come, there was much about these aliens that remained intriguing unknowns. She had divided the main attack fleet into two groups. The first, with about one hundred and fifty ships, would jump into the target system near the planet's two small moons to engage any forces there. The second formation of roughly fifty ships, including her flagship, would jump into low orbit.

She was not disappointed. The group bound for the moons in high orbit arrived first, and Tesh-Dar could feel in the Bloodsong the thrill of the warriors as they found human warships awaiting them. The fleet the humans had assembled was unimpressive, but would provide her warriors with an acceptable challenge. Tesh-Dar could only be pleased.

As her own group emerged in low orbit, she gasped with pleasant surprise: they had materialized right on top of a formation of human ships!

"Elai-Tura'an!" she called to the shipmistress, the warrior who was the rough equivalent in human terms to the ship's captain. "Send forth the boarding parties, then engage at will!"

"Yes, my priestess!" Elai-Tura'an responded instantly as she carried out Tesh-Dar's orders.

Throughout the ships of the second attack group, hundreds of warriors clad in what were to them primitive vacuum combat suits leaped from airlocks arranged along the ships' flanks, steering toward the human ships that were even now turning to meet them.

* * *

"Primary kinetics, *fire!*" *Capitaine de vaisseau* Pierre Monet, captain of the Alliance heavy cruiser *Victorieuse* ordered over the orchestrated chaos of the bridge. The ship was rocked down to her keel as a set of twenty rounds of two hundred millimeter armor-piercing shells was fired from the ship's five main gun turrets. While the current generation of lasers were generally more effective, kinetic weapons, not too far removed from the shells fired by wet navy ships centuries before, were far less expensive and could still be extremely lethal.

Just after the main guns fired, a low humming sound echoed through the ship, one of the smaller close-in defense lasers firing at incoming Kreelan projectiles.

Amiral Lefevre stood silently on the flag bridge, trying to make sense of the chaotic information on the tactical display. The task force to which *Victorieuse* was attached was involved in the equivalent of a knife fight with the second group of Kreelan ships that had jumped in. While this Kreelan force was only slightly bigger than his own task force, his formation had essentially lost any semblance of tactical integrity. The Alliance datalinks were still up, allowing their ships to coordinate their fire, but the targets were so close that the French ships were now in danger of committing fratricide.

"*Triomphante* reports she's being boarded!" one of the tactical officers shouted.

"*What?*" Lefevre demanded, incredulous. He had heard the report of the Kreelans boarding the Terran survey ship, but had dismissed the notion. It was a ridiculous concept in modern space warfare.

"Boarders, sir!" the officer repeated. "They report aliens in vacuum suits are aboard, attacking the crew."

"Sir," *Capitaine* Monet interrupted, worry lining his face as he looked out from the view screen on the flag bridge, "sensors are showing a cloud of objects directly in front of us, on a direct vector from one of the enemy ships."

Boarders, Lefevre thought again. What kind of enemy are we fighting who would throw away their people in such a fashion? But he didn't hesitate. "Fight your ship, captain."

Monet nodded, then ordered his weapons officer, "Put the forward batteries under manual control. Sweep those damn things from our path."

* * *

Li'ara-Zhurah floated through space with the dozens of other warriors of the attack group she led, trying to reach one of the many human ships that were maneuvering wildly in the fierce melee taking place around her. She hated the primitive vacuum suit she had to wear, but had fought a series of fierce challenges for the honor of wearing it, and would have done so again without a second thought. Her blood sang with the rapture and pain of her sisters who now fought and died in the battle raging above the human planet. Her hands clenched reflexively in anticipation as her chosen target, one of the larger human cruisers, swept toward her, belching fire at the attacking warships of the Imperial fleet.

Some of the warriors in her attack group suddenly cried out in shock and agony as rapid-fire laser bolts suddenly began to sweep through their formation. The ancient design of the vacuum suits incorporated reflective shielding, but even the comparatively small amount of energy it still allowed to bleed through was enough to severely burn or kill the warrior wearing it.

"*Attack!*" Li'ara-Zhurah cried as she fired her small maneuvering thrusters in hopes of throwing off the enemy's aim and getting that much closer to her target. "Move in!"

With a war cry from her surviving sisters, the group surged forward *en masse* toward the human warship that was now speeding directly toward them.

* * *

"They're inside minimum range!" the tactical officer exclaimed as the cloud of targets on the *Victorieuse's* tactical display passed inside the range rings of the close-in defense weapons. The weapons were primarily designed to stop missile and kinetic weapons, and had fared poorly against the alien attackers. The software that controlled the weapons' targeting wasn't expecting such slow moving targets, and while the small laser batteries had killed at least half of the aliens heading for the ship, that still left several dozen alive.

Capitaine Monet hit a button on his command console, opening a channel to the crew. "Prepare to repel boarders!" he barked, feeling mildly ridiculous saying those particular words, despite the potential severity of the situation. The Alliance Navy had no protocols for dealing with hostile boarders, and none of the ships carried marines who could mount an effective shipboard defense. In fact, the Alliance had no space marines at all: such a military force had been seen as unnecessary in the modern age. The only thing they had was a small armory containing light weapons that were used during inspection operations that had the potential to turn violent. Doing a quick calculation in his head, Monet ordered, "Every department is to send five men to the armory immediately to draw weapons! Defend the ship!"

Hearing Monet's orders, Lefevre immediately opened a fleet-wide broadcast. "All ships," he ordered, "be prepared to repel boarders. Repeat, be prepared to repel boarders."

Just then there was the sound of an explosion somewhere aft, followed by an alarm that one of the secured compartments was losing air.

"The hull has been breached," Monet hissed.

* * *

Matching velocity with the human ships that Li'ara-Zhurah and her warriors wanted to attack would have been virtually impossible without the inertial compensator that the builders had discovered far back in the Books of Time. It was on a level of technology comparable to what the humans possessed, so it was allowed by the priestess. Bulky and primitive compared to the energy bubbles used in the current day, the compensator was small enough to be fitted to a suit, and had originally been designed millennia before to allow boarding operations just such as this.

The human ship loomed before Li'ara-Zhurah, approaching faster than she would have thought possible. She could see its forward laser batteries still belching coherent light at her sisters; many had been lost, but many yet remained alive, their fury and bloodlust pounding in her own veins. The dull gray behemoth was nothing but angles and bulky protuberances, the muzzles of its larger weapons flashing with crimson brilliance as they fired. She knew that the ships of her fleet were absorbing a tremendous amount of damage while inflicting comparatively little to give her and her sisters the honor of taking the sword to the enemy. It was greater honor to the Empress to fight eye-to-eye with one's foe than to smash away at them with the guns of warships. Her Children would hardly shy away from such carnage, but their goal was a battle of being against being, not one fought by technology.

Holding her breath, Li'ara-Zhurah fired a magnetic grapple ahead of her, hoping that the hulls of the human ships were composed of ferrous alloys to which the grapple could adhere. *Yes!* she thought triumphantly as the grapple clung to the skin of the human ship as it sailed by, automatically triggering the inertial compensator. Suddenly, almost magically, Li'ara-Zhurah was traveling alongside the ship, her velocity relative to the vessel having been equalized by the compensator.

But there was a price to be paid. The device had to do something with the huge amount of energy it had just absorbed in matching her velocity to that of the ship, and it converted it all to heat. Li'ara-Zhurah cried out as her back was suddenly seared by the red-hot compensator just before it automatically separated from her suit and drifted off into space.

Gasping at the pain, she triggered the miniature winch that reeled her to where the grapple had attached itself to the vessel's metal skin. Once there, she activated the magnetic soles of her boots to anchor her feet to the alien hull. She looked around in wide-eyed wonder at the spectacle around her: ships everywhere, blasting away at one another with kinetic rounds and lasers; clouds of warriors maneuvering through space, trying to find their targets; and periodic eye-searing explosions as ships died. And it all took place in total, utter silence.

Bringing her mind back to the task at hand, she unwound a strip of putty-like material and stuck it onto the hull in a rough circle as big around as her arms spread wide. Walking awkwardly across the hull in her magnetic boots, she put some distance between herself and the putty-like material, then triggered it.

Rather than a conventional explosive, the boarding charges the warriors were using was a chemical compound much akin to thermite used by humans. Once ignited, it burned at a ferociously high temperature and could melt through virtually any metal that human technology could produce. Since the warriors would have no way of knowing if the part of the hull they landed on was merely a thin metal skin or armor an arm's length in thickness, primitive explosives might not be sufficient. But even the thickest metal could be penetrated with enough heat.

She watched as the boarding charge burst into brilliant flame, instantly melting the metal of the hull, which bubbled off into space. The flames sank into the ship's metal skin, eating it away with heat.

A moment later, the entire circle of the hull - plating, electrical conduits, piping - exploded outward from the air pressure in the compartment beneath as the boarding charge breached the interior wall. Two human figures, not wearing space suits, flew past her, ejected by explosive decompression. The flow of air stopped after a few moments.

Ignoring the pain from the burns on her back, Li'ara-Zhurah jumped through the breach, her sword held at the ready.

FOURTEEN

One of the enlisted sailors from engineering, *Second-maître* Emmanuelle Sabourin, led four other crewmen toward the nearest compartment that had been breached. They had been among the first to reach the armory, and had drawn two automatic shotguns and three sidearms, plus a pair of grenades. Sabourin had wanted all of her team to be armed with shotguns or rifles, but the armorer simply nodded over his shoulder at what he had available: three more shotguns, half a dozen assault rifles, and maybe a dozen pistols, plus a dozen grenades. That was it.

Disgusted, she'd taken the weapons the armorer had offered, along with a generous quantity of armor-piercing ammunition. That, at least, was not in short supply. She was actually surprised that the armorer was handing out armor-piercing rounds, as they could wreak havoc if they penetrated the inner walls of the ship and destroyed any of the underlying electrical systems or conduits. But he had told her it was on the captain's direct orders: he believed they would need it to fight the boarders. Unsettled by that bit of information, she led her team aft as another group arrived to pick over the meager weapons supply.

Unlike the other teams, Sabourin's team members were all wearing vacuum suits. While the ship had a plentiful supply of emergency "beach balls" that crewmen could quickly jump into in case of a loss of air pressure, there were only a small number of vacuum suits, which normally were used only for external repair work and the various odd jobs for which an EVA (Extra-Vehicular Activity) was required. There were only half a dozen or so, and they were all kept in engineering. When the chief engineer chose her, his senior enlisted rating, to lead the team from engineering to help repel the boarders, she and her companions grabbed the suits and put them on. The only problem was that they weren't designed for combat: she could puncture one with a screwdriver, and they only had basic communications gear. But it was more than the other teams had.

"This way," she said, turning right and pounding down an auxiliary stairway. The captain had locked all of the ship's elevators. Halfway down, the ship rocked to the side, throwing her off-balance. Losing her grip on the handrail, she chose to jump down the rest of the way rather than tumbling down the remaining steps. She landed on her feet and rolled, only to come face-to-face with an apparition the likes of which she had never seen before.

The Kreelan warrior bared her fangs and lunged forward, thrusting her sword at Sabourin's mid-section.

Caught totally off-guard, Sabourin instinctively swung her shotgun to deflect the alien's attack, the sword's tip barely missing her suit. But the movement put Sabourin off-balance, and she fell backward to the deck as the Kreelan raised her sword, preparing to bring it down in a savage double-handed strike.

But the alien warrior never got the chance. With a deafening blast, the other member of Sabourin's team with a shotgun blew the Kreelan back against the bulkhead. The alien slammed into the wall with a grunt of pain, but then got right back up again: her glossy black chest armor looked like someone had hit it with a fist hard enough to make a deep indentation, scraping the black coating off to reveal the gleaming raw metal beneath. But the shotgun's armor-piercing round hadn't gone through. The warrior was no doubt badly bruised, and may even have suffered some broken ribs, but otherwise was quite alive.

At least she was until Sabourin blew her unarmored head off with the shotgun. "*Salope*," she spat. *Bitch*.

"How did she get in here without a suit?" one of her teammates asked as he helped Sabourin get back on her feet, something that wasn't easy to do in the ship's artificial gravity while wearing the bulky suits. "There are no airlocks in this part of the ship."

"She made one," one of the others called from the nearby hatchway in the direction Sabourin had been leading them. "Look."

The hatch, which automatically closed any time general quarters was sounded, stood open. In the compartment beyond, which Sabourin knew had been breached, the Kreelan had attached some sort of thin membrane to the bulkhead around the hatch coaming that had been large enough for her to stand in. The membrane, however it was attached to the bulkhead (chemically bonded, Sabourin guessed), had formed a makeshift airlock, and the Kreelan must then have simply cut through the bulkhead to short out the hatch controls. With a quick blast of air that filled the bubble that now sealed her away from the vacuum in the compartment behind her, the alien could have then just stepped into the pressurized passageway, where she discarded her vacuum armor. Simple and effective.

Looking closer, Sabourin could see that the membrane was actually *two* membranes, with each one having a barely visible seam down the middle. Suddenly she understood: the outer membrane, which now was loosely draped against the bubble of the pressurized inner one, formed the first part of a double-airlock.

"*Merde*," she muttered.

"What is wrong?" one of the others asked.

"If more aliens enter that compartment," she nodded toward the hatchway and the improvised airlock, "through the hole that the first alien made in the hull, they can enter the bubble through the outer membrane, seal it, then enter the ship through the inner membrane without risking explosive decompression of the passageway on this side." She turned to look at her teammates, her angular face and dark brown eyes grim. "Anywhere they make one of these, they can easily gain access to the pressurized portions of the ship."

"But why?" one of the others asked. "If they just blow holes in the hull, they would eventually kill most of us. Would that not be easier?"

"Yes, it would," she said. The question bothered her, but she had no answer. She had to inform the captain. "Bridge," she called over her suit's comms system.

"Bridge," a communications technician answered immediately.

"This is *Second-maître* Sabourin on deck six at frame seventy-three," she reported. "We killed one of the boarders. But alert the other teams that the armor-piercing rounds from our shotguns will not penetrate their chest armor. Head shots only. Please also inform the captain that the boarders can create their own double airlocks. Wherever one of them makes a penetration, more aliens will be able to enter from the vacuum side without further decompression of the adjoining compartment."

There was a moment of silence, then she heard the captain's voice. "Sabourin," *Capitaine* Monet asked, "are you sure about the airlocks? We had assumed that one of the enemy's primary objectives would be to secure at least one of the ship's airlocks to allow them to get more warriors aboard faster. That is where we were going to concentrate our ship defense teams."

"*Oui, mon capitaine,*" she told him grimly as she and the rest of her team began to back away from the hatch while bringing up their weapons, "I am sure these airlocks work. In fact, more aliens are trying to come through this one now..."

* * *

On the other side of the ship, Li'ara-Zhurah had finished fastening the airlock membrane to the bulkhead of the compartment she had entered. Aside from the two humans who had been blown out when she cut through the hull, the compartment had been empty. Behind her, four other warriors had managed to scramble through the hole and now stood by as she prepared the airlock. She waited for a moment more for the chemical matrix around the edges of the membrane to fuse with the metal of the bulkhead, and then, taking a wild guess, she hit the large green button of what she assumed was the control panel for the hatch. She was right: the hatch slid open, and after a small implosion of air that filled the inner bubble, she stepped through the hatch into the passageway beyond.

She could see in the strange yellow-tinged light that there were no humans about, and she signaled to the warriors behind her to follow. One by one, they entered the outer bubble, then the inner one. Some air was lost as they did so, but it was trivial for a ship this size.

As a second warrior joined her, Li'ara-Zhurah gratefully rid herself of the cumbersome vacuum suit, hissing with the pain as the suit snagged on her backplate and pressed it against her burned flesh. With a growl of anger, she tore the rest of the suit from her body, slashing at it with her black talons. At last free of the encumbrance, she felt like a warrior once again, and not like a piece of meat encased in a tin.

Once the other warriors of her group were through the airlock, they set off in search of the crew.

* * *

While more and more skirmishes broke out in the passageways of *Victorieuse*, Lefevre was desperately trying to extricate the fleet from what could easily turn into a colossal disaster. As the close-in slugging match with the Kreelan ships here in lower orbit intensified, Lefevre recalled the two squadrons that were streaming around the planet to engage the larger Kreelan force in high orbit. He ordered the remaining two squadrons, those that had the misfortune of being closest to the larger Kreelan group, to pull back. His goal was to try and achieve sufficient local superiority that he could smash the smaller Kreelan group *Victorieuse* and her sisters were fighting before facing off against the larger group of Kreelan ships.

Destroying the larger group or forcing them to withdraw, he knew, was little more than wishful thinking. While he had rough parity at the moment with the enemy here in low orbit, they had at least fifty more ships in the larger group near the moons than he had in his entire fleet. It appeared that the Kreelans were perfectly positioned to destroy the Alliance squadrons that were closest to the larger Kreelan force.

However, to his shock and surprise, they didn't. The Kreelans allowed the other Alliance squadrons to retreat back toward Lefevre's position near the planet. Some Kreelan ships pursued them, but only made harassing attacks, nothing more.

"What are they doing?" his flag captain asked.

Lefevre shook his head, completely confused. "I have no idea. Why do they not simply destroy our ships? They have overwhelming superiority."

The *Victorieuse* suddenly rocked with a hit, throwing both men off balance. They should have been in their combat chairs, but Lefevre had perversely always refused to sit in one. More alarms blared, signaling yet more damage to the ship, but Lefevre ignored them. That was *Capitaine* Monet's job.

"Are they simply toying with us?" he wondered aloud.

* * *

Tesh-Dar grunted with satisfaction at the humans' response. Realizing their tactical error, they were now trying to reconsolidate their forces. She would allow them to do as they wished - to a point. But only as it suited her. Much of this first battle was simply to study, to learn. Had this been an enemy that posed a true threat to the Empire, she would have clawed them from the skies in minutes, even with ships of a design as ancient as this.

But the humans were not a threat. They were an opportunity to glorify the Empress. They would die and this system would be taken into the Empire, yes, but she would allow them to fight on even ground. For the first time in several thousand cycles did the Children of the Empress have a worthy enemy, and she would take her time to blood her warriors properly and let the humans learn, as well. For the more they knew, the better they would fight.

She ordered that the formation in high orbit detach half its ships to follow the two closest human squadrons back toward the planet, harassing them without making many outright kills. Ships that could be crippled would be boarded, so her warriors could fight the humans face to face. But it was better for her purposes if the human ships were gathered in more closely together. She was sorely tempted to join the young ones in the bloodletting, but the time would soon come when the battle on the planet's surface would begin. Then she would indulge herself.

With that in mind, she had one of the warriors working a sensor console - Tesh-Dar was still amazed that their forebears had extended the Empire across the stars with the aid of such primitive devices - show her the progress of the human ships carrying troops to the surface. Clearly not designed for war, the odd assemblage of vessels were surrounded by a host of small shuttles that were equally ill-designed for ferrying troops and equipment quickly. It would take many trips for the small craft to carry all the humans aboard those ships down to the surface. And then it would no doubt take them some time to prepare their defenses.

It was just as well, Tesh-Dar thought as the guns of her command ship thundered. She was in no hurry.

* * *

Sabourin and her team stared at the handful of Kreelan warriors who had gathered in the compartment beyond the improvised airlock, and the Kreelans stared back.

But only for a moment.

"*Nique ta mere!*" Sabourin cursed at the Kreelans as she snatched one of the grenades from her utility pouch, mashed down on the activator and hurled it into the airlock bubble. "Take cover!" she cried before ducking behind the stairs.

One of her comrades made it to the safety of the stairs with her, but the remaining three never had a chance: three of the Kreelans threw some sort of weapons through the membrane. Like miniature buzz saws, the weapons whirred through the air and caught the three crewmen in mid-stride as they tried to dash out of the way. The weapons cut through the thick fabric of the vacuum suits as if it was made of rice paper, and did the same to the flesh and bone beneath. One crewman clutched at his chest before he fell to the deck; the second, who was hit in the neck, simply collapsed to the floor like a rag doll. Sabourin could see that he had been decapitated, just before his faceplate was covered in blood that still spewed from the carotid artery. The third weapon caught the last crewman in the back, severing his spine just below the shoulder blades. His screams of agony rang from the speakers in her helmet.

Then the grenade went off, and Sabourin held onto the metal skeleton of the stairs for dear life as the air in the passageway was explosively vented into space. The crewman who had managed to take shelter with her behind the stairs didn't have a firm hold and suddenly found himself carried out through the hatch into the adjoining compartment by the force of the explosive decompression. He would have been carried out into space except for the artificial gravity, which was still strong enough to hold him to the deck. But his good fortune was short lived as one of the surviving warriors leapt upon him, and they grappled with one another even as two more warriors clambered through the hole in the hull, dropping nimbly to the deck in spite of their bulky armored suits. Then another appeared to join them.

With tears of hate and anger clouding her eyes, Sabourin threw her second grenade into their midst.

* * *

Gritting her teeth in pain, Li'ara-Zhurah leaned against the bulkhead, waiting for a break in the weapons fire coming from the humans around the corner and down the passageway. She and her small band of warriors had already killed over a dozen members of the crew when they had run into this determined - and, for once, well-armed - group of defenders. They were proving a worthy challenge, and beyond the pain of the bullet wound in her left arm, her blood sang in blissful fury. She turned to look at one of her companion warriors, who knelt on the deck behind her, blood running from her mouth: one of the human projectile weapons had hammered against her chest armor and shattered several of her ribs, which in turn had punctured a lung. "You must rest, Ku'ira-Gol," she counseled the younger warrior. "This is merely the opening battle in a great war. You need not spend yourself in the first of it. Let the healers tend to you once we finish this. A host of humans yet await the attention of your sword and claws."

Looking up at Li'ara-Zhurah with eyes that bore the pain not of her body, but of her spirit, Ku'ira-Gol shook her head. "No, my sister," she said quietly. She had been a late arrival, and happened to discover the hole Li'ara-Zhurah had made in the hull, then followed her and the others here. "You speak with truth and wisdom, but my sword has not yet been blooded. Many combats did I fight in the arena for the honor to be here. I will not spend a moment in the company of a healer until I have spilled the blood of our enemy."

Li'ara-Zhurah understood completely. Not just the younger warrior's words, but the flame of her emotions, the melody of her Bloodsong. Ku'ira-Gol's answer she had expected, but honor demanded that Li'ara-Zhurah offer counsel as she had. "So has it been-" she whispered.

"-so shall it forever be," the others echoed in a simple timeless prayer to the Empress.

With one last look in Ku'ira-Gol's silver-flecked eyes, seeing that her face was now serene with the acceptance of what was soon to be, Li'ara-Zhurah nodded. "May you find a place among the Ancient Ones, my sister."

"In Her name," Ku'ira-Gol whispered just before she leapt out into the passageway to draw the humans' fire. She rolled nimbly to her feet before leaping into the air, hurling her last *shrekka* at one of the human animals.

The passageway was suddenly filled with the staccato roar of assault rifles as they poured fire into her. The bullets from the rifles, able to penetrate the Kreelan's armor, shattered Ku'ira-Gol's body even as her *shrekka* found its mark, severing the head of one of the defenders.

As Ku'ira-Gol's lifeless body fell to the deck, Li'ara-Zhurah and the four remaining warriors broke from cover and charged down the passageway, hurling their own *shrekkas*. They had not thrown them with the intent to kill, but to force the humans down, to give the warriors a few more precious seconds to get close enough to use their swords and claws. Baring their fangs and roaring with fury, they flung themselves into the group of half a dozen humans, blades flashing and claws tearing.

The humans put up a spirited fight, but it was all too brief. It had been clear to Li'ara-Zhurah from her first encounter with the humans aboard this vessel that even though they appeared to be soulless creatures, many of them had great courage and fighting spirit. But they were ill-trained and poorly equipped to engage properly in battle with Her Children. Perhaps their warriors who fought on the ground would prove more of a challenge. If she managed to survive the battle here in space, she would seek to find out.

Her sensitive nose filled with the unpleasant coppery scent from the human blood that now covered her like haphazardly splashed paint, she continued to lead the remaining warriors to her ultimate destination: the ship's bridge.

* * *

Alone now, the rest of her team dead, Sabourin was also cut off from the rest of the crew. There was no way she could enter the pressurized sections of the ship from here, for there was no airlock: having destroyed the one the Kreelans had made to the adjoining compartment where they had penetrated the hull, she had cut off her own escape route. Now, she had no choice but to head out through the hole the Kreelans had made in the ship's hull and try to find another one of their improvised airlocks, or one of the ship's main airlocks. She would settle for whichever was closer.

Clamping the shotgun to a utility sticky patch on her suit, she stepped into the compartment filled with the bodies of the Kreelans and the member of her team that she had killed with the grenade. She tried to console herself with the thought that there was no way she could have saved her fellow crewman, but another voice quietly reminded her that she hadn't even tried. She hadn't known him very well; she hadn't known any of the people on her short-lived team, as they had all been sent from different sections of engineering. She had killed him, and now she couldn't even remember his name. Kicking the mangled bodies of the Kreelans out of the way, she knelt by his lacerated suit for a moment, looking at his face. His expression was oddly peaceful, although his features were distorted from the swelling of his tissues as the fluids tried to turn to vapor in the pure vacuum of the compartment.

"I'm sorry," she said dully, squeezing his dead hand gently. Then she let go. There was nothing else to say.

Turning to the body of one of the warriors, she took the alien's sword. She had no training in how to use it, but it couldn't hurt to have such a weapon handy, especially since the shotgun didn't seem to do much to their armor. She slid the gleaming weapon into its scabbard, having wrenched it from the belt the alien wore, then attached it to another sticky patch on her suit. After a moment's consideration, she checked the rest of the warrior's belongings. Most of it she either could not figure out or could not use, but she found a small pouch that, when she squeezed it, suddenly popped out and expanded into one of the portable airlocks. *That could be useful*, she thought. Finding another warrior who still had hers, Sabourin took it and stuffed it into the utility pouch on her belt. She also found a wound-up strip of taffy-like material, packed together with a small electronic unit in a pouch. It dawned on her that this must be the explosive material that they had used to make the holes in the hull. She had no idea what she might do with it, but since it was small and no inconvenience, she stuffed that in her utility pouch, as well.

Looking at her suit's telltales in the head-up display on her visor, Sabourin saw that she only had an hour of air left. She had to find a way back into the pressurized parts of the ship.

Getting out onto the hull would be a bit tricky, only because the hole the Kreelans had made was in the "ceiling" of this compartment. And since the artificial gravity was still working, she couldn't just jump. Fortunately, this was one of the ship's many equipment storage areas, and after about fifteen minutes of grunting and heaving, interrupted frequently by either the vibration of the ship's kinetics firing or the compartment shuddering as *Victorieuse* took another hit, she had managed to push together enough pallets and other flotsam to build a platform high enough for her to reach the outside of the hull with her hands.

It took her a couple of minutes of frenzied scrabbling in the awkward suit, made worse by the shotgun and sword protruding at odd angles, but she finally made it. She rolled over on the outside of the hull, panting at the effort and holding on with a magnetized glove to keep from drifting away. The artificial gravity field actually stopped mid-way through the hull's thick skin, and it was a queasy sensation as she lifted herself through the hole to have part of her body still sensing gravity and the rest of it sensing weightlessness.

Looking out, the infinite blackness of space was lit with a cascade of fireworks as ships fired upon one other. While the engagement range for space combat was normally judged in thousands of kilometers, she could see at least two dozen ships - some of them very close aboard, *within hundreds of meters* - with her naked eye. Most were moving far slower than they normally would, either because of battle damage or just to hold formation with their wounded sisters. She saw a pair of ships, one clearly human, the other not, that had collided at some velocity slow enough that they had not been destroyed outright. She saw small shapes swarming over the human ship, and knew with bitter anguish exactly what they were. More boarders.

A shadow suddenly fell across her face, something breaking the glare of the system's star. Glancing to her left, she saw another Kreelan warrior floating through space, drifting directly toward her. With a growl, Sabourin ripped the shotgun from its sticky patch. While the weapon was not exactly optimized for space combat, its designers had at least ensured that the chemical composition of the propellant in the cartridges did not need oxygen to fire. The Kreelan was already reaching for one of the flying weapons attached to the outside of her armored suit, but Sabourin had no intention of letting the alien use it. Bracing the shotgun against the hull, holding it as if she were firing from the hip, Sabourin pulled the trigger.

The heavy shot caught the Kreelan warrior square in the chest. While the heavy shot didn't penetrate her armor, it gave proof to Newton's third law of motion: for every action, there is an equal and opposite reaction. The hit sent the warrior flying backward into space, tumbling head over heels.

Shaking with yet another surge of adrenalin, Sabourin managed to get back on her feet, locking the magnetic pads on her boots to the hull. Trying to ignore the distractions of the silent space battle going on around her, she first tried to spot any more Kreelan warriors on the hull or floating nearby. There were none that she could see. For a moment, she stood there, lungs heaving. Her orders had been clear before, if rather broad: repel the enemy and defend the ship. If her team's experience was any indication, the enemy must be gaining the upper hand, and she wasn't sure which way to go or what to do.

"Bridge," she called as she caught her breath.

There was a long pause, and she was about to call again when the same communications tech as before answered.

"Bridge," the tech said, somewhat breathlessly.

"This is Sabourin. I am outside the hull, roughly forty-five minutes of air remaining." She paused, not wanting to say what must be said. "I...I have lost the rest of my team. I need orders."

"Stand by."

The silence that followed was interminable. At one point Sabourin was nearly knocked to her knees by an explosion near the stern of the ship. The stars and the fireflies that were fighting and dying ships wheeled crazily around her before the ship gradually came back under control. But *Victorieuse* was clearly badly damaged. The ship was still in the fight, but she suffered from a constant starboard yaw and downward pitch that the helmsman must be trying to control with thrusters. That meant the main engines had been very badly damaged, and no doubt the rest of the ship was faring no better. She gritted her teeth in frustration. There must be something more she could do.

"Sabourin," the captain's voice suddenly echoed in her earphones, "you must make for the main starboard airlock and do what you can to hold it against attack. We need to get off what is left of the crew, and the port side is controlled by the enemy."

"We are abandoning ship, sir?" she asked, mortified.

A long pause. "*Oui*," he answered heavily. "I was about to inform the *amiral* when you called. We have no choice."

He paused again, as if unsure what to say next. Her heart bled for him: while she did not know him very well personally, he had been a good and fair captain during her time aboard the ship. And to lose *Victorieuse* - the fleet flagship! - this way must have been horrible.

"Listen, Sabourin," he went on quietly, as if he did not want anyone else near him to hear, "aside from the officers' sidearms, which are useless, you have the only weapon left that can kill these beasts. All the other defense teams are gone. You *must* hold the starboard airlock. If you do not, the crew will be trapped in the ship and at the mercy of these creatures. We have no way of fighting our way past them."

"*Oui, mon capitaine,*" she said grimly, already stalking across the hull to the starboard side. "I understand. And I will not fail you."

* * *

"We're losing the ship, *mon amiral,*" Capitaine Monet reported to Lefevre even as screams, very close now, echoed through the blast doors that separated the flag and ship's bridges from the rest of the ship. The agony in his voice was no different than if his wife lay on an operating table in surgery, dying. "Engineering was under attack and no longer responds, and we have lost maneuvering control. While we still control the ship's weapons, fewer and fewer of the gun crews answer, and our fire has fallen to almost nothing. The aliens now control the port airlock, and we have lost contact with all the defense teams." He still had contact with Sabourin, but despite the young woman's determined vow, he held little hope that she alone could do what he had asked. He knew she would die trying, however, and he could ask no more of any of his crew. He took in a shuddering breath. "I recommend that we abandon ship."

As if to punctuate Monet's litany of doom, *Victorieuse* shuddered from another hit. Lefevre realized now that the fire from the Kreelan vessels was generally not intended to kill his ships, but to wound them enough that the boarding parties would have a better chance to attack. They were like pack animals, one tearing at the prey's legs to bring it down, while others pounced on its back or went for the throat. He found some solace in the knowledge that, once the threat of the boarders had been taken seriously, only three more ships had fallen victim to them by direct attack.

But for *Victorieuse* and a dozen or more other ships, it was too late.

His heart heavy, knowing the pain it was causing Monet to even suggest such a thing, he said, "Very well, *capitaine.*" Turning to his flag captain, he said, "Signal *Jean Bart* to come alongside to take on survivors from the starboard side airlock; I will transfer my flag to her." He turned back to the ship's captain, but Monet was not looking at him.

Behind Lefevre, Monet had seen the port side blast door to the flag bridge suddenly slide open. At the threshold stood a small group of alien warriors. "*Get down!*" he screamed, tackling Lefevre to the deck as the keening of Kreelan flying weapons filled the flag bridge.

* * *

Li'ara-Zhurah once again found herself facing a determined group of humans, and her blood sang with the joy of battle. While they were pitifully armed with small handguns, the accuracy of the shots by one of the humans was making for a challenging fight. The human animal who had been facing the door that opened onto what must be part of the bridge had flung itself and another of its kind down behind a console, avoiding the volley of *shrekkas* that her warriors had hurled at the humans inside. But that same human had suddenly peeked above the console and fired his handgun twice, shooting two of her fellow warriors in the head and killing them instantly.

She looked at the three warriors who remained with her. All of them had sustained injuries of one sort or another, bearing witness to the ferocity of the humans, if not their skill. Truly, they were worthy opponents.

Gripping her last *shrekka*, she quickly peered around the hatch coaming, which was the only cover they had here in the corridor. Her other warriors crouched low to the deck, trying to stay out of sight of the sharpshooter.

She had stuck her head out just far enough to get a glimpse of the console where the two humans had hidden when the human again rose up and squeezed off a round. Had she been just a fraction of a second slower he would have killed her. As it was, she would have a handsome scar across her left cheek where the bullet grazed her. Assuming she survived.

* * *

Monet ducked back down behind the command console. He had surprised the Kreelans with his marksmanship, but he had certainly never expected to use his skills with a pistol, honed during his years of competition while attending university, to defend his ship. He keyed his wrist comm to the ship-wide annunciator circuit. "All hands, this is the captain," he said urgently. "Abandon ship. Repeat, abandon ship. Make way to the starboard side main airlock. Starboard side only. The port side airlock is controlled by the enemy." He paused for a moment. "Good luck and godspeed." Turning to *Amiral* Lefevre, who crouched next to him, his sidearm drawn and ready, Monet said, "It is time for you to leave, *mon amiral*. I will cover your withdrawal as best I can. Take the bridge crewmen through the starboard side path to the airlock."

"Monet..." Lefevre began, then stopped. There was no choice. He hated to leave him here in what could only be a last stand. But Lefevre had an entire fleet to worry about, and every moment counted now if he was to extricate the rest of his ships from certain disaster. "*Bonne chance, capitaine*," he said quietly, gripping Monet's shoulder.

Then, in a crouching run, he made his way forward to the main bridge, gathering the other crewman to him as he went. Only the senior officers had sidearms, and the guns were the only protection any of them had.

With one last look toward where Monet lay waiting for the Kreelans, Lefevre rendered him a salute. The captain returned it with a brave smile and a small wave of his hand.

Once the last member of the bridge crew had crept past him, staying low to keep out of the Kreelans' line of sight, Lefevre closed the blast door and locked it behind him as a volley of gunshots rang out on the other side.

* * *

While the *Victorieuse* was not a huge ship compared to some of the gigantic transports and starliners, the hull seemed to stretch for endless kilometers as Sabourin trudged step by exhausting step toward the starboard airlock. Walking in the suit required careful attention to first demagnetize one foot, set it, magnetize it, then demagnetize the other foot to repeat the process. It was dreadfully slow going, and while she was EVA qualified, almost all of her outside operations in a suit had been with a maneuvering pack. This was torture, and a river of sweat was running down her back and between her breasts, and from her forehead into her eyes where it burned like fire. That was perhaps the most frustrating thing, because she had to constantly look around and above for more Kreelan warriors trying to sneak up on her.

But no more had appeared by the time she reached the airlock. With her shotgun held at the ready, although she was not sure her magnetic boots would hold her to the hull against the weapon's recoil, she opened the outer hatch. It was empty. Stepping inside, she hit the controls to pressurize the lock. She was about to hit the button to open the inner door, then paused. It wouldn't do to have come all this way just to be shot by someone on the other side of the door, thinking she was a Kreelan. Of course, there could be Kreelans on the far side of the door, too.

Again holding her shotgun at the ready, she activated her suit's external microphone and punched the button for the airlock intercom. "This is *Second-maître* Sabourin in the airlock," she said. "Is anyone there?"

She nearly pulled the trigger of the shotgun as the door suddenly slid open, revealing what looked to be a couple dozen of her shipmates.

"*Merde!*" she exclaimed to the first of the people who stepped forward to greet her. "I almost blew your head off!" Then she recognized who it was and lowered the shotgun. "Um. Sir," she added sheepishly.

"You would have been quite right in doing so, petty officer," Lefevre told her warmly. "My apologies. Sabourin, isn't it?"

"*Oui, mon amiral,*" she said, noting how haggard the admiral looked. He had gashes along the side of his face, and his uniform was in tatters.

The admiral glanced down at his uniform and nodded sadly. "We were ambushed by another group of boarders on the way here. We fought them off, but not before they killed another ten members of the crew." He had two bullets left for his sidearm. It had been a very close thing that any of them had gotten away. That and Sabourin's shotgun were all they had left. "*Jean Bart* is to dock any moment, petty officer," he told her. "I must ask you, as you have the only real weapon left among us, to do what you can to give the crew time to get off."

"This is all that is left of us?" she asked in a small voice.

The admiral nodded heavily. "I believe there are more down below, barricaded in some of the engineering spaces. But there are boarding parties between them and us, and we have no weapons to try and fight our way through." While Lefevre knew that his first concern must be the fleet, if he had more weapons for his companions or a marine detachment on board he would have led them in an attempt to rescue the trapped members of the crew. But to do so unarmed was beyond hopeless. "We have closed the blast doors here in the main gangway, and I have used my override to lock them. But we know the enemy can open locked doors, do we not?"

Sabourin nodded grimly. She knew what he was going to ask before he asked it. "I will hold them off, sir," she said quietly.

He put a hand on her shoulder and squeezed tightly. She could barely feel it through the thick fabric of the suit. "I know you will," he told her proudly. "It should not be long now."

Raising her right arm, she saluted him, the gesture awkward in her suit, and he returned it. Then, looking past the crowd of worried faces, she asked him, "Sir, how many doors are there beyond this one that you were able to close and lock?"

"Two," he told her. "I doubt they will hold them long."

She pursed her lips, thinking. "*Amiral*, if you would, please open this door. I believe I have a plan that may buy us a bit more time."

* * *

Now at the tail of a group of a dozen warriors pursuing the remaining human survivors of the crew, Li'ara-Zhurah felt a quickening in her breast. The battle to take the bridge, while brief, had been exquisite. The lone human with a pistol had killed two of the other warriors when they had all attacked. Li'ara-Zhurah fought him in hand to hand combat to honor his skill. Such fighting clearly had not been his strength, but he still fought with spirit, and to her that mattered a great deal more. The outcome of that particular contest had never been in question. But when she finally rammed her outstretched fingers into the human's chest, her talons piercing his heart, it was with regret, for he had allowed Li'ara-Zhurah and the others to bring great glory to the Empress in the fight to overpower him.

And now, the battle to take the ship was almost over. She was exhausted and in great pain from her wounds, but her Bloodsong filled her spirit and merged with the infinite chorus of her sisters. No greater ecstasy had she ever known.

The warriors at the head of the group, senior to Li'ara-Zhurah in their order of the challenges fought for the honor to be in this first great battle, opened yet another door the humans had locked behind them. It was a crude if effective tactic to buy some time, but she did not know what they expected to accomplish: herded now to the ship's main starboard airlock, there was nowhere else for them to run.

She heard the warriors at the head of the group sing out with battle cries: the humans were before them! She let herself be swept along as the group surged forward, swords held high.

* * *

Sabourin stood alone in the passageway as the Kreelans forced open the door in front of her. Behind her, the last blast door in the main gangway stood open, with the terrified faces of the crew's survivors looking past her as they stood with their backs pressed up against the rear wall that held the airlock. She had confirmed through her suit radio that *Jean Bart*, one of *Victorieuse's* sister ships, was moving close aboard to extend a flexible dock. But they still needed just a few more precious minutes.

She held the shotgun at her side. She would use it at the last moment if she had to, but she was hoping that the Kreelans would not decide to send their flying weapons at her if she posed no direct threat. If they did and they killed her off first thing, her plan might not work so well. She grinned at her own morbid humor.

She had wondered if her presence, particularly while still wearing the suit (which was nearly out of air), would give the enemy pause. But it had the opposite effect: with a howl, they charged forward *en masse*, driven to a frenzy by the sight of the helpless crewmen behind her.

And so they never noticed the circle of putty-like material as they ran forward, at least until Sabourin pushed the single button on the electronic device that had been in the pouch with the putty strip. With a flash that seemed as bright as the sun, the boarding charge exploded into white-hot flame, burning the flesh of half the Kreelans still charging toward her.

As the aliens' battle cries turned to screams of agony, she flung herself out of the way, against the bulkhead with the open blast door leading to where her fellow crewmen waited, willing bait for her trap.

Kneeling down, Sabourin brought up her shotgun and began to fire into the mass of burning alien warriors.

* * *

Calling to the warriors ahead of her, trying to find out what had happened, Li'ara-Zhurah could get no answer. All she could see were silhouettes of warriors dancing amid white-hot flame, and her ears were deafened by shrieks of agony. The air was thick with the stench of burning meat, metal, and hair, and she instinctively backed up, away from the carnage ahead of her. Whatever had happened, her sense of honor did not dictate that she immolate herself.

Then she heard the booms of one of the human weapons, and caught site of the lone suited human, kneeling to the side of the open door. She was firing into her sisters, which to a warrior such as Li'ara-Zhurah was a mixed blessing in such a horrid situation: being killed by a weapon such as the human wielded would be no small blessing to those whose bodies were now burning like living torches.

But even had that thought not stayed her hand for a moment, she had no *shrekkas* left. The human was beyond her reach unless she wished to brave the fire.

Then it struck her what the fire truly was: one of the boarding charges. With widening eyes, she looked at the human in the suit again, still firing into the churning mass of her sisters, noting the crudely rigged tether that held the human to the bulkhead. And around the open hatchway that led to the airlock, where the other humans cowered, Li'ara-Zhurah saw the trace of one of their own portable airlocks. Transparent and hardly visible at this distance.

It was a trap.

"Oh, no," she breathed, backing up toward the next blast door. "Pull back, my sisters!" she screamed over the din. "*Pull back!*" Hissing in fear and rage, she grabbed two of the closest warriors and pulled them back with her to the bulkhead behind her. There was no telling how thick the hull was here, and so how long the charge would take to breach-

With a thunderous roar, a two meter diameter section of the deck dropped away, blasted into space by air pressure. With screams of surprise now blending with those of agony, the rest of the warriors who were still alive were sucked out the hole in the deck to their doom.

The two warriors she had just pulled back had failed to grab hold of anything, and both lost their footing and tumbled across the deck to disappear into the infinite void beyond. Li'ara-Zhurah had seized the bulkhead wall with one hand, gripping it so fiercely that her diamond-hard talons dug into the metal. With a supreme force of will, fighting against the pain of her eardrums bursting and the air being sucked out of her lungs, she pulled herself to the door controls and slammed her hand down on the various buttons until, to her great relief, the door began to close.

As it did, Li'ara-Zhurah caught a last glimpse of the human in the suit, who had acted as bait for the trap. The human gave her what appeared to be a salute: she held one arm straight out in front of her, the hand clenched in a fist, before she brought her other hand over onto the extended arm just above the elbow. Then she swung up her clenched fist as the door slammed shut.

* * *

"*Va te faire foutre,*" Sabourin gasped at the lone surviving warrior before she disappeared behind the closing blast door. *Go fuck yourself.*

All the other warriors were gone, swept down through the hole she had burned through the deck and the hull. Sabourin had hated to hurt the *Victorieuse* that way, but there was nothing for it.

Staggering to her feet, she undid the tether, still surprised that it had held when the hull gave way. Then she stumbled to the outer membrane, opening it only with great difficulty. The admiral and crew, while frightened when the air had exploded from the hull and snapped the inner membrane taut, had survived. Her plan had worked.

Her fingers were numb and her breathing was coming in quick gasps now: her suit was out of air. But if she didn't make it through the outer membrane, no one inside would be able to come get her. Glancing through to the airlock, she saw that *Amiral* Lefevre stood there, waiting for her. The other members of the crew had been ushered into the link to the *Jean Bart*, so they were safe, at least for the moment.

After what seemed like days, she finally sealed the outer membrane behind her. But she had strength for nothing more. Her hands reflexively going to her neck, she slumped to the floor, her vision darkening as her brain began to run out of oxygen.

She felt more than heard the *pop* of air as the inner membrane was opened, filling the outer bubble where she lay with air. Then someone undogged her helmet and pulled it off. Taking in huge lungfuls of air, she found Lefevre looking down at her with a warm smile on his battered face.

"Come along, Sabourin," he said kindly, shooing away the crewmen from the *Jean Bart* who had come to help. He lifted her to her feet, draping one of her arms over his shoulders as he gripped her tightly by the waist to help her to the other ship. "I think you have done enough for one day."

FIFTEEN

Admiral Tiernan stared grimly at the tactical data that the crew of *Alita* had brought from Keran. While the information was priceless, it was also dangerously out of date: even in the two hours that it had taken *Alita* to reach the rendezvous point, the battle could have been lost or won. Tiernan was a gambling man, a superb poker player, and he wouldn't have put much money on the Alliance fleet from the replay of the first few minutes of the battle. Even though their ships were good, and he knew the Alliance had many first-rate naval officers, it was clear from the information before him that they were also outnumbered two-to-one, and the French commander had placed himself at a tremendous disadvantage by splitting his forces. Had he kept his fleet intact in high orbit rather than distributing his squadrons around the planet, he would have been able to concentrate enough combat power to fight at even odds with the larger Kreelan task force, and would have been able to completely overwhelm the smaller one. Unless the French admiral had pulled a rabbit out of a hat, he was going to be feeding his squadrons piecemeal to the enemy. And that was assuming that any of them stood a chance in hell against the Kreelans' technology.

"How much longer?" he asked his flag captain as he continued to replay the opening sequence of the battle that *Alita* had recorded, trying to absorb every nuance that he could. This was the only intelligence information they had to work with, their only insights into Kreelan tactics. The decisions he made based on this information would likely decide the outcome of the battle.

"Three minutes and forty-seven seconds, admiral," Captain Hans Ostermann replied quietly, his own eyes fixed on the countdown to emergence that was displayed in every compartment of the ship, and in every ship in the fleet.

Tiernan nodded as he went back to his study of the display, carefully concealing his trepidation. He had allowed himself only five minutes to evaluate the data *Alita* had transmitted the instant she arrived at the rendezvous point. It was immediately clear to him that they had no time to lose if they were to stand any chance of helping the French. It already might very well be too late.

His own plan called for splitting his forces, but not in quite the same way as the Alliance had. He had four assault carriers carrying the two heavy ground divisions. They were to jump in as close as they could to the planet, run like hell for low orbit to disembark their troops, and then jump back out to the safety of the rendezvous point. Tiernan had only detailed four destroyers to escort them on their inbound leg; he knew that he was taking a huge risk with that light of an escort, but he simply didn't have enough ships to go around.

He planned to commit the rest of his force - eight heavy cruisers, fourteen light cruisers, and sixteen destroyers - in two mutually supporting tactical squadrons. That decision had been easy. The more difficult one was how to use his fleet to best advantage. He only had two viable options: support the Alliance squadrons in high orbit that had begun to engage the larger Kreelan force, or link up with the single Alliance squadron that was facing a substantially smaller Kreelan force closer to the planet. Both options assumed that there would be enough Alliance ships left intact to matter, because his own fleet would not stand a chance against even half the Kreelan ships shown by *Alita's* data. His fear was that the Alliance squadrons that had been maneuvering to attack the larger Kreelan force might have already been defeated, since they would have been seriously outnumbered. But the sole Alliance squadron that had been engaged by the smaller Kreelan force was at least on fairly even terms, the unknowns of Kreelan technology notwithstanding.

Gambling is about numbers, luck, and guts, and Tiernan knew that you might have two of the three in any given hand. He knew the numbers from *Alita's* data, at least as of four hours ago, and knew that he and his crews had plenty of guts. The only question was how good their luck might be. He couldn't afford to take the long odds offered by the big fight going on in high orbit, even though a tactical victory there would likely kick the Kreelans out of the system. That left him with one option: his fleet would attack the smaller Kreelan force and pray that this Alliance squadron, and hopefully some of the others, had survived this long. Then they could regroup to take on the larger Kreelan force.

"Emergency jump protocols confirmed," the flag captain reported. If the fleet jumped in and the situation was untenable, Tiernan wasn't going to waste his fleet. They would immediately jump out again to the rendezvous point. And it wouldn't take two minutes for the hyperdrive engines to spool up as on the *Aurora*. That little safety interlock problem had been fixed.

"Stand by for transpace sequence," the ship's navigation computer announced to the crew. "Auto-lock engaged. Normal space emergence in five...four...three...two...one. Sequence initiated. Hyperspace Engines disengaged."

Tiernan suddenly found himself staring out at a scene straight from hell.

* * *

"Priestess!" called Tesh-Dar's First, Kumal-Utai. "More human ships have arrived!"

"Indeed?" Tesh-Dar replied, already feeling the change in tenor of the emotions of her young warriors on the ships around the planet. The Bloodsong had never rung with such fury and passion in her lifetime, and through every member of her race, to the Empress Herself, ran a thread of ecstasy not felt since millennia before. Fighting, killing, and dying in Her name: these were the things for which they all existed.

"Forty-six ships," Kumal-Utai reported. "Eight of them jumped in close to the planet and appear to be heading toward low orbit. The rest appeared near the remains of the human ships we fought upon emergence."

"Those eight must be transports carrying more warriors to defend the surface," Tesh-Dar mused. "Allow them to proceed unmolested. As for the newcomers," she said, her eyes surveying the flat-screen tactical display, "let us see the stuff of which they are made."

"Where do you wish our ship, my priestess?" Elai-Tura'an, the shipmistress, asked. Her blood burned for battle, but her mind understood the necessity of prudence. While Tesh-Dar would likely survive anything that happened to the ship, and Elai-Tura'an worried not about her own death, it would be...inconvenient for the fleet command ship to be destroyed.

The great priestess frowned momentarily. She sensed Elai-Tura'an's emotions, and felt much the same way. Tesh-Dar wanted to face the humans in a direct challenge, but it was not yet time. Instead, she would give the honor to the young ones. It was they, after all, who had fought so hard among the peers for the right to be here. "Assemble the remaining ships here in low orbit to bleed the newcomers. We shall take up a position at the trailing edge of the formation."

"Shall I call in additional ships from the high formation?" Kumal-Utai asked, indicating the larger force of ships that had remained near the orbit of the planet's moons.

Tesh-Dar shook her head. "No. Let the humans have the advantage here for now. Let our blood mingle with theirs."

* * *

"Christ!" Captain Morrison cried as *McClaren* suddenly materialized in normal space over Keran. The twisted and burning stern of a ship - it was impossible to tell if it was human or Kreelan - was hurtling directly for them, spewing air and flaming debris in its wake. "Hard aport, Z-vector minus fifty! All ahead flank!" he shouted at the navigator.

Like everyone else on the bridge, Ichiro Sato stared with unbelieving eyes as the tumbling wreck came closer, filling the bridge display. Had the *McClaren* been one of the larger cruisers, there was no way she would have been able to maneuver fast enough to avoid a collision. While Morrison was an imbecile when it came to leadership and tactics, he at least knew how to maneuver the ship. As it was, even with the navigator sending the ship into a sharp left downward turn and the destroyer accelerating like a greyhound, breaking out of their assigned position in the squadron formation, they barely escaped. Turning his eyes back to his targeting console, he saw that the wreckage cleared them by mere meters. But a near-collision was the least of their problems.

"Multiple contacts close aboard!" Sato called to the captain.

"Identify them, damn you!" Morrison bellowed as he looked at the tactical display, which was now filled with a cloud of yellow icons representing unidentified ships or the remains of ships. A few of them, then more and more, began to turn orange as the computer categorized them as wreckage that could potentially pose a navigation hazard. Sato felt his stomach lurch at what his display was showing: this side of the system was a charnel house of dead and dying ships. Flaming wreckage from at least fifty vessels was strewn through nearby space, and Sato could see what could only be hundreds, possibly thousands, of bodies. His sensors indicated that some of them were in vacuum suits, blasting away at one another with small arms or grappling in zero-gee hand-to-hand combat.

"Trying, sir," Sato replied, "but we don't have the Alliance identification codes and the inter-ship datalink hasn't synchronized yet." That concerned Sato more than anything else. Like the ships of the Alliance fleet, the Terran ships had a datalink capability that, in theory, made the fleet one large virtual weapon. Only it still took time, even if just a few moments, to come up after a hyperspace jump. "We've got to identify the ships visually or by their emissions signatures."

"Well, *that's* not an Alliance ship!" the navigator exclaimed, pointing at the bridge screen. A ship that looked like a huge swept-wing fighter, dark gray with cyan runes painted on the bow, arced toward them from the port side. While it maneuvered smoothly, it had not come through the horrendous battle unscathed: its hull was covered with scorch marks and at least half a dozen ragged holes where kinetic weapons had found their mark.

"Primary kinetics," Sato called out, "hard lock!" The ship's targeting systems had painted the enemy ship and were tracking her. At this close range they could use almost any weapon, but the primary kinetics, the destroyer's main guns, were the best choice for this situation: they could do the most damage quickly.

"Stand by..." Morrison ordered before giving the navigator orders to twist *McClaren* hard to the right, unmasking all the ship's heavy weapons turrets, "Fire as she bears!"

Sato gave the computer firing authority, and it calculated the optimal firing point out to the twentieth decimal. The ship echoed with thunder as ten fifteen centimeter guns rippled off five rounds each in under two seconds.

"Clean hits!" Sato cried. None of the bridge crew needed the tactical display to tell them they'd hit their target: the bridge screen, now nearly filled with the image of the enemy ship, showed a cascade of explosions down her flank, blowing off the starboard wing and sending her spinning out of control.

There was a brief cheer on the bridge before Morrison called out, "Target, designate!" Using the command override on his console, he steered the crosshairs for the pulse cannon onto a distant Kreelan ship, silhouetted against the planet far below, that was roughly the size of a heavy cruiser. To him it appeared to be an easy target of opportunity. As the weapon was fixed along the *McClaren's* centerline, the ship altered course automatically to line up her bows with the target.

"Captain?" Sato asked, not believing what the captain was doing. "Captain, *no, wait-*"

"Firing!" Morrison said almost gleefully as he hit the *commit* button. The lights dimmed and the entire ship thrummed as the pulse gun fired, sending an extremely powerful beam of coherent emerald light streaking toward the target.

Unfortunately, when Morrison used the command override, locking Sato's station out of the weapon control cycle, he didn't realize that it would also bypass the additional target lock cues: he thought that as soon as the commit button was illuminated, the weapon was locked on target and ready to fire. The second half of his assumption, that it was ready to fire, was correct, but the targeting system hadn't established a hard lock on the enemy ship, and the *McClaren's* angular motion from the gentle turn hadn't completely stopped.

But an impending miss wasn't why Sato had tried to stop Morrison from firing. It was the Alliance starliner that was directly in the weapon's path, well beyond the Kreelan cruiser.

Expecting to see the enemy ship burst into a gigantic fireball, the navigator increased the bridge screen magnification so they could make a damage assessment. But the Kreelan warship had passed out of view. Now the only thing that was on the screen was an Alliance starliner and a host of shuttles.

"Oh, my God," someone whispered into the sudden stillness that took the bridge as the blast from the pulse cannon sheared off the drive section of the starliner, splitting the ship in two and sending the wreckage tumbling. Sparks cascaded from severed electrical conduits and streams of air bled from the compartments that were now suddenly exposed to hard vacuum. Hundreds of bodies, clearly visible with the high magnification of the screen, flew from the wreckage, arms and legs flailing as the blood of the hapless victims boiled in vacuum. Most of them were soldiers waiting to be ferried to the surface, and so they had no vacuum suits. Secondary explosions peppered the side of the ship where the civilian shuttles, still trying to get the rest of the troops down to the surface, were swatted like flies as the huge hull twisted out of control.

Sato looked away from the carnage, hating the man who now sat in the captain's chair. Morrison's jaw opened and closed like that of a fish as he fought to come to grips with what he'd just done. *That's one screwup he can't blame on the crew*, Sato thought bitterly.

But they clearly weren't out of it yet.

"*Incoming from starboard!*" Sato cried as he saw a volley of projectiles erupt from one of the dozen or more ships embroiled in a huge gunfight that had broken out to the right of *McClaren*. "Recommend coming to course-"

"Belay that!" Morrison shouted, throwing Sato a disgusted look. "I'll handle the ship." With a brief glance at the display, he said, "There's no way those rounds will hit us."

"But sir-"

"*You are relieved, mister!*" The captain screamed at the top of his lungs. The bridge suddenly became deathly quiet except for half a dozen tactical alarms clamoring for attention.

His face an iron mask, Sato unbuckled from his seat and came to attention. "Yes, *sir!*" he said before stepping away from his console.

"Bogdanova," Morrison snapped, "take over tactical."

Without a word, the young female ensign who normally manned communications unstrapped from her combat chair and rushed across the bridge. She had even less experience aboard than Sato, was terrified of the captain, and had very little time training on the tactical position. She looked up at Sato as she slipped into his still-warm combat chair, her eyes wide with barely-concealed terror.

"Get off my bridge, *lieutenant*," the captain ordered tersely.

Giving Bogdanova what he hoped was a reassuring squeeze on her shoulder, Sato turned to leave.

Morrison took another look at his own tactical display, and came to the sudden conclusion that the incoming enemy shells were getting uncomfortably close after all.

"Counter-battery fire, Bogdanova!" Morrison ordered.

Looking desperately at the tactical display, she replied in a hoarse voice, terrified as much by the captain as the incoming weapons, "We can't, sir."

"Goddammit, what do you mean?" he yelled frantically.

"Because, you fucking idiot," Sato told him, unafraid of the captain's ire with death looming so close, "our close-in defense weapons are all lasers, and you completely drained the energy buffers when you destroyed that starliner with the pulse cannon." Horrified realization dawned on Morrison's face. "That's right, captain," Sato told him quietly. "The lasers are useless until the energy buffers recharge. Congratulations. You've killed us all."

Two seconds later the enemy salvo hit.

* * *

"Admiral!" the flag communications officer suddenly shouted. "We've established contact with Admiral Lefevre aboard the *Jean Bart*."

"About bloody time," Tiernan said, relieved. His fleet had been in-system a full fifteen minutes, and had managed to clear the remaining Kreelan ships from the immediate area. Terran losses, surprisingly, had been very light: the only major casualty had been the destroyer *McClaren*. A part of him, a part he never would have admitted existed, was almost glad: he had seen *McClaren* kill the Alliance starliner. If the destroyer's captain had been alive, he would have been facing the court martial from hell, and Tiernan would have been standing ready with the noose to hang the bastard. But that unpleasantness, at least, was unnecessary: the destroyer's dead hulk was adrift among the other shattered hulls. But Tiernan wasn't looking forward to the formal apology he needed to render to the Alliance commander. "*Amiral* Lefevre," Tiernan said into the vidcom, "this is Admiral Patrick Tiernan of the Terran Navy. We are at your disposal, sir." The last words were hard for him to say, but he had direct orders from the president: unless he had reason to believe that his fleet was about to be defeated and had no choice but to withdraw, he was to place himself under the command of the senior Alliance officer.

The man who looked back at him from the vidcom smiled. Tiernan thought Lefevre looked like he'd been through an infantry battle: his face was a mess, and his uniform was in tatters. But the Alliance admiral's eyes were bright, and his expression showed no loss of determination.

Lefevre wasn't a quitter, Tiernan thought. That's got to count for something.

"*Amiral* Tiernan," Lefevre said, "you have no idea how welcome is the sight of your fleet. We had been told there was a chance of Terran support, but..." He gave a Gallic shrug.

"Sir..." Tiernan began, the next words sticking in his throat, "We have much to discuss, but first I wish to formally apologize for the destruction of one of your troopships by a destroyer under my command. I take full responsibility, and will ensure a thorough investigation-"

"*Amiral* Tiernan," Lefevre said quietly, holding up a hand, "this is a tragedy, there can be no doubt. But we are at war, and must first ensure that some of us, at least, survive to worry about such matters. Let it be enough for now that I accept your apology with the sincerity in which it was offered."

"Thank you, sir," Tiernan said, inwardly relieved. He had only met Lefevre once during a joint exercise the two navies had held several years ago. He had been favorably impressed with him then, and was more so now. He couldn't think of many Terran admirals who would have taken such a loss with the same equanimity. "What are your orders, admiral?"

"Our first objective must be to finish clearing the enemy from low orbit," Lefevre said decisively. "I believe that with your ships, we can now do that. Then, perhaps, we may consider our options against the force in high orbit." He paused, frowning. "But I must confess, *amiral*, that I do not understand the enemy's tactics or their overall objective."

"What do you mean, sir?" Tiernan asked.

"They had enough superiority to sweep us from the skies," Lefevre told him, his voice filled with a mixture of indignation and anger. "Their ships seem to be similar enough to ours, not nearly so powerful or advanced as the information provided us by your attaché indicated from your survey vessel's encounter. But..." he pursed his lips and shook his head. "They had a full two-to-one advantage over us, *amiral*, plus the advantage of surprise. They held the high ground with a superior force. They held every major tactical advantage. Yet...they simply threw it all away. *Pfft.* They fight with great ferocity and spirit, but it is as if we have been in a giant brawl, not a modern space battle. They have taken no more than a one-to-one ratio in any of our engagements, save the first surprise encounter, and seem to prefer to disable our ships rather than destroy them. They have not molested the deployment of our troops to the surface, when they have had plenty of opportunity to do so." He again shook his head. "Tell me, *amiral*, who would possibly turn away from such a target, especially when they must know that I would have to split away forces to defend the transports? Yet they did. It is as if they want those troops to land. But for what purpose, I cannot understand."

That gave Tiernan pause. He glanced at the flag tactical display and saw that his four carriers and their destroyer escorts were nearing the drop zones over Keran. And while there were no Kreelan ships in the immediate vicinity, there were plenty in higher orbit that could easily have made a play for the carriers, not to mention all the Alliance starliners that, even after the hours it had taken Tiernan's fleet to get here, had still not unloaded all their troops. In all that time, the only casualty among them had been the one *McClaren* had destroyed. He tried not to wince at the thought.

"And then there are the boarding parties," Lefevre said, his face darkening. "We did not take this information from your attaché seriously. Who would, in such an age as this? And we paid the price. We lost fifteen ships to those devils, including my flagship." He held fast his expression in front of the Terran admiral, but Lefevre inwardly shivered at the hell the compartments and passageways of *Victorieuse* had become after the Kreelan boarders had breached the hull.

"That, sir," Tiernan assured him, "I believe we are prepared to handle." He thought of Lieutenant Sato, who had suffered so much to give them the information that formed the core of the planning and preparation that had been put into action over the last year, and who now was as dead as the *McClaren*. He felt a deep sense of bitterness at the young man's loss. "Every ship in my task force has Marines aboard, along with a few other surprises for any would-be boarders. I don't think we have enough Marines for all of your ships, sir, but if you like, we have enough to at least put a full platoon aboard each of your cruisers to help provide some on-board defense." He hadn't brought extra Marines for the purpose of helping the Alliance ships, but he could thin out the companies aboard his cruisers by a couple of platoons without compromising the security of his own ships. It was clear from Lefevre's expression that he feared the boarders more than anything else. If giving up some Marines would boost the morale of the French fleet, then it was a small but worthwhile sacrifice on his part.

"Thank you, *amiral*," Lefevre said, his voice nearly cracking with relief. "You have no idea how much that would mean to my crews."

"It's the least we can do, sir," Tiernan told him. "If you'll have your flag captain coordinate with mine, we'll have our cutters start transferring the Marines immediately. And we'd also better see what we can do about integrating our maneuvering orders and fire control..."

SIXTEEN

There had been very few occasions in her career when Steph had questioned her sanity, but this was definitely one of them. Strapped into a sling chair aboard an assault boat deployed from the carrier *Subic Bay*, she felt like she was on the bobsled ride from hell as the boat plunged from the carrier's belly into Keran's atmosphere. She was one of half a dozen journalists embedded with the two heavy divisions Tiernan's fleet had brought along to shore up Keran's defenses, and was attached to the headquarters troop of the 7th Cavalry Regiment under the 1st Guards Armored Division. That division was an odd mix of American and Russian lineage, but together with its sister 31st Armored Division, which had its roots in the old Indian Army, they were the best-trained heavy divisions Earth could muster. The 7th Cav, as it was often known, was famous - or infamous, depending on one's point of view - as the last command of General George Armstrong Custer, who led the regiment to defeat and massacre in the Battle of the Little Bighorn. Traditionally it had the job of providing reconnaissance and security to its parent division. On the modern battlefield, the decision had been made many years before to convert it to a heavy armored brigade. The unit's traditional title had stuck, and it had also retained its reputation as one of the first units sent in to stir up trouble for the enemy.

True to form, the regiment would be the first on the ground on Keran, the lead element brought in by the assault boats that would then return to the carriers for a second load. And since they would be on the bleeding edge of the ground campaign, assuming the Kreelans landed, Steph had immediately decided that she wanted to be with them.

But now, as the assault boat screamed through the atmosphere, bouncing and jarring its occupants and cargo like it was flying through a tornado, she had to wonder just what the hell she had been thinking.

She also wondered about the fleet battle going on above. From the brief exchange she'd been able to have with the regimental commander before the boats deployed, the Terran fleet had jumped into the middle of a naval meat grinder that had already left dozens of burning hulks in its wake. No enemy ships had maneuvered to intercept the carriers as they raced from their in-bound jump points to the drop zones over Keran, for which everyone was thankful. But there were still plenty left that were hitting back at the Terran fleet and what ships were left of the French Alliance, and Steph felt herself uncharacteristically worried about Ichiro.

The thought of him gave her a momentary pause from her contemplations of falling through the atmosphere in the company of a bunch of suicidal cavalry troopers. What exactly did she feel for Ichiro? she asked herself. While the two of them had certainly become more than friends, could she say that she loved him? Even if she did, assuming that both of them survived this, what could they do about it? Ichiro had made it clear that he wanted to stay in the Navy, and the war would almost certainly mean extended service for everyone in the military, and possibly even a draft if the president could get it approved by Congress. Despite the series of events that had linked her fate to Ichiro's over the last year, her own career would no doubt take a separate road from his. Her being aboard this ship and not with the fleet above them was already proof enough of that. Looking beyond any love the two of them might share, even if she decided to settle down and start a family - a bridge she was not yet prepared to cross - did she want to be a Navy wife, with Ichiro off on deployment for months at a time?

She frowned inwardly, for she had no answers to those questions. But she cared enough about him that she felt they needed to have that conversation. If they mutually decided that they were better off as friends, fine. But she didn't want to pass up even a one in a thousand chance that they could be something more. He was as close as she'd ever come to finding someone who really cared about her, and she didn't want to throw it away.

While she was going into harm's way herself, she silently prayed for the Lord of All to keep him safe.

* * *

Lieutenant General Arjun Ray was furious. As the commander of the Terran Army's I Corps, the parent corps of the two armored divisions now plummeting toward the surface of Keran, Ray had been given the task of leading the ground portion of the battle. He was subordinate to Tiernan, who was in overall command of the expeditionary force, but once the admiral's carriers got Ray's troops to the surface he would largely be on his own. His greatest concern had been the threat of Kreelan attack against the carriers before his troops could even hit dirt. But soon after the boats had deployed for the surface he discovered that he had another battle to fight.

"My apologies, general," the brigadier of the Keran Defense Forces repeated sternly, and not sounding very apologetic at all, "but you have no clearance to land your troops. Our diplomatic service is already sending a démarche to the Terran embassy here to protest the presence of your fleet." He shook his head. "We will not allow, under any circumstances, Terran ground forces to land on Keran soil."

"My god, man, do you have any idea what is happening right over your heads?" Ray asked him, trying desperately to rein in his anger. "The Alliance Fleet has taken serious losses and may very well not be able to prevent the enemy from attempting a landing if they should choose to. If we don't get our troops on the ground now and consolidate our defenses, we may not get another chance. I'll speak to the Alliance commander and try to get him to convince you-"

"General," the brigadier rudely interrupted, enjoying the opportunity to tweak a superior officer from another planet's service, "the Alliance has no say in this matter.

They are here simply for exercises with our own navy. We have received no reports of enemy activity-"

"*I can hear the bloody raid warning sirens going off in the background of your transmission, you idiot!*" Ray shouted, finally losing his temper. He had already been in contact with Ambassador Pugacheva of the Terran Embassy and so had some idea of the disarray the Keran government was in at the moment. But this was simply too much. Calmly dickering with this imbecile while strapped into a combat chair in an assault boat as it screamed toward the surface was simply beyond the patience of anyone but a saint. "Brigadier, let me make this clear to you," he said through gritted teeth. "I am landing my troops at the coordinates we sent you earlier, with the intention of taking up positions on the left flank of the Alliance Foreign Legion troops that have deployed on the outskirts of Foshan."

Foshan was the largest population center on the planet, although the planetary capital was a smaller city to the north. It was a bustling metropolis that had a nearly perfect balance between the Arabic and Chinese populations. The city center had an impressive skyline of high-rise office buildings sporting garish video banners, countered by the graceful spires of minarets from the many mosques that lined the downtown area. The city's main roads radiated from the downtown area like spokes of a wheel, serving a colorful hodgepodge of neighborhoods and shopping districts that were a mix of pagoda-style buildings and white- or tan-faced stone structures with intricate scrollwork that were typical of many of Earth's cities in what was once the Middle East.

Ray knew that three more French divisions would be deploying to Foshan, while the remaining five would be divided up among the three other largest population centers. It was scant coverage in terms of defending against a planetary assault, but it was all they had to work with. They would be leavened with men from the Keran paramilitary forces, but that was about all the support the off-world troops could expect. Like their navy, the Keran military had little actual combat capability, amounting to a total of three light infantry brigades and some antiquated aerospace defense systems.

"And let me make sure that you understand something," Ray continued. "You are dealing with the commander of two heavy armored divisions. If my troops or the assault boats transporting them are molested in any way by Keran forces," he growled as he leaned closer to the video pickup, "I will have those divisions blow you little fuckers to bits and grind what's left into fertilizer. Do I make myself clear, *brigadier?*"

The other man's darker skin, be it from Chinese or Arab descent, Ray could not have cared less, visibly paled. Beyond the insult, he must have immediately come to the conclusion that Ray wasn't bluffing. On that count, he would have been quite correct. "I will let my commander know that you intend to force a landing on our sovereign soil," he protested with as much indignation as he could muster, "and convey your threats against our forces. And I will lodge the strongest possible protest with your embassy, general!"

"Go right ahead, you little bastard," Ray spat dismissively as he killed the connection. "Just don't get in my way."

                                                  * * *

Lieutenant-Colonel Lev Stepanovich Grishin, commander of the *Première Régiment étranger de cavalerie*, or *1er REC*, of the Alliance *Légion étrangère* watched with professional interest as the Terran assault boats swept down to their drop sites to the south of his unit's position. He had briefly listened to the local Keran military liaison rant about the Terran "invasion" and orders he had for Grishin to fire on the boats before they landed. Making no attempt to conceal his contempt, Grishin kicked the fool out of his command vehicle and had him escorted out of the regiment's defense perimeter. He knew that not all Keran military officers were idiots, but there were enough in key positions to be causing trouble when they desperately needed to be pulling themselves together. The Legion operations staff had been keeping track of the hammering that the Alliance fleet had taken, and Grishin himself had given up a cheer when the Terran ships had appeared. While the Legion had been his home for nearly twenty years and he fully expected to die in uniform, he would prefer that he and his men not be wasted unnecessarily by incompetent bureaucrats.

"Have we made contact with them?" he asked his adjutant.

"Yes, sir," the man replied immediately. "We can only speak in the clear, *mon colonel*. The communications security systems are not compatible. Their commander is waiting to speak with you."

Nodding, Grishin spoke, his voice picked up by the tiny microphone embedded in his helmet. "Terran ground commander," he said, "this is *Lieutenant-Colonel* Grishin, commander of the First Cavalry Regiment of the Alliance Foreign Legion. To whom am I speaking, please?"

"*Bonjour*, colonel," came a gravelly voice that was unmistakably from the American South. While he appreciated the gesture, Grishin winced at the man's pronunciation of the traditional French greeting, hoping that the Terran officer would prefer to speak English. While his own French carried an unmistakable Russian accent, it was pure Parisian compared to this man's speech. "This is Colonel James Sparks, commanding the 7th Cavalry Regiment, 1st Guards Armored Division. We're going to be operating on your left flank, and I wanted to stop by and coordinate our lines and fire plans with you, if I may."

"Certainly, colonel," Grishin told him. "My command post is at-" he read off some coordinates, "-and I will be waiting for you."

"Thank you, colonel," Sparks said. "I'll be there in ten minutes. Sparks, out."

Grishin looked at his adjutant, who shrugged. "At least they will have tanks," his adjutant said. "That must count for something..."

Exactly ten minutes later, Grishin tried to keep the dismay from showing on his face as the Terran regimental commander dismounted from the wheeled reconnaissance vehicle that had pulled up in front of Grishin's mobile command post. Sparks looked as if he had walked off the set of an ancient American "western" movie. While he was dressed in the standard combat uniform of the Terran Army, the wiry man wore a cowboy-style black cavalry officer's hat replete with an insignia of crossed sabers and a gold acorn band, along with a matching bright yellow ascot showing from the vee of the neck of his combat tunic. And under his left arm, carried in a matte black leather shoulder holster, was the biggest handgun Grishin had ever seen. The huge weapon was nickel plated with contoured grips that he would have wagered a month's pay were made of mother-of-pearl.

But the most ridiculous thing, Grishin thought, aghast, was what the Terran wore on the heels of his boots: riding spurs, which made a *ching-ching-ching* sound as the Terran colonel strode purposefully toward him.

The man was simply outrageous.

"*Mon Dieu*," Grishin's adjutant whispered, desperately trying to hold his face rigid and not burst out laughing.

Grishin shared the sentiment right up until the moment that Sparks took off his sunglasses and tucked them in a pocket as he drew to within hand-shaking distance. While Grishin did not believe that the eyes told everything about a man, in some cases they could tell a great deal. And in this case, Sparks's piercing blue eyes and no-nonsense expression told him what he needed to know. A Hollywood dandy, this man might be. But Grishin suspected, and greatly hoped, that he was a formidable combat commander, as well.

Rendering a sharp salute, Grishin said formally, "On behalf of the men of the *1er Régiment étranger de cavalerie*, I welcome you, sir."

Sparks snapped a salute that was parade-ground perfect, then said, "Thank you, colonel. I appreciate the hospitality." As Grishin lowered his salute and shook the Terran colonel's extended hand, noting how strong the smaller man's grip was, Sparks went on, "But if it's all the same to you, I suggest we get down to business over a glass of whiskey." Like magic, he produced a small silver-plated flask and held it up with a devilish grin on his face.

Grishin could no longer help himself. Laughing, he gestured for Sparks to accompany him into the command post. "Come, colonel," he told Sparks. "If you have whiskey, there's no time to lose..."

* * *

Steph stood in the background, recording the coordination session and making verbal notes as she watched the two commanders and their small staffs huddle around the map display in Grishin's command vehicle. Of the two men, she wasn't sure which one was more unusual. Sparks was outwardly an extreme stereotype of the romantic cavalryman, but even in the short time she had been with his unit she had discovered that the men and women who served in his regiment would go to hell and back for him without a second thought. He was polite, thoughtful, and unquestionably loved the men and women who served under him as if they were family. But he could also be ruthless and absolutely merciless to those he found lacking in the will to do their best, or who in any way dishonored his regiment. And from hearing him speak, ruthless and merciless would be the lead traits of his personality that he planned to direct at the enemy.

Grishin, on the other hand, appeared to be what one might expect of a competent colonel in any army, with a very significant exception: of the twenty regiments of the *Légion étrangère*, he was the only regimental commander not seconded from one of the Alliance armies. One of those exceedingly rare individuals who had worked his way up the ranks from a lowly legionnaire to commander of a combat regiment, Grishin was a veteran of the St. Petersburg war. In fact, he had joined the Legion right after the armistice, and rumor had it that he was one of the few communists who had managed to escape the final destruction of the Red Army. But in the Legion, no one cared. His past, whatever it truly was, was left behind and gone. And if he was good enough to make it through the political battlefield that controlled Legion officer assignments, then maybe he would be a good match for the Kreelans, as well.

Turning her attention back to the discussion around the map table, she heard Sparks say, "Our biggest problem as I see it is intelligence. We have absolutely no idea what we may be up against, or which direction they'll be coming from."

"Surely, sir," said Grishin's adjutant, "they'll have to come from the south, over here." Foshan was situated in a forested area, with the western side of the city along the shore of one of Keran's freshwater seas. On the map, the adjutant indicated a large open area in the forest to the south. "That's the only decent nearby landing zone that's not in direct sight of our weapons here. There just aren't many other choices unless they want to drop right into the city, which..." He shrugged. "That would make no sense to me, but I do not know how they think."

"That is the problem," Grishin sighed. "We have no idea what they might do, what they could do. And what if they do drop directly into the city? Our tanks are made for fighting in the open. In the city they would be very vulnerable without more infantry support. And half of Foshan's streets are too narrow for our tanks, let alone yours." The Alliance-made wheeled light tanks that were used by the *1er REC* were not terribly dissimilar from vehicles used long in the past, for a very simple reason: the combination of mobility, lightness, and firepower was extremely effective for the types of low-tech opponents the Legion typically faced. The Terran heavy armor units, by contrast, were equipped with vehicles that weighed upward of one hundred metric tons and were marvels of every facet of human engineering. They were incredibly powerful, well-protected, and amazingly fast for something so heavy, but were totally out of their element in close-in street fighting.

"Yeah," Sparks agreed grimly. "We'd have to blow half the goddamn city down just to move through it. On the other hand, we're cavalry: if we have to dismount, every trooper in my regiment's got a rifle and he knows how to use it."

Grishin thought it would be ridiculous to use tank crews as infantry, but as far as he could tell, Sparks wasn't joking.

"Mobility has to be the key," Sparks said, finally. "It's the only thing we've got against so many unknowns. And the first thing I'd recommend," he went on, "would be to send a company of tanks forward, with some of your men, colonel, as guides, to this nice open patch your adjutant pointed out. That way if our friends do show up there, we can give them a warm welcome."

Thinking it over, Grishin nodded. It wouldn't cost them anything, since they had absolutely no idea what the enemy might do. If the Kreelans did try to land there, one of the 7th Cav's tank companies could give them a difficult time. "I agree, colonel," he told him. "I will detach one of my reconnaissance teams to you: they have been out to that area several times and know the route and commanding terrain well."

"Outstanding," Sparks told him. "My tanks will be outside your door here in thirty minutes. You'll know they're here when the ground starts shaking." He held out his hand. "Colonel, it's been a pleasure, and I'll definitely be in touch. But I need to get back to get the rest of my regiment squared away."

"My pleasure, sir," Grishin told him, meaning it, as he shook the Terran cavalryman's hand and they once again exchanged salutes. "We will be standing by."

On the brief trip back to the reconnaissance vehicle that had brought them over, Steph walked beside Sparks. The two staff officers who'd accompanied him were walking behind, already setting the colonel's orders into motion over the comm sets built into their uniform harnesses. She saw a look of unusual concern on his face. "Colonel," she asked quietly, "may I ask what you're thinking?"

He glanced over at her. "On or off the record?" he asked sharply.

That took her by surprise. One of the whole points of having journalists embedded with the forward units was that everything was "on the record" unless it might compromise the safety of friendly troops.

"Okay, colonel," she said guardedly as they reached the vehicle and she turned to face him. "Let's start with off the record."

Taking a look around them, with the city behind and the dense forest in front that led to the hills protecting the possible landing zone, he told her, "Unless I'm badly mistaken or the enemy really disappoints me, we may be in for the biggest defeat since Custer got his ass handed to him at the Little Big Horn."

"*What?*" Steph blurted. Sparks's comment was totally out of place from what she'd understood of his conversation with Grishin. "Why?"

"Listen, Miss Guillaume," he told her, beckoning her to the front of the vehicle and away from the droning of his staff officers as they continued issuing orders, "this is probably the first battle in modern history where at least one side - that would be us - knows virtually nothing about the enemy. *Nothing.* We don't know jack about their weapons, tactics, motivations, objectives: zippo. For Christ's sake, we don't even know what they look like aside from what that young boy Sato could tell us. And if you don't understand what your opponent wants, it's pretty damned hard to keep him, or her, in this case, I suppose, from getting it. And because we don't understand them, we can't take the initiative and force the battle on our terms: we can only make assumptions about what they want and try to prepare for it, react to what they do. But all our assumptions could be wrong. For all I know they might just start dropping nukes on the cities here and be done with it. Or what if they use a biological weapon? For the love of God, they attacked the French ships with boarding parties, just like Sato said they did to the *Aurora*. Who the devil would expect such a thing in this day and age? And the French paid the price for it from the reports I saw on the way down: they lost over a dozen ships just to that. And the enemy could do something as unexpected here that will throw us totally off-balance. We just don't know. And that just bothers the hell out of me." He dug his heel in the ground in a sign of frustration. "So we're all just guinea pigs right now, I guess," he sighed. "We just have to wait for them to show up at the party and take the lead."

Steph couldn't say that what Sparks said made her happy, but she understood his point well enough. "Well," she prompted, "how about what you think *on* the record?"

He looked at her, his blue eyes bright and his mouth set in a hard line. "*On* the record, if those alien witches come down here looking for trouble, the 7th Cav will be damned happy to oblige them."

SEVENTEEN

Having bled the humans in low orbit to her content, Tesh-Dar withdrew the remainder of her ships to the larger formation in orbit near the planet's moons. In part it was to give some rest to her crews; in part it was to see what the humans would do. Taking into account the losses each side had suffered, plus the recently arrived human ships, the two fleets had rough parity numerically. She was curious to see if the humans would try and take the initiative and attack her formation. Thus far, they had been content to consolidate their hold of lower orbit space and cover the vulnerable troop transports as they finally finished disgorging their cargoes of warriors and war machines. Tesh-Dar made no effort to intercept the huge ships as they broke from orbit for their jump points: killing them would offer no challenge. Her main interest now lay in the troops they had sent down to the surface.

In the meantime, she had sent some of her smaller warships to recover as many warriors as possible from the hulks adrift in the system, both from Imperial ships that had been destroyed and from human ships her warriors had boarded. Only two of the recovery ships had been molested when they probed overly close to the human formation, but they had escaped easily enough. She was happily surprised to see that so many of her warriors, particularly those who had boarded the human ships, had survived. She was especially relieved to see that Li'ara-Zhurah remained alive. A blood daughter of the Empress, she was a fine warrior who had well-proven her honor this day. Tesh-Dar had known Li'ara-Zhurah since she had arrived from the nursery world to enter training at Tesh-Dar's *kazha*, the school of the Way that focused on the teachings of the Desh-Ka. She had fought well against what was clearly a set of fine opponents on the human ship she had boarded. Tesh-Dar had been most pleased.

"My priestess," Li'ara-Zhurah asked, flexing her arm where the healers had repaired the bullet wound in her arm, "I would request the honor of the first wave to attack the surface."

Tesh-Dar turned to look at her. "Child, have you not had enough this day?" she asked gently. While she wanted to give her warriors every possible chance to prove themselves and bring honor to the Empress, she did not want to waste them needlessly. Despite the power of the Bloodsong and the primal need to fight that was ingrained in her people, she knew quite well the physical toll that combat exacted. And what Li'ara-Zhurah had survived this day had been brutal, even by Kreelan standards.

The younger warrior averted her eyes. "My apologies, priestess," she whispered, her voice quivering. "But my blood burns now as never before, even during the Challenge in the arena. I cannot see or think beyond it. It consumes me."

Tesh-Dar understood quite well. The Bloodsong, the spiritual bond that tied their race together and to the Empress, was normally like the sound of the sea washing upon the shore, a ceaseless background murmuring that every one of Her Children sensed since birth. In times of heightened passion, particularly during personal combat in the arena during one of the many Challenges that the warriors faced in life, the Bloodsong burned like holy fire. It could be harnessed and channelled by some, as if it were a source of spiritual adrenaline. To those like Tesh-Dar, who had a vastly greater understanding, the Bloodsong was far more: it was a spiritual river that bound the living even unto the spirits of the dead. It was through the Bloodsong that those such as she could even sense the Ancient Ones, the warriors of the spirit who had passed from life. For they, too, were bound to the Empress and Her will.

But this feeling of which Li'ara-Zhurah spoke was something more. It was the intensity of so many warriors engaged in life-and-death struggles in such a short time, triggering an emotional tidal wave surging through the Bloodsong that had begun to overwhelm some of the younger warriors. Not just here, but throughout the Empire, for the Bloodsong was universal. The effect of the emotional surge on Tesh-Dar had been profound, but as a priestess gifted with powers that even most of her disciples would not understand, she was easily able to control it. The younger ones would adapt in time, as well, for this war would likely go on for many cycles, but they would need help now that only the senior priestesses and clawless mistresses could provide. The healers who had studied the Books of Time recounting earlier encounters with other sentient species had told Tesh-Dar and the other priestesses that this would likely happen, and had prepared them to deal with it.

"Come to me, child," Tesh-Dar said gently as she stood up from her command chair. "Do not kneel," she said as Li'ara-Zhurah made to kneel down before her. "Stand. Try as best you can to clear your mind."

"I...cannot, my priestess," she said softly, her eyes fixed on the deck at her feet. "My thoughts tumble as if caught in a great storm, beyond my control."

"I understand," Tesh-Dar told her as she brought her hands up to rest on either side of Li'ara-Zhurah's face. The young warrior sighed at her touch, her body shivering involuntarily. Tesh-Dar closed her eyes and focused her concentration on the young woman's spirit, seeing it as a ghostly image, glowing brightly in her mind. Her spirit appeared to be caught in the center of a storm that made it flutter like a pennant snapping in a stiff wind. With the power of her own will, using her control of the Bloodsong, Tesh-Dar forced the storm to quiet, to be still. Her ears heard a shuddering sigh from Li'ara-Zhurah's lips, and her arms felt the caress of the young warrior's hands as the two of them stood locked in a spiritual embrace for but a moment that itself was timeless.

Looking deeper still into the young warrior's spirit in that infinite moment, Tesh-Dar discovered another reason for Li'ara-Zhurah's spiritual confusion: her time for breeding would again soon be upon her. Among their race, the need to mate was far more than a physiological condition, for it had its roots in an ancient curse of the spirit. As decreed by the First Empress many generations before, the clawless ones and those warriors with black talons had to mate every great cycle of the Empress Moon or they would die in terrible agony. Those like Tesh-Dar, who were born sterile, could only stand as silent witnesses to the continuity of their species, at least for the few centuries they had left. A part of Tesh-Dar deeply lamented that she could never bear children. But another part secretly rejoiced, for the act of consummation was not a pleasant affair: the males of their species, cursed along with the females by the First Empress so very long ago, now only existed as mindless tools for mating. And having done so once, they died in great pain, without even understanding what was happening to them, or why.

Pushing away those melancholy thoughts, she brought herself back to the pleasant warmth of the spiritual embrace she shared with Li'ara-Zhurah, letting it wash away the sense of despair that had momentarily taken hold of her heart.

And then it was done. Taking in a deep breath, Tesh-Dar opened her eyes and lowered her hands from the young woman's face, as Li'ara-Zhurah reluctantly released her light grip on Tesh-Dar's arms. The young warrior stood still for another moment, as if meditating, before opening her eyes. She met Tesh-Dar's gaze for a few beats of her heart, then lowered them in reverence.

"Thank you, my priestess," Li'ara-Zhurah breathed, the churning storm in her soul now stilled, Tesh-Dar's power echoing through her veins like the ripples of a great stone cast into a shallow pond.

"It is Her will," Tesh-Dar told her gently. "Go now. Eat and rest to restore your body. Then I will grant your wish." Turning to the display that showed the human deployments on the surface of the planet, at least what could be gleaned from the sensors of her ships in high orbit, she said, "You will accompany me in the attack on the planet."

* * *

Tiernan had no idea why the Kreelans had offered the humans a respite, their fleet now brooding in high orbit, but he and Lefevre had tried to put it to good use. The Terran fleet's Marines had been redistributed to provide some protection for the Alliance ships, and the Marines themselves had sorted out how to get at least a fire team aboard every single French ship, with a short platoon on each of the surviving cruisers. While Tiernan hesitated to use the example, the Terran Marines had been welcomed aboard the French ships like American troops must have been when they helped liberate France herself during the Second World War.

After dropping off the Marines, the cutters began to search through the scattered debris and hulks looking for any survivors. They found a few from some of the destroyed Alliance ships, but not very many.

The senior engineers of the two fleets had been working non-stop on trying to integrate the different data-link systems since the low-orbit battle had been decided. But that was a problem that could only be solved by the system designers working together: there were too many safeguards and security measures built into each system to allow any field expedient integration measures. So the admirals and captains had to rely on basic voice and video communications to relay orders and information to one another. It was a dangerous way to handle things in modern space combat, where the tactical situation could change completely in a matter of seconds, but they had no other choice.

On the ground, things were much the same. Tiernan had just spoken to General Ray, who reported that his divisions had deployed without incident (aside from the diplomatic démarche, which the ambassador was handling planetside), and were taking up defensive positions as best they could, given that they had no idea from where or how the Kreelans might attack. The Legion troops had been very accommodating, even before Lefevre issued their *Général de division* very explicit orders about coordinating with the Terrans.

As with their naval counterparts, the ground forces had been completely frustrated in trying to get the data-link systems to talk to one another. This was perhaps even more critical for the ground units because the Terran forces had heavy artillery and aerospace defense weapons that could be used to help support the neighboring Legion regiments, which themselves had few such weapons. Without effective integration of their combat data networks to share intelligence and targeting information, however, the overall effectiveness of employing the Terran heavy weapons outside of their own formations was going to be significantly degraded.

Tiernan, though, was most concerned about one thing: taking the initiative. Aside from the initial surprise his fleet had given them upon emergence, the Kreelans had largely enjoyed a free ride in how the battle had been fought. Now that the two opposing fleets had rough parity in numbers and tonnage, he and Lefevre intended to take the fight to the enemy.

The Kreelans, however, demonstrated an impeccable sense of timing.

"They're moving, sir!" the flag tactical officer reported, pointing to a sheaf of red icons that was separating away from the main body of the Kreelan fleet.

Tiernan held his breath. The temptation of some would have been to curse that the Kreelans had acted out of turn. But if they were splitting their forces, it might give him and Lefevre an opportunity to defeat them, concentrating their own massed squadrons against either smaller Kreelan force.

After a few minutes of watching the new trajectory traces on the tactical display, Tiernan cursed. It was clear where the Kreelan ships, sixty-seven of them, almost all of them cruiser-sized, were heading: directly for Keran.

* * *

"Fight them as you would, Amar-Marakh," Tesh-Dar said to the image of the senior shipmistress, a warrior priestess of the Ima'il-Kush order who remained with the formation in high orbit as she herself led the other ships in the first wave of the planetary assault. She knew that the shipmistresses had chafed somewhat at not being allowed to fight unfettered in the initial battles; Tesh-Dar was not unsympathetic, but it had been necessary at the time. But now, as the battle was about to open on the ground, she saw no reason to hold back anymore in the fighting that must erupt once more in space. The humans had proven themselves capable opponents, and would be treated as such. "We have bled them to learn what we would, and to give them the opportunity to do so, as well. Now challenge them to survive."

"Yes, my priestess," Amar-Marakh answered, clearly pleased. In the first battles, the ships had been used mainly to get the boarders close to their targets. Now they would be used to their fullest. "We are moving to engage now."

Tesh-Dar nodded. "In Her name, let it be so..."

* * *

"Admiral," Tiernan said, addressing Lefevre, "I believe our best choice would be to move to intercept the enemy ships heading toward the surface."

"I agree, *amiral*," Lefevre said at once over the vidcom. He, too, had seen the opportunity opened by the Kreelans splitting their forces. Attacking the group heading toward the planet was certainly the optimal choice: the human forces would have the advantage of being higher in the gravity well and a nearly three to one advantage in tonnage. Being able to intercept the enemy before they could land troops on the ground was simply icing on the cake. "I recommend that we-"

"Admiral," Tiernan's flag captain said tensely.

Tiernan told Lefevre, "Just a moment, admiral," and turned to see what was going on. His flag captain merely pointed at the tactical display, which now showed the larger Kreelan force reforming and starting to move. "Admiral Lefevre, are you seeing this?" Tiernan asked.

"*Oui*," Lefevre said gravely. "Shall we make a wager that they are headed our way?"

Tiernan snorted. "No takers here on that one, sir. You know bloody well they are." He didn't need the tactical computer's analysis for that. Taking a closer look at the trajectory for the enemy formation heading for the planet and doing some mental projections, he said, "So, do we go meet them head-to-head, or do we play a hand that's a bit riskier?"

Lefevre smiled. He had known Tiernan only this short time, but already had come to like the man. "Tell me what you have in mind, *amiral*."

* * *

Senior shipmistress Amar-Marakh hissed as she saw the human ships begin to deploy. Her reaction was not one of fear, but of annoyance. She had wanted to meet the human fleet head-on, but it was clear the humans had something else in mind. The great staggered wedges of their fleet were arrowing toward the planet, plunging downward with the clear intent of intercepting Tesh-Dar's force.

"I see them," came Tesh-Dar's voice, as if the great priestess had read Amar-Marakh's mind. "They come for us."

"We cannot intercept them before they reach you," Amar-Marakh warned. "They will have superiority."

Tesh-Dar shook her head. "They will not reach us," she reassured her senior shipmistress. "They are thinking in terms of their own vessels, not of ours. Be prepared for them when they realize their mistake and climb to engage you."

Amar-Marakh saluted and said only, "As you command, Tesh-Dar."

* * *

"We're missing something," Tiernan murmured to himself. The combined human fleet was speeding toward the planet on a course that would intercept the Kreelan ships now plunging down for what Tiernan believed could only be a planetary assault.

It was a perfect opportunity: the Kreelan ships would have to sail close to Keran to drop their troops. The human fleet would be in a perfect position to smash the enemy ships as they climbed up away from the planet, struggling against gravity. The combination of superior firepower and tactical positioning should let them pound the Kreelans into scrap, he had thought. Then the human fleet could deal with the larger enemy force still holding near Keran's moons.

It had been a good plan.

Except it wasn't going to work. With a sudden shock he realized why: the Kreelan ships were heading in too low. Tiernan had thought the streamlined nature of the enemy vessels was merely an alien aesthetic preference. Now he realized that they were streamlined for a specific reason: the aerodynamic shape, no doubt combined with more powerful electromagnetic shields and high-heat alloys so the ships could withstand the heat of reentry, would allow them to enter atmosphere and drop their troops without the need for assault boats. Not only that, but they'd likely be able to bring the main weapons of the ships to bear on ground targets, which put the human troops in extreme jeopardy.

"Get me Admiral Lefevre," he ordered the flag communications officer.

"*Oui, Amiral* Tiernan?" Lefevre answered immediately.

"They surprised us again," Tiernan told him. "Those ships are going to enter the atmosphere, possibly even land." Looking at the tactical plot, he shook his head. "I don't think we'll be able to catch them."

Lefevre frowned and spoke to someone off to the side. A moment later he said, "I agree with your assessment of their intentions, my friend," he said, "but not that we cannot catch them. If we depress our trajectory slightly and increase our speed, we should be able to give them a broadside at extreme range as we pass."

Ticonderoga's flag tactical officer, who was speaking at the same time with his counterpart on Lefevre's flag bridge aboard the *Jean Bart*, brought up a new set of navigation traces on the display. Tiernan saw that there was absolutely no margin for error. Even under the best of circumstances, it was likely that at least some of his ships were going to sustain damage from contact with the upper fringes of Keran's atmosphere. "That's cutting it awfully close, admiral," he said.

"It is, *amiral*," Lefevre replied grimly. "But if the Kreelans are able to use their ships to fire directly on our ground forces..." He shook his head: the troops on the planet would not stand a chance.

"Agreed, sir," Tiernan said, the decision made for lack of any better choices. "My navigation officer is uploading the new maneuvering orders to our ships. We'll await your signal to execute."

"Stand by," Lefevre told him as he waited for his own flag tactical officer to do the same. "Now, *amiral*."

Tiernan nodded to his tactical officer, who flashed the instructions to the rest of the fleet over the data-link. As one, the four dozen ships of Tiernan's force and the hundred-odd remaining ships of Lefevre's fleet accelerated and nosed down even further toward Keran.

Satisfied that the maneuver had been executed properly, Tiernan turned to his communications officer. "Get me General Ray immediately," he told him. "There's a lot of bad news headed his way."

* * *

"Sir, let me make sure I understand you properly," Ray said, fighting his disbelief. "They are bringing a force of cruisers and destroyers *into* the atmosphere?"

"That's right, general," Tiernan's image said from the vidcom. "There's no question of it at this point: they have sixty-seven ships inbound, and trajectory projections have a good third of them coming your way."

"Do we have any estimates of how many troops these ships might carry," Ray asked, looking helplessly at his operations and intelligence staff officers, who both had mortified expressions on their faces, "or what weapons they have to hit us with?"

"We don't know anything about troop capacity, general," Tiernan answered, "but the larger ships are roughly the size of the *Ticonderoga* here. If they really crammed warriors in like sardines, they might be able to fit a thousand or so in each ship over and above what we estimate for the crew complement. But that would be a damn tight squeeze. I'm figuring not more than a couple of divisions' worth, and they'll be spread out fairly thin based on the trajectories we're seeing.

"As for the weapons," Tiernan went on grimly, "that we have more information on based on the fighting we've been through up here. At a minimum, expect heavy rapid-fire kinetics in the twenty centimeter range and lasers that can kill destroyers. They have a variety of lighter weapons, but those are the ones to worry about."

Ray sat back at the admiral's understatement. Twenty centimeter shipboard kinetics were equivalent to heavy artillery on the ground, and the naval guns could spit out half a dozen rounds that size in a few seconds. Per tube. And cruisers mounted roughly a dozen such weapons. The lasers were as lethal: any laser that could burn through the hull of a destroyer, even at close range, would be more than a match for his tanks. And he had absolutely nothing that he could fight back with except his tanks in direct fire mode: all of his heavy aerospace defense weapons were intended to hit much smaller targets. He could, and would, fire them against ships in the atmosphere, but they would need incredible luck to get past their point defenses. Even if the weapons hit, they would cause little damage to a destroyer, let alone a cruiser. His real concern was the tanks: if he used them to attack the ships, they would become easy targets themselves. "This will make things a bit more exciting than we had planned, admiral," Ray deadpanned.

Managing a mirthless smile, Tiernan told him, "I know. Listen, Arun, we'll do everything we can to screw up their day as they ingress. But the geometry is against us and a lot of them are going to get through. They're going to have a big advantage in firepower, yes, but hopefully they won't be able to mass enough warriors anywhere to achieve local superiority over your troops."

It was Ray's turn to smile. Like a shark. "Even if they do achieve local superiority somewhere in our sector," he said, "that just gives my tanks more targets to shoot at."

* * *

Tesh-Dar watched as the human ships adjusted their trajectory. "More credit are they due," she murmured approvingly. The human leader was clearly taking a major risk: while she - or would it be a *he*, she wondered? - would temporarily be safe from the rest of Tesh-Dar's fleet, their ungainly ships could easily suffer damage, and possibly destruction, from the upper atmosphere. Their strategy, however, held merit: while they would not be able to force a decisive engagement with Tesh-Dar's ships, they would nonetheless have a single pass where they would be able to bring most, if not all, of their weapons to bear, but Tesh-Dar could not. Her ships would already be committed to reentry and would only be able to employ those weapons mounted on the upper hull.

Her shipmistress *humphed* appreciatively, flexing her fingers, her talons digging grooves into the palms of the armored gauntlets she wore. "Courage, they lack not," Elai-Tura'an, the shipmistress of Tesh-Dar's flagship, said. "It seems we will have to pass through a rain of fire to reach the surface."

"A fitting way to begin the battle on the ground, is it not?" Tesh-Dar said as the ship began to roll and shudder as it kissed the outer fringes of Keran's atmosphere. "Alert the warriors that they may be prepared."

"In Her name," Elai-Tura'an said as she saluted, "it shall be so."

Turning her attention back to the tactical display, Tesh-Dar watched the rapidly approaching human ships, eagerly anticipating the coming clash.

EIGHTEEN

"Shit," Sparks cursed vehemently as he got off the vidcom with General Ray. The Terran ground forces commander had just held a remote conference with his division and brigade commanders. It had been brief and brutally to the point. "We've got incoming heavies, people," he told his staff, nodding toward the tactical display embedded in the forward wall of the command vehicle's tactical center. Traces of the Kreelan ships racing for the surface were being echoed from the *Ticonderoga*, and a good twenty of them were headed toward Foshan where the Terran divisions and some of their Alliance counterparts were deployed. "We need to get our vehicles under cover, pronto, and get the regiment ready for full EMCON on my command."

While the vehicles, particularly the tanks, provided a huge amount of firepower, they had one major tactical drawback: they were so large that they were extremely difficult to conceal. With the sensors carried by warships, the Kreelans would have no difficulty finding armored vehicles out in the open. And if they could find them, they could kill them.

As for going to full EMCON - emission control, or "radio silence" as it was once known - Sparks had argued during the vidcom with General Ray that it would be more advantageous to minimize the electromagnetic signature generated by the various data-link systems that networked the units together. Every single vehicle and soldier was networked to help provide a much greater sense of situational awareness of the battlefield and to coordinate their weapons use. It was a tremendous force multiplier, but it was also a major vulnerability if the enemy could use it to help pinpoint the locations of their units. Worse, many commanders had become so dependent on the rich battlefield detail provided by the networked warfare concept that if the network was lost, they would be, too. That was one of the reasons that Sparks routinely trained his men and women in how to fight under severely degraded network and communications conditions, to the point where his vehicle commanders knew how to use signal flags to communicate basic information and orders to one another. Most of Sparks's contemporaries thought he was insane, but no one could contest his results: his brigade was consistently at the top of the corps' combat readiness ratings.

In the end, General Ray had said, "Sparks, I agree there is a risk. But I feel the advantage we gain from the network outweighs the potential weakness."

And that, as the saying went, was that. Sparks wasn't happy about it, but he was a soldier who knew how to follow orders. But he was going to make sure his troopers were ready to take their data-links off the air if necessary.

"Sir," his operations officer asked, a puzzled expression on his face as he looked at the map display of the regiment's area, "where the devil do we have our people hide? We've got some forest cover to the front, for what little that might be worth. Other than that, the only place to find cover would be to drive into the buildings..." He tapered off, looking at Sparks's expression. "You don't really mean..."

"I do," Sparks said. "Get 'em moving, major. We've got about ten minutes before we're going to have Kreelan ships overhead. And make sure Grishin's gotten the word, too, would you?"

* * *

Staff Sergeant Patty Coyle couldn't keep herself from grinning. Part of her felt bad for what she was about to do, but the tanker in the soul of the petite blonde and blue-eyed woman, the absolute antithesis of what a tank commander might be expected to look like, was having a fucking orgasm. This was one of the things every tank commander dreamed of doing, but so few ever got a chance to do it. And here she was being ordered - *ordered!* - to do it.

Fuckin'-A, she thought as she called to her driver, "Okay, Mannie, back her up, a bit to the left."

Her driver, Corporal Manfred Holman, grunted in reply as he applied more power to the M-87 Wolfhound's tracks, slewing the hundred and twenty-five metric ton vehicle slightly, just as Coyle wanted.

"Perfect," Coyle told him as a crash, deafening even here inside the tank, rang out as the tank backed through the huge front glass window of a bakery. She watched through her cupola's vision displays as the massive hull crushed the displays of neatly arranged cookies, pastries and bread, then proceeded deeper into the shop to pulverize the tables and chairs. Above the din of shattering glass, plastic, and wood, she could hear the hysterical shouts of the shopkeeper and his wife, safe on the street outside.

She couldn't believe it when the operations officer had issued orders for all vehicle commanders to immediately find cover *inside nearby buildings*. The units had to pay for any damage they did to personal property if they deployed outside of their regular training areas. She was sure the Terran Government would pick up the tab for the huge mess the tanks were making, but the promise of a fat paycheck wouldn't have made the locals any happier as they watched the armored monsters drive into their shops and living rooms.

After getting the orders from regiment, Coyle had led her platoon down this street and found a three-story building whose first floor was tall enough to clear the tops of the turrets. Then she and the other tank commanders had gone in and asked - nicely at first, and then not so nicely - the occupants to clear out. Even with the raid sirens still wailing, most of the owners and quite a few patrons were still in the shops, living life as if nothing was different. That changed as soon as Coyle pulled out her sidearm and started shooting into the ceilings of the shops, finally getting her point across. A local cop had come running over to see what the fuss was, brandishing his pistol, but ran away even faster after Coyle's gunner, Sergeant Yuri Kirov, rotated the turret in his direction and pointed the main gun at him.

"Gotta hurry, guys," she said over the platoon push channel. She had a timer running in her cupola vision panel, counting down the minutes left until the enemy ships would be overhead, along with a miniature view of the tactical display showing their inbound tracks. "I'm coming around to check how you look." While her communications procedures reflected a less-than-military bearing in how she led her platoon, it was just one of her quirks. She put on the hard-core military façade when she absolutely had to, but otherwise she tossed it aside: it just got in her way. She'd been upbraided for what she called her own "gurlishness" on more than one occasion, but nobody gave her too much grief: she was the most competent tank commander and platoon leader in the entire regiment. And the reason she was platoon leader right now rather than platoon sergeant was that her company was short a second lieutenant, and the company commander had trusted her to take her platoon and go raise hell. Besides, in a regiment commanded by a man who wore spurs and a cavalry officer's hat, and who used a cavalry saber as a pointer when he gave briefings, her own eccentricities hardly stood out.

Waiting until the sound of tinkling glass abated, she threw open the hatch and carefully crawled out onto the turret roof, crabbing along in the two feet of space between the turret and the building's ceiling, her gloves protecting her hands from the shards of glass and wood covering the top of her tank. Swinging down from the barrel to the steeply sloped front glacis plate of the hull, she dropped to the floor of the shop, debris crunching under her boots. A crowd of civilians started to close in on her, shouting and making gestures that she didn't need translated from Arabic and Chinese. She didn't want to hurt anybody, but she drew her sidearm and held it across her chest where they could all see it: it didn't shut them up, but they backed away quickly.

"Two minutes, sarge," her gunner said tensely.

"Roger," she replied as she ran out into the middle of the street. Turning around, she looked at her tank's position: it was fully concealed from overhead, with two more floors above it that hopefully would mask its heat signature. There wasn't even much debris on the sidewalk in front of the shop: most of it had imploded inward. She ran down the street, ignoring the passenger vehicles that still passed by, honking at her. *Fucking morons,* Coyle thought. *Why aren't they heading to shelter or something?*

She checked the positions for the other three tanks in her platoon, happily noting that they were all fully concealed in the building. The Kreelans wouldn't be able to see them unless they were standing right in front of them. *And if they did that,* she told herself, *my tanks'll blow the living shit out of them.*

"Sixty seconds!"

Coyle sprinted back to her tank, quickly clambering back up to the turret, which had *Chiquita* painted in a flamboyant script in black against the green and brown camouflage paint of the vehicle. Dropping neatly into the cupola, she told her platoon, "Okay, everybody, make sure you're buttoned up in case this building gets knocked down on top of us. The colonel would be really pissed if I lost anybody because they got hit on the head with a brick." She smiled as her quip drew some less-than-respectful responses from her platoon. But they instantly did as she had ordered. They were wired and ready.

Just before she dropped into the turret and closed the hatch, she thought she heard the boom of distant thunder.

* * *

"They are networked," shipmistress Elai-Tura'an informed Tesh-Dar, indicating the display of the land coming up to greet them. It was an unfamiliar term to her people, one that the builders had dug from the Books of Time as they built the ships and weapons to fight the humans. The *Kreela* of this age did not use such rudimentary technology, at least as any human would understand it. Tesh-Dar fully understood the concept, but it was for others to understand the details that made it work. Such technology was built into the ships of this ancient design, but, as with many of the electronic devices the builders had resurrected from those ages long past, the warriors had disdained to use them. Such things were from an age when nation-state warred against nation-state for dominance and resources, before the Unification and the founding of the First Empire. Since then, combat was waged as a means to glorify the Empress: it was a battle of spirit and will as much as force.

Thus had Tesh-Dar come to wage war against the humans face to face wherever possible, not to claw at them through layers of technology. She had allowed the human ships to use their data-links in the first encounter simply to give them an advantage, and because she did not yet have a feel for their skills. Many of their weapons she would allow as a challenge to her warriors, for if a human directed the weapon, it was still the human they fought. But she had no patience to fight the mindless calculations of machines. The humans had proven themselves worthy, and she decided that they did not need such devices in a battle that should be fought mainly with tooth and claw.

"Blind them as we return fire," Tesh-Dar ordered as her ship screamed downward through the atmosphere.

* * *

"Hell," Tiernan cursed as the *Ticonderoga* wallowed in the uppermost reaches of the atmosphere. Even the navigation computers were having a difficult time holding the ship and her sisters steady. His biggest concern now was whether the tactical computers would be able to take the atmospherics into account for the targeting calculations. Something else that they had never been designed to do.

"Thirty seconds!" the fleet tactical officer called out. On the tactical display, the two opposing forces were rushing at one another like out of control freight trains. The Kreelan ships were now thousands of meters below, well within the atmosphere. Some of their ships had broken off to head toward the smaller cities, but most were still arrowing directly for Foshan, head-on to the combined human fleet. "Hard target lock across the board, all weapons synchronized." The data-link systems and tactical computers aboard each ship in the Terran formation had formed a massive distributed processing network that had identified each Kreelan ship and assigned weapons from one or more Terran ships to fire on it. The same was happening in the Alliance fleet that flew to the Terran fleet's starboard side. Since the networks of the two fleets couldn't coordinate their targeting, Tiernan and Lefevre had minimized the potential overlap with a simple expedient: Tiernan took all the targets on their relative left, Lefevre took the ones on the right. The human ships would be shooting right down the Kreelans' throats as they passed below.

"Vampire! Vampire!" the tactical officer suddenly cried out: missiles had been launched from the enemy ships.

Tiernan whipped his head back to the tactical display in time to see a swarm of missiles fly from the Kreelan formation. While the human ships carried some missiles, in the age of laser defenses they were rarely used: their maneuverability and speed had never been able to keep up with laser technology, although missile designers kept trying. The only major exception were the torpedoes carried by the destroyers and some cruisers: they were large weapons that carried their own powerful drives and limited shielding. But a ship of a given tonnage could only carry a few, and even their ability to penetrate point defenses was far from guaranteed.

"Vector?" Tiernan snapped.

"They're all over the place, sir," the tactical officer replied, confused. "Some are heading this way, some to the surface. It looks like-"

His words were interrupted by a series of spectacular detonations that looked like a cascade of exploding balls of lightning that briefly overrode the brightness limits of the main displays on the ship.

"Jesus!" someone gasped.

"Were those nukes?" Tiernan shouted as he closed his eyes and turned his head away from the momentary brilliance of the display. The Terran fleet had no nuclear weapons, at the explicit orders of the president. He had argued mightily to have at least a few to use in space, but the president had been adamant, and so he had none. But that didn't mean the Kreelans couldn't use them.

"Negative, sir," the tactical officer replied, shaken, as the main flag bridge display faded to again show the perilously close surface of Keran. "No indication of ionizing radiation from nuclear weapons. I don't know what those things were."

"I do," Tiernan growled, looking at the tactical display and the handful of icons that remained: just what *Ticonderoga* could see with her own sensors. "They knocked out the damned data-link. Do we still have weapons lock?"

"Only local, sir," the tactical officer reported, quickly coordinating with the tactical officer on the bridge. The *Ticonderoga* still held the targets that had been allocated to her and for which she had her own sensor lock-on. The targets she was to have engaged based on targeting by other ships in the Terran fleet were either gone from the display or were tagged in yellow: the fire control system could see the targets, but didn't have enough weapons available to service them. "The fleet firing solutions just went out the window."

"Do we have communications with the other ships?" Tiernan asked quickly. Only seconds were left before their opportunity would be lost.

"Laser voice and vidcom only, sir," the communications officer reported.

Tiernan held back a vicious curse. "Open a channel, fast," he ordered the fleet communications officer.

"Open sir," the woman replied immediately.

"All ships, this is admiral Tiernan," he said quickly as the countdown on the tactical display spun down to zero and the range rings of *Ticonderoga's* weapons intersected the lead Kreelan ships far below. "Local targeting mode, fire at will!"

He was instantly rewarded with an extended rumble from *Ticonderoga's* heavy weapons turrets on the bottom of the hull. They fired at full rate until they ran out of their basic load, which only took a dozen seconds. As the guns fell silent, the looming horizon of the planet rapidly rotated counterclockwise in the flag bridge display as the ship's captain immediately flipped *Ticonderoga* on her back to unmask the turrets on the top of the hull. As soon as the ship stabilized, those guns belched fire at the rapidly fleeing Kreelan targets. It was an outside chance, at best, that any of those rounds would catch the enemy ships. But in this situation Tiernan was not about to be stingy with his ammunition. *Ticonderoga* had plenty of that. Even now, the gun crews were moving the next loads of shells for their guns from the magazines as the captain brought the ship's bow up toward the reassuring blackness of space, the engines thundering with power to get her clear of the deadly atmosphere.

Tiernan silently watched the tactical display, willing the enemy ships to start falling prey to the human fleet's attack.

"*Inbound kinetics!*" the flag tactical officer suddenly shouted. The collision alarm sounded throughout the ship, and Tiernan and the rest of the crew braced for impact.

* * *

While the fire from the human ships had been far less deadly than it would have been with their data networks intact, more than a few of their rounds had found their mark. Several of them hit Tesh-Dar's ship, causing extensive damage to the engineering sections, and one of them penetrated the hull's armor to explode directly beneath the bridge. The resulting explosion had not been powerful enough to blow completely through the deck plating and vent the bridge to vacuum, but it had buckled the deck with such force that several of the heavy support frames had snapped. Tesh-Dar and several of the bridge crew had been slammed into the bulkheads by the force of the explosion: two of the bridge crew were dead, and three others injured. Tesh-Dar herself had been dazed momentarily.

Elai-Tura'an, the shipmistress, had been pinned to the deck by a thick support beam that weighed as much as ten warriors. Had she not been wearing her armor, she would have been killed instantly. As Tesh-Dar stumbled to her side, still dizzy from the impact and coughing from the dense and acrid smoke that now flooded the bridge, she could see that Elai-Tura'an was bleeding badly inside, with bright arterial blood streaming from her mouth.

Tesh-Dar gripped the lower edge of the beam with her hands, and with a roar of fury lifted it and tossed it aside with a horrendous crash. Kneeling by the woman's side, she placed a hand gently on her shoulder and said, "I will summon a healer."

"No," Elai-Tura'an replied, gripping Tesh-Dar's arm in a fierce grip as she looked into the priestess's eyes. "No...time. Must get me...to the navigation station." She spat out more blood from her pierced lungs, a mixed expression of pain and annoyance on her face. "Then get the warriors...off."

Nodding, Tesh-Dar picked her up and carried her to the navigation station, gently setting her down in what was left of the chair. The warrior who had been serving as navigator was one of those killed by the explosion below, her body and the upper part of the chair having been knocked aside by one of the flying support beams. Kneeling beside her, Tesh-Dar gripped Elai-Tura'an's arms in the way of warriors. "May you find Her light and love for eternity," she whispered.

"And may thy Way be long...and glorious, my priestess," Elai-Tura'an replied, bowing her head. "Now go. I will control the ship from here. Get all the others...away, before we are too low."

Turning her attention to the navigation panel, Elai-Tura'an took direct control of the mortally stricken ship as it continued to plunge toward the surface.

With one last look at her dying shipmistress, Tesh-Dar uttered a silent prayer for her soul to the Empress before she gathered the rest of the bridge crew and made her way quickly to the lower decks where her First had gathered the rest of the warriors. Li'ara-Zhurah awaited her, holding Tesh-Dar's other weapons, which the priestess quickly fastened to her armor. Li'ara-Zhurah offered the priestess a set of the special descent equipment the other warriors now wore, but the great warrior priestess refused: Tesh-Dar had no need of such things.

"As have Her Children for countless ages past," she told the gathered warriors, her voice booming over the howl of the air streaming past the ship's hull, "we go to battle with the enemy, face to face. Fight to honor Her, my children, and seek glory in battle and in death." She paused, looking over the hundreds of faces around her, taking in the Bloodsong that echoed from each of them, pulsing in her own veins. "So has it been-"

"-so shall it forever be," they echoed in a thunderous chorus.

Tesh-Dar nodded to Kamal-Utai, her First, who touched a control on the central console in the large ventral compartment the warriors now occupied. There was a momentary hissing of air as the pressure equalized with the outside atmosphere. Then the side panels of the compartment opened to the air streaming by. Humans would have looked at instruments to tell them the altitude and speed of the ship, to know if it was going too high or low, or too fast. None of the warriors here needed such things: they knew such things by instinct.

"Go now," Tesh-Dar ordered above the shrieking airstream, and instantly the warriors began leaping from the ship, their arms and legs spread wide to control their fall.

Tesh-Dar waited until all but Kamal-Utai and Li'ara-Zhurah had gone, then she ushered them from the doomed ship before it flew too low for their descent equipment to function properly.

Satisfied that they were away safely, Tesh-Dar flexed her hands in anticipation, her great talons drawing blood from her palms. Then she leaped from the ship and was carried away by the roaring winds.

* * *

The grains of sand in the time-glass of shipmistress Elai-Tura'an's life were rapidly running out. With grim determination she kept her ship on course for its glorious ending. Making adjustments to compensate for the failing engines, she guided her last command to its destination.

With a smile on her lips, her heart enraptured by the glory it would bring to the Empress, she slammed her cruiser into the very center of the city of Foshan.

NINETEEN

Of the sixty-seven Kreelan ships that attacked Keran, fourteen suffered serious damage and six were destroyed outright from the humans' daring attack. Seven of those that had sustained damage would have to land, for they were in no shape to climb back into space with the other ships. And, of course, Tesh-Dar's ship had come to its own glorious end as it struck the human city.

The senior surviving shipmistress of the attack wave knew of Tesh-Dar's wishes regarding the humans, and observed over the shoulder of the warrior who served as the equivalent of a human tactical battle officer. While the human data-links had been effectively severed, there were still many human combat units that were broadcasting data, even though their companion units could no longer receive it.

Nodding to herself, the shipmistress designated targets for the tactical officer. "The humans at these locations," she said. "Destroy them."

With a brief flurry of her fingertips over the controls, the guns of the Kreelan ships fired as they flew over the human positions, then began the long climb through the atmosphere to reach open space. While most of their shells and lasers found their targets, the devastation seemed inconsequential after the spectacular detonation of Elai-Tura'an's cruiser.

* * *

One moment, Steph was sitting in the regimental command vehicle as Sparks barked orders to his battalion commanders over the vidcom after the strange Kreelan missiles took down the data-links. The next, she found herself lying on the floor of the vehicle, groggily looking up into Colonel Sparks's concerned and bloodied face. The command compartment was dark except for the red combat lights that shone dimly through swirling dust and acrid smoke. She thought it made Sparks look like Satan.

"Are you hurt, Miss Guillaume?" he said as if from very far away.

Steph's ears were ringing, the sound so loud she could hardly hear a thing. "No," she said, her tongue feeling like it was three sizes too big. She tasted blood. "At least...I don't think so." As she came to, she took stock of her body: aside from some scrapes and bruises, plus a big knot on the back of her head, she couldn't feel anything wrong. "What happened?"

Sparks nodded and helped her to her feet. "The Kreelan ships hit us as they passed over, and one of the bastards crashed right into the middle of the city." He had already been outside and seen the huge mushroom cloud rising from Foshan's center. It hadn't been a nuclear explosion, for there was no trace of ionizing radiation on the command vehicle's sensors, but with a ship that must have massed on the order of a hundred thousand metric tons, with power cores that could propel it through space, it didn't have to be a nuclear weapon. The energy release of something like that hitting the surface, even at a comparatively low velocity, combined with the engine cores breaching would still be measured in hundreds of kilotons of explosive power. "Foshan has pretty much been wiped out," he told her grimly. He felt a terrible rending in his heart at the civilians who must have been killed, the people he and his regiment had been sent to try and save.

But at the same time he was indescribably relieved that his men and women had been deployed on the outskirts of the city. Most of the blast had been absorbed by the buildings between the crash site and here, although the command vehicle had still been tossed around like a toy, and the building they had hidden in had largely collapsed on top of them. Ironically, that had provided some incidental protection from the salvoes the other Kreelan ships had fired at them when they passed overhead. Built on the chassis of the M-87 Wolfhound tank, the command vehicle had been hammered hard, but had managed to protect its occupants from serious harm. "We've also lost contact with everyone, including division and corps, which definitely isn't good news."

"So what do you plan to do?" she asked, taking a drink of water from her canteen.

Sparks looked at her with fire in his eyes, glinting in the red combat lighting. "As soon as I can reestablish contact with at least some of my units and figure out where the hell the enemy is, I plan to attack."

"Sir," the driver called back to him as he struggled out of the cramped forward compartment. "This bitch is history. Oh," he said, embarrassed as he noticed Steph. "Sorry, ma'am," he mumbled.

"I've heard the term before, corporal," she reassured him with a tired smile.

"Uh, yes, ma'am. Anyway, sir," he went on, "the left track is busted and we've got half a dozen faults on the drive panel. Without the guys in the repair track working on this tub for a day, after they haul us out of this rubble, we're stuck. So if we need to go anywhere, we're gonna have to walk."

"Had our horse shot out from under us, have we?" Sparks said, already gathering up his personal combat gear. "Hadley," he called to the vehicle commander, "grab one of the extra rifles and give Miss Guillaume a crash-course in how to use it, then give her a combat harness and ammo. No grenades. You've got five minutes."

"But, colonel," Steph protested, "as a journalist, I can't carry a weapon. I'm legally a noncombatant."

Strapping the belt that held his cavalry saber to his waist, Sparks told her, "Not anymore, Miss Guillaume. Do you think for an instant that the Kreelans are going to give a damn about your legal status? They just nose-dived a starship into the center of the biggest city on the planet. That tells me a lot about their articles of war." He drew the massive pistol from its holster under his left arm and checked that the magazine was full. "I don't expect you to be a trooper, but you need to be able to help defend yourself." Turning to his ops officer, he said, "Do we have contact with *anybody* yet?"

"Yes, sir," the woman told him. "Colonel Grishin just came up on the tac-com." They had just had time to lay a tactical communications line between the 7th Cavalry and *1er REC* command posts before the Kreelans attacked. By a small miracle it hadn't been affected by the weapons the Kreelans had fired or the cruiser's explosion. "He says they have incoming enemy paratroops." She paused, a glint of fear in her eye as she heard a terrified shriek in the background. "They're coming in right on top of his positions."

* * *

The scream had come from one of the crewmen of Grishin's vehicle, who had been bodily wrenched from the rear hatch by what looked like an alien version of what was known as a "cat o' nine tails," a multi-tailed whip. One moment the man was telling Grishin there were alien paratroopers falling on top of them, the next he was gone. Grishin was sure that he had heard the hapless man's skull and legs shatter against the metal hatch coaming, even with the protection of his helmet and leg armor.

Beyond his broken body, which had landed in the dirt a few meters from the vehicle, stood a huge alien warrior that made a mockery out of the verbal descriptions and artist's renderings the Terran military attaché had provided the Alliance. With a snap of her arm the whip's barbed tendrils detached from the dead legionnaire as if they were alive, and her demonic eyes were fixed on him as she bared her ivory fangs and snapped the whip back, preparing for another attack.

"*Go, go, go!*" Grishin shouted through the intercom to his driver, reflexively pushing himself deeper into his seat to get away from the ferocious-looking warrior. The driver didn't need any encouragement: the command vehicle suddenly roared out of the pit the engineers had dug for it, snapping the thin tac-com cable that had connected Grishin with the Terran regimental commander. In any normal battle, being dug-in would have given their vehicle some cover and concealment from an approaching enemy. But when the enemy was literally landing right on top of you, the only thing the pit was good for was a grave.

The command vehicle shared the same wheeled chassis as the light tanks of the *1er REC*'s combat squadrons, but had no turret and no main gun. One of the legionnaires was manning the vehicle's only weapon, the modern-day equivalent of a machine gun on a flexi-mount on the vehicle's roof, and was firing rounds non-stop at the warriors that were now landing all around them.

"Conserve your ammunition, you fool!" the vehicle commander shouted at him. But the legionnaire continued to hold down the trigger. The weapon's barrel was red hot.

Suddenly the firing ceased, and Grishin was relieved that the gunner had come to his senses. If he had kept firing that way, they would be out of ammunition in a matter of a few minutes, if that.

"Putain!" the vehicle commander swore, and Grishin looked up to see the legionnaire gunner slide back into the vehicle. Headless.

Focus, Grishin told himself as he fought back a wave of nausea. It wasn't the headless legionnaire that bothered him, for he had seen that and much worse in his career in the *Légion*. It had been the enormous enemy warrior about to snare him with that hellish whip. *Let the crew fight the immediate battle. You've got a regiment to worry about. You're their leader: so lead!*

That thought brought him back to his senses. Unfortunately, he had no communications right now with anyone: all types of radio communications were out, and the *Légion* did not have the funding for the latest vehicle-to-vehicle laser communications.

That left the old fashioned method. "Turn around," he ordered the driver. To this point, they had been barreling down the road that led toward the rear of the regiment's deployment area, and then to the Terran regiment, if any of them had survived the crazy cavalryman's idea of stuffing their huge tanks into buildings. He could see the mushroom cloud over Foshan through one of the vehicle's armored viewports, the orange and black writhing as if it were a living thing. All around it, the city was burning fiercely, and it was difficult for him to imagine the devastation. He wished Sparks and his troops good luck. But now he had to make some luck of his own. He needed to get back to his regiment.

"Sir?" the driver asked, his voice shaking. While they had all been told that aliens might come, none of them had really believed it. And none of them had been truly prepared for the sight of thousands of alien warriors dropping from the sky.

"Turn us around, *soldat*," Grishin ordered. "Without radio, I must make direct contact with our units. I've got to at least get to the squadron commanders."

The driver made no move to respond to Grishin's order.

"Tomaszewski," the vehicle commander said in a low voice over the intercom, "turn us around or I'll blow your fucking head off."

"*Oui, sergent*," the driver replied shakily, slowing the six-wheeled vehicle around enough to turn it without tipping them over.

Pulling the gunner's headless body out of the way, the vehicle commander took his place at the gun on the roof, hiking up his chest armor to try and protect his neck as they headed back toward the rest of their besieged regiment.

* * *

Tesh-Dar and the other warriors had been badly buffeted by the explosion as the cruiser hit the human city. But like many of the human warriors, they had received some protection as the buildings around the city absorbed much of the blast wave. A number of the warriors had lost control and crashed, with some of them no doubt killed. But the majority from her ship, nearly eight hundred, had survived. Around them, thousands of other warriors dropped by the other ships plummeted toward the human city and its defenders.

As they fell rapidly toward the ground, Tesh-Dar saw that they were almost perfectly positioned against one of the groups of human warriors. Almost all of this group were in large, boxy vehicles that were clearly heavily armed. Her blood thrilled with the challenge, for it would be difficult to kill the humans in vehicles such as these. She did not need to look around her to know that her warriors felt the same way, for their emotions sang from their very blood. But she looked anyway, turning to see Li'ara-Zhurah and Kamal-Utai flying beside her, their fangs bared in excitement.

Then it was time for the warriors to deploy their wings. Similar to a human-designed parafoil, they were actually much more akin to a natural wing: mounted to the warrior's back, with the wing supported by a thin but strong framework much like the bones of a bat's wing, it provided exceptional maneuverability.

While expressions of amazement and disbelief at Tesh-Dar's abilities were nothing new to her since she had become high priestess of the Desh-Ka order, she took some bemused enjoyment from the astonished looks on the faces of her warriors as they deployed their wings and she did not. Yet she continued to fly alongside them as if she did. The powers that she had inherited as part of the acceptance of the ways of the Desh-Ka were not infinite, and were nothing compared to the power of the Empress. But controlling her body above the earth was one of the gifts she had received, as was walking through solid objects. She herself did not understand how such things were possible, only that they were.

By now the humans had seen them swooping down upon their positions and began to fire projectile weapons. A number of warriors fell, stricken, while others fired back with weapons akin to those the humans were using. Tesh-Dar preferred close combat, but in this type of attack she would not have let her warriors be exposed at extended ranges to human weapons without being able to fight back. Challenge, she sought; wanton slaughter of her warriors, she did not.

Easing ahead of the other warriors, she arrowed toward a group of vehicles near the center of the area occupied by larger groups of spread-out vehicles. Touching down lightly near one of the vehicles, her sandals leaving no mark upon the dusty ground, she uncoiled her *grakh'ta*, the seven-barbed whip, from her belt.

A human momentarily stared at her open-mouthed from a hatch in the rear of the vehicle, then he turned away to say something in what was, to Tesh-Dar, one of their incomprehensible languages to someone inside. Baring her fangs, she snapped the *grakh'ta* behind her, then whipped it forward. It was a terribly difficult weapon to handle with precision, but Tesh-Dar had many, many cycles of practice and was expert in its use. The whip cracked as the seven barbed tips reached into the vehicle, wrapping themselves around the hapless human. With a titanic heave, she yanked the alien's body from the vehicle with such force that it smashed its head and legs to splinters against the armored interior.

As she snapped the whip again to clear the barbs from the human's flesh, her heightened senses warned her that danger was near. With a leap to one side that no human who witnessed it would have ever believed, she easily dodged the projectiles fired by the primitive weapon mounted on the vehicle. She watched as the vehicle suddenly burst from the hole the humans had dug for it to head quickly down the road, the human on top still firing madly at her warriors, and missing most of them. One of the warriors finally tired of him and took his head with a *shrekka*.

With her blood roaring a symphony in her spiritual ears, Tesh-Dar coiled her *grakh'ta* and set off toward one of the other vehicles, seeking new prey.

* * *

Grishin stood in one of the hatches, accepting the risk to his neck in exchange for the ability to see more clearly as the command vehicle swept around a bend in the road that passed by the positions of the *1er Escadron de combat*, the regiment's first tank squadron.

"*Merde...*" the vehicle commander cursed just before he started firing the top-mounted gun. There was certainly no shortage of targets.

Grishin looked on in horror as Kreelan warriors clad in black armor swarmed over the wheeled tanks of the *1er Escadron* like black ants. A few of the vehicles had made it out of their firing pits and were trying to keep the warriors at a distance while blasting away at them. Some vehicles had not, and Grishin saw a warrior atop a buttoned up tank stab her sword right through the armored commander's hatch. As she pulled the blade out of the metal, he saw that it was slick with blood.

Impossible, he thought. *No metal blade could cut through steel alloy armor like that!* Granted, it was not nearly so thick as the armor that protected the heavy Terran tanks, but it was simply not possible.

But it was. Other warriors did the same thing, stabbing their weapons through the armor of the driver's and gunner's hatches. Then one of them affixed some sort of bomb to the rear of the vehicle, and the warriors leaped clear as the light tank was consumed by what looked like a massive electrical discharge that left behind a smoldering, charred wreck.

"*Putain!*" the vehicle commander hissed, using one of his favorite curses. He dropped into the vehicle, his right arm hanging by a thread of flesh: most of the muscle and the bone had been cut through halfway above the elbow. "One of those bitches hit me with one of those flying things," he gasped, his face already turning pale from shock.

"Help me," Grishin ordered the last legionnaire left in the rear compartment, who had been firing his rifle at the enemy through one of the vehicle's gun ports. Unlike his Terran counterpart, Sparks, Grishin had his main staff officers in different vehicles, which was both a blessing and a curse. A blessing because if one of them was hit, the entire command staff would not be wiped out, and the most senior surviving officer could take over. A curse because without communications, he had no idea if any of them were even still alive to help get the regiment out of this disaster.

Grishin grabbed the sergeant around his chest, ignoring the blood cascading over his arms as he did so. The other legionnaire grabbed his legs, and together they moved him onto one of the combat seats along the side of the compartment.

"Do what you can for him," Grishin ordered before standing up through the roof hatch and manning the machine gun. He managed to clear some of the warriors off of the top of one of the tanks as it backed out of its firing pit, and he signaled for the commander to join on him. Two other tanks also joined up, and they quickly formed an echelon left, with the three tanks in a staggered line that gave all of them clear fields of fire into the bulk of the rampaging aliens, with Grishin's vehicle following close behind them.

Past their shock now, the legionnaires manning the three tanks began to give a good accounting of themselves as they poured machinegun fire into the groups of warriors attacking other tanks that hadn't had a chance to get out of their firing pits. The tank crews fired antipersonnel rounds, carrying thousands of needle-like flechettes, from their main guns, literally blasting the Kreelans from the backs of some of the tanks in clouds of bloody flesh and shrapnel.

Surely the enemy must be about to break, Grishin told himself as they killed Kreelans by the dozens, even as the warriors charged the tanks with swords raised high and war cries on their lips.

But they didn't break: the alien warriors kept on coming.

While the Kreelans had held the upper hand in the beginning, Grishin's legionnaires were now giving as good as they had gotten. But the enemy did not die easily, nor were they slaughtered without cost. As his formation swept along the rear of each of his companies, rallying the survivors, the enemy warriors fought even harder. They hurled themselves at his tanks, sometimes singly, sometimes in groups, but all as suicidal maniacs, and he could hear their fierce war cries through the chattering of the machine guns and the booming of the tanks' main guns.

When they made it to the rear of the last company, the *5ème Escadron*, and rallied what was left of it, Grishin was momentarily struck by despair. Of the roughly forty-eight tanks of the four tank squadrons, plus the various other vehicles that made up the regiment, he now only had half a dozen tanks and a handful of the other vehicles, most of which were lightly armed as his command vehicle. Suicidal maniacs the Kreelans may have been, but they had effectively gutted his unit. And there were still hundreds left alive behind him.

From here, on the far right edge of his regiment's assigned area of responsibility, he should have been able to see the positions of the *2ème Régiment étranger de parachutistes*, the famous *2ème REP*, next to them. He had heard that the paratroops' commander had been livid at having to deploy his unit as regular infantry in prepared trenches, but those were his orders and he had carried them out. Now Grishin could see nothing of the famous elite unit, only a massive swarm of alien warriors. Looking through his field scope at the ferocious close combat there, he could think of no way to help them: the legionnaires were locked in bitter hand to hand fighting, and he could not use his tanks to good effect without killing his fellow legionnaires.

After a moment he realized that the point was moot: the paratroopers, while clearly fighting valiantly, were also being completely overwhelmed. Their part of the battle was already over.

"*Mon colonel*," the vehicle commander said thickly through the painkillers that the attending legionnaire had pumped into his system after applying a tourniquet and self-sealing bandages. "Behind us."

Grishin turned to look behind them, and was shocked to see a line of Kreelan warriors standing there, clearly waiting for him and his men. There really was nowhere for him to run, not that he was inclined to. The road that had been the baseline for the regiment's deployment had relatively open ground to the front for a few hundred meters, but then swiftly turned into dense woods that would be difficult, if not impossible, for his tanks to traverse. To the rear was another hundred or so meters edged by a steep drainage culvert. He would have liked to deploy his regiment on the other side of that defensive feature, on the "inside" toward Foshan, rather than on the "outside" where he was now, but that had been forbidden by the Keran government because of the high-value property in this area. Grishin suddenly wished he had done what Sparks had, and driven his tanks right into the houses and business buildings there, the local government be damned. But it was too late for that.

Besides, while his motivations were different, he was no less a warrior than the alien creatures he now confronted. And while his personal courage had wavered for a moment after they had appeared, he was no longer afraid.

He knew that there was only one option left: to try and break through to link up with the Terran tank regiment, if it still survived. Against so many warriors, the legionnaires stood little chance of survival. Grishin smiled to himself. He had always wished that he could die in a modern-day Battle of Camarón, where centuries before a small band of legionnaires had held off an army of nearly two thousand men in a battle that had become legend. He had never thought this wish would come true. So few ever had.

Signaling his tank commanders to wheel right and come line-abreast facing the Kreelan warriors who stood patiently waiting for them, Grishin rendered his men a sharp salute, which they returned. Legionnaires, to the last.

"*Camarón!*" Grishin bellowed as the survivors of the *1er REC* charged the enemy line, guns thundering.

* * *

Tesh-Dar had quickly become bored with digging the humans out of their strange vehicles. Leaving Kamal-Utai and Li'ara-Zhurah to lead the warriors who had jumped from their doomed ship, for they could not keep up with her, Tesh-Dar raced along the human lines at an inhuman speed, far faster than any human being had ever run. She had seen in her mind's eye a nearby group of human warriors that had no vehicles, and went to meet them.

As she did, a group of warriors from one of the other ships was dropping onto that part of the human line, and the humans fired their projectile weapons at them. While the warriors preferred their swords and claws, they had no hesitation in unslinging their own projectile weapons and firing back. Tesh-Dar was proud to see that they were far more accurate than the humans, with nearly every round finding its target.

With a final great leap, her heart pounding with anticipation, she landed next to the strange trench they had dug for themselves and unleashed her *grakh'ta* whip.

* * *

Soldat 1e Classe Roland Mills had joined the *Légion étrangère* for the same reason countless others had over the centuries: he was an adventurer and soldier of fortune. Aside from his rugged good looks and muscular build, he was unlike the romantic stereotype of the legionnaire: he wasn't trying to escape his past or avoid pursuit by any authorities. In fact, he came from a very respectable English family back on Earth, and had never committed a crime. While he would have lightly scoffed at anyone who thought him a scholar, he was nonetheless quite well-educated. By all accounts, he would have made an excellent barrister and family man, except for one tiny quirk: he was a hopeless adrenaline junky. He had immersed himself in virtually every extreme and nearly-suicidal endeavor he could find, but eventually they came to bore him.

Then one day, he happened to see a news broadcast that played a bit about the Alliance *Légion étrangère*, and came to see it as a nearly non-stop thrill-ride. Over his family's vehement protestations, he signed up two days later at the recruiting center in Paris.

Nearly eighteen months later, despite having had to adjust his perception of reality of what the Legion really was, he had come to really enjoy it. Learning French had been a snap for him, as had the other basic skills he had been taught.

In the end, he had gotten what he had hoped for: he was selected for the elite *2ème REP* and was given jump training (although he already knew how to jump and paraglide). He had loved every minute of it.

When he found the Alliance was deploying every one of the Legion's combat regiments to Keran to protect it against a possible (if far-fetched) alien threat, he had been elated. He had never seen combat, and was hoping that this would be his chance.

Now, however, elation wasn't the emotion he felt. It was gut-wrenching fear melded with the determination to survive as alien starships thundered overhead, dropping thousands of alien paratroops right on top of the regiment's lines. He had been looking for the ultimate thrill, and he was afraid that he might have found it.

"Fire!" his squad leader shouted, echoing the orders passed along the line of the entire regiment as the aliens flew down on their version of paragliders. Over a thousand legionnaires fired their rifles and automatic weapons nearly straight up at their swarming attackers. A handful of aliens, then dozens, began to fall from the sky, dead and wounded.

But the enemy proved to be far from helpless, even as they glided toward the ground. They had their own rifles, and with inhuman accuracy began to kill legionnaires. Some also dropped what looked like hand grenades where legionnaires had bunched together. But when they detonated they released an enormous electrical flux like lightning, turning everything in a radius of four meters into smoldering carbon.

Easily outnumbered two to one, the legionnaires did what they had done since Camarón: they stood their ground, fought, and died.

Roland Mills, however, wasn't ready to die yet. He was terrified, but this was what he had joined the Legion for, after all: the opportunity to participate in unrestricted mayhem. Combat was the ultimate adrenaline rush.

Taking aim at the nearest cloud of warriors bearing down on their lines, he opened fire, emptying an entire magazine into their formation and taking grim satisfaction at seeing six of them plummet to the ground, out of control.

"Mills, *down!*" one of the other legionnaires in his squad shouted. Mills dropped to the bottom of the trench as a warrior swept down behind him. Three of his squad mates blasted the thing to bits with their rifles, spattering Mills with bloody gore.

Suddenly, over the unbelievable din of men and aliens shouting and screaming and the non-stop firing of rifles by both sides, he distinctly heard a strange *whip-crack!* from just beyond the parapet around the trench. Mills looked up just in time to see what looked like a set of thin, barbed tentacles snap over the top of the parapet to wrap themselves around one of his fellow legionnaires. The man screamed in fear and agony as the metal barbs pierced his flesh and the whip-like tails of whatever the thing was encircled his limbs and torso.

Ignoring the chaos around him, Mills leaped to his feet, drawing his combat knife in the same motion, intending to cut the man free of this thing that attacked him.

But in the blink of an eye and with a howl of terror the legionnaire was bodily snapped over the top of the parapet, as if he were a small fish that a fisherman had snatched from the water.

Trying to erase the image of the man's terrified expression from his mind, Mills ducked in time to avoid having his head taken off by a Kreelan warrior's sword. Marveling for just an instant the he was facing an alien, he lunged forward, blocking her sword arm with his left fist as he drove his knife into her gut below her armored breast plate.

The warrior screamed in pain, but was far from mortally stricken. She slashed at him with the claws of her free hand, tearing the cloth camouflage cover from his back armor. Kneeing her in the groin to throw her off-balance, he pulled his knife from her belly and rammed it up under her throat, the knife's tip burying itself in her brain.

Whip-crack!

Another legionnaire shrieked as he was seized by the devilish weapon and heaved by some unseen force from the trench.

But this time Mills had seen something he had not the first time: he saw where the tendrils had come from over the parapet. Pausing only for a moment to pick up a rifle and shoot a warrior in the back of the head, he threw a hand grenade over the parapet in the direction the legionnaire had disappeared.

* * *

Tesh-Dar bared her fangs in a sort of primal ecstasy that she had not felt since the Change, since the day she was accepted as a priestess into the order of the Desh-Ka. Having trained for combat since birth, she was finally experiencing war in its true form, without any of the rules that governed the challenges in the arena. Great would be the glory she brought to the Empress.

While her warriors occupied the humans in the trench, she allowed herself a minor indulgence. She knew that she should not be standing in the open as she was, focused on her prey. But it was an entertainment that she would allow herself. For now. With the whips wrapped around her next victim, she gripped the *grakh'ta* with both mighty hands and threw her entire body into the motion of snapping the whip back, reeling in the hapless human warrior. The human came flying out of the trench, arcing through the air toward her. As the creature drew to arm's length, her left hand snapped to her short sword in a move no human being could match. Twirling aside as her victim flew by, the sword sang from the sheath at her waist and neatly decapitated the human without the blade touching the tendril of the *grakh'ta* that was wrapped about its neck. She flicked the blade with her wrist, ridding it of most of the human's blood before she replaced the sword in its sheath.

She was just snapping her weapon free of the body when she sensed the small object sailing toward her. Abandoning the *grakh'ta*, she leaped clear as the grenade went off, shredding both the whip and the legionnaire's body. Had she not been a warrior priestess with her heightened senses, she would have been killed.

With her blood singing glory to her Empress, Tesh-Dar leaped into the trench to find the one who had come close to killing her, to honor him with death.

* * *

Mills's world had become a snarling orgy of stabbing, hacking, kicking, and grappling with the alien warriors. Few rifle shots rang out now, as the enemy was in so tightly among the legionnaires that a bullet was as likely to kill a friend as a foe. Besides, the enemy was simply too close: at one point, while Mills was fighting one alien, he suddenly realized that he had his back pressed up against another alien who was doing her best to strangle a legionnaire. Suddenly, all four of them were blown into a struggling heap as a grenade went off nearby. Mills was the only one to get to his feet alive.

In addition to his knife, which was by now soaked with blood and had a blade that was nicked in a dozen places, he held a Kreelan sword. He had never received training in how to use any edged weapons but his knife and bayonet, but he had nonetheless put it to good use. About as long as his arm and slightly curved, the sword had proved to be an excellent weapon in trench fighting.

A Kreelan warrior suddenly came staggering backward toward him, two legionnaires clutching at her arms, and he stabbed the alien in the back of the neck with the sword.

"*Down!*" he yelled at his two newfound companions as he saw another legionnaire, badly wounded, hurl himself into the midst of at least half a dozen warriors who had cornered two more legionnaires and were hacking them to death. Mills had seen that the man clutched a grenade in each hand, and the resulting explosions sent bits of bodies, shredded clothing, and twisted body armor for fifteen meters in every direction.

As he got back to his feet, helping up his compatriots, he saw something that made his skin crawl. Looking down the trench toward the end of the regiment's line, perhaps twenty meters away, was what looked like nothing so much as a living threshing machine. But it wasn't a machine. It was an alien warrior. She was huge compared to the others, and bigger than Mills, who stood a full two meters tall and weighed in at one hundred kilos of solid muscle. In one hand she had a short sword, and both it and the claws of her other hand were soaked with blood.

Eyes wide with disbelief, he watched as a legionnaire emptied an entire magazine from his rifle into her chest. But it was as if the bullets simply passed through her; he could even see the spray of dirt they kicked up from the trench wall behind her.

The warrior strode right up to the legionnaire and with what Mills thought must be a look of contempt stabbed her claws into his chest, right through his torso armor. Screaming in agony, blood spraying from his lips, she lifted him from his feet and tossed him from the trench as if he weighed no more than a piece of paper.

Suddenly, he realized what had been behind the whip-like weapon that had snatched some of the legionnaires from the trench earlier. It had been her.

The other Kreelan warriors moved aside as she passed, rendering what appeared to be some sort of salute. Killing every single legionnaire who stood before her with flashing steel or outstretched claws, she finally came to a stop directly in front of him, her strange cat's-eyes blazing, her entire body spattered with human blood.

As if it were some sort of signal, the rest of the Kreelan warriors in the trench eased away from their human opponents. The exhausted legionnaires used the unexpected respite to catch their breath, wondering just what was happening.

"What does she want, Mills?" one of the legionnaires next to him whispered, afraid to break the spell that had suddenly fallen over them all.

The warrior herself answered, but not with words. Raising her right arm, she pointed at Mills. Then she handed her weapons to one of the other warriors, who took them for safekeeping.

"I think," Mills said slowly, "she wants a bloody duel. But why me?" He wasn't the biggest or toughest man in the regiment, or the best close-in fighter. On the other hand, he was probably the biggest and toughest who was still standing. Of the regiment's roughly thirteen hundred men, he guessed that maybe a hundred, if that, were still alive.

"We'll fight with you," the legionnaire said. Mills didn't remember his name, as he was from one of the other companies.

"No," Mills told him, dropping his own weapons. "Let's see where this leads."

"But-"

"Quiet," one of the others, a *sergeant*, ordered. "Mills, do what you need to do."

You always wanted the ultimate thrill, Mills chided himself. Well, it looks like you finally found it.

* * *

Tesh-Dar knew the one before her had thrown the grenade that had come close to killing her earlier. She had never seen him, did not recognize him by scent, and had not seen him with her second sight. But among the gifts she had was the ability to sense some of the threads of time and action, cause and effect, that were woven together into the river of destiny. She could not read the future and predict where that river might lead. However, she could sometimes see a murky vision of the past that she had not witnessed through her other senses, a place where the river had once flowed. She could not see the river's trace for others, only for those events directly tied to herself.

And so it was that she now stood before this human. She had not had any idea what he would look like, or how fiercely he would fight. She only knew that he was the one she sought.

Around her, the other warriors gave the surviving humans some respite. Few were left now, but they had fought well and with great honor. Many of Her Children had died at their hands, and Tesh-Dar mourned their deaths deeply; not that they had died and were no longer with her, but that they could never again glorify the Empress in battle. For Tesh-Dar's people, death, honorably won, was the completion, the fulfillment, of life in Her eyes, and meant an eternal place in the afterlife among the Ancient Ones.

She pointed to the crude steps leading from the trench to flat ground above and led the human there. What motivated these creatures to burrow like sand-worms she did not know or care to understand. All she knew was that it would hardly serve as an impromptu arena.

* * *

Mills followed the huge warrior out of the trench and onto the ground behind it, his feet leaving small clouds of dust as he walked. He happened to see the alien's feet, shod in sandals, and noticed that she left no tracks at all. Nothing. A chill ran down his spine, wondering if she was some sort of supernatural creature. Perversely, that thought gave him even more of a high. He wasn't afraid, he was completely "juiced" as some of his friends might have said.

Behind him, a silent and altogether unnatural procession followed: the hundreds of Kreelan warriors and the comparative handful of surviving legionnaires, mixed together. The latter did not exactly seem to be prisoners, for the Kreelans did not seem to care if they came along or not, or if they kept their weapons, as long as they did not use them (the few who had were quickly butchered). But the legionnaires went anyway, for they had no idea what else to do, and few wanted to risk trying to take their leave of the Kreelans. As word spread that Mills would be facing off against the big warrior, all of them wanted to see the spectacle as much as the Kreelans apparently did.

The warriors formed a large circle around Mills and his opponent. The legionnaires, somewhat emboldened now by the mere fact of their continued survival, pressed up close behind the warriors who formed the inner edge of the circle so they could see.

Mills stood about two paces from the warrior, who kept her eyes locked on his. He had no idea what to do to get this particular ball rolling, so he simply waited for her to make the first move.

* * *

It was time. The human clearly had no idea what to expect or what to do, which was understandable, as he was not of the Way. He had no way of knowing that this challenge, defined by what may have been nothing more than a lucky throw of a grenade, would determine not only his fate, but that of his fellow animals, as well. She would not show him leniency, but she would show him fairness. She would use none of her special powers, for that would be no challenge in such a match, and would bring the Empress no glory. Even her claws, she would not use, for the human had none. She would not give the match away, for she knew that she could hardly lose, but she would measure him by his determination and will to survive.

Assuming one of many choices of combat stances, she opened the challenge with a restrained open-handed strike against the human animal.

* * *

Mills shook his head to clear his brain as he got to his feet, his ears ringing from the blow the alien had just landed on him. He knew intellectually that it had been little more than an open-handed slap, but it came at him like lightning and felt like a freight train had slammed into the side of his head.

"Get the *salope*, Mills!" one of the legionnaires suddenly yelled, tossing any remaining caution about the warriors surrounding them to the wind. His shout of encouragement led to a groundswell of others, and in but a moment every single legionnaire was shouting for him.

It was what he needed. He didn't expect to win against this alien killing machine, but he would do his best to make her remember the men of the *2ème REP.*

He raised his hands to protect his face, elbows held in tight to his sides, and moved closer to her. One of her arms shot out, but he was ready this time. He managed to grab hold of her arm and pull her slightly off-balance. As she grabbed for him with her other hand - *Damn those claws!* He cursed to himself - he pulled her in even closer and suddenly slammed his forehead into her chin.

With a surprised grunt she roughly shoved him away, and he couldn't escape the feeling that she had simply allowed him to get away with it. He had seen some of the things she could do, and he could hardly accept that his skills were a match for hers. But he didn't care. He moved in again quickly, leaving himself largely open to attack as he concentrated on his own offense.

* * *

While the human was no match for her skills, he was clearly determined, and continued to come after her no matter how many times she batted him away or threw him to the ground. His face was bruised and bleeding now, and he wheezed when he breathed. The knuckles of his hands were bloodied, with both her blood and his own, and no doubt some of his bones were broken.

But the human doggedly continued to attack her, even as he approached complete exhaustion. At one point they were locked in an embrace after he had moved in close to her, sustaining a rain of blows to get close enough to try and throw her to the ground. She had actually found herself holding him up for a moment as he clung to her, panting for breath. Sensing he had regained enough energy to at least stay on his feet, she released him, sending him back with another set of blows to the head that again knocked him to the ground.

The humans intermingled with her warriors, a strange phenomenon that she would never have expected, shouted their encouragement in gibberish, and she had to credit them with spirited support. Soulless creatures they might be, beyond Her love and light, but she could not fault their warrior spirit. Truly, she thought, the Empire had found a worthy race to bring honor to the Empress in battle.

She let the human continue to batter himself senseless against her, until at last, finally, he simply had not the strength to rise again. But even then, exhausted and beaten, he still struggled to rise, to fight.

"Enough," she murmured to herself, bringing the ritual challenge to an end.

* * *

"*Kazh*," the big warrior said softly.

At least that's what Mills thought she might have said, whatever it meant, over the ringing in his head and the sound of his own gasping for air. The legionnaires continued to shout their encouragement, their voices hoarse and frayed from yelling so long. Lying face down in the dirt, his body was totally, utterly exhausted. Every muscle quivered, and he could hardly move at all. He was bruised everywhere, and he knew that at least a few bones must be broken, mostly in his hands where they had hit the Kreelan's jaw, which was as hard as steel plate. Blood was running into both his eyes from cuts on his forehead from where she had hit him or her claws had lightly cut him, and he had dozens of other cuts everywhere that wasn't covered by his body armor. But he knew those cuts were merely incidental: she had clearly not used her claws as weapons, or he would have been dead in the first few seconds of the fight.

"Fuck," he gasped through lips that looked like crushed tomatoes, streaming blood down his chin. He didn't have to poke his tongue along his gums to know that he'd lost a few teeth: one he'd accidentally swallowed right after the Kreelan's fist had knocked it loose; the rest he'd managed to spit out.

He tried to get up, but simply couldn't. Finally, he gave up and simply lay there. There was nothing more he could do.

Suddenly, he felt a hand grip his arm and turn him over. It was the warrior. He offered up a bloody smile, knowing that she, too, had her own set of cuts and bruises, and he was the proud culprit. At this point he didn't care if she had gone easy and let him have some mercy hits against her. He'd managed to bloody her up a bit, and that was all that mattered.

The legionnaires fell silent as they waited for the axe, literally, to fall on Mills.

Much to their surprise it didn't. The big Kreelan merely nodded her head, then reached out with her hands to snip off a bit of his hair, which was no mean feat, considering that it was barely a finger's breadth in length. This she tucked into a small black leather pouch on her belt.

Then, standing up, she said something in her language loud enough for all the gathered warriors to hear. They all said something back in unison, and hammered their left fists against their right breasts.

With that, the huge warrior turned and walked away. The other warriors quietly followed after her, leaving eighty-seven very confused but infinitely relieved Legion paratroopers behind.

TWENTY

After the connection to Grishin had broken, Steph followed Sparks as he led the staff and crew of his command vehicle through the rubble of the building and out into the street. While many of the buildings looked fairly intact, most of them had suffered at least superficial damage from the blast when the cruiser had crashed, and there wasn't a single unbroken pane of glass in sight. The air was still heavy with smoke and dust from the shells the Kreelan ships had fired at his command vehicle and the other vehicles that made up the regiment's field headquarters. But the other vehicles had not been quite so lucky as his: the other three command vehicles of the headquarters company were smoldering wrecks. She looked up as what looked like snow started falling around them, carried by the artificial wind generated by the firestorm that was consuming the inner part of the city.

"Ash," Sparks said in a low voice, answering her unasked question as his eyes warily scanned the street. There had still been a lot of civilians out in the open when the Kreelans struck, despite the best efforts of Sparks and the other members of the company to convince the locals to find some sort of shelter. Sparks himself had been the last one under cover, staying until the very last second in the street to try and convince even a single civilian to get to safety. But all they were concerned about was the damage his vehicles were causing.

The air was filled with the cries and wails of the injured and the bereaved. Bodies were strewn haphazardly along the sidewalks, mostly victims of the Kreelan guns that had targeted the command vehicles. Others were victims of the titanic blast that had torn out the heart of the city, but they were far enough away here that most of those casualties were from flying debris. Still others were curled on the street or wandering, helpless, their hands covering their eyes from the pain of being flash-blinded.

Steph captured it all on video, as always making voice notes. But she noticed that her voice held an uncharacteristic flutter: she had never seen devastation on this scale, and the shock of it had deeply unsettled her. She momentarily focused the view on an Arab-descended woman near the center of the street, next to a car that she must have been in before the attack. She was sitting on the rough cobblestones, cradling a young girl, perhaps four years old, in her lap. Steph didn't know Arabic, but she didn't need to: the woman was shrieking with the anguish only a mother can truly know. From the amount of blood on the child's body, it was clear to Steph that the young girl was dead.

Steph had seen anguish and horror before, but never quite like this. Suddenly, it was too much. Dropping the rifle she now carried, she fell to her knees and vomited.

"Come on, miss," Sergeant Hadley, now her personal bodyguard, told her as he gently took hold of her arm to help her up. "We've got to keep moving."

Nodding, wiping the foulness from her mouth with one hand as she picked up the rifle with the other, Steph got to her feet. On unsteady legs, she let Hadley help her along to keep up with the colonel's pace.

"First Battalion shouldn't be more than half a block from here," the operations officer was saying. "We ought to be seeing tanks popping out of buildings all over the place."

"I'm not so sure, major," Sparks said as he checked the corner of a cross street, peering around the corner to make sure there weren't any enemy waiting for them. "I think the damn Kreelans pounded everything that was-"

"You!"

All of them turned at the sound of the voice. A middle-aged man, bloodied and dressed only in torn rags that once must have been nice clothes of the style the Chinese wore here, stood in the street holding a young man, what was left of him, in his arms.

"It was *you!*" the man cried. "This is your doing!" Then he yelled at them in Chinese, then in Arabic. Other survivors, up and down the street, took notice of the commotion. "*They* came because of *you*," the man went on, moving slowly toward them with his grisly burden. "My son died because of *you!*"

More people were gathering now, their faces ugly as they muttered in a mixture of Arabic and Chinese.

"Shit," Steph heard Hadley whisper. "Get behind me." Without asking questions, she slid behind him, noticing that while he wasn't pointing his rifle at anyone, he wasn't exactly pointing it away, either.

"The aliens were coming anyway," Sparks told the man calmly. Raising his voice so the crowd could hear him, he said, "The aliens have been planning this attack for over a year. We came to help protect you. We-"

"*No!*" The man screamed as he staggered closer with his son's limp form. "Your ship found them and led them to us," he cried. "A *Terran* ship gave away our world to them. You played us for pawns as your kind always has. Then you came with your weapons of war to fight them on our world. *Our world!*"

By now, the crowd had grown to well over a hundred people, with more coming to see what was going on.

"Listen, mister," Sparks tried one last time, frustration clearly evident in his voice. "We've got to reach my tanks before the enemy gets here-"

"*You* are the enemy!" the man cried, and the crowd's murmuring grew to an angry growl.

Steph noticed through her video pickup that people were picking up bricks, broken cobblestones, even big shards of glass. She was holding her rifle with a white-knuckled grip. She had fired a weapon before, but had never actually shot at anyone. And she sure as hell didn't want to shoot any of these poor people.

As the crowd began to close in, a new noise rose above their jeering: screaming. It wasn't the wailing of those who had lost their loved ones, or those who were in agony: it was a scream of fear, echoing from a multitude of voices.

Suddenly a handful of people rounded a corner about a hundred meters down the street in the direction of the city's burning center. All young men, they were running flat out toward where the crowd now surrounded Sparks and his troops. Then a torrent of people, not able to run quite as fast, surged around the corner, all of them screaming in terror. There were hundreds of them, then thousands, a river of terrified people that quickly filled the street.

Sparks knew what was coming. Walking up to the man who led the crowd surrounding them, he grabbed him by the arms and leaned over the man's dead son until their noses nearly touched. "The aliens are coming. Now. Let us go so we can fight them or you're going to all die right here."

The man didn't move, but simply stared at Sparks with accusatory eyes.

But the others crowded around them got the message. Even those who didn't understand English knew that something terrible was behind the crush of people stampeding toward them. Dropping their bricks and bits of glass, they turned to run.

"Get inside!" Sparks ordered as he let go of the man and dashed to the side of the street, kicking down the still-standing door of a shop. The others followed him.

Inside, Steph looked at the man who suddenly stood alone in the street, still holding his son. Then, in the blink of an eye, he was gone, shoved to the ground and trampled by thousands of screaming people.

Somewhere farther down the street, in the direction the mob was headed, a tank's main gun fired.

* * *

"Fuck," Coyle said as she wiped the blood from her lip. The unexpected shock wave that preceded the shells that hit her platoon's position had slammed her head against the commander's miniature control console. Its edges were padded, but even that didn't help when your lips were rammed into it full-force. "Status!" she barked.

"Green," Sergeant Yuri Kirov, her gunner, replied. "Weapons are up and ready."

"We can move," Mannie, the driver, told her, "but I've got two caution lights on the right-hand drive. Shouldn't be a problem unless you want to go flying cross-country."

"Let's just see if we can dig ourselves out of this shit," she told him. She had tried opening the hatch, but couldn't: it was blocked by rubble. Shifting views from her cupola sensors to the gunner's sight, then to the driver's sensors, it was clear that her Wolfhound was completely buried by the building they were in. "Mannie..." she paused. She wasn't sure if it would be smarter to try and move out of the rubble slowly to minimize the risk of damaging the tracks and the other equipment on the outside of the hull, or just gun it and get it over with. Normally, she would have gone slowly, but if there were Kreelans around, she'd be a sitting duck until the turret was clear. "Shit. Mannie, we're going to have to risk throwing a track. If there are bad guys out there, I don't want them to shoot the crap out of us while we're being all careful-like getting out of this dump."

"Roger that," he said, squirming a bit deeper into his seat as he gripped the controls. "Hang on to your hats, boys and girls," he warned as he gently goosed the Wolfhound's accelerator. Less experienced drivers might have just stomped on it, which Mannie knew would have most likely made a spectacular display of spinning the tracks and spewing debris everywhere, while not moving them a whit. Driving a heavy armored vehicle really well required more finesse than most people realized. He felt the meter-wide tracks pull tight, just to the point where the big tank lurched. Then at just the right moment he goosed the accelerator, sending a hundred and twenty-five tons of fighting steel through what was left of the building, scattering bits of brick and glass everywhere into the street beyond.

"Jesus!" Coyle cried as the vision displays showed what was ahead of them: the street was filled with people.

"Oh, fuck," Mannie whispered, slamming on the Wolfhound's brakes, rocking the huge vehicle to a hard stop. "God help me..."

"Take it easy," Coyle said, her voice brittle. "It's my responsibility, Mannie," she whispered as the close-in display showed her the bodies that had been crushed under her tank's tracks. There must have been at least half a dozen. If she listened closely, which she desperately tried not to, she could hear the screaming from at least one person whose legs were pinned under them. "Listen, I'll go out and help-"

"Stay put," Yuri, the gunner, said quietly. "Look at them all. They're running."

"You'd run, too, if somebody had just run over a bunch of your friends with a tank, you bastard!" Mannie shouted at him, tears in his eyes.

"No, Mannie," Yuri said. "They're not running from *us*; they're running from *them*." He hit the controls that echoed his gunsight display to the driver and commander stations. In the magnified view, it was clear that something far more horrible than their tank was stalking the people outside. For the first time, they saw the real-life version of the artist's renderings they had all laughed at during the pre-drop briefings, thinking the female warrior aliens had been a great joke.

But the lewd versions that a lot of the troops had come up with weren't so funny as Coyle and her crewmen watched a line of alien warriors moving along behind a group of two or three hundred people that had been streaming past the building, cutting down any that came within reach with swords and claws.

"Shit," Coyle cursed. "Mannie, move forward slowly. We've got to clear this building and get into a firing position away from those people." Firing the main gun over the heads of the fleeing civilians was out of the question: the overpressure near the muzzle of the barrel when the gun fired was so high that it would kill anyone inside half a dozen meters.

"No!" Mannie shouted, horrified. "I can't. There are more people in front of us!" The crowd had largely run past by now, but there were still dead and wounded lying in the street, most of them casualties of the Kreelan attack against the tanks.

"Mannie, if we don't move, we're going to get our asses kicked!" Coyle shouted at him. "*Move forward slowly, corporal!*"

"Okay," Mannie whispered, taking his foot off the brake and gingerly applying pressure to the accelerator. The tank's massive twin electric motors, powered by an equally huge bank of fuel cells deep in its armored belly, smoothly turned the drive sprockets and put the Wolfhound in motion again.

"Mannie," Coyle said more gently, "adjust the vertical gain on your forward display so you don't see what's down on the street. Just keep us from hitting the buildings, okay?"

"Roger," he managed, doing as she had told him. It wouldn't matter, because the images of the crushed bodies were burned into his brain.

"Shit," Yuri said, keeping the turret aligned in the direction of the warriors. "They see us." A number of the Kreelans looked straight at them and cried out to the others. But they kept coming after the civilians, driving them like cattle right toward the tank that now sat idling uncertainly in the middle of the street.

"They'd have to be blind not to," Coyle said as she scanned all around them in her vision display to make sure nothing took them by surprise. Aside from the still-rising fireball at the city center, all she could see were screaming people being pursued by the line of Kreelans. "Dammit, we're not going to have enough clearance from the civvies for the main gun. Yuri, use the coax."

"I don't have a clear shot," he told her, praying that she wouldn't order him to fire, anyway. In his digital gunsight, human heads bobbed in the sight picture as people ran past: if he fired, he would accidentally decapitate at least a few.

"Crap," Coyle snarled as she tried to bring her own weapon to bear. A three-barreled gatling gun that fired twenty millimeter shells at over a thousand rounds per minute, it was mounted high enough that it cleared the heads of the fleeing civilians in her own remote gunsight display. There was only one problem: it was jammed and wouldn't move. "It must be jimmied with rubble."

"Grenades!" Yuri warned as he saw some of the Kreelans, whose attention was now fixed on the tank, detach some sort of weapon from their belts that could only be some sort of anti-tank grenade. The weapons glowed with electric fire, and he definitely didn't like the look of them.

Coyle had no choice: risk killing some of the civilians or have the Kreelans attack her vehicle. "Close-in mortar," she warned, "danger close." She lifted up a clear cover over a small red button and jammed it with her finger. Her sight display switched to a computer-generated overhead view of what was around the vehicle. Clearly displayed were yellow-colored dots representing the Kreelan warriors, and she quickly drew a box around them with her finger.

In the roof of the massive turret was one of the vehicle's close-in defense weapons: a small mortar that could fire one or more forty millimeter smart grenades. It could rotate and adjust the distance the projectiles would fire, covering the area she had marked on her display.

She hit the glowing "Fire" button on the weapon control panel, and the mortar pumped out eight rounds in two seconds with precisely controlled spurts of highly compressed air. The weapon couldn't reach more than a hundred meters, but that was more than enough for what Coyle needed.

The line of Kreelan warriors suddenly disintegrated as the small but potent mortar rounds exploded among them at waist height, with a shrapnel pattern that expanded horizontally like an opening fan. It was none too soon: a few more seconds and they would have been within throwing range for their grenades. As it was, they were close enough that some of the shrapnel pinged off of *Chiquita's* heavy armor

Amazingly, none of the civilians were injured, the bodies of the Kreelans having absorbed nearly all of the shrapnel.

The civilians safely past, Yuri opened up with the coaxial gun, another twenty millimeter cannon. The tank was suddenly filled with the weapon's growl as it spewed shells into the few surviving Kreelans, who were still dazed by the mortar explosions. The alien bodies exploded under Yuri's withering fire, and in a few seconds there were no targets left to shoot at.

"Sergeant Coyle?" a voice suddenly crackled over her headset. "Can you hear me?"

Breathing a huge sigh of relief that at least one of her platoon's other tanks was alive, she said, "I never thought I'd be happy to hear your voice, Gomez, but we're damned glad to see ya." In her cupola display, she watched as Gomez's tank moved to one side of hers, keeping its turret pointed in the opposite direction from where Coyle's turret was aimed, covering their collective backs. She looked at her console, her suspicion confirmed: the tanks only had communications in line-of-sight mode by laser. The Kreelans must have done something to mess up any radio frequency communications.

"Any word on the other two tracks?" she asked, wondering about the other two tanks in her platoon.

There was a slight pause. "They both bought it," Gomez said somberly. "Ivanova's tank took what must've been a twenty centimeter round from one of those enemy cruisers right on the turret mount. She didn't stand a chance. I don't know what happened to Inoue, but his track was a burning wreck. No survivors."

"Fuck," Coyle hissed, leaning her head against the coaming of the commander's hatch. "Any word from company or higher?"

"Zilch," Gomez said somberly. "We just dug our way out of that crap we were buried in, so you'd have had a better chance than us to hear anything. Only thing working is the fucking lasers, and all the whiskers on our left side got scraped off when we dug out of the building. So we can only talk and hear on the right side."

"Okay," Coyle said as she popped the hatch. She needed to try and free up her gatling gun. "Take up position in echelon left," she said, which would put Gomez's tank to her left so the other vehicle's communications lasers would be able to network with hers, "and let's move back toward the battalion CP to see if we can find anybody else. Surely there must be someone else left alive in this clusterfuck."

"Oh, shit," Yuri whispered as he scanned back and forth with the turret to cover their portion of the street and what lay beyond. "We've got company. And lots of it."

Coyle looked up from hammering at the gatling gun's mount to see what must have been hundreds, if not more, Kreelan warriors come striding around a corner a few hundred meters down the cross street from the intersection where the tanks now sat.

The warriors paused momentarily as they caught sight of the pair of tanks. Then they broke into a run straight toward the two human vehicles, and Coyle's skin crawled as the Kreelans howled their bloodlust.

Hammering one last desperate time at a bent pin that was all that was keeping the gatling gun's mount from moving freely, she grunted in satisfaction as the weapon suddenly slewed around on its mount, centering itself. Coyle dropped back into her seat, the hatch hissing shut behind her. "Jesus," she said in wonder as she looked at the display. "They must not have a fucking clue what they're attacking." The Kreelans were running headlong toward them like a bunch of primitives who had never seen an armored vehicle. "Fine by me," she muttered. "Dumbass alien bitches in the open," she called out her own version of the target type. "Load flechette, area fire."

"Up!" Yuri instantly replied, having already selected the round he knew she'd want.

"Fire!"

The tank rocked back as its twenty centimeter cannon, the same size as those fitted on the Terran heavy cruisers, but not as powerful or fast-loading, fired with a gout of flame. Propelled by a powerful binary liquid propellant that was injected into the breech and ignited, the flechette round wasn't simply a gigantic equivalent of a shotgun round. Much like the close-in defense weapon that could cover an area designated by the tank's commander, the flechette round could cover a larger or smaller area, as necessary. After he'd loaded it, Yuri had swiped his thumb across the line of Kreelan warriors shown in his display, designating the entire mass as a target. The tank's computers did the rest.

As the round sped downrange, miniature explosive charges inside detonated at precise intervals, spreading the thousands of flechettes into a broad horizontal pattern to cover most of the Kreelan line.

The results were horrific. Fully the first three ranks of alien warriors were cut to ribbons in a spray of bloody mist by the finger-length razor-sharp projectiles. Their breast armor was strong, but not strong enough to stand up to flechettes moving at three thousand meters per second. Coyle, as happy as she was to give the enemy a pounding, was sickened at the sight. The street was instantly awash in blood and bits of bodies. While she had fired flechette rounds at the ranges for training, of course, she had never actually used one on live targets. With the exception of a few of the senior officers and NCOs who had served during the St. Petersburg war, none of the soldiers of the Terran units had actually seen combat before this. Despite years of training, it was a rude awakening.

"Oh, God," Yuri said in nauseated wonder.

"That should slow them down..." Coyle said with a shaking voice as she clamped down on her own urgent desire to vomit.

But the alien warriors didn't slow down. If anything, the massacre of their front ranks sent them into even more of a frenzy. Coyle couldn't be sure, but it didn't seem like rage, either: it was like they were all having some sort of alien orgasm. But they weren't stupid: the mass of warriors instantly broke up into groups. Most of them headed for the cover of the surrounding buildings, while a couple of groups continued toward the tanks, running fast and weaving to make harder targets.

As Yuri tried to blast them with his coaxial weapon, Coyle ordered the driver, "Mannie, turn us around and head down the street toward where the battalion CP was. Gomez, echelon left." She needed to get the tanks away from the buildings the Kreelans were swarming into: if they could clamber through the rubble to this side of the buildings, they'd be in great positions to hit her tanks from above with whatever weapons they might have for the job. While the gatling guns on the roof could nail them on the upper floors, the main guns couldn't elevate that far.

Then again, they didn't necessarily have to.

"Target, building," Coyle snapped to Yuri as she moved the pipper on her command console over the nearest building the Kreelans had headed for, showing Yuri the target she wanted serviced. "HE-Thermo."

There was a brief whine as the turret's primary magazine whirred, bringing up the type of round she wanted, then a solid *thunk* as the autoloader rammed it into the breech. A second later, the gun now aligned to the target, Yuri barked, "Up!"

"Fire!"

Chiquita's main gun roared, sending the high-explosive thermobaric round into the already heavily damaged building across the street. Unlike a regular high-explosive round that exploded in much the same fashion, if with more effect, than its progenitor TNT centuries before, the HE-thermobaric rounds used a variety of chemical and metallic compounds, detonated in a precise fashion, to greatly enhance the weapon's explosive blast. They weren't useful in every situation or against every target, but in this case it was just what the doctor ordered: the round streaked through a window to hit the back wall of the room within, and the resulting fiery blast and shock wave blew out the entire front wall. A moment later, the roof sagged and what was left of the three-story building suddenly collapsed into a heap of flaming debris. She didn't see any bodies, but Coyle knew that if any of the enemy were in there, they wouldn't be a problem anymore.

"Punch it, Mannie," she said, keeping a close eye on her displays as the big tank rumbled down the street, with Gomez's alongside. She needed to find the rest of the battalion. Because as powerful as her tanks were, stuck here in the close confines of the city, it was only a matter of time before the Kreelans killed them.

* * *

"Colonel, this is suicide," the operations officer argued quietly. He kept his voice down because he didn't want to embarrass Sparks in front of the others.

Holed up in the shop they'd sought refuge in, the others looked out the remains of the front window, watching the terrified mob. They had barricaded the door to keep the river of people from flooding into their safe haven, but most of the civilians weren't interested in finding a hideout: they were simply trying to flee.

Momentarily ignoring the major, Sparks finally caught a glimpse of what had caused the panic outside: a mass of alien warriors, looking just like Sato had described them, were driving them down the street like cattle. But instead of using prods, the aliens were using swords and other weapons. The Kreelans didn't seem to be intent on massacring the civilians; it was more like they were simply trying to get them out of the way. Even at that, they were still killing dozens every second, hacking their way through the people at the rear of the mob who were penned in by the crush of people in front of them.

He didn't have any illusions about their own chances of survival: while he couldn't see them clearly, there must have been hundreds of warriors, and he only had half a dozen soldiers and a journalist. He knew at least some of his tanks had survived, because he could hear the piercing *crack* of their main guns and the rumbling purr of their gatling guns somewhere in the distance. But he couldn't see a way to reach them without being swallowed up by the mob. And the only way out of the shop was through the front: there was no back exit.

Even if there was a back way out, Sparks would not have taken it. This had gone beyond something that could be dealt with through application of the appropriate tactics and sufficient firepower. For him, it had become a question of honor. "Major," he said, loud enough that everyone could hear him, "when you first came to my regiment and I asked you what you thought your primary job was, you told me it was to help me manage the deployment of my regiment. Do you remember what I told you?"

"Yes, sir, I do," the major replied as everyone's head turned to watch them.

"What was it I said, major?"

"You said, sir," the operations officer managed, automatically bringing himself to attention, "that the first job of every member of the regiment was to kill the enemy."

"That would be correct, major," Sparks growled, turning to him with smoldering eyes. "*To kill the enemy.* That is what we do. *There*, major," he shouted, pointing to the rapidly approaching Kreelans, "is the enemy! If you think for one damned minute," he went on, lowering his voice slightly, "that I am going to simply stand here while those *things* butcher more civilians, you are badly mistaken. If we die, so be it. Nobody joins the 7th Cavalry because they want to live forever. Do you understand me, major?"

"*Garry Owen*, sir," the major said, saluting. The 7th Cav had been known as the *Garry Owen* regiment, the name taken from the Irish drinking song *Garryowen*. The tune had been a favorite of the regiment's most famous commander, General George Armstrong Custer, and *Garryowen* was made the regiment's official song. Since then, the term "Garry Owen" had come to mean a combination of *yes* and *can-do* underscored with the sort of determination that only those who are willing to risk their lives every day in the line of duty can truly understand. It was at once a very small thing, and at the same time a very important thing to those who served in the regiment.

"Good," Sparks said, dismissing the man with his eyes. "Listen up," he said to the rest of them. "This isn't going to be fancy or pretty. As soon as the enemy line reaches us and we have a clear shot down their flank, open fire with everything you've got. Hadley, you've got the best throwing arm: take whatever grenades we have and let fly. Everyone keep shooting until we run out of targets or ammo. Miss Guillaume," he said, turning to her, "this isn't something I can order or force you to do. But in the interests of what is no doubt a very slim chance of your own survival, it would behoove you to use your weapon to good effect."

Gulping, Steph nodded. "Yes, colonel," she said, her voice shaking. Her insides felt like everything had turned to jelly, and she felt like her stomach, bladder, and bowels were all ready to let go at the same time.

"Fix bayonets," Sparks growled as he pulled his own from his combat webbing and attached it to the muzzle of his rifle. The others immediately did the same, although Hadley had to help Steph attach hers, taking the bayonet from the standard combat webbing he'd given her when they abandoned the command vehicle.

She stared at the black blade, the silvery edge of the weapon reflecting the many colors of the people who were still streaming by. But they were getting to the end now, and the screams of fear were being replaced by cries of agony from those who were being cut down by the Kreelans. She thought she might be able to shoot one of the aliens, but to stab one with a bayonet? "Jesus," she breathed.

"Stick next to me," Hadley told her as he moved her behind a counter made of thick wood. After placing a handful of grenades on the floor by his feet, he put his rifle on top of the counter, pointing toward the window. "Remember, the rifle's going to kick some, so don't let it surprise you." He double-checked that her weapon was set for single-shot fire and not automatic: he didn't want her to accidentally spray bullets around the shop and hit the others. "Take your time and remember to breathe."

"Okay," she said in a small voice, trying desperately to rally her confidence. "God, I have to pee," she muttered to herself, then suddenly giggled as she realized that she was still recording everything. *I'd better win the Pulitzer for this one*, she thought giddily.

Sparks and the others had also taken cover where they could find it, some behind the counter, Sparks and the major kneeling on either side of the window. Luckily, the shop was big enough that they could all shoot through the front window without getting in each other's line of fire.

"Stand by," Sparks warned as he peered around the edge of the window, holding his rifle to his chest. The Kreelan line wasn't perfectly straight, of course, but it was close enough. "Steady..." he brought his own rifle up, making sure the muzzle would not protrude into the street. "*Open fire!*"

Half a dozen assault rifles chattered in unison, slamming hundreds of rounds into the flank of the Kreelan line, completely surprising the enemy warriors. Their chest armor saved some of them, but unlike the shotguns that the Alliance sailors had used against the Kreelan boarders, the Terran assault rifles, especially at point-blank range, had a lot more penetrating power.

"Down!" Sparks screamed as he saw a number of the Kreelans throwing something. Everyone ducked but a soldier who hadn't heard over the deafening rifle fire: she suddenly staggered back, a miniature flying buzz-saw having cut right through her combat helmet to embed itself in her brain. With a twitch, she pitched backward, dead.

Sparks and the major resumed firing, and the others joined in, popping up to fire a few rounds, then ducking down as more of the flying weapons sailed through the front window.

Hadley grabbed a grenade and hurled it through the window like a hail Mary pass, then dropped back down to snatch up another one. There was no need to look for a good target: the Kreelans were bunching up out in front of the shop. It didn't matter where he threw the grenades, because he just couldn't miss. The explosions rocked the shop and shook dust and plaster loose from the ceiling to rain down on them.

Steph was holding her rifle in front of her, pointed out the window, but still hadn't fired a single shot. She was staring wide-eyed at the frenzied action, watching it as if she were doing a slow-motion review of her own recording. The Kreelans, throwing any sort of tactics or caution to the wind, trying to rush the window. The cavalrymen, faces locked in expressions of grim determination, pouring rifle fire into the enemy. Two more of the soldiers being killed by the flying weapons, one of them decapitated, the other falling to the floor with one embedded in his chest. Hadley next to her, screaming epithets at the enemy as he bobbed up and down like a lethal jack-in-the-box, hurling grenades into the enemy's midst. The smoke from the rifles, acrid and foul-smelling, mixed with the coppery tang of blood and the dryness of plaster dust, that wreathed the soldiers. Colonel Sparks, his rifle's magazine having run dry, thrusting his bayonet into the neck of an alien warrior who had managed to leap through the window, falling on top of her, driving the bayonet's tip into the wood floor as the alien thrashed and clawed at him. And the terrible, terrible snarling of the enemy warriors, their fangs gleaming as they howled in some terrible ecstasy while they crashed in wave upon wave against the humans' defensive position.

All this she saw in what could only have been a few seconds before another warrior flung herself through the window to land right in front of Steph, the Kreelan's sword raised high and fangs bared in a killing rage. Time was suspended for a moment as Steph realized that there was no one else to help her: Hadley was down behind the counter, reloading his own rifle. Sparks, spattered with blood, was shouting something at her, even as he was trying to pull his bayonet from the Kreelan he had just killed. The others seemed not to have noticed that there was an enemy warrior in their midst as they frantically fired at the endless stream of warriors trying to climb through the window.

Steph tried to scream, but nothing came out: her body was completely paralyzed. She saw the gleaming blade of the sword - so beautiful! - swinging toward her neck, and in that moment she knew that she was going to die.

But before the blade could touch her flesh, the Kreelan warrior unexpectedly flew backward, still in slow motion, and Steph imagined a look of surprise and perhaps even disappointment on her alien features. There was a single round hole in her chest armor, right between her well-proportioned breasts, the black of the armor around the hole now a star of shiny metal.

With no small surprise, Steph saw the swirl of smoke streaming from the muzzle of her own rifle; she had not seen the muzzle flash as the round fired. Perhaps she had her eyes closed, an infinitely long time as she blinked. She felt her right index finger, curled around the trigger and holding it tight. With a conscious effort, she managed to let go: Hadley had told her that the rifle wouldn't fire again until she let up on the trigger.

For the first time in her life, she had killed another creature larger than a fly. A sentient being. An enemy of the human race. A being intent on killing her. She wasn't sure whether she wanted to celebrate or puke. But as her perception of time again sped up as the Kreelan warrior's body fell lifeless to the floor, she realized she didn't have time for either. With newfound determination, she raised the rifle to her shoulder and fired again. And again.

* * *

"What the fuck?" Coyle yelped as a huge stream of people came tearing around a street corner halfway up the block, heading straight toward them. Unlike the first group they had encountered, which had been a few hundred, this was a gigantic mob that filled the entire street. She heard screaming above the low whine of the tank's motors, accompanied by a frenzied volley of weapons fire. She could tell that the firing was from Terran assault rifles from their distinct staccato sound.

Standing up in the cupola so she could see better, she didn't have to tell Mannie to stop the tank. But he hit the brakes so hard that her chest slammed into the metal hatch coaming. Her body armor kept her from being bruised, but it was hard enough to almost knock the wind out of her. Mannie was still shaken by running over the people when they broke free of the building they'd used for cover, and she'd heard him vomit three times. But she didn't have anyone to relieve him.

They had passed by the First Battalion commander's position, and found his command track burned to a crisp with two gigantic holes punched through the armor. Of their own company commander there was no trace, nor had any of the other company commanders survived. Or if they were still alive, they hadn't been able to dig themselves out of the rubble. So Coyle had kept searching.

One tank from another company had joined them, but so far that was it for their entire battalion. It was clear that they had gotten the full treatment from the Kreelan ships as they passed overhead. Coyle couldn't be sure, but she suspected that they must have homed in on anything using a combat data-link, because the command tracks had received special attention. But you didn't have to be a genius to find a tank, she thought, disgusted.

Some tanks had survived the barrage, only to be killed by something else. She had found nearly half a dozen in the street that looked like they'd been incinerated. The sight made her very uneasy: while the streets here were quite wide, this being a newer upscale district, the tanks were still extremely vulnerable to attack by any Kreelans holed up in the buildings they passed.

The only good news was that she'd run into a platoon of infantry that had somehow survived. They were part of the mechanized infantry company that was task-organized to her battalion. Their infantry combat vehicle had been hit by the enemy ships, but had only been disabled. So they went looking for other survivors, and the enemy, on foot.

They soon found that the rest of their company hadn't been so lucky: every other vehicle in the company had been destroyed.

While the platoon was commanded by a second lieutenant, she knew that he was straight out of school and had zero leadership experience. She'd called him and his platoon sergeant, who also outranked her, up on top of her tank and told them quietly but bluntly that she wasn't going to obey any orders that she thought were stupid and would endanger her tanks needlessly, and if the boy had any sense he would listen to what she told him and do it.

Much to her surprise, the lieutenant had agreed. With a wry smile and no small amount of sarcastic wit, he turned to his platoon sergeant and said, "So, is this one of those leadership training opportunities you were telling me about?"

The three of them had a good chuckle at that, and after a brief discussion the lieutenant set about putting Coyle's "suggestions" into action, deploying his squads ahead, behind, and to either side of the tanks to help protect them from bomb-throwing alien wenches that the tankers might not see or be able to react to in time. Coyle was incredibly relieved.

Now, with the screaming horde of civilians flooding toward them, the infantry hurried to get out of the way, flattening themselves against the walls on either side of the street. A few of them - *Idiots!* Coyle cursed - tried to get in front of the mob and wave them to a stop. But at the last moment they all managed to dodge out of the way of the speeding human freight train.

The people surged around her tank, which was at the front of the modified three-tank wedge they had been moving in, and then suddenly started climbing on top of it, clearly with the intention of trying to get into its protective armored shell.

"Oh, no, you don't," Coyle cried as a man did an amazing set of acrobatics up the front glacis plate, over the gun, and onto the top of the turret, reaching for her hatch. She hit the panic bar, dropping her seat down inside the turret and slamming the hatch closed, barely missing the man's fingers. She hoped Gomez and the other tank crew had buttoned up or they were going to have an interesting time.

"What do we do?" Mannie croaked, terrified that she was going to tell him to move forward through this mass of people.

"Sit tight, Mannie," she told him. "Yuri," she said to her gunner, "watch for those bitches coming along behind them." Based on their first encounter with the Kreelans driving the civilians along, she figured there must be a ton of them behind this mob.

After a few minutes, though, the stream of people started to taper off, with no sign of the enemy behind them. The civilians on top of her tank, having decided that she wasn't going to invite them inside, had hopped off and followed their fellow scared-shitless citizens down the street.

"Okay, Mannie," she said, popping the hatch and sticking her head back out into the smoke-filled air again, "let's move it." The firing she'd heard earlier had tapered off drastically, then suddenly stopped. "And let's hurry..."

* * *

Only Sparks, Hadley, and, by some miracle, Steph were still alive. Two Kreelans had reached around the edge of the window and hauled the operations major off his feet: wielding his combat knife, he disappeared in a frenzied mob of tearing claws and slashing swords. Hadley lobbed his last grenade into the scrum of Kreelan warriors tearing at the fallen officer. The two other cavalry troopers had been killed by warriors who had managed to get in through the window, much like the one Steph had killed, and been quicker with their swords than the other cavalrymen had been with their rifles.

"Out!" Hadley cried: he was completely out of ammunition, even what he had gathered up from the other fallen soldiers. Steph was out, too: while she had been shooting non-stop, she had shared her spare magazines with Hadley, and had since then been crouching on the floor behind the cover of the counter, feeling like a coward. No longer worrying about the threat from the flying weapons, which the Kreelans had only used at first, he moved around the counter, holding his rifle now as the base of his bayonet.

"Out!" Sparks called, throwing down his empty rifle as half a dozen warriors clambered through the window. He quickly drew the big pistol he carried and emptied the magazine into them, killing five outright before more warriors came through, forcing him back.

Without time to reload his pistol and unable to reach his rifle now, Sparks had only one card left to play. While it was centuries out of date, an anachronism in this age as he himself was, he drew his saber from the scabbard at his side after dropping the now-empty pistol on the floor.

While a sword was still used as part of Terran Ground Forces ceremonial dress, the weapon Sparks held in his hand wasn't made of the inexpensive low-grade and brittle metal of the ceremonial weapons: it was a faithful replica of the last saber ever issued to the United States Cavalry, the Model 1913 that was designed by a young Army lieutenant by the name of George S. Patton, Jr. Made with a strong and flexible steel blade, it had cost Sparks a small fortune and had always been his most prized possession. He had even paid for formal training on how to use it, both from the back of a horse and dismounted. But even in his wildest dreams he had never thought he would actually use it in battle. Yet here he was.

With a confident thrust, Sparks stabbed the nearest Kreelan, who was turned toward Hadley as he charged from behind the wooden counter. He drove the blade into her armpit where there was a gap in her armor, the weapon's tip going deep into her chest. With a cry of shock, she fell to the floor, dead.

The impact on the other warriors was instantaneous and totally unexpected: they stopped their attack. Had Steph not been peering over the top of the counter, no longer content to cower behind it as Hadley had told her to, she would not have believed it. The half dozen warriors who had already come through the window stepped back away from the two cavalrymen, their swords held in what Steph took to be defensive positions. The warriors outside, having seen Sparks draw his sword, immediately backed away from the window, clambering past their many dead sisters who were stacked up in front of the devastated shop.

Hadley, in what otherwise might have been a comical moment, stopped in mid-charge, his war-cry dying on his lips.

Sparks, after tugging his bloodied sword from the side of the fallen Kreelan, backed farther away from the aliens, unsure of what was going on. He watched with disbelieving eyes as the Kreelans inside the shop warily retreated, moving to join the others who now stood outside in what looked like a wide circle open to the storefront. A Kreelan warrior, bloodied and injured, stepped into the center of the circle. In what he recognized as what must be a universal gesture, she beckoned him forward toward her.

"I'll be damned," he breathed.

"What do we do, colonel?" Hadley asked him.

Sparks glanced at him, then said, "We go kill as many as we can before we die."

* * *

Shanur-Tikhan stood in the circle of the gathered warriors as the humans unblocked the door to their small redoubt, apparently a shop of some kind not unlike those found in the cities of her own people. She was senior among her gathered sisters, and although she was already grievously injured, she would not be denied the privilege of matching her sword against the human's. While the warriors of Her Children were versed in the ways of weapons of many kinds, the sword was the ultimate balance of physical form and spirit. That this human possessed one spoke well of him and his kind, even if he was a soulless animal whose blood did not sing.

She grunted in appreciation as the human bearing the sword emerged from the doorway, walking with dignity instead of clambering awkwardly through the smashed window. Two others, a male and a female, accompanied him. The male, unarmed, stooped next to a fallen warrior to pick up her sword before coming forward to join the male who appeared to be the senior of the two. Shanur-Tikhan and her sisters took no offense at his taking the sword, for it was unbound from the dead warrior's spirit. The female human merely stood by and watched, which Shanur-Tikhan found highly curious.

The two males approached her, the dominant without fear, his subordinate with some obvious trepidation. The former held his weapon confidently, while the latter did not. If they meant to fight her two on one, she would accept such a challenge. Her wounds were serious and would soon kill her if she did not seek out a healer, but that was inconsequential. All that mattered was the challenge.

Opening her arms wide, she invited them to make the first move.

* * *

"Hadley," Sparks asked quietly, "do you have a damn clue what to do with that thing?"

Gripping the alien sword tightly, Hadley answered, "No sir, I don't. But if I'm going to die, I'm not going to die without a weapon in my hands."

"Well-spoken, son," Sparks told him. "For what it's worth, you've been a helluva soldier."

"Thank you, sir," Hadley said, his throat tightening up. He had been with Sparks for two years, and had been given his share of ass-reamings by the colonel. But the man had never done anything, even dressing down a man or woman under his command, without the goal of making him or her a better soldier. And he had always treated his soldiers with respect. "It's been an honor, sir."

Nodding, Sparks said simply, "Shall we, soldier?"

"Garry Owen, sir!"

Together, the two cavalrymen attacked.

* * *

"You saw *what?*" Coyle exclaimed, unable to believe what she was hearing.

"You heard me, sarge," the lieutenant said. "It's the colonel and another soldier fighting one of the Kreelans with swords! And that reporter is there, too. Surrounded by a few hundred hostiles."

The lieutenant's infantrymen had been scouting ahead, peering around the corners to make sure Coyle's tanks didn't get ambushed. They'd been heading as fast as they could in the direction from which they'd heard the firing, but the "crunchies" - the infantry - couldn't go nearly as fast as her tanks, and she dared not leave them behind. The woman on point had come running back to the lieutenant, telling him what she'd seen. Unable to believe what she'd said, he had gone forward himself for a look. And now he was relating the same ridiculous tale to Coyle.

It was so bizarre that it had to be true.

"We've gotta do something, sarge," the lieutenant said earnestly.

And there sat the big, fat and ugly problem: what to do. She had plenty of firepower to blast the Kreelans to bits, but she wanted to rescue the survivors of the headquarters company if she could. If she came in, all guns blazing, there's no way she could keep them from being killed in the crossfire.

Calling up a map of the neighborhood, she had an idea. "Okay, el-tee," she told him, "here's what we do..."

* * *

Sparks was gasping for breath, and his right shoulder was burning like fire from holding and swinging the saber. It wasn't a heavy weapon, but he wasn't used to fighting with it, and his body was exhausted after the frenetic firefight they had just gone through. But he was nothing if not determined, and he ignored the pain, willing his wiry body to stay in the fight.

Hadley, beside him, wasn't in any better shape. While bigger and physically stronger, he had no training at all with a sword in his hand, and had suffered a brutal cut to his upper left arm. He could still swing the sword with his right, but the pain and loss of blood were telling.

Their opponent, Sparks realized, was drawing out the affair. Even gravely wounded, as she clearly was from the amount of blood seeping from beneath her armor, he knew that she probably could have killed both of them in the first few seconds. He merely gave thanks for her sense of fair play, because it just gave him that many more opportunities to kill her.

Steph watched as the two men battled the Kreelan warrior, furious with herself that she was unable to help them. She could try picking up a sword and dive into the melee, but she figured she would last about five seconds. Instead, she focused on doing her very best to capture the battle. She had forgotten about the Pulitzer. This was about posterity, assuming any of them actually survived.

Suddenly, she became aware of something that was totally out of place in this shattered street, filled with hundreds of alien warriors watching an uneven battle of survival: music. It was an instrumental of a song she didn't immediately recognize that sounded like something someone might hear in an old-style Irish pub.

But the effect of the music on the two cavalrymen and the aliens alike was profound: the Kreelans turned to look down the street to see what this strange noise was, while Sparks and Hadley charged their opponent as if they had been shot full of adrenaline.

Then Steph saw the first of the tanks belonging to the 7th Cavalry Regiment round the corner up the street with the regiment's official tune, the *Garryowen*, booming from the lead tank's external speakers.

* * *

Coyle's plan was straightforward: she would take the tanks straight in to try and draw the enemy's attention, which was something tanks were very good at, while the young lieutenant took his infantry platoon down the next street as fast as he could to get in position behind the Kreelans. Her hope was that most or all of the Kreelans would head toward the tanks, giving the infantry a chance to grab the colonel and the others, literally behind the enemy's back.

The tanks made very little noise when they moved, as the electric motors were practically silent. The only thing one could hear from any more than a few yards away was the tracks. Even that, with vehicles maintained as well as those of the 7th Cav, was lost in the background noise of the burning city. And Coyle wanted to make something of a grand entrance that wasn't potentially lethal to the colonel and the others.

So she decided on something a bit unconventional. The colonel loved the damned *Garryowen*, the Irish drinking song that was the regiment's official air, and every vehicle had a copy of it that could be played at his whim. She knew that to Sparks, and most of the rest of the regiment, even if many wouldn't admit it, *Garryowen* was a battle hymn that took him back to the era he wished he had been born in. "And the stupid song gives me goosebumps, too," she confessed quietly to herself. She switched on the external public address system that was standard on all the regiment's vehicles and cranked up the volume.

Rounding the corner, she saw that her efforts had met with good effect: the bulk of the Kreelans were now standing there simply staring at her tank, while the colonel and the other soldier charged the enemy warrior facing them.

With *Chiquita* taking up position in the center of the street, the two other tanks moved up beside her. Taking up virtually the entire width of the street, the three tanks moved forward to meet the Kreelans.

* * *

Shanur-Tikhan was shocked at the sudden surge of strength and determination in the humans she fought as soon as the strange noise washed over them. Breaking contact for a precious moment by shoving them both away, she turned to see three large vehicles moving toward her warriors. Why their war machines made such a noise, she could not imagine, but the threat to her warriors was clear.

The challenge, then, was finished.

* * *

Steph looked on in horror as the warrior, wounded though she was, easily parried a slash from Hadley's sword and then, with a brutal attack with her own weapon, opened him up from his left hip to his right shoulder, the sword cutting right through his armor as if it were made of cloth. With a startled cry, he crumpled to the ground.

Sparks attacked the Kreelan with a series of savage thrusts with his saber, but on the last he slightly over-extended himself, and the Kreelan took full advantage. Knocking his sword aside, sending him off-balance as if he were sprawling forward, she pirouetted and brought down her sword, stabbing him through the back. The colonel gasped in agony as the sword's blade ran him all the way through, the bloodied tip hissing through the armor of his breast plate. As he fell to the ground, the warrior yanked the sword from his body and flicked the blood from it.

* * *

"*Fucking bitch!*" Coyle screamed as she saw the colonel go down. Like the other Kreelans, the one who had just stabbed him had turned to look at Coyle's tanks, and in the magnified view of her combat console it seemed like the Kreelan was looking right into Coyle's hate-filled eyes. Coyle hoped she was, because it was the last thing the warrior would ever see.

Making sure her aiming pipper was on the center of the warrior's body in the targeting display, Coyle pulled the trigger on the cupola-mounted gatling gun. The Kreelan warrior disappeared in a gout of bloody mist as a dozen twenty millimeter rounds blew her apart.

* * *

Steph ignored the chaos that erupted around her as the warriors charged the tanks en masse, sprinting across the hundred meters or so of open street to reach them. The tanks' gatling guns and coaxial guns fired continuously, and she heard the *pop-pop-pop* of the tanks' close-in defense weapons launching grenades, then the explosions that followed. And over it all, the horrible war cries of the Kreelans as they charged and died.

She ignored it all as she crawled over the blood-soaked ground to get to Hadley and Sparks. She reached Hadley first, and was amazed to see that he was still alive. Unconscious, but alive. Gingerly prying the severed plate of his chest armor apart, she saw a great deal of blood and the white gleam of bone in the deep gash over his rib cage, but the sword hadn't penetrated his vitals. If they could keep him from bleeding to death, she was sure he would live.

Then she low-crawled the few meters to where the colonel lay face-down in the street, a pool of blood beneath his body. Gently turning him over, she saw that he was still conscious. She saw his lips moving, but couldn't hear what he was trying to say over the din of the tanks firing and the Kreelans screaming.

Putting her ear to his lips, she heard him say, "Turn me...so I can see..."

Nodding, she pulled him around enough to where he could see the battle, his head cradled in her lap.

As they watched the carnage together, they were suddenly surrounded by infantrymen.

"Medic!" a young lieutenant cried as he knelt next to the colonel, who simply nodded to him, then returned his gaze to the undulating dance of death taking place farther down the street. A medic was instantly at the colonel's side, with two other soldiers tending to Hadley.

There was a sudden *boom*, then another, and again as the tanks' last-ditch close-in defenses triggered: explosive strips with embedded ball bearings that were attached in segments all around the hull.

Steph saw the Kreelans dying by the dozens as they continued their insane assault. And more died as the lieutenant ordered his infantrymen to add their own fire to the mayhem, taking the Kreelans from behind.

It was a massacre.

In the end, the Kreelans refused to yield, they refused to even attempt to retreat. They were killed to the last one. But the regiment paid a high price: two of the three tanks were hit with Kreelan grenades, destroying the vehicles and killing the crews. The only survivor was *Chiquita*, a large patch of its left flank blackened from the intense heat.

Driving through the abattoir that was all that was left of the Kreelans, Coyle's tank, blackened and smoking, the suspension and most of the lower hull covered with Kreelan blood and gore, pulled up close to where the medic was stabilizing Sparks, whose eyes had never left the vehicle that rumbled to a stop in front of him.

Climbing out of the cupola and gingerly making her way down the gore-spattered hull to the street, an exhausted Staff Sergeant Patty Coyle saluted her regimental commander.

"That was good work, trooper," Sparks said quietly through the haze of painkillers the medic had pumped into him. He was hurt badly, but the medic had told him that if they could find a decent hospital or get back to the fleet, he would fully recover.

Her face dirtied with soot and flecks of blood from a Kreelan who had come within arm's length of killing her during the fight, Coyle managed a grim smile. "Garry fucking Owen, sir."

That was all the colonel needed to hear.

TWENTY-ONE

"Lieutenant," a voice said. It was vaguely familiar, but muffled and distant, as if in a dream. The voice itself was pleasant, that of a young woman, but even voicing that single word, she seemed distraught for some reason. "Lieutenant, can you hear me?"

Blinking his eyes open, Ichiro Sato saw a pale blur hovering above him that gradually resolved itself into a face: Natalya Bogdanova. The last few seconds of what happened on the bridge flashed through his mind, when Morrison had relieved him of duty and replaced him with Bogdanova as the Kreelan shells were about to hit.

And hit they had: the last thing Sato could recall was flying across the bridge as explosions wracked the ship. He remembered very clearly the thought that your life was supposed to flash before your eyes before you died, and he had felt cheated that he hadn't been able to see his own life replayed before his body smashed into the bulkhead.

Looking up at Bogdanova, he could still hardly see her face: the bridge was shadowed in darkness, with only a few of the emergency lighting strips working, throwing a ghastly dim red glow through the smoke that swirled slowly in the compartment. But what he could see wasn't good: she had a deep gash across her left cheek, and her face was smudged with blood and darkened by the heavy, acrid smoke. Her cheeks were wet with tears, from pain or the emotional trauma of what the ship must have endured, he couldn't tell.

"Lieutenant," she said again, and now he could feel one of her hands cupping the back of his head, and the faint sense of wetness there. Blood. "Please say something," she whispered desperately.

"Bogdanova," he managed, breaking into a wet cough. His head began to throb. Aside from that and some heavy bruising, he seemed to be well enough. Making a few exploratory movements with his hands and feet, he discovered that nothing was broken.

Hearing her name had an immediate effect on the young ensign. "Thank God," she whispered, lowering her head down to his chest, a sobbing cry sticking in her throat.

"Boarders?" he asked immediately, the nightmare from over a year ago coming back to him in an instant.

"No," she reassured him. "No sign of boarders or anyone else. After we were hit, the fleet moved on toward the planet, and we were just left floating in high orbit. I think the Kreelans must think we're dead."

Levering himself up on his elbows, his eyes stinging from the smoke, he asked her, "Where is everyone?" He couldn't see very far in the haze and dim red lighting, but the bridge should have been bustling with activity, the captain helping the XO direct damage control efforts to make the ship at least spaceworthy, if not ready for combat.

"Only four of us made it," she told him as she helped him sit up. "You, Beale, Akimov, and myself. Everyone else on the bridge is dead."

That tore through his headache and chilled his heart. Out of a combat crew of nearly a dozen men and women on the bridge, all but four had been killed? "The captain?" he asked. Regardless of how much he hated Morrison, he was nonetheless a competent ship's master and would have a good idea of how to get *McClaren* underway again. Not hearing his badgering voice was somehow disheartening.

"Dead," Ensign Drew Beale spat as he came forward through the smoky shadows with Seaman First Class Nikolai Akimov to join them. "The fucking bastard."

"What about the XO and the chief engineer?" Sato asked, his mind rapidly shedding the remaining cobwebs from his close encounter with the bulkhead. "And how's the ship?"

"We don't know if anyone else made it," Bogdanova told him. "We have no communications at all, inside or outside of the ship. The bridge has been holding air well enough, but I heard some venting up forward after we were hit. All the controls and consoles are out." She looked around through the dim red haze at the panels that should be glowing with buttons and information. "But we've still got artificial gravity, so main engineering must still be at least partially on-line. We can't get the hatch open to get to the rest of the ship, though."

"We haven't heard anyone outside in the passageway, sir," Akimov offered tentatively. "No one has come to try and find us."

Sato thought for a moment, then got to his feet with their help. He was still a bit unsteady, but they had no time to lose. It suddenly occurred to him that they all should be wearing respirators, if not full vacuum suits. The smoke in the air would be at least mildly toxic. And if the bridge suddenly did decompress, the respirators would allow them to breathe, even in a full vacuum environment, although they would suffer from the bends as nitrogen bubbles formed in their blood. It was a bad choice between ways to die. "Get your respirators on," he ordered. Something else Morrison, and the XO, by following a bad example, had fallen down on was basic survival and damage control drills. Sato was surprised that the ship had managed to survive at all.

The others quickly moved to the emergency lockers located at strategic points around the bridge, pulling out the respirators and putting them on. Bogdanova handed one to Sato, and after he'd pulled it on handed him a flashlight. Sato was eerily reminded of the first moments aboard the *Aurora* after the alien ship had immobilized them, when the crew had been cast into utter darkness before the strange blue glow began. He involuntarily shuddered, a chill running down his spine as the ghosts of his old ship's crew brushed against his soul.

Trying hard to ignore the bodies strewn about the bridge, Sato told the other survivors, "First, we need to get out of here and find out who else is left, and see what sort of shape the ship is in."

"But we can't open the hatch," Bogdanova said quietly.

"Yes, we can," Sato told her as he knelt down next to the small access panel, much like Yao Ming had done on the *Aurora* after the Kreelans had attacked. Sato had spent a great deal of time studying the *McClaren's* schematics after he had come aboard, and he had learned the trick that Yao Ming had used on their old ship. The mechanism was exactly the same, and he did it the same way Yao had. "I'll just crack the hatch first, in case the other side has been depressurized."

Turning the manual handle, an awkward process at best, the hatch began to slide open. Aside from a very slight hiss of pressure equalizing, it looked like the passageway was still holding atmosphere. Sato cranked it open the rest of the way.

Unlike the bridge, the passageway that led to the rest of the ship was fully illuminated by the emergency strips. Putting away the flashlight for the moment, Sato led the others aft and down. His first goal was main damage control, to see if the XO was still alive. Then on to engineering to find Lieutenant Commander Pergolesi.

It took nearly half an hour to reach the hatch for main damage control. Along the way they found over a dozen sailors still alive. After making sure that they all knew how to open the hatches manually, Sato sent half of them forward to find any other members of the crew who might still be trapped.

When he cracked open the hatch to damage control, he was instantly rewarded with a roar of air being sucked out of the passageway into the compartment on the other side of the hatch.

"It's been breached!" he shouted as he frantically cranked the hatch shut again. He knew there would be no survivors: none of the crewmen in the breached compartment would have had a chance to get into one of the inflatable emergency balls. And even if they had, they would have run out of air by now. With a heavy heart, he again led the others aft toward engineering.

Not long afterward, they turned down yet another passageway.

"Halt!"

Sato, leading the others, froze instantly. He couldn't see anyone else in the passageway.

"Identify!" the voice barked.

"Lieutenant Sato, tactical officer. You're a Marine, I take it?"

Suddenly a man dressed in a specially designed armored vacuum suit stepped into view. The suit was entirely off-white, a perfect match with the ship's interior. While he certainly wasn't invisible, he blended in quite well, and would have been difficult to spot for anyone who wasn't paying close attention or was moving fast.

"Gunnery Sergeant Ruiz, sir," the man answered through his external speakers as he lowered his rifle and made his faceplate transparent so Sato could see him. "Kinda glad to see you, sir," he allowed as several other Marines magically appeared behind him. They all looked huge and menacing in their combat armor.

"The feeling's mutual, gunny," Sato said earnestly, "believe me. How many of your men made it?"

"All of 'em, sir," Ruiz answered as if to say, *Of course they're all still here.* "I got eight here, including me, and the rest are still at their battle stations throughout the ship. Tanner almost caught a Kreelan shell, but he and his team made it okay."

"You've got comms with all of them?" Sato asked, incredulous.

"Yes, sir," Ruiz told him. "Just voice and vidcom over induction, none of the data-link stuff. The radio signals are for shit. But we don't need that to kick alien ass," he went on, gesturing with his enormous weapon, a recoilless rifle that was designed specifically for space combat.

For the first time since this disaster began, Sato managed a smile. The Marine combat suits not only had radio, which was currently useless, but also had the ability to send signals through the metal of the ship from induction sensors in the palms of the armored gauntlets, the soles of their shoes, and even a pickup sensor that could be attached to the ship with a simple magnetic clip. In testing during the hasty development of the suits, they had found that radio was often unreliable in the hull of a ship, so the Marines, ever inventive, had come up with an alternative. Just in case.

Looking down at the young Navy lieutenant, Gunnery Sergeant Pablo Ruiz couldn't help but feel a sense of admiration for him. That was something the big gunnery sergeant, or "gunny," as the rank was known, would say about very few of the Navy officers he'd met in his sixteen years as a Marine.

* * *

Formerly of the United States Marine Corps, or USMC, Ruiz was a plank owner, among the very first members of the recently formed Terran Marine Corps. The USMC had been the last amphibious force to be maintained by any of the former nations under what was now the Terran Planetary Government. Through disuse and the virtual elimination of war on Earth after the final series of conflicts that would have destroyed Mankind had it not been for the advent of interstellar travel, the Marine Corps had been left with no real purpose, and had been reduced to little more than a curious anachronism, a pale reflection of bygone years. In truth, it had been retained not for any military function in the post-Diaspora world, but because so many people who still lived in the former United States steadfastly refused to let go of it as a tradition. During one phase of this long twilight of its history, the Corps was even funded by donations from private citizens.

So the Marines had stubbornly lingered on, an institution with warrior traditions that had no more wars to fight.

In the aftermath of the *Aurora* incident, however, President McKenna had other ideas. Based on the analysis of Sato's information, it was clear that the ships of the fleet she was building would need a force of trained soldiers aboard to defend against Kreelan boarding attempts. Such soldiers should also be able to take the fight right back to the enemy. They would also have to become accustomed to serving aboard ships, rather than just being carried by them. Longer-term plans, assuming the

Kreelan threat actually materialized, even envisioned divisions of troops traveling with the fleet for planetary assaults.

The Terran Ground Forces commander, General Jaswant Singh, naturally felt that this was a function of his arm of the service. Admiral Tiernan, Chief of the Naval Staff, was not so sure. While he and Singh got along well and generally saw eye to eye, he had a hard time believing that soldiers brought up in the Ground Forces could quickly be transplanted into this new role.

As it happened, Tiernan's youngest brother was a colonel in the USMC, and had been at a briefing where some of the fleet plans were being discussed, the topic of "fleet infantry" among them. Two weeks later, he had called his older brother, the admiral, and invited - begged might have been a more accurate, if somewhat demeaning, term - him to come to Quantico to see a demonstration. While Tiernan was loathe to do anything that might smack of nepotism, his brother had made a very convincing argument, and Tiernan had finally given in.

When he arrived at Quantico, he was taken to a large hanger that had once been used to house USMC aircraft, a facet of their force that they had long since lost. Inside, he found that the industrious Marines had put together a life-size mockup of the main sections of one of the candidate destroyer designs, almost entirely from scrounged materials. Tiernan cautiously followed the eager Marines inside for a quick tour. Four stories tall and two hundred feet long, it lacked all the details a real ship would have, but it didn't need them. The twisting passageways, stairs, elevators, and hatches were what mattered, for these formed the "terrain" on which the battle would be fought. Video cameras had been placed at key locations throughout the ship to monitor the action during the demonstration battle. After the tour of the mock ship's interior, they led Tiernan to the improvised control room inside a ramshackle trailer that squatted next to the mockup.

Tiernan's brother explained the demonstration engagement: a platoon of Marines would simulate the Kreelans as closely as they could, based on Sato's information. Inside the mockup, a number of Marines played the role of "helpless" sailors, while a platoon in armored suits, led by one Gunnery Sergeant Pablo Ruiz, defended the ship. The suits worn by the defenders were simple mockups of combat vacuum suits the Marines had designed after several intense brainstorming sessions. While the mockups were rough around the edges, Tiernan had to admit to himself that, if made a reality, such suits would be quite lethal.

The Marines showed him the computer that would keep score, and Tiernan's brother swore that it was as accurate and fair as they could make it. In fact, they had programmed in a level of bias against the defending Marines.

Having been in the military for four decades, Tiernan had seen violence exercised across a wide spectrum, and did not expect to be surprised by a group of what he thought of as little more than highly innovative military enthusiasts. But by the time the simulated attack was over, he had to redefine his concept of "violence," at least as it pertained to close-quarters combat. The defending Marines suffered heavy casualties, but they stopped the simulated Kreelan attack, which was quite spirited, right in its tracks. More importantly, they were able to protect the crew and the ship's vital compartments, which would have allowed a real ship to stay in the fight with the rest of the fleet.

The combat armor, which Ruiz had helped design, was a key ingredient in the success of the first exercise. But even in the second exercise, which Tiernan's brother ran with the defending Marines only wearing standard body armor, the Marines were still able to hold the ship. They suffered far more casualties, and some of the simulated crewmen were also killed, but the determined Kreelan attackers were again defeated.

After a review of the two "battles," Tiernan was ferried out to one of the handful of ships that the Terran Navy still maintained just for the Marines, showing him how the Marines were more than just soldiers carried by ships. They were truly adapted to shipboard life and coexistence with the Navy in a Corps tradition that literally spanned centuries, back to the time of tall-masted sailing ships.

The admiral was sold. Selling the idea to the defense minister through the uproar caused by General Singh wasn't nearly as easy. In fact, the Marines had to stage a second demonstration for the minister himself. Over General Singh's very strenuous objections, the minister took the idea to the president, who after a brief pointed discussion with the minister and all the service chiefs, approved the proposal Tiernan and the Commandant of the Marine Corps had drawn up. She signed an executive order federalizing the United States Marine Corps and officially changing its name to the Terran Marine Corps. As its predecessor had been, the "new" Corps was nominally subordinate to the Navy.

Singh was furious that a "second bloody army" was being formed, but the president was adamant: the Army and the Aerospace Defense Force would mainly be responsible for planetary defense and provide follow-on combat forces, while the Corps would protect the fleet and eventually have responsibility for planetary assaults.

It had been many years in coming, but the Corps had a real mission again. And when the Terran ships sailed for Keran, every able-bodied Marine, save a training cadre at Quantico that was already flooded with volunteers, shipped out with the fleet.

* * *

Standing here now on the stricken *McClaren*, Ruiz realized how much they really owed to Lieutenant Ichiro Sato. He had unknowingly saved the entire Marine Corps. *Should make him an honorary Marine,* Ruiz thought to himself. "Orders, sir?" Ruiz asked.

"Engineering," Sato said immediately. "We need to sort out how badly the ship's damaged. And find Lieutenant Commander Pergolesi." He paused. "Both the captain and the XO are dead. Commander Pergolesi is next in line."

Ruiz's expression darkened. "I got some bad news for you, sir," he said, his low voice dropping even lower. "The chief engineer bought it when the ship got nailed. Broke her neck."

Sato closed his eyes, mentally damning their luck. He had been counting on Pergolesi not only to know how to put the ship back in order, if it was possible, but to take command. Because of the surviving officers...

"As I reckon it, lieutenant," Ruiz finished the thought for him, "that leaves you as the skipper."

"Right," Sato managed. For just a moment, he felt a crushing weight on his shoulders, and in that brief flicker of time, the only thing he wanted to do was to run and hide somewhere, to cower in a closet like a child. He wasn't prepared for this. *But who ever is?* he asked himself.

He suddenly felt a real weight on his shoulder, and opened his eyes to see the Marine gunny's hand there. The older man gave him a brief reassuring squeeze and said quietly, "We're with you, sir. What are your orders?"

"Thanks, gunny," Sato said, and the Marine nodded and stepped back with the others. "Right," the *McClaren's* new commanding officer said, shoving his insecurities into a tiny box in his mind and slamming the lid shut. He had a crew to save and a ship to get back into the fight. "The first thing we have to do is get to anyone else who's trapped and free them. Gunny, that's a job for your Marines, since they're already spread around the ship and you have communications. We'll show you how to get the hatches open manually, but you may have a tough time for compartments where the passageways are in vacuum."

"Naw," Ruiz said, "every compartment has those beach ball survival things. We'll just make sure everybody's in those, then open the hatch and take them to the main starboard airlock. The passageways are pressurized all the way back here."

Sato nodded. "Good. Next is engineering. Can you patch me through to one of your Marines there to talk to whoever's senior?"

"Sure thing," Ruiz said. After a few seconds of talking to the squad leader in engineering, Sato heard the sound of Chief Petty Officer Antoinette DeFusco.

"Lieutenant," she said from the speakers in Ruiz's suit, "you heard about Commander Pergolesi, right?"

"Yes, chief," Sato said. "What about the other officers?"

"They were in the forward engine room with the commander when we were hit, sir," the chief answered. Normally a blindingly perky woman, her voice now was ragged. "A shell punched clean through. Nobody made it."

"Damn," Sato whispered. Not only were the deaths of the officers and crew in the compartment a tragedy, but the forward engine room housed the jump drive. *McClaren* wouldn't be leaving the Keran system without a lot of time in space dock. And unless the battle had gone well, he doubted that was going to happen.

"How are the main drives?" he asked, wanting to cross his fingers.

"The mains are up, sir," she told him. "Everything aft of the forward engine room seems to be fine."

"Up forward is a mess," he told her. "We haven't been able to do a damage control survey yet, but I'm guessing about a third of the main compartments on the port side have been breached, with most of the passageways in vacuum on that side. Starboard's not so bad."

"Let me guess," DeFusco said, "you've got artificial gravity but nothing else?"

Sato and Ruiz looked at each other with expressions of amazement. "Good guess, chief," Sato told her. "How'd you know?"

"Because of that fucking pulse cannon, if you'll pardon my saying so, sir," she explained. "It takes up the central conduit that most of the primary circuits would normally use in this ship design. But they had to move them around to make room for that hog. So they decided to put the main buses for the artificial gravity in the starboard cable runs, and everything else in the port side. The ship should have had redundant circuits, but they dropped that to meet the commissioning schedule."

"Do we still have the pulse cannon?" Sato asked.

"Green as a Christmas tree, sir," she told him, "at least for one shot. After that, who knows? The main energy buffers are in forward engineering, too. They show green, but the way that thing drains them, I don't know."

"Okay, chief, listen," he told her quickly. "That means we've got propulsion and we've even got something to shoot with. We've got to get the other main systems, especially life support, navigation, and sensors, back up. Then communications and the other weapons if we can."

"We'd love to, sir, if we could just get out of here to get forward!"

Sato looked up at Ruiz.

"Consider it done, sir," he said gruffly before barking a string of orders to his Marines.

* * *

Six tension-filled hours later, Sato again stood on the bridge. The bodies of the crew had been laid out under shrouds in the upper galley, awaiting proper burial, assuming the survivors were able to stay alive themselves. The surviving engineers, with the help of the rest of the crew, worked themselves to exhaustion to patch the ship's systems back together. Two of them died when a hatch, weakened by an explosion in an adjacent compartment, gave way. But at last Chief DeFusco, scraped, bruised, and dirty, rasped that she thought they were ready to start bringing the main systems back up.

The bridge was still dark and the stench of the smoke persisted, despite the fans the Marines had hauled up from one of the damage control lockers to try and clear it. Using one of the hand-held induction communicators that the Marines had brought up from the armory, Sato said, "Okay, chief, let there be light."

The bridge lights suddenly flickered on, then quickly died.

"Wait one," the chief said after a flurry of curses. A few minutes later, she came back on. "Hold on to your shorts, lieutenant..."

The dim and gloomy darkness was peeled away as the standard lighting flickered on, then held. On the bridge, the computer displays at the various control stations lit up and began their self-diagnostic routines.

A tired but exuberant cheer went up throughout the ship. The *McClaren* was alive again.

* * *

Sitting in the captain's chair was an experience that Sato had only dreamed of. Even on the rare occasions when Captain Morrison had let him and the other junior officers con the ship, he had never let anyone sit in "his" chair. Now, for better or worse, the ship was Sato's.

Looking around the bridge, it was clear to him that the ship was still terribly wounded: several of the main consoles remained dark, with no one to man them. Only half the crew had survived, and it was no small miracle the ship hadn't been completely destroyed. Of those control stations that were lit and active, every single one had crimson warnings and tell-tales glaring, but there were far fewer than before. Glancing at the navigation display, which right now was based on passive sensors only, he could see the *McClaren's* long ballistic trajectory from where she had been hit, taking her out just beyond the orbit of Keran's moons. The ship had drifted perilously close to the Kreelan force in high orbit, shown on the tactical display as a cloud of red circles where the passive sensors believed their ships to be, but had been ignored as another dead hulk. Sato and the others on the bridge had watched as a much smaller Kreelan force had climbed out of the gravity well of the planet toward high orbit, even as another group split from the main force to head down toward Keran.

As for the human fleet, they were just visible on the far side of the planet, also trying to regain the orbital high ground after what must have been an uncomfortably close run to low altitude. Unless the sensors were off, there were far fewer human ships than when *McClaren* had originally jumped in. It was difficult to tell from what the passive sensors could make out, as they were not nearly as sensitive or accurate as the active sensors, but if he was guessing right, Admiral Tiernan and the Alliance admiral were maneuvering to engage the Kreelan force that was staying in high orbit. Sato couldn't be sure of the number of ships on each side, but he could tell that it was going to be close enough that even a single destroyer might be able to make a big difference. He had no intention of letting *McClaren* miss this fight.

Setting his fears and reservations aside, Sato tightened the straps, the ones that Captain Morrison had neglected to use, on the captain's combat chair. Opening a channel to the crew, he said, "This is Lieutenant..." Then he stopped himself. He was no longer simply a lieutenant of the Terran Navy. As fate had decreed, he was now the commander of a warship. "This is the captain," he told them. "As you know, while we have been able to repair much of the critical damage to the ship, we can't jump into hyperspace and return to the rendezvous point and the repair ships. And even if we could, I wouldn't: our fleet and that of the Alliance have taken heavy losses, and it looks like Admiral Tiernan," Sato assumed the admiral was still alive, "is leading an engagement against the enemy in high orbit. We are going to join in that attack." He paused, thinking about his ill-fated ship's few minutes in action before they were struck. "The enemy thought they killed our ship and that we are no longer a threat. I plan to prove them wrong. Remember our fallen shipmates, and do your best. That is all."

Switching off the ship-wide channel, he said to Bogdanova, whom he had moved to the navigator's position, "Stand by to maneuver." The ship was still on a ballistic trajectory, rotating slowly about its long axis.

"Standing by, sir," she answered. She was still afraid, but wasn't terrified as she had been under Morrison's lashing tongue. Like the others among the crew, she wanted payback from the enemy. More than that, she trusted Sato.

"Maneuvering thrusters," Sato ordered. "Bring her straight and level, helm, zero mark zero."

"Aye, aye, sir." Bogdanova touched the controls, at first with unsure fingers, but she quickly gained confidence as the ship began to respond to her commands.

For Sato, it was a very tense moment, because they hadn't been able to test any of the ship's systems for fear of drawing the enemy's attention before they were ready. But having repaired the primary kinetics - two of the main batteries were fully functional - along with a pair of medium lasers and the close-in defense lasers on the starboard side, the ship could at least mount a credible defense. And with the pulse cannon, if it were properly used, and a brace of torpedoes, she still packed an offensive punch, too. But the maneuvering systems and the main drives, despite Chief DeFusco's belief that everything was functional, were still an uncertainty in his mind.

"The ship is at zero mark zero, system relative," Bogdanova reported. She had stopped the ship's tumbling, and now had her level relative to Keran's orbital plane, pointing toward the system's star.

"Very good, helm," Sato said, nodding. "Let's see if we can't get back into the game. All ahead one quarter, course zero four six mark zero zero seven." He was hoping that by not using any active sensors and keeping his acceleration low, the enemy ships might not notice him for a while, allowing them to get closer. He had not tried to raise the fleet for fear of being discovered prematurely by their signal emissions.

"All ahead one quarter, aye." Bogdanova smoothly advanced the analog control handle, which looked much like a throttle might have in fighter aircraft centuries before, to the appropriate stop. The actual propulsion control system and the underlying calculations behind "one quarter" power and the other standard settings were far more complex than simply moving a handle, but the simpler interface was more efficient for the human part of the control loop. After a moment, Bogdanova reported, "Sir, engineering answers all ahead one quarter, and the ship is now on course zero four six mark zero zero seven."

Sato's tension began to quickly fade as the deep and steady thrum of the ship's drives continued without the slightest indication of trouble. He watched her icon on the tactical display as the *Owen D. McClaren* once again sailed into harm's way.

TWENTY-TWO

"We've got to withdraw whatever ground troops are left, admiral," Tiernan told Admiral Lefevre over the vidcom. "The Kreelans are sending what looks like another strike force down to the surface. After the mauling our troops took from the first Kreelan attack, there won't be much left of them after a second."

While the ships of the combined human fleet had suffered only minor damage from the Kreelan force that had assaulted the planet, both the Terran and Alliance ground troops had suffered heavy casualties. Citing the inhumanly accurate fire from the Kreelan ships and the fearless warriors, General Ray's last report over his tactical laser uplink had painted a grim picture of the situation before the fleet had lost communications with both him and the general commanding the Alliance ground forces. None of the ground forces had been heard from since, although direct observations from the telescopes and other sensors aboard the human ships left little doubt that their troops on the ground were fighting for their lives. And losing.

"I agree, *mon amiral*," Lefevre said. "Recovering your troops must be the priority, as we do not have enough combat-capable lift capacity to retrieve our own." Those words were a heavy burden on Lefevre's soul, for he had just condemned tens of thousands of men and women to death if the combined human fleet failed to win the battle in space.

Tiernan gently contradicted him. "I believe you may be mistaken, sir, based on the projected losses we're coming up with. Unless we're badly mistaken, and I wouldn't mind being wrong on this one, the corps we sent in has maybe a brigade left, if that. And if your units have suffered similar losses, the available carriers may be enough to lift out the survivors."

"*Mon Dieu*," Lefevre whispered. His own operations staff had come to similar conclusions, but he hadn't wanted to believe them. He still didn't. There had been ten Alliance divisions on the surface. To think that the survivors of both forces would now fit into six assault carriers was simply unthinkable. And this after only the first Kreelan assault wave.

"I've already dispatched our courier ship to the rendezvous point to bring back our carriers," Tiernan told him. The four Terran carriers had jumped out to a holding position that was far enough away that they were safe from attack, but close enough in case they needed to be recalled quickly. He just hoped they would be able to return quickly enough.

"I will do the same," Lefevre said. "But I am not willing to concede defeat."

"Nor am I, sir," Tiernan reassured him. "I believe that the enemy is giving us an opportunity in disguise," he went on, eyeing the second assault force, which was roughly a third of the enemy's ship strength, as they began to head toward Keran. The first wave, the one that the human fleet had met head-on in the upper reaches of Keran's atmosphere, had almost rejoined the main group in high orbit. "The timing will be tricky, but if we can engage the second wave as they come up from Keran, we should have at least a two to one advantage in firepower. Of course, that assumes that the remaining enemy ships are content to stay in high orbit."

Lefevre offered a Gallic shrug. "Something we can never count on, the enemy doing what we would like. Still, it is an opportunity we cannot reasonably pass up. My operations officer will coordinate for maneuvering orders, since we still have no data-link connectivity. Then we will see if we cannot teach our blue-skinned friends a thing or two about naval combat."

* * *

Aboard the *Alita*, Amelia Cartwright waited tensely as the ship's navigation computer counted down the remaining seconds to their emergence into normal space. While she certainly didn't mind helping the fleet by acting as their courier, she also was itching to do more than just ferry messages back and forth. But *Alita* wasn't built for combat. In any engagement, the best she could be was a target, albeit a fast one.

"Transpace sequence in three...two...one," the computer announced. "Transpace sequence complete." Suddenly the swirling nothingness of hyperspace displayed on the screen before her dissolved into pinpoints of light and the glowing orb of Keran.

"Shit," Sid, her copilot, whispered as the sensor display stabilized and began to paint the situation in the space around the planet, with the large cloud of blue icons facing off against the red. "The admiral's going to kick some ass."

Cartwright nodded, taking a look at the tactical display as she made sure that the ship had come through the jump in one piece. A Kreelan force had headed down to the planet, and it was clear that Tiernan was maneuvering to try and catch the Kreelans on the flip side as they climbed out of the gravity well after their attack. So far the Kreelans remaining in high orbit were staying put, but she knew that wouldn't last if they had any sense at all.

"Five seconds for the carriers," Sid reminded her as she maneuvered the ship, taking her well forward of the carriers' inbound jump point. She had taken *Alita* in first to scout the situation and have a warning prepared for the carriers in case they were jumping into a hot zone. At this point, they were safe.

"There they are," Cartwright told him, seeing the four blue icons representing the Terran carriers materialize right behind *Alita* on the tactical display. "*Guadalcanal*," she called over the vidcom, "it looks like you're clear for now. We'll proceed ahead of you to make sure there aren't any surprises waiting for you."

"Roger that, *Alita*," the lead carrier's captain said. "We appreciate the assist. I've got to contact Admiral Tiernan. *Guadalcanal*, out."

"You sure you want to do this?" Sid asked her quietly, looking at the swarm of ships ahead of them moving toward a massive clash.

She gave him a determined look. "We can't just run, Sid," she told him. "I know we're not in the Navy, but we've got the fastest ship in the system, and we've got to help if we can."

Sid only nodded and readjusted his cowboy hat as he squirmed a bit deeper in his seat.

With a tingle of fear running down her spine, Cartwright throttled up the engines and led the four assault carriers toward Keran.

* * *

"Dammit!" Tiernan cursed under his breath. "So," he growled at his flag communications officer, "you're telling me that we still have no communication with anyone on the ground?"

"Correct, sir," the commander replied, trying not to flinch. "We haven't been able to get any voice or vidcom signals from the surface. The only way we might be able to get through is a direct laser link, but it's going to have to be a very low orbit pass, and the ship will only have a few minutes over any given location before it passes over the horizon and out of range."

Tiernan wasn't angry at his officer, just at the damnable situation. Whatever weapon the Kreelans had used earlier that had knocked out much of the human fleet's communications capability had completely befuddled the communications experts on both the Alliance and the Terran ships. Absolutely nothing that used the radio frequency spectrum would work. Direct laser communications still worked for basic voice and vidcom, but not for the data-link systems, even though there seemed to be nothing wrong with any of the equipment and software.

Regaining communications with the ground forces was vital in order to get them to assembly areas where the assault boats from the carriers could retrieve them: Tiernan couldn't have the boats wandering across the planet looking for his people. The carriers had to be able to get in and out quickly, as Tiernan couldn't afford to detach even a single destroyer to protect them. Without radio communications, which could be broadcast to a wide area, the only way to talk to the troops on the ground would be by sending a ship in low and praying they could make contact over a laser link, which had an extremely narrow broadcast area.

"What about that courier ship?" his flag captain suggested. "The *Alita*, isn't she? She could haul ahead of the carriers, get in low, and try to regain contact with General Ray."

"It's a civilian ship," the flag operations officer protested. "They're not going to do that, and they shouldn't. They're not trained or equipped for it."

Tiernan looked at the tiny icon on the main display that represented a small ship and its two-person crew. "Do they have laser link capability?"

"All diplomatic courier ships have a basic laser link capability, sir," the communications officer said. "It's not military grade, but it's powerful enough. Some of the diplomatic missions they have to serve are in places with pretty rough environmental conditions, and they need communications that can get through, no matter what. And the tactical sensor package that was retrofitted on all the Keran couriers has an improved laser link detection capability, so if anyone on the ground is calling, they have a better chance of picking it up. Assuming they're in the path of the laser."

That decided it. "Get me *Alita's* captain," Tiernan said.

* * *

"Do you know who that was?" Sid asked, incredulous.

Cartwright threw him a sidelong glance. "Of course I do, Sid," she said, exasperated. He'd said the same thing five times in as many minutes after Admiral Tiernan had given her his "request." As if she would even think of saying no.

Alita was now streaking toward Keran under full acceleration, leaving the fat carriers far behind. Orbital insertion was going to be tricky, not just because of the courier ship's speed, but also because the second wave of Kreelan ships, the ones that Admiral Tiernan was going to pound on, were going to be a lot closer than she would like. Low orbit space was going to be awfully crowded for a while.

The admiral's communications officer had given them coordinates for where the Terran and Alliance troops had been landed, and Sid had programmed the ship's laser link system to broadcast over as wide an area as possible. They had already started an automated broadcast, just on the off chance that someone might pick it up before they entered low orbit: they had nothing to lose but a bit of power. Some might have thought their chances were about as good as finding a needle in a haystack, with the qualification that they were looking for the needle through a straw about as big around as a strand of spaghetti.

* * *

Amar-Marakh, the senior shipmistress of the Imperial ships around the human planet, nodded in approval as the human ships began to deploy against her second attack wave, even as the surviving ships of the first wave rejoined her. Her blood burned that she herself was not in the force heading toward the planet, for the engagement the humans were planning would be fierce and her heart cried out for battle. But that would yet come. For now, it was up to the shipmistresses and warriors of the second wave to bring glory to the Empress.

She knew the humans could not pass up an attack against the second wave, and that Her warships would be greatly outnumbered. She also knew that the animals would not have things all their own way. While the ships of the second wave would be dropping many more warriors to engage the surviving humans warriors on the surface, they would be keeping nearly a third in reserve to send against the human fleet as they closed to engage. The human ships had proven very vulnerable to boarding attacks, which perfectly suited the desires of Her Children.

Her heart beat rapidly as she watched the unfolding battle on her display, the Bloodsong of her sisters a thundering chorus in her veins.

* * *

Tiernan was proud of his crews as the Terran ships slid into position in the new formation he had worked out with *Amiral* Lefevre. Normally, the data-link systems also provided navigational orders, allowing the ships to closely coordinate their movements. With that information gone, each ship had to maneuver independently, and it would have been a challenge under the best of circumstances to form up over one hundred warships from two different navies, all under manual control. But his crews and those of the Alliance made it look like such feats were easy.

After more discussion with Admiral Lefevre, they had decided to put the Terran ships at the head of the formation as they engaged the Kreelans. The Alliance ships had already seen an exhausting fight, and some of them were running dangerously low on munitions. *Ticonderoga* herself was the point ship of the third echelon wedge, with a wedge of cruisers ahead, and a flotilla of destroyers leading the attack. The plan was for the destroyers to fire their torpedoes to help distract and, if they were lucky, break up the Kreelan formation, and then have the destroyers peel away to the flanks so that the heavier guns of the cruisers could hammer the enemy ships into scrap.

As Tiernan watched the red icons of the Kreelan second wave near Keran, he saw the solitary blue icon of the *Alita*, which was now sailing ahead of the Kreelan ships. He nodded in approval: the commander of the tiny ship had both brains and guts. Had she tried an orbit that brought her head to head or even flank-on to the Kreelans, they would no doubt destroy her. But sailing ahead of them, as crazy as it seemed, was also safest: unless the Kreelans showed some of the hideously advanced technology that Sato had reported, there was no way they would be able to catch her.

"Come on, Cartwright," Tiernan breathed. The only chance the ground forces might have of survival rested with Cartwright and her tiny ship. Otherwise, the troops on Keran wouldn't even realize a second attack was on its way, and the carriers would have come back for nothing.

TWENTY-THREE

Coyle was exhausted, but there was no stopping. The 7th Cavalry Regiment, which had started with just over three thousand men and women, had been reduced to a short battalion of a few hundred, including the survivors she had picked up from a few other units. The officers, all of whom had been in or near vehicles that were using the data-links targeted by the Kreelan ships, had been decimated: the senior officer, the *only* combat effective officer, was Lieutenant Krumholtz, the infantry lieutenant she had picked up early on. That would have made him the acting commander, but Sparks had made Coyle a brevet captain once the extent of the disaster for the ground forces had become clear, and she'd found herself in charge of the clusterfuck they were in. After that, Sparks had passed out and had remained unconscious. He was holding on, but only through sheer stubbornness: riding in the back of a civilian vehicle that had been abandoned and put into service as an ambulance, he was being tossed around in what had become an increasingly desperate effort to escape the killing ground of Foshan.

Chiquita, Coyle's tank, was one of only four in the entire regiment to have survived the battle to this point. Since the fight to save the colonel, she had found seven other tanks, but three of them had been destroyed by a small but determined pack of Kreelan warriors. Her unit's progress was slow, both because most of her troops had to move on foot, and because of the successive waves of civilian refugees that were boiling out of the wreckage of the city, usually driven along by more Kreelan warriors. Coyle felt compelled to try and give the civilians as much protection as she could, which further slowed her down and made her tanks easier targets for the Kreelans and their devilish grenades.

She would have headed out of the city where her tanks would have a much easier time keeping the enemy at bay, but she knew they had to link up with any other survivors of the division, if they could find them.

After a nightmarish drive farther into Foshan, where she found the smoking wreckage that had been the division command post, she realized that the division, and the corps as a whole, had effectively been wiped out.

She had picked up a few more troops from some of the division's other brigades, but only a handful. She had no doubt that there were other pockets of survivors. She could hear sporadic bursts of gunfire in other parts of the city, but she wasn't going to expend any more effort or lives trying to find them.

She was going to try and get her people out of the city.

"The corps is well and truly fucked," she told Lieutenant Krumholtz and the senior NCOs who had gathered in front of *Chiquita*. Coyle hated to risk stopping even for a few minutes, which would let the Kreelans who were hunting her tanks catch up, but she didn't have any choice. They needed to get a new game plan together. "We've got to turn around and head out of the city."

"We can't do that," Krumholtz argued. If anything, he was more tired than Coyle was, having had to slog along with his troops through the rubble and past shell-shocked civilians as the Terran column had slowly made its way deeper into the city. "If we can find General Ray, he'll be able to-"

"He's dead!" Coyle snapped. "Look at this, for Christ's sake," she said, sweeping her arm around them. The entire block where the division command post vehicles had been hidden had been pulverized, with every single building reduced to ashes and chunks of brick no bigger than her fist. The hammering her own platoon had received from the Kreelan ships had been a love tap by comparison. She knew that it was remotely possible that someone could still be alive in their vehicle, buried under the rubble. But there was no time to search. "The corps CP won't be any different. Face it, el-tee, we're on our own."

The younger officer was about to make a fiery retort when Yuri, her gunner, shouted from his open hatch in the turret, "Coyle! We've got a laser-link from the fleet!"

"Hot damn," she said as she jumped up on *Chiquita* to reach her cupola. Normally she would have been able to take the call through her helmet's radio, but with all radio communications knocked out she had to physically plug in a cable from the helmet.

"This is Sergeant...scratch that," she said hastily. "This is Captain Coyle of the 7th Cavalry Regiment. Go ahead, over."

"Coyle," a woman's voice said quickly, "This is the *Alita*. I only have about ninety seconds before we lose you. The good news is that carriers are inbound for extraction of Terran and Alliance troops, but you have to reach one of the landing zones. The closest one to you will be..." she read off some coordinates that turned out to be near their original combat positions. "You've got forty minutes until the assault boats land."

"Forty minutes?" Coyle cried. "There's no fucking way we can get back there in forty goddamn minutes!" It had taken over an hour to get this far, wading through the tide of civilian refugees and fighting off the pursuing Kreelans.

"There are two other zones at-" the woman read off more coordinates as if she hadn't heard Coyle's outburst. Neither of them was even close to Foshan. "Forty minutes. Pass the word. Be advised that there is also a second wave of Kreelan ships inbound. Expect them in..."

The signal suddenly broke off.

Yuri was looking at her with disbelieving eyes. Tearing off her helmet, Coyle looked up at the sky, which was still a witch's brew of smoke and ash from the burning city center. "Give us a *fucking break*, will you?" she yelled at any god or God who might be listening.

"What happened?" Krumholtz asked, following her gaze to the dirty gray smoke overhead.

"They've recalled the carriers and are bringing down the boats to extract us," she told him through gritted teeth, "but we've only got forty goddamn minutes to make it back to the landing zone, which is right fucking where we started from. And as if that weren't bad enough, more Kreelans are on the way." She slammed her helmet against the cupola in frustration, then stuck it back on her head. "Have your people ditch everything they don't need, lieutenant. They've got to be able to move fast. Drop everything: body armor, water, and anything else they won't need to survive for the next forty minutes, except for weapons and ammo. Put out a dozen guys up front who can move fast and be our eyes and ears so my tanks don't get bushwhacked. If there are Kreelans around a corner or sneaking around in buildings, I want to know before they start lobbing those fucking grenades of theirs."

"You won't leave us behind, Coyle, will you?" he asked uncertainly.

She looked at him hard. "You've got to keep up, lieutenant." Then, softening slightly, she said, "Listen, I'd have some of your guys ride on the tanks, but we've got to keep the turrets and engine decks clear when we run into Kreelans. Otherwise we'll either kill your guys with the muzzle blast if we have to fire the main guns, or get killed waiting for you to clear off. Now get going. We don't have a second to waste."

"Garry Owen," he replied as he and his platoon sergeant dashed off, frantically shouting orders at the infantry. Many of them hadn't started the battle as infantry, but if you had your vehicle shot out from under you and you were left on foot with nothing but a rifle, infantry is what you became.

Normally Coyle would have asked the other tank commanders how they were doing on ammunition and taken some time to redistribute as best they could. She was down to ten rounds of main gun ammunition, all of them armor piercing rounds that were totally useless against infantry. Worse, the close-in defense mortar was out of ammo, and she only had a couple thousand rounds for the coaxial gun and her gatling gun: enough for maybe twenty seconds of continuous firing. But there was no time now. None at all.

"Frederickson," she said to one of the other tank commanders, "you'll ride shotgun with me up in the front. Have your tank cover the right side of the road and I'll take the left. Hoyt, Gagarin, you guys bring up the rear. We'll keep the bulk of the infantry between us, and I'll have the lieutenant run out a skirmish line of whoever he's got who can move fast to scout in front of us. For God's sake, don't run over anybody, but don't let the infantry guys slow you down, either. Keep 'em moving. If we fall behind schedule, we're gonna miss the bus, and I don't need to tell you what that means with more of those blue-skinned bitches about to fall out of the sky on us. Questions?" There were none. "Then let's haul ass."

* * *

Steph felt like she was in a surreal nightmare as she struggled to keep up with the tanks. The cavalry troopers had offered to let her ride with Colonel Sparks and Sergeant Hadley in the civilian van they'd picked up along the way, but she'd given up her spot for a trooper whose hip had been sliced open by one of the Kreelan flying weapons. There were others who were wounded, but they had to do their best to keep up. They realized that there was no surrender. So they walked, ran, and shuffled as best they could, troopers who were uninjured helping those who were.

She wasn't in the military, but she had seen the elephant, as the ancient saying went, and it had changed her life forever. Her vidcam was still recording every moment, and she even muttered notes now and again when she came across some new vision of horror. But she clutched her rifle to her shoulder, imitating the more experienced infantry soldiers around her, and watched every window and door on her side of the street. She had even killed a number of Kreelans that the other soldiers had missed: being a journalist had given her a lot of experience in noticing small things that others often didn't see. The infantry squad that she had arbitrarily become attached to had at first looked at her as a burden, but after she blew the first Kreelan out of a window as she rose unseen to throw a grenade, they had shown her more than a little respect.

But she was tired, so tired from what seemed like an endless battle. She was tired of trudging through these cursed streets, littered with abandoned cars, dead civilians, glass and rubble, only to reach a dead end, and then to have to turn around and run-walk back the way they had come. She was in decent physical shape, largely thanks to Ichiro's intense interest in fitness, and had been able to keep up so far. But she was winded from this agonizing running shuffle behind Coyle's armored behemoths, her eyes stinging from the smoke and grimy sweat, her tongue feeling like it was coated with dust. Her shoulders burned from holding the rifle, which was like a lead ingot in her hands, and she was constantly stumbling on rubble or other bits of debris. And bodies. So many bodies.

But she refused to stop. She would *not* stop.

* * *

Li'ara-Zhurah paused to catch her breath. Her body trembled, but not from exhaustion or pain: her heart and muscles fluttered from a sense of pure exhilaration, the likes of which she had never known. Leading a small group of warriors, she was hunting some of the massive human vehicles that were shepherding a group of human warriors through the city. Curiously, the humans had come some distance into what was left of the metropolis, but then had turned around and were retracing their steps.

She had been hunting them since shortly after her earlier encounter with a group of different armored vehicles, the smaller ones with wheels, when Tesh-Dar had gone her own way. The humans had fought bravely, and after their last charge a few had even escaped; Li'ara-Zhurah and her warriors could have hunted them down, but she had let them go so that other warriors might have the honor. She was yet young and sometimes impetuous, but was already wise enough to understand the dignity of sharing the honor of the kill with her sisters.

When that battle was over, Kamal-Utai had gone to rejoin Tesh-Dar on whatever mission the priestess had set for herself, leaving Li'ara-Zhurah to seek out new challenges. She had been drawn to the sound of heavy guns firing in the nearby fringe of the city, and had run toward what was clearly a savage battle, marked in her blood by the joyful chorus of Her Children as they fought and died. Other warriors had the same idea, and it had become a spirited race to see who might first reach the source of the excitement.

Li'ara-Zhurah had been bested by several warriors, but her disappointment at losing the foot race was brief: incautiously rounding a corner, focusing more on winning than surviving long enough to take the fight to the enemy, the warriors disappeared in a bone-shattering deluge of weapons fire from a huge armored vehicle, much larger than those they had faced earlier.

Pitching herself behind a sturdy brick wall, Li'ara-Zhurah waited until the vehicle stopped firing. It paused, as if the humans inside it knew she was there and were waiting for her to show herself. But after a while, with much shouting and noise, the vehicle and its accompanying human warriors moved on.

Once the humans had turned a corner down the street, Li'ara-Zhurah stepped carefully out of her hiding place, and stood dead-still as she looked upon a killing ground the likes of which she had never before seen. Some few hundreds of warriors, Children of the Empress, lay slain in the street, their bodies torn as if by a great *genoth*, a species of monstrous dragon that inhabited the wastelands of the Homeworld. She and the other warriors who had followed her walked gingerly through the remains of the slaughter, their sandals awash in blood. They knelt here and there to honor their sisters, and gave the last rites to the few who were badly injured and claimed death as their just reward. For even as the daggers of their sisters pierced still-beating hearts, those who were given the gift of death could hear the call of the Empress to their souls, beckoning them onward to kneel alongside the Ancient Ones, basking in the eternal light of Her love.

Once they had finished the rites, there was no question of what must be done. Splitting up into hunting packs, they followed the human behemoth and its attending warriors. Li'ara-Zhurah felt no grief or anger at the carnage the humans had wrought upon her sisters. She felt instead a suffusing joy and a burning desire to take the beast, not in revenge, but as a prize. As on the Homeworld in ancient times, when warriors killed the *genoth* and won great glory in Her name, so it would be for the warrior or warriors who defeated such a beast as the one they now pursued. It was a challenge from which only the most courageous and ferocious warrior would emerge victorious.

The large group of warriors that had originally dogged the humans had gradually been whittled down, as those who were too young, inexperienced, or simply unlucky were culled from the pursuing pack. The effect had been similar on the humans,

Li'ara-Zhurah knew: while several more of the great war machines had joined the group of humans, some of them were destroyed, and only the true survivors were left.

While other warriors had earned their honor in destroying some of the machines, none had yet survived the attacks. More important, the beast she herself desired, the one that she had first seen, remained alive. Its commander was cunning and skilled, and her death would be a great victory. The more difficult the situation, the greater the challenge, and all the greater the glory in Her eyes and soul. Li'ara-Zhurah's spirit trembled on the threshold of a type of ecstasy that no human being had ever known.

The greatest challenge was to get close enough to use one of the grenades, although she would have much preferred to use her sword. But even the living metal of her blade was likely not a match for the vehicle's thick armor. So a grenade it would be. She only had one, and would not risk throwing it unless she was sure of her target.

Leading her group of half a dozen warriors down a parallel street, she darted into a building ahead of where the humans were. They were moving faster now, as if they had to get somewhere at a particular time, and Li'ara-Zhurah was growing concerned that her opportunity may not come. She was unafraid of death, but she did not want to sacrifice her body without bringing glory to Her name. For Li'ara-Zhurah, more even than her spiritual sisters, this was paramount, for she was born from Her very womb, a blood daughter of the Empress. She had never met her mother in the flesh since the day she had been born, but she did not need to: she knew the Empress in her heart, in the Bloodsong that filled her spirit.

She had just crept up to a shattered windowsill that allowed her to peer down the street unobserved when another group of warriors began their attack.

* * *

Coyle's ad-hoc task force had just entered a narrower street, trying to get around a glut of refugees that blocked their original path, when all hell broke loose.

"*Grenade!*" someone screamed as a glowing cyan ball arced through the air from an upstairs window of a building. It landed squarely in the middle of the engine deck of Coyle's tank and instantly began to glow white hot.

Before it could explode into a shower of blue lightning, one of the infantry troopers following behind the tank threw down his weapon and climbed up onto the vehicle. Grabbing the grenade, the soldier screamed in agony as it seared his hands, but he somehow managed to pry it off before leaping from the back of the tank. The weapon detonated while he was still in mid-air, incinerating his body in a wild cascade of lightning that scorched everyone and everything in a three meter radius. *Chiquita's* rear armor was blackened and even melted in a few spots, but the tank still survived.

As the soldier's charred body slammed into the ground, several dozen Kreelan warriors surged out of the buildings along the right hand side of the street, tearing into the mass of weary infantry.

While Coyle's soldiers were taken by surprise, they had been through this before and reacted instantly, blasting away at their enemies at point blank range as the Kreelans hurled their lethal throwing weapons and slashed and stabbed with their swords.

Steph was just taking aim at a warrior when she was viciously knocked to the ground. She struggled to turn over, but couldn't: a foot was planted in the middle of her back, pinning her to the ground on top of her rifle. She could turn her head just far enough to see the Kreelan, the blade of her sword glinting in the smoky light as she swung it down to take Steph's head from her neck.

The blade never touched her. The Kreelan's chest disappeared in a spray of crimson as three rounds from *Chiquita's* gatling gun blew her to pieces. With a passionate curse, Steph struggled to her feet through the muck that fell on top of her, all that remained of her would-be killer. She moved to the rear of Coyle's tank, trying to offer it some protection from another grenade attack while the nearby infantrymen grappled with the alien warriors and the gatling guns on the tanks growled.

Without warning one of the tanks in the rear was suddenly lit by a corona of lightning after it was hit by a Kreelan grenade. The crew never had a chance to get out. The vehicle exploded, knocking everyone, human and Kreelan alike, to the ground. The turret flipped up into the air like a toy before crashing down on top of a still-wrestling mob of humans and Kreelans.

Steph could see that the other tank to the rear was also in trouble: it had stopped in the street, just ahead of the one that now lay burning. The hatches suddenly flew open and the crewmen scrambled to escape. All three were cut down by a flurry of Kreelan flying weapons.

"*Keep moving, goddammit!*" Steph heard Coyle screaming above the raging chaos. Indeed, *Chiquita* hadn't stopped or even slowed down, and Steph suddenly turned and ran to catch up, shouting at her surviving squad mates to do the same.

* * *

The gatling gun mounted to the top of the turret had never been designed as a sniper weapon, but Coyle was doing the best she could. The Kreelans had become so closely enmeshed with her own people that she couldn't open fire without shooting her own troopers. She killed the Kreelan who was about to lop the head off the reporter woman, and managed to get a few more, but her tank's power had effectively been neutralized: she couldn't use her more powerful weapons without taking out half of what was left of her scraped-up battalion.

As if the enemy weren't bad enough, the clock was still ticking. Coyle could almost hear it in her brain, counting down the minutes until they would be marooned on this world. They couldn't afford to get bogged down. Missing their extraction would kill them as surely as a blade to the heart.

"*Keep moving, goddammit!*" she screamed at the troops behind her. "Mannie," she told the driver, "don't fucking stop for anything. Keep us moving or we're dead."

"Roger," he said shakily. "Garry Owen," he whispered, as if to himself. Coyle thought he was losing it. And she knew she wasn't far behind him.

Chiquita was leaving most of the troops behind: they were too fixated on trying to keep from being killed by the Kreelans among them to worry about dying if they missed the boats.

Coyle turned on the loudspeakers for her tank again, her voice booming out, "Break contact! Break contact!"

Her order was rewarded by a surge of soldiers trying to break away from the close quarters fight. The ones on the fringes of the mayhem were able to turn and run after Coyle's tank. But for many, there was simply no getting away from the Kreelans without killing them first. Most of the infantry soldiers were running desperately low on ammunition at this point, or were completely out, and the Kreelans had a decided advantage in any close-in combat: their swords were infinitely better than the bayonets and knives wielded by their human opponents, and their claws were as lethal as any edged weapon.

Out of the corner of her eye, Coyle saw another, smaller group of Kreelans break out of the cover of one of the buildings, just behind Frederickson's tank, which was driving alongside her. She twisted her gun around as Frederickson was, but the warriors were too close: she couldn't depress the barrels enough to shoot at them. "Shoot them!" she screamed, pointing, hoping that some of the infantry would take them down.

Instead, she heard a rapid popping sound as Frederickson panicked, ripple firing the last half dozen rounds from his tank's close-in defense mortar as a Kreelan ran up and slapped a glowing grenade on the lower side of his tank, behind the track.

"No you stupid fuck!" Coyle cried as she watched the small grenades arc away from Frederickson's tank. She could tell from the dispersal pattern that he must have tried to target not only the ones now hunting his tank, but the others in the street, as well. That would have been just dandy, Coyle thought bitterly, except that most of their own people were in the blast zone.

"Get down!" she shouted over the loudspeakers as she dropped down into the turret and slammed the hatch. "*Incoming!*"

* * *

Steph was firing her rifle steadily, killing any warriors who stood far enough away from the humans around them for her to feel confident in taking a shot.

Then she heard a strange popping sound. She knew all the weapons the tanks carried from interviewing some of the cavalry soldiers before they landed on Keran, and she had heard the tanks use this one already. It just took a moment to register what weapon it was. *The self-defense mortars*, she thought. It took one more second to realize that they were close-in weapons, and that she was probably in the blast radius and completely in the open.

She heard Coyle shouting something over her tank's speakers, but Steph couldn't hear and didn't care. She slapped the nearest soldiers on the shoulder to get their attention before sprinting up the narrow chasm between the left side of Coyle's tank and the nearest building, putting the tank's bulk between her and the mortar rounds. She tumbled to the ground as the rounds exploded at waist height behind her.

As she was trying to get back up, the tank next to Coyle's exploded.

* * *

The explosion of Frederickson's tank slammed Coyle's head against the inside hatch coaming. Had she not been wearing a helmet, her skull would have been fractured. As it was, she got off with little more than temporary deafness from the blast and a massive headache.

Chiquita's systems didn't even flicker, but that was no consolation to the tank's commander. Coyle bit back her tears and the surge of bile that rose to her throat as she saw the carnage in the street. Frederickson's grenades would have been bad enough, detonating in the midst of the melee to kill Kreelans and humans alike. But the explosion of his tank was worse: the Kreelan who planted the grenade had the uncanny luck to have stuck it right over one of the fuel cells. The resulting explosion blew out the right rear of the vehicle in a spectacular fireball that killed most of those who managed to survive the grenades.

Coyle was glad Frederickson was dead. Had the Kreelan grenade not cooked him inside his tank, she would have killed him herself. But the heart of Coyle's cold, bitter rage was the knowledge that she would now have to leave so many behind: not just the dead, but the wounded and those simply too exhausted to keep up. She simply couldn't protect them, and if they continued at a shuffling pace, they were all going to die.

Her driver had kept the tank moving at a pace that would just barely get them to the extraction zone on time, assuming they didn't hit any major obstacles. But the time for that was over.

As *Chiquita* turned the corner about fifty meters down the street, she said, "Stop the tank, Mannie." She popped the hatch and wearily stood up to face the pitifully few soldiers who had managed to survive and stay with her. Ironically, the civilian van that was packed with wounded, including Colonel Sparks and Sergeant Hadley, was still with her. The Kreelans were completely ignoring it, as if it weren't worthy of being attacked, and it had been just far enough away to avoid major damage from Frederickson's tank when it blew.

Coyle could still hear screaming from behind them, whether just the agony of the wounded, or from terror of more Kreelans, she didn't know. She didn't want to know.

"Get on," she croaked through the loudspeakers to the exhausted infantry catching their breath in the tank's shadow.

For a moment, none of them moved. She was about to repeat herself when the female newshound awkwardly slung her rifle and clambered up the left side and onto the top deck of the hull. Turning around, she gestured to the other soldiers around her to climb on, and did her best to help them up. In a minute or two, the survivors of the 7th Cavalry Regiment had crammed themselves on top of Coyle's tank, holding on to any handy protrusion on the hull and turret, hanging on to each other.

"Whatever you do," Coyle shouted at them, "don't let go. If you fall off, we're not stopping for you." She caught the eye of the reporter, leaning against the turret near Coyle's cupola. The woman nodded, one hand holding onto the turret basket that contained all of the crew's gear and spare parts. Her other hand clutched her rifle.

"Yuri," she said through her helmet intercom to the gunner as she slewed her gatling gun to point behind the tank, just over the heads of the infantry crouching on the engine deck, "watch our front. I'll keep an eye on the rear." Then, to the driver, she said, "Go, Mannie. Go as fast as you can. And don't stop for shit."

"We're just going to leave them?" he said, his voice colored as much with relief as with guilt.

"Do you want to go back there, Mannie?" she whispered into the microphone, hoping the infantry clustered around her wouldn't hear.

But of course, they did. Heads turned away, faces clouded with shame. More than a few cheeks were streaked with tears. They were leaving behind friends and comrades, in some cases lovers. But none of them, not one, wanted to go back. They heard what Coyle said, but pretended not to.

Without another word, Mannie started *Chiquita* moving, the quiet whine of the powerful motors lost in the squeaking and clanking of the battered tracks as the heavy vehicle picked up speed.

The last thing Coyle heard, as plain as if he were standing right beside her, was the voice of Lieutenant Krumholtz, who had been hit in the leg and hadn't been able to keep up. He was among those who were now being left behind.

"Goddamn, you, Coyle!" she heard him scream. "*God damn you!*"

TWENTY-FOUR

Tiernan's attention was fixed on the tactical display. For once, the combined human fleet had a clear tactical advantage, and he and Lefevre were determined to make the most of it. They outnumbered the Kreelan force by roughly two to one in ships and tonnage both, and the admirals planned to force a decisive engagement before the remaining Kreelan ships in high orbit could maneuver to interfere. So far those enemy ships had been content to stay where they were, but Tiernan knew that couldn't last forever.

The disposition of the two fleets also clearly favored the humans: instead of the head-on stone throwing contest they had against the first Kreelan assault force, the human fleet would first pass across the head of the second Kreelan formation as it clawed its way up from low orbit, "crossing the T" in old wet navy terms. The human ships would be able to bring all of their main batteries to bear, while the Kreelans would only be able to target the humans with their forward-facing weapons. After that, the plan was to reverse course behind the Kreelans and take them the same way from behind, raking the vulnerable sterns of the enemy ships. Neither admiral expected the plan to go off as planned, as reality always intervened, but it was a good place to start.

"All ships reporting assigned target lock," the flag communications officer reported.

On the display, the range rings of the *Ticonderoga's* guns converged on her assigned target as the wedges of human ships swept across the front of the Kreelan formation.

"All ships," Tiernan ordered, "fire as you bear!" Without the data-link and the networked targeting computers to optimize the fleet's firing solutions, Tiernan had to count on each ship firing when it came in optimal range as the formations passed by one another.

At the head of the formation, the destroyers loosed a volley of torpedoes, the missiles streaking toward the Kreelan formation, twisting and jinking madly to avoid anti-missile fire. Not waiting to see if any of them hit, the destroyers hauled to the side to get out of the way of the larger cruisers as they began to open fire.

"Incoming," the flag tactical officer announced, warning of rounds from Kreelan guns heading toward them. Then *Ticonderoga's* primary kinetic weapons thundered, sending several dozen projectiles in a closely-spaced pattern at her assigned target, one of the leading Kreelan cruisers. "Ships maneuvering," he added as the individual human ships adjusted their courses to try and avoid the Kreelan weapons fire. It was a difficult balance: the human ships needed to try and avoid the incoming enemy salvoes, but still had to stay in formation to maximize the volume of fire they could bring to bear on the Kreelan ships.

Tiernan gave a death's head grin as the tactical display showed the imbalance of fire between the two fleets: for every Kreelan round fired, at least three rounds were going back at them from his and Lefevre's ships.

Kreelan ships suddenly began to dart and weave, but the weight of fire from the human fleet was too great: even if a Kreelan ship dodged the rounds targeted against it, it almost inevitably ran into another stream of projectiles fired at another target. The first echelon of cruisers in the enemy formation suddenly disintegrated, with half of the warships destroyed outright and the other half either damaged or maneuvering so wildly that they were unable to effectively return fire. A number of other enemy ships also suffered damage, which slowed them down and forced them to change course to avoid the withering fire pouring from the human fleet.

A cheer went up through the *Ticonderoga* from everyone who could see one of the tactical displays, and Tiernan felt a tingle run up his spine and gooseflesh pop up on his arms. *Eat that, damn you*, he thought savagely.

"Continue firing!" he ordered as *Ticonderoga* shuddered from a single hit. Alarms went off on the ship's bridge, but they were quickly silenced.

"Enemy is changing course," the tactical officer warned. The enemy formation had swung to the left and accelerated slightly, trying to close the range with the human fleet and at the same time unmask their aft batteries so they could bring more of their weapons into play against the human ships.

This was the part that Tiernan had been dreading. Without networked tactical control of the ships and the inability to broadcast orders to the entire fleet at once (as opposed to direct laser-links to individual ships), any large-scale maneuvering was impossible without the formation falling apart. If they tried to maneuver and keep the Kreelans at a distance, he knew they could pound them to hell and back. But only if the fleet maintained its integrity. If it lost that, if the individual flotillas that formed the wedges of the formation fell out to be left on their own, they could be destroyed.

"Admiral Lefevre," he said, "I recommend we hold course until the designated maneuver point. If we maintain integrity, we maintain our advantage in weight of fire, even if the enemy closes with us."

"If they get close enough," Lefevre warned, "they will try to attack with boarders."

"Let them try," Tiernan said.

* * *

Waiting in high orbit with the rest of the Kreelan fleet, Amar-Marakh watched as the second assault wave was savaged by the humans. She bowed her head in acknowledgement of the humans' ferocity and basic skills in naval combat. Had this been a true fight for the Empire's survival, she would never have committed ships, even as primitive ones as these, to battle this way. But this was not a life or death duel for the Empire. It was a great Challenge, a contest of wills and warrior spirit that Amar-Marakh knew would last for generations. Even being here, at this first great battle, was an honor that would be marked forever in the Books of Time.

The senior shipmistress of the second wave had been killed in the first volley fired by the human fleet, along with many of her sisters. Most of the ships would likely not survive, but enough would come within range to send forth their warriors to wreak havoc on the human ships in the preferred way. They had dropped most of their warriors on the planet's surface near the surviving human warriors, but still had several thousand in reserve.

She turned her attention to a curiosity that she had noticed a short time before: six large human ships that were far from the main human fleet and sailing directly toward the planet. She could not be sure at this range, but she suspected they were transports sent to retrieve the remaining human warriors on the surface.

Closing her eyes to help her concentrate, she listened more intently to the Bloodsong coursing through her, striving to hear the individual threads of some of those who fought on the surface, particularly that of Tesh-Dar. The great priestess's song was no challenge to find, and Amar-Marakh focused on the melody of fire and blood, seeking to divine her will.

After a moment, she opened her eyes, withdrawing her attention from the raging torrent of emotions that welled up from the warriors on the surface of the planet, mingling with the tidal wave of pain and ecstasy of the second wave now being mauled by the human ships.

The will of the Desh-Ka priestess was clear: the human warriors should not be allowed to leave.

With a few words to her equivalent of a flag tactical officer, Amar-Marakh sent four swift warships, about the size of human destroyers, in pursuit of the ungainly transports.

* * *

"Skipper," Ensign Bogdanova said, motioning toward the tactical display on the *McClaren's* bridge, "those ships..."

"I see them," Sato said, noting her use of the term "skipper." No one had ever used the term with Morrison, because he had never earned the crew's respect, only their fear and loathing. It was a small thing on the surface, only a single word, but it warmed Sato and helped him find the confidence to get beyond his insecurities as the ship's captain-by-default. There was so much he didn't know, so much that could get them killed. But he didn't have a choice. None of them did.

On the display, they watched as four Kreelan ships broke off and headed on what looked like an intercept course for six ships, presumably human, that had jumped in a short while before in two groups, and were now heading toward Keran. It was impossible to tell what they were from the passive sensors, but the emissions signatures from their engines indicated that the ships must be big. The devil of it was that *McClaren* was probably the only ship that could intervene: the raging battle now underway between the human fleet and the second Kreelan assault group had moved on toward the other side of, and farther away from, the planet. It would be a long stretch for any of Admiral Tiernan's ships to reach the six ships - carriers, he guessed - in time to help them.

As for the situation with his own vessel, *McClaren* had managed to sail past the Kreelan formation in high orbit unscathed. While the Kreelans hadn't been maneuvering, their natural movement along the orbital plane had carried them farther away as *McClaren* crept behind them. He had no idea if they simply hadn't noticed, or if they decided that a lone destroyer wasn't worth worrying about. If the latter, he hoped to prove them wrong.

"Helm," he said to Bogdanova, "plot an intercept course at your best speed to bring us up behind those four Kreelan ships. Communications," he said to Petty Officer Third Class Stephen Jaworski, a repair technician who was manning the communications console, "see if you can get a laser-link to one of the newcomers. Let's see who they are."

"I've been trying, sir," he said uncertainly, "but it's hard to get a directional lock for the laser at this range using just the passive sensors." He continued to peer at his instruments, and after several more moments exclaimed, "Got it! The signature on the laser says it's *Guadalcanal*, sir. Hard link established. But only voice right now. The link's really weak."

"*Guadalcanal*," Sato said immediately, "this is the destroyer *McClaren*. You've got four Kreelan ships headed your way. We are in pursuit."

"*McClaren*," a voice responded, badly distorted, "understood. We see them."

"Do you have an update on the situation?" Sato asked. "We've been out of communications for quite a while."

"The fleet is engaged with a smaller Kreelan force now. But the ground troops have taken extremely heavy casualties. We've been ordered to extract the survivors, but it's going to be hellishly tight. The boats are already away to the extraction zones. We've got a single orbit to pick them up, then we've got orders to pull out."

The news struck Sato in the gut. *Steph*, he thought. "Do you have any details on the ground forces?" he asked, not sure he wanted to hear the answer.

"*Ticonderoga* reported that they lost contact with General Ray soon after the first assault wave hit the planet," *Guadalcanal's* captain replied. "A diplomatic courier was able to make contact with a number of units on the ground, but nothing higher than company level. They think they can lift out the survivors, ours and the Alliance troops, with our carriers and the two that the French have. Assuming those Kreelan ships don't get us first."

Sato exchanged looks with the others around the bridge. If what *Guadalcanal* said was true, they had collectively lost the equivalent of nine out of twelve divisions, maybe more.

"They won't," Sato promised. "Bring them home. We'll cover you."

"Roger, *McClaren*. Good hunting. *Guadalcanal*, out."

In the tactical display, *McClaren* was cutting across space toward the four red circles representing the enemy ships pursuing the carriers, but he began to doubt they'd be able to engage them in time. They needed to close the range faster, and get the enemy's attention, maybe drawing one or more of them off the pursuit. The carriers had defensive weapons roughly equivalent to a destroyer, but were far larger and less maneuverable. The two French carriers were forming up with *Guadalcanal* and her sisters. They might be able to defend themselves from two, maybe three of the Kreelan ships, but not all four. "Bogdanova," he said, "all ahead flank. Bring our sensors to active status. Let's let the enemy know we're here."

* * *

Just like the warriors on the ground, the Kreelan ships refused to yield. Outnumbered, outgunned, and facing an opponent who held all the cards, Tiernan thought, they still came on.

Half a dozen ships in the human fleet had been destroyed thus far, and another two dozen damaged. It was a heavy price to pay, but Tiernan believed they had gotten a good deal on the butcher's bill: fully half of the Kreelan ships had been destroyed, and all the rest had been damaged.

But the human fleet wasn't out of the woods yet: the Kreelan ships were sailing straight into the human fleet's formation, with ranges so close now that his cruisers could no longer fire their primary kinetic weapons without fear of damage to themselves when the rounds hit the enemy ships. And some of his ships had to maneuver out of the way of Kreelans that were clearly trying to ram.

The Kreelan ships didn't seem to care: they continued to fire their kinetics with total abandon, and both sides slashed at each other with heavy lasers. The beams of coherent light vaporized armor and hull plating, venting the crew spaces beyond to vacuum, or seared off sensor arrays or engine mounts, sometimes sending a ship into an uncontrolled tumble.

"Sir!" the flag tactical officer called. "Multiple new contacts, hundreds, across the sector. Designating as probable boarding parties."

"All ships," Tiernan ordered, "prepare to repel boarders!"

On the vidcom display, Admiral Lefevre aboard the *Jean Bart* pressed his lips into a thin line. Outside of the view of the camera, his hands clenched so tightly the knuckles bled white.

Tiernan had hoped that his own ships would bear the brunt of any boarding attacks, but the reality of the battle had determined otherwise. The cloud of targets, which had by now grown to several thousand tiny icons on the tactical display, blowing through his formation like dandelion seeds, was dispersed along the port side of the fleet. Many of the Alliance ships would again be on the receiving end of boarding attacks, although they had new weapons on board that would help even the odds: Terran Marines.

"Have the First Destroyer Flotilla redeploy here," he told the flag tactical officer, drawing a line on the tactical display along the flank of the Alliance warships that were in the heaviest part of the cloud of targets, "to give the Alliance ships some close-in protection."

Nodding, the tactical officer relayed the order to the communications officer, who ensured that the orders got to the commander of the destroyer flotilla.

Less than thirty seconds later, six Terran Fleet destroyers wove quickly through the formation to take up station between the Alliance cruisers and the rapidly approaching cloud of attackers.

"Engage," Tiernan ordered quietly.

Every Terran ship had been fitted with a set of weapons that were not dissimilar from the close-in defense weapons fitted to the Wolfhound tanks. They were large-bore mortars with a short barrel that could be aimed like most other shipboard weapons, and fired an explosive shell filled with thousands of needle-like flechettes. The mortars had a short range, but they were simple, reliable, and devastating against space suits, armored or not.

"Firing mortars," the tactical officer reported.

Seconds later, the crews of the Terran fleet began to hear a very distinct *crump* echo through the hulls of their ships as the mortars began to fire at the incoming clouds of Kreelan warriors.

* * *

Amar-Marakh, the senior shipmistress of the Kreelan fleet, gasped at the sudden turmoil in the Bloodsong as hundreds of warriors were wiped away, almost in an instant. The anticipation in the thread of the melodies sung by the warriors trying to board the human ships changed to shock and then fierce rage.

A challenge, even a great one, the pursuit of which would almost certainly lead to death, was to be sought to bring glory to the Empress. But to have the warriors slaughtered in such a fashion as this was not a challenge; it was a waste of precious blood. That, she could not tolerate.

"Deploy the fleet," she ordered tersely to her First. "We attack."

* * *

"Admiral," the tactical officer warned, "the Kreelan force in high orbit is moving."

Tiernan glanced up at the display, seeing the red icons of the other Kreelan ships heading on a course that would no doubt lead them into the fray. "Dammit," he cursed.

"It was inevitable, *amiral*," Lefevre told him from the vidcom. "We will only have a few minutes until we must break contact with our current opponents to try and regroup."

"*If* we can break contact, sir," Tiernan said as *Ticonderoga* rocked from another hit. "I think we're going to have to kill every last ship in this formation. They're not going to break contact, and we can't put our sterns to them and let them shoot us in the fantail."

"Then let us destroy them with all haste," Lefevre told him. "Engage with kinetics, danger close, *amiral*."

"Aye, aye, sir," Tiernan replied. Then, turning to his flag officer, "Pass the word: all ships are to engage with everything they have, including primary kinetics. Danger close. We *must* finish off these enemy ships!"

Less than one minute after Lefevre had given the order, every gun in the human fleet opened up on the two dozen remaining Kreelan warships. Four human ships died when their targets, only a few hundred meters away, exploded, taking the human ships with them.

But ten minutes after the order had been given, ten minutes that seemed like an eternal orgy of heavy weapons fire to the crews, every Kreelan ship of the second assault wave had been reduced to a blasted hulk.

The human fleet swept onward, mortar rounds continuing to blast the warriors who still were desperately trying to board the fleeing ships. But the efforts of the Kreelans were in vain: not a single warrior made it through the devastating fire from the defense mortars.

The Marines aboard the ships, who had been anticipating their first chance to prove themselves, were terribly disappointed.

TWENTY-FIVE

Pursuing the huge metal *genoth*, the human vehicle that was in her mind akin to one of the great dragons that prowled the wastelands of the Homeworld, Li'ara-Zhurah had never run as quickly in her life. She was on the ragged edge of exhaustion, as were the four warriors who had accompanied her on this great hunt. But she ignored the leaden pain in her legs and the burning in her lungs, the frantic beating of her heart. That beast was her prize, and she would not be denied it.

After the earlier attack by a different group of warriors that she had watched, with dozens of them wading into the human warriors and their armored escorts, only the single vehicle, the one she wanted so badly, had escaped, its hull crowded with the human warriors who had managed to survive the devastating battle.

But then the machine had fled at great speed, the massive tracks bearing it over the mounds of rubble, small passenger vehicles, and bodies alike. It slowed down only when it was forced to make a turn, and the only time it turned was when a street ended or was choked with unarmed humans that were still streaming out of the devastated city.

Wishing that she had powers beyond imagining as did the great priestess, Tesh-Dar, or even a simple vehicle, Li'ara-Zhurah did the best she could with the natural powers of the body the Empress had given her by birth: she ran. She gave up trying to run a parallel course to the vehicle for fear of losing it should it make a turn along the way. Instead, she simply ran at what she considered a safe distance behind it, "safe" being a relative term. Several times the human warrior whose head poked out of the turret had fired at her with the devastating weapon mounted on top of the vehicle. Some of the humans riding along had also fired at her. But the vehicle was moving so quickly over so much debris that their aim was poor.

A few of the humans on top of the vehicle had fallen off in the course of the pursuit, but the vehicle did not slow down. Li'ara-Zhurah had not expected it to, for Her Children would not have done so in battle. She simply ignored the abandoned humans, leaving the other warriors to tend to them with their blades.

Li'ara-Zhurah shut out the complaints of her body by focusing on the vision of thrusting her blade through the heart of the human female who commanded the vehicle.

* * *

Coyle kept a wary eye on the small group of Kreelans who were hunting her tank. Her gut churned at their single-minded intensity, particularly that of the leader. She had tried to blast them to bits, of course, but after the first few shots had given up: even with her gatling gun's gyro-stabilization giving her a rock-solid sight picture, the Kreelans seemed to almost anticipate Coyle's shots, dodging out of the way. And with as little ammunition as she had left, she couldn't afford to waste it.

The infantry had taken pot shots at their pursuers, but with no more effect. Coyle had ordered them to conserve their ammunition.

"How much longer?" the reporter, Steph something-or-other, asked.

"About five minutes to reach the LZ," Coyle told her, checking her map display for the location of the landing zone, or LZ. "Then about five minutes more until the boats are supposed to land."

"What about all the Kreelans who were there before we left?" Steph asked.

Coyle shrugged. "Hope they went somewhere else. If we can't secure the drop zone, the boats aren't gonna land."

A few minutes later, *Chiquita* passed by the original hide positions used by Coyle's platoon. Then they passed by the last buildings on the outskirts of the city, heading toward the positions originally occupied by the Alliance Legion's 1st Cavalry Regiment, the *1er REC*.

"Jesus," Coyle whispered as *Chiquita* slowed to a halt.

Ahead of them were about a hundred men, legionnaires, who were the only living people as far as she could see. From her vantage point on top of the tank, she could see the positions that had been occupied by the wheeled tanks of the *1er REC*, as well as those next to it that had been dug out for the paratroopers, the *2ème REP*. It was a charnel house, with at least a couple thousand human and Kreelan bodies strewn about, along with the burned-out hulks of the armored regiment's tanks and other vehicles. The smoke from the wrecks wafted away over the nearby forest to join the greater black cloud streaming from the devastated city.

The legionnaires were sitting or laying down, clearly exhausted. One of them, a big man who looked like he'd been on the losing end of a fight with a bulldozer, rose unsteadily to his feet and staggered toward *Chiquita*.

Coyle tried to get out of the turret to go meet him, but suddenly just...couldn't. Her legs, her body, wouldn't respond. "Oh, fuck," she said as she leaned forward and vomited. Nothing came up, as she hadn't had anything to eat or drink for hours. She had been running on adrenaline and fear alone.

She felt a comforting hand on her shoulder, then someone hugging her.

"It's okay," she heard the reporter, Steph, say softly.

After the heaves passed, Steph and one of the other soldiers helped Coyle from the cupola, and she made her way through *Chiquita's* human passengers, finally reaching the ground on shaky legs. Despite the lack of any Kreelan warriors, even the ones who had been pursuing them out of the city, none of the infantry wanted to leave the perceived safety of the tank's menacing bulk.

Coyle tried not to sway too much as she walked to meet the approaching legionnaire. "*Bonjour*," she said, using the only word she knew in French that wouldn't start a bar fight. "Staff Sergeant Patty Coyle, 7th Cavalry Regiment."

The man offered her a smile through his battered face, and extended a paw that was equally mauled, with raw, broken knuckles and at least a couple of broken fingers. His grip, though, was still strong, and he didn't even wince when she applied gentle pressure, not wanting to appear to be a wimpy female to him.

"Happy to see you, Sergeant Coyle," he said in an accent she recognized as British, although he had a bit of a lisp from several missing teeth. He sounded far too perky for someone in his condition, particularly in contrast to the exhausted men around him. Then she realized that he was probably so high on painkillers and other drugs that she could have hit his foot with a sledge hammer and he'd only ask her for more.

"She's a brevet captain," Steph corrected him from where she stood behind Coyle.

The legionnaire raised his eyebrows, or would have if his face had not been so swollen. "Outstanding!" he said, saluting. "*Soldat 1e Classe* Roland Mills and the remainder of the *Légion étrangère* - well, two regiments of it, in any case - at your service. If you might like to meet our commanding officer?"

Coyle returned the salute, then turned around to give Steph her best evil eye. The reporter shrugged unapologetically before following Coyle, uninvited, after Mills.

When they reached the small circle of legionnaires clustered around one who was lying on the ground, Coyle bit back more bile. Both of the man's legs were badly burned, as was his left arm.

"*Mon colonel*," Mills said, "this is brevet Captain Coyle of..." Mills turned to her, leaving the rest of the sentence hanging.

"Of the 7th Cavalry Regiment," Coyle said. "Our commander, Colonel Sparks, is still alive, but very badly injured."

"A common theme among the officers, it would seem," the man on the ground said, a humorless smile touching his lips. "I am *Lieutenant-Colonel* Grishin, commander of the *1er REC*. I am glad your colonel survived. A most interesting man." Peering up at Steph, he added, "And I see the lovely Miss Guillaume survived thus far, as well. I am happy this is so."

"Thank you, sir," Steph replied, not sure what else to say. So many others, trained to be soldiers, had died, and yet she had somehow survived. It didn't make any sense. Then again, this entire war didn't make any sense.

"Our colonel's in very bad shape, sir," Coyle said. "He was run through with a sword and has severe internal injuries. I just hope he can make it back to the fleet." She looked to the sky. "There are boats coming in to pick all of us up, your people, as well. They should be here very soon if they stayed on schedule."

Grishin frowned, almost as if he were disappointed. "We did not know. I had thought this would be our Camarón."

Coyle had no idea who or what Camarón was, but from his tone of voice it sounded like it was the Legion's equivalent of the Little Bighorn for the 7th Cav.

Before she could say anything else, Grishin asked her, "Coyle, I am placing you in command of my men. We have no officers remaining, and I am in no shape to command. Will you do that?"

She looked at the weary hard-faced men around her, then up at Mills, who nodded slightly. "Yes, sir. If they're willing to follow my orders."

"They will," he said with a hint of a smile. "They have not followed the orders of a woman before, but with you commanding the only functional armored vehicle here, they can hardly argue, yes? And Mills will make sure they do not misbehave."

The big legionnaire nodded gravely. Coyle noticed that the other men regarded him with obvious awe. He was an impressive-looking man who had clearly managed to take a savage beating and survived to tell about it, but the expressions on the faces of the others said that there was more to the story. She'd have to find out about it later, assuming any of them survived.

"Then we should get into defensive positions," Coyle said. "All your men are clustered in one spot."

"We have no need," one of the other legionnaires said pointedly through a heavy German accent. "We are safe."

"What do you mean?" Steph said hotly. "Nobody's safe here."

The legionnaire pointed to Mills. "He fought one of the aliens, a huge one. She let us go. The aliens went away, let us live."

"It's true," Mills said. "I know it sounds absurd, but that's what happened. They were slaughtering us, then this giant of a female warrior came and tagged me for a bit of fun." He gestured at his face. "I guess I entertained her well enough. Then after beating me into the bloody ground, she and all her vixen friends trotted off somewhere else. They didn't give us a second thought after that."

"Well, you may be safe," Coyle said, not sure she could buy a story like that, "but we sure as hell aren't. We've been hounded from the start, and there was a group of warriors hunting us all the way out of the city. They disappeared, but I can't believe they followed us all that way to just give up right at the end." She glanced worriedly behind her, noting with some relief that Yuri, as tired as he was, had the foresight to turn the turret around and was constantly scanning the approaches to their position. The infantry on the rear deck had hopped, and in some cases simply tumbled, to the ground as the main gun swept back and forth. "I don't think they're just going to let us walk away when the boats get here."

That's when she heard a sound like thunder: sonic booms from the boats as they made their approach.

"It's about fucking time," she whispered, relief suddenly flooding through her. *We can do this,* she told herself. *Just a few minutes.*

"Coyle," one of the infantrymen called to her. She turned and looked where he was pointing. More uniformed figures were coming down the road, running, shuffling, and staggering. There were hundreds of them. As they got closer, she could see that it was a mix of men and women from the rest of her parent 31st Armored

Division and a sprinkling of Alliance troops. No vehicles. But maybe there would be a real officer who could take charge of this fuckup.

As it turned out, there was. One of the company commanders from a different brigade, someone she had never met before, was the ranking officer. After she briefly explained what she knew, he did exactly what she should have figured would happen: he officially put her in charge of securing the perimeter, using her tank and "her" infantry. In the meantime, he began to organize the rest of the survivors into groups to get onto the boats, and completely ignored the legionnaires.

Coyle had seen that most of the new arrivals had thrown down their weapons after they'd run out of ammunition, so they weren't even armed. She tried to get at least some of them to run over and grab weapons from the dead Legion paratroopers, but they refused. The captain ordered her to attend to her duties, although in not very polite terms.

Disgusted to the point she was sure she would shoot the man, she ordered the survivors of the 7th Cavalry to gather weapons and ammunition. And like the professionals they were, they obeyed. But if looks could kill, the nameless captain would have died a hundred deaths.

As the cavalrymen trotted toward the paratroopers' former positions to hunt for weapons, Mills said to his comrades, "Once the boats get here, our blue lady friends will be back, and the honeymoon, lads, will be over." Then, with a nod to Coyle, he led them after the Terran troops to pick up more ammunition for their own weapons. He had no illusions that their survival to this point had been anything more than a stay of execution, and thought the Terran captain was an incredibly ignorant ass for not making sure everyone was armed before the boats arrived.

Coyle was willing to put up with the garbage the captain from the other brigade had dished out to that point, but when he tried to move Sparks, Hadley, and the regiment's other injured soldiers out of the battered civilian van that had carried them out of Foshan and arrange them in the group with the other survivors of his own brigade, she rebelled.

"I am *ordering* you to get your colonel and the other wounded in the first boat," the captain told her. He had been forced to come over and deal with the situation directly after Coyle and the other 7th Cav troopers who hadn't gone with Mills had faced off against the enlisted men the captain had sent over to take Colonel Sparks and the others away.

"Excuse me, *sir*," she told the captain icily from her cupola, "but my colonel stays with his regiment. We'll load him and our other wounded when it's our turn to board. Whenever that may be."

"Are you disobeying a direct order, soldier?" the officer said, his soot-covered face reddening with anger.

Looking down on him from the height of the tank's turret, Coyle thought tiredly, *What a jackass.* "Yes, sir, I am. With all due respect."

"Sergeant!" the captain snapped to the senior NCO of the gaggle of soldiers he'd brought over to take the wounded and deal with any insubordination. "Place this woman under arrest and escort her to the boat."

"Yes, sir," the sergeant said, saluting smartly, a grin on his face.

The grin vanished as he turned and found himself staring down the muzzles of a dozen assault rifles. Looking up, he saw that Coyle's gatling gun was pointed straight at him.

"This is mutiny," the captain breathed. "Sergeant, take her!"

"Sir," the NCO said quietly, staring at the tense 7th Cav troopers, "we don't have any weapons. You ordered us to ditch them all when we ran out of the city."

The captain, his face turning a deep purple, turned back to Coyle. "I'll have you shot for this, soldier," he grated.

"You know, captain," she told him, "that would probably be a relief for me right now." Her finger was shaking over the controls of the gatling gun. Part of her really wanted to shoot him, just for being such a prick. But another part didn't want to waste the ammunition, because she knew they'd need it. Soon. "But I think it'd just be best if you and your crunchies just left us alone so we can save your asses when the Kreelans come after us. *Sir.*"

Without another word, the captain turned and stalked off, shouting orders at his troops, taking out his frustrations on them.

Meanwhile, the cavalry troopers and legionnaires worked quickly to pick up weapons and enough ammunition to try and defend the LZ. When they were finished, Coyle had about a hundred and twenty troops altogether, about the size of an infantry company. The survivors of the equivalent of two combat brigades.

Without bothering to consult the captain, she had her NCOs break the group down into ad-hoc squads that took up positions around the LZ, facing in the direction of the smoldering city.

"I wish we had more ammo," Yuri lamented as he redistributed the rounds between the tank's coaxial gun and Coyle's gatling gun, giving her most of it. "We're going to be nothing but a pissed-off pillbox pretty soon." They hadn't fired any more rounds from the main gun, so they still had ten left in the magazine. But the anti-tank rounds were useless for killing anything but other armored vehicles.

"We'll do what we can," she said, hearing the roar of the boats as they came in. She couldn't see them yet, as they were making a low approach over the forest behind them, trying to stay masked by the terrain as long as possible.

"There they are!" someone shouted, and everyone stood up and whooped with joy as the dark gray Navy assault boats came in to land in the open area in the rear of the position originally occupied by the *1er REC*.

Steph snorted. "We don't have enough people to fill up one of them," she said. "Why'd they send two?"

"Without comms," Coyle told her, shouting now over the deafening scream of the boats' engines, "they wouldn't have any idea how many survivors there might be. Better there's too much room than too little."

Steph nodded, shielding her eyes from the dust kicked up by the big assault boats. "Boat" was perhaps a misnomer, as the vessels now settling down on their massive landing struts massed roughly two thousand tons and were over half as long as a football field. Each could carry a full company of Wolfhound tanks or an entire battalion of mechanized infantry. Despite their size, they carried no armor or weapons, sacrificing those traits for more lift capacity.

As the ships settled low to the ground, the boats' engines throttled back to a muted howl. The main rear ramps began to descend and the side personnel doors opened, with ladders sliding from the hull to drop to the ground. The loadmasters came out to help get everyone aboard.

"Coyle!" she heard Yuri shout from the top of the turret. She turned and saw him pointing in the direction of the city.

As if they had simply appeared out of nowhere, hundreds of Kreelan warriors stood on the slight rise, just over a hundred meters away, between the landing zone and the outer edge of Foshan. In the center stood a huge warrior, her body and face an odd maroon color.

It took Coyle a moment to realize that it was blood. Human blood.

"*Open fire!*" she screamed as the shock of adrenaline once more hit her system and she bolted for *Chiquita*.

The infantry nearest to her, the only ones who had been able to hear her order, began to fire.

With the first shot the Kreelans, all but the huge warrior and two others, charged.

* * *

Tesh-Dar held back Li'ara-Zhurah and Kamai-Utal from the massed attack, not to deny them glory, but to have them learn and, in Li'ara-Zhurah's case, to rest for a moment. The young warrior had given glory enough to the Empress simply in the passion of her pursuit of the human machine and its wily crew, and the great priestess would not see her blood spent here. Not yet. The charging warriors knew that the vehicle was to be left to Li'ara-Zhurah, and they ignored it, concentrating on the other humans.

Seeing some of the humans she had let live after her own small Challenge earlier with the solitary human, she felt a surge of relief: they were fighting back. Tesh-Dar had not intended it this way, but she would have been bitterly disappointed had they used her earlier magnanimity as an excuse to simply watch as their fellow animals were butchered, thinking themselves safe. Had they done so, they all would have died by her own hand.

As it was, she reconsidered her original plan to not let any of the humans go. Her thoughts were driven not by pity, for she felt none, but by the knowledge that some of them had proven such worthy adversaries that they might be used another day to bring glory to the Empress. It was a small enough sacrifice for Tesh-Dar to make.

She watched the line of her warriors surging forward toward the humans, and made her decision: if any of the humans were able to fend off her warriors and make their escape in these ships, she would allow them to leave the surface. From there, fate would have to favor them.

One of the humans, however, she would not allow to leave: the one who commanded the armored vehicle. That one's life belonged to Li'ara-Zhurah.

The warriors howled past the great vehicle to attack the humans who sought to leave without first offering battle.

* * *

Yuri had dropped back down in the turret after alerting Coyle and was firing nonstop at the rapidly approaching mass of howling alien warriors.

"Where the fuck did they come from?" Coyle asked frantically as she trained the gatling gun around to fire at the enemy.

"I don't know!" he said, pausing momentarily as he swiveled the turret slightly to try and keep up with the Kreelan line. He'd fired hundreds of rounds already, but the damned warriors seemed a lot more nimble than before, half of them dodging out of his line of fire at the last instant. "It's like they bloody stood up right out of the ground!"

Coyle squeezed the trigger for the gatling gun, sending a spray of twenty millimeter rounds through a section of the Kreelan line. Half a dozen of them were cut down: it wasn't easy to avoid being hit by a weapon that fired a hundred rounds per second.

"Shit!" Yuri shouted. "They're too close! I can't hit them!"

The Kreelans swarmed past her tank and the defensive positions of the infantry, ignoring them completely as they headed straight toward the first assault boat.

"Jesus, they're going right for the first boat!" Coyle cried as she spun the gatling gun around. She watched in horror as the wave of Kreelans reached the ship. The loadmasters had gotten everyone aboard and had closed the side personnel doors. Now they were frantically trying to bring up the rear ramp, which took nearly twenty seconds to close.

It was halfway shut when the Kreelans got there, and Coyle watched in horrified wonder as the lead warriors suddenly turned into acrobats, with a pair of warriors instantly stooping down to act as a jumping platform for a third. They did it smoothly, as if they practiced such a move all the time. Several groups did this, and half a dozen warriors were vaulted over the top of the closing ramp to disappear inside.

Other warriors, again propelled by their sisters, tried to climb up the hull, using their talons to gain purchase in the metal. All of them failed except for one, a smaller warrior who steadily climbed all the way to the cockpit window and began to batter away at the clearsteel with a long dagger. Coyle had no idea if she'd be able to get through, but she wouldn't have traded positions with the pilots for anything. She'd already had more than her fair share of close encounters.

Around her the legionnaires and infantry from her regiment fired at the enemy, but many of them were now on the far side of the assault boat, protected by its hull.

Coyle decided that there was no point in just sticking around. She felt sorry for the poor slobs in the first boat who were no doubt being cut to ribbons, since most of the fools had no weapons, but she'd take whatever advantage she could. "*Run for it!*" she screamed over the loudspeakers. "Get to the other boat! Mannie, move toward the boat, but don't run anybody over!"

The squads of her ad-hoc command leaped from their positions and dashed for the second boat, which had already closed the rear ramp and was spooling up its engines. The loadmasters were closing the personnel doors, the ladder already retracting from the ground.

"Don't leave us, you fuckers!" Coyle shouted at them as she blasted a few more Kreelans with her gatling gun. In her mind she could hear Lieutenant Krumholtz's voice, begging the same of her. She brutally shoved the thought to the back of her mind.

Suddenly Mills was at the boat. The big legionnaire jumped up and caught the bottom rung of the ladder as it retracted, then managed to reach up and grab the loadmaster's ankle as the ladder slid into the hull. The loadmaster tried to shake him off until another legionnaire leaped up and grabbed onto Mills' legs, their combined weight pulling the loadmaster halfway out of the boat.

"Take us right up to the hatch, Mannie!" Coyle ordered her driver.

"Shit, look!" Yuri cried.

The other boat, carrying the bastard captain and his gaggle of survivors, was taking off, but only made it a few meters into the air before it began to wobble. The Kreelans on the ground surrounding it ran toward the forest, trying to avoid the heat of the hover engines. Coyle thought for a moment that the pilots were maneuvering intentionally to kill the enemy, until the boat yawed drunkenly and she could see the small cockpit above the forward clamshell doors. The Kreelan who had been there had fallen off, but the inside of the windshield was spattered with blood. Then one of the personnel hatches opened and people started flinging themselves out. The boat wasn't very high yet, but it was certainly high enough that jumping wasn't an option. The bodies hit the unyielding ground and lay still.

The boat hit the trees and paused for just a moment, almost as if it might gently rebound to drift back over the LZ. Then it suddenly tipped over and crashed to the ground, its lift and drive engines still roaring, setting the forest on fire.

Mannie swiveled *Chiquita* around and brought her rear engine deck right under the personnel hatch of the second boat where Mills and the other legionnaire still dangled. The legionnaire released his grip and rolled to the ground, dashing out of the tank's way, as Mills flailed his feet, finally gaining purchase on the vehicle's rear deck. Then he hauled the loadmaster out of the boat and hammered him once in the face with an already bloodied fist. The man crumpled to the hot armor plate, holding both hands to his face to stem the blood from his shattered nose before Mills grabbed him by the scruff of the neck and tossed him off the tank. Then Mills ordered two other legionnaires, weapons at the ready, up into the boat.

Coyle couldn't hear what he said to them over the growing roar of the boat's lift engines: the pilots were trying to take off, the loadmaster and the rest of them be damned. She could see it start to rise, the landing struts extending as the boat's lift engines went to full power.

Suddenly the boat stopped going up, then settled back down. Coyle looked at Mills, who grinned and put his index finger to his temple, his thumb raised in the air to mime a pistol.

"Get aboard!" she shouted through the loudspeakers at the others, who were now clustered around *Chiquita*.

The first ones up were the two injured colonels, who were handed up as carefully as was possible in such a ludicrous situation, followed quickly by the rest of the injured.

Mills kept order on the back deck of the tank when it came time for everyone else to board the boat, making sure nobody pushed or shoved to try and get aboard ahead of someone else. The couple who tried that were tossed off the tank to wait their turn at the end of the line.

"Mannie, Yuri," she said, "up and out. Get in the boat!"

"We're not leaving you," Yuri said stubbornly. Mannie said nothing, but he didn't open his hatch to get out.

"Goddammit, get out of the tank!" she yelled at them. "You can't do anything else here."

"Fuck off, Coyle," Yuri told her, turning around as she dropped back into the turret. Looking her in the eyes, he told her, "We've come this far together. When you're ready to leave, we'll go with you. Not before."

She didn't know whether to punch him or kiss him. In the end she settled for saying, "You're both dumb fucks, you know that? But I'm glad you're here."

Looking back out the cupola, she saw that Mills had almost everyone aboard and was gesturing at her to come. "Okay, you idiots, I think it's our turn to get on the bus. Let's-"

Suddenly the huge warrior was simply *there*, right on the tank's engine deck next to Mills, right in front of the open hatch to the assault boat.

His eyes wide with disbelief, Mills lunged at her, trying to knock her off the tank. She did something - Coyle wasn't sure what, because it happened so fast her eyes couldn't follow it - and Mills was down on the deck, lying very still.

"No!" Coyle screamed, as a legionnaire standing in the boat's hatchway fired a full magazine from his rifle into the alien apparition. The rounds simply passed through her to ricochet off the tank's armor.

Baring her fangs, the alien reached up with one arm and plucked the legionnaire who had fired on her from the boat, sinking her talons into his chest before hurling his body to the ground. Then she did something even more unexpected: she picked up Mills like a huge rag doll and handed him up to the disbelieving soldiers crowded into the hatchway.

Coyle didn't want to believe that she had seen the legionnaire's bullets pass right through the big warrior, and was tempted to try and blow her away with the gatling gun. But she would've hit the boat, and that wouldn't do. Not after all this.

The warrior stood there, looking at her, then pointed past the front of the tank. A lone warrior stood there, waiting. Coyle recognized her as the leader of the group that had been hunting *Chiquita* during the regiment's escape from the city.

With a sinking feeling, Coyle suddenly understood. "Yuri, Mannie," she said in a brittle voice, "get out of the tank and get on the boat. Now."

"But-"

"*Now*, boys," she told them. "There's no more time." With that, she took her helmet off and dropped it on the ground beside the tank. She wouldn't need it anymore.

Yuri and Mannie opened their hatches uncertainly, then climbed out on top of the tank. Seeing the hulking warrior at the rear, next to the hatch to the boat, they stopped.

"It's okay," Coyle shouted. "Ignore her. Get in the damned boat."

"What about you?"

"Don't worry about me. I'll be fine," she lied.

She almost had a good laugh at the looks on their faces as they sidestepped past the warrior, who studiously ignored them, her interest focused only on Coyle.

"Goodbye, guys," she whispered into the roar of the boat's idling lift engines as her crew climbed into the boat. Mills looked out at her from the hatch, and she nodded to him. She hadn't believed his tale before, about dueling with the big warrior, but she did now. He nodded back, his face grim, before he hit the button to close the hatch.

The last face she saw as the hatch slid shut was that of the reporter woman, Steph, whose cheeks were wet with tears. Coyle raised her hand in farewell.

With a sigh of resignation, she climbed down from the tank as the boat's lift engines spooled up again, sending up a storm of dust and debris. After a few seconds the landing struts parted company with the ground, and the ship began to climb quickly. She watched it go, flying low over the burning forest in the direction it had come. The pilots weren't taking any chances against Kreelan air defense weapons. *Good luck*, she thought.

Then she turned to face the warrior who apparently wanted her head for a prize. It was a small enough price to pay for the safety of the others, Coyle thought.

As the big warrior looked on, Coyle's opponent approached and handed Coyle a sword. Coyle looked at it, having to admire the beauty of the craftsmanship and thinking that the Kreelans could get rich by making jewelry if they could only get over their urge to kill everyone in sight.

With a shrug, she held the sword up in a salute, whipping it up so the grip was a hand's breadth from her chin, the sword's tip high in the air, then lowering it to her right side, pointing it off at a forty-five degree angle at the ground. It was parade-ground perfect, and she knew that Colonel Sparks would have been proud.

Holding the sword at the ready, her attention focused on the Kreelan as the warrior moved forward into the attack, Coyle never felt the ten centimeter-long sliver of hull plating that killed her as the first assault boat finally exploded, scouring the landing zone with flame and metal debris.

TWENTY-SIX

"We're in range, sir," Bogdanova said as the tactical display showed the range ring for the pulse cannon intersect the Kreelan ships that were gaining on the Terran and Alliance carriers.

"Chief," Sato called to Chief DeFusco in engineering, "I'm going to bring up the pulse cannon."

"Go ahead, skipper," she said. "The damn thing should fire. The only thing I'm really worried about is the structural damage we've taken. Running the ship at flank speed is starting to stress what's left of the keel ahead of the forward engineering spaces. I've checked the alignment of the central conduit where the pulse cannon is mounted, and it looks okay for now. But I can't guarantee that it'll hold when we start maneuvering."

"I'll keep it in mind, chief," Sato told her. Then, to the rest of the bridge crew, "Stand by to engage." They were trailing the enemy ships now, slowly gaining on them as they closed with the carriers. *It's going to be close*, Sato knew. With no one available to man the tactical station, he had to take care of the weapons himself. "Pulse cannon, target, designate," he announced. Aligning the targeting pipper of the pulse cannon with one of the enemy ships, the *McClaren* turned slightly to starboard. Unlike the ill-fated Captain Morrison, Sato waited until the ship had steadied and the targeting computer confirmed a hard target lock and that the ship was slaved to the targeting computer. "Firing."

As when Morrison had fired, the ship thrummed as the energy buffers dumped their stored power into the pulse cannon, drawing on every non-critical system in the ship to feed the hungry weapon. The lights again dimmed as the *McClaren* was joined for just an instant with the target ship.

Unlike when Morrison fired, Sato's shot hit the intended target right between the twin flares of its engines. Designed to pierce the armor of a cruiser's hull, the emerald beam instantly vaporized tons of metal in the enemy warship's vulnerable stern. The resulting explosion obliterated the entire propulsion section, sending what was left of the forward part of the ship tumbling end over end, spewing air, debris, and bodies as it quickly fell behind the other three warships.

"Stand by kinetics!" Sato warned. He wasn't firing to try and hit the other ships, although he wouldn't pass on a luck shot, but to try and distract them from the carriers, which were now running in low orbit, waiting to pick up the assault boats that were even now coming back from the surface. He prayed that Steph had somehow made it onto one of them.

They had only been able to repair two of the ship's primary kinetic weapons. The aft ventral turret was of no use in a trailing fight like this. But the forward dorsal battery, mounted on the "top" of the forward part of the hull, was tracking the enemy ships and was locked on for barrage fire. Sato had programmed it to fire a brace of projectiles in a box pattern that would hit the lead ship if it didn't maneuver out of the way.

"Firing!" he said as he hit the *commit* button. The ship echoed with thunder as the big cannon fired half a dozen rounds.

The hull suddenly made a screeching shudder, an undulating vibration that shook the entire ship and made Sato's blood run cold.

"Captain!" DeFusco suddenly shouted over the ship's intercom from engineering. "We're losing the keel! I've got structural warnings on every frame from forward engineering halfway to the bridge. If we don't reduce speed, we're going to lose her, and for the love of God don't fire the forward kinetic battery again!"

"Can we fire the pulse cannon?" he asked her, ignoring her warning to slow the ship. The weapon display indicated that the energy buffers were still cycling. Twenty seconds remained.

For a moment, DeFusco said nothing. "Sir," she said quietly, "the ship is going to break up if we don't slow down. Doing anything else is about as good as detonating a torpedo amidships."

"Answer the question, chief," Sato ordered her, eyeing the weapon status. Ten more seconds. None of the remaining enemy ships had reacted to the death of their sister vessel, and he already had the target reticle locked on the trailing warship.

"The cannon might work properly, sir," DeFusco said stiffly. "Should I pass the word to abandon ship?"

"Stand by to fire," Sato said, ignoring her. Bogdanova and the others glanced at him as if he were slightly mad. "Those carriers are helpless unless we even the odds for them," he said. "One of them is worth half a dozen ships like this. Or more. And they're the only way our surviving troops can get home." *And the only chance Steph might have, if she's still alive,* he thought without a trace of guilt.

The weapon display flashed green: the energy buffers had recharged.

"Firing," he said, again punching the *commit* button.

Again the emerald beam flared from the *McClaren's* bow, and again it took the next target directly in the stern. The pulse cannon hit one of the ship's engines, resulting in a massive fireball that sent the ship tumbling around all three axes. It hadn't suffered fatal damage, but it was enough to take her out of the fight, and that was all Sato cared about.

Another shudder wrenched at the hull, more violently this time, and alarms began to blare on the bridge.

"Hull breach!" one of the crewmen manning the life support section cried. "The main torpedo room is in vacuum. Containment alarm in tubes one, three and four!"

"Dammit," Sato hissed. He had been hoping to use the torpedoes to take out the other ships if the pulse cannon failed. But the hull had wrenched itself out of line enough, twisting such that some of the torpedo launch tubes themselves had become warped, and three of the big missiles had been ruptured in their tubes. "Can we jettison them?"

"Negative, sir," the crewman said. "I can't even get the outer doors open, for any of the tubes."

The hull suddenly shook so hard that Sato's head was flung down against his chest. His jaw slammed shut, his teeth biting deep into his tongue.

"Bridge!" DeFusco's panicked voice called. "We're losing everything ahead of frame fifty-eight! *Get the fuck out of there!*"

"All stop!" Sato ordered, blood streaming from his lips from where he'd bitten his tongue. Hitting the control to open a channel to the entire ship, he said, "Crew, this is the captain. Move aft beyond frame fifty-eight! *Now!*" With that, he unbuckled from his combat chair and began ushering the bridge crew down the passageway aft.

"Sir, look!" Bogdanova exclaimed as she turned to look one last time at the tactical display. The Kreelan ship that was the target for the kinetic rounds flashed three times and began to lose way, falling out of formation with her surviving sister ship.

Got her, Sato thought as he managed a blood-smeared grin. There's only one left, now. The carriers can manage that much.

As he turned to run after the others, he saw the remaining Kreelan warship change course. He bit off a curse as he realized what she was doing: going after the unarmed assault boats that were rising from the surface.

* * *

Steph sat silently by herself in the cavernous bay of the assault boat, her senses withdrawn from reality, insulated by the dull roar of the ship's engines as it rose through the atmosphere. It was eerie, seeing so much space for so few people. The boat she had ridden down to the planet with the men and women of the 7th Cav had been packed full of soldiers, weapons, and equipment. It seemed like a lifetime ago.

She held her video array in one hand, amazed that, like her, it had survived. She wasn't yet sure what she would do with the footage she had recorded. After reviewing the last few moments before the boat had taken off, watching Coyle wave goodbye as they abandoned her to the Kreelans, Steph had broken down and wept uncontrollably. So many had died. So very many. She realized that what she had recorded wasn't news, or a story that might lead her to a Pulitzer prize. It was the death of whatever precious innocence Mankind had left, stabbed through the heart by an alien sword.

"Some coffee, miss?"

Unwillingly breaking from her melancholy reverie, she looked up at the big legionnaire, Mills. He sat down next to her in the ridiculous sling chairs that hung on the walls around the bay, handing her the steaming cup. "Be warned, though," he said, a smile shining through his battered face, "I almost had to beat that fucking loadmaster again before he'd hand over his thermos, and I think the bastard pissed in it."

Despite herself, Steph had to grin at the big Brit-turned-legionnaire. She took a sip, and was glad for the warning. "Jesus," she sputtered as the incredibly strong brew hit her tongue, "I think this tub's entire crew pissed in it."

Mills laughed. "Compliments of our Colonel Grishin, by the way," he told her, nodding at the coffee. "Went out like a light, he did, right after ordering me to poison you with it. But he's a tough bugger. He'll make it."

Suddenly there was a stir up front, and several of the NCOs came back looking for Mills and Steph. While they weren't in charge by rank, they had both earned a special sort of respect from the others.

"We've got a laser link to *Guadalcanal*," one of them said. Steph recognized the name as one of the four carriers the Terran fleet had brought; the carrier the 7th Cav had originally deployed from had been the *Inchon*. "They say we've got trouble heading our way..."

* * *

"We've got to risk one more shot, chief," Sato told a disbelieving Chief DeFusco. "That Kreelan ship got wise and isn't going to bother with the carriers: it's going to pick off the assault boats coming up from the surface. We've got to stop it."

"With all due respect," she said, not sounding very respectful at all, "you're fucking crazy. Sir. The ship can't take it. If somebody so much as farts in the forward section, let alone fires the main guns, we lose the forward third of the ship. We can't fire the torpedoes because the hull's warped. We can't fire the pulse cannon for the same reason: the optical path is out of alignment and we'd blow ourselves up. Did I miss anything?"

Sato saw Ruiz, a giant in his armored suit, stiffen beside him at the chief's remarks. Sato waved him back. "I'm not asking you, chief," he said icily. "I'm ordering you. *Now.*"

"Fine," she snapped. "Just fucking fine. *Captain.* You might want to have everybody get into their beach balls before you try this stunt, because if the hull warps anymore aft of forward engineering, we're going to lose integrity and atmosphere here, too." She set up one of the engineering consoles to echo the tactical display. "You realize that you'll lose all the forward tactical sensors, too? What are we supposed to aim with?"

Sato ignored her as he quickly set in the targeting commands for the forward main gun. He was aiming for the Kreelan ship, but didn't really expect to hit her. What he really needed the guns for was to do just what the chief was afraid of: break the ship's back. Even with the engines stopped, he could feel a sickening twisting motion in the ship as the hull flexed around her devastated mid-section and weakened keel. To Bogdanova, who had taken over one of the other engineering consoles, he said, "Stand by to maneuver."

"*What?*" DeFusco gasped.

"No time to explain, chief," Sato told her. "Stand by...firing!"

The forward main kinetic battery fired a full volley. Then another. And a third. The magazine ran dry as a horrible screech of metal, more akin to a human screaming in agony, echoed through the ship as the forward third began to break away.

"Engines, aft one quarter," Sato ordered quickly. "Hard a-starboard."

"Aye, aye, sir," Bogdanova said uncertainly as she did as she was told.

Sato called up one of the external cameras and watched as *McClaren* literally tore herself in two. The forward section, nearly a third of the ship, had been pushed to starboard by the firing of the main forward battery, which was aimed to port. Sato's maneuvering order put even more stress on the fractured hull, bending the metal further until finally, with a terrible banging and tearing noise from the rending metal, the front section broke free.

"Rudder amidships!" Sato snapped at Bogdanova. The ship, of course, did not have an actual rudder, but it was yet another wet navy term that had carried over into space, a shorthand order to stop the turn.

"Aye, sir," she said, amazed that they were still alive. "Rudder amidships."

"Status?" Sato barked at DeFusco.

"I don't believe it," she said as she scanned the engineering tell-tales. There were plenty that were in the red, but most of them were for the now-gone forward part of the ship. "She's holding, sir. Slight loss of pressure in some of the compartments aft of frame fifty-eight, but nothing critical."

Sato nodded, then ordered, "All ahead flank. Make your course..." he eyed the tactical display, which was now blank. All of the primary sensor arrays were in the forward part of the ship. Activating one of the remaining external cameras he quickly found what he wanted: a circular storm formation over Keran to use as a reference point they could navigate by. In the middle of it was a tiny speck. The Kreelan warship. "Bring her fifteen degrees to port, ten degrees down," he ordered. "Then just keep the target centered in the screen."

McClaren accelerated like a greyhound, freed of nearly a third of her mass. Sato knew that the severely weakened hull would not long stand the strain, but she only had to last long enough to catch the Kreelan warship. Then Sato planned to use the only weapon he had left that could still be brought to bear: the *McClaren* herself.

* * *

"You've got a Kreelan warship on your tail," the tactical controller aboard *Guadalcanal* told the pilot of the assault boat over the laser link. Mills, Steph, and the ranking NCOs were plugged into the comms system to listen. "The destroyer *McClaren* tagged three others that were coming after us before the last one thought better of attacking the carriers. But now it looks like that last Kreelan ship is hunting the boats."

Steph leaned her head against the cold metal of the bulkhead near the cockpit where she was standing, relief washing over her as she ignored the danger she herself was in. *Ichiro was alive*, she thought, wanting to cry again. God, she wanted to hold him. She would have given anything to be in his arms right now.

"What should we do?" the pilot asked, trying to mask his fear. He knew the Kreelan ships could operate in atmosphere, so there was no point in trying to run for the surface. They also couldn't outrun the enemy ship in space. They didn't have any other options.

"Maintain course," *Guadalcanal* ordered. The boat's trajectory happened to be in the same direction the Kreelan ship was heading, which would help hold the range open as long as possible as this boat and the others caught up to the orbit of the carriers. If they could escape the Kreelan now closing in on them. "The maniac commanding *McClaren* lost the forward part of his ship, but he's pursuing the Kreelan, anyway."

That certainly doesn't sound like Captain Morrison, Steph thought with a sinking feeling, at least from what Ichiro said about him.

"How long before the Kreelan ship can fire on us?" the pilot asked.

A pause. "We estimate five minutes."

"What about *McClaren*? When can she engage?"

A longer pause. "She'd be able to attack by now if she still had her forward weapons," the controller finally answered. "It looks like they're going to try and ram."

Steph slumped down to the deck, wanting to vomit up the bitter coffee in her stomach as she imagined Ichiro's destroyer slamming into the Kreelan ship, both of them disappearing in an expanding cloud of white-hot plasma. "No," she whispered. "Please, God, no..."

* * *

The only reason *McClaren* survived as long as she did was that she was directly astern of the Kreelan ship, in her baffles as the wet navy sailors used to say. While the analogy was inexact, the same basic principles applied: almost every ship had reduced sensor effectiveness directly behind it due to interference caused by the drives. The stern was also usually the weakest area in terms of weapons that could be brought to bear, and it was also generally highly vulnerable.

In the case of the Kreelan ship, either they had nothing mounted in the stern to shoot with, or they hadn't seen *McClaren*. Sato couldn't credit the latter notion, and so he kept his fingers crossed that they didn't have any weapons that could be trained directly aft. On the other hand, maybe they wanted *McClaren* to come close so they could fling boarders at her. If they tried, they'd be in for a very unpleasant surprise.

"We've got two minutes, sir," Bogdanova said nervously. They were measuring their closure rate by having one of the Marines, perched in the wreckage at the front of the ship, take range readings to the Kreelan vessel at intervals with a laser rangefinder. Combining the distance readings and information from the ship's chronometer told them how fast they were approaching, and how long they had left before impact.

"Remember the plan," he told Ruiz, who only nodded in his armored suit. While the crew originally thought Sato was just going to make a suicide attack, he had a different idea. "We've got to hit hard enough to damage her drives so she can't pursue the boats. That's the main objective. If we manage to survive that, Ruiz will lead the Marines aboard to take out her weapons or, better yet, destroy her completely. We can't get away from her while her weapons are still functional, since all we have to fight back with is the aft ventral battery. She'll blow us to pieces if any of her weapons are intact." He looked at the others, then said, "Any questions?"

"What if they send boarders at *us?*" DeFusco asked pointedly.

"That's why I had all of you draw weapons," Sato said grimly, conscious of the weight of the assault rifle slung over his shoulder, and the *katana* hanging at his side. Miraculously, his quarters hadn't suffered any damage and he had been able to retrieve it. And the newly commissioned warships that had come on this expedition, unlike the *Aurora*, had well-stocked armories and weapons lockers in several key locations, not just a handful of weapons concentrated in one place. "The Marines have to take the enemy ship. We have to defend our own."

"Any more questions?" Sato asked. Heads shook all around. "Then let's do it."

* * *

Ruiz thought the idea the lieutenant - *captain*, he reminded himself - had come up with was bug-fuck crazy, but he had to admit the boy had style. And as far as dim-witted stunts that could get you killed went, it appealed to his inner nature. Perched here among the twisted beams and torn plating that was now the "bow" of the ship, watching the Kreelan ship's drives grow ever larger as the *McClaren* charged right up her ass, he didn't doubt that he'd be smashed into paste before he had a chance to shoot one of the aliens. He hoped otherwise, but he'd never been a Pollyanna optimist. He hated people like that.

In the meantime, it was an awesome view. The planet below was a gorgeous blue and brown ball that got bigger as he watched, studded with swirling white clouds in the halo of the atmosphere. The stars shone like a million tiny beacons, and even the Kreelan ship was in its own way beautiful, her flowing lines an elegant contrast to the pragmatic ugliness of her human counterpart. Ruiz hardly thought himself a renaissance man, but seeing a sight like this made him appreciate how someone might be captivated enough to become an artist and put scenes like this on canvas with a brush.

But he'd leave that to others. His art was killing, and his preferred brush was the recoilless heavy assault rifle he clutched in his right hand.

"Stand by," he told his Marines on the platoon channel as he watched their approach to the enemy ship. They were dispersed in the wreckage of *McClaren's* fore end on the side opposite where they hoped to smash into the Kreelan vessel. He had divided them up into eight combat teams of four Marines each, hoping they could reach the hull of the enemy ship quickly after impact, spread out, then plant explosive charges on her gun mounts and anything else that looked vital. And if the enemy wanted to come out and play, the Marines were more than ready to oblige.

Then he switched over to a secondary channel on the induction circuit that linked him back to engineering. "We're ready, sir," he reported. "Jesus, we're getting close." The Kreelan ship was growing at an alarming rate. Ruiz had spent plenty of time in open space, training both for assaults on other ships and to repel boarders.

But this was a lot closer than they'd ever come in training, and the alien ship suddenly seemed a lot bigger than he'd thought it would be.

"Hang on, gunny," Sato's voice, tinny-sounding over the induction circuit, said.

"Three hundred meters," one of his Marines reported from a check of his laser rangefinder. "One-fifty..."

"Oh, Christ!" Ruiz cursed as the *McClaren* slammed into the other ship with the force of thousands of tons of mass moving at nearly ten meters per second. There was no sound, of course, but he could feel the screeching of the hulls grinding together through his hands and feet as he clung desperately to a pair of girders that had once been part of the ship's central conduit.

He saw that somehow the navigator, Bogdanova, had yawed *McClaren* to starboard at the last second so they didn't run right up the Kreelan ship's stern, then reversed the yaw to slam into the target. None of his men flew off into space, so he figured they all managed to survive.

"*Go, go, go!*" Ruiz yelled to his Marines. He could see that a number of protruding girders from what was left of *McClaren's* bow had impaled the other ship through its thin armor. But there was no way to tell how long the unholy union would last. They had to get aboard the Kreelan ship fast and do as much damage as they could. Everything else was gravy.

"Heads-up, gunny!" one of his men shouted. "Here they come!"

Dark shapes had begun to emerge from what must have been one of the enemy ship's airlocks in the shadow of *McClaren's* battered hull. Ruiz knew then that the enemy must have seen *McClaren* coming all along. Knowing she was impotent after losing her forward section, the Kreelans had been waiting for the human ship to get close enough, probably figuring they were trying to ram. *Holy Christ*, he thought to himself. *They could have blown us out of space a hundred times, but pulled this shit, instead.*

"Take 'em!" Ruiz ordered, dropping any attempt to comprehend idiotic alien behavior as he brought up his rifle. The head-up display, or HUD, in his helmet was painting over two dozen targets in red, with his Marines highlighted in blue. He took aim at the nearest Kreelan and fired, watching as the projectile streaked toward its target.

A specialized weapon, the type of rifle the Marines were using had been rushed into production from a hurriedly fabricated prototype. In testing it had turned in an outstanding performance, and Ruiz wasn't disappointed now. Firing small rocket projectiles to minimize recoil that could send the Marines spinning out of control in space, the weapons packed a much bigger punch than the standard assault rifles carried by the Ground Forces troops. The projectiles didn't travel as fast as bullets, and so weren't as accurate over longer ranges against moving targets, but this range, less than a hundred meters, was right in the middle of their sweet spot.

He watched with satisfaction as his round hit his target square in the chest, the semi-armor piercing projectile punching through her suit's armor before exploding inside. The suit instantly puffed up from the pressure of the small detonation, the faceplate turning red with blood as the Kreelan's body was blown up from the inside. "Die, motherfucker!" he hissed.

"Ruiz!" Sato's tinny voice interrupted his concentration as he picked out another target, a Kreelan who had just shot one of his Marines. "You've got to get to the ship! She's starting to pull free!"

With a start, Ruiz snapped his head up to look at where the two ships were joined, and sure enough, the Kreelan was trying to pull away to port. "Fuck," he cursed to himself. "Yes, sir!" he told Sato. Switching to the platoon channel, he boomed, "Marines! *Follow me!*"

Coiling his legs beneath him, he leaped toward the upper hull of the struggling enemy ship, firing at any warriors he saw as he flew over them. Most of his Marines jumped after him, but he could see more than a handful of suits bearing the names of his men and women spinning away, lifeless, from the battle.

Without warning, he was surrounded by three or four warriors that in his eyes looked more like giant black spiders than humanoids. They had him by the arms and legs, pulling at him as if they were trying to draw and quarter him. One of them drew a sword, his eyes couldn't credit the sight, and was about to try and run him through when all four of the aliens suddenly exploded in a cascade of gore as a fusillade of recoilless rifle fire tore through them.

"Christ, gunny!" he heard one of his Marines said as two of them grabbed his arms and propelled him with their micro-thrusters to the Kreelan ship, while two more provided covering fire. "That was too fucking close."

Shaking free of his Marines as he settled close to the hull, annoyed with himself for letting the Kreelans surprise him more than anything else, Ruiz said, "Get those damn charges planted! We don't have time to fuck around!"

"Check," the team leader said, and they took off toward the stern of the ship, skimming over its surface like bloated dark gray birds.

Other Marines tried to break contact with the Kreelans and get to the enemy ship. Some made it, some didn't. Others were simply fighting for their lives as more Kreelans poured out of the ship's airlocks. Ruiz's targeting system was painting at least four dozen enemy targets swarming his people who were still pinned down in the wreckage of *McClaren's* bow.

"Oh, *shit!*" one of his female Marines cried out. "Gunny, the ship-"

Her signal broke off as the *McClaren* sheered away, stripping away a fifty meter long piece of hull plating from the Kreelan ship and venting the enemy vessel's guts to vacuum. Atmosphere exploded in icy clouds into space, carrying along several dozen of the ship's crew, none of them wearing vacuum suits, and other debris.

"Ground!" he ordered as he used his micro-thrusters to slam his suit down on the already-shifting hull of the enemy ship. "Latch on or you'll get left behind!" He activated the magnetic grips in the palms of his armored gloves and the soles of his boots, praying that the ship's skin had enough ferrous metal to hold onto. Luckily, it did.

The good news, such as it was, was that he had good communications with his men and women again. It was a small consolation as he watched the ship pull away from the *McClaren*, most of his Marines left tumbling in her wake. The few Marines left defending *McClaren* went down fighting under a swarm of enemy warriors. Ruiz wondered if Sato's luck had just run out.

"Gunny," one of the team leaders said after Ruiz had taken a head count of the dozen Marines who had made it across, "we don't have enough charges left to take out half the weapon mounts on this bitch. What are we gonna do?"

"Get in close and fuck with 'em," he said. Then he led them over the side of the hull and into the ship through the section ripped open by *McClaren* as she had pulled away.

TWENTY-SEVEN

Admiral Tiernan watched the tactical display with quiet admiration as the *McClaren* took down the three Kreelan warships that had gone after the carriers, then drove off and pursued the fourth. *Morrison*, he thought about the ship's captain, whom he'd had the displeasure of knowing from a previous command, *as much of an asshole as you are, I'll pin the Medal of Honor on you myself for pulling off that stunt.*

They hadn't even realized *McClaren* was still with them until the *Ticonderoga's* sensors picked up her drive signature not long after the destroyer had quietly sailed behind the Kreelan fleet. Tiernan had wanted to contact her, but had decided not to risk drawing any more attention to her than necessary after it became clear that she was headed after the Kreelans pursuing the incoming carriers. That would have been what Tiernan ordered Morrison to do, anyway. The admiral only hoped that the destroyer would be able to keep the last Kreelan ship from doing too much harm to the carriers or the boats that were now rising from the surface with whatever was left of the ground forces.

"Engagement range in two minutes, admiral," his flag captain reported quietly.

On the tactical display, the two opposing fleets raced toward one another and what Tiernan knew would be a final orgy of destruction that would decide the outcome of the battle for Keran. He knew he was taking a huge risk: he was under direct orders not to lose his fleet as a fighting force, but was counting on more than a little luck to favor him in this engagement. He knew that he might very well lose everything in the next few minutes. But as the old saying went, "who dares, wins." An entire planet and millions of people were at stake. Neither he nor *Amiral* Lefevre were about to abandon them.

His only real concern was the ammunition stocks of the Alliance ships. They didn't have much left, and they hadn't been able to take the time to jump out to rearm. So, once again, the Terran ships were in the lead, with *Ticonderoga* in the center of the third wedge that was arrowing for the enemy formation's heart.

"Nothing fancy," he had told the flag staff officers as he had quickly sketched out the maneuvering orders after the Kreelan fleet had begun to come down from high orbit to attack. "We sail through their formation doing as much damage as we can. All ships are to fire at will as soon as the enemy's in range. Then we'll see where we stand." *And how many of our ships are left.*

Turning to the vidcom, Tiernan said, "Good luck, admiral." They didn't expect the laser links to be stable in the upcoming storm of ships and weapons.

"You, as well, my friend," Lefevre told him. "It has been an honor."

"Indeed, it has, sir," Tiernan said as the leading waves of the two fleets collided in fire and rending steel.

* * *

Thousands of kilometers away, Ichiro Sato and the surviving crew of the *McClaren* were fighting an altogether different kind of battle, although one every bit as deadly. The Kreelan warship had managed to free herself from the *McClaren's* embrace and was still closing on the helpless shuttles that were now rising in a loose formation to loop around Keran to rendezvous with the carriers. Sato could only hope that Ruiz and his Marines would be able to stop her.

Like a returning nightmare, there were once more Kreelan warriors aboard Sato's ship. The Marines in what was left of the forward section fought tenaciously, but in the end were simply overwhelmed by superior numbers. None of the crew had actually seen one of the enemy before, and had never really expected to up close. Fear was written on their faces as they ran in teams to defend the key passageways leading aft. They didn't have to worry about defending the main airlocks, as those had been carried away with the forward section when it broke away from the ship. The only airlock left was the auxiliary located aft of engineering.

"How'll they get in, sir?" one of the women in Sato's team asked as he led them forward to defend the ship. He had left DeFusco in charge of maneuvering *McClaren*, with very simple orders: try to catch up with the Kreelan warship, and slam what was left of *McClaren* into her drives.

"I don't know," he told her truthfully. The Kreelan ships were nothing like the massive vessels the *Aurora* had encountered, and he had no idea what other surprises might be in store. "But they'll find a way. Listen," he said, turning to the dozen men and women on his team, "the enemy is tough and extremely well-trained. But they can be killed. We just have to try and-"

He was interrupted by an explosion as the hatch at the end of the passageway disintegrated into white-hot fragments that blew inward toward them. There was a sudden, brief, gust of air down the passageway, and Sato's ears popped with the change in pressure. Two similar explosions sounded from elsewhere in the forward part of the ship.

"Get ready!" he ordered, and the men and women with him took up positions on the floor and behind the hatch coaming, trying to make themselves into the smallest possible targets as they aimed their rifles at the still-smoking hatchway.

As the smoke cleared, Sato saw a pair of Kreelans worming their way into what looked like a set of transparent membranes, clearly some sort of airlock, at the end of the passageway.

"Hold your fire," he said, a tingle of fear creeping down his spine. He had assumed the Kreelans would use the same advanced technology they had when they boarded the *Aurora*. But this was nothing more than a simple, if effective, set of membranes that could certainly be pierced or torn by the human weapons.

"Sir?" one of the sailors asked, his finger tensing on the trigger of his assault rifle.

"If we fire and damage that thing they're coming through, we're dead," Sato told him as he got to his feet. "None of us have vacuum suits."

As if to punctuate his warning, they could hear the staccato firing of several assault rifles, followed by a hollow *whoomp* as a grenade went off in one of the other passageways. That was followed by the shriek of air venting into space, one of the sounds that spacefaring sailors feared as much as fire. The screams of the crewmen as they were blown out of the ship were muted by the intervening compartments, but tore through his heart nonetheless.

"Get back," he told the others as he turned and quickly led them back down the passageway as the Kreelans stripped out of their vacuum suits. Their eyes were fixed on the humans, but otherwise they were not yet prepared to attack. *They know the score, too*, Sato thought. "Let them come," he said. "Once they're out of their suits, we're on even ground."

"If you say so, sir," one of the enlisted men said dubiously as he followed Sato through the hatch, closing it behind him as more alien warriors made their way through the airlock.

* * *

Gunny Ruiz grimaced in pain as he blasted yet another Kreelan out of his path. He had been hit with one of the flying weapons the enemy used: one of the blades was embedded in the thick pectoral muscles of his chest. His suit was leaking air, but he figured he'd have enough to finish the job before he asphyxiated.

He was down to only four Marines in the short time they'd been inside the Kreelan ship. The enemy warriors were beyond fanatical in their defense. They were completely outclassed by the Marines in their combat armor with their recoilless rifles, and still they were murderous opponents. Even after the Marines blew a compartment open to the vacuum of space, the female warriors, without suits, attacked them with swords and claws as they were blown out into space. Two of his people had died that way, their suits slashed open as the enemy went flying past.

The Marines had blasted their way through the hatchways of the ship as they moved aft as quickly as they could, trying to reach the ship's engine room. Ruiz had figured the bridge was probably much farther forward, and at the rate his people were being killed, they'd never make it. And they didn't have time. He knew the ship would be in range of the fleeing shuttles any moment now.

"Down, gunny!" one of his men shouted as a warrior wearing a combat suit hurled herself at Ruiz from around the bend in a passageway.

Ruiz dropped to the deck, but it was the wrong move: he landed right on the Kreelan weapon still embedded in his chest and drove it even deeper. He was momentarily paralyzed with agony as the Kreelan fell on top of him.

His Marines couldn't shoot for fear of hitting him, but he wasn't important. "Forget about me!" he ground out through the pain as he fought to roll over so he could fight the alien. "Find the goddamn engine room! No time left!"

The four other Marines paused only for a second before following their orders, blasting their way through the passageways leading aft.

Using his massive upper body strength, Ruiz managed to push himself up off the deck, the warrior still writhing on top of him, and flip over, slamming his right elbow as hard as he could into her midsection. The warrior's armor absorbed the blow, but it gave him what he really wanted: just a few extra centimeters of room. He rolled back in the opposite direction, careful to keep his chest and the protruding weapon clear of the deck, then leapt on top of her before she could regain her feet. He clung desperately to her armored gloves, which were made to allow her razor-sharp talons to show through the fingertips of the metal and fabric. Using his superior weight, he shoved her to the floor, howling in pain as the throwing weapon was again driven deeper into his chest, the tip burying itself in the bone of his sternum.

Ironically, the inhumanly sharp blades that were sticking out were equally effective against Kreelan armor, and he watched with satisfaction as they sliced through his opponent's armor as well as his own. The blades didn't penetrate deep, but far enough: he suddenly yanked himself backward, pulling the blades out of the alien's suit.

Air rushed from her suit, crystals of water forming as the moisture in the suit's air froze almost instantly. He pinned her to the deck until she stopped twitching.

As he struggled to get up, he found two more suited warriors waiting for him, swords drawn.

He was just bringing up his rifle when a churning wall of fire exploded through the passageway from the aft end of the ship, testimony to the handiwork of his Marines.

* * *

"You're clear," the controller on the *Guadalcanal* informed the assault boat pilots. "The enemy ship that was on your tail is losing way."

The pilots didn't need to hear it from the carrier, as the enemy warship had gotten close enough for them to track it on the boat's sensors. Both pilots breathed a heavy sigh of relief when they saw the ship's icon suddenly slow down, rapidly falling behind them.

"We're actually going to make it," the pilot murmured, holding his hand down to his side out of sight and crossing his fingers. "Tell the *McClaren* that we're good for the bar tab in any port," he told the controller on the carrier. On the sensor display, he saw the icons representing the other shuttles climbing toward the still-invisible carriers. By his count, all but two had made it.

"Nice thought, but it looks like there are going to be some empty chairs around the table," the controller told him, his voice tinged with regret. "The *McClaren* rammed the other ship, then they separated and it looks like her drives have failed. She's not going to make it."

Hearing the words of the controller, Steph sat bolt upright from where she had slumped down to the deck. "We have to go back," she told the pilots. "We have to go back to the *McClaren*."

Both pilots stared at her. "Are you crazy?" the boat's command pilot said. "You see that?" he said, pointing to a blue icon just at the edge of the boat's forward sensor display that had *Guadalcanal* marked under it. "That's our carrier. They're going to leave us behind if we aren't aboard in about ten minutes."

"The people on that ship saved our lives," she argued. "We can help them. This boat has plenty of room for the survivors-"

"There's no time!" the pilot told her. "I'm sorry," he said, his apology utterly sincere. "I appreciate their sacrifice and what they did to save us. I really do. But it won't help them if we mount a rescue only to have all of us get left behind." He glanced at the other faces looking into the cockpit hatch and listening, the few surviving NCOs of the Legion and the 7th Cavalry. "*Guadalcanal* and the other carriers have direct orders from Admiral Tiernan that they are not to wait for stragglers."

"Please," she said, turning to Mills for support. "I know it's a risk, but we've got to go back. Ichiro Sato is on that ship along with the rest of the crew. None of us would have had a chance at all in this fight if it weren't for him."

Sato's name had an immediate effect on everyone who could hear Steph's voice. He was the prophet who had brought warning of the coming invasion. As with most prophets, few had believed his prophecy, and most had scorned and ridiculed him. The haggard men and women on the assault boat, however, had become true believers after coming face to face with the Kreelan nightmare.

"I think we'll go back, then," Mills said casually. "Shouldn't leave a lad like that go to waste. What say you, *sergent chef?*" he asked the ranking Legion NCO standing next to him.

The man answered without hesitation. "*Oui.* We go back."

Nodding their heads in agreement, the other NCOs representing the 7th Cavalry gave their support.

"This isn't a fucking democracy," the pilot told them hotly. "I'm the commander of this boat, and we have orders to return to *Guadalcanal.* And that's what we're-"

He froze as Mills smoothly raised his assault rifle and pressed the muzzle against the pilot's helmet. "Look, mate," he said in a low voice, "the more you flap those gums of yours the less time we have to pick up those fellows on that ship back there. If you or your friend here," he glanced at the copilot, who was staring down the muzzle of a weapon held by one of the 7th Cav NCOs, "utter one more word before you turn this tub around, I'll blow your bloody fucking head off. And please don't make the mistake of thinking I won't pull the trigger."

The pilot's mouth worked for a moment, but in the end he decided that discretion was the better part of valor. With a helpless, angry look at his copilot, he turned back to the ship's controls and turned them around.

Steph watched the starfield turn beyond the ship's cockpit window, praying that Ichiro was still alive.

* * *

Aboard *McClaren*, a very one-sided battle raged in the passageways and compartments of the stricken ship. While the crew fought bravely, they weren't trained as Marines. And without Ruiz and the others in their armored vacuum suits, the Kreelan warriors held the advantage. The *McClaren's* crewmen were killing the aliens, but not fast enough, and too many of the defending sailors were dying in the process.

Sato's team had managed to hold off the advance of the Kreelans who were trying to come down the passageway his men and women were defending, but he was suspicious: they hadn't been trying as hard as he thought they might. His sailors had killed three or four as they tried to force themselves around a turn, but aside from occasionally peering out to see if the humans were still there, they were staying put.

From the sounds coming from other parts of the ship, the same was clearly not true. Sato had sent two men as runners to find the other teams and report what was happening; neither had returned. The bark of automatic weapons and the explosion of grenades echoed through the metal of the bulkheads and the deck, clear indications of savage fighting.

Then he heard something that was at once familiar, and totally unexpected: the distant mechanical *clank* of docking clamps.

"Jesus," one of the crewmen cried, "one of their ships has docked with us!"

"They couldn't," one of the others said. "The only airlock that's left is the auxiliary in the after engine room. They couldn't dock with it."

"They can do anything," Sato whispered, more to himself than to the others, as one of the Kreelans quickly peered around the corner, then darted back as she was met with another fusillade of rifle fire; Sato's team had already run out of grenades.

He felt a change in the tempo of the fighting in the other parts of the ship, mostly aft of where they were. "Engineering," he said. "They've broken through to engineering!" Turning to the senior rating, one of the ship's computer engineers, he said, "Take the team back to help DeFusco. If they take engineering..." He didn't bother finishing the sentence.

"Aye, aye, sir," she said. "But what about you? You're coming with us, aren't you?"

"No," he said, shaking his head as he stood up and handed her what was left of his ammunition. He dropped the empty rifle to the deck. "I'll buy you a little time."

"But..."

"Go on," he told her quietly. "Save our ship."

Tears brimming in her eyes, the sailor turned and led the others back down the passageway toward the thundering fight that was raging near the engineering section.

Sato drew his *katana*, then placed the lacquered scabbard carefully on the deck. It would be destroyed with the rest of the ship when the enemy overpowered the crew, but even in his final moments he would never dream of treating it with disrespect by thoughtlessly casting it aside.

The *katana* held confidently in his hands, he stepped forward into the passageway to face the warriors awaiting him.

* * *

The first men and women to board the *McClaren* were almost cut down by the skeleton crew in engineering who expected nothing other than a flood of enemy warriors, that they themselves had not yet seen in the flesh, to come streaming through the airlock. They stared in open-mouthed surprise and wonder at the ragged legionnaires and cavalrymen who quickly marched aboard.

"Heard you could use a bit of a hand," Mills told a female engineer, a petty officer, who looked to be in charge.

"Jesus," DeFusco said, shaking her head. "I just don't believe it."

"Let's get a move on, shall we? *Allez!*" Mills said, and the legionnaires began to move to the forward end of the engine room, their weapons ready, the cavalrymen right beside them. They didn't need anyone to steer them through the ship. They could clearly hear the sounds of the fighting going on, and did as many soldiers have done through history: they marched toward the sound of the guns.

"Get your people aboard," Steph said, gesturing toward the waiting airlock.

"I can't leave," DeFusco told her bluntly. "I won't leave the ship until we've got everyone back."

"Then get your people into the boat and wait by the airlock," Steph told her, knowing exactly how she felt. "We don't have much time. I'll stay with you in case the Kreelans poke their heads in here." She gestured with her rifle, and DeFusco could tell she must have used it plenty already. The woman's hands were nearly black with dirt and residue from firing the weapon's caseless cartridges, and the rest of her wasn't much better. She was a complete mess, and judging from the sunken look of her eyes must have been running on nothing but fumes.

"You're that reporter woman, aren't you?" DeFusco suddenly realized. "The one that Lieutenant...I mean, Captain Sato was, um..."

Steph offered her a tired smile. "You can say it," she said. "We were dating. But *captain?* And did he...did he make it?"

"Yes on both counts," DeFusco said, a look of concern shadowing her face as she hustled the remaining members of the engineering crew past her into the waiting boat, "at least when I saw him last, leading a team forward to defend the ship. A ship's captain. And a damn good one, at that."

* * *

Mills and the other soldiers didn't have far to go to find the enemy. While none of the men and women who now swarmed through the passageways out of engineering and into what was left of the forward part of the ship had any experience in shipboard fighting, it was close enough to urban combat, with which most of them did have experience, that they adapted quickly. They also had the advantages of surprise and weight of numbers.

As they reached the survivors of the crew's defense teams, which were now down to a handful of men and women, the soldiers sent them aft to the assault boat.

Then the legionnaires and cavalrymen began to mercilessly cut down the boarders, blasting them into bloody pulp through sheer weight of fire from their assault rifles.

* * *

Sato was ready. He was prepared to die and join the ghosts who still haunted his dreams from the *Aurora*, where part of his soul had been lost forever. He had no regrets, save that he had never told Steph how much he really loved her. He knew she would understand, and hoped with all his heart that she had survived the disaster that had befallen the troops on the ground. He would have given anything to be with her now, but he knew that wasn't his destiny.

Four warriors stood before him in the passageway, having left their bulky armored vacuum suits behind. Two stepped forward, their black armor and the silvery blades of their weapons gleaming, while the others held back.

Standing in a ready position, his legs spread forward and back and bent slightly, ready to spring, Sato held his sword in a two-handed grip, down low on his right, the blade's tip pointing diagonally toward the deck. He knew his skills could not compare to the warriors he faced, but he would go down fighting. His *sensei* had given him that much.

That was what he thought up until the moment that the warriors, all of them, knelt down before him.

* * *

Taylan-Murir was a well-seasoned warrior with skills and scars from the many Challenges fought during her life. Like all others who had come here, save the great priestess and the senior shipmistress of the fleet, she had fought many for the honor to face the Empire's latest enemy.

But *this* honor was entirely unexpected. As she and her three sisters came upon this particular group of human defenders, she sensed something in one of the animals.

They had come upon the Messenger.

She and her sisters would not have been able to explain how they knew this, for, as with many things for their ancient race, what once might have required thought and understanding or visible technology to achieve now simply *was*. He carried no mark, nor did she recognize his face, homely and pale as it was to her eyes. But Taylan-Murir knew that this human was the Messenger as surely as she knew her own name. So did her fellow warriors, and so, too, did every member of the fleet - indeed, her entire race - as her Bloodsong echoed her wonder and surprise. It was a great honor to be in the presence of a Messenger, and it was forbidden to bring one to harm. Indeed, it was unthinkable. Thus they had been careful to hold the humans at bay, but had not pressed their attack for fear of harming him.

This Messenger, she knew, was different from all others who had come before in her civilization's half-million year history: he held a sword and clearly understood how to use it, and to die by his hand would be a very great honor.

Trembling with pride, she and her sisters knelt before him, waiting for his blade to fall.

* * *

"No," Sato whispered as the Kreelans kneeled on the deck, their heads bowed in respect as if he were a lord come to call. He knew this wasn't just a coincidence. It couldn't be.

While most might have felt relief at such a reprieve, Sato felt a burning anger that rose into a fiery rage. He wanted a chance to prove himself, to take himself back to the sands of the arena where his shipmates from the *Aurora* had fought and died. He wanted to avenge their ghosts. "Get up!" he shouted at them, not caring that they couldn't understand his words. "*Get on your feet and fight!*"

The four warriors made no move, but were still as statues carved from the deepest ebony.

Rushing forward to the first one, the one he took to be their leader, he grabbed her by the arm and hauled her to her feet. "Fight me, damn you!" He slammed the guard of his sword into her chest, knocking her back a step, trying to force a reaction from her.

But she again sank to her knees, and never met his gaze.

With a roar of anger and frustration, he yanked her to her feet once more, and put the blade of his sword to her throat above her collar and its glittering pendants, the razor sharp blade drawing a line of blood. Grabbing her chin, he forced her face up to look at his, and for a moment their eyes met. He knew he couldn't read her body language and expressions, but he had no doubt of what he saw in those cat-like eyes that were at once totally alien, yet had a sense of captivating beauty: pure, utter ecstasy, as if she were enjoying a high from some alien drug.

He pressed the sword's blade harder against her neck, deepening the wound, her blood running over her collar and down her chest under the breast plate. "Fight me," he hissed once more.

She only sighed as she stood there, trembling not with fear, but with pleasure, her weapon held loosely at her side, here eyes locked on his.

Finally, Sato let her go. The warrior sank to her knees, and then bowed her head to the floor. He thought briefly about trying to provoke the others into attacking, but knew it would be fruitless.

He also considered simply killing them, slicing through their necks with his sword, just like he had practiced under his *sensei's* supervision, chopping cleanly through targets of tightly woven fiber wound around a bamboo pole. Tightening his grip on his *katana*, he raised it over his head, preparing to kill her.

But he couldn't do it. He wanted to kill her, wanted to kill every last one of her kind for what they had done, but not in cold blood. He felt his rage dissipate like an ebbing tide, and the strength went out of his arms. Lowering the sword to his side, he slumped to the deck on his knees in front of the warrior, dispirited, empty.

Apparently intrigued by his refusal to kill her, she lifted her head from the floor and again met his gaze.

"Are you Lieutenant Sato?" a voice with what could only be a British accent whispered from behind him, pronouncing his rank as *leftenant*.

With a surprised start, Sato turned around to see a large soldier peering carefully around the hatch coaming in the passageway behind him, aiming his assault rifle at the aliens. He hadn't heard anyone come up behind him.

"Yes," he said. "Who the devil are you?" That was when Sato noticed that there were no longer any sounds of fighting coming from the other parts of the ship.

"The cavalry, you might say, lieutenant," Mills told him. "*Soldat 1e Classe* Roland Mills of the *Légion étrangère*, at your service. Sent by one Miss Stephanie Guillaume. And might I ask, sir," he went on, "just what the devil is going on here?"

Sato turned to look back at the warriors, who had taken absolutely no notice of Mills or the other men who now spread out behind him, aiming half a dozen assault rifles at the Kreelans. Their leader, blood still seeping down her neck from the cut he had given her, still watched him with her strange feline eyes, almost as if she were afraid or sad to see him go.

"I...don't really know," Sato told him honestly as he struggled to his feet, suddenly overwhelmed by physical and emotional exhaustion. He felt Mills' powerful hand take him under the arm to help him up, the big soldier smoothly moving Sato behind him as the legionnaire kept the muzzle of his rifle pointed at the lead Kreelan's head.

Mills tensed to pull the trigger, but felt a hand on his arm, gently but insistently pushing his rifle down.

"Leave them," Sato said quietly. "Just leave them be."

Pausing only to recover the scabbard for his sword, Sato headed back toward engineering, Mills and another legionnaire covering his back. Just before he turned the corner in the passageway, Sato glanced back to see that the Kreelan, still on her knees, was staring after him.

* * *

As soon as she caught sight of him, Steph threw herself in Sato's arms, not giving a damn about military etiquette, protocol, or anything else. "Ichiro," was all she could say before their lips met. She kissed him hard, and he returned every bit of her passion, holding her off her feet in a tight embrace.

"Sorry to dampen the reunion," Mills said, exchanging a tired grin with his NCO, "but I think we'd best be off, lieutenant."

Reluctantly letting go of Steph, Ichiro nodded. "Is everyone aboard the boat?"

"Yes, sir," DeFusco answered, stepping forward to salute him.

He returned it with a smile. "Then let's get the hell out of here."

Following DeFusco and Steph, he and the two legionnaires stepped through the auxiliary airlock into the boat, and Sato watched with sad but relieved eyes as the hatch closed on his first, and probably his last, command.

* * *

Taylan-Murir and her three companions followed the Messenger and his escorts to where the humans had left, no doubt from a boat that had come to rescue him. She put a hand to her neck, feeling the sticky track of blood that had now stopped flowing, and shivered at the memory of looking into his face as he had held her at his mercy. Her fellow warriors were not jealous of her experience, for they had sensed it in their own veins: the *Kreela* were not all of one mind, but they were bound in spirit. And what one sensed, the emotions one felt, was a stream that fed the timeless river of the Bloodsong.

After pausing for a time where the humans had left the ship, they circulated through the other compartments that were not in vacuum, gathering up what few of their sisters who remained alive. They gave the last rites and ritual death to those who were too severely injured to leave the ship, for there were no healers here. They all had brought the Empress much honor this day, and their deeds would be duly recorded in the Books of Time.

Once they were finished, the warriors again donned their vacuum suits and left the ship, taking refuge in the nothingness of space high above the human-settled world. Staying together in a group, they awaited the imminent arrival of the second fleet they sensed that the Empress had sent forth to continue the conquest of this world.

* * *

"Not that it's a big surprise, but we're not going to make it," the boat's pilot said in a matter-of-fact voice as he watched the chronometer that had been running, marking the time remaining until the carriers were to jump.

The copilot had been frantically trying to establish a laser link with the big ships, but so far hadn't had any luck. "There they are," he said as the carriers suddenly flashed onto the extreme edge of the boat's tactical display. "Okay, I've got a laser lock on *Guadalcanal...*"

The icons for the carriers suddenly disappeared from the screen.

"Oh, shit," the copilot hissed.

"What's wrong?" Sato asked him, leaning over his shoulder to see the display. As the ranking Terran Navy officer, he now found himself in command again, albeit of a much smaller vessel. After speaking with the legionnaires, he had checked on Colonel Grishin, but he was barely lucid. If they didn't get him to a sickbay soon, he would die. Colonel Sparks was worse, his pulse weak and erratic. He was bleeding badly internally, and while every soldier had basic first aid skills, none were medics: all of them had been killed during the running battle on the planet.

"The carriers jumped," the pilot told him bitterly. "We're stuck here."

The soldiers and the survivors of *McClaren* were disappointed, but not surprised. The soldiers had known the risks of trying for a rescue, and had taken them anyway. The crew of the *McClaren* was grateful for even a few more minutes beyond the reach of the enemy's swords and claws.

"Well, that's that, then," Mills said with a sigh.

"Not quite," Sato told him, looking out the window to starboard, where a deadly dance of fireflies was taking place in the near space between the planet and its moons: lasers and the flares of explosions as the human and Kreelan fleets collided.

TWENTY-EIGHT

Ticonderoga shuddered as she took another hit from an enemy kinetic weapon, and her hull screamed as an enemy laser raked her flank, vaporizing tons of hardened steel alloy in an instant.

Tiernan and the rest of the flag staff did the only thing they could: they held on tightly, strapped into their combat chairs, and prayed. There was no point in giving orders: all semblance of cohesion in the fleet had vanished as they had slammed headlong into the onrushing Kreelan warships. Half the laser links had been lost in the snarling chaos of the battle, and effective control was impossible.

The ships fought in a swirling pass-through engagement that was more like a massive dogfight from the long-ago Second World War than a fleet space engagement. But there had never been a fleet battle in space nearly as big as this, and the reality of it had thrown half a century of modern naval thinking out the window. Tiernan knew the Navy was going to have to start from square one on tactics and strategy, because this enemy simply didn't act human, for the most obvious of reasons.

Cruisers and destroyers on both sides hacked away at one another in a knife fight at ranges of hundreds of meters, using weapons that were designed for combat at hundreds or thousands of *kilometers*. Kinetic guns ripple-fired until their magazines were empty, sometimes sending an entire salvo into the hull of an enemy vessel as it flashed by on an opposing course. Lasers slashed across hull plating, vaporizing armor and often penetrating into the target ship's vitals, sending streams of air and doomed crew members into space. Ships of both sides that were gutted and dying tried to ram the nearest enemy. In a few cases, the ships survived the collision, with the crews fighting each other hand to hand.

"Once our ships pass through the enemy formation," Tiernan told his flag communications officer, "they're to jump out to the rendezvous point. We can't fight like this and hope to win without losing most of the fleet."

"Admiral!" the fleet tactical officer called out, "*Jean Bart* is losing way - she's falling behind!"

Tiernan looked down at the vidcom and punched the control to ring up *Amiral Lefevre*. There was a long pause before the system connected, the laser array having to search through the cyclone of wildly maneuvering ships to find the *Jean Bart*.

When Lefevre's image at last appeared on Tiernan's console, the Terran admiral suppressed a grimace at his Alliance counterpart's appearance. Lefevre's face was covered in blood from a deep gash that ran from above his left eye to his left ear, and there was also a line of blood from the corner of his mouth. His uniform was tattered and scorched. Behind him, the video monitor showed a scene of chaos and smoldering devastation on the *Jean Bart's* flag bridge.

"*Mon ami,*" Lefevre wheezed, a weak smile on his face, "I fear I will not have the opportunity to beat you at a game of poker. Our ship is nearly finished."

"Sir, if one of your ships is unable to reach you, I'll send a destroyer to take you and your crew off-"

"No, *amiral*. You must not risk any more ships." He paused, gathering his breath as the *Jean Bart* shook from another hit. "I am sure the fleet that is here now is not all the enemy has. They would not send everything to invade another system. They must have reserves. And if our two fleets are destroyed here, our homeworlds will not be able to defend themselves."

"I'm not sure it would matter, admiral," Tiernan told him. "The Kreelans don't seem to care about their losses. Fighting like this, they could take Earth with a fleet half this size."

"Which is why you must save every ship that you can," Lefevre emphasized. "The loss of Keran will be a terrible tragedy. But if we lose Earth or any of the other core worlds like La Seyne, we will lose the industrial capacity to defend ourselves-"

In the background of the vidcom, *Jean Bart* shook furiously as she took a full broadside from an enemy warship, the impact sending Lefevre sprawling from his combat chair.

The signal broke off.

Tiernan looked at his tactical officer, but didn't have to ask the question: the man's expression told him what he needed to know. *Jean Bart* and all aboard her were gone.

"Contact every Alliance ship you can reach in this mess," Tiernan ordered his communications officer, "and let them know that we're jumping out as soon as we're clear of this furball. I have no idea who may be senior after Lefevre, but if they have any sense at all they'll get the hell out of here."

Ticonderoga shuddered again, and more alarms sounded from the bridge.

* * *

Tesh-Dar stood in the burned-out clearing where so many warriors had been killed by the small human ship when it had crashed. It was an irony of war that the actions of a few of their fellow warriors, in reaching for glory for the Empress in attacking the crew of the vessel, accidentally took many of their sisters' lives. At this, she grieved, but not as a human would understand it: she did not lament the loss of their company in this life, for even in death were they bound to Her will, and Tesh-Dar could yet sense their spirits. She mourned their loss because they could no longer serve the Empress in the most glorious conflict the Empire had seen in millennia, in what Tesh-Dar had begun to think of as the Last War. The humans had proven themselves to be worthy enemies, and they would be given many cycles to bleed among the stars to see if one among them had blood that would sing.

Or so Tesh-Dar hoped. The knowledge that her race had only a few human centuries left before it would die out in a single generation was a heavy weight upon her soul. That all her species had accomplished in half a million human years of civilization, and all the more that had been done in the last hundred thousand since the founding of the Empire, would disappear into dust and ash in an uncaring cosmos was a fate she dared not contemplate. Her great fists clenched in anxiety at the thought, her ebony talons piercing the flesh of her palms, drawing blood.

Pushing away her fears for the future, Tesh-Dar turned her attention back to Li'ara-Zhurah. The young warrior had built a traditional funeral pyre for the human female who had commanded the metal *genoth*, just as the other warriors had built similar pyres for their fallen sisters. She gathered the wood from the nearby forest and stacked it precisely as custom demanded, often staggering in pain. She would not let other warriors help her, nor would she let the healers, who had been sent by the Empress from the Homeworld in an act of will, their bodies materializing here out of thin air, treat her injuries. The explosion of the human ship that had killed Li'ara-Zhurah's human opponent had nearly killed her, as well. A shard of metal, not unlike that which killed the human warrior, had stabbed through Li'ara-Zhurah's abdomen, and was still lodged there. Tesh-Dar sensed the great pain she was in, but was more concerned about her spiritual distress, the discord of her Bloodsong. It was more than mere disappointment at not being able to claim victory over the human after pursuing her so ardently. It was almost as if Li'ara-Zhurah had lost her *tresh*, one to whom she was bound for life as a young warrior. The death of one's tresh was one of the most traumatic events in the life of Her Children, a time of great mourning.

Again Tesh-Dar tore herself away from such melancholy thoughts. They were difficult to avoid, for while her race had conquered this part of the galaxy, spreading across the worlds of ten thousand suns, their Way, the spiritual path of their existence, was a difficult one.

She thought of the Messenger, and the curious twist of fate that had brought him here. Knowing that he was on the tiny human ship that now approached the still-raging battle in space, the warriors of the fleet knew that the craft was not to be molested. Tesh-Dar could not directly assist him in returning home, but the fleet would not interfere in any attempts to join with one of the other human vessels now fighting for their lives.

* * *

Li'ara-Zhurah set the last bundle of wood in place. She fell to her knees for a moment, the loss of blood from her wound taking its toll. She did not understand the depth of her sense of loss over this human animal. The mourning marks, where the skin of her face had turned black under her eyes, flowed as if she had shed tears of ink. It was how her race displayed inner pain, unlike the wetness she had seen streaming down the cheeks of some of the humans. Including this one.

Waving away the warriors who came to assist her, she struggled to her feet, willing her body to obey, controlling the pain with the discipline of many cycles spent training in harsh conditions.

Steadying herself, she reached out a hand to touch the face of the human woman who had sacrificed herself for the others, the cool flesh so alien to her touch, yet so achingly familiar. Perhaps the creature was an echo of her own soul, she thought. If so, then Li'ara-Zhurah had done well in honoring the Empress.

Reverently, she took a lock of the human's hair, cutting it cleanly with one of her talons. She carefully placed it in the leatherite pouch at her waist. It was traditionally used to carry trophies earned in combat, almost always a lock of hair. These strands of light colored hair, too, were a trophy, but one to remember and honor this human and those like her. They may not have souls that could sing to the Empress, but their warrior spirit was no less than that of Her Children.

Stepping back, she took the torch held out by one of the younger warriors. Walking slowly around the pyre, she set the wood alight. Then she moved away to the side, facing the rising flames, close enough that the heat nearly scorched her face.

She did not feel the priestess's arms fold around her as she collapsed into unconsciousness.

* * *

"You're out of your fucking mind, *sir!*" the pilot cried, looking at Sato with wide, disbelieving eyes. "I don't care if you monkeys stick a gun to my head again, but we are not flying into the middle of a goddamn fleet battle."

"If you want to get home, we have no choice," Sato told him, too tired to argue anymore. The fact of his own survival had come to feel like a millstone around his neck. "The enemy won't fire on us."

"How do you know?" Mills asked, his voice carrying no trace of argument, only curiosity.

"Because..." Sato struggled for words as he looked out the cockpit window, his eyes lost in the glare and flash of hundreds of ships trying to destroy one another. "Because for some reason I'm not to be touched." He looked at Mills. "They let me go from the *Aurora*, and somehow that made me special to them. I don't understand how or why. But those warriors on the *McClaren* recognized me somehow. They let us go because of it. And I'm convinced that they know I'm on this boat, and they won't do anything to harm us. Besides," he looked at the pilot, who was staring at him as if he were a rabid dog, frothing at the mouth, "we have no choice. Keran is lost, at least for now. If we want to leave, we've got to link up with one of the fleet's ships before they jump out. And that's going to be soon."

The fleet battle was still on the edge of the boat's sensor array, but Sato could tell that Admiral Tiernan had suffered heavy losses. He would have no choice but to jump out before the fleet was completely gutted. Sato knew that the Kreelans could sustain the loss of the fleet they had sent here, which he suspected had been "dumbed down" to the current level of human technology. Otherwise they probably could have destroyed the human fleet with just one of the gigantic ships that had met the *Aurora*.

"It's our only chance," Steph told the pilot. "I don't want to go back to Keran." She tightened her grip on Sato's hand as the sight of Coyle waving at her as the boat lifted off rose again in her mind, unbidden.

The pilot and copilot exchanged glances. "Fuck," the pilot said. "Why the hell not. It wouldn't be any more nuts than everything else that's happened today."

Ramming the boat's throttles to the stops, he turned and accelerated toward the cascade of explosions that marked the silent battle in space that was rapidly drawing to its conclusion.

* * *

Ticonderoga was streaming air from half a dozen hits that had penetrated her armor, but she was still making full speed as she burst out the far side of the Kreelan formation. There were other ships behind her, but not many: Tiernan had ordered several of his heavy cruisers, including his flagship, to turn and help a number of the Alliance ships that had run out of ready ammunition and were being mercilessly hammered by the Kreelans. He had lost two of his own cruisers, but saved nearly a dozen Alliance vessels. In the massive butcher's bill being rung up over Keran, he had to consider it a good trade.

The enemy was already turning to consolidate and regroup for another attack, but Tiernan had had enough. He knew it was time to fold. The war wasn't over, not by a long shot, but this battle certainly was.

"Stand by to jump," he said stonily as the *Ticonderoga* and two of her sister ships blasted a Kreelan destroyer that had pursued them out of the swirling engagement. Ahead of the flagship, most of the surviving ships had already jumped out. He had given them very explicit orders to jump as soon as they were clear. They would worry about regrouping at the rendezvous point.

"Sir," the flag communications officer suddenly called, "there's an assault boat calling in a mayday. They didn't make the rendezvous with their carrier."

"We can't risk stopping for them," Tiernan told him. The words tore at his heart, but he simply couldn't risk it. The fleet had already bled far too much.

"It's Lieutenant Sato on the line, sir," the communications officer told him in the sudden silence of the flag bridge, the guns and alarms now quiet, the bridge crew focused on the jump sequence.

Tiernan sucked in a breath through his teeth. He knew it was wrong to even consider wavering in his decision simply because it was Sato: he knew that the life of every other person aboard the boat was as precious.

But Sato was also a strategic asset. His knowledge and understanding of the enemy had been critical leading up to the battle, and his insights into them now might be even more so. On that basis, he convinced himself, and on that alone, could he justify one more risk to the *Ticonderoga* and her crew.

"Captain," he called over the vidcom to the ship's commander, who was busily engaged in monitoring the jump sequence, "suspend the jump. We need to pick up that assault boat."

The captain blinked at him, then said crisply, "Aye, aye, sir," before issuing maneuvering orders to get to the boat before the Kreelans had a chance to catch them.

As *Ticonderoga* sped forward, the remaining Terran and Alliance ships jumped out.

* * *

"I don't believe it," the pilot said, shaking his head in wonder. "*Ticonderoga's* on her way to pick us up." He looked back at Sato, who still stared out the viewscreen. "You know, sir, you might be considered lucky if you didn't seem to attract so much trouble."

Sato couldn't help but smile. He had forgotten the pilot's insubordination. He had forgotten everything but the enemy, and those who had died fighting them. More ghosts, but ones that now he could live with, that he could help avenge.

Steph stood next to him, her shoulder pressing against his side. He looked down and saw her smile, her grimy, soot-covered face the most beautiful thing in the universe at that moment.

Ticonderoga was only a few minutes away when the second Kreelan fleet arrived.

* * *

"Good, God!" someone exclaimed on the flag bridge as the tactical display suddenly filled with new yellow icons that immediately began to turn an ugly red.

"*Enemy close aboard!*" Tiernan heard the ship's tactical officer shout at her captain. In the flag bridge's main display, he could see half a dozen Kreelan warships, all clearly heavy cruisers like *Ticonderoga*, that had materialized within tens of meters of the flagship. Even in the swirling fight they had just been through, no ships had come that close. Every detail of the sleek Kreelan warships was clear without any magnification as they slid through space next to *Ticonderoga* like the predators they were.

"Stand by to fire!" the captain called out.

"Belay that!" Tiernan ordered on an impulse. The cruisers surrounding *Ticonderoga* were among what must have been at least another hundred warships that had just jumped in-system. And his flagship was right in the middle of the formation. "If they were going to fire, they would have already," he said, not quite believing his own words, but hoping they were true.

"The boat's approaching the starboard main airlock, sir," the tactical officer reported shakily, his eyes darting from ship to ship in the tactical display. There was utter and complete silence on the bridge and flag bridge. The only thing Tiernan could hear was the deep thrum of the ship's drives.

"Get them aboard," Tiernan ordered, "and then let's get the hell out of here."

* * *

"Come on, let's go!" Sato told the others as he ushered them forward through the airlock into the wounded cruiser. As soon as they had opened the hatch to the ship's main airlock, which opened directly to the passageway, since both ships were pressurized, smoke streamed into the boat, along with a dozen of the ship's crewmen who had been sent to help.

"These men need to get to sickbay immediately," Sato told the ship's surgeon and her brace of nurses and Marine medics. They quickly but carefully gathered up Sparks, Grishin, Hadley, and the others, lifting them onto stretchers and moving them quickly to sickbay.

"Lieutenant Sato?" one of the crewmen, an ensign, called. "The admiral wants to see you right away, sir."

Nodding, Sato told him, "As soon as my people are off this boat." He stood near the hatch, giving a pat on the back or a helping hand, whichever was most needed, to the soldiers and sailors who streamed past.

Steph stood next to him, clutching her rifle to her chest. Not for fear of anything on the *Ticonderoga*, but for fear of what could happen any moment: she and the others had seen the Kreelan warships jump in all around them, and she knew they would be boarding at any second. Sato had assured her it wouldn't happen, but she wasn't about to hand her rifle to anyone. And even now, her battered and grimy video array was still recording.

"But sir," the ensign protested, "the admiral said *right away.*"

"He can wait a couple minutes," Sato said as he hustled his charges off.

In three minutes, everyone was off the boat. After a quick check of the little ship's cavernous interior to make sure they hadn't left anyone behind, Sato grabbed Steph by the hand and dashed through the airlock into *Ticonderoga*. A crewman slapped the emergency disconnect control, and the airlock doors slammed shut. Then the docking collar was released, and the assault boat fell behind as the big cruiser pulled away.

Together, Sato and Steph ran after the ensign toward the flag bridge as *Ticonderoga* jumped to safety.

* * *

On Keran, watching as the healers tended to Li'ara-Zhurah's wounds, Tesh-Dar's mind was simultaneously tens of thousands of kilometers away, her second sight watching as the ships of the second fleet arrived. Her mind's eye saw the small vessel bearing the Messenger dock with one of the surviving human ships, sailing bravely under the many guns of her Imperial consorts, and he was borne to safety when the human ship jumped away.

She sighed in contentment, drawing her mind fully back to her body. She had decided she would take Li'ara-Zhurah back to the *kazha*, the school of the Way, where Tesh-Dar was headmistress. For there could the injury to her soul be mended.

Looking around her, she frowned at the devastation that the opening battle had wrought. The Children of the Empress would have much preferred personal combat without the use of such weapons as had been used this day, but the humans did not understand. Tesh-Dar knew that they would try and develop greater weapons, but hoped that someday they would see that it made little sense outside the arena of space: there, yes, let the great ships fight on. But on the ground, they would not be allowed to use much of what they had long taken for granted. She shrugged inwardly. They would learn. They had no choice.

"She is ready, my priestess," one of the healers told her, head bowed as she gestured toward Li'ara-Zhurah, who still lay unconscious.

Tesh-Dar bowed her head in thanks as she knelt and picked up Li'ara-Zhurah in her arms, an easy burden to her great body, but one that yet troubled her soul. With one last look at the human's funeral pyre, its flames rising high in the smoke-filled sky, Tesh-Dar closed her eyes as the power of the Empress surged through her, bending the laws of space and time to return the two of them to the Homeworld.

* * *

Aboard the *Ticonderoga*, now safely away in hyperspace, Admiral Tiernan turned at the sudden commotion at the entrance to the flag bridge.

"Lieutenant Sato, reporting as ordered, sir." Ichiro stood at rigid attention, holding a perfect salute for the admiral. Beside him stood Steph, still clutching her rifle.

"Lieutenant," Tiernan said, returning the younger man's salute. "Miss Guillaume." He was quiet for a moment as he looked at the two of them. Their uniforms (as an embed, Steph wore one, but without any rank) were filthy and torn, and their faces and hands were no better. "I take it that it was you who took *McClaren* up against those Kreelan ships that went after the carriers," he said to Sato.

"Yes, sir," Sato told him. "Captain Morrison was killed soon after...soon after he destroyed the Alliance troopship and we were hit. I was the senior surviving officer. I...did the best I could, sir, but...I lost my ship."

Tiernan saw the young officer's eyes mist over with a kind of grief that the admiral understood all too well. He saw Steph take Sato's hand and grip it tight.

"Son," Tiernan said, stepping closer and putting a hand on Sato's shoulder, "I lost a lot of ships today, and a lot of good men and women. You may have lost your ship, but you saved the carriers and their crews, and the soldiers from the planet. That's not a bad day's work for any ship's captain." He offered Sato a proud smile. "You and your crew did a damned fine job, Ichiro. A *damned* fine job."

EPILOGUE

President McKenna sat in a room deep in the heart of the presidential complex. It was surprisingly small and unassuming, considering the importance of the conversations that took place around the oval table at its center.

With her sat Minister of Defense Joshua Sabine, Admiral Tiernan, General Singh, and Secretary of State Hamilton Barca. General Sharine Metz, commander of the Terran Aerospace Defense Force, was also present. Metz was still angry that her service had been unable to participate in the defense of Keran, but part of her couldn't help but be relieved after hearing of the losses the other services had suffered.

This was the first unofficial debriefing that had been called by the president upon the fleet's return. The summary of the battle that Tiernan delivered had been more than sobering.

"So, you lost a third of your ships, admiral," McKenna said, looking at the room's display screen and the brutal list of losses it showed in stark text.

"Yes, Madam President," Tiernan said tightly. He was ready for the axe to fall. While the inevitability of being relieved had eaten at him like acid, he knew there was far more at stake than just his career or his pride. Had he been in McKenna's shoes he would not have hesitated to cashier an officer who had lost a full third of his fleet. The president had given him very strict instructions that he was not to sacrifice his fleet as a fighting force, but that's essentially what he had done when he and Lefevre had decided to go after the Kreelan force in high orbit. He had been appalled at how many ships were missing when *Ticonderoga* arrived at the rendezvous point. He had taken a high stakes gamble and lost.

She fixed him with her gaze, and the others in the room suddenly found other things to look at. They knew what was coming, too.

But, as she had on other occasions, McKenna surprised them. "Under the circumstances, Admiral, you and your crews did an amazing job," she told him. "I would have expected you to have lost far more of the fleet. And had you been given the ships and resources we had originally planned on, I suspect the battle might have gone a bit more in our favor."

Tiernan blinked, taken completely off-balance. "Ma'am, I've already prepared my resignation and retirement papers," he said automatically, as if he hadn't heard a word she had just said. He had practiced this conversation so many times on the trip home that his brain simply hadn't caught up with the reality.

"I don't think that will be necessary, admiral," Sabine, his direct boss, told him with a smile. "The president and I are of one mind on this. The losses suffered by the expeditionary force were extremely heavy. No one can dispute that. But you, and General Ray's troops in the ground battle, carried out the spirit of the president's orders."

"You might have been able to preserve more of your ships had you pulled out of the system before the final engagement with the Kreelan fleet," McKenna told him, "but that would have left our relations with the Alliance in a shambles. I'll say this only in this room, and it is never to be repeated: as great a tragedy as losing Keran might be, it is one we could diplomatically and politically afford in terms of Earth's standing in the human sphere. But we could not afford to leave the Alliance fleet hanging. That would have been an unmitigated disaster in this situation. Admiral," she told him, "I want you to know that the sacrifice of your ships and crews, and the sacrifice of General Singh's troops, was not in vain."

As if on cue, the door opened quietly and one of her aides poked his head in.

"He's here, Madam President," he said.

"Show him in, please." McKenna watched her companions as they all looked toward the door, curiosity evident on their faces.

Ambassador Laurent Navarre of Avignon stepped into the room, and the others came to their feet in surprise. All but President McKenna, of course.

"Mr. Ambassador," Barca said, taking Navarre's hand, "what a pleasant surprise." With a slight but unmistakeable emphasis on the last word, he glanced over his shoulder at the president, who remained silent.

"Please, Hamilton," Navarre told him as he took the big man's hand and shook it, "you may blame me for the cloak and dagger antics. I specifically requested that President McKenna keep my presence here a secret, even from you."

"Especially from me, you mean," Barca told him with a smile as Navarre shook the hands of the others.

"Madam President," he said as he came to McKenna. She stood, and he took her hand and kissed it. "Always a great honor."

"The honor is all mine," she told him, smiling despite herself at the man's charm. *You can take the Frenchman out of France*, she thought, *but you can't take France out of the Frenchman*. "But I have to admit we're all curious about the, as you put it, 'cloak and dagger antics.'"

"Yes," he said heavily as he waited until she had regained her seat, then sat down with the others around the table. He glanced at the information on the wall display, but only briefly. What it showed came as no surprise to him. "I come unofficially as a representative of the Alliance," he told them. "I am here so soon because my government arranged for a series of couriers to relay news as quickly as possible. Very expensive, but in this case a bargain." He licked his lips, clearly upset about what he had to tell them. "Madam President, my friends, the Alliance is in a state of near-panic. As you know, the fleet led by *Amiral* Lefevre was the greater part of our space combat power, and the ground divisions that were lost on Keran were our best troops. The opposition in the parliaments of every planet of the Alliance is calling for a vote of confidence against the Alliance Prime Minister, saying that the current government has left the entire Alliance open to alien invasion."

"But the opposition parties were the strongest proponents of sending the fleet in the first place!" Tiernan blurted, looking at Barca, who was shaking his head, not in disbelief, but in disgust. The opposition's reaction came as no surprise to him.

"Too true, *amiral*," Navarre said, "but they are equally free to blame the current government for any disasters. And what happened to *Amiral* Lefevre's fleet and the ground forces can only be considered a disaster. The greatest defeat in a single battle, perhaps, since Napoleon's defeat at Waterloo."

"How many ships did you lose?" McKenna asked.

"Lefevre sailed with just over one hundred and fifty warships, including half a dozen resupply ships," he told her, the pain of Lefevre's loss clearly written on his face. "Only fifty-seven returned, most of them damaged. And all ten ground divisions were virtually wiped out, although the *Légion étrangère* suffered the worst: of the twenty combat regiments deployed to Keran, only a few hundred legionnaires survived."

"It wasn't just about the numbers," Tiernan interjected. "We did the right thing, making a stand there and not just letting the enemy walk in with their swords swinging. Even with the second fleet the Kreelans sent in at the end, if we had only had a few dozen more ships and a better idea of what to expect before we went in, I think we might have been able to hold them off. Our two fleets worked extremely well together, even without tightly linked command and control."

"No one would agree with you more than me, *amiral*," Navarre reassured him. "And that, truly, brings us to why I am here." He looked at the faces around the room, his gaze finally settling on the president. "The Alliance Prime Minister would like to establish a new government, an interplanetary government that goes beyond the Francophone worlds, beyond the existing *Alliance Française*."

"Earth constituencies would never agree to become part of the Alliance," Barca interjected, shaking his head. "No matter how much sense it may make. We went through hell years ago just to form the planetary government."

"You misunderstand, *mon ami*," Navarre corrected him gently. "What we propose is the formation of a completely new interplanetary government, a confederation of all humanity, if you will, based on the original principles of the Human Sphere Defense Agreement proposal. In the aftermath of Keran, all of the planetary prime ministers of the Alliance support this, although in secret - for now. We believe that if Earth and the *Alliance Française* formally unite, other planetary governments will follow suit." He paused. "Especially once word of the Keran disaster reaches all the governments. There is likely to be an interstellar panic, and we must avoid it as much as possible, and concentrate our efforts on building up our defenses."

"Ambassador," Tiernan interjected, "with all due respect, before the deployment to Keran we couldn't even get your government to accept or even consider, even though it was *gratis*, critical hardware and software that would have helped our fleets work together."

"I assure you," Navarre told him, "that situation no longer pertains, *mon amiral*. Let me put it to you plainly: both the planetary and Alliance governments - majority and opposition, both - are terrified. And with good reason. We stand no hope of defending ourselves unless we can rebuild our fleet, and quickly. And a unified government with Mankind's homeworld right now makes a great deal of political sense." He gave them an ironic grin. "Fear opens many doors that before were firmly shut."

"It's going to be a hard sell to the Terran Congress," Barca told her.

"No, it won't," the president said coldly. "I've assured every member of Congress who voted against the appropriations bills for the expeditionary force that I'll make sure every human being on this planet knows that they were against building the fleet that might have saved Keran and held the Kreelan menace at bay. I don't expect this lovely honeymoon to last long, but for now we can count on a great deal of support from Congress. Right now they're tripping over themselves to build out our original appropriations, more than tripling the size of the *original* fleet we wanted to build over the next three years. Assuming we have that long." She turned back to Navarre. "But there will be problems setting up a government such as you propose, the same ones that killed the Human Sphere Defense Agreement proposal."

"Namely," Barca said, "who runs the show, and how to keep the leadership position from becoming a political plum for the 'haves' in the eyes of the 'have-nots.'"

"We have a solution for that much of it, I believe," Navarre said. "We propose that the new government's leader - president or prime minister - should be nominated from Earth alone. Earth has the greatest industrial capacity of any single planet in the human sphere, and, despite the differences among the various planetary governments, it is a symbolic home to us all. This will not be a hard sell, as you say, in the current climate. The Alliance will need some concessions, of course, but on that point agreement has already been made." He turned to President McKenna and smiled. "Madam President, I believe you may be in for a promotion."

"Now that we've sorted out that minor detail," Tiernan said quietly, an uncharacteristically worried expression on his face, "we only have one other thing to worry about." The others turned to him with questioning looks. "Where, and when, are the Kreelans going to strike next?"

* * *

Colonel Sparks was still in a great deal of pain from his injuries, but it paled in comparison to the sorrow he had endured in the weeks before he was able to bull his way out of the hospital. He had spent the time writing letters, by hand with pen and paper, from dawn until dusk, to the kin of his dead soldiers. Two thousand seven hundred and twenty-three, all told. Most of the letters had been brief; some had not. All of them had been heartfelt. Sparks was in many ways a hard and difficult man, but his soldiers were his family, and he refused to rest until he had reached out and touched the family or loved ones, or in some cases simply a friend, of every man and woman who had died under his command. He had written letters for all of them. All but one.

Among all the 7th Cavalry troopers who had made their final stand on Keran, there was one to whom they all owed their very lives. Standing now at the front porch of an old-style farm house surrounded by acres of golden wheat, in what had once been the American state of Iowa, he knocked on the sturdy but time- and weather-worn front door. In the window next to the door hung a small flag with a white background and red trim around the edges. In the center was a single gold star.

Sparks wore his dress blues, which as fate would have it was of a design loosely based on the uniform worn by cavalrymen when horses were the standard mode of transportation. Today there were no spurs, no flamboyant cavalry officer's hat. But there was a sword, held reverently in his white-gloved hands.

With him stood Sergeant Hadley, also wearing his dress blue uniform, and Stephanie Guillaume in a trim black dress. She wasn't here as a journalist, over the vehement protestations of her editor, who went ballistic at her snubbing what he had claimed was a once-in-a-lifetime human interest story. Steph knew that this would hardly be the only opportunity for someone who wanted to follow a story like this: the war would be filled with countless opportunities to report on stories of personal tragedy. She was here purely out of respect for a woman she had known only a very brief time. And to give her thanks to someone she had never met.

After a moment, movement could be heard inside. The door opened, swinging inward on well-oiled hinges. A man in his early fifties, as sturdy and weather-worn as the door to the house, looked out at them through the screen door.

"Mr. Coyle?" Sparks said, trying to force his voice to be clear. But despite his best efforts, his throat had choked up on him.

The man blinked at the uniforms, and then said quietly, cocking his head toward the flag with the gold star hanging in the window, "The Army already notified us."

"I understand that, sir," Sparks told him. "I was Patty's commander. I was only released from the hospital today, or I would have come to deliver the news myself."

"Who is it, John?" said a woman's voice from deeper in the house. Her face appeared beside her husband, and Steph could barely hold back her tears. Like her husband, the woman was in her fifties, and time hadn't treated her kindly. But her face was unmistakably that of her daughter.

"I'm Colonel James Sparks, ma'am," Sparks said through the screen door. "Your daughter, Patty, was under my command when she...when she died." He bit his lip, trying to stave off his own tears. He had delivered the news of the deaths of his men and women to many other parents and loved ones, but for some reason this was different. "This is Sergeant Jason Hadley and Miss Stephanie Guillaume," he went on, introducing his companions. "We wanted to come by and pay our respects to you and your husband. The other soldiers of the regiment...well, they all wanted to come, but I figured it had best be just a few of us. I know this must be a terribly difficult time for you, but your daughter...your daughter was a very special woman. A very special soldier."

John Coyle just stood there staring at them, saying nothing.

Gently pushing past her husband, she opened the screen door. "I'm Elaine," she told him. "Please, colonel, do come in." As she led them in, passing by her husband, she told Sparks in a quiet voice that echoed her own pain, "I apologize for my husband, colonel. Patty was always his little girl, even after she joined the Army. And he...he hasn't been able to grieve for her. He's still in shock, and I worry about him. I don't know that he's really accepted that she's gone."

Inside the house, sitting in the living room, Mrs. Coyle offered them something to drink, but they all declined. She sat down beside her husband on a sofa that, like them, had seen better times than these.

"We already know she's dead," John Coyle said woodenly.

"I know that, sir," Sparks told him, holding his gaze steadily. "I didn't come here to tell you that she died. I simply wanted to tell you about how she lived. How she saved hundreds of her fellow soldiers. Had it not been for your daughter, not a single one of the soldiers of my regiment, including the three of us, would have made it home alive. Us and the survivors of two regiments of the Alliance Foreign Legion. She saved us all."

Elaine Coyle had her arm around her husband's shoulders, and she nodded appreciatively at what Sparks was saying. Her eyes misted over, but she had come to grips with Patty's death.

John Coyle simply stared at the coffee table.

"I realize that it's no consolation, but your daughter is being submitted for a Medal of Honor," Sparks went on. "Lord knows she earned it.

"But I have something more personal I wanted to give you to honor her memory." He held out the saber he had brought, an exact duplicate of the one he had fought with and lost on Keran. Every bit of the sword and its scabbard had been polished until it gleamed. "This is a cavalry saber, the very same as those last used by the horse soldiers of the 7th Cavalry Regiment centuries ago. Like me, it's an anachronism, but it's the most fitting thing an old cavalryman could think of to represent your daughter's spirit and determination."

Elaine smiled uncertainly as she made to take the weapon, but suddenly her husband reached out to grasp it, taking the scabbard in both hands. He held the sheathed sword in his lap and stared at it, running a hand along its glossy surface.

Then, for the first time since being told about his daughter's death, the tears came. Cradling the saber as if it were his little girl so many years ago, yet only yesterday, John Coyle wept with grief.

* * *

On La Seyne, Emmanuelle Sabourin saw the news about the formation of a new interplanetary government, the Confederation of Humanity, that would bring together the Alliance with Earth, and any other worlds that wanted to join for mutual protection against the Kreelan menace.

Sitting in a café on a side street in the capital city of Rouen, sipping at a cup of strong coffee, she watched the reaction of the people around her as the news was broadcast over the planetary web. Most, she saw, were happy about the news. It gave them some hope that humanity might have a chance against the aliens.

Of that, Sabourin was not so sure. She herself should not have been here, relaxing like a tourist. She should be dead with the rest of the crew of the *Jean Bart*. But in an ironic twist of fate, when *Amiral* Lefevre was distributing the Terran Marines among the Alliance ships, someone had miscounted and the team earmarked for one of the destroyers was short by two people. Sabourin had volunteered to go with them. Emotionally drained as she had been, she wasn't about to sit by and leave one of their ships with a weak ability to defend itself against the horrid boarders. As fate would have it, the destroyer, while damaged by enemy fire, had managed to survive the last frantic engagement and had jumped to safety.

What caught her eye in the news report was the proposal to formally merge the combat forces of all constituent planets into a unified Confederation military, including a navy, ground forces (which people had begun to talk about as a Territorial Army), an aerospace arm, and a marine force that would fight from the ships of the fleet as the Terran Marines had at Keran. As she herself had. The report said that the new Confederation Marine Corps (the name had not been officially blessed, as the new government did not technically exist) was in desperate need of any personnel with combat experience to help train the wave of volunteers that was flooding into military recruiting centers across Earth and the Alliance worlds.

Sabourin only considered the thought as long as it took her to finish her coffee. Then she picked up her satchel and headed down the street toward the naval headquarters building where she had been temporarily posted. Her new commander had told her in no uncertain terms that she could have whatever assignment she wanted. But she had been unable, unwilling, perhaps, was more accurate, to decide on what her next posting should be.

Until now.

* * *

Sergent Chef Roland Mills felt very conspicuous wearing the red ribbon of the *Légion d'honneur (Commandeur)* on his uniform as he strode off the Earth-orbit shuttle from Africa Station onto the tarmac at the newly renamed Confederation Marine Corps Headquarters at Quantico in what was once the United States. The *Légion d'honneur* was the highest award the Alliance had for gallantry in the face of the enemy, much as the Medal of Honor was for the Terran military forces. Precious few legionnaires had won it in recent history, and few of those had been awarded a class higher than *Chevalier*. The reason Mills felt self-conscious about it was that he really had no other decorations to speak of, other than a couple of deployment medals. The bright red ribbon blazed from the drab camouflage of his battle uniform.

He was among the advance party, led by Colonel Grishin, sent by the Legion to coordinate its incorporation as a regiment in the new Marine Corps. Mills knew that the bureaucratic battles fought to keep the Legion as a separate entity had been every bit as fierce in their own way as the Battle for Keran, as it was now known. But in the end the Legion's leadership had been given a simple choice: become part of the new Marine Corps and continue to fight as an elite unit, or be dismantled and absorbed into the new Territorial Army formations that were being formed for homeland defense on every planet that was planning to join the nascent Confederation Government.

Faced with such an ultimatum, and after suffering the near-total loss of every single existing combat regiment, they had chosen for the Legion to become part of the Corps.

Mills shook hands with the greeting party, a group of Marines who, like him and most of the other legionnaires present, were veterans of Keran. But the term "veteran" was relative: none of the Marines here had actually fought the enemy, while Mills and the other legionnaires had seen more than their fair share of combat against the Kreelans. The Marines - *the* other *Marines*, Mills corrected himself - were eager to make up for that shortcoming, and wanted to take advantage of the legionnaires' experience.

As with nearly everyone he had met who knew what had happened on Keran, the very first thing they wanted to hear about was the famous hand-to-hand battle Mills had fought against the huge Kreelan warrior.

Mills had always thought that telling the tale would get easier over time through sheer mindless repetition of his greatest adrenalin rush. But it hadn't. It had only gotten more difficult with every telling. He had never been one to have nightmares, but after returning home the warrior began to haunt his dreams. More often than not, he woke in a cold sweat, breathing as if he had run a marathon, with the memory of her snarling blue face and ivory fangs fading like an afterimage in his eyes. He was smart enough to know that he was suffering from post-traumatic stress, but he was too proud to seek counseling. He also knew that the Legion and the Corps needed him and those like him who had survived, and there simply wasn't time to waste kibitzing with a head doctor. And he would lose any chance he might have to go back into combat. Of that, more than anything else, was he afraid.

As he began to tell his latest group of eager listeners of his exploits, he put his hands on his thighs under the table so no one could see how badly his tightly clenched fists were shaking.

* * *

Lieutenant Amelia Cartwright, now an officer of the Terran (soon to be Confederation) Navy, sat in the pilot's chair of the recently commissioned military courier *Nyx*. Her hands tensed on the controls as the navigation computer went through its litany of announcements prior to the ship's reemergence into normal space. This would be the sixth mission she had flown in as many weeks from a support ship that had been positioned roughly a day's jump from Keran: far enough to hopefully avoid detection by Kreelan ships in the system, yet close enough to minimize the travel time for the couriers.

The design of the *Nyx* and her sisters emphasized speed and maneuverability above all else, and they were being used to monitor what was happening to Keran. The news they brought back was increasingly grim.

Any hopes the human sphere had of retaking Keran any time soon, if ever, had quickly been dispelled after the first few reconnaissance missions had returned. Keran was being transformed with frightening rapidity. While the changes being made appeared to be compatible with human life, the fundamental features of the planet were being reshaped by alien hands. The atmosphere was being altered with a combination of compounds that gave it a slight magenta hue. On the ground, large areas of the planet's deserts were turning dark, as if they were being transformed into black seas whose composition eluded every attempt at analysis.

It was increasingly difficult to ascertain the fate of Keran's people, but everyone expected the worst. Every reconnaissance mission brought back fewer and fewer recordings of transmissions from the surface, and every single one of them was a cry of agonizing despair. The Kreelans were killing them. All of them. As best anyone had been able to piece together, the aliens herded groups of them into arenas built for the purpose, to fight and die exactly as the crew of *Aurora* had. Men, women, children: it made no difference. They were forced to fight, and if they didn't, they were simply killed. Humanity was now in a war for survival, and the loser would become extinct.

"Standby for transpace sequence," the navigation computer purred. Cartwright had programmed a very close emergence this time, using the data from her last jump to refine the coordinates. It would be right on the theoretical edge of where the planet's gravity well would pose a major danger during their reemergence.

As the computer counted down the last seconds, Cartwright wondered how many ships would be in-system this time. The average had been a hundred ships, about half of them cruisers and the rest destroyers. What no one had been able to figure out was how the Kreelans were managing to change the planet so quickly without having a huge number of ships hauling in the necessary materials and machinery. It was as if they were simply doing it by magic. And that wasn't possible. Was it?

"...three...two...one," the computer said. "Normal space emergence."

Hyperspace dissolved into a panorama of the deepest black, and where Keran should be was...

"Holy Mother of God," Sid, now a lieutenant, junior grade in the Navy, breathed beside her.

The surface of Keran, the outlines of its continents where land met the sea, had changed. The deserts that had been turning dark were now gone, replaced by plains of grass. The ship's telescope array hunted the unfamiliar landscape for the major cities. Even during the last mission, they had still been clearly visible, even as burned out scars in the landscape. Now...they were gone, erased as if they had never existed.

"Jesus," Cartwright whispered. "How is this possible?"

"I don't know," Sid told her, his eyes wide, frightened by the changes in the planet below. "And it looks like they have more ships."

The tactical display showed nearly two hundred ships in near-Keran space and around its moons. The ship's telescope array took images of them, as well. As with the planet's deserts earlier, both moons were being consumed by a sea of blackness, some unknown and unfathomable material that denied its secrets to human science.

"Just a suggestion," Sid told her tightly as *Nyx* sped ever closer to the planet and the warships sailing around it, "but wouldn't it be a good idea to jump out?"

"Not yet," she said, adjusting the ship's course minutely. "I want to get all the data we can. Are you picking up any signals?" On previous missions, they had always been able to contact someone on the surface.

Sid didn't answer her right away as he worked the ship's instruments. After a few precious minutes, he said, "Nothing. Not a goddamn thing."

They shared a glance, then looked back at the globe of the planet, now alien and forbidding. Cartwright's hands clenched as she fought to keep her emotions under control. She knew that there were most likely still survivors on the planet, fleeing or fighting for their lives. But during the last reconnaissance mission they had picked up *hundreds* of different transmitters, radio and laser-links. Now there was nothing but shattering silence. Survivors there might yet be, but the silence on the airwaves told how effective the Kreelans had been in hunting them down.

Nyx flew onward for another minute, then two, when half a dozen of the cruisers that were headed to intercept her were almost close enough to fire.

"Time to go, boss," Sid reminded her.

"Yeah, I guess so," Cartwright said grudgingly as she hauled the ship around in a tight chandelle turn.

Five long minutes later they reached their jump point, and *Nyx* disappeared into hyperspace.

* * *

Tesh-Dar stood upon the central dais of one of the arenas on this, the newest world to be claimed for the Empire. Reshaping this planet was a a reflection of the compulsion of her race to bend the universe to their will. It was not for want of more living space: the Empire was so vast that Tesh-Dar could have traveled most of her life in the swiftest of starships, and still not reached from one far frontier to the other. The Empire spanned ten thousand suns and even more planets. When there had been need of a world for a particular purpose, or in a particular place as suited the Empress, often as not the builders had simply created it. Such was the power of Her Children.

But her race lived and breathed for battle. And here on this planet, in this arena, the final battle was being fought, pathetic though it had become. A brace of her warriors, using only the weapons they had been born with, faced off against the last human survivors. They had been very adept at evading their hunters, but at last Tesh-Dar had called an end to the game. Great wheels were turning in the heart of the

Empire, and this first great combat between humans and Her Children was to be brought to a final ending.

The humans before her were dirty and starving. A ten of males and half as many females were all that remained of the planet's original population. In the many matches Tesh-Dar had watched as the humans had been sacrificed to the demands of the Way of her people, she had seen many fight bravely; some had clearly cried for mercy, of which there was none; others stood with what she admired as a quiet dignity, refusing to fight, until they at last were painlessly put to death. None were tortured or forced to endure pain beyond what was experienced in battle in the arena. Tesh-Dar understood the concept of cruelty, but did not believe it applied to her people. Their Way was extraordinarily difficult, and death came all too easily. But pain was never inflicted needlessly, or as an end unto itself.

One by one, the humans fell to her warriors. But these humans, the last upon this planet, did not give up, and did not surrender. They fought to the last, and died with honor.

* * *

In the capital city on his home planet of Nagano, Commander Ichiro Sato ignored the veiled stares he received as he made his way along a crowded street that led to his childhood home. He wore his dress black uniform, which made him stand out even more among the dour salarymen in cheap suits and the women in colorful kimonos, eyes downcast, who streamed past him. Around his neck he wore the Terran Medal of Honor, the only one to be granted for the battle of Keran that wasn't posthumous. He hadn't known most of those who had received "The Medal," as it was often called. But his own decoration served to remind him of the one he had: Gunnery Sergeant Pablo Ruiz. Sato's recommendation to award Ruiz The Medal had been taken up-chain almost without comment, followed by Silver Stars for bravery in the face of the enemy for every man and woman of *McClaren's* Marine detachment. Ensign, now Lieutenant, Bogdanova and Senior Chief Petty Officer DeFusco also wore Silver Stars, and every single survivor of the *McClaren* had received at least a Bronze Star. They had all earned it. And more.

Walking beside him, Stephanie held an exquisitely wrapped gift. She and Sato had spent nearly an hour getting the wrapping just so. She had thought it a fun but ultimately wasteful use of time, until he explained how important the wrapping of a gift was in Nagano's culture, and that it was as important as the gift itself.

And the gift? Two fresh pineapples in a box. She had laughed at him when he had first suggested it, but he was completely serious. "Listen, I know you don't believe this," he had told her, "but this is perfect! She absolutely loves pineapple, and they're almost impossible to get on Nagano. My uncle managed to get some a few times - that's where she first tasted it - but he must have paid a fortune."

"She," of course, was his mother, whom he hadn't seen since he had left for the Terran Naval Academy. Steph had suggested some gorgeous jewelry, but he only shook his head. "She doesn't wear any." It was hard for Steph to conceive of any woman not wanting to wear jewelry, but she had let it ride and trusted Ichiro's advice. He hadn't steered her wrong yet.

A few weeks before, they had both been at the commissioning of the first of the new shipyards that were being built in Earth orbit, where the keels of a dozen new warships were being laid down in a fast-build program that would have the new ships undergoing their first space trials in three months. One of them, the heavy cruiser *Yura*, would be Ichiro's to command.

The ceremony had been held on Africa Station, which, like the other orbital transfer points, was being radically enlarged to accommodate more traffic. While most of the attention had been riveted on the massive yards and the ships that were even now beginning to take shape, Sato had spent a considerable part of the ceremony staring out at the hulk of the *Aurora*, which rode quietly at anchor in the original space dock. The Navy had decided that she would never sail again, and would eventually be broken up. Part of him would have exchanged his new heavy cruiser for the old *Aurora* in an instant; another part was horrified at the thought of ever again setting foot on her decks.

Despite the maudlin thoughts about his old ship amid the martial pomp of the commissioning ceremony for the shipyards, the gathering on Africa Station was also one of joy: to a great deal of well-wishing and cat-calling, he and Steph announced their engagement and plans to marry. After returning from Keran, they quickly came to the conclusion that they were meant for each other. With him in command of a warship and her helping the government get people behind the formation of the Confederation, their married life would be difficult, to say the least. But they were determined to make it work. They knew now that the universe was not a hospitable place, and it was an immense comfort just knowing that they had each other to love and hold onto.

They arrived at the drab apartment building and rode up the cramped elevator to the fifteenth floor. Everything here was clean, almost antiseptic in appearance. And quiet. Their footsteps echoed as they walked down the tiled hall until they reached a certain door.

Looking one last time at Steph, who only nodded, Ichiro pressed the illuminated button that would let the occupants know they had visitors.

After a brief moment, the door opened to reveal a middle-aged woman of Japanese descent, not so different in appearance from a million others in the city. Physically she was still in the prime of beauty for those of her age, her face showing few wrinkles and only faint traces of gray in her otherwise lush raven hair. But her expression and eyes were blank, her thoughts and emotions carefully concealed, a defense mechanism developed over a lifetime of emotional and physical abuse.

"Greetings, Mother," Ichiro said in Japanese, bowing his head.

For a moment, she said nothing, did nothing. She made no reaction at all. Then the veneer that had been her shield against the pain of her life, built up over decades, suddenly shattered and fell away.

In that moment, she did what no self-respecting Nagano woman, even one who had been widowed only a week before when her hated husband had died of a burst aneurysm, would ever have admitted to: she burst into tears and took her only son in her arms.

LEGEND OF THE SWORD

TWENTY-NINE

Tesh-Dar, high warrior priestess of the Desh-Ka, strode quietly along the paths of the Imperial Garden. Protected by a great crystalline dome that reached far into the airless sky of the Empress Moon, the stones that made up the ages-old walkways had come from every planet touched by the Empire. The paths wove their way in a carefully designed pattern for leagues: had Tesh-Dar been of a mind and had the luxury of time, she could have wandered in contemplative peace for an entire cycle and still not fully explored it all. Cut from lifeless rocks adrift in deep space to planets teeming with the fruits of galactic evolution, each stone was a testament to the glory of the Empire and the power of the Empress. Rutted sandstone to crystalline matrix, each told part of the Empire's long and glorious history.

In Tesh-Dar's mind, each step also brought her people closer to their End of Days.

Like the stones, the flora of the Garden was made up of every species of plant that flowered from across the Empire. From gigantic trees that reached up to the top of the great dome to tiny algae, all were preserved for the pleasure and the glory of the Empress. Even species that were incompatible with the atmosphere natural to Her Children were here, protected by special energy bubbles that preserved them in their native atmosphere and soil, carefully tended by the army of clawless ones whose lives were devoted to this task.

Many of the stones she trod upon were from worlds that had been one-time enemies of the Empire, including the dozen or so species Her Children had fought in past ages since the *Kreela* had attained the stars. Now the stones and flora the gardeners tended here were all that was left of them. Some of those ancient civilizations had fought to the last against the swords of Her Children, and were now remembered with honored reverence. Others, broken and beaten, consigning themselves to defeat, had been obliterated by the will of the Empress, their worlds left as nothing more than molten slag, barren of all life. The last such war had ended thousands of generations before Tesh-Dar was born, and some living now thought the records of them in the Books of Time were only legend. Tesh-Dar, greatest of the living warrior priestesses and elder blood sister to She Who Reigns, knew better. There was much in the Books of Time that she fervently wished was nothing more than legend, but wishing did not make it so.

She strolled to a part of the path that was newly added, made up of stones from the planet the humans had called Keran. The rocks and the flora from that world were no more or less remarkable than the other specimens in the Garden, save that they had been taken in a war whose birth she had witnessed, a war in which she would likely die. Now Keran, too, was part of the Empire. The many humans who had lived there, and many who had come from other worlds to aid them, had died at the hands of Tesh-Dar's warriors, and the builder caste had since reshaped the planet in a way more pleasing to Her Children. The reshaping had been done more out of habit than out of need: the Empire had enough worlds on which to live, for as long as her race had left.

Tesh-Dar paused as she stood upon these tokens of Keran in her sandaled feet. The humans had impressed the great priestess: even at the last — exhausted, desperate, and afraid — they had resisted. And those who had come from across the stars to help them, sailing in primitive vessels and fighting with weapons the Empire had retired tens of thousands of cycles before, had fought tenaciously for a world that was not their own. The Empress, too, had been greatly pleased. Yet it did nothing to ease the worry in Tesh-Dar's heart. As the highest-ranking warrior of her entire race, standing only two steps from the throne, Tesh-Dar bore the greatest responsibility for helping to preserve her people and carry out the will of the Empress. But their greatest enemy was not the humans. It was time.

"Why is your heart troubled so, priestess of the Desh-Ka?" the Empress said quietly from behind her.

Tesh-Dar turned and knelt before her sovereign. She had sensed the Empress approaching, of course. While they were sisters born of the same womb, although many cycles apart, She Who Reigned was Mother to them all. United by the ethereal force that was the Bloodsong, the members of their species were both individuals and part of a greater spiritual whole, of which She was the heart. Their purpose for existence was driven by the will of the living Empress, who contained the souls of every Empress who had lived since the founding of the Empire a hundred thousand cycles before. Her body held all of their souls, save one: the First Empress, the most powerful of all, and the one they sought for their very salvation.

"My Empress," Tesh-Dar said reverently as she saluted, bringing her left fist in its armored gauntlet against her right breast, the smooth black metal of her armor ringing in the quiet of the Garden. She had been in the presence of the Empress many times over her long life, but each time was as the very first. She felt a surge of primal power, as if she were standing close to a spiritual flame, which, in a sense, she was. "The humans have given us hope," she said, "yet I fear that we will not find what we must in the time we have left."

"Walk with me, daughter," said the Empress, holding out her arm. Tesh-Dar gently took it, careful not to mar her sovereign's flawless blue skin with her long black talons, and they walked slowly together along this section of the path that was now a remembrance of their first conquest among the humans.

The two were a study in contrasts. While Tesh-Dar had the smooth cobalt blue skin and felinoid eyes shared by all of her race, she stood more than a head taller than most warriors and was wrapped in powerful muscle that made her the most powerful of her species, equal in raw strength to half a dozen warriors. She was clad in traditional ceremonial armor that was as black as night and yet shone like a mirror, with the rune of her order, the Desh-Ka, emblazoned in cyan on the breastplate. Her hair, black as was the norm for her people, hung in elegant braids, so long now that they were carefully looped around her upper arms. That was the only way any of Her Children wore their hair, for it was more than simply a legacy from some long-forgotten biological ancestor who needed it for warmth and to protect the skin: their hair was the physical manifestation of a complex spiritual bond with the Empress. At her neck she wore the ebony Collar of Honor, a band of living metal that all of Her Children came to wear in their youth, when they were ready to accept the Way. Every child wore at least five pendants of precious metal or gemstones that proclaimed their given name. As the child matured, more pendants were added to display her deeds and accomplishments in glorifying the Empress. Tesh-Dar wore more than any other of her kind save one, with rows of pendants flowing across the upper half of her chest. As with all the high priestesses of the warrior orders that served the Empress, she also wore a special symbol at the front of her collar: an oval of glittering metal in which had been carved the rune of the Desh-Ka, echoing the larger image that blazed from her breastplate.

By comparison, the Empress was was typical in size for a Kreelan female. Her dress was as simple as Her spirit was complex: much like the healer caste, all She wore was a simple white robe with no adornments. Around Her neck, unlike the black collar worn by the others of Her race, was a simple gold colored band. It, too, was living metal, far more resilient than gold, and was the only surviving relic of the First Empress, their only physical link to Her. Passed from Empress to Empress upon each new Ascension, if there was anything that embodied the spirit of the Empire, it would be this simple object.

The most striking feature of the Empress was that her hair, braided but not as long as Tesh-Dar's, was pure white. It was not a random anomaly or an indicator of age: every Empress since the First Empress, Keel-Tath, had been born with white hair. It was part of their ancestral bloodline from those days of legend. Once every great cycle, roughly seven human years, a female warrior child was born with white hair and ebony talons. Not all would ascend to the throne, but the collar of the Empress could only be worn by a warrior who had those two traits. For the white hair proclaimed them as direct descendants of Keel-Tath, and the ebony talons signified that they were fertile.

"I share your fears," the Empress said simply, as they continued walking along the path. There were no lies told in the Empire, no exaggerations or deceit to misdirect or conceal, no factions battling for control. These things had been left behind long, long ago, cut away from their civilization by the wisdom and sword of the First Empress. "Long have we searched for the One who shall fulfill the ancient prophesies, just as we have searched for the tomb of the First Empress among thousands of stars in the galaxy. Much of interest have we found, but not that which we so desperately need."

The Empress's words chilled Tesh-Dar. She did not need to hear them to know they were true, but it was one thing to believe such a thing on one's own, and quite another to hear them from Her lips so plainly spoken.

"There is no hope, then?" Tesh-Dar asked quietly, the hand not holding the arm of the Empress clenching so hard that her talons pierced the armored gauntlet she wore, and the skin beneath. She did not notice any pain.

Stopping in the middle of the path, the Empress turned to her, lifting up Her hand to caress Tesh-Dar's face. "Do not despair so, Legend of the Sword," She said, using the nickname She had given Tesh-Dar long ago, when she had been a child and under Tesh-Dar's tutelage at the priestess's *kazha*, or school of the Way. It was not merely a token of affection, for Tesh-Dar was the greatest swordmistress the Empire had ever known in all its history. Even before she became the last high priestess of the Desh-Ka and inherited her current physical form and the powers that were the legacy of that ancient sect, she had had no rival in the arena. Among Her Children, Tesh-Dar was indeed a living legend.

She gave the Empress a shy smile, something few of the peers had ever seen, her ivory fangs momentarily revealed through parted dark red lips. While her nickname was well-known throughout the Empire, none of the peers — save one — had ever addressed her as "Legend of the Sword."

"Even with all the powers at My command," the Empress went on, "I cannot see the river of time that flows into the future. Our own time among the stars grows short, yes. Yet we have been blessed with an enemy that may provide us the first key to the prophecies: one born not of our blood, yet whose blood sings."

"And the tomb of the First Empress?" Tesh-Dar asked. The prophecies foretold that their race could only be redeemed, the ancient blood curse undone, if Keel-Tath's soul returned to take its place among the thousands of other souls inhabiting She Who Reigned. The curse left by Keel-Tath had doomed their race to eventual extinction, condemning the clawless ones and the warriors with black talons to mate every great cycle or die. Over time, the Empire's population had become unbalanced, with more males and sterile females being born. If the trend continued, in only a few more generations their species would no longer be able to procreate. "How are we ever to find it?"

"That, My priestess," the Empress said, turning to resume their walk along the path, "even the prophecies do not reveal. Yet, I believe that if we find the One, we are also destined to find Her tomb. The fates of the two are intertwined, inseparable. I must believe that the humans are the key."

"You believe that the One is among them?"

"We must hope, Tesh-Dar," the Empress said heavily. "For if not..." She did not have to finish the sentence. If the One was not found among the humans, the *Kreela* would join the races they had destroyed over the ages in dark oblivion. The chances of them finding another sentient race in what time remained to them was infinitesimal. "The One may not yet have been born," She went on. "We shall give the humans as much time as we may to find him."

Him, Tesh-Dar thought. She found it disquieting that the prophecies foretold that their race would be redeemed by a male. That thought led to another as they strolled along, and Tesh-Dar said, "Thy daughter, Li'ara-Zhurah, is to have her first mating. I have tended to her spirit, yet she remains deeply disturbed over what happened to her at Keran." She paused. "I fear her mating will be difficult."

The Empress looked up at the Homeworld, shining full above the great crystalline dome of the Garden, but her mind's eye was on a far away nursery world where Li'ara-Zhurah waited for her mating time. The Empress knew well of what Tesh-Dar spoke, for while She could sense the feelings of all Her Children through the Bloodsong, She was even more attuned to those born from Her own body, as was Li'ara-Zhurah. From when their spirit first cried out in the womb to beyond death in the Afterlife, She could sense the feelings of all. Their joy, their pride. Their fear, their pain. Their sorrow, their anguish.

"I have no doubt it will be difficult," She whispered. "It always is."

* * *

Many light years away, Li'ara-Zhurah lay in her temporary quarters on one of the Empire's many nursery worlds. To such worlds were the fertile warriors and clawless ones taken to mate and give birth once every great cycle. For if they did not, they would die in horrible agony that even the healers could not avert.

Any other time she would have found a room such as this a place of unaccustomed comfort. It was not large, but it was certainly more expansive than a warrior's typically spartan quarters on a warship or in one of the many *kazhas*. It was well appointed with a thick pallet of soft skins for a bed, and a low table where she and any companions — should she have them — could kneel as was customary to eat and drink. A window of intricately stained transparency, made of material thinner than a hair's breadth, yet strong as steel, was set into the smooth granite walls, flooding the room with serene light from the artificial sun that warmed this planet.

A construct of the builders, the caste responsible for creating anything the Empress called for, this world had been created from an airless rock drifting in deep space, far from any star. The planet was surrounded by a vast cloud of particles, a derivative of the matrix material that the builders used to create whatever the Empress required. The cloud was the planet's primary defense and also what gave it the necessary light and heat to support life, in measure that was identical to the star of the Homeworld. Although every nursery world was zealously guarded by warships of the Imperial Fleet, should one of the nurseries be threatened, the thick but seemingly insubstantial cloud of wispy white matrix material would form into a shell that was impenetrable by anything short of the energies released by a star gone nova. The Empire's mothers and newborns, valued beyond all measure, would not easily fall prey to an enemy.

Even thought this place was warm and comfortable, her body shook from alternating hot and cold flashes. It had already been her time before the attack on the human world, Keran, but she had refused to go to the nursery world before the campaign had ended. She had fought too many challenges for the right to be there, and was willing to risk death from her rebellious body rather than give up her right to be among the first to do battle with the humans.

She had been wounded, her back burned during an attack on a human ship and her side pierced by shrapnel from an exploding human assault boat, but her true scars were inside, upon her soul. Tesh-Dar had been able to excise much of the anguish and confusion Li'ara-Zhurah had felt in the aftermath of the battle. Yet some wounds still lay open, beyond the reach even of the great priestess and, Li'ara-Zhurah feared, even the Empress herself.

The torment of her body from the growing imbalance in her reproductive hormones, however, was as nothing next to the painful fear of the mating ritual. It was not fear of physical pain, but fear of emotional emptiness. Fear arising from the certain knowledge that the creature she was soon to be joined with, one of the males of her species, was barely self-aware. As part of the curse that was the legacy of the First Empress, the males had been reduced to mindless breeding machines that only functioned a single time before dying in agony.

It had not always been so, Li'ara-Zhurah knew, for the Books of Time spoke of the ages before the Curse, when the males were proud warriors and artisans who lived alongside the females. There had once been a time when they mated with physical love, bonded for life as *tresh* who lived as two individuals, yet were one. In the time since the Curse, her people bonded together in pairs, female to female, a bond that was only broken by death. They often might serve the Empress far apart, but their spirits were always entwined in the Bloodsong. And when one's *tresh* died, it was a soul-wrenching experience. Li'ara-Zhurah's *tresh* had died some years ago, and her soul had never entirely recovered. Even now, she would awaken at night with her *tresh's* name on her lips. She could feel a glimmer of her *tresh's* spirit from the Afterlife, but that was all, and it was not enough to ease the pain.

The room she occupied now had two doors: one that led to the corridor outside and the rest of the complex, and one through which the male would be brought when it was time. She nervously glanced from one door to the other, part of her wanting to get on with the ordeal, while the rest of her shamefully wished she could escape.

A gentle knock at the smaller door startled her, and she gasped in fright.

"Come," she called through the haze of fear that clouded her senses, berating herself for being unable to control her emotions. *You have fought in a true battle*, she told herself, *and proved yourself worthy. Be not afraid!*

Telling herself to not be afraid was one thing, but didn't stop the fear from clutching her heart in a tight and icy grip.

A pair of healers entered, closing the door softly behind them. One was senior, as indicated by the many pendants hanging from her collar, and the other was junior. Like all of their caste, they could heal nearly any injury or disease. The specialty of these healers, however, was in understanding what Li'ara-Zhurah was feeling now and helping her cope with what was to come.

They knelt beside her on the soft skins, and the elder healer opened her arms to Li'ara-Zhurah, offering to hold and comfort her.

With a whimper of despair, Li'ara-Zhurah threw herself into the healer's arms, burying her face in the elder's shoulder. The other healer, the apprentice, wrapped her arms around Li'ara-Zhurah, adding her warmth and empathy, helping to soothe the frightened young warrior through the Bloodsong. Mourning marks, a display of inner pain, turned Li'ara-Zhurah's skin black below her eyes, as she moaned and shivered in the arms of the healers.

"Be still, child," the elder healer whispered as she gently rocked Li'ara-Zhurah. She could feel the young warrior's torment in the Bloodsong, sharp and bitter. "Be not ashamed. What you feel now is what each of us feels the first time. Even the Empress Herself."

Li'ara-Zhurah's only response was to tighten her grip on the elder healer. She did not realize it, but her claws had drawn blood from the healer's sides, staining the pure white robes with streaks of bright crimson.

The healer was accustomed to such pain and ignored it. Her attention was focused solely on her young ward. "When you are ready, we will prepare you," she whispered as she gently stroked Li'ara-Zhurah's hair. "It will be difficult, child, but will not last long. You shall endure."

I do not wish to endure, Li'ara-Zhurah railed silently. *I do not wish for any of this!*

But there was no use putting off the inevitable. She was a warrior who had faced the fires of battle against worthy foes and survived. She could not allow herself to succumb to cowardice and dishonor now.

"Let it be done," she rasped, reluctantly pushing herself from the healer's embrace.

The healers helped her to her feet, then carefully undressed her, peeling away the black undergarment that was worn beneath armor, for the warriors, and the robes of the clawless ones like the healers. Then they removed her sandals. She then stood shivering, wearing nothing but her collar.

"Here, child," the elder healer said, pointing to the center of the bed of skins.

Li'ara-Zhurah knelt down as she was shown, then leaned forward on all fours, placing her elbows on the skins, her head close to the edge near the wall. Before her were a set of soft leather cuffs bound by slender but unbreakable cables that were attached to the floor. Her stomach turned at the sight, for they reminded her of the shackles of the *Kal'ai-Il*, the place of punishment that was at the center of every *kazha* throughout the Empire. Without thinking, she pushed herself away, back up to her knees.

"It is so you do not accidentally injure the male," the apprentice healer, even younger than Li'ara-Zhurah, explained as she and the elder healer gently pushed her back down onto the skins. "You will...not be yourself for a time."

"It is for the best, child," the elder healer said as she fastened the cuffs around Li'ara-Zhurah's wrists, making sure they were fixed firmly but not over-tight. "And I will tell you this, even though I know you will ignore my words: it is best not to look at the male when we lead him in. They, too, are Children of the Empress, but they are different from us in more than just gender."

Li'ara-Zhurah had heard the stories, of course, but she had never seen a male of her race. They were kept only on the nursery worlds such as this, never to be seen elsewhere in the Empire. She knew the healer's words were well-intended, but they left her even more frightened. She shivered uncontrollably.

"Imagine how you would like him to appear," the junior healer advised. "And do not fight against what must be. Your body will understand what to do. Close away your mind and let your body take control."

"Do you understand, child?" the elder healer asked.

"Yes," Li'ara-Zhurah said through gritted teeth. Her hands, bound now by the cuffs, fiercely gripped the skins of the bed, her talons cutting all the way through to scrape against the unyielding stone beneath.

"We shall return momentarily," the junior healer told her before the two of them left through the door through which they had entered.

Li'ara-Zhurah squeezed her eyes shut, burying her face in the warm skins, trying desperately to gain control of her fears. Her breath was coming quickly, too quickly, as if she were still running after the great human war machine that had become her obsession during the battle on Keran.

She heard a sound at the door. Unable to help herself and just as the healer had known would happen, she turned to look. There, standing between the two healers, was a male. It - he - was clearly young, judging from the length of his braided hair, for there was no use for males other than breeding, and they were bred as soon as they were of age. And once they bred, they died. She had seen images of the male warriors during the time of the First Empress, from ages-old legend, but aside from the blue skin and black hair typical of her race, there was little in this creature that she could recognize from those ancient scenes. He only stood as tall as the healers' shoulders, was dreadfully thin, and had a body that clearly had never endured the physical rigors of the *kazha*. Standing there without clothes, his maleness was alien to her, for she had never seen such, even in the ancient images.

The real shock was his face and head. While his eyes were bright and looked normal, they were set in a face that betrayed no sign of intelligence, with a forehead that sloped steeply back, part of a small skull that housed an undersized brain. From his lips began a high keening sound, for his body understood what his tiny brain did not: his purpose for existence was now before him.

Then she noticed his hands: the talons had been clipped from his fingertips, no doubt to keep him from injuring her in his witless passion.

She turned away in revulsion, fighting to keep hold of her sanity as the male eagerly moved toward her. The apprentice healer held Li'ara-Zhurah's shoulders, trying as best she could to comfort her, while the senior healer guided the male's efforts.

Li'ara-Zhurah's thoughts faded to blackness as her body responded to the male's pheromones. She cried out at the momentary pain, whimpering in her heart for the love of her Empress, and begging the First Empress — wherever She was — to return and lift this curse from them all.

What came after was blessed darkness.

* * *

Tesh-Dar stood in her quarters, part of the complex of buildings that made up the *kazha* of which she was headmistress. Having returned to the Homeworld from her audience with the Empress on the Empress Moon, her thoughts remained fixed on Li'ara-Zhurah. She could clearly hear the melody of the young warrior's Bloodsong that carried her fear and pain, and she ground her teeth at the thought that she was powerless to aid her. Tesh-Dar did not even truly understand what the young warrior was going through, for she herself had never mated. Being born sterile was both a blessing and a curse: she was not subject to the need to mate every great cycle to continue living, but she was a bystander in the continuity of her species, standing a world apart from those who could give birth.

She allowed herself a moment of guilt, for she did not feel this way for all of her wards. She cared deeply for all of them, every warrior of every generation she had helped to train here, but for a very few she found that she cared more. Li'ara-Zhurah was among them. It had nothing to do with her being a blood daughter of the Empress, for such things as favoritism had been bred out of her race eons before when the Bloodsong took hold and one's feelings were exposed to all. That had triggered the age of Chaos, when her species was torn apart by countless wars before the First Empress and Unification.

No. She felt strongly for Li'ara-Zhurah because of who she was in her heart and spirit. A part of Tesh-Dar fervently wished that this young warrior would be the one with whom she could share her inheritance from the Desh-Ka order, who could follow in Tesh-Dar's footsteps as high priestess. For Tesh-Dar was the last of her kind: after the death of the First Empress, the warrior priestesses of the ancient orders were only permitted to select a single soul as a replacement, transferring their powers to their acolyte in a ceremony that dated back tens of thousands of cycles before the Empire was founded. If Tesh-Dar died before passing on her knowledge, the powers of the Desh-Ka, the greatest of all the warrior sects in the history of her race, would be lost forever. She was already older by fifty cycles than was normal for her kind, and old age gave little warning before death would take her. There was no gradual descent into infirmity over the course of years for the warriors, no time to make considered choices for an acolyte: when a warrior's body reached the time appointed by Fate, death came in days, weeks at most. Even the healers could not predict when it was time to pass into the Afterlife until a warrior's body began to shut down.

Dying without an heir was one of the few things Tesh-Dar had ever truly feared in her long life. But she could not choose an heir out of fear, for it was a choice she could make only once. After she surrendered her powers to her successor, there was no turning back.

"Do not let your heart be troubled so, great priestess," a voice said softly from behind her.

Tesh-Dar turned to see Pan'ne-Sharakh standing at the open door. Of the many souls Tesh-Dar had known in her life, Pan'ne-Sharakh was unique. The greatest living mistress of the armorer caste, she was among the oldest of their race, far older even than Tesh-Dar. Such were her skills that she had served as the armorer of the reigning Empress and the Empress before Her, eventually retiring from Her personal service as age took its toll. Pan'ne-Sharakh's collar was the only one in all the Empire that bore more pendants than Tesh-Dar's, with rows hanging down nearly to her waist, shimmering against the black of her robes. Tesh-Dar had known her since Tesh-Dar was a child, but much of their lives had been spent on opposite sides of the galaxy. After Tesh-Dar had taken over as headmistress at this *kazha* several dozen cycles ago, Pan'ne-Sharakh had joined her, and since then they had been nearly constant companions whose personalities complemented each other: Tesh-Dar was the embodiment of physical power and ferocity, while Pan'ne-Sharakh represented wisdom and faith.

"Forgive me, mistress," Tesh-Dar told her with a warm but troubled smile, "but much weighs upon my heart."

"As it must in this time of war," Pan'ne-Sharakh replied as she shuffled into the room. "Something to ease your troubles, great priestess," she said with an impish grin as she held up two mugs of the bitter ale that was a favorite drink among their kind.

"You will put the healers to shame," Tesh-Dar told her, gratefully accepting one of the large mugs. After she took a long swallow of the warm, bitter drink, she said, "It is not the war with the humans that troubles me, mistress. It is my own mortality. I do not fear death, but if it comes before I have found a successor..." She shrugged. "Then my life — and that of all those who came before me — will have been without meaning, without purpose. I believe Li'ara-Zhurah is the one I would choose, but her soul is yet stricken with grief, and anguished all the more by her first mating. She is the closest I have ever found to a worthy successor, yet I am unsure." She paused, staring out the window of her quarters at the Empress Moon. "*I must* be certain. I can make no mistake." She would rather face a *genoth*, a great and deadly dragon native to the Homeworld, with her bare talons than endure the bitter emptiness of failure. She fought to keep the rising tide of trepidation in her soul from gaining a firm hold, for the strength of her Bloodsong carried her emotions to every soul in the Empire like tall waves upon the ocean, and it was irresponsible of her to let her worries so taint the great river of their race's collective soul.

"To my words, you will listen, child," Pan'ne-Sharakh said in an ancient dialect of the Old Tongue that was rarely spoken anymore. She lifted a hand to the center of Tesh-Dar's chest, gently placing her palm on the cyan rune of the Desh-Ka that blazed from her shimmering black armor, and said, "In all the cycles of my long life, never have I known a greater soul than yours, save for the Empress Herself. Upon the second step from the throne do you stand, high priestess of the Desh-Ka, but not merely for your feats of courage and glory. What has made you great is here, in your heart, a heart that is known throughout the Empire. I know not if Li'ara-Zhurah is to be your chosen one. But know it *you* will, when the time is upon you. No doubt, no uncertainty will there be. All that has come to pass in the thousands of generations since the First Empress left us has been for a purpose. The strength and powers you received after the Change, when you became high priestess of the Desh-Ka, was for a purpose." Her eyes blazed as she stared up at Tesh-Dar, radiating an inner strength that Tesh-Dar could feel pulsing through the Bloodsong. "Yes, the End of Days for the First Empire looms. *Yet even this has a purpose.*"

"But what?" Tesh-Dar asked in frustration. "The end of all that we have ever done, all that we have ever created? Leaving behind nothing but dead monuments to half a million cycles of the Way?"

"No, my child," Pan'ne-Sharakh said, a knowing look on her face, as if she had already seen the future. "The death of the First Empire shall herald the birth of the Second."

THIRTY

The conference room was small and sparsely furnished with a faux wood table and a dozen comfortable but well-worn chairs. Several vidcom units that had seen better days were spread out over the table top. A large wall display, the only device in the room less than ten years old, glowed with brilliant images. The carpet, once a regal blue, had long since faded, with the deep pile worn through to the nap in several places. The odors of caustic cleaners, furniture polish, and air fresheners competed with the reek of stale cigarette smoke for dominance in the room's confines. The air handlers had never worked properly, and there were no windows to air out the smell, for this room was buried a hundred meters below the surface. And it was always either too hot or too cold here.

The room's hand-me-down appearance was ignored by the men and women who sat around the table. Like the room itself, they were shabby and worn. Their eyes, however, reflected hope and determination as they focused their attention on the wall display.

"Turn it up, please," said the man seated at the head of the table. In his mid-fifties, he had the distinguished look of a scholar, with a patrician nose and high cheekbones that set off a pair of blue eyes sparkling with intelligence. His well-trimmed hair had been brown, but was now mostly gray, and had receded little over the years. He had taught English literature at a university on Earth for a number of years before he had been compelled to return to his home planet of Riga, eventually becoming President of his home world's government. It was a grandiose-sounding position that, in reality, left him little more than a figurehead, a lackey to the greater power that controlled his planet and its people. He tried to suppress the hope that the words he was about to hear from a woman he had never met would mean the release of his planet from bondage and tyranny. Although a man who was well acquainted with disappointment, he found that he was unable to hold back a tingle of excitement. His name was Valdis Roze.

A young man with deep circles under his eyes quickly manipulated the controls for the wall display, bringing up the volume, and the recording of what had taken place on Earth three weeks ago began to play. Roze had asked the young man to skip forward past the pomp and ceremony and go straight to the speech. He wanted to see, to hear, the words of the first President of the Confederation of Humanity. He knew she had intended for everyone in the human sphere to hear her words, but not all humans were allowed such privileges. Information access for the citizens of Riga was tightly controlled by their masters on the neighboring planet of Saint Petersburg.

A rarity among the great numbers of stars in the galaxy, the Saint Petersburg system had two habitable worlds. The system had been settled in the first wave of the Diaspora, the great exodus from Earth that occurred after the series of wars that had shattered governments and killed several hundred million people. The colonists had been ethnic Russians, plus many people from Russia's immediate neighbors, including the Baltic states. The colony had done well for half a century until the government, controlled by the Russian majority, turned to tyranny. Most of the non-Russian groups were eventually forced to resettle on the system's other habitable planet, which had been named Riga. But "habitable" did not necessarily mean comfortable, and Riga's bitter winters and devastating storms during the summer months made survival a challenge.

The government on Saint Petersburg retained tight control for the next couple of centuries until a visiting dignitary of the *Alliance Française*, investigating allegations of genocide on Riga, was assassinated by the Saint Petersburg secret police. That had triggered the Saint Petersburg War, with Earth and the *Alliance Française* leading a military coalition that had as its goal the liberation of Riga and the institution of a democracy there. The ruling government had not gone down easily, and it took six years of bloody fighting before they were finally defeated.

The victory left a weak Saint Petersburg government in its wake, and in the years that passed after the weary coalition forces returned home, old habits began to reemerge. Roze thought about how, over the last half dozen years, the Saint Petersburg government had quietly reasserted its hold on its former possession. Their secret police no longer murdered Rigan citizens in the middle of the night, but the oppression was no less real. While Riga still enjoyed diplomatic relations with many worlds, Saint Petersburg controlled all inter-system communications. They also held Riga's economy in an iron grip of outrageous taxation and open corruption, and none of the worlds that had helped Riga before seemed inclined to challenge Saint Petersburg a second time on their behalf.

Now alien invaders had come to the human sphere, apparently bent on little but death and destruction.

Roze thought of his reaction — stark incredulity — at the news that the *Aurora*, a Terran survey vessel, had made first contact with a sentient species that had murdered the ship's crew. Then came the annihilation of the colony on Keran, which threw most of the human sphere into a panicked uproar. The Saint Petersburg government, in typical fashion, had flatly labeled the entire affair a hoax, but in Roze's eyes, that only served to increase the odds of it being true. The video reports of the battle that his agents had smuggled past Saint Petersburg's censors were too surreal to be even a Bollywood production. Saint Petersburg jealously controlled the communications buoys that stored and received information from the courier ships that carried information from star to star. While the Rigans could officially send and receive only what the Saint Petersburg government allowed, a well-established web of spies and informants ensured that the Rigan leadership was well-informed.

"That's fine," President Roze said when the young man brought the volume up. The audio was just as impressive as the image display: Roze felt like he was standing right next to Natalie McKenna, former President of the Terran Planetary Government and now President of the Confederation, as she began to speak.

"Citizens of the Confederation," she began, her strong voice a reflection of the will that had carried the Terran Planetary Government from a state of denial to a fierce determination to survive in the aftermath of the Kreelan invasion and destruction of the human colony on Keran. "*Citizens of the Confederation*," she repeated. "While there are and have been governments in the human sphere made up of more than one world, for the first time since the Diaspora have we truly begun to look beyond our differences, to unite for a common purpose. That purpose, my fellow citizens — my fellow *humans* — is our survival as a species.

"You have all seen the reports of what happened on Keran," she went on, her voice dropping lower in pitch. "Millions of people were wiped out, exterminated. The fleet of the *Alliance Française* was nearly destroyed, and Earth's fleet severely mauled. Yet our combined forces were almost enough to stop the invasion. *Almost*. We did not believe then. And there will never again be another *almost*. Never again will we give less than our all to defend our people, to defend humanity itself. If the Kreelan Empire has come looking for a fight, we will give it one. And we will emerge victorious!"

The crowd, several million people lining the streets of old New York City on Earth, roared in support. While it would take months for the recording to reach the farthest human settlements, McKenna's speech would eventually be heard by the twenty billion humans living among the stars.

"Yet the battle fought at Keran showed us the crucial importance of unity. Our fleets and ground forces could not communicate properly. Our weapons and equipment are not standardized. Most important of all, we have had no unified military or political leadership." She shook her head slowly. "My friends," she said, "the Kreelans do not care about our differences. They do not care about our history. They do not care about any of our problems, any more than they care about our dreams and aspirations. They have come for one thing, and one thing only: to kill us. If Keran is an example of what they plan for our species, every man, woman, and child of our race is under a threat of death. Unless we unite, unless we can pull together and form a common defense, *we will not survive*." Drawing herself up to stand even taller, she went on, "In that spirit, and as my first official act as President of the Confederation of Humanity, I extend an open invitation to every world to join the Confederation. There will be commitments necessary for the common defense of human space, but your planetary sovereignty will be respected. The Confederation's purpose, reflected in its charter, is not to subdue or absorb its member worlds, but to defend and protect them. As president, I offer that protection unconditionally to any world that chooses to join us..."

Roze signaled the young man to stop the playback. He had heard enough. Looking around the room, he saw the answer to his unasked question — *Should we risk joining?* — written on every face. For there was much risk, particularly for the men and women in this room. Officially, there were no Saint Petersburg military forces currently on Riga, as that had been banned under the armistice twenty years ago. But everyone around the table knew that this was a hollow truth. "Military advisers" were garrisoned near vital installations, including the bunker they were meeting in. Worse, Saint Petersburg had rearmed in blatant violation of the armistice treaty, building heavy weapons and expanding their "coast guard" into a potent navy that Roze believed could challenge even the new Confederation. They also had enough interplanetary lift capacity to land a large occupation force on Riga or any number of other worlds quickly. Riga, by contrast, had only a token paramilitary force of policemen who also trained as militia, armed with weapons controlled by Red Army detachments from Saint Petersburg.

Roze and the others had no illusions about what the "St. Petes" could — and would — do if sufficiently provoked. Riga petitioning to join the Confederation would certainly be provocative. The only question was how strong their response might be.

On the other hand, if Riga's government did nothing, Roze was sure Riga's lot would only become worse. Political pressure from Earth and the Alliance to keep Saint Petersburg in line had evaporated years ago, long before the threat from the Kreelan Empire loomed. Saint Petersburg would have a free hand to deal with Riga however they chose.

"It is our best chance, Valdis," his interior minister, who also doubled as defense minister, told him. "At worst, we will only accelerate whatever the bastards plan to eventually do with us. At best..." he shrugged.

"At best," Roze finished for him, "we may at last have true independence." He looked across the table at his foreign minister. "Send an envoy to Earth with a petition for Riga to join the Confederation."

As the room filled with discussion of fears and opportunities, Roze silently wondered how long he had before the Saint Petersburg secret police would come for him.

* * *

President Natalie McKenna hated the new presidential complex, particularly her main office. She appreciated that it was new and intended to support the needs of the leader not of a world, but of a union of worlds larger than any other formed in post-Diaspora history. It was huge, over four times the size of the White House that had been the home of the presidents of the old United States, with dozens of rooms and a staff that numbered in the hundreds. Fitted with every conceivable gadget, all the latest and greatest of everything she could imagine and many that she couldn't, the complex was a marvel of technology and engineering. Everything was so high-tech, in fact, that at first she was afraid of using the vidphones for fear of not being able to figure out how to work them.

No, she decided, the only thing she liked about the new complex was the view. Built on Governor's Island, the ten-story complex provided a grand view of modern New York City, including the hallowed ground of what had once been the twin towers of the World Trade Center and the fully restored Statue of Liberty, which had been badly damaged during the wars before the Diaspora. McKenna had arranged her office so that her desk faced toward the window wall that framed the statue in the distance. The sight of Lady Liberty brought her comfort and gave her strength. Today she needed that more than usual.

"How the *hell* could we have let this happen?" she cursed. "I shouldn't have to find out about a resurgent militant government on Saint Petersburg from a Rigan envoy! We should have known!"

Secretary of State Hamilton Barca, who could easily have been mistaken for a football linebacker who happened to be wearing an expensive suit, frowned. President McKenna only cursed when she was extremely upset. Looking across the coffee table at the woman who had been his friend and boss as they had climbed up the political ladder, he was worried for her. An African-American from the old American state of Georgia, Natalie McKenna had grown up poor, owning nothing more than an unconquerable sense of determination, and eventually rose to the most powerful position on Earth as the president of the Terran Planetary Government. Now, with the formation of the Confederation to rally humanity's colonies to a common defense against the Kreelan menace, she had become the most powerful individual in the entire human sphere. Such power, however, was an unthinkable burden of responsibility for a single human being, and he knew the strain was slowly killing her. She had lost far too much weight in the months since the battle for Keran, and her skin was now tightly stretched over her cheekbones. Her hair — raven black only two years ago — had turned almost completely gray. Her face was lined from worry, and there were dark rings beneath her eyes from a constant sleep deficit. Those intense brown eyes, however, were as clear and sharp as ever. Right now they were looking out at the Statue of Liberty, for which he was grateful. Had she turned them on him, he was half afraid he would ignite from her anger and be burned to a cinder.

"It's not Hamilton's fault, Madam President," Vladimir Penkovsky, former head of the Terran Intelligence Agency and now the director of the new Confederation Intelligence Service, said quietly. "We have been reporting for several years on the rearming of Saint Petersburg and the quiet return to power of people who still hold the ideologies and policies that led to the war twenty years ago. The armistice left a power vacuum in its wake that was filled by a weak government, and over time that government has been suborned by the survivors of the old guard. There can be no doubt. Our sources have been excellent; the information is very detailed and we believe it to be quite reliable."

Penkovsky wished he had intelligence half as good on the other problem areas he faced. Saint Petersburg was a special case: there was a great deal of yearning by many of the ethnic Russians there to have the freedoms that their Terran cousins enjoyed, and many Saint Petersburg citizens had secretly provided information to the TIA.

Like the other major powers of the time before the Diaspora, Russia had been devastated by the wars that had led to a frenzy of interstellar colonization missions as the world teetered on the brink of total annihilation. China, its natural resources guttering out, launched a massive invasion of Russian Siberia to take by force what it needed, with a simultaneous attack against northeastern India to secure that strategic theater. Totally overwhelmed, the Russians fought back the only way they could: they obliterated the invading Chinese armies with nuclear weapons. The Indians, also reeling from China's attack, followed suit. Once the mushroom clouds had dissipated, half the major cities in India and Russia were burning nuclear pyres. In China, no city with a population over a hundred thousand people was left standing.

After the war, the Russians who were left banded together politically with the other major survivors of the wars, notably the United States and India, and the resulting unlikely melting pot had, by and large, been extremely successful. It had been a long road back from the brink, but since then Earth's inheritors had enjoyed a kind of global peace that modern humankind had never before known.

Saint Petersburg, on the other hand, had gone the opposite direction. The colonization mission had been led by a small oligarchy of powerful men and women who had been able to muster the resources to finance the mission. Their vision was to create their ideal of "Mother Russia" on a planetary scale, free of the external influences and threats that Terran Russia had suffered. Paranoid, ruthless, and power-hungry, successive generations fell into tyranny in a variety of guises. At last, a form of neo-Communism arose that fostered atrocities that would have made Josef Stalin proud, and eventually led to war with Earth and the *Alliance Française*. The armistice had ended the ordeal twenty years ago, but old ways often died hard. Sometimes, they didn't die at all.

"If we had that much intelligence information," McKenna growled, "then why didn't we do anything about it. Why the *hell* wasn't I informed?"

"You were, Madam President," Barca told her as gently as he could, deciding to dive with Penkovsky into the vat of boiling oil, figuratively speaking. "We got the reports, and plenty of the information showed up in your daily briefings over the last several years. But none of us, least of all me, was going to make more of an issue out of it than was absolutely necessary."

"My God, Hamilton," McKenna said, turning to face him, her face a mask of shocked anger, "why didn't you?" She turned her glare on Penkovsky. "Why didn't *both* of you?"

"Economics," Barca answered bluntly. "After the war, Saint Petersburg was an economic disaster. But Korolev, the new bastard in charge, managed to turn things around by exporting strategic minerals and other raw materials that are always in critical demand. Everybody lined up for the peace dividend."

"Including us," McKenna said softly, closing her eyes. She had been in the Terran Senate then, and had voted for the trade treaty with Saint Petersburg. It had seemed like such a good idea at the time.

"And the Alliance, as well," another voice sighed. Laurent Navarre looked down at the polished wood surface of the coffee table. The former ambassador from the *Alliance Française* to the Terran Planetary Government, he was now McKenna's vice president. Intelligent, charming, and extremely competent, he was a much-valued addition to McKenna's leadership team. "As you may recall, our economy, and Earth's, was in a very bad state in the years after the war. Korolev's government made such a handsome offer to all of us that it was impossible to refuse." He shrugged. "Without that agreement and access to their resources, it would have been at least another decade before our economies would have recovered."

"We made a deal with the Devil," McKenna grated.

"It was not the first time, Madam President," Navarre told her levelly, "and it will not be the last. It is the nature of what we must do sometimes. You know this."

"Yes, I do," she said tiredly as she sank down into the wing-back chair at the end of the coffee table, facing the others. Barca and Penkovsky had been part of her cabinet since her first administration in the Terran Planetary Government. The other key member she had brought along was Joshua Sabine, the Defense Minister, who was away with the Chief of Naval Staff, Admiral Phillip Tiernan, to review the new ships coming off the ways in the orbital shipyards. Navarre was a recent addition, having been the Alliance ambassador to Earth prior to the Confederation's founding. "So, it seems we have a bit of a quandary," she told them. "Saint Petersburg has rearmed in violation of the armistice: so do we go after them, or ignore them and focus on the Kreelans?" She sighed. "I suppose we could count that on the good side of things, in that it potentially gives us more firepower against the Kreelans."

Penkovsky snorted, shaking his head. "They would defend their own world, Madam President," he told her, "but they would never send forces to the aid of another system. I doubt they would even bother to defend Riga. There would be no tears shed by Korolev if Riga shared Keran's fate."

McKenna frowned. "Which brings us to the next problem: if we accept Riga into the Confederation, how is Saint Petersburg going to react?"

"Saint Petersburg's reaction is almost immaterial," Navarre pointed out, "because we do not really have a choice about accepting Riga. The Confederation charter is explicit: membership is open to every world that is willing to help provide for the common defense of humanity. If Riga is willing to meet the requirements of raising a Territorial Army and provides the designated per capita quota of manpower and resources for combat units and shipbuilding, which their envoy indicated that they can, they must be accepted. The Confederation will then be obligated to help train, arm, and equip them. There are some stipulations to keep out the rogue worlds, but not many: a planet led by anything short of an outright dictatorship can meet the basic political requirements." He shrugged. "Saint Petersburg could join if they wanted, and we would be obligated to give them the same benefits."

"Okay," McKenna conceded, "we don't have any choice about accepting Riga. That still doesn't answer my question: how will Korolev's government react?"

"Despite the armistice conditions that made Riga independent," Barca told her, "Saint Petersburg has never really accepted it. They've made placating noises and done the minimum required to observe Rigan sovereignty, but that's it: they still believe that Riga is nothing more than a breakaway state that will someday be brought to heel." He scowled. "Frankly, I'm surprised Riga was able to get an envoy here. If Korolev had known..."

"There would have been no envoy," Penkovsky finished for him.

"Just how far is Korolev willing to go on this?" McKenna asked. "We can't afford to have a second front, a civil war, going on while we're trying to save ourselves from the Kreelans!" Fortunately, the enemy had made no further major moves against human space in the months since the fall of Keran. There had been unverified reports of Kreelan ships in many sectors, but most of them were thought to be either erroneous or even fabricated. The only attacks on shipping had been from pirates, and none of the colonies had reported anything unusual. In some quarters, this long lull was being called the "phony war," and an increasing amount of the Confederation government's efforts were being devoted to keeping the Kreelan threat foremost in the mind of a public that was easily distracted. McKenna, however, didn't believe that this lull was going to last much longer: she thought of it more as the calm before the storm.

"If we arm Riga and provide them a guarantee of protection — which applies to *any* external threat, not just the Kreelan Empire — as written in the Confederation charter," Penkovsky said with a look at Barca, "Korolev will simply not allow it."

Barca nodded in agreement.

"He's willing to go to war with the Confederation over this?" she asked Penkovsky.

"I believe so, yes."

"Bloody hell," McKenna breathed.

"There may be worse," Penkovsky ventured, clearly uncomfortable about what he was about to say. "I happened to have a report flagged for my review this morning that we recently received from a new source on Saint Petersburg. I...can barely credit the information, but in light of this discussion I cannot in good conscience not mention it."

"Spit it out, Vlad," McKenna ordered tersely.

"You must keep in mind that we have not yet had time to validate this source or the content of the report," he went on hesitantly. "The source indicates that Saint Petersburg has been secretly building a stockpile of thermonuclear weapons."

There was stunned silence around the room. Terran forces had nuclear weapons, as did the Alliance, but the stockpiles amounted to only a few hundred weapons. None had been used, anywhere, since the last wars on Earth before the Diaspora. After the devastation Earth had suffered, the hundreds of millions who had died, no one had ever wanted to unleash them again. With the threat from the Kreelans,

McKenna had very reluctantly given authorization to increase the Confederation's weapons stockpile, but only slowly. If the Kreelans used them first, she would give the Navy all the nukes they wanted. But she would not be the first one to open Pandora's Box in this war.

"I do not believe it," Navarre said carefully. "Saint Petersburg has very little in the way of accessible uranium deposits, and what nuclear material they import for their power industry — virtually all of it from the Alliance in the form of pre-manufactured fusion cores — is carefully tracked by an Alliance regulatory commission. I do not see how Saint Petersburg could be getting the uranium and plutonium they would require without smuggling it in. That would be extremely difficult, if not impossible, with the tight controls over uranium mining and production of fissile materials."

"That is what I thought, too," Penkovsky told him, "until I read this report. Tell me, Laurent," he said, "with a power industry that has been based on fusion, solar, and wind generation for generations, why would they have built a few dozen massive coal-fired power plants in the last seven years? And why put them in out of the way locations that must make getting power to the grid extremely costly and difficult?"

Navarre sat back, thinking. He knew a great deal about the planet, having been stationed there as part of the peacekeeping force after the armistice. "Saint Petersburg has a great deal of coal, formed just as it did on Earth, and with very similar qualities. It is easy, if ecologically devastating, to mine it. But I cannot think of why they would need coal power plants: the fusion plants alone give them a net excess of electrical power. As for why they would put them in odd places, I cannot say."

"I must have missed something," McKenna interjected drily. "I thought we were talking about nuclear weapons here, not fossil fuel for electricity."

"Madam President," Penkovsky said, "a fact that was previously unknown to me is that coal typically contains between one and ten parts per million of a particular element that, theoretically, can be captured from the fly ash, which is a byproduct of burning coal." He looked her in the eyes. "That element is uranium. And of that, just under one percent is uranium-235, which is the key ingredient for making nuclear weapons. They would need to burn a lot of coal to get what they need. But if the source's information is correct, the coal burning facilities they have could produce several metric tons of uranium-235 per year. They would still need to refine it, but based on the enormous quantity of coal these plants are reportedly burning, and assuming they have been producing uranium-235 for at least the last three years, they may already have a stockpile of several hundred weapons." He grimaced before he went on, saying, "My analysts also say that this is a very conservative estimate. The information also suggests they are manufacturing tritium, which is a key ingredient for making fusion weapons, but the source did not know where or how they were doing it."

"Good God," Barca breathed.

"Vlad," McKenna said, careful to keep her voice level, "we simply *cannot* have a nuclear war in the human sphere. I would say that under any circumstances, but especially with the Kreelan Empire stalking us." Penkovsky made to speak, but McKenna silenced him with a raised hand. "I know the information isn't verified. I understand that. But you've got to pin this down. If the Confederation has to defend Riga against Saint Petersburg, I don't want our forces facing nuclear weapons. Nor do I want to give Korolev the chance to use them to terrorize other worlds beyond Riga. Pull out all the stops on this one, Vlad. We have *got* to know if this is true and how far they've gotten. And if it's true, we've got to find a way to stop them in their tracks."

Penkovsky, his face grim, nodded. "Yes, Madam President."

Turning to Navarre, McKenna said, "Get with Defense Minister Sabine and Admiral Tiernan on this right away and put together a contingency deployment plan. If we get hard confirmation that this information is true, I want a Navy task force and Marines ready to go in right away..."

* * *

Lost in thought as his limousine whisked him from the presidential complex back to the newly constructed Confederation Intelligence Services headquarters building, Penkovsky came to the rapid conclusion that their best chance of finding out what was happening on Saint Petersburg lay with a particular special asset.

Her codename was Scarlet.

THIRTY-ONE

"So, what trouble are you going to get into while I'm gone?" Confederation Navy Commander Ichiro Sato said as he ran a finger down his wife's nude back.

"Who says I'm going to let you go?" Stephanie Sato — Steph to her friends — purred as she arched against her husband's chiseled body, goosebumps breaking out over her skin at his touch. He wrapped his arms around her and pulled her close, her back to his chest, burying his face in her hair. "And I never get into trouble," she said primly.

"Liar," he said, playfully nipping her shoulder.

She laughed, but then settled back against him, quiet. Thoughtful. "I'll miss you," she whispered.

"I'll miss you, too," he breathed.

The two of them were an unlikely pair in some ways, but had been brought together by events that had shattered humanity's view of the universe forever. Ichiro had been a young midshipman aboard the survey ship *Aurora* when Mankind made its first contact with another sentient species: the Kreelans. He was the only survivor of that encounter, and had been sent back in his ship by humanity's new enemy to warn his people of the coming war. A year and a half later, the Kreelans had attacked the human colony on Keran, occupying it after a brief but vicious battle with the human defenders. Ichiro had been there, too, on a destroyer of the Terran fleet in the battle that had raged in space. And there he had again lost most of his shipmates, and again the Kreelans had spared his life when they could easily have taken it. It was something he had managed to come to grips with, but he had never truly decided which troubled him more: having so many others die around him, or the enemy letting him live. He had gone to see several counselors to help him come to grips with all that had happened, but in the end the best therapy had been Steph.

She had been a journalist hungry for the big break she needed to make it into the major leagues. Before she met him, Steph had thought nothing of shamelessly using her body to advance her career as a journalist. When then-Midshipman Sato came back to Earth on a ghost ship with his improbable story of bloodthirsty aliens, she had been at the right place to get an exclusive story from the Navy, and his fame had taken her higher than she had ever imagined. She could have taken terrible advantage of him, but that temptation had fallen away when she first met him as a lonely, guilt-ridden soul. They soon became friends, and just before the battle of Keran, they became lovers. After the nightmare of that battle, which she had experienced first-hand as a journalist embedded with the ground troops, they had returned home to Earth, marrying soon thereafter.

Ichiro was Japanese by descent, born and raised on Nagano. Five centimeters shorter and nearly ten years younger than Steph, he was a handsome young man with a lean muscular body and a mind that had been keen enough to record everything he had learned of the enemy on his long, lonely return to Earth aboard the ill-fated *Aurora*. His knowledge had not saved Keran, but it had given humanity the only edge it had in preparing for the coming war. His body was young, but his eyes might have belonged to someone far, far older.

Prior to the war, he would have been considered absurdly young to hold the rank of commander in the Terran Navy. But his performance under fire and the heavy losses among command qualified officers at Keran had changed the rules, and rapid promotion of promising junior officers had been necessary to fill the many new critical positions opening up as the new Confederation's fleet rapidly expanded. Ichiro had also had the benefit of the sponsorship of the Navy's Chief of Staff, Admiral Phillip Tiernan. Some might have thought that Ichiro's rank had been bestowed by the admiral as an act of favoritism. But the Medal of Honor on Ichiro's uniform told a different story.

Based on his actions at Keran that had earned him "the medal," he had been given command of one of the Navy's newest heavy cruisers, the *Yura*. The ship had finished her shakedown trials and was in the yards where the yard hands were making some last minute adjustments while she took on provisions. Ichiro was scheduled to take *Yura* out on her first war patrol the next morning. It was something most of him looked forward to, hoping he could give the Kreelans some of the death that they had come looking for. The rest of him wanted to stay here, holding close the woman he loved.

Steph, too, would be leaving their home here on Africa Station, one of the massive orbital transit stations for people and cargo traveling to and from Earth. She had accepted a completely unexpected offer by President McKenna to be her press secretary. That had been an incredibly tough decision for Steph: she wanted to go where the big stories were as a journalist. Yet after being around McKenna, she had come to realize that she had an opportunity to become part of something far larger than herself, something that could be vitally important to all of humankind. For her, it was a sacrifice to give up her field work, but after the first few weeks on the job it was a sacrifice she had seen as being a worthy one.

"How long until you have to get ready?" she asked him quietly, kissing one of his hands as she stretched her body slowly, suggestively, against his back.

Ichiro grudgingly eyed the clock display. "An hour," he sighed.

"Then let's not waste it," she told him as she turned over, kissing him hard as she straddled his body in one smooth movement.

Ichiro didn't argue.

* * *

A few hours later, Commander Ichiro Sato, captain of the *CNS Yura*, stood on his ship's bridge as his crew completed preparations to depart Africa Station. He and Steph had said their goodbyes, swearing they wouldn't cry, then crying, anyway. After they parted and before he stepped through the gangway hatch to board his ship, he paused a moment. Closing his eyes, he took one last look at Steph's image in his mind, then reverently put it away in a mental box that he closed and locked. He would set aside time to think of her — and write her letters, even though they probably wouldn't reach her through the slow inter-system mail system until *Yura* returned home — when he was alone in his quarters. Except for those special moments, he would think only of his ship and her crew, and the perils that might await them. That was the best insurance he could provide that he would return home to the woman he loved.

"All umbilicals and gangways have been cast off, sir," Lieutenant Commander Raymond Villiers, Sato's executive officer (the XO) reported. "Africa Station has given us clearance to maneuver. Engineering is ready to answer all bells."

"Helm," Sato said as he settled back into his combat chair in the center of the bridge, "give me ten seconds on the port-side thrusters."

"Ten seconds, port-side thrusters, aye," Lieutenant Natalya Bogdanova answered instantly. She had served with Sato aboard his previous ship, the *TNS Owen D. McClaren*, which had been destroyed at Keran. They had become good friends while serving together aboard *McClaren*, and he was more than glad to have her aboard.

The *Yura* slowly moved away from her berth in the newly-built docks on Africa Station. Over six hundred meters long, *Yura* was a radical departure from previous heavy cruiser designs. Instead of having a collection of several modules and numerous protrusions and appendages attached to a rigid latticework keel, *Yura's* hull was formed of armor plate that encased her entire internal structure. While she was not aerodynamic (a feat the Kreelans had somehow mastered with their ships), and so could not enter atmosphere, her shape was very streamlined. Her profile reminded Sato of a shark, a likeness that he found intensely satisfying. Like a shark, she had teeth: four triple turrets mounting twelve fifteen-centimeter kinetic guns, another six turrets with single heavy lasers, and enough close-in defense weapons and anti-personnel mortars to cover every approach to the ship, save directly astern because of the drive mountings. To round out her armament, she had ten torpedo tubes and twenty-two torpedoes: large, self-guided and highly maneuverable missiles that had proven effective in the fleet battles at Keran.

Yura and her eleven sister ships had been built in just over three months in the emergency construction program begun by President McKenna after the Keran debacle. It had taken three more months to get her ready for combat, and Sato had done his best to use every minute of it to the fullest to prepare his ship and crew. He had mercilessly drilled the men and women who served under him, but always ensured they understood that their survival and ability to carry out their mission depended on how well they could do their jobs, even under the worst conditions. Following the example of his first commanding officer aboard the old *Aurora*,

Captain Owen McClaren, for whom the ship he served on at Keran had been named, he forged his officers into a well-oiled team of leaders that quickly earned the respect of the enlisted ranks. Sato knew that they still had to improve in many areas, but he was intensely proud of his crew. He knew that many of his fellow commanding officers doubted — some quite vocally — that he was fit for command. Yet Sato had no doubts that his ship and crew were ready for battle.

Watching the tactical display, which was toggled to a mode optimized for departure and showed only the local space around Africa Station, he ordered, "All ahead one-quarter. Make your course two-eight-three mark zero-seven-five."

Bogdanova echoed his command as her fingers confidently moved over the controls.

While the inertial dampeners theoretically removed any sensation of motion, Sato certainly felt like he was moving as the ship accelerated away from Earth, the great blue marble of Mankind's home rapidly dwindling behind them.

"Captain," Villiers informed him as they reached their planned jump point well out of Earth's gravity well, "the jump coordinates for the squadron rendezvous are verified, and the hyperdrive engines are green for jump. All hands are at jump stations."

This jump, in addition to being the initial leg of their first combat patrol, was also the final test in the squadron's operational readiness evaluation trials. Each of the six ships of the 8th Heavy Cruiser Squadron had jumped from Earth separately over the last three days, with *Yura* being the last. It was a very complex navigational exercise with the ships leaving at different times, briefly patrolling different sets of star systems, and then making a squadron rendezvous at Lorient during a fifteen minute window in twenty-one days.

Sato smiled to himself. It was an incredibly challenging navigation problem that was typical of his squadron commander, Commodore Margaret Hanson. She was something of an odd bird in the Navy, having crossed over from the Terran Army years before. She was as outgoing as she was outspoken, which Sato knew had cost her more than one promotion in the past. Keran, however, had changed things: she had held the rank of commander before that disastrous battle, and had her commodore's rank pinned on little more than three months later. If there had been any silver lining from the Keran disaster, it was the rapid promotion of competent officers like Hanson.

Sato knew that she had been very skeptical about his command abilities when he took over *Yura*. She had been very frank with him in their first meeting when he had joined the squadron.

"Handing over a brand new heavy cruiser — of a completely new design, at that — to someone with no real command experience doesn't make a lot of sense to me," she had told him bluntly. "Admiral Tiernan passed over a lot of fully qualified officers to give you your ship, Sato. He obviously had his reasons, but I don't need to tell you that you're probably not the most popular officer in the Navy at the moment, at least among the officers who've been waiting in line for a command slot."

Sato knew quite well that Tiernan's decision had caused a huge uproar among the command-rank officers, but he was honest enough with himself to admit that he didn't care what they thought. It wasn't that he felt entitled to the ship after what he'd gone through on the *Aurora* making first contact with the Empire, or after what had happened aboard the *McClaren* during the battle of Keran. He would have been happy and honored to serve on any ship that would take the war to the Kreelans. Yet when Tiernan had given him this unique opportunity, there was no way he would have turned it down. He knew that he could fail and be replaced — Tiernan had made that perfectly clear — but he also knew that he could succeed. It would give him one of humanity's greatest weapons against the aliens that had murdered the crew of his first ship and an entire planet of fellow human beings.

Despite her misgivings, after seeing his ship perform in her squadron's exercises, Hanson decided that maybe Admiral Tiernan hadn't had a screw loose when he put Sato in command of *Yura*.

"Sato," she had told him later, "you're probably the best tactician I've ever seen, and *Yura* beat every other ship in the squadron combat evaluations." That was the good news. The bad news came next. "But your ship's administration, commander, is an outright disaster."

He had no good answer for that, other than he simply had not had the time or the training to learn all the things ship captains had to know. Beyond tactics and ship handling, where he excelled, lay paperwork, policies, procedures and much more: even in war, these things persisted, and a ship could not function without them.

He knew that many officers in Hanson's position would have been happy to see him fail, for no other reason than because he hadn't served his time like his peers before getting a command. That, however, was not the sort of officer Hanson was. She saw in him a highly capable junior officer who had the capability to be an outstanding one, and decided to rescue him before he drowned in paper. Taking him under her wing, she brought him up to speed in the more mundane but necessary skills needed to keep a ship running. Sato smiled, remembering some of the commodore's lessons. Hanson was a tough teacher, and he was a determined student.

When the bridge chronometer being used to log their exercise time counted down to zero, Sato turned to Bogdanova and ordered, "Helm, commence jump."

Thirty seconds later, *Yura* vanished into hyperspace, bound for her first patrol station.

* * *

Roland Mills was fighting for his life. His regiment had been annihilated in an orgy of hand-to-hand fighting with the aliens, with but a hundred or so survivors left when the huge warrior had chosen him for single combat. It was the ultimate adrenaline rush that might even help save a few of his fellow legionnaires.

He knew from the start that he could never beat her. He had seen what she had done in the trench where they had fought viciously against the other warriors, watched as her sword and claws tore his comrades apart like a killing machine. He had seen her snatch others from the trench with some sort of whip with several barbed tails, and heard the terrified screams of her victims as they were yanked from the trench like fish from a pond.

Of all of the trained killers his regiment had to offer, she had chosen him. Setting aside her weapons, she fought him hand-to-hand. She battered him to the ground time and again, and each time he regained his feet and charged her. He had landed his share of blows, bloodying her face. He knew that it was only because she had let him, but that was enough. He kept charging her until he could no longer stand. Then he crawled until he could no longer lift himself from the mud.

It was enough. She would spare his fellow survivors. She would spare him. She rolled him over and he looked up, offering her a bloody smile, a measure of defiance. She looked down at him, her blue face bearing an inscrutable expression, her cat's eyes taking in the measure of his soul.

She should have just walked away with the rest of her warriors. That was what was supposed to happen. But she didn't.

Instead, one of her massive clawed hands closed around his neck and she lifted him from the ground. Her dark crimson lips parted in a snarl to reveal long white fangs, and an icy chill threaded its way through his heart, eclipsing the pain of his battered body. He suddenly felt a horrible, tearing pain in his chest. Looking down past the alien hand clamped around his neck, he saw his ribs cracked and broken, the flesh torn and bleeding where she had shoved her other hand into his chest. With a smooth motion, she tore out his still-beating heart, holding it up for the other warriors to see, as she bellowed an alien cry of victorious rage. The other warriors howled their approval, and Mills watched in silent horror as they butchered the surviving legionnaires.

He watched the carnage, knowing that he was dead, must be dead, yet he wasn't. His eyes locked with hers as she turned back to him, and the hand that had been holding his heart — where had it gone? — reached back into his shattered chest. Not for another part of his body, but for his very soul...

"Roland!"

Mills snapped his eyes open. His body was drenched in sweat, his heart — still with him, thank God — hammering in his chest, blood pounding in his ears. He had rolled out of his bunk onto the metal deck, shaking so badly that his teeth chattered. Looking up, he saw Emmanuelle Sabourin kneeling next to him, her eyes wide with concern.

"Roland," she said again, softly this time. She helped him sit up, then wrapped her arms around him, holding him tight. "The dream again?"

"Yes," he shuddered, burying his face in the hollow of her shoulder.

Sabourin stroked his hair with one hand as she continued to hold him with the other. Both of them were veterans of Keran, survivors of close and bloody combat. Mills had been serving in the *Légion étrangère* of the *Alliance Française*, which had fought on the surface, while Sabourin had been an engineering technician on the

Alliance fleet's flagship. He had fought a now-legendary hand-to-hand battle with a seemingly unstoppable Kreelan warrior, and Sabourin had fought the Kreelan boarders who had taken her ship, saving the few members of the crew who managed to survive. Both had wound up joining the new Confederation Marine Corps. The Legion, what little was left of it, had been transferred in its entirety to the newly formed service, and Mills had gone along with it. Sabourin had joined the Corps through an inter-service transfer from the former Alliance Navy. They had wound up here on the *CNS Yura* as part of the cruiser's Marine detachment because Sato had known Mills and made a by-name request for him from the transition team that had been integrating the legionnaires into the new Marine Corps. As for Sabourin, she had been given her choice of assignments as a reward for her performance at Keran. After learning that Sato was commanding a ship with a Marine detachment, she requested to serve under him.

Mills had assumed the post of first sergeant of the ship's company-sized Marine detachment, and Sabourin was the platoon sergeant for one of the detachment's platoons. Being the only two veterans in the detachment who had actually fought the enemy, they had immediately gravitated toward one another, and had become lovers not long afterward. They were as discreet as they could be in the confines of a warship, which meant that everyone knew about their relationship, but pretended not to. They both knew that the detachment commander wasn't happy about their affair, but he had made it clear that as long as they did their jobs and kept their personal lives out of the detachment's business, he would be willing to turn a blind eye.

"I wish I understood why this is happening," he whispered. "I wasn't afraid when I fought her. I wasn't afraid during the entire battle. It was such a *rush*. Then when we got back to Avignon the dreams started. They've become so...so *real*. It's bad enough when she tears my heart out." He tried to laugh, but it came out a strangled sob. "But when she reaches for me again..." He shuddered. "I could understand having nightmares about something that happened to me, but what's in the dream didn't. I just don't understand."

"If you were not such a pig-headed bastard and would see a psychologist, they might be able to do something for you," she chided him. It was an old argument they had gone over many times. She was convinced it was post-traumatic stress. He was convinced it wasn't.

"I won't let them pull me from duty," he said stubbornly.

She held him away just far enough to look into his eyes. "If the dreams keep getting worse, my love, the CO will relieve you, anyway. He would be derelict in his duty if he did not." She kissed him, then said, "Roland, you are exhausted and irritable much of the time. You have been losing weight, and you use far too many stimulants." He started to protest, but she put a finger on his lips. "You can lie to the commander, you can lie to yourself, but you cannot lie to me. Do not even try, because I know you too well. Listen to me, first sergeant: you owe it to our Marines to do something about this. If — when — we again go into combat, you must be ready. If you are not, it is not only your life that is at risk. You risk all our lives. Including mine."

She braced herself for the argument to start getting ugly as it always did, and waited for him to trot out the same tired and illogical reasons that he had used before to avoid treatment.

"I'll see the ship's surgeon next watch," he said quietly, completely surprising her. She saw the stark fear in his eyes as he looked at her. "If the dream gets any more real, it's going to kill me."

* * *

"How many stim packs a day did you say you are taking?" the ship's surgeon asked, eyebrows raised. "I am not sure I heard you right."

"Twelve," Mills told her sheepishly. He already regretted his decision to come to see her. Commander Irina Nikolaeva was the oldest member of the crew, and from her expression Mills suspected she'd seen it all, including stim addiction. Stims were normally included in combat rations to help troops stay awake during extended periods of combat, and the temptation to pilfer and abuse them was the reason that ration packs were normally kept under the lock and key of a responsible junior officer or senior NCO like Mills.

"Twelve," she repeated in her thick Russian accent, shaking her head. "I am surprised you can stand still. Stims are not normally addictive, but taken in such quantities they can be. There are also other negative side effects." She looked at him pointedly. "Cardiac arrest is among them."

"I know all that, commander," he grated. "I wouldn't be taking the bloody things if I didn't feel I had to."

"The dreams," she said.

Mills nodded. He had tried as best he could to explain his recurring dream to her. It had been an uncomfortable, humiliating experience. He knew it wasn't the surgeon's fault; it was simply that he had never before felt compelled to confide in someone like this. Even telling Sabourin had been extremely difficult for him.

"Normally I would say it was nothing more or less than post-traumatic stress," Commander Nikolaeva told him. She saw Mills roll his eyes and did something others rarely saw: she grinned. "I will not insult your intelligence, Mills," she went on. "You already know this. That is the most likely answer, the one we fall back on when we believe it to be true. Or when we have no other explanation."

That caught his attention.

She nodded. "No one else except the captain" — Commander Sato — "has experienced anything like you did on Keran. I have carefully read his account of first contact with the Kreelans, and I believe the warrior you faced may have been the same one he did."

That came as a surprise to Mills. He had first met Sato on the assault boat that had rescued him and the rest of the survivors of Sato's destroyer at Keran. As the senior NCO of *Yura's* Marine detachment, Mills saw Sato fairly frequently. While they had talked about the events at Keran, neither had made the connection about the huge warrior: Sato had never mentioned her from his own experiences, and the dreams had driven Mills to stop talking about his fight with the warrior long before he'd come to the *Yura's* Marine detachment.

"Does the captain have dreams like this?" Mills asked hopefully. He would have been incredibly relieved if someone else was having a similar experience.

"You know I cannot answer that, Mills," she said as she turned to one of the medicine cabinets lining the walls. She pulled out two packets. "This one you already recognize," handing the first one to him.

Mills looked and was surprised to see that it was a package of stims. He looked back up at her, confused.

"These will keep you from raiding the ration packs," she said sternly. "If you need more, come see me. And I want you to replace the ones you took."

He nodded, his face flushing with embarrassment. It was an old trick to pilfer stims out of rations, but it left whoever received those ration packs with no stims if they really needed it. Replacing all the ones he'd taken was going to be a bit of work. *Consider yourself lucky, mate,* he told himself. *She could have just as easily turned your arse into the captain on formal charges.*

"And these," she said, handing him the other packet, "are tranquilizers. You will take one — *only* one — before you sleep. These should knock you out for at least six hours and suppress your dreams. If they do not work, do not take more: come back to see me. Unlike the stims, these can be very addictive, and if you take too many at one time, they will kill you."

"How long can I take them?" he asked.

She shrugged as she tapped out something on her console. "I hope you will not need them more than a week. That should give you plenty of time to see if the rest of my prescription works."

"And what is that?" Mills asked, suddenly suspicious.

"A talk with the captain," she replied.

* * *

Mills had thought Sato would get around to seeing him at some point during the week. He didn't expect to see him immediately after his visit to Nikolaeva.

"I've got some free time right now," Sato had told Nikolaeva when she had commed him. "Send him to my cabin."

A few minutes later, Mills stood nervously at Sato's door. He had talked to the captain any number of times during the normal briefings held for the ship's command staff, which included the commander and senior NCO of the Marine detachment. But he had never been in Sato's quarters or spoken to him alone. It shouldn't have bothered him, he knew, but the nervous apprehension wouldn't go away.

He nodded to the Marine on guard duty outside the captain's door, standing at parade rest. The Marine nodded back and palmed the control to open the door.

"The skipper's expecting you, First Sergeant," was all he said.

Mills stepped through the doorway into the captain's private quarters, not knowing what to expect. At that moment, he was frightened more than anything else of the captain thinking he was a coward. There was no getting out of it, however. Commander Nikolaeva had made sure the captain knew what the topic of conversation would be.

He snapped to attention and saluted, "First Sergeant Mills, reporting, sir!" The *sir* came out sounding more like *sah* from his British accent.

"At ease, Mills," Sato said, returning his salute. "Please, come in." Sato gestured to one of the chairs arrayed around a small table that would have been the perfect size for playing cards, but as far as Mills knew the captain didn't play.

Dropping his salute, Mills said, "Thank you, sir." He sat down, but remained rigid as a post.

"Mills," Sato said as he fished around in a wall locker, "relax. If it helps, that's an order. Ah!" He held up a bottle and a pair of tumblers that he'd pulled from the locker. "Pure contraband, of course, but rank hath its privileges, as the saying goes."

When Sato set down the bottle on the table, Mills saw it was a very expensive brand of rum. He knew the captain didn't drink, and his expression must have given away his surprise.

"I normally only drink tea," Sato said darkly as he opened the bottle and poured the liquor into the tumblers, "but the topic of this conversation calls for something stronger." He handed Mills a glass, then leaned back in his chair, his dark eyes fixing the Marine with an intent gaze. "So. Commander Nikolaeva told me you're having a recurring nightmare about the alien warrior you fought on Keran. Let's hear it."

Managing to get over his embarrassment, Mills told the tale of his battle with the alien warrior, describing her carefully, especially the strange ornament on the collar at her throat. Then he spoke of how his dreams had begun, and had recently worsened.

After he had finished, Sato was silent for a moment, looking into his glass as if the answers to all the questions in the universe could be found swirling in the amber liquid. "A good friend gave me some advice once," he finally said, just above a whisper, "just before he died. He said, 'There is no dishonor in living.'" He looked up at Mills with haunted eyes. "I agree with Nikolaeva: the warrior you fought, the one you dream about, is almost certainly the same one that I encountered when *Aurora* was captured."

Taking a gulp of the rum, barely noticing as it burned its way to his stomach, Mills leaned forward. "Do you have dreams, too, sir? Nightmares like this?" he asked, desperate for company in his misery, in his quest for understanding.

"I have plenty of nightmares, Mills," Sato replied, "but none quite like yours. I dream of what happened to me, of events that actually took place, but not of things that didn't happen, or an attack on my spirit or soul."

"You think I'm going around the bend, do you, sir?" Mills asked, anticipating that Sato's next words would be to relieve him of duty.

Sato shook his head slowly. "No, I don't," he said frankly. "Mills..." he struggled for a moment, trying to find the right words. "Mills, a lot of people think the Kreelans are like us, simply because they're humanoid in appearance. In the case of the regular warriors, that might be true. But not *her*. She's something else entirely. Mills, I watched her walk through a wall that must have been a meter thick, and she acted like she'd been pricked with a needle when she let me run my sword through her."

"She *let* you, sir?" Mills asked, incredulous.

"Of course she let me," Sato said disgustedly. He took a tiny sip of the rum, managing to force it down. The burning sensation took his attention away from the memory of the warrior looking down at him as he stood there, his grandfather's *katana* sticking through her side. Then she had simply pulled it out and handed it back to him. "Otherwise I'd have been dead with the rest of my old crew. She could probably kill an entire planet single-handed."

"I don't like to give anyone that much credit, sir," Mills said uneasily, fearing that it might actually be true. "I know bloody well that she let me go after having her fun. But I didn't stick it to her with a sword. And we know they're not immortal. We killed plenty of their warriors at Keran."

Sato shook his head. "The only way she's going to die," he said, "is if she wants to. And I think that's what makes her so different. It's not just her physical abilities. There's something more to her that I've never been able to put my finger on, something that goes beyond our experience."

"That doesn't exactly reassure me, sir, if you know what I mean," Mills said quietly before he finished off his rum.

"I know, and I'm sorry," Sato replied. "But we can't control our fears unless we seek to understand them."

Mills nodded, distinctly unhappy. "So where does that leave me, sir?" he asked. "Are you going to relieve me of duty?"

"Not unless you request it or Commander Nikolaeva recommends it," Sato told him firmly. "I agree with the surgeon's assessment that they're probably not a form of post-traumatic stress."

"If not that, then what?" Mills wondered. "Is it some sort of hocus-pocus psychic link from when she was beating my brains out?" He had meant it as a joke. Sort of.

Sato smiled, but a sudden chill went through him. *What if it was?* He was terrified of the possibilities.

THIRTY-TWO

Tesh-Dar slept. She had no true need of it since the Change that had transformed her body when she became high priestess of the Desh-Ka many cycles ago, but after some time, she had found that she missed dreaming. In dreams she found a curious sense of comfort that eluded her while awake, the Bloodsong within her calming from an irresistible river torrent to the gentle swell of an infinite sea. As time wore on, she found that she could sometimes manipulate her dreams to reveal things in the present that were beyond even the reach of her second sight, and sometimes even give her glimpses into the future. And, of course, there were also dreams that were memories from her past.

Not all such dreams were pleasant.

* * *

"Someday your sword may even best mine, Tesh-Dar," said Sura-Ni'khan, high priestess of the Desh-Ka and mistress of the *kazha* where Tesh-Dar had grown from a child to a warrior nearly ready to formally begin her service to the Empire. "Yet you shall fall — by my own hand if need be — if you do not learn patience when teaching the young ones. Your talent with a blade, with any weapon you have ever held, is far beyond even most of the senior warriors of the Empire. It is because of your skills that I made you a senior swordmistress here. Your duty is to instruct, to pass on to the *tresh*, the young warriors-in-training, what you know. You may do it as you see fit within the bounds of tradition, but this is a duty you are bound to, daughter. It is not something you may choose to ignore."

Kneeling on the cold stone floor of the priestess's quarters, Tesh-Dar's heart was torn between shame and anger. Shame that the priestess's words were true, and anger that she should be so burdened. The Bloodsong did not simply echo the chorus of her sisters' spirits, it burned and raged when she took a weapon in her hand, when she entered the arena. She should not have to teach others, who could not understand what she was able to do; even she did not know exactly how she mastered weapons so quickly and so well. It simply *was*. Born to a race bound to warrior traditions, she was among the best-adapted for the art of killing. She had never taken a life in the arena, for she had no intention of cutting down her sisters. She had fought several ritual combats outside of the arena, but after the last one her reputation was such that no one would challenge her. That in itself was another source of frustration: the only warriors who could face her were the priestesses, and she knew that it would have been a great dishonor to provoke any of them into a ritual battle. She had no peers worthy of her skills, she thought sullenly, and she had not even completed her final Challenge at the *kazha*, this school of the Kreelan Way, after which she would be declared an adult warrior and be free to serve the Empress as She willed.

It was maddening, but Sura-Ni'khan's word was law, and Tesh-Dar had no choice. She would do as she must, biding her time until she was free to seek out her destiny, expanding the frontiers of the Empire in the name of the Empress.

"Yes, my priestess," she said, trying mightily to inject a note of humility into her voice and calm the fire that raged in her veins. She did not wish to disappoint her mentor, but she felt chained away from her destiny.

"My child," Sura-Ni'khan said quietly. "I believe you have the makings of greatness about you. Someday...someday I believe you may be worthy of wearing one of these."

Tesh-Dar glanced up to see Sura-Ni'khan's fingers touching the dazzling ruby-colored eyestone, taken from a monstrous *genoth* she had killed long ago, in which was carved the rune of the Desh-Ka order. It was affixed to her collar, the rune matching the one on her breastplate that blazed in luminous cyan. Of all the warrior sects their civilization had known, even before the founding of the Empire, the Desh-Ka was the oldest, its priestesses the most powerful. But after the Curse laid upon their race by the First Empress, the great orders were dying out.

"I am the last of my kind, Tesh-Dar," the priestess said sadly, "and my time grows short before I must pass into the Afterlife. But I would rather the order end its existence and take my leave to join the Ancient Ones than surrender my powers to one who was not ready, or unworthy." She paused. "Do not disappoint me, young swordmistress."

"I will obey, priestess," Tesh-Dar told her, tightly clenching her silver-taloned hands.

After brooding over the priestess's words that evening, Tesh-Dar had an epiphany: she would do what the Desh-Ka and the other warrior priestesses did, and take up a single disciple. She would train a promising young warrior to a level of mastery that would see them easily through their next Challenge, when the *tresh* fought amongst themselves for the honor of besting their peers. That would see her through her own final Challenge, after which she could leave this place and be free to seek the glories that lay beyond the confines of the Homeworld.

"Your Bloodsong rejoices," a soft and welcome voice said from behind her.

Quickly getting up from her bed of animal hides, Tesh-Dar knelt and saluted. "Mistress," she said happily. Seeing Pan'ne-Sharakh never failed to lift her heart.

With a sigh, the old armorer slowly knelt down on the young warrior's skins. "The priestess spoke with me about you, young one," she said. Her voice was serious, which was unusual for her. "I am concerned."

Tesh-Dar again felt a wave of burning shame, a sensation that was alien to her. Disappointing the priestess was bad enough. Disappointing this ancient clawless one, who stood so high among the peers and had played a major role in Tesh-Dar's young life, was far worse. "I have a plan, mistress," she said humbly. She explained what she planned to do. "I will choose Nayan-Tiral," she went on. "I believe she has great promise. I shall teach her all that I can."

Pan'ne-Sharakh was silent for a time, considering. Then, she said, "It is not unheard of, to train a *tresh* in such fashion. Yet careful you must be, child," she warned gently. "Teach her, yes, but mind the power of your sword hand, the fire of your Bloodsong. You must stay in the here and now, and not let your spirit merge with your sword, or lost shall you be."

Tesh-Dar nodded in understanding. When the most talented warriors fought, they lost all sense of self beyond their weapon and the battle. It was the ultimate state of mind for combat, but could be deadly in the wrong circumstances. Tesh-Dar fell into such a state almost instantly, using the power of the Bloodsong as a source of strength and speed. It was an ability of which she was exceedingly proud, for few warriors had ever attained this state at any age, let alone as a youth. "I shall not fail, mistress," she promised.

Pan'ne-Sharakh nodded, then offered Tesh-Dar her characteristic mischievous grin. "Then come, child," she said, "it is time for us to eat."

* * *

With the next dawn, after the morning rituals were complete and training was to begin all around the *kazha*, Tesh-Dar took Nayan-Tiral aside and explained her plan.

"Honored am I," the young warrior, whose next Challenge would be her third, said gratefully as she saluted Tesh-Dar.

"Then let us begin," Tesh-Dar told her, anxious not so much to teach Nayan-Tiral, but to prove to the priestess that she could indeed train the young *tresh*, and do so better than anyone at the *kazha* other than the priestess herself.

As the days passed, Tesh-Dar's talents at teaching were revealed in the dramatic improvements Nayan-Tiral made in her swordcraft. Both the priestess and Pan'ne-Sharakh were impressed: it seemed that the headstrong young swordmistress had found her path to enlightening others. It was not the traditional way of teaching those of Nayan-Tiral's age, but it was certainly not unheard of, and Sura-Ni'khan let the pair be.

Then, just as Pan'ne-Sharakh had originally feared, it happened. With the priestess and many of the *tresh* looking on, as was often the case these days, Tesh-Dar began sparring with Nayan-Tiral, demonstrating a new technique with combat weapons that bore a sharp deadly edge. This in itself was no cause for concern, for *tresh* at Nayan-Tiral's level began to train with such weapons; it had its dangers, but danger was the constant companion for any warrior. While Nayan-Tiral was well below Tesh-Dar's skill level, she had learned much from her young mentor, and her pride and love for Tesh-Dar echoed in her Bloodsong. The two danced a deadly ballet, with the younger warrior pressing her attacks with impressive skill and aggression.

So well did Nayan-Tiral do that Tesh-Dar momentarily forgot where she was and what she was doing, the "here and now" that Pan'ne-Sharakh had once spoken of. It only took a single shard of time for Tesh-Dar to fall into the state of mind that so many of the peers sought, yet failed to achieve, merging her mind perfectly with her weapon. It was not a conscious decision; it was simply a momentary lapse of control and an unforgivable act of negligence by a warrior with her skills.

A heartbeat later, Tesh-Dar found herself staring at the blade of her sword, buried in young Nayan-Tiral's chest, the tip having speared the child's heart. The young *tresh's* bright eyes were wide with shocked disbelief as she slumped to the ground, dead, and Tesh-Dar felt a faint flutter in the chorus of the Bloodsong as Nayan-Tiral's spirit passed from this life to the next. Then Tesh-Dar fell to her knees, cradling the young warrior's body in her arms.

"No," she whispered as mourning marks began to flow down her cheeks, turning her smooth cobalt blue skin pitch black. "*No.*" Shivering with grief and shame, she held the young *tresh*, her soul torn by Nayan-Tiral's dead eyes, still staring up at her mentor. Her killer.

* * *

Her mind returning to the present, Tesh-Dar opened her eyes, willing the dream away. It did not come to her often now, for many cycles had passed since that dark and horrible day. Part of her mind shied away from what came after, but she seized upon the memory, forcing it upon herself in what had become a ritual act of atonement. The night after she had killed Nayan-Tiral, she had faced punishment on the *Kal'ai-Il*. It was a massive stone construct at the center of every *kazha* in the Empire that served as a living reminder of the price for failing to walk the Way, for falling from Her grace. Nude, shackled hand and foot, Tesh-Dar had hung above the massive central dais as the warriors and the *tresh* of the *kazha* looked on from the great stones that circled the *Kal'ai-Il*. Sura-Ni'khan had lashed her with the *grakh'ta*, a seven-tailed barbed whip that was one of the most brutal of all weapons, with all her strength. Eight times the weapon struck Tesh-Dar's back, flaying skin and muscle to expose the bone beneath. She grunted in agony, but never cried out. She had shamed the Empress, her priestess, her peers, and herself with her laxity; she would not further shame them by whimpering during her punishment.

When it was over, she was released from the chains, falling to the dais in a bloody heap. But her punishment was not over until she had staggered down the steps and along the stone walk to reach Sura-Ni'khan, who waited for her across a polished stone threshold. Had Tesh-Dar not reached her by the time the gong of the *Kal'ai-Il* had sounded twelve times, the priestess would have killed her.

Recovering from her wounds had been worse than being lashed, for the healers were not permitted to assist one who had been punished on the *Kal'ai-Il*. They could cover the wounds in sterile dressings, but that was all. Tesh-Dar writhed in blinding agony for two days. On the third, she forced herself to her feet, donned her armor, and staggered step by step to the arenas to train. In the days that followed, she nearly died from infection, something that was unheard of among her race in these times. Yet, her body eventually healed itself, and Pan'ne-Sharakh and Sura-Ni'khan had helped as best they could to heal her soul.

With a sigh, her ritual self-punishment now at an end, she pushed aside the thick animal hides of her warm bed and rose like Death's shadow in her night-shrouded room, ignoring the chill of the air around her. She stepped to the window that filled most of one wall of her quarters, staring out at the snow-covered landscape that glimmered from the light of the Empress Moon that hung high above. It was winter now in the Homeworld's northern hemisphere, and the outside temperature was so low that anyone trapped at night without a shelter would almost surely perish.

"Only a few steps," she murmured to herself. It was only a few steps to the door leading to the outside and winter's eager embrace. Such thoughts had come to her often after her punishment so long ago, but they were only fantasy. If she had learned nothing else on the *Kal'ai-Il*, she had learned the true meaning of duty. As often as Death had called to her, promising to take away her pain, as comforting was the thought of such release, she could no more kill herself than she could bear children.

That thought brought her to Li'ara-Zhurah. Rather than remain on the nursery world until her child was born, as tradition held, she had requested to return to Tesh-Dar's side as the Empire made its next move against the humans. It was unusual for one to be released at such a stage in the mating process, but not unprecedented, and Tesh-Dar could find no reason to deny the young warrior's request. Tesh-Dar's own First, the warrior who had served as her sword hand to assist in the many things the priestess did each day, had moved up another step toward the throne in the rankings of the peers, and was ready to lead her own *kazha*. Tesh-Dar had decided that Li'ara-Zhurah would make an excellent replacement. When the child was near birth, Tesh-Dar would send her back to the nursery world. In the meantime, Tesh-Dar vowed to herself that she would allow no harm to come to her.

Sighing softly, Tesh-Dar knelt to add more wood to the embers of the fire that kept her quarters from freezing, wishing that it could warm her soul.

* * *

"We have allowed the humans time to recover from the first blow. Now, it is time to begin the true Challenge," Tesh-Dar said from where she stood at the center of one of the many enormous chambers in the Imperial Palace on the Empress Moon. Like all things built by Kreelan hands, it was in its own way a work of art: the floor was a great mosaic depicting the tragedy of the Curse, while the walls and ceiling were made of clear crystal panels that let the light of the Homeworld shine through. Around her, sitting on thick animal hides, were the last of the Empire's warrior priestesses. In the time of the First Empress, they had numbered in the thousands. Now, there remained only a handful more than a hundred. There had not been a council of war such as this for millennia, and it had shocked Tesh-Dar to the core to see that so few priestesses remained. It was a clear and bitter illustration of the plight of her species.

As the highest among them on the steps to the throne, Tesh-Dar led the council. The Empress was not present, for she was content to leave the details of war in Tesh-Dar's hands. "We have shown them our power in the transformation of the world they called Keran, which we took from them," she went on, "and also have we granted them fair combat by adapting our technology to theirs. We do not know how they have reacted as a species, but we will soon find out."

She closed her eyes and summoned an image in her mind of the systems occupied by the humans. They had taken the navigational charts of the first human ship they had encountered and added to it the knowledge from the wreckage of the human ships left in Keran space. It was a convenience, for now that they knew of the humans' existence, the second sight of the Empress could reach into every corner of their domain.

As Tesh-Dar opened her eyes, the image that had been in her mind shimmered into existence in the air next to her. "Now we will begin to bleed them. Our deeds shall bring great glory to the Empress, but we also search for the One," she explained. "There are two hundred and thirty-seven human-settled worlds. These," a cyan halo appeared around sixteen of the planets, including Earth, "shall not be molested for now. They are critical to the humans for producing ships and weapons, and are the largest population centers. Instead, we will make widespread attacks against shipping and smaller colonies, forcing the humans to give battle while not destroying their ability to wage war."

"Would it perhaps not be wiser, Tesh-Dar," said Mu'ira-Chular of the Alun-Kuresh order, "to do the opposite? To bleed their heart worlds first? Where there are more humans, are we not more likely to find the One? Or should we simply attack all of their systems at once?" It would be a trivial matter for the Empire to do so: the human realm was minuscule against the ten thousand suns of the Empire.

"We strike a precarious balance between fate and time," Tesh-Dar explained. "We do not know if the One has yet been born. The prophecies say that we will know him when his blood sings, but little more." Looking at the images of the worlds suspended above her, she went on, "If we attack all their systems, we may exterminate them before he has taken his first breath. If we prolong the war as long as we are able, the Empress believes there is a greater chance of finding him. And thus may we bring Her more glory across the few remaining generations we have remaining."

Mu'ira-Chular nodded, as it was the will of the Empress to follow this course, but her face betrayed her concerns, not least of which was how close was the Empire's end of days. That their race was dying was not a secret, but few beyond the priestesses who had direct contact with the Empress truly understood how closely extinction loomed.

"My sisters," Tesh-Dar told them, "there is no certainty in what we do. There is only certainty in our fate should we fail to find him. And if we find the One, the Empress believes we are also fated to discover the tomb of the First Empress, Keel-Tath. Then...then may the Curse be lifted and our race redeemed in Her glory."

In chorus, the other priestesses murmured, "In Her name, let it be so."

"What are your commands, my priestess?" One of them asked.

"We shall begin by attacking their ships," Tesh-Dar said as bright cyan lines joined the images of the human worlds. "We do not want to sever their lifeblood, merely bleed them and bring them to battle. I leave detailed planning for this to the Ima'il-Kush," she nodded to one of the priestesses, whose domain was the Imperial Fleet. "Then we will attack these worlds," seven planets were highlighted with cyan halos, "using those warriors of our orders who have earned the privilege by right of Challenge. Unlike Keran, these will be extended campaigns that will take many cycles, giving our warriors many opportunities for combat, and hopefully making the humans even more challenging adversaries. At a time of our choosing, we will expand our attacks against additional human worlds. For now, we will wait and see what comes to pass."

The other priestesses spoke amongst themselves for a time, dividing the human worlds among them in such a way that there would be glory enough for all. Their only disappointment was that so many warriors in the Empire would never get the chance to be properly blooded in battle before the humans were exterminated from the galaxy.

As they discussed their strategies, Tesh-Dar looked at the target worlds. Of the seven, none had any particular features that appealed to her more than any other, so she simply picked one at random that would receive her personal attention.

That one, she thought to herself, looking at a heavily forested world with expansive oceans. It had a sizable human population, far larger than Keran, and a great deal of industry, according to the files extracted from the human computers. Had she cared to ask one of the keepers of the Books of Time who were now the holders of knowledge about things human, she could have learned the planet's human name.

Saint Petersburg.

* * *

In the armory of Tesh-Dar's *kazha*, Pan'ne-Sharakh sat at a low table, her attention focused on an ornate sword. The blade was so long that the tip would touch the ground if she held the handle at chin height. Gracefully curved so that it could be drawn in an instant from its scabbard, the blade shimmered in the light of the torches that illuminated her work. The crystal handle with inlaid gemstones was large enough for the massive hands that wielded the weapon. It belonged to Tesh-Dar, and was one of the many weapons Pan'ne-Sharakh had fashioned for her in their long acquaintance.

The weapon rested in a carefully padded cradle, the edge facing up toward her. With reverent hands she stroked the gleaming silver metal, fashioning its form as an act of will. Much like the builder caste and the matrix material from which they created anything that was necessary to suit the will of the Empress, the armorers had the gift of working the living metal that made up their edged weapons and the collars that all who walked the Way wore around their necks. It was the hardest, most durable substance in the galaxy, yet was malleable as clay to the gentle touch of a skilled armorer. Kreelan blades were not made with the fires of a forge and the hammer upon the anvil, although their body armor was still made in such a fashion. Pan'ne-Sharakh smiled inwardly at the strength she still possessed, even at her advanced age, to wield a hammer to bend such metal as she would.

They were created from ingots of metal, carefully grown over the span of many years. The ingots were smoothed and shaped by the armorer's vision and touch, their spirits in communion with the metal as they stroked the blade into existence. The handles and the hand guards were generally created by more mundane means, although armorers of Pan'ne-Sharakh's skill — of which there had been few over the ages — could form them as an act of will from virtually any material. The form was always functional first, yet every weapon was also a work of art. The warriors brought glory to the Empress in battle, but Pan'ne-Sharakh and her sisters glorified the Empress through the perfection and beauty of their craft.

She lovingly stroked the sides of the blade with her hands, barely brushing it with her fingertips, as her mind focused on its essence. The metal reacted instantly, the molecular structure realigning as she willed. This was an old weapon, one she had fashioned for the priestess after the Change, after Tesh-Dar had become the last of the high priestesses of the Desh-Ka order. In Tesh-Dar's hands, the weapon could slice through a brace of enemy warriors. Even if the blade was nicked, it would reform on its own back to a killing edge. In Pan'ne-Sharakh's mind, her fingers not only formed and sharpened the blade, but infused it with her love. While she did not lavish this much attention on every weapon, there were a select few such as this one that always received her gentle touch before and after a challenge. Or a battle.

She absently hummed an ancient hymn to the Empress, a harmony to the Bloodsong that was a soothing warmth in her ancient veins. The clawless ones did not feel the same fire as the warriors, yet in some ways they could read the eddies and currents of their race's spiritual river far better than their taloned sisters.

For Pan'ne-Sharakh, applying her craft always allowed her to see more clearly the things in her mind. She knew that something deeply troubled Li'ara-Zhurah, who had begged to return from the nursery world. It was something more troubling than even the priestess believed, but exactly what was beyond Pan'ne-Sharakh's understanding, and perhaps even that of the Empress. She feared that Li'ara-Zhurah might be one among their race, exceedingly rare, who might choose to depart the Way, to fall from Her grace. It would break the heart of Tesh-Dar, who had pinned such high hopes upon the young warrior. Pan'ne-Sharakh had spoken to Tesh-Dar about her concerns, and while the great priestess listened carefully as she always did, she saw no reason to change what was. If anything, it had made her more insistent that Li'ara-Zhurah accompany her on the new campaign against the humans, in hopes that Tesh-Dar could assist the young warrior through the pain that yet wracked her soul.

Switching to a hymn that was an ancient plea for intercession from the Empress, Pan'ne-Sharakh poured her soul into the metal of Tesh-Dar's sword. It was all she could do to help shield the heart of one she so loved.

* * *

Li'ara-Zhurah stood by Tesh-Dar's side as her new First, watching hundreds of proud warriors filing past, each one rendering a salute to Tesh-Dar. They moved quickly up the massive ramp of the heavy cruiser that would serve as Tesh-Dar's flagship for this new campaign. They did not march in step, nor was there music or speeches to celebrate the mission of carnage on which they embarked. They needed none of these things, for the Bloodsong echoed in their hearts, and it carried them joyfully to war.

The emotional river of fierce anticipation that flowed through Li'ara-Zhurah's own veins left her strangely unmoved. She yearned for battle, yes, but as a form of release for her soul, and not simply to honor the Empress by slaying Her enemies. Li'ara-Zhurah's spirit had been torn during the first battle with the humans on Keran, and just as it had begun to heal, it again had been torn by her first mating.

She shivered as she brutally shoved the memory aside, not noticing how Tesh-Dar suddenly glanced at her, the great priestess's eyes narrowed with concern. Li'ara-Zhurah had been desperate to leave the nursery world: the thought of having to remain there through the entire half-cycle of a child's gestation had been agonizing. It was not that the nurseries were unpleasant, other than the mating experience itself: indeed, in a race that created beauty in all things with the same passion they applied to personal combat, the nurseries were among the most beautiful worlds of the Empire. The warriors and clawless ones awaiting the birth of their children had no duties, no obligations save the normal daily rituals of dressing, meditating, and preparing for sleep. It was a time of unaccustomed luxury and contemplation, with many of the expectant mothers studying passages from the Books of Time or, particularly popular among the clawless ones, practicing one of the many forms of art known to their civilization.

None of this held any appeal for Li'ara-Zhurah. She was not interested in the Books of Time, and cared not for the arts. Her only desire was to grapple with the humans again, to finally gain the spiritual release that had been denied her on Keran. She had sent an urgent message to Tesh-Dar, praying fervently to the Empress that the priestess would not abandon her to the comfortable prison of the nursery.

Li'ara-Zhurah had been shocked when the priestess summoned her to act as her First. While it was an incredible honor, Li'ara-Zhurah's deepest reaction was relief, not gratitude. She boarded a ship for the Homeworld the same day that Tesh-Dar's response arrived, eager to leave the nightmare of the mating ritual behind her.

Now, waiting to board another ship that would again take her to make war on the humans, her hand, as if by its own accord, strayed to her belly. She thought of the life growing within her, and fervently prayed that it would be a female. A sterile female. The thought of bringing forth one of the misshapen males was unutterably vile, and she would not willingly see the torture of mating inflicted upon any fertile offspring. The child was now nothing more than a small but rapidly growing collection of cells, a tiny nub of tissue inside her womb. There would come a time, soon, when its spirit would awaken. It was then, long before even the healers could determine what the child's gender was to be, that she would know if it was to be male or female. She knew the souls of the males formed part of the Bloodsong; but if the songs of the females formed an ever-churning river of emotion, the songs of the males were little more than tiny pebbles at the bottom of the river over which the water flowed. She would know the birth of a female's spirit from its strength and clarity; from a male, she would sense little but its existence. Yet her apprehension about the nature of her child remained. In her darkest dreams she plunged a dagger into her belly, but to do so would have cast her from the grace and love of the Empress to spend eternity in the infinite Darkness.

She knew such thoughts were tantamount to heresy; thus they remained unspoken, especially to Tesh-Dar. She trusted the great priestess with far more than her life: Tesh-Dar had touched Li'ara-Zhurah's spirit in a way that was rare among her people, a gift possessed by only a few of the great warrior priestesses. That was before Li'ara-Zhurah's mating, during the battle for Keran. She would never willingly allow Tesh-Dar to so openly probe her spirit now. Tesh-Dar had the authority and the power to do so if she wished, but Li'ara-Zhurah hoped that the priestess's respect for her would hold her curiosity at bay should she sense anything amiss.

Li'ara-Zhurah knew that her emotions were transparent to the peers, and particularly to Tesh-Dar, but none of her sisters could fully glean the focus of her fears. They believed her soul to still be grief-stricken over what had happened to her at Keran, and she was content to allow their misperceptions to continue. For herself, deep in her heart, she wished for death before the turn of the next great cycle when she would again have to mate. The war with the humans offered her a convenient solution: there would be many opportunities to die with honor for the glory of the Empress.

THIRTY-THREE

Dmitri Andreevich Sikorsky sat in a small booth in one of the many nondescript cafés that were scattered about the city of Saint Petersburg, the capital of the planet that bore the same name. The founders had tried to recreate some of the ornate majesty of the original city in Russia on Earth, but had only succeeded in producing a tawdry imitation of Peter the Great's vision. The only thing they had duplicated with uncompromising success was the tyranny and despotism that had characterized so much of the history of their ancestors' motherland.

In times long past, in a nation on Earth that had once been known as the Soviet Union, Sikorsky would have been known as a dissident. He was a member of a quiet underground movement yearning for political change, but unable to openly express it without suffering severe reprisals. More active demonstrations of political discontent, such as armed rebellion, were simply impossible, as the government controlled all the weapons. Even street rallies were tantamount to suicide. The secret police rarely kicked down doors in the middle of the night anymore because they did not have to: most of the real "threats to the state" had long since been imprisoned, exiled to Riga, or executed. That did not keep them from periodically terrorizing the populace to remind them of the true power of the state, but Sikorsky and his underground companions were thankful for what few blessings came their way.

Unable to confront the power of the state in any other fashion, Sikorsky had done the only thing he could to fight back: he had become an agent for the *Alliance Française*. Sikorsky considered himself a patriot, but after he had experienced first hand the excesses of the government and the Party that controlled it, he had to do something, no matter the risk.

After the armistice ended the war and he was released from military service, he managed to get a job as a foreman of a construction firm (which, like all commercial ventures, was owned by the state). He was involved in the reconstruction of the Alliance Embassy, which had been burned to the ground when the war started, and had made a number of friends on the embassy staff. Over the years, he had been required to maintain and repair a number of the buildings on the compound, which gave him continued opportunities to maintain contact with them.

Years later, when the provisions of the armistice that ended the war expired and the Alliance and Terran inspection teams returned home, the true power behind his own government came out of hiding, and a new cycle of repression began. Sikorsky had looked the other way, trying to ignore the truth, until the secret police came for his son-in-law. Like many citizens of Saint Petersburg, the young couple could not afford their own place to live, so Sikorsky and his wife had taken them in until their fortunes improved. Sikorsky had never viewed this as a bad thing, as he cherished his daughter and loved having her around, and her husband was a good young man who treated her well and was respectful toward her parents.

Then, one night, the secret police came. Sikorsky had never thought it would happen to him. Why should it? He had always been loyal. He had fought in the war. He did his job and kept his mouth shut, and his family did the same. Or so he thought.

Roused from sleep when the apartment's flimsy front door was kicked in, he tried to protest. He shut his mouth quickly when a cold-eyed man wordlessly shoved a gun in his face. Without any explanation, without even a single shout, a dozen members of the secret police swarmed into the apartment, beat his son-in-law unconscious, then dragged him out. Sikorsky's daughter, Natalia, was taken out, too. She was not beaten, but was bound with handcuffs. She had looked at Sikorsky as they paraded her out, while he looked on in wide-eyed shock. Her expression had been calm, even proud. The look in her eyes told him that this had not come as a surprise, and that there was a reason the secret police were here. She and her husband had been members of the underground. Dissidents.

Sikorsky would never know what it was that she and her husband had done, for the government did not bother explaining its actions to the great unwashed of its citizenry. He never saw or heard from her or her husband again.

Two months later, the Alliance Embassy's water supply was having problems, and Sikorsky was sent to direct repairs. Knowing that there would be secret police informants on his repair team, he managed to get a moment alone with an embassy military attaché whom he had met years before as a junior Alliance officer right after the armistice. After a very brief greeting, Sikorsky discreetly passed the man a small envelope when he shook his hand goodbye. On the small piece of paper the officer found inside the envelope was written Sikorsky's contact information and the location of a munitions factory that his company had helped build that was illegal under the long-term provisions of the armistice. He had hoped that the Alliance would come and shut down the factory and hold the government accountable. It would not bring back his daughter, he knew, but it was something. For the first time since his military service, he felt like he was *doing* something.

Unfortunately, the French did nothing about the factory that he had risked his life to show them. The inspection teams had long since left the planet, and the Alliance was far more concerned about the state of their economy than an illegal munitions factory. Sikorsky had been devastated, wondering if he had risked his life for nothing.

Even though the Alliance government decided not to act, their intelligence services were very interested in Sikorsky. The information he had provided was the first evidence they had seen that Saint Petersburg was blatantly violating the long-term provisions of the armistice. After verifying the factory's existence using other sources they already had on the planet, they decided to develop Sikorsky as an agent. As a spy.

That had been ten years ago. Ten years since Sikorsky's daughter had disappeared, most likely raped and then murdered. Ten years of watching his wife go from being in a state of near-catatonic depression to becoming a fanatic member of the Party, Saint Petersburg's ruling elite, in some manifestation of guilt-driven insanity that Sikorsky would never understand. Yet even that, in its own way, had served a purpose, for her rabid support for the Party had led to minor but significant promotions for him that had given him access to more people and information that the Alliance had found useful. His construction work put him in touch with many people who were. The latest was a scientist working on a special project to develop coal as a power source. Sikorsky had no idea why anyone off-world would care about such things as coal power plants, but the information provided by the scientist — one of the many informants Sikorsky had recruited over the years — had clearly gotten the attention of the Alliance.

The Confederation, he corrected himself with an inward smile. He was not sure he believed in the ridiculous tale of aliens attacking human space, but the formation of the Confederation was real, and it was an event that he welcomed. In the last few months, Earth had closed its embassy, consolidating its mission in a newly constructed wing of the Alliance Embassy, that was then officially redesignated as the Confederation Embassy to Saint Petersburg. Then the new ambassador of the Confederation Government, who was the former ambassador of the Alliance, presented his credentials to Chairman Korolev. From what Sikorsky's wife had heard from her Party friends, Korolev had been livid about this new development,but had been powerless to do anything about it.

To Sikorsky, anything that the Party did not like was good for his people and his world.

The Confederation's unexpected interest in these strange coal power plants was why he was sitting here in this café. Sikorsky was a frequent visitor here, often holding informal interviews for people looking for a job, and so his presence would not be unusual in the eyes of any secret police informants. He had received a coded message from his Confederation controller to meet someone here who needed the cover of a job in his company. All he had been told was that he was to meet a woman, and her name was Valentina Tutikova. He was to treat her as he would any candidate, reviewing her credentials and interviewing her as he normally would, hiding the cover aspect of their relationship in plain sight of the secret police.

His controller had never had him meet someone like this before, and it had made him nervous. His nervousness had turned to shock when his wife confided in him that one of her Party friends had told her that the daughter of a well-placed bureaucrat was looking for a job, and Sikorsky had been highly recommended. The girl's name was Valentina Tutikova.

Fortunately, he had been making dinner, and when he spilled hot soup all over his pants in reaction to his wife's revelation, she had thought his shouts of pain and annoyance were only the result of some clumsiness on his part. He had been stunned that the Confederation would go so far and risk so much to establish their agent's credentials. It certainly impressed upon him the importance of the person he was to meet. He only hoped that the Confederation was not pulling the proverbial tiger by the tail: the Party and the secret police might have been fooled for now, but he doubted it would last for long.

In the booth, he sipped his tea and consciously avoided looking at his watch as the appointed time for the meeting arrived, trying instead to focus on the morning edition of the latest Party propaganda displayed on the view screen built into the tabletop.

He only looked up when the bell on the door jingled and a young woman walked in.

* * *

While the documents that every citizen on Saint Petersburg was required to carry said that her name was Valentina Mikhailovna Tutikova, the young woman's true identity, if one could call it that, was Scarlet.

Born Mindy Anne Black, she had joined the Terran Intelligence Agency, or TIA, at the age of twenty. She was a talented linguist, was superbly fit, extremely intelligent and a fast learner, and had nerves to cope with the most extreme situations. TIA had a very special program for such talented people, and it did not take long for her to come to the attention of the powers-that-be.

Two years later, Mindy Black died in a staged vehicle accident. At least that's what the coroner's report said. Since then, the closest she had to a real name was her codename, Scarlet. She had trained for two more years in the skills she would need to survive in the field as one of a handful of special operations agents. They were only assigned the most difficult missions, ones where the value of their objective was only matched by the difficulty in achieving it. Only five people in the entire Confederation knew who and what she was, and only two of them knew she was on Saint Petersburg. One of them was Director Penkovsky. The other was her controller, a man — or woman — she had never met, but whose coded messages sent her across the human sphere to risk her life.

Her mission now was to follow up on the information the Confederation had received that Saint Petersburg was building nuclear weapons and, if she could, verify if it was true. The Alliance had built an extensive network of informants here, one of whom had turned out to be an innocuous construction manager who had turned dissident, and then had become an asset, an informant. He would help her by providing the information, contacts, and access she required for her mission.

The setup with her contact had been arranged through another set of Alliance-turned-Confederation agents, who also arranged for the proper documentation for her when she arrived. The really hard part had been actually getting planetside: it was virtually impossible for any ship, even a small one, to get to the surface without drawing the attention of the planet's coast guard. Getting through customs was also virtually impossible, as the customs teams were led by secret police informants who pried apart every box and container.

Her only option had been an experimental sub-orbital insertion system being developed by the Confederation Marine Corps, and a merchant ship was hastily fitted with a concealed launcher. The timing of the operation was critical: the ship had to arrive at precisely the right time and place in orbit for one of the periodic meteor showers that lit up the skies over much of Saint Petersburg. It had been a divine coincidence that would help cover her arrival; a single brilliant streak across the sky might have drawn unwanted attention. The ship's crew managed to hit the launch window just right, and she was quietly jettisoned from the ship to join a host of other shooting stars. She had never ridden in a deployment pod, which was a grandiose name for a human-sized can covered with ablative material that both absorbed radar tracking signals and acted as a heat shield. She also hoped to never have to use one again: the ride down had been a roaring, bone-jarring experience, and it had taken all her nerve to remain calm as the pod howled down to an altitude of only three hundred meters before it suddenly disintegrated around her. From there it had been a comparatively unexciting, and very brief, parasail ride to the ground.

After carefully burying her chute and other gear that she would not be taking with her for now, she changed into what passed for casual wear in Saint Petersburg City, carrying what she needed with her in a rucksack that could quickly be altered to look like a well-used soft-sided travel bag.

She had landed a few kilometers from a town to the north of Saint Petersburg, and quickly made her way to the train station there under cover of darkness. Arriving in early morning, just as the first rust-streaked commuter train pulled into the station, she made a quick stop in the women's rest room. There, carefully tucked behind the broken toilet paper dispenser in one of the stalls, were her documents. A rumpled white envelope contained a passport, work permit, a visa to live in Saint Petersburg City, an inter-city travel permit, money card, a Party membership card, and an electronic ticket showing that she had boarded a train yesterday in Vasilevsky, a town further to the north and her home of record as shown in her papers, before transferring to this commuter train. It would not stand up to intensive scrutiny, but it would get her past any militiaman who happened to check her travel itinerary.

After quickly changing into a poor-fitting dark gray pantsuit that was typical of the other women she had seen, she grabbed her bag and boarded the train like everyone else, blending in with the other drab and morose commuters heading to the worker's paradise of Saint Petersburg.

* * *

Sikorsky watched as the young woman casually glanced around the café. He was about to get up and hail her when the waiter, whom Sikorsky suspected of being a secret police agent, walked over to her. After a brief exchange of words, he pointed at Sikorsky, and the young woman thanked him and headed back to the booth.

"*Gospodin* Sikorsky," she said with an eager smile, "it's so nice to meet you. I am —"

"Valentina Tutikova," Sikorsky said, standing and offering his hand, "of course. It's very nice to meet you, as well." He shook her hand, and watched her as she settled herself into the booth. With drab brown hair cut in the haphazard style typical of the capital city's women and wearing very little makeup, dressed in clothes that half the other women in the city had in their tiny wardrobes, with ugly black pumps to match, she gave the impression of being just another ordinary citizen looking for a job. Even her eyes were a muddy brown as they looked at him eagerly. She appeared to be in her mid-twenties, but he could not pin down her age: he thought she could easily be older, and perhaps younger. She was not ugly, nor was she particularly attractive. She was outwardly unremarkable by any measure, and would have been invisible in a crowd. Even the waiter, who was infamous for ogling the women who came to the café, did not give her a second glance. She made him think of a creature he had once heard about that was found on Earth: the chameleon, able to change the color of its skin to suit its environment. He wondered what she was really like, but decided that it was probably best not to know.

The only sign he had that she was something other than a daughter of a middling Party bureaucrat had been her handshake: his knuckles had cracked under the pressure of her grip. That was saying something, considering that Sikorsky had worked with his hands in construction all his adult life and his upper body was built like a bear. He took it for the silent signal that it was meant to be, before shoving the fact that she was a Confederation agent aside and getting down to business.

"So, Miss Tutikova, let us go over your background, shall we?" he began as he normally did for such interviews. He asked bland questions about her family and education, her Party standing and participation in Party-sponsored events. She gave equally bland answers that, like her train ticket, would never survive a real investigation, but would be good enough for a casual information scan. Together, they fed the eyes and ears of those who cared to listen with mindless drivel.

Sikorsky realized that Tutikova — or whatever her real name was — answered everything so naturally and played her part so well, that after a while he lost all trace of his own nervousness. "Well," he said as he came to the end of his interview questions, "your background is certainly impressive, young lady. I believe we can get you started right away."

"Thank you, comrade," Tutikova told him earnestly. "That is such good news!" She paused a moment, obviously embarrassed. "Would you happen to know where I might find a hotel?" she asked. "I have a city visa, so I can live here, but of course I have not had time to find an apartment."

Sikorsky smiled. "Do not trouble yourself, dear," he told her. "If you wish, you can stay with my wife and myself until you find something." It was a very typical practice: the Sikorskys had an extra room, where their daughter and her husband had lived, and would frequently put up people just like Tutikova to help make ends meet. It was another bit of fortunate timing that the extra room was currently empty.

Putting on a picture-perfect display of gratitude, Tutikova shook his hand again, slipping him a small wad of money as she did. The move was meant to be seen by prying eyes for what it appeared to be: a gray market deal. In a state where everything was controlled by the government, where citizens were expected to aspire to political perfection, it was a supreme irony that anyone who wasn't making small deals on the side was viewed with deep suspicion. The government wasn't concerned about the gray market economy, which worked far better than the "real" economy run by the government. The Party simply wanted its citizens to be doing something incriminating to make the job of the secret police that much easier.

"Wonderful!" Sikorsky said as he clumsily pocketed the money. Gathering up his papers, he ushered Tutikova out of the café. A block down the street, they got in his battered car and he headed for his apartment, the little electric vehicle humming loudly.

"What do we—" Sikorsky began before she cut him off by putting a finger to her lips.

Tutikova — Scarlet — twisted one of the buttons that was inside her jacket and was rewarded with a green glow. It was a counter-surveillance device that would detect any eavesdropping devices or signals in or aimed at the car. "It's safe to talk," she said.

Sikorsky was shocked at the change in her voice, even in those simple words. She was no longer the eager young Valentina Tutikova, but something else entirely. He just was not sure what. "What are we to do?" he asked quietly. "There is no way I can get you into the coal plants without a full security check. That would take time, and..."

"And my cover would never hold," she finished for him, nodding. "We don't need a security check, because the coal plants aren't what I'm after, Dmitri. I need to know where they're taking the slag and fly ash after the coal is burned. We believe they must be transporting it from the plants to some central facility. That's what I'm interested in. We need to find it and figure out a way to get me inside, but finding it will do." If the government was indeed gathering uranium from the waste byproducts of the massive coal plants, there would have to be a large facility where the uranium-235 was being extracted and processed. She hoped the bombs were built at the same facility, but she would not know that until, or if, she got that far.

Sikorsky frowned. "I don't know where they may be taking the waste," he said, "but I know it is carried away by special trains, at least some of it. It is odd, actually: the basic design of the plants has a very large chemical separation complex to break down the waste products. This was a very expensive and difficult part of the plants to build. Then, of what comes out, the majority is slag that is simply dumped next to the plant in mountainous piles. That is what I would have expected them to do, without bothering with the chemical separation processing. What comes out of that, though...that is hauled away in sealed container cars in much smaller trains." His frown deepened. "I always thought that was odd," he went on, "that they would bother sealing up the waste for transport. They told us that it was for environmental safety. I should have known then that there was something wrong." Protection of the environment, or keeping people safe from environmental hazards, had never been high on the list of the government's priorities. He glanced over at her as he made another turn, drawing out their time in the car where they had some privacy. "What is in those trains, Valentina?"

She momentarily debated whether she should tell him. In most operations, the less one knew, the better. There were some cases, though, where everyone was in so deep it didn't matter. If Sikorsky was caught and interrogated now, he would reveal her interest in the coal plants and where the waste products were being taken. That in itself would be enough to lose the game, so telling him what was really going on wouldn't truly matter. "Believe it or not," she told him, "we believe they're extracting uranium and other fissile materials out of the coal ash. We think Korolev is building an arsenal of nuclear weapons."

A horn suddenly blared and Sikorsky cursed as he steadied the car. He had been so shocked he had nearly run into a car coming the opposite way.

"*Bozhe moi*," he whispered. "My God. Is such a thing possible?" The thought of the rulers of this world in control of even one nuclear weapon was terrifying.

She shrugged. "The scientists — including your contact — seem to think it is, at least in theory. I'm here to find out if it's true. Which brings us around again to our problem: we need to find out where those special trains are going."

"I know someone who might be able to help us find out," he told her. "I have an acquaintance, let us say, who has access to the central train scheduling system. We pay him *na levo*, under the table, to help make sure that the trains we use to transport heavy equipment and materials to construction sites reach their destinations on time, or at least not too late. He is not one of us — not a dissident — but he is not a Party man. He is also a fool for attractive young women." Glancing over at her, he said, "But that can wait for later. You must be exhausted. I should get you home and introduce you to Ludmilla, get some food into you, and let you get some rest."

Tutikova shook her head. "We don't have time for rest, Dmitri," she told him gravely. "I only have six days before I'm extracted. After that..." She trailed off, staring out the passenger-side window.

"After that, what?" he asked.

She turned to look at him, and he was shocked at the glimpse of what she really was behind her disguise. Her eyes were hard, and her voice even more so. "Dmitri, they only send me in where things might get very bad. I can't tell you exactly what's going to happen, because I wasn't told. But if I were you, I would make sure to be on a nice visit to the countryside a long way from here in six days." What she didn't tell him was that she was to be extracted by Confederation Marines. And that was if things went well. If things went badly, she wouldn't be extracted at all. Ever.

Sikorsky felt his stomach clench. *Six days.* Punching a small keypad on the steering wheel, he said, "I'll give him a call right now."

THIRTY-FOUR

"All hands, prepare for normal space emergence in two minutes," the XO's voice sounded through the compartments and passageways of the *Yura*.

On the bridge, Sato watched his crew in action as the indicators for the various stations throughout the ship changed from amber to green on the status board, signaling the readiness of the various departments for the jump back into normal space. *Yura* was on the third leg of her patrol route, which would take her to Kronstadt, a rapidly growing Germanic colony that boasted fifteen million people and was on a popular trade route between the Confederation worlds and the Rim colonies.

Kronstadt had a small but efficient coast guard, but no true warships — yet. The colony had long produced merchant ships of every size, and after joining the Confederation had shifted over two-thirds of its yard capacity to warship production, while retaining the other third for badly needed transports. On top of that, they had implemented a massive building program to double their shipbuilding capacity in eighteen months. While many in the Kronstadt government had still not accepted that Mankind was under serious threat, especially since the Kreelans had not ventured further into human space beyond Keran, there was universal agreement that if the Confederation wanted to finance a major building program, Kronstadt would be happy to reap the benefits of it. The tradeoff was that the colony had to raise a minimum of one Marine assault regiment per million people, and arrange for the training of Territorial Army forces that included every able-bodied male and non-pregnant female of at least seventeen years of age. The Confederation would pay for their weapons and provide the cadre to train them, but the colony had to provide the bodies. For Kronstadt this was not terribly difficult, for they already had a large and well-trained national guard force.

"All stations report ready for emergence, sir," Lieutenant Commander Villiers, his XO, reported. "I suggest that we—"

Sato silenced him with a slight shake of his head. Glancing over at the life support station, Sato saw Midshipman Michelle Sanchez looking at him. Seeing that he was looking at her, she nervously turned back to her console.

"Did you have something on your mind, midshipman?" he asked her.

"No...no, sir," she said stiffly.

Sato suppressed a smile. Sanchez, a black-haired beauty who could melt half the crew with one glance from her deep brown eyes, was bright and competent. If she had a weakness, it was her lack of self-confidence. She consistently had the right answer in any given situation, but was too afraid of making a mistake, of making herself look foolish, particularly when speaking in front of the captain. As her senior mentor aboard ship, he had been helping her overcome this weakness, and had just set her up for a learning experience. This was the first time she had been on the bridge during a normal space emergence, so technically it was unfair to expect her to know all the various protocols. There was one regulation, however, that was immutable, that every officer and rating on the ship should know.

He waited a few more seconds to see if she would react before saying, "Navigation, begin the transpace sequence," he ordered.

"Excuse me, captain," he heard Sanchez say. Her voice was clear, but obviously forced.

"Yes, Sanchez?" he said casually, turning to her.

"Sir...forgive me for saying so, but aren't we supposed to go to general quarters before normal space emergence?"

He gave her something that he rarely gave to anyone beyond Steph and a few close friends: a wide smile. "Very good, midshipman," he told her. Then, with mock reproof in his voice as he glanced at Villiers, he said, "The XO must've forgotten to tell me."

Villiers threw up his hands in mock surrender, which drew smiles and a few chuckles from around the bridge.

"Well done, midshipman," Sato told Sanchez, his voice serious now. "I expect my officers and crew — each and every one of them — to think and, as necessary, to act in the ship's best interests. Going to general quarters before normal space emergence is one of our most important regulations, and for good reason: the enemy could be waiting for us, and we have to be ready to come out fighting. It's unlikely a captain or XO would ever forget to do it, but unlikely things sometimes happen, and it's up to you to ask questions when you think something might be wrong. I'll never penalize you for thinking. Always remember that."

"Yes, sir," she said, sitting up straighter in her combat chair, obviously proud of herself. "I will, sir."

Sato nodded. "In that case, Sanchez, you get the honors: bring the crew to general quarters. Navigation, start the transpace sequence."

"Aye, aye, sir!" Sanchez replied before hitting the general quarters alarm. "All hands, general quarters!" her voice boomed over the piercing hoot of the alarm. "Man your battle stations!"

Villiers started a timer as he himself dashed off the bridge to reach his own battle station in the auxiliary bridge halfway across the ship. The Marines, who were always in their combat armor for any planned normal space emergence, pounded through the passageways to get to their anti-boarding stations, making sure all the airtight hatches were closed behind them.

The status console now showed the "Christmas tree" for general quarters, with all the departments of the ship reporting their readiness. All of the amber lights quickly changed to green and the general quarters klaxon turned itself off.

"Forty seconds flat, skipper," the XO reported breathlessly from the auxiliary bridge as the last indicator turned green. "Not half bad."

Sato nodded his head, inwardly grinning at the thought that Villiers must have broken a world speed record to get to his position in time. He normally would have been at the auxiliary bridge, anyway, but he had wanted to see how Sanchez did first-hand.

As for the crew's time, forty seconds was a huge improvement. At their first emergence, into the Sandoval system, the crew had taken over ninety. They had done a lot of drills between then and now to help them improve. "Agreed," he said. "But we can do better, XO. I'd like to shave at least five seconds off of that next time."

"Will do, skipper," Villiers said. He did not take Sato's comment as a rebuke, but as a challenge. They had a good crew, and they would only get better over time. Like Sato, he wanted to have the ship combat-ready as quickly as possible, since speed was life.

"Navigation auto-lock engaged," the computer's synthesized female voice interjected over the ship-wide intercom. "Transpace sequence in five...four...three...two...one...Transpace sequence initiated. Sequence complete. Emergence into normal space...now."

The main bridge display suddenly lit up with a visual of the Kronstadt system, with the shining crescent of the planet itself directly ahead.

"Navigation confirmed, Kronstadt system," the navigator announced. "Emergence deviation negligible. We're—"

"*Contact!*" the tactical officer shouted. "Four bogies at three-three-eight mark eight-nine relative. Distance fifty thousand kilometers." Four yellow icons appeared on the tactical display to the left of the ship's current heading. Several dozen other icons, all green, also appeared.

Sato didn't hesitate. "Maintain course, all ahead flank!" If the four unidentified ships were friendly, he would just be giving them a good show of how fast *Yura* could accelerate. And if they weren't friendly ships, *Yura* would have the advantage of surprise. "Communications, get a positive ID on those ships."

"All ahead flank, aye," Lieutenant Bogdanova reported tersely as she smoothly brought the ship's acceleration up to maximum. She could feel the deep thrum of the sublight drives vibrate through the deck beneath her feet as *Yura* leaped forward.

"Forward kinetic batteries and heavy lasers locked on and tracking all bogies, sir," the tactical officer reported. "Recommend closing to ten thousand kilometers to engage."

On the bridge tactical display, the green icons representing known friendly ships were clearly scattering away from the yellow icons like a school of fish fleeing from a predator.

"Sir, I'm picking up multiple mayday signals," the communications officer reported. "Eight ships report they've been hit and are losing air. Three of them are Kronstadt coast guard cutters."

The four yellow icons suddenly changed to red.

"Hostile contacts confirmed," the tactical officer reported. "All four appear to be Kreelan warships, destroyer category."

Sato had to commend the Kronstadt coastguardsmen. They had incredible courage to go up against Kreelan destroyers with their lightly armed cutters.

"Request that any surviving Kronstadt coast guard vessels form on us," Sato ordered. "And try to get the merchantmen to all turn toward us. If we can get the Kreelans to head our way, we'll close the range more quickly."

"Assuming they don't jump out," Villiers said through the vidcom terminal on Sato's combat chair.

"They won't," Sato shook his head. "They'll never run from a fight, even when they're completely outmatched." He knew that the actual odds in this battle were against him: four destroyers, competently handled, could take a single heavy cruiser. But not *his* heavy cruiser. Not the *Yura*.

As they watched the display, most of the green icons turned in *Yura's* direction. The merchant captains were desperate for help, and were more than eager to get closer to the only real human warship in the entire system. They weren't fast enough to get far enough from Kronstadt to jump, and were far too slow to run from the enemy ships in normal space. Three of the ones that had sent mayday signals suddenly vanished, destroyed.

"The enemy is just firing indiscriminately, sir," the communications officer said, trying to hold her emotions in check. "Some of the ships are even broadcasting their surrender, but the Kreelans are just ignoring it."

"The Kreelans don't take prisoners," Sato said flatly. "Take my word for it."

* * *

Riyal-Tiyan tensed as the tactical display showed another human ship jump into the system. As the senior shipmistress of the small squadron of destroyers, her mission had been simple: wreak havoc among the human shipping lanes in this area of space. She was specifically not to attack planets or any orbital complexes, only ships. Her purpose was to test how well the humans had developed their defenses and to rekindle their respect for and fear of the Empire.

This was the second system her squadron had visited. In the first one, they had destroyed six merchant ships and three lightly armed defense vessels before the other merchantmen had jumped away. Some smaller craft, armed only with small kinetic weapons, had risen to challenge her destroyers. She had saluted their courage by allowing them to live as she took her warships on to the next target.

In this system, which the humans had named Kronstadt, her ships had jumped into the midst of a small fleet of merchant vessels, which tried to run away from them like terrified steppe beasts before the claws of a *genoth*. With guns hammering and lasers singing, her ships tore at the fat merchantmen, then turned with equal ferocity on the small human warships that bravely sped into the attack. Like those Riyal-Tiyan had encountered at the first system — Andover, the humans called it — these were only lightly armed and hardly worth calling warships. They put up a spirited fight, however, and succeeded in diverting her attention long enough for the merchant ships to try and race for their jump points.

Now a new ship had appeared, and it immediately began to race directly toward her squadron. Not a merchant vessel, then.

"Ah," she sighed with anticipation as the tactical display showed the targeting systems emanating from the human vessel. "A true warship. Ayan-Kulil," she said to her tactical officer. "Let our ships form in pairs and flank the human warship. Ignore the merchant ships for now."

A moment later the other three destroyers turned from hammering the defenseless merchant ships and sped to their places in the designated formation to greet their new opponent.

* * *

"They've formed up in pairs, sir, trying to flank us," the tactical officer reported tensely.

Sato eyed the display, silently calculating his options as the range rings showing the maximum effective range of his weapons quickly converged on the charging Kreelan warships. He was under very strict orders not to let *Yura* suffer heavy damage while she was operating solo: the Confederation Navy was still tiny compared to the number of systems they were tasked with defending, and every ship, particularly the new heavy cruisers like *Yura*, were precious. Each captain on solo patrol had discretion on whether to engage the enemy, but they were not to risk destruction of their ships for any reason, even if the Kreelans were mounting an invasion. In that scenario, a single ship would not be able to make a substantial difference, anyway.

His main problem was preventing the Kreelans from raking him from two sides at once, which could be lethal to *Yura*. "Tactical," he ordered, "prepare torpedo tubes one through five for salvo fire at the left pair of targets on my mark." Sato didn't expect the torpedoes to hit their targets, but he hoped it would distract that pair of destroyers. "Then engage the right pair with kinetics and heavy lasers. Helm," he turned to Bogdanova, "when I give the order, I want you to come forty degrees to starboard. Let's try to keep them from flanking us on both sides as we pass by."

On the tactical display, *Yura* raced toward the two pairs of Kreelan destroyers, the range rings overlapping. Sato let them close, then close further.

"Enemy kinetics, inbound!" called the tactical officer.

"A little closer," Sato whispered to himself. The destroyers were now close enough to be picked up on visual display, their rakish hulls unmistakable. "On my mark, people...stand by...*mark!*"

Yura shuddered as five torpedoes leaped from their launch tubes and streaked toward the farther pair of Kreelan destroyers. In the same instant, two of the main triple-gun turrets volleyed fifteen centimeter projectiles at the nearer pair of enemy ships, while three heavy laser turrets fired, flaying tons of metal from the sides of the nearer destroyers.

At the same time, *Yura* made a sharp turn to starboard, missing all but a few of the projectiles the Kreelan ships had fired. As the ready rounds in the first two gun turrets ran out, Bogdanova skillfully rolled *Yura* to bring the other batteries to bear.

"Cease fire," Sato ordered as the nearer pair of destroyers disappeared in twin balls of flame and debris, struck by a full salvo of heavy shells. One of the other pair of enemy ships disintegrated under the impact of three torpedoes.

The fourth destroyer escaped unscathed.

"Turn and pursue," Sato ordered, setting aside his pleasure at his ship's performance for later.

Bogdanova brought the ship around, even as the crew belowdecks were reloading the guns and torpedo tubes.

* * *

Riyal-Tiyan was both shocked and pleased. Shocked that the human ship's weapons had been so effective, and pleased that the humans had apparently not been idle in the time since Keran had been taken by the Empire.

She mourned the loss of her ships and their crews, that they could no longer bring glory to the Empress. She and her own crew would have preferred to turn and charge the pursuing human ship, but Tesh-Dar's orders and the will of the Empress had been clear: the squadrons such as Riyan-Tiyal's were not to sacrifice themselves. In such a situation as this, any surviving ships were to return with information on what they had encountered, and how well the humans were fighting back.

"Prepare to jump," she ordered her navigator, failing to mask her disappointment. They would rendezvous with the fleet heading toward the human world of Saint Petersburg.

* * *

"They jumped, sir!" the tactical officer said incredulously.

For a moment, Sato didn't believe it. He simply couldn't accept that the Kreelans would run away from a fight. But there was no denying that the surviving Kreelan destroyer had escaped. *Could it be a trick?*

That didn't fit any better, he decided. While he couldn't deny what the tactical display showed him, he knew deep in his soul that the Kreelan hadn't run because the captain was afraid of challenging his ship. It was something else, some other reason he didn't understand, and it gave him a bad feeling in his gut.

"Very well," he said finally. "Helm, bring us around toward Kronstadt. XO," he told Villiers through the vidcom, "prepare the cutters for launch: let's see if we can't help the coast guard with search and rescue."

"Aye, aye, sir," Villiers said before he disappeared to carry out his orders.

Sato continued to stare at the place on the tactical display where the Kreelan destroyer had disappeared, wondering where she had gone. And why she had run.

* * *

After helping to rescue the surviving crew members of the merchant ships and turning them over to the Kronstadt coast guard ships, Sato had placed *Yura* in a high defensive orbit over the planet. Before this battle, he would have been sure that the

Kreelans would return in force, but the Kreelan destroyer's sudden departure had shaken his confidence in his assessments of their actions. He knew there must have been a reason other than just "running away to fight another day." That would have been a very reasonable action were it a human destroyer facing off against a heavy cruiser, but was totally out of line with all he knew, or thought he knew, about the enemy.

His decision now was whether to proceed on schedule to the next leg of his patrol, or delay here in Kronstadt in case the Kreelans returned. He knew that, unless the enemy returned only with a token force, his single ship would hardly be able to hold off an invasion fleet. Yet showing the Confederation flag to new signatories like Kronstadt was vitally important. *Yura* had already made a lasting impression, but he was worried about leaving the colony if there was a chance the Kreelans might return soon.

He set that matter aside for the moment. They still had seven hours left before they would have to jump out on their next leg to stay on their patrol schedule. Commodore Hanson had built some time into the navigation exercise for her ships to actually patrol, rather than just jumping from system to system. With the other responsibilities, particularly repairs to the light damage the ship had suffered, taken over by the XO for now, Sato had some time to relax.

Sitting on the side of his bunk, he pulled out a shiny black lacquer box that Steph had given him just before they'd parted at Africa Station. She hadn't told him what was in it, and made him promise not to look until after his first jump. He smiled as he opened it.

Letters. She had written him three dozen letters, each lightly scented with perfume. He had only read three so far, and it had almost been enough to make him want to turn the ship around and head for Earth. Neither of them were terribly good at expressing their emotions face to face. They could talk about things, certainly, but there seemed to be a limit to those conversations, something that held them back. Steph's letters broke through that barrier, cast it aside. The words on those slips of stationery were really *her*. He had read the first one at least a dozen times, then sat down and wrote his own. He had grinned to himself at writing his words of love on ship's letterhead, but that was the only real paper (even if it wasn't actually made out of wood pulp) he had aboard ship. In a way, though, it was fitting: his ship, the Navy, was part of him. And even though it kept them apart much of the time, she had made it clear that it was a part of him that she loved.

He had just begun to read the fourth letter when his alert chime sounded. "Yes?" He tried to conceal his irritation.

"My apologies, captain," the communications officer said, "but a courier just jumped in, broadcasting a coded message for us."

"What does it say?" he asked, knowing she would have already decoded it.

"It's a recall from headquarters, sir," she said. "The entire squadron is ordered to rendezvous at an assembly point for a possible assault on Saint Petersburg."

"Damn," Sato spat as he carefully folded Steph's letter and put it back in the box. "Have the navigator plot us a least-time course, then ask the department heads, Marine commander, and the senior NCOs to meet in my ready room in five minutes."

If nothing else, he thought grimly, he no longer had to worry about making a decision about extending their stay in Kronstadt.

THIRTY-FIVE

"You do well, child," Tesh-Dar told Li'ara-Zhurah after they completed their latest sparring match in the ship's arena. Even the smallest ships of the Imperial Fleet had one aboard, for the arena was not just an affectation of their civilization, it was a fundamental institution of their civilization since before the founding of the Empire. As the fleet made its way toward the human world of Saint Petersburg, Tesh-Dar worked each day with Li'ara-Zhurah, trying to ease the pain from her soul and guide her along the path that the priestess so hoped she would choose to take.

Tesh-Dar not only remembered Pan'ne-Sharakh's words of caution about the young warrior, but had used them as a guide to further build her relationship with Li'ara-Zhurah. She had come to believe that there was indeed something the young warrior was shielding in her heart, and had sought to gently sway her into revealing it of her own accord. Tesh-Dar could have simply ordered her to do it, and while that would have revealed the truth of the matter, it would also likely have destroyed the bond between them. That was the one thing Tesh-Dar was loathe to do, for if Li'ara-Zhurah was to follow in her footsteps and become a priestess of the Desh-Ka, her faith and trust had to be complete, without reservation.

"I am honored by your words, my priestess," Li'ara-Zhurah said as she quickly stilled her breathing after their latest round of fierce swordplay. She knew that she would never be a tenth as good as was Tesh-Dar with any weapon, but she found herself proud of her own abilities: she was no warrior priestess, but knew she could defeat any of her peers. Tesh-Dar pushed her beyond the limits she had set for herself, and Li'ara-Zhurah was openly surprised at how much her combat skills had improved, even in the short time since returning from the nursery world. And much as part of her wished to deny it, the gentle spiritual ministrations of the great priestess had allayed the worst of the melancholy that had so distracted her since the battle of Keran. It had not changed her loathing about bearing a male child, or her fears for any fertile female children, but she had set aside the thoughts of sacrificing herself in battle simply to avoid future matings. Early in the voyage, she had gathered her courage enough to speak to one of the other young warriors who had recently suffered through her first mating. Li'ara-Zhurah was surprised to learn that the warrior had felt much the same as she herself had: the warrior had been greatly distraught by the experience and had suffered similar thoughts of casting her life away before another mating could be consummated. Yet, after a time, the warrior told her, these feelings had passed; mating would never be a pleasant experience, but like with all things in the Empire, it was a duty to the Empress that could not be set aside. Honor would not allow it.

"Come, then, child," Tesh-Dar said as she sheathed her sword. "Walk with me."

Li'ara-Zhurah bowed and saluted before following the great priestess from the arena. Walking behind Tesh-Dar as they passed the next group of challengers set on honing their skills before fighting the humans, Li'ara-Zhurah was again amazed, as she had been every time she had witnessed it, that Tesh-Dar left no footprints in the sand behind her. While the priestess possessed a soul in a vessel of flesh and blood as did all of Her Children, there was so much more to her. The powers she possessed, glimpsed here in the grains of sand that were left untouched by her passing, were both frightening and reassuring. Frightening, because Li'ara-Zhurah could not imagine any enemy, no matter how terrible, standing against her, and reassuring for the same reason: as long as Tesh-Dar lived, the Empire and the Empress would endure, would be safe. The other warrior priestesses were great in their own right, yet they could not compare to the high priestess of the Desh-Ka. If the Empress was the body and soul of Her Children, Tesh-Dar was the physical manifestation of their sword and shield. Li'ara-Zhurah had once heard Pan'ne-Sharakh refer to Tesh-Dar as *Legend of the Sword*, and she had come to understand the truth of that name in the time she had spent with the priestess.

Walking in Tesh-Dar's path was truly a humbling experience.

"You could be more than simply a witness to the powers of the Desh-Ka," Tesh-Dar said quietly as Li'ara-Zhurah moved up to walk beside her, once they were clear of the arena. "I would show you the temple where our order has passed on our knowledge from generation to generation, from priestess to priestess."

Li'ara-Zhurah stopped and stared at Tesh-Dar, her eyes wide with surprise. "My priestess..." she began, unsure if she had heard correctly what Tesh-Dar had said. "Did you just say..."

"Yes, I did, child," Tesh-Dar said, turning to face her young disciple. "Your Bloodsong sings to me in a way that very few have over the many cycles of my life," she explained. "You have suffered in a way that few of our warriors have, and you have shown the strength of will to control, and I hope to conquer, your inner fears. At Keran you brought great glory to the Empress in battle, and showed your courage in the face of a worthy enemy." She looked deeply into the young warrior's eyes, into her soul. "One of my greatest honors, one of my greatest responsibilities as high priestess, is to choose a successor, a warrior who shall inherit the powers passed down to me, whom I shall teach all that I know. I have chosen you. You may choose to accept, or not, as it pleases you."

Li'ara-Zhurah closed her eyes and bowed her head. In a shaking voice she said, "Great priestess, I am unworthy of such an honor." She was suddenly stricken with a deep sense of guilt for the thoughts that had clouded her mind earlier, thoughts of casting away her honor even as Tesh-Dar was considering granting her the greatest gift that she could give, a gift nearly as great to one of her kind as life itself.

She suddenly felt Tesh-Dar's hand against her cheek. "Be not ashamed of your earlier thoughts," she said, as if reading Li'ara-Zhurah's mind. "You have endured much in Her name, child. Our Way is never easy, from the moment we emerge from the womb until the instant our spirits pass into the Afterlife to join the Ancient Ones. To honor Her, we each seek perfection in our craft, as warriors or clawless ones. Yet what we aspire to is something we can never achieve; perfection is a state of grace that only the Empress knows."

"I cannot imagine imperfection in you, my priestess," Li'ara-Zhurah noted humbly.

Tesh-Dar gave an ironic *humph*. "Child, I was punished upon the *Kal'ai-Il* when I was young, before my Seventh Challenge, and wear the scars of my disgrace upon my back, even now."

Li'ara-Zhurah looked up at her, shocked. "You...were punished upon the *Kal'ai-Il?*" She shook her head. "Then how..." She looked at the great cyan rune on Tesh-Dar's breastplate that was the twin of the one engraved in the oval disk on her collar. The rune of the Desh-Ka, that only priestesses were allowed to display.

"How did I become a priestess after suffering such dishonor?" Tesh-Dar asked as she turned and began walking down the passageway of the ship toward her quarters, Li'ara-Zhurah falling into step beside her. "Because, like you, daughter, I learned what it truly means to bear the burden of Her honor."

* * *

While her punishment on the *Kal'ai-Il* was complete absolution of her sin in the eyes of the Empress and the peers, Tesh-Dar was unable to rid herself of a deep sense of guilt. With Sura-Ni'khan's very reluctant blessing, Tesh-Dar left for what was to be a long and lonely sojourn on the frontier. For nineteen cycles she sought out every challenge that her people faced in the deep unknowns of space and the many worlds they sought to conquer. While there were many perils to be found, there were few that truly tested her.

She served on survey vessels that extended the Empire's domain and probed for any threats to Her Children. Along the way, she taught swordcraft in several *kazhas* in the frontier settlements, astounding even the most senior warriors with her mastery of every weapon. She fought in spectacular Challenges, at times taking on five or more highly skilled opponents and never suffering defeat.

She visited worlds that the Empress had left untouched, planets where mere survival was a challenge. She saw and battled amazing beasts that were far more deadly than the *genoth* of the Homeworld, and even learned to survive vegetation that could kill and maim. These worlds were reserves where the more seasoned warriors of the Empire could embark upon the very kind of spiritual quest on which Tesh-Dar found herself. She visited each of the worlds that were thus preserved, hunting and killing the most vicious creatures in the galaxy, sometimes in company with other warriors, but more often hunting on her own.

Over the cycles that passed, the Legend of the Sword indeed became a legend on the frontier, yet this only served to heighten Tesh-Dar's sense of loneliness. As more pendants were added to her collar in recognition of her feats of skill and courage, as she ascended the figurative steps toward the throne that defined her social standing, so did the peers became more reverent, more distant. It gave her some painful insights into how Sura-Ni'khan, who was only five steps from the throne, and the other warrior priestesses and senior mistresses among the clawless ones must feel. It was a great achievement to reach such a lofty height among the peers, yet it brought a kind of social isolation that Tesh-Dar had never suspected as a young *tresh*.

She corresponded regularly with Sura-Ni'khan, as well as Pan'ne-Sharakh, and their words of hope and praise helped to gradually ease the pain Tesh-Dar felt in her heart. The shame and guilt of killing Nayan-Tiral never left her, but eventually she came to terms with it in the great emptiness of the frontier where she planned to spend the rest of her life if the Empress so allowed.

Tesh-Dar's travels eventually took her to Klameth-Gol, a primordial world that had been left by the Empress as a massive game preserve, where some of the most vicious forms of life in all the Empire could be found, from invisible microbes that challenged the skills of the healers to massive sea creatures half a league in length, and predators on land that made a mockery of the most dangerous creatures that had ever walked upon the Homeworld. These great predators were what Tesh-Dar had come for. Yet, as she and her fellow warriors were to discover, on this planet the largest and most fearsome beasts were merely prey themselves.

Tesh-Dar was returning from a solo hunt in the jungle, where she had been tracking a particularly large predator for the last several days, when she heard an eruption of screams from the hunting encampment. Screams of terror. Screams of pain.

Dashing forward along the trail she had earlier hacked through the dense undergrowth, she burst into the encampment's clearing. With a shock, she saw the dismembered bodies of several warriors strewn about the bare, soggy ground, with seven survivors standing back-to-back in the center, swords drawn. They were terrified, which drove a spike of fear into Tesh-Dar's heart. For these were not young *tresh*, inexperienced and untrained. They were seasoned warriors and hunters who had long cycles of experience on worlds much like this. She could not imagine what would frighten them so.

"Tesh-Dar!" one of them warned. "Beware! There is—"

Suddenly, Tesh-Dar sensed something to her left, very close. Her eyes saw nothing, yet she knew with certainty that there was something there: a disturbance in the air that caressed her skin, a strange scent, very faint, wafting toward her. She did not have Sura-Ni'khan's special powers or second sight as a warrior priestess of the Desh-Ka, but her own senses were naturally keen, and had been refined by many years of training and experience.

With a lightning-quick draw, her sword sang from its sheath. Using a powerful two-handed cut, she slashed the air where her senses told her something was approaching, even though her eyes still saw nothing other than the bodies of some of her companions on the blood-soaked ground.

She cringed as her sword found its mark and a demonic shriek pierced the air. Watching in fascination, she saw a wound open in her sword's path, as if the skin and flesh of the air itself had parted and was left exposed and bleeding.

Bringing her sword overhead in a fluid motion, she slashed downward in a move that could cut through stone. The creature shrieked again, but that was its last act as Tesh-Dar's sword cleaved it in two. The thing collapsed to the ground in a heap of bloody meat and bone.

It was not alone. She whirled just in time as she sensed something behind her, and her slashing sword must have caught this beast at the neck. A cross-section of its body, roughly as big around as her thigh and spouting a torrent of blood, was suddenly revealed at her own shoulder's height. She was knocked to the ground as the thing's body continued forward before it collapsed, making a deep indentation in the ground.

Two of the other warriors suddenly screamed, and Tesh-Dar watched in horror as their bodies were plucked from the defensive ring they had formed and were carried into the forest, caught in the jaws of the invisible creatures. The warriors slashed at their attackers with sword and claw, but it was for naught: a maw suddenly opened out of thin air to bite off the head of one of the warriors. The other warrior was simply carried onward into the jungle, still screaming.

Tesh-Dar stood there for several minutes, reaching out with her senses to see if she could detect any more of the creatures in their midst. While she knew she could not be sure, she did not think there were any more. Yet, she had no doubt they would return.

Cautiously, she joined the five remaining warriors. They were even more terrified now, and Tesh-Dar did not blame them: she was only barely able to suppress her own fear. Kreelan warriors were accustomed to being the hunters, not the hunted.

"What are these things?" Tesh-Dar whispered as the group carefully moved toward one of the creatures she had killed. Even now, all that could be seen of it was the bloody wound left by Tesh-Dar's sword; even in death, the creature's body was completely invisible.

"We do not know, Tesh-Dar," one of them said, trying to control the tremor in her voice. "There are no records of such beasts on this world. I have hunted here before several times, from this very encampment."

"Let us see, then, what we face," Tesh-Dar said as she knelt to the ground. Gathering up handfuls of dirt, she sprinkled it over the creature's invisible body. Gradually, an outline of their menace was revealed.

"In Her name," one of the others whispered.

It looked to be a type of saurian creature, with two powerful hind legs and two smaller, yet still powerful arms, that stood a head taller than herself. As Tesh-Dar continued to sprinkle dirt over the body, she saw that it had a long tail and a ridge of long, sharp spines along its back. Its head was oversize, as large as her torso, and after she found its mouth and pried it open, she and the others could see that the creature had a massive jaw filled with an impressive array of razor-sharp teeth and fangs.

While it would have been an impressive opponent without its invisibility, it was still nothing compared to an adult *genoth* on the Homeworld, which was far larger and more powerful. In fact, the creature Tesh-Dar had been hunting the last several days was far larger and more dangerous even than a *genoth*.

The *genoth* was adept at the art of camouflage, but it could not make itself invisible. That was what made these beasts, which were also small and agile enough to move about the jungle silently, truly dangerous. And even worse, unlike the *genoth*, they clearly hunted in packs.

There were no warrior priestesses with this hunting party, and of the survivors, Tesh-Dar was now senior; the lives of the others rested in her hands. It did not take her long to decide what to do. While the warriors of the Empire sought challenges of the body and spirit, there was no honor in sacrificing themselves to mindless beasts. "We must leave," she told them. "Now. Gather up water and any weapons you need, and then we leave for the ship." Their ship, a small craft designed for such forays, was in a clearing several leagues from the hunting camp. Tesh-Dar could have summoned it to them, but there was nowhere for it to land, and it had no means to cut through the canopy of trees above them. The path leading there was well-worn and easily followed, but the jungle pressed close along the entire distance, and there were several streams to cross. They could be easily ambushed anywhere along the route.

"Tesh-Dar," one of the warriors said, "it grows dark. Should we not light a fire and wait until morning?"

Tesh-Dar eyed the monster under the thin coating of dirt. "Night or day makes no difference when we cannot see what comes to kill us," she said grimly. "If it is only a small pack of beasts, they may be content with their kill for a time, but I have no doubt they will return." She warily eyed the jungle surrounding them. "Gather your things. I will attend to the last rites of the fallen."

As the five other survivors ran to collect weapons and water, praying to the Empress that the creatures would not ambush them again here, Tesh-Dar quickly moved among the fallen warriors. Muttering a quiet prayer for each, she gathered up their collars and reverently placed them in a leatherite pouch. The Collar of Honor worn by all of Her Children from the time they came of age was made of living metal that did not part from its owner until death. She would return them to the *kazhas* where the warriors had served, assuming she survived to do so.

In a few minutes, they were ready. "I will lead," Tesh-Dar told them, "and try to give warning if I sense any of the creatures around us. Keep careful watch on the trail behind us for footprints appearing in the earth. That should give you warning of their approach."

"What if they attack from the flank?" one of the warriors asked. "We will not be able to see them with the jungle so close to the trail."

Tesh-Dar offered her a grim smile, her white canines glistening in the fading light. "Then hope they choose not to attack that way." With one last look around, she said, "Come, let us go."

After that, they ran, threading their way along the path as quickly as they could. They did not need lights to see in the darkening forest, for the eyes of the *Kreela* are well-adapted to see in near-total darkness. Tesh-Dar had debated the merits of moving quickly versus more slowly and cautiously, but in the end had decided upon speed: not knowing how many more of the creatures might be out there, she felt that moving at a slower pace would simply give their enemy more opportunities to attack. She would slow for the stream crossings, which she felt were the most likely ambush sites, but otherwise she planned to move as quickly as their feet would carry them.

Sword in hand, Tesh-Dar led the others at a fast pace. They were all experienced warriors in prime condition, and had no trouble keeping up. Even though she was well-accustomed to the sounds and smells of the jungle from having spent weeks here, fear clutched at her heart with every grunt and groan from the forest around her, with every rustle of vegetation.

They were nearly halfway to the ship when the first attack came. The trailing warrior called out a warning when she saw tracks suddenly appear in the ground close behind her. Loosing a *shrekka* at the invisible beast, she was rewarded with a gout of blood and a pain-filled cry before the creature crashed into the vegetation beside the path where it fell to the ground.

"*On the right!*" Tesh-Dar shouted as she sensed something moving in the jungle beside them. One of the other warriors slashed outward with her sword, but was not quick enough: long, serrated teeth appeared out of thin air above the foliage to clamp around her face, and with one vicious shake of its massive jaws the creature yanked her head from her body. Tesh-Dar hurled a *shrekka* at the beast, but only wounded it. Hissing in pain, showing a trail of blood down its side that illuminated part of its body in crimson, the creature quickly moved away into the forest with its grisly prize. One of the other warriors paused just long enough to snatch the fallen warrior's collar from the ground before they ran onward.

The warrior directly behind Tesh-Dar cried out as a beast snapped at her from the other side of the trail, but she was quicker than her attacker: with a cry of fear and rage, she stabbed her pike into the creature's flesh. It roared in pain, slashing at her with one of its forelegs. The claw crashed against her chest armor, sending the warrior flying into Tesh-Dar and knocking both of them to the ground. The other warrior screamed as the beast stepped on her legs and opened its jaws wide.

Rolling clear, Tesh-Dar hurled her sword directly into the thing's open mouth, burying the blade in the back of its throat. It fell to the ground, writhing, and the other warriors hacked and stabbed at its invisible body until it lay still in a blood-covered heap.

As suddenly as the attack had begun, it was over: Tesh-Dar could hear several more beasts moving quickly through the forest away from the trail.

Panting heavily, she turned her attention to the warrior who had been pinned by the legs.

"My left leg is broken," she hissed. "Leave me here, I will draw them away from you for a time."

"Nonsense," Tesh-Dar told her as she waved two of the others to help the wounded warrior to her feet. "I will leave none of you behind. Kuirin-Shuril," she told the remaining warrior, "watch our trail. Let us go."

It was a desperate, agonizing trek over the last league and a half to the clearing where the ship lay waiting. The two warriors carrying the one with the broken leg were fighting for every breath as they trotted and stumbled to the ship, their arms and legs burning and exhausted. The nerves of Tesh-Dar and Kuirin-Shuril were worn and raw from watching the jungle around them, expecting an attack to come at any moment.

"In Her name," one of the warriors whispered in relief as they emerged into the clearing.

That was when the second attack came, but in an entirely unexpected way. With an ear-shattering roar, a beast like the one Tesh-Dar had been hunting the last several days suddenly lunged into the clearing. So tall that its spined head crested the lower trees, it was in many ways a much larger cousin of the invisible creatures, except that its thick — and quite visible — hide was dappled in greens, yellows, and browns that helped it blend in with the jungle vegetation. Normally it would silently lay in wait for its prey, which made it difficult to hunt: ambushing a creature that specialized in ambushes was no small feat.

For a moment, the warriors simply stopped and stared at this latest horror that charged across the clearing directly for them, disbelieving their incredible misfortune. That was when Tesh-Dar noticed that the creature was badly wounded, with deep slashes down its flank and thigh.

It suddenly whipped its head to one side and snapped at thin air, but its jaws closed on something more substantial: one of the invisible creatures appeared in a cascade of blood as the leviathan crushed it in its powerful jaws.

The jungle behind the great beast suddenly parted in over a dozen places, and the air was torn by the high-pitched shrieks of more of the invisible hunters.

"*Run!*" Tesh-Dar screamed above the din, pushing the other warriors toward the ship. As Kuirin-Shuril passed her, she said, "Your sword! Give it to me!"

"But..." Kuirin-Shuril stuttered, her eyes wild with fear.

Tesh-Dar reached out and took the sword from her hand before shoving her toward the ship. "Take the others and go!"

Kuirin-Shuril made to say something else, but Tesh-Dar ignored her and began to run toward the massive animal thundering across the clearing, bellowing in agony and rage. The other warriors would need a few seconds to reach the ship, but the great beast would be upon them before they could make it unless Tesh-Dar could somehow slow it — and its pursuers — down. She had no plan, no strategy, other than to become one with her weapons and let the will of the Empress guide her fate. Once the others were safely in the ship, they could bring the small vessel's weapons to bear on the animals.

Yet, in a cold place in her soul, Tesh-Dar hoped they did not. After all that she had been through in these last nineteen cycles, she realized that this would be her true atonement, not for the peers or even the Empress, but for herself. She knew that she would die here, but it would be a death worthy of a warrior, a death worthy to end her own passage in the Books of Time.

For the first time since her sword had taken Nayan-Tiral's life, Tesh-Dar's Bloodsong rang out in a melody of pure joy.

The huge beast charged straight over her, ignoring the puny two-legged creature in its path until Tesh-Dar's swords sliced deep into the flesh of its inner thighs, cutting the muscles and tendons there. With a deafening howl, it stumbled and crashed to the ground.

One of the invisible creatures suddenly crashed straight into her, and she was knocked from her feet and sent flying, one of the swords torn from her grip. She landed heavily in the soft soil, but before she could roll to her feet to defend herself, one of the invisible creatures clamped its teeth onto her sword arm, making her drop the other sword. Grunting in agony as the powerful jaws ground together, tearing her flesh, she gouged the talons of her free hand into its head, hoping to find its eyes.

The creature hissed in pain and released her, its teeth disappearing into its invisible mouth. She sensed others closing in around her, and she was determined not to die on her knees. Regaining her feet, she drew her dagger and was about to stab at the air where she thought the nearest creature might be when she felt an ice-cold wind upon her back.

Turning around in surprise, she saw Sura-Ni'Khan standing behind her.

The great priestess, clad in shimmering black ceremonial armor, stood with her arms outstretched, but with no weapons other than the claws she had been born with. "Kneel, my child," she ordered, "and shield your eyes!"

Tesh-Dar, not understanding, nonetheless did as she was told. She knelt before the priestess and brought her good arm up to protect her eyes, even as she knew half a dozen animals must be rushing toward them for the kill.

Cyan lightning exploded from Sura-Ni'khan's outstretched hands. Tesh-Dar fell to the ground, her skin tingling as if tiny insects were crawling all over her body. Even with her eyes closed and shielded by her arm, she was nearly blinded by the sun-bright bursts of energy that lanced out across the clearing. Through the deafening thunder, she could hear the squeals of terror as the attacking beasts were vaporized, and her nose filled with the stench of burned flesh and hide. She suddenly realized that this was no weapon fashioned by the hands of the armorers, but was among those special gifts Sura-Ni'khan had received when she became the last high priestess of the Desh-Ka.

The lightning storm raged for several minutes, for there were far more of the creatures than Tesh-Dar had suspected: it was not merely a pack, but a herd of predators that had swept through the area like a plague, converging in pursuit of the mammoth beast that Tesh-Dar had brought down.

She dared to look up in the silence that had suddenly descended, just in time to see Sura-Ni'khan slowly fall to her knees.

"My priestess!" Tesh-Dar exclaimed as she moved to Sura-Ni'khan's side, holding her up with her good arm while ignoring the pain of her own injuries. The priestess's skin was burning hot, and the metal of her armor even hotter. Tesh-Dar lay Sura-Ni'khan on her side and slashed the bindings of her armor, pulling the burning hot metal away from her, cringing as wisps of smoke rose from the black cloth garments beneath.

"My priestess," Tesh-Dar repeated worriedly as she held one of Sura-Ni'khan's hands with her own, "answer me!" Tesh-Dar looked up at the sound of approaching footsteps, and was relieved to see Kuirin-Shuril and the two other uninjured warriors, armed now with heavy energy weapons, running toward her.

Sura-Ni'khan's eyes flickered open, and Tesh-Dar felt the priestess's hand squeeze her own. "My time draws near, child," Sura-Ni'khan whispered. "I had almost given up hope of finding a successor, for there could be no other but you. All this time I waited, and at last heard your blood sing with joy. The Empress sent me here to join you, to protect you, for you are my chosen one." She paused for a moment, looking deeply into Tesh-Dar's eyes. "It is time for you to choose, Tesh-Dar, while I yet have enough days to teach you before I join the Ancient Ones: would you accept the way of the Desh-Ka?"

Lowering her gaze, bowing her head, Tesh-Dar knew in her heart that she was ready. She had faced many challenges and stared Death in the face, yet this was the first time she had felt her soul finally break free of its bonds of guilt and shame. Her heart and spirit were whole again. "I accept, my priestess," she said quietly.

As the words escaped her lips, she and the others vanished from the planet, brought home by the will of the Empress.

THIRTY-SIX

Despite his best efforts, it had taken three precious days for Sikorsky to set up a meeting with his contact from the train dispatch center, Pyotr Medvedev. After a great deal of wrangling, Sikorsky and Valentina — Scarlet — had agreed to meet him at an underground dance bar in a run-down industrial district of Saint Petersburg City. Accessible through a battered metal door in an equally battered warehouse, it had no sign out front, no parking, no indication of what it was other than the people who trickled in and out. Even in a police state, there were places such as this that were officially outlawed, but unofficially sanctioned. Frequented by dissidents and Party members, men and women, young and old, it was a social relief valve that also served as a venue where needs of every description were satisfied and deals were made. The undergrounds offered a modest amount of protection from the secret police, for the children of senior Party officials were often to be found at such places late at night, and their arrest could prove awkward.

In a back corner booth, vibrating with the deafening beat of the music to which hundreds of young men and women gyrated on the dance floor, they sat with Medvedev. They had tried asking him questions, at first indirect, and then very direct, shouting to be heard above the roaring music.

He had simply waved aside their questions, shouting back that they had plenty of time for business. "Pleasure comes first," he yelled over the music, his eyes firmly fixed on Valentina. Taller than Sikorsky, Medvedev also boasted a lean, muscular body. With slicked-back black hair and deep blue eyes, he would have been considered handsome were it not for the constantly calculating expression he wore. While his official job was as a lowly train dispatcher, his true vocation was making deals in the underground. And dominating women. He considered himself a gift to the opposite sex, and it was clear from the look on his face that he believed that his next conquest was sitting before him: Valentina.

Sikorsky was across the table from Medvedev, knowing quite well what the man was thinking. While he was useful in his own business dealings, Sikorsky had always hated having to deal with him: he was scum. He would make a deal with anyone for anything if it served his purposes. He was also known to be more than a so-called lady's man: he was a beast with a reputation for violence. Sikorsky knew that he himself was no angel, but at heart he was an honest and scrupulous man, and those like Medvedev sickened him. He had told all of this to Valentina, and hoped that she really understood what she was getting herself into by using her body as the currency for this transaction.

Valentina, he thought, inwardly shaking his head, *you have no idea what this man is capable of.* Yet he knew that he was probably underestimating her. He had been shocked at the transformation she had undergone with the aid of some of the clothes and makeup she had brought in the traveling case with her, from wherever she had really come from. Gone was the inconspicuous mouse of a woman who could be mistaken for a thousand others and easily disappear into a crowd. Instead, when she reappeared from the rest room at the back of the restaurant where they had waited until meeting Medvedev, Sikorsky found himself looking at a gorgeous brunette wearing a black leather outfit that looked like it was painted on, hugging her generous curves, with the blouse exposing a generous amount of cleavage.

Clicking across the floor in stiletto heels, he didn't even recognize her until she came right up to him and asked with a wry smile, "What do you think?"

Red-faced with embarrassment, for he had been staring at her open-mouthed, he looked away and muttered, "I think that will work."

Now, sitting between them, he could feel an emotional current running between the two that made him increasingly uncomfortable. He watched as Medvedev stared at Valentina, and wondered who was truly baiting whom as she stared back, shifting in her seat to give him a slightly better look down her blouse. A clear and dangerous invitation.

Sikorsky was just about to get up and announce they were leaving when Valentina suddenly leaned over to Medvedev and shouted something in his ear. Then she got up and disappeared into the writhing mass of people on the dance floor, her hips swaying suggestively.

After a few seconds of staring after her, completely ignoring Sikorsky, Medvedev got up from the booth and followed in her wake.

* * *

The women's bathroom was about what Valentina had expected: large, ridiculously upscale, as if it were in a luxury hotel, loud — although not nearly as loud as the dance floor — and crowded. While most of the occupants were women, there were plenty of men, too, engaged in everything from polite discussion with their partners, wine glasses in hand, to unabashed sex.

Her most pressing concern was privacy: she could not do what she needed to do out in the open. Several people looked up as she walked in, with a few giving her more than a casual glance. She strutted over to the row of stalls, prepared to yank one of the other women out if she had to. Fortunately, a woman made her exit from the stall at the end, dragging another woman, only half-dressed, behind her, and Valentina moved quickly to take it. She waited, holding the door open until Medvedev walked into the bathroom. Seeing her instantly, he sauntered over, a broad smile on his face.

Without a word, he came into the oversize stall with her, and she closed the door behind him.

After that, things did not go quite as Medvedev probably had expected. When he reached for her, a leering grin on his face, she leaned forward as if she were going to kiss him before viciously slamming a knee into his bulging crotch. As he doubled over, gagging, she slapped a syrette against his neck, then slammed him against the back wall. He slumped down onto the toilet, still gasping for breath as the drugs rushed through his system, carried by his carotid artery. She held his head down between his knees, effectively immobilizing him until he stopped struggling. A moment more and his body clearly relaxed, fully under the influence of the drugs she had given him.

"Now, my friend," she said in a conversational voice that he would be able to hear, but that would not carry beyond the stall over the background of music and the other goings-on in the bathroom, "we're going to play a little game. I'm going to ask you questions, and you're going to give me answers."

"Sure," he said groggily as she lifted his head up and shoved his body against the wall again. The syrette she had injected him with contained a powerful cocktail of muscle relaxants and a psychological uninhibitor that would loosen his tongue about anything he knew.

"Pyotr," she asked him, "where do the special trains, the ones from the big coal-fired power plants, go? What are they carrying?"

"Why do you want to talk about that when you could be—" He tried to clumsily grab for her again.

"Where do the special trains go?" she hissed, grabbing one of his hands and twisting it back in an extremely painful grip.

Medvedev opened his mouth to shriek, but she silenced him with a blow from her free arm, hitting him in the jaw with her elbow. One of the side effects of the drugs she had given him was that they amplified the sensation of pain, and between the wrist lock and the blow to his jaw, he was shivering in agony.

"Tell me what I want to know, and quietly," she said in his ear, "and I'll make the pain stop."

He nodded quickly, desperate for her to make the pain go away. "They just carry waste from the plants, that's all I know," he rasped. "There is a place, a disposal facility, thirty kilometers due north of here. All the special trains go there."

"There's nothing north of the city but forest, Pyotr," she told him, twisting his wrist a bit more. The ship that had dropped her off had also carried a full reconnaissance package. The makeup compact in her tiny purse was in actuality a microcomputer that contained, among other things, a complete download of all the information the ship had recorded, and she had studied it intently before she had landed, and studied it more in the two evenings she had stayed with Sikorsky and his wife. There was nothing north of Saint Petersburg but an endless stretch of forest. Yet it was possible she missed something.

"No, wait!" he said, panting. "The facility is not easy to find. There is no need for people to go there. But it is there. There is a track that leads north from the main ring around the city, near the Chornaya Rechka station. Dmitri will know where it is; he helped to build the station. There is a track from the north that isn't marked, that goes to the main space port. The special trains from the coal plants all take that northern spur. It will take you to the facility."

As Medvedev talked, she took out her makeup case with her free hand and activated the computer it contained. It projected a ghostly overhead image of Saint Petersburg City on the wall, and with a few whispered words the tiny but intelligent computer displayed what she wanted.

"There!" Medvedev panted, pointing at a rail line that went north from the main ring, just as he had said. "That is the one!"

"It only goes a few kilometers north and then ends, Pyotr," she said, her voice holding an edge that made him cringe. The image on the wall showed a rail line that could easily hold a large mag-lev train, but after a short run northward it simply ended in the trees.

"It must be camouflaged," he pleaded. "I *know* it goes north to the facility. It is a priority line, and we control the switches at the facility. It is *there*, I tell you!"

Quickly zooming out to show a larger view of the area, the computer projected where the facility might be and then began a rapid search to find it. In under a minute she found what she was looking for.

"*Chyort voz'mi*," she cursed quietly. "Damn it." Deep in the forest was a set of drab buildings behind a tall concrete wall topped by several guard towers. There were military vehicles, including heavy tanks, inside the compound, with a large landing area for vertical take-off aircraft. And at the base of the mountain against which the compound was sited, a massive concrete apron, carefully painted to make it look like a large forest meadow, lined with cargo vehicles led into a cavernous tunnel that disappeared into the mountain. She had recognized it during her earlier studying of the area as a military facility, of course, but had never suspected that this would be what she was looking for.

The facility was indeed there, and it was underground.

"How do I get in, Pyotr?" she asked him, twisting his wrist again as she slipped the makeup compact back into her purse with her other hand.

"I don't know, I swear!" he whimpered. "It doesn't matter, anyway."

The way he said the last words sent a chill through her. "What do you mean?"

"The secret police are coming for you." He looked up at her, tears in his eyes, "I just wanted to fuck you before they took you away. Such a waste," he sobbed, shaking his head. The drugs were running their full course in his system now. "I tell them things I hear, things they want to know, and they leave me alone. Dmitri told me that he was very interested in the train schedules from the big coal power plants. Not *to* the plants, but *from* the plants. I thought that was interesting, and so did the secret police."

"Is that why you took so long setting up this meeting?" she asked him quickly. "You were waiting for the secret police?"

"Yes," he nodded. "They said they needed some time to arrange things, and that I was to meet you here tonight and have a good time with you. Past that, they did not tell me, and I didn't care. Oh, come here, *dorogaya*, while we still have time!" He suddenly reached for her with his free hand, groping at her breasts.

She was out of time, and so was Medvedev. Letting go of his hand, she put one of her hands on the back of his head and locked the other around his jaw, then gave his head a sharp, vicious twist. His neck broke with a wet *snap* and his body went limp. She carefully propped him up against the wall to make it appear as if he had passed out from too much of a good time. As crowded as this place was, he wouldn't go undiscovered for long, but comatose bodies were commonplace here, and few who weren't comatose were in full control of their faculties. No one would realize that he was dead before she and Dmitri got away.

Her only worry now was how to escape this place without being taken by the secret police.

* * *

Dmitri was growing increasingly worried. Valentina and Medvedev had been gone what seemed like hours, but he knew from the frequent glances at his watch had only been minutes. He hated this place, and couldn't understand how anyone could find enjoyment here: music so loud that he couldn't hear himself scream, women and men propositioning each other shamelessly. He had gotten half a dozen invitations from both men and women in the few minutes that Valentina had been gone, and he had done his best to not act offended: he already felt completely out of place here, and didn't want to call any more attention to himself than was absolutely necessary. He nursed his drink, trying to give the impression of drinking a lot more than he actually was. And most of all, he forced himself to ignore the overpowering urge to follow after Valentina and find out what was happening. On that, however, she had given him very explicit instructions when they took this booth.

"No matter what happens, Dmitri," she had told him earlier, "do not follow me if I get up to leave and Medvedev follows after me."

"Why not?" he had asked.

She had given him a searching look. "You don't want to know," she had finally said.

He was holding his hands under the table to keep everyone from seeing how he was clenching and unclenching them, a nervous habit since childhood. *If she is not back in another two minutes*, he told himself, *I am going after her.*

A moment later, he saw her emerge from the solid wall of gyrating bodies on the dance floor, heading toward him. Medvedev was nowhere to be seen. She nodded her head in the general direction of the door. It was time to go.

Sikorsky breathed a sigh of relief and tossed back the rest of his vodka. As he stood up, the music suddenly stopped. The crowd instantly howled and jeered, but their voices went silent as the dance lighting, lasers and holographic displays, mostly of nude men and women engaged in lewd acts, disappeared. The entire club was cast into pitch darkness for a moment, which was replaced by the harsh glare of white lights that went on all around the perimeter of the ceiling. If anything, the stark illumination of the club's interior was even more surreal than the light show, exposing the details of the sound and lighting systems, not to mention the deteriorating concrete walls and corroded sheet metal ceiling high above the hushed crowd.

He felt Valentina's hand clamp on his arm.

"This way," she whispered urgently. "Now."

"*Secret police!*" someone suddenly yelled. The effect would have been exactly the same if there had been a fire. The crowd instantly panicked, with nearly five hundred people surging for the single entrance. While there were other doors in the warehouse, most of those now trapped inside didn't know about them, nor did they have the keys to the locks.

Sikorsky fought to follow Valentina through the tide of people stampeding to get out. "We are going the wrong way!" he shouted over the din of screaming voices around them. "The door is back there!"

"Just stay close to me!" she yelled back as she viciously slammed her elbow into the jaw of a wild-eyed man who otherwise would have run right over her, knocking him to the floor. She jumped over him without pausing, dragging Sikorsky behind her.

Finally, they reached the back edge of the crowd. Sikorsky cringed at the screams: they were no longer just of people who were frightened and panicking, they were screams of pain. He knew that dozens were probably being trampled on the floor and crushed to death against the wall near the door.

Valentina ignored the chaos around them. Sikorsky watched as she drew a small case from her tiny purse.

"Makeup?" he asked incredulously. "What..."

His voice died as he saw her flip it open to reveal a miniature computer display.

"Current location," she said into the device. "Emergency exit routes." In a fraction of a second, details of the building they were in and what lay beyond it appeared. She turned the device upside-down, projecting the image on the floor so both of them could see it. Sections of the wall and floor were highlighted in yellow, with dotted paths marked in red from each yellow section into the warehouse district beyond. "This way," she told him after she scanned the map for a few seconds. Then she snapped the device shut and slipped it back into her purse. "Quickly!"

She broke into a run, with Dmitri struggling to keep up with her. She led him to the women's restroom, which was in the right rear corner of the building. Just as they dashed through the door, he heard the doors to the loading docks along the rear wall start to open. As the door to the bathroom swung shut, he looked back just long enough to see men in dark uniforms come pouring through the loading dock doors. They carried clear body shields and wielded electrified truncheons.

"What are we going to do?" he whispered, looking around the room where they were now trapped. "There is no way out of here!"

"Have faith, Dmitri," she said. She stripped off the thin leather jacket, then took out her microcomputer and connected it to a metal tag on the inside of it. With a slight popping sound, the seams of the jacket disintegrated. After quickly pulling the leather apart along the front edges, waist, and the seams of the arms, she was rewarded with several thin ropes of gray material.

"Is that explosive putty?" Dmitri asked, shocked. It looked much like the plastic explosive compound his teams used for blasting out sections of rock or concrete at building sites. It could not be detonated easily, which made it comparatively safe. But he could not imagine wandering around in clothing loaded with it.

"Yes," she said as she pressed the material against the floor, making a dotted circle of small blobs of putty. "Stand back."

There were suddenly shouts outside, very close and clearly audible against the continued screams from the crush of people trying to get away.

"They are coming!" Dmitri warned, pressing his ear against the door to better hear what was going on outside. A simple wooden wedge lay near the corner of the door, a prop to keep the door open when the bathroom was cleaned. He jammed it under the door with his foot, hoping to give them a few extra moments when the men on the other side tried to get in.

Valentina peeled off the small metal plate from her jacket, the one she had temporarily connected the microcomputer to, and put it in the center of the circle of explosives. She ran over to Dmitri, and they both put their faces toward the wall to protect their eyes.

"What are you waiting for?" he hissed as Valentina stood next to him, still holding the microcomputer, which now acted as a detonator.

A shot echoed from outside, then more. The screaming rose even higher, and more shots followed. The voices of the men who had been heading toward them turned to frantic shouts that retreated into the general bedlam beyond the door.

"They're murdering those people!" Dmitri cried.

Valentina said nothing as she pushed him against the wall, then activated the detonator. Behind them, sounding much like the gunshots booming beyond the door, the explosives went off, blowing a ragged hole through the floor into a dark, cramped corridor filled with pipes dripping condensation.

Without another word, she grabbed Dmitri and, now using the tiny microcomputer as a glorified flashlight to illuminate their way, jumped into the darkness below.

THIRTY-SEVEN

"I know I don't have to say this, but I'm going to say it, anyway," Commodore Hanson said grimly to the ship captains gathered around the conference table in her flagship, the heavy cruiser *CNS Constellation*. "Make sure you review all the nuclear combat protocols with your crews. We've never fought a war in space with nuclear weapons, so the procedures are all theoretical, but they're all we've got."

"Most of the protocols cover weapon handling, launch procedures, and targeting, commodore," Sato said quietly. "They don't have much on what to do if someone is shooting nukes at you, other than to keep the ships spread wide apart and to destroy the incoming weapons before detonation. If possible," he added, with an ironic grin.

His comment drew a few muttered comments from around the table.

"I know, Sato," Hanson said, nodding, "but review the damn things again. All of you. The flag operations officer is working up formation options for us that will be downloaded to your ships, then we'll work on those in simulation exercises before we have to jump in. By then the rest of the task force will be here. I hope."

Needless to say, the orders to prepare for an assault on Saint Petersburg had come as a complete surprise to everyone. Naval couriers had managed to catch up with all the ships of the squadron, directing them to this isolated volume of space that was a day's jump from the target system. Hanson had been gratified and relieved to see that all six ships of her squadron had made the rendezvous, all within twenty-four hours of one another. A flotilla of ten destroyers and a pair of Marine troop carriers were already there when *Constellation*, which was the first of Hanson's ships to arrive, jumped in. The fleet orders said that another heavy cruiser squadron and destroyer flotilla were assigned to the task force, but they hadn't arrived yet. They were to have sailed from Earth with a single patrol stop at Edinburgh, but according to the schedule in the operations orders transmitted by the couriers, they were a full day late. Based on what Sato had reported from Kronstadt about his encounter with the Kreelans there, Hanson suspected that the other ships may have run into trouble at Edinburgh.

"We're also going to set up contingency orders and simulations for an assault with the forces we have on hand," she said. "You've all read the orders we received: I have absolutely no discretion in terms of action. If we receive the go order, we *must* deploy. That one comes straight from the commander-in-chief."

While she didn't show it to her subordinates, Hanson was deeply worried. Not because she was the ranking officer of the naval forces here and would be leading the mission, rather than the two-star admiral who was with the missing cruiser squadron, but because their intelligence information on Saint Petersburg military forces was so sketchy. And that was never a good thing when nuclear weapons were potentially involved. "Intel," she said, turning to a lieutenant commander sitting on her left, "what have you got for us?"

The man grimaced. "Not a hell of a lot, ma'am," he said as he stood up, taking a position next to the briefing room's main screen. Information suddenly flashed into existence, bright text and diagrams showing various types of military vessels and their vital statistics. What few were known. "This is what we have on the Saint Petersburg Navy," he said. "As you can see, a lot of the information is either unavailable, very dated or considered unreliable. I guess after the war, nobody thought we'd have to worry about this particular problem again." That elicited a few grumbles from around the room. Two of the captains at the table had been junior officers during the Saint Petersburg war, and they had been among the few who were not surprised by what was happening. The focus of intelligence gathering after the war was on political and economic concerns; there had been little interest in or resources assigned to monitoring Saint Petersburg's military capabilities. "The main problem is that Saint Petersburg built new naval facilities on their moon after the main demilitarization provisions of the armistice expired. No inspection teams could be sent there, and according to what little I've got, foreigners aren't exactly welcome, anyway. We know that they have shipbuilding facilities there, but have almost no information on what those facilities have been doing. And since they don't conduct any joint exercises with any other navies or invite naval visits, there's been virtually no direct observation of Saint Pete naval units. Just their coast guard vessels, which are about the size you'd expect, but are armed to the teeth." The main screen changed to show an ugly, bulbous vessel that was a quarter the size of the *Constellation*, but that packed a punch roughly equivalent to one of the new Confederation destroyers. "So I think it's highly likely that they have more and better ships than what this," he gestured disgustedly to the sketchy information on ship types and numbers that had replaced the image of the ugly coast guard ship, "is showing."

"That would be a safe assumption," the task force Marine commander said with a slight Russian accent. Colonel Lev Stepanovich Grishin, formerly of the *Légion étrangère* and a veteran of Keran, was in command of the Marine expeditionary force that was made up of four battalions from the new 12th Marine Regiment, and that was deployed aboard the two assault carriers. Grishin was a native of Saint Petersburg, and had fought in the war twenty years before: on the wrong side. He had escaped the final destruction of the Red Army by Coalition forces and the ensuing witch hunt by the winning side, the White Army, to root out any remaining neo-communists. He had eventually found himself in the Legion, where he had risen from a lowly recruit to become the commander of an armored regiment that had been wiped out at Keran.

The irony of the current situation had not escaped him: in the intervening twenty years since the war, the Whites had lost the battle to rebuild the economy. In the resulting social chaos they had been replaced in a quiet and outwardly bloodless revolution by "rehabilitated" communists. Grishin even knew many of the ruling senior Party members, including Chairman Korolev, under whom Grishin had served when Korolev had been a junior political commissar. Over the years since then, Grishin had received subtle entreaties from several of his one-time comrades to return to his former motherland. These, he had studiously ignored, never returning their messages. He had given up his nationality and his past for the Legion, and had willingly given his loyalty to the newly formed Confederation Marine Corps, which now incorporated what little was left of the Legion after the debacle on Keran. The Legion was redesignated as the 12th Marine Regiment, and six battalions had already been formed and trained. While it did not apply to new recruits, one important caveat that had applied to all former legionnaires who transitioned to the new Marine Corps was that they would not be required to take the Confederation service oath. Like most of his surviving comrades, Grishin would never again give his allegiance to any nation or government. His true loyalty was now to the Corps, as it had been to the Legion, and to the men and women who served with him. He knew that many of the officers around the table did not trust him, both because of the side on which he had fought during the war, and because he was from the Legion: the legionnaires, while respected for their sacrifices and combat prowess, were nonetheless the black sheep of the new Confederation military.

"Would you care to elaborate, colonel?" Commodore Hanson asked coolly.

Grishin knew that she had her doubts about his loyalty: she had flat out told him her misgivings when he had first come aboard *Constellation*, but she had no grounds to take any action against him. *Piss on her*, Grishin thought, making sure his face did not betray the inward smile he felt. Her feelings did not anger him. He had endured far worse. "I have no specifics, commodore," he said. "As you well know, I have not been to the planet of my birth since the end of the war. Yet I know some of the men in power there: they are heartless, ruthless bastards. Just like me." He offered up a humorless smile. "Behind their propaganda of equality and brotherhood, they are unapologetic imperialists. They hold Riga under their thumb, and they aspire to claim more worlds as their own. They wish to become a great star nation, superior to the Alliance, and no doubt superior to the Confederation, as well." He glanced around the room, his gaze settling on Sato, whose expression was not clouded or veiled by suspicion: Sato had helped save Grishin's life and those of his legionnaires at Keran, and he owed the young commander a great debt of honor. And Sato was probably one of the few people in this room who did not doubt Grishin's loyalty or question his motivations. "As you all know, the key to becoming a star nation is to have a superior navy. Korolev has been in power now for a number of years, and I am sure has not wasted his time in this arena. While he served as a political commissar during the war and has no naval experience, he well understands what is necessary to build an empire." He turned his gaze back to Hanson. "You have not seen the true face of their navy because they do not wish you to see it. If we have to jump in, however, you will. Even if we bypass Saint Petersburg and sail directly to Riga, they will fight, for they consider Riga their territory; I believe that an image of Korolev's expression when he found out that Riga had applied for Confederation membership would have been priceless." No one smiled at the joke. With a sigh, he went on, "I fear that our naval encounter will not be pleasant, commodore, even under the best of circumstances."

"Don't they realize that the Kreelans are out there?" one of the ship captains asked quietly. "They should be joining forces with us, not fighting us!"

Grishin shook his head sadly. "I am sure that Korolev and his minions believe that the Kreelan threat is merely Confederation propaganda, designed to draw in gullible worlds like Riga," he replied. "The men in power on Saint Petersburg live in fear and suspicion of all that is beyond their control, my friends. They do not see the same reality that we do."

"So what can we do about their navy, *colonel?*" one of the other captains asked hotly.

"Not a damn thing," Hanson interjected before Grishin could say anything more. The last thing she needed was an open conflict among her commanding officers. "Remember, ladies and gentlemen, we have zero leeway in this one. When the mission clock counts down to zero, if we haven't received the order to abort, we jump in, weapons hot. It doesn't matter if they have a hundred heavy cruisers waiting for us: we still go." Turning back to Grishin, she said, "So, colonel, now that we have such a reassuring understanding of their viewpoint, perhaps you'd care to outline the operations plan for the Marine contingent?"

Grishin realized that Hanson probably hadn't intended to come across as being sarcastic, but she certainly sounded that way. He shrugged inwardly. If she wanted to become an expert at sarcasm, she should take lessons from the French officers he had once served under in the Legion. "Certainly, commodore," he said easily as he stood and replaced the intelligence officer at the front of the room. "As you know, our primary mission is to capture or destroy any nuclear weapons Saint Petersburg may possess," he began. "In the task force, we have an entire brigade of Marines, in addition to the shipboard contingents, which we can call upon to form an additional ad-hoc battalion, if necessary. The basic plan is to conduct a rapid exo-atmospheric assault on their storage site or sites, employing enough Marines and shipboard fire support to achieve overwhelming local superiority. Each Marine assault group will have a technical team whose responsibility will be to assess whether the weapons can be rendered safe and extracted, or whether they need to be destroyed *in situ*. If the latter, the teams have a wealth of demolitions available, and we are also authorized to employ orbital bombardment, if necessary."

"Once the weapons are secured or destroyed," Hanson interjected, facing her ship captains, "we are to take up defensive positions around Riga. We are *not* to engage in battle with Saint Petersburg naval forces unless we have no other choice. I want to make this very clear: we are not here to make war on Saint Petersburg. We are here to take care of the nukes and then defend Riga from any potential punitive action. That's it. Even if the Saint Petes have nothing more serious than a dozen coast guard cutters to throw against us, I don't want a major naval battle. Stick to the job at hand." Turning to Grishin, she said, "Thank you, colonel."

"The real problem," the intel officer said as Grishin took his seat, "is that the entire operation for going after the nukes is based on intelligence information that we're supposed to receive shortly *after* we jump into the system." He rolled his eyes, showing what he thought of that part of the plan, eliciting a few snickers from the others.

"If we don't receive that information," Hanson added, shooting the intel officer a mild glare, "the nuke part of the mission is scrubbed. We can't search the entire system, and we're not going to provoke Korolev by taking up orbit around Saint Petersburg if we don't have anything firm to go on. So, if we don't get the intel we've been promised, our mission is to sail straight to Riga and take up a defensive posture. Any questions?"

Around the table, heads shook to a chorus of "No, ma'am." There would be questions in the next hours before the task force jumped, but right now everyone wanted to get back to their ships.

"That's it, then," Hanson said. The other officers stood to attention as she got up from her chair. "We've got less than twenty-four hours, people. Let's make the most of it."

* * *

"It's good to see you again, sir," Sato said as he walked beside Grishin on the way to the boat bay to return to their respective ships. The last time Sato had seen Grishin was when he was taken off the *Ticonderoga* after the Battle of Keran: Grishin had been on a gurney headed for the sickbay on Africa Station for the severe injuries he had received.

"It is good to see you, too, Sato," Grishin said warmly. "I also appreciate your...quiet support in there," he nodded back toward the briefing room, "for lack of a better term. It seems that former residents of Saint Petersburg are not in the running to win today's popularity contest."

"I know, sir, and I apologize for that," Sato replied, rather embarrassed. He had felt extremely uncomfortable at the way Grishin had been treated. Sato could sympathize: most of the other ship captains did not want to have anything to do with him, either, "ship thief" that he was in the eyes of some. "Sir," he went on tentatively, "may I ask you something?"

"Of course, Ichiro," Grishin said, smiling. "Asking is always free, but I may not give you an answer."

Sato grinned, but it quickly faded from his face. "Sir, how well do you know First Sergeant Mills?"

"Roland Mills?" Grishin asked. Sato nodded. "I knew of him when we served in the Legion, but he never served under me, and you know of our time on Keran. But I got to know him quite well when the Legion was being merged into the Marine Corps: he was one of the senior transition NCOs and worked for me until you stole him away." He nudged Sato good-naturedly. "He is a good man, and an outstanding legionnaire...and Marine. Why do you ask?"

"Well, sir..." Sato began, then hesitated. He did not want to inadvertently put Mills in a bad light with a senior Marine officer, but he had to ask. "Sir, do you know if Mills ever suffered from chronic nightmares after Keran?"

"We all suffered nightmares after Keran, Ichiro," Grishin said quietly as he came to a stop, turning to face Sato. "I would be concerned about anyone who did not."

"Yes, sir, I agree," Sato told him. "But his nightmares, I believe, are different. They are not just of what happened on Keran, but dreams of him being killed by the big warrior who let us go, of something that did *not* happen. And with a more...spiritual meaning: in the dream she is taking his soul, and it has deeply disturbed him. He was having them with increasing frequency until he finally saw the ship's surgeon because he was on the verge of stim addiction. She prescribed a series of sedatives that initially knocked him out and allowed him to sleep and get some rest." He frowned. "But in the last two days, the nightmares have returned, even through the sedatives, and appear to be even more intense. He woke up screaming before the morning watch. He woke up half the Marine company, sleeping in their bunks. I'm very worried about him." *And I can't have a senior NCO who doesn't have all his wits about him taking men and women into combat,* he didn't add.

Grishin thought a moment. "I cannot recall that he had dreams, exactly, Ichiro," he said slowly. "I know there were times when he clearly had not slept well, but that is not necessarily unusual for soldiers, especially veterans, and I thought nothing of it."

"Do you dream, sir, of her? The big warrior? Or any of the other Kreelans?"

Shaking his head, Grishin answered darkly, "I dream of electric fire, Ichiro, and the smell of burning flesh." He shivered inwardly, remembering how one of the Kreelan warriors had flung a grenade at his command vehicle. The alien grenades did not explode, exactly: they seemed to spawn a confined electric storm that could destroy a heavily armored battle tank, lacing it with electric bolts that were like lightning, and that could burn right through armor plate. His command vehicle was hit by one, and he could clearly recall the screaming of his crew as they were simultaneously burned and electrocuted to death. Grishin only survived because the vehicle hit the edge of a weapon emplacement and flipped over after the driver lost control, sending Grishin flying from his hatch in the top of the vehicle. He had survived, but had been grievously injured. "I do not remember much after that until Africa Station. Why, do you think his dreams are significant, something more than a stress disorder?"

Sato shrugged in frustration. "I don't know, sir. I don't want to make it sound mystical, but...there is just something strange about it, and I wish I understood what it was, what it means."

Grishin snorted, then put a hand on Sato's shoulder. "It means nothing, Ichiro," he told him. "The human mind is a complex thing that often plays tricks on itself. We are victims of our own cruel nature and God's poor sense of humor. And this is made worse by our desire to understand everything, even though some things were made to never be understood. Do not worry yourself about Mills, my friend. He is a tough bastard, as tough as they come. He will be all right, and will do whatever needs to be done."

* * *

At that moment First Sergeant Roland Mills was inspecting every one of his company's Marines to make sure they were ready for combat, before the detachment commander's formal inspection. He hoped they would be called upon to help the battalions that would be deploying to the surface, because he didn't want to sit out a battle up here in a ship the Saint Petes would want to use for target practice when he could be getting his hands dirty planetside.

He was doubly glad they were so busy now, because the dreams had come back. Even through the knockout drugs the surgeon had given him, the huge warrior had reached through his subconscious to tear out his heart and reach for his soul. Now the dreams were even more real, if that was possible, as if they were a mental signal whose strength was rapidly increasing. He didn't need the stims yet, but had asked the ship's surgeon for some extras, anyway. With her usual warnings of gloom and doom about the risks of addiction, she gave them to him. He was far more terrified of what lay waiting for him when he slept than becoming addicted to stims.

As he expected, there were only a few minor things amiss as he went from Marine to Marine with their respective platoon sergeants and squad leaders. The most important things — weapons, ammunition, armor, and communications — were perfect. Those few things that weren't in order were quickly straightened out. The company had five platoons: four regular platoons and a heavy weapons platoon. Their commander had ordered that they would make ready to support the ground campaign with the four line platoons, while the heavy weapons platoon would remain aboard for ship defense. That had made for some major disappointment among the heavy weapons troops, Mills knew, because everyone doubted that the Saint Petersburg Navy would try any boarding stunts like the Kreelans had. They would likely be stuck in their vacuum combat armor in a battle — if there was one — that would be decided by the guns of heavy cruisers, while their fellow Marines would be down on the surface raising hell. They all hoped.

He grinned inwardly, trying to set aside the dread that had settled over him like a chill mist. *Poor left-behind buggers*, he thought.

* * *

Sato watched the mission clock steadily wind down toward zero. "Stand by to jump," he ordered. In a task force jump, it was technically unnecessary for a ship's captain to give the jump order, for the sequence of events had already been programmed in to the ship's systems, slaved to the navigation computers aboard the flagship *Constellation*. But tradition demanded it, and Bogdanova had her hand on the manual override controls just in case.

Sato frowned as he thought of the task force's composition. The other cruisers and destroyers that were supposed to join them had never arrived, and the mission orders left no discretion as to the mission profile: they had to jump on time, no matter what. He was distinctly uncomfortable about the lack of intelligence information they had on the Saint Petersburg Navy, particularly in light of what Grishin had said, but there was nothing they could do about it, other than to hope for the best.

"Autolock sequence engaged," the navigation computer announced. "Transpace sequence in five...four...three...two...one...jump initiated."

In the blink of an eye, the ships of Commodore Hanson's task force vanished.

THIRTY-EIGHT

The fleet was coming. That was the only thing that Valentina could think about. She didn't know the details of how many ships would be coming, but she knew when they would jump in-system, and she had to be ready for them: not just for her own retrieval, but to get them the information she had been sent here for in the first place. She knew that she didn't have all the information she would have liked, but she had found out the main things the Confederation needed to know. Now she just had to get them the data, and hopefully survive.

That was going to be a bit difficult from where she had been imprisoned in the secret police headquarters.

She and Sikorsky had escaped from the underground club, but it had been a near thing. A *very* near thing. They had run for their lives through the filthy sewer and utility service tunnels that snaked under the industrial district, finally emerging through a sewer manhole cover behind a grim, gray apartment complex that was at the edge of the adjacent residential district. They had been able to hear people in the tunnels pursuing them, but none of the tracking devices their pursuers had could function through the stench, moisture, and flowing muck in the tunnels and sewers. The secret police had fired random shots and even thrown a few grenades to try and frighten them and draw them out, but after nearly an hour of running through the tunnels, the sounds of pursuit began to fade: the secret police did not have enough men to sweep the entire tunnel network at once, and fortuitously they headed off in the wrong direction.

While Sikorsky was a strong man, he was not used to such running. Nearing exhaustion by the time they exited the sewer tunnel, she had to help him up the ladder to ground level. Once there, they used water from one of the outdoor faucets protruding from a nearby work shed to rinse the muck from their shoes and the cuffs of Sikorsky's pants.

Then there was the question of what to do next.

"I must return to my wife," Sikorsky argued quietly but forcefully. "She will be worried, and if what you say is true, I need to get her to safety."

Valentina shook her head. "They'll be waiting for you, Dmitri," she explained. "You'll be walking right into their arms."

"Perhaps not," he said. "If Medvedev did not tell them—"

"Dmitri," she hissed, "he told them everything! They know it was you who was asking about the trains. That's why they raided the club: to catch us. It wasn't just a random act. The entire thing was Medvedev's doing." Her voice softened slightly.

"The best thing you can do for your wife now is to try and distance yourself from her. Perhaps the secret police will believe she had nothing to do with all this." She couldn't see his expression in the darkness, but she could tell that he was brooding. "Listen, we only have to stay hidden for another eight hours," she told him, revealing more operational information in that one brief sentence than she would have liked. "After that...if you want, I'll try to get you and your wife out."

"What do you mean, *out?*" he asked, curious.

"The Confederation will be willing to grant you asylum for what you've done here," she explained. "You can get a new identity, a new life on a different world. Even Earth, if you want."

"I am a patriot," he said quietly, "not a traitor. I did what I did to bring about changes here, to my homeland. Why would I want to leave? I—"

"Shh," Valentina whispered. She had heard something outside. She had already prepared an act in case they were discovered: she was a prostitute with a client, and the work shed had been a convenient spot for their business transaction.

Such was her surprise, then, when the door flew open and half a dozen men holding automatic weapons burst in, shouting, "*On the ground, now!*"

She had a fraction of a second to decide to fight or surrender. She was confident that she could win a close-in fight with the men who had come into the shed. It was the additional dozen outside that gave her pause.

No way out, she thought. Her first objective had just become survival. Without a word, she got down on the ground, face-down, next to Dmitri. His face was turned to hers as the secret police cuffed their hands and shackled their feet before roughly hauling them out of the shed.

From his expression, he was not at all surprised.

* * *

"The Confederation spy and her accomplice have been captured," Vasili Morozov, head of the secret police, announced as he put away his secure vidphone. The call had come at a most opportune time: just when the chairman himself was calling into question Morozov's competence in dealing with the situation that had first been brought to light a few days before by the now-dead informant, Medvedev.

"At last," Chairman Iosef Korolev said with just a hint of sarcasm as he leaned back in his plush leather chair, glowering at Morozov. Around the polished antique wooden table that was worth more than ten thousand times the average annual income on Saint Petersburg sat the planet's ruling body, the Supreme Council. It was a loose coalition of vicious predators who ruled a world, and who dreamed of ruling much more. As its leader, and the most powerful man on the planet, Korolev was the most dangerous predator of them all. Yet he only retained his superior position by playing his colleagues and subordinates against one another. It was this skill, more than any other, that had seen him rise from the disgrace of being a "rehabilitated communist" to the position he now held.

Morozov had always been a threat to Korolev, but he was also a key to Korolev's own power: Morozov and the secret police held the military in check and cowed the populace. In turn, Korolev made sure there was constant friction between the military and the secret police to counter Morozov, using the other ministers as necessary to add the perfect amount of weight to each side of the political equation. It was a balancing act in which only true masters of the art could participate. While Korolev periodically derided Morozov in council, he was acutely aware of the man's intelligence and political cunning. Were he not so effective at his job, he would have been "retired" some time ago.

"I would have thought that between the information from your informant and that provided by Sikorsky's wife you would have been able to bring them in far earlier," Korolev said in a voice that was quiet but far from pleasant. "And without the needless deaths of dozens of citizens. That was sloppy, Vasili. Very sloppy."

The others around the room fixed their eyes on Morozov. All of them knew that Korolev cared as little about those who had died in the raid as they themselves did. That is to say, not at all. It was merely an easy and effective way to embarrass Morozov before the council. It was a game, albeit with the highest possible stakes.

The chief of the secret police, however, was unfazed. "Regrettable, but let us be honest, comrades," he said, looking around the table. "Those who died and those who were arrested were clearly engaged in illegal acts. And the shooting only started after a gunman in the crowd opened fire, killing one of my men." He did not add that the gunman had actually been a secret police operative whose specific job was to provoke violence during the raid. He had succeeded quite well, and his reward had been a bullet to the head once the raid was over. Morozov lived, and others died, by the motto that dead men told no tales. "You will also notice that there were no...potentially embarrassing deaths or arrests."

Korolev's expression did not change, but he could feel a rush of heat to his face. His grandson, the only one he had and a young and impudent fool, had been at that underground club. So had the sons and daughters of a number of other powerful Party members. But Korolev was the only member of the council with a family member involved. It was an inexcusable embarrassment, but its resolution would have to wait until later.

Shying away from the bait, he merely grunted. Turning to the defense minister, he said, "And how, comrade, does your expensive space navy fare? Is it ready to protect our world from this so-called *Confederation?*" He said the word as if it were a particularly vicious expletive.

Marshal Issa Antonov nodded. "Yes, comrade chairman," he said in a deep baritone voice. "Our navy is not yet ready to meet their entire fleet head-to-head—" Korolev shot him a frigid glare "—but unless they send the majority of their fleet, we will enjoy a significant advantage. Their newest ships are better in some respects than our own, particularly in targeting and navigation systems, but ours are far more heavily armed." He paused significantly, glancing around the table, making eye contact with everyone except Morozov, before saying, "And all of our heavy cruisers are armed with torpedoes tipped with special weapons."

"Do not be ridiculous," Morozov chided. "Call them what they are: *nuclear* weapons. Everyone in this room knows about them. Everyone in this room gave up resources to fund the program. Stop playing silly word games."

Antonov only glared at him, clenching his fists. "*You—*"

"Enough," Korolev interjected. "We must assume that there are Confederation forces on the way," he went on, "coming to protect those spineless traitors on Riga."

"But when?" Antonov asked. "I do not doubt that we can defeat them, but I cannot keep the fleet at peak readiness indefinitely."

"It must be soon," Morozov said quietly as he studiously examined his fingernails. "We know from Sikorsky's wife that he was very adamant that they should take a holiday by a particular date, something that was very out of character for him. I suspect that may be a clue."

"And when is that supposed to be?" Antonov asked, his hands clenched into fists on the table.

Morozov looked up and smiled. "Why, today, of course," he said pleasantly.

Antonov looked about to explode.

"Vasili," Korolev said carefully, leaning forward, his gaze locked with Morozov's, "when, exactly, did you discover this insignificant bit of information?"

With a shark's smile, Morozov told him, "Only this morning before this meeting, comrade. When we brought in the two fugitives, I thought it prudent to bring in Sikorsky's wife, as well."

"You interrogated her?" Korolev asked, surprised. While Sikorsky's wife, Ludmilla, was not a high-ranking member, she had gained a wide circle of supporters. Her rise to a modest level in the Party had been a marvel of social engineering in the wake of her daughter's arrest and subsequent execution.

"Of course," Morozov said, shrugging. "She is married to a spy. He has not yet divulged anything of interest. She, however, told us what little useful information she knew immediately. The only thing that required any time was...verification."

Torturing her to make sure she was telling the truth, you mean, Korolev thought. *And this is the man who tells us to not play games with words?* "And what of the Confederation spy?"

Morozov frowned. "She has been difficult, I must admit," he said grudgingly. "She *will* break, comrade. I assure you of that. We will know what she knows. She was obviously interested in the nuclear weapons program, and no doubt learned of its location from our now-deceased informant. But it will take time to learn what we wish to know."

"Perhaps that is not the best use of her," Antonov mused.

"You have a momentous thought for us, marshal?" Morozov said with a bored sigh.

Ignoring him, Antonov turned to the chairman. "I suggest we use her as bait," he said. "She clearly came here to learn of our *nuclear*," he glanced sourly in Morozov's direction, "weapons. Perhaps the Confederation fools hope to find them still in their storage bunkers at the Central Facility." *The place where the weapons were built and* stored, a massive underground labyrinth of nuclear labs and storage bunkers deep in the mountains to the north, had never been given a name, only a bland project number. Yet everyone who knew about its true function simply called it the Central Facility. It was an underground fortress, protected by a full division, over fifteen thousand men, who were stationed inside the facility and in several well-concealed garrisons nearby. If there was an impregnable location on the entire planet, that was it. "I say, let them find the Central Facility. Let them come for the weapons. Let them *try*."

* * *

Valentina lay naked on the frigid bare concrete of the cell, eyes closed, feigning unconsciousness. She was handcuffed, with the cuffs chained to a ring bolt set in the floor. Her face and body were badly bruised and bloodied from the beatings she had received. Her interrogators had been quite professional about it, and no doubt would have been disappointed had they gotten any information out of her so soon. They had not raped her yet, but she knew that would not be far off. The pain she had endured thus far was hardly trivial, but it was something she had been conditioned to in her training: they would not break her through mere physical torture.

She was surprised that they had not already tried to use drugs on her, although that would also do them little good: she had chemical implants that had been inserted into her body at several key locations, deep in the muscle tissue. Transparent to modern medical imaging technology, they would react to a variety of drugs that were typically used for interrogation purposes, counteracting their effects. It would be up to her acting skills to convince her tormentors that she was under the influence of whatever drugs they chose to use, while keeping her wits about her, prepared to take advantage of any opportunity to escape. If that moment never came, one of the implants was a failsafe device: once the level of certain chemicals in her bloodstream reached a critical threshold, the implant would automatically release a poison that would kill her almost instantly. She would tell her captors nothing other than what she might choose to say to further her own goals.

She assumed they were at the headquarters of the secret police in Saint Petersburg City, but could not be sure, as they had been transported in a box-bodied vehicle that had no windows. Sikorsky had initially been terrified, his eyes bulging with fear as they shoved the two of them into the van. By the time they arrived at their destination, however, his expression reflected only grim resignation. The two of them had been separated after that, although they had probably received their introductory interrogations — and beatings — at the same time: she could hear a man that sounded like Sikorsky screaming somewhere down the dim corridor from where she was being beaten in her own cell by a pair of burly guards and an interrogator.

Sikorsky. For a brief moment, she allowed herself to feel guilty about him. He obviously had his own reasons for being involved, but having to face what would most likely be death by torture was more than most people would be able to deal with. She had the benefit of her training and experience, and being tortured and killed was also an accepted, if not particularly pleasant, risk of her job. *I'll get him out*, she vowed to herself. *I'm not through yet. Not by a long shot.*

Her opportunity arrived only a few minutes later. The same pair of guards, minus the interrogator this time, came into the cell, slamming the door shut behind them. She could sense the change in their breathing, heavy with expectation, rather than exertion, and their pause before they acted tipped her off to their intentions. This would be the rape, she knew. Or might have been, had they brought at least two more men.

One of them stepped forward and delivered a vicious kick to her stomach that sent her limp body sprawling across the floor. His only reward was a grunt from the air expelled from her lungs. For all he could tell, she was completely unconscious. Of course, she knew that they would be much happier with her conscious so that she would understand what was happening to her. These were not the sort of men who would be finicky about such things: raping an unconscious woman was perfectly acceptable, especially since they knew they would be doing it quite a few more times when she was conscious before her suffering — and their entertainment — was ended with a bullet to her brain.

Valentina expected them to take her while she was still handcuffed and chained to the floor, and she stifled an exclamation of amazement when one of them undid the chain to the eye bolt in the floor. Apparently they wanted a bit more freedom to position her the way they pleased than the short chain allowed. After rolling her over on her back, they undid their pants and knelt down on the floor, almost panting now. One took up position between her legs, while the other knelt to one side near her head, clearly intending to gain some oral satisfaction from his unconscious victim.

Sorry, boys, she thought acidly, *not today*. As the guard between her legs was propped up on one arm, using his other hand to guide his manhood to its intended destination, she twisted her body and brought her knee on that side up in a lightning swift strike to his head, shattering his skull and knocking him off of her. She used her momentum to continue rolling in the same direction, which happened to be the same side that her other would-be tormentor was on. Before he could manage a shout of surprise, let alone anything more threatening, she rose to one knee, balancing herself with one hand, and landed a kick to his throat. He fell forward on his face, clutching his smashed larynx and gagging for breath. She pulled the small chain of her handcuffs around his neck and strangled him, finishing the job.

Quickly searching the bodies, she found what the electronic keys to her cuffs and the guards' badges. Unfortunately, she needed one more thing, which forced her to resort to a grisly expedient. The cells used biometric sensors that scanned the guards' thumbprints. Since neither guard had a knife, she had to use her hands and teeth to liberate the guards' thumbs.

Her next problem was clothing. One of the guards was a fairly small man, not much larger than she was. Quickly stripping him, she donned his uniform and boots, doing her best to tuck in the extra material in such a way as to minimize its obviously poor fit. Fortunately, he had small feet for a man, only a size or two larger than her own. She couldn't do anything about the bruises on her face, but she cleaned off the blood with a combination of spit and the tail of her "new" shirt.

Hoping against hope that she could quickly find Sikorsky, and that he was in sufficient shape to mount an escape attempt, she stripped the other guard of his clothes, believing that his uniform might be a close-enough fit for Sikorsky.

Ready now, she placed the thumb of one of the guards — Petrovsky, his name had been — against the biometric scanner and swiped his badge over the magnetic reader. The door instantly opened.

Peering carefully outside, she could see no one else in the dimly lit hallway. The cell block seemed to be a single corridor with cells on both sides and a monitoring station and a personnel elevator at one end, and a large freight elevator at the other. The monitoring station was presently unattended. Presumably the guards she had just sent on their way to Hell had been manning it before they had taken a few minutes off for a casual bout of rape. Since only the guards had come to her cell, she assumed that their visit hadn't been authorized; otherwise, they would certainly have called for more guards to man the monitoring station. That left her wondering how much time she had before their superiors became alarmed by the guards' absence: certainly more than just a few minutes, but probably not more than half an hour. She would have to move quickly.

Each cell had a small one-way window of armorglass set in the door, and she peered quickly into each one as she went, looking for Dmitri. She saw that all of them held one to three prisoners, most of whom lay in fetal positions in a corner of the cell. Some of the prisoners were sitting dejectedly against a wall, and a few were on their feet, pacing the small perimeter of their cell.

She finally found Dmitri in the second to last cell on the right. Again using the bloody thumb and electronic ID card, she opened the door.

"Dmitri," she said quietly to the bloodied mass of flesh sprawled on the floor. If they had beaten her badly, they had beaten him far worse. For a moment, she thought he was dead. She knew that would have made her mission that much easier, but it was a death that would never have rested easily on her conscience.

"Valentina?" he whispered hoarsely, turning his head to look at her with the eye that wasn't swollen shut. "How...?"

Closing, but not latching, the door behind her, she quickly knelt beside him. "Don't worry about that now, my friend," she said. "We need to get out of here. Can you walk?"

"Help me up," he grunted.

Working together, she got him to his feet. His face was a wreck of cuts and contusions, and he was extremely unsteady on his feet. Just getting the uniform on him would be a struggle, and he would never be able to pose as a guard. Her original plan had been to try and escape by masquerading as a pair of guards and simply walking out of the building, hoping that no one would notice their ill-fitting uniforms. But Dmitri's injuries would call immediate attention from anyone they passed, so she had to come up with something else. After a moment of feverish consideration, she had an idea. She hated herself for it, but there was no time for anything else.

She managed to get the other uniform on Dmitri, who had drawn strength from her presence, and had recovered somewhat by the time he was dressed. She handed him one of the two submachine pistols she had taken from the guards.

"Now what?" he asked.

"Here," she said, handing him the other thumb and ID badge. The thumb he took with undisguised revulsion, but took it nonetheless.

She went to the adjacent cell and showed him how to use the thumb and badge to open the door. "Open all of the cells," she told him. "We're going to stage a breakout."

Dmitri grinned at her, and it was hard for her not to wince at the four bloody stumps where some of his front teeth had been knocked out.

* * *

"Not bad," said the secret police colonel who, along with several others, had watched the Confederation spy kill the two guards and "rescue" her compatriot from the miniature video sensors in their cells. He regretted somewhat that the guards had not made any progress in their amorous pursuits with her, for she was extremely attractive and it would have made for some enjoyable viewing. But he had to admit to himself that her martial arts performance, though extremely brief, had also been quite exciting in its own way.

"Should we not sound the alarm, comrade colonel?" one of the junior officers asked, his hand hovering above the alarm button.

The colonel said, "No. We are to allow them to escape, then follow them. Those two," he nodded at the naked bodies of the dead guards, "were a necessary sacrifice. We did not want this to appear too easy." He shrugged. "She and her friend will no doubt try to impersonate guards and leave the complex. Our job is to make sure this happens, then follow them."

Nodding dutifully, although with an expression on his face that was clearly intended to conceal his doubts, the junior officer returned his attention to the displays. "Now what is she doing?" he asked quietly.

The colonel leaned closer, a slight chill creeping up his spine. "I am not sure..."

* * *

Valentina and Dmitri quickly opened all twenty cells in the block and uncuffed the prisoners. Those who weren't catatonic, she herded out into the corridor and toward the freight elevator. She had not bothered trying to tell them that she was trying to save them, because she wasn't: while in her heart she hoped that some might escape, or at least survive, the cold-hearted truth was that they were nothing more than a tool she was using to help her — and Dmitri — escape. For all they knew, she and Dmitri were taking them out to be shot. Which was probably exactly what was going to happen to most of them in the course of the next few minutes. Thousands of lives, perhaps millions, hung in the balance if she failed.

She used her stolen thumb and badge to open the freight elevator, and forced in the nearly thirty terrified inmates at gunpoint. Then she and Dmitri squeezed themselves in. Pushing the button for what she hoped was the ground level, she noticed that there was a second door to the elevator, in the back, that the indicators showed would be opening at the floor she had chosen.

"Get out when the door opens!" she bellowed menacingly. As the elevator slowly ascended, she tightened her grip on the submachine pistol and worked her way to the new "front" of the elevator.

* * *

"Dammit!" the colonel hissed as the doors closed on the freight elevator, shutting the escapees away from their view; there was no monitor in the elevator, although the "escapees" would be under the eyes of more monitors when they emerged from the elevator, regardless of which floor they chose. The two spies simply marching out of secret police headquarters was one thing. Staging a major breakout — or using it to mask their own escape — was something else entirely. "That *suka* is going to make this complicated," he muttered.

Unfortunately, he had little discretion in the matter. None, in fact. The chairman himself had sanctioned this operation, which the colonel had thought outrageously risky, although he would never admit it. On top of that, he had received the orders directly from Morozov. In the secret police, such rare face to face orders either meant an opportunity for a major promotion, in the case of a successful operation, or a bullet to the brain for failure. There was no in-between, and no excuses.

"Colonel?" the young officer asked. "What should we do?"

After an agonizing moment, the colonel said, "Nothing, for now. Let us see how this plays out..."

* * *

When the door of the freight elevator rattled open, retracting upward, Valentina shouted, "*Prisoner escape!*" She had no idea if there was a way to escape on this floor, but they only had one chance at this. She just prayed that there would be a way out.

For a moment, the prisoners just stood there, blinking at each other. They were so terrified, drugged, or simply so far gone mentally that they didn't move.

Then Dmitri loosed a deafening volley from the submachine pistol, blasting holes in the ceiling of the elevator. "*Get the fuckers!*" he bellowed.

That got the message across. With shrieks and screams, the thirty-odd prisoners burst from the elevator and swarmed into what Valentina saw must be the headquarters morgue. Not surprisingly, it was quite large, with at least fifty refrigeration bays for bodies, and a dozen gurneys lined up with their grisly cargo in various stages of post-mortem examination.

There were half a dozen men and women in medical gowns around the bodies, along with two guards. The shocked expressions on their faces would have been priceless had Valentina had the time to appreciate them.

"Watch out!" Valentina shouted to the two stunned guards, "they have weapons!"

She knew that the room was almost certainly monitored, and the words were only for the benefit of anyone who might be listening. She fired her submachine pistol, making it look like she was shooting into the mass of prisoners, with the first two bursts taking the guards in the chest. Then she slaughtered the medical examiners with tightly spaced shots, careful to avoid shooting the panicked prisoners.

One of the examiners managed to reach a double door at the rear of the morgue. The woman was able to scan her thumbprint and swipe her badge in time to avoid being crushed by the prisoners fleeing toward her, but she couldn't avoid the bullets from Sikorsky's weapon. She fell in a bloody heap, the prisoners trampling her lifeless body as they fled outside, Valentina and Sikorsky close behind.

* * *

"*Chyort voz'mi*," the colonel choked as he saw the catastrophe unfold in the headquarters morgue. The situation became even worse when he saw one of the examiners open the door *to the outside*. The prisoners would still be contained inside the compound, but there was only a single checkpoint at the rear of the facility and four guards. The two spies were supposed to escape, yes, but having the entire staff of medical examiners wiped out had not been part of the plan.

"Colonel," the young officer asked him again, quite urgently, "should we not sound the alarm?"

"No," the colonel said grimly. "Come with me. All of you." Drawing his sidearm, he led the young officer and three guards at a run to the other side of the complex. He doubted he would be able to reach the morgue in time to salvage this disaster.

* * *

Valentina and Sikorsky herded the prisoners like cattle toward the only visible guard post that sat astride the gate through the wall surrounding the headquarters complex. She could see that Sikorsky was having a difficult time keeping up, and moved over to help him, but he waved her away impatiently. "I am fine," he rasped. "Let us finish this."

Nodding, she moved back over to the side of the screaming mob in time to see the guards at the checkpoint, four of them, raising their weapons. Valentina waved, drawing their attention. "Be careful!" she yelled. "They're armed!"

A rifle barked and one of the prisoners dropped, then the other guards began firing. Every shot tore through Valentina's heart, but she had to get close enough to make sure she could kill all four guards. Sikorsky was falling behind, clutching his ribs, and would be no use in this battle.

Half a dozen of the prisoners had been cut down when she finally judged she was close enough. Pulling far out to one side, she leveled her submachine pistol and held down the trigger, fanning the bullets across the four guards. Two were hit in the head, the others took rounds to the chest. They were wearing body armor, so she put an extra bullet into their heads.

Dead men tell no tales, she thought savagely. Then she fired her weapon into the air, getting the prisoners to flee back the way they had come, away from the check point and past their fallen comrades. Then she went to Sikorsky, wrapping one of his arms around her shoulders and helping him to the small military utility vehicle parked next to the gate. After putting him in the passenger seat, she used her stolen thumb and ID badge one more time to open the gate. Then she hopped in the driver's seat and headed out of the facility, just as the alarm siren went off.

As she was driving out, a platoon of secret police troops ran toward her from their barracks outside the compound walls. She brought her vehicle to a stop and waved their commander, a very young lieutenant, over.

"The prisoners have escaped, and they have weapons!" she said, panicked, as she grabbed him by the lapel of his uniform. "My comrade has been shot," she went on, jerking her head toward Dmitri, who sat beside her, moaning. "Do you have a medical kit in your barracks?"

"Of course," the lieutenant said, as if she were a simpleton. "Get him there and take care of him. We will take care of those scum." He glared in the direction of the gate and the confused screaming beyond it.

"Thank you, comrade lieutenant," she said gratefully.

He nodded once before taking off at a run with his men, weapons at the ready.

Watching them in the rear-view mirror as she turned onto the road that led toward town, ignoring the nearby barracks, Valentina held back her tears as she waited for the massacre to begin.

* * *

The colonel and his men burst into the courtyard just as the first volley of gunfire *cracked* through the air and bullets whizzed by their heads.

"*Govno!*" one of the men cried as he took a round in the leg. "Shit!"

"Cease fire!" the colonel screamed at the secret police troops he glimpsed beyond the mass of prisoners who were running directly toward him and his men, only a few meters away now, screening them from the view of the other troops. "*Cease—*"

Thirty-four weapons, firing on full automatic, cut down the rest of the prisoners. It was only afterward, as the men of the quick reaction platoon sorted through the bodies, that the colonel and his troops were discovered.

They were the only ones other than Morozov himself who knew of the secret orders regarding the Confederation spies, and the secret died with them. By the time anyone in authority realized the two high-value prisoners were missing and had not been followed, it would be far too late.

* * *

Valentina drove through the city, using the intrinsic authority of a secret police vehicle to bypass the normal traffic stops and other encumbrances Saint Petersburg drivers normally had to contend with. She was headed toward where she had originally landed a week, a lifetime, ago. Having lost her microcomputer when they were captured, she had to reach the cache of equipment she had left behind: it contained a backup secure transmitter with which she could communicate with the fleet.

"How do you do it?" Sikorsky said. He had been quiet for a long time after their escape. She had thought it was simply from the injuries he had suffered which, while certainly serious, did not appear to be life-threatening. From the tone of his voice, however, it was clear that he had also been doing a great deal of thinking.

"How do I do what, Dmitri?"

He turned his face, now covered with bandages she had applied from the vehicle's medical kit, and gave her a cold, appraising look. "How do you live with yourself, after doing such a thing?" He looked away. "You knew those poor fools would be slaughtered," he went on quietly. "They never stood a chance. You used them. Even Medvedev, pig that he was, was nothing more than a tool to you. And that is all I am, as well."

She bit back her emotions. *Focus on the mission,* she told herself, knowing that there was almost certainly a special spot in Hell waiting for her for all the things she had done. Medvedev certainly did not bother her conscience. And sending those prisoners to be used as cannon fodder was not the worst of her misdeeds, nor — if she survived — would it be the last. What Sikorsky had said about himself, if anything, hurt far worse. Not because it wasn't true, but because it was.

"We had no choice, Dmitri," she told him bluntly. "And what did you think was going to happen to those people, anyway? That the secret police were going to suddenly forgive them and let them go? They were all dead men and women who happened to be still breathing. Every one of them was bound for the grave." She paused a moment, trying to convince herself that it was all true. Even if it was, it would still be a huge burden on her soul. "If there had been any way for me to save them without endangering my mission, Dmitri," she finally said, "I would have. If we had been given more time, and I had more information to make a better plan, things might have been different. But..." She shook her head helplessly.

Sikorsky said nothing, but simply stared out the passenger side window.

Sighing, Valentina glanced up to the clear blue sky. "I only hope we're not too late," she whispered to herself.

THIRTY-NINE

Li'ara-Zhurah stood beside Tesh-Dar, who sat in the command chair of the assault fleet's flagship. Their force, fifty-seven ships headed toward the human planet of Saint Petersburg, was not nearly as large as the one used against Keran, where the Empire's warriors first engaged in battle with the humans. Unlike the attack on Keran, which was intended to frighten the humans, to shock them into action that would make them a more potent and effective enemy, the attacks here and against several other human systems were to be long-term battles of attrition. The Empire would allow the bloodletting here to go on for cycles before the humans were finally extinguished from this world. In this way a great many warriors could be blooded to bring honor to the Empress.

And in that time, or the cycles that would come after, when the Empire attacked yet more human worlds, perhaps Her Children would find the One whose blood could sing, the One who could save them all from extinction.

Throughout the assault fleet, now was a time for contemplation. All the preparations for combat had been made, and the warriors and shipmistresses were ready to open the great battle that lay ahead. Anticipation swirled in their blood like a hungry predator in a deep ocean, but it was yet far from the surface, barely registering on their consciousness. Instead, they turned inward, reflecting on their lives, their sisters, and their bond to the Empress.

Li'ara-Zhurah closed her eyes, seeking to shed the last remains of the melancholy that had plagued her since Keran. It no longer held sway over her heart, but she was determined to expunge it from her soul: she refused to shame Tesh-Dar's legacy by being anything less than completely worthy of the honor that the elder priestess sought to bestow upon her. Relaxing her mind and body, she gave herself up completely to the power of the Bloodsong. She lost her sense of self in the ethereal chorus from the trillions of her sisters. It was a timeless, infinite melody containing every emotion her race could express, and running through it all was the immortal love of the Empress.

As she felt the great river gently wash away the last of the pain and uncertainty from her soul, she suddenly sensed something that had not been there before, a new voice in the chorus of souls. She gasped at the power of this new voice, at the purity of its song as it joined with the many others of its kind. Opening her eyes wide with wonder, she looked down at her body, gently placing a hand over the armor protecting her abdomen.

There, in her womb, her child's spirit had awakened.

She felt someone touch her arm, and looked up to see Tesh-Dar, smiling at her.

"Her Bloodsong is powerful, child," Tesh-Dar said proudly, "much like her mother's."

Li'ara-Zhurah could only nod her head, still overwhelmed by the sensation of a second spirit singing together with, yet unique from, her own. *A girl child*, she told herself. *Thank you, my Empress.* She knew now that she would bear any male children that might result from future matings, that her earlier misgivings could not deter her honor and duty. Yet she was thankful that this, her first, was a female child. A part of her yet hoped that this child would be sterile, that she would not have to endure the agony of mating. Regardless, Li'ara-Zhurah realized that she would cherish her daughters, of black talons or silver, fertile or sterile. She would bear any male children that fate demanded of her, but in her heart of hearts she would never consider them sons. They were tools necessary to preserve the Empire, but no more. It was part of the heart-rending tragedy that was the Curse, the final act of a heartbroken First Empress.

Beside her, Tesh-Dar's heart swelled with love and pride: Li'ara-Zhurah's Bloodsong was strong and pure, just as that of her newly awoken daughter. Soon, once Li'ara-Zhurah's role in opening the battle at Saint Petersburg had played out, Tesh-Dar would take her to her appointed nursery world to give birth. From there, she would lead Li'ara-Zhurah to the temple of the Desh-Ka, just as Sura-Ni'khan had taken Tesh-Dar many cycles ago. Once she had bequeathed her powers to her young acolyte, Tesh-Dar would spend her remaining days helping Li'ara-Zhurah learn the full extent of her powers.

In one sense, Tesh-Dar was saddened that she would be diminished once she and Li'ara-Zhurah performed the ritual that would make the young warrior high priestess of the Desh-Ka. No longer would Tesh-Dar be able to call upon the powers she had inherited from Sura-Ni'khan; she would still be a force to contend with in the arena and in battle with the humans, but only because of her great strength and skill with weapons. No longer would she be able to walk through walls, or cast herself into the air and float along as she willed, or see far beyond the senses of her body with her second sight. All these things that she had come to treasure, would she lose.

Yet part of her also yearned for release from the crushing sense of responsibility she bore upon her shoulders. For nearly a hundred cycles now had she worn the rune of the Desh-Ka upon her collar as high priestess, and her soul was weary. To spend the remainder of her days teaching Li'ara-Zhurah in the ways of the Desh-Ka and helping the *tresh* at her *kazha* — including, she hoped, Li'ara-Zhurah's daughter, should the Empress bless it — to become warriors were her only ambitions. She had always thought she would die in battle (*And that may yet come to pass*, she thought), but she would welcome a quiet death in a warm bed of animal hides just as well. She was the supreme warrior of a race that lived for battle, but she would not be disappointed if, like Pan'ne-Sharakh, she could live out her remaining days among the arenas of the *kazha*.

Sighing in contentment, her hand on Li'ara-Zhurah's, she watched the ship's displays as her fleet moved inexorably closer to its objective.

* * *

Sato sat rigidly, strapped in his combat chair on *Yura's* bridge. Beside him, in a special sheath the ship's engineers had fixed to his chair, was his *katana*. Left to him by his grandfather, the weapon had been with him during the most traumatic moments of his life. He knew in his heart that he would die with it in his hands, fighting the Kreelans. *For a warrior*, he thought, *was there any other way to die?*

"Transpace sequence initiated," the navigation computer announced. "Normal space in ten seconds...five...four...three...two...one...now." The main bridge display suddenly resolved into a panorama of stars, with Saint Petersburg's sun a blazing white disk off the port side. "Transpace sequence complete."

They had jumped into the system very close to the planet of Saint Petersburg, barely outside the orbit of its moon. If the task force received the intelligence information they were expecting about the nuclear weapons, they would deploy the Marines or conduct an orbital bombardment. Or both. If they didn't get the information, they would sail directly to Riga, which lay further in-system.

It was just a question of waiting.

"Jump engines off-line and respooling for contingency jump," the bridge engineering officer called out. In case the task force got into too much trouble, the ship would be ready to jump out on thirty seconds notice. "Engineering is ready to answer all bells, captain."

"All ahead, one quarter," Sato ordered. "Keep us in tight formation, helm."

"Inter-ship datalink acquired, captain," the young tactical officer announced, and information on the nearby planets and ships suddenly blossomed into life on the display. The sensors of all the ships in the task force were linked together, with each ship sending what it "saw" to the other ships. The datalink would do the same for targeting information, allowing the task force to fight as a tightly integrated weapons complex, rather than individual ships. It was a wonderful system, but the Kreelans had proven at Keran that it could be disrupted, with devastating effect. Since then, while it was still used on a regular basis, every crew and squadron trained to function effectively without it.

"Any hostiles?" Sato asked, carefully filtering the tension from his voice.

"Negative, sir," the tactical officer reported. Unlike Sato, his voice wavered slightly, betraying how tense he was. Like most of the crewmen aboard *Yura* and the other ships of the task force, this was his first combat patrol. "I see three Saint Petersburg coast guard cutters in low orbit, but that's it for ships in the order of battle database. Everything else is either a freighter or an unknown. None of the vessels has changed course or activated additional sensors. No new emanations from the planet or the moon. There's no reaction at all that we can see."

Sato frowned. Something was wrong. Any planet, particularly now that humanity was at war with the Empire, would react to a fleet of warships appearing in their system. They would be insane not to.

He stared at the display, searching for clues. The ships of the task force appeared as blue icons, while every other ship in the system was painted in yellow: not hostile, but not confirmed as friendly, either. If a ship was later confirmed to be a friendly vessel, it would change to green on the display.

And that's not bloody likely, Sato thought grimly as the Confederation task force moved in closer to the planet.

* * *

Valentina sped through the forest as fast as she dared. If the fleet had stayed on schedule, they were already in-system, waiting for her signal. She was late.

"Damn it," she muttered venomously as she gunned the vehicle across a small creek, the oversized drive wheels clawing for purchase in the soft soil of the opposite bank. The distance from the road to where she had buried her cache of equipment had seemed much shorter when she had walked into the train station after she arrived. They had made good time getting here, thanks to everyone's fear of anything having to do with the secret police, but these last few kilometers had been nerve-wracking.

Then she saw it. She had buried her equipment container near a dead tree that had been split by a lightning strike. "*Slava Bogu*," she said. "Thank God."

"God has nothing to do with this," Sikorsky said as she pulled the vehicle to a stop.

Ignoring him, she jumped out and ran to the spot, seven paces due south from the trunk of the tree, where she had buried her gear. The vehicle they'd stolen had no utility tools like a shovel, so she simply dropped to her knees and began to claw at the ground. "Help me," she pleaded. "We've got to hurry."

Sikorsky simply stared at her for a moment. Then, with a sigh of resignation, he got down on his knees and began to dig.

In five minutes they pulled a cylindrical container about as long as Valentina's arm and as big around as her leg from the ground. Sikorsky put his hand on the small control panel that was inset into the casing.

"No!" she cried, batting his hand away.

"What?" he asked angrily. "I help you, and this is—"

"It's booby-trapped, Dmitri," she explained quickly as she moved her hands in a peculiar way over the casing, pressing gently at several points. "The access panel you see here is a fake. If you'd tried to open it that way, it would have exploded and killed you. And me."

With a faint popping sound, the cylinder opened. She reached in and extracted a black device that was as thick as her little finger and fit neatly in her palm. Swiping a finger across one edge, the face lit up in a small display.

Sikorsky noticed that the finger she had used to touch the device had come away bloody.

"It's validating that it's my DNA," she breathed as the face of the device suddenly glowed amber. Then she said in English, "The standard four square is hex.

Copernicus. Execute." Glancing up at Sikorsky, she explained, "It's a randomly generated code phrase. That, plus my voice print and DNA will enable it."

The face of the device suddenly glowed green. There were no numbers or other data displayed, just a monochrome green.

Closing her eyes in concentration, Valentina began dictating a stream of numbers that would tell the fleet about the hidden nuclear weapons facility and where to find it.

* * *

"We are taking a tremendous risk, comrade." Korolev's voice was soft, but the threat was clear.

Marshal Antonov nodded. Despite Korolev's implicit threat, he was not nervous. It was not that he doubted what would happen to him if his plan failed, it was simply that he knew his plan could *not* fail. "It will work, comrade chairman," he said confidently. "As long as our friends in the secret police managed to do their job." He shot a sideways glance at Morozov, who sat quietly at his place at the table. "The Confederation ships that just arrived will either surrender or be destroyed."

"What if they try to jump out when your trap is sprung?" one of the other ministers asked.

Antonov shook his head. "If what we know about their naval procedures is true, they will not have time. I believe they will try to engage the force of warships we will soon send to greet them. When they do, they will be within range of the *special*," he glanced sourly at Morozov, "torpedoes. These weapons are very fast, far faster than the Confederation designs: their ships will not have time to cycle their jump engines before they are destroyed."

Korolev nodded, satisfied. Then he turned to Morozov. "And were you, comrade, successful in your part of this grand scheme?"

"Quite, comrade chairman," he said with a carefully controlled expression. He had no doubts that Antonov already knew of the disaster at Morozov's own headquarters, but the defense minister apparently was holding back that bit of news from the chairman to use at a future time when it would prove particularly detrimental. In the end, however, it would do Antonov little good: the goal had been for the two Confederation spies to escape and not be suspicious that their getaway had, in fact, been planned. Morozov had intended for them to be followed so they could be quickly rounded up after they had done whatever they needed to do to contact the Confederation, but that part had not come to fruition. *Obviously*, he thought, cursing the dead colonel who had let things get so out of hand. The fool's family was already on their way to a labor camp in the far south, where they would spend the rest of their miserable lives. "The spies are away, just as we planned," he said in a half-truth. "If what we suspect is true, you should see the result soon enough from the actions of the Confederation ships."

They did not have long to wait.

* * *

When she had finished dictating the stream of numbers, Valentina quickly set the device down on the ground and grabbed Sikorsky with one hand, holding the cylinder in the other. "Come with me," she said as she quickly walked away. "You don't want to be near it when it transmits."

"Why?" Sikorsky asked, stumbling after her as she quickly pulled him along. He kept glancing over his shoulder at the small device, wondering what could be so—

The forest behind him where she had placed the device suddenly lit up, blindingly bright. He shut his eyes and turned away, only to be knocked to his knees by a powerful blast.

"Does *everything* you brought with you explode?" he demanded as she pulled him back to his feet.

"The ship that dropped me off left some microsats in high orbit to relay any messages to the fleet," she said as she led him back to their stolen vehicle. "With a device as small as that transmitter, the only way to generate the power for a strong enough signal is to create a small explosion and a pulse wave." She looked at him. "Does that make sense?"

"I understand the concept," he grumbled, "but what if you have to tell them something else? You no longer have a way to communicate."

"I have a shorter-range transmitter," she said, showing him the watch she had taken from the cylinder and strapped to her wrist. "It won't reach the fleet, but when my extraction team comes..."

She stopped as they reached the vehicle, and she turned to Sikorsky. "Dmitri," she told him, "you can come back with me. The Confederation will grant you asylum, give you a new life."

He said nothing for a long moment as he stared out at the forest around them. "I cannot leave, Valentina," he said quietly. They had gone over this earlier, but it would have been a lie to say that he had not been thinking about it. The final answer, however, had not changed. "I am disgusted by what our leaders have done to our people, to my family. I helped you in hopes that, in some small way, it might change things for us, make things better, even if not for me." He turned to look at her. "I could not live with myself if I simply walked away. That would make me feel like a traitor, and that is something I am not. And what sort of life would I have somewhere else? I know our world is not listed in many tourist guides of the human sphere, Valentina, but this is where I was born and where I have lived my life. It is my home."

"They'll kill you, Dmitri," she said quietly. "And what about your wife? I doubt she's going to be happy about all this."

"What about her, indeed," he sighed.

* * *

Commodore Hanson was in her command chair on the *Constellation's* flag bridge, which was a special compartment adjoining the ship's bridge from where her staff could control the actions of the task force.

The door behind her suddenly swished open, and a tall, well-muscled man in civilian clothes stepped quickly to her side. She knew little about him other than his name, Robert Torvald (which she suspected was a pseudonym), and that he was the controller for the Confederation agent whose mission was to get Hanson the information she needed to snatch Saint Petersburg's nuclear weapons. He had arrived in a special courier at the task force's rendezvous point, coming aboard *Constellation* at the last minute, when it had become clear that the rest of the task force and the designated mission commander, a two-star admiral, would not be making the party. Hanson had initially been irked at the man's presence, for he was the only one authorized to make contact with the source, the Navy apparently not being sufficiently trustworthy. He had brought along special communications gear that had been locked away in a small arms locker under the control of two Marine guards. That's where he had been since two hours before the task force's emergence here, crammed into the tiny room with his mysterious equipment.

"Here it is," he told her quietly, handing her a data chip. "I've sanitized the information to a classification level that will allow you to use it in any of the ship's systems."

"And what did you leave out?" she asked sharply.

"Nothing that will affect your mission, commodore," he answered softly, returning her gaze levelly.

She held the tiny chip in her hand, looking at it for just a moment, wondering at the guts of whomever had obtained the data. And how accurate the information was. The lives of her crewmen and the Marines now depended on it. With a scowl, she called over her flag operations officer. "Here," she said, handing him the chip. "This is the data on the nuclear weapons. Get this analyzed and update our operations plans, pronto."

"Aye, aye, ma'am," he said, taking the chip and hurrying back to his station.

"Commodore," the flag communications officer said, "we've got an incoming message from planetside."

Hanson frowned. She had wanted to take the initiative in making contact with the Saint Petersburg government or military, but she had been forced to wait until she had the information on the nuclear weapons. "Put it on the main screen," she ordered tersely, wondering who she would be dealing with.

* * *

"This is Commodore Margaret Hanson of the Confederation Navy," the woman on the screen said formally. "To whom am I speaking?"

"Commodore, this is Iosef Korolev, Chairman of the Ruling Party Council of Saint Petersburg," he said amicably. "May I ask why the newly formed Confederation has sent a fleet of warships to our peaceful system?"

"Mr. Chairman," the woman said evenly, "I was sent here on the orders of the President of the Confederation to carry out an inspection of several facilities on Saint Petersburg. This inspection is in accordance with article fourteen of the long-term armistice provisions, citing that Saint Petersburg may not develop, construct, or possess weapons of mass destruction. My secondary orders," she went on, "are to conduct a training exercise with the Rigan coast guard and provide supplies and personnel to assist them in forming Territorial Army detachments for common defense. This is required and was agreed to, as stated in the Confederation Constitution, when Riga became a member."

Korolev relaxed back into his chair. "Well, commodore," he said, his Russian accent barely evident in his New Oxford-educated English, "welcome to Saint Petersburg. If you would please have your staff coordinate with our naval personnel, we will be happy to arrange for your inspection parties to land.

"As for your proposed exercise with the Rigan coast guard, however," he went on, wincing slightly, as if the idea gave him indigestion, "I believe your government misunderstands the situation. Riga is a *semi*-autonomous world under our governance. Any claim they may have made to independent status or membership in your interplanetary government is neither legitimate, nor legal. Their defense is well in hand, I assure you, without any involvement by Confederation forces. Please, commodore, I strongly urge you to seek further counsel from your government — preferably with clarification from an envoy I would be happy to send with you — before carrying out those orders. Your ships are welcome in orbit around Saint Petersburg, but we will consider any deployment of your vessels further in-system toward Riga to be an...unfriendly provocation." He smiled, conveying just the right mixture of warmth and menace.

Hanson paused a moment. "Mr. Chairman, I suggest we consider the two issues separately for now," she finally said. "I'll maintain my task force in orbit around Saint Petersburg while we conduct our inspections. Once that is taken care of, we can further discuss the situation with Riga."

"There is not really any more to discuss on that point," Korolev told her, "but for as long as your ships stay in orbit here, we have no quarrel. If there is nothing else, commodore, my naval personnel will contact you with the necessary information to coordinate your inspections."

"Thank you, Mr. Chairman," Hanson said. "You're most gracious."

Korolev nodded, then killed the connection.

"Fools," Marshal Antonov said, aghast. "They cannot believe that we would just let them walk into our facilities. The armistice conditions expired years ago!"

"Not entirely true, marshal," Morozov said. "Technically, the provisions of article fourteen, and article fourteen alone, were to remain in effect in perpetuity: the good commodore does indeed have legal right to inspect our facilities if they have reasonable suspicion that weapons of mass destruction are present or being produced. No doubt she will land her troops and then stay in close orbit to protect them. Of course, this is exactly what we wanted." He smiled. "So, you see, even though it caused us much pain at the end of the war, today the armistice will serve our purposes nicely, and will allow us to firmly put the Confederation in its place."

Almost grudgingly, Antonov returned Morozov's smile.

* * *

"Do not be deceived, commodore," Grishin said with uncharacteristic vehemence, "This is a trap."

Commodore Hanson had called a final commander's meeting over the inter-ship vidcom immediately after she got off the link with Korolev. All of the ship captains were virtually present, their images displayed on the main viewscreen in her ready room. Around the table with her sat her flag staff and the *Constellation's* captain. As the senior Marine commander, Grishin also participated, the vidcom projecting his image from the cramped cockpit of his assault boat. It was ready to be launched with the rest of the boats carrying the Marines from the two assault carriers, as soon as the commodore gave the word.

"Colonel," Hanson's intelligence officer said in a neutral voice, "we're not seeing any indications of a hostile reaction. We've identified every ship in the system as either some sort of transport or a coast guard vessel. There's not a single sign of any warships. We've also not detected any unusual emissions — search or targeting systems — from the planet." He turned to Hanson. "Ma'am, I'm not saying that Korolev may not have a surprise in store for us, but if he is, he's concealing it bloody well."

Grishin shook his head. "*Maskirovka* — deception — is a specialty of theirs. If you review the history of the conflict twenty years ago, you will clearly see this: the Terran and Alliance forces suffered several major defeats and the loss of many troops because of it."

"Colonel," Hanson said, "even if it is a trap, there's very little I can do other than spring it while keeping our eyes wide open. We have confirmation that they have nuclear weapons, and we have details on where they're produced and stored. Our orders are clear on what we have to do next: get down there as quickly as possible to seize them before they can be moved." As she spoke, the task force was taking up position in a series of polar orbits. This would allow Hanson to have at least a few ships passing over the primary target area at any given time in low orbit to provide support to the Marines, while allowing her to also keep an eye on the rest of the planet. "If I knew what their deception was, we could try to disrupt it. Unfortunately, we don't, so we've got to go with what we've got." She paused, looking each of her commanders in the eye. "Let's do it, people."

FORTY

"You don't have to do this, Valentina," Sikorsky said for the third time as she drove him back into Saint Petersburg City. After she had sent the signal to the fleet, he had wanted to return home, to try and get his wife out of the city before the Confederation Marines came. Before the next war started.

"If you say that one more time, Dmitri," she told him with a wry smile, "I'm going to break your arm. I'm coming with you. So get used to the idea and stop worrying about it."

Sikorsky nodded, an unhappy expression on his face. As he turned to look out the window, however, she saw in the side mirror a small smile form on his lips.

What she was doing was explicitly against her orders. She was supposed to sever any ties with the locals and wait in a secure location for pickup. It was something she had done before, many times. One of those times, she had even been forced to kill her contact, a woman she had worked closely with and befriended over a three month-long mission that had gone bad, literally, at the last minute. Valentina had been known as Consuela then, just one of the many false identities behind which Scarlet had concealed herself. Outwardly, her contact's death did not appear to affect her; she told her controller that it was simply part of the mission, and that the woman had been an asset or, as Dmitri had said, a tool to be used and discarded as necessary.

But she had become so adept at the art of deception that she had deceived herself. It took her several months to realize that part of her soul had died the day that she had turned to this woman, her contact and friend, and wordlessly snapped her neck before she could be captured and interrogated. The two of them had been cornered, trapped, and the woman had simply known too much to fall into the wrong hands. There had been no way for both of them to escape, and so Consuela — Scarlet — had killed her friend. She managed to escape after a vicious fight with her pursuers, but the emotional wound was deep, and had never truly healed. There had been other missions since then, but she had never allowed herself to become close to any of the contacts she had made. Nor to anyone else.

Until Dmitri. He was an anomaly in her experience. There was nothing outwardly special about him. While he certainly was not a homely man, she was not physically or emotionally attracted to him. He didn't play the role of a hero, although he clearly had courage. He wasn't rich or powerful. Had she called him a simple and ordinary man, with simple and ordinary ways, he would no doubt have heartily agreed and poured the two of them some vodka to drink together.

No. Her bond to Dmitri, the sense of loyalty she felt to this human tool, who would be used and discarded as necessary for her mission, was simply because he was a good man, with a good heart. There were few enough of those in the universe, she knew from painful experience, and she had decided that if she could help him, she would. It wouldn't be a full atonement for her past sins, but it was a start.

Now that her primary mission objective had been met and the target information conveyed to the fleet (she hoped, for there was no way for her to know if the fleet had actually received it, or if the Navy had even arrived), the only harm that could come from her helping Dmitri was to herself. She realized that she was an asset to the Confederation in the same way that Dmitri was to her, but the difference was that the Confederation was not here to enforce the rules. What she did now was up to her, and she had chosen to help him.

On the way back to the city, they had stopped at the small town where Valentina had boarded the train to Saint Petersburg only a week earlier. It was risky, but she needed some civilian clothes to do what they had planned. Assuming the arrogant attitude typical of the secret police, she had marched into the shabby local clothing store and bought what she needed using the credit disk of the soldier whose uniform she wore. That caused the clerk to raise her eyebrows, but looking up into Valentina's cold eyes was enough to avert any questions. Valentina knew that there was a chance the woman would report her, but Sikorsky dismissed the notion.

"No one will question you," he said. "You wear a secret police uniform, are driving one of their vehicles, and have a comrade with you, all in plain sight. It does not matter if the name on the credit disk does not match. People do not delve into the affairs of the secret police, because they do not want them knocking on doors, asking questions, and taking people away, never to return. If you look like secret police, to them you *are* secret police."

They had made a second stop, this time at a small deli that was completely empty except for the elderly man behind the counter. Sikorsky bought some questionable looking cold cuts and bread, which actually looked good and smelled delicious, and two bottles of mineral water. In the meantime, Valentina disappeared into the disgustingly dirty rest room to change. She put on her civilian clothes, a pair of black pants and a dark brown blouse that were both shapeless and common, and then put her baggy uniform back on over top. She had also bought a set of sandals that were typical summer casual wear for women here, which she left in the vehicle. So, for all the proprietor of the deli knew, she had simply gone to the bathroom while her comrade had procured lunch.

As they got back on the road and headed toward Saint Petersburg, they saw contrails, high in the sky, spiraling downward.

* * *

Grishin struggled to keep from gritting his teeth in frustration. *I should not be surprised*, he told himself harshly. *It is exactly what I would do, just before springing the ambush.* The Saint Petersburg government had waited until the Marine boats were away before they had a sudden "unexpected systems failure" that caused all of their planetary defense arrays to activate. Fearing an attack, Hanson had called the boats back and regrouped her ships in higher orbit in a better defensive position, with every vessel poised to repel the as-yet unseen Saint Petersburg Navy.

Not surprisingly — at least to Grishin — no attack had materialized. The whole farce, he knew, had been both to test the Confederation task force's reactions and to gather information on their weapons systems. On top of that, their entire operation had effectively been disrupted. Hanson had been forced to make an agonizing decision: take the time to reposition her ships as she had before, which would have provided optimal support to the Marines, or send the assault carriers in with minimal protection while keeping the bulk of her ships further from the planet where they had more maneuvering room for combat.

Knowing that the tactic had been nothing more than a play for time, no doubt to move as many weapons and incriminating equipment as possible out of the huge mountain facility, Hanson had sent the carriers in with Sato's ship, *Yura,* and one of her sister heavy cruisers for protection and fire support for the Marines, if they needed it.

After the targeting systems had been shut down, the Russians had been extremely obliging in guiding the boats down and effusive in their apologies. Hanson had accepted their regrets with admirable diplomacy, but Grishin was not fooled: he had planned a small bit of deception of his own.

His original plan, after analyzing the information the Confederation agent had transmitted, had called for a battalion of troops to land at the mountain facility, and two companies each to land at the coal burning facilities (he refused now to call them "power plants"). After the game the Russians had played, however, he knew that the only facility of any true value would be the mountain facility: the locations of the coal burning facilities were known now, and their outward details had been confirmed from orbit. They may be producing uranium, but that was all. The real prize, if there was one, was the massive bunker in the mountains.

Once Hanson finally gave clearance for the landing to recommence, Grishin had his boat pilots follow their original courses, with one small deviation: the boats bound for the coal burning facilities simply did a quick flyover of their targets before turning to join Grishin's main force at the mountain bunker, concentrating the entire Marine brigade at the main objective. The boats dove low, skimming the treetops, to avoid the planetary defense radars as best they could.

* * *

In a deep underground bunker five kilometers south of Saint Petersburg City that served as the military command center and survival shelter for the planet's leaders, Marshal Antonov grunted in satisfaction.

"All too predictable," he murmured as the Confederation boats that had been heading for the coal plants suddenly disappeared from the defense network displays, no doubt as some sort of ruse. He could have ordered his aerospace fighters up to engage and destroy them, but that would have given away the game. They could only be heading toward one place. "Let them concentrate at the Central Facility where we can apply overwhelming force," he said to Korolev, who stood beside him at the massive map table, whose surface showed the known and projected tracks of the enemy boats as they raced toward the Central Facility, "and we will be done with these fools." The map showed the forces that now awaited the Confederation Marines: in addition to the division that was normally garrisoned in and around the facility, two more divisions had been deployed in concealed positions in a ring around the massive bunker. The Confederation troops would be outnumbered six to one. He glanced at the wall display, which showed the disposition of the Confederation task force's ships, hovering in high orbit not far from the moon. He shook his head in disgust at the sight of the vulnerable carriers, now escorted only by a pair of heavy cruisers. "Then we will formally introduce them to the Saint Petersburg Navy."

Beside him, Korolev could not help but smile as he looked at the icons representing the seventy-three ships of his planet's secretly built navy, including thirty-eight powerful heavy cruisers, all armed with highly advanced nuclear-tipped torpedoes. Carefully concealed in deep fissures in the small moon's surface, they were perfectly positioned for a surprise attack on the Confederation task force.

* * *

"Roland, are you all right?"

Mills snapped his eyes open at the sound of Sabourin's voice. She had opened a private channel to him so no one else could hear. Two of the *Yura's* Marine detachment's platoons had been prepared as a quick reaction force to help support the surface operation, with a platoon in each of the two cutters the cruiser carried. The two other platoons, along with the detachment commander, had been ferried to one of the assault carriers, and — if the mission called for it — would be taken down in one of the carrier's assault boats that would soon be returning from the surface after deploying the Marines there. The detachment commander had left Mills in charge of the force waiting aboard *Yura.*

"Yes," he rasped, "I'm bloody fine."

After a brief pause, Sabourin said softly, "You should know better than to lie to me."

Mills looked up at her. "My head has been aching like a bloody bitch," he confessed. "And..." He stopped, shook his head.

"And you're still seeing the Kreelan, as in the dream?" she finished for him.

Unwillingly, he nodded. "It's like it's getting stronger by the fucking minute. Damned if I know why or what it means."

"Could they be coming here?" Sabourin wondered.

Mills laughed mirthlessly, shaking his head. "Now wouldn't that be a capital cockup? As if the Russkies aren't trouble enough."

"I think we should tell the captain, Roland," she said. "Maybe it's nothing, but if —"

"No," he said, cutting her off. "He probably thinks I'm off my fucking nut with this dreaming business. I'm not going to give him cause to pull me off the line now, Emmanuelle."

"But what if it *does* mean something, Roland?" she pressed.

"It doesn't," he snapped. Then, after a moment, he added softly, "Please, just drop it?"

Fearing that he was making a potentially grave mistake, Sabourin nodded and settled back into the combat seat, her worried eyes fixed on her lover.

* * *

"Okay," Valentina breathed, "let's go."

A secret police vehicle parked on the street during daylight was highly unusual; like cockroaches, the secret police normally came out at night to swarm through the city. Unfortunately, there was no convenient place to park it out of sight and still be close to Sikorsky's apartment building. On the other hand, anyone who saw the vehicle or its two occupants would just as quickly pretend they hadn't.

A few minutes earlier, Sikorsky and Valentina had stopped the vehicle in an alley, where Valentina stripped off her secret police uniform to expose her civilian clothes, and swapped places in the vehicle with Sikorsky, who then drove them to his apartment building.

"Do you think this will work?" he asked quietly as they got out of the vehicle and climbed the worn concrete stairs to the main entrance.

"I don't know," she said, "but we don't have time for anything else." She knew that the Marines must be close to their objectives by now, and was surprised that an orbital bombardment hadn't already begun. Some Marines would be detailed to pick her up: they just had to find her. One of the items in her retrieved cylinder was a special emergency retrieval beacon. She should have activated it as soon as she knew the boats were inbound. She hadn't, because she wasn't going to leave this planet without making sure that Dmitri and his wife were safe.

Valentina led the way, following Sikorsky's quiet instructions to reach his apartment. Her hands were bound by cuffs, although they were loose enough that she could quickly get free if she had to. Sikorsky held his submachine gun trained on her back to round out the image of her being his prisoner.

When they arrived at his door, Sikorsky knocked. "Ludmilla!" he called. He would have let himself in, of course, but his key — along with his clothes and other items he had when they were captured — was still sitting somewhere in secret police headquarters.

After an agonizing moment, the door swung open.

"*Ludmilla*," Sikorsky gasped, horrified.

There stood his wife, her face battered and bruised, with deep cuts in her forehead and on both cheeks, with her lips still bleeding and swollen. Her left arm was in a sling, her wrist and fingers in a poorly made cast. She stumbled back from the door, trembling in fear of her husband, who now wore a secret police uniform.

Valentina instantly realized that they had made a terrible miscalculation. Neither she nor Sikorsky had thought of the possibility that Ludmilla might have been brought in for questioning. In retrospect, she knew that had been an amateurish mistake. *Of course they would have interrogated her*, she berated herself. And now here the two of them were, Dmitri ready with a story that he had been working undercover for the secret police to bring this Confederation spy to justice, hoping that would fool his devoted Party wife long enough to get her away from the city, and Valentina playing the role of captured villainess.

Worse, now that she was thinking more clearly, she realized that the secret police no doubt had Ludmilla under surveillance on the chance that Sikorsky would return home. They had walked straight into a trap.

Dropping his weapon to hang limply at his side, Sikorsky reached for his wife, but she stumbled backward before collapsing to the floor, a cry of terror on her lips. "No," she begged him, holding up her good arm, trying to ward him off. "*Please, no more...*"

"Ludmilla," he said, kneeling down and reaching for her, "it is me, Dmitri..."

"No," his wife whispered, turning away.

Valentina put a hand on Dmitri's shoulder, drawing him back. "Listen to me," she told him. "Go change into civilian clothes — quickly. I'll look after her."

With a questioning look, but without argument, Dmitri turned and shambled down the short hallway to the bedroom, his own battered face a mask of shocked pain that went far deeper than his physical wounds.

Valentina knelt next to Ludmilla and said softly, "Ludmilla, he's not one of them. He would never, ever hurt you. We didn't know they had taken you in for interrogation."

After a moment, Ludmilla, tears running down her face, whispered, "I have been such a fool. After they took away my daughter, my only child, I was convinced it was something I had done, some terrible wrong for which I was responsible. I tried to be good after that, to do everything the Party wanted. I know...I know that it hurt Dmitri, but I could not help myself. Then...then they came for me, just as they did my daughter. They said terrible things, that Dmitri was a spy, helping you — a Confederation spy — and that I must also be guilty, that I was a traitor to my planet, to my people. They beat me..." She moaned, curling into a fetal position, shivering.

"Your husband is a good man, Ludmilla," Valentina told her fiercely, gently pulling the older woman into her arms. "It is the Party that is twisted and evil. They have used you, just as they have used everyone, torturing and murdering anyone who dares to defy them. People like your daughter and her husband. People like Dmitri. He has been risking his life, trying to change that."

"I don't know what to believe now," Ludmilla said, choking on the words.

"Believe that I love you, and that if I ever catch the fucking bastards who did this to you, I'll kill them with my bare hands," came Dmitri's savage voice from beside her.

Ludmilla turned to see him, now dressed in his customary plain, ordinary clothes. His eyes, staring from his bandaged face, were wet with his own tears. "Dmitri," she cried softly as she finally reached for him, "what are we to do?"

Suddenly there were shouts from down the corridor outside, and the sound of pounding feet, growing louder, nearer.

"What is that?" Ludmilla cried, her face a mask of terror.

Valentina snatched up Dmitri's weapon and handed it back to him. "Don't worry," she said grimly. "Dmitri, take this." She handed him a tiny device with a numeric code lit in red, blinking. "It's an emergency beacon. I've already activated it: help will be coming soon. But in case something happens to me, they'll take you and Ludmilla to safety." He took it and shoved it into his pocket. "Now, take her back to the bedroom and stay there, behind whatever cover you can. If any secret police troops make it past me..." She shrugged. "Just stay alive until help arrives."

"What about you?" he asked as he pulled Ludmilla to her feet and began to move her to the back of the apartment. "Don't you need a weapon?"

"I've got plenty," she said cryptically. "Now get going!"

As he and Ludmilla hurried down the hall to the bedroom, Valentina turned and bolted for the kitchen. Fortunately, Ludmilla was a very good cook and kept her kitchen and its contents, as humble as they might be, in good order and condition.

Especially the knives. The secret police were almost to the door, so she had no time to be choosy. She grabbed a meat cleaver and shoved it into her waistband, then took the two butcher knives protruding from the simple wooden knife block, noting with satisfaction that they had a fresh, sharp edge. She would have preferred to have some knives that she could throw, but there wasn't time. She would have to work close-in.

She darted back into the main room just as the door burst open and the first of seven secret police troops stepped in, weapons raised. In a blur, Valentina moved toward him from the opposite side of the door, knocking his weapon down toward the floor with one hand as her other slashed one of the knives across his throat. She slammed into him with one shoulder, sending him cartwheeling backward into the others. Blood spurted from his neck, splattering his surprised comrades as his finger spasmed on the trigger of his weapon, sending a hail of bullets into the ceiling.

Then she was among them, spinning, kicking, and slashing, her face frozen into a cold mask of merciless hatred.

* * *

"Commodore!"

Hanson turned to see Robert Torvald, the Confederation agent's controller, burst onto the flag bridge, the pair of Marines who stood guard on the hatch during battle stations both pointing their weapons at him.

"Bloody hell, man!" she snapped. "We're at general quarters! What the devil are you doing—"

"I've picked up the emergency recall beacon," he said urgently as he came to stand close by her command chair.

"Ma'am?" one of the Marines asked tensely. Few people on the ship had even seen Torvald on this patrol, and the Marines were very uneasy about letting this man stand so close to their senior-most officer.

"It's all right," she said quickly. "Thank you, gentlemen. Return to your posts."

"Aye, aye, ma'am," they said in unison before leaving the flag bridge, but not without a surreptitious glance back at the stranger in civilian clothes.

"The recall beacon," Torvald said again. "You must send a team to retrieve our asset. Now."

Hanson hated it when the spooks talked like that, like there weren't actual people involved. "I'll send a team as soon as Colonel Grishin secures—"

"I'm sorry, commodore, but that won't do," Torvald interrupted her. "If you'll recall the special section of your orders, retrieving our asset becomes your first priority once the beacon is activated. You have no discretion in the matter."

She stared at him a moment, debating in the back of her mind how much trouble she would be in if she recalled the Marines standing guard and had them frog-march this mouth-with-legs to the brig.

"That section of the orders was undersigned by the president herself, commodore," he added.

"I realize that," she told him acidly, grudgingly conceding that she wouldn't be able to throw him in the brig after all. She punched a button on her control console. "Captain Zellars," she called to her flag captain. "We need to get a Marine assault team down to the surface on a...special mission. Right now. Who do we have that's ready to go and in the best position?"

"*Yura* would fit the bill, commodore," Zellars said immediately. "She has two Marine platoons prepped as quick reaction teams, already in the ship's cutters. They just need a frag order to go."

Hanson looked at Torvald. "Give them the coordinates and tell them what they need to know to bring your *asset* back," she said, "then get the hell off my flag bridge."

"I'm sorry, commodore," he shot back, "but that's impossible. I have to go with the Marines on the cutter—"

"That, Mr. Torvald," she interrupted him this time, "is distinctly *not* in my orders. If you want your asset picked up, give my people the information they need to get the mission done. Otherwise, get your ass out of my sight."

Up until then, Torvald had been disquietingly cool. But she could see that she had cracked his armor. She wasn't quite sure what mix of emotions were showing through, but she could tell they didn't include love or joy.

"Here," he said tersely, handing her a data chip. "This has everything they'll need to find..." He paused before finishing, almost reluctantly, "...her."

* * *

"Mills," Sato said through his bridge vidcom, his face betraying his concern, "we'll be over the horizon and out of support range for ninety minutes. You'll be on your own."

"Understood, skipper," Mills told him as the cutter slipped away from the *Yura*. Outside of her parent ship's gravity field now, he was overtaken by the familiar but queasy sensation of weightlessness. Ahead loomed their destination, the glowing surface of Saint Petersburg. Sato had called him only a few minutes ago to brief him on their new mission, to rescue a Confederation agent in Saint Petersburg City. It was a completely insane mission that fit perfectly with Mills's thrill-seeking personality. *If only the fucking headache would go away*, he cursed to himself, *this might even be fun*. None of the meds he had taken had made a dent in it. He shrugged inwardly. He would have to make do. "Don't worry, sir," he said. "We'll make the grab and be back for more fun before you sail 'round again."

Sato nodded, but did not smile. "Godspeed, Mills," he said before terminating the connection.

"Okay, Faraday," Mills said to the warrant officer who piloted the cutter, "let's get on with this little party, shall we?"

FORTY-ONE

Even though everything appeared to be calm and orderly, every hair on the back of Grishin's neck was at stiff attention, screaming that there was something wrong. Here he was with a brigade of troops deployed in a hasty defensive perimeter around a gigantic concrete apron, painted to blend in with the forest, that easily accommodated all of his assault boats at one time, exchanging pleasantries with the man who claimed to be the commandant of the facility. A storage facility, yes, the man, a brigadier, had told him.

"But not for nuclear weapons," the brigadier said, laughing, as if Grishin was mad to even think such a thing.

Grishin had sent the special teams, men and women trained in disarming nuclear weapons, into the gigantic tunnel, accompanied by an entire battalion of Marines. He could have sent a smaller escort, but he had plenty of troops and had no idea how big the complex was. He intended, however, that if they ran into any trouble, they would be able to defend themselves.

He had arranged the rest of his Marines around the inside of the huge wall. He had been sorely tempted to take over the walls and the security positions there, but without any sign of resistance from the "host" military, he under very strict orders to avoid provoking them without cause.

Fuck, he thought savagely. There is something wrong here, but—

"Colonel!" one of his men cried, pointing toward the tunnel entrance. The door, a gigantic plug of hardened steel that was easily three meters thick, was closing. The Marines inside would be cut off, trapped.

"Brigadier," he said, turning to the alleged commandant, "what is the meaning of this?"

"My apologies, colonel," the man said calmly as he drew his sidearm with one hand and with the other casually rolled a hand grenade onto the ground in the midst of Grishin's nearby staff. Unbelievably, he made no attempt to escape.

"*Alarm!*" Grishin screamed as he knocked the Russian officer's gun arm to the side, then stabbed his right hand, fingers held rigid like a knife, into the brigadier's throat, crushing his larynx. Grishin grabbed him by the collar and web gear, and with a desperate prayer and a massive heave, threw the gagging Russian to the ground on top of the grenade just before it exploded. His body didn't absorb the full force of the explosion, for two of the staff officers were riddled with shrapnel and killed instantly. But Grishin's quick reflexes had saved the lives of the others. For the moment.

In those few seconds, bedlam erupted around the facility. The formerly peaceful Russian soldiers atop the massive wall turned inward and opened fire on the Marines, who were now caught out in the open with nowhere to hide across hectares of bare concrete. A volley of hypervelocity missiles lanced out, almost too fast to follow with the unaided eye, from points along the wall, obliterating most of the assault boats on the ground in massive fireballs. Two boats actually managed to get airborne, struggling skyward amidst the flames, smoke, and debris from the others that had been destroyed outright. One of them only made it a dozen meters above the concrete before it was skewered by a missile. The other, piloted by either a genius or a maniac, managed to avoid four missiles before it was destroyed. The four boats that Grishin had on patrol overhead were hit simultaneously. Three exploded, while the last plummeted toward the ground, trailing smoke. That boat's pilot guided her stricken craft over the heads of her fellow Marines and straight into the closed gate at the entrance to the facility, blasting a huge hole in it.

That may be our only way out, Grishin thought quickly as he surveyed the carnage around him. The surprise assault on the boats had resulted in a shower of flaming debris that had crushed or burned to death dozens of his Marines, and scores more had already fallen to the murderous fire from the walls.

"Return fire!" he barked over his comm set to his battalion commanders, although most of the Marines had already begun to return fire on their own. He got acknowledgments from all of his commanders except the one who had been swallowed up by the mountain: they didn't have any communications gear that was powerful enough to penetrate the mountain's shielding. They were on their own.

Around the facility, the Marines fought back fiercely, blasting away at their attackers with everything they had.

Grishin knew that it would not be enough. They were totally cut off and surrounded, with the only possible way out being the hole blown in the main gate by the suicidal boat pilot. And judging by the increasing amount of fire coming from the wall, he suspected that there were fresh troops being brought up from some subterranean barracks.

"*Camarón.*" He breathed the name of the famous last stand, from centuries before, of the French *Légion étrangère* that had been his family and country for the last twenty years before the Confederation was founded. He had said it once before during the Battle of Keran when he was sure he was about to die. He had never expected to say it a second time. "Follow me!" he ordered the surviving members of his headquarters staff as he snatched up a rifle from a fallen Marine and headed toward the burning wreckage of one of the assault boats, trying to find some cover from the withering hail of fire from the enemy soldiers on the walls. "And patch me through to Commodore Hanson!"

"Colonel," one of his staff shouted, pointing at the pile of wreckage that was all that was left of their ad-hoc command post, "the FLEETCOM terminal is gone..." Without the terminal or the boats, they had no way to contact the fleet.

"*Merde,*" he said savagely. Grishin knew that their chances of survival had just dropped to near-zero.

* * *

"We've lost contact with Colonel Grishin, commodore," the flag communications officer reported suddenly. The icons for Grishin's units deployed on the surface suddenly became transparent on the display that showed a map of the underground facility: the real-time feed that updated the information from the sensors the Marines carried was gone.

Hanson took a closer look at the display. Losing all communications with the Marines on the surface should be nearly impossible: even if the FLEETCOM units were destroyed, any of the boats could relay Grishin's transmissions. The bulk of the task force was in a stand-off orbit, far enough from the planet that no planetary defense weapons could reach them without fair warning. The carriers and their two escorting heavy cruisers, including Sato's *Yura*, were in low orbit, now on the far side of the planet. The single small moon was also on the far side of Saint Petersburg, effectively screened from the sensors on the ships with her here, but visible to the carriers.

She suddenly felt a sickening sensation in the pit of her stomach. Losing communications with the Marines was no coincidence. *They were going to hit the carriers first,* she thought, a cold spear of dread lancing up her spine, *from the goddamn moon!* "Contact the carriers and have them get the hell out of there—"

It was too late. A sudden bloom of yellow icons erupted from the moon, echoed by the sensors on board the carriers and their cruiser escorts, and in only a few seconds all of them turned to red: warships, believed to be hostile.

Hanson held her breath as the tactical computer counted the enemy ships and did its best to identify them by class. *Seventy-three warships,* she told herself, shocked. Worse, thirty-eight of them were classed as heavy cruisers. Hanson's entire force amounted to only six heavy cruisers and ten destroyers, plus the two carriers. It would be a slaughter.

"*Radiological alarm!*" her flag tactical officer shouted as the lead Russian ships fired a brace of what could only be torpedoes at Hanson's carriers and their escorts, now frantically trying to escape Saint Petersburg's gravity well so they could jump into hyperspace and escape. "Nuclear warheads, inbound!"

"Extend the fleet formation," Hanson snapped. "Stand by for emergency jump."

"What about the Marines, commodore?" her flag captain asked quietly.

She turned to him, a stony expression on her face. "I said to stand by for emergency jump."

"Aye, aye, ma'am," the flag captain said, turning away to issue the necessary orders.

Hanson stared at the screen, her gut churning at the butcher's bill if they were forced to jump.

On the display, as the carriers accelerated hard away from the inbound torpedoes, *Yura* and her sister turned to fight.

* * *

"Stand by point defense," Sato ordered. Inside, he was quivering from adrenalin, both from fear and excitement. But his voice only gave away a faint trace of what he was feeling. He was the captain, and his crew would follow his lead. He wanted them calm and level-headed as they charged directly into the teeth of the torpedo salvo, knowing they were fitted with nuclear warheads. *We can do this*, he told himself. "Main batteries, engage on my mark..." The range rings showing the effective range of the ship's main guns intersected the rapidly approaching torpedoes. "Fire!"

With the data-link connecting *Yura* with her sister ship *Myoko*, the two ships became a single virtual weapon, able to more effectively coordinate their targeting and firing. With a measured cadence, their fifteen-centimeter guns began to fire. Unlike the projectiles they normally fired at other ships, which were armor piercing explosive rounds, these shells contained thousands of ball bearings surrounding a large explosive charge. At a distance determined by the targeting computers, the shells detonated, sending a hail of metal into the path of the incoming weapons.

The designers of the torpedoes, however, had anticipated this. The torpedoes were smart weapons, and began individual rapid evasion patterns to confuse the defending targeting systems and dodge around defensive fire.

At a point designated by the targeting computers, *Yura* and *Myoko* did a hard turn-about. Now, instead of heading directly toward the torpedoes as they fired, they were running away from them, continuing to fire astern. The torpedoes were significantly faster, but this maneuver ensured that the two cruisers had the maximum amount of time for defensive fire before the torpedoes caught up to them or, worse, passed them by to strike the nearly helpless carriers.

The Saint Petersburg ships had fired ten torpedoes, and all but two fell to the defending fire of the two cruisers before their basic load of ammunition ran out and the main guns fell silent. The ships' laser batteries thrummed as they fired, but the wildly maneuvering torpedoes were nearly impossible to hit.

"Godspeed, Sato," *Myoko's* captain suddenly said through the vidcom terminal on Sato's combat chair, just before his ship disappeared in a blinding fireball. In space, there was no atmosphere to transmit shock waves that could tear a planet-bound structure or ship to bits. Nor were there thermal effects that could incinerate people or structures, as there was no air for the explosion to heat. There was only a massive blast of neutron and gamma radiation that seared *Myoko* and her crew into oblivion. The blast from the torpedo itself was overshadowed by the detonation of the cruiser's main drives.

"*Sir!*" Sato's tactical officer cried. One torpedo remained, just pulling abreast of *Yura* and clearly locked onto the fleeing carriers.

"Helm, bring us ten degrees to starboard, all ahead flank!" Sato ordered, telling Bogdanova to steer the ship closer to the weapon. "Ready point defense!"

"Point defense, standing by!" the tactical officer reported, his voice tight.

The entire bridge crew waited in tense silence as the next few seconds brought them closer to what they knew was almost certain destruction. The tactical computer had generated an estimated yield of twenty kilotons for the weapon that had just destroyed *Myoko*. The torpedo had managed to penetrate the ship's close-in defenses and detonate at a range of two kilometers, spearing the ship with over ten thousand roentgens of radiation; as few as five hundred were required to incapacitate, and sometimes kill, a human being.

Yura would not be that close, but she would be close enough.

"Stand by..." Sato said. Then: "Point defense, *fire!*"

The lasers and gatling guns of the cruiser's close-in weapons systems spat beams of coherent light and streams of explosive shells at the wildly maneuvering torpedo. The weapon danced across the star field as it tried to avoid the incoming fire, but with *Yura* sailing on a parallel course, the torpedo had lost its speed advantage. In one brief moment, three laser bolts converged on the weapon.

Sato suddenly saw a blossoming of new ship icons, all of them red, on the tactical display, just before the universe went white.

* * *

The fleet was just making its transition from hyperspace to the target human system when Tesh-Dar sensed it: the massive spike of energy and radiation that heralded the detonation of an atomic weapon. Such weapons, of course, had been known to the *Kreela* for ages, since long before the First Empire. They were far from the most powerful weapons the Empire had at its disposal, but like its far more destructive cousins, it was a class of weapon that the Empress disdained to use. Were the Empire seriously threatened, She would not hesitate to use everything at Her disposal to protect it. Yet, even the greatest of the Empire's weapons and warships were as nothing compared to the power that dwelt within the Empress Herself.

The *Kreela* had encountered such weapons as these before in the course of the Empire's expansion across the stars: all of the races the Empire had fought and vanquished in the ages-long search for the First Empress had used atomic weapons — very briefly. While the Empress condoned combat with ship-board weapons as long as they were, in essence, controlled by the enemy's warriors, such weapons of mass destruction were an abomination in Her eyes: they took away the opportunity a warrior had to bring Her glory in battle, and to seek the One who might save them all.

Tesh-Dar did not need a sensor suite or computers to tell her what had just happened. She was finely attuned to the space around her, and could in fact pilot a starship by second sight alone.

And what she felt, the Empress felt.

"Prepare yourselves, daughters," she warned the others on the bridge, "for we shall be Her sword hand this day, and shall feel Her power in our flesh."

Then a second nuclear detonation occurred.

"Priestess!" her tactical officer cried as the ship's sensors localized the two detonations and what appeared to be a mortally stricken human ship, and the vaporized remains of a second one, not far from the target planet.

As Tesh-Dar watched, what she assumed was a second volley of torpedoes was fired from a larger human fleet at a smaller one, to which the two ships that had been destroyed apparently belonged.

"They battle one another," she said in confused wonder, shaking her head. Here sailed a battle group of the Imperial Fleet to challenge the humans, and they were destroying one another. She could not understand these creatures.

"The missiles are armed with atomic warheads," the tactical officer announced.

Tesh-Dar only nodded absently: she already knew. And she could feel a sudden strengthening of the Bloodsong, like a massive storm surge through their souls. "Prepare yourselves," she whispered as she gave herself up to the power that soared higher, ever higher, in her veins.

* * *

"Whose ships are *those?*" Admiral Lavrenti Voroshilov demanded sharply.

"Unidentified!" his flag tactical officer barked. On the main display, fifty-seven ships had just jumped into Saint Petersburg space and were displayed in a glaring crimson: assumed hostile. To the Saint Petersburg fleet, any ship that was not known to be theirs was first considered an enemy. "Configuration unknown. They do not appear to be Confederation vessels." According to the display, the new arrivals were much closer to Voroshilov's fleet than were the Confederation ships.

"Give them a full salvo of torpedoes," Voroshilov ordered.

* * *

"Holy shit," someone muttered on the *Constellation's* flag bridge in the silence that fell immediately after the new arrivals had been identified by the tactical computers.

A Kreelan battle fleet, Hanson thought acidly. *Could this mission get any more fucked up?* The only good news was that the carriers finally reached their emergency jump points and disappeared safely into hyperspace. At the cost of two of her heavy cruisers.

"Twenty seconds to jump," the fleet navigator announced.

On the flag bridge tactical display, there was now a second — and much larger — salvo of torpedoes heading toward Hanson's ships, and the Russians had just launched yet another salvo at the newly-arrived Kreelans. *How many of those bloody torpedoes do they have?* she wondered.

"Fifteen seconds..."

Her ships would be well away before the torpedoes were close enough to present a danger, but she now desperately wanted to see how the Kreelans reacted. While she knew that President McKenna was dead-set against using nuclear weapons, if they would help turn the tide against the Kreelans...

* * *

It took all of Tesh-Dar's will to keep herself from writhing in the agony and ecstasy of the power unleashed by the Empress through her and the senior shipmistresses in the fleet. The other warriors, even those senior among them, felt only the passing tidal wave, but were not chosen to directly channel it: they would not have survived.

For a mere instant that was drawn out into eternity, Tesh-Dar could sense what the Empress sensed, glimpsed all that the Empress knew, sensed all that the Empress was, in mind and spirit, and it drove her to the brink of insanity. As great as her own powers were, Tesh-Dar was reminded of how insignificant they were beside those of the Empress. The most shocking thing was that she knew that what the Empress did now was merely a shadow of Her true power.

Tesh-Dar's body shook and trembled as the Empress reached out through the space around the fleet, to the human ships and missiles, to the planet and its moon, and bent the physical world to Her will.

* * *

"Jesus!" someone on Hanson's flag bridge shouted as all the ship's systems, even the artificial gravity, suddenly flickered.

"Status report!" Hanson demanded.

"There's no damage to the ship," the flag captain told her quickly after conferring with the ship's captain, "but the emergency jump sequence automatically aborted and had to be restarted."

"Fleet data-links are down," the communications officer reported. "Voice and vidcom backup are on-line."

"So what the devil happened?"

"Some sort of energy spike, commodore," the flag tactical officer reported. "I've never seen or heard of anything like it—"

"Commodore, look!"

Tearing her eyes away from the swarm of torpedoes heading toward her own ships on the tactical display, she saw that the torpedoes fired at the Kreelan warships were almost in range.

* * *

"Weapons malfunction!" Voroshilov's flag tactical officer reported, confused, as the first torpedo to reach the new set of enemy ships detonated. Or should have. The Saint Petersburg fleet had just recovered from a bizarre mass electrical problem that had affected all shipboard systems, but that apparently had caused no major damage except for taking down the inter-ship data-links. More torpedoes reached their targets. And failed to detonate properly. "Multiple malfunctions!"

On the screen, he watched as one by one the torpedoes detonated under the control of their proximity fuses, which told the weapons when a target was at the optimal range. The fuses then triggered a sort of "gun" that slammed two chunks of uranium-235 together to produce a fission reaction and the desired nuclear explosion. It was a primitive, but quite effective, design. The fleet's sensors told Voroshilov that the weapons were fusing properly and the so-called guns inside the warheads were firing, but there were no nuclear detonations. In fact, there was no further trace of radiological emissions from any of the warheads. Every single torpedo was a dud, and these new enemy ships did not even bother to waste any of their point defense fire on them.

"Comrade admiral," the tactical officer told Voroshilov, "this is simply not possible!"

Voroshilov barely heard. His attention was focused on the other torpedoes that had been streaking toward the Confederation ships, and that now were just coming into range.

* * *

Hanson stared at the torpedoes bearing down on her task force, thinking about what she had just seen happen to the Kreelans. Or, rather, what had *not* happened to them. *Could it be?* She wondered. *And can I take that kind of risk?* She thought of Grishin and his Marines, and Torvald's precious "asset," all stranded on the planet. Grishin, no doubt, had fallen into a trap similar to the ones the Russians had sprung on her task force. She hated the thought of leaving them behind, and if there was even a chance of getting them back, she wanted to take it. It was a horrible risk, but she didn't get paid to make easy decisions.

"Emergency jump sequence complete! Fifteen seconds to jump, stand by!"

"Belay that!" she shouted over the organized bedlam of the emergency jump sequence. "Terminate jump sequence. Stand by point defense!"

Several of her officers gaped at her for a moment before they scrambled to change the fleet's orders, a process made much more difficult with the data-links out of commission. The jump countdown timer stopped with four seconds left.

Hanson outwardly kept her cool, but rivulets of cold sweat were running down her spine as the tiny icons representing the torpedoes closed with her formation. *Please, God*, she prayed, *let me be right.*

Suddenly the point defense batteries of her ships began to fire, and torpedoes began to die. Several of them got through, and one exploded near enough to the *Constellation* that she could hear fragments of it ping off the ship's armor.

But there was not one single nuclear detonation: all of the torpedoes were either destroyed by the point defense systems or produced very small explosions when their nuclear triggers — which were mere conventional explosives — fired.

"Commodore," her flag tactical officer said, shaking his head, "there's no longer any trace of radiological elements in those torpedoes. If our calculations are right, the uranium-235 in the weapons is now nothing but...lead. We had solid radiological readings on every single one before that energy spike. Then after that — nothing. It's like something just changed the uranium into lead, like magic. It's just...impossible."

"Well," Hanson breathed, enormously relieved to be alive, "thank God for Kreelan alchemy." Then, turning to her communications officer, she said, "See if you can get a channel open to the commander of the Saint Petersburg fleet. If we can convince him to join forces, I think we can knock the Kreelans on their collective asses."

* * *

Voroshilov stared at Commodore Hanson on his vidcom with undisguised contempt. "Under no circumstances, *commodore*," he spat, "will we join forces with you, our enemy. This is a trick: those other ships are simply more Confederation vessels. And after we deal with them, we will finish with *you*, if you are foolish enough to remain in our sovereign system. If you want to live, you will depart immediately." He terminated the connection before the woman could respond.

"Comrade admiral," the ship's chief engineer said, a small image of his worried face appearing in Voroshilov's vidcom terminal.

"What is it, Stravinsky?"

"We have checked the remaining nuclear warheads aboard this ship, sir," Stravinsky reported. "All of them have been rendered inert. The uranium cores have been...converted to lead. I believe the other ships will discover the same thing."

"Sabotage?" Voroshilov demanded.

"No, comrade admiral," Stravinsky said, shaking his head. "Such a thing, replacing the uranium cores with lead, could only be done at the Central Facility. I have no explanation for what has happened. It is simply not possible!"

"It was the energy spike," mused the flag captain.

"*Da*," Stravinsky agreed. "I do not understand how, but that must have been the cause. The timing was no coincidence, for we know that the first salvo of weapons worked against the two Confederation cruisers we destroyed."

How could the Confederation have developed such a weapon? Voroshilov wondered, terrified at the possibilities. If they could neutralize Saint Petersburg's arsenal of nuclear weapons so easily, the plans of the Party leadership would come unraveled quickly, indeed.

"Your orders, admiral?" his flag captain asked.

Voroshilov glared at the tactical display, quickly weighing his options. *My fleet does not need nuclear weapons to fight and win its battles*, he thought savagely. "We shall destroy the newcomers," he said. "Then we shall deal with our friend Commodore Hanson."

FORTY-TWO

"Son of a bitch!" Warrant Officer John Faraday swore above the roar of superheated air that flamed around the cutter as it dove through Saint Petersburg's atmosphere toward the surface.

"What is it?" Roland Mills asked him over the small ship's intercom. His head was now pounding so fiercely that it was difficult for him to do anything, even speak. The pain had become so intense that he had bitten his tongue to keep from crying out, and his mouth was now awash with the taste of blood.

"We lost contact with the *Yura*," Faraday, the cutter's pilot, told him grimly. He punched a couple of buttons on his console. On the small display that was part of Mills's combat seat, Mills watched the last few moments of the battle in space, transmitted to the cutter over *Yura's* data-link before the signal was lost. There was no mistaking the nuclear detonation that killed the cruiser *Myoko*, and the track Captain Sato had taken toward the remaining torpedo left little to the imagination. "I think she's gone."

"Fuck," Mills hissed. "That just made my bloody day." He was not by nature a sentimental man, but he had to make an enormous effort to keep tears from welling in his eyes. The loss of Sato himself was a huge blow, not to mention the rest of his Marines and the ship's company. *Bloody hell*, he thought. *I'll save that news from the others until we've made our pickup.*

"It's going to get a lot worse," Faraday assured him. The display in front of Mills cleared, then changed to show the planet's surface, below. Angry red circles pulsed all around the city toward which they were heading: radars that were tracking them, that were now locked on. There were also several tell-tale icons of aerospace interceptors streaking toward them. Faraday wasn't too worried about interceptors: the cutter's weapons would be more than a match for them, unless they attacked in large numbers. Heavy ground-based defenses, however, were another story. "Their planetary defense systems are nearly in range. I'm not sure what anybody was really thinking when they ordered us down here, but without the ships upstairs to provide suppressing fire, this is gonna be a really short ride."

Just when Mills thought things couldn't get any worse, his headache seemed to explode in his skull. Crying out in agony, he hammered his fists against his temples, writhing in his combat harness.

"*Mills!*" Sabourin shouted as she began to unbuckle her harness to reach him.

"Stay in your goddamn seat!" Faraday, the pilot, yelled at her. "You'll be killed when we have to maneuver to avoid ground fire!"

With her heart breaking, she watched helplessly as Mills thrashed around in his seat and cried out, his screams carried over the platoon channel for everyone to hear.

"*Fuck!*" Faraday cursed as a sudden energy spike surged through the cutter. Every system flickered for a moment, and he nearly lost control of the ship in the roaring slipstream around them before the attitude control computers came back on-line. The cutter rolled sickeningly on its back and began to yaw, but he managed to wrestle the craft back on course before it went out of control. Looking at the tactical display, he saw that all of the radars had suddenly gone down, and the tracks of the interceptors had also disappeared, as if they had simply vanished. "Thank you, God," he whispered as he pushed the throttle forward as far as he dared, desperate to get into the ground clutter where the ship would be far more difficult to track.

He had no idea where he was going or even why. All that mattered, he had been told — personally — by Commodore Hanson, was to guide on a very peculiar beacon signal and get the Marines on the ground. After that, Hanson had told him cryptically, he would receive further instructions from someone on the ground.

Sabourin had her eyes glued to Mills. At the same instant the ship's systems had flickered, Mills had grunted as if someone had bludgeoned him, then he passed out. He now hung slack in his combat harness, his head lolling from side to side as the atmosphere bounced and jolted the little ship. She normally would have been able to tell from her tactical readout what his vital signs were, for every Marine carried equipment that monitored their physical status, but the energy surge had apparently fried the electronics built into her gear. Everything associated with her weapons and basic communications seemed to be fine, but the technology-based "combat multipliers," the most critical of which was the inter-Marine data-link network, was gone.

Switching over to a private channel that she and Mills used, she said, "Mills, can you hear me?" More urgently, she said, "Roland? Roland, answer me!"

"I...I hear you," he rasped. As he lifted his head up to look at her, she gasped as she saw blood streaming from his nose, with bloody tears in his eyes. It looked as if every capillary in both eyes had ruptured. "Christ, I can't see a fucking thing," was all he managed before he vomited over the front of his uniform.

"Two minutes!" Faraday barked from the flight deck as he suddenly pulled the ship out of its screaming dive, bringing it level just above the massive trees of the endless Saint Petersburg forests.

The copilot, who also doubled as the cutter's weapons controller, stared intently at the ship's defense displays. The ground radars were coming back up, but the cutter was so low now that they couldn't lock on. There was no sign that the interceptors were still on their way, but that could be good news or bad: they had either been destroyed by the energy spike, or were now playing hide and seek at treetop level, just as the cutter was, or running with their active sensors off, so the cutter's sensors couldn't detect them.

The ride was still incredibly rough, and Sabourin ignored the pilot's curses as she finally unstrapped herself and carefully made her way across the aisle to Mills.

"Well," he said, attempting his trademark devil-may-care attitude, "at least my frigging headache is gone." He made an attempt at a cheerful smile, his teeth covered in blood from having bitten his tongue again.

"You are a mess," she told him, ripping open a field dressing and using it to wipe the blood from his eyes. She followed it up with some water from her canteen, half of which she spilled in his lap when the cutter jolted upward, then sharply down again.

"Well, that'll help clear the puke away, then," he muttered, looking at the mess running down the front of his uniform before hissing at the pain as she poured more water into his eyes. "That's enough, luv!" he said, gently batting her hands away. "I'm okay."

She scowled at him as only a Frenchwoman can. "*Imbecile*," she chided, finally putting away her canteen.

Putting a hand over his tiny helmet microphone, he leaned close to her ear. "She's here," he whispered. "Don't ask me how I know, but that huge bitch of a warrior is here, somewhere on the planet or in the system."

Sabourin's eyes flew wide. "An invasion? *Here?*"

He shrugged helplessly. "I don't know. Let's just get this job done and get the hell back to the fleet as quick as we can." Whatever had been plaguing him in his dreams and that had brought on the awful headache was gone now, as if a balloon had suddenly burst, finally relieving the horrible pressure in his skull. Despite the residual pain, he felt much better than he had in days, if not weeks. And as he had told Sabourin, he knew the Kreelans were here somewhere. He was sure of it.

"One minute!" the pilot called out.

"Jaysus!" Mills cursed, shoving aside his thoughts about the Kreelans. There were more pressing matters afoot, and Sabourin should have been getting the platoon ready instead of fussing with him. He would have to talk to her about that later. In bed. Assuming they survived this harebrained operation.

Unstrapping his harness and getting unsteadily to his feet, using one arm to support himself on the forward bulkhead against the cutter's still-violent flight, he boomed, "First Squad, *up!*"

The men and women of First Squad got to their feet in a flurry of clinking buckles and the tell-tale sound of weapons being checked one final time. They shuffled forward toward the two front personnel doors.

"Second Squad, *up!*" Second Squad did the same, taking up position behind the Marines of First Squad.

"Third Squad, *up!*" The remaining squad stood and faced to the rear and the larger cargo door in the cutter's starboard side. Their exit would be a little easier, as the door would drop down to act as a ramp. The first two squads would have to jump a bit over a meter to the ground.

"Thirty seconds!" the pilot called.

"Bloody hell," Mills cursed as he leaned forward into the flight deck to look at the tactical display. But what caught his eye was the view through the forward windscreen. "We're going right fucking downtown, you fool!"

"Hey, Top," Faraday said tightly as he maneuvered the cutter between buildings, the ship's belly a mere two stories above the ground and its sides nearly scraping the buildings on either side. "My orders were to go to the goddamned little bug on this screen, quick like a bunny," he nodded toward the main tactical display and the glowing green icon representing the beacon they were after. "Nobody told me the fucking thing would be in the middle of the capitol city!"

Mills got a glimpse of a street flashing by below. It was crammed with people, all staring up at the passing ship with comic expressions of disbelief on their faces. They were flying that low. "So where is the damned beacon?" he asked as Faraday quickly slowed the ship as they approached their destination. With the Marine data-link out of action, there was no way for the pilot to echo the beacon's location to Mills for him to follow.

"Looks like it's on maybe the sixth floor of this building," the copilot said quickly, pointing to what looked like a run-down apartment complex. "And I think it's moving."

"Disembark!" Faraday shouted as he brought the cutter into a hover above the street. The forward doors slid open and the rear door quickly lowered. The Marines leaped to the ground, forming a defensive perimeter around the ship.

Mills followed Sabourin and the First Squad out the forward doors. "First Squad, on me!" he bellowed above the roar of the cutter's engines as he charged toward the apartment building, with the other two squads and the cutter guarding their backs.

* * *

Sikorsky felt like a coward, hiding in the bedroom while Valentina fought for their lives and her own. But he was Ludmilla's last defense, and he was determined, more than at any other time in his life, that she would come to no further harm. Keeping his submachine pistol aimed at the doorway, he felt no fear, only rage, and his hands kept the weapon's stubby barrel steady.

He cringed at the sounds coming from the front room: the growls, grunts, and screams of a pitched battle at close quarters. There had been gunfire in the first few seconds, but then only a few sporadic shots after that. He remembered the sounds of combat during the war years ago, and this was little different. Ludmilla whimpered as the wall to the front room shook violently with the impact of a body hurled against it, the wet smacking sound punctuated with the dry snapping of bone. She huddled close to him, shivering in fear.

He heard a noise that he did not recognize, a drone that quickly became a roar just outside the building. The little device Valentina had given him now glowed a solid green.

"Help is here, *dorogaya*," he shouted to Ludmilla over the roar, just as the ferocity of the fighting in the front room suddenly peaked in a flurry of what could only be savage blows and crashes as the combatants flung themselves about the front room in a final killing orgy.

After one last crash, there was only the roar of the engines outside. Sikorsky tightened his grip on the submachine pistol, his finger easing in more pressure on the trigger, preparing to fire.

"Dmitri!" a woman's voice — Valentina's voice — called wearily from the front room. "It's clear! Come on, we have to go!"

"*Slava Bogu*," Sikorsky whispered. *Thank God.* "We are coming!" He gathered up Ludmilla in his arms and helped her into the front room. He was totally unprepared for the sight that greeted him.

The apartment looked as if it had been struck by a bomb. Every piece of furniture was overturned, with the dining chairs reduced to splinters. The bookshelves had been smashed and their contents, most of it Party propaganda and novels by sanctioned authors, spread like confetti across the floor. The kitchen was a disaster, with shattered dishes and glassware everywhere. There were holes punched through the thin drywall by fists and feet, with blood streaked and spattered haphazardly across the walls and floor. He gaped at one of the secret police, whose head had been rammed completely through one of the walls, a spear-tipped leg from one of the demolished dining chairs stabbed through his back. The bodies of half a dozen more secret police were scattered throughout the wreck of their small home, their bodies bloody and broken.

In the middle of it all stood Valentina. She had a deep gash across her right cheek and a bloody welt across her left arm where a bullet had grazed her, but otherwise she seemed unharmed. Sikorsky shook his head in wonderment: she wasn't even breathing hard.

"Let's go," she told them, helping him guide Ludmilla through the mess and around the bodies. She paused only long enough to snatch up one of the submachine pistols, slinging it quickly across her shoulder. "Downstairs."

As they moved down the hall toward the elevator, they heard the sound of heavy footsteps hammering up the stairwell.

"Get behind me," she said grimly as she pointed her weapon toward the stairwell door.

The footfalls suddenly ceased, and the door creaked open slightly. "Confederation Marines!" someone called in a voice with an unmistakable British accent. "I was told to ask if you might be Scarlet," the voice said.

"That's me," she said in Standard, smiling tiredly at the camouflaged face that carefully peered through the door. "We could use a bit of help here. I've got two civilians with me. Friendlies."

With that, a massive man in Marine combat armor, holding an equally massive pistol that he pointed safely toward the ceiling, burst through the door. He held it open as more Marines charged through. Two of them slung their weapons and began to help Ludmilla and Sikorsky, with the rest forming a protective cordon around them and Scarlet.

Up and down the hallway, a few doors cracked open and wide, disbelieving eyes peered out before the doors slammed shut.

"First Sergeant Roland Mills, at your service, miss," the big Marine said, quickly shaking her hand. "Let's get on the road, shall we?"

The young woman offered no objections as the Marines bundled her and the two bewildered civilians down the stairway. Behind them, Mills and Sabourin paused, peering through the door to the apartment.

"Jesus fucking Christ," Mills said, impressed with the devastation.

"Do not piss her off," Sabourin advised with a wry grin as she turned and double-timed after her squad.

"No worries about that," Mills muttered as he quickly followed after her.

They had just pushed through the front doors of the apartment building when a volley of small arms fire cracked down the length of the street toward the cutter, clearly audible through the roar of the ship's hover engines.

"Return fire!" Mills shouted. "But watch for the civilians!" The last thing he wanted on his hands was a bloodbath of innocent people who got caught in the crossfire.

The Marines immediately unleashed a barrage of accurate rifle fire that quickly silenced their attackers, who turned out to be a pair of militiamen who normally directed traffic, but who were armed with pistols and unwisely decided to try and defend their motherland with them.

The Marines got Sikorsky and his wife aboard, and covered Scarlet as she darted up the rear ramp.

"Time to go, Marines," Mills said on the platoon common channel. Instantly, the three squads reversed their deployment order to board the cutter, with the only difference being that they all piled in through the rear ramp. Faraday already had the cutter gliding forward before the hatch hummed closed.

"Well," Mills said to no one in particular, "that was unexpectedly easy."

"Glad you think so, Top," Faraday told him grimly, "because we've got new orders, straight from the commodore."

"Okay, let's have it," Mills said, wanting to kick himself for his comment about the mission having been easy. *Jinxed yourself, you wanker.*

"The fleet's lost contact with Colonel Grishin's force," Faraday told him. "They want us to do a recon to see if we can regain contact. I've got the coordinates, and that's where we're heading now for our first stop."

"Our first stop?" Mills asked, wondering what would top that.

"Yeah, you'll love this," Faraday said as the cutter accelerated hard, shooting down the street as it gained just enough altitude to skim the tops of the buildings. "The Kreelans have just joined the party upstairs—" Mills and Sabourin exchanged a look, "—and the commodore and some civilian guy on the *Constellation* thought it might be a good idea to send us to go talk some sense into the not-so-saintly leadership of this garden planet about working together against the Kreelans."

"The commodore's off her bloody nut!" Mills exclaimed. "What the devil are we supposed to do? Go to their government buildings and hold the chairman and his minions hostage?"

Faraday took a precious moment to turn around and look at him. "How'd you guess?"

From the expression on the pilot's face, Mills knew he wasn't joking. "What a bloody cockup," he moaned as he slid into an open combat seat, strapping himself in as the cutter bucked and jolted through the air, headed toward where Colonel Grishin's Marines had disappeared.

* * *

At that moment, Grishin was still trying to find a way out of the trap in which he and his Marines were caught. The irony of the boats all having been destroyed was that the wreckage had provided his people some cover from the Russian soldiers on the wall, but there was no way to escape from the massive killing field. Some of his people had taken a run at the main gate that had been blown open by one of the boat pilots, but the Russians had cut them all down. Assaulting the wall itself was out of the question, because they had nothing to scale it with to reach the enemy soldiers along the top. The Marines had at least been able to take out the heavy guns in the towers, using some of their anti-armor weapons to blow the towers to bits. Even with the losses his Marines had inflicted, however, the Russians still enjoyed massive superiority in firepower.

Worse, he knew from imagery the Marine force had received prior to landing that there were armored units garrisoned not far from here. If the Russians sent in tanks, the Marines' only real hope was to knock them out right as they entered through the main gate, blocking the path for other armored vehicles. If even one or two tanks got inside the wall, this battle could be over very quickly.

There was an explosion along the wall near one of the entrances to the underground barracks from where fresh Russian soldiers had been appearing. It was followed by a fierce roar from many voices, punctuated by a massive flurry of firing that, from the distinctive sound, could only be coming from Marine rifles.

Unwilling to believe he could be that lucky, Grishin risked raising up enough to train his field glasses on that part of the wall. "*Merde!*" he exclaimed. "It's the other battalion!"

The battalion of Marines he had originally sent into the massive bunker complex, and that had been trapped when the Russians had closed the massive door and sealed them in, had obviously not given up. Somehow, they had made their way through whatever maze lay in the mountain to find the underground barracks area, and from there had fought their way to the wall surrounding the compound. From what Grishin could see, it was clear that the Russians on the wall had been taken completely by surprise. Charging across the top of the wall, the Marines poured fire into the enemy soldiers. Those Russians who managed to survive the rifle fire were brought down in vicious hand to hand combat.

"Concentrate fire on the center and left flank!" Grishin ordered to his operations officer. The Marines on the wall were to his relative right, and would be vulnerable to fire coming from Russians on other parts of the wall. "We must keep the enemy pinned down so they cannot—"

Grishin's explanation was drowned out by a flight of four Russian aerospace fighters that thundered in low. He watched as the bomb bay doors slid open, the smooth curves of the weapons clearly visible.

It is over, he thought, certain that the weapons were the modern equivalent of the napalm that had once been a popular air to ground weapon on Earth. The walls and the concrete apron would contain the heat, effectively incinerating his entire force.

As the slow-motion movie in his mind continued rolling, he saw streaks of tracer fire from Marine rifles pass by the fighters, and even an anti-armor missile that some industrious Marine had fired. He smiled, proud that his men and women were still fighting, then closed his eyes. He had seen enough death in his time, and had seen the effects of these weapons during the war twenty years ago. He did not want to see them again.

The weapons never fell. Grishin snapped his eyes open again as four explosions shook the ground. Where the four fighters should have been were fireballs that burned through the air to slam into the far wall of the facility, instantly incinerating the Russian soldiers along the top.

That miracle was followed by the appearance of a Confederation warship's cutter, which proceeded to blast the remaining Russian soldiers from the wall. The Russians tried to shoot it down with their hypervelocity missiles, but unlike the assault boats, the cutter carried point defense weapons that were more than adequate to defend it against the non-maneuvering missiles. The ship swept along the wall at low altitude, firing at everything that moved or fired back. Then the cutter's pilot swung the ship outside the wall near the massive entry gate and attacked whatever Saint Petersburg forces were there.

Finally, satisfied that the area was secure for the moment, the pilot brought the ship in to land in the center of the apron, picking a spot that was relatively clear of debris from the hapless assault boats. The rear ramp dropped down and a platoon of Marines charged out, led by someone he instantly recognized.

"First Sergeant Mills," Grishin said as the big Brit rushed over, "I am very, *very* happy to see you!"

"Likewise, sir!" Mills replied with a smile. "Bit of tight spot you were in, sir, it looks like."

"How soon until we can get enough transports to get us back to the fleet?" Grishin asked as he watched Mills's people moving quickly across the apron, gathering up the wounded and moving them to a makeshift aid station close to the cutter where the surviving corpsmen could treat them.

"That's a bit of a problem, sir," Mills said, his smile quickly fading. "We've got orders from the commodore, but they don't include leaving. In fact, she told me that if we found you alive, you're to come with us on our next little joyride."

"And just what might that be?" Grishin asked, sure from Mills's expression that he didn't want to know.

Mills said, "Would you believe we're going to go pay a visit to Chairman Korolev, to see if he would kindly help us with a pesky little Kreelan fleet that's popped into the system?"

FORTY-THREE

"Status," Sato breathed, trying to control the nausea that gripped him. *Radiation poisoning.* Every crew member carried a dosimeter, a device that tracked any exposure to radiation. Normally green, his and those of the other bridge crewmen had turned an ominous amber tinged with red. The situation with much of the rest of the crew was far worse. The bridge was located toward the center of the vessel's hull to help protect it against enemy fire. There were many compartments and systems, however, that were closer to the ship's skin, and far more exposed to the blast of radiation from the nuclear torpedo. While the ship was designed to protect its crew and systems from the radiation typically found in space travel, *Yura's* design specifications had not included providing protection against the torrent of ionizing radiation from nuclear weapons. When the torpedo they had been chasing detonated, the electromagnetic pulse had fried half of the ship's electronic systems, while the radiation had devastated the crew. Sickbay could administer a full scope of treatment for radiation poisoning, but the supplies were limited: they were primarily intended to help crewmen in the engine room should there be an accidental radiation leak from the ship's propulsion systems. There was enough medication to treat a dozen cases of moderate radiation poisoning, but Sato was faced with nearly three hundred, many of them severe.

"We've got auxiliary navigation control back on-line, captain," Bogdanova reported weakly. She had already vomited several times and could barely stand without bracing herself against something. Besides Sato, she was in the best shape of those still functioning on the bridge. Most of the ship's crew was worse, totally unable to function, and Sato had ordered the worst ones taken to their quarters. There was no point in taking them to sick bay: half the crew was already there, vomiting and physically too weak to function. "We've patched enough of life support back together to keep us alive for at least the next forty-eight hours, maybe longer."

"Communications?" he asked.

She shook her head. The movement threw her off balance and she almost fell to the deck. Sato grabbed her arm and held her up. The movement left him weak, his head spinning.

"No luck, sir," she said. "Every component we've swapped in has been burned out. We've tried everything, even the Marine radios, but nothing works." She took a labored breath before continuing. "I've got some people in engineering trying to put together a radio that doesn't use solid state electronics. It's all basic theory, it'll work, allowing us to transmit and receive, but I don't know if anyone will pick it up. Scanning the electromagnetic spectrum for analog radio signals is something survey crews do as part of their survey missions, searching for atomic-era civilizations. Fleet communications officers don't normally look for that sort of thing." Exhausted, she suddenly sat down on the deck, leaning back against one of the bridge support pylons.

Kneeling down beside her, Sato patted her gently on the shoulder and said, "Good work, Bogdanova. You keep this up and you'll have your own command pretty soon." He managed a tired smile, which she wanly returned. "Come on," he told her, forcing himself back to his feet. "We've got to get that radio working." Gripping her hands in his, he pulled her upright. She fell against him momentarily, as if they were in a romantic embrace, but Sato could think of few things less romantic than acute radiation poisoning. "Get back with those engineers and get that radio put together. It's the only thing that might save us."

"Yes, sir," she whispered. Then, gathering up her strength, she stood tall and made her way unsteadily off the bridge, heading for engineering.

Sato collapsed into the combat chair at the navigation console. The other four members of the bridge crew who were still functional glanced up at him to make sure he was all right. "Carry on," he told them, and they turned back to their tasks, swapping out electrical components or jury-rigging analog equivalents to get more of the ship's systems back on-line. "Any luck with the sensors, Avril?" he asked one of the men who was half-buried in an access panel.

"Just a minute, sir, I think I've almost got it..." he rasped. Then, "There! Give that a try, skipper."

Sato activated the controls on the navigation console, and was immediately relieved when the main bridge display lit up.

"We don't have anything but visual right now, sir," Avril told him. "We were able to replace some of the external cameras and get some video feeds going. But the main sensor arrays..." He shook his head. "Going to need some time in dry dock for those. Every relay, amp, and signal processor between the main arrays and the computer core is fried."

"It will do, Mr. Avril," Sato told him. "It will do quite nicely. Damn fine work."

"Thank you, sir," Avril said with a tight smile, one arm clamping around his stomach. "Jesus, captain," he said through clenched teeth at the nausea that tore at his gut, "make sure the galley doesn't serve any more of those damned burritos, will you?"

Despite his own increasing discomfort, the nausea and a pounding headache, the weakness he felt, Sato couldn't help but chuckle. "I'll do that, Mr. Avril," he promised. "I promise."

In the meantime, using the just-repaired navigation controls, Sato brought the ship to a gentle stop. She had been drifting for the last hour, after the torpedo had detonated. Even with the main navigation systems off-line, he knew roughly where they were from basic spacial astrography using Saint Petersburg and its star as reference points. They weren't too far from the planet in astronomical terms, but he wasn't comfortable with navigating blind. Knowing where they were in the system was only half the problem: he needed to know where the task force was, not to mention the Saint Petersburg fleet. There was also the question of the flurry of red target icons that had appeared on the tactical display just as the torpedo exploded, but he was no longer sure if he had seen them or if he had been imagining things. None of the other members of the bridge crew remembered seeing them.

"Captain, this is Bogdanova." Her tinny voice came from a small speaker in a crude metal box that had been insta-glued to the navigation console. Bodganova had brought it up with her from engineering before she updated Sato on the ship's status. It was another analog contraption they had somehow cobbled together, a crude intercom system.

Sato pressed the switch on the jury-rigged device. "Sato here."

"We're ready, sir," she said. He could tell from the sound of her voice that she must be dead — almost literally — on her feet. That only served to make him more desperate to get his people back to the fleet. He had already lost half a dozen people to extreme radiation poisoning, and he would lose many more if they didn't get medical attention soon. "We don't have a lot of options with this. We can pump in plenty of power, so range isn't an issue, but it'll be voice only and totally unencrypted, so friendly or enemy alike will be able to hear it. We can also only transmit on one frequency at a time, so I picked an old emergency navigation frequency that was standard on Earth and is still used on some other worlds."

"It'll work, Bogdanova," he reassured her, praying that it really would. "Let's do it." He had already decided that if the Saint Petersburg fleet responded first, he would put his crew into lifeboats and then scuttle the ship. There was no point in offering battle: *Yura* would require weeks in the yards before she was combat-ready again.

"Okay, sir," she said after a brief pause, "you're live. Just push the button and speak into the intercom like you have been. Whatever you say will be broadcast. Just make sure you let up on the button or you won't hear any reply."

"Understood," he told her, nausea and anticipation warring for supremacy in his stomach. Taking a deep breath, he said, "Mayday, mayday. This is Captain Ichiro Sato of the *CNS Yura* in the Saint Petersburg system, calling any Confederation vessel. We require immediate assistance. Please come in, over."

He heard nothing at all until he remembered to let up on the transmit button. Feeling foolish, he released it and was rewarded with the hiss of static.

He waited a moment, then began his call again. "Mayday, mayday. This is Captain Ichiro Sato of the *CNS Yura...*"

* * *

"Bleed the humans and their ships wisely, my sisters," Tesh-Dar counseled the senior shipmistresses of the fleet, most of whom had not been with her at the battle of Keran. "Remember: we come now to do battle over many cycles, not merely to win a swift victory. More ships come behind us, so you need not worry about being overwhelmed. Give the humans advantage where you so choose, that your combat may bring greater glory to the Empress. They are worthy opponents, and will challenge you and your warriors." She looked around at the projected images of the shipmistresses, all of whom knelt on the command decks of their ships, heads bowed. "Go in Her name," Tesh-Dar ordered. The shipmistresses saluted her, bringing their left hands up to crash against the armor of their right breasts before the images faded.

The fleet had been maneuvering against the larger of the two human forces, not quite letting them get into range as Tesh-Dar tested them, seeking to understand these new opponents. It seemed that humans had many clans, at least one per world, and perhaps even more, and this was reflected in the combat style of their ships and warriors. The group her fleet now faced used little finesse, but instead charged forward like a massive bludgeon. Their ships were powerfully armed, more so than the ships she had faced at Keran, and she would have to inform the builders to upgrade the next crop of ships they were growing. She was willing to confer tactical advantage to the humans, but would not allow her warriors to be needlessly slaughtered in obsolete vessels.

Still, the human who commanded this fleet was clumsy, as if she had never before wielded her — or *his*, she reminded herself, remembering that both female and male humans were sentient — fleet as a unified weapon. The human ships charged forward in a great mass, guns blazing, while her own ships, like a school of gigantic predatory fish, raked the enemy vessels with fire before darting gracefully away.

Turning her attention for a moment to the other, smaller group of human ships, she recognized some of their designs from the battle of Keran. It was incomprehensible to her that the two human groups would have been fighting one another in the face of the Empire's invasion. On the other hand, she consoled herself, they were alien, with alien thoughts and beliefs. Understanding them was not her mission; it was likely she could never understand them, even if she tried. Finding the One whose blood would sing was why she was here, why they brought what would be many cycles of warfare to the humans. And if the One were not found, Tesh-Dar and her sisters would eventually exterminate the humans from the galaxy, just before the light of the Empire itself was extinguished.

"My priestess," Li'ara-Zhurah spoke suddenly from behind her. "We are picking up a strange signal from one of the human ships, located away from the two main groups."

Tesh-Dar turned in her chair just as a salvo from her command ship thundered, sending a broadside of heavy kinetic rounds toward their human opponents. The star field in the main display whirled as the shipmistress maneuvered the ship to clear some of the humans' incoming fire. "What type of signal?" she asked, curious. The human communications systems were far more complex than anything the Kreelan ships of a similar technology level had ever used; the Bloodsong communicated far more information between Her Children than any human could ever imagine. Tesh-

Dar's ships used mainly voice and a primitive type of holographic display, normally transmitted — in the time when these ships were first designed, over a hundred thousand years ago — by basic electromagnetic waves.

"It is a radio signal," Li'ara-Zhurah said, perplexed. "These ships on which we now sail commonly use such signals, but we have not seen such a basic emanation from a human ship before. It is a human voice that repeats the same message."

Frowning, Tesh-Dar rose from her chair and came to stand beside Li'ara-Zhurah, who looked over the shoulder of the warrior who worked the communications console. "Play it for me," the priestess ordered.

Over the speaker she could hear words spoken in a human language. She could not understand the words, but the lilt of the creature's speech, the timbre of the voice, sounded familiar, and a sense of trepidation mixed with excitement suddenly flooded through her. "I recognize that voice," she whispered. The signal was strong and clear, and while the human male who spoke clearly must be injured or exhausted, to judge from the sound of its voice, she nonetheless knew beyond a shadow of a doubt who it was. "It is the Messenger."

Li'ara-Zhurah snapped her head around to stare at Tesh-Dar for a moment before she realized what she was doing and lowered her eyes in respect. "Fools, they are," she hissed, "to risk him yet again!"

Tesh-Dar *humphed*. "Indeed, daughter," she said. "Is it so surprising? They do not understand the Way." In the Way of their people, from a tradition that was born in the mists of time long before the founding of the First Empire a hundred thousand years earlier, the Messenger was held sacred, sacrosanct in a way that few other things were among Her Children.

Closing her eyes, Tesh-Dar reached out across space with her mind, her second sight taking in the human ships, then speeding beyond them. She could see the signal in her mind like gentle ocean waves. Following them to their source, she found the Messenger's ship. Passing through the hull, she was distraught when she saw the condition of the crew. They were dying, all of them, from the radiation released by one of the nuclear weapons the larger human force had fired upon them before the Empress intervened. Many would live for a few weeks, at most, but all would die unless they were treated, and quickly.

She found him then, sitting at a console on his ship's command deck. He looked so much older now than when she had last seen him, when she had returned him to his people, the sole survivor of his crew and the bearer of tidings of war. She could see and hear him speak into a small, ungainly box, his voice eventually reaching her ears here. She could not understand what he said, but she knew that, like any shipmistress, he would be trying to save his ship, his crew.

With a great sigh, her second sight faded and she opened her eyes to the reality around her. "He is dying," she said with great sadness.

Li'ara-Zhurah, too, was deeply saddened. "Can we do nothing?" she whispered softly.

Tesh-Dar settled her gaze on Li'ara-Zhurah, her heart swelling with pride that her young successor would even consider, let alone say, such a thing. Truly, she had come far in her spiritual journey since the dark days her soul faced after Keran. "I shall give you a ship," Tesh-Dar told her. "Healers are forbidden here, but you may take some of the healing gel we carry with us to care for him." She was not worried about the potential harm to Li'ara-Zhurah or her unborn child from any residual radiation in the Messenger's ship. The Children of the Empress were highly resistant to radiation poisoning, and any ill effects they suffered could be cured by the healers who remained in the support ships that waited well behind the assault fleet.

"Yes, my priestess," Li'ara-Zhurah said, kneeling to the floor. Tesh-Dar had given her a very great honor. Command of a ship for as junior a warrior as she was honor enough. But to protect the Messenger was far, far beyond it.

Tesh-Dar put her hand on Li'ara-Zhurah's shoulder. "Take care, my daughter," she said. "You are not to risk yourself, even for him. For you are not only my chosen successor, but you are with child, and I forbid you to put yourself in danger."

"I understand, Tesh-Dar," the young warrior said, bowing her head deeper, her heart open to her priestess and the Empress, to her entire race, through the Bloodsong. "It shall be as you say."

Tesh-Dar nodded, satisfied. "Go then, my child, in Her name."

Li'ara-Zhurah saluted, then turned to leave the command deck, bound for a boat that would take her to her first command and the greatest honor of her young life.

* * *

"...Please come in, over." Sato let up on the transmit button for the last time. He had been transmitting over and over for the last half hour with no response. Unable to help himself, he leaned forward, resting his head on the navigation console, exhausted. He had vomited twice since starting his radio vigil, but had kept at it until he simply couldn't utter another word. The other bridge crewmen lay on the deck, resting from their exertions trying to get the bridge functional again.

Just a quick break, Sato told himself. *A short rest. Then you have to start again.* He was terrified that if he stopped for more than a few minutes, he wouldn't have the strength to resume the mayday calls.

After taking in a few deep breaths and forcing himself to ignore the worsening nausea tearing at his insides, Sato looked up at the main bridge display.

"Captain," came Bogdanova's voice from the intercom. "Are you seeing what I'm seeing on the primary display?" She was obviously looking at one of the monitors in engineering that echoed the video feed on the bridge.

"Yes," Sato said, the nausea in his gut quickly overtaken by an even more unpleasant sensation: the cold knife of fear. "I see it." He stared stupidly at the intercom box. "Bogdanova, is there any way I can address the crew on this?"

"No sir," she said apologetically. "It only works from the bridge to here, and to the radio transmitter. We haven't had time to rig anything else yet."

"It's not a problem," he reassured her. "You and the rest of the crew have done a great job." He paused, looking again at the display, his hands clenching in frustration. *As if things weren't bad enough already*, he thought. "We'll just have to do this the old fashioned way," he told her. "Pass the word among the crew: stand by to maneuver."

"Stand by to maneuver, aye," she echoed. "You have maneuvering control from the navigation console there, sir," she reminded him.

"Understood," Sato said, the adrenaline pumping into his system now helping to offset the effects of the radiation poisoning. For a time. "Avril," he called as he began to move the *Yura*, "pass the word along from here to anyone who can hear you down the passageways: the ship is maneuvering." Taking another look at the image on the main display, he added, "And have every crewman who can move get to their battle stations."

Plainly visible now against the velvet black of space and the glowing disk of Saint Petersburg was the unmistakable silhouette of a Kreelan warship, sailing directly toward them.

FORTY-FOUR

"Dammit," Commodore Hanson breathed as she watched the Saint Petersburg fleet try to close with the Kreelans. Again. They were inflicting some damage, but the alien ships had an almost uncanny ability to dance out of the way of incoming fire, preventing the Russians from making a decisive engagement. This was totally unlike the Kreelan tactics — if that was the term — used during the battle of Keran, where they simply bored in, all guns blazing (much as the Russians were doing now, she noted). In comparison, this was death by a thousand paper cuts.

The political situation contributed to her frustration. She had already tried twice to assist the Russian fleet, but each time they had fired on her task force as soon as they had come into range. While she was sorely tempted to fire back, to earn some payback for the loss of *Myoko* and *Yura*, if nothing else, she restrained the urge. The lives of millions of people were at stake: she *had* to find a way to make the Saint Petersburg government cooperate. She had tried to convince them peacefully through reason when she had spoken with Chairman Korolev. Now, using the Marines on the planet who had survived the devastating ambush Grishin had reported from *Yura's* cutter, she was trying something that the Russians were perhaps better prepared to understand.

* * *

"This is nuts," Faraday muttered as he guided his cutter at treetop height through the middle of Saint Petersburg City. The threat display was showing a dozen crimson icons, ground defenses and inbound fighters, that were trying to find them. The only thing saving them thus far was that they were literally lost in the clutter of the buildings of downtown. Navigating through the tight turns necessary to follow the streets, while keeping them alive, also had him in a cold sweat. "If we had an extra coat of paint, colonel, we'd be scraping the sides off these buildings."

"You are doing just fine," Grishin told him calmly, standing in the aisle, leaning against the bulkhead at the rear of the flight deck, seemingly impervious to the sharp turns the cutter was making. "It is not much further."

The threat display chirped for attention. "Standby point defense," the copilot said tensely. A pair of fighters had found them. "Firing!"

The hull was suddenly filled with a deep ripping sound as the point defense lasers fired. The two icons of the inbound fighters suddenly disappeared.

"Targets destroyed," the copilot reported. "We can hold them off as long as they send in their fighters a few at a time and we don't get too close to any ground defenses, but sooner or later somebody's going to figure that out and they'll swarm us."

"We will be finished long before that happens," Grishin assured him.

Faraday glanced at the colonel, turning over in his mind the very different possible meanings of what Grishin had said. He grimaced as he turned his attention back to flying.

In the rear, the Marines were strapped in but anxious to get off of the wildly maneuvering ship. Near the front, next to Grishin, sat Valentina, with Sikorsky and Ludmilla across from her. Both of them were wide-eyed with fear. Valentina had asked them to stay with the larger force of Marines that was now rushing into the city from the base where they had been ambushed, using trucks and armored vehicles they had liberated from the Russian garrison. The two had refused, however, both declaring in no uncertain terms that they felt their best chance of survival was with Valentina.

Looking at the two of them, Valentina felt a deep pang of regret. Despite the tragedies that had rocked their lives, Sikorsky and Ludmilla were still deeply in love. They held on tightly to one another, most of the time with their eyes closed. But when they were open, they were looking at Valentina. And every time they did, a little more of their fear seemed to fall away. She felt unworthy of their trust and confidence, and prayed that she wouldn't fail them.

As if reading her mind, Sikorsky reached across the aisle and took her hands in one of his. Squeezing them tightly, he gave her a brave smile.

Valentina did her best to smile back, but her expression faltered. She was surprised: lying and deceit were second nature to her as part of her profession, but for some reason she was unable to put on one of her many masks for Sikorsky. What he saw now was the unvarnished truth of her, a face that she had shown to precious few people, a face that now betrayed uncertainty.

Standing in the aisle ahead of them, Grishin stared out the cutter's massive windscreen, watching as the ship finally broke free of the last ring of buildings and the city center appeared. Here was the government complex, a poor copy of the old Kremlin in Moscow back on Earth, only uglier, Grishin thought. The original Kremlin and the city in which it had stood had been destroyed in the wars before the Diaspora, but its oppressive architectural ideals, particularly from the time of Josef Stalin, had somehow been preserved. Growing up here, Grishin had loved the monolithic majesty of the massive skyscrapers surrounding the center of government. As a young man, he had happily, almost deliriously, embraced the tenets of the Party and joined the Red Army. His happy delirium had lasted for a brief five years before being transformed into barely suppressed horror at what he had been called upon to do during the war with Earth and the Alliance. Yet he had done his duty, and suffered the consequences in the war's aftermath. One of many accused — with just reason, he thought guiltily — of war crimes, he had managed to escape off-planet, eventually starting a new life in the Alliance Foreign Legion.

Looking out at the monolithic structures that surrounded the faux Kremlin, he felt a wave of hatred wash over him for the men and the ideas that had turned his planet into a war zone twice in as many decades, and had forced him from his home.

As they approached the walled fortress, flying low over the massive square that had hosted gigantic military parades before the last war, and surely before this one, Grishin was surprised that Korolev had not erected a mausoleum in which to entomb himself upon his death and preserve his carcass for the benefit of future generations. Of course, Grishin thought darkly, perhaps Korolev thought himself immortal. If so, that was a delusion that Grishin would be quite happy to dispel.

"Stand by," he told his Marines as the cutter soared over the impressive wall of red brick surrounding the government buildings themselves. The point defense lasers ripped again, sweeping a dozen surprised but heavily armed ceremonial guards from the top of the wall and the entrance to the Central Chamber where the Party Council met.

His plan was absurdly simple: the cutter would put down in the open square in front of the Central Chamber, then Grishin would lead his Marines in, hoping to catch Korolev and the senior members of the Party and bring them to their senses. He knew that the buildings were guarded by a battalion of ceremonial guards who were extremely well-trained and equipped. Normally that would have made odds that were nothing short of suicidal for a single platoon of Marines, but with the fire support from the cutter and the element of surprise on his side, he believed they had a fighting chance. They only had to hold out for thirty minutes: that was how long it would take for the survivors of his brigade to reach them.

Turning around, he looked at Sikorsky and his wife, then at Valentina. "Are you sure about this?" he asked. While he understood the sentiment all too well, he thought the idea of taking the two Sikorskys in with them was utter madness. "I cannot detail any Marines to protect them."

"I'll take care of them, colonel," Valentina replied, meeting his gaze. She understood that he wasn't making it a personal issue; it was simply a tactical reality. "And we'll help watch your back." She held a shortened heavy assault rifle that looked far too large for her hands, and at her feet lay a sniper rifle in a case that, when the weapon was assembled, was a full two meters long.

Any doubts Grishin may have had about her ability to use either weapon had been dispelled by Mills's quiet account of the devastation she had wrought on the secret police squad in the Sikorskys' apartment. He thought her embellishment of his little attack plan was insane, but in a very Russian way. Despite himself, Grishin smiled. He liked this woman. "*Khorosho*," he said before bellowing, "On your feet, Marines!"

As one, the platoon, led by Mills and Sabourin, got to their feet and readied their weapons.

"Stand by!" Faraday said tensely, and the Marines held on tightly to their grab bars as he swung the cutter — a small ship by Navy standards, but huge compared to most aerospace vehicles — in tightly next to the Central Chamber building. "Now!"

The doors hummed open, and the Marines quickly filed out, followed by Valentina and the Sikorskys, with Dmitri clutching a submachine pistol and carrying Valentina's sniper rifle and extra ammunition.

The pilot waited until the last Marine had one foot on the ground before closing the hatches and lifting off into a protective orbit low around the government buildings.

In a break from their normal tactics, the Marines did not bother to form a protective perimeter around the cutter as they debarked, but simply raced inside the building, trying to keep up with Grishin.

Behind them, Valentina led the Sikorskys in the opposite direction, heading for the huge clock tower that rose above the wall's main gate.

* * *

"Marshal Antonov!" one of the communications technicians called, his voice urgent.

"What is it?" Antonov said, grudgingly turning away from the display of the indecisive battle still raging in space.

"The Ceremonial Guards commander reports that the Central Chamber is under attack."

"Put him on vidcom," Antonov snapped.

Instantly the Red Army colonel in charge of the Ceremonial Guards came on. "Comrade Marshal," he reported breathlessly, "the entire government complex is under attack by Confederation Marines."

"What happened?" Antonov asked.

The colonel hesitated before answering. Antonov could hear a sudden burst of automatic weapons fire, followed by screaming. "We are under attack by Confederation Marines, comrade marshal. We thought at first it was just the Central Chamber," he said. "Then my quick reaction force came under fire from Confederation troops somewhere on the wall. Many of my men are still pinned down, but I have called for reinforcements from the local garrisons."

Korolev had been listening intently. "They think we are there," he thought aloud. "The Confederation fools are trying to capture us!"

Antonov nodded. They are courageous, he thought, if not terribly bright.

"Kill them," Korolev ordered. "Kill them all, colonel. Do not bother with prisoners. We do not need any."

"Understood, Comrade Chairman," the colonel said, his expression on the vidcom conveying both relief and satisfaction. "It will be my pleasure."

"Carry on," Antonov ordered before closing the connection.

"Sir," a tactical controller called out a moment later, "there is a Confederation ship that is separate from their main group, heading on a bearing toward orbit." He paused a moment, looking at fresh data that was being provided by the orbital sensor stations. "It appears to be one of the ships we had believed destroyed by Admiral Voroshilov's nuclear torpedoes in the first engagement. It is being followed by one of the newcomer ships."

Antonov frowned at the mention of the "newcomer" ships. Korolev was firmly convinced they were nothing more than additional Confederation vessels, but Antonov had been having second thoughts after watching the ongoing space battle and discussing the situation with Voroshilov over vidcom. These newcomers were totally different in design from the known Confederation ships, and their tactics were certainly nothing like what Saint Petersburg's intelligence services had reported. He was not sure what they were, but he was sure what they were not, and they were *not* Confederation ships. He was not ready to challenge Korolev's assessment, however. At least, not yet.

"Voroshilov's forces are fully engaged," Antonov mused. "Do we have anything else available to intercept?"

"There are five orbital defense vessels on patrol, comrade marshal," the controller replied, highlighting the ships on his display. "They are not fast, but are well-armed. Together they may be able to engage both ships." He looked up at Antonov. "The lead enemy vessel, the one that we believe was damaged by one of the nuclear torpedoes, must have taken severe radiation damage, comrade marshal. Unless its hull was specially shielded, the crew is almost certainly suffering from severe radiation poisoning, and many of the electronic components will have been destroyed or damaged. That ship should be an easy prize. The other vessel following it is roughly the same size, but its configuration is unknown."

"Have the defense vessels depart their stations and engage both ships," Antonov ordered without hesitation. "Order them to capture the lead vessel if they can, but they are not to take unnecessary risks."

* * *

Neither the Russian nor French languages had sufficiently potent curses to express Grishin's sentiments as he burst into the Committee Chamber, weapon drawn and a full squad of Marines behind him.

It was dark and empty.

"*Fuck!*" he hissed, settling on an ancient English expression out of helpless frustration. "Have you found anyone upstairs?" he asked urgently into his comm set.

"Negative, sir," said the squad leader who had taken his Marines upstairs to the main cabinet offices. "This place is a ghost town. None of the leadership is here, no gofers, not even secretaries. We found a few cleaning crews, but that's all." He paused, then said, "Orders, sir?"

"Regroup by the main entrance," Grishin told him, "and prepare for extraction." *Korolev must have a wartime bunker somewhere*, he thought, *something they built since the last war*. Something Grishin knew nothing about.

"Sir?" Mills asked from behind him.

"It is time for us to leave, Mills," Grishin told him. "They are not here." They had fought a brief but intense battle with the Ceremonial Guard troops in the building, losing three Marines in the process. All for nothing. "Let's go."

He followed Mills and Sabourin back toward the main entrance, the other Marines moving watchfully beside them.

"What is the situation outside?" Grishin asked the second squad leader, whose Marines were stationed near the main entrance.

"Scary as hell, sir," the squad leader reported, "at least for the Russkies. Whoever that bitch is with the sniper rifle, she sure knows how to use it. We got tired of counting her kills, and none of my folks have had to fire a shot yet..."

* * *

Valentina knew their luck would soon run out, but she was determined to give Grishin what he needed more than anything else right now: time. She had nearly two companies of Russian troops pinned down around the open square leading to the Central Chamber building. The massive rifle she now held snugged up tight to her shoulder was a distant descendant of the famous Barrett Model 82A1 that had been widely used by United States military forces through most of the first half of the twenty-first century. Unlike the now-ancient Model 82A1, however, the rifle she now used fired not massive .50 caliber bullets, but tungsten sabot rounds, fired by a powerful liquid propellant. The projectiles were small enough that a single magazine held fifty, yet they were incredibly dense and packed a devastating punch. Combined with an advanced thermo-optic sight and targeting computer, she could kill targets at ranges of nearly five kilometers if she had clear line of sight. The men she had been killing today, however, were much closer: mere hundreds of meters, which was just far enough to put her out of their effective range. She could kill them at will, but they could only hope that one of their bullets would get lucky, if they wanted to risk shooting at her in the first place. Since she had plenty of ammunition — Sikorsky was carrying four additional magazines — she had been able to effectively neutralize the enemy troops who had not been inside the buildings. If one of the soldiers exposed so much as a hand or a foot, she fired, and the resulting damage to the target was generally lethal.

Her only real worry was that enemy troops might try to swarm the clock tower from along the wall, or that an air strike would get past the cutter that patrolled above.

"To the left, behind the fountain," Sikorsky told her. He was looking through the spotting scope that had been in the rifle's case, helping her look for targets.

Behind them, Ludmilla watched the entrance to the clock tower behind them, nervously holding the submachine pistol that Sikorsky had brought. Valentina had booby-trapped the stairwell leading up to their position, but it never hurt to have a set of human eyes watching.

Following Sikorsky's cue, she shifted her aim slightly, the big weapon's electronic sight immediately picking up the thermal signature of the three soldiers who were trying to low-crawl their way toward the Central Chamber building, using a small decorative wall for cover. They had not yet learned that her weapon was powerful enough to shoot through a foot of reinforced concrete and kill a man on the other side.

"Firing," she announced before holding her breath and stroking the trigger. The weapon fired with a deafening boom, the recoil against her shoulder shoving her back a few centimeters.

Sikorsky watched as the three soldiers disappeared in an explosion of stone and flesh. Unlike a standard rifle, which usually simply punched holes through the human body, the rounds from this weapon literally blew them apart. Having been an infantryman during the war against Earth and the Alliance, he could imagine the terror of the men down there in the square, knowing that they would not merely be shot, but blown to bits, if they were not behind solid cover, and if they did not *stay* there. Valentina's aim was supernatural, and her eyesight must also have been exquisite, for she had seen movement and picked out targets that he had barely seen with his more powerful spotting scope. In all, Valentina had killed fifty-six enemy soldiers in the brief time since they had taken up residence in the clock tower, including what he believed must have been virtually all of the enemy battalion's officers and senior NCOs. Leading their men headlong across the square to the Central Chamber building as part of the quick reaction force called in against the Marines, Valentina had massacred them.

The butchery, while gruesome, had reinforced his faith that she was the best chance of survival he and Ludmilla had.

Valentina was scanning for more targets when she heard Grishin's voice in her earphone.

"Scarlet," he said, "they are not here. This was all for nothing."

"Shit," she said in response.

"*Da*," he said. "Exactly so. I am ordering the rest of the brigade to not bother coming here, but to head to the main spaceport to secure it if they can. They will need to find a ship we can use to get back to the fleet. We will pull out from here using the cutter, and then provide the brigade with fire support as they assault the spaceport." He paused. "With the enemy troops now so close to the building here..."

"Don't worry, colonel," she promised. "I'll cover you as you load up the cutter. We'll be ready to hop on board as you cross over the wall."

"Be careful, *dorogaya*," he said. "And good hunting."

"Dmitri, Ludmilla!" Valentina called out. "We're pulling out of here. We have to cover the Marines as they move from the Central Chamber building to the cutter, then they'll pick us up on the way out." She turned to look at each of them in turn. "The Ceremonial Guards will do everything they can to stop us. Be prepared."

"We are ready," Sikorsky answered, and Ludmilla nodded before turning back to watching the door behind them.

Above them, the drone of the cutter's engines suddenly became louder, just before its point defense lasers ripped through the sky.

* * *

Grishin cringed as the sky around the government complex suddenly seemed to explode. The Russians had fired a volley of anti-aircraft missiles at the cutter, trying to saturate its defenses. The point-defense lasers were up to the task, but barely. He could see where the ship's hull was pitted and scored by shrapnel from one of the missile warheads, and he hoped the hull hadn't been penetrated. If it had, the cutter would no longer be spaceworthy until it could be patched.

The ship dove over the wall surrounding the complex, the lasers firing at any enemy troops who were exposed. The pilot managed to maneuver the ship right up next to the Central Chamber building, the ramps already down.

"Get aboard!" Grishin ordered. "Quickly!"

The Marines needed no coaxing. In a fast but orderly manner, they ran up the ramp, diving into their seats inside.

The Russian troops huddling around the fountains, concrete benches, and other bits of cover afforded in the square suddenly came to life. Even with most of their officers gone, they knew that this was their last and probably best chance to kill the Marines. As one, they knelt and stood up and began to pour fire into the cutter, with those who were in throwing distance preparing their grenades.

The cutter's point defense lasers sent a cascade of emerald beams across the square, vaporizing half a dozen men. But the geometry was bad: the weapons simply couldn't be brought to bear against most of the now-berserk Russians, half of whom had gotten to their feet and were charging toward the vulnerable rear of the cutter, their enraged howling nearly as loud as the cutter's hover engines.

Amid the bedlam, two Russian soldiers calmly readied hypervelocity missiles that could obliterate a heavily armored tank.

* * *

"Firing!" Valentina hissed as she pulled the trigger, blasting a Russian soldier who had been cocking his arm to throw a grenade. The grenade fell to the ground and exploded, sending several other soldiers flying. She selected another target and fired, then again and again. "*Blyad*," she cursed, "they're rushing the ship!"

She whipped her head to the side as an assault rifle went off right next to her: it was Dmitri, using the rifle she had carried up here, doing what he could to help stop the attacking Russians. He could not fire accurately at this range, but he didn't have to: if a bullet landed almost anywhere in the square down there, it would hit a Russian soldier.

"Keep shooting!" he shouted at her as he fired short bursts into the mass of screaming Russian troops that were now surging toward the cutter.

Putting her eyes to the electronic scope again, Valentina tried to sort out the most important targets in the swirling mass of bodies. She caught another soldier about to throw a grenade, blowing his torso to pieces, the tungsten needle continuing on to shred three other soldiers before it stopped. She had to be careful, because if one of those slugs hit the cutter, it would punch right through the hull. *Boom*. Another grenade thrower went down. *Boom*. Four soldiers who had lined up in a perfect row as they ran now lay together in death.

Her first magazine empty, she quickly changed it, keeping her eyes glued to the cutter. She watched in amazement as several small objects arced over the top of the cutter from the far side where the Marines were dashing aboard: grenades they had blindly tossed over the ship into the attacking Russians. They exploded almost simultaneously, wiping away most of the lead rank of attackers, but there were more behind them. Many more.

"Reloading!" Dmitri cried as he popped out his weapon's empty magazine and slammed another home.

Valentina did the same, ramming the massive magazine for her weapon into its slot and pulling the charging handle to chamber a round. There was a brief hissing sound as a tiny amount of liquid propellant was vaporized in the weapon's breech, and a tiny green ready light glowed.

"Firing!" she announced again, beginning a rapid series of shots that echoed among the government buildings like God's own thunder. Attacking soldiers were blown apart one after another. Just as the first Russians got close enough to the cutter that Valentina dared not fire on them, the attack faltered, her continued hammer blows having literally gutted their advance.

At last, after what had seemed a lifetime but was really less than a minute, the cutter lifted off, the pilot shearing the top from an old oak tree that stood near the Central Chamber building. Free now of the intervening obstacles that had kept them largely silent while the ship was on the ground, the cutter's point defense lasers tore through the Russian troops who now stood in the middle of the square, firing up at the ship's belly as it passed overhead.

"Valentina!" Sikorsky shouted desperately. "*Missile launcher, behind the main fountain!*"

Cursing under her breath, Valentina lowered her muzzle, searching for the target Dmitri had called out. She only saw troops standing, blazing away at the cutter. She didn't see any missile...there! The two soldiers were blocked by several others; she could only see the tip of the missile in its launcher tube, slowly tracking the cutter. As if in slow motion, she saw a plume of white smoke from the ejection charge puff to the rear, boosting the missile out of the launch tube just as she pulled the trigger.

"*No!*" Sikorsky cried as the missile's motor ignited and it raced through the air like lightning toward the cutter.

Valentina had lost sight of the launcher when she fired, her weapon's recoil knocking her back. She lowered the big rifle to stare at the scene: she could see that the launch crew was dead, along with the soldiers in front of them, but she realized that she had been just a fraction of a second too late. "*Nam konets,*" she said, her heart in her throat. "We're fucked."

The missile streaked toward the cutter, blowing off one of its horizontal stabilizers in a cascade of sparks and flying metal shards.

In that instant, Valentina realized that her last round had made a difference: the missile's aim must have been knocked off by just a hair when her shot vaporized the man's torso.

The ship wobbled, but remained steady as it headed directly for them. She knew it would not be spaceworthy, but would get them at least as far as the spaceport. Probably.

"Dmitri!" Ludmilla suddenly cried as a hollow boom echoed from the stairwell behind them: someone had set off Valentina's booby-trap.

"Get behind me!" Valentina cried as she got to her feet. Moving away from the courtyard side of the wall, which was now being hit by a hail of gunfire as the angry Russian mob below fired at the approaching cutter, she knelt next to one of the pillars supporting the huge clock above them, aiming the big rifle at the door. Ludmilla crouched on the other side of the pillar, with Sikorsky standing next to Valentina. "You get her on the boat!" Valentina ordered him.

"We are not leaving without you!" he told her angrily as the cutter swung parallel to the wall, the pilot clearly wrestling with the controls after the loss of the stabilizer.

The door exploded outward with the force of several grenades that had been thrown by the troops coming up the stairwell. Valentina did not even bother to wait for a target: she just began to fire rhythmically into the smoke-filled doorway. Parts of a man flew out of the smoke, then more.

Then one of them low-crawled through the doorway, below her line of sight. He fired his weapon at her on full automatic, and her body flew back against the red brick of the pillar, dancing like a marionette as the bullets slammed into her. She slumped to the ground, leaving wide streaks of blood on the brick pillar.

The soldier's success was cut short by a vicious burst of rifle fire from the cutter: Mills hung out of the open hatch, Sabourin holding onto his utility belt to keep him from falling, smoke swirling from the muzzle of his rifle. One of the other Marines pumped a magazine of rifle-fired grenades down the stairwell, blowing apart the other Russians still inside.

Sabourin let go of Mills as the cutter bounced against the side of the wall, and he jumped to where Dmitri and Ludmilla knelt next to Valentina. He moved to scoop her up, but Dmitri pushed him away.

"I will take her," he said, tears running down his face. "I will carry her."

With Ludmilla weeping beside him, he gathered up Valentina's shattered body in his arms and carried her aboard the cutter, a grim-faced Mills covering his back.

FORTY-FIVE

"The Messenger moves away from us," the senior warrior at the tactical station reported, "toward the planet."

"He fears us," Li'ara-Zhurah replied from her position in the ship's command chair. She was in many ways junior to most of the other warriors on the ship, but they acceded to her authority both because she was Tesh-Dar's chosen one, and because the pendants she had earned in battle placed her higher on the steps to the throne. Her own self-confidence had wavered slightly when she had first come aboard the ship, after Tesh-Dar had given her permission to assist the Messenger and heal him. Yet after a few moments in the command chair, her fears of any inadequacy faded away: she was a blood daughter of the Empress, and to this she had been born. "He does not understand the Way, nor his place in it, Ulan-Tyr."

Ulan-Tyr nodded understanding, although the emotions flowing in her Bloodsong betrayed her skepticism. She did not doubt the Messenger's place or importance, only the concept that he could not comprehend it himself.

They continued to pursue the fleeing human ship, gradually closing the range. At first, Li'ara-Zhurah had been surprised that the humans had not fired on their pursuers, but then remembered that nuclear detonations could destroy the primitive electronic components that were critical to the functioning of ships of this technological epoch. The Messenger's ship apparently had some sensors remaining that could detect other ships, but no functioning weapons with which to engage them. This made Li'ara-Zhurah's mission much, much easier: otherwise, the human ship would have been able to fire on her with impunity, for she could not return fire without fear of harming the Messenger whom she had come to save. The nature of her mission also required her to board the other ship, to take the healing gel to the Messenger. She suspected that the ship's crew would be largely incapacitated from radiation poisoning, but she knew enough about humans after fighting them on Keran not to underestimate them. Her mission of mercy would not be bloodless.

"Mistress!" Ulan-Tyr suddenly called for her. "Five human vessels are breaking from low orbit and moving to intercept the Messenger's ship!"

Li'ara-Zhurah got up from the command chair and moved closer to the tactical display. "Are these ships native to this world, of the fleet that launched the nuclear weapons?"

"They were not part of the main body, mistress," Ulan-Tyr said as she analyzed the information the ship's computer provided, "but they appear to be of this world, not of the Messenger's fleet."

"All ahead flank!" Li'ara-Zhurah ordered. She had been closing on the Messenger's ship gradually, in hopes he might understand that she meant him no harm. Had any of her warriors been able to speak his language, she would even have attempted to communicate with him. As it was, there was no point: each of them would only hear gibberish from the other. This was clearly a case where action would speak far louder than words; she hoped he would understand her intentions.

* * *

"Captain! *Captain!*"

Sato heard a familiar voice as if he were at the bottom of a deep well and they were shouting down at him from the opening far above. Unwillingly, he forced his eyes open. He was still on the bridge, slumped in his command chair, the combat straps holding him in place. He turned to see Bogdanova, now sitting at the navigation console. She looked terrible, just like he felt. "What is it, Bogdanova?" he asked, nearly choking on the taste of blood in his mouth. Only through a supreme effort of will was he able to keep himself from throwing up.

"The Kreelan ship following us must have gone to flank speed, sir," she rasped. On the main display, the enemy ship was quickly closing the gap between them.

"Are they in firing range?" Sato asked, confused.

"Sir, they've been in range of our weapons — if they were working — for at least ten minutes, maybe more. So I assume they could have hit us, too."

She suddenly doubled over, groaning, as a wave of nausea hit her. Sato empathized with her, but there was nothing he could do. There was nothing any of them could do. Every one of them was a dead man or woman walking. Even if they could get to a major planetside hospital, he doubted that most of his crew could be saved.

"I wonder why they suddenly accelerated," Sato mused as Bogdanova pushed herself back upright, panting.

"Because of these...I think, captain," she managed. On the main screen two bright objects, clearly ships, were heading straight for them, the glowing disk of Saint Petersburg behind them. "There are ships coming up from Saint Petersburg, sir," Bogdanova rasped. "It's hard to tell without the main sensors, but I think they may be some of the coast guard vessels. I can only find two, but it's possible there may be more. Coming right for us."

"Is this radio still rigged up?" Sato asked suddenly.

"Yes, sir," she said, nodding.

Sato pushed the radio transmit button. "Saint Petersburg vessels approaching CNS *Yura*, be advised that we surrender. Repeat: we surrender! Our crew is suffering from acute radiation poisoning and needs medical attention—" He broke off as he saw flashes winking from the two ships visible on the screen, and then flashes from three more ships that were in the planet's shadow, hidden in the darkness. "Damn them!" he hissed. "All hands, brace for impact," he shouted. "Pass the word!" As the crewmen relayed his warning to the rest of the ship, he ordered, "Helm, bring us to two-three-six mark one-six-five. Can we get any more speed out of engineering?"

"We're at redline now, sir," Bogdanova reported as the ship began to turn sluggishly to port, her bow raising up over Saint Petersburg's north pole.

Sato gritted his teeth in frustration as he watched the scene on the display move all too slowly.

"Engineering could only get one fusion core operating and stable," she explained, "so we're only at twenty percent of full power."

Sato had known that, of course, but something didn't add up. *The Kreelan ship,* he suddenly realized. *We were a sitting duck. Why hadn't they closed the range and finished us off,* he wondered, *instead of creeping up behind them until the Saint Petersburg ships showed up?*

"Estimated time to impact?" Sato asked. The Russian ships had continued to fire, pouring a steady stream of shells in their direction. Sato had no doubt that no matter how he maneuvered, *Yura* would be heading into a solid wall of steel, and there wasn't a damn thing he could do about it.

Bogdanova and the other handful of bridge crewmen turned to him with pained expressions on their faces.

"Without the sensors, or at least some way of gauging the range to the enemy ships, we have no way of knowing, sir," Avril said quietly. "But probably soon."

"Look!" Bogdanova cried as the main display suddenly filled with the bulk of the sleek Kreelan warship as it pulled alongside *Yura*, matching her course and speed with uncanny precision. "What are they doing?"

Sato clenched his hands on the arm rests of his combat chair, waiting for a cloud of warriors to spring forth from the enemy vessel, warriors they would be powerless to repel with most of the ship's combat systems inoperative and its crew, including the Marines who had remained aboard, largely incapacitated.

He waited, but they didn't come. Then, in a moment of utter clarity, he understood that the Kreelan ship had placed itself between *Yura* and the Saint Petersburg ships. "Good, God," he breathed. "They're shielding us!"

As he spoke, the Kreelan ship was surrounded with a halo of crimson and emerald fireworks as the weapons on her far side began to fire at the incoming Russian shells and the ships that had fired them.

* * *

Tesh-Dar gasped as she saw what Li'ara-Zhurah was doing on the tactical display. "No, my daughter," she breathed as tiny icons representing the inbound human shells fell like rain upon Li'ara-Zhurah's ship. Many were stopped by the ship's point defense weapons, yet it was inevitable that some would get through. Li'ara-Zhurah was furiously returning fire at the attacking human vessels, which had immediately begun evasive maneuvers. While there were more of them, and they were clearly heavily armed, they were small and could not take much damage. Torpedoes arced out from Li'ara-Zhurah's ship, vaporizing first one, then another of the attackers. Then the remaining three closed in, firing non-stop as they came. "Maneuver," she whispered, willing Li'ara-Zhurah to get out of the way of the incoming bombardment. "You must move clear!"

Li'ara-Zhurah's ship did not move, but stayed abeam of the Messenger's ship, shielding it from the rain of fire from the other human vessels. Tesh-Dar did not have to reach out with her second sight to see the battle: she could feel it all in the Bloodsong of Li'ara-Zhurah and the others on her ship. She did not have to know exactly what they thought, for she could sense their fear or trepidation. There was none. Only fierce pride and joy that they would bring great glory to the Empress.

In that moment, Tesh-Dar realized that Li'ara-Zhurah would not hesitate to give her life and that of her unborn child for the Messenger. It was an epiphany bound in pride for the young warrior whom she had chosen as her successor, and fear that Fate would somehow snatch her away.

For one of the very few times in her life, Tesh-Dar, high priestess of the Desh-Ka and the Empire's most-feared warrior, was captured by indecision. She considered sending other ships to assist Li'ara-Zhurah, but the senior shipmistresses were fully engaged with the large human force here. Moreover, it would not do to coddle Li'ara-Zhurah: if she were to become what Tesh-Dar hoped, she must be able to face and survive the challenges placed before her; she must find her own Way. She would also resent Tesh-Dar's interference, and rightly so.

At last, doing her best to force aside her mounting anxiety for Li'ara-Zhurah and the child she carried, the child that Tesh-Dar had allowed to be carried into battle instead of being safely sequestered on a nursery world, Tesh-Dar decided to simply watch the situation closely, content in the knowledge that she could yet intervene, if necessary.

Having decided that internal struggle for the moment, she decided that the next phase of the battle for this planet was to begin. Perhaps it would draw the attention from the three ships clawing at Li'ara-Zhurah as she sought to defend the Messenger. Closing her eyes, she sought out the thread in the Bloodsong of one of the other warrior priestesses who waited nearby with a special fleet. The streams of their spirits touched and briefly entwined, and in that moment Tesh-Dar's emotions conveyed a simple message: *It is time.*

* * *

"My Marines are marching on the main spaceport now," Grishin said through the vidcom. "We hope to find a ship that can transport us back to the fleet."

"We could send our cutters down to ferry you back," Hanson told him.

Grishin shook his head. "We will not last long," he explained. "We no longer have the element of surprise, we are low on ammunition, and our cutter is badly damaged. Korolev's troops will finish us long before we could get everyone ferried back. We will either find a ground to orbit freighter with which we can link up with you, or a ship with jump drive. If the latter, we will need additional crewmen to man it, assuming the cutter pilots can get it off the ground."

"You'll have them," Hanson promised. "Just get your butts into space, colonel."

"New contacts!" cried the flag tactical officer on *Constellation's* flag bridge. "Eight...ten...no, shit..." He paused, a look of disbelief on his face as he stared into his console display. Turning to Commodore Hanson, he said, "*One hundred and seventeen* new contacts just jumped in-system, ma'am. So far."

"Are you sure...?" Hanson's voice died away as she studied the tactical display. The count spiraled upward until it finally stopped: two hundred and forty-three ships. She looked at the data displays next to each of them, almost unreadable because there were so many ships. Half of them appeared to be warships in the heavy cruiser class. The others were huge. "My God," she exclaimed. "Two kilometers long, massing half a million tons? Those numbers can't be right!"

"I think they are, commodore," the flag captain interjected. "Look." The ship's main telescope was now focused on the mass of ships that had jumped in, dangerously close to Saint Petersburg's gravity well. Their markings, large cyan runes over a brilliant green on the sleek hulls, left no doubt as to whose ships they were.

"The small one there," the flag captain highlighted a vessel that was perhaps an eighth the size of the larger ones around it, "is about the size of a heavy cruiser. If I had to guess, I'd say these are troop transports. Massive ones."

"Colonel, did you catch all that?" she said urgently to Grishin.

"Yes, commodore," he told her. "It appears that a Kreelan invasion force has just joined our quaint little party. Do not worry about us. Fight your ships, and we will contact you when we are on our way." He paused. "I truly hope to not have to fight them on the ground again. Not now."

"I understand, colonel," Hanson told him. "Good luck."

"Godspeed, commodore," Grishin said just before his image faded to black on her console.

Hanson sat back, stunned at the size of the enemy fleet. She watched, speechless, as the armada moved in, taking up orbit around Saint Petersburg.

"Orders, ma'am?" the flag captain asked quietly.

Hanson heard his voice as if in a dream. She had kept the task force at arm's length from both the original Kreelan fleet and the Russians, firing at the former when she could while trying to avoid being fired upon by the latter. It was like sparring in a boxing match, but with three boxers in the ring, all fighting one another. *Saint Petersburg is lost*, she thought. *There's no way we could help them, even if they let us. Even if every warship from Earth and the Alliance were here, they still wouldn't be enough.*

"You can't run now," a vaguely familiar voice said quietly. "You have a duty to the men and women on that planet who need you to get them out of this, to bring them home."

She turned to find Torvald, her resident spymaster, standing beside her combat chair, staring at her. His words snapped her out of her dark reverie. "I don't get paid to *run*, mister," she told him angrily, "but I'll also be damned if I'm going to lose my entire goddamn task force! In case you can't add, we're slightly outnumbered here."

The flag bridge became utterly silent, with every member of her staff, even the flag captain, studiously looking anywhere but toward her and Torvald.

"I'll do everything I can to get my people — including your agent — off the planet," Hanson went on in a quieter voice, forcing the words through gritted teeth as she jabbed a finger into Torvald's chest, "but I don't need the likes of you to remind me of my duty. Now, if there's nothing else, get the hell off my bridge before I have the Marines throw you in the brig."

Torvald looked at her impassively, then quietly turned and left the flag bridge.

Orders, she thought, pushing Torvald from her mind. What orders can I give in a situation like this?

Before she could say anything, the flag tactical officer said, "The Saint Petersburg fleet is trying to disengage with the first Kreelan force, commodore. It looks like they're trying to come about to intercept the invasion fleet."

Hanson nodded. That gave her something to work with. "Communications," she ordered, "try to raise Admiral Voroshilov from the Saint Petersburg fleet again. Let's see if he might like our help *now*."

* * *

"The sensors cannot be correct. This must be some sort of electronic *maskirovka*, a deception by the Confederation fleet," Korolev's image said decisively.

"Comrade chairman," Admiral Voroshilov said, fighting to restrain his anger, "the sensor readings you see are correct. We have verified the size of these massive vessels with every type of sensor, including optical measurement. *There is no doubt*. And from their design and markings, they are clearly nothing like the Confederation ships. The Kreelan threat is real, and they are here. I believe these ships to be troop transports. You must have Marshal Antonov activate the military reserves immediately, and bring the remaining orbital and planetary defense sites to full readiness. We should also activate Riga's defense forces—"

"Limit yourself to things you understand, admiral," Korolev said, the threat in his voice plain. "Marshal Antonov shall handle the planetary defenses as he sees fit. *You* will concern yourself with dealing with this new *Confederation* threat."

The vidcom suddenly went blank.

Voroshilov sat in his command chair, seething. Even now, with the enemy at the gates, Korolev was in complete denial. He looked up at the tactical display and the icons of the massive enemy ships encircling his planet like a string of bloody pearls. He was a Party man and always had been, but he was also a patriot who had devoted his life to the military and fervently believed in the oath he took to defend his people. These aliens, whatever they were and wherever they were from, had come to destroy his motherland and his people. They, not the Confederation, were the enemy. The path of his duty was crystal clear, even if it would cost him his life in front of a firing squad. Korolev did not look favorably upon those who committed treason.

"Is the Confederation flagship still hailing us?" he asked his communications officer.

"Yes, sir, continuously." the officer said. "I have ignored them as you instructed."

"Tell them that I wish to speak to Commodore Hanson at once," Voroshilov ordered.

The officer gaped at him for a moment before turning his attention back to his console, quickly obeying his orders.

In seconds, Hanson's face appeared on the secondary viewscreen. "Admiral Voroshilov," she said formally.

"Commodore, let us dispense with any formalities," he said bluntly. "I am committing treason merely by speaking with you, but I have no choice if I am to have any chance of saving my homeworld...if it can be saved. I would like to accept your offer of assistance against the aliens, if it still stands."

Hanson frowned. "Admiral, your fleet has repeatedly fired on us when we tried to assist you earlier. What assurance do I have that you're not pulling us into a trap?"

"Commodore, I give you my personal word of honor," Voroshilov said earnestly. "There is nothing else of substance that I can provide."

Hanson nodded. "I'll accept that, admiral, but I want assurances that your ground forces will not launch any further attacks on our Marines on the planet, and will let them depart peacefully."

"I can give you no such assurance, commodore," Voroshilov said grimly. "Our leaders believe the invaders are Confederation ships in disguise, bringing yet more of your Marines, and I have not been able to convince them otherwise. Your people will have to fight their way to safety if they are to survive." He paused. "Commodore, I have not informed the chairman that I am asking for your assistance. Assuming I survive the rest of this battle, I will most likely be shot for my troubles. In that way," he glanced around the flag bridge at his officers, who were watching the discussion with expressions ranging from utter surprise to quiet resignation, "my subordinates may be spared the same fate."

After a brief moment's consideration, Hanson said, "Very well, admiral, I agree. If I may, I suggest that we attempt to break contact with the first group of Kreelan ships you have been fighting and focus our efforts on disrupting the invasion force. Our sensors indicate that they're already deploying smaller vessels to the surface. We don't have much time..."

FORTY-SIX

Li'ara-Zhurah held on to her combat chair, the restraints digging into her shoulders and waist as the ship shuddered violently beneath her. The command deck was wreathed in smoke from a fire in the electrical system, the acrid stench of burning metal and plastic still burning in her nose.

"We are heavily damaged, mistress," the tactical controller reported, fighting to keep her voice level. Her hands had been badly burned when her console had exploded from a short-circuit of the electrical system that had started the fire. Li'ara-Zhurah had pulled her away from the burning console, while others had put out the flames. The controller had refused to leave her post, and had managed to reroute the controls to another station on the bridge. "We cannot long survive unless we destroy the human ship." To retreat, she well knew, to abandon the Messenger, was unthinkable.

The human ships, while small, had been most worthy adversaries. Armed to the teeth and far more resilient than Li'ara-Zhurah had given them credit for, the five human ships had crippled her own vessel. The cost had been high: four of them had been destroyed, and the fifth was damaged. Li'ara-Zhurah was impressed with the fortitude of its commander: even though the ship had clearly suffered grievous damage in the fight, she — or he — had not given up. Apparently grasping that Li'ara-Zhurah's ship was protecting the Messenger's vessel, he had changed his tactics, maneuvering to use it as a shield from Li'ara-Zhurah's guns. They were at knife-fighting range in space, the three vessels locked in a deadly orbit around one another at a range of no more now than a few ship lengths.

"Send forth the warriors," Li'ara-Zhurah ordered. Over a hundred of the ship's crew had been preparing for boarding operations as the human ship had drawn closer. It did not appear to have the deadly close-in defense weapons that ships such as the Messenger's vessel mounted, and that had proven so devastating in the battle for Keran. She only hoped that the Messenger understood what her warriors were doing, and did not fire on them himself.

At a word from the tactical controller, airlocks in the ship's flank cycled open and warriors in space armor poured into the utter silence of the raging battle, their thruster packs propelling them toward the remaining human attacker.

* * *

"Captain!" Bogdanova cried. "Warriors!"

Sato looked up at the visual display and his blood ran cold at what he saw. "No..." he breathed. A cloud of Kreelans in space combat armor left the alien ship, speeding toward them across the few hundred meters of empty space that was all that separated the badly wounded vessels.

Yura rocked again as the Russian ship pounded her with another broadside, even as the Kreelan ship swept over, trying to protect Sato's command. He didn't understand what was happening, but he could only be thankful for the Kreelan's intervention.

"Preparing close-in defense mortars," Bogdanova said, her hands now flying over the console's controls, the effects of radiation sickness be damned. The weapons were a cheap but incredibly effective innovation that had saved the then-Terran ships from the menace of Kreelan boarders during the battle for Keran. Nothing more than large-bore mortars, they fired projectiles up to a few hundred meters from the ship. The mortar bombs then exploded in a cloud of shrapnel that would tear any warrior, even wearing space armor, to shreds, but not cause any significant damage to any ships, even at very close range. While none of the weapons that required more sophisticated sensors were working, the mortars, which were "dumb" weapons, were still functional.

"Standing by to fire, sir," she said, her voice shaking. She had been aboard Sato's first command, the destroyer *Owen D. McClaren*, when it had been badly damaged and boarded by Kreelan raiders. It was an experience she did not wish to relive. "Firing..."

"Belay that!" Sato snapped, looking carefully at the warriors as they swarmed across their field of view. "They're not coming for us," he said. "They're going after the Russian ship!"

Bogdanova's hand didn't move from the firing console. "Captain," she asked, her voice quavering, "are you sure?"

"Yes," he reassured her. "Look at them! They're sweeping right past us!"

On the screen, they watched as the warriors jetted past *Yura's* torn hull, some of them coming to land on the ship for an instant before pushing off again, using *Yura* to adjust their trajectory.

The Russian ship began to fire at them, but it was too little, too late. Unlike larger warships, she had no close-in defense weapons, and the Kreelan warriors attacked her hull like black-clad locusts. Sato saw the flare of the boarding charges the Kreelans used to blow entry holes in the hull of the target ship. But they weren't content with making one hole: they made dozens. The ship's outer hull was being flayed from her keel, with chunks of hull being blown outward by the air pressure within, with everything — including the crewmen — being blasted out into space. Then the warriors crawled inside, and Sato could well imagine the carnage that followed. Even though the Russians had tried to kill him and his ship, he didn't wish on anyone what he knew was happening to them now.

He closed his eyes as the Kreelan ship that had been protecting them slid beside *Yura*, blocking their view just as the captain of the Russian vessel detonated his ship's self-destruct charges.

* * *

Dmitri Sikorsky sat in the rear of the cutter, still cradling Valentina's body. Ludmilla was next to him, leaning on his shoulder, her eyes firmly closed against the horrors around her. The Marines were crammed into the ship, sitting in the combat chairs or standing in the aisle, their uniforms blackened and dirty, many of them wounded. Their bodies swayed in time with the sickening roll of the badly damaged cutter as if they were on a ship at sea. Their faces, streaked with camouflage paint and sweat, betrayed nothing but numbed exhaustion.

He stared at Valentina's face, haunted by the last image he had of his own daughter when she was hauled away by the secret police. Proud. Defiant. How much Valentina reminded him of her. He had already cried all the tears his body had to give, but he felt a crushing burden of grief and guilt. It should have been him who died, he thought over and over again. It should have been him the secret police had taken, not his daughter. And would it not have been better for him, who had lived a long and full life, to have died, rather than Valentina?

He squeezed his eyes shut, trying to force away the bitter waste of his life. Ludmilla was his only comfort now, but he feared they were both among the walking dead. Either the secret police or the Red Army would kill them, or the Kreelans would. Were it not for his determination to get Ludmilla to safety, he would have welcomed death.

He felt a hand touch his face, and a soft voice spoke, barely audible over the rumble of the cutter's engines.

"Dmitri..."

He opened his eyes and his heart leaped into his throat as he saw Valentina looking up at him, her mouth curled up in a gentle blood-smeared smile.

"Valentina!" he cried. "You...you were dead! They checked you!"

Ludmilla sat up at his exclamation, her eyes wide with shock.

"*Pomogitye!*" Sikorsky shouted. The colonel, Grishin, snapped his head around, but then Sikorsky remembered that the others probably did not understand Russian. "Help!" he cried in Standard. "Help me! She is alive!"

The female sergeant, Sabourin, was at his side instantly. With one look at Valentina, she shouted, "*Medic!*"

"How is this possible?" Dmitri asked hoarsely, looking again at Valentina's body. She had been hit by at least half a dozen rounds in her chest and abdomen. "You were dead, *dorogaya.*"

"What the fuck?" the medic cursed as she knelt next to Valentina, already checking the readouts on her field medical scanner. Addressing Sabourin, she said, "I checked her out carefully when she was brought on board, staff sergeant. But she must have some sort of implants that activated: I'm reading a ton of stimulants in her bloodstream." Turning to Valentina, she asked pointedly, "Were you augmented?"

Valentina offered a weak smile. "Let us just say that I'm not like other girls," she whispered before passing out.

Quickly moving to where Grishin stood, Sabourin told him, "The agent, that Valentina woman. She is alive."

"How is that possible?" Grishin asked, shocked.

"Some sort of augmentation, according to the medic," Sabourin said, shaking her head. "She does not know how, but the woman is very much alive."

"Unbelievable," Grishin whispered, looking again at where the Sikorskys and the medic hovered over Valentina. "Thank you for letting me know, staff sergeant."

With a nod, he dismissed her before turning his focus on other matters: directly ahead lay the spaceport.

"Fighters inbound!" the copilot reported. "Firing..." The point defense weapons again blasted coherent light at the attacking aircraft, wiping them from the sky. The copilot shook his head. "Let's hope they keep playing the game that way," he said. "Aerospace fighters are dead meat against our lasers."

"As long as we can pick them up at a distance," Faraday reminded him. "If they can get in close enough with enough weapons, we're toast."

"Surface-to-air defenses?" Grishin asked, his eyes scanning the console displays.

"Several heavy missile emplacements, sir," the copilot reported, "but I don't think they can hit us. We're too low. Looks like the defenses were designed more to fend off a large-scale exo-atmospheric attack."

"There's the field!" Faraday exclaimed as the cutter roared over the outer barriers and the massive earthen berm that had been put in place as part of the port's security features. Several dozen ships squatted on the enormous landing apron, with men and equipment — ant-like against the bulk of the big ships — busily at work next to most of them. "Let's go shopping."

He flew down the orderly rows of ships, scattering the ground crews below and ignoring the frantic calls from the control tower. "I don't recognize most of these types," he said. "A bunch of them must be locally built. I'd really rather not have to try our hand at figuring out controls in cyrillic..."

"Wait!" the copilot said. He had been scanning the ships with his sensors, trying to find matches in the cutter's ship recognition database. "There's a La Seyne-built light freighter in the next row to the right. According to this, she should have jump capability and only needs a flight crew of four." He turned to Grishin and said, "They're designed for a hundred passengers and five thousand tons of cargo. It'll be a little tight for the Marines, but should work to get us off this rock." Shaking his head as he looked at the other ships, most of which were far too large to get into space with only two pilots. "It's really the only option out of all this other space junk."

"Let us check it out, then," Grishin said, nodding. "Mills," he went on, "how much time until the rest of the brigade arrives?"

"One moment, sir," Mills told him. After a brief conversation over the vidcom with the acting commander of the Marine forces now speeding through Saint Petersburg City toward the spaceport, he reported, "Major Justin estimates another thirty minutes, sir. The Russkies must have figured out what our game is and have started trying to put up blocking forces in the city, and the Major's had to make few side trips."

Grishin frowned, momentarily considering getting on the vidcom and reiterating to Justin the vital importance of the brigade getting here as quickly as possible. Then he set it aside. Justin, his senior surviving officer, was a competent leader and knew what he was supposed to do. "Give the major my compliments, Mills, and tell him we'll have a ship ready and waiting by the time he gets here."

"Yes, sir," Mills said before passing the word along.

"There she is," Faraday said as he hauled the cutter around into the next row and headed for the French-built ship. "*Mauritania*," he read from the rust-streaked letters of the ship's name painted on the hull. "What the hell kind of a name is that?"

"She's in the ship registry database," the copilot said after a moment. "She's La Seyne-flagged, and according to this was impounded four months ago for alleged smuggling."

"That's not good," Faraday said as he nosed the cutter toward the tarmac in front of the much larger ship. "If she's been sitting here for four months without maintenance, we may be screwed."

"What other options do we have?" Grishin asked.

"None, sir," the copilot answered as he checked his threat display again. "This is the smallest ship here that can carry the whole brigade. The rest of them are too big for us to even have a chance of getting off the ground by ourselves."

"Then let us hope the Saint Petersburg government was kind enough to keep it in running condition for us," Grishin told them. "Mills!"

"Sir!" Mills barked.

"We'll need a team to clear the ship," Grishin told him, "with the rest of the platoon in a defensive perimeter."

"Yes, sir!" Mills replied before turning around and barking orders to the platoon's team leaders.

As Faraday was setting the cutter down, it yawed unexpectedly to port as the damaged stabilizer finally failed completely, sending the cutter's stern swinging dangerously close to the bow of the *Mauritania*. "Shit!" he cried as he and the copilot struggled with the controls. "Hang on!" Terrified of damaging their only possible way off the planet, he cut the hover engines and dropped the cutter the last few meters to the tarmac. They missed smashing the *Mauritania's* bow by centimeters before it slammed into the ground, collapsing the nose gear.

The cutter was filled with screams of fear and surprise as everyone not strapped down suddenly found themselves weightless, then were smashed to the deck when the cutter hit the unyielding reinforced concrete of the tarmac.

* * *

Tesh-Dar felt an electric jolt pass through her as the Bloodsong of the warriors Li'ara-Zhurah had sent forth to attack the human ship bedeviling the Messenger were snuffed out of existence when the vessel exploded. She knew Li'ara-Zhurah remained alive, but her ship had been close — very close — to the human vessel, again shielding the Messenger's ship from harm. Both ships likely suffered even more severe damage.

"Can you reach Li'ara-Zhurah?" she asked her communications controller, fighting to keep the fear from her voice. She could tell much from the Bloodsong, but needed the reassurance of hearing Li'ara-Zhurah's voice.

"Yes, my priestess," the warrior answered instantly, and Tesh-Dar was rewarded with Li'ara-Zhurah's image on the secondary view screen.

The bridge behind her was a shambles, looking much like that of Tesh-Dar's ship before it crashed during the battle of Keran. Li'ara-Zhurah was wreathed in smoke, with fire flickering from half the consoles in Tesh-Dar's view. Several of the bridge crew lay on the deck, quite still, and she knew that they, and many others aboard, were dead.

"My priestess," Li'ara-Zhurah said, bowing her head. She had a deep gash in her left cheek and blood was seeping from beneath the armor of her right arm, but other than that she appeared to be uninjured. "We have grappled with the Messenger's ship. Our vessels are now joined. I was just about to take a party across and give him the healing gel and whatever other aid that we may."

Tesh-Dar had been about to tell her that she was to leave the Messenger, and that she was sending other ships to retrieve her, but Li'ara-Zhurah's words gave her pause. She was so close now to her objective, and despite the terrible risks she was taking, Tesh-Dar could not force from her own lips the words she had intended to speak, words that would keep her young disciple from the glory she and the warriors aboard her ship had already sacrificed much to earn.

Running in the current of the Bloodsong, too, were the deep notes of the melody of the Empress, and Tesh-Dar could tell that she was watching her blood daughter closely, and approved of her actions.

Gritting her teeth as she clenched her fists so tightly that her talons drew blood from her palms, she told Li'ara-Zhurah, "Do what you must, child, but I am sending ships to watch over you and retrieve you when the Messenger is safe." She looked deeply into the younger warrior's eyes. "I will not lose you, child, you or your daughter-to-be."

"In Her name," Li'ara-Zhurah said, "it shall be so." She looked a moment longer at Tesh-Dar before saying, "Thank you for believing in me, my priestess."

Her words touched Tesh-Dar's heart. Yet the rush of warmth the great priestess felt only partly offset the lingering chill of fear as she nodded one last time and closed the communications channel between them.

Aboard her crippled ship, Li'ara-Zhurah waited until Tesh-Dar's image faded before she allowed herself to succumb to the coughing fit that had taken monumental control to suppress.

"Mistress," the senior surviving bridge controller told her, "you are bleeding."

Li'ara-Zhurah put her fingers to her lips; they came away bloody. She had been hit in the chest by a flying piece of debris from the bridge support structure when the human vessel had exploded. If she had not been wearing her armor, she — and her child — would have been killed. "It is a trifle," she said, forcing her body back under control. At the look the other warrior gave her, she explained, "A rib has pierced my lung, nothing more. I have experienced worse." She stood up, ignoring the lancing pain in her chest. "Come. We must take those who are left and cross over to the Messenger's ship. We must render him what aid we might to satisfy Her honor, and await the ships the priestess is sending to take us back to the fleet."

* * *

"Are you sure about this, admiral?" Hanson asked tensely as *Constellation's* guns fired another salvo at the pursuing Kreelan fleet. She had agreed to use her task force to try and help Voroshilov's ships break contact with the first group of Kreelans, so the Russians could try to attack the invasion force now in low orbit over Saint Petersburg.

The problem was that the Kreelans were having none of it. While they still seemed to be sparring, rather than seeking a decisive victory, the human ships needed to somehow escape and regroup. The Kreelans, however, stayed close on their heels, their ships at least as fast as the human vessels. As they had been doing with Voroshilov's fleet, they played with Hanson's forces, charging into range to fire a salvo or two before retreating beyond effective range. Hanson liked to think that her handling of her task force was far more polished than Voroshilov's had been, but the end result had been the same: a stalemate, which was something Voroshilov and Hanson could not afford.

"*Da*, commodore," Voroshilov answered. "We have practiced this many times during in-system exercises as a tactic to defeat Confederation ships attempting to defend Riga." He gave her a mirthless smile. "It will work."

"But the proximity to the system's gravity wells..." Hanson cringed inwardly. Voroshilov had proposed that they use what was often referred to as a micro-jump, a very, *very* brief trip through hyperspace. While such jumps had been demonstrated in the past in deep space, no one had ever done so in a planetary system. If a ship came out into normal space within a certain threshold in the gravity well of a body like a star or planet, it would be torn apart.

"We have extremely refined calculations for many jump point pairs," Voroshilov reassured her. "I know it is much that I ask of you to trust in me this way, commodore, but this is the only path that offers some hope of retrieving your people from the surface, and of trying to stop the alien invasion force."

Her mouth pressed into a thin, worried line, Hanson nodded. "Very well, sir. We'll jump on your mark." Turning to her flag captain, she asked, "Have all of our ships verified their calculations and reported readiness to jump?"

"Aye, ma'am," he said, equally worried. "The ship captains aren't too thrilled with this, but everyone's ready."

"I'm not thrilled with it, either, believe me," she told him. Turning back to Voroshilov, she said, "We're ready, sir. Our jump systems have been advanced through the interlock stage, bypassing the normal jump cycle procedure. Once you give the order, we'll be jumping out immediately."

"Very well. Stand by, commodore," he told her. "We approach one of our pre-plotted jump positions. Stand by...three...two...one...now!"

As one, the ships of the Saint Petersburg and Confederation fleets vanished.

FORTY-SEVEN

Grishin came to at the sound of Emmanuelle Sabourin's voice as she desperately sought to wake him.

"*Mon colonel!*" he heard her say. "Colonel Grishin! Can you hear me?"

"*Da,*" he managed. Remembering that Sabourin was French, he added, "*Oui.* I am fine." He opened his eyes, but suddenly wished he hadn't. He was staring up at the deck of the cutter, and was taken by a sudden bout of vertigo until he realized that the ship must have rolled onto its back when the pilot brought it down and the landing gear collapsed. The troop compartment was dark, lit only by the red emergency lights, and filled with smoke and the stench of burning electrical components. He heard moans of pain from both fore and aft, and saw that three Marines still hung from their combat chairs, unconscious or killed by heavy equipment and weapons as the craft tumbled over. Other Marines were trying to cut them down. "*Bozhe moi,*" he breathed as Sabourin helped him up. "Casualties?"

"Four dead, sir," she reported wearily. "Three more seriously injured — broken bones — and several with minor injuries. Mills is trying to get one of the hatches open. Right now we are trapped in here."

"Watch your eyes!" Mills called from the rear hatch. A moment later a dazzling light lit the compartment as Mills, wearing a protective mask, turned an electric arc cutter on the hatch's hinges and lock. Sparks flew through the dark compartment, tiny fireworks in the smoky gloom. In the eerie light, Grishin caught a glimpse of the three civilians and the platoon's medic, all of whom appeared to have survived.

He wondered why the compartment was so dark: it should still be daylight outside, and there should be light streaming in through the flight deck windscreen. When he turned around, he understood why: the flight deck had been crushed when the ship rolled over. With a sickening sensation in the pit of his stomach, he asked Sabourin, "Did either of the pilots make it?"

She glanced at the mangled wreckage of the flight deck, then looked at one of the figures nearby, lying back against the curve of the hull, moaning. "The pilot got out, sir," she answered quietly. "He is shaken up, but will be all right. The copilot is dead. We could not even get to his body." The copilot's side of the flight deck was nothing more than gnarled wreckage. He hadn't stood a chance.

"*Merde,*" he cursed.

"Bloody..." they looked up as Mills cursed, kicking at the jammed hatch with all his might. "...fucking..." Another kick, and a tiny sliver of light shone through. "...*hell!*" With one final kick and a rush by several other Marines throwing their weight against it, the big hatch groaned open, letting in both light and fresh air. "First and second squads," Mills called, "form a perimeter around the freighter! Third squad, board and search her. Do *not* shoot anyone unless they shoot at you first. Maybe we'll get a bit of luck and some old sod on board can help us get that bucket off the ground. *Move!*"

The Marines piled out of the overturned cutter and immediately ran to carry out Mills's orders.

"Do we have contact with the rest of the brigade?" Grishin asked Sabourin.

She shook her head. "*Non, mon colonel,*" she said. "The cutter's systems are out, and I have not been able to raise anyone outside of our own troops on our gear. The equipment seems to be working properly, but I cannot raise anyone. I suspect we are being jammed."

"Better and better," he grumbled. "Do we have any anti-air weapons aboard?"

"Yes, sir," she told him, nodding toward several crates that still remained tightly strapped down to the deck above them, all the way aft. "Six Viper missiles."

"Put together an anti-air team and have them set up on the top hull of the freighter," he ordered. "Our Russian friends will not leave us be for long, and they will certainly not be happy when we try to take off." He looked again at the pilot, Faraday, who seemed to be recovering his wits. "If we take off."

"Yes, sir," she said, immediately moving aft toward the missile crates as she called Mills to let him know.

"Pilot," Grishin said, kneeling next to the man, "how do you feel?"

"Like I got flattened by a goddamn bus, colonel," Faraday rasped, grimacing. He was holding his right arm protectively against his chest. "Think I broke a rib or two."

"Can you still fly?"

Faraday grinned. "Are you giving me a choice, sir?"

"No," Grishin said, offering a smile in return. "I wish I could, but it appears that you are not going to get out of work so easily."

"In that case," Faraday said quietly, looking at the crushed remains of the flight deck and the blood that was the only trace of the copilot, "I can fly, sir. I just hope that tub out there is spaceworthy."

"As do I," Grishin agreed, fervently wishing that the rest of the brigade arrived soon.

* * *

Tesh-Dar did not know what to make of the disappearance of the human fleet. From what she had learned of the humans since first contact, she suspected they would be back, and soon. Tactically, it was a good move, and the same that she would have made had she been in their position: jump away, regroup, and then reenter the fight. Depending on the timing, it would work out well, for the invasion force would only be in orbit just long enough to drop the warriors and their supplies. After that, the great ships would return to the Empire, while Tesh-Dar's ships would remain here to do battle with the humans.

The temporary lull afforded her an opportunity to go planetside, and she took one of the ship's shuttles — like the ships themselves, very primitive affairs compared to the Empire's modern starships, but necessary to allow a fair fight with the humans — and docked with one of the many assault craft that had been disgorged by the gigantic transports. With another check on Li'ara-Zhurah through her spiritual second sight, Tesh-Dar noted that she was well, if injured, and was continuing on her quest to save the Messenger, Tesh-Dar boarded the assault craft that would take her to the planet.

Not content to join the many warriors dropping into the unpopulated areas to establish the roots of a wartime colony, she ordered her pilot to join in the assaults against the planet's population centers, choosing to participate in the attack against the largest city.

Flexing her massive hands in anticipation, she looked forward to again facing human warriors in battle. Humans, even many at a time, were not a challenge in combat against a warrior priestess such as she. Her powers, greater than any other living warrior priestess, were not understood among her own people; to the humans they were nothing less than magic.

* * *

"We must sound the invasion alert, comrade chairman!" Marshal Antonov stated flatly to a stunned Chairman Korolev. The display screens in the underground command center were painted with red icons, showing the massive enemy fleet that was now sending forth a torrent of landing craft.

"I do not believe these are aliens!" Korolev grated. "It is simply a ruse!"

"It does not matter, sir," Antonov persisted, "if they are aliens or Confederation troops. We are being invaded by *someone*, and we must prepare!"

With that, Korolev could not argue. "Very well," he said. "Initiate the invasion protocols. And find out where that bastard Voroshilov and his expensive fleet disappeared to!"

"Yes, sir," Antonov said before moving over to the control center's communications section. "Sound the invasion alert," he told them. "All Red Army units are to report to their invasion defense positions, and recall all reserve personnel immediately." Every able-bodied man, along with women who had no young children, were part of the reserve, from age fifteen on up. If they could stand and hold a weapon of any kind, they met the necessary qualifications. "Notify all commands that they have full authority to engage enemy forces at will: weapons free. The Air Force and surface-to-air elements are to engage the landing craft."

"What about the Confederation Marines at the spaceport and the others trying to join them?"

With a sideways glance in Korolev's direction, Antonov lowered his voice and said, "Let them be. Call off the pursuit. If the invaders are who and what I think they are, every human being who can hold a weapon may be of use. Let them spill their blood for our cause."

"Sir, what should we do if they are successful in stealing a ship?"

"Do nothing. Conserve our weapons," Antonov answered, gesturing toward the display and the mass of red icons for enemy ships. "Where could they go? Which brings us to the next question: have you had contact with Admiral Voroshilov?"

"No sir," one of the other controllers answered. "We have had no contact since the fleet jumped. But we do know that they jumped from a pre-designated jump point that corresponds to one of the positions near Riga."

Antonov nodded, considering. "Very well. Notify me immediately when you regain contact. And update the tactical display as our forces come to full readiness."

"Yes, sir!" they chorused in response.

With that, he turned and headed back to join Korolev, thinking, *Voroshilov, you old bastard, I hope you know what you are doing.*

* * *

"*Collision alarm!*" Hanson heard someone shout as the *Constellation's* klaxons bleated their warning tones through the ship. In the tactical display, just moments after emerging from the micro-jump, she saw that the combined human fleet had indeed emerged on the far side of Riga, but their formation — or, rather, the Confederation ships' formation, she thought bitterly — was a deadly mess. Untrained in the peculiarities of this type of jump, there had been small inconsistencies in their formation and velocity that had been magnified tremendously during the micro-jump, putting some of the ships in dangerously close proximity.

"Task force base direction zero-nine-zero mark zero!" she shouted at her flag captain, ordering her ships to turn to the same heading to help avoid colliding with one another. "All ships reduce speed to station-keeping until we get this sorted out! Communications," she barked to the flag communications officer, "get me Admiral Voroshilov!"

"Aye, commodore!"

On the main display, her ships quickly wheeled around to their new heading and reduced speed, and in a few moments were starting to slide back into their assigned positions in the formation.

"Damage report?" Hanson asked.

"None, commodore," her flag captain reported, relieved. "Some close calls, but not so much as any scraped paint. We made it."

Hanson nodded, greatly relieved. It could easily have been a disaster, but certainly no worse than going up against a vastly superior Kreelan fleet. *On the other hand*, she thought acidly, *Voroshilov could have given us some warning as to the dangers.*

"Commodore," Admiral Voroshilov's image suddenly appeared on her vidcom, "welcome to Riga, an autonomous republic under Saint Petersburg's beneficent protection." He gave her another one of his mirthless smiles. "I congratulate you on your successful jump, commodore, and my compliments to your crews. On our first task force micro-jump during an exercise, we lost two ships to interpenetration. You did very well."

Hanson choked down the hot remarks she had been about to give the admiral. The Russians had made it look easy, their ships still in perfect formation. But many had obviously died in the perfection of their technique. *Maybe we didn't do so badly, after all*, she consoled herself. Instead of biting his head off, she said, "Thank you, sir, I'll do that. What do we do now?"

"We must regroup quickly, before we move out of Riga's shadow and again come under direct observation of the enemy," he told her. The jump point had left them on the far side of Riga from Saint Petersburg, temporarily shielding them. "I believe that the large transports will stay only long enough to deploy their troops, then they will leave. After that, we may stand a fighting chance against the remaining covering forces. In the meantime," he went on, "I must make contact with the Rigan government: they must prepare as best they can." While the Party had decreed that the Kreelan menace was nothing more than Confederation propaganda, Voroshilov had seen more than enough to convince him the alien threat was real.

"What about Chairman Korolev?" she asked him.

Voroshilov shrugged. "I am already a dead man in his eyes, I am sure. Giving him one more reason to have me shot is a worthwhile trade for saving human lives." He paused. "My wife is from Riga. Something tells me she would not be happy if I did not warn them of what is coming. While I am doing that, get your ships in order and prepare to reengage the enemy, commodore."

"Aye, aye, sir," she said. "We're with you."

* * *

After closing the connection with Hanson, Voroshilov told his communications officer, "Get me President Roze." The officer merely gaped at him. "Did you hear me, comrade?"

"Yes...yes, comrade admiral," the man answered uneasily, turning away to his console, his face bearing a fearful expression.

"Sir," his flag captain asked quietly, "may I ask what you are doing? Some of the officers are not..." He paused and looked around quickly before whispering, "Some of the men are beginning to be concerned over your actions, comrade admiral. You have so much as declared that you are committing mutiny by allying us with the Confederation fleet. And now contacting Roze directly?" He looked at Voroshilov with undisguised concern. "The crews in the fleet know your wife is Rigan, sir, and they will think you are doing this only for her sake. You know this is a political decision that must be made by the Party leadership, comrade admiral. Please, I beg you to reconsider!"

Voroshilov looked at him. "Yuri Denisovich, my friend," he answered quietly, "I am doing what I feel I must. Yes, my wife is Rigan, but that is not why I must speak with Roze. It is because Riga is part of our small star nation that is under attack. It will not help our cause to leave Riga blind and deaf when the invaders turn their attention to them: if Riga is prepared, they will be able to kill far more of the enemy than if they are not. Chairman Korolev does not see this, any more than he believes the invaders are aliens. Tell me, Yuri, do you still believe the invaders come from the Confederation after seeing their ships?"

Captain Yuri Denisovich Borichevsky had known Voroshilov most of his adult life, and had served under him his entire career. More than anyone beyond his immediate family, he trusted Voroshilov. "No, comrade admiral, I do not believe they are from the Confederation," he said. "That does not help with the crews, however. They are losing faith in you."

Voroshilov turned again to his communications officer. "Open a channel to the fleet," he ordered tersely.

"Including the Confederation ships?" the man asked.

"*Nyet*," Voroshilov told him. "Only our own."

"Yes, comrade admiral," the man answered quietly. "Channel open."

"Comrades of the Red Navy, men of the fleet!" Voroshilov said. "Some of you no doubt are wondering at the course of the actions we have taken, why we have joined forces with the Confederation ships that we initially fought, and why now we have jumped to Riga while enemy forces surround Saint Petersburg, the motherland to most of us." The "most of us" was for the benefit of the fleet's crewmen — mostly officers — who were Rigan. "Many of you have no doubt heard that I took these actions without the consent of the Party leadership, that I acted on my own authority. This is true."

Around him, every man in sight turned to stare at him. In the last twenty years, since shortly after the war with Earth and the Alliance had ended, such a thing would have been considered unthinkable. The Party had been everything, particularly to the younger officers.

"I assure you, comrades," he went on, steadily meeting the stares of those around him, "these are not actions that I have taken lightly. Comrade Chairman Korolev and Marshal Antonov are fully occupied with organizing the ground and air defenses of our motherland. I know the chairman still believes that the ships attacking our world are humans from the Confederation. However, I cannot accept this in light of what we have seen with our own eyes and sensors: these ships that have come to our system are not of human design. With our world under attack, we cannot blind ourselves by what we want to see, ignoring what truly is. Our families, our people, are depending on us to save them, and the only way we can hope to do that is to understand what we are up against. In the past, the Party has often tried to shield us from unpleasant truths; in this hour, we cannot afford such a luxury.

"For those who are concerned about why we are now above Riga, it is not because it is the world of my wife's birth." Some of the faces around him looked away with embarrassment. Like Flag Captain Borichevsky, they had all served with Voroshilov most of their careers, and had come to know him well. When faced with such a blunt statement, their unvoiced thoughts about him acting purely out of personal desires were shown to be hollow and untrue, yet another manifestation of the negative side of human nature. "We are here because Riga is part of our *kollektiv*, and we have an obligation under the constitution to protect her. This is indisputable, even by the Party. I cannot now spare any ships to stand guard over her people, but I will provide them with information and what encouragement I can by speaking with President Roze.

"Once that is done and we are again fully prepared for battle," he continued, "we will mount another attack against the invaders. And *this* time," he promised, "they will not simply dance away from our guns like ballerinas!

"Comrades," he concluded, "do your duty to protect the motherland and the Party. Our world depends on it."

With that, he snapped the connection closed. *And if that does not mollify them,* he told himself, *they can all go to hell.*

"Comrade President Roze is on the vidcom, comrade admiral," the communications officer informed him.

Voroshilov glanced at the man and noticed that there was indeed a change in his expression. He was perhaps yet unsure of this strange path they were taking, as in a way was Voroshilov himself, but he was no longer acting like a dog afraid of being whipped. "Thank you, comrade lieutenant," he said. Then, turning to the face that had appeared on his vidcom, he said, "Hello, Valdis." Voroshilov had known Valdis Roze for many years: the man's sister was the admiral's wife.

"Lavrenti," the president of Riga answered cautiously. "This contact is a bit...unusual, is it not?"

"It is," Voroshilov told him bluntly. "Valdis, have your military people been monitoring what has been going on in-system?"

Roze hesitated a moment, clearly wondering if Voroshilov was trying to entrap him. Then, thinking better of it only because he knew that Voroshilov was a man of honor, even if the Party he served held such a quality as a vice, he said, "Our astronomers noted that there were two energy spikes that conform with nuclear detonations in space. Other than that, we have little to go on: we were totally cut off from the datasphere a few hours ago. And, as you know, we have little in the way of sensors that can see in-system."

Voroshilov frowned. He had repeatedly argued with Marshal Antonov to upgrade Riga's defenses, but he had steadfastly refused, even with the suggestion of keeping Saint Petersburg military personnel in charge. Now it was too late. "Valdis, we are being invaded," he told his brother-in-law. "The Confederation reports of an alien attack on Keran were true; now they have come here. Over two hundred enemy ships are dropping troops all over Saint Petersburg, and it is only a matter of time before they come to you."

"And what are we to do?" Roze asked hotly. "The only military forces here are yours, and are intended to keep us in our place, not to defend from invasion. We are helpless."

"No," Voroshilov corrected him. "I know that you have an extensive underground militia, a resistance. I recommend that you have them and as many of your people as possible evacuate the cities. From the account of the battle of Keran, the enemy seems to concentrate on the cities. I will give orders to the garrison commander that he is to place himself under your command."

Roze scoffed. "He is a Party lapdog, Lavrenti. I know you are doing this without Korolev's permission, and so will he. He will spit in your eye."

"Indeed." Turning to Borichevsky, Voroshilov said, "You will detach the destroyer *Komsomolskaya Pravda* to provide early warning coverage for Riga, on my direct orders. The ship's captain is to place himself under the direct command of President Roze. He is also to send a party to the garrison commander and deliver my orders that he do the same. Let them understand that if the commander refuses, they are to shoot him on the spot. If the garrison resists, the *Komosomolskaya Pravda* is to destroy it from orbit." The ships of the Saint Petersburg fleet were equipped with weapons that were designed for orbital bombardments, for occasions just such as this. "Is that clear, flag captain?"

"Perfectly, comrade admiral!"

Voroshilov nodded, and Borichevsky began barking orders to the fleet controllers. "I know that is a token effort, Valdis," he said, "but it is all I can do for now. We have Confederation ships with us, and I will ask their commander to ensure that one of them is sent back to their government to request that supplies and, if possible, troops be sent as quickly as possible. I would detach more ships to defend Riga, but I fear we already do not have enough ships to defeat the force that faces us."

"I...I appreciate what you've done," Roze said. "You are a good man. I can imagine what it will cost you in the end."

Voroshilov gave him a wry smile. "I have much to survive before Korolev can shoot me," he said. "Good luck, Valdis."

"You, too, Lavrenti."

FORTY-EIGHT

The two ships, joined now by the grapples Li'ara-Zhurah's crew had fastened to the human vessel, turned slowly together in space like dreaming lovers. In her armored space suit, she led her surviving warriors to the Messenger's ship. She ignored the spectacular scenery around her: the millions of stars, the brightly colored disk of the human planet below, and the shimmering spears of flame that were the hundreds of assault craft penetrating the planet's atmosphere. She had seen things like these before at Keran, and shut them from her mind: they brought her only unpleasant memories.

The crossing between ships was merely a matter of jumping across the few body lengths of space separating the vessels where the hatch opened. The hulls would have been even more closely bound were it not for the profusion of unsightly antenna arrays, turrets, and various other protrusions with which the humans chose to encumber their ships.

Had they been making a combat boarding, she would have simply found a patch of hull and burned a hole through it to the interior compartments, but that was not an option in this case. She had no idea where the Messenger might be inside the ship, and thus had to exercise caution.

Instead, they moved across the hull of the Messenger's ship toward one of the holes that had been blown in it by the attacking human vessels. The damage there was already done. She led her warriors inside the blasted compartment, noting that it had contained the force of this particular shell's explosion: there were no major breaches in the interior bulkheads or the hatch. She approached the latter, carefully placing a boarding airlock — essentially a double membrane with sealable flaps down the middle — around the scorched hatch coaming. The edges stuck to the metal with a molecular glue that fused the membrane material to the steel.

Once that was accomplished, she stepped inside the airlock, sealed the membranes behind her, and then carefully cut a small hole in the hatch with a small cutting torch. The membrane suddenly inflated with a loud pop as air from the other side of the hatch flowed through the hole she had cut, pressurizing her side of the airlock. She used the torch to cut the hatch's jammed lock, then swung it open to reveal a red-lit corridor beyond.

Darting her head through the hatch to check in both directions, she saw that the way was deserted. "Come," she told her accompanying warriors, "we must move quickly now."

After gratefully shedding her armored suit, she stood guard while her warriors entered through the double airlock in pairs. In a few minutes, all had entered the ship.

"Which way, mistress?" one of the warriors asked. Li'ara-Zhurah was the only one among them who had ever been on a human ship, another of her experiences during the battle of Keran.

Li'ara-Zhurah considered: they had entered the hull roughly two-thirds of the way aft. If this ship was anything like the ship she had boarded at Keran, they were near the engineering section. The command deck, which is where she assumed the messenger would be, should be somewhere forward of that. The corridor they were in ran fore-and-aft. "This way," she said, leading them in the direction of the bow, the front of the ship.

At the first turn, they came upon several humans who lay slumped against the walls and sprawled on the floor. All had vomited profusely, and had blood streaming from their mouths. She did not have to see their faces to know that the Messenger was not among them: she had never seen his face, and had only heard his voice the one time over the radio. Yet she knew instinctively that she would recognize him when she saw him. It was a paradox that she did not understand, nor did she try to: it was as elemental to her as breathing.

One of her warriors raised her sword to kill the humans, but Li'ara-Zhurah signaled with her hand to leave them be. "Leave them," she said as she moved onward. "We must find the Messenger."

They moved forward as fast as they dared in the eerie red lighting, skirting around the many damaged areas of the ship. The passageways were filled with swirling smoke and the bitter reek of burned metal and plastic, along with the stench of bodies that had lost control of their digestive systems. Li'ara-Zhurah momentarily regretted leaving her vacuum suit behind, for her species had an extremely acute sense of smell, and the stink was nearly overwhelming.

They came upon more humans, unconscious or dead in the passageways. She surmised that those whose stations were out here, close to the outer hull, must have absorbed a great deal more radiation than those further in toward the ship's central core. She prayed to the Empress that the Messenger had been deep in the ship, protected as much as possible.

Descending a ladder, she suddenly came face to face with two humans who, if not healthy, were nonetheless able to move about. They stared at Li'ara-Zhurah, and she stared back as her warriors quickly formed up behind her. The humans began to edge backward, eyes wide with fear.

Suddenly, they turned and began to run away, screaming in their native tongue. Three of her warriors instantly had *shrekkas*, deadly throwing weapons, in their hands ready to throw, but she said, "No! Follow them, for they may lead us to the Messenger. Let any humans alone unless they resist or interfere."

Her warriors obeyed, putting away their weapons as Li'ara-Zhurah led them quickly along the path taken by the screaming humans, who shuffled down the passageway, their bodies too weak to carry them faster.

As they passed an open doorway, an unexpected *boom* filled the passageway and one of her warriors was flung against the opposite wall, a massive hole punched in her chest armor. Three of her other warriors pounced on the human, one of their warriors in vacuum armor, and slashed him to pieces before he could fire another shot.

They encountered more humans in what Li'ara-Zhurah could only think of as a bizarre situation: here they were, warriors of the Empire, marching by the humans in the haze-filled passageways, holding their swords toward the aliens to ward them off, but otherwise offering to do them no harm. Except for one more of the armored warriors, who was killed before he could attack, the humans shrank back and offered no resistance. Li'ara-Zhurah knew this was not because they lacked the warrior spirit, but because their bodies were so weakened from radiation poisoning that most of them could barely move.

At last they reached what she hoped was the command deck. Forcing the door open, she surveyed the humans within. Four of them were conscious, all of them staring at her in amazement; the rest were unconscious or dead, sprawled on the deck. Of the four, one held a weapon, a pistol, pointed at her chest.

The Messenger.

She knelt to the deck before him and saluted, bringing her left fist against her right breast. Normally to salute one not of the Way was forbidden, but a Messenger was an exception. Her warriors in the passageway did the same.

As they did, the Messenger spoke in words that she could not understand.

* * *

"Bogdanova," Sato croaked, "are you seeing what I'm seeing?" Sato was afraid he was having a hallucination.

"If you mean a bunch of Kreelan warriors, sir," she replied, shivering from the pain in her abdomen and the fear of seeing Death kneeling a few meters away, "then yes, sir, I am."

"None of you move a muscle," Sato ordered. He held his sidearm, unsteadily pointing it at the lead warrior. It felt incredibly heavy, and he was sure that if he tried to fire it the recoil would send it flying from his hand.

The Kreelan simply knelt there, head bowed, and made no move to attack. *I'm either incredibly blessed or incredibly cursed*, Sato thought tiredly. He almost wished the warrior would kill him with the sword and get it over with. It would be better than the agonizing death he faced from radiation poisoning. He lowered his weapon and let it fall to the deck. He simply had no energy left to fight. All he wanted was to try and save his crew, but knew that virtually all of them were going to die, no matter what happened. The ship's surgeon had analyzed the radiation absorption data, and they had all absorbed far more radiation than he had initially believed. More than any of the anti-radiation medicines carried by the fleet could deal with. That was before the surgeon himself had collapsed into a coma.

"What do you want?" he asked the warrior. He knew she would probably not understand him, but it was all he could think of to say.

She tentatively raised her eyes, as if she was in awe of him, and then gracefully came to her feet. The other warriors behind her remained on their knees. Approaching him slowly, her head again bowed down, she knelt before him in his command chair. Then she removed a smooth black tube, about as long as her forearm and as big around, from her belt. It looked much like the black scabbard for his sword, and Sato imagined it was some sort of weapon, something special just for him. He nodded, relieved. *It will be over soon*, he thought. He tried to focus his last thoughts on Steph, calling up an image of her in his mind, but even that much effort was too much. He simply sat there, staring at her as she opened the tube.

What he saw inside was not at all what he expected.

* * *

Li'ara-Zhurah had to concentrate on holding her hands steady as she opened the special vessel containing the healing gel. She wished that she could speak with the Messenger, to reassure him that she meant him no harm. She hoped he would remember the healing gel, for she knew from Tesh-Dar's recounting of their first contact with the humans that all of them had been treated with it. Normally it was physically bound to a healer until just before it was used, but this was an unusual circumstance, and a vessel such as this could preserve it for a period of days before the gel, a living symbiont, perished.

As she opened the top, revealing the swirling pink and purple mass inside, she glanced up at the Messenger. Even without understanding human body language, she could tell that he was repulsed by it, feared it. She paused, unsure of what to do.

* * *

When he saw what was in the tube, Sato instinctively pushed back in his command chair, his eyes wide with revulsion. He would have tried to turn and run, anywhere, but his body was far past that now. He doubled over, his abdomen a writhing mass of pain as he vomited again. The only thing that came up was blood, and the pain was excruciating. Clasping his arms around his stomach, gasping in agony, he passed out, collapsing into the Kreelan's outstretched arms.

* * *

Li'ara-Zhurah gently caught the Messenger as he fell, writhing in great pain, and she gently laid him onto the deck. "Alar-Chumah, Kai-Ehran!" she called. "Assist me!"

The two warriors dashed forward, followed quickly by the others, who formed a tight defensive ring around the Messenger and the others trying to save him. The watched the conscious humans on the bridge, who stared open-mouthed at what was happening, but there was no sign of any threats from them or down the passageway leading to the command deck.

"Hold him down and help me remove his clothing," Li'ara-Zhurah ordered. "Be gentle, and beware your talons against his skin; they do not wear armor as we do."

In but a moment, using their razor sharp talons, they had stripped his clothing from his body, discarding it to the side. Li'ara-Zhurah upended the vessel with one hand, catching the oozing mass of the healing gel in the other. It shimmered and writhed with life, and she noted absently that the three other humans who were still conscious were clearly repelled by its appearance. She did not understand their aversion, nor did she care. With her heart hammering with the importance of what she was doing, and the glory it brought the Empress, she began to knead and thin the healing gel on the deck, trying to expand its area to cover as much of the Messenger's body as possible. It was difficult, both because she had no experience doing this, and because she had talons, unlike the clawless healers.

After a few moments of effort, she decided that she would never be able to duplicate what the clawless ones did, covering the entire body with a single thin film of gel. Instead, she carefully cut it into sections, flattened them out, and then draped them over different parts of the Messenger's body. It was not perfect, but it did not have to be: half a million cycles of evolution and — in the early ages of her civilization's recorded history — genetic engineering ensured that the gel would itself know what to do, even without a healer to guide it. She watched as the pulsating mass penetrated the Messenger's skin, completely disappearing into his body after only a few moments.

Normally, the healing gel worked very quickly on nearly any injury, but the healers had warned her that this would take longer, for the gel had to repair every cell that had been damaged or destroyed by radiation. The gel was also not fully attuned yet to human DNA, and she hoped that no unforeseen complications arose: only a healer could interact with the gel to guide it in what to do.

With the other three humans looking on in frightened awe, she waited silently next to the unconscious Messenger as the healing gel did its work.

FORTY-NINE

"No one was aboard her, colonel," Mills reported to Grishin after getting the information from the squad that had boarded the light freighter they planned to steal. "The ship has power from the field umbilicals," he glanced at the massive cables that snaked from a terminal on the tarmac near the ship's forward landing gear and were plugged into various power receptacles, "and looks like she's had at least some maintenance work done."

"So what's the bad news?" Faraday asked. He hurriedly walked between Grishin and Mills, ignoring the pain in his left leg and back from the crash.

"Nothing," Mills told him matter-of-factly, "except that the sodding buggers physically removed the navigation core."

Faraday stopped in his tracks. "They pulled the whole core, not just the memory cells?"

"Yes," Mills confirmed grimly. "There's nothing but a fucking hole where the core should be. That's how my chaps found it, not being too clever about such things normally. Whoever pulled it didn't even bother to seal the socket to keep out the dust."

"Fuck," Faraday exclaimed, balling his fists in anger. "*Fuck!* Well, colonel, even if everything else on this ship is hunky-dory, we've just made this trip out here for absolutely nothing."

"Why?" Grishin asked. He realized that this was a serious problem, but was smart enough to understand that he didn't know everything. "Can you not still take off and make orbit without it? Our ships may be able to pick us up if we can make it that far."

"I might, if they'd only taken the memory cells, which contain all the star charts." He shook his head. "The navigation core itself, though, that's the brain behind the operation, the processing unit that translates the information we give it through the controls into machine-level language that the ship's systems understand. Without it..." He shrugged. "Trying to fly without it would be like trying to drive a skimmer on manual without a steering wheel or any other controls. If we had a full crew, we might be able to manage on full manual, although that would be dangerous as hell. But with just me...I'm sorry, sir, but it just can't be done. It's just not physically possible."

"Brilliant," Grishin muttered.

"Sir?" Mills asked.

"It is a perfect way to ground a ship," Grishin told him. "It does not matter if you can fire up the engines or other systems manually. If you cannot control them, it makes no difference." He sighed.

"What now, sir?" Mills asked quietly as Faraday wandered over to the pile of equipment that had been salvaged from the cutter and flopped down, dejected. "We can't let the troops give up hope."

"No, Mills, we can't," Grishin told him. "Yet I do not have any bright ideas. This ship was our only hope of getting off-planet unless more Confederation ships arrive, which is most unlikely. Even then, I doubt they would be able to fight their way to the surface to retrieve us. We're going to have to think of something else."

"Yes, sir," Mills said, pressing his mouth into a thin line. *Dammit*, he thought, *we came so bloody close!*

He and Grishin both looked up at the sound of distant gunfire from near the spaceport's entrance.

"Well," said Grishin, "there is some good news, at least. It appears that Major Justin has arrived with the rest of the brigade."

"And not a moment too soon," Mills told him, pointing skyward. "We have visitors, I'd say."

Grishin looked up to where Mills was pointing and his heart sank even further, if that was possible. He saw the tell-tale streaks of inbound assault craft in the high atmosphere, hundreds of them, swarming toward the surface.

Missiles suddenly rose from the ground on pillars of fire and smoke, streaking away toward their targets. They only made it a few kilometers into the air before they were vaporized by defensive fire from the incoming enemy boats. More missiles fired, then more. Saint Petersburg was ringed with dozens of surface-to-air missile emplacements that were now belching missiles into the sky. A few of them actually got through the torrent of defensive fire from the boats, blasting a few of them into fiery shards, but not enough to make any difference.

As the boats came closer, ground-based defense lasers began to fire. Similar to the point defense lasers carried on Confederation warships, these had roughly the same amount of power, but their range was far more limited because of the interference from the atmosphere. But where the missiles had failed miserably, the lasers achieved some success: there was no defense against them except armor or reflective coatings, neither of which the attacking craft had. In ones and twos they began to die. Some exploded in huge fireballs, while others simply spun out of control.

Yet the Kreelans were not content to let the defenders have things their own way. Grishin watched in awe as several waves of what looked like shooting stars blazed through the sky from space, kinetic weapons that passed straight through the weaving cloud of assault boats toward the ground. While most of them impacted on the defense positions on the far side of the city, one group hit a site only a few kilometers from the spaceport: thunder boomed across the landing field, so loud that the men and women who stood outside had to cover their ears. As the alien-made thunder died away, giant clouds of smoke and debris rose above the targets.

"Good God, colonel, what was that?" Major Justin had to shout for Grishin to hear him.

Grishin turned to him, not having heard the final approach of the column of vehicles as he watched the fireworks display unfold. "That, major," he shouted back, "was the Kreelans suggesting that we find a way off this planet."

* * *

Inside the ship, Valentina lay quietly in one of the beds in the small but well-equipped sick bay, Dmitri and Ludmilla by her side. The medic tended to her and the seriously injured Marines, thankful that the stocks of plasma and blood expanders had not gone bad. The ship's autodoc had managed to improve on her field dressings, fully sealing the wounds and even extracting the bullets. It had also managed to isolate and cauterize the arteries and veins that were the most serious contributors to her internal bleeding.

"I'll be damned if I know how," the medic said, "but I think she'll actually live if we can get her to a real surgeon fairly soon."

"She is yet in danger?" Sikorsky asked worriedly just before Valentina woke up from the surgery.

"Yes," the medic said, "but I'd say her chances are good. The autodoc fixed the worst of the trauma, and we've got plenty of plasma and even whole blood for more transfusions if she needs it. She definitely needs a real surgeon, but..." She shrugged. "It's a freakin' miracle, my friend. That's all I can say."

A miracle, Sikorsky thought, just as Valentina opened her eyes.

"Don't look so sad," she whispered.

"I am not sad," he told her, wiping his eyes. "I am so happy you aren't..." He refused to say the word that threatened to come to his lips. "That you are still with us." He ran a hand over her forehead, brushing her hair back, and the gesture gave him a sudden sense of déjà vu: he had done the same for his daughter many years ago. Ludmilla held one of Valentina's hands, squeezing it gently.

Sikorsky glanced up as someone else entered the sick bay: the cutter's pilot. He limped in and slumped into an unoccupied chair. Closing his eyes, he leaned his head back against the wall as if to sleep. Sikorsky noticed that the medic and a couple of the injured Marines give the pilot a long look, then they turned away, stony expressions on their faces.

"Why are you not preparing the ship to leave?" Sikorsky asked.

Faraday sighed in resignation before opening his eyes and turning his head toward him. "Because we're not going anywhere in this tub," he said flatly, his usual flippant attitude having evaporated.

"What does that mean?" Sikorsky demanded. "Why not?"

"Because the Russkies took the fucking navigation computer core," Faraday snapped. "The nav system is nothing but an empty goddamn box. Without it, I can't control the ship. We're stuck here."

"Those explosions we heard outside," Ludmilla said, her Standard thickly laced with her Russian accent. "Are Red Army troops coming for us?"

Faraday gave her a death's head grin. "No, nothing that easy. The Kreelans are invading. What you heard were the city's air defenses being blasted to bits by a huge wave of Kreelan assault boats. We're probably next on the menu. They won't pass up a nice, juicy spaceport for long."

"Did you inspect the nav core?"

Sikorsky was shocked to hear Valentina's voice, and saw that she was looking intently at Faraday.

"What's to inspect, lady?" the pilot snapped. "The damn thing is gone. They pulled it."

"No," she said tiredly, "not the module they removed, but the housing itself."

"Of course I did, for what that was worth." He looked at her more closely, noting that she was obviously intent on something he wasn't picking up on yet. "What difference does it make?"

"Does it have an RP-911 interface?" she asked, ignoring his question.

"Sure," he said, curiosity and irritation both evident in his voice. "That's a standard connector for uploading data and doing system troubleshooting using an external terminal. Why the hell are you asking about it?"

"Because," she told him in an unsteady voice, as if she had suddenly been chilled by a bone-deep dread, "I can help you fly the ship."

* * *

"There," Tesh-Dar said, pointing out the assault craft's forward window at what could only be a spaceport. "We shall land there and disable the ships."

"Could we not simply destroy them from the air, my priestess?"

Tesh-Dar shook her great head. "And what challenge would that be?" she chided gently. "What glory to the Empress would it bring? No, destroying ships is the work of the fleet. Ours is to meet the enemy in close combat when we may. With the ships disabled, the humans cannot use them to flee, and there shall be more for us to fight, and more glory to bring to the Empress."

The young warrior bowed her head in submission.

"It is not a violation of the Way to enjoy great explosions," Tesh-Dar consoled her with a gently touch on the shoulder, "but we have other work this day."

As they approached the spaceport, with a dozen other assault craft flying a loose formation around them, Tesh-Dar sensed something else, an odd stirring in her soul that she did not immediately recognize. It was as if she were looking at a face she had not seen in years, and now was unable to recognize its owner.

Closing her eyes, she reached out with her mind, her second sight taking her spirit ahead of the ship her body rode. Slowing time to a standstill, she searched the spaceport, seeing the humans frozen as they were in that instant. Through the buildings, across the great expanse of the landing apron, through the ships, she searched.

Suddenly, she found him. A face that she recognized. He stood before one of the smaller ships, near a craft much like an assault boat that had crash-landed. Larger and, she knew, fiercer than his fellow warriors, he stood a head taller than most of the camouflage-dressed humans around him. She did not know or care to know his name, nor did he have any special standing as did the Messenger. Yet she knew more of him than most of his human companions, for she had fought him in ritual combat on Keran. She had let him live then, for he had fought bravely and well, and it would do the Empress no service to cull from among the greatest of the warriors the humans had. Tesh-Dar knew that his blood did not sing, and he was not the One they sought. Yet she relished the thought of fighting him again, to see if he had learned anything new.

Drawing her spirit back to her body, time resumed its normal course, and she clenched her fists in anticipation of the combat that was to come.

* * *

"You can't be serious," Faraday said, clearly dismayed. "Colonel, this is nuts!"

Colonel Grishin heard the pilot, but his attention was focused on Valentina. She still lay in the bed in sick bay, her haunted eyes staring back at him. "Valentina," he said, figuring that was as good a name to use as Scarlet, "is this even truly possible?"

"Yes, colonel," she told him, "it is. I was specially augmented for black operations, and one of the...modifications was an organic RP-911 interface."

"There's nothing odd that showed up on the autodoc scan," the medic interjected, not sure to believe what the young woman was saying, wondering if she was suffering from some sort of dementia. "There would have to be connectors, something..."

"There are," Valentina breathed. "Believe me, there are. But that's why the interface is organic: so it doesn't show up on medical scans."

"Then how do you use it?" Faraday asked, looking at Grishin like she was nuts.

"You have to apply a small electrical current to a specific location at the base of my skull," she explained in a small voice. "There is a matrix of special material there that will realign to form the interface. Then I just...plug in." She closed her eyes and shivered.

"What are you not telling us, Valentina?" Sikorsky demanded, his eyes full of concern. "Why are you frightened of this so?"

"Because..." she whispered, looking up at him. "Because the machines are so cold, so inhuman. I had to do it once before. I don't remember much..." She lied, shaking her head, trying to force away the horrible memories. "We have to get out of here, and without the nav core we have no choice."

"Let's see this interface," the medic demanded. She dug through the medical equipment, coming back with an electrical cauterizing unit. "What sort of current do you need to make this work?"

"Thirty-seven volts at two point five milliamperes, alternating at one hundred and five kilohertz," Valentina whispered, her eyes fixed on the cauterizing unit as if it were a dreadful monster.

The medic looked at her, then at Grishin. The pilot shook his head, circling an index finger around his temple: *she's nuts*. Grishin shrugged.

"That's, um, a bit of an odd setting, don't you think?" the medic said as she dialed in the settings. Surprisingly, the instrument accepted them.

"It was intended to be," Valentina explained quietly. "You wouldn't want an interrogator to torture you with electrical current and accidentally discover the interface, now would you?"

Sikorsky looked up at Grishin and said, "Colonel, stop this! Valentina, I do not doubt that you have this...thing in your body. But this is madness! It is—"

"It is our only chance, Dmitri," Valentina pleaded, squeezing his hand tightly. Turning to the medic, she said, "You will find a small mole on the nape of my neck. Apply the current there and you will see."

"Well, the current certainly won't hurt her much," the medic muttered as she stepped up to the bed and gently turned Valentina's head. She touched the tip of the cauterizing probe to the designated spot and pressed the button on the instrument. It began to hum. "Nothing's happen...ing. Oh, *Jesus!*"

Before her eyes, a small patch of Valentina's skin began to reshape itself into the form of a non-metallic electrical interface: instead of metal, it was moist organic tissue, but quite hard and shaped just like a standard jack interface. Looking up at the autodoc's display of Valentina's real-time body scan, she could see it taking form. It was not simply an interface, however: tendrils quickly formed from the external connector that led to various areas in Valentina's brain like a dark, malignant spider.

"*Bozhe moi*," Grishin breathed. He had never had any idea that such things were even possible.

"Does it hurt?" Sikorsky whispered as he watched the awful thing take shape.

"No," Valentina said, "not really."

He could tell she was lying.

"Do we have to keep this current applied?" the medic asked, still unable to believe what she was seeing.

"Only until the jack is inserted," Valentina told her. "After that, the auxiliary power lead in the jack will provide enough power to hold the matrix in place. It will remain until the jack is removed."

"No," Sikorsky said angrily, standing up to face Grishin. "This is monstrous, colonel! I will not allow it!"

Grishin faced him calmly. In Russian, he said, "My friend, she is our only hope. If she does not do this, we will all die. Every one of us, including her. The Kreelans take no prisoners, and this planet will soon be a graveyard: there were no survivors left on Keran after the aliens finished with them. They have come here to exterminate us. You do not wish that for her, do you?"

"No," Sikorsky breathed, feeling utterly helpless. "No, I do not."

In English, Grishin said to the others, "Let us get her up to the flight deck and
—"

"Colonel!" Mills's voice suddenly burst over Grishin's helmet comm unit, "We've got Kreelan assault boats coming in over the spaceport perimeter!"

"Understood!" Grishin told him. "Get going!" he ordered the others in the sickbay. "We are out of time!"

He ran down the passageway toward the loading ramp, just as the anti-air team perched on top of the freighter began to fire their missiles at the inbound enemy boats.

* * *

Tesh-Dar hissed as three assault boats in her formation disappeared in fiery explosions, victims of hypervelocity missiles fired from the ship where she knew her human opponent waited. "Land!" she ordered the pilot tersely.

The boat instantly plunged toward the ground, followed instantly by the others. The pilot flared her landing at the last moment, bringing the nose up just in time while the jump doors along the boat's flanks slid open. Warriors leaped to the ground even as the pilot set the ship down on its thick landing claws. The boat's pilot would not be staying with her craft, but would go with the other warriors: fighting face to face brought greater glory to the Empress.

Tesh-Dar led the others across the flat landscape of the landing field. The warriors took cover where they could behind the massive landing struts of the ships that now stood between them and their objective. They moved as quickly as possible over the flat, open landing apron to avoid the torrent of weapons fire now pouring from the humans surrounding the ship that was their goal. Tesh-Dar did not bother trying to shield her body, for she had no need to: the projectiles from the human weapons simply passed through her without leaving a trace. She strode toward the humans, her mind's eye fixed on the one that she wanted, the one she had come for.

* * *

"Mills!" Sabourin gasped. "Is that her?"

Next to her, crouching behind the relative safety of the cutter's wreckage, Mills felt his insides turn to ice. The huge warrior, the one he had fought on Keran and who had let him live, the one who had been the focus of his nightmares, was walking straight toward him.

"She knew," he murmured into the cacophony around him as hundreds of Marines fired at the advancing Kreelans. "She bloody *knew!*" And so had he, he realized. When his headache had abruptly stopped, it was because she had entered the system. He suddenly wondered if the headache itself had been caused by her being in hyperspace, aboard whatever ship that had brought her here. He pushed the thought aside: it was nothing more than idle, useless speculation for a man who had been living on borrowed time. He knew that the sand had just run out of his life's hourglass.

"Knew what?" Sabourin asked, her eyes filled with fright. She grabbed him by the arm and pulled him to her, breaking him away from the advancing alien horror. "Knew what, Roland?"

"She knew I'd be here," he told her. "Somehow, she knew. She came for me." He tried to put on his famous devil-may-care smile for her, the smile she had always thought made him look so young, but it faltered, failed. Pulling her close and putting his lips to her ear, he told her, "I love you, Emmanuelle." He held her for a moment, kissing her with a passion he had only ever shown during their lovemaking.

Then he was gone, sprinting across the tarmac toward his destiny.

"Roland, no!" Sabourin screamed after him, feeling as if her heart had been ripped from her chest. "*Come back!*"

* * *

From his vantage point behind the main forward landing gear of the ship, Grishin saw Mills suddenly break cover and dash straight for the Kreelans. Or, rather, straight for the huge warrior who stalked across the tarmac toward the human positions, totally impervious to their weapons.

"*Chyort voz'mi,*" he whispered, instantly recognizing her. She had killed one of his crewmen on Keran, snatching him out of his command vehicle's rear hatch with an alien version of the cat-o-nine tails, a dreadful multi-barbed whip. Grishin could still hear the wet smacking sound the legionnaire's body had made when it hit the metal coaming of the vehicle's open hatch, smashing the skull and leg bones, just before Grishin's driver had panicked and driven away.

"Colonel," Major Justin shouted over the firing, "look!"

The Kreelans had stopped, taking cover as best they could behind the landing gear and ground equipment of the nearest ships. Only the huge warrior was out in the open now, standing. Waiting.

"Cease fire!" Grishin called through the brigade command net.

"Cease fire!" His command was repeated by his surviving subordinate commanders and NCOs, and in only a few seconds there was a sudden silence as the Marines stopped firing.

Grishin felt more than heard a deep rumble behind him. The Mauritania's engines were spooling up. He switched over to another channel, linked to Faraday in the ship. "How long?" he asked tersely.

"Jesus, colonel," the pilot said, "I don't know! Five, maybe ten minutes if we're lucky."

"I hope it's closer to five than to ten," Grishin told him grimly as he watched Mills warily approach the huge alien warrior. "We may not have that long."

* * *

"I'm doing my best, sir," Faraday told him. He was panting from having run back and forth twice between the bridge and engineering on his injured leg. "Your Marines are trying to be helpful, but they don't know shit about running a ship, and I'm having to figure all this crap out on my own." *And it's a fucking good thing I know some French,* he told himself. *Otherwise I wouldn't be able to understand what the hell anything was.* Since she was a ship out of La Seyne, all of Mauritania's instrumentation was in French. Slipping into the flight command chair, he frantically typed in a series of commands into the main control console, and was rewarded with a series of green indicator lights on the ship's main status panel. "All right! We've got the main drives up, jump drives check out, and thrusters are green. Sir, if you can get someone to disconnect the umbilicals, that'd be a big help."

"Consider it done," Grishin's voice informed him.

"All we need now is navigation," Faraday said quietly as the medic and the Sikorsky's appeared, carefully carrying Valentina. They strapped her down in the navigator's chair, leaning it back as far as it would go. She was white as a sheet, and shivering as if she were freezing. "Are you going to be okay?" he asked her. He had never claimed to have much emotional depth, but his heart ached when he looked at her. *Talk about having guts*, he thought.

"Just get us out of here," she rasped. Turning to the medic and the Sikorskys, she grabbed Dmitri's arm. "Whatever happens to me after the medic plugs in the jack," she told him in Russian through teeth that were now chattering with fear, "*do not unplug it*. No matter how badly you may want to. Do you understand me?"

Dmitri glanced at Ludmilla, with both of them wearing terrified expressions. They were not afraid of death so much as what was about to happen to Valentina. They could tell she was petrified.

"Promise me!"

"We promise," he whispered.

Satisfied, Valentina relaxed her grip, sliding her hand down to hold onto his. "Let's get this over with," she told the medic, turning her head to the side, toward Dmitri, to expose the back of her neck. "Please hold my hand," she whispered to him as she felt the tingle of electricity from the cauterizer begin to tease the interface into existence, "and don't let go."

"Okay," the medic said, simultaneously fascinated and repelled by the interface as it formed in Valentina's skin, "here we go." She took the slender cable and gently inserted it into the receptacle, then took away the cauterizer.

Valentina suddenly stiffened as if she'd been hit with a massive electric shock. Just as suddenly, her body relaxed and stopped shivering. The fearful expression fell from her face, replaced by limp placidity.

Sikorsky took a deep breath, leaning against Ludmilla. *That was not so bad as I had feared*, he thought, just before Valentina began to scream.

FIFTY

Mills stood facing the warrior of his nightmares, the warrior he had faced on Keran a lifetime ago. The firing around him had stopped, but he barely noticed. She was his universe now, and he knew they had now come full circle, and she would be the end of him. Part of him was bitter at the thought, not just because he hated the thought of dying, but he had actually found someone he truly loved, a love born in the most unlikely of circumstances. *I'll miss you, Emmanuelle*, he thought. But he dared not look back at her. It was too late for that.

"Well," he said casually, "let's get to it, shall we?" She had beaten him to a bloody pulp the last time he had faced her, and he doubted today would be any different. For some reason, that thought eased much of the tension out of his body. Facing one's destiny was sometimes easier when the outcome was crystal clear.

Without another word, he launched himself at her.

* * *

Tesh-Dar was pleased with the human animal, that he had lost none of his fighting spirit since she had last seen him. He had also learned from their last encounter: he was much better at feinting, trying to conceal his true intentions from her as he attacked.

She began sparring with him, careful not to injure him severely, again enjoying the thrill of single combat. She did not use any weapons other than her body, for she had no need. Nor did she wish the combat to be over too soon. She did not yet know if she would allow him to live as she had last time: much would depend on how well he fought.

So focused was she on the human that she failed to sense what was taking place far above, in space.

* * *

"They're leaving!" the flag tactical officer reported excitedly. On the flag bridge display aboard Constellation, the swarm of red icons orbiting Saint Petersburg suddenly thinned.

"Recall the cutter!" Hanson ordered. The ship had deployed its cutter to the limb of Riga, allowing its sensors to peer past the planet at Saint Petersburg while the human warships sheltered behind the planet, waiting for the right moment to strike.

"Aye, ma'am!" the communications officer reported. "The cutter is on its way. ETA three minutes."

"Commodore," Voroshilov's image said on Hanson's vidcom terminal, "you see the change in the enemy fleet's disposition, *da?*"

"Yes, admiral," she said. "It looks like our time has arrived. My ships are ready to jump on your command, sir, once our cutter is back aboard."

"Do you have any questions about our strategy, commodore?" he asked.

"No, sir," she said. "We make a micro-jump back to Saint Petersburg," she continued, quickly recapping his instructions, "make a slashing pass against the enemy fleet, and then micro-jump away again before we can become decisively engaged."

Voroshilov nodded. "Yes, commodore. Just so. Our opponents are not foolish, however," he told her. "Do not be surprised if they attempt to follow us, for our exit point for the second jump will leave us in a position visible to them. I do not expect them to let us have a 'free ride,' as you might call it, again."

"If they do, admiral," she told him gravely, "we'll be in serious trouble. The Kreelans have incredible navigation capabilities." She remembered the reports of the return of the Aurora, the ship that had made first contact with the Kreelans. It had emerged from hyperspace within meters of Africa Station in orbit over Earth after the ship had been traveling in hyperspace for months. It should have been impossible, but it happened. "Even without having carefully mapped the space in this system for any perturbations as you have, if they want to jump after us, they will."

"I am counting on it," Voroshilov said with a cunning smile. "Our comrades on Saint Petersburg's moon have not been idle in our absence, commodore. They have been launching a steady stream of mines to saturate the space surrounding the emergence point for our second jump."

"Will our ships be safe?" Hanson asked. The last thing she needed was to jump into a mine field and have half her ships blown apart — by human-made mines.

"Yes, commodore," Voroshilov reassured her. "The mines have been programmed to ignore your ships as well as ours. The Kreelan ships may get an unpleasant surprise, however. It is a trick we may use only once, but once might just be enough."

"Very well, sir," she told him. She glanced over at the flag captain, who gave her the thumbs-up sign as the status board indicated the cutter had been brought aboard and was secured. "We're ready on your mark."

"Stand by..." Voroshilov said tensely from the vidcom terminal. "In three...two...one...mark!"

As they had once before, the ships of the combined Confederation-Saint Petersburg fleet disappeared into hyperspace.

* * *

For a moment, no one on *Mauritania's* flight deck could move as Valentina's screams pierced their ears. Her eyes were open, her face completely slack except for her lips, which were parted wide as she screamed.

"Valentina!" Sikorsky cried, panic-stricken. "*Valentina!*" He reached for the interface cable, intent on pulling it away from her.

"Dmitri, no!" Ludmilla told him, grabbing his hands. "You must not!"

"I cannot let this happen," he shouted, tears in his eyes. "I will not..."

"You promised her, Dmitri," she told him, her face etched in anguish at the young woman's torment. "You promised!"

"Nav systems are coming up!" Faraday suddenly shouted. "We don't have any star charts, but we can get this fucker off the ground." He tapped a few buttons on the console. "I've got control."

Just then Valentina's screams stopped, as if the last button Faraday had pushed turned them off. She simply lay slumped in the navigator's seat, her eyes vacant, her body completely limp. Her mouth still hung open, as if she were still screaming.

"Is she dead?" Sikorsky asked.

The medic shook her head. "No," she managed, her skin still crawling from seeing Valentina's vacant expression as she'd screamed. "Her pulse and respiration are fast, but she's alive. I don't know how much of this she can take, though. I had no idea there would be this kind of psychological trauma."

"She tried to warn us," Sikorsky whispered, desperately holding Valentina's hand. "May God forgive us."

"Colonel!" Faraday called over the comm link. "We're up! Get your asses on board and let's get this tub off the ground!"

* * *

"Understood!" Grishin told Faraday, not daring to take his eyes off the drama that was playing out before him between Mills and the alien warrior. "Major Justin!" he called.

"Sir!"

"Start loading everyone aboard, as quickly as you can. Have Bravo Company of Third Battalion provide cover until the rest are aboard." That company was actually more like a reinforced platoon in strength after it had been decimated by the Russian ambush when they'd landed, but it was in better shape than the other companies were. He hoped that the distraction Mills was providing would be enough to get most of his Marines aboard before the Kreelans started shooting again.

"What about Mills, sir?" Justin asked.

Grishin gave him a hard look. "Carry out your orders, major."

"Yes, sir!" Justin nodded his understanding, then moved along the line of Marines, getting them moving toward the ship's massive loading ramp.

* * *

She hasn't lost her touch, Mills conceded as the Kreelan warrior landed another blow. He had fought his fair share of men in both combat and in barroom brawls, and it amazed him how bloody *hard* she was. He expected that of her metal armor, of course, but the few blows he'd managed to land on her face or the parts of her body that were not protected by metal felt like he was hitting a granite boulder. And, when she hit him, it felt like he was being hit by one.

He had his combat knife, but was hesitant to use it. To this point, she seemed content to play by the same rules as their little engagement on Keran: fists and feet only, with her essentially toying with him for her alien pleasure. He was afraid that if he pulled out his knife, she might do the same. And the smallest bladed weapon he saw on her was nearly as long as his arm, which would put him at more than a slight disadvantage.

He ducked and just managed to avoid another open-handed strike she made to his face, then darted in and landed a hard right jab to her gut, just below her breastplate. *Bloody hell*, he thought, *how does someone get abs that hard?* She grunted from the blow, however, so he gave himself a brief mental pat on the back for at least hitting her hard enough for her to notice him, just before she brought a huge fist down on his shoulder, knocking him flat on the concrete tarmac. His head slammed into the unyielding surface, and he lay there, momentarily dazed.

He didn't see Sabourin sprint from cover toward them, her knife drawn and a look of cold hatred on her face.

* * *

"Enemy ships, close aboard!" the flag tactical officer shouted as *Constellation* emerged into normal space from the fleet's first micro-jump.

"All ships, commence firing!" Hanson ordered, her spine tingling with a dreadful mixture of excitement and fear as she checked the tactical display. All her ships had made it, and their formation, while not as good as the Russians, at least had all of her vessels pointing in the same direction. They had landed on top of the bulk of Kreelan ships that remained in Saint Petersburg space, and that now circled the planet in low orbit. The huge transports and most of their smaller consorts had left, although the human fleet was still considerably outgunned.

Jesus, admiral, you cut it close, she thought as a Kreelan warship — *Constellation's* current target — showed on the view screen. Even with no magnification, the sleek shark-like shape nearly filled it. Her flagship's main batteries went to continuous fire mode, pouring shells into the Kreelan warship at point-blank range. She heard the ship's captain order the secondary and point defense weapons to fire, as well: it was a knife fight.

She watched as the lasers etched the enemy ship's hull, vaporizing armor plate, just before the shells from the main guns hit. The Constellation's gunners were spot on: a dozen flashes lit the enemy ship's flank as the shells hit home, all of them concentrated amidships. In a spectacular flash, the enemy ship's midsection exploded, her back broken, sending the remaining bow and stern sections tumbling in opposite directions, both of them streaming air and bodies behind.

The Kreelan ship had not fired a single shot in return.

A cheer went up from the ship's bridge crew even as the captain called for a shift in targets, and the *Constellation* poured fire into yet another Kreelan warship that was only slightly further away.

"Prepare for jump!" Hanson ordered. This first part of their plan was only to get the Kreelans' attention, to poke them with a sharp stick in hopes of getting them to follow after the humans as they fled. If they stayed here any longer, her ships would be gutted.

"Coordination signal from the flag!" her navigation officer called out. Voroshilov's flag navigation officer was coordination with his counterpart on

Constellation directly, while Voroshilov and Hanson concentrated on keeping their ships alive. Their level of trust had matured at least this far, their officers were cooperating directly as fellow professionals. It was difficult for Hanson to believe that she had originally been sent here to blow the Russians out of space.

"All ships, secure for jump!" she ordered in the din of *Constellation's* continued firing. The ship rocked from several shells that hit almost simultaneously. The lights dimmed ominously for a moment and several electrical panels overloaded, sending sparks flying across the flag bridge.

"Jump execution..." the navigation officer called as the center of the human formation tracked exactly over the pre-designated jump point, "...*now!*"

The *Constellation* disappeared along with the rest of the human fleet as a hail of heavy shells passed through the space where she had just been.

* * *

Li'ara-Zhurah knelt quietly, her eyes fixed on the Messenger, her warriors formed around her in a protective circle. Perhaps they need not have done so, for there was certainly no threat from the human crew: they were all but finished. Only one of the handful on the command deck who had still been conscious when she had arrived remained so, a female warrior who was clearly near death. The others had already slumped lifelessly to the deck.

She did not envy them the death that they faced. While they may have been soulless creatures in the eyes of the Empress and Her Children, Li'ara-Zhurah knew better than most of her sisters that the humans were worthy of respect. They had certainly earned hers during the attack against Keran. She would never understand their species or the peculiar things they did, like fighting among one another here in this system, even as Her warships descended upon them, but understanding was not required. In the end, there was only duty to serve Her honor and glory, for nothing else truly mattered. It had taken her a great deal of pain and much help from Tesh-Dar to fully understand that, but now it was a source of deep contentment.

She thought about the child she now carried in her womb, the song of its spirit strengthening hour by hour. Its melody was simple, yet strong: she would be a great warrior or clawless mistress one day, she knew, placing a hand reverently over her abdomen where she knew the child's tiny heart had begun to beat. In time, the child's song would grow as rich and complex as that of the countless others that flowed in the river of the Bloodsong of her race.

The Messenger's body suddenly began to twitch, and she knew that the healing gel had run its course. Being treated with it was sometimes not a pleasant process, but her race had not suffered from disease for millennia, and virtually any injury short of destruction of the brain could be repaired, if She so willed it. His body suddenly convulsed, and the gel flowed from his mouth, out of his lungs. It had penetrated the various layers of his body, repairing the damage left behind by the radiation, or so she hoped, and at last had gathered in his lungs before exiting through the mouth.

She reverently took the gel, now laced with sickly yellow streaks, and placed it back in the tube, where it pulsed weakly. It could normally be reused after it had bonded with a healer, but this symbiont would never again know such a bonding. She would take it back with her, but it would perish long before they could return it to the Empire: treating radiation sickness was a terribly rare thing, and one of the few applications that for some reason sickened the symbionts. It was a great loss, for the healing gel was one of the most valued things in their civilization, but its sacrifice was for a worthy cause.

The Messenger lay back on the deck, his eyes fluttering open. He looked at her, his strangely-shaped eyes, narrower than most of the other humans she had seen, as if he were born squinting, then sat up to face her. She bowed her head low to honor him.

* * *

As Sato woke up, he felt wonderful. It was not simply that he was still living and breathing, but he felt truly alive, his body completely refreshed.

Opening his eyes, he saw that there was a Kreelan kneeling in front of him, head bowed, and with sudden clarity he remembered what had happened. She had used the awful goo that the Kreelans he had encountered on first contact had used to heal him, to eliminate the radiation poisoning. It would also have "fixed" anything else that was wrong with his body, something that was far, far beyond the dreams of modern human medical science.

He sat up, and she raised her eyes to meet his. He had not come across this warrior at Keran, but she obviously knew him. They all seemed to. It had been maddening during the battle of Keran, when he faced a group of warriors aboard his now-dead destroyer, and they had simply knelt before him as this warrior was now. He had been so enraged that he had wanted to kill them all, and they would have let him. In fact, it had almost seemed as if they wanted him to kill them. In the end, despite all that he had gone through, all the Kreelans had done, he couldn't. He simply was not capable of killing in cold blood, even the aliens who had invaded the human sphere.

"Captain," he heard a voice rasp weakly.

With a shock, he saw Bogdanova on the deck, looking up at him with glassy eyes.

"No," he moaned, suddenly noticing the state of the bridge crew, which he knew would be reflected in the rest of his people. They were dead or dying. All of them. "Bogdanova!" He got up and made his way toward her, and the Kreelans parted to let him pass, the group of surrounding warriors melting and flowing to reform around him where he knelt next to Bogdanova. "I'm going to get you out of here," he promised her fervently, holding her hand and brushing the hair from her eyes. Her skin was cool, far too cool, to his touch. She had seemed to be faring better than many of the others, but the radiation poisoning had clearly caught up with her. She was dying, as was the rest of his crew. "I'm going to get you out of here, all of you. You're going to be okay."

Turning to the warrior, he pointed to the slowly pulsating mass of goo in the tube next to her, then at Bogdanova, then the other members of the bridge crew. "Please," he pleaded with her, "help them. Save my crew."

The warrior gestured toward him, then the goo, holding it up for him to inspect more closely. It wasn't the grotesque purple and pink color he remembered from the first time he had been subjected to it. This specimen was clearly damaged or diseased, leprous in appearance.

"Can't you get more?" he demanded, pointing at the goo, then at Bogdanova again. "Goddammit," he shouted angrily, "you saved me, why can't you save them?"

The Kreelan simply stared at him, her silver-flecked feline eyes fixed on his. He had no idea if there was no more of the healing substance to be had, if she refused to get more, or if she simply had no idea what he was asking.

He suddenly felt a fiery rage building inside, a manifestation of his complete helplessness and his fear that, as on his first voyage when humanity had made contact with the Kreelans, he would again be left alone, the sole survivor of his crew. It was a possibility that he could not, would not accept. *Not again*, he thought bitterly. *Please, not again.*

His attention was brought back to Bogdanova as she squeezed his hand, her grip little stronger than an infant's.

"They saved you, Ichiro," she whispered. He and Bogdanova had been together since before the battle of Keran, and while they had never been anything more than friends and shipmates, it tore his heart out to see her like this. Tears welled up in his eyes as he watched the life slip away from her. She smiled one last time. "I'm glad they did..."

Then she was gone.

Ignoring the Kreelans, Sato picked her up and held her in his arms, tears flowing freely. "No," he moaned. "God, why do you hate me so much?"

He was still weeping when the ship was suddenly torn apart.

* * *

"Direct hit!" cried the tactical officer aboard the *CNS Southampton* as her shells slammed into the Kreelan warship at point blank range. About twice the size of a heavy cruiser and already badly damaged, it was an easy mark for their first target upon emergence in the Saint Petersburg system. It had an extremely odd configuration, but no one noticed in the heat of the moment: if it was Kreelan, you shot first and didn't bother to ask questions.

Too goddamn bad for you, Captain Moshe Braverman, the *Southampton's* captain, thought savagely as the ship's engines exploded, sending what was left of the forward hull spinning away. He turned his attention to the other three Kreelan warships that were close aboard. It had been only blind luck — whether it was good or bad depended on your point of view — that had put their task force's emergence point right on top of the Kreelans. *Southampton* was assigned to the second flotilla of cruisers that was supposed to have rendezvoused with Hanson's force before jumping into the system to take the nuclear weapons away from Saint Petersburg and to defend Riga. Unfortunately, they and their escorting squadron of destroyers had been ambushed at Edinburgh by Kreelan raiders, who had put up enough of a fight to delay the task force's arrival until now. Braverman certainly hadn't expected to find Kreelans here, as well, but he had made sure that everyone had been fully prepared for the unexpected.

After blowing *Southampton's* first target into pieces, Braverman ordered his tactical officer to shift fire to one of the other Kreelan warships that were furiously fighting back. All three of them were making full speed toward the one that *Southampton* had just finished off, which put them right in line with Braverman's guns.

"Fire!" he ordered, and the ship thundered as the main batteries blasted another salvo of twenty-centimeter shells at their next target. "Anti-boarding, units, stand by," he ordered as the enemy ships drew closer. He had been at Keran and had seen the devastation Kreelan boarding parties could wreak upon a ship, and he had no intention of letting that happen to *Southampton*. Just as another Kreelan cruiser exploded, he said, "Continue firing. Let's show these Kreelan bitches how it's done."

Blazing away at the remaining pair of Kreelan ships, *Southampton* and her sisters sailed by the remains of *CNS Yura* and the Kreelan warship that had been bound to her.

FIFTY-ONE

Tesh-Dar was enjoying the challenge posed by the human warrior. While she could easily have killed him, giving him a chance such as this to fight brought greater glory to the Empress, and also served as a useful lesson for her warriors, who watched the combat with rapt attention.

She had noticed the second human warrior approaching, of course, but was unconcerned: two of them would pose a more interesting contest, especially since the second human had drawn a knife. Tesh-Dar had no intention of drawing a weapon other than those her body possessed, but she might consider indulging herself in the use of her talons. Her warriors did not interfere, for they knew that two humans, a dozen, could not harm a priestess of the Desh-Ka.

After blocking a blow to her face by the human male, she was just preparing to make a counter-strike when there was a terrible surge in the Bloodsong, one of pain and fear from a dozen among the billions of spiritual melodies.

"Li'ara-Zhurah," she gasped, feeling as though a bolt of lightning had pierced her heart. She staggered with shock, nearly falling to her knees. The human warrior wasted no time, throwing himself upon her, but she brutally shoved him away.

Then she was seared by white hot pain as the second human warrior, about whom she had completely forgotten as she considered Li'ara-Zhurah's plight, plunged her knife into Tesh-Dar's back, just below her armored backplate.

* * *

"Emmanuelle," Mills shouted, "no!"

It was too late. He had seen her rush from the cover of the downed cutter toward him, but had been unable to wave her back as he staggered back to his feet after the Kreelan had knocked him to the ground. And now, just as the enemy warrior mysteriously stumbled, temporarily losing her focus on the fight, Sabourin had dashed forward the last few meters, her combat knife held at the ready.

Mills threw himself at the warrior, trying to hold her and keep her from turning on Sabourin. Even as addled as she clearly was, however, she was still far too strong for him. With an angry growl, she flung him half a dozen meters across the tarmac, where he landed hard, breaking his right arm and scraping his face on the rough concrete. "Emmanuelle," he cried desperately. "*Get back!*"

* * *

The Messenger's ship suddenly exploded around them, the force flinging warriors and humans alike across the bridge as the hull was torn apart. The lights flickered, then went out, plunging the command deck into total darkness. The artificial gravity failed, leaving the living and the dead flying through the compartment like ricocheting bullets before they were sucked into the screaming torrent of the ship's air as it vented into space through the shattered hull.

Sato flailed his arms and legs, trying desperately to find something to cling to as he was sucked toward the bridge hatchway, but in the total and utter darkness it was impossible. His lungs felt like they were about to burst, and he forced himself to exhale to relieve the pressure. It wouldn't matter in another few moments, he knew, but that is what he had been trained to do, and that is what he did.

His leg slammed into something hard, making him gasp with pain, his lungs venting what little air they had left. For just an instant while he tumbled, he could see down the passageway from the bridge: ten meters down the passageway, *Yura's* hull was simply gone. There was nothing left of the rest of the ship, and he could see the stars whirling outside as the chunk of her that he was on spun out of control.

Steph, he thought. I'm sorry. I'm so sorry I won't be coming home...

A clawed hand suddenly grabbed his arm like a vice, and he felt himself being pulled against the quickly subsiding rush of air. Before he could react, he was forcibly stuffed head-first into something that felt like a bag made of metallic cloth. He struggled, his lungs totally out of oxygen now, but the owner of the clawed hands had both strength and leverage. The Kreelan, whichever it was, finished cramming his body in and sealed his malleable sarcophagus shut.

* * *

Li'ara-Zhurah was in agony. Her punctured lung had collapsed and one of her legs had shattered when she had been flung across the compartment when the ship's aft section exploded. She realized that more human ships must have come, and had fired on her abandoned ship, not realizing that it was tied up to one of their own.

Yet in defeat, she could still find victory. Even though her warriors had perished, sucked into the vacuum of space, the Empress had graced her one last time, for she had found a spot to anchor herself near the hatch leading from the command compartment. As the air howled into space, taking everything in the compartment with it that was not locked down, the human ship had automatically released what she knew must be survival devices, cloth-like bags that probably had emergency air supplies and more inside them. Even without the ship's lighting, she could see quite well by the starlight that entered the compartment from the torn hull behind them. She had snatched one of the survival devices as it sailed past her, careful not to puncture the device with her talons. Holding it between her thighs, ignoring the pain in her broken leg, she pulled the Messenger from the airflow as he passed her. She had to wait a moment until the air was nearly gone before she could stuff his struggling body into the safety device, hoping it was smart enough to function automatically.

With one final effort, she forced his feet through the opening in the bag, then sealed the flap shut behind him.

* * *

It's a beach ball, Sato thought. *I'm in a beach ball.* They were life preservers in space, cheap but effective devices that were stored in every compartment of the ship in case the hull was breached. While they had a long-winded official designation, the spherical survival bags were traditionally called "beach balls" because of their shape.

As soon as the Kreelan sealed him in, a small tank filled the beach ball with life-giving air, its shape snapping from a formless bag into a tight sphere. An emergency beacon began to transmit, and a set of small lights came on, providing him with gentle illumination of the ball's interior, along with bright lights on the exterior to help rescuers see it. A section of the ball was transparent, allowing him to see out.

And there, in the beach ball's external lights, was the face of the warrior, looking in at him. She placed a hand against the transparency, and he raised his hand to meet hers.

"Why?" he asked. "Why me?"

But there was no answer. She took her hand away and reached around the back of her neck, releasing her collar. She attached it to one of the handholds on the outside of the beach ball, and with one final look at him, she let him go.

* * *

The living metal of Li'ara-Zhurah's collar would normally never have unclasped until she was dead, but the collar knew in its own way that she had reached the end of her Way in this life; all that remained was for the spirits of her and her unborn child to leave the dying vessel that had carried them. She watched as the ship's last remaining breath of air carried the Messenger into space.

May thy way be long and glorious, she thought one last time before closing her eyes.

Willing her body to relax, she focused on the Bloodsong of her child, calming it. For even the unborn had a place in the Afterlife, and together the two of them crossed the infinite bridge from the darkness to the light.

* * *

Tesh-Dar shuddered, then fell to her knees as she felt Li'ara-Zhurah and her unborn child pass on to join the Ancient Ones.

"No," she whispered, her eyes wide with pain and disbelief. "No!" A warrior's death in battle was something in which her people normally rejoiced, for that was their Way. A part of her understood this, but only a part. The rest of her was overcome with anguish so great that it sent a shock wave through the river of souls that sang the infinite melody of the Bloodsong, echoing her pain throughout the Empire. The young warrior she had come to love like a daughter was gone, along with her unborn child. The child that Tesh-Dar had looked forward to training after she had passed on the honor of the Desh-Ka to Li'ara-Zhurah, in a time that would leave behind the crushing responsibilities of being who and what she was now.

Her mind stared into the future, realizing that it was now empty, her entire existence pointless. She was far older than all but one other among her race, and she knew that Death would come for her, if not today, then soon. It must. And she would have no successor, no legacy. All that she had accomplished, all for which she had suffered, had been for nothing. "My Empress," she whispered in prayer, "please let it not be so."

And yet it was. For even the Empress, with all Her powers, could not bring the dead back to life. Only Keel-Tath, the First Empress, had such power in the times of legend, but She had been lost to Her people for a hundred millenia.

Tesh-Dar, Legend of the Sword and greatest warrior of the Empire, knelt on the field of battle, her heart broken by Fate.

* * *

The warrior suddenly fell to her knees as if she had been struck a great blow, and stayed there, gasping and clearly in distress.

Sabourin wasted no time. Rushing up behind the warrior, she put the force of her own body behind her attack, plunging her knife up to the handle into the Kreelan's back, just beneath her armor near where a human's kidney might be. The warrior made no reaction at all, as if she had not even noticed.

Furious, Sabourin yanked out the knife, covered now with alien blood, deftly changed to an overhand grip, and plunged the blade through the gap at the top of her chest armor, deep into the Kreelan's flesh where her shoulder met her neck.

As if suddenly coming to life again, the Kreelan roared in pain and rage. She grabbed Sabourin's hand, still clinging to the handle of her knife, and yanked her over her shoulder so hard that Sabourin's arm popped out of its socket. The alien stood fully upright now, holding Sabourin in the air, gasping in pain, their faces mere centimeters apart.

Sabourin spat in the alien's face. "*Nique ta mere!*" she shouted defiantly as she slammed her free fist into the warrior's mouth, then brought a foot up and slammed it into the alien's stomach.

Having managed to get back on his feet, Mills watched helplessly as the huge warrior plunged her free hand into Sabourin's chest, right through her armor and ribs, and ripped out her heart.

* * *

Tesh-Dar let the dead human's body slip from her grip to fall to the ground. Then she crushed the creature's still-beating heart in her fist before flinging it away. The other warrior, the large male, made to charge at her, but he was tackled to the ground by yet another human.

She ignored them, ignored the warriors who stared at her in shocked disbelief as they felt the depth and intensity of her loss. Ignored the pain from her wounds and the blood that poured from them. She simply stood there, the torn body of the human at her feet, feeling nothing, caring for nothing.

In the Bloodsong, she felt the empathy of the Empress pour into the great river as if a dam had broken, but it washed against Tesh-Dar as a wave might break against a mountain. She sensed it, yet she was not moved by it. She could have blamed the Empress for not saving Li'ara-Zhurah, for certainly that might have been within Her power, but that was not their Way, nor was it entirely true: Li'ara-Zhurah had given herself for a higher purpose, bringing great glory to the Empress and Her Children through her sacrifice. Had it been any other warrior in the Empire, Tesh-Dar's heart would now be singing praise and joy at such a feat as saving not just a Messenger, but a Messenger-warrior, a thing never documented in all the Books of Time.

But there was no joy to be found in Tesh-Dar's heart now, and part of her wondered if there ever would be again.

Instead, she felt the stirrings of a primal rage at Fate, at the humans, at the Universe around her.

* * *

"No, Mills!" Grishin shouted as the *Mauritania's* engines roared to life. "She's gone!"

Mills struggled against his commander, determined to get to Sabourin's lifeless body. "I'm not going to leave her!"

"If you do not, her sacrifice was for nothing," Grishin yelled at him. "Nothing!"

"Emmanuelle!" Mills cried, reaching for her even as he realized that Grishin had spoken the truth. She had bought him his life, paying for it with her own. "I love you," he whispered as he let Grishin help him to the ship.

The Kreelans made no move to stop them as two other Marines ran down and carried Mills up the massive loading ramp, which slowly closed behind them.

"We've only got one little problem," Faraday said as Grishin made it to the flight deck. "This tub doesn't have any armor. If those Kreelans fire at us..."

"They will soon have other things to worry about," the colonel told him, fighting to keep the emotional exhaustion out of his voice. "There is a Saint Petersburg combat regiment coming right toward them." He had seen a stream of armored vehicles and personnel carriers pour through the spaceport entrance and head across the massive landing field while Mills was sparring with the alien. He suspected the troops had originally been sent to kill him and his Marines. *Even that fool Korolev must have realized by now that the invaders were not human*, he thought. In any case, it did not matter: either the *Mauritania* would make her way to safety, or she would not. Grishin was almost too tired to care anymore which it would be.

He looked at Valentina, then quickly looked away. He had seen enough death for one day, and there was certainly nothing to be gained by looking at the inhumanly empty expression she wore.

"Here we go," Faraday muttered tensely as he manipulated the controls, ordering *Mauritania* to lift off, the commands mysteriously translated by Valentina's human-machine interface.

The ship rumbled and shook, then slowly began to lift. A cheer went up from the hundreds of exhausted Marines on the passenger deck and in the cargo hold as they heard the whine of the ship's landing gear cycle into flight mode.

As *Mauritania* took flight, Grishin caught a last glimpse of the huge alien warrior, standing still as a statue over Sabourin's body even as the approaching Russian troops opened fire on her and the other warriors.

Then they were gone as Faraday flew away from Saint Petersburg toward the surrounding forests, trying to get away from any Kreelan ground defenses before they made their climb toward the relative safety of space.

* * *

Tesh-Dar was not sure how long she had been standing there. It was as if she had fallen into the deepest level of meditation that she had been taught to achieve in the many cycles she had spent at the Desh-Ka temple, cycles that had passed in but a few hours of time to the rest of the Empire.

She knew that her injuries were severe, and that she should seek the attention of a healer, but she no longer cared. She felt nothing, save a cold fire that had taken root in her now-empty soul.

As if in a dream, she saw the warriors around her fighting, firing their weapons at the enemy. At humans. She could sense the bullets the humans fired streaking past her, others striking her armor and flesh. Some had actually hit her, for the power that let her walk through solid objects and let other objects pass through her was a conscious one. She glanced down at her feet, her gaze passing over the human warrior she had killed, to see a pool of blood, her own, spreading at her feet.

The humans, she suddenly seethed. Within her, a power began to build, one that she had never had cause to use. Until now.

Fully aware now, using the powers she had inherited and trained to use over many long cycles, she turned toward the humans. She saw that many of her warriors were dead, others wounded, as the humans fired their primitive rifles and larger weapons from their war machines. One of the latter had its massive cannon aimed directly at Tesh-Dar. Firing with a great gout of flame and smoke, she instantly slowed the flow of time, examining the dart-like projectile that was pointed at her. Letting time begin to flow again, but slowly, she waited until the projectile was just in front of her before she batted it away as if it were an offending insect. Then she let time speed up to its normal rate, and watched with satisfaction as a number of the humans gaped at what she had just done.

"You have seen nothing yet, animals," she snarled to herself.

The humans began to focus more of their fire on her, and she let the projectiles pass through her. Inside, she felt the surge of power begin to peak, a wave of heat rushing through her body, her soul, like the core of a long-dormant volcano about to erupt.

All around her, the surviving warriors threw themselves to the ground. They did not know what was about to happen, but they could feel Tesh-Dar's power in the Bloodsong rising higher, a tide the power of which none had ever felt since the time of Sura-Ni'khan, Tesh-Dar's predecessor as high priestess of the Desh-Ka.

Tesh-Dar spread her arms wide, fists closed, and opened her soul and her body to the energy that eagerly sought release. Had anyone been close enough, they would have seen electric sparks dancing in her cold eyes. At last judging the moment to be right, she opened her hands, her palms facing the enemy.

The warriors around her cried out in fear and shock as bolts of lightning suddenly exploded from Tesh-Dar's hands, accompanied by a deafening barrage of thunder. Hotter than the surface of a star, the bolts lanced through the humans and their machines, melting, burning, and vaporizing all that they touched. The electric storm danced along the human line, blasting the animals to cinders, leaving nothing behind of the individual warriors but ash and black scars on the landing field. As the bolts touched the war machines, the metal turned white hot and began to flow, baking alive the creatures within who were not already dead from electric shock.

The humans stopped firing at her and tried to flee, but none would escape her wrath. There were nearly a thousand of them that had come to die here, and she disappointed none of them. By the tens, then the hundreds did she kill them. All of them. Using her second sight, she knew that there were other humans on the landing field, some in the ships, some in the buildings near the ships, and others caught out in the open, running between the two.

Her own warriors fled from the field as her lightning struck the ships containing humans, the electrical surge electrocuting those who were not insulated from the hull. Some yet survived, but not for long: her rage now a rampaging beast in her soul, she poured electrical fire into the ships around her, probing to their power cores, overloading them. One by one they blew up, exploding in tremendous fireballs that could be seen by Her warships in orbit. Their fire and debris washed over her, passed through her, and she let the winds of the storm she created lift her from the ground and carry her toward the large human city nearby. She did not need wings to fly, for she could control the fall of her body above the ground, another of the powers she had inherited. As the roiling clouds from the explosions carried her higher and higher, she looked out over the human domain, her second sight sensing the thousands, millions of souls below.

She would kill them. All of them.

FIFTY-TWO

"Damage report!" Hanson snapped after the fleet emerged on the near side of Saint Petersburg's moon, the same one that Voroshilov's fleet had originally launched their ambush from. *It seems like a lifetime ago*, she told herself wonderingly.

"One moment, commodore," the communications officer told her. Then: "All ships are combat-ready, with none reporting anything more than minor damage."

"We got a lucky break, admiral," she said to Voroshilov's image in her vidcom terminal.

"Yes, commodore," he said. "And I am hoping for another one, although that is perhaps too much to hope for. By my estimate, we destroyed at least six ships outright and damaged eighteen more. The Kreelans will not be happy with us. I hope." He paused, looking at something off-screen. "Ensure your ships are radiating as much as possible, commodore," he told her. "We want the Kreelans to know exactly where we are."

"I don't think you have to worry about that, admiral," she told him. "If they want us, they'll find us."

"New contacts!" her flag tactical officer reported. "Eight new contacts, classify as Confederation heavy cruisers, and twelve destroyers just jumped in!" On the tactical display, a group of yellow icons flashed into existence, then quickly turned blue as the ships were identified by their transponder signatures. "They're right on top of a group of three Kreelan cruisers, commodore..."

Hanson nodded absently as she used her console controls to zoom in on the section of the tactical display that showed the new arrivals. *It's about goddamn time*, she told herself, seeing the *Southampton* and the other ships that should have been with her since the beginning.

"One Kreelan cruiser's been destroyed!" the tactical officer cried.

"That didn't take long," her flag captain murmured.

"It shouldn't," Hanson said quietly. "Southampton has the best gunnery scores in the entire fleet." She often thought that Captain Braverman, the *Southampton's* captain, could be a real asshole, but no one could argue about his ship's combat capabilities.

A few moments later and that fight was finished. "Scratch a total of four Kreelan ships," the tactical officer reported.

"Commodore," the flag communications officer said, "we have an incoming hail from *Southampton*."

"Let's have it," Hanson said.

Braverman's image appeared on the secondary display screen on the flag bridge. "Commodore Hanson," he said formally, "my apologies for not making our rendezvous sooner, but we were attacked during our patrol stop at Edinburgh."

Hanson frowned. "With all due respect, Captain Braverman," she said, "where's Rear Admiral Assad?" He had been designated the overall force commander when the mission had been put together, and should be taking over command of the Confederation forces here.

"Dead, ma'am," Braverman said bluntly. "He went down with the *Bayern*. There were only seven Kreelan ships, but they concentrated their fire on her. She was lost with all hands. As the senior officer, I took command of our task force and got here as quickly as we could."

Assad's death left Hanson in charge. "Very well, captain," she told him, sensing that Braverman was being overly defensive about how long it had taken him to arrive. "Moshe," she said, trying to reassure him, "you and your people did well to get here as quickly as you did. And that was damn fine work on those enemy ships you killed on arrival."

"Thank you, commodore," he said, relaxing slightly. "May I inquire as to the tactical situation, ma'am? I see from your proximity to what I assume are Saint Petersburg ships that things have changed somewhat since the operations plan was drawn up."

Hanson offered him a wry smile. "Indeed they have, captain," she said. "The planetary government still seems to think we're the invaders, but Admiral Voroshilov, who commands the fleet, has—"

"*Multiple contacts, close aboard!*" the flag tactical officer suddenly shouted. "Enemy ships!"

"Execute plan alpha!" Hanson ordered. Then, turning back to Braverman, she said hurriedly, "Captain, we'll try to form up as soon as possible. For now, you're in charge of your ships. Take the fight to the enemy as you see fit, but do not — repeat, *do not* — become decisively engaged or sacrifice your command. Give them hell, Moshe."

"Aye, aye, ma'am," Braverman said gravely before he signed off.

Turning to her vidcom terminal and Voroshilov's seemingly ever-present image, she said, "It looks like your plan worked, admiral."

"*Da*," he replied stonily. "Perhaps too well. Most of their ships emerged inside our safe area." The Saint Petersburg Navy forces on the moon that had launched the mines had created a spherical minefield centered around one of the pre-designated jump points. At the very center was a cleared area where the human ships could jump in without fear of emerging right on top of a mine, which would be fatal to a ship. Their assumption had been that the Kreelans would jump in close by, but not quite *this* close. Some of them had appeared within a hundred meters of one or more of the human ships.

Red icons ringed the blue icons of her and Voroshilov's ships at what was, for space combat, stone-throwing distance. Her ships and those under Voroshilov's command were already firing, but the Kreelans weren't firing back. They were closing in.

"Dammit," Hanson hissed. "Admiral! They're going to try and send boarding parties across to our ships! We've got to maneuver away from them!" Her ships had Marines and effective anti-boarding weapons. Voroshilov's ships did not.

He gaped at her for only a moment, the universal reaction of commanders who had been told that the Kreelans actually boarded starships, and preferred that over simply firing at them. "Scatter your ships, commodore," he ordered. "Lead the enemy through the minefield in as many directions as you can. We shall do the same." Turning to someone off-screen, he barked a rapid series of commands in Russian. "We will rendezvous with you once this is over." He paused. "It has been an honor, Commodore Hanson. *Udachi*. Good luck."

"You, too, sir," she said. Scattering their ships into the minefield was a desperate move. While the mines had been programmed to recognize their ships, that was something that no ship commander who wished to live very long would ever trust. The fact that mines were inherently dangerous to any ships near them, not just their designated targets, added to the adrenaline surge in her system. Turning to the fleet communications officer just as a cloud of tiny icons — warriors in armored vacuum suits — erupted from the enemy ships, she ordered, "All ships: scatter! Repeat, scatter, and prepare to repel boarders!"

Clenching the arms of her combat chair, she kept her eyes riveted to the main display screen as *Constellation* wheeled to a random bearing and surged forward into the minefield and away from the approaching warriors at flank speed, every weapon aboard blasting at the enemy ships that turned to pursue her and her sisters.

* * *

"Captain," *Southampton's* tactical controller called out. "Sir, you need to see this."

Scowling, Braverman got up from his combat chair and went to stand next to the controller, looking at her console. "What the hell?" he muttered. "Is that right?"

"Yes, sir," she said. "I confirmed it. It's a survival beacon from the *Yura*."

The blue icon on her display flashed, calling for urgent attention. It was well astern now, but was directly along the bearing where they had engaged the Kreelan cruisers.

"Recall the data from the engagement," he ordered.

The woman quickly called up the ship's logs of the sensor and weapons data, starting at their emergence point. In just a few seconds, she had forwarded it to where they had opened fire on the first Kreelan warship.

Braverman studied the information, which was now displayed on three separate screens: non-visual sensors, visual data from the ship's external video arrays, and weapon pointing and ammunition expenditure.

"Son of a *bitch!*" he cursed. He had thought something was peculiar about the first target, but there had been no time to think or ask questions. That, however, did nothing to lessen the burden of guilt and responsibility he felt. Now, looking at the data again, he could clearly see what they had really been firing at: the Kreelan warship that was their intended target was grappled to what was clearly a Confederation cruiser. While none of the sensor data he had could tell him which one, other than that it was the newest class that had been launched, he could add two and two. The emergency transponder was coded for the *Yura*. Ichiro Sato's ship. He had never cared for Sato, and thought he had been brought up to command level far too quickly. *But he wasn't the one who fucked up and fired on a friendly ship, now was he?* Braverman told himself harshly. He could have made excuses for himself about the fog of war or the heat of battle, any one of a dozen valid reasons why he fired on that ship. But Braverman would never have tolerated such an excuse from one of his crew, and he certainly would never tolerate it from himself. That simply was not the kind of man he was. As soon as this battle was over, he promised himself, he would report himself to Commodore Hanson and await the inevitable court-martial.

"Are there any enemy vessels behind us?" he asked, clearing the past from his mind so he could focus on the mission at hand.

"Negative, sir," the tactical officer replied. "We have multiple targets rising from orbit to engage us, but nothing astern."

Braverman punched the button to activate the vidcom link at her console. "XO," he barked.

"Yes, sir?" the ship's executive officer immediately responded from the ship's alternate bridge.

"I want you to take the ship's cutter and a team of Marines on a SAR mission," Braverman said. SAR was short for Search And Rescue. "The first ship we fired on wasn't one ship, it was two: a Kreelan and the *Yura*, Sato's command, grappled together. We've got an emergency locator beacon, probably a beach ball, that lit up astern. Go recover it."

"On my way, sir," the XO replied and instantly signed off.

On the tactical display, eleven enemy ships were rising to meet him, while the rest of the Kreelan fleet in the system was after Hanson and Voroshilov.

"Come on, then," he growled at the approaching enemy ships. "We'll kick your asses, too."

* * *

Pan'ne-Sharakh hurried through the antechambers of the Great Palace to the throne room, moving as fast as her ancient legs could carry her. Normally she would have *chuffed* with good humor at her pace, so slow that a sleeping warrior could move faster. There was no humor in her soul now, however. Only pain, fear, and dread.

More than any other, save the Empress, Pan'ne-Sharakh was attuned to the Bloodsong. It was a random gift of birth that she had honed over her many cycles into a tool that had served her uncommon wisdom. And none of the threads of the great song that echoed in her veins had ever been stronger than that of Tesh-Dar. Savage and primal it had always been, for that was at the core of the great priestess's soul. But it had changed with the death of Li'ara-Zhurah, and Pan'ne-Sharakh feared that Tesh-Dar might stray from the Way, that she might fall into the Darkness that consumed those who fell from grace. While she trusted in the might and wisdom of the Empress, she had to be sure. Not only because she loved Tesh-Dar as a daughter, but because she was sure that the Empire's greatest warrior had a greater role to play in the Way that lay ahead of Her Children than merely slaughtering humans. But to play that part, she had to keep her soul.

As Pan'ne-Sharakh entered the throne room, she paused. Even in this hour of need, the sheer grandeur of what her forebears had worked in this place was breathtaking. Located at the apex of a huge pyramid, the largest single construct their race had ever conceived, the throne room stood above the city-world of the Empress Moon. Made of transparent crystal, one could see the stars and the glowing disk of the Homeworld, above. The soaring walls, inlaid with precious jewels and metals, were decorated with tapestries that told of the birth of the Empire and the fall of Keel-Tath, the First Empress. While Her Children were born first for war, they also understood the concept of beauty, and nowhere in all the Empire was there a better example than this.

High above her, on a great dais atop a sweeping staircase of hundreds of steps, was the throne. Even with her aging eyes, she could see the Empress sitting upon it, her white hair shining in the glow of the light that shone from the Homeworld and the sun. It was a trek she had made many times in her life, but the last time had been many cycles ago. Looking at the steps before her, for once she wished for a return to her youth or a mechanical conveyance to whisk her to her destination. She had not the time to waste, but her body was not what it once was, and fantasizing that she could wish herself to the top would not get her there any faster.

The Empress, of course, knew she was here, and no doubt also knew why. And while she on rare occasion would use Her will to move one of Her Children through space and time, Pan'ne-Sharakh knew that this would not be one of those times. Like everything else that was of the Way, this was a trial, a test of self, a test of her love for the Empress.

Her face creased with grim determination, she shuffled across the enormous fresco-covered floor that led to the great steps, hoping she would survive the climb to the top.

And praying that she would not be too late.

* * *

Tesh-Dar floated free above the human world, carried now by her will and momentum more than the roiling clouds of smoke and flame that were all that was left of the human ships at the spaceport.

While she still sensed the Bloodsong, it was like a painting devoid of color, lifeless and faded. Powerless over her. She had given in to her rage, embracing it, letting it fill her heart and mind. Her strength, her true strength, was drawn from a core of animal passion that she had always had to rigidly control. But no longer. She knew that her rage, her anger, surged from her through the Bloodsong, overwhelming many of Her Children with its power, but she no longer cared. All she wanted was to kill.

She had seen several human aircraft and a few small ships rise from the surface, trying to escape the onslaught of Her Children: she had destroyed them all with the power that boiled within her soul, blasting them with lightning, tearing them from the sky.

The city lay before her, and her mind's eye knew where every human was. She could sense the beating of their alien hearts, almost as if she could hear them, and was eager to silence every single one. By the powers that had been passed down to her, by the sword or by claw, it did not matter. She was Death, coming for all of them.

Her wounds still bled, and a distant part of her mind realized that she would soon die if she did not seek out a healer. The rest of her, the animal that had taken over her soul, did not care.

As she came lower to the ground, she noticed a group of warriors battling against a mass of humans in a large compound not far from the edge of the city. The place was strange: it was little more than a great open field, surrounded by several sets of fences with strange coiled wire along the top, with watchtowers along the fence line. In the center, next to a large landing pad strewn with destroyed aircraft, stood a squat, ugly structure of concrete. Not large enough in itself to house anything substantial, her second sight told her the truth: like a burrowing *kailekh*, a rare serpent on the Homeworld, the thing above ground was merely a portal to tunnels the humans had dug beneath the ground.

She paused, considering. The fraction of her mind that remained rational managed to convince her animal consciousness that she would likely bleed to death before she could destroy the inhabitants of the city. She decided to expend her remaining wrath on these humans.

Landing gracefully ahead of the young warriors who surrounded the place, all of whom hugged the ground in fear of her, she marched toward the line of humans behind their defensive barriers. They fired their weapons at her, and she snarled as their bullets and rockets passed through her, as if she were no more than shadow and smoke.

Drawing her sword, she charged their line. With a deafening howl of rage she slaughtered the humans at a pace almost too fast for her terrified sisters to see. It was a gruesome spectacle that none of them had ever seen, or would ever see again.

When it was over, the human defensive positions were awash with blood. Tesh-Dar herself was painted in crimson, and the coppery smell was lodged so deeply in her senses that she doubted she would ever be rid of it. Yet she was not finished.

Trembling now, her great body on the verge of succumbing to her wounds and the strain for using her powers so intensely, she moved toward the mound of concrete. A short tunnel led her to a massive metal blast door that, she knew from her second sight, was nearly as thick as she was tall.

Baring her fangs in contempt, she brought up her sword, holding it ready as she stepped forward into the door, her body merging with the metal as she crossed through it toward the other side.

* * *

Constellation's hull shook as her main batteries fired off yet another salvo at a nearby target that had already been severely damaged by a mine. The Kreelan warships that had jumped into the minefield after them had not fired on the human ships at first, apparently hoping that their boarding parties would be successful in attacking their targets. Fortunately, Voroshilov had accepted Commodore Hanson at her word when she warned him about boarding attacks, and the Saint Petersburg ships joined their Confederation counterparts in diving into the minefield before the Kreelans could close the range.

Looking at the tactical display, Hanson smiled grimly at their conundrum, temporary though it might be: the Kreelan ships either had to pause and pick up their warriors, which would put them at a severe tactical disadvantage, or pursue the human ships with only a skeleton crew aboard, which also worked in the humans' favor.

For once, she knew, the Kreelans had made a major tactical blunder: some ships stopped to recover their warriors, and others didn't. It was as if they had suddenly become confused or preoccupied with something she could not even guess at.

Whatever works, she thought as the Kreelan ship that was *Constellation's* target exploded. A few seconds later she could hear the debris rattling against her flagship's hull like metal rain.

"I'm not sure I believe this," her flag captain said tensely.

"We're clobbering them," she said, hoping the words would not jinx the battle. The tactical display, however, told the story: between the mines, her ships, and Voroshilov's fleet, the Kreelans were being pounded. They had already lost twenty ships with as many more damaged, for the price of only three destroyers and two cruisers of what she had come to think of as the Combined Fleet.

"Captain Braverman reports that he's engaging enemy ships coming up from Saint Petersburg orbit," the flag tactical officer told her.

"Show me," she ordered, and a secondary display lit up with a depiction of Braverman's fight. The Kreelans had a slight advantage in tonnage — all of their eleven ships were heavy cruisers, whereas Braverman had only seven pre-war cruisers and ten destroyers — but her money was on Braverman.

She watched as he split his destroyer escort into a ring forward of the conical formation of his cruisers, pointed right at the center of the enemy formation. The cruisers began to fire their main batteries on a continuous cycle, and at just the right moment the destroyers ripple-fired their torpedoes so they would reach the Kreelan formation at the same time as the first wave of shells from the cruisers. It was a masterful display of precision gunnery.

It was a massacre. The Kreelan formation's point defense weapons were saturated with far too many targets at once, the rain of shells allowing more than half of the far more powerful torpedoes to get through to their targets. In less than a minute, all eleven Kreelan ships had either been totally destroyed or were nothing more than flaming hulks that were finished off by the destroyers.

A cheer went up among her staff as *Constellation* fired her own salute, finishing off yet another Kreelan ship.

"Damn," her flag captain said.

"I wish every engagement could be like that," Hanson told him, opening a channel to Braverman. "Captain Braverman," she said as his image appeared in her vidcom terminal, "that was absolutely superb. My compliments to your captains and crews."

"Thank you, ma'am," he told her. "I'll do that. And commodore..." He paused, and Hanson prepared herself for bad news. "Commodore, I've sent a cutter to our emergence point where we destroyed several Kreelan ships. I regret to inform you that..." He grimaced before going on, "...that I believe *Yura* was grappled to one of them, and we destroyed her. I'll submit myself for court-martial as soon as conditions permit."

Hanson sat up in her chair amid the thunder of another salvo fired from Constellation. "What? Captain, *Yura* was destroyed by a russian nuke when we first arrived," she told him. "What you fired on was nothing more than a lifeless hulk. In fact, if a Kreelan warship was grappled to her, I would have ordered you to destroy her anyway, to keep her from falling into enemy hands." She paused to let those words sink in. "There will be no court-martial, captain."

"That's...that's good to know, ma'am," he said, an expression of relief washing over his face. "But she wasn't a completely lifeless hulk: there was at least one survivor. We picked up an emergency transponder beacon, we think from a beach ball, and I sent the ship's cutter to retrieve whoever it is."

Hanson thought of the radiation the ship must have received, what it must have done to the crew. She doubted the cutter would find anyone alive. "Very well, captain," she said. "Let me know immediately about any survivors. And now that you've cleared out the enemy ships from orbit, how would you like to come up here and join our little party in the minefield?"

"With pleasure, commodore," he answered with a cold smile.

* * *

Pan'ne-Sharakh was in agony by the time she reached her designated place on the great stairway, the fourth step from the throne. She paused for a moment, turning her mind inward to calm her racing heart and burning lungs. Even more than the warriors, the clawless ones such as she were trained in deep meditation techniques, for control of their minds was essential to carrying out the tasks assigned to their caste, and control of the mind extended to control of the body. It would not keep her ancient muscles from being terribly sore come the morning, but the task at hand made such concerns nothing more than trivialities.

"Pan'ne-Sharakh," the Empress called to her softly.

She opened her eyes to see her sovereign standing on the step above her. Kneeling down in reverence, saluting just as did the warriors, she said, "My Empress, to thee I come for Tesh-Dar's sake."

"This I know, my child," She said. "I have tried to reach out to her, but she does not hear Me." Her voice lowered. "I fear forcing My will upon her in her present state, for if she raised her hand against Me, I would have no choice but to cast her away her soul."

The mere thought sent a tremor of fear through Pan'ne-Sharakh. The Empress loved and commanded both the living and the dead. Those who fell from Her grace and were cast into Darkness lived in eternal agony, lost to Her love and light. Tesh-Dar could not be allowed to suffer such a fate.

The Empress took Pan'ne-Sharak's hands. "Together, perhaps," She said, "we may bring her back to the Way. She is too important to the future of the Empire to risk her falling into Darkness. I cannot see into the future, yet I know to the depths of My soul that she yet has a great role to play in what time our race has left. But we have not much time: powerful as she is, her body, badly wounded, grows weaker by the moment."

"Then let us begin, my Empress," Pan'ne-Sharakh said, firmly clasping her hands, intent on bringing home the daughter of her heart.

FIFTY-THREE

"Okay," Faraday said nervously, glancing back at Valentina, who still lay comatose in the navigator's chair, "this is where it might get interesting." He had flown *Mauritania* away from the spaceport, staying as low as he dared in hopes of avoiding any Kreelan forces that might be lurking in the area before climbing toward orbit. No one had fired on them, but they had seen the destruction of the ships back at the spaceport through the electronic eyes of the ship's sensors, and he had no wish to have his ship experience a similar fate. He had gotten intermittent locks on ships in orbit, but the Mauritania did not have military grade tactical sensors, and could tell him nothing about whether they were enemy or friendly. "It's time to head upstairs."

"Take us up, Faraday," Grishin told him, now sitting in the copilot's seat. He avoided looking at Valentina: the sight of her gave him what he knew Mills would have called the heebie-jeebies. The Marines were settled in as well as they could be, with the wounded in the passenger cabins and the rest in the otherwise empty main cargo hold. He hadn't given Mills any choice about taking over the job of assisting Major Justin in getting things organized: having no idea of where they might wind up at the end of this lunatic caper, Grishin wanted his Marines ready to fight again if need be. What was left of the brigade had to be reorganized, weapons and ammunition redistributed, and the available food and water inventoried. The *Mauritania* could carry them through space, but its food processing capability was far too small to support all of his people. They had to find a refuge, and without any star charts to plot hyperspace jumps — even assuming that Valentina could stand such a strain — there was really only one option: Riga.

Looking out the flight deck's massive windscreen, Grishin saw the horizon fall away as Faraday brought the ship's nose up, climbing toward the clouds.

After only a few seconds, the ship's sensors displayed two groups of ships in near space above them, heading directly toward one another.

"I don't like the looks of this," Faraday muttered as he watched the game play out between the two sets of amber icons on the screen.

Suddenly the ships of one group, the one higher in space, began to change to blue, with ship data displayed next to each one.

"Hot damn!" Faraday cried. "Those are ours!"

He and Grishin stared as the two groups closed the range, gasping in surprise as the yellow icons representing the eleven Kreelan ships were wiped out.

"Holy shit," Faraday said, looking at the colonel. "We certainly kicked their asses that time."

"Indeed," Grishin said, impressed. "Can you raise them on vidcom?"

"Should be able to," Faraday said. "They should still be monitoring the merchant GUARD frequency." He glanced around the ship's console, finally finding the communications controls. Putting on the headset, he tapped in the frequency he wanted and began calling. "Any Confederation vessel, this is the merchant vessel *Mauritania*, please respond." He paused, waiting.

He was just about to repeat his call when a clipped voice answered. "*Mauritania*, this is CNS *Southampton*. You are in an active combat zone. Clear this area immediately."

"Let me talk to them," Grishin said, and Faraday handed him a headset. "*Southampton*, this is Colonel Grishin, Confederation Marines. I would like to speak to your commanding officer, please."

There was a pause before another voice came on. "This is Captain Braverman, commanding *Southampton*," a male voice said. "I take it that you're aboard the merchant vessel rising toward our formation?"

"Yes, captain," Grishin replied. "All of our assault boats were destroyed by the Russians, and then the Kreelans tried to finish the job. We had to...borrow an impounded ship to get into space. Unfortunately, we do not have enough provisions aboard to make a hyperlight jump, and our navigation system is, shall we say," he looked at Valentina's limp form, "not fully functional. I would be greatly obliged if you could provide an escort to guide us to Riga."

"I appreciate your situation, colonel," Braverman said grimly, "but I can't detach any of my ships right now to provide an escort. We're moving at flank speed to join Commodore Hanson near Saint Petersburg's moon to see if we can finish off the Kreelan fleet here."

"I understand that, captain," Grishin said, "but I have five hundred and seventy-three men and women aboard. Over one hundred of them are seriously injured. We have no star charts or navigation aids aboard; we are flying blind." While Riga was in the same system, the ship's sensors were not designed for survey work: finding a planet in a star system was much easier said than done.

Aboard *Southampton*, Braverman paused, scowling. He could not in good conscience leave Grishin and his people to fend for themselves, but the Kreelans — while taking a serious beating at the hands of Hanson and Voroshilov — were far from finished. He simply could not part with even a single destroyer.

Then the solution struck him. "Colonel," he said, "we detached a cutter a short while ago on a SAR mission. I'll order them to rendezvous with you and guide you to Riga. I'm sorry, but that's the best I can do right now."

"Thank you, captain," Grishin said, relieved, "that would be most appreciated."

"I'll give the orders immediately," Braverman told him. "Continue to climb toward our formation and stay on this vector. Your instruments should pick up the cutter soon."

"Understood, and thank you. Grishin, out." Taking off the headset, Grishin sat back in his seat, thanking God that Braverman had been able to help them. He had not relished the thought of Mauritania wandering about the system looking for Riga. At least fifteen of his Marines were wounded badly enough that they would die in a day, maybe less, if they did not receive proper medical attention. The ship's autodoc had helped stabilize them, but that was all it could do. And for those with burn injuries, it could do little more than temporarily deaden the pain.

As Braverman's ships sailed away at top speed, Faraday and Grishin kept their eyes glued to the navigation console, looking for the promised cutter.

* * *

Ichiro Sato looked through the transparent pane of the cramped survival beach ball that imprisoned him, staring at the stars and the world of Saint Petersburg as he slowly tumbled through space, utterly and completely alone. More than once he had reached for the tab that would open the beach ball and vent the air it contained into space. The only thing that stayed his hand was the thought of Steph. Yet even that, as much as he loved her, was only barely enough.

His emotions, were a confused kaleidoscope of guilt, anguish, and helpless rage. Twice, now, he had been the sole survivor of a ship aboard which he served. The first time, when humans had first encountered the Kreelans, the aliens had slaughtered his fellow crewmen and sent him, alone, back to Earth to bring word of the coming war. This time, fellow humans had killed his ship and his crew, but the "enemy" — the Kreelans — had saved his life, sacrificing themselves, an entire ship and its crew, for him.

He thought, too, of the warrior who had saved him as he was being swept from the *Yura's* shattered bridge and into space, saw her hand against the beach ball, feeling his own pressed up against it as he looked into her eyes. He wept for her as he watched the wreckage containing her body spin away into the darkness, thanking and cursing her in the same breath. He had endured a crushing sense of survivor's guilt after the Kreelans had sent him back to Earth after killing the rest of the crew of the *Aurora*, but that had been nothing compared to this. Then, he had only been a midshipman, the youngest member of the crew, on his first interstellar mission. This time, *Yura* had been *his* ship, *his* command. He had been responsible for her and every man and woman aboard, and he felt as if he had failed them all. As much as he wanted to see Steph again, he would have gladly traded his life and the miracle of Kreelan healing for any one of his crew, Bogdanova most of all. Her loss, more than any other single person aboard, tore at his heart. The part of his mind that clung to logic knew that he had done the best he could, had done his duty, and that fate and the enemy — humans and Kreelans alike — had dictated the rest. Yet that was little consolation in light of a destroyed ship and a dead crew.

As he stared into the void, he caught glimpses of bright flashes, orange and crimson against the black of space near the limb of Saint Petersburg's moon. *No doubt they're Kreelan warships*, he thought gloomily, *hammering our own into scrap.*

He let such dark thoughts take him as the fireworks continued, then intensified into a non-stop chain of brilliant, if distant, flashes. There was no way for him to know who might be winning, human (Confederation or Russian) or Kreelan, but he felt a sudden flush of pride. Even if the human fleet was losing, it was obviously fighting back hard. That thought penetrated to the heart of the warrior that lay inside of him. He couldn't help them, but the least he could do, he realized, was to cheer them on, even if his only audience was himself.

"Come on," he growled angrily, clenching his fists as he leaned forward, wishing the beach ball would stop spinning so he could see better. *"Fight, damn you!"* he shouted as a pair of explosions, larger than the others, lit the dark side of Saint Petersburg's moon.

And that was how the crew of *Southampton's* cutter found him, yelling at the top of his lungs as if he were watching the game-deciding play of an Army-Navy game, damning the enemy and cheering for his own kind.

* * *

Colonel Yuri Rusov, the commander of the bunker's internal security detachment, stared in unabashed awe and disbelief as the alien warrior systematically killed every one of the troops defending the bunker's entrance on the surface. He had never seen anyone or anything move as fast as she had, her sword nothing more than a brilliant disk as it cut down the men outside. Their weapons had no effect on her at all, as if they were nothing more than movie props that gave one the impression of being lethal, but that only produced a loud bang and a satisfying flash.

When she was finished with the men outside, she approached the blast door at the entrance, and Rusov breathed a sigh of relief. *She cannot get through that with her sword*, he thought. He watched the security monitor as she looked at the door. Then, with barely a pause, she stepped into it, her body disappearing into the two-meter thick metal.

"*Tvoyu mat'!*" one of the men on the security monitoring team choked, his eyes wide with disbelief. "That is impossible!"

"Get the reserve company to the main entrance!" the colonel snapped. "And sound the intrusion alarm!"

One of the other controllers flipped open a clear plastic cover over a large red button and slammed down on it with his fist. Throughout the massive underground complex, a klaxon began to bleat it's warning. Another controller spoke urgently into his headset, ordering the commander of the reserve company of troops to double-time to the entrance.

"What is going on?"

Rusov turned to find Marshal Antonov standing at the threshold of the darkened security room, glaring at him.

"Comrade marshal," Rusov reported quickly, "I believe an alien has somehow penetrated the facility."

"Don't be ridiculous, colonel," Antonov told him, stepping toward the large bank of security monitors. "That door and the entrance tunnel can hold against a nuclear strike. What did the alien do, walk right through it?"

"Yes, sir," Rusov answered, holding his ground, "she did." He gestured for one of his men to play back the video of the alien stepping into the door, her body eerily disappearing into the thick steel, as if she had stepped through a wall of liquid.

Antonov said, "It is a trick, comrade colonel. *Maskirovka*. This..." he gestured at the video monitor, "this is a charade."

The both turned suddenly as they heard a sound like a string of firecrackers going off, but heavily muffled by distance and many tons of reinforced concrete. Gunfire.

"Sir!" one of the controllers cried, as he quickly changed to a different video feed. "The guard detachment at the main door reports they are under attack!"

The camera view switched just in time to see the alien warrior finishing off the last of the eight men assigned to guard the inside of the blast door. She then turned and moved on down the massive entrance tunnel, her sword at the ready.

"The reserve company is moving to block her," Rusov informed Antonov, "although I doubt they will fare no better than the troops outside."

"I will not tolerate defeatism, colonel," Antonov warned sharply.

"It is not defeatism, comrade marshal," Rusov told him, looking him squarely in the eyes. "It is the simple truth." He played back part of the battle on the surface, again watching as the alien butchered his men.

Antonov visibly paled. "You must stop that creature, colonel," he ordered. "Use every man you have, including yourself."

"Yes, sir," Rusov said quietly, trying to keep the resignation out of his voice. He had faced his share of danger during his service in the military, and had even been in situations where he had faced the possibility of dying. But this was the first time that he knew with complete and utter certainty that he would not survive. "Men, get your weapons and come with me," he told the controllers as he headed for the door, drawing his sidearm from its holster.

They quickly followed him out, each of them taking a last fearful glance at the alien apparition on the security monitors as it tracked her movements.

* * *

Tesh-Dar was breathing heavily now, her heart racing to keep enough blood pumping through her system. She was still bleeding heavily from the wounds the human warrior had given her at the spaceport, but her own blood would have been indistinguishable from that of the humans she had killed, covering her from head to toe in wet crimson. Her muscles burned, weakened to the point where her entire body was vibrating like a taut string that was being repeatedly plucked.

Inside the human hive, she continued to slaughter the soulless creatures, but the passionate fire to kill that had burned so brightly only a brief time before was guttering, dying. As was she. Yet this last thing — killing the humans here in this underground warren — would she accomplish before her life ended. The rest she had killed in murderous rage; these she killed to honor the Empress and, in a small way, pay for her lack of obedience. A sliver of her mind, the rational part that was slowly reasserting its dominance as she grew weaker, was cloaked in the fearful certainty that her soul would rot in the Darkness for all eternity: she had stepped from the Way, essentially defying Her will and falling from grace.

More of the human warriors charged at her, a large group this time, and she began to kill them, but not as before, when the fire in her was at its peak. Then she had been a raging *genoth*, a great dragon and the most-feared creature that dwelled on the Homeworld. Now, her powers drained, she was only an extraordinarily powerful warrior. Even her ability to pass through objects, and let objects pass through her, was waning. Their bullets stung as they passed through her, and soon they would pierce flesh and shatter bone.

Baring her fangs in rage, at herself as much as the humans, she swept her sword through their ranks. They closed with her, throwing themselves upon her, until her sword was useless. Dropping the weapon, she resorted to the weapons she had been born with, and reached for them with her talons.

* * *

Voroshilov stared, disbelieving, at the vidcom and its projection of Chairman Korolev's panicked image. "Comrade chairman," he said, "what you ask is impossible. Our ships — all of them — are engaged in battle near lunar orbit. Even if I could detach a destroyer and with a microjump closer to you, it could not possibly reach you—"

"Stop making excuses, comrade admiral," Korolev hissed at him. "*You* will come here, right now, or you will face the most severe repercussions! We have been monitoring your communications, even as you ignored our calls, and know that you have been in collusion with the Confederation enemy that even now comes to kill us!" He paused in his tirade, before suddenly shouting, "*I will have your family shot!*"

Voroshilov turned away to look at the tactical display, an uncharacteristically stony expression on his face. There were very few red icons left now, the combined human fleet and the minefield having done their work. He was deeply surprised that the enemy ships chose to stay and fight to the death, rather than jump to safety, where they could live to fight another day. It was as if they simply did not care, or perhaps is was a point of honor that they fight to the bitter end.

A point of honor, he thought coldly, was something that the likes of Korolev would never understand.

Turning back to his so-called superior, he said quietly under his flagship's still-thundering guns, "Your threat is an empty one, comrade chairman. As I am sure you and that *chekist* in charge of the secret police know, my wife and children are on Riga, visiting her brother's family. I doubt that President Roze will let any harm come to her." Glaring at Korolev, he told him, "The Confederation commander has some ships that are not yet engaged with the enemy. I will ask that she send one to your aid, with the understanding that if you fire on them, they should fire back with everything they have and leave you to rot. If you survive, you can have me shot, should you wish. Yet even you should see now that your time is over." He paused, a scowl deeply etched on his face. "I do this not because you threaten me, comrade, but because saving some of our planetary leadership may allow us to better repel the many aliens that now roam free on our world. Remember that."

Korolev, his face contorted in cold rage, was just opening his mouth to speak when someone off-camera screamed, followed by a sudden eruption of gunfire close by. The chairman looked up at what was happening, then turned back to the vidcom, his face a mask of terror. "The alien is here!" he screamed.

Voroshilov watched silently as the last few seconds of Korolev's life played out before him.

* * *

Korolev turned away from his argument with Voroshilov as someone screamed. He turned to see the giant alien drop what was left of one of the communications technicians, blood pouring from his throat where she had ripped it out with her huge claws. She had not come through the door, which was locked and guarded: she had come right through one of the reinforced concrete walls!

Standing behind Korolev, who was now frozen with fear in front of the vidcom terminal, Marshal Antonov calmly drew his sidearm and fired at the alien, which focused her attention on him. Every round hit her, but she simply shrugged them off and kept coming.

Terrified, Korolev turned back to the vidcom and Voroshilov, screaming, "The alien is here!"

* * *

Tesh-Dar was running now on nothing more than force of will. She had finally dug her way out of the mass of humans who had tried to overwhelm her, stabbing and slashing them to death with her talons, biting them with her fangs, ignoring the revolting taste of their blood.

This room, the last in this warren that she was able to find with her rapidly failing mind's eye that contained living humans, was her last challenge. She knew the door was guarded, so she chose to penetrate the wall. She almost did not make it: the power within her that made such things possible was now little more than a flickering spark. She was halfway through the thick wall when she nearly lost control. Had that happened, she would have been entombed there, dead, the molecules of her body interspersed with that of the concrete.

Yet with one last agonizing push, she emerged into a large room, brightly lit with many screens and consoles, with a small number of humans. The closest to her was the first to die as she snatched the surprised human from his chair and slashed his throat before tossing him aside.

Another drew a gun and began shooting at her while the handful of others panicked. For the first time, her powers failed completely and the bullets slammed into her. Slowed and deformed by the strength of her armor, they still had enough energy to penetrate her skin and rend her flesh. She ignored the pain as bullet after bullet found its mark in her chest and abdomen, struggling forward the last few lengths to reach the human shooting at her.

With a roar of fury, she grabbed his gun hand as he was trying to reload and ferociously yanked it up and back toward her, tearing the arm from its socket. She slammed her other fist with all her remaining might into the human's skull, crushing it and driving his body to the floor.

The human next to him, who might have been able to get away had he not clearly been paralyzed with fear, babbled at her in one of the incomprehensible human tongues. She stood there for a moment, observing with disgust what she thought must be a form of supplication, perhaps begging for mercy.

"No mercy shall you be shown, animal," she hissed before driving the talons of her right hand into the creature's rib cage, piercing its heart. She hurled the still-writhing body against one of the nearby control consoles. She was rewarded with a cascade of sparks as his body smashed into the console, shorting out the circuits within and starting a fire that began to blaze fiercely.

Such is my funeral pyre, she thought sadly, knowing that it was the closest to the death ritual she would receive now. When her spirit passed from her body into the Darkness, there would be no one to take her collar. She felt the love of the Empress crashing upon her through the Bloodsong, but Tesh-Dar turned away from Her call, shame filling her heart for having lost sight of the Way, of losing control of her rage after the death of Li'ara-Zhurah. She could not bear the thought of again facing her sovereign.

Taking one last look around the room, now quickly filling with smoke and flames, she saw that the remaining handful of humans had escaped. *No matter*, she thought. *It is done.* She wanted now only to die, for her life to be finished.

As her eyes closed and she collapsed to the floor, Tesh-Dar opened her spirit to the cold of the Darkness that she knew awaited her.

* * *

"*Now*," the Empress whispered.

Pan'ne-Sharakh held her eyes firmly closed. This was not the first time she had been whisked across the stars by Her will, but it was a mode of transport that she had never been entirely comfortable with. She much preferred the feel of her sandaled feet against the earth.

She sensed infinite cold and dark around her for an instant that seemed to stretch forever, yet was only a tiny stitch in the fabric of time. She felt the air change around her, and when she breathed in her sensitive nose was assaulted with the vileness of smoke from burning plastics and metal, intermixed with the unmistakable scent of blood, Kreelan and — she surmised — human.

Opening her eyes, she saw that Tesh-Dar lay deathly still upon the cold floor, her body laying in a pool of blood that glittered with reflections of the flames that roared from the strange bank of devices next to her.

Rushing to her side, Pan'ne-Sharakh knelt beside her. She was aghast at the damage that had been done to Tesh-Dar's body, the many holes piercing her armor and her flesh. Pan'ne-Sharakh still sensed Tesh-Dar's Bloodsong, but it was fading quickly. Lifting the great priestess's head, holding it to her breast, Tesh-Dar opened her eyes. Pan'ne-Sharakh could clearly see the dark streaks of the mourning marks under Tesh-Dar's eyes in the flickering light of the flames.

"Pan'ne-Sharakh," the priestess whispered, her voice nearly lost to the crackling of the fire burning around them. "This is...no place for you, ancient one."

"I come in Her name," Pan'ne-Sharakh said urgently in her ancient dialect of the Old Tongue, lovingly stroking Tesh-Dar's battered and blood-smeared face, "for She feared forcing you to come home, that you would spite Her and truly fall from grace. Neither of us could let that happen, child. Too important are you."

Tesh-Dar groaned, both in physical and spiritual agony. "I have already fallen from Her grace...I am...lost."

"No, child," the ancient armorer said, gazing deep into Tesh-Dar's eyes. "Do you believe that the Empress would forsake you, among all of Her children? That She would send me here to you if She did not want you to return home? There will be penance for what you have done, priestess of the Desh-Ka, but only to prepare you for the future. For on you shall our race someday depend, Tesh-Dar."

Tesh-Dar said nothing, her face twisted in indecision and pain as she fought for breath, a trickle of blood spilling from her mouth from her pierced lungs.

"Let Her take us home," Pan'ne-Sharakh begged, taking one of Tesh-Dar's hands. "I will not leave you here, alone to die."

"Will She forgive me?" Tesh-Dar whispered.

"She has already forgiven you, child," Pan'ne-Sharakh said. The fire was now so hot that it was scorching her ancient skin, but she would not move from Tesh-Dar's side, even if the flames took her and she burned alive. "Surrender to Her love."

Tesh-Dar finally nodded, opening her spirit to the power of the Bloodsong.

Her heart stopped beating just as the two of them disappeared in a swirl of smoke and flame as the Empress brought them home.

EPILOGUE

Former Commander, now Captain, Ichiro Sato came down the gangway of the *CNS Oktyabr'skaya Revolyutsiya* where she had tied up to Africa Station in Earth orbit. Six months had passed since he had taken *Yura* to Saint Petersburg, months in which a great deal had happened.

With the decapitation of the planet's government, Voroshilov had taken command of the Russian military forces in an effort to exterminate the tens of thousands of Kreelans who had been seeded across Saint Petersburg by the alien invasion force. He was, however, unwilling to accept the role of leader of the government. "I was a Party man because I had to be to serve as I wished in the military," he had explained to Commodore — now promoted to rear admiral — Hanson after the last Kreelan ships in the initial attack had been destroyed. "I am not suited for it. But I know someone who may have some interest in the job, and would certainly be well qualified."

That is how his brother-in-law, Valdis Roze, President of Riga, found himself elevated from leading a planet struggling for political survival, to leading a star system that was immediately accepted into the Confederation under a hastily drawn-up charter as the Pan-Slavic Alliance. Riga, formerly Saint Petersburg's dumping ground, suddenly became both a safe haven for Russian refugees fleeing their parent world, and a base for the Confederation's efforts to eradicate the Kreelans. Roze had managed to masterfully set the formerly at-odds populations working together toward a common goal: survival.

The long-term outlook for Saint Petersburg was uncertain. Despite the generous terms of the Confederation charter for supporting member worlds with training, weapons, and equipment, the bureaucracies and industries to support those terms were still being put into place. For now, aside from shipments of smaller weapons and light equipment, of which there were plenty in stock and more quickly made, the Russians and Rigans in the system largely had to make do with what they had. This was the only silver lining to Korolev's despotic rule: Saint Petersburg had built and stockpiled a tremendous quantity of weapons over the years. These were now being put to good use.

While the Confederation fleet, which now incorporated Voroshilov's forces, had retained control of the system, the Kreelans continued to make what Sato considered probing attacks. Unlike the attack on Keran, where they came and quickly subdued the system and eliminated the human populace in a matter of months, with Saint Petersburg they seemed content to play cat and mouse. Kreelan squadrons would appear in the system, drop more warriors to the surface, and then brawl with the human ships. But each attack seemed to be slightly stronger, and Sato wondered if there would come a tipping point when the Kreelans would finally put enough into their attacks to drive the human fleet out.

A further oddity was that they had left Riga completely alone. Not a single Kreelan ship had ventured there. It was as if they wanted to give the humans a safe base to operate from, and were using Saint Petersburg as the designated battleground.

"It's nothing more than a gigantic arena where they can fight us," he had told Hanson before he left the system to return to Earth. It was like a massively upscaled version of the arena aboard the first Kreelan ship humanity encountered, where Sato's shipmates from the *Aurora* had died.

They had received news from courier ships that six other systems had been attacked in a similar fashion, although none of them had suffered the spectacular damage that had been inflicted on Saint Petersburg's primary spaceport. There had also been no reports of any incredible feats by the Kreelans like the tale told by Voroshilov about Korolev's death. The senior officers and civilian leadership listened to him intently, but quietly dismissed what they heard. It was simply too fantastic.

On Riga, Sato had not had any time to get depressed over the loss of *Yura*. With the blessing of Admiral Phillip Tiernan, Chief of Naval Staff, Hanson had promoted Sato to captain, and Voroshilov had promptly given him a ship to command: the *Oktyabr'skaya Revolyutsiya (October Revolution)*. Voroshilov had been forced to remove a number of ship captains who were Party hard-liners and had refused to accept the "new order" after Korolev's death. That had left a number of slots open with too few officers to fill them. *October Revolution's* captain was both highly competent and loyal to his people above the Party, and Voroshilov had promoted him to take a squadron command. The ship needed a new captain, and Vorishilov had felt that Sato would be an excellent choice.

"You commanded your ship, *Yura*, bravely against my fleet," Voroshilov had told him, "and your commodore speaks very highly of you. I cannot bring back your dead, but I can give you a new ship to command."

Sato had misgivings about the crew accepting him, but as it turned out, he need not have worried. Despite the information control exerted by Korolev's government, many Russians — and virtually every Rigan — knew of him as the only survivor from first contact with the Kreelans. His handling of *Yura* during the battle that led to her destruction had also earned the Saint Petersburg Navy's respect. The worst he had to contend with was learning as much Russian as quickly as he could.

He still felt the ghosts of his dead shipmates with him, especially Bogdanova, but he had never spiraled into depression as he had feared he would. "You can rest when you're dead, Sato," Hanson had told him once. "Until then, I've got too much work for you to do."

Sato smiled at the memory. He liked Hanson.

Pushing those thoughts aside, he began to quicken his pace down the gangway. He had brought his ship here for a weapons upgrade, but that would be mostly in the hands of the shipyards, and his XO had shooed him off the ship. He had free time now, at least for a while.

At the threshold there was a gaggle of civilians, mostly reporters, and military personnel waiting to catch a glimpse of him. But there was only one he cared about. Standing there in the red dress she had been wearing when he had first met her was Steph, his wife. While they had been in touch as often as possible, President McKenna had been keeping her press secretary — Steph — as busy as Hanson had been keeping him, and Steph hadn't been able to come see him for those long months.

But that was all in the past now. Running to him, her face streaked with tears of joy, she leaped into his arms. As he twirled her around, his own heart rejoicing in the feel of her warm body against him, her scent, in the sound of her tearful laughter, their lips met in a passionate kiss.

Captain Ichiro Sato was finally home.

* * *

Dmitri and Ludmilla Sikorsky were living a life that they could not even have dreamed of on Saint Petersburg. For the service that Dmitri, in particular, had rendered to the Confederation, the Confederation Intelligence Service had offered them a chance at a new life. They owned a small horse farm in what had once been the state of Virginia, with Ludmilla working from their new home as a consultant for relations with the Pan-Slavic Alliance, while Dmitri tended the farm. It had been a bittersweet decision for the Sikorskys: on the one hand, both of them were patriots, and wanted to do what they could to help Saint Petersburg repel the alien invaders. On the other hand was a very personal consideration for both of them: Valentina.

After Faraday had landed *Mauritania* on Riga, they had disconnected her from the ship's computer interface, but she had never regained consciousness. Her eyes and mouth had closed, as if she were asleep, but that was all. The Rigans had taken her to a local hospital, but before any doctors could evaluate her, President Roze himself had called and, obviously with great unwillingness, told them she was to be given what she needed for her body to stay alive, but otherwise was not to be examined or treated.

Dmitri had been furious, but there was nothing any of them could do. A day later, a man named Robert Torvald came for her, giving orders to the hospital staff that they were to prepare for transport back to Earth aboard a special courier ship.

"What is to become of her?" Dmitri, standing over her like a sentinel, asked him pointedly.

"That, Mr. Sikorsky," Torvald said with cold detachment, "is none of your business. She is a Confederation Intelligence Service asset, and that's all you need to know."

Unlike Valentina, Torvald had never been a special operative, only a field handler, and had no special self-defense training. He was totally unprepared for

Dmitri's work-hardened fist slamming into his mouth, followed by a powerful uppercut that lifted Torvald from the ground and slammed him against the wall of Valentina's hospital room.

"Listen, *svoloch*," Dmitri growled as he grabbed Torvald by the neck and hauled him up from the floor, slamming him against the wall again as the hospital staff looked on in stunned silence. "She is not a machine! She did all she was sent to do, saved all of our lives, and was shot for her trouble. Then she suffered the horror of whatever that thing is that you put in her head to get us here. And you treat her — and us — like we are cattle? I do not know or care who you are, but if you want to walk out of this room alive, you will do as I tell you."

"I think you might want to seriously consider it, Mr. Torvald," Colonel Grishin said casually from the doorway. Many of his wounded Marines were on the same floor, and he had come to see what the commotion was about. "She is a very special young lady," he said sadly.

Mills stood behind him, his face an expressionless mask as he glared at Torvald. His hand rested on the pistol that was strapped to his hip.

Eyes darting from the two Marines and back to Dmitri, Torvald said through bleeding lips, "Just what is it that you want, Sikorsky?"

And Dmitri had told him.

Even now, there were days when Dmitri was unable to believe that he had gotten his wish. But thanks to the intervention of Grishin with Commodore Hanson and Admiral Voroshilov, Dmitri's "request" had been granted on Hanson's authority as the senior Confederation representative in the system.

Torvald had been livid, but there was absolutely nothing he could do about it until he returned to Earth. He had the political clout to browbeat President Roze into not having any doctors poke and prod at Valentina, but he had no leverage over the military chain.

Dmitri's request had been simple: he wanted to take care of Valentina. Torvald had finally explained that she would probably never come out of her coma. The cerebral implant she carried was a one-of-a-kind prototype that had only been tested once before. Valentina — Scarlet — had suffered so much neurological trauma that she had been hospitalized for weeks afterward. After a thorough and quite secret review, the program had been abandoned as a failure. The implant had never been removed, Torvald had confessed, because it couldn't be done without causing her irreparable brain damage.

"As long as the implant was dormant," he had explained, "there was no danger to her. But as soon as you plugged her into the ship's navigation system..."

Torvald had wanted to take her home by himself to try and keep the implant's existence as secret as possible. He had quickly learned from Grishin while Sikorsky held Torvald pinned to the wall that there was no longer any point: every soul aboard *Mauritania* knew, and they had passed on the tale to the hospital staff, who in turn had gotten a copy of the *Mauritania's* autodoc scans.

Dmitri forgot all about Torvald as he headed back to the house after feeding their three horses, two mares and a young colt. He had always enjoyed stories and movies involving horses when he was a boy, and it just so happened that CIS's suggested relocation plan for Ludmilla and himself was here. He could not have planned it better.

Washing his hands of the dust and grime of the stables, he went to see Valentina. The CIS would not tell him her real name, and he did not feel right calling her Scarlet. So she was Valentina until she told him otherwise.

His spirits fell at the thought, because she would probably never say another word as long as she lived. *I will not give up hope*, he admonished himself. At least three times a day, every day, for the last six months he had come to spend time with her. They had a live-in nurse, a pleasant older woman who cared for all of the medical necessities, but she could not tend to the young woman's mind and soul. Dmitri knew beyond a shadow of a doubt that Valentina was still there, trying to escape the damage done by the implant. He hoped that every day would be *the* day, the day she came back. He would not stop trying to guide her and comfort her. Never.

He came in and nodded at the nurse, who smiled and left to give them some privacy. Dmitri gently brushed Valentina's hair and fluffed up her pillow, then sat down and took her hand in his. Sometimes he would read to her, sometimes tell her about the latest antics of the horses, or just chat about anything that came to mind. He grinned at himself, knowing that he probably spoke more to Valentina than he did to Ludmilla.

There were other times, like this one, when he simply came to be with her, to hold her hand and let her know that someone was there for her. He gazed out the window at the horses (he had made sure that her room had a good view of the corral), thinking only idle thoughts as time passed. As he sometimes did, he sat back in his chair, still holding her hand, and fell asleep.

When he opened his eyes again, he was still holding her hand, except that something was different: her other hand was gently stroking the back of his. Holding his breath, not daring to hope, he shifted his gaze to her face to see her eyes open, looking at him. She was smiling.

"Dmitri," she said, the sound of her voice filling him with joy, "I knew you wouldn't leave me..."

* * *

Roland Mills stood on the spot where Emmanuelle had died. Beneath his boots, the scorched and blackened concrete of the landing field was a reflection of his soul. This was the only monument, the only remembrance of her death other than some electronic forms filed by the Corps. There was no monument, no headstone or other marker that others might know that she had died here.

While the Marines had taken back the spaceport months ago, there had not been enough engineers available to clear the wreckage from the field until an engineering regiment had been sent from La Seyne. This was the first time he had been able to come here. There was no marker, nothing special about this patch of concrete, but he knew it was the place where she had given herself up to save him. As hardened to the horrors of war as he had become in the last six months, as dead as he had thought his heart to be, he found himself kneeling down. Just this once, he didn't try to fight it, but let the tears come. She deserved at least that much.

Still serving under Grishin, Mills had been one of the first Marines to return to Saint Petersburg, and had been fighting there ever since. The battles had ebbed and flowed as they rooted out the Kreelans who had been dropped across the planet. But he held out little hope that they would ever succeed in fully driving back the enemy: it seemed that every time they cleared out one area, more Kreelan ships would arrive to drop in more warriors somewhere else.

That was fine with him. It gave him more of them to kill. He knew that even if he killed every single one of them, it would not bring Emmanuelle back to him. But it was all he had left.

"I love you," he whispered, placing his palm on the ground where she had fallen.

Then, wiping the tears from his face, he stood up and silently walked away.

* * *

President McKenna set down the stylus pad and the electronic copies of the reports she had retrieved earlier. Of necessity, her staff controlled every minute of her day, ensuring that she met the right people and made the necessary decisions to keep the Confederation running. One thing that she had insisted on, however, was at least a full hour each evening that she could spend doing the one thing she had little time for during the rest of the day: thinking.

She rubbed her eyes and then rose from her desk, stretching out the stiff muscles of her legs and back. Another casualty of the war, she thought ruefully as she massaged her aching neck, was her daily exercise routine. Moving over to stand before the windows that looked out on the gleaming lights of New York City, she silently pondered the information she had just reviewed.

Let's review the bad news first, she told herself. A total of fifteen human colonies had been attacked in the six months since the Kreelans reopened their offensive against humanity with the invasions of Saint Petersburg and six other worlds. The number of casualties was uncertain, but Penkovsky's intelligence analysts put the figure at roughly half a million dead. That was a horrible figure, but still paled in comparison to the millions who had died on Keran in the first attack.

Unfortunately, the enemy seemed bent on a long-term war of attrition, committing just enough warriors and ships to keep the humans fully engaged in a multi-front war, but without delivering any knockout blows. As Ichiro Sato had told his commanding officer in a report that had eventually reached McKenna's desk, it seemed as if the Kreelans intended to make the entire human sphere a collection of arenas in which they could satisfy their alien bloodlust.

McKenna wanted to push the enemy back, to give them a brutal kick of strategic proportions, beyond simply defending the worlds under attack. But there had not been enough ships or trained personnel available to do anything more than to throw them into desperate local defensive actions. Under enormous pressure from Joshua

Sabine, her defense minister, she had grudgingly authorized the use of nuclear weapons in the hope that what had happened at Saint Petersburg had been a design flaw in the Russian weapons. But in three separate engagements where Confederation ships had used them, the Kreelans had somehow disabled the warheads. Forensic examination of six recovered warheads confirmed the unbelievable findings reported by Admiral Voroshilov: the fissile material had somehow been changed into ordinary lead. It was impossible, yet it had happened. Once those reports reached her, she decided to recall the remaining weapons from the fleet and had them returned to storage. If they were no threat to the Kreelans, she wanted to at least make them protected from potential loss or even theft by some of the colonies that steadfastly refused to join the Confederation.

In the meantime, the military high command had been working out the details for a strategic offensive. She had been impatient for them to finalize their plans, but they had needed time to build the infrastructure necessary to provide the Confederation with the weapons and ships it needed, and time to train the men and women who would use them.

And that brought her to the good news: the military and the industrialists who had been charged with putting the Confederation on a war footing had used those intervening months well. Beginning with Earth and the Alliance worlds, they had transformed the peacetime industrial base, and now several dozen worlds were churning out enough weapons to fully arm the Territorial Army units that were being formed on the Confederation's one hundred and thirty-seven member planets. The Marine Corps was growing at a rapid pace, with a massive new training facility established on a previously unsettled world that was now called Quantico, named in honor one of the training facilities used by the old United States Marine Corps.

Best of all, she thought, were the ships. Just two weeks before, the first of a new class of warship had been launched from the orbital shipyards annexed to Africa Station. The *Lefevre* class battlecruisers were twice as large as the latest heavy cruisers like the one Ichiro Sato had commanded at Saint Petersburg, and had nearly four times as much firepower, plus berthing for a full battalion of Marines. Twenty three more battlecruisers were under construction in various shipyards across the Confederation, and would be launched within the next two weeks. Over one hundred smaller warships, from frigates to heavy cruisers, were being built at the same time, and the shipyards were still being expanded.

Two more months, Admiral Tiernan, her Chief of Naval Staff, had promised her, and the Confederation would be ready to launch its first major strategic offensive campaign against the Empire. McKenna knew that throwing the aliens out of human space would not be easy, nor would it be done quickly.

But by God, she promised herself, we'll do it. However long and whatever it takes, we'll do it.

* * *

Tesh-Dar rode silently on her *magthep*, a two-legged beast that had been used as common transportation by her people since before the first Books of Time had been written. Save for her mount and two others of its kind that carried provisions, she was alone on this trek, as alone as any of her kind could truly be. For the Bloodsong in her veins was a link to her sisters across the Empire. And to the Empress.

Making the decision to return to the Empire had been the most difficult thing Tesh-Dar had ever done in her long life. The wounds to her body, while grievous, were yet trivial for the healers to mend. The injury she had done to her honor was far worse, or so she had thought.

When she regained consciousness, wrapped in a cocoon of soft and warm animal skins in the *kazha* in which she had grown up, Pan'ne-Sharakh had been at her side. As was someone else.

"My Empress," Tesh-Dar whispered, averting her eyes. "Please...forgive me."

The woman who had once been her blood sister gently stroked her face and held her hand. "All is forgiven you, priestess of the Desh-Ka," She said softly. "The powers within you are great, Tesh-Dar, greater, perhaps, than any of your forebears, yet you have never had cause to tap them to the full. You could not have known what would happen; you were not prepared to control it."

"I did not want to," Tesh-Dar told her. "I *chose* not to."

"This, too, I know," She said. "Obedience and duty, even to the Way, may sometimes waver when one's heart is broken."

Her spoken reminder of Li'ara-Zhurah's death sent a fresh wave of anguish through Tesh-Dar's heart. "You could have saved her," she whispered.

"With great honor did she die," the Empress told her. "It would have been a disservice to Li'ara-Zhurah to deny her sacrifice. You know this."

Unwillingly, Tesh-Dar nodded, realizing that her thoughts had become so clouded by her own emotions that she had completely lost sight of the path, of the Way. "I am lost, my Empress," she said.

"No, my child," the Empress told her, "you have merely come to a part of the Way that you have never before traveled, where the path is *not* clear. Children can follow the Way as a path of stones laid out in a line, but they could not find their way in a dark forest. It is this forest that you must enter now, Tesh-Dar, a place where your wisdom and faith will be tested. Few have reached so far as you; even Sura-Ni'khan, powerful as she was, had not come this far.

"What must I do, my Empress?" Tesh-Dar asked.

"You must return to your roots," She told her, "to the temple of your order. There shall you learn how to follow the Way, not as would a child in spirit, but as the great warrior that you are."

"How long?" Tesh-Dar asked.

"You will know," She said, "when my heart calls to thee." With one last caress of Tesh-Dar's face before She turned to leave, the Empress said softly, "May thy way be long and glorious, Legend of the Sword."

Throughout the exchange with the Empress, Pan'ne-Sharakh had stood in reverent silence. Now, she said, "A gift for you, I have," she said proudly as she reached down from where she knelt next to Tesh-Dar. In her hands, as she raised it up where Tesh-Dar could see it, was a sword.

"Oh, mistress," Tesh-Dar breathed. The black scabbard gleamed like a dark mirror. The handle, wrapped in matte black leather, was studded with diamonds that spelled out Tesh-Dar's name in the Old Tongue. Tesh-Dar felt a deep pang of guilt, suddenly remembering that she had lost her sword, the one Pan'ne-Sharakh had made for her earlier, on the human planet.

Knowing exactly what Tesh-Dar was thinking, the old armorer told her, "The other sword was but a toy compared to *this*." With a smile, Pan'ne-Sharakh drew the blade partway out of the scabbard, exposing the living metal into which she had poured her soul since Tesh-Dar's return. It did not simply gleam in the light, it shimmered, as if the metal reflected the water of a pond, its surface driven by the wind. "This is the greatest level of my craft," she said, "the finest that any of us, in all the ages, has ever done. This, to you, is my gift, that it may see you through the challenges you will face where you now are bound..."

The sword hung as a welcome weight on Tesh-Dar's back as she rode, with the ancient short sword of the Desh-Ka in its scabbard at her side.

She brought the *magthep* to a halt for a moment, letting it and its companions catch their breath from the climb up the mountains. It was a long trek from the *kazha*, over thirty days' travel, to reach this place. Above her, on a massive overhang that jutted out beneath the peak of the mountain, stood the temple of the Desh-Ka. She had last been here when Sura-Ni'khan passed on the stewardship of the order to Tesh-Dar, and the site of it sent a tingle of anticipation down her spine as she urged her *magthep* onward.

The temple was a collection of massive structures built from green stone that once had boasted carvings depicting warriors in battle, telling the tale of the ancients who had first formed the order. The temple had been erected so long ago that the carvings in the hard stone were worn nearly smooth from the work of wind and rain, and most of the structures had fallen into ruin.

Yet the stone was merely a façade, for the true temple was formed by the spirits of her forebears that yet dwelt here. When she had first come with Sura-Ni'khan, many cycles ago, she could feel a presence in the place, could hear the quiet murmur of the Ancient Ones in the Bloodsong.

Now, she could sense them clearly. Among them, she heard the melody of her own priestess, Sura-Ni'khan, beckoning to her.

Guiding her animals to the entrance to the only part of the temple that had not succumbed to time, a great domed arena, the largest of the structures in this ancient place, she dismounted. After quickly removing the packs she had brought, she freed the animals of their bridles and harnesses.

"Go where you would," she told them, gently slapping the rump of her mount, sending it trotting off, its companions close behind. She had no need of them here, and she suspected she would be here for quite some time before the Empress called for her.

Time, she thought, *in this place has no meaning.* Pushing open the massive door to the ancient enclosed arena, she stepped into the darkness and the embrace of the spirits that awaited her.

DEAD SOUL

FIFTY-FOUR

Three Years After First Contact

"Happy Birthday, Allison!"

Allison Murtaugh, now fourteen years old, smiled as her friends and parents clapped and shouted happily. Even her older brother, Shaun, who was nearly ancient at the age of seventeen and almost always a grouch, smiled and slapped his hands together.

Kayla, Allison's mother, gave her a tight hug. "Blow out the candles, honey!"

Allison looked at the cake her mother had made, now blazing with fourteen flames. The candles danced in her inquisitive green eyes and added highlights to her wild copper-colored hair as she leaned closer to the cake and drew a full breath.

"Don't forget to make a wish, Ali!" Elena, Allison's best friend, held both hands up, fingers crossed.

She'd thought a hundred times of what to wish for, but still wasn't sure. It was hard to wish for anything more than she already had. It was a perfect day, with clear weather and a light breeze that carried the scents from the fields around the farmhouse to the big porch where they'd gathered. Her parents and brother were here with her, as were her friends, and they'd all had a great time that morning, playing and riding horses.

She'd even gotten everything she'd wanted for her birthday, and more. A new reader to replace the one she'd worn out. Shaun's favorite hunting rifle, which she'd always wanted but had never expected to have, especially freely given as a gift. And best of all, she'd gotten a brand new saddle, her very own, for her horse, Race, to replace the worn out hand-me-down saddle that had been Shaun's when he was a little boy.

It was the best birthday she'd ever had, and had been an awesome day so far.

But it was one awesome day out of an endless string of days that were carved from sheer boredom. Her family made ends meet on the farm, but that was about it. They didn't have money to take trips, and you couldn't just up and leave a farm to take a nice vacation for a week or more.

Her family didn't even have a vid in the house, let alone a virtual gaming system or any of the other cool things that some of Allison's friends had.

Then there was school. It was utter torture, and she was always relieved when school went out of session for the harvests, even though that was really hard work. But she'd rather help her parents in the fields or go hunting with her brother than be cooped up in a stifling class room with Mr. Callaway. They had virtual teachers for many of their subjects, but old Callawag, as the kids called him, felt compelled to comment on nearly everything the virtual teachers said.

Allison would have preferred to live in one of the cities, or maybe even sail through space on a starship, traveling to faraway exotic planets, or maybe even visit Earth. She wouldn't want to go anywhere the Kreelans might be lurking, of course, but they couldn't be everywhere.

That's it, she knew. That's what my wish is, for a little excitement around here.

"Come on, Ali!" Elena was leaning forward, her face only inches now from the flickering candles and the glistening cake icing. Allison knew why she and the other girls were so eager. Allison's mother made the best cakes in the province, and won first place every year at the fair.

Before Elena could get any ideas about blowing out the candles herself, Allison released her pent-up breath and snuffed the flames to a thunderous round of applause.

As the applause tapered off and Allison's mother moved in with the knife to cut the cake, an unfamiliar, eerie sound reached them.

"What's that?" Allison looked up at her father, Stephen.

"That's not what I think it is..." Kayla set the knife down and moved beside Stephen, taking hold of his arm. They both stared in the direction of Breakwater, a few kilometers away.

"It is." Stephen, his brow knitted in concentration, turned to Shaun. "Get the truck, son. Right now."

"Yes, sir." Shaun had rarely heard his father speak that way, but when he did, Shaun knew to obey right away. He vaulted over the porch railing and ran for the vehicle shed behind the house.

"Daddy?" Allison's voice seemed like that of a little girl to her ears, and she didn't like it. Not at all. "Daddy, what is it?"

"It's nothing, honey." Her mother said, turning and taking Allison's hands. "Don't worry..."

"It's the invasion alert." Her father glanced at her mother, who glared at him. "She needs to be worried, Kayla. That might help keep her and the others alive." He knelt down in front of Allison and gathered the five other girls closer. "You remember the tests of the new emergency sirens we had last month?"

They all nodded, and Allison said, "But those were in case there was a fire in town."

Stephen frowned. "That's what they told you. But that's not the truth." He glanced up at his wife. "The mayor told everyone to say that because he didn't want to scare folks. But you girls are old enough to know the truth, aren't you?"

They all nodded, although Allison thought the others were nodding just because they respected her father. The looks in their eyes told her they were all afraid.

She was worried, but unafraid. She was her father's daughter, and had learned to ride a horse, to fish and hunt. She'd even been with him when he'd killed a neo-bear, one of the few indigenous predator species, that had come after the horses.

And from her brother she had learned how to defend herself at school from a couple of bullies who had tormented her last year. She'd been suspended for breaking both their noses, and had been grounded at home for a month. But she had overheard her parents talking, and both of them had secretly been proud of her. When she'd asked Shaun about it, he'd only smiled.

"The truth is, that's the alarm in case the Navy thinks the Kreelans might be coming." Her father squeezed Allison's hand. "It's to give us a heads-up so we can get ready for them, and get you kids to safety."

They all looked up as three light utility trucks came tearing down the road that led toward town. One of them turned into the long drive to the house, while the other two, both packed with men and women who briefly waved, raced toward Breakwater and the still-screaming sirens.

"Elena, girls," Kayla called, gathering them up when she recognized who was driving the truck. It was Elena's older sister, Danielle. "Time to go."

"We'll see you soon," Elena said, hugging Allison as Danielle brought the truck to a skidding stop, sending up a cloud of dust. Allison hugged the other girls, who all lived right next to Elena's house, as they filed off the porch and climbed into the open truck bed.

"What news, Danielle?" Allison's father called.

Danielle's father was the fire chief and the mayor. His house had one of the new network communication systems the Confederation had brought, but most of the rest hadn't been installed yet, and the local communications network had never worked properly. There was little profit to be made from it here from farmers like Stephen who didn't see the sense in spending money on it, and the only places that had reliable communications were the government and volunteers who manned the local fire station.

"Daddy only told me that it's not a drill." She glanced at the dust trail left by the trucks. "And us *kids*," she spat the word, "have to stay behind." Danielle was old enough to drive on Alger's World, where the legal license age was fourteen, but wasn't old enough for the Territorial Army training or equipment, which the Confederation had mandated was for ages seventeen and older. "It's not fair."

"Let's just hope it's a false alarm, shall we?" Stephen didn't hold out much hope that would be the case, but miracles were always possible. His older brother had seen combat on Saint Petersburg over twenty years before, and had returned home with his left arm and leg missing and his mind caught in an endless nightmare. Stephen had thanked God every day since then that he himself had never had to see combat. He prayed now that his streak of luck would hold.

"Not likely." Danielle glanced in the mirror to make sure the girls were all sitting down in the old truck's cargo bed. "Daddy said the alarm would only be triggered by the Navy defense station."

Stephen's hopes sank. The defense station was the first and, so far, only orbital weapons platform defending the planet. It was manned by regular Confederation Navy personnel and supported by two corvettes. If they had sounded the alarm, it was for real.

"Damn." Stephen turned to see his own battered truck pull up, a grim-faced Shaun at the wheel. "Get going, then, and good luck to you, Danielle. You, too, kids," he called to the other girls. "You be damn careful!"

"Yes, Mr. Murtaugh," they echoed in unison as Danielle backed away. Putting the truck into drive, she spun the wheels and kicked up a huge cloud of dust as she raced back down the drive to the road, then turned back the way she'd come toward home.

"Maybe we should have sent Allison with her." Kayla gave him a worried glance.

"No, she's better off here where she knows her way around." He looked down at his only daughter. "And we've got a better storm shelter than just about anybody, don't we?"

Allison nodded. The family had always had a storm shelter, because this part of Alger's World sometimes suffered from tornadoes and violent storms.

But after the stories of the Kreelans had come across the news channels, after the Confederation had formed to help protect humanity from them, Stephen had taken some precious time from the fields to build a new one. He and Shaun had disappeared into the barn one day with a backhoe, where they dug a tremendous hole in the ground that was nearly four meters deep. Then they built a framework of molds using wood, and filled them with concrete to make a structure that was a third of a meter thick throughout. Steps led toward the surface, with the entrance capped by a ten-centimeter thick steel door operated by an ingenious counterweight mechanism, so even Allison could open it easily. Her father had thought of everything, even a bathroom that only used a little water, pumped in through a pipe from the creek that ran behind the barn.

After backfilling over the top of the structure, about two meters below the surface, the dirt floor of the barn was packed down and again ready for use. Then they stocked the new shelter with enough food, water, and other supplies to last the family at least a month.

Once it was finished, the shelter had instantly become Allison's favorite hangout. It had annoyed her mother for a while, but her father had said, "Let her be. If we ever need it, she'll feel comfortable there."

Reluctantly, her mother had relented, not happy with her daughter spending her free time with her friends, playing in the shelter like it was some sort of entertaining dungeon.

But now, while the rest of her family went into town to draw their weapons and equipment, the last thing Allison wanted to do was cower in the shelter.

"Daddy, can't I go with you? Just to get your weapons and stuff?"

"I wish you could, baby. But you've got to stay here. We've talked about this."

Allison nodded, unhappily giving in. "We've talked about this" was her father's way of saying that he wasn't going to tolerate any further discussion or argument on the subject. He rarely said it, but when he did, nothing short of a supernova would move him.

"Yes, Daddy." She looked down, afraid he might see the tears that threatened to run down her face.

"Don't worry, Ali," he told her softly, drawing her into a tight embrace. "You'll be fine. We'll only be in town for a bit to get our gear and find out what's going on, then we'll make sure we let you know what's happening."

His warmth and strength comforted her, and her nose filled with the scent that was uniquely his, a mix of sweat, earth, and all the many other things that were part of the farm, part of him. She hated feeling like a little girl, but at that moment she was.

"Come on, now." He let go of her and lifted her chin with a callused hand. "You get to where you need to be. We've got to get going." He kissed her on the forehead before taking the steps to where Shaun waited in the truck. "Love you, big girl."

"I love you, too, Daddy."

"We'll be back soon, honey," her mother said, giving Allison a fierce hug, and Allison wrapped her arms tightly around her mother's neck. "Just be careful and keep the door on the shelter locked until we get back, okay?"

"I will, Mom." Allison was crying now, but no longer ashamed of it. Fear took hold of her heart, which felt heavy in her chest, as her father held the door open for her mother. "I love you."

"I love you, too, baby."

They squeezed into the cab next to Shaun, who leaned out the window and said, "Don't forget the present I gave you if you need it." He pointed at the table next to her that held the cake and her presents, including the hunting rifle he'd given her. "And you better not eat all the cake before we get back or I'll paddle you!"

He gave her a big smile and a wave before he pulled away.

* * *

Two hours had passed since her parents and Shaun left for town. A parade of trucks and cars had streamed down the road behind them, and Allison had felt more abandoned and alone with each one.

She'd gone to the shelter as soon as her parents had left, but after sitting there alone for what could only have been ten minutes, she couldn't stand it anymore.

"I'll know when the Kreelans come. I'll have time to run back." Even knowing that her father and mother would be angry, it had been an easy rationalization. Stomping up the stairs, she opened the heavy metal door that was located in the front right corner of the barn. She checked on her horse, Race, who wasn't at all concerned about an alien invasion, but was content to munch on the hay in his feed trough, before she went back to the porch.

After carving a huge piece of her birthday cake, even though she had no appetite to eat it, she had sat there and watched everyone else head to town.

The last of them had gone by nearly half an hour ago, and most of her cake still sat on the table, uneaten.

She knew some of the families had left a parent or older sibling behind to care for the younger children, and part of her was jealous. She wanted more than anything right now for her father or mother, or even Shaun, to be here with her.

But her parents trusted her to take care of herself, and so she would. Her new rifle, the one that Shaun had given her, sat across her knees, the ten-round magazine loaded and a round in the chamber. She wasn't as good a shot as her older brother, but she could hit what she was aiming at, and had brought down her share of the deer that lived in the woods, one of the many Terran species that had been released into the wild when the colony had first been founded here on Alger's World.

She was about to force herself to eat a huge bite of cake that would have brought an indignant rebuke from her mother about poor table manners when she saw them. White trails in the sky, streaking across the horizon.

The invasion alert siren continued its mournful wail, the changes in pitch eerily in step with the wide S-turns made by the white streaks.

Dropping the fork, she stood up and moved to the porch railing for a better look. Some of the streaks were moving north and south, quickly fading from view. Another group, maybe a dozen, spiraled in toward Breakwater.

The house was shaken by what sounded like explosions, but she realized were sonic booms as some of the streaks passed right overhead.

It dawned on her what those streaks were. Kreelan ships, coming in to land. The only other time she'd seen streaks in the sky like that was when her father had taken her to one of the space ports when her uncle had come to visit a few years ago.

A few moments later, the streaks that circled high over the town in graceful arcs resolved into tiny specks as the ships lost their contrails and dove for the ground.

Allison gasped as three small pillars of fire rose from where the town was, each followed by a crackling roar. The anti-air missiles flew unbelievably fast, aimed at three separate landing ships. Two of the missiles exploded well short of their targets, the noise loud enough to force Allison to put her hands over her ears.

The third missile found its target, tearing one of the stubby wings of one of the incoming ships. The craft tumbled out of control, and as she watched a group of smaller things fell away from it like seeds from a pod.

Parachutes fluttered from the tiny things, and they began gliding toward the town, following the other ships that had passed out of view beyond the low rise between the Murtaugh farm and Breakwater.

Over the roar of the ships' engines, Allison heard a sudden eruption of pops from the direction of town.

Rifle fire.

"Oh, no." She stood there, gripping her new hunting rifle, uncertain about what she should do. If her parents were here right now, she knew they would be terribly upset that she wasn't hunkered down in the shelter with the door bolted shut. But they weren't here. They were over there. In trouble.

Before she even realized she was doing it, she was running for the barn. Not for the shelter, but for her horse.

"Easy boy," she soothed as she quickly slipped the bridle on old Race. He was a nine year-old Percheron with a midnight black coat who'd carried Allison since her father had first set her in a saddle when she was four. Race was descended from the genetically modified stock brought by the original colonists to help with clearing and working the land. While most farming tasks were now done with machines, horses still had abundant uses on Alger's World, especially on small farms like this one.

Not to mention they were fun for young girls to ride.

Allison didn't bother with a saddle. There wasn't time. Slipping the rifle's sling over her shoulder, she grabbed a handful of Race's thick mane and jumped up, folding herself over his broad back before sitting up, her legs on either side of his wide rib cage.

Race huffed and tossed his head up and down as the sound of a thunderous explosion rolled across the farm, making the timbers of the barn shake.

"I know, boy," she said as she signaled him forward. "Don't be afraid. I've got to know what's happening."

With one last toss of his head, as if telling her this was a terrible idea, Race dutifully trotted out of the barn, then hit a full gallop as Allison squeezed him with both legs and leaned forward on his back.

She gasped as she looked toward town. Smoke billowed upward, black greasy snakes that curled and undulated into the sky.

The roar of the ships' engines died away as the aliens shut them down, and Allison's ears were filled with the non-stop pops and cracks of even more rifle fire.

Race flew across the fields, taking the shortest route to where Allison could get a glimpse of the town.

To her left, a truck roared over the small hill on the road from town, so fast that the wheels momentarily lost touch with the ground as it sailed over the top.

It was burning. As Allison watched, a web of what looked like lightning arced across the vehicle's body. There were three people in the cab and five in the back, desperately holding on. All of them wore Territorial Army uniforms.

When the lightning touched them, they screamed.

The scene played out like a slow-motion horror vid as the web of lightning grew more intense, wrapping around the entire vehicle. The body of the truck began to melt, and the people writhed in agony as they were electrocuted and charred black.

She was shaken from the horrific scene when the truck finally swung off the road into one of the fields, rolled over and exploded.

"Oh, God. Oh, God." She murmured the words over and over as Race took her up over the rise, where she brought him to a sudden stop with a firm pull on the reins.

The alien ships were in a rough ring around the town, and dozens of black-armored figures were making their way along the streets and alleyways. She immediately saw that almost all the gunfire was coming from her people. None of the Kreelans even seemed to have rifles. Instead, as the news reports had said, they held swords and strange throwing weapons.

She witnessed just how deadly the throwing weapons were when she saw a man poke his head around a corner, rifle at his shoulder. He got off a shot at a warrior, who crumpled to the ground. But before the man could duck back behind the corner, another warrior threw one of the things at him.

Allison saw it pass by him, but it didn't seem to hit him. The man stood there for a moment, as if stunned. Then his face and the front half of his head simply fell away as the warrior who'd killed him ran by, snatching up the weapon she'd thrown before moving deeper into the town.

The horror was overwhelming, and for a moment Allison simply sat there, tears streaking down her face and her mouth open in numb disbelief.

Then she saw them. Two men and a woman lay near one of the missile launchers. Dead. She remembered Shaun bragging about how important his job was, loading one of the fancy missile systems the Confederation had brought in. The helmet of one of the men had come off, and while the body was covered in blood, she could see enough of her father's red hair to know it was him. Her father, her mother, and her older brother. All dead.

"No." The word caught in her throat as she saw a warrior near one of the ships happen to turn her way.

Only then did she realize that she was completely exposed, silhouetted on the top of the rise. And sitting astride a horse, yet. Every warrior in town would be able to see her.

But at that moment, she didn't care. A flare of rage, the likes of which she'd never known, flowed through her at the thought of her murdered family.

The warrior called to one of the others near the ship, and the two of them bolted toward where Race and Allison stood.

"Come on, then." Allison raised the rifle Shaun had given her. It wasn't fancy, but it was incredibly accurate out to three hundred meters. It was also powerful enough to stop a neo-bear.

She had never fired from horseback before, but knew that Shaun had fired his rifle while riding Race, and the big horse had barely flinched.

Laying the sights on the chest of the first alien, who was running flat out toward her, Allison let out her breath and stroked the trigger.

Sitting on Race without a saddle or stirrups, she had no way to absorb the rifle's recoil, and it nearly knocked her backwards off the horse's back. She grabbed his mane just in time and managed to pull herself upright.

"Good boy!"

Race had stood rock-steady, but snorted at her compliment, clearly unhappy to be there.

Her target was down, a crumpled heap of black armor and blue skin on the ground. But the second one was gaining fast, and other warriors had turned around at the sound of the shot.

Allison aimed and fired.

This warrior was smarter, pitching herself to the side at the last instant.

Allison fired again and missed, then once more. Another miss.

The warrior grabbed one of the throwing weapons from her shoulder and cocked her arm back as Allison squeezed the trigger a fourth time, cringing as the warrior's head exploded in a shower of blood and gore.

More warriors were now heading her way.

Time to go, she thought.

"Come on, boy!" She turned Race around and squeezed him hard with her legs. The big horse ran as fast as Allison could ever remember him moving.

She wasn't heading back toward the farm and the safety of the barn and the shelter. Not yet. As fast as the warriors ran, they'd be able to see where she was going if she went straight back home. Her only chance was to make it to the woods that lay a couple hundred meters to the north, then work her way back home.

Glancing behind her, praying that the aliens wouldn't top the rise before she made it into the trees, she urged Race on.

She was almost to the woods when she heard one of the ships starting its engines.

Looking back, a shiver of fear ran up her spine as she saw the black ship, its shimmering black sides covered with strange alien writing in the same color as the lightning that had killed the people in the truck, rise above the hill and turn toward her.

"Come on, boy! Come on!"

She didn't see the laser blast that killed Race. She only heard a brief thrumming sound before the horse make a strange grunt and he fell. Allison went sailing over his head as he went down, and the rifle flew from her hand.

Rolling as she hit the ground, just as her father had taught her, she quickly got to her knees and looked back at her fallen horse.

Race stared at her with dead eyes. His body had been sheared in half, just behind where she'd been sitting. Smoke rose from the blackened ends of his severed body, and she smelled the stench of burning meat and hair. His rear hooves twitched.

The tree next to her crackled with heat and burst into flame as the ship fired again, and she caught sight of several warriors running toward her. She couldn't see how the ship could have missed her with the laser as she knelt there. They must have killed Race just to keep her from getting away.

"Goodbye, boy," she whispered before she turned and fled into the woods.

* * *

It took Allison nearly six hours to make her way home. Kreelans were scouring the area, and Allison had been forced to hide in a secret spot along the creek until the aliens went away. Waist deep in the burbling water of the creek, she cowered in a tiny cave formed by a group of rocks. Before her father had built the shelter, it had been her favorite hideaway when she played with Elena and the other girls, although her parents and Shaun knew perfectly well where it was.

But the Kreelans didn't. She heard them moving around in the woods outside, but stayed put until late at night, long after the voices of her alien pursuers had faded away.

There, in the dark, she had listened to the continued sounds of gunfire coming from town. The defenders weren't giving in easily. She didn't know anything about armies and fighting, but she knew the Territorial Army, her townsfolk, would probably lose. A lot of Kreelans had come out of those boats.

At last, she forced herself out of the little cave. She was afraid that if she didn't go now, she never would.

After looking and listening carefully for any sign of the aliens, she made her way along the creek that formed the northern boundary of the farms on this side of town, careful not to make any noise.

Finally reaching her own farm, she paused again. Kneeling in the gently burbling water, she carefully watched the barn, which was only a short run from the creek, and listened.

There was nothing but the sounds of battle coming from town. She also heard more shots being fired from the west and south.

Getting up, Allison crept across the open ground to the rear of the barn, then slipped inside. The other animals were still there, and after a moment's deliberation, she freed them. The four cows and two horses wandered out the open doors and began grazing, unconcerned that aliens had invaded their world.

Opening the door to the shelter, Allison entered the stairwell, then closed and locked the door behind her, shutting away the awful sounds of the fighting.

Leaving the lights off, as if the aliens could somehow see them here underground, she crawled into the small bed that was hers. She didn't bother to take off her wet clothes.

After a moment, shivering with cold and the agony of all she'd lost that day, Allison quietly wept in the darkness.

FIFTY-FIVE

Ku'ar-Marekh, high warrior priestess of the Nyur-A'il, walked alone on an airless world whose existence in the cosmos was unworthy of an entry in the Books of Time, save that she had set foot upon it.

She stopped a moment and looked up at the protostar that was forming far above, an accretion of gas and dust that someday would achieve sufficient mass for fusion to begin, for a star to be born. It was a swirling, glowing cloud whose beauty had never been witnessed by any sentient being other than herself.

Her armor, a light-drinking black that was so smooth it could be used as a mirror, except for the cyan rune of the order of the Nyur-A'il in the center, reflected the subtle hues. The reds and yellows and blues that she could see, but whose beauty could not touch her soul.

Her jet black hair, woven into the braids that were an ancient tradition of her people, hung down to her waist, glistening in the ghostly light. Her eyes, flecked with silver, looked at the scene through slitted pupils. Her skin, a cobalt blue, in this light was so dark as to be nearly black. Black as the empty space around her, a reflection of the emptiness within her.

Around her neck she wore the black collar of living metal that every one of Her Children wore, the many rows of pendants that hung from it proclaiming her accomplishments for the peers to witness. The front of the collar also bore an oval device of glittering metal, the same living steel from which Kreelan swords were made, with her order's rune etched into the surface. It proclaimed that she was a priestess, although the warriors around her knew who and what she was through their very blood. They could sense her spirit in the Bloodsong that united their people across the ten thousand suns of the Empire, and across the boundary that separated life and death.

Indeed, she was a high priestess, but it was an empty honor, the name of her order ash on her tongue. The Nyur-A'il was not the oldest of the orders that served Her, the Empress, for that honor was accorded to the Desh-Ka and its last living disciple, the great priestess Tesh-Dar.

But while the Desh-Ka might be considered the most powerful in the Empire, it could be said that the Nyur-A'il were the most feared.

Yet fear was an emotion that Ku'ar-Marekh no longer felt. Nor was love, joy, or anger. Among the peers she had heard whispers of a name that some had for her. They called her Dead Soul.

Had they spoken the name to her, she would not have taken them to task for it, for it was too close to the truth.

Reaching out her hands toward the protostar, she yearned to touch it, to become one with it over the ages yet to come. The invisible energy bubble surrounding her body flexed, matching her movement. It held the air she needed to breathe and shielded her from the radiation of the star-to-be, but it was not an artifact of technology. It was an act of will, a gift of the Change that had made her far more than a mere warrior, just as was the ability to flit among the stars, merely by wishing it so. Few high priestesses had that particular power, for the sacred crystals which powered the Change were fickle, their gifts not easily predicted.

For her, the Change had not been as expected. While it had brought her powers that made her greatly feared, even among the other warrior priestesses, it had robbed her of much more.

She knew she could not touch the cloud, but yearned to be part of it, to be reborn. To have been chosen to take her place as a warrior priestess among the Children of the Empress had been a great honor, the greatest to which any of the peers could aspire.

But for Ku'ar-Marekh, it had been the end of her happiness. The great cloud of glowing dust at which she longingly stared would know more of happiness than did she.

For long cycles after the Change, after she had become her order's highest and last priestess, she had wandered the galaxy far beyond the Empire's vast domain. She had walked upon a hundred worlds such as this, had floated through great rings of fire and ice, and had seen sights among the stars that no other of her race had ever glimpsed. She sought to find something, anything, that would kindle the faintest emotion in her heart, the tiniest sense of wonder or awe. Even fear or loneliness.

Yet she had felt nothing. Views that would have paralyzed her sisters with their celestial grandeur left her unmoved.

All she could do was live, to survive from day to day without hope or solace. She breathed the air she took with her during her leaps through space. She ate and drank when her body demanded, rested when her endurance was at an end. She existed. No more.

Even the Bloodsong, the emotional river that flowed from the Empress and bound Her Children together, was like a fire that cast light but not the warmth that Ku'ar-Marekh remembered from before the Change. She could sense her sisters, their joys and sorrows, the fierce ecstasy of those fighting the far-distant humans. But their fates were bound to the Universe around her, and in the end did not matter to Ku'ar-Marekh. Nothing did.

Nothing...except the Empress Herself. From Her alone could Ku'ar-Marekh sense in the Bloodsong a trace of the love that she had once known, as if the Empress were a great star, now far distant. That was the only reason Ku'ar-Marekh had not surrendered her honor and taken her own life. Even the eternal dark beyond the love of the Empress could not be worse than the dark and empty torment of her existence.

Ku'ar-Marekh lowered her arms, letting them fall to her side. All she felt now was a great weariness. It was a familiar sensation, and meant that it was time to move on yet again.

That was when she felt a sudden surge in the Bloodsong, a great upwelling that could only have one source, the Empress Herself. Ku'ar-Marekh sighed as she opened herself to her sovereign's power.

She knelt and closed her eyes as she felt space and time whirl around her, bending to the will of She Who Reigned. There was but a brief moment of freezing emptiness as she crossed the vast span of the galaxy to her destination. Toward the home of her race.

"Rise, priestess of the Nyur-A'il."

Ku'ar-Marekh opened her eyes to find the Empress standing before her. She wore only a simple white robe and a golden collar around the deep blue skin of her neck. Unlike the peers, Her collar bore no embellishments, no testimony to her feats from the time before she had surrendered her Collar of Honor and her birth name, things every Empress gave up when ascending to the throne.

The braids of Her hair, unlike that of the peers, was white, not black. It was a rare trait among Her race, and only those warriors born with white hair could ever become Empress.

She Who Reigned had once been a powerful warrior, but since ascending to the throne had become far, far more. She was the heart and soul of the Empire, and embodied the souls of all those who had reigned before Her. All except for Keel-Tath, the First Empress, and the most powerful. The Empress who had cursed Her Own people in a fit of rage and anguish, and whose spirit Her successors had sought for tens of thousands of generations.

Ku'ar-Marekh and the Empress were alone in a corner of the Imperial Gardens that were part of the palace on the Empress Moon orbiting the Homeworld.

Ku'ar-Marekh did as the Empress commanded and rose, yet kept her eyes downcast in respect.

"Walk with me, child." The Empress turned to follow the winding path made of stones taken from all the worlds the Empire had ever touched. Somewhere, Ku'ar-Marekh knew, there was a stone from each of the dead worlds she herself had set foot upon in her travels, and that someday the Empress would touch those stones with Her feet as she guided the Empire with Her words and the power of the Bloodsong.

The thought of how long Ku'ar-Marekh had been away, how she had intentionally shunned the peers, even the Empress herself, should have made her feel great shame. She knew this, but did not feel it.

"It has happened before." The Empress walked slowly, one hand on her belly. She was heavy with child, one of many she had borne. She was older than most of the peers, but would yet outlive nearly all of them, and would bear children for many cycles more. For She was bound by the same curse as were the others of Her people.

Fertile adult females had to mate every cycle or they would die. Powerful as She was, the living Empress, too, fell under the same Curse.

"What has happened before, my Empress?"

"What happened to you, child." The Empress stopped and turned to face Ku'ar-Marekh. "I know the emptiness you feel, priestess of the Nyur-A'il. It is a rare thing, for when a priestess passing on her legacy dies in the Change, as did yours, the disciple nearly always dies, as well. But sometimes..."

"Yes, my Empress?"

"Sometimes, the body lives."

"I..." Ku'ar-Marekh stopped, her mind grappling with the unpleasant possibilities. "I do not understand."

"Your soul is caught between life and death, child. That is why you feel no fire in your heart from the Bloodsong, why joy and sorrow have no meaning. Why even pain has no sting. Why you do not feel this."

The Empress raised Her hand to Ku'ar-Marekh's face, and as their flesh touched, Ku'ar-Marekh was flooded with the power of the Bloodsong as she remembered it, with feeling, emotions. With life. It was as if one of the great tapestries that hung in the throne room, drained of color, was returned to its original glory.

"Oh," she gasped, instinctively covering the Empress's hand with her own, pressing it firmly against her cheek, never wanting to let Her go.

Ku'ar-Marekh fell to her knees, and it took all her will not to cry out in joy that she could feel again, and in anguish at the knowledge that this was but a fleeting moment that would vanish as soon as the Empress took away Her hand.

She bit her tongue, one of her fangs piercing it clean through, to keep from begging the Empress to take her life, to not consign her to another moment of living death. For Ku'ar-Marekh was a warrior priestess, and she could not dishonor herself or her order. She would not.

"Your Way is a difficult one, child." The Empress gently ran the fingers of Her other hand over Ku'ar-Marekh's black braids. While the priestess was not a child of Her body, she was a child of Her spirit, and the Empress felt the fear and anguish in her heart now. Yet She was warmed by Ku'ar-Marekh's strength and her refusal to give in, to beg for mercy. "It is a path that very few have been fated to walk during the long ages of our history. Yet it is a path that you must follow to its end, where you shall find peace."

Slowly, the Empress took away Her hands, and Ku'ar-Marekh felt the warmth fade from her heart. In but seconds, her soul was as it had been since the terrible day of the Change. Dead. Empty.

"What must I do, my Empress?" Ku'ar-Marekh's tongue felt heavy, wooden in her mouth.

"You are a warrior priestess, and the Empire is again at war. We know the measure of the enemy, the humans, and they are worthy opponents." She paused. "And if we are to find the One who shall release us from the Curse, we must find him among these animals. For if we do not, in but a few generations our race shall perish from the stars."

Ku'ar-Marekh merely nodded, for the ancient prophecy was no secret among the priestesses and the elder mistresses of the clawless ones.

"A scout force has landed on one of the smaller human colonies, but they have no priestess attending them. Your presence there will redress this."

"As you command, my Empress." Ku'ar-Marekh saluted, hammering her gauntleted fist, her silver talons clenched, against the armor of her breast. The silver signified that she was sterile, barren. Another legacy of the change, and one whose irony had not escaped her.

"I will deliver you to the command ship." The Empress paused, looking at Ku'ar-Marekh with great sorrow. "May thy Way be long and glorious, my child."

To Ku'ar-Marekh, the ancient words of parting were a curse that echoed in her mind as the Empress again sent her across the stars.

FIFTY-SIX

Her name was Valentina. It was not the name she had been given at birth, and she had gone by many others in her life. Those few who knew her true identity called her only by her old codename, Scarlet. But Valentina was her chosen name, the one she planned to carry with her to the grave.

A year of agony, sweat and tears had passed since she had awakened from her coma to endure a brutal physical therapy regimen designed to rebuild her body and recover her strength. Beyond the psychological trauma from the implants, she had been hit five times at point blank range by an assault rifle, and only the implants she had been given as a special operative, the ones that could inject painkillers, adrenaline, and hormones into her blood stream, had kept her alive.

As her body mended, so did her mind. She had brought under control the soul-numbing coldness of the machines that she had merged with, that had nearly driven her insane. She had not banished the frigid darkness entirely, for it still haunted her dreams, but it no longer ruled her mind.

Now, her dark brown hair was pulled back in a tight ponytail, and her face was dripping sweat as she hammered at a well-worn punching bag with her hands and feet. Where she had once cried with joy at being able to hold her arms up from the bed for an agonizing thirty seconds, she now worked out hard every day for at least two hours, kicking and punching the bag with lethal moves taken from a variety of martial arts before she went running through the surrounding woods. She was not as strong or as fast as she had been before she had been shot, for there was some damage to her body that the surgical team had not been able to fully repair. Even at that, once again she was a lethal weapon, even though there was no one for her to kill.

Her days were spent with Dmitri and Ludmilla Sikorsky, her adopted parents, in peaceful pursuits on their horse farm in what had once been the American State of Virginia. During the days and in good weather they were mostly outdoors, working the garden, tending the horses and riding, and enjoying the beauty of the surrounding woods. Inside, especially during the winter, reading had become a favorite pastime. The Sikorskys had grown up on a world where the only books allowed were those published by government-approved authors, and with their sudden immersion in a society where they could read whatever they wanted, where authors could write whatever they pleased, reading had become an instant addiction. Valentina had always loved to read, but never had the time, and had happily gone along with this new family tradition.

Valentina - Scarlet - found that she was, for the first time in her life, at peace.

She had just landed another low kick against the bag, a hit that would have shattered the leg of a human opponent, and was about to follow up with an open-hand strike when her wristcomm chimed.

"Security alert." It was the soft female voice of the house's central security system. It had been installed by the CIS to protect Valentina and the Sikorskys from anyone who might have somehow learned her true identity and come to take revenge for her previous operations. "An unidentified vehicle is approaching."

Valentina immediately went from the workout room to the front door. Next to it was a cabinet on the wall. Opening the cabinet, she pulled out a large-bore pistol that could put a hole through centimeter-thick armor plate. She and the Sikorskys had some local friends who periodically came to visit, but no one ever came to the house unannounced. While she considered herself out of the death-dealing business, she would never hesitate to defend herself or her adopted parents, and there was an impressive arsenal hidden throughout the house.

Taking a look at the video monitor that was tracking the vehicle's progress along the lengthy driveway toward the house, she did a double-take.

It was a Marine utility vehicle.

"What the hell?" She wondered who it could possibly be. While she had been in a coma, she had received a pile of get well cards and flowers from the Marines she had helped to save from the Saint Petersburg debacle, but none of them had ever stopped by to see her. Most of them, she knew, were either still in combat zones or had been killed in action. Very few had been able to return home, and most probably never would.

The dark green- and brown-painted vehicle, an ugly, angular beast on four oversized tires that could drive through or over virtually any terrain, pulled to a stop in front of the house, about a dozen meters from the front door.

The driver side door opened, and a big, broad-shouldered man with close-cropped dark blond hair stepped out. He was wearing a Marine dress uniform that was a stark contrast to the dark forest colors of the vehicle's camouflage paint: a dark blue coat with polished brass buttons and crimson piping over slightly lighter blue trousers sporting a broad crimson stripe down the leg, with the bright red and gold stripes and rockers on the sleeve proclaiming him a first sergeant.

He carefully placed his white "wheel" cap on his head with his white-gloved hands, the black visor shielding his eyes from the bright sun, before he headed toward the house.

With a warm smile, Valentina opened the door and stepped outside to meet him.

"Mills." She was unable to keep the tears from her eyes. "Roland Mills."

"Valentina!" His handsome face turned up in a devilish grin. "Bloody hell, woman," he said in his public school English accent, "but you're looking good!"

She wrapped her arms around his muscular frame, hugging him. He returned her embrace with rib-cracking force.

"It's good to see you." She pulled away, looking up into his intensely green eyes.

"Were you, ah, expecting someone?" He cocked his head at the pistol she was still holding.

"Well, a girl can't be too careful these days." She set the safety on the pistol and hooked an arm through his and led him into the house. "Come on. Let me make you some tea."

When they reached the kitchen, Valentina made some tea from an ornate samovar perched on one of the counters. She smiled every time she looked at it, thinking of how excited Dmitri and Ludmilla had been when they had come home one day and found it there. They had always wanted a nice samovar, which had long been used by Russians to boil water for tea, but had never been able to afford a good one. Valentina had this one custom made for them in Tula, Russia, where samovars had been made since the late sixteenth century. It was ridiculously ornate by modern standards, with an intricate floral design in silver over a bright blue enamel surface, and had cost her a small fortune. But it had been worth every credit for the joy it had brought to her adopted parents.

She turned around to look at Mills, who now sat at the cozy wooden table where the Sikorsky family normally ate breakfast. Having taken off his hat and gloves, he was giving her an openly appraising look.

"I'm not in the market, Roland." She frowned at him as she handed him the glass of hot tea.

"Pardon?"

She stood there, hands on hips, and stared at him. "If you came here looking for some female companionship while you're on shore leave, you came to the wrong place."

He sat there for just a moment, dumbfounded. Then he covered his face with his hands, and she could see his shoulders begin to quiver. She thought he was crying until he threw his head back and roared with laughter.

Valentina, unable to help herself, started laughing, too, as she sat down next to him.

"No, girl." He finally brought himself under control, wiping tears from his eyes after laughing so hard. "Christ, no, I'm not here to try and crawl in your knickers, although Lord knows a lad could do worse."

She took the complement for what it was, and knew that plenty of women would gladly have welcomed the attentions of Roland Mills. He was unarguably good looking, with a ruggedly handsome face bearing a mouth that could light the room when he smiled, and a scowl that could make hardened Marines shrink away in fear when he was angry. Nearly any man would be frankly envious of his body. He was big, tall and broad-shouldered, with a tight waist and powerful arms and legs, his muscles perfectly defined under his lightly bronzed skin. While he often enjoyed giving others the impression that he was an ignorant ape, he had a keen mind and a big heart, a heart that she knew had been gravely wounded when the woman he loved, Emmanuelle Sabourin, had been killed by the Kreelans on Saint Petersburg.

Valentina had only met him briefly before she had been shot during the battle, but he had been one of the few visitors she had received during her recovery from her coma. He had been on temporary duty to Earth and had made special arrangements to see her, appearing in his dress uniform, just as he had today, to thank her in person for what she had done to get him and his Marines to safety.

She had still been bedridden then, her muscles so atrophied that she could barely lift up her hands to hold his. They had talked for a long time, and even managed a few jokes, but she could tell that the pain he felt inside, just like her own, would take a long time to heal. They had become friends that day, and she still remembered the feeling of his lips on hers as he had gently, like a shy schoolboy, kissed her goodbye before starting the long trip back to the ongoing battle for Saint Petersburg. They had exchanged emails since then, but getting anything other than military communications into or out of the spreading war zones was hit or miss, at best.

Looking at him now, she could tell that he had come a long way from the last time they had spoken, despite what must have been an incredible strain from having been engaged in nearly non-stop combat operations. She knew there was still a reservoir of pain under the surface, but he could smile now without forcing it, just as she herself could.

"Seriously, Valentina," he told her, "you're looking fantastic. When I came to visit you that first time, I...I didn't think you'd ever even be able to walk again. You were a bit of a fright, you know."

She laughed. "Thanks for the compliment! You really know how to impress a woman, you know that?" Then, more seriously, she asked, "And how about you? How are you doing?"

He shrugged, an uncomfortable look on his face. Like most men, she was sure he hated talking about his emotions, but he hadn't shied away from it when he visited her last time, or in their correspondence.

"Okay, I suppose." He looked down into his tea as he slowly spun the glass around on the table. "Still in one piece, as you can see." He was silent a moment, then went on softly, "I still think of her, Emmanuelle, but I guess I've moved on, mostly. Combat has a way of focusing your attention on more immediate matters." He sighed. "But for most of us there isn't much beyond that now, is there?"

Valentina had a sudden premonition that his last words were more significant than he had meant to let on. Understanding the truth behind a casual statement was a talent she had honed into a useful skill that had saved her life on more than one occasion.

After taking a sip of tea, she set the glass down and looked the big Marine in the eyes. "All right, Roland, you didn't come here just for another social visit, did you?"

Mills had to look away for a moment, a feeling of guilt knotting up in his stomach.

Bloody idiot, he cursed himself. You should have just gotten to the point right from the start. She's not a damn fool.

He turned back to her, once again stunned by the transformation she had undergone in the months that had passed since he had last come to visit her. Where there had once been a bullet-riddled body housing a tormented mind, he now saw a strikingly beautiful woman in superb physical and, from what he had read from her files before he had come here, mental shape. With muscles that were lithe and strong as any champion athlete, even without the additional strength her implants might offer, she remained profoundly feminine, with a full bust and invitingly curved hips, her features accentuated by her tight black workout clothes. Valentina's face was graced with sensuous lips and deep brown eyes that were now locked with his own.

Despite his earlier joking about not wanting to get into her knickers, he couldn't deny the attraction he felt toward her. He hadn't been with another woman since Emmanuelle had died, and he felt a warm shiver ripple down his spine.

Now's not the time, you fool, he counseled himself. She'd kick your arse.

He couldn't suppress a grin at his own foolishness. Valentina cocked an eyebrow at his change of expression, but she didn't offer up a smile in return.

"Fair enough." He let out a sigh. "You caught me. The truth is, I did come here to pay a social visit, but it's...business, as well." His grin disappeared and his expression grew serious. "I'm putting a team together, Valentina. It's a special recon team that's tasked to go in ahead of an assault force to scout Kreelan positions and report back. The Kreelans keep defeating our technology, or at least selective bits of it, and they completely bugger every kind of technical reconnaissance, seemingly at will. Satellites, drones, even the stealth microsats the CIS has come up with. They just stop working. Poof. The boffins don't have a clue how the blue girls are doing it."

"All of them fail?" Valentina leaned back as she considered the dreadful implications of what Mills was saying. Any combat force that was blind to what the enemy was doing was already halfway to being defeated.

"No." Mills shook his head. "That's what makes it even stranger. Sometimes they work fine, but if they seem to touch on something the enemy doesn't want them to see, the sensor or weapon just dies. Drones fall from the sky. Satellites just stop working. Guided missiles lose their guidance and merrily sail off course.

"And sometimes things don't really go dead, but just stop working for a while. Data-links will drop, then come back on sometime later. It's like the Kreelans just wave some sort of magic wand when they don't want us peeping in on them or don't like the weapons we happen to be using," he snapped his fingers, "and we're bollixed."

"Jesus." Valentina hadn't fought the Kreelans on Saint Petersburg, as she had been injured before they aliens had attacked. She had heard of their seemingly supernatural powers, but that had only been rumor. Until now.

"Ships can help a bit from orbit," Mills went on, "as the Kreelans don't seem to hamper them so much, but our Navy is usually too busy trying to beat back Kreelan warships to help much with the ground battle. But on the ground, our boys and girls are dead without decent battlefield intel."

"So what is it that you have in mind?"

"We need boots on the ground," he told her firmly, "people who can put eyes and ears on the target area, sort out what's going on and report back, and who can move quietly and quickly through enemy territory without being seen. I also need people who are good enough to fight their way out of a tough scrap if things turn–"

"I'm not going back to Saint Petersburg." She said it before he could finish, a haunted look shrouding her face. She would never go back there.

Mills shook his head. "It won't be Saint Petersburg. The target for the first operation hasn't been announced yet, but I know it won't be there, or any of the six other worlds the enemy attacked in the first round after the invasion of Keran."

"Why not?"

"Because," he went on grimly, "those worlds are as good as lost. That's obviously not being trumpeted from the Presidential Complex, but it's the truth. The fighting will probably go on for some time yet, maybe even a few more years, but the Kreelans are too well entrenched on the ground, and the Navy can't prevent the enemy from bringing in reinforcements."

He took a sip of tea, noting Valentina's shocked expression. "Every so often a Kreelan task force appears and drops another big load of warriors to the surface. The big transports jump out, while their warships rough up the Navy until our ships finally wipe them out. Meanwhile, the warriors they leave behind continue hacking and chopping away at us on the ground.

"Don't get me wrong. We kill them in droves, even without using the really high-tech weaponry that they somehow bedevil. But there are always more of them to kill, and they have to be killed, because they don't surrender. Ever. We haven't had one single prisoner, Valentina, in all the battles being fought now across over a dozen worlds. Not one. And we haven't been able to break them psychologically, get them to rout or retreat in a single battle. All the things we've always taken for granted as part of warfare amongst humans," he flicked his fingers in the air, "is good for nothing at all. They come at us like they're berserkers and just go on fighting until they die. Then more come to replace them."

"This operation you're talking about, is it part of the strategic offensive that President McKenna has been alluding to?"

Natalie McKenna was the first president of the newly formed Confederation. Working under incomprehensible pressure and driving herself mercilessly, she had managed to forge a working interstellar government amidst a massive alien invasion, using the industrial might of Earth and the worlds of the Francophone Alliance to forge an arsenal that could defend humanity.

"Yes." Mills nodded. "It was originally going to be launched months ago, but the second wave of attacks set back the timetable. And now there's been a third."

"How many colonies have been hit so far?"

"Fifteen," Mills told her. "The Empire attacked seven, including Saint Petersburg, in the first wave of invasions after Keran was wiped out. A few months later, while you were still in a coma, they attacked six more. And just last week they attacked two, Alger's World and Wuhan. The couriers came in this morning with that news.

"McKenna's tired of letting the blues having the initiative, and she's given the green light for a full counteroffensive to take back one of our worlds so we'll have some good news. So we can give people hope. Because frankly, love, we're getting our arses pounded."

He took a long sip of tea, then set the glass down. "Now we're just trying to put the last pieces together. I'm to lead one of the recon teams that'll be first on the ground." He paused, looking at her pointedly. "I have one slot on my team left to fill. I need a sniper, and God strike me dead if you're not the best shot I've ever seen, with that circus shooting you did on Saint Petersburg.

"On top of that, you know all about intel, and I know you've had extensive training in first aid and communications. Plus," he added with a playful leer, "you'll bring up the average for good looks on the team by quite a few points."

"How much do you know about my background?" Valentina narrowed her eyes at the mention of her background in intelligence. Only two people had ever seen her complete file and knew everything about her. One was Vladimir Penkovsky, the Director of the Confederation Intelligence Service. The other was her controller, Robert Torvald. There was information in there that she would never want anyone else to know, information that was dangerous enough that she would kill someone, even a friend, to keep it secret.

Mills held up his hands toward her, seeing the change in her expression and the sudden tension in her body that he knew could erupt into lethal violence. He was far larger than she was, but despite his size advantage and experience in close combat against the Kreelans, he wouldn't have wagered money on his own survival in a fight against her. From what he had been told and seen in her file, she could tear him to pieces without breaking a sweat.

"Hold up, Valentina. Your old friend Torvald briefed me on your training and abilities that were pertinent to our mission needs. That was all. Nothing about your past or what you've done; nothing about any of that spooky stuff from your former life. I don't care, and I don't want to know. Confirm it with him if you like." He chuckled. "Director Penkovsky had to order Torvald to talk to me, and even then it was like pulling teeth to get the bugger to tell me anything useful. He's a bit of a constipated sod, isn't he?"

With that, Valentina relaxed. She would double-check what Mills had told her with Torvald, with whom she'd kept in periodic contact, but she could tell Mills wasn't lying. And thinking about his ribald description of Torvald, she couldn't help but chuckle herself. It was too close to the mark.

"All right. I guess I won't have to kill you. This time."

"Whew!" Mills puffed some air through his lips and theatrically wiped a hand across his brow, but inwardly he was relieved. Torvald had warned him that if he lost "Scarlet's" trust and she thought Mills knew too much about her past, she wouldn't hesitate to kill him. "So that brings us to the big question of the day. Will you do this?"

Valentina looked out one of the kitchen windows at the woods beyond, considering. She had given up everything for her career with the CIS. She had traded away her true identity and had made a profession of spying on and killing other human beings. Sometimes it had been justified, sometimes it had simply been necessary.

But with every life she had taken, she had felt like a piece of her soul had been carved away and cast into Hell. Even now that she was no longer officially in the employ of the CIS, her past guaranteed that she would never be able to live the ordinary, normal life that so many others took for granted. She was still young, and often wished for a man to share her life and her bed, but that, too, had been something she had decided could never happen. She could never expose anyone else to the risks that she and the Sikorskys already lived under, the perpetual fear that her identity might be compromised and the demons of her past deeds would come to claim their vengeance. She did not have to worry about such threats to any children she might have, for the bullets that had ravaged her body at Saint Petersburg had put an end to that possibility.

She had more than paid her dues to the Confederation government, she knew, and to the Terran government before that. She had even paid the price for getting Mills and his fellow Marines away from Saint Petersburg, spending months in a coma that wasn't dreamless, but had been a never-ending nightmare until the day she finally awakened. She owed nothing more to humanity.

But the threat now was not from another group of human beings with which her star nation was in competition or conflict, but from an alien menace that seemed determined to wipe her kind from the Universe.

Turning her eyes to the beautiful samovar on the counter, she realized that everything good that humanity had ever done was now at risk. Humanity had a dark and ugly side, and she had seen far more than her share of it. But she believed there was far more that was good, that was worth saving. Things of beauty like the samovar, and things that money could not buy, like the love and devotion of Dmitri and Ludmilla as they waited for her to wake from her coma.

If the Kreelans had their way, all of that, and so much more, would be erased, gone forever.

She knew that she couldn't prevent that from happening single-handed. But standing on the sidelines, comfortably tucked away on this little horse farm in the deep woods, wouldn't help win the war.

And Mills was right. There was probably no one, anywhere, who was more qualified for what he needed than she was.

With a deep sigh, Valentina turned back to him. "Okay, Mills, I'm in."

FIFTY-SEVEN

Allison spent the first three days after the invasion in the shelter. She heard strange sounds on the second day, muffled and indistinct through the concrete and earth above her. The third day was quiet.

By the fourth day, she had to get outside to take a look before she went crazy.

Waiting until the clock told her night had fallen, she crept up the steps to the thick shelter door and tried to open it, but it was stuck. She checked the counterbalance mechanism to make sure it wasn't jammed. As far as she could tell, it looked fine.

That meant that something was blocking the door.

It took her nearly fifteen minutes of desperate pushing and shoving before she finally managed to get the door open far enough to see what was blocking it.

Charred wood. It wasn't hot or smoking, but the smell of it was so strong it made her cough.

An hour of hard, messy work later, she had cleared the wood away by poking and prodding it through the slim opening with long screwdrivers and the pry bar.

Finally able to open the door enough to stick her head outside, she could see in the starlight that the barn was nothing but a burned out ruin. The front half had collapsed, with some of the rafters falling across the door to the shelter. That's what had been blocking her way.

She suppressed a gasp when she saw someone sprawled on the dirt floor toward the rear of the barn, which still stood.

Letting the door close quietly behind her, Allison crept over to the person.

"Hello? Can you hear me?"

She flicked on the tiny flashlight she carried, and bit back a cry of

It was a man wearing a Territorial Army uniform. She didn't recognize him, but he was clearly dead, a deep gash through his throat. His eyes stared, unseeing, at the underside of the ruined barn's loft.

She looked around with her flashlight, but couldn't see any other bodies. Afraid now that one of the aliens might see the light, she switched it off and sat there in the dark, shivering.

Some soldiers must have hidden in the barn, she thought, and then the Kreelans found them. That would explain the noises she'd heard earlier. They were the sounds of a battle taking place right over her head. A battle that the humans had again lost, and during which the barn had been set ablaze. She was only amazed that the whole structure hadn't burned to the ground.

Moving back toward the front of the barn, picking her way carefully through the wreckage, she found a spot that had a clear view of the house.

Or where the house should have been. She stared open-mouthed at the sight of her home. It looked like it had been destroyed by a tornado of fire. There was wreckage everywhere, like the house had blown up, and everything was singed and blackened.

Moving slowly, she made her way to what was left of the porch where she'd been sitting only a few days ago, enjoying her birthday party.

Clambering up on the burned and broken wood, she could only get as far as where the door would have been, because it ended in a big hole that had once been the basement.

Allison sat down, her legs dangling into the hole, wanting to vomit from the smell of smoke.

After sitting there a while, she thought of the body back in the barn, and knew she couldn't just leave the man as he was.

"That wouldn't be right." Her father spoke those words when he used to talk to her about making choices, and she fought back a sudden hot flash of tears as she thought of him.

As she returned to the barn, she saw with dismay that the vehicle shed, too, had been destroyed. Moving to the rear of the barn, which was still largely intact, she looked and listened for any signs of the enemy.

Nothing moved in the starlit darkness between the barn and the nearby creek, beyond which lay the woods. The night creatures made their normal chirruping and occasional hoots, and she knew that nothing was hiding out there, waiting for her.

Already exhausted from prying open the door to the shelter, she knew that what had to be done would only be harder the longer she waited. The body hadn't begun to smell yet, but she knew it would.

Taking hold of the dead man's wrists, she pulled him outside the barn and into the nearest corner of the family garden where the earth was soft.

After retrieving a shovel from the mess in the barn, she began to dig.

* * *

Not content to stay put in the shelter and wait for rescue that she now doubted would ever come, Allison ventured out at night to learn what she could of the enemy. While many children her age were still afraid of the dark, especially in the woods, she had spent enough time hunting with her father and brother that the woods held no fears for her other than the packs of Kreelan warriors that sometimes passed by.

The first night, she was able to reach a place where she could see into the town. There wasn't a single light shining from any of the buildings. The power was out, which didn't surprise her.

But it wasn't completely dark. In the town square she could see the flickers of what must have been a number of fires, and off in the woods beyond the town she could see the faint glow of what must have been many more. The dark shapes of warriors moved here and there, the glow of the firelight sometimes glinting from their shiny black armor.

She also noticed that the landing ships had all gone.

"At least they can't go around shooting horses." She thought bitterly of poor Race.

She stayed in the shelter on the second night when a storm passed through. Allison had cracked the door to the shelter, but rain was pouring down outside. After a moment's consideration, she closed the door and went back inside.

On the third night she had reached the edge of town when she was stopped cold by a Kreelan patrol. She had come around the corner of a big storage building where the town kept its communal equipment, which was the farthest building that was generally considered part of the town itself, when she ran into them.

She had reached the back of the building and moved toward one of the corners. Stopping, she listened for any sounds, and after about thirty seconds she rounded the corner.

And there they were. For a moment, she just stood there, stupefied, while not ten paces away three alien warriors stood facing her, dark shadows against the star light.

The warriors stiffened, and two of them began to move toward her. But the third uttered something in their strange language, and the others stopped, flexing their claws in their armored fists.

Afraid to so much as breathe, Allison backed slowly around the corner, then turned and ran.

Terrified as she had been, she came back the next night and made it into the town proper, sneaking down the alley behind the town's small theater.

She paused a moment near the back door, remembering how the theater's owner, Mr. Bernson, always gave the kids free popcorn during the matinees. Allison knew that he was almost certainly dead, and the thought brought with it more sadness than she'd expected. Mr. Bernson had been a very nice man who had loved the town's kids. She would miss him.

On a whim, she tried the door handle. It was unlocked. Opening the door just a few centimeters, she looked inside, but couldn't see anything. It was pitch black.

She waited a moment, listening for any sign of movement, then quickly stepped inside. She pulled the door closed behind her, wincing as it clicked shut.

Then she waited, trying to muffle the sound of her own breathing as she listened. She was in the small store room where Mr. Bernson kept the supplies for the refreshment stand. Flicking on the pocket flashlight she'd brought, she saw that she was surrounded by neat stacks of cups and containers holding popcorn bags and candy.

With a vague sense of guilt, she reached out and took a package of her favorite candy from one of the boxes. Then two more.

The store room had another door that led to the main hall where the refreshment stand and the entrance to the theater were. As she was pocketing the candy and considering taking more, she heard something out there.

Whispers.

Quickly switching off her light, she moved to the hallway door, which stood ajar.

She heard something else now, too. Footsteps on the carpet beyond the door. Slow and stealthy.

Allison had no weapon. She had looked near where Race had been killed, but hadn't been able to find her hunting rifle, and her father hadn't been able to afford a separate set of weapons just to store in the shelter. The guns had all been in the house, and had been lost when the house was blown up.

With the furtive sounds of the footsteps growing steadily closer, she backed up behind the door next to one of the stacks of boxes.

The door was pushed open, very slowly. A dark shape, then another, came into the room, illuminated by the ghostly starlight glow from the theater's front windows down the hall.

"It should be in here," one of the shadows said softly, just above a whisper.

It was Vanhi, a girl from her school. She was only eight, but Allison had spoken to her a few times in their small school's cafeteria. Vanhi had a very distinctive singsong voice that Allison instantly recognized. The other shadow with her, about the same size, must be her twin brother Amrit. They lived on a small farm on the far side of town, and had only arrived on Alger's World a year ago, immigrants from Earth.

"Vanhi," Allison whispered, reaching out a hand to touch the girl's shoulder.

Both Vanhi and Amrit screamed in fright, jumping away from Allison to crash into a floor to ceiling stack of plastic cups that clattered to the floor.

"Be quiet!" Allison turned on her flashlight and held it up to the ceiling to provide a little illumination without blinding any of them. It was a trick her brother had shown her.

"Allison?" Amrit's voice trembled, his dark brown eyes wide with terror.

"Allison Murtaugh?" Vanhi lay on the floor amongst the jumble of cups, staring up at the older girl.

"Yeah, it's me." Allison reached out her free hand to help Vanhi up. "It's okay. But we've got to get out of here. Now." She knew that the racket they'd just made would have alerted any Kreelans who might be nearby. "Come on. Follow me." Reaching into a box of chocolate bars, she stuffed a bunch into her jacket, then took Vanhi's hand.

Allison pushed the outside door open just a crack, then looked and listened for any signs of patrolling warriors. There was nothing.

"You've got to be really quiet." Allison's whisper broke the silence of the darkened alley, and she quickly glanced around.

They were still alone.

Behind her, the twins nodded their heads side to side in a way that some of the other kids in school had thought funny, but that Allison had always found endearing.

Allison led the way out, with Vanhi holding tightly to one of her hands, and Amrit holding onto Vanhi's other hand to make sure they didn't get separated in the dark. They followed Allison down to the end of the alley.

Once there, she had the twins sit down and gave them each a chocolate bar from her pocket. She was shocked to see how they both ripped off the wrapper and devoured the bars in but a few bites.

"We're starving."

Allison could barely understand what Amrit said, his mouth was so full of chocolate, but the message was clear. She gave them both a couple more bars.

The twins sat right next to each other as if they were freezing, even though it was a warm spring night. Allison sat cross-legged across from them, and their foreheads almost touched as they leaned in close to talk.

"What were you doing in there?" Allison asked.

"Looking for food." Vanhi's singsong voice was flat, desperate. "We haven't had anything to eat since the aliens came."

"Nothing at all? Didn't your family have a storm shelter or anything?"

"We didn't have a chance to get to it." Amrit's voice quivered, and Allison reached out a hand and took his to reassure him. "One of the alien ships landed right next to the house. Our parents..."

Vanhi let out a quiet sob, and it was a moment before Amrit went on in a raspy voice. He was a small boy, no bigger than his sister, but he didn't lack for courage. Allison had seen him stand up to one of the class bullies once. The older boy had nearly beaten Amrit to a pulp before the teachers could intervene, but Amrit had stood his ground.

"The aliens killed them and set fire to the house. We were playing in the barn." He paused. "We saw everything."

"I'm sorry." Allison couldn't think of what else she could say. After a moment, she asked, "How did you get away?"

"There is a big pipe under the drive between the barn and the main road for water to run through."

"We hid there for two days," Vanhi added. "We got some water from a sprinkler line that still held some water, but that was all. Without power, the well pump stopped working."

"Since then we've been trying to get to Mr. Bernson's theater, because we knew there would be some food and things to drink there. And we wouldn't have to go far into town to where the restaurants are." Amrit paused. "Because there are lots of *them* there."

Nodding, Allison understood their reasoning. She had noticed that, too. After the initial battle, the aliens seemed to have concentrated in the center of Breakwater. She'd heard strange things and seen weird lights, like flickers of lightning coming from the town square area, but she hadn't yet mustered the courage to investigate any further.

"Well," she told them, "you won't have to worry about a place to stay. I want you to come back with me. I've got lots of room in a nice shelter back at our farm."

"You have food and water?" Vanhi's voice had taken on more of its singsong quality, and it made Allison smile.

"Yes, I've got plenty for all of us."

* * *

Over the next week, Allison's optimistic appraisal of the food situation radically changed as she found seven more children, all younger than herself, who were desperate enough for food to brave the dangers of being caught by the aliens. All of them had been starving, and one had been so weak that she'd had to carry him to the shelter on her back.

Ravenous as they were, they had quickly eaten their way through most of the food supplies in the shelter. Allison had gone to look for food at the adjoining farms, but without exception the houses, barns, and any other buildings had been destroyed.

Foraging in town was the only option. Deciding that they needed something more than the candy in the town theater (and the popcorn was useless, as she had no way to cook it), she began to explore deeper in the town. While many of the buildings had suffered heavy damage, the contents were still largely intact, especially the market and the hunting store, which had prepackaged food they could eat. She had tried to get a gun at the hunting store to replace the rifle she'd lost, but had given up. While she could get to the guns in the display cases, the ammunition was locked in a big safe.

While gathering food and looking for other children had become her main goals in her nightly forays, Allison's expeditions into town also made her feel like she was doing something useful. She didn't have a weapon to fight back, but just learning what she could of the aliens and finding out what they were up to, aside from simply killing humans, made her feel good.

But it wasn't easy sneaking past the Kreelans who had set up their main base in the town square and the warriors constantly moving in and out of the area. Like the third night after the attack when she had run into a group of warriors who had just let her go, she was sure that warriors had seen her more than once on her nighttime runs, but had simply ignored her. They must have only been concerned with older humans. Every once in a while she heard the distant sound of gunfire, so she knew there were still people fighting back.

While the aliens didn't seem all that interested in her, she wasn't taking it for granted. She did everything she could to move unseen and unheard.

Now, almost two weeks to the day since the attack, she was deep into the town, moving down an alleyway, probing toward the town square. It was the focus of whatever the aliens were doing here, and she wanted to know what it was.

She paused, then put her back against the wall as a pair of Kreelans walked by a few meters away, their black armor and talon-like fingernails glistening in the bonfires that the aliens kept burning at the center of the town square each night. They strode right past her, unaware that two hateful young eyes were boring holes in them, wishing them dead and gone back to whatever hellish world had spawned them.

The two warriors had just reached the end of the alley and Allison took a step away from the wall when she heard the aliens make a slight gasp. Quickly backing up to the wall again, she saw that the warriors were rooted to the ground, their eyes staring up at the sky, as if they could see something among the stars that was invisible to Allison's gaze.

A moment later the two warriors turned around and ran back toward the square, and Allison could hear alien cries and the sound of more running feet and the clatter of weapons and armor as the entire Kreelan garrison came alive.

This can't be good, she told herself. Deciding to take advantage of the situation, she darted into the market and stuffed her backpack full of packaged food, napkins (that were used mainly for toilet paper), and the short list of other essential items she had come for.

Back out in the alley, she paused. The Kreelans in the square, hundreds of them, if not more, were making a lot of noise in their guttural language. She hadn't seen them act this way before, and knew that whatever was happening must be important.

Reluctantly setting down her backpack and concealing it in a pile of empty boxes, she crept down the alley toward the end that opened onto the main street and the square beyond to see what was happening.

The aliens had formed themselves into a military-style formation, the warriors arrayed in semicircular rows facing an open area of the square. There were hundreds of them, maybe even a few thousand. It was hard to tell. She hadn't realized there were so many, and an involuntary shiver ran up her spine at the sight of the orderly ranks of alien killers.

A warrior who stood in front of the formation bellowed a command, and the warriors fell silent and stood ramrod-straight.

Allison looked up as she heard the growing roar of an approaching shuttle, and watched with slitted eyes as it settled to the grass in the square, its hover engines blowing dust and debris in a swirling cloud that swept through the Kreelan ranks.

As the shuttle's engines spun down, a ramp extended from the rear. Allison had a clear view, as the ramp faced directly toward her, and watched in frightened awe as the Kreelan warriors knelt and hammered their right fists against their left breasts as one, the sound of their armored gauntlets against their chest armor echoing through the square.

* * *

Ku'ar-Marekh stepped down the shuttle's gangway into the smoke-shrouded square. She had chosen to arrive in the shuttle because she knew that many of the warriors found her more accustomed means of appearing out of thin air...disturbing.

She looked upon the ranks of kneeling warriors with silver-flecked eyes, her gaze taking in everything, missing nothing.

Unlike the peers who knelt before her, the porcelain-smooth blue skin of her body bore not a single scar. Scars were considered a prize among her people, trophies of combat or great deeds done in service of the Empress. Ku'ar-Marekh had seen more than her share of battle from the time she was a young *tresh* learning the Way of Her Children, and had gathered an impressive collection of scars through the cycles before she had become a priestess.

But the Change that took place when her mentor had passed on her powers to Ku'ar-Marekh had stripped her skin bare of her trophies. While she still wore a sword and dagger, and three *shrekkas* on her left shoulder, the powers she had inherited when she became a priestess had made combat by sword and claw largely irrelevant.

She looked out upon the warriors the Empress had put in her care, and could barely see them through the swirling dust kicked up by the shuttle's engines.

With a gentle wave of her hand, the gusts of air stilled, and the tiny particles fell to the ground in a silent rain. Some of the warriors bowed their heads even further, for they could sense the power of her spirit in their blood like a great, frigid wind.

Ku'ar-Marekh could of course sense the warriors, but she also sensed something else, and stopped at the bottom of the ramp, casting her second sight into the world around her.

A human.

While the blood of the animals did not sing as did that of Her Children, priestesses such as Ku'ar-Marekh could see beyond the senses of the flesh. She turned to stare at the creature, which cowered in the shadows of a nearby building. It was plainly visible to Ku'ar-Marekh's eyes, for her race could see well in the dark. She knew that the warriors could only have overlooked the tiny human simply because it posed no challenge to their skills. Killing it would have brought no honor to the Empress, and no doubt they thought it better to leave it die of starvation.

Ku'ar-Marekh was not concerned with honor, but thought instead that killing the human would bring the Empire one step closer to exterminating these unworthy animals from the universe. Its blood did not sing, so it could not be the One the Empress so eagerly sought.

Staring at the creature, Ku'ar-Marekh reached out with her mind, seeking the human's heart. She could feel it, beating rapidly with fear in the tiny chest, and in her mind she imagined her fist gripping the pulsating organ, her talons sinking into the muscle. Then she began to squeeze...

* * *

Allison felt a shiver pass through her as the warrior walked down the ramp. The Kreelan looked much the same as the others, but there was something about this one that was different. She didn't know why, but a sudden surge of fear swept through her.

The alien stopped and turned to stare right at her.

She can see me! Allison realized, and her stomach fell away into a dark abyss as terror took hold and she turned to run.

It was then that she felt an uncomfortable pressure in her chest. She gasped as the sensation turned into icy needles that speared her heart, and she collapsed to the ground, gasping in agony.

She felt as if her heart was being torn, still beating, from her chest.

* * *

"My priestess?" Ri'al-Hagir said quietly. She was to serve as the First to Ku'ar-Marekh, to act as her right hand in all things. She had never before met the priestess, although she had heard many fearful tales from other warriors, and of course could sense the priestess through the Bloodsong.

Ri'al-Hagir glanced at where the human child writhed, perplexed as to why one such as Ku'ar-Marekh, who stood twelfth from the throne among all the souls in the Empire, would trifle with such a thing.

"We decided to leave the pups be," she explained as the human writhed in torment. "We have hopes that those that are resourceful may survive to be warriors worthy of our attention, as the adult human animals of this planet have been."

For a moment she was unsure if Ku'ar-Marekh had heard her words, for the attention of the priestess remained fixed on the human child, whose struggles were rapidly weakening. Ri'al-Hagir could sense the power flowing from the priestess, and was not so proud to admit, at least to herself, that it caused her fear such as battle never had.

Then, with a barely audible sigh, the priestess turned to look at her, and Ri'al-Hagir quickly lowered her gaze.

"I meant no offense, my priestess."

"Had any been taken, you would now be with our ancestors in death." Ku'ar-Marekh barely breathed the words, but every warrior kneeling before her heard them. Each and every one bowed her head even lower. In a louder voice, cold as any machine could be, she went on, "However, I honor your wisdom. If such as that can grow to pose a challenge to us, then I shall allow it to live."

* * *

Allison heaved a desperate gasp of air into her lungs as the icy spikes that had been crushing her heart disappeared. She lay on the hard pavement of the alley, her body wracked with tremors as her heart sluggishly returned to its life-sustaining duty.

She managed to turn on her side just before she vomited.

Looking up, spitting the awful taste from her mouth, she could see the Kreelan who had come on the shuttle, moving through the ranks of warriors, who still knelt before her.

"Get up," Allison told herself. She was afraid that if she didn't leave now, paralyzed by pain and fear, she never would. "Get up!"

She pushed herself to her knees, and then to her feet, leaning against the outside wall of the market for support. With unsteady steps she went to where she had hidden her backpack and hoisted it onto her shoulders, wincing at the weight.

After she'd gone a short way down the alley, Allison looked one last time at the Kreelans.

The newly-arrived warrior was staring at her. She pulled her lips back in a silent snarl that revealed a set of glistening ivory fangs.

Allison turned and ran.

FIFTY-EIGHT

"We're ready."

Those simple words, spoken by Fleet Admiral Phillip Tiernan, commander of the Confederation Navy, sent a wave of excitement through every person sitting in the briefing room in the Presidential Complex.

At the head of the conference table sat President Natalie McKenna. The dark skin of her face that was a gift of her African heritage was deeply lined from stress and worry, but the hard look from her dark eyes was proof of indefatigable determination to defeat the Kreelan Empire and save her people.

"Go ahead, admiral." McKenna nodded. "Let's hear it."

"Yes, Madam President." Tiernan turned to the wall-sized display at the front of the room that showed a star map of the human sphere. Not all human-settled worlds had yet joined the Confederation, but there were very few holdouts after the latest wave of Kreelan invasions. "Just to recap the strategic situation, there are now a total of eighteen colonies currently under attack by forces of the Kreelan Empire. Only one, Keran, where the enemy struck us first, has been completely...assimilated."

According to the last intelligence information the Navy had been able to obtain, the Kreelans had likely exterminated every human soul on Keran, then had begun to terraform the planet to better suit their needs.

What had happened there had driven home to everyone in the government that humanity was not simply in a battle for territory, riches, or ideology. Humanity was fighting for its very existence.

"The other planetary campaigns," Tiernan continued, "are essentially long-term battles of attrition. From what we can tell of the enemy's intentions, it's basically to try and kill as many of us at close quarters as possible. They don't seem interested in simply taking our worlds from us, because we know from the information we gained during the first contact encounter that they're radically more advanced than we are, or at least some portion of their Empire is. Our assessment is that if they wanted to simply take something from us, or just wipe us out, they could. But for some reason, they're taking their time about it."

"So, you're saying we have no chance against them?" Secretary of Trade Raul Hernandez asked the question of Tiernan, but his eyes darted to the President.

"Not at all, Mister Hernandez. Perhaps the best thing for me to say is that we simply don't understand their intentions. We understand some of their potential capabilities from what Commodore Sato," he nodded to a man with Japanese features who sat at the table, looking absurdly young compared to the other flag officers around him, "brought back from first contact, but we don't understand why they do what they do, or what their strategic goals are, other than killing us one by one." He looked around the room, finally resting his gaze on the president. "They've kicked us hard, and if they wanted to they could take us down.

"But I didn't come here," he went on, his voice deepening with resolve, "to tell you that we don't have a chance, or that we're just going to roll over and let them have their way."

Hernandez, clearly not convinced, simply nodded and rested his chin on his hands, focusing on the map of humanity's outposts among the stars, eighteen of which were displayed in red.

"What's the target, admiral?" McKenna asked.

"Alger's World."

The screen zoomed in on one of the red-flagged planets, and data appeared in a pop-up. It was a rare cousin of Earth, capable of supporting human life without domes or respiration equipment. It had a population of just over five million, with a planetary economy that was based primarily on agriculture. Before the arrival of the Kreelans, Alger's World had been a quiet, modestly successful colony in a location that had no particular strategic significance.

"Why Alger's World?"

The question had come fromVice President Laurent Navarre, who was leaning forward, studying the information on the screen. The former ambassador of the Francophone Alliance to the Terran Government, he had been the logical choice for McKenna's right-hand man. He had been of inestimable help to her in both forging the Confederation government and in setting in motion the largest industrial mobilization in the history of humankind to provide the weapons and material with which to fight humanity's enemy. "Not to belittle the suffering of any of our citizens, but Alger's World doesn't strike me as a strategic target. Its entire population is less than some of the major cities on some of the other besieged worlds, and it has no industrial capacity to speak of. I do not ask this to sound heartless, admiral, Madam President," he turned and nodded his head to McKenna before turning back to Tiernan, "but what do we gain strategically by mounting a major operation there?"

"In short, our plan for Alger's World gives us the best possible chance of winning a decisive victory, Mr. Vice President." Turning to McKenna, he went on, "Madam President, your orders to me were to find a way to strike back at the enemy and give the Confederation a success in the wake of so many invasions. The battles being fought on every planet other than Alger's World are battles of attrition that we will likely lose in the end." He paused, glancing momentarily at a naval officer who was new to the Confederation Navy, but who wore the stars of a full admiral. "As an example, I'm sure Admiral Voroshilov can tell you that we have very little hope of mounting a successful counteroffensive against the Kreelan forces on Saint Petersburg."

"Our world is lost." Lavrenti Voroshilov confirmed Tiernan's statement without preamble. He had been the commanding officer of the Saint Petersburg Navy when

Confederation forces had come to confiscate his government's illegal nuclear weapons, and he had fought the Confederation Navy before the Kreelans had arrived.

Now, Saint Petersburg was a charnel house, and the surviving units of his fleet had been merged with that of the Confederation. Most of Saint Petersburg's surviving population, those the Confederation had been able to evacuate, had been sent to the colony of Dobraya, where even now a massive industrialization program was underway to help build more ships that the Confederation needed to survive.

"We could send in the entire fleet and every Marine, and still we would lose. The battle is not over, but it has already been decided."

Tiernan nodded, his expression grim. "The other larger colonies under attack are in similar straits. In a two years, if we can ramp up production of the new ship designs fast enough and expand the Marine Expeditionary Forces as rapidly as our plans are calling for, we could think about trying to take back a world like Saint Petersburg. Now..." He shook his head. "We had to choose a smaller colony that had not been completely overrun, did not have an enormous number of Kreelan warriors, and was still central enough to our primary fleet elements that we could mass an overwhelming number of ships quickly, get the job done, and then get them back on station as rapidly as possible. We've been waiting for this opportunity for months, and Alger's World is it. We don't expect that a victory there is really going to hurt the Kreelans in a strategic sense, but it will give us some good news to tell the people."

"It will not hurt the morale of the fleet and Marines, either," Voroshilov added.

"So this is like the so-called 'Doolittle Raid,' is it not?" Navarre asked.

Tiernan nodded, impressed at the vice president's historical knowledge, but there were blank looks from everyone else around the table.

"Forgive my dredging up ancient history," Navarre apologized. "It was during Earth's Second World War, when the United States was reeling from a succession of defeats by the Empire of Japan. Then-President Roosevelt needed a victory to give the American people hope, and the United States Navy and Army Air Corps came up with a plan to bomb Japan using land-based bombers flown from a naval aircraft carrier. The raid caused little real damage, but was a blow to Japanese morale as much as it was a boon to that of the Americans." He gestured toward the map. "This strikes me as similar, at least in terms of our morale. The effect on the Kreelans, we may never know."

"Ladies and gentlemen," McKenna told them, "what the vice president said cuts to the heart of what we're trying to accomplish here. The success of this operation is vital from a political perspective, regardless of any military gains. Many of the planetary governments, not to mention their citizens, are near panic. After the last wave of attacks, there has even been talk of secession, with some people believing that the formation of the Confederation has somehow encouraged the Kreelans to attack more of our worlds."

"Rubbish!" Voroshilov spat.

"I agree, admiral, but people everywhere are terrified, with every one of them wondering if their world will be the next to sound the invasion sirens. And that's without the knowledge of how thinly spread the fleet really is. With the current campaigns underway, there aren't enough ships to mount a credible defense against more than half a dozen worlds, including Earth."

Tiernan and Voroshilov exchanged a look, then Tiernan nodded unhappily.

"We're not just fighting the Kreelans now," McKenna went on. "We're fighting the worst enemy mankind has ever known: unreasoning fear. And I have very little with which to fight it. The Confederation has no deep-rooted traditions or other social fabric to hold it together, no historical flag around which I can rally our people. Right now the Confederation is still a relatively loose alliance of worlds brought together by the need for common defense, and it's held together by little more than treaty and this government's commitment to help member worlds build up their defenses.

"We're doing that, but the chronic fear our citizens are suffering, especially after the most recent attacks, is leading to irrational beliefs that can't be defeated by reason. Secession may sound like a crazy idea from where we sit, but if people don't believe the Confederation can protect them, cutting their ties and trying to lay low starts to look like an attractive option." Her expression hardened. "Make no mistake. If the Confederation splinters and breaks apart, our species is doomed. That's why this operation *must* succeed, because a victory, even on a small, backwater colony world, will show our people that all is not lost and give them hope. And hope is a weapon I can use to combat their fears."

"We will succeed, Madam President," Tiernan assured her. "I can't say at what price, and I hope I don't sound arrogant when I say this, but we're going to win this one." He turned and gestured toward Sato. "And I'd now like to introduce Commodore Ichiro Sato, who's going to go over the details of how we're going to do it."

McKenna watched as the young commodore moved to the podium and stood at attention. Sato had become a household name throughout the Confederation. The sole survivor of the ill-fated ship that had made first contact with the Kreelans, he had gone on to have two more ships shot out from under him, one at Keran and the other, his first command, at Saint Petersburg. Unlike most of his peers, who wore several rows of ribbons, Sato only had two. The lower one held his campaign decorations for Keran and Saint Petersburg, while the top one held the ribbon for the Medal of Honor, which McKenna had presented to him.

Sato was fifteen years younger than the next youngest flag officer in the room, and had gone from a midshipman aboard the ill-fated *Aurora* to commodore in a mere three years. Many senior officers had complained about Sato's rapid promotion to commander, but none had complained about him receiving his first star as commodore. Most of his detractors had died in combat.

Looking at the younger man as he stepped up to the podium, Tiernan knew that Sato didn't have everything a peacetime flag officer needed to be successful. But this wasn't peacetime, and Tiernan needed warriors. More importantly, he needed leaders of warriors. And that's exactly what Sato was.

"Madam President," the young commodore began, bowing his head slightly, "Admiral Tiernan, ladies and gentlemen. As the admiral already noted, our target is Alger's World, which the Kreelans invaded nine days ago. Most of the human population is settled in small towns distributed through open country that is well-suited for agricultural production, which was another important consideration for the ground phase of the battle plan, which we'll cover shortly.

"Navy reconnaissance missions into the target system have indicated that the Territorial Army probably no longer exists as a cohesive force, but radio transmissions clearly show that there is continued organized human resistance. We have no idea how many survivors there may be, but based on projections derived from the assimilation of Keran, we believe that the majority of the population is still alive."

"How old is this information?" McKenna asked.

"Six days, Madam President. The emergency courier departed for Earth as soon as the naval detachment there sounded the invasion alert, and we dispatched a reconnaissance vessel as soon as we received the alert at Naval HQ."

Courier ships were used to route communications between star systems, storing up batches of data in one system before jumping to another to download it to a relay and upload another batch for the next jump. It was a huge hindrance for military planning, because some of the star systems under siege were weeks away by hyperlight travel.

Fortunately, Alger's World was much closer.

"Please continue."

Sato turned to the map on the wall, which now showed a glowing green icon that moved in a graceful arc toward Alger's World. "The first part of the operation involves the covert insertion of several ground reconnaissance teams. The Kreelans are able, through means we do not yet understand, to selectively defeat or disrupt our high technology weapons and sensors, apparently at will. We're hoping that these teams will be able to provide the reconnaissance we need for the ground phase of the operation without involving high-technology assets that may not work.

"The ships transporting the teams are modified courier vessels that are already on their way to the system. We sent them in as quickly as possible so they'll be able to get the teams on the ground with as much lead time as possible."

"You sent them in before the operation was approved?" McKenna asked.

"Yes, ma'am." Sato made no attempt to dodge what some might have considered a freight-train sized bullet. "You see, we have another courier standing by that will deliver your 'go' order to the reconnaissance teams. If for any reason the teams don't receive that order, they'll automatically abort the mission and return home."

"Very well, commodore. I applaud the initiative, and as Admiral Tiernan can confirm," she smiled, "I try very hard not to micromanage the fleet's operations."

That earned a number of grins and a few chuckles from those around the table.

"Then what happens?"

"Concurrent with the deployment of the scout teams," Sato continued, "we'll be sending couriers with orders for Fleet elements from fourteen systems. Those ships will deploy from their current duties to participate in the assault." A list of ships appeared on the display, with lines connecting them to the fourteen different systems. "As you can see, we are taking only a handful of vessels from each system to minimize the impact on operations, as eleven of these systems are currently under siege.

"The main drawback is that the assault fleet will not have had the opportunity to train as an integrated unit, but this will allow us to bring a very potent force to bear at Alger's World quickly. Based on reconnaissance data, we should initially have a ratio of at least four to one in warships, and nearly ten to one in total tonnage."

He paused as the map display showed a depiction of the courier ships heading out from Earth with orders for the other systems, then the warship flotillas jumping in sequence to Alger's World.

"I must point out that the most critical aspect of the operation is the sequencing of the jumps for the assault fleet. We intend to have all of our warships arrive over Alger's World within a window of only sixty seconds. The main risk factor is that they'll be jumping deep into the planet's gravity well using techniques pioneered by Admiral Voroshilov at Saint Petersburg." He nodded toward the Russian admiral, whose attention was fixed on the screen. "This should give us complete tactical surprise and allow us to deploy the Marine assault force under a solid shield of warships." He paused. "But I must advise you that this is the first time, during war or peace, that any navy has attempted such a complex navigational maneuver."

"Admiral Voroshilov," McKenna asked quietly, "you don't look very happy."

"I am not," Voroshilov replied, turning to look her in the eye. "Do not misunderstand, please. The plan is a good one, and Commodore Sato and his planning staff have done an amazing job of bringing it together.

"The danger is that we are pushing right to the limits of our computational capabilities for navigation. After a long and lively debate, we decided not to stage the fleet closer and then jump in. That would take precious additional time to reach Alger's World, and would also prolong the time the ships are away from their other vital duties, as well as lead to further civilian casualties on Alger's World.

"But there is great risk, Madam President. If the fleet arrives out of sequence, we run the risk of being defeated in detail by Kreelan forces and newly arriving warships interpenetrating with existing ones when they come out of their jumps.

"I also worry about the accuracy of our navigational data for jumping so deep into the gravity well. We were able to test and verify our mapping many times in Saint Petersburg before the Confederation fleet arrived. This time we will have only the remote sensor data from surveillance vessels. It will be difficult. And that is not all." He frowned.

"Admiral?" McKenna prompted.

"We will also be taking nearly two-thirds of the ships from Home Fleet. Earth's defenses will temporarily be greatly weakened."

McKenna looked to Tiernan. "Are we taking too much of a risk here, admiral? I want to hit back at the enemy, but I don't want to wipe out the fleet in the process or leave Earth open to invasion."

"Ma'am," Tiernan said, "as Admiral Voroshilov noted, there was a great deal of debate over how we should do this. But what it boiled down to in the end was that we're past the time for half-measures. We haven't thrown caution or prudence to the wind. Thousands of hours have been spent in very meticulous planning for this operation. We started this as a contingency plan months ago, using it as a framework. That's why Sato was able to bring it together so quickly.

"But we're not going to win this war by being careful. We're going to win it by taking daring, calculated risks." He gestured to the map. "As you know, I named Admiral Voroshilov as the fleet commander for this operation because he has unique expertise in the navigation aspect, and a significant number of the fleet units involved were formerly of the Saint Petersburg Navy, all of which have seen combat. And I told Lavrenti straight up that if he didn't think this mission would succeed to say so. He's frowned a lot, but hasn't said he wouldn't lead it."

Voroshilov only grunted, but the others in the room visibly relaxed.

"As for the invasion threat to Earth," Sato interjected darkly, "if the Kreelans wanted to invade, they would have. They know exactly where we are."

A round of quiet murmurs swept through the room. Sato, as the sole survivor of the ship that had made first contact, had unique first hand experience with the Kreelans. When the aliens had finished massacring his crew, they had sent him alone in his ship back to Earth in a feat of navigation that humans had thought to be impossible.

"That may be, commodore," McKenna said, "but there is a political dimension beyond any military realities. There would be a panic if Earth's population felt their defenses had been stripped. We have to at least keep up the appearance that Home Fleet can stop the enemy."

"That appearance, and the reality," Tiernan told her firmly, "will remain, Madam President. Aside from some of the Francophone Alliance worlds, Earth is the most heavily defended planet in human space, even without the Home Fleet units we plan to detach for this operation. We've taken this into account by putting ships that would normally be in dry dock on extended defense patrols until we can bring the deployed ships home. If the Kreelans come calling, they'll be in for the fight of their lives."

Still concerned, but satisfied with Tiernan's reasoning, McKenna nodded. "Very well, admiral."

"Go on, Commodore Sato." Tiernan gestured for the younger man to proceed.

"Yes, sir." Sato again turned his attention to the president. "Once the fleet has jumped in, its first mission will be to gain orbital supremacy to protect the assault carriers and, if possible, to destroy any Kreelan ships in-system. Once that is accomplished, the battleships and cruisers may also be tasked to provide fire support for the ground operation.

"And with that, I would like to hand the briefing over to Lieutenant General James Sparks, the ground force commander."

"Thank you, commodore." McKenna smiled at Sato as he took his seat.

She caught Tiernan's sigh as a wiry officer stood up from a chair along the wall. The man wore a Marine dress blue uniform with the three stars of a lieutenant general, but something was...odd about it.

It took her a moment to realize that rather than the regulation gloss black shoes, he was wearing calf-high black leather boots that made a clinking sound with each step. She nearly guffawed when she saw that he was wearing riding spurs, as if he was expecting to go and hop onto a horse as soon as the briefing was over. He also wore a saber strapped to the gold belt of his uniform. And his cap, which was held by an aide sitting behind him, wasn't the regulation cap of the Confederation Marines, but was a wide-brim black hat with gold braid around it and an insignia with crossed sabers at the front.

She couldn't suppress a smile, thinking that while he was clearly out of regulation, the unusual attire seemed to suit him perfectly.

Her smile quickly faded as she realized that while the man might be a bit of a theatrical dandy, he was one of the few survivors of the disastrous defense that had been mounted against the enemy at Keran, the first world that had been attacked. She had read the full report of the battle, and Sparks had acquitted himself well. Like Sato, he was a leader of warriors. Also like the much younger commodore, Sparks had been rapidly promoted to flag rank.

"Ma'am," he began without preamble in a heavy drawl from the American South, looking at some hand-written notes on crumpled paper he'd taken from a pocket inside his uniform, "we've allocated three full divisions, each with roughly eighteen thousand Marines, to conduct the ground campaign. We'll be using the most advanced weapons and systems we have available, but we're also going into this battle prepared to lose them."

McKenna frowned. "I'm not sure I understand that, general."

"Ma'am, it's because of the Kreelans' ability to selectively defeat our technology. This has had a huge impact on how we wage war. It's hard to emphasize just how much. And weapons and sensors aren't the only things the enemy has meddled with. They do the same thing to the command, control, and communications systems that we normally rely on. I've read reports of some combat units having to resort to voice communications over radio using equipment that they've had to cobble together in the field, because their normal comm systems and data-links inexplicably die on them. The Kreelans don't seem to have a problem with us using radio."

"Radio?" Navarre didn't try to conceal his amazement. "But that technology is, well, practically ancient!"

"Yes, sir," Sparks told him, "it is. But I believe in using what works. We haven't had any reports of the Kreelans jamming or disrupting radio where it's been put into use, so I've had radio equipment retrofitted on all of our vehicles and infantry gear."

"We have also installed radio equipment in the ships and assault boats so they can communicate with the ground forces in case our primary systems go down," Tiernan added. "The Kreelans sometimes still let us use the data link systems, but most of the time they limit us to voicecomm in the fleet. It seems to depend on their mood."

McKenna shook her head in dread and wonder. She'd been briefed on this before, and knew that the best and brightest minds of humanity were trying to figure out how the Kreelans were interfering with the technology that humanity had long taken for granted. But so far there was no news. It was as if the Kreelans were using magic. "Go on, general."

"Our units will be deployed based on the intelligence information we receive from the forward recon teams once the fleet jumps in." Drawing his saber (which caused some momentary consternation among the presidential protective detail) he used it as a pointer, jabbing the tip at illuminated areas of the wall display, which now showed a map of the main continent. "We believe these will be the most likely areas, as they hold the greatest population concentrations, and we'll deploy units tailored to the size of each threat. We can drop a single battalion or a whole division in any given area, depending on the situation, with the assault boats providing close air support unless we need to call on the Navy for heavier firepower."

Sparks looked over the attendees, his eyes focusing on each face in turn before he locked eyes with the President. "We're going to kick their asses, ma'am. That's all I have."

With that, Sparks sheathed his saber and left the podium, his spurs making a ching-ching-ching sound with every step until he sat back down.

Tiernan turned to the president from his seat at the table. "After we've destroyed the Kreelan ground forces, transports will bring in defensive equipment and support personnel that will make it very expensive for the Kreelans to try and come back to Alger's World any time soon. We're hoping to give them such a bloody nose in this operation that they won't want to try."

"Wouldn't it make more sense to just evacuate?" Everyone turned to Secretary of Industry Johann Thurmond, whose question had several others around the room nodding their agreement.

"It's going to be a huge additional burden on the fleet and the Territorial Army to fortify Alger's World to the point where they might stand a chance against another attack." With a look toward Voroshilov, he added, "Its population is much smaller than many of the other colonies. We should consolidate so we can better concentrate our forces."

Tiernan opened his mouth to answer, but didn't get the chance.

"No." McKenna hadn't raised her voice, but that single word echoed through the room like a gunshot. "No. The Kreelans have already taken too much from us.

Eighteen worlds are under siege and millions have already died, with more dying every day. We're not going to give them anything without a fight, and we're going to take back everything we can. We're also going to rapidly build up the survey arm of the fleet so we can find more habitable worlds and establish more colonies. We need to expand our presence in the galaxy, not withdraw, because every time we do that we move one step closer to extinction."

McKenna looked around the room at her cabinet members and the other attendees, her eyes cold and hard. "We'll fight them on every planet, give up nothing that we aren't forced to, and kill every last one of them if we must to achieve victory."

The president turned to Tiernan. "The operation is a go, admiral."

* * *

"Madam President?" Stephanie Guillaume-Sato, President McKenna's press secretary, stood at the door to McKenna's office.

"Steph!" McKenna looked up from the pad on her desk where she'd been making notes for an upcoming speech. "Please, come in."

Closing the door behind her, Steph crossed the office's dark blue rug to stand in front of McKenna's mahogany desk. The wall behind the president was armor glass that looked out over the Hudson River from where the Presidential Complex stood on Governors Island. From where Steph was standing, the Statue of Liberty was just behind the president. It was an image captured more than once by the president's official media artist.

"You wanted to see me, ma'am?"

"Yes, I did, Steph. Please, sit down." McKenna gestured to one of the armchairs in front of her desk, and Steph sat down. "You read the briefing on the Alger's World operation, didn't you?"

"Yes, Madam President, I went through the entire briefing." Steph suppressed a rush of guilt. She should have attended, but had been on an assignment on the west coast and had been delayed by a foulup in her transportation arrangements, a foulup she had purposely engineered. The truth was that she had known Ichiro was going to be at the briefing, and she hadn't wanted to see him. *Not exactly*, she amended to herself. *He wouldn't want to see me.* "And let me apologize once again for not making it. It won't happen again."

McKenna waved the apology away. "I'm sure it won't."

Looking into the president's eyes, Steph could tell that McKenna knew the truth. It wasn't any secret that Steph and Ichiro had parted company a few months before, and Steph was ashamed that she had let her personal situation interfere with her job.

"Yes, ma'am." She dropped her gaze.

McKenna paused a moment before asking, "Steph, are you tired of this job?"

Looking back up at her boss, Steph said, "Tired of it? No. No, of course not."

A glint of anger flared in McKenna's eyes. "Don't tell me two lies in a row."

"Madam President..." Steph was momentarily at a loss for words. She had loved the job as press secretary for most of the two years that she'd held it, but McKenna was right. It had become a grind, a chore. More and more, Steph was just going through the motions, and she'd been growing increasingly restless. "I'm sorry, ma'am. I didn't mean for it to sound like that. I...I don't want you to think I'm disloyal. You gave me an incredible opportunity, and I can't tell you how much I appreciate what you did for me by giving me this position. But if you put it like that, then yes, I'm getting tired of it."

"Good." McKenna sat back and smiled, enjoying the confused mix of emotions on Steph's face. "Because I have a job that I think is right up your alley." She leaned forward, completely serious now. "Steph, you know as well or better than anyone else how the Confederation is faring. So you know just how fragile things are now."

Steph nodded. "If the Kreelans breathe hard against one more planet, the Confederation is finished." While the members of the president's cabinet had access to channels of information that Steph didn't, no one in McKenna's entire administration had a better handle on the pulse of the Confederation's citizenry than Steph. She was plugged into every news service for every human-settled world that was part of the interstellar courier network. She had seen how the political landscape had transformed from one of hope and optimism in the aftermath of the Confederation's formation to weariness as the war dragged on, and near-hysteria after the latest round of Kreelan invasions. "If we don't pull a rabbit out of the hat," she told McKenna, "the only thing we'll have left is what we started with, Earth and the Francophone Alliance."

"That's right. That's why this operation is so important. And that's why I want someone in on it from the start to document what I hope and pray will be our first decisive victory."

Stunned, Steph sat there for a moment. Her mind suddenly filled with the nightmare images of the Battle of Keran, where she had been an embedded journalist with the 7th Cavalry Regiment. She was incredibly lucky to have survived.

At the same time, she felt her pulse quicken, not in fear, but anticipation. She also realized that it wouldn't have been long before she would have resigned her position to return to being a journalist in the field. That was her passion, and she was one of a very few journalists who had not only survived, but had helped fight.

"I want to be clear," McKenna went on, "that this is strictly a volunteer assignment. There will be other journalists going in with the main force, but I've given a lot of thought to something I hadn't considered earlier. I want someone to tell the story from the very beginning of the operation, which means going in with one of the reconnaissance teams and documenting what they find. There aren't many people who could do that, and I wanted to give you first crack at it."

Steph didn't have to think about her answer. "When do I leave?"

McKenna pressed a control on her desktop pad. Five seconds later a Marine staff sergeant opened the door and stood at attention beside it. "The courier's waiting for you. It's the one taking the execution orders to the teams. I've already ordered your field equipment and travel bag loaded on the shuttle you'll be taking up to Africa Station. You just have to decide which team you want to go with."

That was another easy answer. Steph had studied the operations files long before the briefing and had seen some familiar names. "I'll go with the team led by First Sergeant Roland Mills."

"Done. Now get going, and good luck." McKenna stood and offered her hand.

"Thank you, ma'am!" Steph stood up and shook the president's hand, then turned to go.

As she boarded the shuttle on the roof of the complex, she thought about contacting Ichiro to let him know, but decided against it. *He went his own way*, she told herself. *I don't care if he knows.*

It was the third lie she'd told that day.

FIFTY-NINE

Ku'ar-Marekh strode toward what had been the open center of the human town. She could not abide what passed for human architecture, where all the structures were square and blocky, bereft of the pleasing curves inherent in all the works of Her Children and the graceful script of the New Tongue. While she knew that she should be hoping that the One would be found soon, she could not help wishing the humans gone from the universe. They were unsightly creatures, whose ugliness was reflected in all they made.

Her warriors were building the first *Kalai-Il* to be erected on this world, making the first step in reshaping the planet for the pleasure of the Empress.

A massive stone edifice, the *Kalai-Il* comprised a large central dais surrounded by two rings of stone pillars that supported enormous capstones. It was central to Kreelan society, and was a place of atonement for those who had fallen from Her grace. Rarely was it used, for few were the transgressions of the peers severe enough to warrant such punishment. It stood as a reminder to all of the terrible price of dishonor.

She watched as hundreds of warriors labored, hauling the stones from a nearby quarry cut into the rock by the landing ships. Beyond that, no modern machines were used. The *Kalai-Il* was built on every world of the Empire the same way as it had been since before the time of the First Empress, with simple machines of wood and stone, powered by the straining muscles of the warriors who served Her will.

Around the *Kalai-Il*, hundreds more warriors hauled in smaller stones to build the five arenas that tradition demanded for ritual combat. Once they and the *Kalai-Il* were complete, contests between her warriors and the humans would commence, and would continue through all hours of the day and night until no humans remained, or the One had been found.

When the last of the humans was gone, this world would be turned over to the builder caste, who would fashion it into whatever form the Empress required.

There had been a time when that knowledge had thrilled Ku'ar-Marekh, knowing that her people could shape the face of a world, or even create a planet in the void of space. Or destroy one, or even an entire star system. These things and more had the Empire done in the long ages since the First Empress, Keel-Tath, had forged it.

But the wonder of what was in the power of the Empress to accomplish, to create or destroy, was gone.

All that remained to her was duty.

Ri'al-Hagir strode up to Ku'ar-Marekh and knelt as she saluted. "My priestess, the *Kalai-Il* and the arenas will be finished in another three turns of the sun."

"And have you made arrangements to hold the humans who will await their turn in the arenas?"

"Yes, my priestess. Pens are being constructed for the animals."

"When are the first humans due to arrive?"

"This evening. A column of the animals is being marched from the south."

"How many are there?" Ku'ar-Marekh ran her eyes across the arenas, watching as warriors hauled the sand on which the combats would be fought.

Ri'al-Hagir glanced up, then returned her eyes to the safety of the ground. "Thousands, my priestess. That is just in this first catch. There are many, many thousands more that we can take at our leisure."

"So many allowed themselves to be captured?"

"There were few warriors here, it seems. Some still fight on in small groups, but most are as our clawless ones, unable to defend themselves."

Ku'ar-Marekh grunted in surprise. The clawless ones of her race, those such as the builders and the healers, the armorers and many more, were never allowed in harm's way, for they were precious beyond their skills. They were the sacred legacy of those priestesses who had cut off their talons as a proclamation of faith and honor to the First Empress after She had been betrayed, over a hundred thousand cycles ago.

To leave any such as their own clawless ones undefended, vulnerable to attack, was unthinkable to any warrior.

"Animals, indeed." Ku'ar-Marekh made a flicking gesture with her talons, indicating disgust. "Be they human clawless ones or merely untrained warriors, they will fight and die in the arenas."

"As you command, my priestess." Ri'al-Hagir again saluted, then stood and hurried away to fulfill her duties.

* * *

That evening, Ku'ar-Marekh found herself restless despite a long day of accompanying some of the hunting parties that ranged across the planet, looking for humans to capture.

It had been a dull, empty day in a lifetime of such days since the Change.

Despite her weariness from covering many leagues on foot and whisking herself from place to place across the planet, she found that sleep eluded her.

With a sigh, she finally got up from her bed of animal hides and, on her knees, began to dress. Like everything else that was of the Way, there was a ritual to guide it. Unlike many of the peers, she normally slept in the nude, wearing only the collar about her neck and the pendants that hung from it.

Now she knelt beside her bed and carefully unfolded the black gauzy undergarment that was worn by all Her Children. It fit close to her skin, molding itself to her as she stood to put on the bottom, then the top, and she sealed it closed with a stroke of her hand.

Kneeling again, she began to put on her armor, drawing each piece in sequence from the neat stack she had made when she undressed. First came the sections of black leatherite that formed a layer covering her body from her ankles to just below her collar, and along her arms to her wrists. Then came her sandals which, like everything else, had been created by a senior armorer to fit her body perfectly. She tied the leather laces around her calves.

Last came the armor plate, which always gleamed like a black mirror, the cyan rune of the Nyur-A'il at the center of her breastplate glowing in the darkness. She put on the armor protecting her shins and thighs, then her upper and lower arms. She attached her breast and back plates, which molded themselves to her body. Then she put on her armored gauntlets, which had openings in the ends of the fingers for her black talons.

She cinched the leatherite belt around her waist and slid her sheathed sword into the holding ring. Her dagger was already attached, the deadly blade shrouded by the scabbard. Last, she attached three of the deadly *shrekkas*, throwing weapons, to her left shoulder.

Standing up, she pulled aside the white cloth that formed the door of her temporary quarters, which was little more than a large domed tent. Like all things, it was traditional, but she would have much rather slept in the open so she could see the stars before sleep took her away into blissful darkness for a few hours. Sleep that had passed over her this night.

Walking past the warriors who continued to labor on the *Kalai-Il* and the nearby arenas, she nodded her head as they saluted her, even though she felt completely isolated from them.

Ku'ar-Marekh did not know or care where she was going. It did not matter. Her warriors had the situation on this world well in hand, and the ships of Her fleet in space above were vigilant. All was quiet.

Too quiet.

She wandered the dark streets of the human settlement, her footsteps making no sound and leaving no mark, marveling at how ugly it was. Wishing she were of the builder caste, she imagined how she might remake it to be more pleasing.

Then she sensed it. The same small human she had seen the night she had arrived on this world. She did not need to cast forward her second sight to know it was the same creature, for she could sense its heartbeat, which was as unique to Ku'ar-Marekh as a face.

Curious, she silently glided toward the young animal.

* * *

Allison crept down the street along the side of the market, heading toward the front of the building. The back door was locked, and she hadn't wanted to risk trying to break in.

She felt guilty for having gone out tonight, because they really didn't need any more food right now. But the truth was that Allison needed some breathing room, some freedom from being cooped up with the kids all day, and it wouldn't hurt to have a little extra.

A quick smile crossed her lips as she thought of the word. Kids. She wasn't a kid anymore, she knew. She was an adult. For a moment she was proud of that, before she remembered how it had come to be. The smile faded as she thought of the contrails in the sky and the sirens, of her family, dead in the street.

The bodies, both human and Kreelan, had all been removed, along with all the weapons. Allison had planned to go see the bodies of her parents and brother, but they and all the others had been taken away before Allison had first ventured into town.

She didn't know what the Kreelans had done with them. The vids she had seen about the aliens had only made clear how little humans really knew about them. No one had said for sure that they didn't eat people, and their fangs made it pretty clear they were meat eaters.

Allison shuddered and shoved the grisly thought aside as she moved up to the corner of the market, crouching low. The building didn't face onto the town square where the Kreelans were busy with their construction project, but it was close enough that warriors passed by frequently. She always had to be careful here.

She took a quick peek around the corner, then pulled back. It was clear.

Taking a deep breath, she took the corner quickly, still staying low.

There, right in front of her, was the warrior who had landed that night. The one who had absolutely terrified Allison, and who somehow had grabbed her heart.

Even though the street was pitch dark and the warrior's features were indistinct, a shadow that blocked the glow of the star light, Allison knew it was her. A faint glow shone from the strange rune on her chest armor, as if it was lit from within.

Allison knew she couldn't get away if the alien wanted to get her. She had no idea where the Kreelan had even come from in the second between when Allison had checked that the coast was clear and when she turned the corner. There had been nowhere for the alien to hide. She was simply...there.

"What...what do you want?" Allison cursed herself for asking such a stupid question, but she wasn't sure what else to say. What was the proper thing to ask a member of an alien race that was bent on annihilating humanity?

The Kreelan, of course, said nothing. She simply stood there, unmoving, starlight glinting from her eyes.

Allison tensed as she saw the alien clench her hands, and felt a sudden stab of fear at the sight of the Kreelan's claws. They were five, maybe six centimeters long, and Allison knew they were wickedly sharp.

"Can't we talk about this?" She could barely hear her own whisper above the blood pounding in her ears.

Then the alien did something Allison never would have expected in a million years. The Kreelan stood aside, and made a clear gesture for Allison to pass, holding her hand out, palm up, in the direction Allison had intended to go.

Stunned, Allison simply stood there a moment, wondering if it was some sort of trick. But she quickly realized that the alien had no need to trick her. Allison's life was entirely in the alien's hands. Or claws.

Biting her lip, Allison was tempted to turn and run, but didn't. Not so much because of what the warrior might do, but because running would be like surrendering. And one thing both her parents had taught her was that the worst thing you could ever do was give up.

"Okay, then." Steeling herself, she took a step forward. Then another, which drew her up next to the warrior, who kept her eyes fixed on Allison, but otherwise made no move.

With the next step, Allison passed the Kreelan. She wanted to turn around to keep her eyes on the alien and back away from her, but resisted the urge.

Instead, she walked slowly to the market's front door, which had been blasted from its hinges. Shards of glass still littered the walkway, and the sound of it crunching under Allison's shoes sounded like a long string of gunshots in her ears. Her nose wrinkled at the sickening smell at the threshold, but she knew it was only spoiled food.

Glancing over her shoulder to see if the warrior was still there, Allison saw that the alien was following right behind her, barely an arm's length away.

Growing a bit bolder now, Allison asked, "So, I guess you're hungry, too?"

* * *

Ku'ar-Marekh was intrigued by the industrious human. While obviously little more than a pup, the animal had repeatedly come into the human settlement, no doubt seeking sustenance for the other pups that Ku'ar-Marekh knew had taken refuge at a destroyed homestead beyond the settlement. The young animal had taken great risks to do so, even coming back after an encounter with a group of patrolling warriors.

Through the numbness in her soul, she felt a tiny sliver of warmth: respect. It would not change the eventual fate of the pup and those sheltering with it, for when they were old enough to pose a credible threat to her warriors, or when Ku'ar-Marekh grew tired of their existence, they would be put to the arena.

For now, however, the young animal provided an interesting diversion.

It stood at the entrance to what must have been an indoor market for food, much of which had spoiled. The reek was overpowering to Ku'ar-Marekh's sensitive nose, but it was hardly the worst thing the priestess had endured.

The human said something in its incomprehensible language.

Ku'ar-Marekh again gestured with her hand in a way that she hoped the human would understand, urging it onward.

* * *

Allison saw the alien raise her hand again, palm up, simultaneously nodding toward the market's dark interior.

She found herself nodding back, then took out her flashlight and flicked it on. There was no reason to be stealthy, now that she had a Kreelan chaperone.

"Unreal," she breathed as she moved into the market. She moved quickly down the aisles, stuffing her backpack with boxes of breakfast bars, freeze-dried food packets, and some medicine that she hoped would cure what she knew was an infection in the hand of one of the kids. With every step she hoped that the warrior wouldn't decide to kill her. But every time Allison glanced back, the warrior was right behind her, intently watching everything she did like a curious but deadly puppy.

With the backpack nearly full, Allison tried to jam in a package of dried fruit. As she did, one of the closures on the pack flew opened and everything spilled out.

None of it hit the floor. Allison stood there, mouth agape, as the spilled contents of her backpack floated in the air as if they were in zero gravity in space, reflecting the light cast by the tiny flashlight that was clamped in her teeth.

Looking up at the Kreelan, she saw that one of the warrior's hands was out, fingers spread, as if she were going to pluck the items from the air. With a graceful turn of the warrior's wrist, everything magically flew back into the pack as Allison's shaking hands held it open.

As the troublesome dried fruit joined the other items, the pack closed itself, sealing tight. Then, as Allison stared at the warrior, she felt the pack lift up and seat itself on her shoulders.

Allison gulped. "Thank...thank you," she stuttered.

The Kreelan just stood there.

Carefully, as if she were stepping past a tame but hungry tiger, Allison moved toward the market's entrance. Glancing behind her, she saw that the warrior was gone. The Kreelan had disappeared as mysteriously as she had appeared in the first place.

"Oh, my God." Allison sighed with relief as she moved quickly along the front of the store and turned the corner back the way she had come.

And there stood the warrior, waiting for her.

"You know, that's really getting annoying." Allison didn't try to mask the anger in her voice. It was a more comforting feeling than unbridled fear, and even a tiny bit of jealously. She wished that she had powers like the alien did. It was like - she hated to use the word - magic. It was impossible.

But Allison knew that she wasn't just seeing things. She didn't imagine it. She wondered if all the aliens possessed such powers. If they did, what chance did humans have?

Not wanting to take that line of thought any further, she hastened down the street, heading toward home. The only difference was that she didn't take her normal route along the creek to try and stay out of sight. She walked right down the road, this time ignoring the aliens who passed by.

The alien warrior stayed right behind her the entire way.

* * *

Ku'ar-Marekh padded silently behind the human, marveling at the animal's courage as it marched right past the warriors moving through the night on their appointed tasks.

Other than a curious glance, the warriors paid the human no mind, seeing that Ku'ar-Marekh was with it. She felt intense curiosity from them through the Bloodsong, but they only saluted her as they continued on. Warriors did not question the affairs of a high priestess, especially of the Nyur-A'il.

When the human reached the path to the homestead that led from the main road, it stopped and turned to her. The animal held out its clawless hands toward her, as if pushing Ku'ar-Marekh away. The meaning was clear enough. Come no farther.

Ku'ar-Marekh pondered the peculiarities of the situation. Save the Empress and those who stood higher upon the steps to the throne than Ku'ar-Marekh herself, she would have instantly killed any other member of her race for such an egregious act. She would never even have given it thought before striking. She would have demanded ritual combat from any of the priestesses who stood above her had they done such a thing.

And yet, this human, this tiny thing that Ku'ar-Marekh could slay with the barest thought, gave her pause. The pup must eventually die in the arena, if Ku'ar-Marekh or another of her warriors did not kill it first. So why let it live?

The realization came to her with sudden clarity. She saw in this human something of what she herself had once known as a young warrior, fiercely proud. This animal clearly was not the One, for Ku'ar-Marekh could tell it was female and its blood did not sing.

Yet for the first time she gave some credence to the belief that the salvation of Her Children might be found among the humans. While she did not entirely accept the notion as fact, she no longer dismissed the possibility.

The human said some more words, shaking Ku'ar-Marekh from her reverie. Looking deep into the human's strange eyes, she bowed her head slightly.

* * *

Allison stood there, her arms still raised to ward the Kreelan off, hoping that the alien wouldn't become angry and decide to kill her.

The warrior shifted her gaze momentarily, as if looking at something beyond Allison. Glancing over her shoulder, Allison couldn't see anything behind her.

Looking more carefully at the warrior, who stood just beyond arm's reach, Allison thought the alien must have been deep in thought. Even in nothing but the starlight, Allison could see that the Kreelan's eyes, which looked much like those of a cat and in their own way were beautiful, were empty. Dead. Allison had seen enough of other warriors, had seen their expressions through the binoculars, to know that this alien was different. The other aliens showed expression, even if Allison couldn't read them. This one didn't. Her face was an unmoving mask, her eyes lifeless mirrors.

And if she was entertaining herself by following a human child around, rather than going to kill other humans, she was probably alone, too. Perhaps an outcast, even though she was clearly the leader here from the way the other warriors acted around her.

For a moment, Allison felt an unfamiliar sensation toward the warrior. Pity. She could never forgive the Kreelans for what they had done, but she couldn't help but feel sorry for this one, all alone out here, with no one for company but Allison.

But she wasn't about to invite the warrior in for dinner. "Go away, now. Please."

The warrior refocused her attention on Allison, spearing her with a gaze that sent a cold rivulet of fear through Allison's stomach.

Then, much to Allison's astonishment, the warrior bowed her head.

Not trusting herself to say anything, Allison slowly backed away, then turned and began walking down the drive toward the ruined house and barn.

After half a dozen paces, she threw a glance back at the warrior, but she had already vanished.

SIXTY

Valentina wiped her face with the waterless cleansing cloth, then stared into the mirror of the tiny lavatory, savoring a few precious moments alone.

She, Mills, and the other four members of the recon team had been crammed aboard a hastily modified courier ship that had originally been designed for a crew of two. The two pilots kept mostly to the cramped cockpit, leaving the Marines to fend for themselves in the midships area, which had been stripped of equipment and expanded with some welded-on sections that held the Marines' bunks. There was enough room in an aisle to move around, if you could make your way past the crates of equipment and weapons that were bolted to the walls and floor. There was no exercise equipment and nothing with which to entertain themselves but the ship's library of vids and books, and the Marines' imaginations, of course.

The ship reeked of stale sweat and unchecked body odor. Aside from the waterless wash towels, which never got their bodies truly clean and left an oily residue, they had no way to clean up. There was enough water aboard for drinking, and that was all. The deodorants the pilots tried to use to mask the smell only made it worse, and after some dire threats from the Marines, they wisely chose to stop using them.

They had only been cooped up in the courier for three days, but the overly close quarters, complete lack of privacy, and the stress of the high stakes mission had made the trip seem like weeks. Tempers were running high, and Mills had been forced to break up arguments that had threatened to erupt into potentially lethal violence.

The Marines were counting the nanoseconds until they could get off what they had begun calling the "pig boat."

The only place anyone could have any privacy was in the tiny lavatory, which some naval architect had the foresight to modify to accommodate the extra waste produced by the tiny ship's oversize crew.

Both of the courier's pilots were women who kept largely to themselves in the cockpit, and Valentina was one of only two women on the recon team. The other woman, Ella Stallick, who was the team's demolition specialist, was built like a champion wrestler and had a face to match, replete with a scar and twice-broken nose.

That left Valentina to deal with the brunt of the overdose of testosterone from the men on her team. In an effort to avoid any unpleasantness, she had taken to spending most of her time out of her bunk in the door to the cockpit, standing silent vigil with the pilots as the point of light that was Alger's World slowly grew brighter.

Almost there, she thought. Soon they'd be making their final approach to the planet, with the courier darting in to land the team.

The biggest question was what the Kreelans had in the system. So far, it was all good news. There were only seven destroyers, all in orbit over the planet. A heavy cruiser had appeared the day before, but had quickly departed.

The pilots were confident that they would be able to dodge the destroyers easily enough, drop the Marines, and then jump to safety.

Now all they needed was the final execution order. It was a failsafe in case the mission had been called off or delayed. If they didn't get the final go order within the next twelve hours, they would jump back to Earth space and terminate the mission.

Part of Valentina wanted desperately to go home, to be out of this stinking sardine can and be back in the safe and sweet-smelling woods around her home in Virginia.

Another part of her, the part that had defined most of her adult life, wanted to get on the ground and do nothing but kill Kreelans. Unlike the Marines (she had refused to formally join the Corps, but had deployed as a civilian contractor), she had never fought the aliens, only humans. But she had no doubt she could kill them better than any of the Marines could.

The door to the lavatory, which was only a glorified closet with a waterless toilet, mirror, and a small medicine cabinet, opened. The door wasn't equipped with a lock or occupancy indicator.

"I'm not done yet-" was all she managed to say before a large hand roughly clamped down on her mouth.

It was Ely Danielson, the team's communications technician. He had been extremely persistent in his amorous pursuit of Valentina until Mills had finally put him in a painful headlock and threatened to break his neck.

"Just keep your mouth shut," Danielson breathed as he shoved her backward against the bulkhead, using his other hand to close the flimsy door behind him. "I just want to-"

Her right hand shot upward in a sword strike, the rigid fingers jabbing into the vulnerable spot under his jaw, then drove her knee into his unprotected groin.

Gagging, he let her go and sagged to his knees, his hands instinctively going to his groin.

Valentina wasn't quite finished with him. She shoved both thumbs into his mouth and stretched it open so violently that the skin at the corners split and began to bleed.

Danielson screamed.

"When a girl says no," she said softly, her breathing barely above its normal slow rhythm, "she means no. The only reason I'm going to let you live is because we need you for this mission. But if you ever try to touch me or the other women again, I'm going to kill you. Do you understand?"

He nodded emphatically, or gave the impression of doing so as best he could. She was still holding his mouth stretched open with her thumbs while her fingertips dug into the nerves behind his ears.

Letting one side of his mouth go, she reached for the door latch.

Before she could touch it, the door flew open. Mills stood there, his face red with fury. He held a combat knife in his hand.

"No need." She shoved Danielson out of the lavatory. He fell backward into a groaning heap in the narrow aisle.

Putting his knife back into its scabbard, Mills shook his head. "Danielson, you have no idea how far out of your league you are, mate."

"I...just...had to pee." Dannielson wheezed out the words as he struggled to get to his knees. "She was hogging the head."

That caused Valentina, who wasn't easily given to laughter, to chuckle. "Well, sorry, then." She hoisted him up by the belt and shoved him into the lavatory before closing the door. "It's all yours."

"Jesus," Mills muttered. "What a fuckup. I'm sorry."

"It's not your fault. He's here for the mission, not his personality. He just needs to grow up a little."

"Well, after what you did to him, we may not have to worry about him propagating his genes."

That brought a big smile to Valentina's face, and Mills threw back his head and laughed.

"Mills," the courier's senior pilot called, "we've got the go order!"

"About time!" He grinned at Valentina.

"That's not all," the pilot went on, a strain of worry creeping into her voice. "We've had a last minute change in plans."

"What kind of change?" Mills didn't like last minute changes in missions. They had a tendency to get people killed.

"The courier that laser-linked the orders to us is coming in to dock. It looks like someone else is going to be joining your little party."

* * *

Ku'ar-Marekh crept silently through the woods two dozen leagues from the human town where her warriors had made their main encampment. She was alone, save for the unfamiliar forest creatures around her and the sense of the humans who lay ahead, those she was hunting.

She could have found them easily enough with her second sight, casting her spirit from her body to search the world around her.

Yet she chose not to, for that would have given her unfair advantage. It was for the same reason that she was making her final approach in daylight, for she knew the humans had poor night vision. While she could also slaughter the animals without ever coming in sight of them, this would bring no honor or glory to the Empress. That one thing, that duty to honor and glorify Her, was the closest thing she had left to any feeling.

She paused behind a large tree and knelt to the ground, closing her eyes. She listened to the sounds of the woods around her and smelled the air, her sensitive nose picking out the scents of the animals, the different varieties of trees. The faint stench of human body odor.

She could not entirely tune out the sense that the humans were near, for the powers she had inherited when she became priestess of the Nyur-A'il were as much a part of her as the heart that beat in her breast. Some of those powers she used or not, as she willed. Others simply fed her mind, as did her sight or hearing.

Opening her eyes, she found herself staring down at the cyan rune that graced her breast plate, thinking of the great honor it had been to accept the Way of the Nyur-A'il, and also of what it had cost her. She remembered, as if it were yesterday, kneeling in the ancient temple of her order, her hands locked with those of her priestess as the blazing light from the sacred crystal first touched her flesh, consummating the Change. Even with all her years of training and discipline, it was all she could do to not scream in agony as every cell in her body seemed to burst into flame. For to have done so, to have screamed or shown weakness, would have invited instant death.

When she had awakened, her priestess lay dead, and Ku'ar-Marekh's own clothing and armor was burned to ashes. Her skin, once proud with the scars of many contests of sword and claw, was now flawless, unblemished. While she did not then know how to control them, she could sense the powers that she had inherited from her now-dead priestess. She could tell instantly that she was more than she had been before.

And yet, something else that she had once had, like the scars on her skin, had vanished. Looking at the body of her priestess, who had stood on the sixth step from the throne in the rank of Her Children, she had felt...nothing. No anguish at her death, no pride that she had gone to join the Ancient Ones in the afterlife. Not even a shard of self-pity that she would not be able to teach Ku'ar-Marekh about her new powers. All emotion, all feeling, was gone. Her memories, even of the ceremony of the Change, when she had never been more honored, elated, and frightened, did not stir her soul or quicken her heart. It was as if they were the memories of someone else, gray and empty.

The Bloodsong, which bound together the Children of the Empress, still flowed in her veins, but only as a source of power. The tide of emotions from her sisters in blood that ebbed and flowed within it were no more to her now than the rise and fall of the waves of a long dead sea. All the feelings that made up the complex tapestry of her soul were gone.

Even the knowledge that all the Children of the Empress, every soul in an empire that spanned ten thousand suns, would die if they failed in their search for the First Empress and the One failed to move her. That their race was within but a few generations of extinction had become nothing more than a dry fact.

Drawing her mind away from what she could not change, Ku'ar-Marekh focused on the present. Somewhere ahead was a small band of humans that had proven particularly adept at inflicting serious losses on her warriors before melting away into the woods. They were well-armed with weapons of which the Empress would approve, without any of the more advanced systems that made the battle more between machines than true combatants.

She had tracked them this far mainly by scent. The humans, for all their cunning, could not completely mask their odor, or that of the weapons they used. She could identify eleven unique human scents, along with traces of oil and chemical residue of weapons that had been recently fired. They had covered their tracks extremely well, and...

She heard the faint mechanical sound of a trigger being pulled back ever so slightly. In a blur of motion, she drew one of her three *shrekkas* and hurled it at a patch of leaves on the ground at the base of a pile of large rocks not far ahead of her. As the weapon left her hand, she leaped into the air toward where the human animal lay in ambush, her body sailing between the trees as if she were borne on the wind.

The *shrekka* tore into her prey, and Ku'ar-Marekh was rewarded with the animal's shriek of agony as the *shrekka's* blades ripped down the human's spine.

She drew her sword in mid-air and did a graceful forward flip. Landing with her legs astride the writhing human, she stabbed the sword downward, the gleaming tip spearing the creature through the heart.

Ku'ar-Marekh snatched another *shrekka* from her shoulder and hurled it at a human whose head had poked out from among the rocks above her. The creature had no time to cry out as the whirling blades took its head from its neck in a spray of crimson.

She leaped again, this time to the top of the rock outcropping where she found two more humans armed with rifles. She took the head from one with her sword, and simply grabbed the other one and tossed him bodily from the rock, ignoring his scream as he fell to the ground below.

Four. Ku'ar-Marekh mentally tallied the kills, knowing there were at least seven more. She could feel the surge of power in the Bloodsong, but the elation, the ecstasy she had once felt were missing. It was a bright light that flared in her heart, but brought no warmth to her soul.

Four humans emerged from where they had been sheltering in the rocks. All of them opened fire on her with their rifles.

The bullets came within an arm's length of her body and simply fell from the air, so hot that they instantly melted into small pools of metal that set the leaves smoldering.

Pausing to gape at what their eyes told them, yet clearly not believing what they saw, the humans continued to fire, and the other three she had knew must be here stepped from behind the rocks and joined in.

Between them, they fired hundreds of rounds at her, until their magazines ran dry and a pool of molten metal sizzled on the ground before Ku'ar-Marekh.

Two of the humans tried to run, and she was upon them in an instant, her sword flashing as she leaped beyond the ring of fire that now surrounded her.

Another charged at her, brandishing a knife, and in the blink of an eye she slammed her sword back into its scabbard and faced her opponent with only her claws. He was skilled and fearless, but was no match for her. After toying with him enough to satisfy her honor, she clawed the knife from his hand, then drove the talons of one hand into his throat.

She whirled as the remaining four humans attacked her. She did not bother to draw her sword. One of them came at her with a knife, but only used it as a diversion. When the human was close enough, he simply grabbed her in a bear hug and shoved her backward, no doubt hoping to pin her to the ground while the remaining humans finished her off.

Using the animal's momentum, she leaped backward, sailing into the air with the human clinging to her, terrified. She grasped its head and twisted it until the neck snapped, then tossed the animal away before landing on her feet.

Looking up, she saw that the surviving humans, which she had expected to try and run, were instead coming straight at her, bellowing what must have passed for war cries.

Then she noticed what they held in their hands. Explosive grenades.

A fair contest, then, she told herself. Focusing on them, she reached out with her spirit and found their hearts. Then she began to squeeze.

The three humans collapsed in mid-stride, the grenades, all of them armed, rolling from their twitching hands.

Ku'ar-Marekh released her hold on their hearts and watched just long enough to see the realization dawn in their eyes of how their lives would be ended.

By their own grenades.

Then she leaped away, gliding to the ground below.

Behind her, the three humans were consumed by thunder and flame.

* * *

"I don't fucking believe this." Mills stood between the pilots as they guided the ship to rendezvous with the incoming courier. "If the Kreelans don't pick up on this stunt, I'll eat my drawers."

"You're probably safe on that count, Mills." The pilot's voice was tense as she watched the head-up display that showed the soft-dock approach of the other ship. "Our buddies here had good timing. The ESM sensors aren't chirping at us."

The Electronic Surveillance Measures, or ESM, suite on the ship was designed to warn the crew if any signals from enemy ships were strong enough to detect them. When they were near the detection threshold, the system warned the crew with a variety of chirps and automated voice warnings.

"I don't give a bloody damn. We're exposed as hell and on a tight timeline now. Whoever comes aboard had better have a good reason or I'll wring his neck for putting us and the mission in such danger."

A few moments later, the two ships were flying side-by-side, and there was a gentle thunk outside the airlock as the soft-dock tubes linked up. They didn't bother to pressurize it.

"The link's good." The pilot confirmed the hookup to her counterpart in the other ship. "Send over your cargo."

A few minutes later a figure in a vacuum suit moved awkwardly though the tube to enter their air lock, then turned to hit the control to close the outer door.

When the lock indicator showed it was pressurized, Mills slid the hatch open and stood in the doorway, glaring at the suited figure.

Whoever it was fumbled with the helmet catches, but Mills didn't offer to help. He was furious.

As soon as the newcomer managed to undo the catches and began to take off the helmet, Mills lit into whoever it was.

"I don't give a fuck if you're the goddamn Chief of Naval Staff," he said coldly. "Your coming here may have put the knife to all of us, and..."

"Oh, my God." Valentina, who stood beside him, put a hand up to her mouth in surprise as the face behind the helmet was revealed.

"And here I thought you two would be happy to see me." A woman with brunette hair handed her helmet to a stunned Roland Mills.

Mills heard someone behind him blurt, "Who the fuck is that?"

"That," Valentina said, unable to suppress a smile, "is Stephanie Guillaume-Sato, Commodore Ichiro Sato's wife."

SIXTY-ONE

"What the devil are you doing here, Steph?" Mills helped Steph strip out of her vacuum suit, revealing combat fatigues identical to his own, but without any badge of rank.

The other members of the team grabbed the suit and the small case she'd brought along as the courier accelerated away from the rendezvous point, racing now toward Alger's World.

Behind them, the ship that had brought Steph leaped away into hyperspace.

Mills had met Steph during the battle of Keran on the assault boat that had extracted them from the disastrous ground battle. She had been one of the embedded journalists attached to the 7th Cavalry Regiment, and Mills had been in what had been the Francophone Alliance's Foreign Legion, the remnants of which had been absorbed into the new Confederation Marine Corps after being decimated at the battle of Keran. It had been designated as a regiment in the Corps, but had taken on the unofficial name of the Red Legion for the blood that had been spilled from its ranks in its final battle.

While Steph had started out in the battle as a journalist, by the time she and the other handful of survivors had escaped the abattoir the Kreelans had made of the planet, she had also become a combat veteran.

After her return to Earth, she became something of a celebrity, and that had helped catapult her to a position she had never even dreamed of, President McKenna's press secretary. That's the role she'd been playing in service of the Confederation.

Until now.

"The president decided that we needed a unique view of this operation to give the public." She met his glaring gaze without the slightest trace of guilt. "She wanted someone on one of the recon teams, and I wanted to go. When I found out you were leading one, it was pretty much a given which team I'd choose."

"And she just let you go, did she?" Mills didn't try to mask his sarcasm as he folded his tree trunk-sized arms across his chest.

"Yes, Mills, she did. In fact, she asked me to go." She stepped closer to him, tilting her head back to stare up at him. "You were going to be stuck with someone, regardless. So just go ahead and name another journalist who has my qualifications for this type of assignment, or that you'd rather have with you."

Mills glared at her a moment more, then broke out into a grin. "Well, I guess better you than some fat-headed dolt who doesn't know how to handle a weapon when the Kreelans get in sword range." He slapped her on the shoulder, nearly knocking her off her feet. "Welcome aboard, then, girl."

"Speaking of weapons," Steph said, rubbing her shoulder as she regained her balance, "I take it you've got a spare rifle for me?" While Steph was a journalist first, she would never again go into a combat zone unarmed.

"I think we can arrange that. Do you know the op?"

"Yes, I've been fully briefed. I can also be a backup for Danielson." She nodded to the comms specialist, who had just emerged from the lavatory, where he'd been trying to recover from Valentina's knee smashing into his groin. "I went over the information for your communications gear and procedures on the trip out."

"All right, then." Mills sighed, not happy about the situation but resigned to the reality of it. "I just hope your surprise appearance didn't give us away too early."

"Maybe not too early," the pilot called, having listened in to the conversation over the intercom, "but they're definitely on to our game. Four of the ships in orbit are changing course."

"Are any after us yet?" Mills called.

"I can't tell, but they're definitely hot and bothered now. Some of them look like they're going after the drones, but we're still too far away to be sure."

The courier ships carrying the Marine recon teams weren't the only ones that had been sent to the system. There were another two dozen smaller vessels, drones, that were programmed to follow flight profiles similar to the real ships. They were decoys designed to appear identical to the real ships to the enemy's sensors. It was hoped they would give the couriers a better chance to slip into their insertion positions.

"Well, let's get ready for the big game, then, shall we?"

As the others began unpacking their equipment and double-checking their weapons, Mills cornered Steph and asked quietly, "Does the commodore know you've come along?"

Steph looked up at him, and he saw a brief flash of pain in her expression before she could hide it. "I don't know, Mills." She averted her eyes, looking down at the deck. "We...we haven't spoken in the last couple months. We separated not long after he came back from Saint Petersburg."

"Oh." Mills felt a fool, not quite sure what to say. "Sorry for that."

Steph looked back up into his eyes. "Ichiro was different after he came back. The only thing he could focus on was the Kreelans, and how we could defeat them. He lost himself in working on the new ship designs. Nothing else seemed to matter. Nothing. And no one."

Mills was feeling increasingly uncomfortable, hearing of the marital problems between a commodore and his former press secretary wife. But he couldn't just walk away. He hadn't known Steph all that well, but the survivors of Keran, both those who'd fought on the ground and in space, shared a special bond. There had been few enough of them.

As if reading his mind, Steph smiled, masking her inner pain. "And why am I telling a big lug of a Marine about all this? Aren't you supposed to be yelling at people or something?"

Mills mustered a smile, but his eyes betrayed his concern for her. The mission was going to be tough enough without someone with a lot of emotional baggage weighing them down.

"Don't worry, Mills." She touched his arm to reassure him. "I've got it together."

"Right, then," he said, nodding. "Come on, let's get you fitted out with proper kit. Valentina?" he called. "Could you give our, ah, journalist extraordinaire a bit of a hand?"

"Sure." Valentina took Steph back to the crowded center aisle where the Marines were busy getting ready. She shot a glance at him over her shoulder when Steph wasn't looking, and Mills gave her the thumbs-up sign.

She's okay.

Valentina, who hadn't known Steph personally, shrugged as she turned back around and helped Steph pick out weapons and other combat gear.

Mills made his way to the cockpit. "How long?"

The luminous disk of Alger's World was huge now in the forward viewscreen. He saw a sudden bright flash against the black of space to the left.

"One of the drones just bought it." The pilot shook her head as a green icon flickered and died on her display. A red icon depicting a Kreelan destroyer swept through the space where the drone had been just a moment before.

"Have any of the other insertion ships bought it?"

"None, yet. But...oh, shit."

"What is it?"

The pilot pointed to a pair of red icons on the head-up display, or HUD. They were two Kreelan destroyers that had appeared from around the far side of the planet. Even Mills, who didn't understand the trajectory data displayed on the HUD, could see that they were coming at his ship on a converging course.

The pilot turned to glance up at him. "Looks like we've got company."

* * *

After killing the group of humans, Ku'ar-Marekh spent the rest of the day gathering wood from the forest to build funeral pyres for their bodies. It was an ages-old tradition to honor worthy opponents who had fallen in battle, and she had judged these to be worthy. They had inflicted many casualties upon her warriors since the Children of the Empress had come to this world, and had acquitted themselves well in the brief battle she had fought with them.

That they had never stood a chance against her was irrelevant. She nonetheless honored their sacrifice as tradition demanded.

As with most things, she did this alone. She realized that the warriors placed in her charge were deathly afraid of her, for she was not given to tolerance of the slightest flaw and had taken the lives of many who had displeased her. It was not an uncommon thing for a warrior priestess to act so, for their place among the peers of the Empire was only below the Empress Herself. But some would say that Ku'ar-Marekh's lethal punishments were...excessive. It was yet another reason why she had spent as much time as she could alone, among the stars.

None, however, even the other warrior priestesses, had ever said as much to her, save one: Tesh-Dar, the last priestess of the Desh-Ka, the oldest order that served the will of the Empress.

Of all the priestesses who still lived, she was the only one who did not fear Ku'ar-Marekh. Tesh-Dar had once counseled Ku'ar-Marekh against being so heavy-handed with her warriors. It had been in private, as much as anything could be private when their entire race was linked through the Bloodsong, for Tesh-Dar's intention had clearly been to instruct, rather than humiliate.

But Ku'ar-Marekh, high priestess of the Nyur-A'il, was not about to be lectured by anyone, even such as Tesh-Dar.

Ku'ar-Marekh could have issued a challenge to the elder priestess, but had instead settled for giving the great priestess of the Desh-Ka a taste of the Nyur-A'il's power. Ku'ar-Marekh no longer felt fear herself, but she knew how to instill it in others.

She reached out with her mind to take hold of Tesh-Dar's heart.

Such was her surprise when she discovered that her ethereal claws collided with a solid wall of power. She could sense Tesh-Dar's heart, feel it beating in the great warrior's chest, but try as she might, Ku'ar-Marekh could not reach it.

"Try as you may, child," Tesh-Dar whispered, "you shall fail. Issue a challenge for combat in the arena, as that is your right, but do not play such childish games with me."

Knowing that she should feel shame, but unable to taste even those bitter ashes in her mouth, Ku'ar-Marekh knelt before Tesh-Dar and offered her neck to the elder warrior's sword. She knew that she had disgraced herself, and that death was the only possible reward. In the cold place that was her heart, she silently wished for it. Her only hope was that in the Afterlife she might recover what the Change had taken from her.

"Take my life," she begged. "I offer it freely."

"No, child." Tesh-Dar, a giant among Her Children, placed a great hand upon Ku'ar-Marekh's head to stroke the braids of the younger priestess's raven hair. "I can sense the emptiness in your heart, the chill of your spirit. The peers call you Dead Soul, and with good reason. I would grant your wish out of compassion, but this is not the will of the Empress. And that, above all else, must we obey. Even you, I know, can sense that much."

Ku'ar-Marekh nodded, then stood to face Tesh-Dar. "I will not thank you for your kindness, priestess of the Desh-Ka."

Then she had turned and left.

That had been many cycles ago. Now, kneeling before the burning pyres of the humans, Ku'ar-Marekh stared into the flames, replaying Tesh-Dar's words. Of all those in the Empire, save the Empress Herself, Tesh-Dar was the only one who had understood Ku'ar-Marekh's pain, a pain she herself could not feel for the emptiness inside her.

And now Tesh-Dar was gone, locked away in the ancient temple of the Desh-Ka, perhaps forever.

Fire and flame. It would be so easy to simply hurl herself into one of the flaming pyres and purge herself of this empty life. Yet she could no more do that than feel the long-gone warmth of the love of her sisters in the Bloodsong. She remained subject to the will of the Empress, a yoke around her spirit, binding her to this life.

As the flames licked higher into the sky and the bodies of the humans were gradually consumed in the fire, Ku'ar-Marekh knelt on the ground and fell into a deep meditative state. Focusing her concentration inward, she slowed her breathing until it stopped, then stopped her heart. It was the closest she could come to death, and she sought this state as often as she could, hoping to force time ahead to the moment of her blessed demise. Her only lament was that she could not hold herself in this state indefinitely.

But there, in the depths of the nothingness that shielded her from herself, she felt a sudden stirring in the Bloodsong, a surge in the excitement of her sisters. Casting her mind's eye outward, following the strands of the chorus of the song, she found herself among the orbiting warships.

The humans had sent tiny ships into the system.

Unlike the sensors of the warships, which had intentionally been made to match the primitive capabilities of the human vessels, Ku'ar-Marekh's second sight could tell which ships held living beings and which did not.

She would never have revealed that information to the warriors aboard her own ships, of course, for that would have violated the will of the Empress. The humans had proven themselves worthy opponents, and would be given equal or better advantage in any combat. Priestesses had more leeway in the matter in their own personal challenges, but the peers would never confer undue advantage upon themselves.

Fastening her attention upon a single human vessel that was closer than the others, Ku'ar-Marekh watched as its fate was decided.

* * *

"They've got us," the pilot called back to where Mills now sat, strapped into one of the fold-out seats against the inner wall of the hull.

"Damn." Mills shook his head, looking at Valentina. The plan had called for the courier to set down on the planet. If that wasn't possible for any reason, the Marines were to jump from high altitude using parasails. Mills had made the decision to prepare to jump, but had hoped they could land. They had the bulky packs strapped to their chests, with their equipment stuffed into backpacks. They also had face masks and oxygen cylinders. If they had to jump at high altitude, they would need oxygen to breathe.

"Mills," the pilot shouted, "we have to abort! We haven't gotten too far into the gravity well that I can't jump out-"

"No!" Mills barked through the microphone in his face mask. "There's no aborting this one, missy. The fleet and Marines are coming in behind us and they need to know what the hell they'll be facing here. We either make it or we die trying. Got that?"

The pilot muttered a string of curses as she and the copilot fought to get the courier into the atmosphere. If they could make it that far, the Kreelan destroyers wouldn't be able to follow them, as the sensors suggested that these particular ships weren't designed to operate in the atmosphere.

The courier lurched. Then it began to roll, the arc of the planet below spinning in the forward view screen. Mills felt a wave of nausea as his inner ear went crazy. The gravity compensators were failing.

The pilot shouted something just before everything went to hell. There was an explosion at the rear of the main cabin that sent shards of metal and plastic flying, but the screams of the men and women of his team were drowned out by the roar of the ship's air streaming through the hole punched into the engineering section by a Kreelan shell.

The explosion had weakened part of the hull wall, and the seat of Staff Sergeant Rajesh Desai, the team's heavy weapons specialist, tore loose. Still strapped to his seat, the NCO tumbled through the cabin, screaming. His screams were cut off as he slammed into the torn metal in the aft bulkhead. Mills watched in horror as the man was pinned there for a moment, then in a spray of blood was blown out through the hole, which was much smaller than Desai.

The ship was wallowing in the atmosphere now as the pilots fought the controls, and the only thing that kept them alive were the shields. If those failed, they would burn up in an instant.

"Is anyone injured?" Mills bellowed through the face mask comm system. "Sound off!"

"Ephraim is gone." Valentina spoke loud enough to be heard through the scream of the air still streaming out, but her voice was completely calm.

Mills turned to look to where Jeremy Ephraim sat. The upper half of the man's body had been torn to ribbons by shrapnel from the shell hit. "Bloody hell. Anybody else hit?"

He received a brief volley of no's from Valentina, Steph, Ella Stallick, and Danielson.

"Mills!" the pilot shouted. While the air had by now vented out, the cabin was filled with the whistling roar of the atmosphere through which the courier was now tumbling, out of control. "You have to jump!"

"Are you off your nut?" Mills shouted back, his mask fogging up slightly as he did. "We're not even close to our release altitude! We'll burn up out there!"

"We're through the worst of it! We redlined our descent, using the shields as a brake. We're high but not too fast now. You don't have any choice! If you don't jump now, you-"

The pilot's words were brutally cut off by a brace of Kreelan shells that blew the nose from the courier. Mills stared in horror as the entire forward part of the ship sheared away, the pilot and copilot carried with it. He could hear the pilot screaming as she fell, her voice echoing in his earphones from the comm system, when he looked up to find Valentina in front of him, clinging to his chair.

"Come on! We've got to go! Now!"

Fighting against the roller coaster motion of the courier's hulk, Mills pushed away his fear and focused on what had to be done.

Taking hold of a nearby conduit running along the wall, he unstrapped himself with his free hand and got to his feet. Stallick and Danielson followed his example, but Steph was still in her chair, struggling with her seat harness.

"Go on!" Mills shouted at Valentina and the others. "Get out! I'll help her!"

"No!" Valentina grabbed his arm. "I'll get her. You get the others and the weapons!"

Mills didn't argue. He understood Valentina's intent. He was the mission leader, and the mission was the most important thing. Everything else was secondary, and he didn't have the luxury now for any heroics.

"Stallick! Danielson! Get one ammo and both supply containers!" Aside from their personal weapons and other gear that was on each Marine's weapons harness, the team's equipment was in a set of containers that had their own parachutes. Mills would have liked to take everything, but having enough to eat and at least some ammunition were the top priorities.

The two Marines nodded. Fighting the tumbling motion of the courier, they began to unstrap the containers from the deck.

In the meantime, Valentina had made her way to where Steph still struggled. The former spy could see Steph's mouth moving, but couldn't hear anything.

"Steph!" She leaned closer to better see Steph's face. "Can you hear me?"

Steph nodded, then pointed to her face mask. A tiny sliver of shrapnel from the hit that had taken the courier's forward section had damaged the microphone's electronics. Had it been a few centimeters to either side, it would have sliced into her mask and her face.

Looking down at the buckle of Steph's harness, Valentina saw that shrapnel had done its work there too. Another shard had bent the buckle's latch mechanism, somehow glancing away from Steph.

"God, you're lucky." Valentina pulled her combat knife from its scabbard and quickly sawed through the tough straps. "Come on!"

Valentina turned to make her way forward toward Mills after Steph was free.

But Steph didn't follow her. Instead, she headed aft.

Valentina was about to go after her when she saw that Steph was going after the small case she'd brought aboard, and which had been stowed in one of the lockers near the smoking wreckage of the lavatory.

Steph grabbed the case and strapped it to her side.

While Valentina waited for her, she told Mills, "Steph's all right, but her mic's not working. She can receive but not transmit."

"That's not a bad thing for a woman sometimes," Mills quipped as he helped Danielson move the second supply container.

"Fuck you, Mills." Stallick, who was silhouetted against the spinning planet in the opening at the front of the hull, was holding down the first supply container and the ammo container.

The ship lurched again, and Stallick reached out to brace herself, taking hold of some bent conduits. The Kreelan destroyers had given up the chase, but the air currents were tossing the ship around as it plummeted toward the surface. "If you-"

The ship dropped, and the container that Mills and Danielson had been shepherding down the aisle toward Stallick got away from them.

"Down!" Mills tried to warn Stallick, but it was too late.

With a single bounce, the fifty kilo container caught Stallick right in the face and carried her out of the ship. Unconscious or dead, she silently spiraled out of sight.

"Goddammit!" Danielson turned to Mills, his eyes wide behind his oxygen mask. "That one had our commo gear!"

Mills slammed a fist into the bulkhead. "Fuck!" Not only had they lost Stallick, they'd also probably lost the container. She had been the one setting the automatic parachute deployment systems, and obviously hadn't been able to take care of that container. It would just fall to the ground like a rock, smashing everything inside it.

We'll have the devil's own time trying to communicate with the other ground teams and the fleet when it arrived, Mills thought bitterly, but he knew that was something they'd have to sort out later. If they survived.

"Come on!" He gathered the others close together. "Let's get off this bitch!"

Danielson checked that the chute controls for the other two containers had been set before kicking them out. Then Mills grabbed the three survivors of his team and leaped out the gaping hole where the cockpit had been.

As they fell away, Mills and Danielson spread their arms to control their fall, moving slightly apart. Valentina did the same, but held onto one of Steph's hands to help stabilize her. Steph had said she'd made a few jumps in simulators before shipping out here, but had never made a real jump, and certainly not one like this.

The four of them fell toward the ground, keeping their eyes fixed on the black dots that were the two containers. They could also see Stallick's body, still spinning lazily below them.

The hulk of the courier tumbled away from them, finally smashing into an empty field where it exploded.

"Stallick!" Danielson called. "Stallick, can you hear me?"

"She's gone," Valentina told him quietly. "Mills, how far from the target are we?"

"We're in bloody bumfuck!" Mills fought to bring his anger under control. "We're not even close to our planned drop zone. I think we're over the right continent, but that's about it."

Looking down, Valentina could see orderly patches of farmland far below. The neat patches of the farms were interspersed with large stretches of forest.

"Well, at least we're not falling into the ocean."

"Now there's a bright side." Mills looked at the digital map display in the face mask. "At least there's a town near here. Breakwater, it's called. Maybe there are some Territorial Army blokes we can hook up with to help get us to where we need to be."

They saw the chutes for the containers open below them. They were set to open at two hundred meters.

Stallick's body continued to plummet downward, and Mills winced when it hit the ground. "Damn."

"Altitude," Valentina called. They were nearing three hundred meters. They could open the chutes lower, but she didn't want to risk it with Steph never having made a combat drop before, and not being able to communicate.

Mills gave the thumbs-up. "Go!"

Danielson activated his chute, and it fluttered out of his pack to form a graceful camouflage-colored parasail.

Valentina let go of Steph and moved away to give her chute room to open. She watched as Steph hit the control to release it...and nothing happened.

Steph frantically worked the chute control again. Nothing. Wide-eyed with terror, she looked up at Valentina, who was already arrowing in toward her.

"Mills, Steph's chute failed. I'm going to double up with her."

"You're too bloody low!" Mills warned. "Valentina!"

Ignoring him, she grabbed Steph and quickly hooked their harnesses together.

"Hang on," she said grimly as she hit her chute's controls. If hers didn't work... well, they wouldn't have to worry about it for very long.

"Valentina!" Mills shouted again. Cursing in frustration, he deployed his own chute. He was too heavy to risk going any lower, or the chute wouldn't be able to slow him enough before he hit the ground.

Valentina's parasail blossomed from her pack and snapped full open. She guided it toward a field not far from where the two containers had fluttered to the ground on their chutes.

Steph clung to her like a terrified child, her eyes fixed on the ground. They were coming down fast, really fast.

Valentina judged the distance. It was going to be close. Really close. "Okay Steph, roll with me when we hit. Ready...ready...now!"

They slammed into the ground. Valentina took the brunt of it as the two of them awkwardly collapsed and rolled into the soft earth of the field. Steph wound up on top, panting heavily.

Valentina undid the buckle that linked them, and Steph rolled off onto her back before tearing off her face mask and throwing it aside.

"Jesus," she gasped. "And to imagine that some idiots pay good money to do this sort of thing."

Valentina, taking off her own mask, couldn't help but laugh. "Actually, for something like this, you'd have to pay extra."

That had them both laughing, happy to be alive.

"I'm glad you two girls are getting along so well," they heard Mills call from where he was busy gathering up his chute about fifty meters away, "but it's time to stop socializing and get to work, dearies. Go get the containers and haul them into the woods, then inventory what we've got and divide up the ammo we need. Danielson, you're with me."

"What are you going to do?" Valentina asked.

Mills turned to her, his expression grim. "We've got to bury Stallick."

* * *

Ku'ar-Marekh withdrew her second sight from watching the humans fall from the sky, returning her spirit to the sanctum of her body.

Her heart again began to beat, and her chest slowly rose and fell as she began to breathe. After a moment, she opened her silver-flecked feline eyes.

With the pyres still burning brightly, she moved off into the forest, toward where the humans had landed.

SIXTY-TWO

Commodore Ichiro Sato stood on the flag bridge of the newly commissioned battleship *CSS Orion*, intently watching the combat information display that took up the entire forward wall of the compartment.

Orion and her three sister ships, *Monarch*, *Conqueror*, and *Thunderer*, made up the Confederation Navy's First Battleship Flotilla, and were the most powerful warships humanity had ever built. Yet even as the four ships were being launched, larger and more powerful ships were being designed.

For their main armament, *Orion* and her sisters had twelve thirty centimeter main guns, able to fire a variety of munitions ranging from basic armor-piercing to what amounted to a gigantic shotgun shell to repel Kreelan boarding parties. While their rate of fire was slower than the fifteen centimeter guns carried by most heavy cruisers, the shells were nearly fifteen times larger by mass, packing an incredibly massive punch.

The battleships also had a pulse cannon running along the keel that could spear even a heavy cruiser. Having learned both the power and the limitations of the weapon through bitter experience during the battle of Keran, Sato had worked with the shipwrights who designed the *Orion* class to maximize the weapon's advantages and minimize its limitations.

The ships had an impressive secondary armament of both kinetic weapons and lasers, which by themselves would be more than a match for any Kreelan warship the humans had yet encountered.

But even as powerful as the new ships were, Sato knew that the enemy had vessels that were vastly beyond humanity's technology. He had seen them with his own eyes. For reasons of their own, the Kreelans had chosen not to use them, instead preferring to match the humans, "dumbing down" their own weapons and systems.

He knew the advantage that *Orion* and her sisters would enjoy during their first battle would be short-lived, for the Kreelans would soon build ships to match them. But he believed that for at least this once, the four battleships would reign supreme.

Half of the display he was watching showed the bright blue and white curve of Earth as the battleships and their escorts maneuvered away from the naval base at Africa Station. The other half showed a tactical map with the icons of the ships of Home Fleet, including *Orion* and her sisters, that were preparing to jump.

The formation, Sato saw with satisfaction, was perfect. All the crews had trained hard for this mission, and Sato had drilled the battleship crews nearly to the point of mutiny.

The battleship captains, all of whom were senior to Sato in time in service, finally complained that he was driving their crews too hard.

"Let me make something perfectly clear," Sato had told them, his voice cutting through the conference room when he'd finally called the captains together to hear their complaints. "This is the first time since the war began that we may have a chance to beat the Kreelans. You've all seen combat and you know some of what the enemy is capable of." He paused, his mind replaying the nightmare visions of the first contact encounter with the Kreelans, of which he had been the sole survivor. Their giant warships had technology that centuries, and perhaps more, beyond what his own people had. "They are relentless, merciless killing machines, and the only way we stand any chance of winning this war..."

He paused in spite of himself, knowing in his heart of hearts that it simply wasn't possible that humanity could win against the Empire. Just the few gigantic, fantastic ships the Kreelans met the *Aurora* with during the first contact encounter would have been more than enough to obliterate the entire Confederation fleet.

"The only chance we have," he went on, "is to be like them in combat. To be the blade of a sword, forged in the hottest flame. And that is what these ships are, the true swords of the fleet. We can't afford to be easy on our crews, because the outcome of the coming battle may very well depend on what those men and women do when all hell is breaking loose around them. We have to be merciless with them, and they have to be merciless with themselves. They must be ready. And they will be, no matter the cost."

No matter the cost. Sato's own words echoed dully in his mind as he considered the price that he himself had paid. After his return from the battle at Saint Petersburg he had become obsessed with the war. He had spent every waking moment at Naval Headquarters or in the yards at Africa Station, working on the new ships and the tactics to employ them, focusing on the day that he knew must eventually come, the day when he would again be able to sail into harm's way. For that, he had given up everything. Even his wife.

A dull pain welled up inside him as he thought of Steph. He hadn't simply drifted away from her, but had intentionally isolated himself, pushing her away, so he could focus his entire being on the fight against the Empire. It had broken his heart when she finally told him that she was leaving him.

The cold, calculating part of his brain considered this a step forward, while the man and husband inside him wept bitter, lonely tears. She had begged him to help her understand what was going on inside him, but he couldn't, wouldn't, tell her.

Part of it was the illogical pursuit of vengeance for what had happened to the crews of all three ships he had served on since encountering the Kreelans. The *Aurora*, the unlucky ship to make first contact; the *McClaren*, named after *Aurora's* captain, which had been destroyed in the battle for Keran; and the heavy cruiser *Yura*, Sato's first true command, which had been destroyed at Saint Petersburg.

Many in the fleet thought he was an incredibly lucky man. He thought he was cursed.

Sato knew he carried an enormous amount of grief and guilt inside him, but he had used it to help forge the weapons that would now finally strike a decisive blow against the enemy. He knew that in the interstellar war the Kreelans had begun, his own personal feelings weren't important. But that didn't keep him from feeling the pain in his heart every time he thought of Steph, which seemed like every minute of every day.

At least she's safe on Earth, he consoled himself, knowing that she was doing vital service as the president's press secretary. She was as safe as anyone could be.

He only wished that he'd had the courage to at least call her before he again sailed into battle. He had told himself every day since this operation had been announced that he would. Every day his hand had hovered over the comm unit as he sat at his console in his cabin, wondering what he would say.

And every day he had taken his hand away, then gone to the flag bridge, his heart a cold stone in his chest.

"Admiral," the operations officer called, breaking him from his reverie, "*Guadalcanal* has initiated the jump timing sequence."

"Very well," Sato told him, shoving his regrets aside. "First Battleship Flotilla," he said over a communications circuit that repeated his voice to the crews of the four battleships under his command, "prepare for jump. *Guadalcanal* has primary control."

While each ship did its own jump calculations, the assault carrier *Guadalcanal*, which was Admiral Voroshilov's flagship, made the primary calculations that were fed into each ship's navigation systems to help ensure that their jump emergence would put every ship where it was supposed to be. Across human space, other groups of warships were going through the same process, with all of them timed to appear over Alger's World.

The ships would be using a single jump, with no mid-course correction or staging points. The navigation for every ship had to be perfect to avert disaster over the target.

Sato could tell that the crew was tense, and with good reason. Nothing like this had ever been attempted before, and everything now rode on this one calculated risk.

"Standby for transpace sequence," an automated female voice announced over the *Orion's* public address system, and Sato could sense a slight change in the tremor of the ship's rhythm, a deepening of the thrum that was the beating of her metal heart. "Transpace sequence in five... four... three... two... one...Jump."

Humanity's four most powerful warships and the bulk of Earth's Home Fleet vanished into hyperspace.

* * *

It had taken four days of slow and deliberate movement for Mills and the others to make their way to the outskirts of Breakwater. They had been forced to lay low for hours at a time to avoid groups of patrolling Kreelan warriors. And the closer the team moved to the town, the larger and more frequent were the patrols.

Mills was convinced that there was some sort of a buildup in the town, and they had finally found a spot on a wooded hill a few kilometers away that had a view into the town center.

"Okay, I see the town square." Mills zoomed in more with his binoculars, the digital stabilizer keeping the image steady. "Or what's left of it. Looks like they've cleared out more buildings." He took the binoculars away from his eyes, then looked again. "A couple of the surrounding buildings look like they've been partially sliced away, like someone hacked them apart with a knife."

"What are they building?" Valentina was looking at the town through the scope of her sniper rifle. "Have you ever seen anything like that?"

"I've never seen anything like this from any of the combat footage that's come in." Steph was looking at the town through her vidcam, while Danielson lay prone beside her, his own binoculars fixed on the town and a grim look on his face. "I feel like we're looking at something through a time tunnel back into ancient history."

They watched as well over a thousand straining warriors moved huge stone blocks with primitive cranes and winches made of trees, using thick rope and block and tackle rigs to lift and tilt them into position. More stones, resting on wooden sleds rolling over cut logs, were being moved into position.

The construct was circular in shape, maybe twenty meters across, with some stones, each of which must have weighed hundreds of tons, placed vertically, while others were being raised to bridge the tops.

"Where the hell are they getting the stones?" Valentina checked her mission data. If it was up to date, the nearest quarry was nearly three hundred kilometers away.

"They must have dug a new quarry nearby." Mills lowered his binoculars. "It must be taking thousands of them to quarry and move those bloody things. The warriors we see here can only be the tip of the iceberg."

"Well, I don't know what that twin of Stonehenge is," Steph said quietly, "but I know very well what those are around it. They're a perfect match for what Ichiro," it almost hurt to say his name, "saw during the first contact massacre. They're dueling arenas."

Mills and the others shifted their view slightly. Not far from the ponderous structure was a set of five circular rings that the warriors had built from much smaller rough-cut stones. Each ring was perhaps thirty meters in diameter and looked to be about chest high, with pillars that rose to about two meters and were evenly spaced around the circumference. In the center of each ring was a raised dais of stone, and there was a single entrance to each ring that faced the larger structure, with the two linked by a stone walkway. White sand covered the ground in each one.

"Bloody hell," Mills breathed. "I'll take your word for it."

Valentina lowered her rifle and turned to look at him. "Maybe it was lucky we landed here after all."

"Why?" Steph asked as she filmed both the Kreelans below and the other members of the team. The miniaturized and combat-hardened vidcam that she'd taken from the case she'd brought with her was strapped to her helmet and followed the movement of her head.

"Because we want to find out where the bitches are concentrated," Danielson chimed in. Glancing at Mills, he added, "I doubt anybody ever would have expected there'd be so many here in a podunk little town."

Mills grunted agreement. "We were supposed to land near one of the major cities. Or at least as major as they are on this planet, because we expected most of the enemy would be concentrated there. They probably only needed a few dozen to take this town, but there's at least a thousand, maybe two, in the town alone."

"You can probably double or triple that," Valentina said, aiming her rifle at the woods on the far side of the town. "I can't make out specifics, but I'm picking up a lot of thermal signatures over there through the trees. A few that look like fires, and a bunch that I'll wager are more warriors. They're all over the place over there."

"Look!" Danielson hissed, pointing off to their left. "Down there!"

Along the main road that passed through Breakwater and linked it to two much larger towns to the north and south, a column of figures came into view, marching around the base of the hill the team occupied.

"Oh, my God." Steph focused on the tiny figures, her vidcam able to zoom in more than even Mills's binoculars. "Prisoners."

There were a few thousand people being marched along by at least as many enemy warriors. Men, women, and even children were in the mass of ragged, shuffling figures. She could see their tattered clothes and dirty faces, the helpless defeat in their expressions. The warriors walked along the side of the road, content to leave the humans alone as long as they kept moving.

"We've had reports of civilians being rounded up like this, but never had any hard intel on what happened to them." Mills bit his lip as he looked over the prisoners, his stomach knotting with anger. "We assumed they were killed, but..." He broke off, not sure what else to say.

"Well," Valentina said woodenly, resisting the urge to take out some of the warriors with her rifle, "now we know what the arenas are for."

"What are we going to do?" Steph asked.

"Not a bloody thing," Mills grated, "but take note of what we see and be ready to pass on our information when the fleet jumps in."

"But we can't just leave them!" Steph argued. "They'll be slaughtered!"

"Listen to me," Mills said coldly, turning to face her. "In case you lost count, there are four of us. Just four. I'd sacrifice myself in a heartbeat to help those poor buggers if it would make the slightest difference, but we'd be throwing our lives away.

"Worse, we'd be throwing away their only chance, which is to make sure the fleet knows what they'll be facing down here so the Marines coming in behind us can blow these bitches to hell." Steph turned away, and Mills went on more softly, "Don't believe for a second that I don't want to do something, but-"

"Listen!" Danielson hissed, holding his hand up for silence as he turned to look behind them, up the slope of the hill.

They fell silent, listening intently. For a moment, they heard nothing but the gentle rustling of the leaves.

It was quiet. Too quiet.

Then Mills saw dark shadows moving among the trees, coming toward them. With a silent curse, he made a hand signal for Danielson to take point. The comms specialist moved out, heading silently down the hill to the right, toward a burned out barn and farmhouse in the middle of a patchwork of tilled fields.

Gripping her assault rifle, Steph followed close behind him. Then came Valentina, who slung her big sniper rifle, which was unwieldy for close-in work, over her shoulder. Then she drew her pistol.

Mills hung back for a moment, watching the dark figures as they approached. He knew that if his team was forced into a fight now, they wouldn't stand a chance. Even if they defeated the warriors coming at them, they'd be cornered and wiped out by the warriors now moving down the road.

He'd fight if there was no alternative, but the only real chance they had was to get away.

Hoping the Kreelans weren't very good trackers, he turned and quickly followed after Valentina.

* * *

Ku'ar-Marekh had been watching the humans for hours when a small group of patrolling warriors stumbled upon their trail.

She could have simply killed the alien animals, of course, but watching them had provided an entertainment, of sorts, in which she chose to indulge herself.

The warriors, unaware of her presence, had been hunting for more humans believed to be in this area when they came upon the tracks of those who had fallen from the sky.

These particular warriors had not yet seen battle, and they were eager to prove themselves against some humans to bring glory to the Empress.

Ku'ar-Marekh held back as the warriors excitedly began to follow the trail, and was curious now to see what the humans would do.

* * *

"Follow the creek." Mills pointed as they reached the bottom of the hill. "If we can move along it far enough, it should cover our trail."

"It's going to slow us down," Danielson cautioned, looking at the water that was running shin-deep.

"Yes, but it's either that or make a break for it across the open fields to the barn over there." Mills nodded toward the burned-out structure. "If we can make it around to the woods behind the barn, maybe we can-"

"Down!" Valentina shouted as one of the Kreelan flying edged weapons came whistling through the air at them.

She shoved Steph aside and Mills dropped flat into the water. Danielson tried to dodge the thing, but it clipped his left arm, slicing deep into the muscle. With a grunt of pain, he fell into the creek, which began to run red with his blood.

Four alien warriors emerged from the woods, moving toward them with swords drawn.

Mills raised his assault rifle, but never got a chance to fire. He heard a sound like a mechanical cough that came four times in under a second.

One after the other, all four warriors collapsed into the creek, each with a hole drilled neatly between the eyes.

Whipping his head around, he saw Valentina, still aiming her pistol at the woods in case any more aliens appeared. The weapon now had a large cylinder attached to the muzzle. A suppressor.

"Good God, woman," Mills said, the amazement plain in his voice. Aside from her incredible shooting, he had no idea how she'd gotten the suppressor onto the weapon so quickly. "That was a neat bit of work."

Before anyone could say anything else, a groan got their attention.

"Danielson!" Mills got to his feet, soaking wet now, and went to where the other man was trying to sit up in the creek.

Danielson was holding the wound in his arm with his free hand, but blood was streaming from between his fingers and his face had already turned pasty white.

"Come on, mate, it's only a scratch."

But when Mills pulled Danielson's hand away to take a quick look, he saw why the man was going into shock. The Kreelan throwing star, which is what it was called sometimes, had cut Danielson's arm right down to the bone, almost completely severing the biceps muscle.

"Here," Steph said, kneeling next to Danielson and wrapping a field dressing around the wound. "I got some basic first aid training before I deployed for the Keran operation," she explained. "Don't expect me to take out your appendix or anything, but I can apply a field dressing with the best of them."

"Thanks." Danielson gave her a weak smile after she'd finished wrapping his arm.

"I think we'd better go." Valentina knelt behind them, her pistol held level and steady. While she didn't see or hear anything unusual in the woods behind them, she felt certain there was someone there.

"Capital idea." Mills hauled Danielson to his feet. "Can you move?"

"Yeah," Danielson rasped, grasping his assault rifle in his right hand. "Let's get the fuck out of here."

"I'll take point," Mills said. "Valentina, cover our asses, if you please."

Mills turned around to start moving along the creek again when he found himself staring at a teenage girl, peering at him from around a rock near a bend in the creek a few yards away.

All four of the adults just stood there, dumbstruck with surprise.

"*She's* following you," the girl said cryptically, just barely loud enough for them to hear over the gurgling water of the creek. "I can't save you from her if she wants you. But if you come with me, the others won't bother you."

Then she turned and disappeared along the creek toward where the wrecked farmhouse stood.

Still stunned speechless, Mills and the others followed quickly behind.

* * *

After the adult humans had followed the young animal, Ku'ar-Marekh stepped from the shadows of the trees to where the four warriors had been slain by the single human female. That one, she knew, would be worthy of her personal attention. But Ku'ar-Marekh had decided that she would save these particular humans for later.

In the meantime, the first batch of survivors of the larger population centers were being brought here. There was no special reason for her having chosen this place over any other for the Challenges soon to be fought; it had merely been convenient.

Soon, the humans and her warriors would fight and die in the arenas for the glory of the Empress.

SIXTY-THREE

"Lord God." Mills sat back against the cold concrete wall, unable to keep the awe from his voice after Allison Murtaugh finished her tale.

They were in the shelter under the barn, where Allison had taken him and the others after the encounter with the alien warriors. He looked at the dozen children who were clustered around him and his team. Neither the adults nor the children could quite believe that the other was actually real.

"And you not only survived, but gathered up these other children here and saved them." Steph stared in rapt fascination at Allison, her vidcam having captured the girl's every word. While Steph didn't really care anymore about such things, she knew that what she was recording now would be in the running for the next Pulitzer Prize.

Making the grand assumption, of course, that she and the footage survived.

"Yes," Allison answered simply, nodding her head while offering Steph a shy smile.

The other children voiced their assent, and one by one told their own story of how Allison had saved each of them. By the end, Mills and the other three adults were in tears.

One thing still wasn't quite clear to Mills. Allison had explained it, but he still couldn't quite believe it. "Allison, you said that the Kreelans don't come here to your little hideout. I'm still not clear on that."

"They don't bother us because *she* seems to like me."

"That's this other warrior you mentioned at the creek when you found us?" Valentina asked. "The one who you said would get us if she wanted to?"

Allison visibly shivered. "She looks the same as the others, except she has more of the jewel or bead things hanging from the collar around her neck. Oh, and there's some sort of round or oval thing on the front of her collar that none of the others have, and some fancy bright blue design on her chest."

Mills and Steph simultaneously stared at one another. They had both seen another warrior with a special collar and a bright blue design on her chest armor. The warrior had beaten Mills twice, apparently purely for entertainment, and had killed the woman he loved.

"Is she big?" Mills clenched his huge fists to focus his rage. "As big or bigger than me, much taller and stronger-looking than the others?"

Allison shook her head. "No, not at all. Other than those two things, you couldn't tell her from any of the others." She paused. "Well, except for her eyes. They're dead."

"What do you mean by that?" Steph asked.

"Since the night she landed, the night she did...whatever it was that she did to me, when I felt like she was driving ice picks through my heart, I've seen her a number of times. She's followed me around, watching what I do." She wrapped her arms around herself as if to ward off a chill, even though the shelter was quite warm. "One time, when I was hunting for food in town, I went around a corner and she was right there." She held out her arm and touched Mills on the chest. "That close. I thought, 'That's it, Allison. You're dead.'

"But she just stood there and stared down at me. And her eyes, her face...she's not like the others. The others have expressions, you know? I don't know what all of them mean, but their faces change, a lot like ours do when we're happy or sad. But looking into her face is like looking into nothing, like her eyes are empty wells that just go down forever, but there's no water in them. I don't know how to explain it."

"And she just let you go that time, too?" Valentina was having as difficult a time as Mills believing it.

Allison nodded again. "Yes. I figured that I was still alive, so I'd better get moving. I could've just run back here, but then figured I may as well still get the food. I knew she could find me whenever she wanted. She followed me all night after that, even when I came back here, and she's followed me around other times, too."

"Oh, great!" Danielson blurted. "So you lead us back here so the enemy knows exactly where we are? Brilliant!"

"She already knew where you were," Allison told him bluntly. "She was in the forest, following you."

"How do you know that?" Mills asked her.

"Because I was following her when I saw you escape down to the creek, and I came to help you," Allison explained. "I've followed her before." Mills and the others exchanged a disbelieving glance. "No, really! I think she enjoys it, like I'm a pet or something, trotting after her.

"Don't get me wrong, she terrifies me, but after she followed me that first time and didn't do anything, I decided that fair's fair." She paused, looking defiantly at Danielson. "I don't like being bullied."

Valentina covered up her smile with one hand and Steph suppressed a giggle as Danielson turned red.

Mills shook his head. "You've got some guts, girl. I'm not so sure about your smarts in following a warrior around like that, but I'm glad you did. You saved our lives."

Allison beamed at the big Marine's praise.

"But now I'm hoping you can help us solve a little problem we've got."

"If I can," she told him eagerly, nodding her head.

"Is there anywhere in town where we might find some communications gear? An electronics shop or network node, anything like that? The kit we need to talk to the other ground teams and the fleet when it comes in was lost when our ship was destroyed. We've got to find another way to get in touch with them about what's happening here."

"Sergeant Mills?" A girl, Vanhi, Mills remembered, interrupted quietly. "Just what is happening here? What about all those people on the road that you saw? What's going to happen to them? You're here to help them, aren't you?"

Mills exchanged an uncomfortable glance with the other members of the team. "Yes, love," he told her, avoiding the question of what was going to happen to the prisoners. "We're going to help them. But to do that, we've got to get the gear we need to talk to our friends."

"The communications exchange?" Amrit, Vanhi's brother, suggested.

Allison shook her head. "The exchange building is still there, but almost everything inside is burned and wrecked. I think our soldiers tried to destroy it."

"That would make sense. They wouldn't want the enemy to get access to it." Danielson glanced at Mills, who nodded agreement.

"There's a gadget shop in town," Allison said slowly, her face a mask of concentration. "A place that has the kinds of things you might need. Comm units and stuff. But it's along Main Street, right across from the town square and whatever those things are the Kreelans are building." She looked up at Mills. "I could get there..."

"But you won't know what we need," Danielson finished. "And I'm in no shape to go with this fu...um, messed up arm."

Allison scowled at him, making it clear that she wouldn't want him with her, anyway.

"I'll go." Valentina smiled at Steph. "I'm the real backup comms specialist, anyway."

Mills nodded. He knew she was the best choice in any case, even had Danielson not been wounded. "All right, then, we'll go in tonight. In the meantime, we'll start keeping a lookout. If that warrior knows where we are, it's only a matter of time before she comes for us herself or sends her dogs after us. I don't want to be caught without any warning."

"We'll help!" one of the children chirped.

Mills grinned. "Is that so?"

All the children nodded emphatically.

"All right, then, we can always use some extra eyes and ears. I'll take the first watch, then Steph and Danielson. Once it's fully dark, Allison and Valentina will head into town, so you two had better get a bit of rest now."

Later, Mills lay prone in some of the barn's wreckage, watching an endless stream of people moving along the road, escorted by yet more enemy warriors.

Valentina came and silently lay down next to him. A young boy, Evan, lay an arm's length from Mills on the opposite side, facing toward the rear of the barn and the fields there, diligently watching for any enemies that might approach from the woods.

The sun was just beginning to droop over the gentle hills to planetary west.

"You're supposed to be getting some sleep," Mills chided.

"Like that's going to happen." She held out her hand for his binoculars. "Anything new?"

He shook his head as he handed them over. "Nothing good." He leaned closer and whispered so Evan couldn't hear. "There's been a constant stream of civilians being herded down the road from the north toward town. And more warriors. Christ, but there's a lot of them."

Valentina frowned as she looked back and forth along the procession moving slowly along the road. There were thousands of people, and their moans and cries sent a shiver down her spine. "My God, where are they going to put them all?"

"I can't see it from here, but if you take a gander over that way," he pointed to a small rolling hill about a kilometer away, "you can see a stretch of road rising up behind that hill just before town. None of the prisoners have passed that way, so the Kreelans are moving them off the road somewhere before that, out of sight from where we are. I'm thinking they're turning off near where you saw all that thermal activity before we were chased down from the hill earlier. I'm wagering the Kreelans have some sort of concentration camp set up there to hold all our people until..."

He couldn't finish the rest. Not just because he didn't want Evan to hear it, but because he had a hard time bearing the burden of being totally helpless when so many people were about to die. He had already seen so much death in this war, but most of those had been in combat, men and women who'd been trained and armed, who could fight back. These poor souls being marched along the road were just regular everyday people who wouldn't stand a chance against the warriors who'd be sent into the arenas with them.

He couldn't do a thing about it. Nothing. And unless Valentina and Allison were successful tonight, he wouldn't even be able to tell the fleet to land Marines here to mount a rescue operation.

He felt Valentina's hand on his arm.

"Don't be so hard on yourself." She understood the anguish he was feeling. While the scale had been vastly different, she had been in more than one situation when she worked as an agent for the Terran Intelligence Service where she hadn't been able to help someone who had been in desperate trouble. Those people had died, some of them under long and agonizing torture. "Take it from me, you can't save everyone, no matter how hard you try."

"I know, but..." He looked away for a moment, wiping at his face, and Valentina saw the glistening of tears.

She'd come to the conclusion over the course of the mission that there was a lot more to Mills that she had ever realized. He would have everyone believe that he was nothing but a big ape, an ignorant jarhead, but that wasn't him at all.

"We won't be able to save them all, Mills," she told him, "but we'll be able to save some, maybe most, if the fleet comes in time. That's what you need to focus on. Not how many we'll lose."

Mills grunted. "And what makes you so worldly-wise, all of a sudden?"

She was silent for a moment, and he was wondering if he'd managed to insult her when she said softly, "Do you know how many people I've killed, Roland?"

"Not if you're going to add me to the list after you tell me." It wasn't quite as much of a joke as he might have liked, and it unnerved him that she was talking about anything related to her operations as a covert agent. It was an extraordinary measure of the trust she'd placed in him.

"I've killed eighty-seven human beings, not counting anyone I killed in the firefights we were in on Saint Petersburg and a few other places I won't mention. But those eighty-seven, they were people I killed face to face. People whose names I knew. I knew everything about them, almost as if we were longtime friends. And do you know how many I've saved?"

"How many?"

"None." It was her turn to look away. "Not a single one. Some of my contacts who were in danger were extracted by other agents. But my own personal salvation score? Zero."

Mills stared at her. "You know, for someone who's supposed to be a brilliant super-spy, you're as dense as a bloody brick."

"What?" Valentina turned to him, a perplexed look on her face.

"We wouldn't be having this conversation if it weren't for you. My mates and I would all be dead back in the government complex on Saint Petersburg had you not shot up half the Russians coming after us. Oh, and let's not forget that minor miracle of how you got all of us off that rock by doing that freaky mind-meld thing with the navigation computer that left you a vegetable for six months." He shook his head in wonder. "My God, woman. Yes, we'll all have to answer for our sins in the end. You've got yours, and Lord knows I've got my own list of dirty deeds. But don't ever tell me again that you never saved anyone, or I'm going to turn you over my knee and spank your bottom."

She grinned. "You'd like that, wouldn't you?"

Mills grinned back. "I could think of worse ways to spend my time."

They were quiet for a while after that, turning their attention back to the stream of people marching down the road.

After a while, Valentina said, "Mills?"

"Yes?"

"Do you know what I'd like?"

Mills snorted. "That's a bit of a loaded question, dearie, but I'll take the bait. What would you like?"

"I'd like a frozen margarita with real strawberries. On a nice beach somewhere under a cloudless sky and a warm sun. I want to be able to just enjoy myself and not be there to kill someone." She glanced at him. "And I don't want to be alone."

Unable to help himself, Mills felt his jaw drop open as he turned to look at her. "Lord Almighty. Are you asking me on a date?"

"Don't get a fat head about it," she told him with a wry grin. "But yeah, I guess I am."

"Bloody hell, woman," he choked, glancing over to see if Evan heard him cursing. "I think I might take you up on that."

"You'd better, or I'm going to do to you what I did to Danielson on the ship and you'll be squeaking like a school girl."

Mills had to bite his tongue to keep quiet. It wouldn't do for the Kreelans to find them because he was laughing his head off. "Well, I guess it's a deal, then. Assuming we get out of this mess."

"Yeah, I guess there's always that." She sighed. "I guess I'll go check on Allison to see if she's getting any rest. I might try and close my eyes, too. Talking to you is exhausting."

"Smart arse." As she began to get up, he reached out and took her arm. "Just promise me you'll be damn careful tonight. Both of you."

"I promise. Allison and I'll take care of one another."

"Okay, then." Mills reluctantly let her go.

Without another word, she got up and returned to the shelter, leaving him to his worrying.

With a sigh, he turned to watch the column of people again, but instead looked up to the sky as he heard the faint but growing roar of an approaching ship.

* * *

Ri'al-Hagir, the First to Ku'ar-Marekh, masked her fear. But inside she trembled, for she knew that Death was very close. Very close indeed. She did not fear dying in itself, for that was the worthy and hoped-for ending for any warrior who served the Empress.

No, she was afraid of what would come after. Or, more precisely, of what might not. To die with honor meant basking in the Afterlife, to take one's place among the spirits who dwelled beyond death in the love of the Empress.

To die without honor, to perish in disgrace, meant that one's soul would be cast into eternal darkness beyond Her love, without hope of redemption. From birth, Her Children sensed the Bloodsong in their veins, an emotional bond with the Empress that was just as real as the blood in their bodies. It was as natural to Her Children as taking a breath.

But that bond could be broken, the lifeline to the river of the Bloodsong severed, both in life and in death. It was rare, yet it did happen. No mere warrior could mete out such a punishment. Only the Empress had that power...and the high priestesses such as Ku'ar-Marekh.

Ri'al-Hagir knelt now before the cold-hearted priestess of the Nyur-A'il, a silent prayer to the Empress on her lips.

"I entrusted you with a simple matter." Ku'ar-Marekh's voice was, as always, empty of all emotion.

Shivering at the words, Ri'al-Hagir braced herself for the eternal agony that would soon befall her. She had been summoned moments earlier by Ku'ar-Marekh to the *Kalai-Il*, the place of atonement that the warriors had been struggling mightily to complete. The sun had long since given its place to the stars, and the great stone edifice was lit by a ring of torches, their orange light flickering in the darkness.

Were it any other than Ku'ar-Marekh, Ri'al-Hagir would have feared only the pain of the lash up on the *Kalai-Il*. Agonizing and potentially lethal as it was, it was a mortal pain. Even if her body died, her spirit would live on.

Yet, Ri'al-Hagir knew that her priestess had never inflicted punishment to any warriors on the *Kalai-Il*. She had either tortured them to death with her powers, or severed their bonds to the Bloodsong.

She could easily accept the former, but greatly feared the latter.

"My life is yours, my priestess," Ri'al-Hagir said, forcing strength into her voice through the fear in her heart. "The *Kalai-Il* is not yet finished as you had commanded. I offer no excuse."

In fact, the delay had been from having to quarry the stones farther away than they had expected. Transporting them to this place using the ancient ways, as custom demanded, had taken more time. The builder caste could have created this monument to Kreelan discipline in but moments, but that was not the Way of their race. The *Kalai-Il* was found on every world of the Empire, and in all of the great warships built in the last fifty millennia. It was built only by the hands of Her Children, using ingenuity and backbreaking labor. For that was the Way, as it had been even before the Empire had been founded a hundred thousand cycles before.

The priestess stood over her, Ku'ar-Marekh's right hand holding the hilt of her sword. "I do not take you to task for the *Kalai-Il*. It is of the humans that I speak."

This so surprised Ri'al-Hagir that she involuntarily glanced up at the priestess, then quickly cast her eyes down again. "I do not understand, my priestess."

"Behold." Ku'ar-Marekh placed a hand on the braids of Ri'al-Hagir's raven hair.

Ri'al-Hagir gasped as she felt herself flying from the *Kalai-Il* to the woods where a great encampment had been built for the warriors streaming here, and the corrals where the humans were being kept.

Not intending any cruelty to the humans, the corrals were nonetheless horrific affairs. Thousands of the human animals had been crammed into the pens, and more were on the way. Many hundreds of those who had been strong enough to survive the march here, a winnowing process to eliminate those unworthy to fight in the arenas, had died, trampled to death by their fellow animals or from lack of food and water.

The stench of their waste and wretchedness reached a full league here to the *Kalai-Il*. In what Ri'al-Hagir knew was the view of the priestess's second sight that she somehow was sharing, the smell was unbearable, and she could sense through the powerful Bloodsong of the priestess how the warriors guarding the animals suffered their duties.

"We do not treat our food animals in such a fashion, let alone those we would face in the arena or in open battle." Ku'ar-Marekh released Ri'al-Hagir, bringing the warrior back to the here and now atop the *Kalai-Il*. "There are millions of the aliens left on this world, and I summoned more warriors here to challenge them and bring glory to the Empress. And this is what they would find when the fleet bearing them arrives on the morrow."

Ku'ar-Marekh paused. Ri'al-Hagir could feel a tingling sensation around her heart, and she shivered in fear.

"The Way of our people is difficult, yet we do not revel in cruelty. We have dishonored Her and ourselves by letting humans we have captured, especially those who survived the difficult trek to this place, die needlessly and in such a fashion, without the chance to fight," Ku'ar-Marekh continued. "What would I tell your sisters when they arrive and see this? What would I tell the Empress? This is not Her will."

Ri'al-Hagir hung her head low, clenching her fists so tightly that her talons drew blood from her palms. "I give my life in dishonor," she whispered, hoping that the priestess would choose to end her life with a blade, and not with the other powers that dwelt within her.

Ku'ar-Marekh's sword sang from its scabbard, moving too quickly to see as it severed the first braid of Ri'al-Hagir's hair. The braids of Her Children were not merely a form of style or ornamentation, but formed a very tangible bond with the Empress. The first braid was the key, for it linked the owner's spirit with the Bloodsong. Were it severed, the bearer might survive physically, but would be doomed upon death to an eternity of darkness beyond Her love.

Ri'al-Hagir cried out as the braid parted, but her voice died as Ku'ar-Marekh's blade flashed again, slicing through the warrior's neck. The severed head fell to the dais of the *Kalai-Il* with a wet thud, and Ri'al-Hagir's body collapsed on top of it in a clatter of metal on stone.

The priestess could sense the sudden silence of her First's Bloodsong as she was carried away into the depths of the cold darkness of eternity. It brought her no satisfaction, but honor had been satisfied.

Ku'ar-Marekh calmly flicked the blood from her blade and slid it back into its scabbard. The warriors around her knelt low to the ground, their left fists over their right breasts in salute. They were terrified.

"Place her body in the forest as a feast for the wild animals," Ku'ar-Marekh ordered. "Then make right what she allowed to go wrong, or you shall suffer the same fate."

As she strode down the wide steps of the *Kalai-Il*, the warriors moved quickly to obey.

* * *

Allison pressed a hand to her mouth to stifle an involuntary gasp as the strange warrior with the dead eyes killed one of her own warriors on the huge stone platform they'd been building.

"What is it?" Valentina whispered from behind her. They'd made better time getting into town than Valentina had expected. The frequent Kreelan hunting parties that had been wandering across the countryside earlier had vanished, and Valentina suspected they were all congregating for the slaughter that must soon be about to start for the prisoners being marched into Breakwater.

"She killed one of them!" Allison hissed. "Cut her head right off!"

"A prisoner?" Valentina sidled up beside Allison where the girl crouched near the blasted-out front window.

"No." Allison shook her head and pointed to where the strange warrior was now walking down from the stone platform. "One of the other warriors. It looked like they were talking for a while, with the other one kneeling. Then Dead Eyes just whipped out her sword and lopped the other one's head off."

"Well," Valentina said grimly, "I guess that's one less that we have to kill ourselves."

"How can they do that, Valentina? How could they just...kill one another like that?"

"Don't think that humans haven't done the same to one another, and worse." Valentina fought to keep a host of unpleasant memories from surfacing. "Let's just be thankful that our friend there is occupied with her own problems instead of coming after us."

"I guess so." Allison watched the warrior disappear from view behind the stone. As she did, the other warriors around her ran to take the body away, then they all disappeared down the street that led toward the woods on the south side of town where the human prisoners were being taken.

In an effort to deflect Allison's thoughts, Valentina said, "You picked a good place here. It'll take me a while to put something together, but I think we've got all the parts for both a radio and a comm link."

"What's a radio?" Allison asked, finally turning from the window.

"Something people used to use a long time ago to talk across distances, before we had comm links. In a way they're the same sort of thing, just that what we have nowadays can carry a lot more information a lot farther."

"Then why don't we just use that?"

"Because sometimes the Kreelans don't let us. We don't know how they do it, but they can make it stop working. They don't do it all the time, but when they do, it's usually at the worst possible moment."

"But they don't bother the radio thing?"

"No, at least not so far as anyone knows. So I want to make sure we have both, just in case." Patting Allison on the shoulder, she said, "I've got just a couple more things to find, then we'll get out of here."

"Okay."

Allison continued to watch, peering out from the corner of the window and keeping as much of her face concealed as possible. The flickering fire from torches illuminated all five of the big rings, arenas, Valentina had called them, and the big stone thing. The sight made her shiver, and she hoped that Valentina would finish soon. She hated just sitting here.

She looked up at the growing roar of an approaching ship, and followed it as it lowered into the woods on the far side of town. Valentina said that while she wasn't sure, she suspected it probably carried more human prisoners. The ships had been coming about every fifteen minutes since Mills had seen the first one a few hours ago.

"Let's go," Valentina whispered from behind her, and Allison nearly jumped out of her skin.

"It's about time."

Together, they crept out the back of the store and through the dark, deserted streets as yet another ship roared overhead.

SIXTY-FOUR

"Shit." Danielson looked up, wondering if the children had heard him curse. It had taken him four hours of frustrating labor to try and piece together the device from the parts and tools Valentina had brought back, while she focused on trying to build a radio.

Her task had been just as challenging, as it was difficult to put together a primitive device like a radio with modern technology.

"What's wrong?" Steph had been helping Danielson. She didn't have the technical knowledge to build the equipment, but she could provide a pair of extra hands.

"There's nothing." Danielson glared at the fist-sized collection of electronic components he had managed to fuse together. Two lights glowed on a small panel that was connected to the device. One was green, the other was red. Pointing to the green one, he said, "The thing's broadcasting. I can tell that much. But it's not connecting to anything, not even our headsets." He held up one of the headsets they'd been wearing. They hadn't had to use them much since they jumped down to the planet's surface, as they'd been together most of the time and within easy talking distance.

"Is it just not synchronizing?" Valentina picked up her own headset and working the tiny controls.

"No," he told her, shaking his head. "Those have stopped working, too. The hardware checks out okay, but there's no carrier signal for them to pick up. The network's just gone."

"He's right." Steph was looking at her vidcam. While she hadn't connected it to the team's net, it could see the headset nodes. Now it couldn't. "The Kreelans must have done whatever they do to kill our comm and data links."

"Well, I guess that's that for this piece of crap." Danielson shoved the makeshift comm unit away from him, a look of utter disgust on his face.

"How do they do that?" Steph wondered quietly.

"I think the question we should be asking is why they did it now?" Valentina frowned. "I just spoke to Mills a few minutes ago on my headset."

"Who the hell knows?" Danielson snapped. "I sure hope you had better luck than I did."

"Let's find out." Valentina tapped a few more commands into a small console that she had connected to her own collection of oddball bits and pieces of tech from the gadget store. "Let me have that, would you?" She pointed to a connector attached to the end of a cable that she had run outside the shelter to a wire antenna outside. Steph handed it to her, and Valentina plugged the connector into the makeshift radio.

They were rewarded with the sound of static from the small speaker unit. Valentina touched a control on the console, and the static disappeared.

"I programmed in the alternate radio frequencies we were given" she explained. "All the teams were issued radio beacons. If the other teams have their beacons on, we should be able to pick them up."

"We don't have a beacon, do we?" Steph asked.

"No," Danielson answered bitterly. "It went down with the ship, along with most of our other stuff."

They all stared at the speaker, waiting to hear something.

"What are we listening for?" Steph whispered.

"Bursts of static," Valentina answered, keeping her eyes glued to the console. "It won't sound like anything to us, but I built in a decoder that will break out any transmissions. The beacons are just to let other teams know you're still on the mission. If we pick up a beacon and respond, we'll be patched through to the team and be able to talk to them."

They watched and listened, but heard nothing but silence. One minute passed, then two.

"Are you sure it's working?" Danielson leaned in for a closer look at the device.

Valentina nodded. "We don't have a transmitter that I can use to test it, but at certain frequencies there are natural radio sources like lightning, and gas giants like the one in this system produce a lot of radio signals." She looked up at him. "Those were my test sources. The radio's working, there's just no one out there transmitting."

"Maybe they're too far away?" Steph asked.

Both Danielson and Valentina shook their heads.

"No," Danielson told her. "The beacons were tailored for Alger's World, and all the teams are here on the same continent. If they were broadcasting, we'd hear them."

"And if they're not broadcasting..." Steph looked at Valentina.

"They're gone," Valentina answered with brutal finality.

The three of them sat silently, staring at the equipment on the small table. Behind them, the children slept in a mass of pillows and blankets spread across the shelter's floor. Allison had refused to go to bed after returning from town with Valentina, and had instead gone outside to keep Mills company.

Valentina grinned inwardly. She suspected Allison was quickly developing a crush on the big Marine.

They looked up with a start as the door opened. Mills.

"Why aren't any of you answering your bloody headsets?" he hissed angrily, glancing at the mass of sleeping children.

Danielson held up one of the headsets. "The comm links are out. The hardware's okay. We think it's the Kreelans locking us down."

"They shut down the network only a few minutes after I last spoke to you," Valentina added.

"And none of you thought to clue me in to that little fact?" Mills raised his voice. "Maybe it's because there's a file of warriors from town heading right toward us!"

"Oh, Christ." Danielson closed his eyes and banged his head back against the concrete wall, a small measure of his anger at his own stupidity.

"Get them up," Mills ordered, nodding at the children. "We've got to get them out of here, right now."

"There's something else you need to know," Valentina told him as Danielson gathered up the two comm units and carefully put them into a satchel, while Steph rushed to wake up the rest of the children. "There aren't any beacons from the other teams. They're gone."

"We're it." Danielson gave Mills a sick look as he hurriedly crammed some other essential gear into a pack.

Mills muttered something dark under his breath, not wanting to say out loud what he was thinking in front of the children, who were now all awake and alert.

"Bloody perfect." He fought to calm himself. The children were looking at him with wide, terrified eyes, and he knew that he needed to give them some confidence. Being angry or panicking wouldn't do. "They're probably just busy," he said. When Danielson opened his mouth to say something, Mills cut him off, managing to muster a smile. "I'm sure they're all heading here, as this is clearly where all the real action is. We might even leave a few warriors for them to clean up."

"Uh, yeah," Danielson managed to say, finally catching on. "Yeah. But only if they move their asses and get here soon. I'm not going to hold back just to leave 'em some."

"Valentina, Steph," Mills said, "get the kids out of here. Lead them back to the creek and into the woods and try to get clear. Danielson and I will try to buy you some time."

"Send Danielson with Steph. I'm not leaving you." Valentina stared at him, defiance shining in her eyes. "You know that I can fight better than the rest of you put together."

"Why the bloody hell do you think I want you with the children?" Mills reached out and took her arm. "You may be the only chance they have."

Valentina stared at him for a moment, then slowly nodded. "Damn you, Mills. I..."

"I know," he whispered. "I know." He turned to Danielson. "Give her the comms gear." Turning back to Valentina, he said, "Now you and Steph get your arses and the children out of here. We don't have any more time."

Taking the satchel with the comm units from Danielson, Valentina quickly gathered up her pistol and the extra assault rifle that had belonged to Stallick. "I'm leaving you the sniper rifle. It won't be any good to me in the woods, but you might be able to get some use out of it."

"That I will," he agreed as he held up her pack. She stuck her arms through the straps and cinched them tight. Danielson did the same for Steph.

They were ready. The children stood, behind them, quiet but tense.

"Get going." Mills nodded toward the door.

Allison stood in the stair well, his assault rifle in her hands.

"And what do you think you're doing?" Mills put his hands on his hips, giving the girl a severe look.

"I'm staying to help you." Allison flicked a glance at Valentina.

"Good Lord!" Mills glanced at Valentina, who shrugged helplessly. With a sigh, he bent down so his face was level with Allison's. "Girl, you can't stay with me. You've got to help Valentina and Steph."

"But what will you do if *she* comes?"

Mills's expression hardened. "Don't worry. I've dealt with her type before. Now," he gently took the rifle from her, "we've wasted enough time. Get the devil out of here."

"Here, take this for me, would you?" Valentina handed her the satchel with the comms gear. "We can't let anything happen to it."

Allison, pouting, took it.

Mills slung the assault rifle over his shoulder before taking the big sniper rifle that Valentina held out to him. Then he led the way out the narrow door and up the steps to the burned out barn.

Holding out a hand to stop Allison for a moment, he took a quick look through the sniper rifle's scope toward where he and Allison had seen the warriors approaching.

The Kreelans were about where he'd expected them to be, except now they had fanned out into a skirmish line, swords drawn.

"Come on," he hissed urgently, and Allison quickly ran up the last of the steps and headed toward the back of the barn.

Valentina followed her, pausing until the rest of the children were out before taking the lead as they moved out across the dark field toward the creek.

Then Steph appeared, with Danielson right behind her. Steph knelt next to Mills and squeezed his shoulder. "Good luck, Mills," she said quietly. "And thank you."

"Take good care of yourself, Steph." He grinned, his smile splitting the darkness. "I'll see you in the next turn of the wheel."

She nodded solemnly, then followed after the children, who were moving fast behind Valentina.

"How many of our friends are coming to dinner?" Danielson wriggled into a pile of collapsed timbers from the barn's roof that offered him some cover and a good field of fire.

"About two dozen," Mills told him casually as he snugged the sniper rifle up to his shoulder and put his eye to the scope. The warrior in the center was the same who had been leading the column of warriors when he had first seen them, and he figured she was the leader. She was easy to recognize, as her right ear was gone.

That won't be the only thing you'll be missing in a minute, he thought as he centered the scope's target bead on her forehead.

"Let me know when." Danielson stared through the low-power scope on his assault rifle. "I'll start on the right and work left." He shifted his aim to the warrior who was on the right end of the line.

"I'll take the leader and work left," Mills said. "Good luck, mate."

"You, too, Mills." Danielson's finger tensed on the trigger.

Mills took a deep breath, then let it out. "Let's get to it, shall we?"

He stroked the sniper rifle's trigger, the shot shattering the quiet darkness.

* * *

Steph turned to look back at the farmhouse as the first shot was fired. The building was nothing more than a black shadow against the darkness of the pre-dawn hours, an angular shape that blocked out the stars. She could see flashes of light reflected from the far side of the barn as Mills and Danielson began to fire on the approaching warriors. She could have used the light amplification of her vidcam to see better, but the small projection lens gave off enough light to stand out in the darkness. She knew the Kreelans could see well in the dark, and she didn't want to give herself away.

"Come on!" One of the children took her hand and pulled her along.

Bringing up the rear made Steph feel isolated from the others, but Valentina needed to be at the front in case they ran into trouble, and someone had to make sure none of the children got left behind.

Trying to ignore the frenzied firing now coming from the barn, the rapid staccato of Danielson's assault rifle punctuated with the heavier booms of the sniper rifle, Steph hurried after the young girl who was still holding her hand.

Other shadowy figures shimmered ahead of them as the line of children moved quickly toward the creek, where Valentina gathered them in a circle around her.

"I'll cross first," she told them in a whisper as Steph knelt beside her, "and I'll whistle if it's clear. If you hear anything else, run. Everyone understand?"

There were nods from the ghostly faces, and Steph could see them glance back nervously toward the barn as the alien warriors let loose a bone-chilling war cry.

"If anything happens to me," Valentina whispered into Steph's ear, "get Allison and protect the radio. It's already pre-set to the fleet broadcast frequency. Everything depends on it."

With that, she turned and moved silently into the burbling creek, crouched down low and holding her rifle at the ready.

* * *

"Out!" Danielson ejected another spent magazine and slammed a fresh one into his rifle.

Mills fired again at something moving in the field, but wasn't sure if he hit it. The two of them had taken down at least half the approaching warriors, but he knew that at least some of them must be getting close. Every time he fired, he lost his sight picture and was partially blinded by the rifle's muzzle flash, and he was losing track of his targets without a spotter.

"Check behind us!"

That's when he heard the strange keening sound that the Kreelan flying weapons made. He ducked down just as the thing flew right through his makeshift firing port, making a heavy thunk as it embedded itself in something behind him.

Danielson shoved himself backward with his elbows and peeked up over some of the fallen trusses from the barn's roof to see behind him.

A warrior leaped at him from the darkness.

"Christ!" He fired, the muzzle flashes dancing along the shining blade and gleaming fangs of the alien. The slugs stopped her in midair, and she fell to the ground in a bloody heap.

Four more of the snarling humanoids attacked. Mills barely rolled away in time as a sword slashed right through the timber he'd been next to, and he lost his grip on the sniper rifle.

A warrior was standing right over him, raising her sword again for an overhand cut, the fangs in her mouth gleaming as she roared in triumph.

He kicked one of her legs out from under her, and she fell on top of him, trying to stab him with the sword.

Mills managed to block it, knocking the blade to the side as she fell.

Letting go the sword, she slashed him across the chest, her talons cutting deep into his body armor before he caught hold of both her wrists.

They rolled and writhed until Mills settled for the simple expedient of repeatedly smashing his forehead against her nose and mouth. That stunned her long enough for him to slip his combat knife from its sheath on his belt. He shoved it through the base of her jaw, driving the tip into her brain.

Danielson screamed.

Mills rolled the still-twitching Kreelan away, ignoring the blood that had poured onto him from her punctured throat. Getting to his knees, he saw three of the aliens slashing and stabbing at Danielson. He was holding his rifle, its magazine now empty, by the muzzle with his good hand, using it as a club.

The Kreelans weren't making a concerted effort to kill him, but were taking the time to make him bleed.

Mills grabbed his assault rifle from the black ash and dirt of the barn's floor and fired, killing two of the Kreelans instantly.

The third seemed to somehow dance out of the way of his bullets, moving closer to Danielson. Mills watched in slow-motion horror as the warrior easily parried Danielson's desperate swing with his rifle, then plunged her blade into his chest.

"No!" Mills screamed as he emptied the rest of the magazine into her. The bullets pinned her body to the remains of the barn's wall until his gun fell silent and she crumpled to the floor.

Without thinking, he dumped the empty magazine and shoved a new one in as he crawled through the debris to reach his fellow Marine.

"Stay with me, mate." Mills knelt down next Danielson.

"If my arm hadn't been hurt," Danielson breathed, a froth of blood seeping from his mouth, "I could've whipped all of them."

"No doubt," Mills told him as he moved his hands over Danielson's chest to feel the wound, then reached around to probe gently along his back. The sword had run all the way through the right side of his chest, perilously near his heart. There was nothing Mills could do. "And you'll have a chance to prove you're a macho bastard again after we get you patched up."

"Don't fuck with me, Mills. I'm done, and I'm okay with it." Danielson took Mills's bloodied hand and held it tight. "Just go. Take care of the brats." He coughed, a wet, ugly sound from deep inside his chest. "And good luck with the spy chick, you lucky...bastard."

"Thanks, mate." Mills said quietly, blinking away the wetness from his eyes.

But Danielson couldn't hear him. He was gone.

Mills waited a few minutes, scanning the approaches from town to make sure there were no more Kreelans about. Then he wearily gathered up the remaining rifle magazines from Danielson's combat gear. As an afterthought, he took his grenades, as well.

Picking up the sniper rifle, Mills slung it over his shoulder. Then, holding his assault rifle at the ready, he moved out the rear of the barn and followed after the others toward the creek.

He wasn't quite halfway there when he heard the sound of gunfire and children screaming.

* * *

Valentina waded silently through the water, looking into the forbidding darkness of the woods on the other side of the creek. She stepped slowly onto the soft soil on the opposite bank, taking care that the water in her boots and trousers made no noise.

After she reached the other side, she moved about ten meters into the trees. She paused for a moment behind one of the larger trees and opened up her senses to her surroundings. Nothing suspicious appeared in the computer-generated image of the night vision optics as she looked around, nor did she hear anything unusual over the hammering of Mills and Danielson firing their weapons. Her nose wasn't attuned to the unique smells of the plant and animal life on Alger's World, but she couldn't pick out anything like the faint musky scent ascribed to the Kreelans.

It looked clear. And yet...

The firing at the barn stopped, and she knew that she'd run out of time. If Mills and Danielson survived, they would catch up. The analytic part of her mind told her that she'd probably never see Mills again. Her heart wanted to tear her mind to pieces.

"No time," she whispered to herself. Then she whistled, a low, soft sound amazingly similar to one of the species of birds she'd heard the morning before, welcoming the sun.

Looking back toward the creek, she saw small shadows crossing the water. They stopped and looked back toward the barn as alien screams echoed across the field before a larger shadow, Steph, urged them onward.

Faster now, the children crossed the creek, and Valentina gestured for them to kneel down behind her. She wanted to gather them all together before they moved farther into the woods and make sure she didn't lose any of them.

Seeing that Allison was crossing the creek, followed by Steph, Valentina turned to lead her charges deeper into the woods where they might find a defensible position.

That was when the warrior with the dead eyes appeared right in front of her, out of thin air.

Valentina didn't allow surprise to overcome her. She simply reacted. With barely a conscious thought, she squeezed the trigger on her rifle, whose muzzle was a mere hand's breadth from the warrior's armored chest.

The gun spat rounds at the alien, but the bullets simply fell to the ground in small bubbling pools of molten metal.

Forcing herself to accept the impossible as fact, Valentina swung the rifle in a brutal butt stroke that would have shattered the jaw of a human opponent.

The Kreelan warrior danced out the way, barely, and then held out her hand as if she was going to place her palm on Valentina's chest.

"Oh!" Valentina gasped as she felt her heart pierced by frozen spikes. To anyone else, the pain would have been unimaginable and instantly debilitating, but few human beings had ever endured pain such as Valentina had and survived. It slowed her down, but didn't stop her.

She lunged at the alien, feinting with a lightning-fast open hand strike to her armored chest with her left hand before lashing out with her right elbow at the Kreelan's head.

The alien was taken by surprise, apparently convinced that Valentina would go down from the ethereal attack on her heart. The warrior parried the feint and tried to dodge the strike to her head, but didn't move quite fast enough.

Valentina grinned savagely through the searing pain in her chest as her elbow smashed against the Kreelan's temple, knocking her backward.

But the warrior moved with the force of the blow, pirouetting around to again face Valentina, and the icy grip around Valentina's heart intensified.

Despite all that the implants given her by the Terran Intelligence Service when she had become a covert agent could do, she was still a mortal human. Her heart constricted so far now that it was barely beating at all, Valentina collapsed into the loamy soil, unconscious.

Behind her, the children ran screaming, but they didn't get far. A line of warriors appeared from the woods, clawed hands outstretched toward their victims.

Still in the middle of the creek, Steph watched in horror as Valentina went down and the children were taken. The warriors had some sort of stunning device, and the children crumpled to the ground after being touched with it.

Allison, who had stayed back with Steph to let the younger children cross, was the first to react. Grabbing Steph's hand, she ran back the way they had come, in the direction of the barn, which had fallen disturbingly silent.

Without a word, Steph followed her, the two of them splashing noisily through the water as they ran. In half a dozen steps they had reached the shore.

Then *she* appeared out of nowhere, right in front of them. Steph raised her rifle to fire, but dropped it as her heart felt as if it was being ripped from her chest by an icy hand.

With a cry of agony, she collapsed to the ground and lay still.

"No!" Allison screamed in terrified rage as she charged right into the warrior. She had no weapon, nothing to fight with except the satchel with the precious radio, which was now useless. There would be no one to operate it.

Taking the strap off her shoulder, Allison threw the satchel at the warrior, who simply plucked it from the air and tossed it aside.

Screaming in fury at the loss of her parents, her world, the children she had saved, and now the friends who had come to save them, Allison hammered against the warrior's armor with her fists until they bled.

The Kreelan simply stood there, looking down at Allison her face a dark mask against the night sky.

Finally spent, Allison fell to her knees, sobbing.

She didn't see the warrior take a small wand from her belt. Leaning down, the warrior touched it to Allison's shoulder, and she slumped to the ground beside Steph, unconscious.

* * *

"Lord God, no," Mills breathed as he watched the warriors wade through the water from the woods, bearing Valentina and the children.

Two more picked up Steph and Allison from near the feet of the warrior that he knew must be *her*.

He had dropped to the ground in the field behind the barn as soon as he'd heard the gunfire from across the creek. He quickly exchanged his assault rifle for the larger sniper rifle and its advanced scope while his gut churned with fear and something worse. Self-loathing. He knew the right decision was to stay alive. But it took all his will not to pull the trigger and kill as many of the Kreelans as he could, starting with the warrior who had taken down Steph and Allison, before they came for him.

The thing that stayed his hand was that he had seen the strange warrior toss aside the satchel that contained the precious radio. That was the key to everything, and was more valuable than his honor or his life, because it represented the only chance for Valentina and the others, for any of the surviving humans on this planet.

He watched the aliens through the sniper rifle's scope as the warriors formed a line and slowly marched off through the field to his left, bearing the children and the two women.

When he turned back to look for the warrior with the dead eyes, he found her standing where she had been on the bank of the creek. Except now she was staring right at him.

He pulled his eye away from the scope for a moment to make sure he wasn't imagining things, then looked again.

She was still there, looking right at him, and a shiver of dread ran down his spine.

He had fought another warrior like her who had one of the strange devices affixed to her collar, which seemed to signify some sort of special warrior or class of warriors. That warrior had been huge, nearly a giant compared to Mills, who himself was a big and powerful man. He had fought her twice in hand to hand combat, once on Keran and once on Saint Petersburg. He knew that she had only been toying with him, but he had learned that any warrior wearing a device like that on her collar was one to be feared. This one perhaps more than the big warrior he had fought before. Just as Allison had said, this one seemed to be completely devoid of expression, and looking into her face made him want to turn and run.

She continued to stare at him, but when he blinked his eye, she was gone. He pulled his eye away from the scope, thinking that she was rushing toward him across the field, but there was nothing. No one. She had just vanished.

"Bloody hell." He got to his knees to get a better look, sweeping the scope along the creek and the woods.

There was no sign of her.

His heart in his throat, he turned to watch the line of warriors bearing away their captives. They were heading in the direction of where Valentina had thought the Kreelans had a big encampment in the woods on the far side of town.

After they disappeared down the road, he wearily got up and trudged to the creek to retrieve the satchel. Taking out the cobbled-together radio and the small console, he breathed a sigh of relief as he turned it on and the indicators glowed green. The radio was working, and when the fleet arrived, he would hopefully be able to communicate with them.

Checking his chronometer, he saw that only fourteen hours remained before the fleet was scheduled to jump in.

Switching the radio off and carefully replacing it in the satchel, he strapped the bag to his combat belt and then slung the sniper rifle over his shoulder.

Picking up his assault rifle, he stood for a moment, alone in the empty field, feeling like he was the last free human on the entire planet.

He needed to find a place to hide so he could plan his next move. After a moment's hesitation, he broke into a jog, following a parallel path to the ones the Kreelans and their captives had taken.

* * *

From her vantage point in the shadows of the charred ruins of the human building where the skirmish line of warriors had earlier fought the two humans, Ku'ar-Marekh watched the large human warrior move at a fast trot across the open field.

He had Tesh-Dar's mark upon him, something that the rank and file warriors could not discern, but that to a warrior priestess such as herself was like a mental scent. That he had fought Tesh-Dar in personal combat did not mean that Ku'ar-Marekh could not challenge him. It simply meant that he might prove more worthy of her skills.

She had let him go as an entertainment, to see what the human warrior might do, just as she had indulged herself by following and being followed by the female pup. Such indulgences were all that she had left.

As for the rest of the human pups taken this night, Ku'ar-Marekh had come to the conclusion that her First had been misguided in believing that they should not be put to the arena until they had matured. If the One they sought were here, he - for it had to be a male, Ku'ar-Marekh knew - would stand out in the arena. They sought one not of their race, but whose blood would sing.

There was no trace of the Bloodsong in any of these creatures, and there was no reason to spare them from the blade. Perhaps they would be more worthy to die by a warrior's hand if they were older and stronger, but Ku'ar-Marekh was not inclined to make the conquest of this world into an experiment.

After reaching that conclusion, she had ordered that the children and the humans who had come from the sky be gathered up from their hideout. Unless their blood sang, they would die in the arenas, for that was the will of the Empress.

Waiting until the big human had crossed the road, Ku'ar-Marekh closed her eyes, imagining her spartan quarters in the woods near the *Kalai-Il*.

Then her body vanished, leaving behind only the silent darkness that would soon give way to dawn.

SIXTY-FIVE

Lionel Jackson watched through hooded eyes as the alien warriors continued to sweep through the concentration camp in a whirlwind of building and cleaning.

They had come late the night before, hundreds of them, seemingly hell-bent on a sudden "do right" campaign to ease the suffering of their human prisoners, and had worked tirelessly by torchlight. The warriors mucked out the human waste and built proper latrines, quadrupled the size of the camp by extending the fences, brought in a supply of fresh water, and now were building what passed for primitive housing.

They'd also brought in a great deal of food, an odd assortment of vegetables and fruits that they must have collected from the farms around the town, along with game animals that they distributed throughout the compound. They even built fires over which the meat could be cooked.

But what came as the greatest shock was that they dropped a few knives, every one of which looked to be unique and with the incredibly sharp blades shared by all of their edged weapons, with each animal they brought, apparently expecting the humans to use them to gut and skin the carcasses.

Of course, a few enterprising souls had gotten the idea that they could use the knives as weapons to fight the Kreelans.

Unfortunately for them, the aliens enjoyed this development immensely. Every time someone had tried to attack one of the warriors, other warriors formed a ring around the combatants, who then fought in a battle to the death.

In two cases, the humans had won, and the Kreelans let them go about their business after hauling away the bodies of the dead warriors.

As for the humans who weren't so lucky, their bodies were hauled out along with the rest of the waste.

The first glow of the rising sun was just visible on the horizon when the gates swung open and a group of warriors entered, carrying two women and eleven children.

Curious, Jackson made his way toward them. He ignored the bustling alien warriors, just as they ignored him.

The warriors shooed away some people who had occupied one of the newly built shelters and carefully, almost gently, lay the two women down on the bed of leaves, then lay the children down beside them before turning and marching away, back through the gate.

Pushing his way through the sudden crowd that had gathered around the new arrivals, Jackson felt his pulse quicken as he looked at the two women. They were wearing Marine combat uniforms.

The fleet's here, he thought, or it's coming. Has to be.

He knelt down beside one of them, a blond, and did a double-take as he got a better look at her face in growing light.

"I don't believe it," he whispered.

Someone else pointed at the woman. "Isn't that Stephanie Guillaume?"

A low murmur ran through the circle of people, expanding through the camp as more people came to see what was happening.

"What's she doing here?"

Steph's eyes fluttered open at the sound.

"Miss Guillaume?" Jackson asked. "Can you hear me?"

"Yeah," she groaned, rubbing her temples. "My head's killing me."

Jackson grinned, but there wasn't any humor in it. "It'll pass in half an hour or so." He reached toward the woman next to her, intending to give her a gentle shake to wake her up.

Steph grabbed his hand, stopping him. "Bad idea." Mills hadn't been the only one to read Valentina's psych profile. With Steph's clout and habit of always getting what she wanted, she'd actually seen more than Mills had. "Let her wake up on her own. Otherwise you're likely to wind up dead."

Propping herself up on her elbows, she wrinkled her nose and muttered, "My God, what's that horrible smell?"

"Us." Jackson gesturing at the filthy clothes, rags really, that he and the other prisoners were wearing. While there was now enough to eat and drink, and latrines had been dug, there weren't any showers or other means to wash their clothes or their bodies.

Beside her, Valentina shot to her feet with a startled cry, instantly assuming a combat stance. Everyone around her stumbled backward in surprise.

"Easy," Steph told her quietly as Valentina looked around, wild-eyed. "Easy. We're in a prison camp, it looks like."

"You're okay," Jackson added, impressed and not just a little frightened at the dark-haired woman, her body tight as a steel spring. "You're safe. For the moment."

After taking a deep, shuddering breath, Valentina relaxed. Slightly. "We're in the camp near Breakwater, aren't we?" Her eyes flicking rapidly across the faces around her, then settling on a group of warriors that marched by, carrying yet another load of materials to build more shelters. "My God," she whispered.

"That's doing the Almighty a bit of an injustice." Jackson favored her with a wry smile as he followed her eyes.

"Work of the Devil's more like it," someone in the crowd spat.

Steph took a closer look at Jackson. She judged him to be in his mid-fifties, with close-cropped hair and a body that, despite the deprivations he'd suffered, was lean and tough. It matched the look in his eyes. "Former military?"

He nodded. "Twenty-six years in the Terran Army. I saw enough during the first war with Saint Petersburg and some other actions, and Alger's World looked like the perfect place to start a quiet new life. The homesteading provisions let me settle down on a nice chunk of land." He looked wistful. "It was a nice place until the Kreelans burned it to the ground."

"You weren't in the Territorial Army here, were you?"

"Yes, I was. I was the first sergeant for one of the companies up north, near Gateway." He shook his head. "We killed a lot of warriors, but there were just too many. We got as many people out of the city as we could before it was surrounded and cut off. Most got away, but not all."

He paused a moment, remembering the screams and pleas for help of those who'd been trapped, an eerie, distant keening of the doomed. "The corridor we were holding was the last passage out of the city. But we finally had to get out of there. There were a few more lucky souls who somehow managed to break through the enemy cordon and followed us out, but that was it." He gestured at the people around them in the camp. "I thought everyone we'd left behind had been slaughtered, but they weren't. They're bringing them here."

"What happened to you after that?"

"They began to hunt us down. After we finally broke contact and retreated from Gateway, I had five-hundred people with me who wanted to fight. I divided them up into five smaller groups and sent them out to cause trouble for the enemy in the nearby towns." He shrugged. "I never heard from any of them again.

"Our group did well for a while. We killed warriors in droves, but they just kept coming at us, like they enjoyed the idea of getting killed." He shook his head in disbelief. "Once a group of them made contact with us, they'd stay after us until we wiped them out. They never broke or ran like humans normally would. You know, live again to fight another day? Not them."

"So how did they get you?"

He laughed. It was a bitter sound. "I guess they finally decided they'd had enough. There were only forty-seven of us left, out of the hundred and sixty-five that I started with after I sent the other groups off. They surrounded us and just came charging in.

"But they didn't come to kill us. They came to capture us, just like you. They hit us with those stun batons of theirs and that was that. Then they stripped us of our weapons and had us join that little procession down the main road. Most of those folks are from Gateway and the other towns north of here, although there are a lot of people here from Caitlin, the other big town to the south.

"We marched for three days, day and night," he went on. "The Kreelans left you alone if you kept up. If you couldn't and fell out of line, they just killed you. No whips or yelling. There was just one type of motivation. Some of the folks here had to march longer than that."

About a third of the people in the circle around them nodded, their faces haunted by the horrors they'd seen on the march.

"And that's when the real fun began." Jackson looked at a party of warriors that was hauling in fresh dirt to cover up the sodden, waste-strewn areas of the camp. "They shoved us all in here, into what was nothing more than a huge livestock pen with a crude wooden fence. There were at least eight, maybe ten thousand people here when we arrived, literally with room only to stand. There weren't any latrines, nothing. It was reeking, filthy mass of desperate people. The Kreelans just shoved us in and started closing the gates, and anyone who was in the way, they started cutting them down. That started a stampede, and I don't have any idea how many were trampled to death." He took a deep breath. It was the worst experience, even in combat, he'd ever endured. "And a lot of folks couldn't take it anymore, and decided it would be better to hop the fence and have the warriors put them out of their misery."

Steph turned to look at the fence that surrounded the camp, beyond which stood a cordon of warriors, their attention riveted to the humans in the camp.

"That's when I gave up hope," Jackson went on quietly. "I could feel it dying inside me. I lost my wife and two sons. My friends. Everything that I'd tried to build here. And I knew I was going to die in this stinking cesspool." He looked at Steph. "It took me a day to work my way to the edge of the crowd. I was going to have the warriors work their sword magic on me, too.

"And then, last night, everything changed." He gestured around him. "There were shuttles coming in all night. Some of them brought more humans, but most of them carried warriors. They and some of the others who were already here started cleaning up this pit." He managed a smile. "I guess it must've been for your arrival."

"It doesn't matter," a woman said as she ceaselessly twirled a lock of her dirty hair through her fingers. "We're all dead, anyway."

Everyone else was silent. They looked down at their feet, each a study in total defeat.

Steph turned to her. "That's not true. The fleet's coming."

Only a few people looked up at her words. She glanced at Valentina, who shrugged.

"Didn't you hear me?" Steph said, louder now. "The fleet's coming!"

More looked up at her now, out of curiosity, not out of hope. Steph glanced at Valentina again and saw her frown. "What?"

Valentina didn't speak until another party of alien warriors had passed, then said, "They may not be able to find us, remember?"

"Goddammit!" Steph got unsteadily to her feet. She stumbled, still suffering from the after-effects of the stun, and Jackson caught her arm to steady her.

"People, listen to me!" Anger was burning inside her. The children began to wake up from her shouting. "The most powerful fleet the Confederation has ever assembled is coming here!" She wasn't worried about the Kreelans hearing her. In all the encounters with them so far, there had been no indication that any of them understood any human language, or cared. "It's on its way right now, and..." She glanced at her chronometer. "...it's going to arrive in less than six hours. They're going to wipe the Kreelan fleet from orbit, and then three assault divisions are going to land and do the same to the warriors here on the planet."

"Why didn't they come already?" A man in the crowd shouted angrily as he stepped forward to confront Steph. Valentina moved slightly closer in case he decide to get violent. "Look at us!" he shouted. "Just look at us! Look at what they made us go through, how many of us have died at the hands of those beasts!" Tears were running down the man's face now. "Why should we believe the bloody fleet's coming now?"

"Because," Steph said evenly, stepping right up to the man and placing her hands on his shoulders, "my husband is in that fleet." She looked around at the other faces near her. "Some of you may have heard of him. His name is Ichiro Sato."

Recognition dawned on almost every face. Sato's name was one of the most well-known in the Confederation. While she was estranged from him, she hadn't lost track of what he had been doing. She still loved him. And believed in him. "He's commanding the most powerful ships we've ever built, battleships that are more than a match for anything the Kreelans have. And he's not going to leave until every one of these blue-skinned bitches is dead."

"But why didn't the Confederation come earlier?" the man asked. "Why did they wait so long, until now?"

"Because they couldn't," Valentina answered. "We've been fighting and losing battles on almost two dozen colonies. President McKenna is taking a terrible gamble on this attack by pulling ships away from every one of those systems to put together an assault fleet big enough to beat the Kreelan forces here. She's even stripped Home Fleet over Earth down to the bone." She stared into the frightened, desperate faces around her. "If the Kreelans attacked Earth in any real force, we could lose it. That's the risk she's taking."

"Too bad for them," someone sneered. "They've had it easy."

"Too bad for humanity, you mean," Valentina answered icily. "If we lose Earth, we lose the war. And you should know better than anyone what that would mean. Every colony would be exterminated."

"So what are we going to do?"

The question came not from the crowd of adults, which by now had become a thick ring of hundreds of people, trying to hear and see what was going on, but from the voice of a tired teenage girl. Allison.

"There's nothing we can do," Jackson said quietly. "We just have to..."

"Bullshit," Steph snarled. "We didn't go through hell getting down here just to give up."

"Steph," Valentina interjected, "we don't have a lot of options. The radio's gone. There's no way to communicate with the fleet. Mills and the others..."

She bit her lip, unable to say what she knew must be true. That Mills was gone.

"I don't care," Steph rounded on her, eyes blazing. "I am not just going to be herded into one of those rings and slaughtered like Ichiro's first crew was!" More than anyone else, she understood the nightmare that her husband had endured as a young midshipman when humanity had made its first contact with the Kreelans. He still had nightmares, at least the last time they had shared a bed, months ago now. She bitterly shoved the memory aside, wishing more than anything else that he was here right now to hold her.

But she knew he was coming. And that was enough.

"If we're going to die," she went on, "then let's die doing something worth dying for." She looked at Allison and the other children who were riveted to the ongoing discussion. "At least we can try and get the children out of here."

"*She* won't let us go now." Allison's face, for once, displayed outright despair. While it had been a nightmare in many ways, it had been nothing compared to this awful-smelling place, surrounded by warriors, and knowing that death awaited all of them.

Steph moved over and wrapped her arms around the girl, who returned the gesture, holding on tightly.

"It doesn't matter what that warrior wants," Steph said, her conviction growing with every word. "Somehow, we're going to-"

At that moment a deep gong reverberated through the camp. It was a mournful sound, and it sent a shiver down Steph's spine.

A cry arose from near the entrance to the camp as the gates opened and a phalanx of warriors marched in. Without further ceremony, they grabbed the nearest twenty people before they could run, then herded them out, the gates closing behind them.

Running to the fence near the gates, Valentina, Steph, and Jackson watched the prisoners and their escorts move down the trail that led to the arena complex at the town square. From where the three stood, the top of the large stone construct at the center was just visible through the trees, but they couldn't see the arenas themselves.

Then they heard it, the low murmur of a great number of voices, coming from the direction of the arenas. It had been masked by the moaning and bustle in the camp. But the humans had fallen silent after their fellows had been taken, not wanting to draw attention to themselves as they moved toward the rear of the camp's enclosure.

The Kreelan warriors in the camp continued to work, but all of them periodically glanced in the direction of the arenas.

Fifteen minutes later, as the sun rose full above the horizon, the gong sounded again. Valentina, with her sharp eyes, could see that it was affixed to the top of the stone structure, rung by a single warrior.

Another warrior stood there, silhouetted against the brightening horizon, a cloak fluttering in the light morning breeze. Valentina knew without a doubt who it was. The warrior, the one who had nearly torn Valentina's heart from her chest with nothing but a thought, was looking right at her.

As the sound of the gong faded, the warrior turned away to face the arenas, and a bone-chilling roar from thousands of warriors, unseen beyond the trees, filled the air.

SIXTY-SIX

Ku'ar-Markekh stood upon the *Kalai-Il*, her eyes fixed upon the unusual human female who held much promise as a challenge to Ku'ar-Marekh's skills. She had decided to face the human animal with only sword and claw, for this would bring the Empress the greatest glory, and would also give Ku'ar-Marekh a chance for an honorable death.

But she would save her own combat until her most junior warriors had blooded themselves against other humans. Those of Her Children who had not yet had a chance to fight one of the animals had been cast first in the lottery of the Challenge. Once they had fought, Ku'ar-Marekh would take to the arena against the female warrior and perhaps some of her companions. Anything less would be no contest at all.

Turning away from the human who stared back at her from inside the holding pen, Ku'ar-Markh faced into the rising sun as the last echoes of the gong faded.

The warriors roared, their excitement over the coming combats pulsing through the Bloodsong.

She gave them a moment to express their anticipation, for Challenges such as this were rare in the Empire outside times of war. The battles fought here would be to the death, and every warrior wanted her chance to fight for the honor of the Empress.

At last raising her arms, Ku'ar-Marekh commanded them to silence. Thousands of warriors knelt as one, crashing their armored left fists over their right breasts.

The litany the priestess spoke was older than the Empire itself. Its words were simple and brief, the core of every warrior's heart.

"As it has been," she began as the human prisoners were brought forth, four of them to the entrance of each of the five arenas where the first challengers already waited, "and so shall it always be, let the Challenge begin."

"In Her Name," the warriors echoed solemnly, "let it be so."

A single human was forced into each arena. They were shown a table that held a variety of edged weapons, and the waiting challenger was honor-bound to choose a similar weapon. They only had a single turn of the small hour-glass that Ku'ar-Marekh's new First, Esah-Kuran, held to decide upon a weapon.

Two chose swords, two refused to decide, and one tried to flee the arena. The one who tried to run was cut down by a *shrekka*.

This prompted the two humans who had not chosen weapons to do so.

Ku'ar-Marekh nodded in approval. They could die like meat animals, or they could fight for their honor. Should a human survive, they would be allowed to rest until the other humans had taken a turn in the arena. Then the survivors again would have to fight.

All would eventually die, unless The One came forth. But Ku'ar-Marekh did not believe that would happen here.

Nor, in her cold heart, did she care.

Another human was brought forward to take the dishonored one's place. This one, seeing its companions in the other arenas, made the choice of honor and chose a sword.

Stepping down from the *Kalai-Il*, Ku'ar-Marekh took the place that tradition demanded atop the dais at the center of the middle of the five arenas.

Looking out upon her warriors and their reluctant human challengers, she bellowed, "Begin!"

* * *

After Valentina and the others had been taken, Mills had taken the risk of running across the fields to beat the group of warriors carrying the women and children.

As he neared the woods, he could hear the pitiful moans and cries of the human prisoners, and his nose was overpowered with the stench of human waste. He forced himself to slow down as he entered the treeline, moving slowly to remain silent.

When he came within sight of the camp, he unslung the sniper rifle and took a closer look. He saw what must have been thousands of people milling around inside an enclosure bounded by a very crude wooden fence. Outside of that stood a cordon of warriors.

As he watched them, he noted that they never turned around to look back into the woods. Their attention was entirely fixed on their prisoners, thinking there was nothing to fear behind them.

"You've got that a bit wrong, dearies." During the run from the barn, Mills had been thinking of different plans he could set into action to help free the prisoners, depending on what he found.

Looking at the camp, he settled on one of those options. A little explosive diversion that he would light off when the time was right.

He had eight grenades, which could be set to detonate a variety of ways, including by remote. He had used them against the Kreelans before during the fighting he'd seen after the original Saint Petersburg operation, and the aliens had never interfered with the detonation signals like they did with other tech like the comm and data links.

Leaving the sniper rifle behind a tree, he crept forward to the trees nearest the Kreelan guards. Moving parallel to what he took to be the rear of the conpound's fence, he set seven grenades at roughly equal intervals, keeping a single grenade in reserve. He didn't expect they would kill many of the warriors, but it would give them a nasty surprise.

He placed the last grenade and was making his way back to where he'd left the sniper rifle when he heard a commotion at the far side of the camp near the entry gates.

Taking out his binoculars, he watched as warriors brought in Valentina and the others, setting them down under one of the newly built shelters. His stomach knotted up at the sight of their limp bodies carried in the aliens' arms, but he told himself that they must still be alive.

Forcing himself to stop lingering and watching for movement from the women and children, he focused on finding a spot in the woods that gave him a good view into the camp, but that wasn't right on top of the Kreelans.

It wasn't easy, but at last he found a small knoll a couple hundred meters from the camp that had a narrow but clear view through the compound up to the gates. He could see the shelter that Valentina and the others were in, and watched tensely through the scope on the sniper rifle the crowd that had gathered around the newcomers. He saw a rustle of movement among the people around the shelter, then saw Steph's face briefly through the mass of bobbing heads.

Then the crowd seemed to flinch back, with some of those closest to the women and children actually falling backward. Mills couldn't help but chuckle as he saw Valentina leap to her feet, her hands raised, ready for a fight.

"That's my girl." He felt like a spring steel band had just been removed from around his chest, such was his relief that she was alive.

He saw the two of them talking to a black man for quite some time, then Steph became agitated and was shouting something at the people clustered around them.

He could only wonder what was going on, but he felt another wave of relief as he saw the children awaken, and smiled when he caught a glimpse of Allison.

Then the gates opened and a group of warriors came in, seizing a bunch of people who were unlucky enough to be in easy reach. The unlucky prisoners were frog-marched out the gates, which closed behind them, disappearing along the trail that led toward the big stone structure and the arenas.

"Hell," Mills whispered. *This is what must have happened at the end on Keran,* he thought. The survivors of the initial slaughter were used as unwilling opponents in the arenas. And when the last had been killed...

Shoving that thought aside, he checked his chronometer. A little less than six hours were left until the fleet jumped in. There wasn't much time. He needed to let Valentina and Steph know he was here, but had no idea how to do it.

Watching through the scope, he saw them return to the shelter from where they had run to the fence. He had a much clearer view now, because almost everyone else in the camp had moved toward the back of the enclosure, closer to him. Valentina was talking to the black man, and Steph leaned down and picked up her helmet. He saw her detach something that looked like a set of eyeglasses and put them on. Then she went to stand a bit behind Valentina, and Allison came up to hold her hand.

She put her vidcam gear back on, Mills realized.

An idea was forming at the back of his brain, but it didn't gel until he pulled his eye away from the big rifle's scope. One of the controls on the tiny panel was for a laser designator that was normally used to provide the exact range to the target. It could also be used to direct guided rounds fired from the rifle or larger weapons from another platform. Unfortunately, it was one of the technologies that the Kreelans frequently nulled out in battle through whatever mysterious means they used.

Mills turned it on, and in the scope an indicator lit up. He put the crosshairs on the head of one of the warriors guarding the camp pulled the trigger back just enough to activate the laser.

The display read 187 meters. The laser was working.

The only trick was that it was completely invisible to the unaided eye.

But Steph's eyes weren't unaided. She was looking at the world through the artificially enhanced view of her vidcam display.

* * *

"Good God." Steph looked toward the commotion coming from the Kreelans gathered around the arenas. She couldn't see anything, for the complex was masked by trees and the buildings on this side of the town square, but she could hear them. Her flesh crawled at the roar of what must be thousands of alien voices.

She felt a small hand take hold of hers, squeezing it tightly. Allison. Her eyes were wide and her face stricken with fear. She had been strong, incredibly strong for someone her age, but she was smart enough to know what awaited them down the dirt path that led from the gates. And she knew that her special relationship with the warrior leader wouldn't spare her.

"Don't worry, honey." Steph had to raise her voice to be heard above the din. Her vidcam was running now, and she planned to just leave it on to record whatever was to come. She would never get the chance to edit it or be able to tell the story of the people here, but with a little luck perhaps the Marines who landed would eventually find it.

She thought of Ichiro and wished more than anything that she could speak to him one last time, just to tell him how much she still loved him. She bit her tongue to take her mind away from the tears she felt welling up in her eyes. "We'll be all right." She squeezed Allison's hand. "I promise."

Allison nodded in jerky movements, and her face twitched in an attempt at a smile, but that was all. She accepted Steph's words for what they were, a comforting lie.

Looking up again as the sound of the alien voices peaked, movement on Valentina's back caught her eye. She was standing just ahead of Steph, and at first Steph thought it was some sort of insect.

Then she realized it couldn't be. It was a small, bright green dot, and it pulsed rhythmically as it moved up and down Valentina's spine.

"What the..." She flipped up the tiny visor that projected an enhanced view of the scene she was recording.

The mysterious dot vanished.

Flipping the vidcam visor back down, the dot reappeared. Now, instead of moving up and down Valentina's spine, the dot was moving slowly from one of her buttocks to the other, pulsing on and off, on and off.

"Oh, my God." Turning around, she looked across the mass of people crushed into the back of the compound, trying to avoid being the next ones to be taken to the arenas.

At first she saw nothing, and then there it was. A bright flash, aimed at her now, coming from somewhere in the woods. "Mills?" Then, realizing that whoever it was couldn't hear her, she said his name again, over-emphasizing the movement of her lips and tongue.

Two flashes.

"You're alive?"

Again, two flashes.

"Blink once."

One flash.

"Valentina!" Steph said, a surge of joy and adrenaline shooting through her system as she stepped backward and reached for the other woman, not wanting to lose sight of the spot in the forest where Mills was hiding. "Valentina!"

"What is it?" Valentina was beside her.

"You're not going to believe this," Steph snatched off her vidcam and carefully placed it on Valentina's head, "but Mills is alive!"

She stepped behind Valentina and gently turned her head toward the spot in the woods. Steph didn't want to draw unwanted attention from the warriors who were still working in a frenzy throughout the camp by simply pointing.

"Steph, you know as well as I do that he's gone." Valentina's voice was wooden with pent-up grief, but she was enough of a realist to know that Mills was dead. She thought Steph had gone off the deep end, even as Steph's hands guided her to look toward the woods. "He couldn't have..."

She stopped, her mouth hanging open as she stood still, staring.

"Do you see it?"

"Yes." A smile lit up Valentina's face as she watched the merrily blinking light coming from the woods. "Oh, God, yes! He must be using the laser designator on my rifle!"

"What is it?" Jackson was looking in the direction that the two women were looking, but couldn't see anything.

"Our team leader." Steph leaned over to speak closer to his ear over the tumult from the arenas. "We were sure he was dead, but he's alive!"

"Thank God." Valentina began to play a game of twenty questions with Mills, who could only answer "yes" or "no."

* * *

Mills gritted his teeth in frustration, wishing that they had a better way of communicating, that he could tell Valentina what he needed to say. He had once heard of an ancient communications code, Morse, he thought it was, that would have worked well for this situation, but neither he nor Valentina knew it. So he had to be content with Valentina mouthing questions in hopes that he could lip-read what she was saying, then he would answer yes or no, two pulses of the laser or one.

Valentina immediately realized that he wasn't there just to let them know he was alive, but that he had a plan to help get them out. After what had seemed like forever, but had only taken about five minutes, she had figured out what he had in mind.

"Beautiful and brilliant." He grinned as Valentina blew him a kiss before turning to Steph and the black man, who had the look about him of someone who'd been in the military, and began to tell them what she'd learned.

Steph made her pause for a moment, then took the vidcam gear from Valentina and put it on Allison. Then she aimed Allison's gaze toward Mills, and he shot her a few blinks with the laser.

The girl put her hands to her face and burst into tears. But when she took her hands away a moment later, he could see that they were tears of joy, and her mouth kept forming his name.

Then Steph took the vidcam gear from Allison and put it back on herself. She gave Mills the thumbs-up sign as Allison gathered the other children around her and began to tell them what was happening, her hands gesticulating wildly. All of them turned to look toward the woods. Toward him.

"Hang in there, sweeties." Mills prayed the fleet would be on time, and that he could contact them. "Just a few more hours."

* * *

"We've got to make sure everyone knows," Valentina told Jackson. "Mills thinks that when the fleet arrives, the Kreelans will be distracted. When that happens, he's going to try to contact the fleet to let them know where we are. That's his first priority. Then he's going to take down as many of the warriors along the back fence as he can."

"Then we make a break for it," Jackson finished for her. He looked around at the people who were still crowded fearfully at the back of the compound. "I don't know how far we'll get with this many warriors guarding us, but it's better than being slaughtered like cattle."

As he spoke, there was a sudden spike in the volume of the nearby Kreelans watching the arenas. Then the huge gong sounded again, and the warriors instantly fell silent.

"Uh-oh." Steph wasn't sure what the silence meant, but doubted it was anything good.

"Get the children back." Valentina took Allison's hand and pulled her toward the rear of the enclosure. As she approached the people at the edge of the crowd, she shouted, "Let the children move to the back!"

"Go to hell." A well-muscled man who stood a head taller than Valentina gave her the finger.

She stepped closer, still holding Allison's hand, and stabbed her free hand, flattened like a blade, into his throat in a lightning-fast thrust. It was a blow that could easily have killed him, but she only intended to make a point. Literally. He collapsed to the ground, gagging. "Let the children through!" "Now!"

Those nearby, many of whom looked at the man with undisguised contempt, stepped aside and offered welcoming hands to help the children.

"No!" Allison begged as Valentina tried to guide her after the younger children. "I want to stay with you!"

"Allison," Valentina told her, kneeling down to look Allison in the eyes, "you can't. What I have to do now..."

"Look!" Steph pointed toward the gate. Everyone looked up.

The warriors who had taken the people earlier had returned. To everyone's shock, one of the men who'd been taken in the first group was with them. He was bloody and battered, but alive.

The gates opened, and they marched in, stopping just inside. One of them motioned for the man to continue inside, and as one the warriors bowed their heads as he moved through their ranks and into the relative freedom of the compound.

The warriors remained where they were.

Valentina waited to make sure the warriors weren't going to rush forward to seize more victims before she ran to where the man collapsed under the nearest shelter. Steph and Jackson were right behind her. As was Allison.

The rest of the crowd hung back, still fearful of being taken by the warriors.

"What happened?" Valentina asked the man, who was slim and wiry, his head clean-shaven. Steph rushed over from where she had grabbed a container of water in another shelter and handed it to the man, who drank from it greedily.

"They made us fight," he explained after chugging down half the water. He had a gash in his scalp and a set of puncture wounds in his left side. Valentina pulled out her medical kit and began applying an antibacterial salve to the wounds as he went on, "It's one on one, to the death. No point in trying to run. If you don't fight, they just kill you and bring up someone else."

"What style of combat are they using?" Jackson asked grimly.

The man laughed. "You choose your own poison, Swords, knives. Other stuff I don't have a name for. Just hands and feet if you like, I suppose. But no guns or anything like that."

"What did you do?"

"I used a knife." He grinned. "That's what I was in for."

"What do you mean?" Valentina asked.

"Prison. I was in for murder. Stabbed a guy. Did the same thing to that warrior bitch in the arena, although she put up more of a fight." He shrugged. "Sort of ironic, huh?"

"I guess you could say that." Valentina accepted the cold logic of it. A killer would stand the best chance of surviving against the Kreelans. In this war there wasn't much of a distinction between killers such as Mills and herself, and a murderer such as this man. Their fight was for more than morality or justice, it was for the survival of the human race. "I can't say that you've atoned for your sins, my friend," she said as she finished with the first aid kit, "but it certainly didn't hurt."

"They're waiting." Steph eyed the warriors, who stared back. The leader stepped forward, a hand on the handle of her sword.

Valentina stood up and looked at them, then at the mass of people muttering nervously behind her. She held up her hand to the warriors, hoping they'd understand, before moving close enough to the crowd that they could hear her.

"I need volunteers," she shouted. "People who can fight hand to hand. The fleet will arrive in a few hours, and we've got to buy some time. If you fight and win," she gestured toward the former inmate who gave them a wave, "you'll get to live." *At least for a while*, she thought darkly, doubting that the Kreelans would simply let go any survivors. "If we don't choose to fight, they'll choose for us!"

A young man, deeply tanned and with shoulders as broad as Mills, stepped forward. Then two more. A woman moved up from behind the front row. Then more.

There was hope now, Valentina knew, seeing the determination in their eyes. Most of those who stepped forward had been fighting the Kreelans since the invasion began.

Valentina took the first nineteen volunteers, then turned and strode toward the warriors, pausing momentarily to talk to Steph. "Get as many of the others as you can organized into groups of twenty for when the warriors come back." Looking at the survivor of the first round, she added, "Hopefully we'll do a bit better than one out of twenty."

"God, Valentina," Steph said, squeezing Valentina's hand. "Be careful."

"Don't go." Allison threw her arms around Valentina. "Please."

Valentina gently pushed Allison away and put a hand on the girl's cheek. "This is the only way we have any control over this. And I have no intention of dying. Not today."

She leaned forward and kissed Allison on the forehead. Then she turned and looked toward the woods where Mills lay hidden.

"I'll be back." She waved at him before turning away and leading the others to where the Kreelans stood waiting.

SIXTY-SEVEN

Ku'ar-Marekh watched as the next group of humans was brought forth. She noted that the female human warrior, the one who was of special interest to her, was in this group.

She was pleased, or as close to being so as her empty heart allowed. Ku'ar-Marekh also saw that this group of humans, led by the dark-haired female, whose gaze was fixed on Ku'ar-Marekh, walked with heads held high, clearly proud and showing no fear. They carried themselves like warriors, come to do battle, and were not mere beasts waiting to be slaughtered like most of the animals in the first group.

Around the arenas, the gathered warriors who awaited their turn to fight the humans were quiet in respect, curious as to how this group of opponents would fare.

Warriors gestured for the humans to divide into five groups of four and guided them to the arenas, with the dark-haired female stepping forward onto the sands of the central one. She barely took her eyes from Ku'ar-Marekh.

The first challengers of each of the other groups moved into the other arenas to face the warriors who awaited them on the bloodied sands.

While the priestess could have taken this challenge for herself, a junior warrior had already been chosen by the lottery, and Ku'ar-Marekh would not dishonor her by claiming first right of combat.

Instead, she watched with cold eyes as the warrior, Ayan-Ye'eln, strode toward the human, then gestured toward the table where the weapons were arrayed.

The human glanced at the table, then turned to face the young warrior. Shaking her head in a gesture Ku'ar-Marekh had come to understand as a sign of negation, she raised her hands toward Ayan-Ye'eln, then clenched them into fists.

Tooth and claw.

Interesting, Ku'ar-Marekh thought to herself as Ayan-Ye'eln, understanding the human's intent, bowed her head in acceptance.

With a brief glance at Ku'ar-Marekh, the young warrior began to remove her armor, placing it carefully on the table beside the weapons arrayed there. In a moment she wore only the black garment that formed the under-layer for the armor.

She strode back to her place near the dais, then turned toward the human, flexing her hands, her black talons glittering in the sun.

The greater honor is yours, child, Ku'ar-Marekh thought approvingly. Ayan-Ye'eln was trying to even the odds for the human as best she could by removing her armor, something that was never demanded by tradition.

The human moved forward, coming to stand a few paces away from Ayan-Ye'eln, but her attention remained on Ku'ar-Marekh.

The priestess returned the human's gaze as she again raised her arms, signaling her warriors to kneel and render their salutes.

Then Ku'ar-Marekh once more spoke the words that preceded every Challenge.

"As it has been," she said, her voice carrying across the five arenas and the *Kalai-Il*, "and so shall it always be, let the Challenge begin."

"In Her Name," the warriors echoed once more, excitement plain in their voices, "let it be so."

* * *

Valentina listened as the lead warrior on the dais at the center of the arena spoke, then the other warriors answered in unison.

As they finished speaking, the huge gong sounded again and the warriors rose to their feet.

Unlike with the first group of human victims, when the Kreelans had immediately broken out in a huge uproar at the sound of the gong, this time they remained quiet.

They know we're different, Valentina thought, sensing their curious anticipation. *We're not lambs to the slaughter. Not this time.*

The warrior opposing her turned side-on with one hand extended forward and the other back, both with fingers spread. Her nails, vaguely similar to the claws of a bird of prey like an eagle that Valentina had seen once on Earth, glistened, and Valentina knew they were incredibly sharp.

Have to watch those, Valentina cautioned herself. She knew she could have chosen one of the many weapons arrayed on the table when she entered the arena, but decided not to. She had plenty of experience with knives and had trained with swords in various styles, but for one on one combat, the weapons she knew best were those that were already part of her body.

She suspected that the opposite was true for her opponent. Everything Valentina had read and seen during her brief time here indicated that the Kreelans greatly preferred edged weapons in combat. While hand to hand fighting wasn't unheard of in combat reports, it was rare.

She hoped fighting hand to hand without weapons would help achieve her main goal, which was to draw out the fight as long as she could. She felt confident she could kill the warrior quickly if she wanted to, but the longer the fights went on, the fewer people would have to set foot in the arenas before the fleet arrived.

She stood still, her body relaxed but ready, waiting for the warrior to attack.

* * *

Ku'ar-Marekh watched as Ayan-Ye'eln lunged at the human, trying to grab the animal with her leading hand before impaling her with the talons of her trailing hand. It was a basic attack that typically worked well against the humans, who seemed universally afraid of the talons of the warriors.

The priestess was impressed with the speed of the attack, but was more impressed with the human's response. In a smooth motion, the human animal sidestepped Ayan-Ye'eln's strike.

Then with one hand the human grasped the warrior's leading arm, immobilizing it, before slamming the elbow of her free arm into Ayan-Ye'eln's head.

That probably would have been enough to put the dazed warrior on the ground, but in a seamless continuation of the elbow strike, the human wrapped that arm around Ayan-Ye'eln's head, twirled her halfway around, and flipped her backwards onto the ground in a spray of sand.

It was a fluid, beautiful move, the likes of which Ku'ar-Marekh had never seen.

The human, who clearly hadn't even exerted herself, backed away a few paces as the young warrior fought to regain her senses.

A roar went up from the gathered warriors, not of anger, but of approval. Like Ku'ar-Marekh, none of them had ever seen such a fighting style, and they knew that whoever bested this human, who was clearly a formidable warrior, would bring great glory to the Empress.

That honor shall be mine, my children, Ku'ar-Marekh thought, for she did not believe that any of the warriors here could beat the human in a fair match.

Ayan-Ye'eln got to her feet, and with a roar of anger charged the human again.

* * *

Valentina continued to spar with the warrior, who became increasingly frustrated at her inability to inflict even the slightest injury on her human opponent.

The Kreelan had stopped charging like a bull, but no matter what she did, she always found herself up on the ground, spitting sand from her mouth.

Valentina had no idea how much time had passed, but she knew that the other combats for her group had ended. Seven men and women stood near the entrance to her arena, the survivors of the nineteen who had come with her to fight.

The other warriors, too, had moved in as close as they could, trying to get a glimpse of what was happening in the central arena.

The warrior, her lungs heaving now from exhaustion, came again at Valentina, and again Valentina easily deflected her attack. She hammered the warrior twice in the face with her fists, further bloodying the Kreelan's mouth and nose, before sending the warrior flying face-first into the sand.

"*Kazh!*" The warrior leader bellowed as she raised her arms in the air, and the warriors watching the fight instantly fell silent.

* * *

"Stop!" Ku'ar-Marekh called as the human flung Ayan-Ye'eln to the ground yet again. She did not understand why the human had not simply killed the young warrior.

A strange creature, this one, she thought. But they were all strange to her, their motivations well beyond her understanding or caring.

But it was time for honor to be measured. "Ayan-Ye'eln."

The young warrior pushed herself to her knees, bloodied and exhausted. Her head bowed in reverence to her priestess, and in humiliation, as well. She had fought as best she could, but in this Challenge there was but one acceptable outcome.

"You may choose."

"I choose by her hand, my priestess." Ayan-Ye'eln mustered some pride into her voice as she spoke through her battered lips. Blood ran from them and her shattered nose down her bruised and swollen face as she gestured toward the human.

It was as Ku'ar-Marekh expected, and she nodded her affirmation. "You honor the Empress, my child." She stepped from the dais and strode toward the human, her ceremonial cloak fluttering behind her.

As she drew near the animal warrior, Ku'ar-Marekh drew her sword.

* * *

Valentina tensed as the warrior leader approached, drawing her sword. This one, she knew from her very brief encounter the night before, would be an incredibly hard fight, assuming Valentina was given a chance at all and the alien didn't use her strange powers as she did before.

But fighting now wasn't the alien's intention, Valentina saw. The warrior held out her sword, handle first, toward Valentina, and nodded her head toward the young warrior, who had remained kneeling.

"Kill her!" One of the men shouted from where he and the other six survivors stood, watching the spectacle.

Valentina reached out and took the sword, whose blade shimmered in a way that she had read was peculiar to Kreelan edged weapons. Metallurgists had tried to replicate the metal, which had proven to be far stronger than any man-made alloy, but thus far had been unsuccessful. It was similar in shape to the Japanese katana, with a long, gently curved blade and a long handle intended for two-handed use, although the sword was light enough and so exquisitely balanced that it could easily be wielded in a single hand. The handle itself was a work of art, made of a clear crystal, perhaps even diamond, with golden fibers woven within it. While it looked smooth and should have been slippery, it wasn't. Even with her sweating hands, she could grip it easily. The handle also had an unusual shape, and as she changed her grip slightly, she realized that it was instantly reforming itself to give her the best possible hold, as if it were alive, anticipating how she would hold the weapon.

"My God." She wondered at what magical technology must be at work inside what one could easily mistake for a mere sword.

She looked up at the warrior leader, the one with the dead eyes, who again gestured toward the kneeling warrior, making a chopping motion with her hand.

"Do it!" One of the surviving women called out. "That'll be one less we have to kill when the fleet gets here!"

In her mind, Valentina knew that the woman was right. And while she had killed plenty of human beings, some of whom had been as helpless as the battered warrior now kneeling before her, she had given up a small piece of her soul with every life she had taken that way.

The young warrior who had tried to fight her, if Kreelans aged anything like humans, looked to be little beyond her teens. She would almost certainly die when the fleet arrived and the Marines landed to retake the planet. But she wouldn't die now, at least not by Valentina's hand.

"No." She held out the sword to the warrior leader, who reluctantly took it back.

* * *

Ku'ar-Marekh took back her sword from the human, who stepped beyond the reach of the blade.

The other humans, the survivors of this round of the Challenge, made noises in their language, clearly displeased.

"The animal does not understand the Way," Ku'ar-Marekh told Ayan-Ye'eln as the warriors around the arena again fell silent, straining to hear her words. "She refuses to take your life. She does not understand the honor she would render upon you, if she understands the concept of honor at all."

Ayan-Ye'eln looked up at the human, then reached out a hand to her, palm up. Moving forward on her knees, she came close enough to touch the alien's hand. The alien tensed, but did not move away. Ayan-Ye'eln took the human's hand in hers, then reached out to the priestess for the sword. Ku'ar-Marekh gave it to her, and Ayan-Ye'eln placed the handle in the alien warrior's hand, closing the human's pale fingers around the gleaming living crystal.

Looking up one last time into the human's unreadable gaze, she bent forward, offering her neck. She shivered not with fear, but with anticipation, for when alive all of Her Children, even the males, felt the power of the Empress through the Bloodsong. But in death they became one with it, immersed in Her power and love.

And to die at the hand of a worthy opponent, one who might even challenge the high priestess of the Nyur-A'il, was an honor that few among her race had known since the last great war, fought among the stars many millennia before.

She steadied her breathing, awaiting her release.

* * *

Valentina stood over the warrior, the alien sword now clenched in her hand. She looked up at the other survivors, who had fallen as silent as the alien warriors around them.

How can we fight a race of warriors that wants to die? Valentina wondered. Did winning a battle even matter to them, or did they simply fight until they finally found someone who could beat them.

What if, to them, death was the ultimate victory? What if territory, resources, ideology, or any of the other reasons humans had traditionally fought one another had no meaning to them? How, then, could humanity win, other than by killing every single Kreelan in the universe?

The thought chilled her, more because no one had any idea how large the Empire might be. Even if the Confederation could somehow manage to kill the Kreelans at a ratio of hundreds to one, what if the aliens had thousands, or tens of thousands, of warriors for every human, warriors who simply wouldn't stop until they died?

Valentina looked at the warriors who were intently staring at her, waiting to see what she would do. She realized that in this war, even on as grand a scale as it was being fought, every life would count in the end. On both sides.

With one last glance into the warrior leader's dead eyes, Valentina gripped the sword in both hands and brought it down in a slashing arc, cutting cleanly through the kneeling warrior's neck.

The warriors around them roared their approval as the Kreelan's head fell to the sand and her body toppled beside it. Valentina flicked the blood from the blade before handing the sword back to the warrior leader.

The huge gong sounded again. This round was over.

The warrior leader bowed her head slightly, then gestured with one hand toward the entrance to the arena as she replaced the sword in its gleaming black scabbard with the other.

With a last look at the dead warrior's body, still pumping blood onto the white sands of the arena, Valentina rejoined her fellow humans for the march back to the camp.

Behind her, five other warriors reverently lifted the body of their fallen sister and carried her to a nearby field where the funeral pyres were already burning.

* * *

"Valentina!" Steph shouted as the warriors appeared at the gates and released the eight survivors of the second group. Steph wrapped her arms around Valentina and hugged her fiercely. The men and women of the third group gathered around the survivors, peppering them with questions about how the Kreelans fought.

"I'm okay." Valentina returned Steph's hug briefly. "How long? How long were we gone?"

"Almost thirty minutes. You were gone almost half an hour."

"That was all?" Valentina felt sick. Combat had a time dilation effect, where seconds could seem like hours, and minutes stretched on to eternity. She looked past Steph to the next few groups of fighters lined up, waiting for their turn in the arenas. "We're going to need more people."

Steph ignored her last comment. "What do you mean, 'That was all?' Thirty minutes against them? That's incredible! The first group was gone only ten minutes, and only one survived!"

"The next group will do even better." Jackson came to stand next to Valentina, giving her a brief pat on the shoulder. "It's made up mostly of my people, and all of them have fought hand to hand before." He looked at the warriors, who waited expectantly. "We'll give a good accounting of ourselves, I think."

"You're going?"

Jackson nodded. "I'm not a young buck anymore, but I think I can hold my own in a reasonably fair fight. I'm not just going to sit here on my ass."

"Have one of your people sit out." Valentina headed back toward the waiting warriors, as both Steph and Allison opened their mouths to protest. "I'm going back in."

"Sorry, Valentina." Jackson matched her stride, gesturing for the others in the next group to move up. "You can come along if you like, but none of these folks are going to back out."

The other nineteen people moved past Jackson into the box formed by the warriors, and Jackson joined them.

Valentina walked forward to join them, but the warrior in charge put her hand on Valentina's chest, holding her back while bowing her head.

"I'm going." Valentina's growl did not dissuade the warrior, who held fast while the others turned about and marched out the gates with Jackson's group.

"Don't be a fool, Valentina." Steph took her by the arm and gently pulled her back. "I know you can fight better than any of us, but you can't save us by yourself. That's something we all have to do together. And we're going to need you when Mills gets ready to break us out of here."

Valentina shrugged off Steph's hand. After a moment more of glaring at the warrior who still stood there, barring her way, she turned away and walked back toward their shelter, a silent Allison and Steph following close behind.

The warrior watched her for a moment, then turned and followed her sisters back toward the arenas.

"Here, take this." Steph handed Valentina her vidcam headset. "Mills is talking again."

Valentina put it on and looked out into the woods, where she saw the laser light blinking.

* * *

The half hour that Valentina had been in the arena had been one of the longest of Mills's life. He had cursed her for a fool the entire time using every foul word he could conjure up, knowing all the while that she was doing it to buy time for the others.

Steph and Allison had waited for her along the fence by the gate, now that they weren't afraid of the warriors picking people out at random.

For thirty minutes Mills held still, his eye to the scope as he trained the sniper rifle on the gates. His gut churned, his stomach alternately filled with butterflies and acid.

When Valentina and the others were marched back, he breathed a long, ragged sigh of relief until he saw the altercation between her and the black man. He didn't have to guess what it was about, and he started cursing her again when she tried to join the next group to go to the arenas. Between one of the warriors and Steph, she had her mind changed and turned back to walk deeper into the camp, toward one of the empty shelters.

That's when he started flashing the laser at Steph to get her attention, and Steph gave Valentina her vidcam.

* * *

Valentina tried to smile at the quick pulses of the laser, but couldn't. Instead, she felt an unfamiliar moist warmth in her eyes, and a moment later tears were rolling down her face. She felt Allison's arms wrapping around her, and Valentina hugged the girl tight.

"I'm sorry," she said softly to Mills, taking care to form her words slowly in hopes he would understand what she was saying. "I want to save them. I want to save all of them. But I can't, can I?"

A pause, then one blink of the laser. No.

That was when the gong sounded once more, its deep tone echoing across the camp to signal the next round of bloody combat.

SIXTY-EIGHT

"Stand by for transpace sequence in sixty seconds." The artificial female voice of *Orion's* navigation computer echoed through the ship.

Sato was strapped into his command chair, his eyes fixed on the flag bridge displays that showed the computer's estimates of where the other ships in the fleet were in the hyperspace around them.

To the crew on the flag bridge he appeared calm, but his heart was hammering and his stomach churned. He had served aboard three ships that had been lost, two with all hands other than himself. He knew that *Orion* and her sisters would perform well, and that, unless he had completely underestimated the Kreelans, the battleships would outmatch anything the enemy could throw against them. Yet the ghosts of his dead shipmates haunted him still, a peculiar feeling that he hadn't been able to dispel.

His crews thought him a slave-driver, but he had also heard the scuttlebutt, the rumors, that he was a lucky sailor to have survived all that he had. His lips curled up slightly at the thought, wondering if the crew would still think that if they knew how many men and women had died on those ships. In a different age, he might have been considered a Jonah, a curse to his ship and crew.

Not this time, he told himself sternly. *This time it's going to be different.* The ships and crews were the finest in the fleet and the Kreelan forces awaiting them would be terribly outnumbered. This engagement wouldn't be decided by luck or blind fate. It would be decided by superior planning and overwhelming weight of fire.

"Ten seconds." The tension on the flag bridge rose even higher. "Transpace sequence in five...four..."

"Stand by!" Sato's hands tightened on the grips of his chair. The 1st Battleship Flotilla and its escorts were scheduled to jump in first, with the rest of the fleet right behind them.

"...three...two...one..." The computer voice paused. "Transpace sequence complete. Normal space emergence."

The computer generated display on the main flag bridge screen changed to show the actual view of the system, with Alger's World a bright disk taking up nearly half the screen. Green icons representing the other ships of the task force appeared around *Orion* and the three other battleships. They had all made it, and were in tight formation.

"All ships accounted for," the flag tactical officer reported.

"Data links...are working." The communications officer was surprised. "Links are up with the other ships of the flotilla and the escort group."

Sato frowned. "Take advantage of the connectivity, but be ready to cut over to voice and vidcom immediately. Let's not count on something we're almost sure to lose."

"Aye, sir."

"Enemy ships identified, commodore." Sato's flag captain highlighted eight red icons on the tactical display. "Two cruiser class and six destroyer class, just rounding Alger's World on a converging course."

"Inbound contacts!" The tactical officer looked up. "Classify as...friendly! It's the rest of the fleet, commodore. Right on schedule."

Sato watched intently as a cloud of green icons appeared on the display. One of them was a brighter green. It was *Guadalcanal*, Admiral Voroshilov's flagship. The assault carrier group had materialized right where they were supposed to be, in low orbit over Alger's World.

The Kreelan warships altered course, heading toward the carriers and their escorts. Sato saw that his task force was in a good position to intercept the enemy ships before they reached the assault group.

"Inform Admiral Voroshilov that the 1st Battleship Division will engage the enemy formation," Sato said formally to the flag communications officer. Then, to the flag captain, he said, "Have the task force alter course to intercept the enemy. Let's give them a taste of what *Orion* class battleships can do."

* * *

"Acknowledge Commodore Sato's signal," Admiral Voroshilov said to his tactical officer, "and wish him godspeed." He turned to the communications officer. "Is there any word from the ground reconnaissance teams?"

"Nothing yet, sir." She frowned at her console as she worked the controls. "The spectrum's clean. There's nothing from the automatic beacons, no voice contact, no civilian broadcasts. Nothing. We're transmitting the fleet beacon over the normal comm channels and then radio, but..." She shrugged her shoulders helplessly.

Voroshilov's comm panel chimed, and he looked down to see an incoming call from General Sparks, who was with his troops in the assault boats in the carrier's hold. "Yes, general?"

"We're ready to deploy, sir."

"We have nothing yet from the reconnaissance teams, my friend. I will not release the boats until we have targeting information."

"At least let us clear the carriers, admiral. The boats can tag along in formation until we hear something. If enemy warships come calling in strength, I'd rather my troopers...Marines...have a chance to get to the surface than be useless ballast aboard your carriers."

The admiral frowned, considering. The assault force had eight carriers, and had enough boats to drop all three divisions in one pass. While he was reluctant to deploy the boats on the chance that an overwhelming Kreelan fleet appeared, he hadn't come to Alger's World to lose. And when all was said and done, the Navy was here primarily to support the ground operation. Only Sparks and his Marines could actually save the people of the colony, and to do that they had to get on the ground. "Granted, general. I will issue the necessary orders. Prepare your Marines for immediate deployment."

"Thank you, sir!" Sparks was clearly relieved.

As his face disappeared from the small comm screen, Voroshilov looked up again to his communications officer, who shook her head.

Still no contact. His worry grew by the second as he turned his attention to the developing encounter between Sato's battleships and the Kreelan warships.

What had happened to the reconnaissance teams?

* * *

Mills watched the chronometer on his wrist, counting the seconds until the scheduled arrival of the fleet. The last hours had been agonizing as successive batches of people had been taken to the arenas. The longest any of them had lasted after Valentina's fight had been fifteen minutes, and while the first few groups had almost a fifty percent survival rate, the latter ones hadn't fared so well.

Despite Steph's best efforts at rallying their spirits, people were panicking.

"Bloody hell," he hissed, "where the devil's the fleet?" His worry was compounded by gnawing discomfort from the aches in his shoulders, arms, and neck from being stuck in the same position for so long. A trail of native insects, akin to large ants, had made a trail through his hide position, and he could feel a sick tickling sensation as they marched across his back. Fortunately, none of them had decided to take a bite of him. Even if they had, he wouldn't have been able to move.

He held the radio unit that Valentina had cobbled together. When he wasn't staring through the rifle scope to watch the activity in the camp, he was alternately stared at radio and his chronometer.

The fleet's past due. He wondered if the operation had been called off at the last minute. If so, he would still go through with the breakout plan, although the end game would still have every human on this world dead.

The gates opened up again and the warriors returned for more victims. This time they brought four survivors, one of whom was being carried by two of the others.

The people in the crowd surged back toward the rear fence of the camp. There weren't any more orderly groups of twenty people ready to face their doom. The returning survivors had been the last such group that Steph and Valentina had been able to organize. He had watched as Valentina had tried to go with every single group that went, but the warriors always refused her.

The two women, Allison, and the black man went to help the survivors.

The warriors stood waiting, but no one was volunteering to come forward.

"It's time, mate." There was no point in waiting any longer before putting his plan into action. If he didn't do something now, even more people would die, killed by the Kreelans or trampled in a panicked stampede like trapped animals. At least if they were freed from the camp they would have some small chance at freedom.

He pulled the remote detonator for the grenades from a pouch on his combat belt. Flipping up the arming cover, he was just easing pressure onto the button that would trigger the grenades when the radio console blinked.

Looking down quickly, he saw that it was displaying a beacon signal from *Guadalcanal*, the fleet's flagship.

Setting down the detonator, he pressed the transmit button on the console.

"*Guadalcanal*, this is Echo-Six," Mills whispered, hoping the radio had the power to reach the fleet. He knew Valentina wouldn't have put together a hunk of junk, but everything else for this mission had gone wrong, and he was expecting yet another disaster. "Come in, *Guadalcanal*."

His hopes sagged as he heard nothing but silence, and was about to call again when a voice boomed in his ear.

"Echo-Six, this is *Guadalcanal*. Fleet is in position and awaiting targeting information, over."

"Thank you, God." Mills didn't consider himself much of a believer, but he figured it couldn't hurt. He pressed the transmit button. "*Guadalcanal*, target concentration is in the town of Breakwater, located at..." He read a string of coordinates. "Note that we have several thousand civilians being held here. I'm going to try and break them out, but will need help fast to keep the enemy from hunting us down."

"Understood, Echo-Six. Have you had any contact with the other teams?"

"Negative." Mills tensed as saw movement in the camp. Putting his eye again to the rifle scope, he saw that the Kreelans were beginning to move toward the crowd of people to take the next victims. "We've had no contact with them since the drop and assume they've been neutralized. We have no other information on other Kreelan concentrations, but there's a bloody trainload of them here."

Valentina, Steph, and the black man made to intervene between the warriors and the terrified people, but the Kreelans waved the stun wands at them, forcing them to back off.

"Listen, mate, just send a bloody division here to Breakwater as fast as you please. Tell them to expect a very hot reception. I've got to go. Echo-Six, out."

Shutting down the radio and carefully putting it back in its makeshift case, Mills grabbed up the remote detonator and held it in his left hand. Then he snugged the big rifle into his shoulder with his right hand, staring through the scope at the disaster about to unfold in the camp.

Taking a deep breath, he pushed the button on the detonator.

* * *

Ku'ar-Marekh looked into the sky as she felt it, a wave of excitement and bloodlust from the warriors of the ships orbiting above.

Casting her mind's eye upward, she found the human ships that had come to do battle. She sensed the elation of the shipmistresses as they saw that they were not only outnumbered, but that the humans had with them a new class of warship, far more powerful than any of the Imperial ships in this system. They stood no chance of survival, but their deaths would bring great glory to the Empress.

She also sensed…something else. Expanding the reach of her spirit as she slowed time, she flowed through the human ships until she found it. Him.

The Messenger.

Ku'ar-Marekh considered this for a long moment. A Messenger had never been killed, in all the ages recorded in the Books of Time, even in the age of chaos before the Empire.

It was also true that one who had been so marked had never again engaged in battle, for that was part of the Way. Yet this Messenger, as was well known among all the priestesses and many warriors, had fought after he had been marked, and in his last battle had been shown a great mercy by Li'ara-Zhurah, a disciple of Tesh-Dar.

It had brought great honor to the young warrior, but Ku'ar-Marekh was not inclined to be charitable. If the Messenger had again taken up the sword, then he was willing to die by it. It was not the Way of the Empress, but perhaps it was for the humans.

"In Her name," Ku'ar-Marekh whispered, "let it be so."

She turned to the warriors surrounding the arenas, who had also felt the stirring in the Bloodsong. "More humans have come to give battle to our sisters in the fleet. Let us continue the Challenge until the arrival of their warriors."

The peers gave a horrendous roar of joy even as they felt the ecstatic pulses in the Bloodsong of the warriors in orbit as they began to die.

Their roar of blood lust was drowned out by rippling explosions coming from the direction of the holding pen.

* * *

"Targets in range, commodore." The flag tactical officer looked up at Sato, nodding.

On the main screen on *Orion's* flag bridge, icons representing the battleships were joined with the rapidly approaching Kreelan warships with thin lines indicating the targets designated for each ship.

Sato leaned back in his command chair. "Open fire."

As one, the guns of the four battleships spoke. Each ship was precisely aligned along the projected track of four of the six enemy destroyers. A moment after Sato's command was relayed, four beams of intense light stabbed out from the bow of each ship, and an instant later the four destroyers disappeared in titanic fireballs.

Sato felt a sense of deep satisfaction. The pulse cannons had been largely ineffective when mounted in smaller vessels because of their huge energy requirements. The battleships, on the other hand, had power to spare from their four massive fusion plants, and the energy drain on other systems in the ship was negligible. The recycle time was less also than ten seconds before the ship could fire the weapon again.

The remaining two enemy destroyers and the pair of cruisers didn't disappoint Sato. Instead of trying to run, they began a complex evasion pattern as they tried to work their way closer to the carrier strike group.

"Kinetics firing...now."

The twelve thirty centimeter main guns of each of the four battleships fired, sending their massive shells toward the volume of space through which the Kreelan ships had to pass to reach the carriers. The hull of the *Orion* echoed with man-made thunder as the guns salvoed five rounds each.

"Magnify the view, if you please." Sato wanted to see the effects of the weapons on the enemy ships. The optical station at the fore end of the ship zoomed in on the enemy vessels, capturing their rakish lines and haunting runes that adorned their flanks.

The entire flag bridge crew stared at the tactical display, watching the rounds trace their way through virtual space to finally intersect with the four remaining Kreelan warships.

The shells fired by the battleships each contained fifteen submunitions, smaller shells inside the larger casing. Once they reached a certain range from the enemy ships, the larger shells split open, ejecting the submunitions. It was much like a titanic shotgun, and the effect was dramatic.

The Kreelan ships were blasting away at the inbound shells and managed to destroy over half of them, but that still left hundreds inbound.

A cascade of explosions erupted from the enemy ships. One of the two destroyers turned into the storm of shells in what Sato credited as the only reasonable maneuver, as there was some slim possibility it might avoid them altogether. Its point defense weapons were firing desperately until a submunition punched right into its bow. The munitions were set to detonate a fraction of a second after impact, allowing them time to penetrate into a ship's vital areas. In this case, the shell found something vital indeed, as a massive explosion amidships tore the ship in two.

The second destroyer must have run into a closely-packed cluster of munitions. One minute it was there, the next it was gone. There was no spectacular explosion, only the flares of the submunitions as they detonated. The ship was simply torn apart. The debris twirled away, and some of the hull fragments were hit by even more submunitions.

The cruisers fared little better. A hail of explosions marched across their hulls, and while they could absorb more punishment, no cruiser could absorb that much. Both ships lost way and began to stray off course. One of them ran into a chunk of the second destroyer and disappeared in a massive explosion that left only her drive section visible beyond an expanding cloud of gas and debris.

The remaining cruiser simply drifted along, its shattered hull streaming air and debris, its drives torn apart.

Looking at the projected trajectory for the hulk shown on the tactical display, Sato saw that it would eventually enter the atmosphere and burn up. Any members of her crew who might still be alive would come to a fiery end.

Good enough, he thought with grim satisfaction.

The flag bridge crew broke into a cheer that was echoed throughout the battleships. It was the most one-sided engagement, favoring humans, that had yet been fought in the war.

"Incoming from the flag, sir." The communications officer was smiling.

Sato answered the call on his vidcom. "Yes, admiral?"

"I simply wanted to pass on my compliments, commodore." An unusual smile lit up his face. "Please pass on to your crews my thanks for a truly superb performance."

"Thank you, sir." Sato nodded, unable to resist a slight smile himself. "The crews will appreciate that. As do I." He paused a moment. "Sir, what's the situation on the ground?"

That wiped the smile from Voroshilov's face. "It is grim, commodore. We were only able to contact one of the ground teams very briefly. From their report...it is unclear how many survivors there may be, but at least several thousand are in immediate peril. General Sparks is deploying the 10th Armored Division to the contact position indicated by the reconnaissance team, while we hold the other two divisions in reserve. Beyond that...we can only hope."

"Yes, sir," Sato agreed quietly. "Your orders, admiral?"

"Maintain high orbit over the carrier group. I suspect that our blue-skinned friends will bring in reinforcements soon."

"We'll be ready, sir." Sato looked at the bright disk of Alger's World, wondering at the horrors that must have taken place there, and perhaps still were.

SIXTY-NINE

"It should be time." Valentina looked at her chronometer, then at where Mills was in the woods. She was wearing Steph's vidcam, but the laser was silent. "Everyone will need to be ready. Whether the fleet comes or not, we're going to break out of here."

"God, I hope they come." Jackson had suffered a few cuts and bruises in his fight before defeating the warrior he'd faced. In a way he'd felt guilty, because she looked like nothing more than a teenager. But his guilt was assuaged by his need to survive. Teenager or not, she'd been determined to kill him.

"They will." Steph looked up, as if she could see the fleet's ships in orbit. *Ichiro will come. I know he will.* "I'll tell the others."

"Is Mills going to get us out?" Allison trailed behind Steph, leaving Valentina to alternate between watching for a signal from Mills and waiting for the warriors to bring back any survivors.

"Yes, honey. You like him, don't you?"

"Yes. He's funny, especially the way he talks. And big. I just wish he were here now."

"It won't be long."

They came close enough to the crowd huddling at the back of the pen for Steph to be heard. "Listen to me!" Her shout got their attention. "The fleet should be here any time now. Some Marines-" She glossed over the fact that there was only one, Mills. "-are going to create a diversion so we can break out of here. When the time comes, go as fast as you can. And if any warriors are in your way, mob them! Even unarmed, there are a lot more of us than them."

"But they'll kill us!" The cry came from deep within the crowd, but was echoed on many faces.

"Yes, they'll kill some of us. But would you rather take a chance dying on your way to freedom, or be killed in there?" She pointed in the direction of the arenas. "Those are you choices! When it's time, head into the woods toward the fields east of town." She and Valentina had decided to send everyone there, as that seemed the most likely place for the Marines to land.

"What about all the warriors guarding us?" Someone asked.

"The diversion will take care of some of them. We just have to take our chances with the rest."

"Steph!" Valentina called. "The warriors are coming back!"

With Allison right behind her, Steph ran back to where Valentina and Jackson stood. The warriors marched back through the gates, but this time there were only three survivors. One of them was so badly injured that the other two had to carry him.

Jackson took the weight of the injured man, with Allison wrapping her thin arm around the man's waist to help, while Steph and Valentina helped the other two, a man and a woman.

"It was a slaughter." The woman was gasping, and there was a deep cut in her side. "Most of the others were finished in a few minutes. God, that hurts."

"I know it hurts," Steph told her, "but you'd better be ready to run. The fleet should be here any minute, and Marines out in the woods are going to start a diversion to help get us out of here."

"Don't worry." The woman managed a smile that quickly turned to a grimace. "You'll have to run fast to catch up to me."

Valentina helped the other survivor, a man whose leg had a long gash but was otherwise uninjured, to one of the shelters. She looked back at the warriors, and could tell that something was different. Their demeanor had changed, as if they were agitated.

I wonder if they know something. Several of them glanced up at the sky, and she looked up herself just in time to see four miniature suns ignite, low on the western horizon.

The crowd of people murmured behind her. They, too, had seen the flashes.

"They're here, by God!" Jackson shouted. "Somebody in low orbit just bought it."

"The warriors!" Allison cried as the aliens began to move farther into the camp, toward the crowd of people.

Valentina, with Jackson and Steph beside her, moved forward to try and intervene. The Kreelans didn't threaten them with lethal weapons, but the leader and several others pulled out the stun batons they had used to take them captive.

"Damn." Jackson pulled Valentina and Steph back. They couldn't afford to be stunned and helpless. Not now.

The warriors were just moving past them to take the next group of victims when the forest along the rear fence of the camp was ripped apart by a series of explosions.

* * *

Mills watched in satisfaction as the grenades detonated, tearing through the line of warriors guarding the rear of the camp. He hadn't actually expected many of the warriors to be killed or wounded, but at least half of them went down under a hail of shrapnel and wood splinters.

He cringed as some of the people lining the fence went down, too, screaming as they were cut and slashed.

There was nothing he could do for them now, and he shifted his attention to the warriors who had come for more victims, and who now were momentarily dazed by his little diversion.

Centering the crosshairs right between the breasts of the leading warrior, he stroked the big rifle's trigger. It fired with a deafening crack, jolting him back with the massive recoil. When he adjusted his aim to where the warrior had been standing, what was left of her body below the midriff was just collapsing to the ground. The rest of her was gone.

He didn't celebrate the shot, but took aim on a line of three warriors, swords drawn, who were running straight at the civilians.

He fired. Two of them went down and the third spun off to the side, all victims of the same shot.

The people along the fence recovered from the shock of the explosions and, following the instructions that Steph and Valentina had given them, tore down the fence and began to run.

"Damn." His sight picture was blocked by the escapees, and he had to take careful aim at the blue-skinned faces working their way toward the mass of civilians.

He fired and fired again, and kept firing until he'd expended the twenty-eight rounds he had for the sniper rifle, dropping at least one enemy warrior with every shot.

After he fired the last round, he looked through the scope, desperately hoping to see Valentina.

He shook his head in wonder when he found her. Covered in the blood of the enemy, she was wielding a sword in each hand, battling the few warriors who remained standing. Even in that brief moment, he saw other people taking up the weapons of now-dead warriors and joining her, hacking and slashing at the warriors.

Tossing the now-useless sniper rifle to the side, Mills grabbed up his assault rifle and charged forward to help them.

* * *

"Now!" Valentina screamed at the top of her lungs to the other prisoners after the booms of the grenades had faded. "Take down the fence and run for it!"

The people along the fence who hadn't been badly hurt by shrapnel from the grenades reacted instantly, tearing the fence apart and running headlong into the woods.

Valentina was just about to go after the leader of the warriors who had come for the next victims, and who was leading her cohorts after the defenseless civilians, when the Kreelan's upper body simply exploded, covering Valentina with blood and gore.

Ignoring the blood bath, she snatched the sword from the warrior's hand as the severed arm fell. Then she pirouetted, driving the blade into the belly of another warrior who was charging past her.

Taking that warrior's sword, as well, she turned, ready to fight. For a moment she had no targets, for the warriors in the camp were systematically being cut down by the sniper fire coming from the woods.

You're almost as good as me, Mills, she thought with a blood-stained smile as one of the few surviving warriors charged her, bellowing a challenge.

Valentina blocked the warrior's overhand cut with an upward block with her left sword before cutting deep into the warrior's thigh with the sword held in her right hand. The warrior went down, and Valentina finished her with a quick stab to the throat.

Jackson was at her side, a sword in his hands, followed by Steph, who held her own captured weapon.

More people armed themselves and joined them, trying to fend off the warriors who swarmed around from the sides of the enclosure to cut off the retreat of the civilians.

Steph watched in horror as the children Allison had saved, every one of them, burst from the stampede of people, heading right toward her and Valentina.

"No!" Steph cried as a group of Kreelans broke through and charged right toward the children. They screamed in terror as the swords flashed down in deadly arcs.

The blades never touched their intended victims. A burst of fire from an assault rifle hammered the warriors backward, revealing the grimy and exhausted form of Roland Mills.

"Good to see you again, girls." He flashed a bright smile as his eyes continued sweeping the area for nearby threats.

"Mills!" A chorus of young voices sounded above the bedlam of the escaping prisoners as the children clustered around the big Marine, as if he were a rock in the middle of a raging river.

"When we get out of this," Valentina said, pausing as Mills blasted a pair of warriors who were getting too close, "I'm going to take you and-"

"Where's Allison?" Steph asked. "She was right next to me!"

All of them looked around, trying to spot the girl in the chaos swirling around them.

"There she is!" Jackson said, pointing.

There was Allison, about twenty meters away, helping a young man who was bleeding badly from his side, the victim of one of the Kreelan flying weapons.

"Allison!" Steph shouted, sprinting toward her.

"Steph, wait!" Mills cried, catching sight of more warriors who had come through the woods and were now vaulting the fence into the camp. "Christ!" Taking careful aim, he fired past Steph, Allison, and the injured man, who were right in between him and the oncoming warriors.

Jackson ran over and relieved Allison of her burden, putting the injured man's arm across his shoulder and his own arm around the man's waist.

Allison had just turned toward Steph, reaching out her hand, when the injured man and Jackson both cried out and pitched forward to the ground. The injured man was now dead, a Kreelan flying weapon embedded in his spinal column. Jackson had one of the weapons protruding from his lower back, but managed to get to his feet using the sword as a crutch, a grimace of agony on his face.

"Run!" Steph screamed, shoving Allison ahead of her, shielding the girl with her body as more of the flying weapons hissed toward them.

Steph's left leg collapsed under her. As she fell to the ground, she could see a deep line of scarlet across her leg where one of the weapons had cut deep into her thigh. She didn't feel any pain yet, so sharp was the blade.

Looking up, she saw Allison stop and turn back toward her. "No, Allison! Run!" Then she fainted.

Without a thought, Allison ran back to her, falling to her knees and catching Steph by the shoulders as she slumped to the ground.

"Allison!" Mills shouted. "Get out of there! Run!"

With an agonized look on her face, Allison shook her head as she cradled Steph, trying to hold the unconscious woman's head and shoulders out of the churned-up soil. "I can't leave her!"

"Oh, God." Mills saw warriors pouring through the gates from the direction of the arenas. A number of Jackson's people tried to fight them off, but there were too many. He fired his assault rifle into the mass of aliens as Valentina ran forward to help Jackson. She tossed him over her shoulder as if he were a young child and ran back to Mills while he held the Kreelans at bay.

"Take him!" She quickly set the groaning Jackson on his feet next to Mills, who wrapped a powerful arm around Jackson's waist as he fired the assault rifle with his other hand.

Then the rifle's magazine ran out.

"Shit!" Mills looked helplessly at Valentina. "That was all the ammo!"

"Put me down," Jackson wheezed. "Put me down, dammit."

The children, who looked around wide-eyed at the cataclysm unfolding around them, made room as Mills set Jackson down.

"Grenade." Jackson held out his hands.

"Aye, mate." Mills snatched the last grenade from his combat belt and handed it to Jackson. His eyes met the other man's and held them for a long moment.

"Now get these kids out of here." Jackson gave Mills a bloody smile as he popped the safety cap off the grenade.

"He's right." Valentina had to shout in Mills's ear, as her voice was drowned out by the sonic booms of assault boats from the fleet. "You've got to get the children to safety."

"No!" Mills stared at her, his heart hammering with dread. The only other woman he'd ever loved had died in front of his eyes at the hands of one of these alien beasts, and he wasn't about to let it happen again. "I am not leaving you behind!"

"We don't have time." She pulled him down and kissed him hard on the mouth. Pulling away, she said, "I'll see you on that beach someday, Mills."

Then she was gone. Sprinting inhumanly fast, she ran to protect Steph and Allison just as they were about to be overrun. The blades of her crimson-stained swords caught the afternoon sun as a tide of howling warriors swarmed over them.

His heart a cold, dead stone in his chest, Mills gathered up the children and led them away just as Confederation assault boats roared overhead, coming in to land.

* * *

Jackson ignored the agony in his back. He could feel blood pouring from the wound. He'd been hit in the kidney. His vision was fading quickly, but he had time enough.

Warriors had surrounded the women, and more were heading right toward him in pursuit of the fleeing civilians.

Noticing that he was still alive, one of the aliens paused just long enough to raise her sword as the others sped around him.

"Fuck you, bitch." Jackson smiled as he pressed the detonator with his thumb.

* * *

No other human being could do what Valentina was doing, because none had the special implants that poured adrenaline and other chemicals into her system, speeding up her reaction time, increasing her strength.

She wasn't invulnerable, and the warriors could have overwhelmed her had they worked together. Instead, they swept around her, Steph, and Allison to form a ring, an arena bounded by warriors, as more continued to chase after the fleeing civilians.

The warriors took turns, seemingly at random, dashing into the makeshift arena to challenge her. One after another they came, and one after another she killed them, her swords whirling, slashing and stabbing as she danced around Allison and Steph, protecting them.

She had no idea how long she had been fighting when they stopped coming at her. Looking up from where her latest victim was collapsing to the ground, she saw that the surrounding warriors were now kneeling.

"Valentina!" Allison was pointing. "It's *her*."

The warrior leader stood a few paces away, somehow having appeared out of thin air. She was staring at Valentina with her silver-flecked, vaguely feline eyes.

Raising her swords, Valentina prepared to fight.

The warrior held out her hands, and the swords were torn from Valentina's grip, flying as if by magic to the warrior, who deftly caught them. She held them out, and another warrior dashed forward to take them. The warrior leader said something in her language, and eight warriors rose to their feet and came forward.

Valentina tensed, ready for the worst, but none of the aliens drew their weapons. Instead, six came to stand before her, briefly bowing their heads, while the other two knelt next to Steph and carefully lifted her from the ground. The ring of warriors parted as they carried her in the direction of the arenas, and the warrior leader gestured for Valentina to follow.

"Come on." Valentina held out her blood-covered hand for Allison.

"What are they going to do?" Allison got up and clutched Valentina's hand, ignoring the blood.

"I think they're going to let us live. At least for now." The two of them followed after the warriors who carried Steph, and the six other warriors fell in behind them.

Valentina glanced back as she heard the rumble of hover engines from the assault boats in the fields beyond the woods.

The warrior leader was staring off in the same direction as another warrior came up and began to speak to her.

* * *

"My priestess." Esah-Kuran bowed her head and saluted, raising her left fist to her right breast. "The humans land in force around us. We await your command."

Ku'ar-Marekh knew this, of course, for beyond the obvious senses of sight and sound that told her of the human craft landing their warriors, her mind's eye had cast about them, seeing all there was to see, knowing all there was to know.

She saw the many warriors and the great metal machines that were such treasured prey for her warriors descend from the landing craft, even as the tide of humans who had escaped from the pen began to reach them.

"Make sure these humans," she gestured to where the three had been taken to the *Kalai-Il*, "are well-kept until I return."

Then she closed her eyes and opened her mind to the Bloodsong so that her warriors would know her will.

* * *

"Marines!" Mills ran through the field from the woods, panting as he carried two of the younger children, one in each arm.

He had reached the Marines' defensive positions around the landing zone. The empty fields he had crossed the night before were now a beehive of activity as dozens of assault boats disgorged Marines, tanks, and other vehicles and equipment that were part of the 10th Armored Division. Hundreds of Marines were trying to gather up the panicked civilians and get them into boats that were empty of their cargos and ready to return to the carriers.

He was surrounded by Marines offering helping hands, gently taking the children and leading them to a nearby boat.

"First Sergeant Mills." One of the Marines recognized Mills's rank insignia and his name patch and had called it in. "General Sparks wants to see you ASAP."

"Where is he?"

"There, sir." The Marine pointed to a massive M-90 Wolverine tank about a hundred meters away that had a pennant waving wildly from a mast on the turret. "Just look for the guy wearing the biggest damn pistol you ever saw."

"I know him." Mills started off, but paused as a hand gripped his.

It was Vanhi, one of Allison's friends.

"Thank you, Mr. Mills." Then she hugged him. He returned it, biting back the urge to burst into tears.

"Get on the boat, young lady."

She nodded, then turned and went with the boat's loadmaster.

Running to where Sparks's Wolverine squatted on the field, Mills climbed up the track skirt onto the engine deck, then onto the turret.

Sparks was kneeling on the turret roof, surrounded by his staff officers and the commanders of the 32nd Armored Brigade, the first unit to hit dirt.

"Mills." The general's intense blue eyes glittered in the sunlight. "You did a damn fine job. A damn fine job!"

"Thank you, sir." Mills bobbed his head in acknowledgement as he tried to bring his breathing under control.

Sparks held up a display pad that showed a large red swath, like an intense thunderstorm on radar, that circled most of the way around the town of Breakwater, with a large red patch right in the middle of the town. "This is a thermal plot we got of the enemy from orbit. Does this match up with what you've seen on the ground?" With the Kreelans interfering with human technology, seemingly at will, Sparks had very little trust in what any electronic sensors told him.

"Yes, sir." Mills pointed to a spot on the screen where the red was particularly intense. "They built some sort of temple or something in the town square, along with arenas where they were making the civilians fight them. And in the woods around the town there are thousands of warriors." He shook his head. "It's hard to know how many, sir, but I'd say at least five thousand. Maybe more."

"What about the cities to the north and south?" Sparks zoomed out on the map. "Any idea of enemy concentrations there, or how many civilians may be left?"

"We weren't able to find out anything about any other Kreelan forces, sir, but from what we heard from some of the civvies, there are still quite a few people around the cities. But it seems like most of the Kreelans are concentrated here."

Sparks zoomed out more, with the display now showing the entire continent. "We've got recon boats searching all the other major population centers, but so far they haven't reported back."

"Sir..."

Sparks pinned him with his eyes. The general was a thin, wiry man of average height, but the intensity of his gaze commanded respect from every man and woman who encountered him. "Spit it out, first sergeant."

"One of the warriors here, sir. The leader, has...I don't know how to describe it without sounding like I've lost my mind, sir, but she's like a bloody witch."

"Like the one who rearranged your face on Keran and again on Saint Petersburg?"

Mills nodded. "Yes, sir, but not the same one. I don't know much of what she can do other than what one of the civilians..." He had to bite his lip at that point, thinking of Allison's face, looking back at him as the Kreelans swarmed over her. "...what one of the civilians told me. That she can pop out of thin air right next to you. But I believe her."

"Is there anything I can do about this warrior except blow her to bits?"

"No, sir. I just wanted you to know."

Sparks nodded. "Then we'll have to hope that a frag round will do the job when the time comes."

"There's something else."

Sparks stared at him.

"Valentina Sikorsky and Stephanie Guillaume-Sato were..." Mills hesitated, unable to say the word that he knew had to be said. *Killed.* He couldn't say it, because doing that would have somehow made it real, and it was a reality he simply wasn't prepared to deal with, a reality that he refused to acknowledge.

Sparks saved him from having to cross that abyss. "Damn. I'm sorry, son." He looked toward the town, his expression hard as the armor of the tank on which they knelt. "I guess I'll have to inform the commodore. And Valentina...I'm sorry."

"Yes, sir." Mills felt himself choking up. "General, if it wouldn't be too much trouble-"

An alarm sounded, a piercing siren that wailed from several of the boats and brought all activity in the landing zone to a dead stop.

His comm unit chimed before his operations officer came on. "Sir, we've got an inbound air attack!"

A wave of red dots appeared on the miniature tactical display Sparks was holding.

Then the sensor feed went dark and the red icons disappeared.

Disgusted, Sparks tossed the display into its bin inside the turret and keyed his comm unit. "All units, air action west, I repeat, air action west!"

That broke the spell. Everyone in the landing zone leaped into action, trying to get the last of the Marines unloaded before cramming in the civilians. Boats began to lift off, staying low as they turned away from the approaching Kreelan ships.

The Wolverine tanks of the brigade's armored regiment moved forward, turning to face the threat. The muzzles of their fifteen centimeter guns elevated as the crews prepared for the attack.

The Marine infantry around them fanned out, aiming their own weapons in the same direction. Every one of them knew that their assault rifles probably wouldn't scratch the Kreelan boats, but they would fire if he or she got the chance.

Sparks turned to Mills. "You've done enough here, first sergeant." He gestured to the nearest boat. "Hop aboard and get the hell out of here."

"Yes, sir!"

As Sparks turned his attention to managing the battle, Mills quickly climbed down the Wolverine's flank and headed in the direction of the assault boat.

They're dead. The words kept ringing in his head as he trudged toward the boat. He was tortured with the image of Valentina disappearing into the mass of warriors, trying to defend Allison and Steph as warriors swarmed around them like water flowing past a rock in a river.

The scene played over and over in his mind. He slowed his pace, then finally stopped, staring at the boat's gaping hold as Marines continued to stream out of it.

You didn't see them die. It was an easy rationalization to make, even if it made no sense at all. Steph was down, Allison helpless beside her, and Valentina couldn't have fought so many warriors. It was impossible. There was no reason the warriors swarming into the compound wouldn't have killed them.

No reason...except for the warrior leader. She had let Allison live. She must have known that Mills and his team were hiding at the farm, but she didn't come for them right away. When she did, she took the women and children prisoner when she could have easily killed them all.

It didn't make any sense.

Then his encounters with the huge warrior on Keran and Saint Petersburg came back to him. He had never really understood why she had let him live when she could so easily have killed him any time she pleased, both times they'd fought. The fights had almost been like Saturday night brawls in a pub.

Then it dawned on him. The Kreelans didn't care about winning as humans thought about it. For them, the pleasure was in how the game was played, and the tougher the opponent, the better.

And who could be a more formidable opponent for the warrior with the dead eyes than Valentina?

"You're just making this up, you fool."

Perhaps. But looking at the hold of the boat, he realized that he had nothing to live for, no future but a violent death. He wouldn't have any cushy retirement, reminiscing at the pub with a bunch of other old codgers. No one would in this war. His pension would be the blade of a Kreelan sword through his gut.

He accepted that he was going to die in this war. But if he was going to give his life, he wanted it to be for something that mattered to him. Even if it was only a lunatic idea about an alien's motivations.

"Move it, Marines! We're lifting!" The boat's loadmaster was windmilling one arm as if he were making an underhand softball pitch, urging the Marines to get off. His eyes were glued to the western horizon.

Mills made his decision. Turning and running after the last batch of Marines that had passed by, he caught up to the one he wanted. The platoon's sniper. If his lunatic speculation about the warrior leader was right, there could be only one place she'd take Valentina and the other women. The arenas. And for him to help, he'd need a weapon with a long reach.

"You there, Marine!"

"First sergeant?" The Marine, a sergeant, stepped out of line, his eyes darting to the west as the defensive barrage opened up. Tracers from the Marines' weapons and point defense lasers from the boats arced toward the small but rapidly approaching shapes of the Kreelan ships.

The sniper's squad leader turned and was about to give Mills an earful when he saw that Mills was a first sergeant. Not only that, he was covered in mud, blood, and had a wild-eyed look.

The young Marine snapped his mouth shut.

"Your rifle." Mills pointed at the sniper's weapon, a twin of the one he had used earlier. "Give it to me. And your ammo. Now."

The Marine turned to his squad leader, a helpless look on his face.

"Now, old son. I don't have time to argue or explain." Mills held out his hands.

"Do it." The squad leader had to shout over the racket of the gunfire and roar from the engines of more assault boats as they rose into the air, trying to flee. "I hope you know what the hell you're doing, first sergeant."

"I do, too, lad." Mills took the weapon and slung it over his shoulder, then clipped the ammo bandolier to his combat belt. "Believe me, I do, too."

With that, he turned and ran through the formation just as dozens of Kreelan attack ships screamed in over the trees from the direction of town.

SEVENTY

Ku'ar-Marekh opened her eyes after blinding the humans' electronic eyes. It was not something she could accomplish on her own, but she acted as a conduit for the power and will of the Empress. It was a role that only high priestesses such as herself could fulfill, for the surge of raw power through the Bloodsong would kill even the hardiest of her warriors.

Other than the small force guarding the humans for whom Ku'ar-Marekh had special plans, all the warriors here had gathered to welcome the human warriors.

Sensing the approach of her attack ships, Ku'ar-Marekh turned to Esah-Kuran. "Let it begin."

As the attack ships soared overhead, ten thousand warriors charged from the tree line along the edge of the landing zone.

* * *

Lasers and cannon fire from the incoming Kreelan ships tore through the assault boats that were still on the ground, turning half a dozen into flaming pyres of debris in mere seconds. Three more boats were shot down as they tried to lift, and a fourth was brought down just before it reached the relative safety of the low hills to the east.

Sparks stood on his seat in the turret of his tank so he could see out the commander's cupola. He had always preferred to see the battlefield directly, and hated it when he had to button up and close the hatch.

"Anti-air round, up!" The tank's gunner, who was also acting as its commander while Sparks worried about the conduct of the battle, was tracking one of the wasp-like Kreelan ships with his main gun. "Firing!"

The tank rocked back on its tracks as the gun fired with a deafening roar and a huge tongue of flame from the muzzle.

The anti-air round the tank had fired was a huge shotgun shell that was set to go off when it came close enough to a target. It was a relatively primitive weapon compared to the much smarter missiles that the tanks were designed to carry, but Sparks had insisted that each tank carry some. In this war, he had discovered, simpler was often better.

The other Wolverines fired the standard anti-air rounds, small smart missiles that were almost impossible to evade or spoof.

"Son of a bitch." He watched as every one of the missiles followed a ballistic trajectory from the tanks, flying "dumb." None of them maneuvered or came close to hitting any of the Kreelan attackers. "All units, use the anti-air rounds!"

The attacking ships were now close enough that the smaller weapons like the gatling guns mounted on the tops of the tanks and some of the other vehicles began to open up.

One of the ships, then more, started taking hits. The anti-air round Sparks's gunner had fired went off, and they were rewarded with a bright yellow fireball as the target ship exploded.

Sparks was sure the enemy ships would try to evade, but they didn't. They flew straight into the curtain of fire from his Marines.

A chill ran down his spine as he realized what they were doing. "Kamikazes!"

He was partly correct. A third of the ships didn't make it through the defensive fire, and Sparks grimaced as they plowed into the landing zone, killing dozens of Marines and reducing eight Wolverines to burning slag.

The rest of the ships, most of them damaged and streaming smoke as the Marines continued to fire at them, streaked overhead.

Sparks thought they were pursuing the departing assault boats. Then he saw a cloud of black objects leap from the ships, which were about half the size of the assault boats.

Warriors.

His Marines didn't need any orders from their general. The air over the landing zone was filled with thousands of weapons firing at the aliens gliding on thin parasails toward the ground. The enemy wasn't content to just use swords this time around. They had rifles, too, and were lethal shots.

The tanks and infantry combat vehicles swept the sky with their gatling guns. Firing at over a hundred rounds per second, they killed warriors by the dozens while they were falling toward the ground.

A few hundred warriors managed to reach the ground alive, but they wouldn't enjoy the sort of victory they had over the human forces deployed to Keran in the first major battle of the war. Most of the men and women with Sparks had seen combat, and weren't surprised or terrified by the aliens. They met them with blazing assault rifles and, when the Kreelans got too close, unsheathed combat knives.

That's when Sparks heard a roar like the rising wind before a storm.

"General!" His deputy commander was calling over the radio. He was in the command vehicle near the center of the landing zone. It was his job and that of the combat controllers with him to make sure that orders and reports made it to where they were supposed to go. "The southern flank, sir!"

Sparks turned and looked, and for one of the few times in his life, even during the desperate hours of the Battle of Keran, he felt a stab of fear. A massive line of warriors had emerged from the trees and was charging toward the brigade's positions, the warriors howling as they ran, their swords drawn.

That wasn't what frightened him. It was the warrior who led them, who was floating above the ground like a ghost, her arms extended out to her sides as if they were wings. As he boosted the magnification on the vision block in his cupola, it looked like she was staring right at him.

The entire brigade opened up in what should have been a hailstorm of death. Instead, every round, whether fired from assault rifles or the tanks, made a bright flare about a meter short of the line of warriors, then simply fell to the ground, molten or burning. The warriors, incredibly nimble in the black armor they wore, bounded over or danced around the spatters and pools of sizzling metal.

The Marine infantry moved forward while the Wolverines maneuvered back, trying to keep their distance from the oncoming alien horde. Had it not been for the strange shield protecting the warriors, the tanks could have gutted the alien charge. But now the huge vehicles were rapidly coming into range of the hellish Kreelan grenades and would be slaughtered if Sparks couldn't get them clear, and the Marine infantry now had to protect the tanks.

Led by their own angel of death, the warriors ran behind their protective shield right up to the outermost Marine positions, when the shield disappeared. The line of warriors slammed into the Marines like a steel curtain, the air filling with the screams of the dying and those doing the killing, the crash of metal on metal and non-stop weapons fire.

Sparks knew there was no choice. He had to play their game. For now. He looked back toward the middle of the landing zone where the Kreelans had airdropped in. There was still a snarling fight going on, but a company of Marines could finish it. It had only been a diversionary attack.

He contacted his deputy commander. "Move every Marine who isn't involved in the contact inside the LZ to the southern flank and get them into the fight."

"Understood, sir." His deputy's voice was tight. "But if we get hit by more warriors on either end of the line, they could turn our flank. Or worse."

"I'm counting on it, colonel." Sparks saw with approval that the infantry units in the LZ were already moving forward toward the massive brawl. Part of the defensive line was already sagging where the lead warrior was cutting his Marines down like paper dolls, but more Marines piled in, fighting with assault rifles, knives, entrenching tools, and fists. "Just move our infantry forward so I can maneuver my tanks." After a pause, he added, "And get me through to Commodore Sato in the fleet."

* * *

With space above Alger's World secured, most of the crew on *Orion's* flag bridge was watching the secondary display showing a computer-generated depiction of the ground battle. Few could make heads or tails of it, because it resembled nothing so much as a battle between a huge force of red ants and a larger force of blue ants.

Sato allowed them that indulgence because he knew that the tactical and communications officers were fully focused on monitoring the fleet and the space around it, which was blissfully, almost disturbingly calm. For one of the few times since the war had begun, a human fleet had complete and total space supremacy, at least for a time.

He saw the flag communications officer stiffen, then turn to look at Sato. Then he got up and handed Sato his headset.

"It's a direct comm from General Sparks on the surface, sir."

Frowning, Sato put on the headset. "General Sparks, sir?"

"A moment, commodore." Sparks's voice was calm, but Sato could hear a riot of sound in the background, voices shouting orders and reports, punctuated by the unmistakable crack of a large caliber weapon, a tank's main gun. "We're in full contact down here and I don't have much time."

Sato glanced up, seeing the entire flag bridge crew now staring at him. He pointed at the tactical officer and gestured him over. "We're standing by to provide orbital bombardment, general, but it will be terribly dangerous until you can break contact and-"

"Your wife's dead." Sparks paused. "Sorry to sound like a heartless bastard, but there's no easy way to say it."

"General, I don't understand." *Steph, dead?* He couldn't get his mind around the words. Even if it were true, how would Sparks know? Steph was back on Earth.

"She was on one of the recon teams as an embedded journalist, just like she was with my unit at Keran. First Sergeant Roland Mills just informed me that the enemy...got her. I'm sorry, commodore. Damn sorry."

"Yes," Sato answered weakly as the color seemed to drain from the universe around him. "Thank you for letting me know, general." Forcing himself to put some steel back into his voice, he asked, "We're standing by to support you, sir. Just give us the word."

"I appreciate that, son, but right now this is a good old-fashioned slugfest. Godspeed, commodore. Sparks, out."

"Sir?"

Looking up, Sato found his flag captain looking at him, a concerned expression on his face.

"Commodore, is something wrong?"

"No," Sato lied. "I'm fine." He forced himself to his feet, ignoring the vertigo that threatened to take him. "I'll be in my day cabin."

"Yes, sir."

Crossing the flag bridge to the hatch that led to his day cabin was one of the longest treks Sato had ever made in his life. It took every shred of willpower to maintain the appearance of a leader, of a man in control not only of himself but thousands of others. He couldn't allow his crew to see what was happening to him. He couldn't.

As the hatch slid shut behind him, closing him away from the flag bridge, he staggered and barely caught himself on his desk. One of the perquisites of being a commodore was that he had a small private viewport and a couch on which to enjoy the view outside. Slumping onto the couch, he stared through the clearsteel window at the bright disk of Alger's World. At any other time, it would have been a beautiful sight.

"Steph." Her name caught in his throat as his heart hammered in his chest. "It's my fault," he whispered to the world below where the woman he loved had died.

And he hadn't even known that she'd been involved in the mission. "If I hadn't pushed you away, you never would have done this. Or if you had, at least you would have told me. I would have known." He clenched his fists so hard the knuckles bled white. "I could have told you how much I loved you one last time."

The beautiful clouds of Alger's World were reflected in the tears of the man who commanded humanity's most powerful warships as he wept, his heart broken.

* * *

After leaving Sparks, Mills had hoped to make his way back to the woods that led toward the camp when the Kreelans attacked. Their air assault trick had given him the shakes, remembering what had happened to his old Legion regiment on Keran, but fortunately he had been clear of that little dance.

He had nearly made it to the edge of the landing zone when the mass wave attack had come from the woods, and he had been caught up in the melee. Luckily, he was on the very edge of the Kreelan line, but he hadn't been able to break contact as he had intended. The senior NCOs and handful of officers in this part of the Marine line had been killed. The Marines were still fighting valiantly, but they had no one to lead them and were quickly giving ground. In only a few more minutes the Kreelans would have been in a position to break through and attack the Marine line from the rear.

Mills had glanced longingly at the woods, then turned his attention to rallying the Marines.

"Stand and fight!" He bellowed over and over again as he waded into the enemy, his head and shoulders standing above most of the warriors. His only weapon was the sniper rifle, and it was useless in a close-in fight.

So he'd unslung it and, holding it by the barrel, began using it like a huge baseball bat. He wasn't killing any warriors with it, but he was able to knock them off balance, giving the other Marines a chance to dive in to blast and hack away at the enemy.

"Bleeding Christ!" Two warriors lunged at him at once. He knocked the first one senseless with the butt of the rifle, but the second used the opportunity to thrust her sword at him. He twisted to the side, managing to keep the tip from running him through, but the blade sliced through the muscle of his right side, just above his hip.

Hissing with pain, he pivoted around, closer to the warrior, too close for her to use her sword effectively. Using the bulk of his body to shove her off-balance, he viciously slammed the rifle butt into the side of her head, sending her flying to the side. He didn't bother finishing her off, trusting the Marines behind him to take care of that little detail.

Another group of Marines had pushed forward, joining Mills and his group in the fray. One of the newcomers had the black bar insignia of a first lieutenant.

"Lieutenant!" Mills's voice was raw, and it was hard to shout loud enough for anyone to hear him beyond a few feet amid the raging shouts and screams around them. "Lieutenant!"

The man turned his head, glancing at Mills, just as a warrior leaped over the top of a trio of Marines and came flying at the lieutenant, her sword pointed at his neck.

Mills could only be impressed as the young officer calmly raised his rifle and blasted her in mid-air.

"Can I help you, first sergeant?" He looked over at Mills as the bullet-riddled corpse of the warrior landed at his feet.

"Would you mind taking over this lot?" Mills nodded at the Marines he'd brought with him. "I have a little something special I'm supposed to be doing with this." He held up the sniper rifle, then jabbed the barrel into the ear of a warrior who was about to get the upper hand against one of his Marines. Thrown off balance, she tumbled to the ground, where the Marine finished her off with a bayonet thrust to the gut.

"Roger that. I relieve you, first sergeant!"

"Thank you, sir!"

After a few close calls, Mills was able to work his way around the end of the melee without drawing undue attention from the Kreelans, who now had their clawed hands full with the Marines.

Fighting against gnawing exhaustion and the pain from the wound in his side, he finally made it back to the woods from which he so recently had escaped.

SEVENTY-ONE

Valentina, Steph, and Allison had been taken to the dais in the middle of the central and largest arena. There, they awaited their fate, surrounded by alert warriors.

"I think I finally got the bleeding stopped." Valentina wiped her forehead, leaving a smudge of blood. She'd been trying to staunch the blood from the wound in Steph's leg, but all she had to work with was the material from their uniforms. The Kreelans had taken everything else.

She'd torn up the cleanest sections of her uniform blouse to use for bandages to stop the bleeding, then used the lower half of her undershirt and the now-empty combat belt as a final clean bandage, wrapping it around Steph's leg and cinching it tight. "The throwing star must have clipped a vein, but that's the best that I can do."

"Thanks." Steph was conscious again, but very pale and weak, both from the loss of blood and the pain.

"Does it hurt?" Allison knelt behind Steph, letting Steph's head rest on her legs, rather than on the cold stone of the dais.

"Only a little." Steph smiled at her own lie and reached up to take one of Allison's hands, giving the girl a little squeeze that proved to be a herculean effort. Then she turned back to Valentina and nodded her head toward the warriors guarding them. "What do you think they're going to do?"

"Them? Nothing. They're just making sure we stay put."

"They're waiting for *her*." Allison looked in the direction of the landing zone and the sounds of the battle that raged there. The sky beyond the trees lit up with glares and flashes of weapons being fired. She turned to Valentina. "When she's done with the Marines over there, she'll come back here. For you."

"I hate to say it, Allison, but I think you're right." Valentina took a closer look at the warriors around them, gauging her chances.

"Don't even think about it," Steph whispered. "You're good, Valentina, but you're not that good. And Allison and I wouldn't stand a chance."

"You're assuming we have a chance either way."

"All I know is that as long as you're alive, we've got a hope of making it out of this. But if something happens to you..."

"We're dead." Allison finished the thought.

"What about when the warrior with the dead eyes comes back? You know I can't beat her."

"Maybe, maybe not." Steph grimaced as a sudden lance of pain shot through her leg. "But we still might teach the king's horse to sing."

Valentina couldn't help herself. She laughed.

"What does that mean?" Allison had no idea what Steph was talking about.

"She means that she believes in miracles." Valentina smiled and shook her head. "Even now."

"Yes." Steph looked up into the darkening sky as a set of bright points of light that she knew must be Confederation warships passed overhead in low orbit. "Yes, I do."

* * *

Ku'ar-Marekh's warriors surged forward, smashing into the human warriors with a ring of steel on steel, punctuated with the staccato fire of the human weapons.

While some priestesses allowed their warriors to use rifles and other such weapons, Ku'ar-Markeh held them in contempt. The far greater challenge was to close with and slay a superior enemy with sword and claw. Many more warriors died than might have otherwise, but simple victory was not the Way of the warrior. The warriors among Her Children were born to glorify her in battle, and to die with honor.

As she moved forward toward the battle line to blood her own sword against the humans, she sensed the arrival of the fleet bearing the additional warriors she had summoned days before. The new warriors would be pleased to know there were now many human warriors here to fight, assuming the shipmistresses could hold off the human fleet long enough to land the warriors.

It will be an interesting challenge, she thought as she lunged into the melee, her sword drawing its first blood against the humans.

* * *

"Commodore to the bridge!"

Sato sat bolt upright, then got to his feet. The tears were long gone. His heart was dead and his soul was empty, and the computing machine that his brain had become filled the void with a cold yearning for vengeance on the creatures who had taken everything from him.

"Status?" He strode onto the flag bridge, his eyes immediately going to the main tactical display.

"One of the destroyers on picket duty just reported that enemy ships have emerged on the far side of the planet." The flag tactical officer came up beside him. "Ten destroyers, eight cruisers, and four large vessels that appear to be transports."

"Orders from the flag?" Sato focused his attention on the four transports, imagining the massive shells of the *Orion* venting its troop compartments to space and annihilating the thousands of warriors who must be aboard.

"The admiral ordered that we maintain position covering our carriers, sir. He's ordering the cruisers and destroyers from Home Fleet to engage."

Restraining the urge to clench his fists in frustration, Sato only nodded. *Orion* and her sisters were in formation above the precious carriers and the remaining assault boats that had yet to drop to the surface. They had not received any additional targets, only the enemy force that Sparks was engaging near Breakwater. "Very well. Maintain condition two throughout the flotilla and-"

"Emerging contacts!" The tactical officer's call was punctuated with a flurry of yellow icons appearing on the tactical display. "Contacts close aboard!"

The display that showed a video feed looking out over the bow of the ship was filled with a Kreelan cruiser that the *Orion's* captain just barely managed to avoid. The enemy ship's luminous green flanks and rune markings slid past on a reciprocal course, her guns and lasers flashing as she fired. *Orion* shuddered as the shells struck, but her thick armor shrugged them off.

The cruiser had plenty of company. Over thirty enemy vessels had emerged from hyperspace right on top of the battleships and their escorts.

Sato quickly took in the situation on the tactical display as the *Orion's* captain opened fire with the battleship's secondary weapons on the cloud of enemy warships.

But the nearby Kreelan ships weren't what he was most concerned about. A dozen enemy cruisers were pulling away, heading straight for the carriers and the cloud of assault boats, which began to dive toward the surface like a school of terrified minnows.

The destroyers and cruisers escorting the carriers turned to engage, but would be hard-pressed to stop the attacking enemy ships before they were in weapons range of the carriers.

And the carriers were too low in the planet's gravity well to jump away, and were too slow to run.

Sato didn't have any good choices. He could take his battleships after the cruisers pursuing the carriers, which would leave the other enemy warships around him free to overwhelm his escorts and pour fire into the exposed sterns of the battleships as they turned. Or he could fight the Kreelan ships here and hope that the carrier escorts managed to carry the day.

Looking at the balance of power in the looming engagement, the escorts were going to be badly outgunned.

There was one other possibility that he was loathe to do, but there was little choice. He had to split the battleship flotilla. It would divide his combat power, but if he could pin down the enemy ships here with two of the battleships, the other two would be able to maneuver to help the carriers.

Sato turned to his flag captain as the ship staggered under a heavy hit and alarms began to blare. "Order Captain Abdullah to take *Monarch* and *Conqueror* to help protect the carriers. *Thunderer* is to follow us in trail, with our escorts covering her stern."

"Aye, aye, sir." The flag captain's expression made it clear he wasn't at all convinced of the wisdom of Sato's orders, but he obeyed.

Sato called up the *Orion's* captain on his comm panel. She was on the ship's bridge two decks below. "Captain Semyonova, *Orion* is now in the lead of the first division. *Thunderer* is behind us. Make your heading zero-four-three mark seven-zero."

A trajectory line appeared on the tactical display, which was now zoomed in to show the action around the two battleships as their sisters pulled away. The white line curved right through the center of the Kreelan formation, a cloud of red icons.

Sato was going to take the battleships right down the enemy's throat. "*Monarch* and *Conqueror* are maneuvering to protect the carriers, and we need to pin down the enemy here. The flag tactical officer will provide you targeting cues so we don't fire on the same targets, but use your discretion. Fight your ship, captain."

"Aye, aye, sir." The small image of Semyonova's face nodded once, then disappeared.

The ship rang and boomed as enemy shells slammed into her heavy armor, and were answered in turn by her own fire. The secondary guns, as big as those fitted on cruisers, fired non-stop, punctuated by the hum of the point defense lasers as they sought to blast enemy shells before they hit.

As the formation split, *Orion* and *Thunderer* opened fire with their main batteries at the more distant targets of the Kreelan formation, tongues of flame shooting hundreds of meters from the muzzles of the thirty centimeter guns as they sent their massive shells toward their targets.

The space outside the view screen was an enormous pyrotechnic display, with shells and lasers streaking across the darkness, flaring into explosions as they hit their targets.

Sato looked out the forward view screen at the beautiful, yet terrible sight as *Orion* and *Thunderer* advanced with all guns blazing, seeking to tear out the enemy's heart.

* * *

Ku'ar-Marekh's sword whirled and slashed, killing the human warriors who swarmed toward her. She had never been a great swordmistress among the high priestesses. Nonetheless, her skills were far superior to that of the peers. Here, now, her warriors watched in awe as their priestess laid low their enemies in the time-honored tradition.

She had to keep moving or she would have had to reach over a pile of corpses to continue killing. Many of the humans fired their primitive weapons at her, but the projectiles simply melted and fell to the ground. It was a power she could not consciously control. Had she been able, she would have abandoned it, for it might have brought an honorable death sooner.

The humans were indeed worthy opponents, she admitted to herself. Ferocious and fearless, they grappled with her warriors, and with her. Great would be the funeral pyres for the fallen after this day, for even though the humans were soulless creatures whose blood did not sing, she would see that these were honored in death.

To her left, she saw a sudden blaze of lightning as one of her warriors finally reached one of the huge battle machines that were so prized as a kill among her warriors. She felt the warrior's dying ecstasy through the Bloodsong as the machine took her life. Then the humans inside it died in their turn, burned alive by the cyan energy that swept through the machine's metal body.

Emboldened and encouraged, more warriors surged forward, struggling to break through the line of humans who sought to hold them back.

"Forward, my children!" Her bellow carried over the storm of shrieks and curses, the gunfire and explosions that echoed across the smoke-shrouded battlefield.

With a final, massive surge, the warriors broke through the human line. First in a trickle, then in a torrent of swords and claws they broke onto the hallowed ground where the war machines had squatted, useless unless they wished to kill their own kind.

She watched as the things began to back away, their ungainly metal tracks creaking as they sought to escape. They could move faster than her warriors could run, but they would not be able to escape the droves of new warriors who even now were making their final approach to join this battle.

Hurling a *shrekka* and beheading a human who had strayed too close, she stayed where she was, allowing her warriors the honor of the kill as the quickest among them readied their grenades to attack the great machines.

* * *

"Now!" Sparks had his attention focused not on the rapidly approaching wave of howling warriors, but on the Marines they had passed by.

As one, the Marines dropped to the ground, most of them seeking what shelter might be given by their fallen comrades and dead aliens.

Like the other Wolverines, Sparks's tank was backing up, moving erratically, hoping to give the impression they were panicking. The vehicles were moving just fast enough that the warriors dashing toward them were gaining on them.

The timing was going to be close.

Dozens of cyan glows appeared along the approaching line of alien warriors as they readied their hellish grenades.

"Steady..." Sparks's voice was calm, even though his own gut was clenched in a steel vise. He had seen up close what the Kreelan grenades could do to a tank and its crew, but he wanted to let the enemy get in close, to point-blank range. "Steady..."

The nearest warriors cocked their arms back, preparing to throw.

"Now!"

The weapons on every vehicle of the brigade opened up on the Kreelan line in a deafening barrage. The main guns of the tanks spewed flechette rounds that ripped the warriors to pieces dozens at a time, while the gatling guns on the tanks and personnel carriers killed more. Anti-personnel mortars from the tanks popped non-stop, lobbing the small but lethal grenades among the closest attackers, who disappeared in a string of detonations like the climax of a fireworks display.

Even some of the Marine infantry behind the Kreelan line, bravely or foolishly, rose from cover and began firing into the warriors, adding to the carnage.

It was a bloody massacre.

A small measure of what we owe you, Sparks thought. He had not a shred of compassion for the enemy. Were it in his power, he would have killed them all.

Everywhere. Because he knew in his heart that would be the only way humanity would win this war. By extinction.

Still, he had to concede the enemy's courage, or stupidity, in refusing to withdraw. Even against the hail of fire that cut them down by the dozens, a few warriors managed to get through. He watched with grim resignation as five of the lightning grenades sailed through the air. Three infantry fighting vehicles and two Wolverines died, consumed by cascades of electrical discharges that left the thick armor plating red hot and cooked the crews.

The firing trailed off, then stopped. It was over. Not because the Kreelans had broken and run, or because they had surrendered, but because there were none left to kill.

"Thank you, God." Sparks surveyed the carnage before him, his eyes taking in the thousands of bodies, most of them enemy warriors, that littered the battlefield. Some were still whole, while others had been blown to pieces. The stench of flesh, blood, and shredded entrails would have been overpowering were it not for the acrid smoke pouring from the burning tanks and the reek of gun propellant that filled his nose.

One of the destroyed Wolverines cooked off, its ammunition exploding from the heat of the flames that consumed its interior. The heavy turret was blown from the hull to twirl twice in the air like a toy before it slammed into the ground, upside down.

Then another sound came, one he hadn't heard before.

It was his Marines, the battered and weary survivors of this brief but desperate battle, who had gotten to their feet beyond the sea of dead Kreelans. Holding their weapons above their heads, they gave voice to the joy of their survival, to victory.

Sparks's heart melted at their spirit, and at how few remained. While he had not lost many of the armored vehicles, the two Marine infantry regiments had been decimated. He guessed from those who were now standing that they'd lost at least half their strength. Nearly six thousand men and women, gone.

It had been a steep price to pay.

"But we won, by God," Sparks whispered softly. He keyed his comm unit to reach his deputy in the command vehicle. "Get the medevacs in here."

"Boats are inbound." His deputy commander's voice carried an edge that immediately worried Sparks. "But they're not medevacs, general. The fleet's under attack, and Admiral Voroshilov is sending the rest of the assault force down to us." He paused. "*Guadalcanal* is also reporting that more enemy warriors are heading our way. Looks like multiple division strength from the number of landing craft heading toward us from some transports that just arrived in orbit."

Sparks's mouth compressed to a thin line under his mustache at the news as he watched infantry fighting vehicles moving toward the line of exhausted Marines to pick them up.

It would be a race between the remainder of his three divisions and the Kreelans. "Damn."

A sudden crack from the direction of town made him look up. It was the unmistakable sound of a heavy rifle being fired. More shots rang out in short order.

The Marine infantry reacted instantly, diving to the ground and turning their weapons toward the sound.

That's when they all noticed her. A solitary warrior, the one who had led the enemy charge and shielded the warriors like some sort of witch, stood behind the Marine line. Unmoving, still surrounded by a wall of dead Marines, she again seemed to be staring at Sparks.

He felt an unaccustomed tightness in his chest, a momentary prickling of needles around his heart.

Then she vanished.

* * *

Ku'ar-Marekh watched as Her Children died in a blaze of glory under the guns of the humans. The challenge posed by the armored vehicles was irresistible, regardless of the odds. Both the hunt and the devastation among the warriors hearkened back to the tales told in the Books of Time from before the Empire, when warriors hunted the wild genoth, the great dragons of the Homeworld. The ancient tales told of battles with the great beasts every bit as horrific as this, and she watched as thousands of warriors ran to their doom, the Bloodsong echoing the ferocity of their joy.

And for those few who survived long enough to attack the great metal machines, even Ku'ar-Marekh could sense their intensity of their ecstasy as they hurled their grenades, just before the humans released them from the bonds of this life.

Great was the glory these warriors had brought the Empress this day, Ku'ar-Markekh knew as the battlefield was lost to smoke and flame. She did not even notice the occasional projectile that immolated itself against the shield of her spirit.

At last, it was over. As the smoke gradually cleared, she saw the human warriors stand and voice a great war cry at their victory.

She looked at the animal she believed to be the leader of the human warriors, sensing the beat of his heart, feeling it in the grip of her mind. It would be so easy, she knew, to take the creature's life.

But what glory would be given the Empress from such a trivial feat?

The loud report of a weapon sounded from the direction of the *Kalai-Il*, and she felt the Bloodsong tremble as two of her warriors died. More shots were fired, and more warriors died.

Casting her mind's eye to the great stone edifice, she saw her human prizes in the central arena and watched as the last warriors guarding them perished.

Guiding her spirit through the nearby woods, then the human settlement, she quickly found the attacker. It was the large human warrior who carried the mark of Tesh-Dar, atop one of the buildings.

Sighing in satisfaction, the gesture more of habit than of any true feeling, Ku'ar-Marekh hoped that together the humans would pose a worthy challenge for her when the time came.

But satisfying her personal indulgence would have to wait a short time longer, for she could sense the approach of both the new warriors and the human reinforcements. All were converging here in what would be a glorious and mighty battle.

Closing her eyes, she focused her mind on the leading attack ship, then disappeared.

SEVENTY-TWO

Mills was gasping with exhaustion as he ran through the woods, bearing the heavy sniper rifle. He prayed with every step that Valentina, Steph, and Allison were still alive, and that the warrior with the dead eyes had taken them for her own reasons and temporarily kept them safe. He wanted to believe that he would have known inside if they had been killed, but he had been a solider for far too long, and he knew it was only wishful thinking. Yet his heart told him they still lived, and he had to believe it was so. He had to.

"I'm not going to lose you." The words were a ragged whisper through his lips, but were the focus of his entire being.

He ignored the continued roar of the battle now well behind him and instead concentrated on finding a clear view of the arenas and the huge stone construct.

Unable to find a good spot in the woods, he had to run even farther, praying that he didn't blunder into any enemy warriors along the way as he circled to the edge of town nearest the arenas.

He needn't have worried. The town was utterly deserted. He wove his way through the buildings until he was at the central communications exchange, which had a direct line of sight to the town square and the arenas.

Climbing up the service access ladder in the rear, he low crawled on his belly to the mass of antenna supports at the center of the roof.

After unslinging the sniper rifle, he set out the spare magazines so they'd be in easy reach.

Putting the rifle's scope to his eye and aiming in the direction of the arenas, he slowly, carefully, levered himself up along one of the antenna pedestals until he could just see over the parapet around the building's flat roof.

"Thank you, Lord." Relief flooded through him when he saw them all in the center arena, still alive. Steph was on her back, her head on Allison's knees, and Mills grimaced at Steph's blood-soaked leg. Valentina knelt next to them.

They were surrounded by a circle of nine warriors, who were standing at what Mills thought of as parade rest, their attention fixed on Valentina. Even with the thundering racket of the battle raging on the far side of the woods, they never flinched or took their eyes from her.

"They've got your number, love." He grinned as he lined up the crosshairs on the chest of his first target, with another warrior right behind her.

He stroked the trigger, and the big rifle kicked against his shoulder as it fired.

* * *

Valentina happened to be looking right at one of the warriors when the Kreelan's upper body exploded, her arms and head sailing away from the crimson spray that was all that remained of her torso. From the corner of her eye, she saw the warrior who stood beside the first one crumple to the ground, a fist-sized hole in her abdomen.

A deafening crack followed, and Valentina recognized the sound of a sniper rifle. Part of her wanted to turn and see where the firing was coming from, but she had more important things to attend to.

The other warriors reacted instantly. Three of them bolted toward the sound of the firing, while the other four closed in around Valentina. Before they moved more than a pace, she darted forward and pried the sword from the amputated arm of the sniper rifle's first victim.

Another shot rang out, and the warrior who was closest to Valentina died.

Turning back toward Steph and Allison, Valentina leaped forward, raising her sword in time to block an overhand cut by another warrior aimed at Allison. Valentina let her momentum carry her forward, slamming her body into the alien and knocking her off the stone dais and onto the sands of the arena. The Kreelan's sword went flying, landing a few paces away.

As Valentina rolled to her feet, the big rifle fired again, and two of the warriors heading for the sniper's position exploded in a fountain of gore.

"Valentina!" Allison's scream sent an electric shock through Valentina's heart as a warrior grabbed the girl by the hair and stabbed down with her sword, the tip aimed at the juncture of the girl's neck and shoulder.

"No!" Valentina cried as the warrior she had just knocked to the ground sank her claws into Valentina's leg and dragged her down.

Allison's scream ended as the Kreelan's head disappeared in a spray of blood and bone, followed by the now-comforting sound of the sniper rifle's thunder. The blade of the alien's sword grazed Allison's neck as the dead warrior crumpled to the stone dais behind her.

With a roar of fury, Valentina smashed her foot into the face of the warrior who still had her claws in Valentina's calf muscle. Then Valentina twisted up on one knee and with both hands drove her sword into the alien's chest, the glittering blade easily slicing through the black armor, pinning the warrior to the sand.

The fourth warrior who was moving in to attack screamed in agony as the rifle fired again. She only had time to look down and see that one of her legs was gone before she collapsed.

Valentina was just about to write her off as a threat when she saw the warrior pry one of the throwing stars from her shoulder. Valentina was too far away to kill her first, and the sniper - Mills, she knew - was now focused on killing the last Kreelan still dashing toward his position. He was firing round after round at the warrior, who was dodging his aim with stunning agility.

The Kreelan facing Valentina snarled as she levered herself up on her side to throw, and Valentina readied her sword to try and deflect the hellish weapon.

With a scream of rage, Allison was there, swinging a sword at the alien's neck.

Caught totally by surprise, the warrior tried to deflect the blow with the throwing star still clutched in her hand, but she was too late.

Allison's aim was poor, but with a Kreelan blade it made no difference if it encountered flesh or bone. The glittering metal flashed through the warrior's skull, and the top half of her head fell to the ground like a slice of ripened fruit. The body fell back to the bloody sand and twitched.

Allison fell to her knees and vomited just as a shot found the last warrior heading for Mills, blowing the alien apart.

Getting to her feet, ignoring the pain in her calf, Valentina fell to the sand next to Allison and hugged the girl fiercely.

"Are you all right?" They turned to see Steph, who had rolled onto her side and was trying to drag herself toward them.

Valentina and Allison struggled to their feet and went to her. Lifting Steph up to a sitting position, they hugged each other, overjoyed to be alive.

All three of them looked up at a sound like an ape howling. It was so loud that it stood out from the continued thunder of battle beyond the woods.

There, on top of a building with a maze of antennas, stood a familiar figure, a big man wearing a camouflage uniform, brandishing a huge rifle over his head and whooping in obvious joy.

"Mills," Valentina said, shaking her head as she smiled, "you magnificent bastard."

* * *

The *Orion* shuddered as a deafening boom echoed through the flag bridge, jolting Sato so hard that his teeth cracked together. Blood flooded into his mouth from where he'd bitten his tongue. He spat it out before calling to the flag captain. "Status report!"

"The bridge isn't responding, sir!"

Sato hit the button on his comm console. "Captain Semyonova!"

Nothing.

"Get a runner to the bridge to see what's going on. I'm taking the con. Eldridge, you've got navigation. Tactical, assume control of the ship's weapons. Communications, relay our status to *Thunderer* and Admiral Voroshilov."

"Aye, sir!" Eldridge had commanded two cruisers before becoming Sato's flag captain. It had been a long time since he'd been a navigation officer, but he hadn't forgotten how. Sato had despotically drilled him and the other members of the flag bridge crews in emergency procedures, and now Eldridge was glad for it.

The officers acknowledged their orders even as *Orion* reeled from more heavy blows, and her firing slacked off noticeably. While she and *Thunderer* had destroyed at least a third of the Kreelan ships swarming around them, there were still many left that were either undamaged or still able to fight. *Thunderer* had also suffered two ramming attempts, one of which actually hit her, but didn't cause serious damage.

"Commodore, we've got severe damage to the port side." The engineering officer was a young woman whose face was colored scarlet by the reflection of the red status indicators from her display. "We've lost all but one of the secondary turrets on that side, and four of the point defense lasers."

As if to punctuate the statement, the ship shuddered again, and another set of alarms sounded.

"Sir," the communications officer turned to him, her face pale, "the runner reports that the bridge is gone. One of the secondary magazines detonated..."

"Understood." Sato set aside his grief for Semyonova and the others. There would be time to grieve later, if they all survived. "Order *Thunderer* to pull up along our port side and protect our flank, and have her rotate her weakest side to us."

"Aye, aye, sir."

On the tactical display, a trio of enemy cruisers veered toward them on a collision course. All three were seriously damaged, streaming air and debris from earlier hits inflicted by their human foes.

"Tactical, concentrate fire on those ships, if you please." Sato didn't have to point out which ones he meant. "And alert the Marines that we may have company coming."

Everyone glanced at him. The Kreelans had stopped flinging warriors through space at human ships soon after the introduction of the anti-personnel mortars that had proven utterly devastating to boarding attacks. The Kreelans spent their lives easily, but even they didn't have the stomach to waste their warriors that way.

Instead they used warships that had suffered serious damage to ram their human opponents. The warriors then swarmed through the resulting hull breach. It was more effective for the Kreelans, because it was harder for the humans to mount a defense against them before the warriors boarded.

But in most cases, boarding wasn't a concern. The ships were generally moving so fast when they collided that both were totally destroyed.

"Firing, sir."

Sato looked at the main viewscreen, which was now trained to port, following the muzzles of the ship's main guns. *Orion* shuddered again, not so violently, as she began ripple firing a broadside at the approaching enemy ships as *Thunderer* approached from astern.

"Rotate us fifty degrees to port." Sato watched the approaching battleship, whose forward main guns were also firing at the three approaching cruisers. *Thunderer* matched *Orion's* rotation, slipping into place next to her sister to cover her badly wounded flank.

Behind them, the three remaining cruisers and four destroyers of the support flotilla, supported by fire from the battleships' secondary guns, fended off attempts by Kreelan ships to attack the vulnerable sterns of the battleships. It was a desperate battle of attrition, but on balance the humans were winning. Barely.

Sato allowed himself a grim smile, his lips still smeared with blood from his bitten tongue, as he watched the results of the ship's gunnery. The cruiser at the center of the approaching trio bloomed into a gigantic fireball as she was struck simultaneously by no fewer than six main gun rounds from *Orion*, the huge shells tearing deep into the enemy ship before exploding.

A second cruiser exploded, then the third, both the victims of *Thunderer's* guns.

"What's our ammunition level?" Now that *Orion's* mauled flank was protected by *Thunderer's* armored bulk and the most immediate threats had been eliminated, Sato could turn his attention to the ship.

"Twenty-two percent for the main guns, sir. If we maintain our current rate of fire, we're going to be out in another ten minutes." The tactical officer paused. "We're at fifty-seven percent for the secondaries, but that includes the guns on the port side that are out of action. I'm having the ammunition from their magazines shifted to the starboard guns, so we should be in good shape for at least another thirty minutes, even maintaining the current rate of fire."

"And *Thunderer*?"

"She reports thirty-two percent for her forward main guns; the aft guns are out of action. Forty-three percent for her secondaries."

Sato pursed his lips. He knew they could win this fight, but they'd be extremely vulnerable if additional Kreelan ships showed up. "Restrict main gun fire to cruisers or ships attempting to ram. Engage all smaller targets with the secondaries."

"Aye, sir."

On the tactical display, there were still six enemy cruisers and a dozen destroyers left in this group of enemy ships, but nearly all of them were damaged. They had stayed alive thus far by concentrating their efforts on the battleships' escorts in a running fight astern of the big ships where they were comparatively safe from the battleships' main guns and pulse cannons.

Zooming out, he saw that *Monarch* and *Conqueror* had mopped up the cruisers that had tried to attack the carriers, and that the ships from Home Fleet were getting the upper hand in the separate battle against the Kreelan ships on the far side of the planet.

Returning the view to the immediate surroundings and the desperate fight going on around them, he turned to Eldridge. For the first time, it looked like a ship he'd been aboard would not only survive, but emerge victorious from battle. Even at the steep price the ship had paid in the losses of Semyonova and the other members of the crew, it would have been a heady feeling were it not for the knowledge that Steph was dead. He couldn't bring her back, but he could kill as many Kreelans as he could.

"Bring us about as tight as she'll turn with *Thunderer* alongside. Tactical, stand by with the pulse cannon." He paused, his dark eyes taking in the positions of the Kreelan ships. "Let's finish this."

* * *

"We've got to hurry." Mills puffed as he jogged along the road, carrying Steph in his arms. Allison ran beside him, carrying the same sword she'd used to kill one of the guards. Valentina ran a few yards ahead of them, a Kreelan sword in its scabbard tucked into her combat harness and the sniper rifle across her shoulders.

After dealing with the Kreelans, Mills had run from the communications center to meet the trio. After lifting both Allison and Valentina off the ground in an unrestrained bear hug, he had quickly applied a combat dressing to Steph's leg and gave her some painkillers. Then he picked her up and started off for the nearest Marine positions.

Ahead, the pillars of smoke rising from the fields marked the positions of dead ships and armored vehicles, just over the rise outside of town.

"Bloody hill." Mills was struggling, every muscle in his body quivering from exertion as he forced his body up the incline.

Valentina kept an eye all around them, periodically running backward so she could look behind them and make sure they weren't being followed. There wasn't a single warrior in view. *Good*, she thought. "Come on. It's not too much farther."

"Steph, darlin', you need to go on a diet." Mills's dirty, blood-spattered face crinkled briefly into a grin.

"Fuck you, Mills." Steph gave him a weak hug, trying not to wince. Even with the painkillers, her leg hurt like the devil. She also didn't tell him that her wound was bleeding again, the dressing separating from her skin from the rough treatment it was getting.

"Don't let the commodore hear you propositioning me."

Beside him, Allison rolled her eyes theatrically.

Valentina spun around again to check behind them, and stopped in her tracks, her eyes widening at what she saw. A cloud of black specks, just above the flat farmland beyond the town, was heading right for them.

Enemy attack ships.

"Down!" She grabbed Allison and threw her to the ground as Mills, not bothering to ask what Valentina had seen, dropped to his knees beside them, putting Steph down as gently as he could before covering her with his body.

The air was shattered by the screech of dozens of boats, larger ones than had attacked Sparks's Marines earlier, flying over them. The ships were so low that they kicked up a huge cloud of dust and debris from the fields as they passed.

Wave after wave flew overhead. Mills looked up, and could clearly see the garish markings on the alien craft and make out every detail of their wasp-like hulls. While not as large as the assault boats the Marines typically used, he guessed they were still big enough to hold a couple hundred warriors each. Just the ones he counted after the first waves had passed would have amounted to nearly a division's worth of warriors. And there were more, a lot more.

As they passed overhead, the ships climbed higher into the sky.

He glanced over at Valentina, who looked back. She shook her head, grimacing.

After the final wave finally passed over and the roar faded, Mills could hear the unmistakable thrum of gatling guns and the sharp crack of tank main guns firing.

"Come on." Valentina helped him up, then made sure Allison was all right.

Picking up Steph, they walked the rest of the way up the rise to where they could see the battlefield where the Marines had annihilated the warriors earlier.

"Bleeding Christ." Mills felt his hopes of rescue die as the scene came into view.

The landing zone the Marines had used earlier was a scene right out of hell. Hundreds of Kreelan assault ships flew through what looked like a solid flaming wall of defensive fire. Many of the ships began to stream smoke and crashed, while others simply exploded.

But most got through. Seconds later Mills saw the sky fill with clouds of warriors falling from the Kreelan ships.

Beyond them, he could just make out the glint of what must have been Confederation Navy boats, now caught in a brutal slugging match with the Kreelan ships.

"I guess we're not getting out of here yet."

Mills and Valentina exchanged a glance at Allison's words.

"Looks that way, hon." Mills knelt down, and Valentina and Allison helped him put Steph, unconscious again, carefully on the ground.

The big man was overcome by a wave of exhaustion, and nearly fell over before Valentina caught him.

"I'm fine," he rasped, trying to push her away.

"No, you're not, you idiot." She undid his equipment harness and pulled his uniform tunic aside to look at the wound in his side from the battle earlier. "You've lost a lot of blood."

"Give me a pint or two of beer to make up for it." He tried to laugh, but it ended up little more than a cough. He felt Allison's arms around his neck, hugging him tightly. "I'll be okay," he told her.

Valentina, frowning at his bravado, quickly did what she could for the wound, slapping a coating of the liquid bandage over it and hitting him with a painkiller and some stims while silently cursing Mills for not having done it himself earlier. "Idiot."

Then she checked on Steph, noticing that her leg was bleeding again. She'd lost too much blood, and if they couldn't get her to a corpsman or sickbay soon, she was going to die.

"What are we going to do, Mills?" Allison, her arms still around his neck, was watching the fireworks over the battlefield, her voice nearly lost in the booms and cracks that followed the explosions and gunfire.

"We're going to hope that General Sparks kicks their little blue arses. And soon."

SEVENTY-THREE

After the fleet had informed him he could expect more Kreelans, Sparks had quickly gathered his staff officers and regimental commanders to his tank to regroup after the battle and get ready for the one that was yet to come.

"This is good ground, right here." Sparks pointed to a spot on a laminated map he'd pulled out of a tube and unrolled on the back of his Wolverine's turret. The location he was pointing to was a huge expanse of farmland that was only broken by a few scattered stands of trees. The farms around Breakwater were bordered fairly close-by with woods, but five kilometers from town, where Sparks was indicating on the map, the gently rolling farm land opened wide like a river delta.

"The main thing is going to be who gets here first, our reinforcements or theirs." The operations officer looked up. "It's going to be bloody close."

"And we have no idea where the Kreelans are going to come from. It's not like they have anyone left here to reinforce. They could approach however they please, so we don't have a known axis of attack." The intel officer's observation failed to add any cheer to the conversation.

Sparks nodded. "That's true, but the Kreelans seem to do things very direct." He took a pen from his pocket and set it down on the map, near the margin, in the upper left corner. The tip pointed in the direction of the area where Sparks wanted to deploy, the imaginary line passing right over Breakwater. "The fleet intel pukes said the enemy boats were coming from roughly this direction, did they not?"

The intel officer nodded. "Yes, sir. Their approach vector is a steady one-four-zero degrees toward us. But they could break off at any point and encircle our position."

"They could, but I don't think they will. I think they're going to come straight down our throats and play their favorite little air drop game." Sparks took another pen and set it down on the map in the rough center of the open expanse of farmland, turning the point to face the direction of the Kreelans' approach. "This is our center point and axis, ladies and gentlemen. I want our forces here, facing the enemy's approach vector. It's a risk, but we don't have enough firepower to cover the entire LZ, we're going to need to get the rest of our folks on the ground."

"It's going to be a madhouse." The logistics officer shook her head. "Has anyone ever landed three divisions simultaneously?"

"At Kirov they landed six," the operations officer replied. "But they had weeks to plan the op and there weren't any Kreelan reinforcements inbound to screw things up." He glanced skyward. "We've just got a big gaggle of boats coming down in a race to see who gets here first."

Sparks looked at the logistics officer. "I want a straight up answer. Are you going to be able to get those boats down without making a big charlie foxtrot?"

The young woman returned his gaze evenly. Charlie foxtrot was the phonetic term in military-speak for a cluster-fuck, and she had served under Sparks long enough to know that he never tolerated bullshit. "Yes, sir. We can handle this. We'll get them down."

Satisfied, Sparks nodded. "Good. I want the center of the LZ to be right here." He pointed to a small stand of trees on the map, and the logistics officer noted down the coordinates. "Any questions?" The young woman shook her head. "Then get in your track and get over there to set up the welcoming committee."

"Yes, sir!" She climbed down the flank of the Wolverine, then ran to her own track, which was a field support vehicle based on the same tank chassis, but with a much larger superstructure and no turret. It was only armed with a gatling gun on the commander's cupola. Shouting a warning to the nearby infantry, she climbed into the cupola and in a few seconds was off, the tank's tracks throwing out big rooster tails of mud and dirt as it sped away.

"I want the rest of the brigade on this line here." Sparks turned his attention back to the map, drawing a line along a slight rise that was perpendicular to the Kreelan's approach vector. "Space out the two armored regiments evenly, and I want a company-size reserve...here." He made an X near another stand of trees about two kilometers behind the main line. "I'll be with the brigade on the center. XO, I want you with the reserve."

His executive officer nodded as he jotted a note on his data pad.

Sparks turned to the man who was the commander of what was left of the Marine infantry. The brigade had started the day with two mechanized infantry regiments, but had lost over half their total strength in the first fight. The highest ranking officer who had survived was a captain, who stared at the map with bloodshot eyes.

"Captain, I want you to divide your Marines evenly along the line. Don't worry about making it clean, just divide up your folks as best you can and get them moving, pronto. We don't have much time."

"If I may, sir?"

Sparks glanced at the intel officer, a young man who had graduated from college only six months before, but had already made two previous combat deployments. Sparks had given the youngster a hard time during training, but only because he had respected him and had great expectations for the him as an officer, assuming he lived long enough to make his next promotion. "Shoot, son."

"If the Kreelans do try another one of their air drop runs, I'd suggest deploying some of the empty infantry combat vehicles forward of the main line..."

He took a pen and drew a line on either end of the line where Sparks wanted the armored regiments, forming a squared U shape with the open end pointing toward the Kreelans' expected approach vector. "They can provide some flanking anti-air fire with their gatling guns, then pull back through these depressions here and here."

Sparks looked up at his operations officer. "Thoughts?"

"I like it. Anything coming through that corridor would hit a solid wall of lead, and we've got plenty of empty ICVs." He saw the Marine infantry officer wince. There were a lot of empty vehicles because so few of the infantry had survived the earlier attack. "Sorry, Hermann."

The captain made a dismissive gesture with his hand, but said nothing.

"Agreed." Sparks turned to the intel officer and nodded in approval.

"Anything else from anyone?"

There wasn't. Sparks ran his eyes around the tight circle, meeting the gaze of each of his officers in turn.

"Good. But let me remind you of something, ladies and gentlemen. We are not retreating. Either we beat the Kreelans here or we die. Make sure your people know that."

"With our shields or on them, sir?" The operations officer, who had a love of ancient literature, paraphrased Plutarch.

Sparks did something he rarely did in the field. He smiled. "Damn right. Now saddle up."

* * *

Selan-Kulir stood silently next to the high priestess of the Nyur-A'il as their attack ship streaked through the sky toward where the humans awaited them. As tradition demanded, Selan-Kulir had offered to become the First to Ku'ar-Marekh when the priestess materialized on their ship. The priestess had declined her offer with no more than a shake of her head.

To some, it would have been a great dishonor to have been denied the duties of First.

To Selan-Kulir, it brought not shame, but relief. She had sensed the fate of Ri'al-Hagir, the echo of fear in the Bloodsong as her soul was cast into the pit of darkness. Esah-Kuran, who had followed in the ill-fated Ri'al-Hagir's footsteps, had not long survived, but at least had met an honorable end in the great charge against the human warriors who had landed on this world, and against whom she herself would soon fight.

She glanced at Ku'ar-Marekh, who stood as still and cold as the stones of the *Kalai-Il* beside her. Her Bloodsong, as with all the priestesses, was strong, powerful. But instead of providing the warm fire that would ignite into flame during battle, it was a frigid wind that blew upon the souls of the peers.

Shivering involuntarily, Selan-Kulir returned her attention to the ship's forward view port, looking beyond the craft's pilot. Their ship led the entire formation, which stretched out for half a league on either side, and as much again behind them. She knew that the transport ships that had brought them had already been destroyed by the humans in orbit, and that while the battle still raged in space above, the Imperial warships were doomed to die under the guns of the human fleet.

This, too, brought no shame, for the warriors of the fleet had fought valiantly and well against a worthy foe, and had brought much glory this day to the Empress. Their deaths were merely the next step in the Way of Her Children. Death was a part of life, and for a warrior, to die for Her in battle was to have lived well, earning a place in the Afterlife, basking in Her love.

"That is what I, too, desire."

Selan-Kulir snapped her head around to look at Ku'ar-Marekh, who was staring at her. Realizing the breach of protocol, Selan-Kulir lowered her eyes. "I beg your forgiveness, priestess."

Ku'ar-Marekh went on as if she hadn't heard, shifting her eyes to look well beyond the young warrior, to something only she could see. "To die with honor in Her glory, to awaken on the other side of death and join those who have gone before. To feel again, and be warm..."

Selan-Kulir bowed her head and saluted, mystified by Ku'ar-Marekh's words. She had never known a priestess to act so.

Turning to look out the view port, Ku'ar-Marekh watched as the ship flashed up over a sharp rise. Off to their right, she caught a glimpse of four tiny figures collapsing to the ground as the landing force passed overhead. She sent forth her second sight to confirm her suspicion, and a moment later a cold smile graced her lips, revealing her ivory fangs.

It was her humans, the ones she wished to face in personal combat. They had survived.

"Good," she murmured to herself. She would attend to them soon.

Ahead, she could see the positions the force of human warriors had taken along a slight rise in the terrain. Beyond them was a cloud of human assault ships, racing in to land.

With a last glance at Selan-Kulir, she turned to the warriors gathered in the hold of the ship. "Prepare yourselves!"

Beyond the view screen, the fiery streaks of cannon fire rose to greet them.

* * *

With the rough battle plan made, Sparks's officers dispersed to their own vehicles to rush off to their units.

The tanks didn't wait, knowing that the infantry could quickly catch up in their fighting vehicles. After their orders were passed down, the big vehicles spun around in place and tore their way across the farms and fields toward their new positions, the air filled with the sounds of the racing turbine engines and the creaking of hundreds of tracks.

A few minutes later, half the infantry vehicles followed, carrying the Marines who had survived the first battle.

The infantry vehicles manned only by the drivers and vehicle commanders divided into two groups and headed toward their positions to form the mouth of the

U, into which Sparks hoped the Kreelans would fly. Their orders were simple. Train their gatling guns toward the center of the formation, elevating them high enough that the shells would fall beyond the vehicles on the far side if they didn't happen to hit a Kreelan ship, and open fire on order.

"About time." Sparks squinted into the sky as he heard the rumble behind him, heralding the arrival of the rest of his Marines. The assault boats were streaking down toward the landing zone the logistics officer had set up five kilometers behind the line of tanks facing the Kreelans, right where he'd wanted.

"Looks like we beat them." The voice of his XO, who was now with the reserve tank company behind the main line, said in his headphones as the first boats, still smoking from the heat of their reentry, set down and quickly began disgorging their troops and vehicles.

"Incoming!" The operations officer broke in from his command vehicle. "One of the forward observation posts has sighted incoming enemy ships."

Sparks had sent out three infantry fighting vehicles well ahead of the main battle line to give warning of the Kreelans. The ships in orbit had been providing the intel officer with a rough plot of the Kreelan attack ships, but being voice only, it lacked the clarity of the datalink-fed displays. Besides, Sparks liked to have human eyeballs on the target, not just orbital sensors.

"Count?" Sparks demanded.

"Stand by..."

There was a sudden series of explosions in the direction of the approaching Kreelan ships.

After a long pause, the operations officer said, "Sir, the OPs just went off the air."

"Damn."

At the landing zone, the first wave of assault boats lifted while more came in to land. The sky beyond the LZ was thick with the ungainly ships, but somehow the logistics officer was keeping them organized. Vehicles quickly formed up into their company formations and headed off at full speed to their assigned combat positions along the edge of the landing zone.

But there were so many more boats to get down. So many.

"Sir! Look!" Sparks's gunner had been keeping watch in the direction of town. The general looked at the display in his cupola, which was slaved to the tank's main gun sight.

Hundreds of enemy ships were now streaking toward them, their rakish prows and gaudily painted flanks reflecting the glow of the afternoon sun.

"Well," Sparks muttered to himself, "at least they're coming from the direction we wanted." He just hadn't anticipated so many of them. *Just more to kill*, he told himself.

Thumbing his radio control to the corps command frequency, which would broadcast to every vehicle in the formation, he said one word. "Fire."

The land echoed with thunder as the brigade's guns opened fire.

* * *

"Fire." Ku'ar-Marekh's order to her pilot was not relayed through the formation by voice or data, for there was no need. Every warrior sensed her will.

As one, even as they entered the curtain of steel thrown up by the defending human vehicles on the ground, the attack ships began firing. Not at the enemy warriors on the ground, or even the boats bringing in more humans, but at the ships leaving the battlefield. It was a small honor compared to besting a foe with sword and claw, but it gave those who piloted the attack ships an extra chance to bring Her glory while the humans landed more of their own warriors.

Around her, ships and warriors died. The cannon fire the humans were putting into the sky was brief but incredibly intense. Many of the attack ships were destroyed as they passed through the stupendous barrage, but those that survived were free to wreak havoc among the humans behind their main battle line.

Those ships that were mortally wounded found glory in destroying their foes on the ground, guiding their ships in as they might a sword, striking at the enemy's heart. Three tens of ships fell in the brief span of time the formation passed through the humans' fire, but nearly all of them destroyed at least one of the greatly prized human vehicles.

Ku'ar-Marekh caught Selan-Kulir's look of exhilaration.

On impulse, she reached out to the young warrior, gripping Selan-Kulir firmly on the shoulder. Selan-Kulir's eyes widened in surprise. "May thy Way be long and glorious, my daughter."

Then Ku'ar-Marekh turned to the pilot. "Now!"

The sides of the craft disintegrated except for the framework. The warriors, a fierce battle cry on their lips, leapt into the air. Moments later, flying wings sprouted from packs on their shoulders, and they began to glide rapidly to the ground.

Ku'ar-Marekh leapt with Selan-Kulir, but when the younger warrior's wing deployed, the priestess simply vanished from the sky to reappear on top of a human war machine on the ground below, and the priestess again began to kill.

* * *

"Move, move, MOVE!"

On Sparks's shouted order over the radio, the tanks and infantry fighting vehicles turned and began racing away from the cloud of warriors descending on top of them.

Sparks was tense, but unafraid that this battle would devolve into a debacle as had been suffered by the *Légion étrangère* on Keran.

This type of attack had become typical for the Kreelans when making assaults from orbit against massed human defenses, and Sparks had been counting on them repeating it here. While the tactic had proven devastating in every instance thus far, it had one major weakness. The parawings could only carry the warriors so far before they reached the ground. Once the Kreelans jumped from their ships, always at low altitude, their ability to maneuver was extremely limited. The descending warriors couldn't cheat gravity.

Most of the fighting in the war thus far had been in urban areas on more populated worlds, because the Kreelans attacked where they could find the most people. Unfortunately, the most powerful human land weapons, the tanks, were highly vulnerable in the confined streets of a city.

But here, outside a small town on a backwater planet, Sparks had found a near-perfect fighting ground for his tanks, and he intended to make the most of it.

His head sticking out of the cupola as his tank tore across the fields, he watched with satisfaction as the other vehicles around him maneuvered at breakneck speed away from the center of the Kreelan drop zone.

Every gatling gun and assault rifle in what was now over a division, with more boats coming every minute, swept across the sky to kill enemy assault ships and warriors before they could touch the ground. Dozens of Kreelan ships fell in flames, and Sparks gritted his teeth in anguish as many of them became lethal weapons, guided by their dying pilots to destroy his tanks and infantry fighting vehicles.

A swirling battle involving the assault boats developed as the Kreelan ships that had dropped their load of warriors swept in to attack.

Massive explosions shook the battlefield as ships on both sides died.

Above, warriors spun crazily in the air, trying to avoid the streams of cannon and rifle fire coming from the ground. Those warriors who were close enough hurled their lightning grenades at the fleeing armored vehicles. Some hit their targets, turning tanks and fighting vehicles into flaming pyres.

But most missed their mark, and the warriors found themselves landing in a field that was empty, save for the ships that had crashed and a couple dozen destroyed vehicles.

Sparks took it all in, his mind tallying up the butcher's bill as his driver guided the big Wolverine to their destination. The gunner kept up a steady stream of fire from the top-mounted gatling gun, firing it remotely. He punctuated the gatling's fire with shots from the main gun, flechette rounds aimed into the densely packed cloud of descending warriors.

The sky rained blood as the enemy was ripped to shreds.

"They're committed now, by God," Sparks told his operations officer as the last of the Kreelan ships dropped its warriors, then turned to attack an assault boat.

The boat's defensive lasers fired, and the Kreelan ship dove straight into the ground, sending up a tremendous pillar of flame. Warriors who had been coming down nearby burned like mosquitos on an electric grid.

Sparks keyed his microphone again. "Have the logistics officer shift our remaining boats to land three kilometers to the east. That'll keep them from taking too much fire, and we'll use those troops as a reserve. The rest of the formation here is to keep moving outward from the LZ until we're clear of the Kreelans' drop radius. Then we're going to turn back on them in a full envelopment and blow these blue-skinned bitches to hell."

"General, we've just gotten word that the fleet can provide direct fire support from *Conqueror* and *Monarch!*"

That news sent an electric shiver of relief through Sparks. "Are our people clear of the center of the LZ?"

"Aside from a few stragglers, yes sir. All units have made it beyond where the warriors landed."

Sparks spared a quick prayer for the few Marines who might be left in the ant's nest of warriors the former landing zone had become. They'd likely be dead long before the first shells from the fleet arrived.

"Have the fleet open fire on the center of the drop zone with a kill radius of three kilometers." Sparks raised his field glasses to his eyes, thankful that the driver had stopped. The Wolverine now stood facing the landing zone. It was swarming with thousands of warriors, running toward the iron ring encircling them.

Surrounded by two Marine heavy divisions, the enemy was being systematically annihilated.

Sparks was pleased. But he was also a man who believed in using all available firepower. He wanted the enemy dead.

"Have the fleet open fire."

* * *

Ku'ar-Marekh beheaded the human who had been sitting half-out of a hatch in the vehicle she'd chosen to land on. Kicking the corpse down into the bowels of the machine, she sheathed her sword and leaped down after it. Using only her claws, she made short, bloody work of the humans inside, even as the vehicle continued to race across the land.

Climbing back out, her armor covered in blood and the scent of it filling her sensitive nose, she jumped from the vehicle just before it went over a small hill and overturned, its tracks thrashing at the empty air.

Rolling gracefully to her feet, she surveyed the carnage around her. While some of the human vehicles were burning and tremendous pyres marked the final resting places of many ships, both human and her own, precious few humans remained in the kill zone.

The ones being killed now were her warriors. Nearly twenty-thousand had been dropped over the human positions, but the animals had run away as her warriors drifted down from the sky. And as the warriors descended on the flying wings, the humans raked them with fire.

On the ground, her warriors were trapped within a ring of weapons. The circle of human vehicles and troops surrounded them like an armored hand that would squeeze the life from Ku'ar-Marekh's legions.

Over the ceaseless roaring of the human guns, Ku'ar-Marekh heard the screams of pain from the dying, and rage from those who even now charged toward the humans, spending their lives fruitlessly. The Bloodsong echoed their feelings, a bright stream of cold light in Ku'ar-Marekh's heart.

"My priestess." Selan-Kulir appeared at her side, gasping. A hunk of flesh was missing from her right shoulder, and she shivered with pain and loss of blood.

Ku'ar-Marekh saw that there was blood on the young warrior's blade, as well, and nodded in satisfaction. She had found at least one human to kill.

"There is no honor in this!" Selan-Kulir dodged behind Ku'ar-Marekh as a fiery stream of cannon shells swept over their position, blasting divots of dirt from the ground. Three of the shells fell to the ground in front of the priestess, sizzling and burning.

"I agree." Ku'ar-Marekh did not feel fury or anger. It was merely duty that motivated her. It was honorable to give advantage to the enemy in battle, to prove one's worthiness against a superior opponent; this was a fundamental part of the Way by which Her warriors lived.

But there had to be balance. Just as the warriors of the fleet had learned when making boarding attacks against ships armed with the hellish anti-boarding weapons, Ku'ar-Marekh had to redress the overwhelming advantage the humans had, just as she did during their initial attack against the human forces earlier in the day.

Honorable advantage was one thing. Even waves of warriors dying for the honor of slaying the monstrous vehicles was a worthy way to die, as long as the warriors had at least a slim chance.

Slaughter, without a chance to even come within sword range of the enemy, was something entirely different.

Raising her hands out to her sides, palms up, Ku'ar-Marekh closed her eyes. Unlike the Empress, her own powers were finite. Even Tesh-Dar, great as she was, nearly died when her powers failed in her last battle with the humans. She would have died, had the Empress not intervened by sending Pan'ne-Sharakh to save the great warrior.

Ku'ar-Marekh silently prayed that the Empress would not show her the same mercy when Death's hand closed around her own heart.

Selan-Kulir watched in awe and fear as the smoke and dust around them stopped swirling upon the wind and began to move outward. Above, the sky darkened as the tiny motes in the air gathered together, blocking out the sun.

The circle of the wall of smoke and dust expanded. Slowly, at first, and then with gathering speed, darkening with every passing moment as it grew less transparent, more opaque. The warriors it passed felt nothing more than a brush of air, but the shells fired by the human weapons simply fell to the ground when they touched the expanding wall.

Sensing in their blood what their priestess was doing, the warriors ran as fast as they could toward the humans, whose weapons were now all but useless.

Dozens of streaks appeared in the sky, falling toward the battlefield like fiery meteors.

Selan-Kulir hissed as she realized that they were massive shells from the human ships in orbit. She held her hands up to her ears in anticipation of the sonic booms before closing her eyes, awaiting death.

But neither sound nor destruction came. Looking up again, she saw the shells, each as big as a several warriors, stop as they hit the darkening shield Ku'ar-Marekh had spawned over the battlefield. The weapons did not explode or even melt, they simply fell from the sky, great lumps of inert metal that the warriors easily evaded as the shells dropped to the ground.

Looking back at her priestess, Selan-Kulir saw that blood now trickled from Ku'ar-Marekh's nose and eyes, and her body trembled.

While she knew that the priestess might have considered it an affront, Selan-Kulir knelt beside Ku'ar-Marekh and reverently placed a hand on one of her sandaled feet.

The physical contact brought a surge of power through the Bloodsong from the priestess that overwhelmed Selan-Kulir. The young warrior cried out, lost in an ecstasy that she had never before felt, and never would again.

* * *

"What the devil?" Sparks whispered as he saw the dust and smoke that shrouded the battlefield begin to move toward him. As it did, moving faster and faster, it became opaque, a black wall expanding outward from the center of the Kreelan positions. It was like the shield the alien warrior witch had used in the previous fight, and the rounds from the Marines' weapons fell to the ground as the wall swept onward.

Behind the wall, he knew with chilling certainty, would be the warriors. He switched to the corps broadcast frequency. "Marines, prepare for close contact! The warriors are going to be right behind that..." He was at a loss for words. What exactly was that thing?

"General, fleet reports incoming fire!" The voice of his operations officer, coming to him over the staff channel, diverted his attention.

Sparks looked up as the contrails from the shells fired by the battleship guns signaled their imminent arrival. He raised his field glasses again, hoping he could see the shells when they detonated. They would be submunition rounds, the big shells nothing but containers for thousands of smaller bomblets that would turn any living thing in the target zone into mincemeat.

The shells came in...and stopped in mid-air. Then they just fell toward the ground. He couldn't see them hit because of the ever darkening wall that was racing toward him.

"Dammit!" To his crew, he said, "Be ready. There's going to be a lot of pissed-off warriors right on top of us when that thing blows past. We'll have to be quick."

After one last look to either side, seeing that the crews in the other tanks and fighting vehicles had buttoned up, he reluctantly gave in to his own apprehension and dropped into the cupola, slamming the hatch shut above him.

The wall was racing at them now, so thick it was nearly black. He only hoped that his theory was correct and the thing would pass by them, rather than simply smashing them to pieces.

"Steady, now..."

Closer it came.

Sparks could feel the big tank trembling as the ground shook, and tightened his grip on the handholds inside the turret, wondering what could possibly create such a phenomenon.

"Steady..."

His last thought was that the dark, swirling mass looked as if it were alive.

SEVENTY-FOUR

"That's the last of them, commodore. We did it."

Sato watched the last red icon representing a Kreelan warship blink and disappear from the tactical display as *Orion's* final salvo echoed in the flag bridge. No Kreelan warships were left in the entire system, only tumbling heaps of metal and frozen bodies that even now clanged off of the battleship's armor as she changed course, *Thunderer* still alongside, to rendezvous with their twin sisters.

"Yes, we did." Sato's voice held an air of satisfaction mixed with sorrow. The Confederation had won the battle and the new battleships had certainly proved their mettle. But the cost had been high. Eight cruisers and thirteen destroyers had been lost, most with all hands.

"Sir," the communications officer called, "incoming from Admiral Voroshilov."

"On the main display, if you please."

The Saint Petersburg admiral's bearded face appeared on the forward viewer. "My congratulations on a battle well fought and won, Commodore Sato."

"Thank you, sir." Sato bowed his head, wincing as he looked back up.

"You are injured, commodore?"

"Minor burns, admiral." Sato gestured with his left arm, where the sleeve was still smoking and his left hand was heavily bandaged. An electrical fire had broken out on one of the command consoles, seriously injuring his engineering officer. Sato had dragged her away and batted out the flames covering the woman's upper body with his hands while other members of the flag bridge crew extinguished the fire. His hand was covered with second degree burns, but he barely felt it now after the surgeon had injected him with painkillers. "It's nothing, sir. We've lost far more."

"Which brings me to the next question, commodore. What is the status of your ships?"

"*Monarch* and *Conqueror* suffered only minor damage and no casualties, and remain fully combat capable. I've ordered them to rendezvous with the munitions ships to rearm. That should take roughly four hours."

Voroshilov nodded. "Very good. Go on, please."

"*Thunderer* suffered moderate damage. Half of her main batteries are out of action and she's lost her secondary sensor array. She's also very low on ammunition. I've ordered her to detach and head for the resupply ships as soon as *Monarch* and *Conqueror* are finished. As for casualties, she suffered twelve dead and fifteen wounded, sir."

"And your flagship, commodore?"

Sato's expression hardened. "*Orion* is no longer fit for combat, admiral." Those words hurt him, but he was buoyed by the knowledge that at least *Orion* had survived. "Two of our main batteries are out of action, along with half our secondaries and point defense lasers. The armor along the starboard side has been compromised, and the hull has been breached in five places. Damage control parties have contained the damage and are shoring up the hull around the breached sections.

"Casualties..." Sato paused, thinking of the smoking wreckage that was all that was left of the ship's bridge, and the silent vacuum-filled tomb of engine room number three. "Casualties were high, sir. We lost eighty-seven members of the crew, including Captain Semyonova and the other personnel on the ship's bridge. My condolences, sir."

Voroshilov closed his eyes for a moment. Semyonova had served under him while they were in the Saint Petersburg Navy. "Thank you, commodore."

"Admiral, if I may ask, what's happening on the ground? I know that *Monarch* and *Conqueror* conducted a direct fire bombardment, but we haven't heard what happened."

"Absolutely nothing happened, commodore." Voroshilov's mouth twisted as if he were about to spit. "The shells did not detonate. Tracking indicated they were precisely on-target. But optical sensors showed them simply...stopping, and falling toward the surface."

"Impossible," Sato breathed, knowing even as he said it that it that anything seemed to be possible for the Kreelans. He knew that better than anyone.

"Yes, just like neutralizing radioactive isotopes as they did during our battle at Saint Petersburg. Impossible. Yet it happened."

"And there's been no word from General Sparks?"

"None since just after the bombardment commenced."

No one else on the flag bridge would have caught it, but Sato had worked long enough with Voroshilov that he could tell the admiral was worried.

"The combat zone has become obscured and we have lost all contact with the general and his Marines."

* * *

With a cry of agony, Ku'ar-Marekh collapsed.

Selan-Kulir, her body tingling from the power of the priestess's Bloodsong, still had the presence of mind to grab hold of the priestess's armor and help to ease her fall.

"My priestess?"

Ku'ar-Marekh stared at the eerily darkened sky as the shield she had woven began to rapidly disperse. Blood now ran freely from her nose and eyes. She coughed, and droplets of blood sprayed from her lips. The pain in her body was nearly as bad as the fire that had engulfed her during the Change when she had become a priestess.

"I will get you to a healer." Selan-Kulir closed her eyes to focus her need through the Bloodsong, but felt Ku'ar-Marekh's hand take her wrist.

"No, child. There is no need."

"But..."

Ku'ar-Marekh shook her head. "There is no need." Gently pushing the young warrior's hands aside, she managed to get to her feet.

Selan-Kulir stood close beside her, uncertain. She forced herself to keep her hands at her sides as her priestess swayed on her feet.

"The battle is again an honorable one." Ku'ar-Marekh could see her warriors charging the humans that surrounded them. The humans still held a decisive advantage if they could recover in time, but her warriors would no longer be slaughtered like meat animals with no chance for glory.

The two stood there, alone among the screaming wounded and the silent dead, the smoke from the destroyed ships and vehicles again wafting across the field of battle.

Above, the sky began to clear. Ku'ar-Marekh cast her second sight upward to the human ships, and quickly saw that their weapons were no longer prepared to bombard her warriors, for they were too close now to their human opponents.

In the distance, all around them, the howl of the warriors grew as they came within striking distance of the human animals. The sound was slowly punctuated by weapons fire as the humans regained their senses. Their rate of fire picked up quickly, but no one would know until the battle was over if it would be quick enough.

"You will return to the fleet," Ku'ar-Marekh ordered quietly.

"But, my priestess, what of the battle?" Selan-Kulir could conceal neither her confusion, nor deep disappointment. She had been wounded, yes, but could still wield a sword. "I wish to fight!"

Ku'ar-Marekh turned to her. "And fight you shall, child, but not this day. Our lives are spent easily in war, but do not waste yours. This," she gestured around them, "will be over before you could reach the battle line, and if the humans win, you will simply die an empty death. I do not wish this, and it brings neither honor to yourself, nor glory to the Empress."

Selan-Kulir, chastened, bowed her head as Ku'ar-Marekh went on. "You did the Empress great honor by standing by my side this day. The last day..."

She faltered, and Selan-Kulir reached out to steady her.

"...the last day a high priestess of the Nyur-A'il shall walk among Her Children. After me, there shall be no more, for all eternity. You are my last witness, and I wish you to live until you can die with honor. Do you understand?"

"Yes, my priestess." Selan-Kulir looked up, the skin under her eyes black with mourning for what the Empire was about to lose. Ages before the foundation of the Empire, all of the martial orders had maintained unbroken lines of high priests and priestesses. After the passing of Keel-Tath, there were only priestesses, for the males had been left barely sentient by the Curse.

But the most ancient orders, such as the Nyur-A'il, had fewer and fewer disciples since those ancient days. Two of the orders now had only a single priestess, Tesh-Dar of the Desh-Ka, and Ku'ar-Marekh of the Nyur-A'il.

And this day would see the passage of the Nyur-A'il from history, something that had never happened in all the ages since the first Books of Time.

Holding out her hands, Ku'ar-Marekh took the young warrior's forearms in a tight grip, the formal greeting, and parting, of warriors. "May thy Way be long and glorious, Selan-Kulir."

And then she was gone.

* * *

Sparks shook his head, trying to clear his vision. The last thing he remembered was his helmet slamming against the heavy metal frame of the cupola display.

The Wolverine was dark and deathly quiet. All the displays were out. The engine must have died and the power had somehow failed.

"Crew! Status?" He didn't bother with the intercom, but shouted so his crew could hear him through their helmets.

"Christ, sir, what was that?" The driver was still disoriented.

"I don't know and I don't care," Sparks snapped. "Can we move or is the tank dead?"

"Hang on, general..." Sparks relaxed slightly at the change in the driver's tone of voice. He was snapping out of it.

The interior lights snapped back on, and Sparks heard the whine of the starters for the tank's twin turbine engines.

"Gunner?"

"Sir, primary fire control is off-line, but we've still got optical." He paused, then looked up at Sparks from where he sat, below and ahead of the general. Sparks could have reached out and tapped the man's helmet with his foot. "Jesus, sir, they're right on top of us!"

"Hell!" Sparks popped the hatch. Shoving it open, he stuck his head out and looked to their front. His skin crawled at not only the sight, but the blood-curdling screams of thousands of alien warriors who were now less than a hundred meters away. "Do we have radio?"

"Negative, sir." The driver muttered a curse. He couldn't move the Wolverine until the turbines had reached operating temperature. It didn't take long, only a minute, but it was a minute they didn't have. He could see the cyan glow of lightning grenades held by some of the approaching warriors. He was a veteran of the ongoing campaign against the Kreelans on Saint Petersburg, and knew painfully well what those hellish weapons could do to his vehicle and its crew.

"Guess we'll have to wake everybody up the old fashioned way." Sparks manually aimed the gatling gun at the approaching horde. "Open fire!"

The gun spat a solid stream of shells that tore into the front ranks of the warriors, mowing them down by the dozens. Other tanks and fighting vehicles, their crews recovering from the strange phenomenon that had hit them, began firing, as well.

The Wolverine's main gun spoke, sending a flechette round straight into the Kreelan line. Normally a devastating weapon, the enemy was so close now that it simply punched a deep but narrow hole into the mass of warriors that was quickly filled by more.

"Driver!" Sparks paused momentarily in his firing so he could hear his driver's response. "Back us up! Fast!"

"The turbines aren't up yet, sir!"

Sparks cursed as he fired again, sending over a hundred cannon rounds every second into the enemy in a desperate attempt to keep the Kreelans away.

Next to him, the antipersonnel mortar began to fire, sending the small bombs arcing into the alien horde.

The first volley of lightning grenades rose from the approaching warriors, and the tanks on both sides of Sparks were hit. Webs of cyan energy engulfed the weapons as soon as the weapons touched the metal, the flickering tendrils leaving white-hot scars across the armor. The commander of the Wolverine on the left managed to get out. His uniform was on fire, and he only lasted a few seconds before a Kreelan flying weapon cut him down. The other members of his crew and that of the tank on the right were burned alive.

A pair of lightning grenades sailed up from warriors in front of Sparks's tank just before his gunner blew the Kreelans apart with another round from the main gun.

"Driver!" Sparks gritted his teeth in resignation as he kept on firing, waiting for the lightning to take him.

"Hang on, sir!"

Sparks barely had time to reach out a hand to brace himself after the driver's warning when the Wolverine lurched in reverse, throwing up a huge geyser of dirt into the faces of the attacking warriors.

"Please, God." Sparks prayed as he watched the two grenades arcing down toward them. He mashed down the trigger again, blasting more warriors into oblivion.

One of the grenades missed completely, sending out a flurry of lightning bolts as it hit the ground.

The other hit the edge of the glacis plate, the very front armor of the tank.

"Oh, shit." The driver's words echoed the thoughts of all three men as the grenade began to arc against the tank's armor.

But as the metal around it began to melt, the grenade fell away to sizzle harmlessly on the ground.

"Driver, we're running out of room!" Sparks glanced behind them. The tree line was approaching fast. The woods here were too thick for the tank to drive through without the risk of throwing a track and being immobilized. Right now, mobility was life. "Spin us to the right and get moving forward. We'll run parallel to their line and pour fire into 'em!"

"Yes, sir!"

As the driver answered, the Wolverine did exactly as Sparks had wanted, coming to a skidding stop before spinning in place in a perfect turn that lined them up parallel with the approaching aliens.

The gunner turned the turret to the left and began raking the enemy with the tank's guns. Behind and ahead of him, the other surviving tanks and infantry fighting vehicles were doing the same, following the lead of the Wolverine that flew a red pennant with three gold stars.

Sparks shook his head in grudging admiration at the endurance showed by the alien warriors. Even wearing armor and carrying weapons, they had sprinted almost half a dozen kilometers and were still coming on strong.

"General, we're going to run out of room."

Looking to his right, toward the tree line, Sparks saw that the driver was right. They wouldn't be able to keep far enough away from the Kreelans without going into the woods.

"Just keep firing." Sparks figured that if he had to die, this was as good a place and as good a way as any for an old cavalry soldier like him.

That's when he heard a sudden, massive barrage of cannon fire.

Looking up, he saw a line of tanks and infantry fighting vehicles burst over a rise just to the east, in the direction they were heading, every gun hammering at the mass of alien warriors.

"The reserve," Sparks whispered, relief flooding through him. These were the Marines his logistics officer had brought down farther away from the LZ, and they had been beyond the range of the strange...phenomenon. "Driver, wheel around as they pass and join their line."

"Yes, sir!"

For the first time, Sparks knew for certain that this battle was theirs. More of his Marines would die before the day was through, but he knew they were going to win.

SEVENTY-FIVE

Mills, Valentina, and Allison watched the strange dark wall consume the battlefield like a sandstorm.

Above, they saw the unmistakable streaks of incoming shells from an orbital bombardment, and clapped their hands over their ears at the deafening sonic booms.

Mills knew the shells were from the new battleships, which had special munitions that Commodore Sato had helped design. Mills had witnessed the gunnery tests over a deserted expanse of Siberia on Earth. The effects on the target area, which had been covered with dummies designed to simulate the alien warriors, had been devastating.

"Come on! Blow them to bloody kingdom come!"

The shells simply stopped in mid-air. He could see the glint of the metal casings, red-hot from reentry, hanging above the target.

Then they simply fell toward the ground, out of sight behind the rapidly expanding darkness.

"My God! That's bloody impossible!"

The dark cloud, whatever it was, swept over the Marine positions surrounding the landing zone.

Then, as suddenly as it had appeared, it began to dissipate.

Taking his hands from his ears, he could hear the voices of the warriors, tens of thousands of them. A mass of black-clad bodies ran through the clearing smoke as they charged the human encirclement.

"Start shooting, you buggers!" Mills bellowed at the top of his lungs.

As if the distant Marines heard him, a gatling gun growled, followed by the heavy crack of a tank's main gun firing.

In a moment, the battlefield was consumed by weapons fire as the human defenders came alive.

"It's going to be close," Valentina said from beside him. Her eyesight was better, and she could see how close the Kreelans really were. The Marines were mowing them down in droves, but the aliens were right on top of them. "If the Marines don't..."

Right in front of them, *she* was there. The warrior leader.

"Look at her," Mills whispered.

The warrior's face was covered in blood. It ran like tears from her eyes, which themselves were a bright red from burst blood vessels. It dripped from her chin onto the pendants that hung from her collar, then onto her breastplate. Streaks of crimson ran down the bright cyan rune on her armor.

She swayed for just a moment, then steadied herself. She looked at each of them in turn, her gaze lingering on Allison, before she fixed her eyes on Valentina. Then she slowly drew her sword.

Mills began to step forward, but Valentina held out a hand to stop him. "No, Mills. I've got this. Keep Allison and Steph safe."

He wanted to argue, but knew that she was right. He was at the end of his rope physically and could barely stay on his feet. And the only thing he had left as a weapon, besides his massive fists, was his combat knife, although Allison still held onto the sword she'd taken from a dead warrior. "Be bloody careful."

With that, Valentina moved forward, and the warrior took a few paces back to give them both some room.

Drawing her own sword, Valentina fought to clear her mind, hoping only that the warrior wouldn't use any of her supernatural powers. If she didn't, Valentina thought the fight might just be even, especially since the warrior was clearly injured.

With her blade held at the ready, she waited for the warrior to make the first move.

* * *

Ku'ar-Marekh was disappointed. One of the humans was grievously injured, and the others clearly wished to fight her one at a time. She had hoped they would attack her simultaneously to provide more of a challenge. Fighting each of them alone, even as badly wounded as her own body was, could have only one outcome, and would give little opportunity for her to bring the Empress the glory She deserved.

It also allowed for the chance that Ku'ar-Marekh herself might survive.

If that is to be my Way, she thought, then so be it.

With the roar of gunfire echoing from the distant battlefield, Ku'ar-Marekh raised her sword, her hands tightening around the living crystal of the handle, the tip of the blade glinting in the fading sunlight.

Staring into the eyes of the human, she attacked.

* * *

Valentina thought she was ready, but the strength and ferocity of the lightning-swift cut of the alien's blade caught her by surprise. The alien was far stronger than her battered appearance let on.

She managed to parry the attack, the blades singing as they collided, but the force of the blow knocked Valentina off-balance.

Using her momentum instead of fighting against it, she fell backward and rolled, springing to her feet just in time to block a thrust aimed at her heart. The alien missed her intended target, but Valentina hissed with pain as the alien's blade sliced deep into the flesh along the ribs under her left arm.

Baring her teeth and focusing her anger and frustration, she launched herself at the warrior, her sword whirling in a series of strikes that drove the alien back. Adrenaline and stimulants flooded into Valentina's system from her implants, and the sword in her hand was a blur as it slashed and cut at the Kreelan, trying to get past the alien's devilishly fast defense to land a telling blow.

The alien made a sudden overhand cut, and as Valentina blocked it, she whirled to one side, intending to land a disabling kick to the alien's knee when a sudden, white hot pain exploded from her left shoulder.

She turned to see the claws of one of the alien's hands buried in the fragile joint.

With a cry of pain, Valentina shoved the alien back and tried to slash at the Kreelan's exposed wrist.

The alien warrior pulled out her claws and used her armored fist to deflect Valentina's blade.

Then the Kreelan rammed her sword into Valentina's unprotected stomach, shoving it in up to the golden hilt.

* * *

"Valentina!" Allison cried.

"No!" Mills screamed as Valentina froze, her face echoing shock and surprise as she stared down at the sword that had run clean through her body. The blade, glistening with her blood, protruded from her back.

Filled with murderous rage, Mills charged the warrior, armed with nothing but his bare hands.

The Kreelan deftly sidestepped his charge, even as she still held Valentina pinned on her sword.

A victim of his own momentum, Mills tumbled to the ground, but was back on his feet in an instant. Like a bull who'd missed the matador on its first pass, he came at the alien again.

This time, when she looked at him, he felt his heart constrict, pierced by thousands of icy needles.

Gasping in agony and clutching his hands to his chest, Mills sank to his knees.

He saw Allison, a feral snarl on her lips, rise up from beside Steph. Holding the Kreelan sword in both hands, she ran at the alien.

While the girl's attack had spirit, it was no match for the Kreelan. The warrior batted the sword's blade downward with her free hand, then with a powerful backhand blow sent Allison sprawling backward. She tripped over Steph and fell to the ground, still clutching the sword.

Get up, Mills told himself, sensing the pain ease slightly as the alien turned her attention back to Valentina. The warrior stared into Valentina's eyes as she deflected Valentina's weak attempts to strike the warrior with her good arm, the sword having slipped from her grip.

"Get up, you bastard..." Mills forced himself to his feet, his heart desperately trying to work within a constricting cage of ice.

With a wet hiss, the warrior yanked the sword from Valentina, who slowly fell to her knees, a thin line of blood seeping from the corner of her mouth.

Then the Kreelan raised her sword, intending to take Valentina's head from her body.

Grimacing in agony, Mills charged.

* * *

Steph awoke with a start, her heart racing. She'd been having a nightmare, a terrible dream of swords and death. But as her subconscious gave way to conscious thought, the details blissfully faded into oblivion.

She was curled up in bed, surrounded by all the familiar things of home. The scent of freshly brewed coffee drifted in from the kitchen down the hall, where the automatic coffee maker was percolating away.

Early morning. It had always been her favorite time of day, the brief moment out of time when the world hadn't yet intruded, when she had no duties or obligations. A moment when she had time to herself to do absolutely nothing.

Beside her lay Ichiro. She watched the rise and fall of his well-muscled chest, the slow rhythm of his breathing as he slept. She was so happy he was home, that they were together again. She had hated being separated from him, had wanted him back so badly. But he was here now. Everything was again as it should be.

Watching him sleep, she marveled at what a handsome man he was. Despite having what amounted to a sedentary job, he still kept himself in excellent shape, and she smiled as she ran her eyes over his arms and shoulders, his chiseled abs. He was quite a bit younger than she was. It was a fact she never made any to-do about in public, but that she secretly allowed to serve her vanity. And as motivation to stay in great shape herself.

Young though he might be, he had been made far older and wiser by the dreadful experiences he'd had since first contact with the Kreelans. He'd suffered through more than any man should have to endure, having lost so many of his shipmates and his beloved ships to the enemy.

Her mind filled with visions of the blue-skinned horrors rampaging across the human sphere, a plague in shining black armor, killing everyone in their path. She heard the cries of rage and pain as men and women fought the enemy for their lives, defending their homes, themselves, and their children.

They fought, yes. And died under the enemy's sword.

The thought made her shudder, gooseflesh breaking out all over her skin. She snuggled closer to Ichiro, rearranging his arm so she could lay up against him, her head on his shoulder.

But as she clung to him, her visions of the loathsome aliens intensified, and Ichiro's body seemed cold. So cold.

She began to shiver uncontrollably, and one of her legs throbbed with pain.

Propping herself up so she could see Ichiro's face, she saw that it was deathly pale.

No, not pale, she decided. His face was...fading. He was disappearing before her eyes.

"Ichiro?" she whispered, her heart hammering with dread.

His eyes snapped wide open, and he spoke, but it wasn't his voice. It sounded like Roland Mills.

"Valentina!"

* * *

Steph screamed and blinked her eyes open. She lay there in the dirt, disoriented, wondering where she was.

Beside her, she saw a young girl staring at something. Then she heard a man, not Ichiro, bellow "No!"

Turning her head, she saw a huge man in a camouflage uniform running toward an alien warrior, who was standing next to another woman.

"Valentina," Steph whispered, recognizing her. But she realized Valentina wasn't just standing next to the alien. The Kreelan's sword was sticking out her friend's back. "Oh...God..."

The big man - Mills, she realized, fighting through the fog in her brain - ran at the warrior, who dodged aside. He turned around to attack again, but before he took more than two steps he clutched at his chest as if he were having a heart attack, then crumpled to the ground.

Beside her, Allison charged the alien, brandishing a sword. But the Kreelan deflected the girl's sword before knocking her backward. Allison tripped and fell over Steph, sprawling in the dirt beside her.

Grimacing in the pain from her leg and fighting the dizziness that threatened to again leave her unconscious, Steph reached down to her combat harness and pulled out her knife. Her mind had caught up with the reality around her. She didn't expect to survive, but wasn't about to allow the Kreelan to kill her without putting up a struggle.

"Allison!"

The girl was next to her in an instant. "Steph? Oh, God..."

Steph grabbed the girl's hand and held on. "Listen to me. You need to run. Get away."

"No! I'm not leaving you!"

They both looked up as Mills roared.

Valentina was on her knees, the warrior standing over her, sword raised, as Mills ran at the Kreelan. Her blade whistled through the air, and the big Marine grunted as the sword slashed deep through his right shoulder, effortlessly slicing through muscle and bone.

But that didn't stop him. A hundred and twenty kilograms of solid muscle slammed into the warrior.

While the warrior was shoved back, right up next to Steph, she somehow managed to stay on her feet.

Mills grappled with her, his good hand yanking the braids of her hair. He levered her head back and bit into her neck above her collar, his teeth sinking deep into her flesh even as she battered at his head with the handle of her sword.

Shoving Allison out of the way, Steph cried out in pain as she forced herself over on her side, plunging her knife into one of the alien's sandaled feet and pinning it to the ground.

With one final, titanic heave, Mills threw the warrior off-balance, and the two of them crashed to the ground.

* * *

Allison watched in terror as Mills, blood streaming down his chest from the terrible sword wound, clung desperately to the warrior. Behind them, she could see Valentina, still on her knees, watching the spectacle as her life drained away.

Allison gripped the alien sword in her hand, determined not to run, but afraid at the end to die.

That's when Steph shoved her backward, away from the struggling titans, and rammed her knife into one of the Kreelan's feet.

The alien gurgled a cry of pain, half her throat torn out by Mills, before he finally shoved her over, making her fall.

Right on top of Allison.

Without thinking, Allison propped up her sword, the handle on the ground. The blade pierced the alien's back armor as the warrior fell right on top of it, and the glittering tip burst from her chest armor only a few centimeters from Mills's neck.

Allison gasped as the Kreelan and Mills slammed down on top of her, driving the air from her lungs. But Allison didn't have to suffer their full weight. Most of it was supported by the handle of the sword.

After a moment, the weight lifted as Mills rolled off to one side, dragging the Kreelan with him.

"Bloody hell, girl," he gasped as he struggled to his knees. "Bloody hell." Mills grabbed his right shoulder with his left hand, literally holding the flesh together. The sword had cut clean through his collar bone and part of his shoulder blade, and he could tell from the wet rasp of his breathing that his right lung had been punctured, as well.

He looked up as a shadow fell over him, and Valentina, blood soaking the front of her uniform, slowly sank down beside him. Her face was deathly pale. "Ready for that margarita on the beach?"

Then she closed her eyes and slumped against his chest.

"Jesus," Mills whispered, fighting away the darkness that threatened to take him.

"You've got to get help, Allison." Steph pointed toward the battlefield, where the sounds of the guns had reached a crescendo of growls, staccato pops, and booms, mixed with the fading roar of the warriors. "Hurry, honey."

"Just ask..." Mills could barely get the words out as his right lung filled with blood. His heart was as broken as his body as he cradled Valentina, who lay lifeless against him. "Just ask...any Marine...for General Sparks."

"General Sparks," Allison repeated, and Steph nodded.

But as Allison rose to her feet she felt a clawed hand grip her arm.

With a cry of fright, she looked down to see the warrior, staring up at her.

* * *

Ku'ar-Marekh felt the life flowing from her body. She knew the blade held by the human pup had severed one of the major arteries inside her, and she would bleed to death in but moments.

Beyond the pain, the thought gave her a sense of peace.

Instead of the chill she expected as death came for her, she felt a growing warmth. It wasn't simply a trick of her dying body, but was from the Bloodsong. She could sense it more fully as her blood soaked the loose earth beneath her. She began to feel the emotions of her sisters again.

And the Ancient Ones. She could sense them now, as well. All who had lived and died since the days of the First Empress were bound in spirit to She Who Reigned. Ku'ar-Marekh could feel them now, as clearly as those who now fought and died against the humans here on this world.

The humans. She had not expected them to best her, but she did not regret their victory.

The small one, the child who had held the killing blade, was next to her. As the child made to stand up, Ku'ar-Marekh reached out and took her arm.

The young human made a small noise of fear and surprise, but did not attempt to flee.

Ku'ar-Marekh released the child's arm and instead held out her hand, palm up. Much to her surprise, the human slowly took it.

"In Her name, may thy Way be long and glorious, little one."

Giving the human's hand a gentle squeeze, Ku'ar-Marekh let go before closing her eyes and letting the warmth of death enfold her.

* * *

Allison had no idea what the alien had said, but in the moment that she spoke her final words, her eyes changed. Allison saw life in them, just before they closed for the final time.

As the alien's hand slipped away, Allison stood up and ran as fast as she could toward the sound of the guns.

* * *

Many light years away, the Empress stood upon the dais at the top of the pyramid of steps in the great throne room on the Empress Moon. She cast Her eyes upward, beyond the transparent crystal that formed the top of the gigantic pyramid that housed the palace, looking out at the stars.

And at one, in particular. With a second sight that could see beyond time and space, She watched Ku'ar-Marekh's last battle, and felt the priestess's pain as the sword pierced her.

The Empress opened Her heart wide as Ku'ar-Marekh's life bled away, releasing her spirit from the bonds of life, and the last priestess of the Nyur-A'il took her place among the Ancient Ones.

Across the vast stretches of the Empire, a vast wave was cast through the Bloodsong, an echo of the sorrow of the Empress.

SEVENTY-SIX

Allison had never run so far, so fast. Exhausted as she was, she knew that every second counted, and that the lives of her three friends depended on her. Even as she sucked air into her lungs, she bit her lip to drive away the fear that they would all be dead by the time she could get help.

She had never seen so much blood on a person who was still alive as she'd seen on both Mills and Valentina. And while Steph's wound wasn't as bad, she'd been bleeding a long time now. All three of them, Mills especially, looked like something right out of a vid about zombies that she had seen once with her older brother.

God, please don't let them die. She forced herself to go just a little faster, wishing with every step that she had Race, her brave, dead horse to carry her. Wishing the Kreelans had never come to her world. Wishing them all to Hell.

As she ran, heading right down the road past her farm, she came upon more and more bodies. Most of them were Kreelans, but there were many humans, too. Marines, like Mills.

And there were ships, both human and Kreelan. Many of the wrecks still burned, while others were nothing more than smoking piles of melted metal and plastic, surrounded by bits of debris. The stench of it, combined with the smell of blood and other bodily things she didn't want to even think about, made her want to gag.

Around her, there were no cries for help or screams of agony from the wounded or the dying. None here, human or Kreelan, were left alive. The humans had all been killed, and the Kreelans, she had read, committed suicide. None had ever been taken alive.

With a yelp, she dove to the ground as a stream of cannon shells whipped past her, stray rounds from the fight up ahead.

She looked up after a moment, and found herself next to a Kreelan warrior whose dead, sightless eyes were open, as if staring at her.

"Get up, Allison!" She looked away from the nightmarish blue face, mustering the courage to go on. She couldn't stop. Too much depended on her.

With a grimace, forcing herself to not be sick from the horror around her, she pushed herself up from the sticky pool of blood that the road had become and again started running.

Mills, Valentina, and Steph. I have to save them. I won't let them die. She kept repeating that mantra, over and over, with every step through the nightmare landscape around her.

She slowed momentarily as the gunfire, which had become deafening the closer she'd come to the battle, began to taper off, then stopped.

The silence that descended gave her a chill until she heard something she hadn't heard in what seemed like years: people cheering. She could see Marines on their big tanks and on the ground, holding up their arms and giving voice to their victory.

"We've won!"

The thought gave her a new burst of energy, and she ran toward the tank that was nearest her.

* * *

Sergeant Emilio Sanchez sat in a small patch of grass in the shadow of his tank. He was on the side facing away from the gruesome mass of dead aliens, leaning against one of the big road wheels. He could make out the smell of the charred paint and scorched metal from what was left of the tank's skirt, a sheet of relatively thin armor that was meant to protect the vehicle's vulnerable lower hull.

A Kreelan had thrown a lightning grenade that had stuck to it, and Sanchez had been sure they were done for.

They would have been, had not a lunatic commanding an infantry fighting vehicle driven alongside them, shearing off most of the skirt, the grenade along with it, just as the thing detonated. Both vehicles were scorched, but had survived.

Sanchez had every intention of making sure the crazy bastard got a medal and a case of beer as soon as he could figure out who it had been.

Taking another drag on his cigarette, he stared blankly at the original landing zone, toward the town, idly watching the columns of smoke rise from all the destroyed ships and vehicles there. Behind him, his crew and most of the others around them were hooting and hollering, celebrating their victory.

Sanchez just wanted to find a bar somewhere and get drunk, but he knew there probably weren't any bars left open on the entire planet, and Confederation warships were "dry," not allowing alcohol on-board.

"Navy prudes," he muttered, disgusted.

Taking a last drag on the cigarette, he flicked it away. Following it with his eyes, he noticed something moving in the distance, coming closer.

No, not something, you idiot, he chided himself. Someone.

"Pikula!" Standing up, he called out to his gunner, who was sitting on the turret. "Pikula!" he shouted, louder.

The woman turned around. "What is it, TC?" Her smile faltered as she caught the movement. "Holy shit! It's a civilian!"

"It's not just a civvie, it's a kid!" Sanchez was already running toward the grimy, blood-spattered girl, who was gasping for breath as she staggered more than ran toward him. "Get the medikit and some water!"

As he reached the girl, she collapsed in his arms, her chest heaving.

"Take it easy, kid. I've got you." He sat her down on the ground and knelt in front of her. "You're okay now. Nobody's gonna hurt you here."

She shook her head. "Need...to talk...to General Sparks."

He leaned back, shocked that she knew of Sparks. "Well, sure. We'll get you up to see the general when we've got you taken care of. You've been roughed up a..."

"No, now!" She leaned forward and grabbed his combat webbing with both hands and shook him, a look of desperation in her eyes. "I have to talk to him...right now!"

Sanchez rubbed his chin, thinking for a moment as Pikula dropped to her knees beside him, offering the girl a canteen.

Taking her hands off Sanchez, the girl grabbed it and took a single, greedy swig, before handing it back.

"Now," she begged him. "Please, there's no time! My friends are dying, or already dead. They need help."

"Right." Sanchez clicked the control for his unit's general channel. "Captain Kamov, this is Sanchez. I've got a civilian here who needs to talk to General Sparks." Looking into the girl's pleading gaze, he added, "It's an emergency, sir."

"Roger that." Kamov's response was instant. Sanchez had had his disagreements with the man, but one thing the captain wasn't was indecisive. "Stand by."

Barely a few heartbeats had passed when a voice came over Sanchez's headset. "This is Sparks. Go."

Sanchez took off his helmet and gently set it on the girl's head. "Just talk, honey. The general will hear you."

* * *

Hands on hips, Sparks stood at the ragged edge of the killing field where tens of thousands of dead Kreelans lay, his cavalry hat shading his eyes from the sun. While on the whole it had been a massacre, the aliens had managed to kill another three thousand of his Marines. He shuddered to think what they could have done if they had chosen to fight with more modern weapons. In some battles, they did, and others they didn't.

Like everything else about the Kreelans, Sparks didn't understand it, and that bothered him more than anything else. *How can we ever defeat an enemy we don't understand at all?* The thought further depressed him as he looked at the carnage.

"Nothing except a battle lost can be half so melancholy as a battle won." The operations officer, his face bandaged where a piece of shrapnel had sliced his cheek, murmured the words spoken by the Duke of Wellington centuries before.

"At least at Waterloo the end was in sight." Sparks gestured at the mass of bodies that lay sprawled in death. "This here was just a sideshow."

"Maybe so, sir, but we still won. That counts for something."

"I wonder," Sparks murmured. Turning to the other man, he said, "I assume you didn't just come over here to cheer me up, especially since you didn't bring a damn beer with you."

The operations officer smiled. "No, sir. I just wanted to pass on that Commodore Sato's coming down to pay his respects."

"And look for his wife, I imagine." Sparks had worked with Sato during the planning for this mission, but held him in high regard for another reason. Sato had saved Sparks's life, and that of his men and women, during their escape from the Keran disaster. And Sato's wife, Steph, had been right with Sparks and his regiment there, and had in her own way been very much a hero. Sparks planned to render every assistance to Sato to try and find his wife's body. He owed both of them that much. "Damn, that was an awful thing."

"Yes, sir. I won't argue with that." He looked out at the battlefield, following his general's gaze. "God, what a mess that'll be to clean up."

Sparks was about to reply when a voice sounded in his comm headset that was draped around his neck.

"Sir, I think you need to take this," his communications officer told him.

"What have you got?"

"Sir, it's an emergency call for you. I'm cutting you over to Sergeant Sanchez, a track commander in the 47th Armored Regiment."

There was a pause, then a beep, indicating the channel was open.

"This is Sparks. Go."

He was surprised to hear the voice of a young girl.

* * *

"General, sir, my name is Allison Murtaugh..." She paused, not sure how to say the right words to this stranger. The voice on the other end, the man, seemed as hard as steel.

"Go on, honey," the voice said, much softer. Even though his accent was different, one she had never heard before, his voice reminded her of her father's.

"Sir, my friends need help. Sergeant Mills and Valentina are terribly hurt, and Steph is, too. They're dying. Mills told me to run here and get you, so I did. Please help them!"

There was a brief pause before the general spoke again, the steel back in his voice. "You can count on it, Allison. Now please put Sergeant Sanchez back on."

Relieved to be rid of the weight of the helmet, Allison handed it back to Sanchez, who quickly slipped it on.

"General, sir?"

"Sanchez, crank up your track right now. Take Allison and have her show you where Mills and the others are. And if there are any corpsmen nearby, take them, too. If not, have your medikit handy. I'll be with you as soon as I can. Got all that, son?"

"Yes, sir!"

"Then ride hard and fast, trooper! Sparks out."

Sanchez pulled Allison to her feet and headed toward the tank. Pikula was just disappearing down the hatch to her position in the turret.

"Tibbets!" he called to the driver over the tank's comm link, "crank her up!"

As he helped Allison climb up the front of the tank, vibrating now from the power of the vehicle's big turbine engines, he told her, "Little lady, you're about to have the wildest ride of your life."

* * *

Sato sat in the passenger compartment of the shuttle from the *Orion*, desperately trying to shut off his brain, to banish the dark thoughts that clouded his mind.

With *Orion* severely damaged, he would be shifting his flag to *Conqueror*. Before he did, however, he had one last duty to perform as *Orion's* acting captain, burial services for his dead crew members. It was a task he dreaded, but like his other duties, he would perform it to the very best of his abilities. Semyonova and the others deserved no less.

In the meantime, a duty much closer to his heart called. He had to look for Steph's body. He had to bring her home. It would be a grisly task, looking over the thousands of bodies around the town of Breakwater, but he would do it. No matter how long it took or what he might find, he would do it.

He couldn't tell himself that she never would have come here had he not pushed her away, because that wouldn't be true. Steph was an adventurer, as he was in his own way, and she probably would have come, anyway.

"Commodore?"

He turned to see the copilot, standing in the doorway to the cramped flight deck.

The copilot handed him a headset. "Sir, General Sparks is calling for you."

"Thank you." He took the headset and slipped it on. "Sato here, general."

"Ichiro, get your ass down here. Steph and some other members of her team may have survived. I've got some troops on the way to them now. Head toward the western edge of Breakwater, and I'll send you exact coordinates as soon as I have them. You'll have to evac them. We don't have any boats left down here that can fly. You got that?"

Sato sat, staring wide-eyed at the forward bulkhead, not believing his ears.

"Sato?"

"Yes...yes, sir! We're on our way."

"Let's hustle, son. Sparks, out."

"Pilot!" Sato ordered. "Take us down, now! Emergency descent!"

* * *

Allison didn't know if she should be terrified or elated. She was standing in the commander's position in the big tank as it raced along, going so fast it sometimes went completely airborne when they came over a rise in the ground. The commander, Sanchez, stood behind her on the engine deck, clinging to handholds on the turret for dear life.

"A little to the left!" Sanchez had fitted her with an extra helmet so she could talk over the tank's intercom and guide the driver. She pointed to a spot about a hundred meters away now, where a few figures were visible on the ground.

"It's them!" Sanchez told the driver. "Pull up close and stop."

The tank slowed at the last possible moment, then slewed to the side and came to a stop. The driver was careful to make sure that the dust and dirt the vehicle kicked up didn't hit the blood-soaked bodies.

"This is Sanchez. We found 'em." He didn't wait for his company commander to respond before he linked the coordinates to the division's net. Sparks would be able to find them easily now.

Sanchez helped Allison out of the turret, then hopped down to the ground. Pikula and Tibbets, both with medikits, were right behind him.

"Holy Jesus," Sanchez whispered, crossing himself. The blond-haired woman, who he knew by sight was Commodore Sato's wife, lay on her back, eyes closed. The only major injury he could see was her leg, but that was enough. It was a mass of dried and matted blood.

The other two were far worse. A huge Marine - Mills, he must be, from what the girl had said - lay on his back. There was a horrible wound in his right shoulder, as if he'd had a run-in with a bandsaw and lost. His face was covered in blood.

In his left arm he cradled a woman who had been stabbed clean through with a sword, with another set of stab wounds in one shoulder.

There was blood everywhere.

"Sanchez..." The tone of Pikula's voice echoed his own thoughts. They were all dead.

Allison stood there beside Sanchez, shivering as tears brimmed in her eyes. "I was too late."

Sanchez knelt down next to Steph first and reached out with a pair of fingers to her throat to feel for a pulse. "She's alive. Barely." He gestured to Tibbets. "Get a fresh bandage on the wound and shoot her up with some antibiotics and stims."

Then he turned to Mills and the other woman. "What's her name?"

"Valentina." Allison slowly knelt beside her two entwined friends. She had been too slow. Too slow. Steph was still alive, but they were dead. "No."

Again reaching his fingers out, he touched Valentina's throat.

He shook his head and was just pulling his fingers away when he stopped. "What the hell?" He tried again, waiting longer. "Son of a bitch! It's slow as hell, but she's got a pulse! Pikula, get a patch on the wound in her back, then we're gonna roll her off this guy."

Then he checked Mills for a pulse. "I don't believe it. He's still alive, too."

Ripping open the medikits, Sanchez and his crew did what they could to patch up Mills and the two women.

As they worked, Allison heard another sonic boom and looked up. A small ship glinted in the sky, and as she watched, it headed right for them.

Rescue had come.

Smiling, hope rekindled that her friends might yet live, she turned back to watch as the tankers gently rolled Valentina off Mills and put a dressing over the wound in her stomach.

That's when she noticed that the Kreelan who had nearly killed them all, the one with the dead eyes, was nowhere to be seen. Steph's knife was still stuck in the ground where she had impaled the warrior's foot, just as it had been, but there was no sign of the alien's body.

She was gone.

* * *

The first thing Steph noticed was the vibration. It was rhythmic and steady, but seemed...hurried.

After a moment, she realized that she was being carried.

The second thing she noticed was her left hand. Someone was holding it, and she could tell just by touch whose hand it was.

Her eyes fluttered open, and she looked up to see a familiar face looking down at her. It was the face of the man she loved. Beyond him she could make out the interior of a small ship, and the shapes of people she didn't know, carrying her along.

"Ichiro," she breathed as she was gently lowered onto a foldout bunk in the ship. "I knew...you'd come."

"The whole Empire couldn't have kept me away." His hand tightened on hers. "And I'll never leave you again."

Just before she drifted off into a painless, dreamless sleep, she felt the warmth of his lips on hers.

EPILOGUE

On the open plain of Ural-Murir, an island continent in the southern hemisphere of the Homeworld, stood the temple of the Nyur-A'il.

As with all the temples of the seven orders from the ancient times, it had long since fallen into ruin. The stone of which the buildings were made was eroded and crumbling, the runes and glyphs of the Old Tongue long since erased by wind and rain.

The dilapidated state of the temple was an illusion, however. For the true nature of this place, as with the other ancient temples, lay beyond mere stone. It was in the spirit of the Ancient Ones, the high priests and priestesses now dead, whose spirits dwelled here.

The Empress stood on the worn dais of the temple's *Kalai-Il*, Her white robes and hair reflecting the gentle magenta hue of the sky as the sun began to set. Around the edges of the massive central stone base, torches flickered in anticipation of night's fall.

Before Her lay Ku'ar-Marekh's body on a carefully constructed pyre of wood. Each piece had been brought by one of the warrior priestesses and clawless mistresses who now stood upon the weathered stone rings of the *Kalai-Il*. They had come from all over the Empire, brought here by the will of the Empress.

As had Ku'ar-Marekh's body. She was the first high priestess to fall in battle since the last great war with a soulless enemy among the stars. And, as She had done since the time of Keel-Tath, the body of a high priestess would always be given the last rites, and would never be left behind for an enemy.

The difference between this ceremony and those in ages past was that Ku'ar-Marekh was the last of her kind. This had never before happened in the long history of the Empire. There would be no more disciples to follow in her footsteps, to keep alive the Way of the Nyur-A'il.

For this, the Empress mourned, and the skin below her eyes was black with the tears of Her soul.

Around the pyre stood five high priestesses of the surviving orders. The sixth, she who would have stood at the right hand of the Empress representing the Desh-Ka, was absent. Tesh-Dar, the greatest living warrior of the Empire, remained cloistered in her temple, and there would remain until the Empress again summoned her. When it was time.

To the left of the Empress stood Pan'ne-Sharakh, the oldest and wisest of the clawless ones. All of the high priestesses had weapons crafted by the ancient armorer, who could shape the living steel of their blades like no other, and make each a unique work of art worthy of display in the throne room on the Empress Moon.

Her hands clasped in the sleeves of her black robes, Pan'ne-Sharakh stood, head bowed in silent thought. The Empress knew that she mourned for Ku'ar-Marekh, but that the ancient mistress's heart mourned far more the silence in the Bloodsong of Tesh-Dar. The two had long been close, perhaps closer than the Empress had been to the great warrior before ascending to the throne, even though Tesh-Dar and the Empress were sisters by blood, born from the same womb.

Around the high priestesses, filling the dais, were the senior clawless mistresses of the castes from among Her Children. From porters of water to the builders, they represented the spirits of those who had been most loyal to the First Empress in Her darkest hour. All now stood in honor of the fallen high priestess of the Nyur-A'il.

Beyond the massive platform of the *Kalai-Il*, on the concentric raised rings of ancient stone stood the hundreds of warrior priestesses and acolytes of the five orders. There were none from the Desh-Ka, as Tesh-Dar had no disciples.

An even greater tragedy, the Empress thought darkly, before turning Her gaze upon the warriors watching from above, remembering from ages past how there once had been many thousands.

Never would such a time come again, She knew.

And yet, solemn as the occasion might be, the Empress's heart was warmed by Ku'ar-Marekh's spirit. Her soul, complete now, had at last taken its rightful place among the warriors of the spirit.

"My Children," the Empress began, "we grieve the loss this day of the high priestess of the Nyur-A'il, not because she fell in battle, for she did so with great honor, but because she was the last of her kind. Never again shall there be another. For with her death, the ancient crystal that dwelled here, one of the seven that formed the heart of the ancient orders, has become dark and cold. Never again shall a warrior experience the fire of the Change in the temple of the Nyur-A'il."

She paused, looking around the inner circle of high priestesses. "Never before has this happened, in all the pages of the Books of Time. The Nyur-A'il was fated to be the first to pass into the darkness, but it shall not be the last." She glanced at the empty place to her right where Tesh-Dar would have been standing.

"In this, the Last War, all of us shall succumb to the same fate unless we can find the One and the tomb of the First Empress. Even then, most who stand here before Me now shall fall in battle, as is your honor and your right.

"I wish My Children to survive the dark night that is falling over us, borne by the Curse of Keel-Tath. Yet even the ancient prophecies from the oldest of the Books of Time do not speak of our salvation, only what we need to achieve it."

The warriors and clawless ones nodded. All of them knew the peril in which the Empire found itself, and realized that they were all bound to the same fate.

Sensing their darkened spirits through the Bloodsong, the Empress caressed Her belly where Her next child was growing in Her womb. It was a female, for which She was thankful, but would be born with silver talons. Sterile. While the Empress would give birth to new life, She knew that it would only bring Her Children one step closer to extinction.

"The humans," the Empress went on, looking up at the stars. "They are the key. We know much about them from the first of their ships that came to us, and from others since, lost in battle. We have pressed them hard, driving our blade deep.

"Yet, this is not prey we wish to kill quickly. They now build greater, more powerful ships and are training legions of warriors that will bring you much honor in the coming cycles. But we must bleed them slowly; I do not want to overwhelm them and break their courage. And no more shall we take them to the arenas. It is clear they do not understand the honor we accord them."

The high priestesses nodded their understanding. The pace of the offensives against the humans would be slowed. It did not upset them, but gladdened them. For the humans were worthy opponents, and letting their soulless race live longer would give greater opportunity for the warriors of Her Children to bring honor to the Empress. And all of them had seen by now that the arenas were nothing but slaughter pens for most of the humans, slaughter in which there was no honor, nor glory for the Empress.

"The world where Ku'ar-Marekh and her legions fell, we shall leave to the humans in her honor, until the time comes when we have found the One, or until we perish from the cosmos."

"In Thy name," the assembled warriors and clawless ones intoned, "shall it be so."

The Empress watched as the sun set over the distant white-topped mountains, beyond which lay the great sea of Tulyan-Ara'ath. The sky rippled with fiery hues of red and orange, yellow and violet that glittered in her silver-flecked eyes, eyes that opened onto an ageless soul.

"It is time."

Acolytes handed torches to the five high priestesses and Pan'ne-Sharakh, who stepped forward and set alight Ku'ar-Marekh's funeral pyre. As the flames grew, the wood crackling and throwing sparks into the air, they stepped back and watched as their sister's body was consumed.

As the smoke rose into the sky, the Empress focused Her love on the once-tortured spirit of Ku'ar-Marekh, whose soul now rested in the peaceful stillness of the Afterlife.

* * *

The beach was perfect. The sand was white and fine, the water clear blue and warm. A light breeze blew in from the ocean, carrying with it the sound of the gently rolling surf and the voices of the children playing in the waves.

Valentina took a sip of her margarita, savoring the taste of the tequila and strawberries as she sat in a beach chair under a huge umbrella. She watched Allison, hopping up and down in the waves and screaming with delight as she and some other kids she had found to play with splashed each other.

Not having any other relatives on Alger's World, and not wanting to stay there, Allison had come back to Earth. Ichiro and Steph, who had recovered quickly from her leg wound, had taken care of her while Valentina and Mills were in the hospital.

But when Valentina had been well enough for visitors, Allison had asked if she could live with her and Mills. Permanently.

"You two are going to get married, right?" The girl had gone straight for the jugular with an assumption about something that Valentina had only just been giving some thought to. "And well, I thought maybe you could adopt me. I promise I won't be any trouble!"

Valentina had been taken completely off-guard, and the girl's expression tore at her heart.

She was a great kid, and Valentina would never be able to have her own. The injuries she'd sustained in the battle at Saint Petersburg had seen to that. She'd never considered adopting, because she had never really given much thought to being a mother. But after all that had happened...

Adopt Allison? Why not?

Looking into Allison's expectant eyes, Valentina knew she couldn't say no. Instead, smiled and said, "Okay. We will."

Allison had been elated, but that was nothing compared to her delirium after meeting Valentina's parents, Dmitri and Ludmilla Sikorsky. That's when she discovered they owned a horse farm, and Allison could ride as much and as long as she wanted. And she was in complete heaven when they presented her with her very own horse.

Marrying Mills, on the other hand, had been something that Valentina had been a lot less certain about, and so had he.

While they had been living together after they got out of the hospital, they hadn't discussed anything more serious than what Valentina had originally promised him. Some time together on a beautiful, sunny beach, sipping margaritas.

They had Allison along, of course, albeit sleeping in an adjacent room at the hotel. She didn't seem to mind, and was happy to let Valentina and Mills have a little privacy.

"Looks like she's doing well enough." Mills, sitting next to her, was watching the kids, too, and when Valentina glanced at him, she could see a look of fondness on his face. While he was still a bit of a tough guy on the outside, she knew that he couldn't have loved Allison more if she'd been his daughter by birth. "Tough kid."

Valentina smiled, thinking of how happy the three of them were now.

It hadn't been that way at first. Both of them had gone through hell the last few months since returning from Alger's World, but Mills had gotten the worst of it. While her own injuries had been bad enough, her implants had shut down her body's systems after the warrior had stabbed her, preventing her from bleeding out. She had lost a kidney and suffered some other internal injuries, not to mention the damage to her shoulder joint, but had recovered relatively quickly. She still experienced some pain, but knew that over time it would fade away to nothing.

The worst of it, she thought wryly, was that she'd never wear a bikini again. Her body had too many scars.

Mills, on the other hand, almost hadn't made it. Surgeons on the *Guadalcanal* had worked on him for six hours. His heart had stopped three times, and the surgeons would have given up on him the last time, except for Sato's impassioned pleas for them to try to resuscitate him one last time. Just as they were about to give up, his heart started beating.

His survival had been little short of a miracle.

After that he'd had to battle a series of infections, and then the ultimate torture of physical therapy for his right shoulder, which had to be completely reconstructed. Many had been the nights when she'd held him, his body shivering from the pain. He refused to take any painkillers after leaving the hospital. At first she had thought it was because he was trying to be a macho fool, but gradually realized it was because he was afraid of becoming addicted. As a big, powerful man, a trained killer, he had very few fears, but that was one of them.

Finally his condition reached a tipping point. The pain eased off, his strength and range of motion dramatically improved, and after the last of the dressings and restraints had been removed, he was again able to sleep.

Among other things, she thought with a sly smile.

"What's that look for?" He squinted at her, as if trying to read her thoughts. "God, but you're a randy wench."

Valentina couldn't restrain a laugh. "Well, in that case, I guess we needn't have a repeat of last night."

"Well," he said quickly, "you wouldn't want to deprive me of some great physical therapy, would you?" He made a show of moving his right arm, flexing the muscles that, between his physical therapy and increasingly tough workouts, were quickly growing back to their earlier massive size. Unlike her, he had no reservations about displaying his battle scars for all to see. He liked the attention.

His flexing drew more than a few appreciative glances from some of the bikini-clad women nearby.

"You're hopeless." Rolling her eyes, Valentina took another sip of her margarita, turning her attention back to Allison.

"But you love me, anyway."

"Yes, you idiot. God help me, but I do."

* * *

Ichiro came into the apartment and closed the door behind him, puffing a breath out through his lips. It had been a long day at Africa Station, as most days were, overseeing the repairs of *Orion* and the construction of the next batch of new battleships. Eight of them were being built at Africa Station, with another six in the yards at Avignon and four at Ekaterina. The new class was only slightly changed from the *Orions*, but the next battleships that were now being designed would be even larger and more powerful.

It was exhausting work, but it was no longer the focus of his life. He called Steph at least once a day to tell her he loved her, and made sure he did at least one little thing each day when he came home to prove it. And sometimes a big thing or two.

But his work week was over. While he was technically always on call, unless Earth were attacked, he was looking forward to an uninterrupted weekend that he fully expected to enjoy.

His wife, too, had made more room in her life for their marriage. She was back working on the president's staff, but this time as a coordinator for the agency the president was establishing to handle the massive refugee problem. The goal wasn't to simply find a place for refugees to go, but to use those who were willing to establish new colonies on the edge of human-explored space.

While that was an option for adults and families, it didn't help the war orphans like Allison and the other children from Alger's World. That was a much harder problem to solve, and is what Steph concentrated her energies on while at work.

Her first success had been placing the children Allison had saved in foster homes. The children had been on one of the boats that had escaped to reach the fleet, and the kids had first class accomodations in Admiral Voroshilov's living quarters aboard the *Guadalcanal* for the trip back to Earth.

After the story of what Allison had done hit the press, Steph's department had been deluged with thousands of inquiries from people offering to adopt. After personally interviewing the families that seemed most promising, Steph had placed Amrit, Vanhi, and the other children with families on Earth, and had stayed in touch with them to make sure they were getting the love and care they deserved.

"Steph?" He called out again.

No answer.

Frowning, he quickly hung up his uniform jacket in the foyer closet, then walked down the hall toward the living room.

He wasn't worried, although Steph had been acting a bit odd the last couple days. He hadn't been able to put his finger on it, but she'd seemed unusually anxious.

Walking into the living room, he saw her there, seated on the couch. She was leaning over, her elbows on her knees, with her chin propped up by her hands. She was beaming at him, but she had wet streaks down her cheeks.

Ichiro stopped, confused by her behavior. "Steph, are you all right?"

She nodded as she stood up and came over to him, reaching for his hands. "Yes, we're just fine."

Cocking his head, Ichiro asked, "We? You mean..."

"Yes." She nodded, a look of uncertainty on her face. "I'm pregnant. I know we hadn't exactly planned it, but-"

She didn't get a chance to finish as Ichiro threw his arms around her.

"I'm going to be a father!" Lifting her gently from the floor, he whirled her around, his heart filled with joy.

* * *

"It worked, by God." Secretary of State Hamilton Barca's deep voice carried the mixture of pleasure and relief he felt at the news he had brought to the president's cabinet meeting. "Every government that was even whispering about secession before the Alger's World operation has stepped back from the proverbial abyss. They remain concerned, obviously, but nobody can argue now. The Kreelans can be beaten. And the real key to it was the footage that Steph gathered. The stuff with those kids surviving until the Marines got there, and the recounting of the young lady - Allison, correct? - who helped kill the warrior leader..." He shook his head in admiration. "Along with the combat footage, it was some incredibly powerful stuff that really helped turn things around on the diplomatic front." He grinned at the president. "Your speech didn't hurt, either."

At the head of the table, McKenna blew out her breath and leaned back in her chair, a huge weight lifting from her shoulders. The news about the operation had received a lukewarm reception from the Confederation planetary ambassadors until the video footage had been released. It had been heavily edited, of course. Steph's assistant had compiled a documentary from the mass of footage Steph had captured, and McKenna and her defense counsel had been the first to see it. Some of what they had seen had been disturbing, to say the least. In particular, the phenomenon that had nearly led to General Sparks's forces being defeated.

Those things, McKenna had decided, the public did not yet need to see.

With Steph's help from her hospital bed where she was recovering from her leg wound, the raw footage had been transformed into a documentary that had left McKenna with her heart in her throat, overcome with pride in the men and women she had sent there, and in the people of Alger's World who had fought to survive.

Most of the planet's population had survived, although the butcher's bill had still been enormous. Fifty thousand civilians and Territorial Army soldiers had died. Another eight thousand sailors and Marines had been killed in the fighting, with hundreds more wounded.

But it could have been far, far worse.

"The reconstruction effort on Alger's is moving along well," Barca continued. "A number of other worlds have even stepped forward, volunteering to send workers and supplies to assist in the effort." He cocked an eyebrow at the president. "That, Madam President, is a first."

"They feel confident enough to send some of their own resources off-world in troubled times," said Vice President Navarre. "That is indeed a good sign."

"How are things going on the production front?" McKenna turned to Defense Minister Sabine and Admiral Tiernan.

"Aside from some supply problems we're having with certain components, things are actually going amazingly well," Joshua Sabine told her.

"Supply problems?" McKenna leaned forward. "Who do I need to lean on?"

Tiernan and Sabine exchanged grins. "No one this time, Madam President," Tiernan told her. "The problem is simply that our growing building capacity has outstripped our ability to produce certain parts, mainly for the hyperdrive engines.

We had anticipated that problem and were already establishing additional production facilities, but our shipwrights and yard workers have been, shall we say, excessively efficient."

"So what's the projection for the fleet's strength?" McKenna asked.

Sabine smiled. "We'll double the number of ships and nearly triple our warship tonnage in the next eighteen months."

"And that's a conservative estimate," Tiernan added. "More importantly, by that time we'll have naval shipyards established in sixteen systems, four times what we have now. So in case the Kreelans give us another sucker punch, we won't have to worry so much about its impact on our shipbuilding."

McKenna nodded, impressed. "And what about the Marines and Territorial Army?"

"We've found a candidate world that we'd like to set up as a primary Marine training facility," Tiernan told her. "We'll expand the Corps as the Navy builds its transport capacity, as that's really the limiting factor beyond raw manpower. We certainly don't have any shortage of volunteers."

"And the Territorial Army is rapidly expanding, as well." Sabine paused, considering how far they'd come from the chaos three years before. "We've got cadres fully established on every Confederation world now, and some of the bureaucratic interference we were starting to get from the governments considering secession has pretty much vanished since the Alger's World operation."

McKenna nodded in satisfaction. They had bought the Confederation some time to bind itself together and better prepare its defenses. It was time she desperately needed, because she had no doubt that this war, more than any other ever fought by humanity, was going to be a long, bloody affair.

We'll win in the end, she thought. There was no other option. Because in this war, the only alternative to victory for humanity would be its extinction.

WHERE IT ALL BEGAN: EMPIRE!

If you've enjoyed this trilogy from the *In Her Name* series so far, don't miss the story that started it all, *Empire!*

Set one hundred years after *First Contact*, *Empire* begins the tale of the climax of the human-kreelan war.

To give you a taste of what's to come, here's the first chapter of *Empire* — enjoy!

* * *

The blast caught Solon Gard, an exhausted captain of New Constantinople's beleaguered Territorial Army, completely by surprise. He had not known that the enemy had sited a heavy gun to the north of his decimated unit's last redoubt, a thick-walled house of a style made popular in recent years. Like most other houses in the planet's capitol city, this one was now little more than a gutted wreck.

But the Kreelan gun's introductory salvo was also its last: a human heavy weapons team destroyed it with a lucky shot before the Territorial Army soldiers were silenced by a barrage of inhumanly accurate plasma rifle fire.

The battle had become a vicious stalemate.

A woman's voice suddenly cut through the fog in Solon's head as he fought his way out from under the smoking rubble left by the cannon hit. He found himself looking up at the helmeted face of his wife, Camilla. Her eyes were hidden behind the mirrored faceplate of the battered combat helmet she wore.

"Solon, are you hurt?"

"No," he groaned, shaking his head, "I'm all right."

She helped him up, her petite form struggling with her husband's greater bulk: two armored mannequins embracing in an awkward dance.

Solon glanced around. "Where's Armand?"

"Dead," she said in a brittle voice. She wiped the dust from her husband's helmet, wishing she could touch his hair, his face, instead of the cold, scarred metal. She gestured to the pile of debris that Solon had been buried in. The wall had exploded inward a few feet from where he and Armand had been. The muddy light of day, flickering blood-red from the smoke that hung over the city, revealed an armored glove that jutted from under a plastisteel girder. Armand. He had been a friend of their family for many years and was the godfather of their only son. Now... now he was simply gone, like so many others.

Solon reached down and gently touched the armored hand of his best friend. "Silly fool," he whispered hoarsely. "You should have gone to the shelter with the others, like I told you. You could never fight, even when we were children." Armand had never had any military training, but after his wife and daughter were killed in the abattoir their city had become, he had come looking for Solon, to fight and die by his side. And so he had.

"It's only the two of us," Camilla told him wearily, "and Enrique and Snowden." Behind her was a pile of bodies in a dark corner, looking like a monstrous spider in the long shadows that flickered over them. The survivors had not had the time or strength to array them properly. Their goal had simply been to get them out of the way. Honor to the dead came a distant second to the desperation to stay among the living. "I think Jennings's squad across the street may be gone, too."

"Lord of All," Solon murmured, still trying to get his bearings and come to grips with the extent of their disaster. With only the four of them left, particularly if Jennings's squad had been wiped out, the Kreelans had but to breathe hard and the last human defensive line would be broken.

"It can always get worse," a different female voice told him drily.

Solon turned to see Snowden raise her hand unenthusiastically. Platinum hair was plastered to her skull in a greasy matte of sweat and blood, a legacy of the flying glass that had peeled away half her scalp during an earlier attack. She looked at him with eyes too exhausted for sleep, and did not make any move to get up from where she was sitting. Her left leg was broken above the knee, the protruding bone covered by a field dressing and hasty splint that Camilla had put together.

Enrique peered at them from the corner where he and Camilla had set up their only remaining heavy weapon, a pulse gun that took two to operate. Its snout poked through a convenient hole in the wall. From there, Enrique could see over most of their platoon's assigned sector of responsibility, or what was left of it. In the dreary orange light that made ghosts of the swirling smoke over the dying city, Enrique watched the dark figures of the enemy come closer, threading their way through the piles of shattered rubble that had once been New Constantinople's premier shopkeeper's district. He watched as their sandaled feet trod over the crumpled spires of the Izmir All-Faith Temple, the most beautiful building on the planet until a couple of weeks ago. Since the Kreelans arrived, nearly twenty million people and thirty Navy ships had died, and nothing made by human hands had gone untouched.

But beyond the searching muzzle of Enrique's gun, the advancing Kreelans passed many of their sisters who had died as the battle here had ebbed and flowed. Their burned and twisted bodies were stacked like cordwood at the approaches to the humans' crumbling defense perimeter, often enmeshed with the humans who had killed them. Enemies in life, they were bound together in death with bayonets and claws in passionate, if gruesome, embraces.

Still, they came. They always came.

Solon caught himself trying to rub his forehead through his battered helmet. *Lord, am I tired*, he thought. Their company was part of the battalion that had been among the last of the reserves to be activated for the city's final stand, and the

Territorial Army commander had brought them into action three days before. Three days. It had been a lifetime.

"One-hundred and sixty-two people, dead," he whispered to himself, thinking of the soldiers he had lost in the last few days. But they had lasted longer than most. Nearly every company of the first defensive ring had been wiped out to the last man and woman in less than twenty-four hours. Solon and his company were part of the fourth and final ring around the last of the defense shelters in this sector of the city. If the Kreelans got through...

"Hey, boss," Enrique called quietly. "I hate to interrupt, but they're getting a bit close over here. You want me to light 'em up?"

"I'll do the honors," Camilla told Solon, patting him on the helmet. "You need to get yourself back together."

"No arguments here," he answered wearily, propping himself against the remains of the wall. "I'll keep on eye on this side."

Camilla quickly took her place next to the gunner. "I'm glad you didn't wait much longer to let us know we had company, Enrique," she chided after carefully peering out at the enemy. "They're so close I can see their fangs." She checked the charge on the pulse gun's power pack. A fresh one would last for about thirty seconds of continuous firing, an appetite that made having both a gunner and a loader to service the hungry weapon a necessity.

"Yeah," Enrique smiled, his lips curling around the remains of an unlit cigarette butt he held clenched between his dirt-covered lips. He had tossed his helmet away the first thing, preferring to wear only a black bandanna around his forehead. His grime stained hands tightened on the gun's controls and his eyes sighted on the line of advancing Kreelans. "Looks like they think we're all finished, since we haven't shot back at 'em for a while." He snickered, then snugged his shoulder in tight to the shoulder stock of the gun. "Surprise..."

Solon was hunched down next to a blown-out window, looking for signs of the Kreelans trying to flank them, when he noticed the shattered portrait of a man and woman on the floor next to him. He picked up the crushed holo image of the young man and his bride and wondered who they might have been. Saying a silent prayer for their souls, he carefully set the picture out of his way. Somehow, the image seemed sacred, a tiny reminder of the precariousness of human existence, of good times past, and perhaps, hopes for the future. These two, who undoubtedly lay dead somewhere in this wasteland, would never know that their own lives were more fragile and finite than the plastic that still struggled to protect their images.

He turned as he heard the coughing roar of Enrique's pulse gun as it tore into the alien skirmish line. He listened as the gunner moderated his bursts, conserving the weapon's power while choosing his targets. Solon was glad Enrique had lived this long. He was as good a soldier as could be found in the Territorial Army. They had all been good soldiers, and would make the Kreelans pay dearly for taking the last four lives that Solon had left to offer as an interest payment toward humanity's survival.

As he looked through the dust and smoke, the thermal imager in Solon's visor gave him an enhanced view of the devastation around him, the computer turning the sunset into a scene of a scarlet Hell. He prayed that his seven-year-old son, Reza, remained safe in the nearby bunker. He had lost count of the number of times he had prayed for his boy, but it did not matter. He prayed again, and would go on praying, because it was the only thing he could do. Reza and the other children of their defense district had been taken to the local shelter, a deep underground bunker that could withstand all but a direct orbital bombardment, or so they hoped. Solon only wished that he had been able to see his little boy again before he died. "I love you, son," he whispered to the burning night.

Behind him, Camilla hurriedly stripped off the expended power pack from the pulse gun and clipped on another. She had come to do it so well that Enrique barely missed a beat in his firing.

Solon saw movement in a nearby building that was occupied by one of the other platoons: a hand waving at him from a darkened doorway. He raised his own hand in a quick salute, not daring to risk his head or arm for a more dashing salutation.

He made one more careful sweep of the street with his enhanced vision. Although he had spent his life in service to the Confederation as a shipbuilder, not as a hardened Marine or sailor, Solon knew that he needed to be extra careful in everything he did now. His body was past its physical limit, and the need for sleep was dragging all of them toward mistakes that could lead them to their deaths. Vigilance was survival.

As he finished his visual check, he relaxed slightly. All was as he had seen it before. Nothing moved. Nothing changed but the direction of the smoke's drift, and the smell of burning wood and flesh that went with it. He felt more than heard the hits the other side of his little fortress was taking from Kreelan light guns, and was relieved to hear Enrique's pulse gun yammer back at them like an enraged dog.

He glanced back toward the building occupied by the other platoon just as a massive barrage of Kreelan weapons fire erupted on the far side. He watched in horror as the structure began to crumble under the onslaught. The human defenders, sensing the futility of holding on, came boiling out into the street, heading for Solon's position, only to be cut down in a brutal crossfire from further down the lane.

The firing tapered off, and Solon saw shadows rapidly flowing toward the other platoon's survivors: Kreelan warriors silently advancing, swords drawn. They killed with energy weapons when they had to, but preferred more personal means of combat.

"Oh my God," Solon whispered, knowing that his own final stand would soon be upon him: they were surrounded now, cut off. His throat constricted and his stomach threatened to heave up the handful of tasteless ration cake he had eaten earlier in the day. He flipped up the visor for a moment to look at the scene with his own eyes, then flipped it back down to penetrate the smoky darkness.

Suddenly, a lone figure darted across the street, plunging suicidally into the raging battle. Under the figure's arm swung what could have been an oversized doll, but Solon knew that it was not. The little arms clung to the neck of the madly running soldier and the rag doll's little legs kicked at empty air. With a sinking sensation, Solon realized who it was.

"Reza!" he shouted, his heart hammering with fear and joy, wondering how in the Lord's name the boy had gotten here.

With a crack of thunder, the soldier's luck ran out as a crimson lance struck him, spinning him around like a top. He collapsed into the rubble, shielding the boy's body with his own.

Solon roared in the protective fury only a parent can know, his voice thundering above the clamoring of the guns. Camilla turned just in time to see him leap through the blasted wall into the carnage raging beyond.

"Solon!" she screamed, struggling up from her position next to the hammering pulse gun.

"No!" Enrique yelled at her, grabbing for her arm. He was too late to stop her as she bolted from the pit. "Dammit!" he hissed, struggling to change the empty and useless magazine himself. He pried the heavy canister off the gun's breech section with blind, groping hands while his bloodshot eyes tracked the rapidly approaching shadows of the enemy.

Solon suddenly staggered back over the shattered wall. His breath came in long heaves as if he had just finished running a marathon, and his armor was pitted and smoking from half a dozen glancing hits. In his arms was a small bundle of rags. Camilla nearly fainted at the sight of Reza's face, his skin black with soot and streaked with tears of fright.

"Mama," the boy cried, reaching for her.

"Oh, baby," she said softly, taking him in her arms and rocking him. "What are you doing here?" Camilla asked.

Solon collapsed next to her, wrapping his arms around his wife and child.

"What happened to the bunker?" Snowden shouted in between bursts from her rifle as she tried to kill the Kreelans who escaped Enrique's non-stop firing.

"The same thing that's going to happen to us if you guys don't start shooting!" Enrique screamed hoarsely, finally slamming a new – and the last – magazine into his pulse gun. "The Blues are all over the place out here!"

Reluctantly letting go of his wife and son, Solon grabbed up his rifle and thrust its muzzle through a hole in the wall. Gritting his teeth in rage and a newfound determination to survive, to protect his wife and son, he opened fire on the wraiths that moved through the darkness.

Camilla, after a last hug, set Reza down next to Snowden. "Take care of him," she begged before taking up her station next to Enrique.

Snowden nodded and held Reza tightly as the thunder of gunfire surrounded them.

* * *

The sky was black as pitch, black as death, as the priestess walked alone over the arena this world had become. Her sandaled feet touched the ground but left no sound, no footprint. She looked up toward where the stars should be, yearning for the great moon that shone over the Homeworld. But the only sight to be had was the glowing red smears of the fires that were reflected by the wafting smoke and dust.

As she made her way across the field of carnage, she touched the bodies of the fallen children to honor them as they had honored their Empress. They had sacrificed their lives to show their love for Her. She grieved for them all, that they had died this day, never again to feel the flame that drove them to battle, the thrill of sword and claw, never again to serve the Empress through their flesh. Now they basked in the quiet sunset of the Afterlife, someday perhaps to join the ranks of the Ancient Ones, the warriors of the spirit.

She moved on toward her destination. It had once been a human dwelling, but now was a mound of ashen rubble. It squatted impetuously in the wasteland created by weapons the Kreela disdained to use. The humans had never realized that the destruction of their worlds was caused by their own predilection for such weaponry, to which the Kreela sometimes had to respond in kind. The warriors of the Empress sought battles of the mind, body, and spirit, of sword and claw, and not of brute destruction.

Watching the battles rage here for several cycles of the sun across the sky, she had become increasingly curious about these particular humans who fought so well, and at last had decided that perhaps they were worthy of her personal attention. She bade the young warriors to rest, to wait for her return, before setting out on her own journey of discovery.

She paused when she reached the back of the crumbled structure that hid the humans she sought. She listened for their heartbeats, smelled their pungent body odor, and felt for their strange alien spirit with her mind. After a moment she had an image of them, of where they sat and stood within.

Silent as the dead around her, she moved to a chosen point along the wall. Her breathing and heart stilled, she concealed everything about herself that made her presence real. Unless one of the humans looked directly at her, she would be utterly invisible.

Then she stepped through the wall, her flesh and armor melding with the essence of the barrier as she passed through without so much as a whisper.

* * *

"Is that all you remember, honey?" Camilla asked Reza softly, brushing his unruly hair back with her hand, which was temporarily freed from the armored skin she had been wearing for the past several days.

"Yes, Mama," he replied. The fear had mostly left him, now that he was with them again, and that they thought he had done the right thing. "All I remember was lots of smoke. Then someone started to scream. People ran, hurting each other, because they were afraid. Someone, Madame Barnault, I think, led me out, but I lost her after we got outside. I remembered where Papa said you would be, so I came here to find you. I almost made it, except the Kreelans were everywhere. That's when Kerry–"

"That's enough, son," Solon said gently, not wanting to force the boy to describe the death of the soldier, who had been another friend of their family. "It's all right, now. You're here and safe, and that's all that counts." He exchanged a quick glance with Camilla. *Safe* was hardly the word to use, he knew, even though the Kreelans had apparently given up for the day. Reza would now have to suffer whatever fate was in store for the rest of them. Solon could not justify risking someone else's life for the boy's benefit. One had already died for him.

"Reza," Camilla told him, "I want you to stay with Snowden and help her find more ammunition for us." She leaned close to his ear and whispered, "And I want you to watch out for her and protect her. She's hurt and needs a big boy like you to care for her."

Reza nodded vigorously, glancing in Snowden's direction, the horrors of the past few hours fading. He had a mission now, some responsibility that helped to displace his fear. "I will, Mama," he said quietly so that Snowden would not hear.

Later, as his father and mother rested under Enrique's watchful eyes, Snowden kept an eye on Reza as he busied himself with hunting for the things she had told him to look for.

Peering through the darkness, his father having told him that they could not use a light for fear of bringing the Kreelans, Reza spied what Snowden had told him would be a great prize in the game they were playing. A bright metal clip protruded from under a stairway crawlspace, its surface reflecting the occasional flash of artillery fire that showed through the mangled roof. He saw that it was attached to a big, gray cylinder: a pulse gun magazine. Grinning with excitement, he scampered forward to retrieve it. He had heard Enrique say that they didn't have any more of the magazines, and the big gun wouldn't work.

He reached down to pick it up, but found that it was much heavier than he had imagined. He pulled and heaved, but the magazine would not move. He started sweeping the dirt away from around it, to try and dig it out. His hand brushed against something, something smooth and warm, totally different from the rubbery pocked coating of the magazine that was supposed to make it less slippery.

Curious, he reached out to feel what it was. He did not need a light to tell him that he was touching someone's leg, and they had their foot resting on the magazine. Looking up into the darkness above him, he could see only a shadow.

"Who are you?" he asked quietly, curious as to how and why someone would have come into the house without letting his father know about it. "Are you one of Papa's soldiers?"

Silence.

A flare burst far down the street, slowly settling toward the ground. In its flickering glow, Reza saw clearly the monstrous shape above him, saw the eyes that glared down from the dark-skinned face and the glistening ivory fangs that emerged from the mouth in a silent snarl.

Reza stumbled back, screaming at the nightmarish shape, all thoughts of the precious magazine vanished from his mind. He scrambled backward on all fours like a terrified crab, screaming. "Mama! Papa!"

"Reza, what is it?" Solon asked, picking the boy up from the debris-strewn floor as he burst from the hallway. "What's wrong?"

"One of them's in here! By the stairs! There, Papa!" Reza pointed, but the monster had disappeared. "It was right there!" he cried, stabbing at the air with his trembling finger.

Solon peered through the darkness, but could see nothing. "Reza, there's no way anyone could be back there. That's the one place where they can't get in, because it's a solid wall, no doors or windows, no holes."

"Papa, one of them's in here!" Reza wailed, his terrified eyes still fixed on where he knew the monster had been.

Solon hesitated. He knew how tired and confused Reza must be, how much they all were, and he knew he had to humor the boy.

"I'll take a look," Snowden volunteered. In the time since the last wave of Kreelans had attacked, Camilla had finally had time to splint her leg properly and block the nerves. Walking on it would probably do permanent damage, but Snowden had figured that it was better to be alive and mostly functional than just plain dead. She snatched up her helmet and put it on. The shattered interior of the house, enhanced into precise detail by the visor, came into focus. "He's probably just wired over what happened at the bunker," she said. Camilla nodded, but Snowden could tell that she was nervous. "Don't worry, Camilla," Snowden reassured her, hefting her rifle. "I'll take care of him." Then, turning to the boy, she said, "Can you show me, Reza?"

Reza did not want to go anywhere near the stairs or the back rooms again. But everyone was looking at him, and he would not act like a baby in front of them. After all, he was seven years old now. "All right," he said, his voice shaking.

Solon set him down, and then looked at Snowden. "Just be careful, okay?"

"No problem, boss," she replied easily. Her outward confidence wasn't foolish arrogance: even as exhausted as she was, she was still the best sharpshooter in the entire company. "C'mon, Reza." Taking the boy's hand, her other arm cradling the rifle, she led him down the dark hallway toward the back of the house.

Once into the hallway, she became increasingly edgy with every crunch of plaster under her boots, only one of which she could feel, the other having been deadened to stifle the pain. The hairs on the back of her neck were standing at stiff attention, but she could not figure out why. *There's nothing here*, she told herself firmly.

She finally decided that it must be because Reza's grip had tightened with every step. It was a gauge of the little boy's fear. But her own senses registered nothing at all.

Reza moved forward, about half a step ahead of her, one hand clinging to hers, the other probing ahead of him through the murk. He knew he had seen the alien warrior. But as his fear grew, so did his self-doubt. *Maybe I was wrong*, he thought.

Behind them came a scraping sound like a knife against a sharpening stone. Snowden whirled around, pushing Reza to the ground behind her with one hand while the other brought the rifle to bear.

"Hell!" she hissed. A fiber optic connector that had been part of the house's control system dangled from the ceiling, the cable scraping against the wall. She shook her head, blowing out her breath. *Don't be so tense*, she told herself. *Take it easy.* "Reza," she said, turning around, "I think we better head back to the others. There's nothing–"

She stopped in mid-sentence as she saw a clawed fist emerge from the wall in front of her, the alien flesh and sinew momentarily merging with stone and steel in a pulsating mass of swirling colors. The hand closed around Snowden's neck with a chilling *snick*. The alien warrior's hand was so large that her talons overlapped Snowden's spine. Gasping in horror, Snowden was forced backward as the Kreelan made her way through the wall and into the dark hallway.

Snowden's mouth gaped open, but no words came. There was only a muted stuttering that was building toward an uncontrollable ululation of terror. She dropped her rifle, the tiny gap between her body and the alien making it as useless as a medieval pike in a dense thicket. Desperately, she groped for the pistol strapped to her lower thigh, her other hand vainly trying to break the Kreelan's grip on her neck.

His mind reeling from the horror in front of him, Reza backpedaled away, his mouth open in a scream for help that he would never remember making. He watched helplessly as the warrior's sword, free from the wall's impossible embrace, pierced Snowden's breastplate. It burst from her back with a thin metallic screech and a jet of blood. Snowden's body twitched like a grotesque marionette, her legs dancing in the confusion of signals coursing through her severed spine, her arms battering weakly at the enemy's face. The pistol had fallen to the floor, its safety still on.

Satisfied that the human was beaten, the Kreelan let go of Snowden's neck. As the young woman's body fell to the floor, the alien warrior pulled the sword free, the blade dragging at Snowden's insides with its serrated upper edge. She was dead before her helmeted head hit the floor.

Reza bolted for the main room, his scream of terror reverberating from the walls and battered ceiling.

"Reza!" Solon cried as his son burst into the room to fall at his father's feet. "Where's Snowden?"

"Solon," Camilla whispered, slowly rising to her feet as she saw the dark shape silently move from the hallway. A burst from down the street lit the thing's face with a hellish glow, leaving no doubt as to its origin.

The Kreelan stopped just beyond the hallway. Watching. Waiting.

Enrique reacted first. Instinctively he brought up his rifle, aiming it at the alien's chest.

"Bitch!" he cried, his finger convulsing on the trigger.

Solon saw her arm move like a scythe in the eerie display of his helmet visor. The movement was accompanied by a strange whistling noise, like a storm wind howling against a windowpane.

Enrique suddenly grunted. Solon saw the gunner's eyes register disbelief, then nothing at all as they rolled up into his head. His body sagged backward and the gun discharged once into the ceiling before clattering to the floor at his side. Solon saw a huge wet horizontal gash in Enrique's chest armor that was wide enough to put both fists in, as if someone had split him open with an ax.

Camilla reached for her rifle, propped against the wall behind her.

"No," Solon said softly. "Don't move."

She stopped.

Reza lay face down on the floor, his body pointing like an arrow toward where his father now stood frozen. He blinked away the tears in his eyes, his entire body trembling with fear. He felt something sharp under his right hand, and without thinking he closed his fingers around it: a knife. He clung to it desperately, for he had no weapon of his own. A brief glance told him that it was his father's. He knew that his father always carried two, but must have somehow lost this one in the rubble during the fighting. Reza held it tightly to his chest.

"Why doesn't she attack?" Camilla whispered, terribly tempted to reach for her pistol or rifle. The sight of Enrique's gutted body stayed her hand. And then there was Snowden. Undoubtedly, she lay dead somewhere deeper in the house.

"I don't know, but..." Solon hesitated. He suddenly had an idea. "I'm going to try something."

Before Camilla could say a word, he drew the long-bladed knife he carried in his web gear. It was an inferior weapon to the Kreelan's sword, but it was all he had, and he didn't know where his regular combat knife had disappeared to. Then he slowly moved his free hand to the clasps that held his web gear to his armor. With two quick yanks, the webbing that held his grenades, pistol and extra weapon power packs clattered to the floor.

"So far, so good," he muttered. Sweat poured from his brow down the inside of his helmet. "Now you do it," he ordered his wife. "Draw your knife and drop the rest of your gear."

"What about Reza?" she asked, her eyes fixed on the alien as she repeated what Solon had done, her own equipment rattling to the floor around her feet a moment later. "Solon, we've got to get him out of here."

Crouching down slowly under the Kreelan's watchful, almost benevolent gaze, Solon reached down to where his son lay.

"Reza," he whispered, the external helmet speaker making his voice sound tinny, far away, "stand up, very slowly, and look at me."

Reza did as he was told, his body shaking with fright.

"Listen carefully, son," he said, tearing his eyes away from the Kreelan to look at his son for what he knew would be the last time. He fought against the tears that welled up in his eyes. "You must do exactly what I tell you, without question, without being too afraid. You're a young man, now, and your mother and I need you to help us."

"Yes, Papa," Reza whispered shakily as he stared into his father's dirty helmet visor. But instead of his father's face, Reza saw only the dull reflection of the apparition standing behind him, only a few paces away.

Holding his son by both quivering shoulders, Solon went on, "Not far from here, there used to be a really big schoolhouse, the university. Do you remember?"

Reza nodded. His father had taken him there many times to show him the great library there. It had always been one of his favorite places.

"Our people have built a big, strong fortress there," Solon continued. "That's where I need you to go. Tell them your mother and I need help, and they'll send soldiers for us." He pulled Reza to him. "We love you, son," he whispered. Then he let him go. "Go on, son. Get out of here and don't look back."

"But Papa..." Reza started to object, crying now.

"Go on!" Camilla said softly, but with unmistakable firmness. Her own body shook in silent anguish that she could not even hold her son one last time. Fate had held that last card from her hand, an alien Queen of Spades standing between her and her child. "Go on," she urged again, somehow sensing the Kreelan's growing impatience, "before it's too late."

"I love you," Reza whispered as stumbled toward a hole in the wall, a doorway to the Hell that lay beyond.

"I love you, too, baby," Camilla choked.

As her only son crawled through the hole to the street beyond, Camilla turned her attention back to the waiting Kreelan. "All right, you bitch," she sneered, her upper lip curled like a wolf's, exposing the teeth that had once illuminated a smile that had been a young man's enchantment, the man who later became her husband. But there was no trace of that smile now. "It's time for you to die." The blade of her knife glinted in the fiery glow that lit the horizon of the burning city.

Together, husband and wife moved toward their enemy.

* * *

Reza stumbled and fell to the ground when the blast lit up the night behind him. The knoll of debris that had been his parents' stronghold vanished in a fiery ball of flame and splinters, with smoke mushrooming up into the night sky like the glowing pillar of a funeral pyre.

"Mama!" he screamed. "Papa!"

But only the flames answered, crackling as they consumed the building's remains with a boundless hunger.

Reza lay there, watching his world burn away to ashes. A final tear coursed its way down his face in a lonely journey, its wet track reflecting the brilliant flames. Alone now, fearful of the terrors that stalked the night, he curled up beneath a tangle of timbers and bricks, watching the flames dance to music only the fire itself could hear.

"Goodbye, Mama and Papa," he whispered before succumbing to the wracking sobs that had been standing by like friends in mourning.

* * *

Not far away, another lone figure stood watching those same flames through alien eyes. The priestess's heart raced with the energy that surged through her body, her blood singing the chorus of battle that had been the heart and spirit of her people for countless generations.

The two humans had fought well, she granted, feeling a twinge of what might have been sorrow at their deaths. It was so rare that she found opponents worthy of her mettle. The humans would never know it, but they had come closer to killing her than any others had come in many cycles. Had she not heard the *click* made by the grenade, set off by the mortally stricken male while the female held her attention, she might have joined them in the fire that now devoured their frail bodies. Some of her hair, her precious raven hair, had been scorched by the blast as she leaped through the wall to safety.

What a pity, she thought, *that animals with such instincts did not possess souls.* Such creatures could certainly be taught how to make themselves more than moving targets for her to toy with, but her heart ached to give something more to her Empress.

Standing there, nauseated by the acrid stench of the burning plasticrete around her, she heaved a mournful sigh before turning back toward where the young ones lay resting. Her time here was terribly short, but a single moon cycle of the Homeworld, and she had yet much to see, much on which she would report to the Empress.

She had just started back when she heard a peculiar sound, an unsteady pulse under the current of the winds that carried the embers of the fire. It came at once from one direction, then from another as the fickle winds sought new paths over the dying city. She closed her eyes and reached out with her mind, her spirit flowing from her body to become one with the scorched earth and smoldering sky, using senses that went well beyond any her body could provide.

The child.

She hesitated, tempted simply to let it go, to die on its own while she returned to the young warriors who awaited her. But she found herself overcome with curiosity, for she had only seen their children in death. Never had she seen a live one. She debated for a moment what she should do, but in the end her curiosity demanded satisfaction. To blunt the pup's whimpering misery with death would be an indulgent, if unchallenging, act.

* * *

Reza blinked. Had he fallen asleep? He rubbed his eyes with grimy fists. His cheeks were caked with a mortar of tears and masonry dust. He glanced around, unable to see much in the dim glow that filtered into his hideout. Not really wanting to, but unable to help himself, he looked toward where his parents had died.

He sucked in his breath in surprise. A shadow blocked the entrance to his tiny hideaway. With arms and legs that felt weak as stalks of thin grass, he crawled forward a bit to see better.

"Mama?" he whispered cautiously, his young mind hoping that perhaps all had not been lost. "Papa?" he said a little louder, his voice barely rising above the wind that had begun to howl outside.

The figure stood immobile, but for one thing. Extending one arm, the fingers slowly, rhythmically curled back one by one in a gesture he had long been taught meant *come, come to me.*

His teeth chattering with fear and anticipation, he gripped his father's knife, his fingers barely long enough to close around the handle. He crawled forward toward the gesturing apparition, still unsure if it was a man or woman, or perhaps something else. He was terrified, but he had to know.

Coming to the last barrier of fallen timbers that formed the doorway to his hideaway, Reza gathered his courage. He fixed his eyes on the shadow hand that continued to call him, mesmerizing him with the thought that help had arrived and that his parents might yet be saved. Placing his empty hand on the bottom-most timber, the other clutching the knife by his side, he poked his head out the hole.

The shape seemed to shimmer and change in the light. It moved with such speed that Reza's eyes only registered a dark streak before an iron hand clamped around his neck and plucked him from the hole with a force that nearly snapped his spine. He cried out in pain and fear, never noticing the warm flood that coursed down his legs as his bladder emptied.

His cries and struggling ended when he found the cat-like eyes of the Kreelan warrior a mere hand's breadth from his own. Her lips parted to reveal the ivory fangs that adorned the upper and lower jaws.

For a moment, the two simply stared at one other, Reza's feet dangling nearly a meter from the ground as the Kreelan held him. Her grip, strong enough to pop his head like a grape with a gentle squeeze, was restrained to a force that barely allowed him to breathe. His pulse hammered in his ears as his heart fought to push blood through the constricted carotid arteries to his brain. Spots began to appear in his vision, as if he were looking at the Kreelan through a curtain of shimmering stars.

Then the alien closed her mouth, hiding away the terrible fangs. Her lips formed a proud, forceful line on her face, and Reza felt the hand around his tiny neck begin to contract with a strength that seemed to him as powerful as anything in the Universe.

As his lungs strained for their last breath through his constricted windpipe, a voice in his brain began to shout something. The words were repeated again and again, like a maniacal litany, the rhythm surging through his darkening brain. As his body's oxygen reserves dwindled and his vision dimmed, he finally understood.

The knife!

With a strength born of desperation, he thrust the knife straight at the Kreelan's face.

Suddenly she released him, and he fell to the ground. His feet crashed into the brick rubble over which he had been suspended, his legs crumpling like flimsy paper rods. Stunned, he fought to get air back into his lungs, his chest heaving rapidly. His vision returned at an agonizingly slow pace through the fireworks dancing on his retinas. He groped about, desperately trying to get away from the alien warrior.

His hand smacked into something, and he knew instantly what it was. He had felt it before. It was the Kreelan's leg. He looked up in time to see her kneel next to him, her mountainous form overshadowing the world in his frightened eyes. He tried to push himself away, to roll down into the flat part of the street where he might be able to run, but a massive clawed hand grasped him by the shoulder, the tips of her talons just pricking his skin.

His pounding fear giving way to resignation, he turned to face her. He did not want to watch as she killed him, but he had to see her. Whether out of curiosity or to face down the shame of being a coward, he did not know. Reluctantly, his eyes sought hers.

The knife, he saw, even in his tiny hand, had done its work. A vertical gash ran from a point halfway up the brow above the Kreelan's left eye down to the point of her graceful cheekbone. The blade had somehow missed the eye itself, although it was awash in the blood that oozed from the wound. The weapon had fallen from Reza's hand after doing its damage, and he held out little hope of recovering it. Besides, he thought as he waited for the final blow, what was the point?

He sat still as she reached toward him with her other hand. He flinched as one of the talons touched the skin of his forehead, just above his eye. But he did not look away, nor did he cry out. He had faced enough fear during this one night to last a lifetime, and when death came, he thought he might welcome it.

Slowly, she drew a thin line of blood that mimicked the wound he had given her. Her talon cut deep, right to the bone, as it glided down his face. Just missing his left eye, it lingered at last on his cheek.

He blinked, trying to clear the blood away as it dribbled over his eyebrow and into his eye. The flesh around the wound throbbed with the beating of his heart, but that was all. He was sure she was going to skin him alive, and he knew that her claws were as sharp as carving knives.

Instead, the Kreelan's hand drew back, and her other hand released his shoulder. She looked at him pensively, lightly tapping the talon smeared with his blood against her dark lips, her eyes narrowed slightly in thought.

His heart skipped a beat as she abruptly reached forward toward his hair. He felt a small pull on his scalp and instinctively reached to where he had felt the tug, expecting to feel the wet stickiness of more blood. But there was none. He looked up in surprise as the Kreelan held out a lock of his normally golden brown hair, now a filthy black from the dirt and smoke. With obvious care, she put it into a small pouch that was affixed to the black belt at her waist.

A prize, Reza thought, his mouth dropping open in wonder, a faint spark of hope sizzling in his breast. Was she about to let him live?

In answer to his unvoiced question, the huge warrior stood up. She made no sound, not even a tiny whisper, as her body uncoiled to its towering height. She glanced down to the ground at her feet and, leaning down, scooped up his father's knife. Turning the blade over in her hand, she made a low *humph* and put it in her belt. She looked at Reza one last time, acting as if the bleeding wound on her face was nothing, and bowed her head to him.

He blinked.

And she was gone.

If You've Enjoyed In Her Name...

From Chaos Born is the first novel in a series chronicling the founding of the Kreelan Empire.

Set one hundred thousand years before encountering the human race in *First Contact*, *From Chaos Born* begins the epic tale of Keel-Tath, who will someday rise to become the legendary First Empress...

To give you a taste of what's to come, here's the first chapter of *From Chaos Born* — enjoy!

* * *

The sun was just rising over the mountains of Kui'mar-Gol, painting the magenta sky in hues of flame above the three warriors as they rode along the ancient road toward the city of Keel-A'ar, leaving a long trail of dust in their wake.

Kunan-Lohr rode at the lead, periodically lashing his animal to keep up the brutal pace. The beast ran on two powerful rear legs, the taloned feet tearing into the worn cobbles of the road. Its sides heaved with effort, the black stripes over the brown fur rippling as it panted for breath, the small forearms clutching at the air, as if begging for respite.

Not given to cruelty, Kunan-Lohr drove the beast mercilessly because he had no choice. Bone weary himself, he had already killed four other animals by running them to death in the two months he had been traveling. The seven braids of his raven hair were still tightly woven, but like the rest of his body were covered in dust and grit. His silver-flecked eyes were sunken in the dry, cracked cobalt blue skin of his face. His armor, a gleaming black when he had set out two months ago, was beyond any hope of repair by the armorers. The breast and back plates were pitted and creased from battle, and the black leatherite that covered his arms and legs had been cut open and stained with blood. Some was his own. Some was not. His right hand clutched the reins, while his left hung limply at his side, broken. Two of his ebony talons on that hand had been snapped off, and the others, like his armor, were scratched and pitted from desperate fighting against bands of honorless ones who preyed upon travelers in these troubled days.

Of sleep, he had allowed himself precious little. It was a luxury he had not been able to afford. During the fifty-six days that had passed since he had begun his journey home from the east, he had slept only eight times. He had stopped no more than once a day to eat and let his animal graze for the short time he would allow. Every other waking moment had been in the saddle, riding hard.

His pace had been too much for all but the last two warriors who now accompanied him. The rest of the three hundred with whom he had begun this journey had either perished in the battles they had been forced to fight along the way, or were somewhere behind him, making their own way home.

Even with the wind whipping past from his mount's furious pace, the sour reek of his body odor still reached his sensitive nose. Normally fastidious in his grooming habits, he had only allowed himself the luxury of bathing when he had been forced to stop and barter for fresh mounts. It was not the way in which the master of a great city such as Keel-A'ar should arrive home, but time was his enemy now, and he knew he had very little left.

He could feel her more clearly with every pace the *magthep* took toward home, could sense her with every beat of his heart. His consort, Ulana-Tath. They had once been *tresh*, joined in the path of life that was simply called the Way, when they had first entered the *kazha*, or training school, overseen by the great warrior priests and priestesses of the Desh-Ka order.

Despite Kunan-Lohr's discomfort and desperation to return home, he could not help but grin, his white fangs reflecting the fire of the sunrise as he recalled those days. Ulana-Tath had bested him in everything for most of the early years at the *kazha*, beating him soundly in training nearly every day. Be it with sword or dagger, spear or unsheathed claws, she had beaten him. She was the finest warrior among their peers through her fifth Challenge, when at last he had become her equal. While he bested her in the sixth and seventh Challenges before they came of age as warriors, he had always suspected that she had let him win. And he had loved her all the more for it.

While they were already bound, body and soul, as *tresh*, there was no question when they became warriors that they would be consorts, a mated pair. It was often the case with male and female paired as *tresh*, for a deep bond already existed. While the Way did not demand monogamy, *tresh* who mated as a pair typically did so for life.

And so it had been with them. They loved and fought together, seeking perfection and honor on the battlefield and in their lives.

One enemy, however, remained steadfast in its refusal to yield to their most determined efforts: they had been unable to bear children.

Kunan-Lohr's smile faded as he thought of the sad and frustrating cycles they had endured in that singular pursuit. Many times had they tried, and every time had failed to conceive. The healers were confused and frustrated, for they had determined that both he and Ulana-Tath were fertile and entirely healthy. It was a confounding mystery, as if some dark magic had cast a veil between their two bodies, denying them what they most desired.

While it had been a most bitter disappointment, despair was not the way of their kind. The intensity of their love for one another remained undiminished. Indeed, if anything, their bonds grew stronger, matched only by their lust for battle. In the perpetual wars that raged across the face of the Homeworld, the two made their mark in service to the great warrior who was the mistress of Keel-A'ar, and who in turn served the King of the Eastern Lands of the continent of T'lar-Gol.

Over the cycles that passed and the many battles that were fought against opposing kings and roving bands of marauders, Ulana-Tath and Kunan-Lohr rose in the ranks of the peers until Kunan-Lohr won the leadership of the city of Keel-A'ar in a Challenge, defeating the mistress of the city. As had long been customary in their city, the Challenge had been to first blood, not to the death. For the Way, as taught by the Desh-Ka priesthood, held that there was great honor in victory, and no shame in defeat. The only shame for those who lived by the sword was not to step into the arena to accept the challenge of combat. Aside from the non-warrior castes, who lived by a code that was less bloody but just as difficult, the only path to leadership was through the clash of swords in the Challenge.

After that, Ulana-Tath had challenged him, and he had bested her, drawing a thin bead of blood from her shoulder with his sword. She had bowed and saluted his victory, but the smile in her eyes and the joy that echoed from her spirit in his blood told him that, as he had suspected, she had not entered the arena with the intent of winning the contest. She had already won his heart, and had no interest in becoming the mistress of the city.

But she would be his First, his most trusted lieutenant, the sword hand of her lord and master.

Those had been the good days, he thought now, before the rise of the Dark Queen, Syr-Nagath. An orphan and survivor from the Great Wastelands beyond the Kui'mar-Gol Mountains, she had come to their lands wearing armor she had taken from the dead, with the eyestones of a *genoth*, a great dragon that lived in the wastelands, around her neck. Young, little over the age of mating, she had walked the many leagues to the king's city and challenged him the day she arrived. The right of challenge belonged to every warrior, and the only thing anyone had questioned had been her wisdom in choosing such an opponent.

No one had expected her to win. For the king, while growing old, was still a formidable and ferocious opponent.

But against this demon, as Kunan-Lohr remembered all too well, having presided over the Challenge himself, the venerable warrior had stood no chance at all. Syr-Nagath had toyed with the older and much more powerful-looking warrior just long enough to pick apart his weaknesses. Then she killed him.

To fight to the death in a Challenge was an ancient right. But it was relatively rare, and usually occurred only in cases where serious offense had been given. Every group, from the small bands of honorless brigands who haunted the mountains and forests, to the most powerful nations, needed their warriors in order to survive. It was an unwritten code of the Way that mercy was acceptable, even preferable, in the arena.

That changed under Syr-Nagath. As Kunan-Lohr had feared after she had slain the king, warriors had gathered to challenge the young mistress from the wastelands. He would have challenged her himself, had he not known what these new challengers did not: he had seen her fight the king, and knew that she was by far the superior warrior. Those that chose to fight her believed that the old king had lost the Challenge simply because he was old. In that, too, Kunan-Lohr knew they were wrong. Unlike these challengers, he had sparred many times with the king, and knew just how good he had truly been.

Ten of the kingdom's best warriors died at the hands of Syr-Nagath in the day that followed the king's death. By the time the sun had set, she was covered in blood that was not her own.

"*Ka'a mekh!*" Kunan-Lohr had himself given the command for the thousands who had watched the gory spectacle to kneel and render a salute to their new leader.

Their new queen.

Since that day, over ten cycles ago, the continent of T'lar-Gol had run red with blood, more than had been spilled in millennia. Syr-Nagath was bloodthirsty, even for a race that lived for war.

During most of the time since the Dark Queen had risen to power, Kunan-Lohr and Ulana-Tath had been away on campaign, leading their warriors into battle after battle. He would not have thought it unnatural, save that Syr-Nagath demanded that her vassals strip their cities and lands of most of their warriors, leaving the other castes nearly defenseless against the bands of honorless ones who had become bold enough to strike out of the forests and mountains for the rich plunder of the cities. Keel-A'ar had survived unscathed because its ancient walls could easily be defended by a small garrison against anything short of an army, but many other cities and villages across the land were not so fortunate.

Unlike those who followed the Way as taught in the *kazhas*, the honorless ones had no taboo against the ill-treatment or killing of non-warrior castes. Healers, armorers, builders, and the many other castes that were the foundation of life as defined by the Way were murdered or, worse, taken as slaves. It was unthinkable to warriors such as Ulana-Tath and himself to leave the other castes unprotected; it was tantamount to throwing one's own children to the *ku'ur-kamekh*, the ravenous steppe-beasts, to be torn apart and eaten.

But, as Syr-Nagath herself was fond of pointing out, she was not of their Way. No one knew anything of her past, but it would not have surprised Kunan-Lohr if she was one of the rare rejects from one of the ancient orders such as the Desh-Ka. That was the only explanation for her extraordinary fighting skills.

He knew with the same degree of certainty that she was not descended from the Desh-Ka, for he could not feel her, could not sense her emotions. Their race was descended from seven ancient bloodlines, each of which could be traced back over many thousands of years to one of the seven original warrior sects. The descendants of each of those sects had an empathic sense for the others in their bloodline. Those whose blood was mixed were empathic toward all their relations, but the intensity of the sensation was reduced as the bloodlines became diluted. Ulana-Tath and Kunan-Lohr were both pure descendants of the Desh-Ka, and could sense each other over hundreds, even thousands, of leagues. Others from their city, by contrast, were only distant whispers, fleeting sensations that formed an emotional tide in one's blood.

And it was that sense that had brought him home. Ulana-Tath had been summoned back to Keel-A'ar eight months earlier from the bloody campaign in the east to face a set of challengers for her place in the city's hierarchy of peers. To forbid her return was something that was not even in Syr-Nagath's power, much as the Dark Queen would have liked to try. Even honor-bound to her as they were, warriors such as Ulana-Tath and Kunan-Lohr, who were also masters and mistresses of their cities, would not fight if they could not defend their honor at home.

Kunan-Lohr, who had remained with the queen in the east, knew something momentous had happened with Ulana-Tath. It had been three months since she had departed for home, and he sensed a fountain of joy and wonder from her such as he had never before felt. The intensity of the feeling ebbed over time, but was always there, a constant in his heart. Three more months passed when a messenger arrived, sent by his wife with the news: she was with child.

He remembered the moment as if it were yesterday. The courier had arrived in the midst of a major battle, and the young warrior waded through the enemy to Kunan-Lohr's side to tell him that his wife was expecting a girl-child. Overhearing the news, the warriors who had just been trying to kill him lowered their swords and stepped back, rendering him a salute. Kunan-Lohr had a fierce reputation, and fighting him was a great honor for any enemy warrior. Allowing him the privilege of stepping away from the battle to attend to his child had been an even greater honor.

The Dark Queen, however, did not see things that way. After quickly cleaning the blood of the day's fighting from his body and armor, he sought an audience with her. Kneeling before her in the great pavilion that served as her palace, he had begged her to grant him leave, but she had refused.

"I must grant your right to return to defend your honor," Syr-Nagath had told him, her voice as cold as her eyes, "but this trifle is another matter. I command you to stay, and so you shall. Your child shall be given over to the wardresses in the creche, as custom demands. You may see it — her — if you are challenged for your lordship of your city, or when my conquest has concluded and I release you from my service."

To hold him in such a manner was her right, but it few sovereigns in living memory had chosen to enforce it. Warriors who were allowed to return home to visit loved ones returned to war refreshed. Those who did not fought on, but with hearts heavy with yearning.

For five days, he begged her to give him leave to return home, pushing to the very brink of challenging her to fight in the arena.

On the sixth day, she had relented, but her promise of his release had come with a price: to mate with her. While Kunan-Lohr had been disgusted at the prospect, at that time he would have done anything in order to return home.

While it was unusual for a king or queen to demand such a thing, it was not unheard of. There was no dishonor or taboo in doing so, for there were few taboos or strictures in Kreelan life regarding mating.

But mating with Syr-Nagath was a cold, loathsome union that left him feeling soiled, and he carried away long gashes in his back from where her talons raked him in her ecstasy. Unlike the cuts and stab wounds he had received in the fighting on the way home, he would have the healers remove any trace of Syr-Nagath's marks upon his flesh. Not to hide them from Ulana-Tath, but to cleanse himself of the Dark Queen's stain.

Rounding a bend in the road through a stretch of forest, his heart lifted as Keel-A'ar finally came into sight.

"At last," he breathed. His tired *magthep*, as if sensing the end of their journey was near and that food and rest would soon be at hand, quickened its pace.

Keel-A'ar stood at the center of a great plain that was bounded by forests to the south and east, and the mountains of Kui'mar-Gol to the north and west. It was among the oldest and greatest cities of the world. A great wall surrounded it, the seamless surface a tribute to the builders who had created it many generations ago. The walls reflected the sun rising at his back, the light rippling along the serpent-hide texture of the ancient fused stone. The height of six warriors and as thick as three laid heel to toe, the walls had withstood many assaults over the ages. Like everything in the city, it was carefully tended and maintained by the builder caste, so much so that it looked new.

A branch of the Lo'ar River ran beneath the walls through the center of the city, but it was not for the sake of beauty or idle pleasure: in times of siege, it provided fresh water and fish to sustain the defenders. While there was need for vigilance, lest a foe mount an attack from under water, the fish that provided much of the city's food were also part of its defense. The vicious *lackan-kamekh* were bountiful and lethal, with rows of needle-sharp teeth. The wall was surrounded by a moat that could be flooded with water and a host of the terrible fish if the city were attacked. Only in winter, after the river had frozen over and shut away the light of the sun, did the *lackan-kamekh* sleep, hibernating on the river bottom.

Above the wall, he could see the golden domes and spires of the taller buildings rising above the walls to catch the sun's rays. They were a beacon of welcome to his weary eyes.

As he and his two companions drew closer, he looked again at the sun, which rose steadily in the magenta sky behind him toward the great moon. On this day there would be an eclipse of the sun by the moon, an event that only took place every fifteen thousand and seven cycles. It was a momentous omen, and even in his weariness, the thought lifted his spirits. He knew in his heart that today was the day his daughter would be born.

"Faster!" He whipped the *magthep* to a sprint toward the waiting gate, leaving his two companions fighting to keep up.

* * *

Like the *lackan-kamekh*, the killer fish, the city's defenders never slept, particularly in these times. With most of the city's warriors away on campaign in the service of the queen, the small garrison Kunan-Lohr had been allowed to retain never relaxed its guard.

They had been attacked several times by bands of honorless warriors, and had easily defeated the disorganized mobs. But their master and his master before him had taught them well: overconfidence was as much an enemy as those who would destroy the city. They were charged with protecting that which was most precious to those who followed the Way: the children in the creche and the non-warrior castes.

Anin-Khan was the captain of the guard. Aside from Ulana-Tath and Kunan-Lohr, he was the most senior and skilled warrior, having challenged them both to contests in the arena. After they had drawn first blood in the contests he had fought against them, he had accepted with great honor the responsibility of the city's defense. It was a measure of Kunan-Lohr's trust in him and his abilities, for while the city's master was away, it was the most important role a warrior could fulfill.

He spent most of his time on watch, which was nearly every moment that he was not asleep, in the barbican, the defensive structure that jutted out over the city's main gate, or the watchtowers that rose at key points along the wall. From those vantage points, he had a view over the open plain between the city and the surrounding forests.

He happened to be standing watch on the barbican when he caught sight of a trail of dust from the main road leading from the east. His bloodline was not pure Desh-Ka, and so his empathic sense was not terribly strong, but he could always tell the approach of his lord and master.

"Alert the mistress," Anin-Khan told one of the guards. "Our master returns."

The guard saluted and set off at a run for Ulana-Tath's chambers.

While he was certain in his heart that Kunan-Lohr led the trio of approaching warriors, Anin-Khan waited until he could clearly see his master's weary face. Parties of warriors and non-warriors were often welcomed at Keel-A'ar on their travels, but never before Anin-Khan himself had given his approval. The honorless ones had been growing bolder, and had tried to gain entry under the guise of honorable travelers.

Sure now of the approaching warriors, he called to the gatekeepers below. "Open the gate!"

The guards below him shouted their acknowledgement before turning a set of great wheels in the thick walled guard house, grunting and straining with the effort. The massive metal gate, thicker than a warrior stood tall, slowly rose, driven by the wheels and supported by a complex set of thick chains, counterweights, and pulleys.

Kunan-Lohr and his two escorts thundered through, ducking their heads under the ancient metal as it rose.

"Close it!" Anin-Khan favored his master with a salute as the trio of riders sped through the courtyard behind the gate and on into the city proper. He very much wanted to greet his master in person, but would not leave his post. There would be time for that later.

For now, he and the other guards would continue to attend to their duties.

The trio hammered along the streets, which were now lined with thousands of people, kneeling and rendering the *tla'a-kane*, the ritual salute, with their left fists over their right breasts. All but a handful were of the non-warrior castes. Armorers, porters of water, healers, seamstresses, builders, and many more, the colors of the simple robes that defined their castes creating a vibrant rainbow along the gracefully curved streets of inlaid stone.

Ignoring the pain of his broken left hand, Kunan-Lohr returned the salute, holding it as he rode past his people. His eye caught the glint of the armor of the soldiers on the battlements, who also were kneeling.

He ground his teeth together in frustration, not wanting to show his concern on his face. There were so few warriors, now. Too few to properly defend the city from anything more than the most half-hearted attack by anything other than the honorless ones. And how long would it be before they had grown enough in numbers to pose a credible challenge?

May the Dark Queen's soul rot in Eternal Darkness. The curse was one he had thought many times in the cycles since Syr-Nagath had risen to power, but he had never given voice to the thought. His honor would not permit it.

They flew by the central gardens that formed the green, open heart of the city. The main garden, set deep in the earth compared to the surrounding land, was surrounded by terraced levels that were open to the sky above. Unlike most days, it was empty, for the people who would normally be there, enjoying a contemplative moment or tending the garden were lined along the streets to greet him.

Glancing up, he saw the sun and the moon rapidly converging, and felt a quickening of the urgency in the empathic link with Ulana-Tath.

There was little time, only moments, remaining.

He beat the straining *magthep* savagely, at the same time murmuring his apologies to the beast for inflicting such cruelty. He silently promised that the creature would receive every comfort the animal handlers could give as compensation for its valiant service to his cause.

The beast responded, its exhausted legs stretching farther, its taloned feet striking sparks from the stone of the streets as it dashed forward.

After one final, skittering turn, the citadel came into view. At the center of the city, it was a fortress within a fortress, the home of the city's master or mistress. While it was the final defensive structure of the many that had originally gone into Keel-A'ar's design, it was also one of beauty. The walls, which rose even higher than the defensive walls around the city, were of glittering granite, black with white and copper veins, and polished to an exquisite sheen. Like the other structures in the city, it was not a regular shape, formed by mere triangles, circles, or rectangles. It was a work of art in itself, the smooth lines making it look as if it could sail away upon the wind, pulled toward the stars by the great golden spire that rose from its apex.

Home, Kunan-Lohr thought as he brought his exhausted mount to a skidding stop just inside the gate in the wall surrounding the citadel. He quickly slid to the ground among the crowd of retainers who had gathered, filling the courtyard. As one, they knelt before him.

The two other riders arrived just a moment later, barely bringing their beasts to a stop before dismounting.

Many hands, eager to help, reached out to take the reins from the riders.

"Tend them well!" Kunan-Lohr ordered as the animals, gasping for breath, were led off to the corrals where they could rest.

Other hands offered food and drink to the riders, and words of welcome to the lord and master of the city.

Gratefully accepting a large mug of bitter ale, Kunan-Lohr drank it quickly to help slake his thirst. His party had run out of water the day before, giving the last of it to the *magtheps* before making the final run for home.

"My thanks." He handed the mug back to the young porter of water, who bowed, greatly honored.

Then, willing himself not to run, he took long, urgent strides toward the entryway, where stood the housemistress, who was also the senior healer.

"Where is she?"

"In the birthing chamber, my lord." With a look upward at the impending eclipse, the housemistress turned and led him inside through the tall arch and thick, iron-reinforced wooden door of the entryway.

Kunan-Lohr's footsteps echoed in the stone corridors as he followed her to the infirmary wing where the sick and injured of the city were treated, and where the young were brought into the world.

He restrained his urge to sprint to his consort's side, forcing himself to keep pace with the housemistress. To his pleasant surprise, she was moving faster than he would have believed possible without breaking into a run.

Upon hearing a cry up ahead, unmistakably Ulana-Tath's voice, he put paid to decorum and ran, his good hand clenching tightly around the handle of his sword as he sensed her pain.

He skidded to a stop in the birthing room, which had several large stone basins. Only one of them was in use now.

Ulana-Tath, nude, was leaning back in the basin, which was filled with warm water. One of the healers, her white robes bound close to her body while she was in the water, attended her. Two other healers stood close by, should they be needed, along with the wardress who would be responsible for the child in the creche until she was old enough to enter the *kazha*.

"My love." Ulana-Tath reached out a hand for him, and he took it. He hadn't realized it was his left hand, the one that was broken, but ignored the pain as her powerful grip squeezed it. He kissed her briefly, ashamed that he was so filthy from the long, hard ride. His shame quickly receded as he was overwhelmed with her beauty and the miracle of what was taking place before his very eyes.

She cried out again.

"Push, my mistress!" The healer in the basin moved in close between Ulana-Tath's legs, spread wide and trembling. "She is almost here..."

With one final grunt of effort, Ulana-Tath gasped in relief as the baby was finally released from her mother's womb into the healer's gentle hands.

As the midwife held the child under the water, one of the other healers leaned over the basin and carefully laid on the water what looked like a thin layer of dough, whose surface was swirling with blues and purples. It was living tissue that she held in place as the midwife gently brought the child up underneath it. The tissue, healing gel, wrapped itself around the infant's body, completely covering it.

The adults watched intently as the gel disappeared, absorbed into the child's skin as the midwife lowered the child back into the water. Moment's later, it began to ooze out the nose and mouth, and the healer gently gathered it up as it left the girl's body.

The healer closed her eyes as the oozing mass was absorbed into her own skin. With senses developed over thousands of generations, the healer "listened" to what the healing gel, which was in fact a living symbiont, told her of the child's body.

The healing gel was not only a diagnostic tool for the healers, but their primary instrument, as well. Through the healing gel, the healer could visualize and repair any injury, even replace lost limbs, and cure any ill. The infant now had full immunity from every strain of disease on the planet, and any errors in her genetic coding that would have posed a threat to her health would have been corrected.

After a moment, the healer smiled and opened her eyes. "The child is perfectly well, mistress."

All breathed a sigh of relief. While problems with birthing and newborns were very rare, their health was never taken for granted.

The healer carefully lifted the child from the water, placing her in Ulana-Tath's waiting arms. After only a few moments, the infant began to cry, her tiny voice echoing through the birthing chamber.

"She is beautiful, my love." Kunan-Lohr, master of a great city and a veteran of many terrible battles, highest of warriors among those beholden to him, knelt by his consort's side like a child himself, utterly humbled by the miracle before him. His ears could hear his daughter's cries of life, but his heart could also feel the tiny voice that had joined the murmur of souls that bound together the descendants of his bloodline.

Looking up at the wardress, he asked, "What is to be her name?"

Tradition held that the wardress who would be responsible for the child from birth until she was ready to enter the *kazha* would also name her. "In honor of the city whose master is her father, and the family bloodline of her mother, the child will henceforth be known as Keel-Tath."

"An honorable name," Kunan-Lohr told her, "well-chosen."

As if sensing that she was the center of the entire city's attention, Keel-Tath's tiny hands waved in the air, groping blindly. After one of the healers quickly cleansed his free hand, Kunan-Lohr offered his daughter his little finger, careful that she reached only for the flesh, and not the sharp talon.

She wrapped her fingers around his, gripping it with surprising strength. Her own nails, which someday would grow long and sharp, glittered in the steady glow of light that fell from the walls.

He frowned. "Her talons..."

The senior healer bent closer to see, and with a subtle gesture of her hand the light in the room brightened.

"What is wrong?" Ulana-Tath gasped as she saw her daughter's fingers.

Among their race, the nails that grew from their fingers, eventually to form talons, were uniformly black, both on the hands and the shorter nails on the feet. Unlike some of the animal species on the Homeworld, which sported startling degrees of differentiation, there was very little among their race. Black talons, black nails on the toes, cobalt blue skin, and black hair were features of every child born since at least the end of the First Age, four hundred thousand cycles before.

Keel-Tath's tiny nails, both on her hands and feet, were a bright scarlet.

"And her hair!" Ulana-Tath's view was closer than that of the others, and her eyes widened as she looked closer at the wisps of hair on her daughter's head, clear now in the brighter light. She had seen enough newborns to know what she should be seeing. And what she should not. "It is white!"

Without a word, the senior healer held out her hand, and the healing gel materialized out of the skin on the arm of the healer who had wrapped it around Keel-Tath. She wrapped it around the forearm of the senior healer, and the mass sank into her flesh. Closing her eyes, the senior healer focused on the story the symbiont had to tell.

After a long breathless moment, she opened her eyes, focusing on the squirming child. "She is healthy, my lord. Extraordinarily so." She reached out a hand and gently brushed the snow-white wisps on the child's blue-skinned crown. "I have no explanation, but there is nothing amiss. Of that there is no doubt." She paused. "As with your difficulties in conceiving a child before this, I have no explanation."

Ulana-Tath exchanged a look with Kunan-Lohr. Among all else that had ever been accomplished in the ebb and flow of their civilization over the long ages, the art of the healers was without doubt the most advanced. If the healers said the child was healthy, then she was. Clearly different, perhaps, but healthy.

Breathing out a sigh of relief, Ulana-Tath kissed her daughter on the head, gently nuzzling the white hair.

Kunan-Lohr set aside his apprehensions as he gazed with rapt love at his daughter, who still clutched his finger. "A child unlike any other, born under a Great Eclipse, can only be destined for greatness," he said softly. "May Thy Way be long and glorious, my daughter."

SEASON OF THE HARVEST

What if the genetically engineered crops that we increasingly depend on for food weren't really created by man? What if they brought a new, terrifying meaning to the old saying that "you are what you eat"?

In the bestselling thriller *Season Of The Harvest*, FBI Special Agent Jack Dawson investigates the gruesome murder of his best friend and fellow agent who had been pursuing a group of eco-terrorists. The group's leader, Naomi Perrault, is a beautiful geneticist who Jack believes conspired to kill his friend, and is claiming that a major international conglomerate developing genetically engineered crops is plotting a sinister transformation of our world that will lead humanity to extinction.

As Jack is drawn into a quietly raging war that suddenly explodes onto the front pages of the news, he discovers that her claims may not be so outrageous after all. Together, the two of them must face a horror Jack could never have imagined, with the fate of all life on Earth hanging in the balance...

Interested? Then read on and enjoy the prologue and first chapter of *Season Of The Harvest*. And always remember: *you are what you eat!*

* * *

PROLOGUE

Sheldon Crane ran for his life. Panting from exhaustion and the agony of the deep stab wound in his side, he darted into the deep shadows of an alcove in the underground service tunnel. Holding his pistol in unsteady hands, he peered around the corner, past the condensation-covered pipes, looking back in the direction from which he'd come.

Nothing. All he could hear was the deep hum of the electric service box that filled most of the alcove, punctuated by the *drip-drip-drip* of water from a small leak in one of the water pipes a few yards down the tunnel. Only a third of the ceiling-mounted fluorescent lights were lit, a cost-saving measure by the university that left long stretches of paralyzing darkness between the islands of greenish-tinged light. He could smell wet concrete and the tang of ozone, along with a faint trace of lubricating oil. And over it all was the scent of blood. In the pools of light stretching back down the tunnel, all the way back to the intersection where he had turned into this part of the underground labyrinth, he could see the glint of blood on the floor, a trail his pursuer could easily follow.

He knew that no one could save him: he had come here tonight precisely because he expected the building to be empty. It had been. Almost. But there was no one to hear his shouts for help, and he had dropped his cell phone during the unexpected confrontation in the lab upstairs.

He was totally on his own.

Satisfied that his pursuer was not right on his heels, he slid deeper into the alcove, into the dark recess between the warm metal of the electric service box and the cold concrete wall. He gently probed the wound in his side, gasping as his fingertips brushed against the blood-wet, swollen flesh just above his left hip. It was a long moment before he was sure he wouldn't scream from the pain. It wasn't merely a stab wound. He had been stabbed and cut before. That had been incredibly painful. This, however, was far worse. His insides were on fire, the pain having spread quickly from his belly to upper chest. And the pain was accompanied by paralysis. He had lost control of his abdominal muscles, and the sensation was spreading. There was a sudden gush of warmth down his legs as his bladder suddenly let go, and he groaned in agony as his internal organs began to burn.

Poison, he knew.

He leaned over, fighting against the light-headedness that threatened to bear him mercifully into unconsciousness.

"No," he panted to himself. "No." He knew he didn't have much time left. He had to act.

Wiping the blood from his left hand on his shirt, cleaning it as best he could, he reached under his right arm and withdrew both of the extra magazines he carried for his weapon, a 10mm Glock 22 that was standard issue for FBI special agents. He ejected the empty magazine from the gun, cursing himself as his shaking hands lost their grip and it clattered to the floor.

It won't matter soon, he thought giddily as he slumped against the wall, sliding down the rough concrete to the floor as his upper thighs succumbed to the spreading paralysis, then began to burn.

Desperately racing against the poison in his system, he withdrew a small plastic bag from a pocket inside his jacket and set it carefully next to him. He patted it with his fingertips several times to reassure himself that he knew exactly where it was in the dark. His fingers felt the shapes of a dozen lumps inside the bag: kernels of corn.

Then he picked up one of the spare magazines and shucked out all the bullets with his thumb into a pocket in his jacket so he wouldn't lose them. Setting down the now-empty magazine, he picked up the tiny bag and carefully opened the seal, praying he wouldn't accidentally send the precious lumps flying into the darkness. For the first time that night, Fate favored him, and the bag opened easily.

Picking up the empty magazine from his lap, he tapped a few of the kernels onto the magazine's follower, the piece of metal that the bottom bullet rested on. He managed to squeeze a bullet into the magazine on top of the corn kernels. Once that was done, he slid the other bullets into place, then clumsily slammed the magazine into the weapon and chambered a round.

He took the bag and its remaining tiny, precious cargo and resealed it. Then he stuffed it into his mouth. The knowledge of the nature of the corn made him want to gag, but he managed to force it down, swallowing the bag. Crane suspected his body would be searched thoroughly, inside and out, for what he had stolen, and his mind shied away from how that search would probably be conducted. His only hope now was that his pursuer would be content to find the bag, and not think to check Crane's weapon. He prayed that his body and the priceless contents of his gun's magazine would be found by the right people. It was a terrible long-shot, but he was out of options.

His nose was suddenly assaulted by the smell of Death coming for him, a nauseating mix of pungent ammonia laced with the reek of burning hemp.

Barely able to lift his arms, his torso nearly paralyzed and aflame with agonizing pain, Crane brought up his pistol just as his pursuer whirled around the corner. He fired at the hideous abomination that was revealed in the flashes from the muzzle of his gun, and managed to get off three shots before the weapon was batted from his faltering grip. He screamed in terror as his pursuer closed in, blocking out the light.

The screams didn't stop for a long time.

CHAPTER ONE

Jack Dawson stood in his supervisor's office and stared out the window, his bright gray eyes watching the rain fall from the brooding summer sky over Washington, D.C. The wind was blowing just hard enough for the rain to strike the glass, leaving behind wet streaks that ran down the panes like tears. The face he saw reflected there was cast in shadow by the overhead fluorescent lights. The square jaw and high cheekbones gave him a predatory look, while his full lips promised a smile, but were drawn downward now into a frown. The deeply tanned skin, framed by lush black hair that was neatly combed back and held with just the right amount of styling gel, looked sickly and pale in the glass, as if it belonged on the face of a ghost. He knew that it was the same face he saw every morning. But it was different now. An important part of his world had been killed, murdered, the night before.

He watched the people on the street a few floors below, hustling through the downpour with their umbrellas fluttering as they poured out of the surrounding buildings, heading home for the evening. Cars clogged Pennsylvania Avenue, with the taxis darting to the curb to pick up fares, causing other drivers to jam on their brakes, the bright red tail lights flickering on and off down the street like a sputtering neon sign. It was Friday, and everyone was eager to get home to their loved ones, or go out to dinner, or head to the local bar. Anywhere that would let them escape the rat race for the weekend.

He didn't have to see this building's entrance to know that very few of the people who worked here would be heading home on time tonight. The address was 935 Pennsylvania Avenue Northwest. It was the J. Edgar Hoover Building, headquarters of the Federal Bureau of Investigation, the FBI. Other than the teams of special agents who had departed an hour earlier for Lincoln, Nebraska, many of the Bureau's personnel here at headquarters wouldn't leave until sometime tomorrow. Some would be sleeping in their offices and cubicles after exhaustion finally overtook them, and wouldn't go home for more than a few hours over the next several days.

A special agent had been brutally murdered, and with the addition of another name to the list of the FBI's Service Martyrs, every resource the Bureau could bring to bear was being focused on bringing his killer to justice. Special agents from headquarters and field offices around the country were headed to Nebraska, along with an army of analysts and support staff that was already sifting through electronic data looking for leads.

Everyone had a part in the investigation, it seemed, except for Dawson. In his hand, he held a plain manila folder that included the information that had been forwarded by the Lincoln field office. It was a preliminary report sent in by the Special Agent in Charge (SAC), summarizing the few known facts of the case. In terse prose, the SAC's report described the crime scene, the victim, and what had been done by the local authorities before the SAC's office had been alerted. And there were photos. Lots of photos. If a picture was worth a thousand words, then the ones Dawson held in his shaking hands spoke volumes about the agony suffered by the victim before he died. Because it was clear from the rictus of agony and terror frozen on Sheldon Crane's face that he had still been alive when–

"I'm sorry, Jack," came a gruff voice from behind him, interrupting Dawson's morbid train of thought as Ray Clement, Assistant Director of the Criminal Investigative Division, came in and closed the door. It was his office, and he had ordered Dawson to wait there until he had a chance to speak with him.

Ray Clement was a bear of a man with a personality to match. A star football player from the University of Alabama's Crimson Tide, Clement had actually turned down a chance to go pro, and had instead joined the FBI as a special agent. That had been his dream since the age of ten, as he had once told Jack, and the proudest moment of his life had been when he'd earned his badge. Jack knew that a lot of people might have thought Clement was crazy. "I loved football," Clement would say, "and I still do. But I played it because I enjoyed it. I never planned to do it for a living."

Over the years, Clement had worked his way up through the Bureau. He was savvy enough to survive the internal politics, smart and tough enough to excel in the field, and conformed to the system because he believed in it. He could be a real bastard when someone did something stupid, but otherwise worked tirelessly to support his people so they could do their jobs. He wasn't a boss that any of his special agents would say they loved, but under his tenure, the Criminal Investigative Division, or CID, had successfully closed more cases than under any other assistant director in the previous fifteen years. People could say what they wanted, but Clement got results.

When he had first taken over the division, Clement had taken the time to talk to each and every one of his special agents. He had been up front about why: he wanted to know at least a little bit, more than just the names, about the men and women who risked their lives every day for the American Taxpayer. They were special agents, he'd said, but they were also special human beings.

Jack had dreaded the interview. Whereas Clement could have been the FBI's poster child, Jack didn't quite fit the mold. He was like a nail head sticking up from the perfectly polished surface of a hardwood floor, not enough to snag on anything, just enough to notice. Outwardly, he was no different than most of his peers. He dressed the same as most special agents, eschewing a suit for more practical and casual attire for all but the most formal occasions. His well-muscled six foot, one inch tall body was far more comfortable in jeans and a pullover shirt, with a light jacket to conceal his primary weapon, a standard service-issue Glock 22. While he had no problems voicing his opinions, which had sometimes led to respectful but intense discussions with his superiors, he had never been a discipline problem. He was highly competent in the field, and was a whiz at data analysis. At first glance, he seemed like what he should be: an outstanding special agent who worked hard and had great career prospects.

But under the shiny veneer ran a deep vein of dark emptiness. Jack smiled, but it never seemed to reach his eyes, and he rarely laughed. He was not cold-hearted, for he had often displayed uncommon compassion toward others, especially the victims, and their families, of the crimes he was sent to investigate. But he had no social life to speak of, no significant other in his life, and there were very few people who understood the extent of the pain that lay at Jack's core.

That pain had its roots in events that took place seven years earlier, when Jack was serving in the Army in Afghanistan. His patrol had been ambushed by the Taliban and had taken heavy casualties before reinforcements arrived. Jack had been badly wounded, having taken two rounds from an AK-47 in the chest, along with shrapnel from a grenade. The latter had left its mark on his otherwise handsome face, a jagged scar marring his left cheek. That had been rough, but he was young, only twenty-six, and strong, and would make a full recovery from his wounds.

What had torn him apart was what happened back in the States. While he lay unconscious in the SSG Heath N. Craig Joint Theater Hospital in Bagram, his wife Emily was kidnapped while leaving a shopping mall not far from their home outside Fort Drum, New York. Emily had her own home business, and they had no children, so no one immediately noticed that she'd gone missing. Four days passed before a persistent Red Cross worker who had been trying to get in touch with Emily about

Jack's injuries contacted the provost marshal at Fort Drum. Two military policemen went to the house, and when they found it empty, they contacted the local police.

The police located her car that same day: the mall's security center had ordered it towed away after it had sat in the parking lot overnight, reporting it to the police as abandoned. The next day, the fifth since she had disappeared, police investigators found footage on one of the mall security cameras that vividly showed what had happened to her. A man stepped around the back of a nondescript van as she had walked by, laden with shopping bags. With a casual glance around to see if there were any witnesses, he turned as she passed and jabbed her in the back with a stun gun. Scooping her up in one smooth motion, he dumped her into the van through the already open side door, and then collected up the bags that had fallen to the ground. He didn't rush, didn't hurry as he threw the bags into the van. Then he climbed into the back and slammed the door closed. After a few minutes the van backed out of the space and drove away.

It had all happened in broad daylight.

Because it was clearly a kidnapping and so much time had passed since the crime had been committed, the local authorities contacted the FBI.

That was when Jack learned of his wife's disappearance. Immobilized in the hospital bed, still in a great deal of pain, he was paid a visit by his grim-faced commander and a civilian woman who introduced herself as an FBI special agent. His commander told him what had happened, and over the next three hours the FBI agent gathered every detail that Jack could remember about his wife's activities, associations, family and friends. Everything about her life that he could think of that might help track down her kidnapper. It had been the three most agonizing hours of his life. The special agent had assured him that everything was being done to find his wife and bring her back safely. Jack prayed that they would find her alive, but in his heart he knew she was gone.

His intuition proved brutally prophetic. Her body was found a week later, buried under bags of trash in a dumpster behind a strip mall in Cleveland, Ohio. She had been repeatedly raped and beaten before she'd finally been strangled to death. The FBI and law enforcement authorities in Ohio did everything they could to find her killer, but he had covered his tracks well and was never found.

When Jack was well enough to travel, the Army arranged for him to be flown home, where one of his first duties had been to formally identify Emily's battered, broken body. He had seen his share of horrors in Afghanistan, and some might think it would have made the trauma of viewing her body somewhat easier. It hadn't. Thankfully, the family lawyer, an old friend of his parents, who themselves had died in a car wreck a year before Jack had gone to Afghanistan, had made all the necessary arrangements for her burial. Jack simply had to endure the agony of laying her to rest.

After the funeral, Jack had found himself at a loss. His time in the Army was nearly up, and he was tempted to simply lapse into an emotional coma to shut off the pain and the nightmares of Emily's tortured face.

But a cold flame of rage burned in his core at what had happened to her, and the bastard who had done it. He found himself sitting in the kitchen one morning, holding the business card of the female special agent who had interviewed him in Bagram. As if his body was acting of its own accord, he found himself picking up the phone and dialing the woman's number. The conversation that followed was the first step on the path that eventually led him to become a special agent in the FBI.

She had tried to dissuade him, warning him that he wasn't going to find answers, or vengeance, to Emily's death. In truth, while the thought of finding her killer was more than appealing, he realized from the beginning that avenging Emily wasn't what was pulling him toward the Bureau: it was the thought that he might be able to help prevent what had happened to her from happening to others.

When he got to the FBI Academy, one of his fellow agents was Sheldon Crane. Sheldon had an irrepressible sense of humor, and immediately glued himself to Jack. At first, Jack had resented the unwanted attention, but Sheldon had gradually worn through Jack's emotional armor, eventually becoming the Yin to Jack's Yang. Sheldon was a self-proclaimed computer genius, recruited to work in the Bureau's Cyber Division, while Jack's skills in intelligence analysis and experience in combat made him a good candidate for the Criminal Investigative Division.

Jack had done well in CID, but remained an outsider, something of a mystery to his fellow agents. Most of his supervisors knew his background and were content to let it be, but when Clement took over and began his interviews, Jack had heard that he could be very pointed in his questions. Jack didn't want to be interrogated again about his experience in Afghanistan or Emily's murder. He didn't want anyone's sympathy. He just wanted to move on.

Clement had completely surprised him. He didn't talk or want to know about anything related to Jack's past or his work. Instead, he asked questions about Jack as a person outside of the Bureau, what he liked to do in his free time, his personal likes and dislikes. At first, Jack had been extremely uncomfortable, but after a while he found himself opening up. Clement talked to him for a full hour and a half. When they were through, Jack actually found himself laughing at one of Clement's notoriously bad jokes.

After that, while Jack couldn't quite call Clement a friend, he had certainly become a confidant and someone he felt he could really talk to when the need arose.

Now was certainly one of those times.

Clement walked across the office toward Jack, but stopped when his eyes fell on the folder Jack clutched in one hand. "Dammit, don't you know any better than to grab files off my desk, Special Agent Dawson?"

"Yes, sir," Dawson told him. "I took it from your secretary's desk."

"Lord," Clement muttered as he moved up to Dawson. Putting a hand on the younger man's shoulder, he said again, "I'm sorry, Jack. I'd hoped to have a chance to talk to you before you saw anything in that file." With a gentle squeeze of his massive hand, he let go, then sat down behind his desk. "Sit."

Reluctantly, still clutching the folder containing the professional analysis of Sheldon Crane's last moments alive, Jack did as he was told, dropping into one of the chairs arrayed around a small conference table before turning to face his boss.

"Why aren't you letting me go out with the teams to Lincoln?" he asked before Clement could say anything else.

"Do you really have to ask that?" his boss said pointedly. "Look at yourself, Jack. You're an emotional wreck. I'm not going to endanger an investigation by having someone who isn't operating at full capacity on the case." He raised a hand as Jack began to protest. "Don't start arguing," he said. "Look, Jack, I've lost close friends, too. I know how much it can tear you up inside. But you're not going to do Sheldon any favors now by screwing things up in the field because you're emotionally involved. I promise you, *we will not rest* until we've found his killer."

"My God, Ray," Jack said hoarsely, looking again at the folder in his hand, "they didn't just kill him. They fucking tore him apart!"

He forced himself to open the folder again. The top photo was a shot that showed Sheldon's entire body at the scene. It looked like someone had performed an autopsy on him. A deep cut had been made in his torso from throat to groin. The ribs had been cracked open to expose the heart and lungs, and the organs from his abdomen had been pulled out and dissected, the grisly contents dumped onto the floor. Then something had been used to carve open his skull just above the line of his eyebrows, and the brain had been removed and set aside. Another shot that he dared not look at again showed what was done inside the skull: his killer had torn his nasal cavities open.

Another photo showed Sheldon's clothing. He had been stripped from head to toe, and his clothes had been systematically torn apart, with every seam ripped open. In the background, on the floor next to the wall, was his gun.

Jack had seen death enough times and in enough awful ways that it no longer made him want to gag. But he had never, even in the hateful fighting in Afghanistan, seen such measured brutality as this.

The last photo he had looked at had been a close-up of Sheldon's face and his terrified expression. "He was still alive when they started...cutting him up."

"I know," Clement said, his own voice breaking. "I know he was."

"What was he doing out there?" Jack asked, sliding the photos back into the folder with numb fingers. "This couldn't have just been some random attack. What the hell was he working on that could have driven someone to do this to him?"

Pursing his lips, Clement looked down at his desk, his face a study in consideration. "This is classified, Jack," he said finally, looking up and fixing Jack with a hard stare, "as in Top Secret. The kind of information you have to read after you sign your life away and go into a little room with thick walls and special locks on the door. Even the SAC in Lincoln doesn't know the real reason Sheldon was there, and the only reason I'm telling you is because you held high-level clearances in the Army and you can appreciate how sensitive this is and keep your mouth shut about it."

Jack nodded. He had been an intelligence officer in the Army, and knew exactly what Clement was talking about. He also appreciated the fact that Clement could lose his job for what he was about to say. That was the level of trust that had built up between them.

Satisfied that Jack had gotten the message, Clement told him, "Sheldon was investigating a series of cyber attacks against several research laboratories doing work on genetically modified organisms, mainly food crops like corn. The FDA was also hacked: someone took a keen interest in what the Center for Food Safety and Applied Nutrition was doing along the same lines. And before you say, 'So what's the big super-secret deal,' there was also a series of attacks against computers, both at home and work, used by specific individuals across the government, including senior officials in the Department of Defense and the military services. Sheldon was convinced the perpetrators were from a group known as the Earth Defense Society, and that they're somewhere here in the U.S. He's been out in the field for the last three weeks, tracking down leads." He frowned. "Apparently he found something in Lincoln."

"What the hell are they after?" Jack asked, perplexed. It seemed an odd potpourri of targets for hackers to be going after. He could understand someone going after one group of targets or another, but what common thread could run through such a mixed bag, from labs working on how to improve crops to the military?

"That's the sixty-four thousand dollar question, isn't it?" Clement said. "So, now you know what Sheldon was doing. Just keep your mouth shut about it and pretend this conversation never happened."

Standing up and coming around his desk, Clement continued as Jack rose from his chair, "I want you to take some leave. Get out of here for a few days until you've pulled yourself together. Then come back in and we can talk. And I promise you, I'll keep you informed of what we find."

"Yes, sir," was all Jack said as he shook Clement's hand. He turned and walked out of the office, closing the door quietly behind him.

As Jack left, Clement saw that he still had the copy of Sheldon's case file in his hand. With a satisfied nod, he returned to his desk and checked his phone, which was blinking urgently. It hadn't been ringing because he had ordered his secretary to hold all of his calls. Quickly scanning the recent caller list on the phone's display, he saw that the director had called him. Twice.

He grimaced, then pulled out the two smart phones that he carried. He used one of them for everyday personal communication. That one the Bureau knew about. He had turned it off before talking to Dawson to avoid any interruptions, and now he turned it back on.

The other smart phone, the one he flipped open now, was used for an entirely different purpose, and something of which his bosses at the Bureau would not approve. Calling up the web application, he quickly logged into an anonymizer service and sent a brief, innocuous-sounding email to a particular address. Then he activated an application that would wipe the phone's memory and reset it to the factory default, effectively erasing any evidence of how he had used it.

Putting it back in his pocket, he picked up his desk phone and called the director.

A SMALL FAVOR

For any book you read, and particularly for those you enjoy, please do the author and other readers a very important service and leave a review. It doesn't matter how many (or how few) reviews a book may already have, your voice is important!

Many folks don't leave reviews because they think it has to be a well-crafted synopsis and analysis of the plot. While those are great, it's not necessary at all. Just put down in as many or few words as you like, just a blurb, that you enjoyed the book and recommend it to others. Your comments *do* matter!

And thank you again so much for reading this book!

Discover Other Books By Michael R. Hicks

The *In Her Name* Series

First Contact
Legend Of The Sword
Dead Soul
Empire
Confederation
Final Battle
From Chaos Born

"Boxed Set" Collections

In Her Name (Omnibus)
In Her Name: The Last War

Thrillers

Season Of The Harvest

Visit *AuthorMichaelHicks.com* for the latest updates!

ABOUT THE AUTHOR

Born in 1963, Michael Hicks grew up in the age of the Apollo program and spent his youth glued to the television watching the original Star Trek series and other science fiction movies, which continues to be a source of entertainment and inspiration. Having spent the majority of his life as a voracious reader, he has been heavily influenced by writers ranging from Robert Heinlein to Jerry Pournelle and Larry Niven, and David Weber to S.M. Stirling. Living in Maryland with his beautiful wife, two wonderful stepsons and two mischievous Siberian cats, he's now living his dream of writing novels full-time.

CPSIA information can be obtained at www.ICGtesting.com
Printed in the USA
BVOW08s2012261115

428633BV00001B/49/P